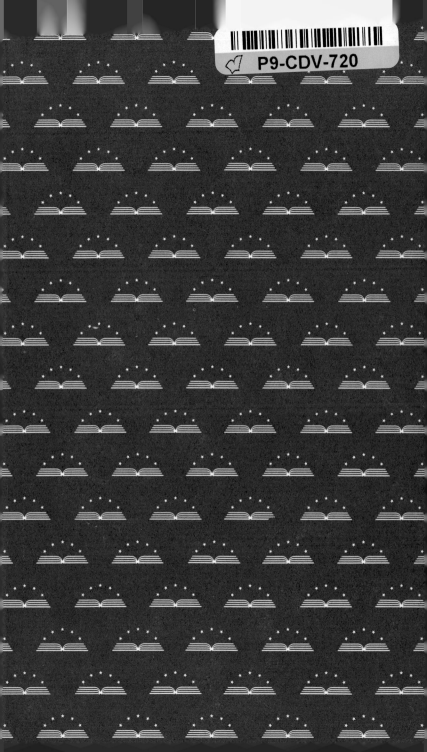

WASHINGTON IRVING

WASHINGTON IRVING

HISTORY, TALES AND SKETCHES

LETTERS OF
JONATHAN OLDSTYLE, GENT.

SALMAGUNDI
or, The Whim-Whams and Opinions
of Launcelot Langstaff, Esq. & Others

A HISTORY OF NEW YORK
From the Beginning of the World to the
End of the Dutch Dynasty

THE SKETCH BOOK OF GEOFFREY
CRAYON, GENT.

THE LIBRARY OF AMERICA

The texts of *Letters of Jonathan Oldstyle, Gent., Salmagundi,* and *The
Sketch Book* are Copyright © 1977, 1978 by
G. K. Hall & Co. All rights reserved.

Distributed to the trade in the United States
and Canada by the Viking Press.

Published in Great Britain by the Press Syndicate
of the University of Cambridge
The Pitt Building, Trumpington Street, Cambridge CB21RP
ISBN   0 521 26116 3

Library of Congress Catalog Card Number: 83-5474
For Cataloging in Publication Data, see end of *Notes* section.
ISBN 0-940450-14-3

First Printing

Manufactured in the United States of America

JAMES W. TUTTLETON
WROTE THE NOTES AND SELECTED
THE TEXTS FOR THIS VOLUME

*This volume prints the texts of Letters of Jonathan Oldstyle, Gent.,
Salmagundi, and The Sketch Book from The Complete Works of
Washington Irving edited by Bruce I. Granger, Martha Hartzog,
Haskell Springer, Henry A. Pochmann, Herbert L. Kleinfield,
Richard Dilworth Rust, and Edwin T. Bowden and
published by Twayne Publishers.*

*Grateful acknowledgement is made to the National Endowment
for the Humanities and the Ford Foundation for their
generous financial support of this series.*

Contents

LETTERS OF
JONATHAN OLDSTYLE
GENT.

Contents

Letter I

Printed in *The Morning Chronicle*, November 15, 1802.

Mr. Editor,

If the observations of an odd old fellow are not wholly superfluous, I would thank you to shove them into a spare corner of your paper.

It is a matter of amusement to an uninterested spectator like myself, to observe the influence fashion has on the dress and deportment of its votaries, and how very quick they fly from one extreme to the other.

A few years since, the rage was; very high crowned hats with very narrow brims, tight neckcloth, tight coat, tight jacket, tight small clothes, and shoes loaded with enormous silver buckles: the hair craped, plaited, queued and powdered: — in short, an air of the greatest spruceness and tightness diffused over the whole person.

The ladies, with their tresses neatly turned up over an immense cushion; waist a yard long, braced up with stays into the smallest compass, and encircled by an enormous hoop: so that the fashionable belle resembled a walking bottle.

Thus dressed, the lady was seen, with the most bewitching languor, reclining on the arm of an extremely attentive beau, who, with a long cane, decorated with an enormous tassel, was carefully employed in removing every stone, stick or straw that might impede the progress of his tottering companion, whose high-heel'd shoes just brought the points of her toes to the ground.

What an alteration has a few years produced! — We now behold our gentleman, with the most studied carelessness, and almost slovenliness of dress; large hat, large coat, large neckcloth, large pantaloons, large boots, and hair scratch'd into every careless direction, lounging along the streets in the most apparent listlessness and vacuity of thought; staring with an unmeaning countenance at every passenger, or leaning upon the arm of some kind fair one for support, with the other hand cramm'd into his breeches pocket. Such is the picture of a modern beau: in his dress stuffing himself up to the dimensions of a Hercules, in his manners affecting the help-lessness of an invalid.

The belle who has to undergo the fatigue of dragging along this sluggish animal, has chosen a character the very reverse: emulating in her dress and actions all the airy lightness of a sylph, she trips along with the greatest vivacity. Her laughing eye, her countenance enlivened with affability and good humor, inspire with kindred animation every beholder, except the torpid being by her side, who is either affecting the fashionable sang-froid, or is wrapt up in profound contemplation of—himself.

Heavens! how changed are the manners since I was young!—then, how delightful to contemplate a ball-room: such bowing, such scraping, such complimenting; nothing but copperplate speeches to be heard on both sides; no walking but in minuet measure; nothing more common than to see half a dozen gentlemen knock their heads together in striving who should first recover a lady's fan or snuff-box that had fallen.

But now, our youths no longer aim at the character of *pretty gentlemen*: their greatest ambition is to be called lazy dogs—careless fellows—&c. &c. Dressed up in the mammoth style, our buck saunters into the ball-room in a surtout, hat under arm, cane in hand; strolls round with the most vacant air; stops abruptly before such lady as he may choose to honor with his attention; entertains her with the common *slang* of the day, collected from the conversation of hostlers, footmen, porters, &c. until his string of smart sayings is run out, and then lounges off, to entertain some other fair one with the same unintelligible jargon.

Surely, Mr. Editor, puppyism must have arrived to a *climax*: it *must* turn; to carry it to a greater extent seems to me impossible.

JONATHAN OLDSTYLE.

Letter II

Printed in *The Morning Chronicle*, November 20, 1802.

Mr. Editor,

Encouraged by the ready insertion you gave my former communication, I have taken the liberty to intrude on you a few more remarks.

Nothing is more intolerable to an old person than innovation on old habits. The customs that prevailed in our youth become dear to us as we advance in years; and we can no more bear to see them abolished, than we can to behold the trees cut down under which we have sported in the happy days of infancy.

Even I myself, who have floated down the stream of life with the tide; who have humored it in all its turnings; who have conformed, in a great measure, to all its fashions—cannot but feel sensible of this prejudice. I often sigh when I draw a comparison between the present and past: and though I cannot but be sensible that, in general, times are altered for the better, yet there is something even in the *imperfections* of the manners which prevailed in my youthful days that is inexpressibly endearing.

There is nothing that seems more strange and preposterous to me than the manner in which modern marriages are conducted. The parties keep the matter as secret as if there was something disgraceful in the connexion. The lady positively denies that any thing of the kind is to happen; will laugh at her intended husband, and even lay bets against the event, the very day before it is to take place. They sneak into matrimony as quietly as possible, and seem to pride themselves on the cunning and ingenuity they have displayed in their manœuvres.

How different is this from the manners of former times!— I recollect when my *aunt Barbara* was addressed by *'squire Stylish*: nothing was heard of during the whole courtship but consultations and negociations between her friends and relatives: the matter was considered and reconsidered, and at length the time set for a final answer. Never, Mr. Editor, shall

I forget the awful solemnity of the scene. The whole family of the Oldstyles assembled in formal conclave: my aunt Barbara, dressed out as fine as hands could make her—high cushion, enormous cap, long waist, prodigious hoop, ruffles that reached to the end of her fingers, and a gown of flame colored brocade, figured with poppies, roses and sun-flowers. Never did she look so sublimely handsome. The 'squire entered the room with a countenance suited to the solemnity of the occasion. He was arrayed in a full suit of scarlet velvet, his coat decorated with a profusion of large silk buttons, and the skirts stiffened with a yard or two of buckram; a long pig-tail'd wig, well powdered, adorned his head, and stockings of deep blue silk, rolled over the knees, graced his extremities; the flaps of his vest reached to his knee-buckles; and the ends of his cravat, tied with the most precise neatness, twisted through every button-hole. Thus accoutred, he gravely walked into the room, with his ivory-headed ebony cane in one hand, and gently swaying his three-cornered beaver with the other.—The gallant and fashionable appearance of the 'squire, the gracefulness and dignity of his deportment, occasioned a general smile of complacency through the room: my aunt Barbara modestly veiled her countenance with her fan; but I observed her contemplating her admirer with great satisfaction through the sticks.

The business was opened with the most formal solemnity, but was not long in agitation. The Oldstyles were moderate—their articles of capitulation few: the 'squire was gallant, and acceded to them all. In short, the blushing Barbara was delivered up to his embraces with due ceremony. Then, Mr. Editor—then were the happy times: such oceans of arrack—such mountains of plumb-cake—such feasting and congratulating—such fiddling and dancing—ah me! who can think of those days, and not sigh when he sees the degeneracy of the present: no eating of cake nor throwing of stockings—not a single skin filled with wine on the joyful occasion—nor a single pocket edified by it but the parson's.

It is with the greatest pain I see those customs dying away, which served to awaken the hospitality and friendship of my ancient comrades—that strewed with flowers the path to the altar, and shed a ray of sunshine on the commencement of the matrimonial union.

The deportment of my aunt Barbara and her husband, was as decorous after marriage as before— *her* conduct was always regulated by *his*—her sentiments ever accorded with his opinions—she was always eager to tie on his neckcloth of a morning—to tuck a napkin under his chin at meal-times—to wrap him up warm of a winter's day, and to spruce him up as smart as possible of a Sunday. The squire was the most attentive and polite husband in the world: would hand his wife in and out of church, with the greatest ceremony—drink her health at dinner with particular emphasis, and ask her advice on every subject—though I must confess he invariably adopted his own—nothing was heard of from both sides but dears, sweet loves, doves, &c. The squire could never stir out of a winter's day, without his wife calling after him from the window, to button up his waistcoat carefully. Thus all things went on smoothly, and my relations *Stylish* had the name, and, as far as I know, deserved it, of being the most happy and loving couple in the world.

A modern married pair will, no doubt, laugh at all this: they are accustomed to treat one another with the utmost carelessness and neglect. No longer does the wife tuck the napkin under her husband's chin—nor the husband attend to heaping her plate with dainties—no longer do I see those little amusing fooleries in company, where the lady would pat her husband's cheek, and he chuck her under the chin: when dears and sweets, were as plenty as cookies on a new year's day. The wife now considers herself as totally independent— will advance her own opinions, without hesitation, though directly opposite to his—will carry on accounts of her own, and will even have secrets of her own with which she refuses to entrust him.

Who can read these facts and not lament, with me, the degeneracy of the present times—what husband is there but will look back with regret, to the happy days of female subjection.

JONATHAN OLDSTYLE.

Letter III

Printed in *The Morning Chronicle*, December 1, 1802.

Mr. Editor,

There is no place of public amusement of which I am so fond as the theatre. To enjoy this with the greater relish I go but seldom; and I find there is no play, however poor or ridiculous from which I cannot derive some entertainment.

I was very much taken with a play-bill of last week, announcing in large capitals

THE BATTLE OF HEXHAM, *or days of old*.

Here said I to myself will be something grand— *days of old!*— my fancy fired at the words. I pictured to myself all the gallantry of chivalry; here, thought I, will be a display of court manners and true politeness; the play will no doubt be garnished with tilts and tournaments: and as to those *banditti* whose names make such a formidable appearance on the bills, they will be hung up, every mother's son, for the edification of the gallery.

With such impressions I took my seat in the pit, and was so impatient that I could hardly attend to the music, though I found it very good.

The curtain rose. Out walked the queen with great majesty, she answered my ideas, she was dressed well, she looked well, and she acted well. The queen was followed by a pretty gentleman, who from his winking and grinning I took to be the court fool. I soon found out my mistake. He was a courtier "*high in trust*," and either general, colonel, or something of *martial* dignity.

They talked for some time, though I could not understand the drift of their discourse, so I amused myself with eating pea-nuts.

In one of the scenes I was diverted with the stupidity of a corporal and his men, who sung a dull song, and talked a great deal about nothing: though I found by their laughing, there was a great deal of fun in the corporal's remarks.

What this scene had to do with the rest of the piece, I

could not comprehend: I suspect it was a part of some other play thrust in here *by accident*.

I was then introduced to a cavern where there were several hard looking fellows, sitting round a table carousing. They told the audience they were banditti. They then sung a *gallery song*, of which I could understand nothing but two lines:

"The Welchman had lik'd to've been chok'd by a mouse,
"But he pulled him out by the tail!"

Just as they had ended this elegant song their banquet was disturbed by the *melodious sound* of a horn, and in march'd a *portly gentleman*, who I found was their captain. After this worthy gentleman had fumed his hour out: after he had slapped his breast and drawn his sword half a dozen times, the act ended.

In the course of the play I learnt that there had been, or was, or would be, a battle; but how, or when, or where I could not understand. The banditti once more made their appearance, and frighted the wife of the portly gentleman, who was dressed in man's clothes, and was seeking her husband. I could not enough admire the dignity of her deportment, the sweetness of her countenance, and the unaffected gracefulness of her action; but who the captain really was, or why he ran away from his spouse, I could not understand. However, they seemed very glad to find one another again; and so at last the play ended by the falling of the curtain.

I wish the manager would use a *drop scene* at the close of the acts: we might then always ascertain the termination of the piece by the *green* curtain. On this occasion I was indebted to the polite bows of the actors for this pleasing information. I cannot say that I was entirely satisfied with the play, but I promised myself ample entertainment in the afterpiece, which was called *The Tripolitan Prize*. Now, thought I, we shall have some *sport* for our money: we will no doubt see a few of those Tripolitan scoundrels spitted like turkeys for our amusement. Well, sir, the curtain rose—the trees waved in front of the stage, and the sea rolled in the rear. All things looked very pleasant and smiling. Presently I heard a bustling behind the scenes—here thought I comes a fierce band of Tripolitans with whiskers as long as my arm.—No such thing—they were only a party of village masters and misses taking a walk for exercise, and very pretty behaved young gentry they were, I assure you; but it was cruel in the manager to dress them in *buckram*, as it deprived them entirely of the use of their limbs. They arranged themselves very orderly on each side of the stage; and sang something doubtless very affecting, for they all looked pitiful enough. By and by came up a most tremenduous storm: the lightning flash'd, the thunder roar'd, the rain descended in torrents; however, our pretty rustics stood gaping quietly at one another, till they must have been wet to the skin. I was surprised at their torpidity, till I found they were each one afraid to move first, through fear of being laughed at for their aukwardness. How they got off I do not recollect, but I advise the manager, in a similar case, to furnish every one with a *trap door*, through which to make his exit. Yet this would deprive the audience of much amusement: for nothing can be more laughable than to see a body of guards with their spears, or courtiers with their long robes *get* across the stage at our theatre.

Scene pass'd after scene. In vain I strained my eyes to catch a glimpse of a Mahometan phiz. I once heard a great bellowing behind the scenes, and expected to see a strapping Musselman come bouncing in; but was miserably disappointed, on distinguishing his voice, to find out by his *swearing*, that he was only a *Christian*. In he came—an American navy officer. Worsted stockings—olive velvet small clothes—scarlet vest—pea-jacket, and *gold laced hat*—dressed quite *in character*. I soon found out by his talk, that he was an American prize master: that, returning thro' the *Mediterranean* with his Tripolitan prize, he was driven by a storm on the *coast of England!*

The honest gentleman seemed from his actions to be rather intoxicated: which I could account for in no other way than his having drank a great deal of salt water as he swam ashore.

Several following scenes were taken up with hallooing and huzzaing between the captain, his crew, and the gallery:— with several amusing tricks of the captain and his son, a very funny, mischievous little fellow. Then came the cream of the joke: the captain wanted to put to sea, and the young fellow, who had fallen desperately in love, to stay ashore. Here was a contest between love and honor—such piping of eyes, such blowing of noses, such slapping of pocket holes! But *old Junk* was inflexible.—What! an American tar desert his duty! (three cheers from the gallery) impossible!—American tars forever!! True blue will never stain!! &c. &c. (a continual thundering among the gods).

Here was a scene of distress—here was bathos. The author seemed as much puzzled how to dispose of the young tar as old Junk was. It would not do to leave an American seaman on foreign ground; nor would it do to separate him from his mistress.

Scene the last opened—it seems that another Tripolitan cruiser had bore down on the prize as she lay about a mile off shore.—How a Barbary corsair had got in this part of the world—whether she had been driven there by the same storm, or whether she was cruising about to pick up a few English first rates, I could not learn. However, here she was—again were we conducted to the sea shore, where we found all the village gentry, in their buckram suits, ready assembled to be entertained with the rare show, of an American and Tripolitan engaged yard arm and yard arm. The battle was conducted with proper decency and decorum, and the Tripolitan very politely gave in—as it would be indecent to conquer in the face of an American audience.

After the engagement, the crew came ashore, joined with the captain and gallery in a few more huzzas, and the curtain fell. How old Junk, his son, and his son's sweetheart settled it, I could not discover.

I was somewhat puzzled to understand the meaning and necessity of this engagement between the ships, till an honest old countryman at my elbow, said he supposed *this* was the *battle of Hexham*; as he recollected no fighting in the first piece.—With this explanation I was perfectly satisfied.

My remarks upon the audience I shall postpone to another opportunity.

JONATHAN OLDSTYLE.

Letter IV

Printed in *The Morning Chronicle*, December 4, 1802.

Mr. Editor,

My last communication mentioned my visit to the theatre; the remarks it contained were chiefly confined to the play and the actors: I shall now extend them to the audience, who, I assure you, furnish no inconsiderable part of the entertainment.

As I entered the house, some time before the curtain rose, I had sufficient leisure to make some observations. I was much amused with the waggery and humor of the gallery, which, by the way, is kept in *excellent* order by the constables who are stationed there. The noise in this part of the house is somewhat similar to that which prevailed in Noah's ark; for we have an imitation of the whistles and yells of every kind of animal.—This, in some measure, compensates for the want of music, (as the gentlemen of our orchestra are very economic of their favors). Some how or another the anger of the gods seemed to be aroused all of a sudden, and they commenced a discharge of apples, nuts & ginger-bread, on the heads of the honest folks in the pit, who had no possibility of retreating from this new kind of thunder-bolts. I can't say but I was a little irritated at being saluted aside of my head with a rotten pippin, and was going to shake my cane at them; but was prevented by a decent looking man behind me, who informed me it was useless to threaten or expostulate. They are only *amusing themselves* a little at our expence, said he, sit down quietly and bend your back to it. My kind neighbor was interrupted by a hard green apple that hit him between the shoulders—he made a wry face, but knowing it was all in joke, bore the blow like a philosopher. I soon saw the wisdom of this determination,—a stray thunder-bolt happened to light on the head of a little sharp-faced Frenchman, dress'd in a white coat and small cock'd hat, who sat two or three benches ahead of me, and seemed to be an irritable little animal: Monsieur was terribly exasperated; he jumped upon his seat, shook his fist at the gallery, and swore violently in bad

English. This was all nuts to his merry persecutors, their attention was wholly turned on him, and he formed their *target* for the rest of the evening.

I found the ladies in the boxes, as usual, studious to please; their charms were set off to the greatest advantage; each box was a little battery in itself, and they all seemed eager to out do each other in the havoc they spread around. An arch glance in one box was rivalled by a smile in another, that smile by a simper in a third, and in a fourth, a most bewitching languish carried all before it.

I was surprised to see some persons reconnoitering the company through spy-glasses; and was in doubt whether these machines were used to remedy deficiencies of vision, or whether this was another of the eccentricities of fashion. Jack Stylish has since informed me that glasses were lately all *the go*; though hang it, says Jack, it is quite *out* at present; we used to mount glasses in *great snuff*, but since so many *tough jockies* have followed the lead, the bucks have all *cut* the custom. I give you, Mr. Editor, the account in my dashing cousin's own language. It is from a vocabulary I don't well understand.

I was considerably amused by the queries of the countryman mentioned in my last, who was now making his first visit to the theatre. He kept constantly applying to me for information, and I readily communicated, as far as my own ignorance would permit.

As this honest man was casting his eye round the house, his attention was suddenly arrested. And pray, who are these? said he, pointing to a cluster of young fellows. These I suppose are the critics, of whom I have heard so much. They have, no doubt, got together to communicate their remarks, and compare notes; these are the persons through whom the audience exercise their judgments, and by whom they are told, when they are to applaud or to hiss. Critics! ha, ha, my dear sir, they trouble themselves as little about the elements of criticism as they do about other departments of science or belles lettres. These are the beaus of the present day, who meet here to lounge away an idle hour, and play off their little impertinencies for the entertainment of the public. They no more regard the merits of a play, or of the actors, than my cane. They even *strive* to appear inattentive; and I have seen one of them perch'd upon the front of the box with his back to the stage, sucking the head of his stick, and staring vacantly at the audience, insensible to the most interesting specimens of scenic representation: though the tear of sensibility was trembling in every eye around him.

I have heard that some have even gone so far in search of amusement, as to propose a game or two of cards, in the theatre, during the performance: the eyes of my neighbor sparkled at this information; his cane shook in his hand; the word, *puppies*, burst from his lips. Nay, said I, I don't give this for absolute fact: my cousin Jack was, I believe, *quizzing* me (as he terms it) when he gave me the information. But you seem quite indignant, said I to the decent looking man in my rear. It was from him the exclamation came; the honest *countryman* was gazing in gaping wonder on some new attraction. Believe me, said I, if you had them daily before your eyes, you would get quite used to them. Used to them! replied he, how is it possible for people of sense to relish such conduct. Bless you, my friend, people of sense have nothing to do with it; they merely endure it in silence. These young gentlemen live in an indulgent age. When I was a young man, such tricks and fopperies were held in proper contempt. Here I went a little too far; for upon better recollection I must own that a lapse of years has produced but little alteration in this department of folly and impertinence. But do the ladies admire these manners? truly I am not as conversant in female circles as formerly; but I should think it a poor compliment to my fair country women, to suppose them pleased with the stupid stare and cant phrases with which these votaries of fashion, add affected to real ignorance.

Our conversation was here interrupted by the ringing of a bell. Now for the play, said my companion. No, said I, it is only for the musicians. Those worthy gentlemen then came crawling out of their holes, and began with very solemn and important phizes, strumming and tuning their instruments in the usual style of discordance, to the great *entertainment* of the audience. What tune is that? asked my neighbor, covering his ears. This, said I, is no tune; it is only a pleasing *symphony*, with which we are regaled as a preparative. For my part, though I admire the effect of contrast, I think they might as well play it in their cavern under the stage. The bell rung a second time; and then began the tune in reality; but I could not help observing that the countryman was more diverted with the queer grimaces, and contortions of countenance exhibited by the musicians, than their melody.

What I heard of the music, I liked very well (though I was told by one of my neighbors that the same pieces have been played every night for these three years;) but it was often overpowered by the gentry in the gallery, who vociferated loudly for *Moll in the wad*, *Tally ho the grinders*, and several other *airs* more suited to their tastes.

I observed that every part of the house has its different department. The good folks of the gallery have all the trouble of ordering the music (their directions, however, are not more frequently followed than they deserve.) The mode by which they issue their mandates is stamping, hissing, roaring, whistling, and, when the musicians are refractory, groaning in cadence. They also have the privilege of demanding a *bow* from *John* (by which name they designate every servant at the theatre, who enters to move a table or snuff a candle;) and of detecting those cunning dogs who peep from behind the curtain.

By the bye, my honest country friend was much puzzled about the curtain itself. He wanted to know why that *carpet* was hung up in the theatre. I assured him it was no carpet, but a very fine curtain. And what, pray, may be the meaning of that gold head with the nose cut off that I see in front of it? The meaning—why really I can't tell exactly—tho' my cousin Jack stylish says there is a great deal of meaning in it. But surely you like the *design* of the curtain? The design— why really I can see no design about it, unless it is to be brought down about our ears by the weight of those gold heads and that heavy *cornice* with which it is garnished. I began now to be uneasy for the credit of our curtain, and was afraid he would perceive the mistake of the painter in putting a *harp* in the middle of the curtain, and calling it a *mirror*; but his attention was *happily* called away by the *candle-grease* from the chandelier, over the centre of the pit, dropping on his clothes. This he loudly complained of, and declared his coat was *bran-new*. How, my friend, said I, we must put up with a few trifling inconveniencies when in the pursuit of pleasure. True said he:—but I think I pay pretty dear for it:—first to give six shillings at the door, and then to have my head battered with rotten apples, and my coat spoiled by candle-grease: by and by I shall have my other clothes dirtied by sitting down, as I perceive every body mounted on the benches. I wonder if they could not see as well if they were all to stand upon the floor.

Here I could no longer defend our customs, for I could scarcely breathe while thus surmounted by a host of strapping fellows standing with their dirty boots on the seats of the benches. The little Frenchman who thus found a temporary shelter from the missive compliments of his gallery friends, was the only person benefited. At last the bell again rung, and the cry of down, down—hats off, was the signal for the commencement of the play.

If, Mr. Editor, the garrulity of an old fellow is not tiresome, and you chuse to give this *view of a New-York theatre*, a place in your paper, you may, perhaps, hear further from your friend,

JONATHAN OLDSTYLE.

Letter V

Printed in *The Morning Chronicle*, December 11, 1802.

[We have to apologize to our friend *Old Style* for the omission of his communication these two or three days back. We shall in future be more punctual.]

Mr. Editor,

I shall now conclude my remarks on the theatre, which I am afraid you will think are spun out to an unreasonable length; for this I can give no other excuse, than that it is the privilege of old folks to be tiresome, and so I shall proceed.

I had chosen a seat in the pit, as least subject to annoyance from a habit of talking loud that has lately crept into our theatres, and which particularly prevails in the boxes. In old times people went to the theatre for the sake of the play and acting; but I now find it begins to answer the purpose of a coffee-house, or fashionable lounge, where many indulge in loud conversation, without any regard to the pain it inflicts on their more attentive neighbors. As this conversation is generally of the most trifling kind, it seldom repays the latter for the inconvenience they suffer, of not hearing one half of the play.

I found, however, that I had not much bettered my situation; but that every part of the house has its share of evils. Besides those I had already suffered, I was yet to undergo a new kind of torment. I had got in the neighborhood of a very obliging personage, who had seen the play before, and was kindly anticipating every scene, and informing those about him what was to take place; to prevent, I suppose, any *disagreeable* surprise to which they would otherwise have been liable. Had there been any thing of a plot to the play, this might have been a serious inconvenience; but as the piece was entirely *innocent* of every thing of the kind, it was not of so much importance. As I generally contrive to extract amusement from every incident that happens, I now entertained myself with remarks on the self-important air with which he delivered his information, and the distressed and impatient

19

looks of his unwilling auditors. I also observed that he made several mistakes in the course of his communications: "Now you'll see," *said he*, "the queen, in all her glory, surrounded with her courtiers, fine as fiddles, and ranged on each side of the stage, like rows of pewter dishes." On the contrary, we were presented with the portly gentleman and his *ragged regiment* of banditti. Another time he promised us a regale from the fool; but we were presented with a *very fine speech* from the queen's *grinning counsellor*.

My country neighbor was exceedingly delighted with the performance, though he did not half the time understand what was going forward. He sat staring with open mouth at the portly gentleman, as he strode across the stage, and in furious rage drew his sword on the *white lion*. "By George but that's a brave fellow," said he when the act was over, "that's what you call first rate acting, I suppose."

Yes, said I, it is what the critics of the present day admire, but it is not altogether what I like; you should have seen an actor of the *old school* do this part; he would have given it to some purpose; you'd have had such ranting and roaring, and stamping and storming; to be sure this honest man gives us a *bounce* now and then in the true old style, but in the main he seems to prefer walking on plain ground to strutting on the *stilts* used by the tragic heroes of my day.

This is the chief of what passed between me and my companion during the play and entertainment, except an observation of his, that it would be well if the manager was to *drill* his nobility and gentry now and then, to enable them to go through their evolution with more grace and spirit. This put me in mind of something my cousin Jack said to the same purpose, though he went too far in his zeal for reformation. He declared, "he wished sincerely, one of the critics of the day would take all the *slab shabs* of the theatre in a body (like *cats in a bag*) and *twig* the whole bunch." I can't say but I like Jack's idea well enough, though it is rather a severe one.

He might have remarked another fault that prevails among our performers (though I don't know whether it occurred this evening) of dressing for the same piece in the fashions of different ages and countries, so that while one actor is strutting about the stage in the cuirass and helmet of Alexander, another dressed up in a gold-laced coat and a bag-wig, with a chapeau de bras under his arm, is taking snuff in the fashion of one or two centuries back, and perhaps a third figuring with Suwarrow boots, in the true style of modern buckism.

But what, pray, has become of the noble marquis of Montague, and earl of Warwick? (said the countryman, after the entertainments were concluded). Their names make a great appearance on the bill, but I do not recollect having seen them in the course of the evening.

Very true—I had quite forgot those worthy personages, but I suspect they have been behind the scene, smoking a pipe with our other friends, *incog*. the Tripolitans. We must not be particular now-a-days, my friend. When we are presented with a Battle of Hexham *without fighting*, and a Tripolitan after-piece without even a *Mahometan whisker*, we need not be surprised at having an *invisible* marquis or two thrown into the bargain.

"But what is your opinion of the house," said I, "don't you think it a very substantial, *solid-looking* building, both inside and out? Observe what a fine effect the dark colouring of the wall has upon the white faces of the audience, which glare like the stars in a dark night. And then what can be more pretty than the paintings on the front of the boxes; those little masters and misses sucking their thumbs and making mouths at the audience?"

Very fine, upon my word—and what, pray, is the use of that chandelier, as you call it, that is hung up among the clouds, and has showered down its favors on my coat?

Oh, that is to illumine the heavens and to set off, to advantage, the little perriwig'd cupids, tumbling head over heels, with which the painter has decorated the *dome*. You see we have no need of the chandelier below, as here, the house is *perfectly well* illuminated: but I think it would have been a great saving of candle-light, if the manager had ordered the painter, among his other pretty designs, to paint a moon up there, or if he was to hang up that sun with whose *intense light* our eyes were greatly annoyed in the beginning of the after-piece.

But don't you think, after all, there is rather a—sort of a—

kind of a *heavyishness* about the house; don't you think it has a little of an *under groundish* appearance.

To this I could make no answer. I must confess I have often thought myself the house had a *dungeon-like* look; so I proposed to him to make our exit, as the candles were putting out, and we should be left in the dark. Accordingly, groping our way through the dismal *subterraneous* passage that leads from the pit, and passing through the ragged bridewell looking anti-chamber, we once more emerged into the purer air of the park, when bidding my honest countryman good night, I repaired home considerably pleased with the amusements of the evening.

Thus, Mr. Editor, have I given you an account of the chief incidents that occurred in my visit to the theatre. I have shewn you a few of its accommodations and its imperfections. Those who visit it more frequently may be able to give you a better statement.

I shall conclude with a few words of advice for the benefit of every department of it.

I would recommend,

To the actors—less etiquette—less fustian—less buckram.

To the orchestra—new music and more of it.

To the pit—patience—clean benches and umbrellas.

To the boxes—less affectation—less noise—less coxcombs.

To the gallery—less grog and better constables—and,

To the whole house—inside and out, a total reformation.—And so much for the theatre.

JONATHAN OLDSTYLE.

Letter VI

Printed in *The Morning Chronicle*, January 17, 1803.

[The following communication from our correspondent, OLD-STYLE, and his friend, will, we hope, induce a number to attend the *benefit* performance this evening, and see the diverting farce alluded to in the latter part of Mr. Quoz's letter.]

TO THE EDITOR OF THE MORNING CHRONICLE

Sir,

As I was sitting quietly by my fire side the other morning, nursing my wounded shin, and reading to my cousin, Jack Stylish, a chapter or two from Chesterfield's Letters, I received the following epistle from my friend Andrew Quoz: who, hearing that I talked of paying the actors a visit, and shaking my cane over their heads, has written the following letter, part of which is strongly in their defence.

To JONATHAN OLDSTYLE, Gent.

My Dear Friend,

I perceive by the late papers you have been entertaining the town with remarks on the theatre. As you do not seem from your writings to be much of an adept in the Thespian arcana, permit me to give you a few hints for your information.

The theatre, you observe, begins to answer all the purposes of a coffee-house. Here you are right: it is the polite lounge, where the idle and curious resort, to pick up the news of the fashionable world; to meet their acquaintances, and to shew themselves off to advantage. As to the dull souls who go for the sake of the play, why if their attention is interrupted by the conversation of their neighbors, they must bear it with patience—it is a custom authorized by fashion. Persons who go for the purpose of chatting with their friends are not to be deprived of their amusement: *they have paid their dollar*, and have a right to entertain themselves as well as they can.

23

As to those who are annoyed by their talking, why they need not listen to it— *let them mind their own business.*

You were surprized at so many persons using opera glasses; & wished to know whether they were all near sighted. Your cousin, Jack Stylish, has not explained that matter sufficiently—for though many *mount* glasses because it is *the go*, yet I am told that several do it to enable them to distinguish the countenances of their friends across our scantily illumined theatre. I was considerably amused the other evening with an honest tar who had stationed himself in front of the gallery, with an air of affected foppishness, & was reconnoitering the house thro' a pocket telescope. I could not but like his notion, for really the gods are so elevated among the clouds, that unless they are unusually strong of vision, I can't tell how they manage to discern with the naked eye what is passing in the little painted world below them.

I think you complain of the deficiency of the music; and say that we want a greater variety and more of it. But you must know that, though this might have been a grievance in old times, when people attended to the musicians, it is a thing of but little moment at present.—Our orchestra is kept principally for form sake. There is such a continual noise and bustle between the acts that it is difficult to hear a note; and if the musicians were to get up a new piece of the finest melody, so nicely tuned are the ears of their auditors, that I doubt whether nine hearers out of ten would not complain, on leaving the house, that they had been *bored* with the same old pieces they have heard these two or three years back. Indeed, many who go to the theatre carry their own music with them; and we are so often delighted with the crying of children by way of glee, and such coughing and sneezing from various parts of the house, by way of chorus—not to mention the regale of a sweet symphony from a sweep or two in the gallery—and occasionally a full piece, in which nasal, vocal, *whistling and thumping* powers are admirably exerted and blended, that what want we of an orchestra?

In your remarks on the actors, my dear friend let me beg of you to be cautious. I would not for the world that you should *degenerate* into a critic. The critics, my dear Jonathan, are the very pests of society: they rob the actor of his repu-

tation; the public of their amusement: they open the eyes of
their readers to a full perception of the faults of our performers, they reduce our feelings to a state of miserable refinement, and destroy entirely all the enjoyments in which our
coarser sensations delighted. I can remember the time when I
could hardly keep my seat thro' laughing at the wretched buffoonery, the merry-andrew tricks, and the unnatural grimaces
played off by one of our theatric Jack Puddings: when I was
struck with awful admiration at the roaring and ranting of a
buskined hero; and hung with rapture on every word, while
he was "tearing a passion to tatters—to very rags!" I remember the time when he who could make the queerest mouth,
roll his eyes, and twist his body with the most hideous distortions, was surest to please. Alas! how changed the times,
or rather how changed the tastes. I can now sit with the gravest countenance and look without a smile on all such *mimicry*:
their skipping, their squinting, their shrugging, their snuffling, delight not me; and as to their ranting and roaring,

> "I'd rather hear a brazen candlestick turned,
> "Or a dry wheel grate on the axle tree,"

than any such fustian efforts to obtain a shallow gallery applause.

Now though I confess these critics have reformed the manners of the actors as well as the tastes of the audience; so that
these absurdities are almost banished from the New-York
stage; yet do I think they have employed a most unwarrantable liberty.

A critic, my dear sir, has no more right to expose the faults
of an actor, than he has to detect the deceptions of a juggler,
or the impositions of a quack. All trades must live; and, as
long as the public are satisfied to admire the tricks of the
juggler, to swallow the drugs of the quack, or to applaud the
fustian of the actor, whoever attempts to undeceive them,
does but curtail the pleasures of the latter, and deprive the
former of their bread.

Ods-bud, hath not an actor eyes and shall he not *wink*?—
hath not an actor teeth and shall he not grin?—feet and shall
he not stamp?—lungs and shall he not roar?—breast and
shall he not slap it?—hair and shall he not *club* it? Is he not

fed with plaudits from the gods? delighted with thumpings from the groundlings? annoyed by hisses from the boxes?

If you censure his follies, does he not complain? If you take away his bread will he not starve? If you starve him will he not die? And if you kill him will not his wife and seven small infants, six at her back and one at her breast, rise up and cry vengeance against you? Ponder these things seriously my friend Oldstyle, and you will agree with me that, as the actor is the most meritorious and faultless, so is the critic the most cruel and sanguinary character in the world. "As I will shew you more fully in my next." Your loving friend,

ANDREW QUOZ.

From the tenor and conclusion of these remarks of my friend Mr. Andrew Quoz, they may not improperly be called the "Rights of Actors;" his arguments are, I confess, very forcible, but, as they are entirely *new* to me, I shall not hastily make up my mind. In the mean time, as my leg is much better, I believe I shall hobble to the theatre on Monday evening, borrow a seat in a side-box, and observe how the actors conduct themselves.

JONATHAN OLDSTYLE.

Letter VII

Printed in *The Morning Chronicle*, January 22, 1803.

Sir,

I mentioned in my last my intention of visiting the theatre on Monday night. I accordingly reached there with the assistance of Jack Stylish, who procured me in one of the boxes an uncomfortable and dirty seat, which, however, I found as good as any of my neighbors. In the pit I was determined never again to venture. The little Frenchman mentioned in my former remarks had adopted the same resolution; for on casting my eyes around the theatre, I recognized his sharp phiz and pinched up cocked hat, peering over the ledge of the Shakspeare. The poor little fellow had not changed his place for the better; a brawny Irishman was leaning with arms akimbo on his shoulders, and coolly surveying the audience, unmindful of the writhings and expostulations of the irritated little Gaul, whose chin was pressed hard upon the front of the box, and his small black eyes twinkling with fury and suffocation. How he disengaged himself I don't know, for my attention was just then called away by a different object, and on turning round some time afterwards, little Monsieur had disappeared.

I found every thing wore its old appearance. The same *silence*, *order* and *regularity* prevailed as on my former visit. The central chandelier hung unmolested in the heaven, setting off to advantage the picture of Mr. Anybody, with which it is adorned, and shedding a melancholy ray into that den in which (if we may judge from the sounds that issue thence) so many troubled spirits are confined.

I had marched into the theatre through rows of tables heaped up with delicacies of every kind—here a pyramid of apples or oranges invited the playful palate of the dainty; while there a regiment of mince pies and custards promised a more substantial regale to the hungry. I entered the box, and looked round with astonishment—not a grinder but had its employment. The crackling of nuts and the craunching of apples saluted my ears on every side. Surely, thought I, never was an employment followed up with more assiduity than that of gormandizing; already it pervades every public place of amusement; nay, it even begins to steal into our churches, where many a mouthful is munched in private; and few have any more objection to eat than laugh in *their sleeves*.

The eating mania prevails through every class of society; not a soul but has caught the infection. Eating clubs are established in every street and alley, and it is impossible to turn a corner without hearing the hissing of frying pans, winding the savory steams of roast and boiled, or seeing some hungry genius bolting raw oysters in the middle of the street. I expect we shall shortly carry our knives and forks, like the Chinese do their chop sticks, in our pockets.

I was interrupted in my meditations by Jack Stylish, who proposed that we might take a peep into the *lounging room*, the dashing appearance of which Jack described in high terms; I willingly agreed to his proposal.

The room perfectly answered my expectations, and was a piece with the rest of the theatre: the high finish of the walls, the windows fancifully decorated with red baize and painted canvass, and the *sumptuous* wooden benches placed around it had a most inviting appearance.

I drew the end of one of them near to an elegant stove that stood in the centre of the room, and seating myself on it, stretched my lame leg over a chair; placing my hands on the head of my cane, and resting my chin upon them, I began to amuse myself by reconnoitering the company, and snuffing up the delightful perfume of French brandy, Holland gin, and Spanish segars.

I found myself in a circle of young gentry, who appeared to have something in agitation by their winking and nodding: at the same time I heard a confused whispering around me, and could distinguish the words smoke his wig—twig his silver buckles—old quiz—cane—cock'd hat—queer phiz—and a variety of others, by which I soon found I was in bad quarters. Jack Stylish seemed equally uneasy as myself, for though he is fond of fun himself, yet I believe the young dog has too much love for his old relation, to make him the object of his mirth. To get me away, he told me my friend Quoz was at the lower end of the room, and seemed by his looks anx-

ious to speak with me, we accordingly joined him, and finding that the curtain was about rising, we adjourned to the
box together.

In our way I exclaimed against the indecorous manner of
the young men of the present day; the impertinent remarks
on the company in which they continually indulge; and the
cant phrases with which their shallow conversation is generally interlarded. Jack observed that I had popp'd among a set
of *hard boys*; yes, master Stylish said I, turning round to him
abruptly, and I observed by your winks and grins that you are
better acquainted with them than I could wish. Let me tell
you honest friend, if ever I catch you indulging in such despicable fopperies, and hankering after the company of these
disrespectful youngsters, be assured that I will discard you
from my affections entirely. By this time we had reached our
box: so I left my cousin Jack to digest what I had just said;
and I hope it may have weight with him; though I fear, from
the thoughtless gaiety of his disposition, and his knowledge
of the strong hold he has in my foolish old heart, my menaces
will make but little impression.

We found the play already commenced. I was particularly
delighted with the appearance and manners of one of the female performers. What ease, what grace, what elegance of deportment—this is not acting, cousin Jack, said I—this is
reality.

After the play, this lady again came forward and delivered
a ludicrous epilogue. I was extremely sorry to find her step so
far out of that graceful line of character in which she is calculated to shine; and I perceived by the countenances around
me that the sentiment was universal.

Ah, said I, how much she forgets what is due to her dignity. That charming countenance was never made to be so
unworthily distorted: nor that graceful person and carriage to
represent the awkward movements of hobbling decrepitude—
take this word of advice fair lady, from an old man and a
friend: Never, if you wish to retain that character for elegance
you so deservedly possess—never degrade yourself by assuming the part of a mimic.

The curtain rose for the after-piece. Out skipped a *jolly
Merry Andrew*. Aha! said I, here is the *Jack-pudding*. I see he

has forgot his broomstick and grid-iron; he'll compensate for these wants, I suppose, by his wit and humor. But where is his master, the Quack? He'll be here presently, said Jack Stylish; he's a queer old codger; his name's Puffaway: here's to be a rare roasting match, and this quizical looking fellow turns the spit. The Merry Andrew now began to deal out his speeches with great rapidity; but, on a sudden, pulling off a black hood that covered his face, who should I recognize but my old acquaintance, the *portly gentleman*.

I started back with astonishment. *Sic transit gloria mundi!* exclaimed I, with a melancholy shake of the head. Here is a *dreary*, but true picture of the vicissitudes of life—one night paraded in regal robes, surrounded with a *splendid train* of nobility; the next, degraded to a poor *Jack-pudding*, and without even a *grid-iron* to help himself. What think you of this, my friend *Quoz*? said I; think you an actor has any right to sport with the *feelings* of his audience, by presenting them with such *distressing* contrasts. Honest Quoz, who is of the melting mood, shook his head ruefully, and said nothing. I, however, saw the tear of *sympathy* tremble in his eye, and honored him for his *sensibility*.

The *Merry Andrew* went on with his part, and my pity encreased as he progressed; when all of a sudden he exclaimed, "And as to *Oldstyle*, I wish him to old nick." My blood mounted into my cheeks at this insolent mention of my name. And what think you of *this*, friend Quoz? exclaimed I, vehemently, I presume this is one of your "rights of actors." I suppose we are now to have the stage a vehicle for lampoons and slanders; on which, our fellow citizens are to be caricatured by the clumsy hand of every dauber who can hold a brush!

Let me tell you, Mr. Andrew Quoz, I have known the time when such insolence would have been hooted from the stage.

After some persuasion I resumed my seat, and attempted to listen patiently to the rest of the afterpiece; but I was so disgusted with the Merry Andrew, that in spite of all his skipping, and jumping, and turning on his heel, I could not yield him a smile.

Among the other *original* characters of the dramatis personæ, we were presented with an ancient maiden; and entertained with jests and remarks from the buffoon and his associates, containing equal *wit* and *novelty*. But jesting apart, I think these attempts to injure female happiness, at once cruel and unmanly. I have ever been an enthusiast in my attachment to the fair sex. I have ever thought them possessed of the strongest claims on our admiration, our tenderness and our protection. But when to these are added still stronger claims—when we see them aged and infirm, solitary and neglected, without a partner to support them down the descent of life—cold indeed must be that heart, and unmanly that spirit, that can point the shafts of ridicule at their defenceless bosoms—that can poison the few drops of comfort heaven has poured into their cup.

The form of my sister Dorothy presented itself to my imagination; her hair silvered by time; but her face unwrinkled by sorrow or care.

She "hath borne her faculties so meekly," that age has marked no traces on her forehead: amiable sister of my heart! cried I, who hast jogged with me through so many years of existence, is this to be the recompense of all thy virtues; art thou who never, in thought or deed, injured the feelings of another, to have thy own massacred, by the jeering insults of those to whom thou shouldst look for honor and protection?

Away with such despicable trumpery—such shallow, worn-out attempts to obtain applause from the unfeeling. I'll no more of it; come along friend Quoz, if we stay much longer, I suppose we shall find our courts of justice insulted, and attempts to ridicule the characters of private persons. Jack Stylish entreated me to stay and see the addition the manager had made to his live stock, of an ass, a goose, and a monkey. Not I, said I, I'll see no more. I accordingly hobbled off with my friend Mr. Andrew Quoz, Jack declaring he would stay behind and see the end of the joke. On our way home, I asked friend Quoz, how he could justify such clumsy attempts at personal satire. He seemed, however, rather reserved in his answers, and informed me he would write his sentiments on the subject.

The next morning Jack Stylish related to me the conclusion of the piece. How several actors went into a wheel one after another, and after a little grinding, were converted into asses, geese and monkies, except the *Merry Andrew*, who was found such a *tough jockey*, that the wheel could not digest him, so he came out as much a Jack-pudding as ever.

JONATHAN OLDSTYLE.

Letter VIII

Printed in *The Morning Chronicle*, February 8, 1803.

[The following communication was received sometime since, but accidently mislaid.]

TO THE EDITOR OF THE MORNING CHRONICLE.

Sir,

I had just put on my spectacles and mended my pen, to give you an account of a visit I made some time since, with friend Quoz and my sister Dorothy, to a ball, when I was interrupted by the following letter from the former.

My friend Quoz, who is what the world calls a *knowing man*, is extremely fond of giving his opinion in every affair. He displays in this epistle more than usual knowledge of his subject, and seems to exert all his argumentative talents to enforce the importance of his advice. I give you his letter without further comment, and shall postpone my description of the ball to another opportunity.

To JONATHAN OLDSTYLE, Gent.

My Dear Friend,

I once more address you on a subject that I fear will be found irksome, and may chafe that testy disposition (forgive my freedom) with which you are afflicted. Exert, however, the good humor of which at bottom I know you to have a plentiful stock, and hear me patiently through: It is the anxious fear I entertain of your sinking into the gloomy abyss of criticism, on the brink of which you are at present tottering, that urges me to write.

I would set before you the rights and wrongs of an *actor*, and by painting, in strong colors, the peculiarity of his situation, call your good sense into action.

The world, my friend Oldstyle, has ever been prone to consider the theatrical profession in a degraded point of view. What first gave rise to this opinion, I am at a loss to conceive;

but I consider it as the reliques of one of those ancient prejudices which the good sense of the world is daily discarding;
and I flatter myself it will in a little time be totally exploded.
Why the actor should be considered inferior in point of respectability to the poet, the painter, or any other person who
exerts his talents in delineating character, or in exhibiting the
various operations of the human mind, I cannot imagine. I
know you, friend Oldstyle, to be a man of too liberal sentiments not to be superior to these little prejudices, and also
one who regards an actor, provided his private character be
good, with equal respect as the member of any other profession. Yet you are not quite aware of the important privileges
solely attached to the dramatic performer. These I will endeavor to point out.

The works of a poet or painter you may freely criticise—
nay, they offer them for that purpose—they listen attentively
to your observations, and profit by your censures. But beware
how you exercise such conduct towards an actor—he needs
no instruction—his own *impartial* judgment is sufficient to
detect and amend all his imperfections. Attempt to correct his
errors and you ruin him at once—he'll *starve* to spite you—
he is like a decayed substance, that crumbles at the touch.

No, sir—when an actor is on the stage he is in his own
house—it is his castle—he then has you in his power—he
may there *bore* you with his buffoonery, or insult you with
his pointed remarks, with perfect impunity. You, my friend,
who are rather apt to be dissatisfied, may call it hard treatment to be thus annoyed, and yet compensate the annoyer for
his trouble. You may say, that as you pay an equivalent for
your amusement, you should have the liberty of directing the
actor in his attempts; and, as the Chinese does his ear-tickler,
tell him when his instrument offends, and how he over-does
himself in the operation. This is an egregious mistake: you
are obliged to him for his *condescension* in exerting his talents
for your instruction; and as to your money, why he only takes
it to lessen *in part* the weight of your obligation.

An actor is, as I before observed, competent to judge of his
own abilities—he may undertake whatever character he
pleases—tragedy—comedy—or   pantomime—however   ill
adapted his audience may think him to sustain it. He may

rant and roar, and wink and grin, and fret and fume his hour
upon the stage, and "who shall say him nay?" He is paid by
the manager for using his lungs and limbs, and the more he
exerts them the better does he fulfil the engagement, and the
harder does he *work* for his living—and who shall deprive
him of his "*hard-earned* bread?"

How many an honest, lazy genius has been flogged by
these unfeeling critics into a cultivation of his talents and attention to his profession!—how have they doomed him to
hard study and unremitting exertion!—how have they prejudiced the public mind, so that what might once have put an
audience in convulsions of laughter, now excites nothing but
a slight pattering from the hands of the little shavers who are
rewarded with seats in the gallery for their trouble in keeping
the boxes. Oh! Mr. Oldstyle, it cuts me to the soul to see a
poor actor stamp and storm, and slap his forehead, his breast,
his pocket-holes, all in vain: to see him throw himself into
some attitude of distraction or despair, and there wait in fruitless expectation the applauses of his friends in the gallery. In
such cases I always take care and clap him myself, to enable
him to quit his posture, and resume his part with credit.

You was much irritated the other evening, at what you
termed an ungenerous and unmanly attempt to bring forward
an ancient maiden in a ridiculous point of view. But I don't
see why that should be made a matter of complaint. Has it
not been done time out of mind? Is it not sanctioned by daily
custom in private life? Is not the character of aunt Tabitha, in
the farce, the same we have laughed at in hundreds of dramatic pieces? Since, then, the author has but travelled in the
same *beaten track* of character so many have trod before him,
I see not why he should be blamed as severely as if he had all
the *guilt of originality* upon his shoulders.

You may say that it is cruel to sport with the feelings of
any class of society: that *folly* affords sufficient field for wit
and satire to work upon, without resorting to misfortune for
matter of ridicule: that female sensibility should ever be sacred from the lash of sarcasm, &c. &c. But this is all stuff, all
cant.

If an author is too indolent or too stupid, to seek new
sources for remark, he is surely excuseable in employing the

ideas of others, for his own use and benefit. But I find I have digressed, imperceptibly, into the "rights of *authors*," so let us return to our subject.

An actor when he "holds the mirror up to nature," may by his manœuvres, twist and turn it so, as to represent the object in any shape he pleases—nay, even give a caricature where the author intended a resemblance; he may blur it with his breath, or soil it with his dirty fingers, so that the object may have a colouring from the glass in which it is viewed, entirely different from its natural appearance. To be plain, my friend, an actor has a right whenever he thinks his author not sufficiently explicit to assist him by his own *wit* and *abilities*; and if by these means the character should become quite different from what was originally intended, and in fact belong more to the *actor* than the *author*, the actor deserves high credit for his ingenuity. And even tho' his additions are *quaint*, and fulsome, yet his *intention* is highly praise worthy, and deserves ample encouragement.

Only think, my dear sir, how many snug little domestic arrangements are destroyed by the officious interference of these ever dissatisfied critics. The honest *king of Scotland*, who used to dress for market and theatre at the same time, and wear with his kelt and plaid his half boots and black breeches, looking half king, half cobler, has been obliged totally to dismiss the former from his royal service; yet I am happy to find, so obstinate is his attachment to *old habits*, that all their efforts have not been sufficient to dislodge him from the strong hold he has in the latter. They may force him from the boots—but nothing shall drive him out of the breeches.

Consider, my friend, the puerile nature of such remarks. Is it not derogating from the elevated character of a Critic, to take notice of clubb'd wigs, red coats, black breeches and half boots! Fie, fie upon it! I blush for the Critics of the day, who consider it a matter of importance whether a Highlander should appear in breeches and boots, or a Otaheitan in the dress of a New-York coxcomb. Trust me, friend Oldstyle, it is to the *manner*, not the *appearance* of an actor, we are to look: and as long as he performs his part well (to use the words of my friend Sterne), "it shall not be enquired whether he did it in a black coat or a red."

Believe me, friend Oldstyle, few of our modern critics can shew any substantial claim to the character they assume. Let me ask them one question—have they ever been in Europe? Have they ever seen a Garrick, a Kemble or a Siddons? If they have not, I can assure you (upon the words of two or three of my friends, *the actors*) they have no right to the title of critics.

They may talk as much as they please about judgment and taste, and feeling, but that is all nonsense. It has lately been determined (*at the theatre*) that any one who attempts to decide upon such ridiculous principles, is an arrant *goose*, and deserves to be *roasted*.

Having thus, friend Oldstyle, endeavored, in a feeble manner, to shew you a few of the rights of an actor, and of his wrongs; having mentioned his constant and *disinterested* endeavors to please the public; and how much better he knows what will please them than they do themselves; having also depicted the cruel and persecuting nature of a critic; the continual restraint he lays on the harmless irregularity of the performer, and the relentless manner in which he obliges him to attend sedulously to his professional duty, through fear of censure, let me entreat you to pause!—Open your eyes to the precipice on which you are tottering, and hearken to the earnest warnings of your loving friend,

ANDREW QUOZ.

My friend Quoz certainly writes with *feeling*: every line evinces that *acute sensibility* for which he has ever been remarked.

I am, however, perfectly at a loss to conceive on what grounds he suspects me of a disposition to turn Critic. My remarks hitherto have rather been the result of immediate impression than of critical examination. With my friend, Mr. Andrew Quoz, I begin to doubt the motives of our New-York Critics; especially since I have, in addition to these arguments, the assurances of two or three doubtless *disinterested* actors, and an editor, who Mr. Quoz tells me is remarkable for his *candor* and *veracity*, that the Critics are the most 'presumptuous,' 'arrogant,' 'malevolent,' 'illiberal,' 'ungentleman-like,' 'malignant,' 'rancorous,' 'villainous,' 'ungrateful,' 'crippled,' 'invidious,' 'detracting,' 'fabricating,' 'personal,' 'dogmatical,' 'illegitimate,' 'tyrannical,' 'distorting,' 'spindle-shanked moppets, designing villains, and upstart ignorants.'

These, I say, and many other equally *high polished* appellations, have awakened doubts in my mind respecting the sincerity and justice of the Critics; and lest my pen should unwittingly draw upon me the suspicion, of having a hankering after criticism, I now wipe it carefully—lock it safely up, and promise not to draw it forth again, till some new department of folly calls for my attention.

JONATHAN OLDSTYLE.

Letter IX

Printed in *The Morning Chronicle*, April 23, 1803.

Sir,

I was calmly enjoying my toast and coffee some mornings ago, with my sister Dorothy and Jack Stylish, when we were surprized by the abrupt entrance of my friend, Mr. Andrew Quoz. By the particular expression of his *knowing phiz*, as cousin Jack calls it, I immediately perceived he was labouring with some important intelligence.

In one hand he held the Morning Chronicle, and with the fore-finger of the other pointed to a particular paragraph. I hastily put on my spectacles, and seized the paper with eager curiosity. Judge my surprize, Mr. Editor, on reading an act of our legislature, pronouncing any citizen of this state who shall send, bear, or accept a challenge, either verbal or written, disqualified from holding any office of honor or confidence, or of voting at any election within this state, &c. &c.

The paper fell from my hands—I turned my eyes to friend Andrew in mute astonishment. Quoz put his finger to his nose, and winking significantly, cried, "What do you think of this, my friend Jonathan?"

"Here is a catastrophe," exclaimed I, in a melancholy tone. "Here is a damper for the mettlesome youths of the age. Spirit of chivalry, whither hast thou flown! Shade of Don Quixote, dost thou not look down with contempt on the degeneracy of the times!"

My sister Dorothy caught a sympathetic spark of enthusiasm—deep read in all the volumes of ancient romance, and delighted with their glowing descriptions of the heroic age, she had learned to admire the gallantry of former days, and mourned to see the last spark of chivalric fire thus rudely extinguished.

Alas! my brother, said she, to what a deplorable state are our young men reduced! how piteous must be their situation—with sensibilities so *easily injured*, and bosoms so *tremblingly alive* to the calls of honor and etiquette!

Indeed, my dear Dorothy, said I, I feel most deeply for

their melancholy situation. Deprived in these dull, monotonous, peaceable times, of all opportunities of evincing, in the
hardy contest of the tented field, that heroic flame that burns
within their breasts, they were happy to vent the lofty fum-
ings of their souls in the more domestic and *less dangerous*
encounters of the duel—like the warrior in the fable, who,
deprived of the pleasure of slaughtering armies, contented
himself with cutting down cabbages.

Here a solemn pause ensued. I called to mind all the tales
I had heard or read of ancient knights; their amours, their
quarrels, and their combats; how, on a fair summer's morning, the knight of the Golden Goose met the knight of the
Fiery Fiddle; how the knight of the Fiery Fiddle exclaimed
in lofty tones, "whoever denies that Donna Fiddleosa is the
most peerless beauty in the universe, must brave the strength
of this arm!" how they both engaged with dreadful fury;
and, after fighting till sunset, the knight of the Fiery Fiddle
fell a martyr to his constancy; murmuring in melodious accents, with his latest breath, the beloved name of
Fiddleosa.

From these ancient engagements, I descended to others
more modern in their dates, but equally important in their
origins. I recalled the genuine politeness and polished ceremony with which duels were conducted in my youthful days,
when that gentlemanly weapon, the *small sword*, was in highest vogue. A challenge was worded with the most particular
complaisance; and one that I have still in my possession, ends
with the words, "*your friend and affectionate servant Nicholas
Stubbs*." When the parties met on the field, the same decorum
was observed; they pulled off their hats, wished one another
a good day, and helped to draw off each other's coats and
boots, with the most respectful civility. Their fighting too was
so handsomely conducted: no aukward movements; no eager
and angry pushes; all cool, elegant and graceful. Every thrust
had its *sa-sa*; and a *ha-hah* lunged you gently through the
body. Then nothing could equal the tenderness and attention
with which a wounded antagonist was treated: his adversary,
after wiping his sword deliberately, kindly supported him in
his arms, examined his pulse, and enquired, with the most
affectionate solicitude, "how he felt himself now?"—Thus

every thing was conducted in a well-bred, gentlemanly manner.

Our present customs I can't say I much admire—a *twelve inch barrell pistol* and *ounce ball*, are blunt, unceremonious affairs, and prevent that display of grace and elegance allowed by the small sword; besides, there is something so awkward in having the muzzle of a pistol staring one full in the face, that I should think it might be apt to make some of our youthful heroes feel rather disagreeable, unless, as I am told has been sometimes the case, the duel was fought by twilight.

The ceremony of loading, priming, cocking, &c. has not the most soothing effects on a person's feelings; and I am told that some of our warriors have been known to tremble and make wry faces during these preparations—though this has been attributed, and doubtless with much justice, to the violence of their wrath and fierceness of their courage.

I had thus been musing for some time, when I broke silence at last by hinting to friend Quoz some of my objections to the mode of fighting with pistols.

Truly, my friend Oldstyle, said Quoz, I am surprised at your ignorance of modern customs: trust me, I know of no amusement that is, generally speaking, more harmless. To be sure, there may now and then a couple of determined fellows take the field who resolve to do the thing in good earnest; but in general our fashionable duellists are content with only one discharge; and then, either they are poor shots, or their triggers pull hard, or they shut the wrong eye, or some other cause intervenes, so that it is ten, aye, twenty chances to one in their favour.

Here I begged leave to differ from friend Andrew. I am well convinced, said I, of the valour of our young men, and that they determine, when they march forth to the field, either to conquer or die; but it generally happens that their seconds are of a more peaceable mind, and interpose after the first shot; but I am informed that they come often very near being killed, having bullet holes through their hats and coats, which, like Falstaff's hack'd sword, are strong proofs of the serious nature of their encounters.

My sister Dorothy, who is of a humane and benevolent disposition, would no doubt detest the idea of duels, did she not regard them as the last gleams of those days of chivalry, to which she looks back with a degree of romantic enthusiasm. She now considered them as having received their death-blow; for how can even the challenges be conveyed, said she, when the very messengers are considered as principals in the offence?

Nothing more easy, said friend Quoz:—a man gives me the lie—very well: I tread on his toes in token of challenge—he pulls my nose by way of acceptance: thus you see the challenge is safely conveyed without a third party.—We then settle the mode in which satisfaction is to be given; as for instance, we draw lots which of us must be slain to satisfy the demands of honor. Mr. A. or Mr. B. my antagonist, is to fall: well, madam, he stands below in the street; I run up to the garret window, and drop a brick upon his head: If he survives well and good; if he falls, why nobody is to blame, it was purely accidental. Thus the affair is settled, according to the common saying, to our mutual satisfaction.

Jack Stylish observed, that as to Mr. Quoz's project of dropping bricks on people's heads, he considered it a vulgar substitute: for his part, he thought that it would be well for the legislature to amend their law respecting duels, and licence them under proper restrictions—That no persons should be allowed to fight without taking out a regular license from what might be called the *Blood and Thunder Office*—That they should be obliged to give two or three weeks notice of the intended combat in the newspapers—That the contending parties should fight till one of them fell—and that the public should be admitted to *the show*.

This he observed, would in some degree, be reviving the *spectacles* of antiquity, when the populace were regaled with the combats of gladiators. We have at present no games resembling those of the ancients; except now and then, a bull or bear bait, and this would be a valuable addition to the list of our refined amusements.

I listened to their discourse in silence: yet I cannot but think, Mr. Editor, that this plan is entitled to some attention. Our young men fight ninety-nine times out of a hundred, through *fear* of being branded with the epithet of *coward*; and since they fight to please the world, the world being thus interested in their encounter, should be permitted to attend and judge in person of their conduct.

As I think the subject of importance, I take the liberty of requesting a corner in the Morning Chronicle, to submit it to the consideration of the public.

JONATHAN OLDSTYLE.

SALMAGUNDI

or
The Whim-Whams and Opinions
of
Launcelot Langstaff, Esq.
& Others

Contents

SALMAGUNDI NO. I

In hoc est hoax, cum quiz et jokesez,
Et smokem, toastem, roastem folkesez,
   Fee, faw, fum.   *Psalmanazar.*

With baked, and broil'd, and stew'd, and toasted,
And fried, and boil'd, and smoak'd, and roasted,
   We treat the town.

Saturday, January 24, 1807.

As EVERY BODY KNOWS, or ought to know, what a Salmagundi is, we shall spare ourselves the trouble of an explanation—besides, we despise trouble as we do every thing that is low and mean, and hold the man who would incur it unnecessarily, as an object worthy our highest pity and contempt. Neither will we puzzle our heads to give an account of ourselves, for two reasons; first, because it is nobody's business; secondly, because if it was, we do not hold ourselves bound to attend to any body's business but our own, and even *that* we take the liberty of neglecting when it suits our inclination. To these we might add a third, that very few men *can* give a tolerable account of themselves, let them try ever so hard; but this reason we candidly avow, would not hold good with ourselves.

There are, however, two or three pieces of information which we bestow gratis on the public, chiefly because it suits our own pleasure and convenience that they should be known, and partly because we do not wish that there should be any ill will between us at the commencement of our acquaintance.

Our intention is simply to instruct the young, reform the old, correct the town and castigate the age; this is an arduous task, and therefore we undertake it with confidence. We intend for this purpose to present a striking picture of the town; and as every body is anxious to see his own phiz on canvas, however stupid or ugly it may be, we have no doubt but that the whole town will flock to our exhibition. Our picture will necessarily include a vast variety of figures, and should any gentleman or lady, be displeased with the invet-

49

erate truth of their likenesses, they may ease their spleen by laughing at those of their neighbors—this being what *we* understand by POETICAL JUSTICE.

Like all true and able editors, we consider ourselves infallible, and therefore with the customary diffidence of our brethren of the quill, we shall take the liberty of interfering in all matters either of a public or private nature. We are critics, amateurs, dillitanti, and cognoscenti; and as we know "by the pricking of our thumbs," that every opinion which we may advance in either of those characters will be correct, we are determined, though it may be questioned, contradicted, or even controverted, yet it shall never be revoked.

We beg the public particularly to understand, that we solicit no patronage. We are determined on the contrary, that the patronage shall be entirely on our side. We have nothing to do with the pecuniary concerns of the paper, its success will yield us neither pride nor profit—nor will its failure occasion to us either loss or mortification. We advise the public therefore, to purchase our numbers merely for their own sakes—if they do not, let them settle the affair with their consciences and posterity.

To conclude, we invite all editors of newspapers and literary journals, to praise us heartily in advance, as we assure them that we intend to deserve their praises. To our next door neighbor "TOWN," we hold out a hand of amity, declaring to him that, after ours, his paper will stand the best chance for immortality. We proffer an exchange of civilities; he shall furnish us with notices of epic poems and tobacco—and we in return will enrich him with original speculations on all manner of subjects: together with "the rummaging of my grandfather's mahogany chest of drawers," "the life and amours of mine uncle John," "anecdotes of the cockloft family," and learned quotations from that unheard of writer of folios, *Linkum Fidelius.*

PUBLISHER'S NOTICE.

This work will be published and sold by D. Longworth. It will be printed on hot-prest vellum paper, as that is held in highest estimation for buckling up young ladies' hair—a purpose to which similar works are usually appropriated: it will be a small neat duodecimo size, so that when enough numbers are written, it may form a volume sufficiently portable to be carried in old ladies' pockets and young ladies' work bags.

As the above work will not come out at stated periods, notice will be given when another number will be published. The price will depend on the size of the number, and must be paid on its delivery. The publisher professes the same sublime contempt for money as his authors. The liberal patronage bestowed by his discerning fellow-citizens on various works of taste which he has published, has left him no *inclination* to ask for further favors at their hands, and he publishes this work in the mere hope of requiting their bounty.

It was not originally the intention of the authors to insert the above address in the work; but, unwilling that a *morceau* so precious should be lost to posterity, they have been induced to alter their minds. This will account for any repetition of idea that may appear in the introductory essay.

FROM THE ELBOW-CHAIR OF
LAUNCELOT LANGSTAFF, ESQ.

We were a considerable time in deciding whether we should be at the pains of introducing ourselves to the public. As we care for nobody, and as we are not yet at the bar, we do not feel bound to hold up our hands and answer to our names.

Willing, however, to gain at once that frank, confidential footing, which we are certain of ultimately possessing in this, doubtless, "best of all possible cities;" and, anxious to spare its worthy inhabitants the trouble of making a thousand *wise* conjectures, not one of which would be worth a "tobacco-stopper;" we have thought it in some degree a necessary exertion of charitable condescension to furnish them with a slight clue to the truth.

Before we proceed further, however, we advise every body, man, woman, and child, that can read, or get any friend to read for them, to purchase this paper:—not that we write for money; for, in common with all philosophical wiseacres, from Solomon downwards, we hold it in supreme contempt. The public are welcome to buy this work, or not, just as they choose. If it be purchased freely, so much the better for the public, and the publisher—we gain not a stiver. If it be not purchased we give fair warning, we shall burn all our essays, critiques, and epigrams, in one promiscuous blaze; and, like the books of the sybils, and the alexandrian library, they will be lost forever to posterity. For the sake, therefore, of our publisher, for the sake of the Public, and for the sake of the Public's children, to the nineteenth generation, we advise them to purchase our paper. We beg the respectable old matrons of this city, not to be alarmed at the appearance we make;—we are none of those outlandish geniuses who swarm in New-York, who live by their wits, or rather by the little wit of their neighbors; and who spoil the genuine honest american tastes of their daughters, with french slops and friccazeed sentiment.

We have said we do not write for money—neither do we write for fame;—we know too well the variable nature of public opinion, to build our hopes upon it—we *care* not what the public think of us, and we suspect before we reach the tenth number, they will not *know* what to think of us. In two words—we write for no other earthly purpose but to please ourselves—and this we shall be sure of doing; for we are all three of us determined beforehand to be pleased with what we write. If, in the course of this work, we edify, and instruct, and amuse the public, so much the better for the public;—but we frankly acknowledge that so soon as we get tired of reading our own works, we shall discontinue them, without the least remorse, whatever the public may think of it.—While we continue to go on, we will go on merrily—if we moralize, it shall be but seldom; and, on all occasions, we shall be more solicitous to make our readers laugh than cry; for we are laughing philosophers, and clearly of opinion, that wisdom, true wisdom, is a plump, jolly dame, who sits in her arm chair, laughs right merrily at the farce of life—and takes the world as it goes.

We intend particularly to notice the conduct of the fashionable world—nor in this shall we be governed by that carping spirit with which narrow-minded book-worm cynics squint at the little extravagancies of the ton; but with that liberal tol-

eration which actuates every man of fashion.—While we keep
a more than Cerberus watch over the guardian rules of female
delicacy and decorum—we shall not discourage any little
sprightliness of demeanor or innocent vivacity of character.
Before we advance one line further, we must let it be understood as our firm opinion, void of all prejudice or partiality,
that the ladies of New-York are the fairest, the finest, the most
accomplished, the most bewitching, the most ineffable
beings, that walk, creep, crawl, swim, fly, float, or vegetate in
any or all of the four elements; and that they only want to be
cured of certain whims, eccentricities, and unseemly conceits,
by our superintending cares, to render them absolutely perfect. They will, therefore, receive a large portion of those attentions directed to the fashionable world;—nor will the
gentlemen, who *doze* away their time in the circles of the
haut-ton, escape our currying. We mean those stupid fellows,
who sit stock-still upon their chairs, without saying a word,
and then complain how damned stupid it was, at miss ———'s
party.

This department will be under the peculiar direction and
control of ANTHONY EVERGREEN, gent. to whom all communications on this subject are to be addressed. This gentleman, by being experienced in the routine of balls, tea-parties,
and assemblies, is eminently qualified for the task he has undertaken. He is a kind of patriarch in the fashionable world,
and has seen generation after generation pass away into the
silent tomb of matrimony, while he remains unchangeably the
same. He can recount the amours and courtships of the fathers, mothers, uncles and aunts, and even grandames, of all
the belles of the present day, provided their pedigrees extend
so far back, without being lost in obscurity. As, however,
treating of pedigrees is rather an ungrateful task, in this city,
and as we mean to be perfectly good-natured, he has promised to be cautious in this particular. He recollects perfectly
the time when young ladies used to go sleigh-riding, at night,
without their mammas, or grand-mammas, in short, without
being matronized at all, and can relate a thousand pleasant
stories about Kissing-bridge. He likewise remembers the time
when ladies paid tea-visits at three in the afternoon, and returned before dark, to see that the house was shut up and the

servants on duty. He has often played cricket in the orchard, in the rear of old Vauxhall, and remembers when the Bull's-head was quite out of town. Though he has slowly and grad-ually given into modern fashions, and still flourishes in the *beaumonde*, yet he seems a little prejudiced in favor of the dress and manners of the *old school*, and his chief commenda-tion of a new mode is, "that is the same good old fashion we had before the war." It has cost us much trouble to make him confess that a cotillion is superior to a minuet, or an un-adorned crop to a pig-tail and powder. Custom and fashion have, however, had more effect on him than all our lectures, and he tempers so happily the grave and ceremonious gal-lantry of the old school with the "hail fellow" familiarity of the new, that we trust, on a little acquaintance, and making allowance for his old-fashioned prejudices, he will become a very considerable favorite with our readers;—if not, the worse for themselves, as they will have to endure his com-pany.

In the territory of criticism, WILLIAM WIZARD, esq. has undertaken to preside, and though we may all dabble in it a little by turns, yet we have willingly ceded to him all discre-tionary powers in this respect. Though Will has not had the advantage of an education at Oxford, or Cambridge, or even at Edinburgh, or Aberdeen, and though he is but little versed in hebrew, yet we have no doubt he will be found fully com-petent to the undertaking. He has improved his taste by a long residence abroad, particularly at Canton, Calcutta, and the gay and polished court of Hayti. He has also had an op-portunity of seeing the best singing girls, and tragedians of China, and is a great connoisseur in mandarine dresses, and porcelaine. He is likewise promised the assistance of a gentle-man, lately from London, who was born and bred in that centre of science and *bon-gout*, the vicinity of Fleet-market, where he has been edified man and boy, these six-and-twenty years, with the harmonious jingle of bow-bells. His taste therefore has attain'd to such an exquisite pitch of refinement, that there are few exhibitions of any kind which do not put him in a fever. He has assured Will, that if mr. COOPER em-phasises "*and*" instead of "*but*"—or mrs. OLDMIXON pins her kerchief a hairs breadth awry—or mrs. DARLEY offers to

dare to look less than the "daughter of a senator of Venice"—
the standard of a senator's daughter being exactly six feet—
they shall all hear of it in good time. We have, however, advised WILL WIZARD, to keep his friend in check, lest by
opening the eyes of the public to the wretchedness of the
actors by whom they have hitherto been entertained, he
might cut off one source of amusement from our fellow-citizens. We hereby give notice that we have taken the whole
corps, from the manager in his mantle of gorgeous copper-
lace, to honest *John*, in his green coat and black breeches,
under our wing, and woe be unto him who injures a hair of
their heads. As we have no design against the patience of our
fellow-citizens, we shall not *dose* them with copious draughts
of theatrical criticism; we well know that they have already
been well physicked with them of late: our theatrics shall take
up but a small part of our paper; nor shall they be altogether
confined to the stage, but extend from time to time, to those
incorrigible offenders against the peace of society, the stage-
critics; who not unfrequently create the fault they find, in order to yield an opening for their witticisms—censure an actor
for a gesture he never made, or an emphasis he never gave;
and, in their attempts to show off *new readings*, make the
sweet swan of Avon cackle like a goose. If any one shall feel
himself offended by our remarks, let him attack us in return—
we shall not wince from the combat. If his passes are successful, we will be the first to cry out a hit! a hit! and we doubt
not we shall frequently lay ourselves open to the weapons of
our assailants. But let them have a care, how they run a tilting
with us—they have to deal with stubborn foes, who can bear
a world of pummeling; we will be relentless in our vengeance,
and will fight "till from our bones the flesh be hackt."

What other subjects we shall include in the range of our
observations, we have not determined, or rather we shall not
trouble ourselves to detail. The public have already more information concerning us than we intended to impart. We owe
them no favors, neither do we ask any. We again advise them
for their own sakes, to read our papers when they come out.
We recommend to all mothers to purchase them for their
daughters, who will be taught the true line of propriety, and
the most adviseable method of managing their beaux. We ad-

vise all daughters to purchase them for the sake of their mothers, who shall be initiated into the arcana of the bon-ton, and cured of all those rusty old notions which they acquired during the last century: parents shall be taught how to govern their children, girls how to get husbands, and old maids how to do without them.

As we do not measure our wits by the yard or the bushel, and as they do not flow periodically nor constantly, we shall not restrict our paper as to size, or the time of its appearance. It will be published whenever we have sufficient matter to constitute a number, and the size of the number shall depend on the stock in hand. This will best suit our negligent habits, and leave us that full liberty and independence which is the joy and pride of our souls. As we have before hinted, that we do not concern ourselves about the pecuniary matters of our paper, we leave its price to be regulated by our publisher; only recommending him for his own interest, and the honor of his authors, not to sell their invaluable productions too cheap.

Is there any one who wishes to know more about us?—let him read SALMAGUNDI, and grow wise apace. Thus much we will say—there are three of us, "Bardolph, Peto, and I; all townsmen good and true"—many a time and oft have we three amused the town, without its knowing to whom it was indebted; and many a time have we seen the midnight lamp twinkle faintly on our studious phizes, and heard the morning salutation of "past three o'clock," before we sought our pillows. The result of these midnight studies is now offered to the public; and little as we care for the opinion of this exceedingly stupid world, we shall take care, as far as lies in our careless natures, to fulfil the promises made in this introduction;—if we do not, we shall have so many examples to justify us, that we feel little solicitude on that account.

Theatrics.
containing the quintessence of modern criticism.
BY WILLIAM WIZARD, ESQ.

MACBETH was performed to a very crowded house, and much to *our* satisfaction. As, however, our neighbor Town has been very voluminous already in his criticisms on this play, we shall make but few remarks. Having never seen KEMBLE in this character, we are absolutely at a loss to say whether MR. COOPER performed it well or not. We think, however, that there was an error in his *costume*, as the learned Linkum Fidelius is of opinion, that in the time of Macbeth the scots did not wear sandals, but wooden shoes. Macbeth also was noted for wearing his jacket open, that he might play the scotch fiddle more conveniently—that being an hereditary accomplishment in the Glamis family.

We have seen this character performed in China, by the celebrated *Chow-Chow*, the Roscius of that great empire, who in the dagger scene always electrified the audience, by blowing his nose like a trumpet. Chow-Chow, in compliance with the opinion of the sage Linkum Fidelius, performed Macbeth in wooden shoes. This gave him an opportunity of producing great effect, for on first seeing the air-drawn dagger, he always cut a prodigious high caper, and kicked his shoes into the pit at the heads of the critics, whereupon the audience were marvelously delighted, flourished their hands, and stroaked their whiskers three times, and the matter was carefully recorded in the next number of a paper called the *flim flam*. (*english*-town)

We were much pleased with MRS. VILLIERS, in lady MACBETH; but we think she would have given greater effect to the night-scene, if, instead of holding the candle in her hand, or setting it down on the table (which is sagaciously censured by neighbor Town) she had stuck it in her night-cap. This would have been extremely picturesque, and would have marked more strongly the derangement of her mind.

Mrs. Villiers, however, is not by any means large enough for the character; lady Macbeth having been, in our opinion, a woman of extraordinary size, and of the race of the giants, notwithstanding what she says of her "little hand," which being said in her sleep, passes for nothing. We should be happy to see this character in the hands of the lady who played *Glumdalca*, queen of the giants, in Tom Thumb; she is exactly of imperial dimensions, and, provided she is well shaved, of a most interesting physiognomy: as she appears likewise to be a lady of some nerve, I dare engage she will read a letter about witches vanishing in air, and such *common occurrences*, without being unnaturally surprised, to the annoyance of honest "Town."

We are happy to observe that Mr. Cooper profits by the instructions of friend Town, and does not dip the daggers in blood so deep as formerly, by a matter of an inch or two. This was a violent outrage upon our immortal bard. We rather differ with Mr. Town in his *reading* of the words "this is a *sorry sight*." We are of opinion the force of the sentence should be thrown on the word *sight*, because Macbeth, having been shortly before most confoundedly humbugged with an aerial dagger, was in doubts whether the daggers actually in his hands, were real, or whether they were not mere shadows, or, as the old english *may* have termed it, ꝰꝑᵹhtes. (this at any rate will establish our skill in *new readings*). Though we differ in this respect from our neighbor Town, yet we heartily agree with him in censuring Mr. Cooper for omitting that passage so remarkable for "beauty of imagery, &c." beginning with "and pity like a naked new-born babe, &c." It is one of those passages of Shakspeare, which should always be retained, for the purpose of showing how sometimes that great poet could talk like a buzzard; or, to speak more plainly, like the famous mad poet, Nat Lee.

As it is the first duty of a friend to advise—and as we profess and do actually feel a friendship for honest "Town," we warn him never, in his criticisms, to meddle with a lady's "petticoats," or to quote Nick Bottom. In the first instance, he may "catch a tartar;" and in the second, the asses head may rise up in judgment against him, and when it is once afloat, there is no knowing where some unlucky hand may place it. We would not, for all the money in our pockets, see Town flourishing his critical quill under the auspices of an asses head, like the great Franklin in his *Monterio Cap*.

NEW-YORK ASSEMBLY.
BY ANTHONY EVERGREEN, GENT.

The Assemblies this year have gained a great accession of beauty. Several brilliant stars have arisen from the east and from the north, to brighten the firmament of fashion; among the number, I have discovered *another planet*, which rivals even Venus in lustre, and I claim equal honor with Herschell for my discovery. I shall take some future opportunity to describe this planet, and the numerous satellites which revolve around it.

At the last assembly the company began to make some show about *eight*, but the most fashionable delayed their appearance until about *nine*—nine being the number of the *muses*, and therefore the best possible hour for beginning to exhibit the *graces*. (This is meant for a pretty play upon words, and I assure my readers that I think it very tolerable).

Poor WILL HONEYCOMB, whose memory I hold in special consideration, even with his half century of experience, would have been puzzled to point out the humor of a lady by her prevailing colors, for the "rival queens" of fashion, Mrs. TOOLE and madame BOUCHARD, appeared to have exhausted their wonderful inventions in the different disposition, variation and combination of tints and shades. The *philosopher* who maintained that black was white, and that *of course* there was no such color as white, might have given some color to his theory on this occasion, by the absence of poor forsaken white muslin. I was, however, much pleased to see that red maintains its ground against all other colors, because red is the color of mr. Jefferson's *****, Tom Paine's nose, and my slippers.

Let the grumbling smellfungi of this world, who cultivate taste among books, cobwebs and spiders, rail at the extravagance of the age; for my part I was delighted with the magic of the scene, and as the ladies tripped through the mazes of the dance, sparkling, and glowing and dazzling, I, like the honest chinese, thanked them heartily for the jewels and finery, with which they loaded themselves, merely for the entertainment of bystanders—and blessed my stars that I was a bachelor.

The gentlemen were considerably numerous, and being as usual equipt in their appropriate *black uniforms*, constituted a sable regiment, which contributed not a little to the brilliant gaiety of the ball-room. I must confess I am indebted for this remark to our friend the cockney, mr. 'SBIDLIKENS-FLASH, or 'Sbidlikens, as he is called for shortness. He is a fellow of infinite verbosity—stands in high favor with himself,—and like Caleb Quotem, is "up to every thing." I remember when a comfortable plump-looking citizen led into the room a fair damsel, who looked for all the world like the personification of a rainbow:—'Sbidlikens observed, that it reminded him of a fable, which he had read somewhere, of the marriage of an honest pains-taking snail, who had once walked six feet in an hour for a wager, to a butterfly, whom he used to gallant by the elbow, with the aid of much puffing and exertion. On being called upon to tell where he had come across this story, 'Sbidlikens absolutely refused to answer.

It would but be repeating an old story, to say that the ladies of New-York dance well;—and well may they, since they learn it scientifically, and begin their lessons before they have quit their swaddling clothes. The immortal DUPORT has usurped despotic sway over all the female heads and heels in this city;—hornbooks, primers and pianos are neglected, to attend to his positions; and poor CHILTON, with his pots and kettles, and chemical crockery, finds him a more potent enemy than the whole collective force of the "North-river society." 'Sbidlikens insists that this dancing mania will inevitably continue as long as a dancing-master will charge the fashionable price of *five-and-twenty dollars* a quarter, and all the other accomplishments are so vulgar as to be attainable at "half the money"—but I put no faith in 'Sbidlikens' candor in this particular. Among his infinitude of endowments, he is but a poor proficient in dancing; and though he often flounders through a cotillion, yet he never cut a pigeon-wing in his life.

In my mind, there's no position more positive and unexceptionable than that most frenchmen, dead or alive, are born dancers. I came pounce upon this discovery at the assembly, and I immediately noted it down in my register of indisputable facts—the public shall know all about it. As I never dance cotillions, holding them to be monstrous distortors of the human frame, and tantamount in their operations, to being broken and dislocated on the wheel, I generally take occasion, while they are going on, to make my remarks on the company. In the course of these observations, I was struck with the energy and eloquence of sundry limbs, which seemed to be flourishing about, without appertaining to any body.

After much investigation and difficulty, I at length traced
them to their respective owners, whom I found to be all
frenchmen—to a man. Art may have meddled somewhat in
these affairs, but Nature certainly did more. I have since been
considerably employed in calculations on this subject, and by
the most accurate computation I have determined, that a
frenchman passes at least three-fifths of his time between the
heavens and the earth, and partakes eminently of the nature
of a gossamer or soap-bubble. One of these jack-o-lanthorn
heroes, in taking a *figure*, which neither Euclid, nor Pythagoras himself, could demonstrate, unfortunately wound himself—I mean his foot—his better part—into a lady's cobweb
muslin robe; but perceiving it at the instant, he set himself a
spinning the other way, like a top; unravelled his step, without omitting one angle or curve, and extricated himself, without breaking a thread of the lady's dress! he then sprung up
like a sturgeon, crossed his feet four times, and finished this
wonderful evolution by quivering his left leg, as a cat does
her paw, when she has accidentally dipped it in water. No
man "of woman born," who was not a frenchman, or a
mountebank, could have done the like.

Among the new faces, I remarked a blooming nymph, who
has brought a fresh supply of roses from the country to adorn
the wreath of beauty, where lilies too much predominate. As
I wish well to every sweet face under heaven, I sincerely hope
her roses may survive the frosts and dissipations of winter;
and lose nothing by a comparison with the loveliest offerings
of the spring. 'Sbidlikens, to whom I made similar remarks,
assured me that they were very just, and very prettily exprest,
and that the lady in question was a prodigious fine piece of
flesh and blood. Now could I find it in my heart to baste these
cocknies like their own roast-beef—they can make no distinction between a fine woman and a fine horse.

I would praise the sylph-like grace with which another
young lady acquitted herself in the dance, but that she excels
in far more valuable accomplishments. Who praises the rose
for its beauty, even though it *is* beautiful?

The company retired at the customary hour to the supper-
room, where the tables were laid out with their *usual* splendor and profusion. My friend 'Sbidlikens, with the native

forethought of a cockney, had carefully stowed his pocket with cheese and crackers, that he might not be tempted again to venture his limbs in the crowd of hungry fair ones who throng the supper-room door:—his precaution was unnecessary, for the company entered the room with surprising order and decorum. No gowns were torn—no ladies fainted—no noses bled—nor was there any need of the interference of either managers or peace officers.

SALMAGUNDI NO. II

Wednesday, February 4, 1807.

FROM THE ELBOW-CHAIR OF
LAUNCELOT LANGSTAFF, ESQ.

IN THE CONDUCT of an epic poem, it has been the custom from time immemorial, for the poet occasionally to introduce his reader to an intimate acquaintance with the heroes of his story, by showing him into their tents, and giving him an opportunity of observing them in their night-gown and slippers. However, I despise the servile genius that would descend to follow a precedent, though furnished by Homer himself, and consider him as on a par with the cart that follows at the heels of the horse, without ever taking the lead; yet at the present moment my whim is opposed to my opinion, and whenever this is the case, my opinion generally surrenders at discretion. I am determined, therefore, to give the town a peep into our divan; and I shall repeat it as often as I please, to show that I intend to be sociable.

The other night, Will Wizard and Evergreen called upon me, to pass away a few hours in social chat, and hold a kind of council of war. To give a zest to our evening, I uncorked a bottle of London particular, which has grown old with myself, and which never fails to excite a smile in the countenances of my old cronies, to whom alone it is devoted. After some little time the conversation turned on the effect produced by our first number: every one had his budget of information, and I assure my readers that we laughed most unceremoniously at their expense;—they will excuse us for our merriment—tis a way we've got. Evergreen, who is equally a favorite and companion of young and old, was particularly satisfactory in his details, and it was highly amusing to hear how different characters were tickled with different passages. The old folks were delighted to find there was a bias in our junto towards the "gold old times;" and he particularly noticed a worthy old gentleman of his acquaintance, who had been somewhat a beau in his day, whose eyes brightened at the bare mention of Kissing-bridge. It recalled to his recollection several of his youthful exploits, at that celebrated pass, on which he seemed to dwell with great pleasure and self-complacency:—he hoped, he said, that the bridge might be preserved for the benefit of posterity, and as a monument of the gallantry of their grandfathers; and even hinted at the expediency of erecting a toll gate there, to collect the forfeits of the ladies. But the most flattering testimony of approbation, which our work has received, was from an old lady who never laughed but once in her life, and that was at the conclusion of the last war. She was detected by friend Anthony in the very fact of laughing most obstreperously at the description of the little dancing frenchman. Now it glads my very heart to find our effusions have such a pleasing effect. I venerate the aged, and joy whenever it is in my power to scatter a few flowers in their path.

The young people were particularly interested in the account of the assembly. There was some difference of opinion respecting the *new planet*, and the blooming nymph from the country; but as to the compliment paid to the fascinating little sylph who danced so gracefully—every lady modestly took that to herself.

Evergreen mentioned also that the young ladies were extremely anxious to learn the true mode of managing their beaux, and miss DIANA WEARWELL, who is as chaste as an icicle, has seen a few superfluous winters pass over her head, and boasts of having slain her thousands, wished to know how old maids were to do without husbands—not that she was very curious about the matter, she "only asked for information." Several ladies expressed their earnest desire that we would not spare those *wooden* gentlemen, who perform the parts of *mutes*, or stalking horses, in their drawing rooms; and their mothers were equally anxious that we would show no quarter to those lads of spirit, who now and then *cut* their bottles to enliven a tea-party with the humors of the dinner table.

Will Wizard was not a little chagrined at having been mistaken for a gentleman, " who is no more like me," said Will, "than I like Hercules."—"I was well assured," continued Will, "that as our characters were drawn from nature, the originals would be found in every society. And so it has happened—every little circle has its 'Sbidlikens; and the cockney,

intended merely as the representative of his *species*, has dwindled into an insignificant individual, who having recognized
his own likeness, has foolishly appropriated to himself a picture for which he never sat. Such, too, has been the case with
DING-DONG, who has kindly undertaken to be my representative—not that I care much about the matter, for it must be
acknowledged that the animal is a good-natured animal
enough—and what is more, a fashionable animal—and this
is saying more than to call him a *conjuror*. But, I am much
mistaken, if he can claim any affinity to the *Wizard* family.—
Surely every body knows Ding-dong, the gentle Ding-dong,
who pervades all space, who is here and there and every
where; no tea-party can be complete without Ding-dong—
and his appearance is sure to occasion a smile. Ding-dong has
been the occasion of much wit in his day; I have even seen
many puny whipsters attempt to be dull at his expense, who
were as much inferior to him as the gad-fly is to the ox, that
he buzzes about. Does any witling want to distress the company with a miserable pun?—nobody's name presents sooner
than Ding-dong's; and it has been played upon with equal
skill and equal entertainment to the bye-standers as Trinity-
bells. Ding-dong is profoundly devoted to the ladies, and
highly entitled to their regard; for I know no man who makes
a better bow, or talks less to the purpose than Ding-dong.
Ding-dong has acquired a prodigious fund of knowledge, by
reading Dilworth when a boy; and the other day, on being
asked who was the author of Macbeth, answered, without the
least hesitation—Shakspeare!—Ding-dong has a quotation
for every day of the year, and every hour of the day, and every
minute of the hour, but he often commits petty larcenies on
the poets—plucks the grey hairs of old Chaucer's head, and
claps them on the chin of Pope; and filches Johnson's wig, to
cover the bald pate of Homer;—but his blunders pass unde-
tected by one half of his hearers. Ding-dong it is true, though
he has long wrangled at our bar, cannot boast much of his
legal knowledge, nor does his forensic eloquence entitle him
to rank with a Cicero or a Demosthenes; but bating his
professional deficiencies, he is a man of most delectable discourse, and can hold forth for an hour upon the color of a
ribbon or the construction of a workbag. Ding-dong is now

in his fortieth year, or perhaps a little more—rivals all the little beaux in town, in his attentions to the ladies—is in a state of rapid improvement; and there is no doubt but that by the time he arrives at years of discretion, he will be a very accomplished agreeable young fellow."—I advise all clever, good-for-nothing, "learned and authentic" gentlemen, to take care how they *wear this cap*, however well it fits; and to bear in mind, that our characters are not individuals, but species: if after this warning, any person chooses to represent mr. Ding-dong, the sin is at his own door—we wash our hands of it.

We all sympathised with Wizard, that he should be mistaken for a person so very different; and I hereby assure my readers, that William Wizard is no other person in the whole world *but* William Wizard; so I beg I may hear no more conjectures on the subject. Will, is in fact, a wiseacre by inheritance. The Wizard family has long been celebrated for knowing more than their neighbors, particularly concerning their neighbors' affairs. They were antiently called JOSSELIN, but Will's great uncle, by the father's side, having been accidentally burnt for a *witch* in Connecticut, in consequence of blowing up his own house in a philosophical experiment, the family, in order to perpetuate the recollection of this memorable circumstance, assumed the name and arms of Wizard, and have borne them ever since.

In the course of my customary morning's walk, I stopped in at a book-store, which is noted for being the favorite haunt of a number of literati, some of whom rank high in the opinion of the world, and others rank equally high in their own. Here I found a knot of queer fellows listening to one of their company, who was reading our paper; I particularly noticed mr. ICHABOD FUNGUS among the number.

Fungus is one of those fidgeting, meddling quidnuncs, with which this unhappy city is pestered: one of your "Q in a corner fellows," who speaks volumes with a wink—conveys most portentous information, by laying his finger beside his nose,—and is always smelling a rat in the most trifling occurrence. He listened to our work with the most frigid gravity—every now and then gave a mysterious shrug—a *humph*—or a screw of the mouth; and on being asked his opinion at the conclusion, said, he did not know what to think of it;—he hoped it did not mean any thing against the Government— that no lurking treason was couched in all this talk. These were dangerous times—times of plot and conspiracy;—he did not at all like those stars after mr. Jefferson's name, they had an air of concealment. DICK PADDLE, who was one of the group, undertook our cause. Dick is known to the world, as being a most knowing genius, who can see as far as any body—into a millstone; maintains, in the teeth of all argument, that a spade *is* a spade; and will labor a good half hour by St. Paul's clock, to establish a self-evident fact. Dick assured old Fungus, that those stars merely stood for mr. Jefferson's red *what-d'ye-callums*; and that so far from a conspiracy against their peace and prosperity, the authors, whom he knew very well, were only expressing their high respect for them. The old man shook his head, shrugged his shoulders, gave a mysterious lord Burleigh nod, said he hoped it might be so; but he was by no means satisfied with this attack upon the president's breeches, as "thereby *hangs a tale*."

MR. WILSON'S CONCERT.
BY ANTHONY EVERGREEN, GENT.

In my register of indisputable facts I have noted it conspicuously, that all modern music is but the mere dregs and draining of the ancient, and that all the spirit and vigor of harmony has entirely evaporated in the lapse of ages. Oh! for the chant of the naiades, and the dryades, the shell of the tritons, and the sweet warblings of the mermaids of ancient days! where now shall we seek the Amphion, who built walls with a turn of his hurdy-gurdy, the Orpheus who made stones to whistle about his ears, and trees hop in a country dance, by the mere quavering of his fiddle-stick! ah! had I the power of the former, how soon would I build up the new City-Hall, and save the cash and credit of the corporation; and how much sooner would I build myself a snug house in Broadway—nor would it be the first time a house has been obtained there for a song. In my opinion, the scotch bag-pipe is the only instrument that rivals the ancient lyre, and I am surprised it should be almost the only one entirely excluded from our concerts.

Talking of concerts reminds me of that given a few nights since by mr. WILSON; at which I had the misfortune of being present. It was attended by a numerous company, and gave great satisfaction, if I may be allowed to judge from the frequent *gapings* of the audience; though I will not risk my credit as a connoisseur, by saying whether they proceeded from wonder, or a violent inclination to doze. I was delighted to find, in the mazes of the crowd, my particular friend SNIVERS, who had put on his cognoscenti phiz—he being according to his own account a profound adept in the science of music. He can tell a crochet at first sight, and like a true englishman, is delighted with the plumb-pudding rotundity of a semi-breve; and, in short, boasts of having incontinently climbed up Paff's musical tree, which hangs every day upon the poplar, from the fundamental-concord, to the fundamental major discord, and so on from branch to branch, until he reached the very top, where he sung "Rule Britannia," clapped his wings, and then—came down again. Like all true transatlantic judges, he suffers most horribly at our musical entertainments, and he assures me that what with the confounded scraping, and scratching, and grating of our fiddlers, he thinks the sitting out one of our concerts tantamount to the punishment of that unfortunate saint, who was frittered in two with a hand-saw.

The concert was given in the tea-room, at the City-Hotel; an apartment admirably calculated by its dingy walls, beautifully marbled with smoke, to show off the dresses and complexions of the ladies, and by the flatness of its ceiling to repress those impertinent reverberations of the music, which, whatever others may foolishly assert, are, as Snivers says, "no better than repetitions of old stories."

Mr. Wilson gave me infinite satisfaction by the gentility of his demeanor, and the roguish looks he now and then cast at the ladies; but we fear his excessive *modesty* threw him into some little confusion, for he absolutely *forgot himself*, and in the whole course of his entrances and exits, never once made his bow to the audience. On the whole, however, I think he has a fine voice, sings with great taste, and is a very *modest* good-looking little man; but I beg leave to repeat the advice so often given by the illustrious tenants of the theatrical sky-parlor, to the gentlemen who are charged with the "nice con-duct" of chairs and tables,—"make a bow, Johnny—Johnny make a bow!"

I cannot, on this occasion, but express my surprise that cer-tain amateurs should be so frequently at concerts, considering what agonies they suffer while a piece of music is playing. I defy any man of common humanity, and who has not the heart of a Choctaw, to contemplate the countenance of one of these unhappy victims of a fiddle-stick, without feeling a sentiment of compassion. His whole visage is distorted; he rolls up his eyes, as M'Sychophant says, "like a duck in thun-der," and the music seems to operate upon him like a fit of the cholic; his very bowels seem to sympathize at every twang of the cat-gut, as if he heard at that moment the wailings of the helpless animal that had been sacrificed to harmony. Nor does the hero of the orchestra seem less affected: as soon as the signal is given, he seizes his fiddle-stick, makes a most horrible grimace, scowls fiercely upon his music-book, and grins every little trembling crochet and quaver out of coun-tenance. I have sometimes particularly noticed a hungry look-ing gaul, who torments a huge bass viol, and who is doubtless the original of the famous "Raw-head-and-bloody-bones," so potent in frightening naughty children.

The person who played the french horn was very excellent in his way, but Snivers could not relish his performance, hav-ing sometime since heard a gentleman amateur in Gotham play a solo on his *proboscis*, or nozzle, in a style infinitely su-perior;—Snout, the bellows-mender, never tuned his wind instrument more musically; nor did the celebrated "knight of the burning lamp," ever yield more exquisite entertainment with his nose; this gentleman had latterly ceased to exhibit this prodigious accomplishment, having, it was whispered, hired out his snout to a ferryman, who had lost his conch-shell—the consequence was, that he did not *show his nose* in company so frequently as before.

SITTING late the other evening in my elbow-chair, indulging in that kind of indolent meditation, which I consider the perfection of human bliss, I was roused from my reverie by the entrance of an old servant in the COCKLOFT livery, who handed me a letter, containing the following address from my cousin, and old college chum, PINDAR COCKLOFT.

Honest ANDREW as he delivered it, informed me that his master, who resides a little way from town, on reading a small pamphlet in a neat yellow cover, rubbed his hands with symptoms of great satisfaction, called for his favorite chinese ink-stand, with two sprawling mandarins for its supporters, and wrote the letter which he had the honor to present me.

As I foresee my cousin will one day become a great favorite with the public, and as I know him to be somewhat punctilious as it respects etiquette, I shall take this opportunity to gratify the old gentleman, by giving him a proper introduction to the fashionable world. The Cockloft family, to which I have the comfort of being related, has been fruitful in old bachelors and humorists, as will be perceived when I come to treat more of its history. My cousin Pindar is one of its most conspicuous members—he is now in his fifty-eighth year—is a bachelor, partly through choice, and partly through chance, and an oddity of the first water. Half his life has been employed in writing odes, sonnets, epigrams and elegies, which he seldom shows to any body but myself, after they are written; and all the old chests, drawers, and chair-bottoms in the house, teem with his productions.

In his younger days, he figured as a dashing blade in the great world; and no young fellow of the town wore a longer pig-tail, or carried more buckram in his skirts. From sixteen to thirty he was continually in love, and during that period, to use his own words, he be-scribbled more paper than would serve the theatre for snow-storms a whole season. The evening of his thirtieth birth-day, as he sat by the fire-side, as much in love as ever was man in this world, and writing the name of his mistress in the ashes, with an old tongs that had lost one of its legs, he was seized with a whim-wham that he was an old fool to be in love at his time of life. It was ever one of the Cockloft characteristics, to *strike* to whim, and had Pindar stood out on this occasion he would have brought the reputation of his mother in question. From that time, he gave up all particular attentions to the ladies, and though he still loves their company, he has never been known to exceed the bounds of common courtesy in his intercourse with them. He was the life and ornament of our family circle in town, until the epoch of the french revolution, which sent so many *unfortunate* dancing-masters from their country to polish and enlighten our hemisphere. This was a sad time for Pindar, who had taken a genuine Cockloft prejudice against every thing french, ever since he was brought to death's door by a *ragout*: he groaned at Ca Ira, and the Marseilles Hymn had much the same effect upon him, that sharpening a knife on a dry whetstone has upon some people—it set his teeth chattering. He might in time have been reconciled to these rubs, had not the introduction of french cockades on the hats of our citizens absolutely thrown him into a fever: the first time he saw an instance of this kind, he came home with great precipitation, packed up his trunk, his old fashioned writing-desk, and his chinese ink-stand, and made a kind of growling retreat to Cockloft Hall, where he has resided ever since.

My cousin Pindar is one of a mercurial disposition—a humorist without ill-nature—he is of the true gun-powder temper—one flash and all is over. It is true, when the wind is easterly, or the gout gives him a gentle twinge, or he hears of any new successes of the french, he will become a little splenetic; and heaven help the man, and more particularly the woman, that crosses his humor at that moment—she is sure to receive no quarter. These are the most sublime moments of Pindar. I swear to you, dear ladies and gentlemen, I would not lose one of these splenetic bursts, for the best wig in my wardrobe, even though it were proved to be the identical wig worn by the sage Linkum Fidelius, when he demonstrated before the whole university of Leyden, that it *was* possible to make bricks without straw. I have seen the old gentleman, blaze forth such a volcanic explosion of wit, ridicule, and satire, that I was almost tempted to believe him inspired. But these sallies only lasted for a moment, and passed like summer clouds over the benevolent sunshine which ever warmed his heart, and lighted up his countenance.

Time, though it has dealt roughly with his person, has passed lightly over the graces of his mind, and left him in full possession of all the sensibilities of youth. His eye kindles at the relation of a noble or generous action, his heart melts at the story of distress, and he is still a warm admirer of the fair. Like all *old bachelors* however, he looks back with a fond and lingering eye on the period of his *boyhood*, and would sooner suffer the pangs of matrimony, than acknowledge that the world or any thing in it, is half so clever, as it was in those good old times that are "gone by."

I believe I have already mentioned, that with all his good qualities he is a humorist, and a humorist of the highest order. He has some of the most intolerable whim-whams I ever met with in my life, and his oddities are sufficient to eke out a hundred tolerable originals. But I will not enlarge on them—enough has been told to excite a desire to know more; and I am much mistaken, if in the course of half a dozen of our numbers, he dont tickle, plague, please and perplex the whole town, and completely establish his claim to the Laureatship he has solicited, and with which we hereby invest him, recommending him and his effusions to public reverence and respect.

LAUNCELOT LANGSTAFF.

TO LAUNCELOT LANGSTAFF, ESQ.

DEAR LAUNCE,

As I find you have taken the quill,
To put our gay town, and its fair under drill,
I offer my hopes for success to your cause,
And sent you unvarnish'd my mite of applause.
Ah, Launce, this poor town has been woefully *fashed*;
Has long been be-frenchman'd, be-cockney'd, be-trashed;
And our ladies be-devil'd, bewilder'd astray,
From the rules of their grandames have wander'd away.
No longer that modest demeanor we meet,
Which whilom the eyes of our fathers did greet;—
No longer be-mobbled, be-ruffled, be-quill'd,
Be-powder'd, be-hooded, be-patch'd and be-frill'd;—
No longer our fair ones their grograms display,

And stiff in brocade, strut "like castles" away.
  Oh, how fondly my soul forms departed has traced,
When our ladies in stays, and in boddice well laced,
When bishop'd, and cushion'd, and hoop'd to the chin,
Well callash'd without, and well bolster'd within;
All cased in their buckrams, from crown down to tail,
Like O'Brallagan's mistress, were shaped like a pail.
  Well—peace to those fashions—the joy of *our* eyes—
Tempora mutantur,—new follies will rise;
Yet, "like joys that are past," they still crowd on the mind,
In moments of thought, as the soul looks behind.
  Sweet days of our boyhood, gone by, my dear Launce,
Like the shadows of night, or the forms in a trance:
Yet oft we retrace those bright visions again,
Nos mutamur, tis true—but those visions remain.
I recal with delight, how my bosom would creep;
When some delicate foot from its chamber would peep,
And when I a neat stocking'd ankle could spy,
—By the sages of old, I was rapt to the sky!
All then was retiring—was modest—discreet;—
The beauties, all shrouded, were left to conceit;
To the visions which fancy would form in her eye
Of graces that snug in soft ambush would lie.
And the heart, like the poets, in thought would pursue
The elysium of bliss, which was veil'd from its view.
  We are *old fashion'd* fellows, our nieces all say:
Old fashion'd, indeed, coz—and swear it they may—
For I freely confess that it yields me no pride,
To see them all blaze what their mothers would hide;
To see them, all shiv'ring, some cold winter's day,
So lavish their beauties and graces display,
And give to each foppling that offers his hand,
Like Moses from Pisgah—a peep at the land.
  But a truce with complaining—the object in view
Is to offer my help in the work you pursue;
And as your effusions and labors sublime,
May need, now and then, a few touches of rhyme,
I humbly solicit, as cousin and friend,
A quiddity, quirk, or remonstrance to send:
Or should you a Laureat want in your plan,

By the muff of my grandmother, I am your man!
You must know I have got a *poetical mill*,
Which with odd lines, and couplets, and triplets I fill;
And a poem I grind, as from rags white and blue
The paper mill yields you a sheet fair and new.
I can grind down an ode, or an epic that's long,
Into sonnet, acrostic, conundrum or song:
As to dull Hudibrastic, so boasted of late,
The doggrel discharge of some muddle brain'd pate,
I can grind it by wholesale—and give it its point,
With billingsgate dish'd up in rhymes out of joint.

I have read all the poets—and got them by heart,
Can slit them, and twist them, and take them apart;
Can cook up an ode out of patches and shreds,
To muddle my readers, and bother their heads.
Old Homer, and Virgil, and Ovid I scan,
Anacreon, and Sappho, (who changed to a swan;)—
Iambics and sapphics I grind at my will,
And with ditties of love every noddle can fill.

Oh, 'twould do your heart good, Launce, to see my mill
    grind
Old stuff into verses, and poems refined;—
Dan Spencer, Dan Chaucer, those poets of old,
Though cover'd with dust, are yet true sterling gold;
I can grind off their tarnish, and bring them to view,
New model'd, new mill'd, and improved in their hue.

But I promise no more—only give me the place,
And I warrant I'll fill it with credit and grace;
By the living! I'll figure and cut you a dash
—As bold as Will Wizard, or 'SBIDLIKENS-FLASH!

PINDAR COCKLOFT.

ADVERTISEMENT.

PERHAPS the most fruitful source of mortification to a
merry writer, who for the amusement of himself and the
public, employs his leisure in sketching odd characters from
imagination, is, that he cannot flourish his pen, but every
Jack-pudding imagines it is pointed directly at himself:—he
cannot, in his gambols, throw a fool's cap among the crowd,

but every queer fellow insists upon putting it on his own head; or chalk an outlandish figure, but every outlandish genius is eager to write his own name under it. However we may be mortified, that these men should each individually think himself of sufficient consequence to engage our attention, we should not care a rush about it, if they did not get into a passion, and complain of having been ill-used.

It is not in our hearts to hurt the feelings of one single mortal, by holding him up to public ridicule, and if it were, we lay it down as one of our indisputable facts, that no man can be made ridiculous but by his own folly. As however we are aware that when a man by chance gets a thwack in the crowd, he is apt to suppose the blow was intended exclusively for himself, and so fall into unreasonable anger, we have determined to let these crusty gentry know what kind of satisfaction they are to expect from us. We are resolved not to fight, for three special reasons—first, because fighting is at all events extremely troublesome and inconvenient, particularly at this season of the year;—second, because if either of us should happen to be killed, it would be a great loss to the public, and rob them of many a good laugh we have in store for their amusement;—and third, because if we should chance to kill our adversary, as is most likely, for we can every one of us split balls upon razors and snuff candles,—it would be a loss to our publisher, by depriving him of a good customer. If any gentleman casuist will give three as good reasons *for* fighting, we promise him a complete set of Salmagundi for nothing.

But though we do not fight in our own proper persons, let it not be supposed that we will not give ample satisfaction to all those who may choose to demand it—for this would be a mistake of the first magnitude and lead very valiant gentlemen perhaps into what is called a *quandary*. It would be a thousand and one pities, that any honest man, after taking to himself the cap and bells which we *merely* offered to his acceptance, should not have the privilege of being cudgeled into the bargain. We pride ourselves upon giving satisfaction in every department of our paper; and to fill that of fighting, have engaged two of those strapping heroes of the Theatre, who figure in the retinues of our ginger-bread kings and

queens—now hurry an old stuff petticoat on their backs, and
strut senators of Rome, or aldermen of London—and now
be-whisker their muffin faces with burnt cork, and swagger
right valiant warriors, armed cap-a-pee, in buckram. Should,
therefore, any great little man about town, take offence at our
good-natured villainy, though we intend to offend nobody
under heaven—he will please to apply at any hour after
twelve o'clock, as our champions will then be off duty at the
Theatre, and ready for any thing. They have promised to fight
" with or without balls"—to give two tweaks of the nose for
one—to submit to be kicked, and to cudgel their applicant
most heartily in return;—this being what we understand by
"the *satisfaction* of *a gentleman*."

SALMAGUNDI NO. III

Friday, February 13, 1807.

FROM MY ELBOW-CHAIR.

As I DELIGHT in every thing novel and eccentric, and would at any time give an old coat for a new idea, I am particularly attentive to the manners and conversation of strangers, and scarcely ever a traveller enters this city whose appearance promises any thing original, but by some means or another, I form an acquaintance with him. I must confess I often suffer manifold afflictions from the intimacies thus contracted: my curiosity is frequently punished by the stupid details of a blockhead, or the shallow verbosity of a coxcomb. Now I would prefer at any time to travel with an ox-team through a Carolina sand-flat, than plod through a heavy un-meaning conversation with the former, and as to the latter, I would sooner hold sweet converse with the wheel of a knife grinder, than endure his monotonous chattering. In fact the strangers who flock to this most pleasant of all earthly cities, are generally mere birds of passage, whose plumage is often gay enough, I own; but their notes, "heaven save the mark," are as unmusical as those of that classic night bird, whom the antients humorously selected as the emblem of wisdom. Those from the south, it is true, entertain me with their horses, equipages, and puns; and it is excessively pleasant to hear a couple of these *four in hand* gentlemen, detail their exploits over a bottle. Those from the east, have often in-duced me to doubt the existence of the wise men of yore, who are said to have flourished in that quarter; and as for those from parts beyond seas—oh! my masters, ye shall hear more from me anon. Heaven help this unhappy town!—hath it not goslings enow of its own hatching and rearing that it must be overwhelmed by such an inundation of ganders from other climes? I would not have any of my courteous and gen-tle readers suppose that I am running *a muck*, full tilt, cut and slash upon all foreigners indiscriminately. I have no national antipathies, though related to the Cockloft family. As to hon-est John Bull, I shake him heartily by the hand, assuring him that I love his jolly countenance, and moreover am lineally descended from him; in proof of which I alledge my invincible predilection for roast beef and pudding. I therefore look upon all his children as my kinsmen; and I beg when I tickle a cockney I may not be understood as trimming an englishman, they being very distinct animals, as I shall clearly demonstrate in a future number. If any one wishes to know my opinion of the irish and scotch, he may find it in the characters of those two nations, drawn by the first advocate of the age. But the french I must confess are my favorites, and I have taken more pains to argue my cousin Pindar out of his antipathy to them, than I ever did about any other thing. When, therefore, I choose to hunt a monsieur for my own particular amusement, I beg it may not be asserted that I intend him as a representative of his countrymen at large. For from this—I love the nation, as being a nation of right merry fellows, possessing the true secret of being happy; which is nothing more than thinking of nothing, talking about any thing, and laughing at every thing. I mean only to tune up those little thing-o-mys, who represent nobody but themselves; who have no national trait about them but their language, and who hop about our town in swarms like little toads after a shower.

Among the few strangers whose acquaintance has entertained me, I particularly rank the magnanimous MUSTAPHA RUB-A-DUB KELI KHAN, a most illustrious Captain of a Ketch, who figured some time since, in our fashionable circles, at the head of a ragged regiment of tripolitan prisoners. His conversation was to me a perpetual feast—I chuckled with inward pleasure at his whimsical mistakes and unaffected observations on men and manners; and I rolled each odd conceit "like a sweet morsel under my tongue."

Whether Mustapha was captivated by my iron-bound physiognomy, or flattered by the attentions which I paid him, I won't determine; but I so far gained his confidence, that at his departure, he presented me with a bundle of papers, containing among other articles, several copies of letters, which he had written to his friends in Tripoli.—The following is a translation of one of them. The original is in arabic-greek, but by the assistance of Will Wizard, who understands all languages, not excepting that manufactured by Psalmanazar, I have been enabled to accomplish a tolerable translation. We should have found little difficulty in rendering it into english, had it not been for Mustapha's confounded pot-hooks and trammels.

LETTER FROM MUSTAPHA RUB-A-DUB KELI KHAN,
Captain of a Ketch,
To ASEM HACCHEM, principal slave-driver to
his highness the Bashaw of Tripoli.

THOU wilt learn from this letter, most illustrious disciple of Mahomet, that I have for some time resided in New-York, the most polished, vast and magnificent city of the United States of America. But what to me are its delights! I wander a captive through its splendid streets, I turn a heavy eye on every rising day that beholds me banished from my country. The christian husbands here lament most bitterly any short absence from home, though they leave but one wife behind to lament their departure—what then must be the feelings of thy unhappy kinsman, while thus lingering at an immeasurable distance from three-and-twenty of the most lovely and obedient wives in all Tripoli! Oh Allah! shall thy servant never again return to his native land, nor behold his beloved wives, who beam on his memory beautiful as the rosy morn of the east, and graceful as Mahomet's camel!

Yet beautiful, oh most puissant slave-driver, as are my wives, they are far exceeded by the women of this country. Even those who run about the streets with bare arms and necks, (*et cætera*) whose habiliments are too scanty to protect them either from the inclemency of the seasons, or the scrutinizing glances of the curious, and who it would seem belong to nobody, are lovely as the Houris that people the elysium of true believers. If then, such as run wild in the highways, and whom nobody cares to appropriate, are thus beauteous; what must be the charms of those who are shut up in the seraglios, and never permitted to go abroad! surely the region of beauty, the valley of the graces can contain nothing so inimitably fair!

But, notwithstanding the charms of these infidel women,

they are apt to have one fault, which is extremely troublesome and inconvenient. Wouldst thou believe it, Asem, I have been positively assured by a famous dervise (or doctor as he is here called) that at least one-fifth part of them—have souls! incredible as it may seem to thee, I am the more inclined to believe them in possession of this monstrous superfluity, from my own little experience, and from the information which I have derived from others. In walking the streets I have actually seen an exceeding good looking woman with soul enough to box her husband's ears to his heart's content, and my very whiskers trembled with indignation at the abject state of these wretched infidels. I am told, moreover, that some of the women have soul enough to usurp the breeches of the men, but these I suppose are married and kept close, for I have not, in my rambles, met with any so extravagantly accoutred; others, I am informed, have soul enough to swear:—yea! by the beard of the great Omar, who prayed three times to each of the one hundred and twenty-four thousand prophets of our most holy faith, and who never swore but once in his life—they actually swear!

Get thee to the mosque, good Asem! return thanks to our most holy prophet, that he has been thus mindful of the comfort of all true musselmen, and has given them wives with no more souls than cats and dogs, and other necessary animals of the household.

Thou will doubtless be anxious to learn our reception in this country, and how we were treated by a people whom we have been accustomed to consider as unenlightened barbarians.

On landing we were waited upon to our lodgings, I suppose according to the directions of the municipality, by a vast and respectable escort of boys and negroes, who shouted and threw up their hats, doubtless to do honor to the magnanimous Mustapha, captain of a ketch; they were somewhat ragged and dirty in their equipments, but this we attributed to their republican simplicity. One of them, in the zeal of admiration, threw an old shoe, which gave thy friend rather an ungentle salutation on one side of the head, whereat I was not a little offended, until the interpreter informed us that this was the customary manner in which great men were honored in this country; and that the more distinguished they

were, the more were they subjected to the attacks and peltings
of the mob. Upon this I bowed my head three times, with
my hands to my turban, and made a speech in arabic-greek,
which gave great satisfaction, and occasioned a shower of old
shoes, hats, and so forth, that was exceedingly refreshing to
us all.

Thou wilt not as yet expect that I should give thee an account of the laws and politics of this country—I will reserve
them for some future letter, when I shall be more experienced
in their complicated and seemingly contradictory nature.

This empire is governed by a grand and most puissant bashaw, whom they dignify with the title of President. He is
chosen by persons, who are chosen by an assembly elected by
the people—hence the mob is called the *sovereign people*—and
the country, *free*; the body politic doubtless resembling a vessel, which is best governed by its tail. The present bashaw is
a very plain old gentleman—something they say of a humorist, as he amuses himself with impaling butterflies and pick-
ling tadpoles; he is rather declining in popularity, having
given great offence by wearing red breeches, and tying his
horse to a post. The people of the United States have assured
me that they themselves are the most enlightened nation under the sun; but thou knowest that the barbarians of the desart, who assemble at the summer solstice, to shoot their
arrows at that glorious luminary, in order to extinguish his
burning rays, make precisely the same boast;—which of them
have the superior claim, I shall not attempt to decide.

I have observed, with some degree of surprize, that the
men of this country do not seem in haste to accommodate
themselves even with the *single* wife, which alone the laws
permit them to marry; this backwardness is probably owing
to the misfortune of their absolutely having no female *mutes*
among them. Thou knowest how invaluable are these silent
companions;—what a price is given for them in the east, and
what entertaining wives do they make! what delightful entertainment arises from beholding the silent eloquence of their
signs and gestures! but a wife possessed both of a tongue and
a soul—monstrous! monstrous! Is it astonishing that these
unhappy infidels should shrink from a union with a woman
so preposterously endowed?

Thou hast doubtless read in the works of Abul Faraj, the arabian historian, the tradition which mentions that the muses were once upon the point of falling together by the ears about the admission of a *tenth* among their number, until she assured them, by signs, that she was dumb, whereupon they received her with great rejoicing. I should, perhaps, inform thee that there are but *nine* christian muses, (who were formerly pagans, but have since been converted) and that in this country we never hear of a tenth, unless some crazy poet wishes to pay an hyperbolical compliment to his mistress; on which occasion it goes hard but she figures as a tenth muse, or fourth grace, even though she should be more illiterate than a Hottentot, and more ungraceful than a dancing-bear! Since my arrival in this country, I have not met with less than a hundred of these supernumerary muses and graces—and may Allah preserve me from ever meeting with any more!

When I have studied this people more profoundly, I will write thee again; in the mean time watch over my household, and do not beat my beloved wives, unless you catch them with their noses out at the window. Tho' far distant, and a slave, let me live in thy heart, as thou livest in mine:—think not, oh friend of my soul, that the splendors of this luxurious capitol, its gorgeous palaces, its stupenduous mosques, and the beautiful females who run wild in herds about its streets, can obliterate thee from my remembrance. Thy name shall still be mentioned in the five-and-twenty prayers which I offer up daily; and may our great prophet, after bestowing on thee all the blessings of this life, at length, in a good old age, lead thee gently by the hand, to enjoy the dignity of bashaw of three tails in the blissful bowers of Eden.

MUSTAPHA.

Fashions,

BY ANTHONY EVERGREEN, GENT.

The following article is furnished me by a young lady of unquestionable taste, and who is the oracle of fashion and frippery. Being deeply initiated into all the mysteries of the toilet, she has promised me from time to time, a similar detail.

MRS. TOOLE has for some time reigned unrivalled in the fashionable world, and had the supreme direction of caps, bonnets, feathers, flowers, and tinsel. She has dressed and undressed our ladies just as she pleased; now loading them with velvet and wadding, now turning them adrift upon the world, to run shivering through the streets with scarcely a covering to their—backs; and now obliging them to drag a long train at their heels, like the tail of a paper kite. Her despotic sway, however, threatens to be limited. A dangerous rival has sprung up in the person of MADAME BOUCHARD, an intrepid little woman, fresh from the headquarters of fashion and folly, and who has burst like a second Bonaparte upon the fashionable world. Mrs. Toole, notwithstanding, seems determined to dispute her ground bravely for the honor of old England. The ladies have begun to arrange themselves under the banner of one or other of these heroines of the needle, and everything portends open war. Madame Bouchard marches gallantly to the field, flourishing a flaming red robe for a standard, "flouting the skies;" and mrs. Toole, no ways dismayed, sallies out under cover of a forest of artificial flowers, like Malcolm's host. Both parties possess great merit, and both deserve the victory. Mrs. Toole charges the highest, but madame Bouchard makes the lowest curtsey. Madame Bouchard is a little short lady—nor is there any hope of her growing any larger; but then she is perfectly genteel—and so is mrs. Toole. Mrs. Toole lives in Broadway, and madame Bouchard in Courtlandt-street; but madame atones for the inferiority of her *stand*, by making two curtseys to mrs. Toole's one, and talking french like an angel. Mrs. Toole is the best looking—but madame Bouchard wears a most bewitching little scrubby wig.—Mrs. Toole is the tallest—but madame Bouchard has the longest nose.—Mrs. Toole is fond of roast beef—but madame is loyal in her adherence to onions: in short, so equally are the merits of the two ladies balanced, that there is no judging which will "kick the beam." It however seems to be the prevailing opinion, that madame Bouchard will carry the day, because she wears a wig, has a long nose, talks french, loves onions, and does not charge above ten times as much for a thing as it is worth.

Under the direction of these High Priestesses of the beau-
monde, the following is the fashionable morning dress for
walking.

If the weather be very cold, a thin muslin gown, or frock
is most adviseable, because it agrees with the season, being
perfectly cool. The neck, arms, and particularly the elbows
bare, in order that they may be agreeably painted and mottled
by mr. JOHN FROST, nose-painter-general, of the color of cas-
tile-soap. Shoes of kid, the thinnest that can possibly be procured—as they tend to promote colds and make a lady look
interesting—(*i.e. grizzly*). Picnic silk stockings, with lace
clocks, flesh-colored are most fashionable, as they have the
appearance of bare legs— *nudity* being all the rage. The stockings carelessly bespattered with mud, to agree with the gown,
which should be bordered about three inches deep with the
most fashionable colored mud that can be found: the ladies permitted to hold up their trains, after they have swept two or three
streets, in order to show—the clocks of their stockings. The
shawl, scarlet, crimson, flame, orange, salmon, or any other
combustible or brimstone color, thrown over one shoulder like
an indian blanket, with one end dragging on the ground.

N.B. If the ladies have not a red shawl at hand, a red petticoat turned topsy-turvy over the shoulders, would do just as
well. This is called being dressed *à la drabble*.

When the ladies do not go abroad of a morning, the usual
chimney-corner dress is a dotted, spotted, striped, or cross-
barred gown—a yellowish, whitish, smokish, dirty colored
shawl, and the hair curiously ornamented with little bits of
newspaper, or pieces of a letter from a dear friend. This is
called the "Cinderella dress."

The receipt for a full dress, is as follows: take of spider net,
crape, sattin, gymp, cat-gut, gauze, whalebone, lace, bobbin,
ribbons, and artificial flowers, as much as will rig out the congregation of a village church: to these add as many spangles,
beads, and gew-gaws, as would be sufficient to turn the heads
of all the fashionable fair ones of Nootka-sound. Let mrs.
Toole, or madame Bouchard patch all these articles together,

one upon another, dash them plentifully over with stars, bu-
gles, and tinsel, and they will altogether form a dress, which
hung upon a lady's back, cannot fail of supplying the place of
beauty, youth and grace, and of reminding the spectator of
that celebrated region of finery, called *Rag Fair*.

> Dat veniam corvis, vexat censura Columbas.
>
> JUV.

> A, *was an archer and shot at a frog,*
> *But missing his aim shot into a bog.*
>
> LINK. FID. vol. CIII. chap. clv.

One of the greatest sources of amusement incident to our
humorous knight-errantry, is to ramble about and hear the
various conjectures of the town respecting our worships,
whom every body pretends to know as well as Falstaff did
prince Hal at Gads-hill. We have sometimes seen a sapient
sleepy fellow on being tickled with a straw, make a furious
effort, and fancy he had fairly caught a gnat in his clutches;
so, that many-headed monster the public, who with all its
heads is, we fear, sadly off for brains, has after long hovering,
come souse down, like a king-fisher, on the authors of Salmagundi, and caught them as certainly as the aforesaid honest
fellow caught the gnat.

Would that we were rich enough to give every one of our
numerous readers a cent, as a reward for their ingenuity! not
that they have really conjectured within a thousand leagues of
the truth, but that we consider it a great stretch of ingenuity
even to have guessed wrong—and that we hold ourselves much
obliged to them for having taken the trouble to guess at all.

One of the most tickling, dear, mischievous pleasures of
this life is to laugh in one's sleeve—to sit snug in a corner
unnoticed and unknown, and hear the wise men of Gotham,
who are profound judges (of horse-flesh), pronounce from
the style of our work, who are the authors. This listening
incog. and receiving a hearty praising over another man's
back, is a situation so celestially whimsical that we have done
little else than laugh in our sleeves ever since our first number
was publisht.

The town has at length allayed the titilations of curiosity, by fixing on two young gentlemen of literary talents—that is to say, they are equal to the composition of a news-paper squib, a hodge-podge criticism, or some such trifle, and may occasionally raise a smile by their effusions; but pardon us, sweet sirs, if we modestly doubt your capability of supporting the atlean burthen of Salmagundi, or of keeping up a laugh for a whole fortnight, as we have done, and intend to do, until the whole town becomes a community of laughing philosophers like ourselves. We have no intention, however, of undervaluing the abilities of these two young men whom we verily believe, according to common acceptation, young men *of promise*.

Were we ill-natured, we might publish something that would get our representatives into difficulties; but far be it from us to do any thing to the injury of persons to whom we are under such obligations. While they stand before us, we, like little Teucer, behind the sevenfold shield of Ajax, can launch unseen our sportive arrows, which we trust will never inflict a wound, unless like his, they fly, "heaven directed," to some conscience struck bosom.

Another marvellous great source of pleasure to us, is the abuse our work has received from several wooden gentlemen, whose censures we covet more than ever we did any thing in our lives. The moment we declared open war against folly and stupidity, we expected to receive no quarter, and to provoke a confederacy of all the blockheads in town. For it is one of our indisputable facts, that so sure as you catch a gander by the tail, the whole flock, geese, goslings, one and all, have a fellow-feeling on the occasion, and begin to cackle and hiss like so many devils bewitched. As we have a profound respect for these antient and respectable birds, on the score of their once saving the capitol, we hereby declare, that we mean no offence whatever by comparing them to the aforesaid confederacy. We have heard in our walks such criticisms on Salmagundi, as almost induced a belief that folly had here, as in the east, her moments of inspired idiotism. Every silly-royster has, as if by an instinctive sense of anticipated danger, joined in the cry, and condemned us without mercy. All is thus as it should be. It would have mortified us very sensibly had we been disappointed in this particular, as we should then have been apprehensive that our shafts had fallen to the ground, innocent of the "blood or brains" of a single numskull. Our efforts have been crowned with wonderful success. All the queer fish, the grubs, the flats, the noddies, and the live oak and timber gentlemen, are pointing their empty guns at us; and we are threatened with a most puissant confederacy of the "pigmies and cranes," and other "light militia," backed by the heavy armed artillery of dullness and stupidity. The veriest dreams of our most sanguine moments are thus realized. We have no fear of the censures of the wise, the good, or the fair; for they will ever be sacred from our attacks. We reverence the wise, love the good, and adore the fair; we declare ourselves champions in their cause—in the cause of morality—and we throw our gauntlet to all the world besides.

While we profess and feel the same indifference to public applause as at first, we most earnestly invite the attacks and censures of all the wooden warriors of this sensible city, and especially of that distinguished and learned body, heretofore celebrated under the appellation of "The North-river Society." The thrice valiant and renowned Don Quixote, never made such work amongst the wool-clad warriors of Trapoban, or the puppets of the itinerant showman, as we promise to make amongst these fine fellows; and we pledge ourselves to the public in general, and the Albany skippers, in particular, that the North-river shall not be set on fire this winter at least, for we shall give the authors of that nefarious scheme, ample employment for some time to come.

"―――― *How now, mooncalf!*"

We have been congratulating ourselves exceedingly on having, at length, attracted the notice of a ponderous genius of this city, Dr. Christopher Costive, L. L. D. &c. who has spoken of us in such a manner that we are ten times better pleased than ever we were before. It shall never be said of us, that we have been out-done in the way of complimenting, and we therefore assure Dr. Christopher Costive that, for a Yankee doodle song, about "Sister Tabitha," "our Cow," and "dandy," and "sugar-candy," and all these jokes of truely *Eastern saltness*, we know no man more "cute" than himself.

If Dr. Costive should find fault with having nothing but

whipt syllabub from us, we promise him that, if circumstances render it necessary, we will occasionally give it a little variety by whipping him up in it as completely as ever a dish of ass's milk was whipt up in this world. Our friend seems rather vociferous in his demand for a dish of "flummery," and as such a dish is not in our bill of fare, we immediately requested our publisher to procure us one that would suit our friend's appetite. He has brought us "Democracy Unveiled, or Tyranny stripped of the garb of Patriotism," by Christopher Costive, L. L. D. &c. &c. &c. &c. &c. &c. &c. We can now promise our friend to serve him up a plentiful dish of flummery from his own shop, whenever he thinks fit to demand it, and garnished with a little Salmagundi for sauce. We hope he will not behave like his prototype, Dr. Lampedo, and gag at his own "patent draught."

Our respected friend appears a little worried that we do not write for money. Now this looks ill of Dr. Costive—not that we thereby mean to insinuate that Dr. Costive is an ill-looking personage: on the contrary, we think him a great poet, a very great poet, the greatest poet of the age, and, considering the excessive gravity of his person, we are the more astonished at the sublime flights of his fat fancy. To convince him that we are disposed to befriend him, all in our power, we take this opportunity to inform our numerous readers that there *is* such a man as Dr. Christopher Costive, and that he publishes a *weakly* paper, called the "Weekly Inspector," some where in this city; and that he writes *for money*. We, therefore, advise "every body, man, woman, and child, that can read, or get any body to read for them, to purchase *his* paper," where they will find the true "bubble and squeak," and "topsyturvy," which Dr. Costive will at any time exchange *for money*.

Upon the whole, we consider him a very modest, decent, good-looking *big* man, who writes *for money*; being but "half a fish and half a monster."

PROCLAMATION,
from the MILL *of* PINDAR COCKLOFT, *esq.*

To all the young belles who enliven our scene,
From ripe five-and-forty, to blooming fifteen;

Who racket at routs, and who rattle at plays,
Who visit, and fidget, and dance out their days;
Who conquer all hearts, with a shot from the eye,
Who freeze with a frown, and who thaw with a sigh;—
To all those bright youths who embellish the age,
Whether young boys or old boys, or numskull or sage;
Whether DULL DOGS, who cringe at their mistresses' feet,
Who sigh and who whine, and who try to look sweet;
Whether TOUGH DOGS, who squat down stock-still in a row,
And play wooden gentlemen stuck up for show;
Or SAD DOGS, who glory in *running their rigs*,
Now dash in their sleighs, and now whirl in their gigs;
Who riot at Dyde's on imperial champaign,
And then scour our city—the peace to maintain;
To whoe'er it concerns, or may happen to meet,
By these presents their worships I lovingly greet.
Now KNOW YE, that I, PINDAR COCKLOFT, Esquire,
Am Laureat, appointed at special desire;—
A censor, self-dubb'd, to admonish the fair,
And tenderly take the town under my care.

   I'm a ci-devant beau, cousin Launcelot has said—
A remnant of habits long vanish'd and dead:
But still, though my heart dwells with rapture sublime,
On the fashions and customs which reign'd in my prime;
I yet can perceive—and still candidly praise,
Some maxims and manners of these "latter days;"—
Still own that some wisdom and beauty appears,
Though almost entomb'd in the rubbish of years.

   No fierce nor tyrannical cynic am I,
Who frown on each foible I chance to espy;
Who pounce on a novelty, just like a kite,
And tear up a victim through malice or spite;
Who expose to the scoffs of an ill-natur'd crew,
A trembler for starting a whim that is new.
No, no—I shall cautiously hold up my glass,
To the sweet little blossoms who heedlessly pass;—
My remarks not too pointed to wound or offend,
Nor so vague as to miss their benevolent end:
Each innocent fashion shall have its full sway;
New modes shall arise to astonish Broadway;

Red hats and red shawls still illumine the town,
And each belle, like a bonfire, blaze up and down.
  Fair spirits, who brighten the gloom of our days,
Who cheer this dull scene with your heavenly rays,
No mortal can love you more firmly and true,
From the crown of the head, to the sole of the shoe.
I'm old fashion'd, tis true,—but still runs in my heart,
That affectionate stream, to which youth gave the start;
More calm in its current,—yet potent in force;
Less ruffled by gales,—but still stedfast in course.
Though the lover enraptured no longer appears—
Tis the guide and the guardian enlighten'd by years.
All ripen'd, and mellow'd, and soften'd by time,
The asperities polish'd which chafed in my prime,
I am fully prepared for that delicate end,
The fair one's instructor, companion and friend.
—And should I perceive you in fashion's gay dance,
Allured by the frippery-mongers of France,
Expose your weak frames to a wintery sky,
To be nipp'd by its frosts, to be torn from the eye;
My soft admonitions shall fall on your ear—
Shall whisper those parents to whom you are dear—
Shall warn you of hazards you heedlessly run,
And sing of those fair ones whom *Frost* has undone;—
Bright suns, that would scarce on our horizon dawn,
Ere *shrouded* from sight, they were early withdrawn:
Gay sylphs, who have floated in circles below,
As pure in their souls, and as transient as snow;
Sweet roses, that bloom'd and decay'd to my eye,
And of forms that have flitted and pass'd to the sky.
  But as to those brainless pert bloods of our town,
Those sprigs of the ton who run decency down;
Who lounge, and who lout, and who booby about,
No knowledge within, and no manners without;
Who stare at each beauty with insolent eyes;
Who rail at those morals their fathers would prize;
Who are loud at the play,—and who impiously dare
To come in their cups to the routs of the fair;—
I shall hold up my mirror, to let them survey
The figures they cut as they dash it away:

Should my good-humored verse no amendment produce,
Like scare-crows, at least, they shall still be of use:
I shall stitch them in effigy up in my rhyme,
And hold them aloft through the progress of time,
As figures of fun to make the folks laugh,
Like that b——h of an angel erected by Paff,
"Vhat shtops," as he says, "all de peoples vhat come
"Vhat shmiles on dem all, and vhat peats on de trum."

SALMAGUNDI NO. IV

FROM MY ELBOW-CHAIR

PERHAPS there is no class of men to which the curious and literary are more indebted than travellers—I mean travel-mongers, who write whole volumes about themselves, their horses and their servants, interspersed with anecdotes of inn-keepers—droll sayings of stage-drivers, and interesting mem-oirs of the lord knows who. They will give you a full account of a city, its manners, customs, and manufactures, though perhaps all their knowledge of it was obtained by a peep from their inn-windows, and an interesting conversation with the landlord or the waiter. America has had its share of these buz-zards; and in the name of my countrymen I return them pro-found thanks for the compliments they have lavished upon us, and the variety of particulars concerning our own country, which we should never have discovered without their assis-tance.

Influenced by such sentiments, I am delighted to find that the Cockloft Family, among its other whimsical and mon-strous productions, is about to be enriched with a genuine travel-writer. This is no less a personage than Mr. JEREMY COCKLOFT, the only son and darling pride of my cousin, Mr. CHRISTOPHER COCKLOFT. I should have said Jeremy Cock-loft *the younger*, as he so styles himself by way of distinguish-ing him from IL SIGNORE JEREMO COCKLOFTICO, a gouty old gentleman who flourished about the time that Pliny the elder was smoked to death with the fire and brimstone of Vesuvius, and whose travels, if he ever wrote any, are now lost forever to the world. Jeremy is at present in his one-and-twentieth year, and a young fellow of wonderful quick parts, if you will trust to the word of his father, who having begot-ten him, should be the best judge of the matter. He is the oracle of the family, dictates to his sisters on every occasion, though they are some dozen or more years older than him-self—and never did son give mother better advice than Jeremy.

As old Cockloft was determined his son should be both a scholar and a gentleman, he took great pains with his education, which was completed at our university, where he became exceedingly expert in quizzing his teachers and playing billiards. No student made better squibs and crackers to blow up the chemical professor; no one chalked more ludicrous caricatures on the walls of the college; and none were more adroit in shaving pigs and climbing lightening rods. He moreover learned all the letters of the greek alphabet, could demonstrate that water never "of its own accord" rose above the level of its source, and that air was certainly the principle of life, for he had been entertained with the humane experiment of a cat, worried to death in an air-pump. He once shook down the ash-house by an artificial earthquake, and nearly blew his sister Barbara and her cat, out of the window with thundering powder. He likewise boasts exceedingly of being thoroughly acquainted with the composition of Lacedemonian black broth, and once made a pot of it which had well nigh poisoned the whole family, and actually threw the cook-maid into convulsions. But above all, he values himself upon his logic, has the old college conundrum of the cat with three tails at his fingers' ends, and often hampers his father with his syllogisms, to the great delight of the old gentleman, who considers the major, minor, and conclusion, as almost equal in argument to the pulley, the wedge, and the lever in mechanics. In fact, my cousin Cockloft was once nearly annihilated with astonishment, on hearing Jeremy trace the derivation of Mango from Jeremiah King—as Jeremiah King, Jerry King! Jerking, Girkin! Cucumber, Mango! In short, had Jeremy been a student at Oxford or Cambridge, he would, in all probability, have been promoted to the dignity of a *senior wrangler*. By this sketch, I mean no disparagement to the abilities of other students of our college, for I have no doubt that every commencement ushers into society, luminaries full as brilliant as *Jeremy Cockloft, the younger*.

Having made a very pretty speech on graduating, to a numerous assemblage of old folks and young ladies, who all declared that he was a very fine young man, and made very handsome gestures: Jeremy was seized with a great desire to see, or rather to be seen by the world; and as his father was anxious to give him every possible advantage, it was determined Jeremy should visit foreign parts. In consequence of this resolution, he has spent a matter of three or four months in visiting strange places, and in the course of his travels has tarried some few days at the splendid metropolis' of Albany and Philadelphia.

Jeremy has travelled as every modern man of sense should do, that is, he judges of things by the sample next at hand—if he has ever any doubt on a subject, always decides against the city where he happens to sojourn, and invariably takes *home* as the standard by which to direct his judgment.

Going into his room the other day, when he happened to be absent, I found a manuscript volume laying on his table, and was overjoyed to find it contained notes and hints for a book of travels which he intends publishing. He seems to have taken a late fashionable travel-monger for his model, and I have no doubt his work will be equally instructive and amusing with that of his prototype. The following are some extracts, which may not prove uninteresting to my readers.

MEMORANDUMS
For a Tour, to be entitled
"THE STRANGER IN NEW-JERSEY;
OR, COCKNEY TRAVELLING."
BY JEREMY COCKLOFT, *the Younger*.

CHAPTER I.

The man in the moon*—preparations for departure— hints to travellers about packing their trunks†—straps, buckles and bed-cords—case of pistols, *a la cockney*—five trunks, three bandboxes—a cocked hat,—and a medicine-chest, *a la francaise*—parting advice of my two sisters—quere, why old maids are so particular in their cautions against naughty women—Description of Powles-Hook ferry-boats—might be converted into gun boats, and defend our port equally well with Albany sloops—BROM, the black ferryman—Charon— River Styx—ghosts—Major Hunt—good story—ferryage

* *vide* Carr's Stranger in Ireland.
† *vide* Weld.

nine-pence—city of Harsimus—built on the spot where the
folk once danced on their stumps, while the devil fiddled—
quere, why do the Harsimites talk dutch?—story of the
Tower of Babel, and confusion of tongues—get into the
stage—driver a wag—famous fellow for running stage
races—killed three passengers and crippled nine in the course
of his practice—philosophical reasons why stage drivers love
grog—causeway—ditch on each side for folk to tumble
into—famous place for *skilly-pots*; Philadelphians call 'em tarapins—roast them under the ashes as we do potatoes—
quere, may not this be the reason that the Philadelphians are
all turtle heads?—Hackensack bridge—good painting of a
blue horse jumping over a mountain—wonder who it was
painted by—mem. to ask the *Baron de Gusto* about it on my
return—Rattle-snake hill, so called from abounding with butterflies—salt marsh, *surmounted* here and there by a solitary
hay-stack—more tarapins—wonder why the Philadelphians
dont establish a fishery here, and get a patent for it—bridge
over the Passaic—rate of toll—description of toll boards—
toll man had but one eye—story how it *is possible* he *may*
have lost the other—pence table, &c.*—

CHAP. II.

Newark—noted for its fine breed of fat musquitoes—sting
through the thickest boot†—story about *Gallynipers*—Archy
Gifford and his man Caliban—jolly fat fellows—a knowing
traveller always judges of every thing by the inn-keepers and
waiters‡—set down Newark people all fat as butter—learned
dissertation on Archy Gifford's green coat, with philosophical
reasons why the Newarkites wear red worsted night-caps, and
turn their noses to the south when the wind blows—Newark
Academy full of windows—sunshine excellent to make little
boys grow—Elizabeth-Town—fine girls—vile musquitoes—
plenty of oysters—quere, have oysters any feeling?—good
story about the fox catching them by his tail—ergo, foxes

* *vide* Carr.
† *vide* Weld.
‡ *vide* Carr. *vide* Moore. *vide* Weld. *vide* Parkinson. *vide* Priest. *vide*
Linkum Fidelius, and *vide* Messrs. Tag, Rag, and Bobtail.

might be of great use in the pearl fishery—landlord member
of the Legislature—treats every body who has a vote—mem.
all the inn-keepers members of Legislature in New-Jersey—
Bridge-Town, vulgarly called *Spank-Town*, from a story of a
quondam parson and his wife—real name, according to
Linkum Fidelius, Bridge-Town, from *bridge*, a contrivance to
get dry shod over a river or brook; and *town*, an appellation
given in America to the accidental assemblage of a church, a
tavern, and a blacksmith's shop—Linkum as right as my left
leg—Rahway-River—good place for gun-boats—wonder
why Mr. Jefferson dont send a *river fleet* there, to protect the
hay vessels?—Woodbridge—landlady mending her husband's
breeches—sublime apostrophe to conjugal affection and the
fair sex*—Woodbridge famous for its crab fishery—
sentimental correspondence between a crab and a lobster—
digression to Abelard and Eloisa—mem. when the moon is
in *Pisces* she plays the devil with the crabs.

CHAP. III.

Brunswick—oldest town in the state—division line between two counties in the middle of the street—posed a lawyer with the case of a man standing with one foot in each
county—wanted to know in which he was *domicil*—lawyer
couldn't tell for the soul of him—mem. all the New-Jersey
lawyers *nums*—Miss Hay's boarding-school—young ladies
not allowed to eat mustard—and why?—fat story of a mustard pot, with a good saying of Ding-dong's—Vernon's tavern—fine place to sleep, if the noise would let you—another
Caliban!—Vernon *slew* eyed—people of Brunswick, of
course, all squint—Drake's tavern—fine old blade—wears
square buckles in his shoes—tells bloody long stories about
last war—people, of course, all do the same—Hook'em
Snivy, the famous fortune teller, born here—cotemporary
with mother Shoulders—particulars of his history—died one
day—lines to his memory, *which found their way into my
pocket-book*†—melancholy reflections on the death of great
men—beautiful epitaph on myself.

* *vide* The Sentimental Kotzebue.
† *vide* Carr and *Blind Bet!*

CHAP. IV.

Princeton—college—professors wear boots!—students famous for their love of a jest—set the college on fire, and burnt out the professors; an excellent joke, but not worth repeating—mem. American students very much addicted to burning down colleges—reminds me of a good story, nothing at all to the purpose—two societies in the college—good notion—encourages emulation, and makes little boys fight—students famous for their eating and erudition—saw two at the tavern, who had just got their allowance of spending-money—laid it all out in a supper—got fuddled, and d——d the professors for nincoms. N. B. Southern gentlemen.—Church-yard—apostrophe to grim death—saw a cow feeding on a grave—metempsychosis—who knows but the cow may have been eating up the soul of one of my ancestors—made me melancholy and pensive for fifteen minutes—man planting cabbages*—wondered how he could plant them so straight—method of mole catching—and all that—quere, whether it would not be a good notion to ring their noses as we do pigs—mem. to propose it to the American Agricultural Society—get a premium perhaps—commencement—students give a ball and supper—company from New-York, Philadelphia and Albany—great contest which spoke the best english—albanians vociferous in their demand for sturgeon—philadelphians gave the preference to racoon,† and splac-nuncs—gave them a long dissertation on the phlegmatic nature of a goose's gizzard—students can't dance—always set off with the wrong foot foremost—Duport's opinion on that subject—Sir Christopher Hatton the first man who ever turned out his toes in dancing—great favorite with queen Bess on that account—Sir Walter Raleigh—good story about his smoking—his descent into New-Spain—El Dorado—Candid—Dr. Pangloss—Miss Cunegunde—earthquake at Lisbon—Baron of Thundertentronck—jesuits—monks—Cardinal Woolsey—Pope Joan—Tom Jefferson—Tom Paine, and Tom the ——— whew! N. B. Students got drunk as usual.

* *vide* Carr.
† *vide* Priest.

CHAP. V.

Left Princeton—country finely diversified with sheep and haystacks*—saw a man riding alone in a waggon! why the deuce didn't the blockhead ride in a chair? fellow must be a fool;—particular account of the construction of waggons, carts, wheelbarrows and quail-traps—saw a large flock of crows—concluded there must be a dead horse in the neighborhood—mem. country remarkable for crows—won't let the horses die in peace—anecdote of a jury of crows—stopped to give the horses water—good looking man came up, and asked me if I had seen his wife? heavens! thought I, how strange it is that this virtuous man should ask *me* about his wife—story of Cain and Abel—stage-driver took a *swig*—mem. set down all the people as drunkards—old house had moss on the top—swallows built in the roof—better place than old men's beards—story about that—derivation of words, *kippy*, *kippy*, *kippy* and *shoo-pig*†—negro driver could not write his own name—languishing state of literature in this country‡—philosophical inquiry of 'Sbidli-kens, why the americans are so much inferior to the nobility of Cheapside and Shoreditch, and why they do not eat plum-pudding on Sundays—superfine reflections about any thing.

CHAP. VI.

Trenton—built above the head of navigation to encourage commerce—capital of the state—only wants a castle, a bay, a mountain, a sea, and a volcano, to bear a strong resemblance to the bay of Naples§—supreme court sitting—fat chief justice—used to get asleep on the bench after dinner—gave judgment, I suppose like Pilate's wife, from his dreams—reminded me of Justice Bridlegoose deciding by a throw of a die, and of the oracle of the holy bottle—attempted to kiss the chamber-maid—boxed my ears till they rung like our theatre bell—girl had lost one tooth—mem. all the american ladies prudes, and have bad teeth—Anacreon Moore's opin-

* *vide* Carr.
† *vide* Carr's learned derivation of *gee* and *whoa*.
‡Moore.
§Carr.

ion on the matter—State-house—fine place to see the sturgeons jump up—quere, whether sturgeons jump up by an impulse of the tail, or whether they bounce up from the bottom by the elasticity of their noses—Linkum Fidelius of the latter opinion—I too—sturgeon's nose capital for tennis-balls—learnt that at school—went to a ball—negro wench principal musician!—N. B. People of America have no fiddlers but females!—origin of the phrase "fiddle of your heart"—reasons why men fiddle better than the women—expedient of the amazons who were expert at the bow—waiter at the city-tavern—good story of his—nothing to the purpose—never mind—fill up my book like Carr—make it sell.—Saw a democrat get into the stage followed by his dog*—N. B. This town remarkable for dogs and democrats—superfine sentiment†—good story from Joe Miller—ode to a piggin of butter—pensive meditations on a mouse-hole—make a book as clear as a whistle!

FROM MY ELBOW-CHAIR.

I have observed a particular intimacy for these few days past, between that dry wag WILL WIZARD and my cousin PINDAR. The latter has taken his winter quarters at old COCK-LOFT'S, in the corner room opposite mine, in order to be at hand and overlook the town. They hardly gave themselves time, on Sunday last, to wait for the family toast of "our absent friends" before they adjourned to Pindar's chamber. In the course of an hour my cousin's enormous mandarine ink-stand was sent down to be replenished;—I began to be seriously alarmed, for I thought if they had exhausted its contents without exhausting their subject, there was no knowing where it would end.

On returning to tea, my cousin Pindar was observed to rub his hands, a sure sign that something tickled his fancy; he however maintained as mysterious a countenance as a seventh ward politician. As to Will Wizard, he took longer strides than usual, his inflexible phiz had an uncommonly knowing air, and a sagacious wink occasionally betrayed that he had

*Moore.
†Carr.

more in his head than he chose to communicate. The whole
family (who in truth are much given to *wonder* at every thing)
were sadly puzzled to conjecture what their two precious
noddles had been bothering about.

In the evening, after I had retreated to my citadel, the elbow-chair, I was surprized by the abrupt entrance of these
two worthies. My cousin opened the budget at once: he declared that it was as necessary for a modern poet to have an
assistant, as for Don Quixote to have a Sancho—that it was
the fashion for poets, now a-days, to write so ineffably obscure, that every line required a page of notes to explain its
meaning, and render its "darkness visible"—that a modern
poem could no more succeed without notes, than a paper kite
could fly without a tail. In a word, Pegasus had become a
most mulish animal, and would not budge a foot, unless he
lumbered along a cart-load of quotations and explanations,
and illustrations at his heels: he had therefore prevailed on
Will Wizard to assist him occasionally as annotator and illustrator. As a specimen of their united labors, he handed me
the following complimentary ode to that king of the buzzards, Dr. CHRISTOPHER COSTIVE, informing me that he had
plenty more on hand whenever occasion required it. I had
been rather surprized lately at the doctor's meddling with us,
as he was sure of gaining more kicks than coppers in return;
but I am told an ass loves to have his muzzle scratched with
nettles. On expressing my surprise, Will informed me that it
was all a sham battle; that he was very intimate with the doctor, and could relate a thousand diverting anecdotes concerning him; and that the doctor finding we were in want of a
butt, had generously volunteered himself as our target. I wish
him joy of his bargain.

In the following poem it will be observed that, while my
cousin Pindar tunes his pipe on the top of the page, Will
Wizard, worries away at his thorough bass below. The notes
of a modern poem being like the sound of a french horn,
bassoon, kettle drum, and bass-viol in our orchestra, which
make such a confounded racket, that they entirely drown the
song; and no man, who has not the sublime ear of a connoisseur, can tell what the devil tune they're playing.

FLUMMERY

FROM THE MILL (1) OF PINDAR COCKLOFT, ESQ.

Being a Poem with Notes, or rather Notes with a
Poem, (2) *in the manner of*
DOCTOR (3) CHRISTOPHER COSTIVE.
"Prick me Bull-calf till he roars." (4)
Falstaff.

THE greatest (5) poet of our day,
From State of Maine to Louisiana; (6)
The hero who did 'sist upon't,
He wouldn't be deputy to Mr. Hunt; (7)
Who rear'd a gallows for each elf, and
Did for *hangman* his own self stand. (8)
And made folks think it very odd, he
Should turn *Jack Ketch* to every body,
This modern mounter of Pegasus,
This clumsy jolter of Jackasses (9)
Who, now the poets dray horse starts on,
Anon, the gibbet hurdle carts on,
Now o'er a poem dozes happy,
And next expertly draws the cap; he
Who cares not though the world should know it
That he's half hangman, half a poet. (10)
Who gibbetted the knaves so knowing,
That kept Democracy a going,
Hung his *fac simile* famed Toney (11)
Pasquin, the friend of Mr. Honé.
Who drags like snail his filthy slime
Through many a ragged hobbling rhyme,
Then calls his billingsgate—sarcastic!
His drabbling doggrel—hudibrastic!
[Good lack, my friends, 'twould make you soon (12) laugh,
To see this jolter-headed moon-calf,
From Hudibras his honors steal
And break Sam Butler on the wheel.] (13)
With other things that I might tell ye on
Performed by this rump-fed hellion (14)
—But not o'er long to dwell upon't,
This man as big as an elephant. (15)

This *sweetest* witling of the age, (16)
This hero, hangman, critic, sage, (17)
This poet of five hundred pound (18)
Has come to grace our hapless town.
And when he entered, every goose
Began to cackle like the deuce;
The asses brayed to one another—
Twas plain—the creatures smelt a brother.

NOTES, BY WILLIAM WIZARD, ESQ.

1 *Mill*] As we are not a little anxious to cultivate the intimacy so happily commenced between the Doctor and ourselves, we feel bound in candor to confess the charge made against us, of having borrowed from him some of the phrazes and ideas of our last number; and we justify ourselves by attributing it to our high regard for his talents: for what can be a greater proof of friendship, now a days, than borrowing? if we were his enemies, we might justify it by the old maxim of "foiling the devil with his own weapons." As to the "mill," which the Doctor so vociferously claims, honest Pindar acknowledges that he borrowed the idea from the Doctor's writings in general, for he never dipped in them without thinking of our nocturnal music-grinder, who continually grinds over and over the same sleepy tune of, "Oh, hard is my fate."

2 *Notes with a Poem*] Whatever merit may appear in this Poem, my friend Cockloft must own that it is entirely owing to his close adherence to his *big* prototype, Dr. Costive. The rhymes are generally *borrowed* from the Doctor's own works, possessing all that quaintness, cuteness and clumsiness, for which he is remarkable. As the lesser thing should always depend upon the greater, we have rather inverted the usual title of such works, and made the poem minor. We recommend the Doctor's mode of *compiling* a book to all the nums of the day—as an example, we instance his "Terrible Tractoration," of which as few buy, and still fewer read it, (a proof that the town are not quite such fools as the Doctor would make them) we shall say little. This book was smothered in notes,

like a goose in onions—some ill-natured cynics have asserted that what little whim the work contained, lay entirely in the notes, which we are sorry to say were not written by the Doctor;—his poem might therefore be said to resemble the *leg of a stool*, dress'd up with *savory sauce*; or, as the Doctor will understand it better, that famous dish called *pumpkin-pie*, where, though the *pumpkin* gives the *name* to the dish, yet the great skill of the cook is to hide the twang of it as much as possible with *spice* and *sugar*.

3 *Doctor*] The Doctor, we are told, was not bred a physician; nor was he indebted for his appellation to a gratuitous donation from any university, as Doctor of Laws—he was humorously so dubbed by his neighbors in Vermont, on account of having once benevolently physick'd a sick horse—his works bear testimony to his drenching abilities; and we may justly apply to him an unlucky epigram, written on a brother quack in physic and poetry:

> *"For physic and farces*
> *His equal there scarce is;—*
> *His farces are physic,—*
> *His physic a farce is."*

4. *Prick bull-calf, &c.*] We had not the least expectation that our notice of Doctor Costive, in the last number, would have put him into such an indecent passion. Bless us how he has roared! and like Falstaff not only roared but "ran and roared"—

> ————*"unpack'd his heart with words,*
> *And fell a cursing—like a very drab!*
> *A scullion!"*

He has given us a most woeful *scolding* through some eight or nine columns, and plainly proved that our work was not worth a fig, because "Salmagundi" had been heretofore given as a title to another work—Launcelot Langstaff was evidently copied from Isaac Bickerstaff, because they both ended with *staff*—"Whim whams" was the same as "Flim Flams"—"Will Wizard" was taken from—the lord knows where, *"Wintry"* was accidentally misspelled or misprinted *Wintery*, and "*Weakly*" was borrowed from his own *Weakly* productions—Oh Midas, Midas, how thine ears do loom through the fog of thy writings—When a man of the Doctor's gumption can write nine columns against our work and discover no greater faults, we may well be vain—were we to criticize our own writings, they would stand a much poorer chance. In spite of the Doctor's crustiness we still love him in our hearts—he may scold like an old woman, but we know it all arises from that excessive irritability common to all men who have " written a book" and particularly a book of doggrel rhymes.—We again assure him of our perfect good will towards himself and his most amiable offspring, that delectable pair of twin brothers, Terrible Tractoration and Democracy Unveiled.—May the whole world in general and posterity in particular know the proper distinction between Hudibrastic and Doggerel, and acquit the Doctor from the imputation meanly levelled against him by sundry nincoms of imitating Hudibras—We are sorry that he should ever have been thought capable of descending to be a copyist, and we challenge the whole world to deny that the Doctor's verse is doggerel, genuine broken winded, rickety doggerel, whatever his enemies may insist to the contrary. The Doctor's waggery, however, like that of many other double headed wits, seems often to have been taken by the wrong end. On the first appearance of his Terrible Tractoration, the critics were absolutely at a loss, such was the delicacy of his wit, to say whether he was the champion or opponent of Perkinism—Thus the Critical Review for 1803, "His real object cannot always be ascertained—we *think* him however the friend of the Tractors." Either the doctor or the critic must have been a dunder head—we charitably suppose the critic. The Doctor afterwards, like "John-a-Gudgeon" in the "pleaders guide" explained, and his explanation proved so perfectly satisfactory that there were very few of the reviewers but could tell, or at least *guess* at his object. The fact was the doctor, good inoffensive soul, did not mean to attack any thing—except common sense—We recommend this work as a soporific specimen of the doctor's skill in *balderdash*.

5 *Greatest poet*.] *Great* is sometimes a positive, sometimes a

figurative term—as we say a *great man*, a *great mountain*, or when speaking of the Doctor, a *great man mountain*—having no allusion here to the mountain which brought forth a mouse. When, however, we speak of the Doctor as a *great* man, or *great* poet, we mean to be understood that he is some six feet six inches high—three feet across the shoulders, nine round the paunch—that he weighs about half a ton, and is withal most clumsily hung together.

6 *Louisiana.*] Though we plume ourselves on adhering closely to the Doctor's rhymes, yet we have taken the liberty of differing a little in the pronunciation of this word—the Doctor gives it in the true eastern dialect, Lousy-anee—but to give it *a-la-costive*—

> "Which late, tis said, in weather rainy,
> Was melted in Louisiana."

Again: for when the Doctor gets hold of a good rhyme, he is a " woundy toad" for harping on it.

> *But please his highness ship, I wont*
> *Be deputy to Mr. Hunt:*
> *No—were it offered 'twould be vain, he*
> *Wont catch me in Louisiana. (or Lousy anee.)*

These two latter lines are truly as musical, as marrow-bones and cleavers, and remind us of that sweet couplet, by the Doctor's rival, the inimitable SEARSON.

> *From this seat I pass'd to Alexandria,*
> *And am pleased through rural scenes to wander.*
> SEAR. Mount Ver.

If our reader wishes for more specimens of the Doctor's knack at rhyming, we'll give him the oft repeated tags of 'rogues and demagogues,' 'brewing and ruin,' ' wildering & children' ' women & common' 'trimming and women' ' well-knows and fellows,' 'comparison and harrass'd-em;' together with an occasional mixture of those attic eastern jingles of 'dandy and handy' and 'sugar-candy.' The Doctor and Sear-

son's poetic contest is similar to one that whilom took place
between two honest tars (we beg the gentle Joe Miller's pardon for *borrowing* an anecdote) one gave as *prize couplet*;

> *As she slips she slides along,*
> *A faithful friend is hard to find.*

but the other *rhymster* beat him all hollow by singing out,

> *"My quart pot holds a gallon,*
> *By zounds!"*

7 *Deputy to Mr. Hunt*] Mr. Hunt was a *little* man and a
young man, the Doctor, although of the same age, feeling the
immensity of his qualifications refuses to second such a governor, urging his *size*, and like Billy Bugby, alledging that
what he wanted in years he made up in *bulk*; and if he lacked
in brains, he atoned for all in *garbage*.

8 *Did for hangman, &c.*] How the Doctor ever came to
stumble on this unhappy idea, we are at a loss to imagine—
it is an odd " whim-wham," for a fellow to dub himself with
the humorous epithet of *hangman*. "We would not have his
enemies say so." Whether the doctor has a *hanging look* or no,
we leave others to determine. We are certain he is in no danger of the gallows himself;—but we warn him to take care
how he visits Connecticut—he may chance to be burnt for a
witch. We give the doctor's own claim to his *Tyburn title*.

> *Now since ye are a ruffian crew,*
> *As honest Jack Ketch ever knew;*
> *No threats nor growling shall prohibit*
> *My hanging you on satire's gibbet.*   *vide* Costive

9 *This clumsy jolter of jackasses.*] As this line partakes of the
true costive obscurity, we beg leave to explain. There is no
intention of calling the Doctor a jackass, we only mean that
he makes an ass of Pegasus, and even when on poor Pegasus
(so degraded) he is but a miserable rider. His trotting, pacing, nigglety-nagglety lines, put us often in mind of that

pious but quaint expression about the "devil riding rough shod over a soul."

10 *Half a poet.*] Oh fie, friend Cockloft, this savors of sheer envy. Were there any doubts of the Doctors being a whole poet—aye, and a *big* poet, the following verse would set them at rest. It shows that he is a complete jockey on Pegasus; and when the poor nag wont pace, he'll cudgel him as soundly as he does his own brains.

> Yes, we were 'raptured when he said
> We're all republican, all fed-
> Ral fellow-citizens, Americans,
> And hoped we'd done with factions' hurricanes!
> > *Costive*

Is this poetic frenzy, (alias idiotism) or is it turgid stupidity? truly it is as smooth as a pine log causeway; it confirms the Doctor's right to his *sir-name*, and can only be matched by a stave from the Doctor's cotemporary bard, and rival *rhymster*, Searson—videlicet.

> *From house to house, soon took my departure,*
> *And to the garden look'd for sweet nature.*
> *The fishing very great at Mount Vernon,*
> *When there with other scenes I look'd upon.*
> *This pleasing seat hath its prospects so high,*
> *That one would think 'twas for astronomy,*
> *'Twould answer for an observatory.*

The reader will perceive the similarity in taste, style, and ear of these rival poets. I have their works bound up together, and Minshull's into the bargain. It shall go hard but that they shall all descend the gutter of immortality together.

11 *His fac simile famed Toney*] The Doctor's abusing poor Toney Pasquin, brought forcibly to our recollection the vulgar cant saying about the pot and the kettle. Perhaps no two of the *great* poets of the day, are more alike, in most particulars, than Doctor Costive and honest Tony. The Doctor is a true poetic blackguard—and so is Toney. The Doctor is an adept in the Billingsgate vocabulary—so is Tony. The Doctor has

bespattered many a poor devil who never offended him—
so has Toney. The doctor has written a book—so has Toney.
It may be said of each of them—

> *"We will not rake the dunghill for his crimes,*
> *Who knows the man will never read his rhymes."*

The only particular in which they disagree is, that Toney
has been occasionally convicted of saying a good thing—the
gentle stupidity of the doctor being entirely innocent of any
thing of the kind.

> "Oh here's another pumpion, the cramm'd son of a
> starved usurer, Cacafogo. Both their brains buttered can-
> not make two spoonsful."   *Rule a Wife*.

12 *Soon*] This word is entirely unnecessary to the sense, and
is dragged in for no other purpose whatever, but to eke out
the line, in humbler *imitation* of a dull, but honest expedient,
frequently made use of by the illustrious Searson, and his
great rival, Doctor Costive.

13 *And break, &c.*] It has for some time been a trick with
many a sleepy scribbler, beside the Doctor, though now it has
grown rather notorious, to break their crabbed lines with a
"fist or stick" or crow-bar, and then term their *chopped hay*
Hudibrastic—thus is poetry daily put on the rack; and thus
is poor Butler crucified every hour!

14 *Rump-fed hellion*] Lest the Doctor should here again accuse us of *borrowing*, a thing, by the by, we strongly suspect
him of, as we think we can discover that many of his
thoughts, and certainly some of his rhymes, are *borrowed* from
the immortal Searson and the inimitable Minshull, we acknowledge that we are indebted for this line to Shakspeare.
Whether the term *rump-fed* applies to the doctor or not, we
cannot exactly tell; but if we were not afraid of swelling our
notes, we would, following the example of the Doctor in his
Democracy Unveiled, give our readers an account of the famous *rump* parliament—and truly 'twould be as much in
point as most of the notes in that celebrated work.

Hellion. A deputy scullion employed in regions below "to

cook up the broth"—Link. Fid.—The doctor, good man, has employed himself, while on earth, as far as his *weakly* powers would go, in stewing up many a woeful kettle of fish.—

> *"Double, double, toil and trouble,*
> *"Fire burn, and caldron bubble."*

Shakspeare must certainly have had the Doctor's weekly mess of *bubble* and *squeak* in view, when he wrote the above.

15 *As big as an elephant*] There is more truth than poetry in this comparison. The following curious anecdote was told me by the Doctor himself, when I breakfasted with him the other morning:—The elephant which travelled lately through our country, was shown in New England;—two simple country girls, desirous of seeing what kind of a beast it was, applied for admittance. On entering the room, the doctor, who was stooping to tie his shoe-string with his back towards them, was for a moment taken for the elephant!—they declared it was a clumsy creature—"they could not make head nor tail of it." No wonder, poor things, the critics were as much puzzled themselves, as we have already shown.

16 *Sweetest witling*] A poetic licence, the Doctor certainly being none of the sweetest of personages. Many a fair flower, however, springs out of a dung-hill—and the Doctor is not the first poet who has written a *sweet* song in "marvelous dirty linen."

17 *This hero hangman, &c.*]

> *All hush'd in mute attention sit,*
> *To hear this critic, poet, wit,*
> *Philosopher, all, all at once,*
> *And to complete them, all this* DUNCE.
> > LLOYD.

18 *Five hundred pounds*] i. e. five hundred pounds weight; or in true avoirdupoise, 4 cwt. 1 qu. 24 lbs.

GENERAL REMARK.

We have endeavored to copy the Doctor's style and manner as correctly as possible throughout this charming poem: the *rhymes* are chiefly "filched" from his own *labors*, and jingle as harmoniously as sleigh bells—like him we have sometimes risen, and sometimes descended, with all his leaden profundity. Some poets sip in the heliconian stream, others dabble in it. The Doctor exceeds them all—he has a true poetic DIVING BELL—plunges boldly to the bottom, and there drabbles in the mud like a flounder. In the *gallows* part of his poem, the doctor may truly be said to *rise*; and in our touch on the Hellion, we have certainly almost equalled those profound sinkings of his genius, where the Doctor even descends *below himself.* We conclude with *borrowing* a speech from old Shakspeare—"Give me thy hand," Doctor, "I am sorry I beat thee; but while thou livest, keep a good tongue in thy head."

NOTICE.

While in a "state militant," waging war with folly and stupidity, and assailed on all sides by a combination of nincoms and numsculls, we are gratified to find that our careless effusions have received the approbation of men of wit and genius. We have expressed heretofore our contempt for the applause of *the million*, but we confess ourselves ambitious of the praises of *the few*; we have read therefore with infinite self-congratulation the encomiums passed on our productions by the learned and liberal editor of the "People's Friend." The attacks of that *billingsgate droll* Dr. Costive, and his whole *North-River fraternity*, could not give us greater delight. We also publish with pride the following card from the authors of "The Echo," a work which we have commended to a conspicuous post in our library; and we do hereby shake its authors by the hand as a set of right merry wags, choice spirits, and what we think better than all, genuine humorists.

CARD.

"The authors of "The Echo" send a copy of it to the writers of "Salmagundi," which they request them to accept, as a mark of the pleasure they have received from their cervantic effusions."

Now we are in the humour of card writing, we would acknowledge the reception of several effusions in prose and verse, which, though they do great credit to the writers, and would doubtless be both pleasing and instructing to the public, yet do not come exactly within the intention of our work, the authors therefore will excuse our not publishing them.

We have likewise received a note written in a french hand, but in villainous bad english. Will Wizard has been at much pains to decypher it, but in vain, it is as unintelligible as an herculanean manuscript. He has discovered however that it is a vindication of dancing, together with a long eulogy on the *pas de chat*.

As a considerable part of this paper is taken up with a stupid subject, viz. the Doctor, and as we do not wish that our readers should pay for "flummery" merely, we have directed our publisher to give them eight pages extra: this will account for the unusual size of the present number. We confess we *borrowed* this idea among many others from the Doctor, who lately finding that his readers were dissatisfied with the *contents* of his *weakly* paper, endeavored to put them in good humor by doubling its *bulk*; this he waggishly enough terms *doubling the dose*—oh the droll dog!

SALMAGUNDI NO. V

Saturday, March 7, 1807.

FROM MY ELBOW-CHAIR.

T HE FOLLOWING LETTER of my friend Mustapha appears
to have been written some time subsequent to the one
already published. Were I to judge from its contents, I should
suppose it was suggested by the splendid review of the twenty
fifth of last November, when a pair of colors was presented,
at the City-Hall, to the regiments of artillery: and when a
huge dinner was devoured by our corporation, in honorable
remembrance of the evacuation of this city. I am happy to
find that the laudable spirit of military emulation which prevails in our city has attracted the attention of a stranger of
Mustapha's sagacity—by military emulation I mean that spirited rivalry in the size of a hat, the length of a feather, and
the gingerbread finery of a sword belt; this being what I understand by *military foppery*.

LETTER
From MUSTAPHA RUB-A-DUB KELI KHAN, *to*
ABDALLAH EB'N AL RAHAB, *surnamed the*
SNORER, *military centinel at the gate of his
highness' palace.*

THOU hast heard, oh Abdallah, of the great magician,
MULEY FUZ, who could change a blooming land, blessed
with all the elysian charms of hill and dale, of glade and
grove, of fruit and flower into a desart, frightful, solitary and
forlorn; who with a wave of his wand could transform even
the disciples of Mahomet into grinning apes and chattering
monkeys. Surely, thought I to myself this morning, the
dreadful Muley has been exercising his infernal enchantments
on these unhappy infidels. Listen, oh Abdallah, and wonder.
Last night I committed myself to tranquil slumber, encompassed with all the monotonous tokens of peace, and this
morning I awoke enveloped in the noise, the bustle, the clangor, and the shouts of war. Every thing was changed as if by

magic. An immense army had sprung up, like mushrooms, in a night, and all the coblers, tailors, and tinkers of the city had mounted the nodding plume; had become, in the twinkling of an eye, helmetted heroes and war-worn veterans.

Alarmed at the beating of drums, the braying of trumpets and the shouting of the multitude, I dressed myself in haste, sallied forth and followed a prodigious crowd of people to a place called the Battery. This is so denominated, I am told, from having once been defended with formidable *wooden* bulwarks, which in the course of a hard winter were *thriftly* pulled to pieces by an *economic* corporation, to be distributed for fire-wood among the poor; this was done at the hint of a cunning old engineer, who assured them it was the only way in which their fortifications would ever be able to keep up a *warm fire*. ECONOMY, my friend, is the watch-word of this nation; I have been studying for a month past to divine its meaning, but truly am as much perplexed as ever. It is a kind of national starvation, an experiment how many comforts and necessaries the body politic can be deprived of before it perishes. It has already arrived to a lamentable degree of debility, and promises to share the fate of the arabian philosopher, who proved that he could live without food, but unfortunately died just as he had brought his experiment to perfection.

On arriving at the battery, I found an *immense* army of SIX HUNDRED MEN, drawn up in a true mussulman crescent. At first, I supposed this was in compliment to myself, but my interpreter informed me that it was done merely for want of room, the corporation not being able to afford them sufficient to display in a straight line. As I expected a display of some grand evolutions and military manoevres, I determined to remain a tranquil spectator, in hopes that I might possibly collect some hints which might be of service to his highness.

This great body of men I perceived was under the command of a small *bashaw*, in yellow and gold, with white nodding plumes, and most formidable whiskers, which, contrary to the tripolitan fashion, were in the neighborhood of his ears instead of his nose. He had two attendants called aid-decamps, (or *tails*) being similar to a bashaw with two tails. The bashaw, though commander in chief, seemed to have little more to do than myself—he was a spectator within the lines and I without—he was clear of the rabble and I was encompassed by them, this was the only difference between us, except that he had the best opportunity of showing his clothes. I waited an hour or two with exemplary patience, expecting to see some grand military evolutions or a sham battle exhibited, but no such thing took place; the men stood stock still, supporting their arms, groaning under the fatigues of war, and now and then sending out a foraging party to levy contributions of beer and a favorite beverage which they denominate *grog*. As I perceived the crowd very active in examining the line, from one extreme to the other, and as I could see no other purpose, for which these sunshine warriors should be exposed so long to the merciless attacks of wind and weather, I of course concluded that this must be *the review*.

In about two hours the army was put in motion, and marched through some narrow streets, where the *economic corporation* had carefully provided a soft carpet of mud, to a magnificent castle of painted brick decorated with grand pillars of pine boards. By the ardor which brightened in each countenance, I soon perceived that this castle was to undergo a vigorous attack. As the ordnance of the castle was perfectly silent, and as they had nothing but a straight street to advance through, they made their approaches with great courage and admirable regularity, until within about a hundred feet of the castle, a pump opposed a formidable obstacle in their way, and put the whole army to a nonplus. The circumstance was sudden and unlooked-for—the commanding officer ran over all the military tactics with which his head was crammed, but none offered any expedient for the present awful emergency. The pump maintained its post, and so did the commander; there was no knowing which was most at a stand. The commanding officer ordered his men to wheel and take it in flank—the army accordingly wheeled, and came full butt against it in rear exactly as they were before: — " wheel to the left!" cried the officer; they did so, and again, as before, the inveterate pump intercepted their progress. "Right about, face!" cried the officer; the men obeyed, but bungled—they *faced back to back*. Upon this the bashaw with two tails, with great coolness, undauntedly, ordered his men to push right forward, pell-mell, pump or no pump—they gallantly obeyed; after unheard-of acts of bravery the pump was carried without the loss of a man, and the army firmly entrenched itself under the very walls of the castle. The bashaw had then a council of war with his officers; the most vigorous measures were resolved on. An advance guard of musicians were ordered to attack the castle without mercy. Then the whole band opened a most tremendous battery of drums, fifes, tambourines, and trumpets, and kept up a thundering assault, as if the castle, like the walls of Jericho, spoken of in the jewish chronicles, would tumble down at the blowing of rams' horns. After some time a parley ensued. The grand bashaw of the city appeared on the battlements of the castle, and as far as I could understand from circumstances, dared the little bashaw of two tails to single combat;—this thou knowest was in the style of antient chivalry:—the little bashaw dismounted with great intrepidity, and ascended the battlements of the castle, where the great bashaw waited to receive him, attended by numerous dignitaries and worthies of his court, one of whom bore the splendid banners of the castle. The battle was carried on intirely by *words*, according to the universal custom of this country, of which I shall speak to thee more fully hereafter. The grand bashaw made a furious attack in a speech of considerable length; the little bashaw by no means appalled, retorted with great spirit. The grand bashaw attempted to rip him up with an argument, or stun him with a solid fact; but the little bashaw parried them both with admirable adroitness, and run him clean through and through with syllogism. The grand bashaw was overthrown, the banners of the castle yielded up to the little bashaw, and the castle surrendered after a vigorous defence of three hours—during which the besiegers suffered great extremity from muddy streets and a drizzling atmosphere.

On returning to dinner I soon discovered that as usual I had been indulging in a great mistake. The matter was all clearly explained to me by a fellow lodger, who on ordinary occasions moves in the humble character of a tailor, but in the present instance figured in a high military station denominated *corporal*. He informed me that what I had mistaken for a castle was the splendid palace of the municipality, and that the supposed attack was nothing more than the delivery of a flag, given by the authorities, to the army for its magnanimous defence of the town for upwards of twenty years past, (that is, ever since the last war!) Oh, my friend, surely every thing in this country is on a great scale!—The conversation insensibly turned upon the military establishment of the nation, and I do assure thee, that my friend the taylor, though being according to a national proverb, but the ninth part of a man, yet acquitted himself on military concerns as ably as the grand bashaw of the empire himself. He observed that their rulers had decided that wars were very useless and expensive, and ill-befitting an economic philosophic nation; they had therefore made up their minds never to have any wars, and consequently there was no need of soldiers or military discipline. As, however, it was thought highly ornamental to a city to have a number of men drest in fine clothes and *feathers*, strutting about the streets on a holiday—and as the women and children were particularly fond of such *raree shows*, it was ordered that the tailors of the different cities throughout the empire should, forthwith, go to work, and cut out and manufacture soldiers as fast as their sheers and needles would permit.

These soldiers have no pecuniary pay, and their only recompense for the immense services which they render their country in their voluntary parades, is the plunder of smiles, and winks, and nods which they extort from the ladies. As they have no opportunity, like the vagrant arabs, of making inroads on their neighbors, and as it is necessary to keep up their military spirit, the town is therefore, now and then, but particularly on two days of the year, given up to their ravages. The arrangements are contrived with admirable address, so that every officer from the bashaw down to the drum-major, (the chief of the eunuchs, or musicians) shall have his share of that invaluable booty, the *admiration of the fair*. As to the soldiers, poor animals, they, like the privates in all great armies, have to bear the brunt of danger and fatigue, while their officers receive all the glory and reward. The narrative of a parade day will exemplify this more clearly.

The chief bashaw, in the plenitude of his authority orders a grand review of the *whole army*, at two o'clock. The bashaw *with two tails*, that he may have an opportunity of vaporing about as greatest man on the field, orders the army to assemble at twelve. The kiaya, or *colonel*, as he is called, (that is, commander of one hundred and twenty men) orders his regiment or tribe to collect *one mile at least* from the place of parade, at eleven. Each captain (or *fag rag* as we term them) commands his squad to meet at ten, at least *a half mile* from the regimental parade—and to close all, the chief of the eunuchs orders his infernal concert of fifes, trumpets, cymbals and kettle drums to assemble at ten! from that moment the city receives no quarter. All is noise, hooting, hubbub and combustion. Every window, door, crack and loop-hole, from the garret to the cellar, is crowded with the fascinating fair, of all ages and of all complexions. The mistress smiles through the windows of the drawing-room; the chubby chambermaid lolls out of the attic casement, and a host of sooty wenches roll their white eyes, and grin and chatter from the cellar-door. Every nymph seems anxious to yield voluntarily, that tribute which the heroes of their country demand. First struts the chief eunuch, or drum-major, at the head of his sable band, magnificently arrayed in tarnished scarlet. Alexander himself could not have spurned the earth more superbly. A host of ragged boys shout in his train, and inflate the bosom of the warrior with ten-fold self-complacency. After he has rattled his kettle drums through the town, and swelled and swaggered like a turkey-cock before all the dingy Floras, and Dianas, and Junoes, and Didoes of his acquaintance, he repairs to his place of destination, loaded with a rich booty of smiles and approbation. Next comes the FAG-RAG, or captain, at the head of his mighty band, consisting of one lieutenant, one ensign, (or mute) four sergeants, four corporals, one drummer, one fifer, and if he has any privates so much the better for himself. In marching to the regimental parade he is sure to paddle through the street or lane which is honored with the residence of his mistress or intended, whom he resolutely lays under a heavy contribution. Truly it is delectable to behold these heroes as they march along, cast side glances at the upper windows, to collect the smiles, the nods, and the winks, which the enraptured fair ones lavish profusely on the magnanimous defenders of their country.

The Fag-rags having conducted their squads to their re-

spective regiments, then comes the turn of the colonel, (a bashaw with *no tails*) for all eyes are now directed to him, and
the Fag-rags, and the eunuchs and the kettle-drummers, having had their hour of notoriety, are confounded and lost in
the military crowd. The colonel sets his whole regiment in
motion; and, mounted on a mettlesome charger, frisks and
fidgets, and capers, and plunges in front, to the great entertainment of the multitude, and the great hazard of himself
and his neighbors. Having displayed himself, his trappings,
his horse, and his *horsemanship*, he at length arrives at the
place of general rendezvous, blessed with the universal admiration of his country women. I should, perhaps, mention a
squadron of hardy veterans, most of whom have seen a deal
of service during the nineteen or twenty years of their exis-
tance, and who, most gorgeously equipped in tight green
jackets and breeches, trot, and amble, and gallop, and scamper, like little devils through every street and nook and corner
and poke hole of the city, to the great dread of all old people,
and sage matrons with young children. This is truly sublime!
This is what I call making a mountain out of a mole-hill. Oh,
my friend, on what a *great scale* is every thing in this country.
It is in the style of the wandering arabs of the desart *El-Tih*.
Is a village to be attacked, or a hamlet to be plundered, the
whole desart, for weeks before hand, is in a buz—such
marching and counter-marching, ere they can concentrate
their ragged forces! and the consequence is, that before they
can bring their troops into action, *the whole enterprise is blown*.

The army being all happily collected on the battery,
though, perhaps, two hours after the time appointed, it is
now the turn of the bashaw, with two tails, to distinguish
himself. Ambition, my friend, is implanted alike in every
heart, it pervades each bosom, from the bashaw to the drum-
major. This is a sage truism, and I trust, therefore, it will not
be disputed. The bashaw fired with that thirst for glory, in-
seperable from the noble mind, is anxious to reap a full share
of the laurels of the day, and bear off his portion of female
plunder. The drums beat, the fifes whistle, the standards wave
proudly in the air. The signal is given!—thunder roars the
cannon!—away goes the bashaw, and away go the *tails*! The
review finished, evolutions and military manœuvres are gen-

erally dispensed with for three excellent reasons; first, because the army knows very little about them; second, because as the country has determined to remain always at peace, there is no necessity for them to know any thing about them; and third, as it is growing late, the bashaw must dispatch, or it will be too dark for him to get his quota of the plunder. He of course orders the whole army to march; and now, my friend, now comes the tug of war—now is the city completely sacked. Open fly the battery-gates, forth sallies the bashaw with his two tails, surrounded by a shouting body-guard of boys and negroes! Then pour forth his legions, potent as the pismires of the desart! The customary salutations of the country commence, those tokens of joy and admiration which so much annoyed me on first landing: the air is darkened with old hats, shoes, and dead cats, they fly in showers like the arrows of the parthians. The soldiers, no ways disheartened, like the intrepid followers of Leonidas, march gallantly under their shade. On they push, splash-dash, mud or no mud. Down one lane, up another—the martial music resounds through every street—the fair ones throng to their windows—the soldiers look every way but straight forward. "Carry arms!" cries the bashaw—"tantara ra-ra," brays the trumpet—"rub-a-dub," roars the drum—"hurraw," shout the ragamuffins. The bashaw smiles with exultation—every Fag-rag feels himself a hero— "none but the brave deserve the fair!" Head of the immortal Amrou, on what a great scale is every thing in this country!

Aye, but you'll say, is not this unfair that the officers should share all the sports while the privates undergo all the fatigue? truly, my friend, I indulged the same idea, and pitied from my heart, the poor fellows who had to drabble through the mud and the mire, toiling under pondrous cocked hats, which seemed as unwieldy, and cumbrous, as the shell which the snail lumbers along on his back. I soon found out, however, that they have their quantum of notoriety. As soon as the army is dismissed, the city swarms with little scouting parties, who fire off their guns at every corner, to the great delight of all the women and children in their vicinity; and woe unto any dog, or pig, or hog, that falls in the way of these magnanimous warriors—they are shewn no quarter. Every gentle swain repairs to pass the evening at the feet of his dulcinea, to play "the soldier tired of war's alarms," and to captivate her with the glare of his regimentals, excepting some ambitious heroes, who strut to the theatre, flame away in the front boxes, and hector every old apple woman in the lobbies.

Such, my friend, is the gigantic genius of this nation, and its faculty of swelling up nothings into importance. Our bashaw of Tripoli, will review his troops of some thousands, by an early hour in the morning. Here a review of six hundred men is made the mighty work of a day! With us a bashaw of *two tails* is never appointed to a command of less than ten thousand men; but here we behold every grade from the bashaw, down to the drum-major, in a force of less than one tenth of the number. By the beard of Mahomet, but every thing here is *indeed* on a great scale!

BY ANTHONY EVERGREEN, GENT.

I was not a little surprized the other morning at a request from Will Wizard that I would accompany him that evening to Mrs. ———'s Ball. The request was simple enough in itself, it was only singular as coming from Will;—of all my acquaintance, Wizard is the least calculated and disposed for the society of ladies—not that he dislikes their company; on the contrary, like every man of pith and marrow, he is a professed admirer of the sex; and had he been born a poet, would undoubtedly have bespattered and be-rhymed some hard named goddess, until she became as famous as Petrarch's Laura, or Waller's Sacharissa; but Will is such a confounded bungler at a bow, has so many odd bachelor habits, and finds it so troublesome to be gallant, that he generally prefers smoking his segar, and telling his story among cronies of his own gender—and thundering long stories they are, let me tell you—set Will once a-going about China, or Crim Tartary, or the Hottentots, and heaven help the poor victim who has to endure his prolixity—he might better be tied to the tail of a Jack-o-lantern. In one word—Will talks like a traveller. Being well acquainted with his character, I was the more alarmed at his inclination to visit a party, since he has often assured me, that he considered it as equivalent to being stuck up for three hours in a steam-engine. I even wondered how he had re-

ceived an invitation—this he soon accounted for. It seems
Will, on his last arrival from Canton, had made a present of
a case of tea, to a lady for whom he had once entertained a
sneaking kindness, when at grammar school; and she in return had invited him to come and drink some of it—a cheap
way enough of paying off little obligations. I readily acceded
to Will's proposition, expecting much entertainment from his
eccentric remarks; and as he has been absent some few years,
I anticipated his surprize at the splendor and elegance of a
modern rout.

On calling for Will in the evening, I found him full dressed,
waiting for me. I contemplated him with absolute dismay—
as he still retained a spark of regard for the lady who once
reigned in his affections, he had been at unusual pains in decorating his person, and broke upon my sight arrayed in the
true style that prevailed among our beaux some years ago.
His hair was turned up and tufted at the top, frizzed out at
the ears, a profusion of powder puffed over the whole, and a
long plaited club swung gracefully from shoulder to shoulder,
describing a pleasing semicircle of powder and pomatum. His
claret colored coat was decorated with a profusion of gilt buttons, and reached to his calves. His white casimere small
clothes were so tight that he seemed to have grown up in
them; and his ponderous legs, which are the thickest part of
his body, were beautifully clothed in sky-blue silk stockings,
once considered so becoming. But above all, he prided himself upon his waistcoat of China silk, which might almost
have served a good housewife for a short gown; and he
boasted that the roses and tulips upon it were the work of
Nang-Fou, daughter of the great *Chin-Chin-Fou*, who had
fallen in love with the graces of his person, and sent it to him
as a parting present—he assured me she was a remarkable
beauty with sweet obliquity of eyes, and a foot no larger than
the thumb of an alderman;—he then dilated most copiously
on his silver sprigged Dicky, which he assured me was quite
the rage among the dashing young mandarins of Canton.

I hold it an ill-natured office to put any man out of conceit
with himself; so, though I would willingly have made a little
alteration in my friend Wizard's picturesque costume, yet I
politely complimented him on his rakish appearance.

On entering the room I kept a good look out on Will, expecting to see him exhibit signs of surprize; but he is one of those knowing fellows who are never surprized at any thing, or at least will never acknowledge it. He took his stand in the middle of the floor, playing with his great steel watch-chain, and looking round on the company, the furniture and the pictures, with the air of a man "who had seen d——d finer things in his time;" and to my utter confusion and dismay, I saw him cooly pull out his villanous old japanned tobacco-box, ornamented with a bottle, a pipe, and a scurvy motto, and help himself to a quid in the face of all the company.

I knew it was all in vain to find fault with a fellow of Will's socratic turn, who is never to be put out of humor with himself; so, after he had given his box its prescriptive rap and returned it to his pocket, I drew him to a corner, where we might observe the company, without being prominent objects ourselves.

"And pray who is that stylish figure," said Will, "who blazes away in red like a volcano, and who seems wrapped in flames like a fiery dragon?" that, cried I, is Miss Laurelia Dashaway—she is the highest flash of the ton—has much whim and more eccentricity, and has reduced many an unhappy gentleman to stupidity by her charms—you see she holds out the red flag in token of "no quarter." "Then keep me safe out of the sphere of her attractions," cried Will, "I would not e'en come in contact with her train, lest it should scorch me like the tail of a comet.—But who, I beg of you, is that amiable youth who is handing along a young lady, and at the same time contemplating his sweet person in a mirror as he passes?" His name, said I, is Billy Dimple—he is a universal smiler, and would travel from Dan to Beersheba, and smile on every body as he passed. Dimple is a slave to the ladies—a hero at tea parties, and is famous at the *pirouet* and the pigeon-wing—a fiddle-stick is his idol, and a dance his elysium. "A very pretty young gentleman, truly," cried Wizard, "he reminds me of a cotemporary beau at Hayti. You must know that the maganimous Dessalines gave a great ball to his court one fine sultry summer's evening; Dessy and me were great cronies—hand and glove—one of the most con-

descending, great men I ever knew. Such a display of black
and yellow beauties! such a show of madras handkerchiefs,
red beads, cocks tails and pea-cocks feathers!—it was, as here,
who should wear the highest top-knot, drag the longest tails,
or exhibit the greatest variety of combs, colors and gew-gaws.
In the middle of the rout, when all was buzz, slip-slop, clack
and perfume, who should enter but Tucky Squash! The yellow beauties blushed blue, and the black ones blushed as red
as they could, with pleasure; and there was a universal agitation of fans—every eye brightened and whitened to see
Tucky, for he was the pride of the court, the pink of courtesy,
the mirror of fashion, the adoration of all the sable fair ones
of Hayti. Such breadth of nose, such exuberance of lip! his
shins had the true cucumber curve—his face in dancing shone
like a kettle; and, provided you kept to windward of him in
summer, I do not know a sweeter youth in all Hayti than
Tucky Squash. When he laughed, there appeared from ear to
ear a chevaux-de-frize of teeth, that rivalled the shark's in
whiteness; he could whistle like a northwester—play on a
three-stringed fiddle like Apollo;—and as to dancing, no
Long-Island negro could shuffle you "double trouble," or
"hoe corn and dig potatoes" more scientifically—in short, he
was a second Lothario, and the dusky nymphs of Hayti, one
and all, declared him a perpetual Adonis. Tucky walked
about, whistling to himself, without regarding any body; and
his *nonchalance* was irresistible."

I found Will had got neck and heels into one of his travellers stories, and there is no knowing how far he would have
run his parallel between Billy Dimple and Tucky Squash, had
not the music struck up, from an adjoining apartment, and
summoned the company to the dance. The sound seemed to
have an inspiring effect on honest Will, and he procured the
hand of an old acquaintance for a country dance. It happened
to be the fashionable one of "the Devil among the Tailors,"
which is so vociferously demanded at every ball and assembly:
and many a torn gown, and many an unfortunate toe did rue
the dancing of that night; for Will thundered down the dance
like a coach and six, sometimes right, sometimes wrong, now
running over half a score of little frenchmen, and now making
sad inroads into ladies cobweb muslins and spangled tails. As

every part of Will's body partook of the exertion, he shook
from his capacious head such volumes of powder, that like
pious Eneas on his first interview with queen Dido, he might
be said to have been enveloped in a cloud. Nor was Will's
partner an insignificant figure in the scene. She was a young
lady of most voluminous proportions, that quivered at every
skip; and being braced up in the fashionable style, with whalebone, stay-tape and buckram, looked like an apple-pudding
tied in the middle, or, taking her flaming dress into consideration, like a bed and bolsters rolled up in a suit of red curtains. The dance finished—I would gladly have taken Will
off, but no—he was now in one of his happy moods, and
there was no doing any thing with him. He insisted on my
introducing him to miss SOPHY SPARKLE, a young lady unrivalled for playful wit and innocent vivacity, and who, like a
brilliant, adds lustre to the front of fashion. I accordingly presented him to her, and began a conversation in which, I
thought, he might take a share; but no such thing. Will took
his stand before her, straddling like a Colossus, with his
hands in his pockets, and an air of the most profound attention, nor did he pretend to open his lips for some time, until,
upon some lively sally of hers, he electrified the whole company with a most intolerable burst of laughter. What was to
be done with such an incorrigible fellow?—to add to my distress, the first word he spoke was to tell Miss Sparkle that
something she said reminded him of a circumstance that happened to him in China—and at it he went, in the true traveller style—described the chinese mode of eating rice with
chop-sticks—entered into a long eulogium on the succulent
qualities of boiled birds nests, and I made my escape at the
very moment when he was on the point of squatting down
on the floor, to show how the little chinese *Joshes* sit cross-
legged.

TO THE LADIES.
FROM THE MILL OF
PINDAR COCKLOFT, ESQ.

THOUGH jogging down the hill of life,
Without the comfort of a wife;—

And though I ne'er a helpmate chose,
To stock my house and mend my hose;
With care my person to adorn,
And spruce me up on Sunday morn;—
Still do I love the gentle sex,
And still with cares my brain perplex,
To keep the fair ones of the age
Unsullied as the spotless page;
All pure, all simple, all refined,
The sweetest solace of mankind.

I hate the loose insidious jest,
To beauties modest ear addrest,
And hold that frowns should never fail
To check each smooth, but fulsome tale:—
But he whose impious pen should dare
Invade the morals of the fair;
To taint that purity divine
Which should each female heart enshrine;
Though soft his vicious strains should swell,
As those which erst from Gabriel fell,
Should yet be held aloft to shame
And foul dishonor shade his name.

Judge then, my friends, of my surprize,
The ire that kindled in my eyes,
When I relate, that t'other day,
I went a morning call to pay,
On two young nieces, just come down
To take the *polish* of the town;
By which I mean no more nor less
Than *a la francaise* to *undress*;
To whirl the modest waltz's rounds,
Taught by Duport for *snug ten pounds*.
To thump and thunder through a song,
Play *fortes* soft and *dolce's* strong;
Exhibit loud *piano* feats,
Caught from that crotchet hero, Meetz;
To drive the rose bloom from the face
And fix the lily in its place;

To doff the white, and in its stead
To bounce about in brazen red.

While in the parlor I delay'd
Till they their persons had array'd,
A dapper volume caught my eye,
That on the window chanced to lie.
A book's a friend—I always choose
To turn its pages and peruse—
It proved those poems known to fame
For praising every cyprian dame—
The bantlings of a dapper youth,
Renown'd for *gratitude* and *truth*;
A little pest, hight TOMMY MOORE,
Who hopp'd and skipp'd our country o'er;
Who sipp'd our tea and lived on sops,
Revell'd on syllabubs and slops,
And when his brain, of cobweb fine,
Was fuddled with five drops of wine,
Would all his puny loves rehearse,
And many a maid debauch—in verse.

Surprized to meet in open view
A book of such lascivious hue,
I chid my nieces—but they say,
'Tis all the *passion* of the day—
That many a fashionable belle
Will with enraptured accents dwell,
On the sweet *morceaux* she has found
In this delicious, curs'd, compound!

Soft do the tinkling numbers roll,
And lure to vice the unthinking soul;
They tempt by softest sounds away;
They lead entranced the heart astray,
And satan's doctrine sweetly sing
As with a seraph's heavenly string;
Such sounds, so good old Homer sung,
Once warbled from the Siren's tongue—
Sweet melting tones were heard to pour

Along Ausonia's sun-gilt shore—
Seductive strains in æther float,
And every wild deceitful note
That could the yielding heart assail,
Were wafted on the breathing gale—
And every gentle accent bland
To tempt Ulysses to their strand.

   And can it be this book so base,
Is laid on every window case?
Oh! fair ones, if you will profane
Those breasts where heaven itself should reign,
And throw those pure recesses wide,
Where peace and virtue should reside,
To let the holy pile admit
A guest unhallowed and unfit;
Pray, like the frail ones of the night,
Who hide their wanderings from the light,
So let *your* errors secret be,
And hide, at least, your fault from me:—
Seek some bye corner to explore
The smooth polluted pages o'er:
There drink the insidious poison in;
There *slily* nurse your souls for sin;
And while that purity you blight,
Which stamps you messengers of light;
And sap those mounds the gods bestow,
To keep you spotless here below;
Still, in compassion to *our* race,
Who joy, not only in the face
But in that more exalted part,
The sacred temple of the heart;
Oh! hide forever from our view,
The fatal mischief you pursue—
Let MEN your praises still exalt,
And none but ANGELS mourn your fault.

SALMAGUNDI NO. VI

THE COCKLOFT FAMILY, of which I have made such frequent mention, is of great antiquity, if there be any truth in the genealogical tree which hangs up in my cousin's library. They trace their descent from a celebrated roman knight, cousin to the progenitor of his majesty of Britain, who left his native country, on occasion of some disgust, and coming into Wales, became a great favorite of prince Madoc, and accompanied that famous Argonaut in the voyage which ended in the discovery of this continent. Though a member of the family, I have sometimes ventured to doubt the authenticity of this portion of their annals, to the great vexation of cousin Christopher, who is looked up to as the head of our house, and who, though as orthodox as a bishop, would sooner give up the whole decalogue than lop off a single limb of the family tree. From time immemorial, it has been the rule for the Cocklofts to marry one of their own name; and as they always bred like rabbits, the family has increased and multiplied like that of Adam and Eve. In truth their number is almost incredible, and you can hardly go into any part of the country without starting a warren of genuine Cocklofts. Every person of the least observation or experience, must have observed, that where this practice of marrying cousins and second cousins prevails in a family, every member, in the course of a few generations, becomes queer, humorous and original; as much distinguished from the common race of mongrels as if he was of a different species. This has happened in our family, and particularly in that branch of it of which mr. Christopher Cockloft, or to do him justice, Christopher Cockloft, esq. is the head. Christopher is, in fact, the only married man of the name who resides in town; his family is small, having lost most of his children when young, by the excessive care he took to bring them up like vegetables. This was one of his first whim-whams, and a confounded one it was, as his children might have told had they not fallen victims to his experiment before they could talk. He had got, from some quack philosopher or other, a notion that there was a complete analogy between children and plants, and that they ought both to be reared alike. Accordingly he sprinkled them every morning with water, laid them out in the sun, as he did his geraniums, and if the season was remarkably dry, repeated this wise experiment three or four times of a morning. The consequence was, the poor little souls died one after the other, except Jeremy and his two sisters, who, to be sure, are a trio of as odd, *runty*, mummy looking originals as ever Hogarth fancied in his most happy moments. Mrs. Cockloft, the larger if not the better half of my cousin, often remonstrated against this vegetable theory, and even brought the parson of the parish, in which my cousin's country house is situated, to her aid—but in vain: Christopher persisted and attributed the failure of his plan to its not having been exactly conformed to. As I have mentioned mrs. Cockloft, I may as well say a little more about her while I am in the humor. She is a lady of wonderful notability, a warm admirer of shining mahogany, clean hearths, and her husband, who she considers the wisest man in the world, bating Will Wizard and the parson of our parish; the last of whom is her oracle on all occasions. She goes constantly to church every Sunday and Saints-day, and insists upon it that no man is entitled to ascend a pulpit unless he has been ordained by a bishop;—nay, so far does she carry her orthodoxy, that all the argument in the world will never persuade her that a presbyterian, or baptist, or even a calvinist has any possible chance of going to heaven. Above every thing else, however, she abhors paganism, can scarcely refrain from laying violent hands on a Pantheon when she meets with it, and was very nigh going into hysterics, when my cousin insisted one of his boys should be christened after our laureat, because the parson of the parish had told her that Pindar was the name of a pagan writer, famous for his love of boxing matches, wrestling, and horse racing. To sum up all her qualifications in the shortest possible way, mrs. Cockloft is in the true sense of the phrase, a good sort of a woman; and I often congratulate my cousin on possessing her. The rest of the family consists of Jeremy Cockloft, the younger, who has already been mentioned, and the two miss Cocklofts, or rather

the *young ladies*, as they have been called by the servants, time
out of mind; not that they are really young, the younger
being somewhat on the shady side of thirty, but it has ever
been the custom to call every member of the family young
under fifty. In the south-east corner of the house, I hold quiet
possession of an old fashioned apartment, where myself and
my elbow-chair are suffered to amuse ourselves undisturbed,
save at meal times. This apartment old Cockloft has face-
tiously denominated cousin Launce's paradise, and the good
old gentleman has two or three favorite jokes about it, which
are served up as regularly as the standing family dish of beef-
steaks and onions, which every day maintains its station at the
foot of the table, in defiance of mutton, poultry, or even venison itself.

Though the family is apparently small, yet like most old
establishments of the kind it does not want for honorary
members. It is the city rendezvous of the Cocklofts, and we
are continually enlivened by the company of half a score of
uncles, aunts, and cousins in the fortieth remove, from all
parts of the country, who profess a wonderful regard for
cousin Christopher, and overwhelm every member of his
household, down to the cook in the kitchen, with their attentions. We have for three weeks past been greeted with the
company of two worthy old spinsters, who came down from
the country to settle a law suit. They have done little else but
retail stories of their village neighbors, knit stockings, and
take snuff all the time they have been here; the whole family
are bewildered with church-yard tales of sheeted ghosts, white
horses without heads, and with large goggle eyes in their but-
tocks; and not one of the old servants dare budge an inch
after dark without a numerous company at his heels. My
cousin's visitors, however, always return his hospitality with
due gratitude, and now and then remind him of their frater-
nal regard, by a present of a pot of apple sweet-meats, or a
barrel of sour cider at christmas. Jeremy displays himself to
great advantage among his country relations, who all think
him a prodigy, and often stand astounded in "gaping wonderment," at his *natural* philosophy. He lately frightened a
simple old uncle almost out of his wits by giving it as his
opinion that the earth would one day be scorched to ashes by

the eccentric gambols of the famous comet, so much talked of, and positively asserting that this world revolved round the sun, and that the moon was certainly inhabited.

The family mansion bears equal marks of antiquity with its inhabitants. As the Cocklofts are remarkable for their attachment to every thing that has remained long in the family, they are bigoted towards their old edifice, and I dare say would sooner have it crumble about their ears than abandon it. The consequence is, it has been so patched up and repaired, that it has become as full of whims and oddities as its tenants, requires to be nursed and humored like a gouty old codger of an alderman, and reminds one of the famous ship in which a certain admiral circumnavigated the globe, which was so patched and timbered, in order to preserve so great a curiosity, that at length not a particle of the original remained. Whenever the wind blows, the old mansion makes a most perilous groaning, and every storm is sure to make a day's work for the carpenter, who attends upon it as regularly as the family physician. This predilection for every thing that has been long in the family shows itself in every particular. The domestics are all grown grey in the service of our house. We have a little old crusty grey-headed negro, who has lived through two or three generations of the Cocklofts, and of course has become a personage of no little importance in the household. He calls all the family by their christian names; tells long stories about how he dandled them on his knee when they were children; and is a complete Cockloft chronicle for the last seventy years. The family carriage was made in the last french war, and the old horses were most indubitably foaled in Noah's ark, resembling marvellously, in gravity of demeanor, those sober animals which may be seen any day of the year in the streets of Philadelphia, walking their snails' pace, a dozen in a row, and harmoniously jingling their bells. Whim-whams are the inheritance of the Cocklofts, and every member of the household is a humorist *sui generis*, from the master down to the footman. The very cats and dogs are humorists, and we have a little runty scoundrel of a cur, who, whenever the church bells ring, will run to the street door, turn up his nose in the wind, and howl most piteously. Jeremy insists that this is owing to a peculiar delicacy in the organization of his ears, and supports his position by many learned arguments which nobody can understand; but I am of opinion that it is a mere Cockloft whim-wham which the little cur indulges, being descended from a race of dogs which has flourished in the family ever since the time of my grandfather. A propensity to save every thing that bears the stamp of family antiquity, has accumulated an abundance of trumpery and rubbish, with which the house is incumbered from the cellar to the garret, and every room, and closet, and corner, is crammed with three legged chairs, clocks without hands, swords without scabbards, cocked hats, broken candlesticks, and looking glasses with frames carved into fantastic shapes of feathered sheep, woolly birds, and other animals that have no name except in books of heraldry. The ponderous mahogany chairs in the parlor, are of such unwieldly proportions that it is quite a serious undertaking to gallant one of them across the room, and sometimes make a most equivocal noise when you set down in a hurry; the mantlepiece is decorated with little lacquered earthen shepherdesses, some of which are without toes, and others without noses, and the fire-place is garnished out with dutch tiles, exhibiting a great variety of scripture pieces, which my good old soul of a cousin takes infinite delight in explaining.—Poor Jeremy hates them as he does poison, for while a younker, he was obliged by his mother to learn the history of a tile every Sunday morning before she would permit him to join his playmates; this was a terrible affair for Jeremy, who, by the time he had learned the last, had forgotten the first, and was obliged to begin again. He assured me the other day, with a round college oath, that if the *old house* stood out till he inherited it, he would have these tiles taken out, and ground into powder, for the perfect hatred he bore them.

My cousin Christopher enjoys unlimited authority in the mansion of his forefathers; he is truly what may be termed a hearty old blade, has a florid, sunshine countenance, and if you will only praise his wine, and laugh at his long stories, himself and his house, are heartily at your service. The first condition is indeed easily complied with, for to tell the truth, his wine is excellent; but his stories being not of the best, and often repeated, are apt to create a disposition to yawn, being

in addition to their other qualities, most unfeelingly long. His
prolixity is the more afflicting to me, since I have all his stories by heart; and when he enters upon one, it reminds me of
Newark causeway, where the traveller sees the end at the distance of several miles. To the great misfortune of all his acquaintance, cousin Cockloft is blessed with a most provoking
retentive memory, and can give day and date, and name and
age, and circumstance, with the most unfeeling precision.
These, however, are but trivial foibles, forgotten, or remembered, only with a kind of tender respectful pity by those who
know with what a rich redundant harvest of kindness and
generosity his heart is stored. It would delight you to see with
what social gladness he welcomes a visitor into his house; and
the poorest man that enters his door never leaves it without a
cordial invitation to sit down, and drink a glass of wine. By
the honest farmers around his country-seat, he is looked up
to with love and reverence—they never pass him by, without
his inquiring after the welfare of their families, and receiving
a cordial shake of his liberal hand. There are but two classes
of people who are thrown out of the reach of his hospitality,
and these are frenchmen and democrats. The old gentleman
considers it treason against the majority of good breeding, to
speak to any visitor with his hat on; but the moment a democrat enters his door, he forthwith bids his man Pompey
bring his hat, puts it on his head, and salutes him with an
appalling "Well, sir, what do you want with me?"

He has a profound contempt for frenchmen, and firmly believes, that they eat nothing but frogs and soup-maigre in
their own country. This unlucky prejudice is partly owing to
my great aunt PAMELA, having been, many years ago, run
away with by a french count, who turned out to be the son
of a generation of barbers—and partly to a little vivid spark
of toryism which burns in a secret corner of his heart. He was
a loyal subject of the crown, has hardly yet recovered the
shock of independence; and though he does not care to own
it, always does honor to his majesty's birth-day, by inviting a
few cavaliers, like himself, to dinner, and gracing his table
with more than ordinary festivity. If by chance the revolution
is mentioned before him, my cousin shakes his head; and you
may see, if you take good note, a lurking smile of contempt

in the corner of his eye, which marks a decided disapprobation of the sound. He once, in the fulness of his heart, observed to me that green peas were a month later than they
were under the old government. But the most eccentric manifestation of loyalty he ever gave was making a voyage to Hal-
ifax, for no other reason under heaven, but to hear his majesty
prayed for in church, as he used to be here formerly. This he
never could be brought fairly to acknowledge; but it is a certain fact I assure you. It is not a little singular that a person
so much given to long story-telling, as my cousin, should take
a liking to another of the same character; but so it is with the
old gentleman—his prime favorite and companion is Will
Wizard, who is almost a member of the family, and will set
before the fire, with his feet on the massy andirons, and
smoke his cigarr, and screw his phiz, and spin away tremendous long stories of his travels, for a whole evening, to the
great delight of the old gentleman and lady, and especially of
the *young ladies*, who, like Desdemona, do "seriously incline,"
and listen to him with innumerable "O dears," "is it possi-
bles," "goody graciouses," and look upon him as a second
Sinbad the sailor.

The miss Cocklofts, whose pardon I crave for not having
particularly introduced them before, are a pair of delectable
damsels, who, having purloined and locked up the family-
bible, pass for just what age they please to plead guilty to.
BARBARA the eldest, has long since resigned the character of
a belle, and adopted that staid, sober, demure, snuff-taking
air, becoming her years and discretion. She is a good natured
soul, whom I never saw in a passion but once, and that was
occasioned by seeing an old favorite beau of hers, kiss the
hand of a pretty blooming girl; and in truth, she only got
angry because as she very properly said, it was spoiling the
child. Her sister MARGERY, or MAGGIE, as she is familiarly
termed, seemed disposed to maintain her post as a belle, until
a few months since, when accidentally hearing a gentleman
observe that she broke very fast, she suddenly left off going
to the assembly, took a cat into high favor, and began to rail
at the forward pertness of young misses. From that moment
I set her down for an old maid; and so she is, "by the hand
of my body." The *young ladies* are still visited by some half a

dozen of veteran beaux, who grew and flourished in the *haut ton*, when the miss Cocklofts were quite children; but have been brushed rather rudely by the hand of time, who, to say the truth, can do almost any thing but make people young. They are, notwithstanding, still warm candidates for female favor, look venerably tender, and repeat over and over the same honeyed speeches, and sugared sentiments to the little belles, that they poured so profusely into the ears of their mothers. I beg leave here to give notice that by this sketch, I mean no reflection on *old bachelors*; on the contrary, I hold that next to a fine lady, the *ne plus ultra*, an old bachelor to be the most charming being upon earth, in as much as by living in "single blessedness," he of course does just as he pleases; and if he has any genius, must acquire a plentiful stock of whims, and oddities, and whalebone habits, without which I esteem a man to be mere beef without mustard, good for nothing at all, but to run on errands for ladies, take boxes at the theatre, and act the part of a screen at tea-parties, or a walking-stick in the streets. I merely speak of these *old boys* who infest public walks, pounce upon ladies from every corner of the street, and like old Tommy Fizgig, worry and frisk, and amble, and caper before, behind, and round about the fashionable belles, like old ponies in a pasture, and strive to supply the absence of youthful whim, and hilarity, by grimaces and grins, and artificial vivacity. I have sometimes seen one of these "reverend youths," endeavoring to elevate his wintry passions into something like love, by basking in the sunshine of beauty, and it did remind me of an old moth attempting to fly through a pane of glass towards a light, without ever approaching near enough to warm itself, or scorch its wings.

Never, I firmly believe, did there exist a family that went more by tangents than the Cocklofts. Every thing is governed by whim; and if one member starts a new freak, away all the rest follow on like wild geese in a string. As the family, the servants, the horses, cats and dogs, have all grown old together, they have accommodated themselves to each others habits completely; and though every body of them is full of odd points, angles, rhomboids, and ins and outs, yet some how or other, they harmonize together like so many straight lines, and it is truly a grateful and refreshing sight to see them agree so well. Should one, however, get out of tune, it is like a cracked fiddle, the whole concert is ajar, you perceive a cloud over every brow in the house, and even the old chairs seem to creak affetuosso. If my cousin, as he is rather apt to do, betray any symptoms of vexation or uneasiness, no matter about what, he is worried to death with inquiries, which answer no other end but to demonstrate the good will of the inquirer, and put him in a passion; for every body knows how provoking it is to be cut short in a fit of the *blues*, by an impertinent question about what is the matter, when a man can't tell himself. I remember a few months ago, the old gentleman came home in quite a *squall*, kicked poor Cæsar, the mastiff, out of his way, as he came through the hall, threw his hat on the table with most violent emphasis, and pulling out his box, took three huge pinches of snuff, and threw a fourth into the cat's eyes as he sat purring his astonishment by the fire-side. This was enough to set the body politic going—mrs. Cockloft began my dearing it as fast as tongue could move—the *young ladies* took each a stand at an elbow of his chair—Jeremy marshalled in the rear—the servants came tumbling in—the mastiff put up an enquiring nose; and even grimalkin, after he had cleaned his whiskers and finished sneezing, discovered indubitable signs of sympathy. After the most affectionate inquiries on all sides, it turned out that my cousin, in crossing the street, had got his silk stockings bespattered with mud by a coach, which it seems belonged to a dashing gentleman who had formerly supplied the family with hot rolls and muffins! Mrs. Cockloft thereupon turned up her eyes, and the *young ladies* their noses; and it would have edified a whole congregation to hear the conversation which took place concerning the insolence of upstarts, and the vulgarity of would-be gentlemen and ladies, who strive to emerge from low life, by dashing about in carriages to pay a visit two doors off, giving parties to people who laugh at them, and *cutting* all their old friends.

Theatrics.

BY WILLIAM WIZARD, ESQ.

I WENT a few evenings since to the theatre, accompanied

by my friend, Snivers the cockney, who is a man deeply read
in the history of Cinderella, Valentine and Orson, Blue Beard,
and all those recondite works so necessary to enable a man to
understand the modern drama. Snivers is one of those intolerable fellows who will never be pleased with any thing until
he has turned and twisted it divers ways, to see if it corre-
sponds with his notions of congruity, and as he is none of
the quickest in his ratiocinations, he will sometimes come out
with his approbation, when every body else have forgotten
the cause which excited it. Snivers is, moreover, a great critic,
for he finds fault with every thing—this being what I understand by *modern criticism*. He, however, is pleased to acknowledge that our theatre is not so despicable, all things considered, and really thinks Cooper one of our best actors. As the
house was crowded, we were complimented with seats in Box
No. 2, a sad little rantipole place, which is the strong hold of
a set of rare wags, and where the poor actors undergo the
most merciless tortures of verbal criticism. The play was
OTHELLO, and, to speak my mind freely, I think I have seen
it performed much worse in my time. The actors, I firmly
believe, did their best, and whenever this is the case, no man
has a right to find fault with them, in my opinion. Little
RUTHERFORD, the roscius of the Philadelphia theatre, looked
as big as possible, and what he wanted in size, he made up in
frowning—I like frowning in tragedy, and if a man but keeps
his forehead in proper wrinkle, talks big, and takes long
strides on the stage, I always set him down as a great tragedian, and so does my friend Snivers.

Before the first act was over, Snivers began to flourish his
critical wooden sword like a harlequin. He first found fault
with Cooper for not having made himself as black as a negro,
"for," said he, "that Othello was an arrant black, appears from
several expressions of the play, as for instance, 'thick lips,'
'sooty bosom,' and a variety of others. I am inclined to
think," continued he, "that Othello was an egyptian by birth,
from the circumstance of the handkerchief given to his
mother by a native of that country, and, if so, he certainly
was as black as my hat, for Herodotus has told us that the
egyptians had flat noses and frizzled hair, a clear proof that
they were all negroes." He did not confine his strictures to

this single error of the actor, but went on to run him down in toto. In this he was seconded by a red hot philadelphian, who proved, by a string of most eloquent logical puns, that Fennel was unquestionably in every respect a better actor than Cooper. I knew it was vain to contend with him, since I recollected a most obstinate trial of skill these two great *Roscii* had last spring in Philadelphia. Cooper brandished his blood-stained dagger at the theatre—Fennel flourished his snuff-box, and shook his wig at the Lyceum, and the unfortunate philadelphians were a long time at a loss to decide which deserved the palm. The literati were inclined to give it to Cooper, because his name was the most fruitful in puns; but then, on the other side, it was contended that Fennel was the best greek scholar. Scarcely was the town of Strasburgh in a greater hub bub about the courteous stranger's nose, and it was well that the doctors of the university did not get into the dispute, else it might have become a battle of folioes. At length, after much excellent argument had been expended on both sides, recourse was had to Cocker's Arithmetic and a carpenter's rule, the rival candidates were both measured by one of their most steady-handed critics, and by the most exact measurement it was proved that mr. Fennel was the greatest actor by three inches and a quarter. Since this demonstration of his inferiority, Cooper has never been able to hold up his head in Philadelphia.

In order to change a conversation, in which my favorite suffered so much, I made some inquiries of the philadelphian concerning the two heroes of his theatre, WOOD and CAIN, but I had scarcely mentioned their names, when, whack! he threw a whole handful of puns in my face; twas like a bowl of cold water. I turned on my heel, had recourse to my to-bacco-box, and said no more about Wood and Cain; nor will I ever more, if I can help it, mention their names in the presence of a philadelphian. Would that they could leave off punning! for I love every soul of them with a cordial affection, warm as their own generous hearts, and boundless as their hospitality.

During the performance, I kept an eye on the countenance of my friend, the cockney, because having come all the way from England, and having se'en Kemble once, on a visit

which he made from the Button manufactory to *Lunnun*, I
thought his phiz might serve as a kind of thermometer to
direct my manifestations of applause or disapprobation. I
might as well have looked at the backside of his head, for I
could not, with all my *peering*, perceive by his features that
he was pleased with any thing—except himself. His hat was
twitched a little on one side, as much as to say, "demme, I'm
your sorts!" he was sucking the end of a little stick, he was
"gemman" from head to foot; but as to his face, there was no
more expression in it than in the face of a chinese lady on a
tea-cup. On Cooper's giving one of his gun-powder explosions of passion, I exclaimed, "fine, very fine!" "Pardon me,"
said my friend Snivers, "this is damnable!—the gesture, my
dear sir, only look at the gesture? how horrible! do you not
observe that the actor slaps his forehead, whereas, the passion
not having arrived at the proper height, he should only have
slapped his—pocket flap? this figure of rhetoric is a most important stage trick, and the proper management of it is what
peculiarly distinguishes the great actor from the mere plodding mechanical buffoon. Different degrees of passion require
different slaps, which we critics have reduced to a perfect
manual, improving upon the principle adopted by Frederic of
Prussia, by deciding that an actor, like a soldier, is a mere
machine, as thus—the actor, for a minor burst of passion,
merely slaps his pocket-hole—good!—for a major burst, he
slaps his breast—very good! but for a burst maximus, he
whacks away at his forehead, like a brave fellow—this is excellent!—nothing can be finer than an exit slapping the forehead from one end of the stage to the other." "Except,"
replied I, "one of those slaps on the breast, which I have
sometimes admired in some of our fat heroes and heroines,
which make their whole body shake and quiver like a pyramid
of jelly."

The philadelphian had listened to this conversation with
profound attention, and appeared delighted with Snivers' mechanical strictures; twas natural enough in a man who chose
an actor as he would a grenadier. He took the opportunity of
a pause, to enter into a long conversation with my friend, and
was receiving a prodigious fund of information concerning
the true mode of emphasising conjunctions, shifting scenes,

snuffing candles, and making thunder and lightning, better
than you can get every day from the sky, as practised at the
royal theatres, when, as ill luck would have it, they happened
to run their heads full butt against a *new reading*. Now this
was a *stumper*, as our friend Paddle would say, for the philadelphians are as inveterate new reading hunters as the cocknies, and for aught I know, as well skilled in finding them
out. The philadelphian thereupon met the cockney on his
own ground, and at it they went, like two inveterate curs at a
bone. Snivers quoted Theobold, Hanmer, and a host of
learned commentators, who have pinned themselves on the
sleeve of Shakspeare's immortality, and made the old bard,
like General Washington, in General Washington's life, a most
diminutive figure in his own book—his opponent chose
Johnson for his bottle-holder, and thundered him forward
like an elephant to bear down the ranks of the enemy. I was
not long in discovering that these two precious judges had
got hold of that unlucky passage of Shakspeare, which like a
straw has tickled and puzzled and confounded many a somniferous buzzard of past and present time. It was the celebrated wish of Desdemona, that heaven had made her such a
man as Othello. Snivers insisted that "the gentle Desdemona"
merely wished for such a man for a husband, which in all
conscience was a modest wish enough, and very natural in a
young lady, who might possibly have had a predilection for
flat noses, like a certain philosophical great man of our day.
The philadelphian contended with all the vehemence of a
member of congress, moving the house to have " whereas,"
or "also," or "nevertheless" struck out of a bill; that the young
lady wished heaven had made her a man instead of a woman,
in order that she might have an opportunity of seeing the
"anthropophagi, and the men whose heads do grow beneath
their shoulders;" which was a very natural wish, considering
the curiosity of the sex. On being referred to, I incontinently
decided in favor of the honorable member who spoke last,
inasmuch as I think it was a very *foolish*, and therefore very
natural wish for a young lady to make before a man she
wished to marry. It was, moreover, an indication of the violent inclination she felt to *wear the breeches*, which was afterwards, in all probability, gratified, if we may judge from the

title of "our captain's captain," given her by Cassio, a phrase which, in my opinion, indicates that Othello was, at that time, most ignominiously *hen pecked*. I believe my argument staggered Snivers himself, for he looked confoundedly queer, and said not another word on the subject.

A little while after, at it he went again on another tack, and began to find fault with Cooper's manner of dying—"it was not natural," he said, for it had lately been demonstrated by a learned doctor of physic, that when a man is mortally stabbed, he ought to take a flying leap of at least five feet, and drop down "dead as a salmon in a fishmonger's basket."— Whenever a man in the predicament above mentioned, departed from this fundamental rule, by falling flat down, like a log, and rolling about for two or three minutes, making speeches all the time: the said learned doctor maintained that it was owing to the waywardness of the human mind, which delighted in flying in the face of nature, and dying in defiance of all her established rules.—I replied "for my part, I held that every man had a right of dying in whatever position he pleased, and that the mode of doing it depended altogether on the peculiar character of the person going to die. A persian could not die in peace unless he had his face turned to the east;—a mahometan would always choose to have his towards Mecca; a frenchman might prefer this mode of throwing a somerset; but mynheer Van Brumblebottom, the Roscius of Rotterdam, always chose to thunder down on his seat of honor whenever he receive a mortal wound. Being a man of ponderous dimensions, this had a most electrifying effect, for the whole theatre 'shook like Olympus at the nod of Jove.' The Philadelphian was immediately inspired with a pun, and swore that mynheer must be great in a dying scene, since he knew how to make the most of his *latter end*."

It is the inveterate cry of stage critics that an actor does not perform the character naturally, if, by chance he happens not to die exactly as they would have him. I think the exhibition of a play at Pekin would suit them exactly, and I wish, with all my heart, they would go there and see one: nature is there imitated with the most scrupulous exactness in every trifling particular. Here, an unhappy lady or gentleman who happens unluckily to be poisoned or stabbed, is left on the stage to writhe and groan, and make faces at the audience, until the poet pleases he should die, while the honest folks of the *dramatis personæ*, bless their hearts! all croud round and yield most potent assistance, by crying and lamenting most vociferously! the audience, tender souls, pull out their white pocket handkerchiefs, wipe their eyes, blow their noses, and swear it is natural as life, while the poor actor is left to die without common christian comfort. In China, on the contrary, the first thing they do is to run for the doctor and *Tchoonc*, or notary. The audience are entertained throughout the fifth act, with a learned consultation of physicians, and if the patient must die, he does it *secundum artem*, and always is allowed time to make his will. The celebrated Chow-Chow, was the completest hand I ever saw at killing himself, he always carried under his robe a bladder of bull's blood, which, when he gave the mortal stab, spirted out to the infinite delight of the audience. Not that the ladies of China are more fond of the sight of blood than those of our own country, on the contrary, they are remarkably sensitive in this particular, and we are told by the great Linkum Fidelius, that the beautiful Ninny Consequa, one of the ladies of the emperor's seraglio, once fainted away on seeing a favorite slave's nose bleed, since which time refinement has been carried to such a pitch, that a buskined hero is not allowed to run himself through the body in the face of the audience. The immortal Chow-Chow, in conformity to this absurd prejudice, whenever he plays the part of Othello, which is reckoned his master-piece, always keeps a bold front, stabs himself slily behind, and is dead before any body suspects that he has given the mortal blow.

P. S. Just as this was going to press, I was informed by Evergreen that Othello had not been performed here the lord knows when; no matter, I am not the first that has criticised a play without seeing it, and this critique will answer for the last performance, if that was a dozen years ago.

SALMAGUNDI NO. VII

Saturday, April 4, 1807.

LETTER
From Mustapha Rub-a-dub Keli Khan,
To Asem Hacchem *principal slave-driver to his
highness the Bashaw of Tripoli.*

I PROMISED in a former letter, good Asem, that I would
furnish thee with a few hints respecting the nature of the
government by which I am held in durance.—Though my
inquiries for that purpose have been industrious, yet I am not
perfectly satisfied with their results, for thou mayest easily
imagine that the vision of a captive is overshadowed by the
mists of illusion and prejudice, and the horizon of his speculations must be limited indeed.

I find that the people of this country are strangely at a loss
to determine the nature and proper character of their government. Even their dervises are extremely in the dark as to this
particular, and are continually indulging in the most preposterous disquisitions on the subject; some have insisted that it
savors of an *aristocracy*; others maintain that it is a *pure* democracy; and a third set of theorists declare absolutely that it
is nothing more nor less than a *mobocracy*. The latter, I must
confess, though still wide in error, have come nearest to the
truth. You of course must understand the meaning of these
different words, as they are derived from the ancient greek
language, and bespeak loudly the verbal poverty of these poor
infidels, who cannot utter a learned phrase without laying the
dead languages under contribution. A man, my dear Asem,
who talks good sense in his native tongue, is held in tolerable
estimation in this country; but a fool, who clothes his feeble
ideas in a foreign or antique garb, is bowed down to, as a
literary prodigy. While I conversed with these people in plain
english, I was but little attended to, but the moment I prosed
away in greek, every one looked up to me with veneration as
an oracle.

Although the dervises differ widely in the particulars above-
mentioned, yet they all agree in terming their government

one of the most *pacific* in the known world. I cannot help pitying their ignorance, and smiling at times to see into what ridiculous errors those nations will wander who are unenlightened by the precepts of Mahomet, our divine prophet, and uninstructed by the five hundred and forty-nine books of wisdom of the immortal Ibrahim Hassan al Fusti. To call this nation pacific! most preposterous! it reminds me of the title assumed by the Sheck of that murderous tribe of wild arabs, who desolate the valleys of Belsaden, who styles himself *star of courtesy—beam of the mercy seat!*

The simple truth of the matter is, that these people are totally ignorant of their own true character; for, according to the best of my observation, they are the most warlike, and I must say, the most savage nation that I have as yet discovered among all the barbarians. They are not only at war (in their own way) with almost every nation on earth, but they are at the same time engaged in the most complicated knot of civil wars that ever infested any poor unhappy country on which ALLA has denounced his malediction!

To let thee at once into a secret, which is unknown to these people themselves, their government is a pure unadulterated LOGOCRACY or *government of words*. The whole nation does every thing *viva voce*, or, by word of mouth, and in this manner is one of the most military nations in existence. Every man who has, what is here called, the *gift of the gab*, that is, a plentiful stock of verbosity, becomes a soldier outright, and is forever in a militant state. The country is intirely defended *vi et lingua*, that is to say, by *force of tongues*. The account which I lately wrote to our friend the snorer, respecting the immense army of six hundred men, makes nothing against this observation; that formidable body being kept up, as I have already observed, only to amuse their fair country women by their splendid appearance and nodding plumes, and are, by way of distinction, denominated the *"defenders of the fair."*

In a logocracy thou well knowest there is little or no occasion for fire arms, or any such destructive weapons. Every offensive or defensive measure is enforced by *wordy battle*, and *paper war*; he who has the longest tongue, or readiest quill, is sure to gain the victory—will carry horror, abuse, and *ink-shed* into the very trenches of the enemy, and without mercy or remorse, put men, women, and children, to the point of the—pen!

There are still preserved in this country some remains of that gothic spirit of knight-errantry, which so much annoyed the faithful in the middle ages of the Hejira. As, notwithstanding their martial disposition, they are a people much given to commerce and agriculture, and must necessarily at certain seasons be engaged in these employments, they have accommodated themselves by appointing knights, or constant warriors, incessant brawlers, similar to those, who, in former ages, swore eternal enmity to the followers of our divine prophet.—These knights denominated editors or SLANG-WHANGERS are appointed in every town, village and district, to carry on both foreign and internal warfare, and may be said to keep up a constant firing "in words." Oh, my friend, could you but witness the enormities sometimes committed by these tremendous slang-whangers, your very turban would rise with horror and astonishment. I have seen them extend their ravages even into the kitchens of their opponents, and annihilate the very cook with a blast; and I do assure thee, I beheld one of these warriors attack a most venerable bashaw, and at one stroke of his pen lay him open from the waistband of his breeches to his chin!

There has been a civil war carrying on with great violence for some time past, in consequence of a conspiracy among the higher classes, to dethrone his highness, the present bashaw, and place another in his stead. I was mistaken when I formerly asserted to thee that this disaffection arose from his wearing *red breeches*. It is true the nation have long held that color in great detestation in consequence of a dispute they had some twenty years since with the barbarians of the british islands. The color, however, is again rising into favor, as the ladies have transferred it to their heads from the bashaw's—body. The true reason, I am told, is that the bashaw absolutely refuses to believe in the deluge, and in the story of Balaam's ass:—maintaining that this animal was never yet permitted to talk except in a genuine logocracy, where it is true his voice may often be heard, and is listened to with reverence as "the voice of the sovereign people." Nay, so far

did he carry his obstinacy that he absolutely invited a professed *anti-deluvian* from the gallic empire, who illuminated
the whole country with his principles—and his *nose*. This was
enough to set the nation in a blaze—every slang-whanger resorted to his tongue or his pen; and for seven years have they
carried on a most inhuman war, in which volumes of words
have been expended, oceans of ink have been shed; nor has
any mercy been shown to age, sex, or condition. Every day
have these slang-whangers made furious attacks upon each
other, and upon their respective adherents, discharging their
heavy artillery, consisting of large sheets, loaded with scoundrel! villain! liar! rascal! numskull! nincompoop! dunderhead!
wiseacre! blockhead! jackass! And I do swear by my beard,
though I know thou wilt scarcely credit me, that in some of
these skirmishes the grand bashaw himself has been woefully
pelted! Yea, most ignominiously pelted!—and yet have these
talking desperadoes escaped without the bastinado!

Every now and then, a slang-whanger, who has a longer
head, or rather a *longer tongue*, than the rest, will elevate his
piece and discharge a shot quite across the ocean, levelled at
the head of the Emperor of France, the king of England; or,
(wouldst thou believe it, oh, Asem) even at his sublime highness the bashaw of Tripoli! these long pieces are loaded with
single ball or langrage, as tyrant! usurper! robber! tyger!
monster! And thou mayest well suppose, they occasion great
distress and dismay in the camps of the enemy, and are marvellously annoying to the crowned heads at which they are
directed. The slang-whanger, though perhaps the mere champion of a village, having fired off his shot, struts about with
great self-congratulation, chuckling at the prodigious bustle
he must have occasioned, and seems to ask of every stranger,
"Well, sir, what do they think of me in Europe."* This is

---

*NOTE, BY WILLIAM WIZARD, ESQ.

The sage Mustapha, when he wrote the above paragraph, had probably in
his eye the following anecdote, related either by Linkum Fidelius, or Jose-
phus Millerius, vulgarly called Joe Miller—of facetious memory.

The captain of a slave-vessel, on his first landing on the coast of Guinea,
observed under a palm-tree, a negro chief sitting most majestically on a
stump, while two women, with wooden spoons, were administering his favorite pottage of boiled rice, which, as his imperial majesty was a little

sufficient to show you the manner in which these bloody, or rather *windy* fellows fight; it is the only mode allowable in a *Logocracy* or government of words. I would also observe that their civil wars have a thousand ramifications.

While the fury of the battle rages in the metropolis, every little town and village has a distinct broil, growing like excrescences out of the grand national altercation, or rather agitating within it, like those complicated pieces of mechanism where there is a " wheel within a wheel."

But in nothing is the verbose nature of this government more evident, than in its grand national divan, or congress, where the laws are framed; this is a blustering windy assembly where every thing is carried by noise, tumult and debate; for thou must know, that the members of this assembly do not meet together to find out wisdom in the multitude of counsellors, but to wrangle, call each other hard names and hear *themselves talk*. When the congress opens, the bashaw first sends them a long message (i.e. a huge mass of words— *vox et preterea nihil*) all meaning nothing; because it only tells them what they perfectly know already. Then the whole assembly are thrown into a ferment, and have a *long talk*, about the quantity of words that are to be returned in answer to this message; and here arise many disputes about the correction and alteration of "*if so bes*," and "*how so evers*." A month, perhaps, is spent in thus determining the precise number of words the answer shall contain, and then another, most probably, in concluding whether it shall be carried to the bashaw on foot, on horseback, or in coaches. Having settled this weighty matter, they next fall to work upon the message itself, and hold as much chattering over it as so many magpies over an addled egg. This done, they divide the message into small portions, and deliver them into the hands of little juntos of *talkers*, called committees: these juntos have each a world of talking about their respective paragraphs, and return the

greedy, would part of it escape the place of destination, and run down his chin. The watchful attendants were particularly careful to intercept these scape grace particles, and return them to their proper port of entry. As the captain approached, in order to admire this curious exhibition of royalty, the great chief clapped his hands to his sides, and saluted his visitor with the following pompous question, "Well, sir! what do they say of me in England?"

results to the grand divan, which forthwith falls to and *re-talks* the matter over more earnestly than ever. Now after all, it is an even chance that the subject of this prodigious arguing, quarrelling, and talking, is an affair of no importance, and ends intirely in smoke. May it not then be said, the whole nation have been talking to no purpose? the people, in fact, seem to be somewhat conscious of this propensity to talk, by which they are characterized, and have a favorite proverb on the subject, viz. "all talk and no cider;" this is particularly applied when their congress (or assembly of all the sage chatterers of the nation) have chattered through a whole session, in a time of great peril and momentous event, and have done nothing but exhibit the length of their tongues and the emptiness of their heads. This has been the case more than once, my friend; and to let thee into a secret, I have been told in confidence, that there have been absolutely several old women smuggled into congress from different parts of the empire, who having once got on the breeches, as thou mayst well imagine, have taken the lead in debate, and overwhelmed the whole assembly with their garrulity; for my part, as times go, I do not see why old women should not be as eligible to public councils as old men, who possess their dispositions—they certainly are eminently possessed of the qualifications requisite to govern in a logocracy.

Nothing, as I have repeatedly insisted, can be done in this country without talking, but they take so long to talk over a measure, that by the time they have determined upon adopting it, the period has elapsed, which was proper for carrying it into effect. Unhappy nation—thus torn to pieces by intestine talks! never, I fear, will it be restored to tranquility and silence. Words are but breath—breath is but air; and air put in motion is nothing but wind. This vast empire, therefore, may be compared to nothing more nor less than a mighty windmill, and the orators, and the chatterers, and the slang-whangers, are the breezes that put it in motion; unluckily, however, they are apt to blow different ways, and their blasts counteracting each other—the mill is perplexed, the wheels stand still, the grist is unground, and the miller and his family starved.

Every thing partakes of the windy nature of the government. In case of any domestic grievance, or an insult from a foreign foe, the people are all in a buzz—town meetings are immediately held, where the quidnuncs of the city repair, each like an Atlas, with the cares of the whole nation upon his shoulders, each resolutely bent upon saving his country, and each swelling and strutting like a turkey-cock, puffed up with words, and wind, and nonsense. After bustling, and buzzing, and bawling for some time, and after each man has shown himself to be indubitably the greatest personage in the meeting, they pass a string of resolutions (i.e. *words*) which were *previously prepared* for the purpose; these resolutions are whimsically denominated the *sense* of the meeting, and are sent off for the instruction of the reigning bashaw, who receives them graciously, puts them into his red breeches pocket, forgets to read them—and so the matter ends.

As to his highness, the present bashaw, who is at the very top of the logocracy, never was a dignitary better qualified for his station. He is a man of superlative ventosity, and comparable to nothing but a huge bladder of wind. He *talks* of vanquishing all opposition by the force of reason and philosophy; throws his gauntlet at all the nations of the earth and defies them to meet him—on the field of argument!—Is the national dignity insulted, a case in which his highness of Tripoli would immediately call forth his forces—the bashaw of America—utters a *speech*. Does a foreign invader molest the commerce in the very mouth of the harbors, an insult which would induce his highness of Tripoli to order out his fleets—his highness of America—utters a *speech*. Are the *free* citizens of America dragged from on board the vessels of their country and forcibly detained in the war ships of another power—his highness—utters a *speech*. Is a peaceable citizen killed by the marauders of a foreign power, on the very shores of his country—his highness—utters a *speech*. Does an alarming insurrection break out in a distant part of the empire—his highness—utters a *speech*!—nay, more, for here he shows his "energies"—he most intrepidly dispatches a courier on horseback, and orders him to ride one hundred and twenty miles a day, with a most formidable army of *proclamations*, (i.e. a collection of words) packed up in his saddle-bags. He is instructed to show no favor nor affection, but to charge the thickest ranks of the enemy, and to speechify and batter by words the conspiracy and the conspirators out of existence. Heavens, my friend, what a deal of blustering is here! it reminds me of a dunghill cock in a farm-yard, who, having accidentally in his scratchings found a worm, immediately begins a most vociferous cackling—calls around him his *hen-hearted* companions, who run chattering from all quarters to gobble up the poor little worm that happened to turn under his eye. Oh Asem! Asem! on what a prodigious great scale is every thing in this country!

Thus, then, I conclude my observations. The infidel nations have each a separate characteristic trait, by which they may be distinguished from each other:—the spaniards, for instance, may be said to *sleep* upon every affair of importance—the italians to *fiddle* upon everything—the french to *dance* upon every thing—the germans to *smoke* upon every thing—the british islanders to *eat* upon every thing,—and the *windy* subjects of the american logocracy to *talk* upon every thing.

Ever thine,

MUSTAPHA.

FROM THE MILL OF
PINDAR COCKLOFT, ESQ.

How oft, in musing mood, my heart recals,
From grey-beard father Time's oblivious halls,
The modes and maxims of my early day,
Long in those dark recesses stow'd away:
Drags once more to the cheerful realms of light
Those buckram fashions long since lost in night;
And makes, like Endor's witch, once more to rise
My grogram grandames to my raptured eyes!
　　Shades of my fathers! in your pasteboard skirts,
Your broidered waistcoats and your plaited shirts,
Your formal bag-wigs—wide-extended cuffs,
Your five inch chitterlings and nine inch ruffs.
Gods! how ye strut, at times, in all your state,
Amid the visions of my thoughtful pate!
I see ye move the solemn *minuet* o'er,
The modest foot scarce rising from the floor;

No thundering *rigadoon* with boisterous prance,
No *pigeon-wing* disturb your *contra dance*.
But silent as the gentle Lethe's tide
Adown the festive maze ye peaceful glide!
   Still in my mental eye each dame appears—
Each modest beauty of departed years;
Close by mama I see her stately march,
Or set, in all the majesty of starch;—
When for the dance a stranger seeks her hand,
I see her doubting, hesitating, stand,
Yield to his claim with most fastidious grace,
And sigh for her *intended* in his place!
   Ah golden days! when every gentle fair
On sacred sabbath conn'd with pious care
Her holy bible, or her prayer-book o'er,
Or studied honest Bunyan's drowsy lore.
Travell'd with him the PILGRIM'S PROGRESS through,
And storm'd the famous town of MAN-SOUL too—
Beat *eye* and *ear-gate* up with thundring jar,
And fought triumphant through the HOLY WAR;
Or if, perchance, to lighter works inclined,
They sought the *novels* to relax the mind,
Twas GRANDISON's politely formal page,
Or CLELIA or PAMELA were the rage.
   No plays were then—theatrics were unknown—
A learned pig—a dancing monkey shown—
The feats of Punch—a cunning juggler's slight,
Were sure to fill each bosom with delight.
An honest, simple, humdrum race we were,
Undazzled yet by fashion's wildering glare;
Our manners unreserved, devoid of guile,
We knew not then the modern monster *style*,
Style, that with pride each empty bosom swells,
Puffs boys to manhood, little girls to *belles*.
   Scarce from the nursery freed, our gentle fair
Are yielded to the dancing-master's care;
And e'er the head one mite of sense can gain,
Are introduced mid folly's frippery train.
A stranger's grasp no longer gives alarms,
Our fair surrender to their very arms,

And in the insidious *Waltz* (1) will swim and twine,
And whirl and languish tenderly divine!
Oh, how I hate this loving, hugging dance,
This imp of Germany—brought up in France;
Nor can I see a niece its windings trace,
But all the honest blood glows in my face.
"Sad, sad refinement this," I often say,
"Tis modesty indeed refined away!
"Let France its whim, its sparkling wit supply,
"The easy grace that captivates the eye,
"But curse their waltz—their loose lascivious arts,
"That smooth our manners, to corrupt our hearts!" (2)
    Where now those books, from which in days of yore
Our mothers gained their literary store?
Alas! stiff-skirted Grandison gives place
To novels of a new and *rakish* race;
And honest Bunyan's pious dreaming lore,
To the lascivious rhapsodies of MOORE.
    And, last of all, behold the mimic Stage
Its morals lend to *polish* off the age,
With flimsy farce, a comedy miscall'd,
Garnish'd with vulgar cant, and proverbs bald,
With puns most puny, and a plenteous store
Of smutty jokes, to catch a gallery roar.
Or see, more fatal, graced with every art,
To charm and captivate the female heart,
The false, "the gallant, gay Lothario" smiles, (3)
And loudly boasts his base seductive wiles,—
In glowing colors paints Calista's wrongs,
And with voluptuous scenes the tale prolongs.
When COOPER lends his fascinating powers,
Decks vice itself in bright alluring flowers,
Pleased with his manly grace, his youthful fire,
Our fair are lured the villain to admire;
While humbler virtue, like a stalking horse,
Struts clumsily and croaks in honest MORSE.
    Ah, hapless days! when trials thus combin'd,
In pleasing garb assail the female mind;
When every smooth insidious snare is spread
To sap the morals and delude the head!

Not Shadrach, Meshach and Abed-nego,
To prove their faith and virtue here below,
Could more an angel's helping hand require,
To guide their steps uninjured through the fire;
Where had but heaven its guardian aid deny'd,
The holy trio in the proof had died.
If, then, *their* manly vigor sought supplies
From the bright stranger in celestial guise,
Alas! can we from feebler nature's claim,
To brave seduction's ordeal, free from blame;
To pass through fire unhurt like golden ore,
Though ANGEL MISSIONS bless the earth no more!

NOTES, BY WILLIAM WIZARD, ESQ.

1 *Waltz*] As many of the retired matrons of this city, un-skilled in "gestic lore," are doubtless ignorant of the move-ments and figures of this modest exhibition, I will endeavor to give some account of it, in order that they may learn what odd capers their daughters sometimes cut when from under their guardian wings.

On a signal being given by the music, the gentleman seizes the lady round her waist—the lady, scorning to be outdone in courtesy, very politely takes the gentleman round the neck, with one arm resting against his shoulder to prevent en-croachments. Away then they go, about and about and about—"about what, sir?"—about the room, madam, to be sure. The whole economy of this dance consists in turning round and round the room in a certain measured step; and it is truly astonishing that this continued revolution does not set all their heads swimming like a top; but I have been pos-itively assured that it only occasions a gentle sensation which is marvelously agreeable. In the course of this circumnaviga-tion, the dancers, in order to give the charm of variety, are continually changing their relative situations—now the gen-tleman, meaning no harm in the world, I assure you, madam, carelessly flings his arm about the lady's neck, with an air of celestial impudence, and anon, the lady, meaning as little harm as the gentleman, takes him round the waist with most ingenuous, modest languishment, to the great delight of numerous spectators and amateurs, who generally form a ring, as the mob do about a pair of amazons pulling caps, or a couple of fighting mastiffs.

After continuing this divine interchange of hands, arms, *et cetera*, for half an hour or so, the lady begins to tire, and with "eyes upraised," in most bewitching languor petitions her partner for a little more support. This is always given without hesitation. The lady leans gently on his shoulder, their arms intertwine in a thousand seducing mischievous curves—dont be alarmed, madam—closer and closer they approach each other, and in conclusion, the parties being overcome with extatic fatigue, the lady seems almost sinking into the gentleman's arms, and then—"Well, sir! and what then?"—lord, madam, how should I know!

2] My friend Pindar, and in fact, our whole junto have been accused of an unreasonable hostility to the french nation; and I am informed by a parisian correspondent, that our first number played the very devil in the court of St. Cloud. His Imperial majesty got into a most outrageous passion, and being withal, a waspish little gentleman, had nearly kicked his bosom friend, Tallyrand, out of the cabinet, in the paroxisms of his wrath. He insisted upon it that the nation was assailed in its most vital part; being, like Achilles, extremely sensitive to any attacks upon the *heel*. When my correspondent sent off his dispatches, it was still in doubt what measures should be adopted; but it was strongly suspected that vehement representations would be made to our government. Willing, therefore, to save our executive from any embarrassment on the subject, and above all, from the disagreeable alternative of sending an *apology* by the HORNET, we do assure, mr. Jefferson, that there is nothing farther from our thoughts than the subversion of the gallic empire, or any attack on the interests, tranquility, or reputation of the nation at large, which we seriously declare possesses the highest rank in our estimation. Nothing less than the national welfare could have induced us to trouble ourselves with this explanation; and in the name of the junto, I once more declare, that when we toast a frenchman, we merely mean one of these *inconnus*, who swarmed to this country, from the kitchens and barbers shops of Nantz, Bordeaux and Marseilles—played games of *leap-frog*, at all our balls and assemblies—set this unhappy town *hopping mad*—and passed themselves off on our tender-hearted damsels for *unfortunate noblemen*—ruined in the revolution! such only, can wince at the lash, and accuse us of severity; and we should be mortified in the extreme if they did not feel our well intended castigation.

3 *Fair Penitent*] The story of this play, if told in its native language, would exhibit a scene of guilt and shame, which no modest ear could listen to without shrinking with disgust; but arrayed as it is in all the splendor of harmonious, rich, and polished verse, it steals into the heart like some gay luxurious smooth-faced villain, and betrays it insensibly to immorality and vice; our very sympathy is enlisted on the side of guilt, and the piety of Altamont, and the gentleness of Lavinia, are lost in the splendid debaucheries of the "gallant gay Lothario" and the blustering, hollow repentance of the fair Calista, whose sorrow reminds us of that of Pope's Heloise— "I mourn the lover, not lament the fault." Nothing is more easy than to banish such plays from our stage. Were our ladies, instead of crowding to see them again and again repeated, to discourage their exhibition by absence, the stage would soon be indeed the school of morality, and the number of "Fair Penitents," in all probability diminish.

SALMAGUNDI NO. VIII

Saturday, April 18, 1807.

BY ANTHONY EVERGREEN, GENT.

"In all thy humors, whether grave or mellow,
  Thou'rt such a touchy, testy, pleasant fellow;
  Hast so much wit, and mirth, and spleen about thee,
  There is no living with thee—nor without thee."

NEVER, in the memory of the oldest inhabitant has there been known a more backward spring." This is the universal remark among the almanac quidnuncs, and weather wiseacres of the day; and I have heard it at least fifty-five times from old mrs. Cockloft, who, poor woman, is one of those walking almanacs that foretel every snow, rain, or frost by the shooting of corns, a pain in the bones, or an "ugly stitch in the side." I do not recollect, in the whole course of my life, to have seen the month of March indulge in such untoward capers, caprices and coquetries as it has done this year: I might have forgiven these vagaries, had they not completely knocked up my friend Langstaff, whose feelings are ever at the mercy of a weather-cock, whose spirits rise and sink with the mercury of a barometer, and to whom an east wind is as obnoxious as a sicilian *sirocco*. He was tempted some time since, by the fineness of the weather, to dress himself with more than ordinary care, and take his morning stroll; but before he had half finished his peregrination he was utterly discomfited, and driven home by a tremenduous squall of wind, hail, rain and snow, or as he testily termed it "a most villanous congregation of vapors."

This was too much for the patience of friend Launcelot; he declared he would humor the weather no longer in its whim-whams, and according to his immemorial custom on these occasions, retreated in high dudgeon to his elbow-chair, to lie in of the spleen, and rail at nature for being so fantastical:—"confound the jade," he frequently exclaims, " what a pity nature had not been of the masculine instead of the feminine gender, the almanac makers might then have calculated with some degree of certainty."

When Langstaff invests himself with the spleen, and gives audience to the blue devils from his elbow chair, I would not advise any of his friends to come within gunshot of his citadel, with the benevolent purpose of administering consolation or amusement; for he is then as crusty and crabbed as that famous coiner of false money, Diogenes himself. Indeed his room is at such times inaccessable, and old Pompey is the only soul that can gain admission or ask a question with impunity: the truth is, that on these occasions, there is not a straws difference between them, for Pompey is as grum and grim and cynical as his master.

Launcelot has now been above three weeks in this desolate situation, and has therefore had but little to do in our last number. As he could not be prevailed on to give any account of himself in our introduction, I will take the opportunity of his confinement, while his back is turned, to give a slight sketch of his character—fertile in whim-whams and bachelorisms, but rich in many of the sterling qualities of our nature. Annexed to this article, our readers will perceive a striking likeness of my friend, which was taken by that cunning rogue Will Wizard, who peeped through the key-hole, and sketched it off, as honest Launcelot sat by the fire, wrapped up in his flannel *robe de chambre*, and indulging in a mortal fit of the *hyp*. Now take my word for it, gentle reader, this is the most auspicious moment in which to touch off the phiz of a genuine humorist.

Of the antiquity of the Langstaff family I can say but little, except that I have no doubt it is equal to that of most families who have the privilege of making their own pedigree, without the impertinent interposition of a college of heralds. My friend Launcelot is not a man to *blazon* any thing; but I have heard him talk with great complacency of his ancestor, Sir ROWLAND, who was a dashing buck in the days of Hardiknute, and broke the head of a gigantic dane, at a game of quarter-staff, in presence of the whole court. In memory of this gallant exploit, Sir Rowland was permitted to take the name of Langstoffe, and to assume as a crest to his arms, a hand grasping a cudgel. It is however a foible so ridiculously common in this country, for people to claim consanguinity with all the great personages of their own name in Europe, that I should put but little faith in this family boast of friend Langstaff, did I not know him to be a man of most unquestionable veracity.

The whole world knows already that my friend is a batchelor, for he is, or pretends to be, exceedingly proud of his personal independence, and takes care to make it known in all companies where strangers are present. He is forever vaunting the precious state of "single blessedness," and was not long ago considerably startled by a proposition of one of his great favorites, miss Sophy Sparkle, "that old batchelors should be taxed as luxuries." Launcelot immediately hied him home and wrote a tremendous long representation in their behalf, which I am resolved to publish, if it is ever attempted to carry the measure into operation. Whether he is sincere in these professions, or whether his present situation is owing to choice or disappointment, he only can tell; but if he ever does tell, I will suffer myself to be shot by the first lady's eye that can twang an arrow. In his youth he was forever in love; but it was his misfortune to be continually crossed and rivalled by his bosom friend and contemporary beau, Pindar Cockloft, esq., for as Langstaff never made a confidant on these occasions, his friend never knew which way his affections pointed, and so, between them both, the lady generally slipped through their fingers.

It has ever been the misfortune of Launcelot, that he could not for the soul of him restrain a *good thing*; and this fatality has drawn upon him the ill-will of many whom he would not have offended for the world. With the kindest heart under heaven, and the most benevolent disposition towards every being around him, he has been continually betrayed by the mischievous vivacity of his fancy, and the good-humored waggery of his feelings, into satirical sallies, which have been treasured up by the invidious, and retailed out with the bitter sneer of malevolence, instead of the playful hilarity of countenance which originally sweetened and tempered and disarmed them of their sting. These misrepresentations have gain'd him many reproaches and lost him many a friend.

This unlucky characteristic played the mischief with him in one of his love affairs. He was, as I have before observed, often opposed in his gallantries by that formidable rival, Pindar Cockloft, esq.—and a most formidable rival he was, for he had Apollo, the nine muses, together with all the joint tenants of Olympus, to back him, and every body knows what important confederates they are to a lover. Poor Launcelot stood no chance—the lady was cooped up in the poets' corner of every weekly paper, and at length Pindar attacked her with a *sonnet* that took up a whole column, in which he enumerated at least a dozen cardinal virtues, together with innumerable others of inferior consideration. Launcelot saw his case was desperate, and that unless he sat down forthwith, be-cherubim'd and be-angel'd her to the skies, and put every virtue under the sun in requisition, he might as well go hang himself, and so make an end of the business. At it, therefore, he went, and was going on very swimmingly, for, in the space of a dozen lines, he had enlisted under her command at least three score and ten substantial, house-keeping virtues, when unluckily for Launcelot's reputation as a poet, and the lady's as a saint, one of those confounded *good thoughts* struck his laughter-loving brain—it was irresistable—away he went full sweep before the wind, cutting and slashing, and tickled to death with his own fun: the consequence was, that by the time he had finished, never was poor lady so most ludicrously lampooned, since lampooning came into fashion. But this was not half—so hugely was Launcelot pleased with this frolic of his wits, that nothing would do but he must show it to the lady, who, as well she might, was mortally offended and forbid him her presence. My friend was in despair, but through the interference of his generous rival, was permitted to make his apology, which however most unluckily happened to be rather worse than the original offence; for, though he had studied an eloquent compliment, yet, as ill-luck would have it, a most preposterous whim-wham knocked at his pericranium, and inspired him to say some consummate *good things*, which all put together amounted to a downright *hoax*, and provoked the lady's wrath to such a degree that sentence of eternal banishment was awarded against him.

Launcelot was inconsolable, and determined in the true

style of novel heroics, to make the tour of Europe, and endeavor to lose the recollection of this misfortune amongst the gaieties of France, and the classic charms of Italy; he accordingly took passage in a vessel and pursued his voyage prosperously, as far as Sandy-Hook, where he was seized with a violent fit of sea-sickness, at which he was so affronted that he put his portmanteau into the first pilot-boat, and returned to town, completely cured of his love, and his rage for travelling.

I pass over the subsequent amours of my friend Langstaff, being but little acquainted with them; for, as I have already mentioned, he never was known to make a confidant of any body. He always affirmed a man must be a fool to fall in love, but an ideot to boast of it—ever denominated it the *villanous passion*—lamented that it could not be cudgelled out of the human heart—and yet could no more live without being in love with somebody or other than he could without whimwhams.

My friend Launcelot is a man of excessive irritability of nerve, and I am acquainted with no one so susceptible of the petty "miseries of human life;" yet its keener evils and misfortunes he bears without shrinking, and however they may prey in secret on his happiness, he never complains. This was strikingly evinced in an affair where his heart was deeply and irrevocably concerned, and in which his success was ruined by one for whom he had long cherished a warm friendship. The circumstances cut poor Langstaff to the very soul; he was not seen in company for months afterwards, and for a long time he seemed to retire within himself, and battle with the poignancy of his feelings; but not a murmur or a reproach was heard to fall from his lips, though at the mention of his friend's name, a shade of melancholy might be observed stealing across his face, and his voice assumed a touching tone that seemed to say he remembered his treachery "more in sorrow than in anger." This affair has given a slight tinge of sadness to his disposition, which, however, does not prevent his entering into the amusements of the world; the only effect it occasions is, that you may occasionally observe him at the end of a lively conversation sink for a few minutes into an apparent forgetfulness of surrounding objects, during which time he seems to be indulging in some melancholy retrospection.

Langstaff inherited from his father a love of literature, a disposition for *castle building*, a mortal enmity to noise, a sovereign antipathy to cold weather and brooms, and a plentiful stock of whim-whams. From the delicacy of his nerves he is peculiarly sensible to discordant sounds; the rattling of a wheelbarrow is "horrible," the noise of children "drives him distracted," and he once left excellent lodgings merely because the lady of the house wore high-heeled shoes, in which she clattered up and down stairs, till, to use his own emphatic expression "they made life loathsome" to him. He suffers annual martyrdom from the razor-edged zephyrs of our "balmy spring," and solemnly declares that the boasted month of May has become a perfect "vagabond." As some people have a great antipathy to cats, and can tell when one is locked up in a closet, so Launcelot declares his feelings always announce to him the neighborhood of a broom, a household implement which he abominates above all others. Nor is there any living animal in the world that he holds in more utter abhorrence than what is usually termed a *notable housewife*, a pestilent being who he protests is the bane of good fellowship, and has a heavy charge to answer for the many offences committed against the ease, comfort and social enjoyments of sovereign man. He told me, not long ago, that he had rather see one of the weird sisters flourish through his key-hole on a broomstick, than one of the servant maids enter the door with a *besom*.

My friend Launcelot is ardent and sincere in his attachments, which are confined to a chosen few, in whose society he loves to give free scope to his whimsical imagination; he, however, mingles freely with the world, though more as a spectator than an actor, and without an anxiety or hardly a care to please, is generally received with welcome and listened to with complacency. When he extends his hand, it is in a free, open, liberal style, and when you shake it you feel his honest heart throb in its pulsations. Though rather fond of gay exhibitions, he does not appear so frequently at balls and assemblies, since the introduction of the drum, trumpet and tamborine, all of which he abhors on account of the rude attacks they make on his organs of hearing—in short, such is his antipathy to noise, that though exceedingly patriotic, yet he retreats every fourth of July to Cockloft Hall, in order to get out of the way of the hub-bub and confusion, which made so considerable a part of the pleasure of that splendid anniversary.

I intend this article as a mere sketch of Langstaff's multifarious character—his innumerable whim-whams will be exhibited by himself, in the course of this work, in all their strange varieties; and the machinery of his mind, more intricate than the most subtle piece of clock-work, be fully explained. And trust me, gentlefolk, his are the whim-whams of a courteous gentleman, full of excellent qualities; honorable in his disposition, independent in his sentiments, and of unbounded good nature, as may be seen through all his works.

On Style.

BY WILLIAM WIZARD, ESQ.

STYLE, *a manner of writing; title; pin of a dial; the pistil of plants.*   *Johnson.*

STYLE, *is* —————————— *style.*   *Link. Fed.*

Now I would not give a straw for either of the above definitions, though I think the latter is by far the most satisfactory; and I do wish sincerely every modern numskull who takes hold of a subject he knows nothing about, would adopt honest Linkum's mode of explanation. Blair's lectures on the subject have not thrown a whit more light on the subject of my inquiries—they puzzled me just as much as did the learned and laborious expositions and illustrations of the worthy professor of our college, in the middle of which I generally had the ill luck to fall asleep.

This same word *style*, though but a diminutive word, assumes to itself more contradictions, and significations, and eccentricities, than any monosyllable in the language is legitimately entitled to. It is an arrant little humourist of a word, and full of whim-whams, which occasions me to like it hugely; but it puzzled me most wickedly on my first return from a long residence abroad; having crept into fashionable use during my absence; and had it not been for friend Evergreen, and that thrifty sprig of knowledge, Jeremy Cockloft the younger, I should have remained to this day ignorant of its meaning.

Though it would seem that the people of all countries are equally vehement in the pursuit of this phantom style, yet, in almost all of them, there is a strange diversity in opinion as to what constitutes its essence; and every different class, like the pagan nations, adore it under a different form. In England, for instance, an honest cit packs up himself, his family and his style in a buggy or tim-whiskey, and rattles away on sunday with his fair partner blooming beside him like an eastern bride, and two chubby children, squatting like chinese images at his feet. A baronet requires a chariot and pair—a lord must needs have a barouche and four;—but a duke— oh! a duke cannot possibly lumber his style along under a coach and six, and half a score of footmen into the bargain. In china, a puissant mandarine loads at least three elephants with style, and an overgrown sheep, at the Cape of Good-Hope, trails along his tail and his style on a wheel-barrow. In Egypt, or at Constantinople, style consists in the quantity of fur and fine clothes a lady can put on without danger of suffocation—here it is otherwise, and consists in the quantity she can put off without the risk of freezing. A chinese lady is thought prodigal of her charms, if she exposes the tip of her nose, or the ends of her fingers to the ardent gaze of bye-standers: and I recollect that all Canton was in a buzz in consequence of the great belle, miss Nang-fou's, peeping out of the window with her face uncovered! Here the style is to show not only the face, but the neck, shoulders, &c.; and a lady never presumes to hide them except when she is *not at home* and not sufficiently *undress'd* to see company.

This style has ruined the peace and harmony of many a worthy household; for no sooner do they set up for style, but instantly all the honest old comfortable *sans ceremonie* furniture is discarded, and you stalk cautiously about, amongst the uncomfortable splendour of grecian chairs, egyptian tables, turkey carpets, and etruscan vases. This vast improvement in furniture demands an increase in the domestic establishment; and a family that once required two or three servants for convenience, now employ half a dozen for style.

BELLBRAZEN, late favourite of my unfortunate friend Dessalines, was one of these patterns of style, and whatever freak she was seized with, however preposterous, was implicitly followed by all who would be considered as admitted in the stylish arcana. She was once seized with a whim-wham that tickled the whole court. She could not lay down to take an afternoon's loll, but she must have one servant to scratch her head, two to tickle her feet, and a fourth to fan her delectable person while she slumbered. The thing *took*—it became the *rage*, and not a sable bell in all Hayti, but what insisted upon being fanned, and scratched, and tickled in the true imperial style. Sneer not at this picture, my most excellent townswomen, for who among you but are daily following fashions equally absurd!

Style, according to Evergreen's account, consists in certain fashions, or certain eccentricities, or certain manners of certain people, in certain situations, and possessed of a certain share of fashion or importance. A red cloak, for instance, on the shoulders of an old market-woman is regarded with contempt, it is vulgar, it is odious:—fling, however, its usurping rival, a red shawl, over the fine figure of a fashionable belle, and let her flame away with it in Broadway, or in a ball-room, and it is immediately declared to be the *style*.

The modes of attaining this *certain situation* which entitles its holder to style, are various and opposite: the most ostensible is the attainment of wealth, the possession of which changes at once the pert airs of vulgar ignorance, into fashionable ease and elegant vivacity. It is highly amusing to observe the gradations of a family aspiring to style, and the devious windings they pursue in order to attain it. While beating up against wind and tide they are the most complaisant beings in the world—they keep "booing and booing," as M'Sychophant says, until you would suppose them incapable of standing upright; they kiss their hands to every body who has the least claim to style—their familiarity is intolerable, and they absolutely overwhelm you with their friendship and loving kindness. But having once gained the envied pre-eminence, never were beings in the world more changed. They assume the most intolerable caprices; at one time address you with importunate sociability, at another, pass you by with silent indifference, sometimes sit up in their chairs in all the majesty of dignified silence, and at another time bounce about with all the obstreperous, ill-bred noise of a little hoyden just broke loose from a boarding-school.

Another feature which distinguishes these new made fashionables, is the inveteracy with which they look down upon the honest people who are struggling to climb up to the same envied height. They never fail to salute them with the most sarcastic reflections; and like so many worthy hod-men clambering a ladder, each one looks down with a sneer upon his next neighbor below, and makes no scruple of shaking the dust off his shoes into his eyes. Thus by dint of perseverence merely, they come to be considered as established denizens of the great world; as in some barbarous nations an oyster-shell is of sterling value, and a copper washed counter will pass current for genuine gold.

In no instance, have I seen this grasping after style more whimsically exhibited than in the family of my old acquaintance, TIMOTHY GIBLET. I recollect old Giblet when I was a boy, and he was the most surly curmudgeon I ever knew. He was a perfect scare-crow to the *small fry* of the day, and inherited the hatred of all these unlucky little shavers; for never could we assemble about his door of an evening to play and make a little hub-bub, but out he sallied from his nest like a spider, flourish'd his formidable horsewhip, and dispersed the whole crew in the twinkling of a lamp. I perfectly remember a bill he sent in to my father for a pane of glass I had accidentally broken, which came well nigh getting me a sound flogging; and I remember, as perfectly, that the next night I revenged myself by breaking half a dozen. Giblet was as arrant a grub-worm as ever crawled; and the only rules of right and wrong he cared a button for, were the rules of multiplication and addition, which he practiced much more successfully than he did any of the rules of religion or morality. He used to declare they were the true *golden rules*, and he took special care to put Cocker's arithmetic in the hands of his children, before they had read ten pages in the bible or the prayer-book. The practice of these favourite maxims was at length crowned with the harvest of success; and after a life of incessant self-denial, and starvation, and after enduring all the pounds, shillings and pence miseries of a miser, he had the satisfaction of seeing himself worth a *plum*, and of dying just as he had determined to enjoy the remainder of his days, in contemplating his great wealth and accumulating mortgages.

His children inherited his money, but they buried the disposition, and every other memorial of their father, in his grave. Fired with a noble thirst for *style*, they instantly emerged from the retired lane in which themselves, and their accomplishments had hitherto been buried, and they blazed, and they whizzed, and they cracked about town, like a nest of squibs and devils in a firework. I can liken their sudden *eclat* to nothing but that of the locust, which is hatched in the dust, where it increases and swells up to maturity, and after feeling for a moment the vivifying rays of the sun, bursts forth a mighty insect, and flutters, and rattles, and buzzes from every tree. The little warblers who have long cheered the woodlands with their dulcet notes, are stunned by the discordant racket of these upstart intruders, and contemplate, in contemptuous silence, their tinsel and their noise.

Having once started, the Giblets were determined that nothing should stop them in their career, until they had run their full course, and arrived at the very tip-top of *style*. Every tailor, every shoe-maker, every coachmaker, every milliner, every mantuamaker, every paper-hanger, every piano teacher, and every dancing-master in the city were enlisted in their service; and the willing wights most courteously answered their call, and fell to work to build up the fame of the Giblets as they had done that of many an aspiring family before them. In a little time the young ladies could dance the waltz, thunder lodoiska, murder french, kill time, and commit violence on the face of nature in a landscape in water-colours, equal to the best lady in the land; and the young gentlemen were seen lounging at corners of streets, and driving tandem; heard talking loud at the theatre, and laughing in church, with as much ease and grace and *modesty*, as if they had been gentlemen all the days of their lives.

And the Giblets arrayed themselves in scarlet, and in fine linen, and seated themselves in high-places, but nobody noticed them except to honour them with a little contempt. The Giblets made a prodigious splash in their own opinion; but nobody extolled them except the tailors and the milliners who had been employed in manufacturing their paraphernalia. The Giblets thereupon being like Caleb Quotem, determined to have "a place at the review," fell to work more fiercely than ever—they gave dinners, and they gave balls, they hired cooks, they hired fiddlers, they hired confectioners, and they would have kept a newspaper in pay, had they not been all bought up at that time for the election. They invited the dancing men and the dancing women, and the gormandizers and the epicures of the city, to come and make merry at their expense; and the dancing men, and the dancing women, and the epicures, and the gormandizers, did come, and they did *make merry* at their expense; and they eat, and they drank, and they capered, and they danced, and they—laughed at their entertainers.

Then commenced the hurry and the bustle, and the mighty nothingness of fashionable life;—such rattling in coaches! such flaunting in the streets! such slamming of box doors at the theatre! such a tempest of bustle and unmeaning noise where-ever they appeared! the Giblets were seen here and there and every where—they visited every body they knew, and every body they did not know, and there was no getting along for the Giblets. Their plan at length succeeded. By dint of dinners, of feeding and frolicking the town, the Giblet family worked themselves into notice, and enjoyed the ineffable pleasure of being forever pestered by visitors, who cared nothing about them, of being squeezed, and smothered, and par-boiled at nightly balls, and evening tea-parties—they were allowed the privilege of forgetting the very few old friends they once possessed—they turned their noses up in the wind at every thing that was not genteel, and their superb manners and sublime affectation, at length left it no longer a matter of doubt that the Giblets were perfectly in the *style*.

"......*Being, as it were, a small contentmente in a never contenting subjecte; a bitter pleasaunte taste of a sweete seasoned sower; and, all in all, a more than ordinaire rejoycing, in an extraordinairie sorrowe of delyghts!*"

Linkum Fidelius.

We have been considerably edified of late by several letters of advice from a number of sage correspondents, who really seem to know more about our work than we do ourselves. One warns us against saying any thing more about SNIVERS, who is a very particular friend of the writer, and who has a singular disinclination to be laughed at. This correspondent in particular inveighs against personalities, and accuses us of ill nature in bringing forward old Fungus and Billy Dimple, as figures of fun to amuse the public. Another gentleman, who states that he is a near relation of the Cockloft's, proses away most soporifically on the impropriety of ridiculing a respectable old family, and declares that if we make them and their whim-whams the subject of any more essays, he shall be under the necessity of applying to our theatrical champions for satisfaction. A third, who by the crabbedness of the hand-writing and a few careless inaccuracies in the spelling, appears to be a lady, assures us that the miss Cockloft's, and miss Diana Wearwell, and miss Dashaway, and mrs. ———, Will Wizard's quondam flame, are so much obliged to us for our notice, that they intend in future to take no notice of us at all, but leave us out of all their tea-parties, for which we make them one of our best bows, and say, "thank you, ladies."

We wish to heaven these good people would attend to their own affairs, if they have any to attend to, and let us alone. It is one of the most provoking things in the world that we cannot tickle the public a little, merely for our own private amusement, but we must be crossed and jostled by these meddling incendiaries, and in fact, have the whole town about our ears. We are much in the same situation with an unlucky blade of a cockney, who having mounted his bit of blood to enjoy a little innocent recreation, and display his horsemanship along Broadway, is worried by all those little yelping curs that infest our city, and who never fail to sally out and growl, and bark, and snarl, to the great annoyance of the Birmingham equestrian.

Wisely was it said by the sage Linkum Fidelius, "howbeit, moreover, neverthelesse, this thrice wicked towne is charged up to the muzzle with all manner of ill-natures and unchari-tablenesses, and is, moreover, exceedinglie naughte." This passage of the erudite Linkum was applied to the city of Gotham, of which he was once lord mayor, as appears by his picture hung up in the hall of that ancient city—but his observation fits this best of all possible cities "to a hair." It is a melancholy truth that this same New-York, though the most charming, pleasant, polished and praise-worthy city under the sun, and in a word, the *bonne bouche* of the universe, is most shockingly ill-natured and sarcastic, and wickedly given to all manner of backslidings—for which we are very sorry indeed. In truth, for it must come out like murder one time or other, the inhabitants are not only ill-natured, but manifestly unjust: no sooner do they get one of our random sketches in their hands, but instantly they apply it most unjustifiably to some "dear friend," and then accuse us vociferously of the personality which originated in their own officious *friendship*! Truly it is an ill-natured town, and most earnestly do we hope it may not meet with the fate of Sodom and Gomorrah of old.

As, however, it may be thought incumbent upon us to make some apology for these mistakes of the town, and as our good-nature is truly exemplary, we would certainly answer this expectation, were it not that we have an invincible antipathy to making apologies. We have a most profound contempt for any man who cannot give three good reasons for an unreasonable thing, and will therefore condescend, as usual, to give the public three special reasons for never apologizing—first, an apology implies that we are accountable to some body or another for our conduct—now as we do not care a fiddle-stick, as authors, for either public opinion or private ill-will, it would be implying a falsehood to apologize:—second, an apology would indicate that we had been doing what we ought not to have done. Now as we never did, nor ever intend to do any thing wrong, it would be ridiculous to make an apology:—third, we labor under the same incapacity in the art of apologizing that lost Langstaff his mistress—we never yet undertook to make an apology without committing a new offence, and making matters ten times worse than they were before, and we are, therefore, determined to avoid such predicaments in future.

But though we have resolved never to apologize, yet we have no particular objection to explain, and if this is all that's wanted, we will go about it directly:—*allons*, gentlemen!—

before, however, we enter upon this serious affair, we take this opportunity to express our surprize and indignation at the incredulity of some people. Have we not, over and over, assured the town that we are three of the best natured fellows living? And is it not astonishing that having already given seven convincing proofs of the truth of this assurance, they should still have any doubts on the subject? but as it is one of the impossible things to make a knave believe in honesty, so, perhaps, it may be another to make this most sarcastic, satirical and tea-drinking city believe in the existence of good-nature. But to our explanation.—Gentle reader! for we are convinced that none but gentle or genteel readers can relish our excellent productions—if thou art in expectation of being perfectly satisfied with what we are about to say, thou mayest as well " whistle lillebullero" and skip quite over what follows, for never wight was more disappointed than thou wilt be most assuredly.—But to the explanation: we care just as much about the public and its wise conjectures, as we do about the man in the moon and his whim-whams, or the criticisms of the lady who sits majestically in her elbow-chair in the lobster, and who, belying her sex, as we are credibly informed, never says any thing worth listening to. We have launched our bark, and we will steer to our destined port with undeviating perseverence, fearless of being shipwrecked by the way. *Good-nature* is our steersman, *reason* our ballast, *whim* the breeze that wafts us along, and MORALITY our leading star.

SALMAGUNDI NO. IX

Saturday, April 25, 1807.

FROM MY ELBOW-CHAIR.

IT in some measure jumps with my humour to be "melancholy and gentleman-like" this stormy night, and I see no reason why I should not indulge myself for once.—Away, then, with joke, with fun and laughter for a while; let my soul look back in mournful retrospect, and sadden with the memory of my good aunt CHARITY—who died of a frenchman!

Stare not, oh most dubious reader, at the mention of a complaint so uncommon; grievously hath it afflicted the ancient family of the Cocklofts, who carry their absurd antipathy to the french so far, that they will not suffer a clove of garlic in the house: and my good old friend Christopher was once on the point of abandoning his paternal country mansion of Cockloft-hall, merely because a colony of frogs had settled in a neighbouring swamp. I verily believe he would have carried his whim-wham into effect, had not a fortunate drought obliged the enemy to strike their tents, and, like a troop of wandering arabs, to march off towards a moister part of the country.

My aunt Charity departed this life in the fifty-ninth year of her age, though she never grew older after twenty-five. In her teens, she was, according to her own account, a celebrated beauty—though I never could meet with any body that remembered when she was handsome; on the contrary, Evergreen's father, who used to gallant her in his youth, says she was as knotty a little piece of humanity as he ever saw; and that, if she had been possessed of the least sensibility, she would like poor old *Acco*, have most certainly run mad at her own figure and face, the first time she contemplated herself in a looking-glass. In the good old times that saw my aunt in the hey-day of youth, a fine lady was a most formidable animal, and required to be approached with the same awe and devotion that a tartar feels in the presence of his Grand Lama. If a gentleman offered to take her hand, except to help her into a carriage, or lead her into a drawing-room, such frowns!

such a rustling of brocade and taffeta! her very paste shoe-buckles sparkled with indignation, and for a moment assumed the brilliancy of diamonds: In those days the person of a belle was sacred; it was unprofaned by the sacrilegious grasp of a stranger—simple souls!—they had not the *waltz* among them yet!

My good aunt prided herself on keeping up this buckram delicacy, and if she happened to be playing at the old-fashioned game of forfeits, and was fined a kiss, it was always more trouble to get it than it was worth; for she made a most gallant defence, and never surrendered until she saw her adversary inclined to give over his attack. Evergreen's father says he remembers once to have been on a sleighing party with her, and when they came to Kissing-bridge, it fell to his lot to levy contributions on miss Charity Cockloft; who, after squalling at a hideous rate, at length jumped out of the sleigh plump into a snow-bank, where she stuck fast like an icicle, until he came to her rescue. This latonian feat cost her a rheumatism, which she never thoroughly recovered.

It is rather singular that my aunt, though a great beauty, and an heiress withal, never got married. The reason she alledged was that she never met with a lover who resembled sir Charles Grandison, the hero of her nightly dreams and waking fancy; but I am privately of opinion that it was owing to her never having had an offer. This much is certain, that for many years previous to her decease, she declined all attentions from the gentlemen, and contented herself with watching over the welfare of her fellow-creatures. She was, indeed, observed to take a considerable lean towards methodism, was frequent in her attendance at love-feasts, read Whitfield and Westley, and even went so far as once to travel the distance of five-and-twenty miles, to be present at a camp meeting. This gave great offence to my cousin Christopher and his good lady, who, as I have already mentioned, are rigidly orthodox; and had not my aunt Charity been of a most pacific disposition, her religious whim-wham would have occasioned many a family altercation. She was, indeed, as good a soul as the Cockloft family ever boasted; a lady of unbounded loving kindness, which extended to man, woman and child, many of whom she almost killed with good-nature. Was any acquaintance sick? in vain did the wind whistle and the storm beat; my aunt would waddle through mud and mire, over the whole town, but what she would visit them. She would sit by them for hours together with the most persevering patience, and tell a thousand melancholy stories of human misery, *to keep up their spirits*. The whole catalogue of *yerb* teas was at her fingers' ends, from formidable wormwood down to gentle *balm*; and she would descant by the hour on the healing qualities of hoarhound, catnip, and penny-royal. Woe be to the patient that came under the benevolent hand of my aunt Charity, he was sure, willy nilly, to be drenched with a deluge of decoctions; and full many a time has my cousin Christopher borne a twinge of pain in silence, through fear of being condemned to suffer the martyrdom of her materia-medica. My good aunt had, moreover, considerable skill in astronomy, for she could tell when the sun rose and set every day in the year; and no woman in the whole world was able to pronounce, with more certainty, at what precise minute the moon changed. She held the story of the moon's being made of green cheese, as an abominable slander on her favourite planet; and she had made several valuable discoveries in solar eclipses, by means of a bit of burnt glass, which entitled her at least to an honorary admission in the american philosophical society. *Hutchin's improved* was her favourite book; and I shrewdly suspect that it was from this valuable work she drew most of her sovereign remedies for colds, coughs, corns and consumptions.

But the truth must be told; with all her good qualities my aunt Charity was afflicted with one fault, extremely rare among her gentle sex—it was curiosity. How she came by it, I am at a loss to imagine, but it played the very vengeance with her and destroyed the comfort of her life. Having an invincible desire to know every body's character, business, and mode of living, she was forever prying into the affairs of her neighbours, and got a great deal of ill will from people towards whom she had the kindest disposition possible. If any family on the opposite side of the street gave a dinner, my aunt would mount her spectacles, and sit at the window until the company were all housed, merely that she might know who they were. If she heard a story about any of her acquaintance, she would, forthwith, set off full sail and never rest until, to use her usual expression, she had got "to the bottom of it," which meant nothing more than telling it to every body she knew.

I remember one night my aunt Charity happened to hear a most precious story about one of her good friends, but unfortunately too late to give it immediate circulation. It made her absolutely miserable; and she hardly slept a wink all night, for fear her bosom-friend, mrs. SIPKINS, should get the start of her in the morning and blow the whole affair. You must know there was always a contest between these two ladies, who should first give currency to the good-natured things said about every body, and this unfortunate rivalship at length proved fatal to their long and ardent friendship. My aunt got up full two hours that morning before her usual time; put on her pompadour taffeta gown, and sallied forth to lament the misfortune of her dear friend.—Would you believe it!—wherever she went mrs. Sipkins had anticipated her; and, instead of being listened to with uplifted hands and open-mouthed wonder, my unhappy aunt was obliged to sit down quietly and listen to the whole affair, with numerous additions, alterations and amendments!—Now this was too bad; it would almost have provoked Patient Grizzle or a saint—it was too much for my aunt, who kept her bed for three days afterwards, with a cold as she pretended; but I have no doubt it was owing to this affair of mrs. Sipkins, to whom she never would be reconciled.

But I pass over the rest of my aunt Charity's life, checquered with the various calamities and misfortunes and mortifications, incident to those worthy old gentlewomen who have the domestic cares of the whole community upon their minds; and I hasten to relate the melancholy incident that hurried her out of existence in the full bloom of antiquated virginity.

In their frolicsome malice the fates had ordered that a french boarding-house, or *Pension Francaise*, as it was called, should be established directly opposite my aunt's residence. Cruel event! unhappy aunt Charity!—it threw her into that alarming disorder denominated the *fidgets*; she did nothing but watch at the window day after day, but without becoming one whit the wiser at the end of a fortnight than she was at the beginning; she thought that *neighbour Pension* had a monstrous large family, and some how or other they were all men! she could not imagine what business *neighbour Pension* followed to support so numerous a household, and *wondered* why there was always such a scraping of fiddles in the parlour, and such a smell of onions from neighbour Pension's kitchen; in short, neighbour Pension was continually uppermost in her thoughts and incessantly on the outer edge of her tongue. This was, I believe, the very first time she had ever fail'd "to get at the bottom of a thing," and the disappointment cost her many a sleepless night I warrant you. I have little doubt, however, that my aunt would have ferretted neighbour Pension out, could she have spoken or understood french, but in those times people in general could make themselves understood in plain english; and it was always a standing rule in the Cockloft family, which exists to this day, that not one of the females should learn french.

My aunt Charity had lived at her window for some time in vain, when one day as she was keeping her usual look-out, and suffering all the pangs of unsatisfied curiosity, she beheld a little meagre, weazel-faced frenchman, of the most forlorn, diminutive and pitiful proportions, arrive at neighbour Pension's door. He was dressed in white, with a little pinched up cocked hat; he seemed to shake in the wind, and every blast that went over him whistled through his bones and threatened instant annihilation. This embodied spirit of famine was followed by three carts, lumbered with crazy trunks, chests, band-boxes, *bidets*, medicine-chests, parrots and monkeys, and at his heels ran a yelping pack of little black nosed pug dogs. This was the one thing wanting to fill up the measure of my aunt Charity's afflictions; she could not conceive, for the soul of her, who this mysterious little apparition could be that made so great a display; what he could possibly do with so much baggage, and particularly with his parrots and monkeys; or how so small a carcase could have occasion for so many trunks of clothes. Honest soul! she had never had a peep into a frenchman's wardrobe, that *depot* of old coats, hats and breeches, of the growth of every fashion he has followed in his life.

From the time of this fatal arrival my poor aunt was in a quandary—all her inquiries were fruitless; no one could expound the history of this mysterious stranger; she never held up her head afterwards,—drooped daily, took to her bed in a fortnight, and in "one little month" I saw her quietly deposited in the family vault—being the seventh Cockloft that has died of a whim-wham!

Take warning, my fair country women! and you, oh ye excellent ladies—whether married or single, who pry into other people's affairs and neglect those of your own household—who are so busily employed in observing the faults of others that you have no time to correct your own—remember the fate of my dear aunt Charity, and eschew the evil spirit of curiosity.

FROM MY ELBOW-CHAIR.

I find, by perusal of our last number, that WILL WIZARD and EVERGREEN, taking advantage of my confinement, have been playing some of their confounded gambols. I suspected these rogues of some malpractices, in consequence of their queer looks and knowing winks whenever I came down to dinner, and of their not showing their faces at old Cockloft's for several days after the appearance of their precious effusions. Whenever these two waggish fellows lay their heads together, there is always sure to be hatched some notable piece of mischief, which, if it tickles nobody else, is sure to make its authors merry. The public will take notice that, for the purpose of teaching these my associates better manners, and punishing them for their high misdemeanours, I have by virtue of my authority suspended them from all interference in Salmagundi, until they show a proper degree of repentance, or I get tired of supporting the burthen of the work myself. I am sorry for Will, who is already sufficiently mortified, in not daring to come to the old house and tell his long stories and smoke his cygarr; but Evergreen being an old beau, may solace himself in his disgrace by trimming up all his old finery and making love to the little girls.

At present my right hand man is cousin Pindar, whom I have taken into high favour. He came home the other night all in a blaze like a sky-rocket—whisked up to his room in a paroxysm of poetic inspiration, nor did we see any thing of him until late the next morning, when he bounced upon us at breakfast

"Fire in each eye—and paper in each hand."

This is just the way with Pindar: he is like a volcano, will remain for a long time silent without emitting a single spark, and then all at once burst out in a tremendous explosion of rhyme and rhapsody.

As the letters of my friend Mustapha seem to excite considerable curiosity, I have subjoined another. I do not vouch for the justice of his remarks, or the correctness of his conclusions; they are full of the blunders and errors into which strangers continually indulge, who pretend to give an account of this country, before they well know the geography of the street in which they live. The copies of my friend's papers being confused and without date, I cannot pretend to give them in systematic order—in fact they seem now and then to treat of matters which have occurred since his departure: whether these are sly interpolations of that meddlesome wight Will Wizard; or whether honest Mustapha was gifted with the spirit of prophecy or second sight, I neither know—nor in fact do I care. The following seems to have been written when the tripolitan prisoners were so much annoyed by the ragged state of their wardrobe. Mustapha feelingly depicts the embarrassments of his situation, traveller like, makes an easy transition from his breeches to the seat of government, and incontinently abuses the whole administration; like a sapient traveller I once knew, who damned the french nation *in toto*—because they eat sugar with green peas.

LETTER
From MUSTAPHA RUB-A-DUB KELI KHAN,
captain of a ketch,
to ASEM HACCHEM, principal slave-driver
to his highness the bashaw of Tripoli.

Sweet, oh, ASEM! is the memory of distant friends! like the mellow ray of a departing sun it falls tenderly yet sadly on the heart. Every hour of absence from my native land rolls heavily by, like the sandy wave of the desart, and the fair shores of my country rise blooming to my imagination, clothed in the soft illusive charms of distance. I sigh—yet no one listens to the sigh of the captive; I shed the bitter tear of recollection, but no one sympathizes in the tear of the turban'd stranger! Think not, however, thou brother of my soul, that I complain of the horrors of my situation;—think not that my captivity is attended with the labours, the chains, the scourges, the insults that render slavery, with us, more dreadful than the pangs of hesitating, lingering death. Light, indeed, are the restraints on the personal freedom of thy kinsman; but who can enter into the afflictions of the mind;—who can describe the agonies of the heart? they are mutable as the clouds of the air, they are countless as the waves that divide me from my native country.

I have, of late, my dear Asem, laboured under an inconvenience singularly unfortunate, and am reduced to a dilemma most ridiculously embarrassing. Why should I hide it from the companion of my thoughts, the partner of my sorrows and my joys? Alas! Asem, thy friend Mustapha, the sublime and invincible *captain of a ketch*, is sadly in want of a pair of breeches! Thou will doubtless smile, oh most grave mussulman, to hear me indulge in such ardent lamentations about a circumstance so trivial, and a want apparently so easy to be satisfied; but little canst thou know of the mortifications attending my necessities, and the astonishing difficulty of supplying them. Honoured by the smiles and attentions of the beautiful ladies of this city, who have fallen in love with my whiskers and my turban; courted by the bashaws and the great men, who delight to have me at their feasts; the honour of my company eagerly solicited by every fiddler who gives a concert; think of my chagrin at being obliged to decline the host of invitations that daily overwhelm me, merely for want of a pair of breeches! Oh Allah! Allah! that thy disciples could come into the world all be-feathered like a bantam, or with a pair of leather breeches like the wild deer of the forest! Surely, my friend, it is the destiny of man to be forever subjected to petty evils, which, however trifling in appearance, prey in silence on his little pittance of enjoyment, and poison those moments of sunshine, which might otherwise be consecrated to happiness.

The want of a garment thou wilt say is easily supplied, and thou mayest suppose need only be mentioned, to be remedied at once by any tailor of the land: little canst thou conceive the impediments which stand in the way of my comfort; and still less art thou acquainted with the prodigious *great scale* on which every thing is transacted in this country. The nation moves most majestically slow and clumbsy in the most trivial affairs, like the unwieldy elephant, which makes a formidable difficulty of picking up a straw! When I hinted my necessities to the officer who has charge of myself and my companions, I expected to have them forthwith relieved, but he made an amazing long face, told me that we were prisoners of state, that we must therefore be clothed at the expense of government; that as no provision had been made by congress for an emergency of the kind, it was impossible to furnish me with a pair of breeches, until all the sages of the nation had been convened to *talk* over the matter, and debate upon the expediency of granting my request. Sword of the immortal Khalid, thought I, but this is great!—this is truly sublime! All the sages of an immense *logocracy* assembled together to talk about my breeches! Vain mortal that I am—I cannot but own I was somewhat reconciled to the delay which must necessarily attend this method of clothing me, by the consideration that if they made the affair a national act, my "name must of course be embodied in history," and myself and my breeches flourish to immortality in the annals of this mighty empire!

"But pray," said I, "how does it happen that a matter so insignificant should be erected into an object of such importance as to employ the representative wisdom of the nation, and what is the cause of their talking so much about a trifle?" "Oh," replied the officer, who acts as our slave-driver, "it all proceeds from *economy*. If the government did not spend ten times as much money in debating whether it was proper to supply you with breeches, as the breeches themselves would cost, the people who govern the bashaw and his divan would straightway begin to complain of their liberties being infringed; the national finances squandered: not a hostile slang-whanger, throughout the logocracy, but would burst forth like a barrel of combustion; and ten chances to one but the bashaw and the sages of his divan would all be turned out of office together. My good mussulman," continued he, "the administration have the good of the people too much at heart to trifle with their pockets; and they would sooner assemble and *talk* away ten thousand dollars, than expend fifty silently out of the treasury; such is the wonderful spirit of *economy*, that pervades every branch of this government." "But," said I, "how is it possible they can spend money in talking—surely words cannot be the current coin of this country?" "Truely," cried he, smiling, "your question is pertinent enough, for words indeed often supply the place of cash among us, and many an honest debt is paid in promises; but the fact is, the grand bashaw and the members of congress, or grand talkers of the nation, either receive a yearly salary or are paid *by the day*." "By the nine-hundred tongues of the great beast in Mahomet's vision but the murder is out—it is no wonder these honest men talk so much about nothing, when they are paid for *talking*, like day laborers:" "you are mistaken," said my driver, "it is nothing but *economy*!"

I remained silent for some minutes, for this inexplicable word *economy* always discomfits me, and when I flatter myself I have grasped it, it slips through my fingers like a jack-o'lantern. I have not, nor perhaps ever shall acquire, sufficient of the philosophic policy of this government, to draw a proper distinction between an individual and a nation. If a man was to throw away a pound in order to save a beggarly penny, and boast at the same time of his economy, I should think him on a par with the fool in the fable of Alfanji, who, in skinning a flint worth a farthing, spoiled a knife worth fifty times the sum, and thought he had acted wisely. The shrewd fellow would doubtless have valued himself much more highly on his *economy*, could he have known that his example would one day be followed by the bashaw of America, and sages of his divan.

This economic disposition, my friend, occasions much fighting of the spirit, and innumerable contests of the tongue in this talking assembly. Wouldst thou believe it? they were actually employed for a whole week in a most strenuous and eloquent debate about patching up a hole in the wall of the room appropriated to their meetings! A vast profusion of nervous argument and pompous declamation was expended on the occasion. Some of the orators, I am told, being rather waggishly inclined, were most stupidly jocular on the occasion; but their waggery gave great offence, and was highly reprobated by the more *weighty* part of the assembly, who hold all wit and humour in abomination, and thought the business in hand much too solemn and serious to be treated lightly. It is supposed by some that this affair would have occupied a whole winter, as it was a subject upon which several gentlemen spoke who had never been known to open their lips in that place except to say *yes* and *no*. These silent members are by way of distinction denominated *orator mums*, and are highly valued in this country on account of their great talents for silence—a qualification extremely rare in a logocracy.

In the course of debate on this momentous question, the members began to wax warm, and grew to be exceeding wroth with one another, because their opponents most obstinately refused to be convinced by their arguments—or rather their *words*. The hole in the wall came well nigh producing a civil war of words throughout the empire; for, as usual in all public questions, the whole country was divided, and the *holeans* and the *anti-holeans*, headed by their respective slang-whangers, were marshalled out in array, and menaced deadly warfare. Fortunately for the public tranquility, in the hottest part of the debate, when two rampant virginians, brim-full of logic and philosophy, were measuring tongues, and syllogistically cudgelling each other out of their unreasonable notions, the president of the divan, a knowing old gentleman, one night slyly sent a mason with a hod of mortar, who, in the course of a few minutes, closed up the hole and put a final end to the argument. Thus did this wise old gentleman, by hitting on a most simple expedient, in all probability, save his country as much money as would build a gun-boat, or pay a hireling slang-whanger for a whole volume of *words*. As it happened, only a few thousand dollars were expended in paying these men, who are denominated, I suppose in derision, legislators.

Another instance of their economy I relate with pleasure,

for I really begin to feel a regard for these poor barbarians. They talked away the best part of a whole winter before they could determine *not* to expend a few dollars in purchasing a sword to bestow on an illustrious warrior: yes, Asem, on that very hero who frightened all our poor old women and young children at Derne, and fully proved himself a greater man than the mother that bore him. Thus, my friend, is the whole collective wisdom of this mighty logocracy employed in somniferous debates about the most trivial affairs, like I have sometimes seen a herculean mountebank exerting all his energies in balancing a straw upon his nose. Their sages behold the minutest object with the microscopic eyes of a pismire; mole-hills swell into mountains, and a grain of mustard-seed will set the whole ant-hill in a hub-bub. Whether this indicates a capacious vision, or a diminutive mind, I leave thee to decide; for my part I consider it as another proof of the *great scale* on which every thing is transacted in this country.

I have before told thee that nothing can be done without consulting the sages of the nation, who compose the assembly called the congress. This prolific body may not improperly be termed the "mother of inventions;" and a most fruitful mother it is let me tell thee, though its children are generally abortions. It has lately laboured with what was deemed the conception of a mighty navy.—All the old women and the good wives that assist the bashaw in his emergencies hurried to head quarters to be busy, like midwives, at the delivery.— All was anxiety, fidgetting and consultation; when, after a deal of groaning and struggling, instead of formidable first rates and gallant frigates, out crept a litter of sorry little gun-boats! These are most pitiful little vessels, partaking vastly of the character of the grand bashaw, who has the credit of begetting them—being flat shallow vessels that can only sail before the wind—must always keep in with the land—are continually foundering or running ashore; and in short, are only fit for *smooth water*. Though intended for the defence of the maritime cities, yet the cities are obliged to *defend them*; and they require as much nursing as so many rickety little bantlings. They are, however, the darling pets of the grand bashaw, being the children of his dotage, and, perhaps from their diminutive size and palpable weakness, are called the "infant navy of America." The act that brought them into existence was almost deified by the majority of the people as a grand stroke of *economy*.—By the beard of Mahomet, but this word is truly inexplicable!

To this economic body therefore was I advised to address my petition, and humbly to pray that the august assembly of sages would, in the plenitude of their wisdom and the magnitude of their powers, munificently bestow on an unfortunate captive, a pair of cotton breeches! "Head of the immortal Amrou," cried I, "but this would be presumptuous to a degree—what! after these worthies have thought proper to leave their country naked and defenceless, and exposed to all the political storms that rattle without, can I expect that they will lend a helping hand to comfort the *extremities* of a solitary captive?" my exclamation was only answered by a smile, and I was consoled by the assurance that, so far from being neglected, it was every way probable my breeches might occupy a whole session of the divan, and set several of the longest heads together by the ears. Flattering as was the idea of a whole nation being agitated about my breeches, yet I own I was somewhat dismayed at the idea of remaining *in querpo*, until all the national greybeards should have made a speech on the occasion, and given their consent to the measure. The embarrassment and distress of mind which I experienced was visible in my countenance, and my guard, who is a man of infinite good-nature, immediately suggested, as a more expeditious plan of supplying my wants—a benefit at the theatre. Though profoundly ignorant of his meaning, I agreed to his proposition, the result of which I shall disclose to thee in another letter.

Fare thee well, dear Asem;—in thy pious prayers to our great prophet, never forget to solicit thy friend's return; and when thou numberest up the many blessings bestowed on thee by all bountiful Allah, pour forth thy gratitude that he has cast thy nativity in a land where there is no assembly of legislative chatterers—no great Bashaw, who bestrides a gunboat for a hobby-horse—where the word *economy* is unknown—and where an unfortunate captive is not obliged to call upon the whole nation, to cut him out a pair of breeches.

ever thine,
MUSTAPHA.

PINDAR COCKLOFT, ESQ.

THOUGH entered on that sober age,
When men withdraw from fashion's stage,
And leave the follies of the day,
To shape their course a graver way;
Still those gay scenes I loiter round,
In which my youth sweet transport found:
And though I feel their joys decay,
And languish every hour away,—
Yet like an exile doomed to part,
From the dear country of his heart,
From the fair spot in which he sprung,
Where his first notes of love were sung,
Will often turn to wave the hand,
And sigh his blessing on the land,
Just so my lingering watch I keep—
Thus oft I take my farewel peep.
    And, like that pilgrim, who retreats
Thus lagging from his parent seats,
When the sad thought pervades his mind,
That the fair land he leaves behind
Is ravaged by a foreign foe,
Its cities waste—its temples low,
And ruined all those haunts of joy
That gave him rapture when a boy;
Turns from it with averted eye,
And while he heaves the anguish'd sigh,
Scarce feels regret that the loved shore
Shall beam upon his sight no more;—
Just so it grieves my soul to view,
While breathing forth a fond adieu,
The innovations pride has made—
The fustian, frippery and parade,
That now usurp with mawkish *grace*
Pure tranquil pleasure's wonted place!
    Twas *joy* we look'd for in my prime—
That idol of the olden time;
When all our pastimes had the art

To please, and not mislead, the heart.
Style cursed us not,—that modern flash—
That love of racket and of trash;
Which scares at once all feeling joys,
And drowns delight in empty noise;
Which barters friendship, mirth and truth,
The artless air—the bloom of youth,
And all those gentle sweets that swarm
Round nature in her simplest form,
For cold display—for hollow state—
The trappings of the *would be great*.
   Oh! once again those days recal,
When heart met heart in fashion's hall;
When every honest guest would flock
To add his pleasure to the stock,
More fond his transports to express,
Than show the tinsel of his dress!
These were the times that clasped the soul
In gentle friendship's soft controul;
Our fair ones, unprofaned by art,
Content to gain *one* honest heart,
No train of sighing swains desired—
Sought to be *loved* and not *admired*.
But now tis form—not love unites—
Tis show—not pleasure that invites.
Each seeks the ball to play the queen,
To flirt, to conquer—to be *seen*;
Each grasps at universal sway,
And reigns the idol of the day;
Exults amid a thousand sighs,
And triumphs when a lover dies.
Each belle a rival belle surveys,
Like deadly foe with hostile gaze;
Nor can her "dearest friend" caress,
Till she has slyly scann'd her dress;
Ten conquests in one year will make,
And six *eternal friendships* break!
   How oft I breathe the inward sigh,
And feel the dew-drop in my eye,
When I behold some beauteous frame,

Divine in every thing but name,
Just venturing, in the tender age,
On Fashion's late new fangled stage!
Where soon the guileless heart shall cease
To beat in artlessness and peace;
Where all the flowers of gay delight
With which youth decks its prospects bright,
Shall wither mid the cares—the strife—
The cold realities of life!

 Thus lately, in my careless mood,
As I the world of fashion view'd,
While celebrating *great and small*,
That grand *solemnity*—a ball,
My roving vision chanced to light
On two sweet forms, divinely bright;
Two sister nymphs, alike in face,
In mein, in loveliness and grace;
Twin rose-buds, bursting into bloom,
In all their brilliance and perfume;
Like those fair forms that often beam
Upon the eastern poets dream;
For Eden had each lovely maid
In native innocence arrayed,—
And heaven itself had almost shed
Its sacred halo round each head!

 They seemed, just entering hand in hand,
To cautious tread this fairy land;
To take a timid hasty view,
Enchanted with a scene so new.
The modest blush, untaught by art,
Bespoke their purity of heart;
And every timorous act unfurl'd
Two souls unspotted by the world.

 Oh, how these strangers joy'd my sight,
And thrill'd my bosom with delight!
They brought the visions of my youth
Back to my soul in all their truth,
Recalled fair spirits into day,
That time's rough hand had swept away!
Thus the bright natives from above,

Who come on messages of love,
Will bless, at rare and distant whiles,
Our sinful dwelling by their smiles!
  Oh! my romance of youth is past,
Dear airy dreams too bright to last!
Yet when such forms as these appear,
I feel your soft remembrance here;
For, ah! the simple poet's heart,
On which fond love once play'd its part,
Still feels the soft pulsations beat,
As loth to quit their former seat.
Just like the harp's melodious wire,
Swept by a bard with heavenly fire,
Though ceased the loudly swelling strain,
Yet sweet vibrations long remain.
  Full soon I found the lovely pair
Had sprung beneath a mother's care,
Hard by a neighbouring streamlet's side,
At once its ornament and pride.
The beauteous parent's tender heart
Had well fulfill'd its pious part;
And, like the holy man of old,
As we're by sacred writings told,
Who, when he from his pupil sped,
Pour'd two-fold blessings on his head,—
So this fond mother had imprest
Her early virtues in each breast,
And as she found her stock enlarge,
Had stampt new graces on her charge.
  The fair resigned the calm retreat,
Where first their souls in concert beat,
And flew on expectation's wing,
To sip the joys of life's gay spring;
To sport in fashion's splendid maze,
Where friendship fades, and love decays.
So two sweet wild flowers, near the side
Of some fair river's silver tide,
Pure as the gentle stream that laves
The green banks with its lucid waves,
Bloom beauteous in their native ground,

Diffusing heavenly fragrance round:
But should a venturous hand transfer
These blossoms to the gay parterre,
Where, spite of artificial aid,
The fairest plants of nature fade;
Though they may shine supreme awhile,
Mid *pale ones* of the stranger soil,
The tender beauties soon decay,
And their sweet fragrance dies away.
   Blest spirits! who enthron'd in air,
Watch o'er the virtues of the fair,
And with angelic ken survey,
Their windings through life's chequer'd way;
Who hover round them as they glide
Down fashion's smooth deceitful tide,
And guard them o'er that stormy deep
Where Dissipation's tempests sweep:
Oh, make this inexperienced pair
The objects of your tenderest care.
Preserve them from the languid eye,
The faded cheek—the long drawn sigh;
And let it be your constant aim
To keep the fair ones *still the same*:
Two sister hearts, unsullied, bright
As the first beam of lucid light,
That sparkled from the youthful sun,
When first his jocund race begun.
So when these hearts shall burst their shrine,
To wing their flight to realms divine,
They may to radiant mansions rise
Pure as when first they left the skies.

SALMAGUNDI NO. X

Saturday, May 16, 1807.

FROM MY ELBOW-CHAIR.

THE LONG INTERVAL which has elapsed since the publication of our last number, like many other remarkable events, has given rise to much conjecture and excited considerable solicitude. It is but a day or two since I heard a knowing young gentleman observe, that he suspected Salmagundi would be a nine days wonder, and had even prophesied that the ninth would be our last effort. But the age of prophecy, as well as that of chivalry, is past; and no reasonable man should now venture to fortel aught but what he is determined to bring about himself:—he may then, if he please, monopolize prediction, and be honored as a prophet even in his own country.

Though I hold whether we write, or not write, to be none of the public's business, yet as I have just heard of the loss of three thousand votes at least to the Clintonians, I feel in a remarkable dulcet humour thereupon, and will give some account of the reasons which induced us to resume our useful labours—or rather our amusements; for, if writing cost either of us a moment's labour, there is not a man but what would hang up his pen, to the great detriment of the world at large, and of our publisher in particular, who has actually bought himself a pair of trunk breeches, with the profits of our writings!!

He informs me that several persons having called last Saturday for No. X, took the disappointment so much to heart that he really apprehended some terrible catastrophe; and one good-looking man in particular, declared his intention of quitting the country if the work was not continued. Add to this, the town has grown quite melancholy in the last fortnight; and several young ladies have declared in my hearing that if another number did not make its appearance soon, they would be obliged to amuse themselves with teasing their beaux, and making them miserable. Now I assure my readers there was no flattery in this, for they no more suspected me of being Launcelot Langstaff, than they suspect me of being the emperor of China, or the man in the moon.

I have also received several letters complaining of our indolent procrastination; and one of my correspondents assures me that a number of young gentlemen, who had not read a book through since they left school, but who have taken a wonderful liking to our paper, will certainly relapse into their old habits, unless we go on.

For the sake, therefore, of all these good people, and most especially for the satisfaction of the ladies, every one of whom we would love, if we possibly could, I have again wielded my pen, with a most hearty determination to set the whole world to rights, to make cherubims and seraphs of all the fair ones of this enchanting town, and raise the spirits of the poor federalists, who, in truth, seem to be in a sad taking, ever since the American Ticket met with the accident of being so unhappily *dished*.

TO LAUNCELOT LANGSTAFF, ESQ.

Sir,

I felt myself hurt and offended by mr. Evergreen's terrible phillipic against modern music in No. II of your work, and was under serious apprehension that his strictures might bring the art which I have the honor to profess, into contempt. The opinions of yourself and fraternity appear indeed to have a wonderful effect upon the town. I am told the ladies are all employed in reading Bunyan and Pamela, and the waltz has been entirely forsaken ever since the winter balls have closed. Under these apprehensions I should have addressed you before, had I not been sedulously employed, while the theatre continued open, in supporting the astonishing variety of the orchestra, and in composing a new chime or Bob-major for Trinity-church, to be rung during the summer, beginning with *ding-dong di-do*, instead of *di-do ding-dong*. The citizens, especially those who live in the neighborhood of that harmonious quarter, will no doubt be infinitely delighted with this novelty.

But to the object of this communication.—So far, sir, from agreeing with mr. Evergreen in thinking that all modern music is but the mere dregs and drainings of the antient, I trust, before this letter is concluded, I shall convince you and him that some of the late Professors of this enchanting art have completely distanced the paltry efforts of the antients, and that I in particular have at length brought it almost to absolute perfection.

The greeks, simple souls! were astonished at the powers of Orpheus, who made the woods and rocks dance to his lyre— of Amphion who converted crotchets into bricks, and quavers into mortar—and of Arion who won upon the compassion of the fishes. In the fervency of admiration, their poets fabled that Apollo had lent them his lyre, and inspired them with his own spirit of harmony. What then would they have said had they witnessed the wonderful effects of my skill? Had they heard me in the compass of a single piece, describe in glowing notes one of the most sublime operations of na-ture, and not only make inanimate objects dance, but even speak, and not only speak, but speak in strains of exquisite harmony?

Let me not, however, be understood to say that I am the sole author of this extraordinary improvement in the art, for I confess I took the hint of many of my discoveries from some of those meritorious productions that have lately come abroad and made so much noise under the title of *overtures*. From some of these, as, for instance, Lodoiska, and the battle of Marengo, a gentleman, or a captain in the city militia, or an amazonian young lady, may indeed acquire a tolerable idea of military tactics, and become very well experienced in the firing of musketry, the roaring of cannon, the rattling of drums, the whistling of fifes, braying of trumpets, groans of the dying, and trampling of cavalry, without ever going to the wars;—but it is more especially in the art of imitating inimitable things, and giving the language of every passion and sentiment of the human mind, so as entirely to do away the necessity of speech, that I particularly excel the most celebrated musicians of antient and modern times.

I think, sir, I may venture to say there is not a sound in the whole compass of nature which I cannot imitate and even improve upon—nay, what I consider the perfection of my art, I have discovered a method of expressing, in the most striking manner, that undefinable, indescribable silence which accompanies the falling of snow.

In order to prove to you that I do not arrogate to myself what I am unable to perform, I will detail to you the different movements of a grand piece which I pride myself upon exceedingly, called the Breaking up of the Ice in the North-river.

The piece opens with a gentle andante affetuoso, which ushers you into the assembly-room, in the state-house at Albany, where the speaker addresses his farewel speech, informing the members that the ice is about breaking up, and thanking them for their great services and good behaviour in a manner so pathetic as to bring tears into their eyes.—Flourish of Jacks a donkies.—Ice cracks—Albany in a hubbub—air, "Three children sliding on the ice, all on a summer's day."—Citizens quarrelling in dutch—chorus of a tin trumpet, a cracked fiddle, and a hand-saw!—allegro moderato.—*Hard frost*—this if given with proper spirit has a charming effect, and sets every body's teeth chattering.—Symptoms of snow—consultation of old women who complain of pains in the bones and *rheumatics*—air, "There was an old woman tossed up in a blanket, &c."—allegro staccato—waggon breaks into the ice—people all run to see what is the matter—air, *siciliano*—"Can you row the boat ashore, Billy boy, Billy boy"—andante—frost fish froze up in the ice—air—"Ho, why dost thou shiver and shake, Gaffer Gray, and why does thy nose look so blue?"—Flourish of two-penny trumpets and rattles—consultation of the North-river society—determine to set the North river on fire, as soon as it will burn—air—"O, what a fine kettle of fish."

Part II.—GREAT THAW.—This consists of the most *melting* strains, flowing so smoothly, as to occasion a great overflowing of scientific rapture—air—"One misty moisty morning."—The house of assembly breaks up—air—"The owls came out and flew about"—Assemblymen embark on their way to New-York—air—"The ducks and the geese they all swim over, fal, de ral, &c.—Vessel sets sail—chorus of mariners—"Steer her up, and let her gang." After this a rapid movement conducts you to New-York—the North-river society hold a meeting at the corner of Wall-street, and determine to delay burning till all the assemblymen are safe home, for fear of consuming some of their own members who belong to that respectable body.—Return again to the *capital*.—Ice floats down the river—lamentation of skaiters—air, affetuoso—"I sigh and lament me in vain, &c."—Albanians cutting up sturgeon—air—"O the roast beef of *Albany*."—Ice runs against Polopoy's island, with a terrible crash.—This is represented by a fierce fellow travelling with his fiddle-stick over a huge bass viol, at the rate of one hundred and fifty bars a minute, and tearing the music to rags—this being what is called *execution*.—The great body of ice passes West-Point, and is saluted by three or four dismounted cannon, from Fort Putnam.—"Jefferson's march"—by a full band—air—"Yankee doodle," with seventy-six variations, never before attempted, except by the celebrated eagle, which flutters his wings over the copper-bottomed angel at messrs. Paff's in Broadway.—Ice passes New-York—conch-shell sounds at a distance—ferryman calls o-v-e-r—people run down Courtlandt-street—ferryboat sets sail—air—accompanied by the conch-shell—"We'll all go over the ferry."—Rondeau—giving a particular account of BROM the Powles-Hook admiral, who is supposed to be closely connected with the North-river society.—The society make a grand attempt to fire the stream, but are utterly defeated by a remarkable high tide, which brings the plot to light—drowns upwards of a thousand rats, and occasions twenty robins to break their necks.*—Society not being discouraged, apply to "Common Sense," for his lantern—Air—"Nose, nose, jolly red nose."—Flock of wild geese fly over the city—old wives chatter in the fog—cocks crow at Communipaw—drums beat on Governor's island.—The whole to conclude with *the blowing up of Sands' powder-house*.

Thus, sir, you perceive what wonderful powers of expression have been hitherto locked up in this enchanting art—a whole history is here told without the aid of speech, or writing; and provided the hearer is in the least acquainted with music he cannot mistake a single note. As to the blowing up of the powder-house, I look upon it as a chef d'ouvre, which I am confident will delight all modern amateurs, who very

*Vide—Solomon Lang.

properly estimate music in proportion to the noise it makes, and delight in thundering, cannon and earthquakes.

I must confess, however, it is a difficult part to manage, and I have already broken six pianoes in giving it the proper force and effect. But I do not despair, and am quite certain that by the time I have broken eight or ten more, I shall have brought it to such perfection, as to be able to teach any young lady of tolerable ear, to thunder it away to the infinite delight of papa and mamma, and the great annoyance of those vandals, who are so barbarous as to prefer the simple melody of a scots air, to the sublime effusions of modern musical doctors.

In my warm anticipation of future improvement, I have sometimes almost convinced myself that music will in time be brought to such a climax of perfection, as to supercede the necessity of speech and writing, and every kind of social intercourse be conducted by flute and fiddle. The immense benefits that will result from this improvement must be plain to every man of the least consideration. In the present unhappy situation of mortals, a man has but one way of making himself perfectly understood—if he loses his speech, he must inevitably be dumb all the rest of his life; but having once learned this new musical language, the loss of speech will be a mere trifle not worth a moment's uneasiness. Not only this, mr. L. but it will add much to the harmony of domestic intercourse, for it is certainly much more agreeable to hear a lady give lectures on the piano, than *viva voce*, in the usual discordant measure. This manner of discoursing may also, I think, be introduced with great effect into our national assemblies, where every man, instead of wagging his tongue, should be obliged to flourish a fiddle-stick, by which means, if he said nothing to the purpose, he would at all events "discourse most eloquent music," which is more than can be said of most of them at present. They might also sound their own trumpets, without being obliged to a hireling scribbler for an immortality of nine days, or subjected to the censure of egotism.

But the most important result of this discovery is, that it may be applied to the establishment of that great desideratum, in the learned world, a universal language. Wherever this science of music is cultivated, nothing more will be necessary than a knowledge of its alphabet, which being almost the same every where, will amount to a universal medium of communication. A man may thus, with his violin under his arm, a piece of rosin and a few bundles of catgut, fiddle his way through the world, and never be at a loss to make himself understood.

I am, &c.

DEMY SEMIQUAVER.

P. S. I forgot to mention that I intend to publish my piece by subscription, and dedicate it to the North-River Society.

D. S.

THE STRANGER IN PENNSYLVANIA
BY JEREMY COCKLOFT, THE YOUNGER

CHAPTER I.

Cross the Delaware—knew I was in Pennsylvania, because all the people were fat and looked like the statue of William Penn—Bristol—very remarkable for having nothing in it worth the attention of the traveller—saw Burlington on the opposite side of the river—fine place for pigeon-houses—and why?—Pennsylvania famous for barns—cattle in general better lodged than the farmers—barns appear to be built, as the old roman peasant planted his trees, "for posterity and the immortal gods." Saw several fine bridges of two or three arches built over dry places—wondered what could be the use of them—reminded me of the famous bridge at Madrid, built over no water—Chamouny—floating bridge made of pine logs fastened together by ropes of walnut bark—strange that the people who have such a taste for bridges should not have taken advantage of this river, to indulge in their favorite kind of architecture!—expressed my surprise to a fellow passenger, who observed to me with great gravity, "that nothing was more natural than that people who build bridges over dry places should neglect them where they are really necessary"—could not, for the head of me, see to the bottom of the man's reasoning—about half an hour after it struck me that he had been quizzing me a little—didn't care much about that—revenge myself by mentioning him in my book. Village of

Washington—very pleasant, and remarkable for being built on each side of the road—houses all cast in the same mould—have a very quakerish appearance, being built of stone, plastered and white-washed, and green doors, ornamented with brass knockers, kept very bright—saw several genteel young ladies scouring them—which was no doubt the reason for their brightness. Breakfasted at the Fox-Chase—recommend this house to all gentlemen travelling for information, as the land-lady makes the best buckwheat-cakes in the whole world; and because it bears the same name with a play, written by a young gentleman of Philadelphia, which, notwithstanding its very considerable merit, was received at that city with indifference and neglect, because it had no puns in it. Frankfort *in the mud*—very picturesque town, situate on the edge of a pleasant swamp—or meadow as they call it—houses all built of turf, cut in imitation of stone—poor substitute—took in a couple of Princeton students, who were going on to the southward, to tell their papas, (or rather their mammas) what fine manly little boys they were, and how nobly they resisted the authority of the trustees—both pupils of Godwin and Tom Paine—talked about the rights of man, the social compact, and the perfectability of boys—hope their parents will whip them when they get home, and send them back to college without any spending money. Turnpike gates—direction to keep to the right, as the law directs—very good advice, in my opinion; but one of the students swore he had no idea of submitting to this kind of oppression, and insisted on the driver's taking the left passage, in order to show the world we were not to be imposed upon by such arbitrary rules—driver, who, I believe, had been a student at Princeton himself, shook his head like a professor, and said it would not do. Entered Philadelphia through the suburbs—four little markets in a herd—one turned into a school for young ladies—mem. young ladies early in the market here—pun—good.

CHAPTER II.

Very ill—confined to my bed with a violent fit of the *pun* mania—strangers always experience an attack of the kind on their first arrival, and undergo a *seasoning* as europeans do in the West-Indies. In my way from the stage-office to Renshaw's I was accosted by a good-looking young gentleman from New-Jersey, who had caught the infection—he took me by the button and informed me of a contest that had lately taken place between a tailor and shoemaker about I forget what;—SNIP was pronounced a fellow of great *capability*, a man of gentlemanly *habits*, who would doubtless *suit* every body. The shoemaker *bristled* up at this, and *waxed* exceeding wroth—swore the tailor was but a *half-souled* fellow, and that it was easy to *shew* he was never *cut-out* for a gentleman. The *choler* of the tailor was up in an instant, he swore by his thimble that he would never *pocket* such an insult, but would *baste* any man who dared to repeat it.—Honest CRISPIN was now worked up to his proper *pitch*, and was determined to yield the tailor no *quarters*;—he vowed he would lose his *all* but what he would gain his *ends*. He resolutely held on to the *last*, and on his threatening to *back-strap* his adversary, the tailor was obliged to *sheer* off, declaring, at the same time, that he would have him *bound over*. The young gentleman, having finished his detail, gave a most obstreperous laugh, and hurried off to tell his story to somebody else—*Licentia punica*, as Horace observes—it did my business—I went home, took to my bed, and was two days confined with this singular complaint.

Having, however, looked about me with the argus eyes of a traveller, I have picked up enough in the course of my walk from the stage office, to the hotel, to give a full and impartial account of this remarkable city. According to the good old rule, I shall begin with the etymology of its name, which according to Linkum Fidelius. Tom. LV. is clearly derived, either from the name of its first founder, viz. PHILO DRIPPING-PAN, or the singular taste of the aborigines, who flourished there, on his arrival. Linkum, who is as shrewd a fellow as any theorist or F. S. A. for peeping with a dark lantern into the lumber garret of antiquity, and lugging out all the trash which was left there for oblivion, by our wiser ancestors, supports his opinion by a prodigious number of ingenious and inapplicable arguments; but particularly rests his position on the known fact, that Philo Dripping-pan was remarkable for his predilection to eating, and his love of what the learned dutch call *doup*. Our erudite author likewise observes that the citizens are to this day, noted for their love of "a sop in the pan," and their portly appearance, "except, indeed," continues he, "the young ladies, who are perfectly genteel in their dimensions"—this, however, he ill naturedly enough attributes to their eating pickles, and drinking vinegar.

The philadelphians boast much of the situation and plan of their city, and well may they, since it is undoubtedly, as fair and square, and regular, and right angled, as any mechanical genius could possibly have made it. I am clearly of opinion that this hum drum regularity has a vast effect on the character of its inhabitants and even on their looks, "for you will observe," writes Linkum, "that they are an honest, worthy, square, good-looking, well-meaning, regular, uniform, straight forward, clockwork, clear-headed, one-like-another, salubrious, upright, kind of people, who always go to work methodically, never put the cart before the horse, talk like a book, walk mathematically, never turn but in right angles, think syllogistically, and pun theoretically, according to the genuine rules of Cicero, and Dean Swift;—whereas the people of New-York—God help them—tossed about over hills and dales, through lanes and alleys, and crooked streets— continually mounting and descending, turning and twisting—whisking off at tangents, and left-angle-triangles, just like their own queer, odd, topsy-turvy rantipole city, are the most irregular, crazy headed, quicksilver, eccentric, whimwhamsical set of mortals that ever were jumbled together in this uneven, villanous revolving globe, and are the very antipodeans to the philadelphians."

The streets of Philadelphia are wide and strait, which is wisely ordered, for the inhabitants having generally crooked noses, and most commonly travelling hard after them, the good folks would undoubtedly soon *go to the wall*, in the crooked streets of our city. This fact of the crooked noses has not been hitherto remarked by any of our american travellers, but must strike every stranger of the least observation. There is, however, one place which I would recommend to all my fellow-citizens, who may come after me as a promenade—I mean Dock-street—the only street in Philadelphia that bears any resemblance to New-York—how tender, how exquisite are the feelings awakened in the breast of a traveller, when his eye encounters some object which reminds him of his far distant country! The pensive new-yorker, having drank his glass of porter, and smoked his cygarr after dinner, (by the way I would recommend Sheaff, as selling the best in Philadelphia) may here direct his solitary steps and indulge in that mellow tenderness in which the sentimental Kotzebue, erst delighted to wallow—he may recal the romantic scenery and graceful windings of Maiden-lane, and Pearl-street, trace the tumultuous gutter in its harmonious meanderings, and almost fancy he beholds the moss-crowned roof of the Bear-market, or the majestic steeple of St Paul's towering to the clouds.—Perhaps too, he may have left behind him some gentle fair one, who, all the live-long evening, sits pensively at the window, leaning on her elbows, and counting the lingering, lame and broken-winded moments that so tediously lengthen the hours which separate her from the object of her contemplations!—delightful Lethe of the soul—sunshine of existence—wife and children poking up the cheerful evening fire—paper windows, mud walls, love in a cottage—sweet sensibility—and all that.

Every body has heard of the famous bank of Pennsylvania, which, since the destruction of the tomb of Mausolus, and the colossus of Rhodes, may fairly be estimated as one of the wonders of the world. My landlord thinks it unquestionably the finest building upon earth. The honest man has never seen the theatre in New-York, or the new brick church at the head of Rector-street, which when finished, will, beyond all doubt, be infinitely superior to the Pennsylvania barns, I noted before.

Philadelphia is a place of great trade and commerce—not but that it would have been much more so, that is had it been built on the scite of New-York: but as New York has engrossed its present situation, I think Philadelphia must be content to stand where it does at present—at any rate it is not Philadelphia's fault nor is it any concern of mine, so I shall not make myself uneasy about the affair. Besides, to use Trim's argument, were that city to stand where New-York does, it might perhaps have the misfortune to be called New-York and not Philadelphia, which would be quite another matter, and this portion of my travels had undoubtedly been smothered before it was born—which would have been a thousand pities indeed.

Of the manufactures of Philadelphia, I can say but little, except that the people are famous for an excellent kind of confectionary, made from the drainings of sugar. The process is simple as any in mrs. Glass's excellent and useful work, (which I hereby recommend to the fair hands of all young ladies, who are not occupied in reading Moore's poems)—you buy a pot—put your molasses in your pot—(if you can beg, borrow, or steal your molasses it will come much cheaper than if you buy it)—boil your molasses to a proper consistency; but if you boil it too much, it will be none the better for it—then pour it off and let it cool, or draw it out into little pieces about nine inches long, and put it by for use. This manufacture is called by the bostonians *lasses-candy*, by the new-yorkers, *cock-a-nee-nee*—but by the polite philadelphians, by a name utterly impossible to pronounce.

The Philadelphia ladies, are some of them beautiful, some of them tolerably good looking, and some of them, to say the truth, are not at all handsome. They are, however, very agreeable in general, except those who are reckoned witty, who, if I might be allowed to speak my mind, are very disagreeable, particularly to young gentlemen, who are travelling for information. Being fond of tea-parties, they are a little given to criticism—but are in general remarkably discreet, and very industrious, as I have been assured by some of my friends. Take them all in all, however, they are much inferior to the ladies of New-York, as plainly appears, from several young gentlemen having fallen in love with some of our belles, after resisting all the female attractions of Philadelphia. From this inferiority, I except one, who is the most amiable, the most accomplished, the most bewitching, and the most of every thing that constitutes the divinity of woman—mem—*golden apple!*

The amusements of the philadelphians are dancing, punning, tea-parties, and theatrical exhibitions. In the first, they are far inferior to the young people of New-York, owing to

the misfortune of their mostly preferring to idle away time in
the cultivation of the head instead of the heels. It is a melancholy fact that an infinite number of young ladies in Philadelphia, whose minds are elegantly accomplished in literature,
have sacrificed to the attainment of such trifling acquisitions,
the pigeon-wing, the waltz, the cossack dance, and other matters of equal importance. On the other hand they excel the
new-yorkers in punning, and in the management of tea-parties. In N York you never hear, except from some young gentleman just returned from a visit to Philadelphia, a single
attempt at punning, and at a tea-party, the ladies in general,
are disposed close together, like a setting of jewels, or pearls
round a locket, in all the majesty of good behaviour—and if
a gentleman wishes to have a conversation with one of them,
about the backwardness of the spring, the improvements in
the theatre, or the merits of his horse, he is obliged to march
up in the face of such vollies of eye-shot! such a formidable
artilery of glances!—if he escapes annihilation, he should cry
out a miracle! and never encounter such dangers again. I remember to have once heard a very valiant british officer, who
had served with great credit for some years in the train bands,
declare with a veteran oath, that sooner than encounter such
deadly peril, he would fight his way clear through a London
mob, though he were pelted with brick-bats all the time.
Some ladies who were present at this declaration of the gallant officer, were inclined to consider it a great compliment,
until one, more knowing than the rest, declared with a little
piece of a sneer, "that they were very much obliged to him
for likening the company to a London mob, and their glances
to brick-bats:"—the officer looked blue, turned on his heel,
made a fine retreat and went home, with a determination to
quiz the american ladies as soon as he got to London.

SALMAGUNDI NO. XI

Tuesday, June 2, 1807.

LETTER
From MUSTAPHA RUB-A-DUB KELI KHAN,
captain of a ketch,
to ASEM HACCHEM, principal slave-driver
to his highness the bashaw of Tripoli.

THE DEEP SHADOWS of midnight gather around me—the footsteps of the passenger have ceased in the streets, and nothing disturbs the holy silence of the hour, save the sound of distant drums, mingled with the shouts, the bawlings, and the discordant revelry of his majesty, the sovereign mob. Let the hour be sacred to friendship, and consecrated to thee, oh thou brother of my inmost soul!

Oh Asem! I almost shrink at the recollection of the scenes of confusion, of licentious disorganization, which I have witnessed during the last three days. I have beheld this whole city, nay this whole state, given up to the tongue and the pen, to the puffers, the bawlers, the babblers and the *slang-whangers*. I have beheld the community convulsed with a civil war, (or *civil talk*) individuals verbally massacred, families annihilated by whole sheets full, and slang-whangers coolly bathing their pens in ink, and rioting in the slaughter of their thousands. I have seen, in short, that awful despot, *the people*, in the moment of unlimited power, wielding newspapers in one hand, and with the other scattering mud and filth about, like some desperate lunatic relieved from the restraints of his strait waistcoat. I have seen beggers on horeback, ragamuffins riding in coaches, and swine seated in places of honour—I have seen liberty, I have seen equality, I have seen fraternity!—I have seen that great political puppet-show—AN ELECTION.

A few days ago the friend, whom I have mentioned in some of my former letters, called upon me to accompany him to witness this grand ceremony, and we forthwith sallied out to *the polls*, as he called them. Though for several weeks before this splendid exhibition, nothing else had been talked of, yet I do assure thee I was entirely ignorant of its nature; and when, on coming up to a church, my companion informed me we were at the poll, I supposed that an election was some great religious ceremony, like the fast of Ramazan, or the great festival of Haraphat, so celebrated in the East.

My friend, however, undeceived me at once, and entered into a long dissertation on the nature and object of an election, the substance of which was nearly to this effect: "You know," said he, "that this country is engaged in a violent internal warfare, and suffers a variety of evils from civil dissentions. An election is the grand trial of strength, the decisive battle when the Belligerents draw out their forces in martial array; when every leader burning with warlike ardour, and encouraged by the shouts and acclamations of tatterdemalians, buffoons, dependents, parasites, toad-eaters, scrubs, vagrants, mumpers, ragamuffins, bravoes and beggers, in his rear, and puffed up by his bellows-blowing slang-whangers, waves gallantly the banners of faction, and presses forward TO OFFICE AND IMMORTALITY!"

"For a month or two previous to the critical period which is to decide this important affair, the whole community is in a ferment. Every man of whatever rank or degree, such is the wonderful patriotism of the people, disinterestedly neglects his business, to devote himself to his country—and not an insignificant fellow, but feels himself inspired on this occasion, with as much warmth in favour of the cause he has espoused, as if all the comfort of his life, or even his life itself, was dependent on the issue. Grand councils of war are, in the first place, called by the different powers, which are dubbed general meetings, where all the head workmen of the party collect, and arrange the order of battle—appoint the different commanders, and their subordinate instruments, and furnish the funds indispensible for supplying the expenses of the war. Inferior councils are next called in the different classes or wards, consisting of young cadets, who are candidates for offices, idlers who come there from mere curiosity, and orators who appear for the purpose of detailing all the crimes, the faults or the weaknesses of their opponents, and *speaking the sense of the meeting*, as it is called—for as the meeting generally consists of men whose quota of sense, taken individually,

would make but a poor figure, these orators are appointed to
collect it all in a lump, when I assure you it makes a very
formidable appearance, and furnishes sufficient matter to spin
an oration of two or three hours.

"The orators who declaim at these meetings are, with a few
exceptions, men of most profound and perplexed eloquence;
who are the oracles of barber's shops, market places and porter houses; and who you may see every day at the corner of
the streets, taking honest men prisoners by the button, and
talking their ribs quite bare without mercy and without end.
These orators, in addressing an audience, generally mount a
chair, a table, or an empty beer barrel, (which last is supposed
to afford considerable inspiration) and thunder away their
combustible sentiments at the heads of the audience, who are
generally so busily employed in smoking, drinking, and hearing themselves talk, that they seldom hear a word of the matter. This, however, is of little moment; for as they come there
to agree at all events to a certain set of resolutions, or articles
of war, it is not at all necessary to hear the speech, more especially as few would understand it if they did. Do not suppose, however, that the minor persons of the meeting are
entirely idle. Besides smoking, and drinking, which are generally practised, there are few who do not come with as great
a desire to talk as the orator himself—each has his little circle
of listeners, in the midst of whom he sets his hat on one side
of his head, and deals out matter of fact information, and
draws self-evident conclusions, with the pertinacity of a pedant, and to the great edification of his gaping auditors. Nay,
the very urchins from the nursery, who are scarcely emancipated from the dominion of birch, on these occasions, strut
pigmy great men—bellow for the instruction of grey bearded
ignorance, and, like the frog in the fable, endeavour to puff
themselves up to the size of the great object of their emulation—the principal orator."

"But head of Mahomet," cried I, "is it not preposterous to
a degree, for those puny whipsters to attempt to lecture age
and experience? they should be sent to school to learn better."
"Not at all," replied my friend; "for as an election is nothing
more than a war of words, the man that can wag his tongue
with the greatest elasticity, whether he speaks to the purpose

or not, is entitled to lecture at ward meetings and polls, and
instruct all who are inclined to listen to him—You may have
remarked a ward meeting of politic dogs, where, although the
great dog is, ostensibly, the leader and makes the most noise,
yet every little scoundrel of a cur has something to say, and
in proportion to his insignificance, fidgets and worries, and
puffs about mightily, in order to obtain the notice and approbation of his betters. Thus it is with these little beardless
bread and butter politicians, who, on this occasion, escape
from the jurisdiction of their mamas, to attend to the affairs
of the nation. You will see them engaged in dreadful wordy
contest with old cartmen, coblers and tailors, and plume
themselves not a little, if they should chance to gain a victory.—Aspiring spirits!—how interesting are the first dawnings of political greatness!—An election, my friend, is a
nursery or hot-bed of genius in a logocracy—and I look with
enthusiasm on a troop of these liliputian partizans, as so many
chatterers, and orators, and puffers, and slang-whangers in
embryo, who will one day, take an important part in the
quarrels, and wordy wars of their country.

"As the time for fighting the decisive battle approaches, appearances become more and more alarming—committees are
appointed, who hold little encampments, from whence they
send out small detachments of tatlers, to reconnoitre, harrass
and skirmish with the enemy, and, if possible, ascertain their
numbers; every body seems big with the mighty event that is
impending—the orators they gradually swell up beyond their
usual size—the little orators, they grow greater and greater—
the secretaries of the ward committees strut about, looking
like wooden oracles—the puffers put on the airs of mighty
consequence; the slang-whangers deal out direful innuendoes,
and threats of doughty import, and all is buzz, murmur, sus-
pense and sublimity!

"At length the day arrives. The storm that has been so long
gathering, and threatening in distant thunders bursts forth in
terrible explosion. All business is at an end—the whole city
is in a tumult—the people are running helter skelter, they
know not whither, and they know not why. The hackney
coaches rattle through the streets with thundering vehemence,
loaded with recruiting serjeants who have been prowling

in cellars and caves, to unearth some miserable minion of poverty and ignorance, who will barter his vote for a glass of beer, or a ride in a coach with such *fine gentlemen*!— The buzzards of the party scamper from poll to poll, on foot or on horeback—and they twaddle from committee to committee, and buzz, and chafe, and fume, and talk big, and— *do nothing*—like the vagabond drone, who wastes his time in the laborious idleness of *see-saw-song*, and busy nothingness."

I know not how long my friend would have continued his detail, had he not been interrupted by a squabble which took place between two *old continentals*, as they were called. It seems they had entered into an argument on the respective merits of their cause, and not being able to make each other clearly understood, resorted to what are called *knock-down arguments*, which form the superlative degree of the *argumentum ad hominem*; but are, in my opinion, extremely inconsistent with the true spirit of a genuine logocracy. After they had beaten each other soundly, and set the whole mob together by the ears, they came to a full explanation, when it was discovered that they were both of the same way of thinking—whereupon they shook each other heartily by the hand, and laughed with great glee at their *humourous* misunderstanding.

I could not help being struck with the exceeding great number of ragged, dirty looking persons, that swaggered about the place, and seemed to think themselves the bashaws of the land. I inquired of my friend if these people were employed to drive away the hogs, dogs, and other intruders that might thrust themselves in and interrupt the ceremony? "By no means," replied he; "these are the representatives of the sovereign people, who come here to make governors, senators and members of assembly, and are the source of all power and authority in this nation." "Preposterous," said I, "how is it possible that such men can be capable of distinguishing between an honest man and a knave, or even if they were, will it not always happen that they are led by the nose by some intriguing demagogue, and made the mere tools of ambitious political jugglers?—Surely it would be better to trust to providence, or even chance, for governors, than resort to the discriminating powers of an ignorant mob.—I plainly perceive the consequence.—A man, who possesses superior talents, and that honest pride which ever accompanies this possession, will always be sacrificed to some creeping insect who will prostitute himself to familiarity with the lowest of mankind, and like the idolatrous egyptian, worship the wallowing tenants of filth and mire."

"All this is true enough," replied my friend, "but after all you cannot say but that this is a free country, and that the people can get drunk cheaper here, particularly at elections, than in the despotic countries of the east." I could not, with any degree of propriety or truth, deny this last assertion, for just at that moment a patriotic brewer arrived with a load of beer, which, for a moment, occasioned a cessation of argument.—The great crowd of buzzards, puffers, and old continentals of all *parties*, who throng to the polls, to persuade, to cheat, or to force the freeholders into the right way, and to maintain the *freedom of suffrage*, seemed for a moment to forget their antipathies, and joined, heartily, in a copious libation of this patriotic, and argumentative beverage.

These *beer barrels*, indeed seem to be most able logicians, well stored with that kind of sound argument, best suited to the comprehension, and most relished by the mob, or sovereign people, who are never so tractable as when operated upon by this convincing liquor, which, in fact, seems to be imbrued with the very spirit of logocracy. No sooner does it begin its operation, than the tongue waxes exceeding valourous, and becomes impatient for some mighty conflict. The puffer puts himself at the head of his body guard of buzzards, and his legion of ragamuffins, and woe then to every unhappy adversary who is uninspired by the deity of the beerbarrel—he is sure to be talked, and argued into complete insignificance.

While I was making these observations, I was surprised to observe a bashaw, high in office, shaking a fellow by the hand, that looked rather more ragged, than a scare-crow, and inquiring with apparent solicitude concerning the health of his family; after which he slipped a little folded paper into his hand and turned away. I could not help applauding his humility in shaking the fellow's hand, and his benevolence in

relieving his distresses, for I imagined the paper contained
something for the poor man's necessities; and truly he seemed
verging towards the last stage of starvation. My friend, however, soon undeceived me by saying that this was an elector,
and the bashaw had merely given him the list of candidates,
for whom he was to vote. "Ho! ho!" said I, "then he is a
particular friend of the bashaw?" "By no means," replied my
friend, "the bashaw will pass him without notice, the day after the election, except, perhaps, just to drive over him with
his coach."

My friend then proceeded to inform me that for some time
before, and during the continuance of an election, there was
a most *delectable courtship* or intrigue, carried on between the
great bashaws, and *mother mob*. That *mother mob* generally
preferred the attentions of the rabble, or of fellows of her
own stamp, but would sometimes condescend to be treated
to a feasting, or any thing of that kind, at the bashaw's expense; nay, sometimes when she was in a good humour, she
would condescend to toy with them in her rough way—but
woe be to the bashaw who attempted to be familiar with her,
for she was the most pestilent, cross, crabbed, scolding, thiev-
ing, scratching, toping, wrong-headed, rebellious, and abominable termagant that ever was let loose in the world, to the
confusion of honest gentlemen bashaws.

Just then, a fellow came round and distributed among the
crowd a number of hand-bills, written by the *ghost of Washington*, the fame of whose illustrious actions, and still more
illustrious virtues, has reached even the remotest regions of
the east, and who is venerated by this people as the Father of
his country. On reading this paltry paper, I could not restrain
my indignation. "Insulted hero," cried I, "is it thus thy name
is profaned, thy memory disgraced, thy spirit drawn down
from heaven to administer to the brutal violence of party
rage!—It is thus the necromancers of the east, by their infernal incantations, sometimes call up the shades of the just, to
give their sanction to frauds, to lies, and to every species of
enormity." My friend smiled at my warmth, and observed,
that raising ghosts, and not only raising them but making
them speak, was one of the miracles of election. "And believe
me," continued he, "there is good reason for the ashes of de-

parted heroes being disturbed on these occasions, for such is the *sandy* foundation of our government, that there never happens an election of an alderman, or a collector, or even a constable, but we are in imminent danger of losing our liberties, and becoming a province of France, or tributary to the British islands." "By the hump of Mahomet's camel," said I, "but this is only another striking example of the prodigious great scale on which every thing is transacted in this country."

By this time I had become tired of the scene; my head ached with the uproar of voices, mingling in all the discordant tones of triumphant exclamation, nonsensical argument, intemperate reproach, and drunken absurdity.—The confusion was such as no language can adequately describe, and it seemed as all the restraints of decency, and all the bands of law had been broken and given place to the wide ravages of licentious brutality. These, thought I, are the orgies of liberty, these are the manifestations of the spirit of independence, these are the symbols of man's sovereignty! Head of Mahomet! with what a fatal and inexorable despotism do empty names and ideal phantoms exercise their dominion over the human mind! The experience of ages has demonstrated, that in all nations, barbarous or enlightened, the mass of the people, the *mob*, must be slaves, or they will be tyrants—but their tyranny will not be long—some ambitious leader, having at first condescended to be their slave, will at length become their master; and in proportion to the vileness of his former servitude, will be the severity of his subsequent tyranny.—Yet, with innumerable examples staring them in the face, the people still bawl out liberty, by which they mean nothing but freedom from every species of legal restraint, and a warrant for all kinds of licentiousness: and the bashaws and leaders, in courting the mob, convince them of their power, and by administering to their passions, for the purposes of ambition, at length learn by fatal experience, that he who worships the beast that carries him on its back, will sooner or later be thrown into the dust and trampled under foot by the animal who has learnt the secret of its power, by this very adoration.

ever thine,
MUSTAPHA.

FROM MY ELBOW-CHAIR
MINE UNCLE JOHN.

To those whose habits of abstraction may have let them into
some of the secrets of their own minds, and whose freedom
from daily toil, has left them at leisure to analyze their feelings,
it will be nothing new to say that the present is peculiarly the
season of remembrance. The flowers, the zephyrs, and the warblers of spring, returning after their tedious absence, bring
naturally to our recollection past times and buried feelings; and
the whispers of the full-foliaged grove, fall on the ear of contemplation, like the sweet tones of far distant friends, whom the
rude jostles of the world have severed from us, and cast far beyond our reach. It is at such times, that casting backward many
a lingering look we recal, with a kind of sweet-souled melancholy, the days of our youth and the jocund companions who
started with us the race of life, but parted midway in the journey to pursue some winding path that allured them with a
prospect more seducing—and never returned to us again. It is
then, too, if we have been afflicted with any heavy sorrow, if
we have ever lost (and who has not!)—an old friend, or chosen companion, that his shade will hover around us—the
memory of his virtues press on the heart, and a thousand endearing recollections, forgotten amidst the cold pleasures and
midnight dissipations of winter, arise to our remembrance.

These speculations bring to my mind MY UNCLE JOHN, the
history of whose loves and disappointments, I have promised
to the world. Though I must own myself much addicted to
forgetting my promises, yet as I have been so happily reminded of this, I believe I must pay it at once, "and there an
end." Lest my readers—good-natured souls that they are!
should, in the ardour of peeping into millstones, take my uncle for an old acquaintance, I here inform them, that the old
gentleman died a great many years ago, and it is impossible
they should ever have known him:—I pity them—for they
would have known a good-natured, benevolent man, whose
example might have been of service.

The last time I saw my uncle John, was fifteen years ago,
when I paid him a visit at his old mansion. I found him reading
a newspaper;—for it was election time, and he was always a

warm federalist, and had made several converts to the true political faith in his time—particularly one old tenant who always
just before the election became a violent anti—— in order that
he might be convinced of his errors by my uncle, who never
failed to reward his conviction by some substantial benefit.

After we had settled the affairs of the nation, and I had
paid my respects to the old family chronicles in the kitchen—
an indispensible ceremony—the old gentleman exclaimed,
with heart-felt glee, "Well, I suppose you are for a trout-fishing—I have got every thing prepared;—but first you must
take a walk with me to see my improvements." I was obliged
to consent, though I knew my uncle would lead me a most
villanous dance, and in all probability treat me to a quagmire,
or a tumble into a ditch.—If my readers choose to accompany me in this expedition, they are welcome—if not, let
them stay at home like lazy fellows—and sleep—or be hanged.

Though I had been absent several years, yet there was very
little alteration in the scenery, and every object retained the
same features it bore when I was a schoolboy; for it was in
this spot that I grew up in the fear of ghosts, and in the
breaking of many of the ten commandments. The brook, or
river as they would call it in Europe, still murmured with its
wonted sweetness through the meadow, and its banks were
still tufted with dwarf willows, that bent down to the surface.
The same echo inhabited the valley, and the same tender air
of repose, pervaded the whole scene. Even my good uncle
was but little altered, except that his hair was grown a little
greyer, and his forehead had lost some of its former smooth-
ness. He had, however, lost nothing of his former activity;
and laughed heartily at the difficulty I found in keeping up
with him as he stumped through bushes, and briers and
hedges, talking all the time about his improvements, and telling what he would do with such a spot of ground, and such
a tree. At length after showing me his stone fences, his famous two year old bull, his new invented cart, which was to
go before the horse, and his Eclipse colt, he was pleased to
return home to dinner.

After dining and returning thanks—which with him was
not a ceremony merely, but an offering from the heart—my
uncle opened his trunk, took out his fishing-tackle, and with-

out saying a word sallied forth with some of those truly alarming steps which Daddy Neptune once took when he was in a great hurry to attend to the affair of the siege of Troy. Trout-fishing was my uncle's favourite sport; and though I always caught two fish to his one, he never would acknowledge my superiority, but puzzled himself often and often, to account for such a singular phenomenon.

Following the current of the brook for a mile or two, we retraced many of our old haunts, and told a hundred adventures which had befallen us at different times. It was like snatching the hour-glass of time, inverting it, and rolling back again the sands that had marked the lapse of years. At length the shadows began to lengthen, the south-wind gradually settled into a perfect calm, and the sun threw his rays through the trees on the hill-top, in golden lustre, and a kind of sabbath stillness pervaded the whole valley, indicating that the hour was fast approaching which was to relieve for awhile, the farmer from his rural labour, the ox from his toil, the school urchin from his primer, and bring the loving ploughman home to the feet of his blooming dairy-maid.

As we were watching in silence the last rays of the sun, beaming their farewel radiance on the high hills at a distance, my uncle exclaimed, in a kind of half desponding tone, while he rested his arm over an old tree that had fallen—"I know not how it is, my dear Launce, but such an evening, and such a still quiet scene as this, always make me a little sad, and it is at such a time I am most apt to look forward with regret to the period when this farm on which "I have been young but now am old," and every object around me that is endeared by long acquaintance—when all these and I must shake hands and part. I have no fear of death, for my life has afforded but little temptation to wickedness; and when I die, I hope to leave behind me more substantial proofs of virtue than will be found in my epitaph, and more lasting memorials than churches built, or hospitals endowed, with wealth wrung from the hard hand of poverty, by an unfeeling landlord, or unprincipled knave;—but still, when I pass such a day as this and contemplate such a scene, I cannot help feeling a latent wish to linger yet a little longer in this peaceful asylum, to enjoy a little more sunshine in this world, and to have a few

more fishing matches with my boy." As he ended, he raised
his hand a little from the fallen tree, and dropping it languidly
by his side, turned himself towards home. The sentiment, the
look, the action, all seemed to be prophetic.—And so they
were—for when I shook him by the hand and bade him
farewel the next morning—it was for the last time!

He died a bachelor, at the age of sixty-three, though he had
been all his life trying to get married, and always thought
himself on the point of accomplishing his wishes. His disappointments were not owing either to the deformity of his
mind or person; for in his youth he was reckoned handsome,
and I myself can witness for him that he had as kind a heart
as ever was fashioned by heaven;—neither were they owing
to his poverty—which sometimes stands in an honest man's
way;—for he was born to the inheritance of a small estate
which was sufficient to establish his claim to the title of "one
well to do in the world." The truth is, my uncle had a prodigious antipathy to doing things in a hurry—"A man should
consider," said he to me once—"that he can always get a
wife, but cannot always get rid of her. For my part," continued he, "I am a young fellow with the world before me, (he
was but about forty!) and am resolved to look sharp, weigh
matters well, and know what's what before I marry:—in
short, Launce, *I dont intend to do the thing in a hurry depend
upon it.*" On this whim-wham, he proceeded: he began with
young girls and ended with widows. The girls he courted
until they grew old maids, or married out of pure apprehension of incurring certain penalties hereafter; and the widows
not having quite as much patience, generally, at the end of a
year while the good man thought himself in the high road
to success, married some *harum-scarum* young fellow, who
had not such an antipathy *to doing things in a hurry*.

My uncle would have inevitably sunk under these repeated
disappointments—for he did not want sensibility—had he
not hit upon a discovery which set all to rights at once. He
consoled his vanity—for he was a little vain, and soothed his
pride, which was his master passion—by telling his friends
and very significantly, while his eye would flash triumph,
"that he might have had her." Those who know how much of
the bitterness of disappointed affection arises from wounded

vanity and exasperated pride, will give my uncle credit for this discovery.

My uncle had been told by a prodigious number of married men, and had read in an innumerable quantity of books, that a man could not possibly be happy except in the marriage state; so he determined at an early age to marry, that he might not lose his only chance for happiness. He accordingly forthwith paid his addresses to the daughter of a neighbouring gentleman farmer, who was reckoned the beauty of the whole world—a phrase by which the honest country people mean nothing more than the circle of their acquaintance, or that territory of land which is within sight of the smoke of their own hamlet.

This young lady, in addition to her beauty, was highly accomplished, for she had spent five or six months at a boarding-school in town, where she learned to work pictures in satin and paint sheep, that might be mistaken for wolves, to hold up her head, set straight in her chair, and to think every species of useful acquirement beneath her attention. When she returned home, so completely had she forgotten every thing she knew before, that on seeing one of the maids milching a cow, she asked her father, with an air of most enchanting ignorance, "what that odd looking thing was doing to that queer animal?" The old man shook his head at this, but the mother was delighted at these symptoms of gentility, and so enamoured of her daughter's accomplishments, that she actually got framed a picture worked in satin by the young lady. It represented the Tomb Scene in Romeo and Juliet: Romeo was dressed in an orange-coloured cloak, fastened round his neck, with a large golden clasp, a white satin tamboured waistcoat, leather breeches, blue silk stockings, and white topt boots. The amiable Juliet shone in a flame coloured gown, most gorgeously bespangled with silver stars, a high-crowned muslin cap that reached to the top of the tomb;—on her feet she wore a pair of short-quartered high-heeled shoes, and her waist was the exact fac simile of an inverted sugarloaf. The head of the "noble county Paris" looked like a chimney-sweeper's brush that had lost its handle; and the cloak of the good Friar hung about him as gracefully as the armour of a Rhinoceros. The good lady considered this picture as a splendid proof of her daughter's accomplishments, and hung it up in the best parlour, as an honest tradesman does his certificate of admission into that enlightened body, yclept the Mechanic Society.

With this accomplished young lady then did my uncle John become deeply enamoured, and as it was his first love he determined to bestir himself in an extraordinary manner. Once at least in a fortnight, and generally on a Sunday evening, he would put on his leather breeches (for he was a great beau) mount his grey horse Pepper, and ride over to see miss Pamela, though she lived upwards of a mile off, and he was obliged to pass close by a church-yard, which at least a hundred creditable persons would swear was haunted! Miss Pamela could not be insensible to such proofs of attachment, and accordingly received him with considerable kindness; her mother always left the room when he came, and my uncle had as good as made declaration, by saying one evening very significantly "that he believed he should soon change his condition," when some how or other, he got a tremendous *flea in his ear*, began to think he was *doing things in too great a hurry*, and that it was high time to consider: so he considered near a month about it, and there is no saying how much longer he might have spun the thread of his doubts had he not been roused from this state of indecision, by the news that his mistress had married an attorney's apprentice, who she had seen the Sunday before at church, where he had excited the applauses of the whole congregation, by the invincible gravity with which he listened to a Dutch sermon. The young people in the neighbourhood laughed a good deal at my uncle on the occasion, but he only shrugged his shoulders, looked mysterious and replied, *"Tut, boys! I might have had her."**

*NOTE, BY WILLIAM WIZARD ESQ.

Our publisher, who is busily engaged in printing a celebrated work, which is perhaps more generally read in this city than any other book, (not excepting the bible)—I mean the New-York Directory—has begged so hard that we will not overwhelm him with too much of a good thing, that we have, with Langstaff's approbation, cut short the residue of uncle John's amours. In all probability it will be given in a future number, whenever Launcelot is in the humour for it—he is such an odd—but, mum—for fear of another suspension.

SALMAGUNDI NO. XII

Saturday, June 27, 1807.

FROM MY ELBOW-CHAIR.

"*Tandem vincitur.*"
TANDEM *conquers!* LINK. FID.

SOME MEN delight in the study of plants, in the dissection of a leaf, or the contour and complexion of a tulip;—others are charmed with the beauties of the feathered race, or the varied hues of the insect tribe. A naturalist will spend hours in the fatiguing pursuit of a butterfly, and a man of the ton will waste whole years in the chase of a fine lady. I feel a respect for their avocations, for my own are somewhat similar. I love to open the great volume of human character—to me the examination of a beau is more interesting than that of a Daffodil or Narcissus, and I feel a thousand times more pleasure in catching a new view of human nature, than in kidnapping the most gorgeous butterfly—even *an Emperor of Morocco* himself.

In my present situation I have ample room for the indulgence of this taste, for perhaps there is not a house in this city more fertile in subjects for the anatomist of human character, than my cousin Cockloft's. Honest Christopher, as I have before mentioned, is one of those hearty old cavaliers who pride themselves upon keeping up the good, honest, unceremonious hospitality of old times. He is never so happy as when he has drawn about him a knot of sterling-hearted associates, and sits at the head of his table dispensing a warm, cheering welcome to all. His countenance expands at every glass and beams forth emanations of hilarity, benevolence and good fellowship, that inspire and gladden every guest around him. It is no wonder, therefore, that such excellent social qualities should attract a host of friends and guests; in fact, my cousin is almost overwhelmed with them, and they all uniformly pronounce Old Cockloft to be one of the finest old fellows in the world. His wine also always comes in for a good share of their approbation; nor do they forget to do honor to mrs. Cockloft's cookery, pronouncing it to be modelled after the most approved recipes of Heliogabulus and mrs. Glasse. The variety of company thus attracted is particularly pleasing to me; for being considered a privileged person in the family, I can sit in a corner, indulge in my favourite amusement of observation, and retreat to my elbow-chair, like a bee to his hive, whenever I have collected sufficient food for meditation.

Will Wizard is particularly efficient in adding to the stock of originals which frequent our house, for he is one of the most inveterate hunters of oddities I ever knew, and his first care, on making a new acquaintance, is to gallant him to old Cockloft's, where he never fails to receive the freedom of the house in a pinch from his gold box. Will has, without exception, the queerest, most eccentric and indescribable set of intimates that ever man possessed; how he became acquainted with them I cannot conceive, except by supposing there is a secret attraction or unintelligible sympathy that unconsciously draws together oddities of every soil.

Will's great crony for some time was Tom Straddle, to whom he really took a great liking. Straddle had just arrived in an importation of hardware, fresh from the city of Birmingham, or rather as the most learned english would call it, *Brummagem*, so famous for its manufactories of gimblets, pen-knives and pepper-boxes, and where they make buttons and beaux enough to inundate our whole country. He was a young man of considerable standing in the manufactory at Birmingham, sometimes had the honour to hand his master's daughter into a tim-whiskey, was the oracle of the tavern he frequented on Sundays, and could beat all his associates (if you would take his word for it) in boxing, beer drinking, jumping over chairs, and imitating cats in a gutter and opera singers. Straddle was, moreover, a member of a Catch-club, and was a great hand at ringing bob-majors; he was, of course, a complete connoisseur in music, and entitled to assume that character at all performances in the art. He was likewise a member of a Spouting-club, had seen a company of strolling actors perform in a barn, and had even, like Abel Drugger, "enacted" the part of Major Sturgeon with considerable applause; he was consequently a profound critic, and

fully authorised to turn up his nose at any american performances. He had twice partaken of annual dinners given to the
head manufacturers of Birmingham, where he had the good
fortune to get a taste of turtle and turbot, and a smack of
champaign and burgundy, and he had *heard* a vast deal of the
roast-beef of Old England; he was therefore epicure sufficient
to d——n every dish and every glass of wine he tasted in
America, though at the same time he was as voracious an
animal as ever crossed the atlantic. Straddle had been splashed
half a dozen times by the carriages of nobility, and had once
the superlative felicity of being kicked out of doors by the
footman of a noble duke—he could, therefore, talk of nobility and despise the untitled plebeians of America. In short,
Straddle was one of those dapper, bustling, florid, round, self-
important *"gemmen"* who bounce upon us half beau half but-
ton-maker, undertake to give us the true polish of the *bon-
ton*, and endeavour to inspire us with a proper and dignified
contempt of our native country.

Straddle was quite in raptures when his employers determined to send him to America as an agent. He considered
himself as going among a nation of barbarians, where he
would be received as a prodigy; he anticipated with a proud
satisfaction the bustle and confusion his arrival would occasion, the crowd that would throng to gaze at him as he
walked or rode through the streets; and had little doubt but
that he should occasion as much curiosity as an indian-chief
or a turk in the streets of Birmingham. He had heard of the
beauty of our women, and chuckled at the thought of how
completely he should eclipse their unpolished beaux, and the
number of despairing lovers that would mourn the hour of
his arrival. I am even informed by Will Wizard that he put
good store of beads, spike-nails and looking glasses in his
trunk to win the affections of the fair ones, as they paddled
about in their bark canoes—the reason Will gave for this error of Straddle's respecting our ladies was, that he had read
in Guthrie's Geography that the aborigines of America were
all savages, and not exactly understanding the word aborigines, he applied to one of his fellow apprentices, who assured
him that it was the latin word for inhabitants. Now Straddle

knew that the savages were fond of beads, spike-nails and looking glasses, and therefore filled his trunk with them.

Wizard used to tell another anecdote of Straddle, which always put him in a passion—Will swore that the captain of the ship told him that when Straddle heard they were off the banks of Newfoundland, he insisted upon going on shore, there to gather some good cabbages, of which he was excessively fond; Straddle, however, denied all this, and declared it to be a mischievous *quiz* of Will Wizard, who indeed often made himself merry at his expense. However this may be, certain it is he kept his tailor and shoemaker constantly employed for a month before his departure, equipped himself with a smart crooked stick about eighteen inches long, a pair of breeches of most unheard of length, a little short pair of Hoby's white-topped boots, that seemed to stand on tip-toe to reach his breeches, and his hat had the true trans-atlantic declination towards his right ear. The fact was, nor did he make any secret of it—he was determined to *"astonish the natives a few!"*

Straddle was not a little disappointed on his arrival, to find the americans were rather more civilized than he had imagined;—he was suffered to walk to his lodgings unmolested by a crowd, and even unnoticed by a single individual—no love-letters came pouring in upon him; no rivals lay in wait to assassinate him; his very dress excited no attention, for there were many fools dressed equally ridiculously with himself. This was mortifying indeed to an aspiring youth, who had come out with the idea of *astonishing* and *captivating*. He was equally unfortunate in his pretentions to the character of critic, connoisseur and boxer; he condemned our whole dramatic corps, and every thing appertaining to the theatre; but his critical abilities were ridiculed—he found fault with old Cockloft's dinner, not even sparing his wine, and was never invited to the house afterwards;—he scoured the streets at night, and was cudgelled by a sturdy watchman;—he hoaxed an honest mechanic, and was soundly kicked: Thus disappointed in all his attempts at notoriety, Straddle hit on the expedient which was resorted to by the *Giblets*—he determined to take the town by storm. He accordingly bought horses and equipages, and forthwith made a furious dash at *style* in a *gig and tandem*.

As Straddle's finances were but limited, it may easily be supposed that his fashionable career infringed a little upon his consignments, which was indeed the case, for to use a true cockney phrase, *Brummagem suffered*. But this was a circumstance that made little impression upon Straddle, who was now a lad of spirit, and lads of spirit always despise the sordid cares of keeping another man's money. Suspecting this circumstance, I never could witness any of his exhibitions of *style*, without some whimsical association of ideas. Did he give an entertainment to a host of guzzling friends, I immediately fancied them gormandizing heartily at the expense of poor Birmingham, and swallowing a consignment of handsaws and razors. Did I behold him dashing through Broadway in his gig, I saw him, "in my mind's eye" driving tandem on a nest of tea-boards; nor could I ever contemplate his cockney exhibitions of horsemanship, but my mischievous imagination would picture him spurring a cask of hardware, like rosy Bacchus bestriding a beer barrel, or the little gentleman who be-straddles the world in the front of Hutchin's Almanack.

Straddle was equally successful with the *Giblets*, as may well be supposed; for though pedestrian merit may strive in vain to become fashionable in *Gotham*, yet a candidate in an equipage is always recognized, and like Philip's ass, laden with gold, will gain admittance every where. Mounted in his curricle or his gig, the candidate is like a statue elevated on a high pedestal, his merits are discernable from afar, and strike the dullest optics.—Oh! Gotham, Gotham! most enlightened of cities!—how does my heart swell with delight when I behold your sapient inhabitants lavishing their attention with such wonderful discernment!

Thus Straddle became quite a man of *ton*, and was caressed, and courted, and invited to dinners and balls. Whatever was absurd or ridiculous in him before, was now declared to be the *style*. He criticised our theatre, and was listened to with reverence. He pronounced our musical entertainments barbarous; and the judgment of Apollo himself would not have been more decisive. He abused our dinners;

and the god of eating, if there be any such deity, seemed to speak through his organs. He became at once a man of taste, for he put his malediction on every thing; and his arguments were conclusive, for he supported every assertion *with a bet*. He was likewise pronounced by the learned in the fashionable world, a young man of great research and deep observation; for he had sent home as natural curiosities, an ear of indian corn, a pair of moccasons, a belt of wampum, and a four leaved clover. He had taken great pains to enrich this curious collection with an Indian, and a *cataract,* but without success. In fine, the people talked of Straddle, and his equipage, and Straddle talked of his horses, until it was impossible for the most critical observer to pronounce, whether Straddle or his horses were most admired, or whether Straddle admired himself or his horses most.

Straddle was now in the zenith of his glory. He swaggered about parlours and drawing rooms with the same unceremonious confidence he used to display in the taverns at Birmingham. He accosted a lady as he would a bar maid; and this was pronounced a certain proof that he had been used to better company in Birmingham. He became the great man of all the taverns between New-York and Haerlem, and no one stood a chance of being accommodated, until Straddle and his horses were perfectly satisfied. He d——d the landlords and waiters, with the best air in the world, and accosted them with true gentlemanly familiarity. He staggered from the dinner table to the play, entered the box like a tempest, and staid long enough to be *bored* to death, and to *bore* all those who had the misfortune to be near him. From thence he dashed off to a ball, time enough to flounder through a cotillon, tear half a dozen gowns, commit a number of other depredations, and make the whole company sensible of his infinite condescension in coming amongst them. The people of Gotham thought him a prodigious fine fellow; the young bucks cultivated his acquaintance with the most persevering assiduity, and his *retainers* were sometimes complimented with a seat in his curricle, or a ride on one of his fine horses. The belles were delighted with the attentions of such a fashionable gentleman, and struck with astonishment at his learned distinctions between *wrought scissors*, and those of *cast-steel*; together with his profound dissertations on buttons and horse flesh. The rich merchants courted his acquaintance because he was an *englishman*, and their wives treated him with great deference, because he had come from beyond seas. I cannot help here observing that your salt water is a marvellous great sharpener of mens wits, and I intend to recommend it to some of my acquaintance in a particular essay.

Straddle continued his brilliant career for only a short time. His prosperous journey over the turn-pike of fashion, was checked by some of those stumbling-blocks in the way of aspiring youth, called creditors—or duns—a race of people who, as a celebrated writer observes, "are hated by gods and men." Consignments slackened, whispers of distant suspicion floated in the dark, and those pests of society, the tailors and shoemakers, rose in rebellion against Straddle. In vain were all his remonstrances, in vain did he prove to them that though he had given them no money, yet he had given them more *custom*, and as many promises as any young man in the city. They were inflexible, and the signal of danger being given, a host of other persecutors pounced upon his back. Straddle saw there was but one way for it; he determined to do the thing genteelly, to go *to smash* like a hero, and dashed into the limits in high style, being the fifteenth gentleman I have known to drive tandem to the—*ne plus ultra*—the d——l.

Unfortunate Straddle! may thy fate be a warning to all young gentlemen who come out from Birmingham to *astonish the natives!*—I should never have taken the trouble to delineate his character, had he not been a genuine cockney, and worthy to be the representative of his numerous tribe. Perhaps my simple countrymen may hereafter be able to distinguish between the real english gentleman, and individuals of the cast I have heretofore spoken of, as mere mongrels, springing at one bound from contemptible obscurity at home, to day light and splendour in this good natured land. The true born, and true bred english gentleman, is a character I hold in great respect; and I love to look back to the period when our forefathers flourished in the same generous soil, and hailed each other as brothers. But the *cockney!*—when I contemplate him as springing too from the same source, I feel ashamed of the relationship, and am tempted to deny my origin. In the character of Straddle is traced the complete outline of a true cockney, of english growth, and a descendant of that individual facetious character mentioned by Shakespeare, *"who, in pure kindness to his horse, buttered his hay."*

THE STRANGER AT HOME;
OR, A TOUR IN BROADWAY
BY JEREMY COCKLOFT *the younger.*
. . . . . *Peregre rediit.*
He is returned home from abroad.
DICTIONARY.

PREFACE.

Your learned traveller begins his travels at the commencement of his journey; others begin theirs at the end; and a third class begin any how and any where, which I think is the true way. A late facetious writer begins what he calls, "a Picture of New-York," with a particular description of Glen's Falls, from whence with admirable dexterity he makes a digression to the celebrated Mill Rock, on Long-Island! now this is what I like; and I intend in my present tour to digress as often and as long as I please. If, therefore, I choose to make a hop, skip, and jump to China, or New-Holland, or Terra Incognita, or Communipaw, I can produce a host of examples to justify me even in books that have been praised by the english reviewers, whose *fiat* being all that is necessary to give books a currency in this country, I am determined, as soon as I finish my edition of travels in seventy-five volumes, to transmit it forthwith to them for judgment. If these transatlantic censors praise it, I have no fear of its success in this country, where *their* approbation gives, like the tower stamp, a fictitious value, and makes tinsel and wampum pass current for classick gold.

CHAPTER I.

Battery—flag-staff kept by Louis Keaffee—Keaffee maintains two spy-glasses by subscriptions—merchants pay two

shillings a-year to look through them at the signal poles on
Staten-Island—a very pleasant prospect; but not so pleasant
as that from the hill of Howth—quere, ever been there?—
Young *seniors* go down to the flag-staff to buy peanuts and
beer, after the fatigue of their morning studies, and sometimes to play at ball, or some other innocent amusement—
digression to the Olympic, and Isthmian games, with a description of the Isthmus of Corinth, and that of Darien: to
conclude with a dissertation on the indian custom of offering
a whiff of tobacco smoke to their great spirit Areskou.—Return to the battery—delightful place to indulge in the luxury
of sentiment.—How various are the mutations of this world!
but a few days, a few hours—at least not above two hundred
years ago, and this spot was inhabited by a race of aborigines,
who dwelt in bark huts, lived upon oysters, and indian corn,
danced buffalo dances, and were lords "of the fowl and the
brute"—but the spirit of time, and the spirit of brandy, have
swept them from their antient inheritance: and as the white
wave of the ocean by its ever toiling assiduity, gains on the
brown land, so the white man, by slow and sure degrees has
gained on the brown savage, and dispossessed him of the land
of his forefathers.—Conjectures on the first peopling of
America—different opinions on that subject, to the amount
of near one hundred—opinion of Augustine Torniel—that
they are the descendants of Shem and Japheth, who came by
the way of Japan to America—Juffridius Petri, says they came
from Friezeland—mem. cold journey.—Mons. Charron says
they are descended from the gauls—bitter enough.—A Milius from the Celtæ—Kircher from the egyptians—L'Compte
from the phenicians—Lescarbot from the canaanites, alias the
anthropophagi—Brerewood from the tartars—Grotius from
the norwegians—and Linkum Fidelius, has written two folio
volumes to prove that America was first of all peopled either
by the antipodeans, or the cornish miners, who he maintains,
might easily have made a subterraneous passage to this country, particularly the antipodeans, who, he asserts, can get
along under ground, as fast as moles—quere, which of these
is in the right, or are they all wrong?—For my part, I dont
see why America had not as good a right to be peopled at
first, as any little contemptible country of Europe, or Asia;

and I am determined to write a book at my first leisure, to prove that Noah was born here—and that so far is America from being indebted to any other country for inhabitants, that they were every one of them peopled by colonies from her!—mem. battery a very pleasant place to walk on a sunday evening—not quite genteel though—every body walks there, and a pleasure, however genuine, is spoiled by general participation—the fashionable ladies of New-York, turn up their noses if you ask them to walk on the battery on sunday— quere, have they scruples of conscience, or scruples of delicacy?—neither—they have only scruples of gentility, which are quite different things.

CHAPTER II.

Custom-house—origin of duties on merchandize—this place much frequented by merchants—and why?—different classes of merchants—importers—a kind of nobility— Wholesale merchants—have the privilege of going to the city assembly!—Retail traders cannot go to the assembly—Some curious speculations on the vast distinction betwixt selling tape by the piece or by the yard.—Wholesale merchants look down upon the retailers, who in return look down upon the green grocers, who look down upon the market women, who don't care a straw about any of them.—Origin of the distinction of ranks—Dr. Johnson once horribly puzzled to settle the point of precedence between a louse and a flea . . . good hint enough to humble purse-proud arrogance. . . . Custom house partly used as a lodging house for the pictures belonging to the academy of arts . . . couldn't afford the statues house room, most of them in the cellar of the City hall . . . poor place for the gods and goddesses, . . . after Olympus . . . Pensive reflections on the ups and downs of life . . . Apollo, and the rest of the sett, used to cut a great figure in days of yore.—Mem. . . . every dog has his day . . . sorry for Venus though, poor wench, to be cooped up in a cellar with not a single grace to wait on her! . . . Eulogy on the gentlemen of the academy of arts, for the great spirit with which they began the undertaking, and the perseverance with which they have pursued it . . . It is a pity however, they began at the wrong end . . . maxim . . . If you want a bird and a cage, always buy the cage first . . . hem! . . . a word to the wise!

CHAPTER III.

Bowling green . . . fine place for pasturing cows . . . a perquisite of the late corporation . . . formerly ornamented with a statue of George the 3d. . . . people pulled it down in the war to make bullets . . . great pity, as it might have been given to the academy . . . it would have become a cellar as well as any other. . . . The pedestal still remains, because, there was no use in pulling *that* down, as it would cost the corporation money, and not sell for any thing . . . mem . . . a penny saved is a penny got. . . . If the pedestal must remain, I would recommend that a statue of somebody, or something be placed on it, for truly it looks quite melancholy and forlorn. . . . Broadway . . . great difference in the gentility of streets . . . a man who resides in Pearl-street, or Chatham-row, derives no kind of dignity from his domicil, but place him in a certain part of Broadway . . . any where between the battery and Wall-street, and he straightway becomes entitled to figure in the beau-monde, and strut as a person of prodigious consequence! . . . Quere, whether there is a degree of purity in the air of that quarter which changes the gross particles of vulgarity, into gems of refinement and polish? . . . A question to be asked but not to be answered. . . . New brick church! . . . what a pity it is the corporation of Trinity church are so poor! . . . if they could not afford to build a better place of worship, why did they not go about with a subscription? . . . even I would have given them a few shillings rather than our city should have been disgraced by such a pitiful specimen of economy . . . . Wall-street . . . . City-hall, famous place for catch-poles, deputy sheriffs, and young lawyers, which last attended the courts, not because they have business there, but because they have no business any where else. My blood always curdles when I see a catchpole, they being a species of vermin, who feed and fatten on the common wretchedness of mankind, who trade in misery, and in becoming the executioners of the law, by their oppression and villainy, almost counter-balance all the benefits which are derived from its salutary regulations. . . . Story of Quevedo, about a catchpole possessed by a devil, who in being interrogated, declared that he did not come there voluntarily, but by compulsion, and that a decent devil would never of his own free will enter into the body of a catchpole . . . instead therefore of doing him the injustice to say that here was a catchpole be-devilled, they should say it was a devil be-catchpoled . . . that being in reality the truth. . . . Wonder what has become of the old crier of the court, who used to make more noise in preserving silence than the audience did in breaking it. . . . If a man happened to drop his cane, the old hero would sing out silence! in a voice that emulated the "wide-mouthed thunder" . . . . On inquiring, found he had retired from business to enjoy *otium cum dignitate*, as many a great man had done before. . . . Strange that wise men, as they are thought, should toil through a whole existence merely to enjoy a few moments of leisure at last! . . . why don't they begin to be easy at first, and not purchase a moments pleasure with an age of pain? . . . mem . . . posed some of the jockeys . . . eh!

CHAP. IV.

Barber's Pole—three different orders of *shavers* in New-York—those who shave *pigs*, N. B.—Freshmen and Sophomores—those who cut beards, and those who *shave notes of hand*—the last are the most respectable, because in the course of a year, they make more money and that *honestly*, than the whole corps of other *shavers*, can do in half a century—besides, it would puzzle a common barber to ruin any man, except by cutting his throat; whereas, your higher order of *shavers*, your true blood suckers of the community, seated snugly behind the curtain in watch for prey, live on the vitals of the unfortunate, and grow rich on the ruin of thousands.—Yet this last class of *barbers* are held in high respect in the world—they never offend against the decencies of life, go often to church, look down on honest poverty walking on foot, and call themselves gentlemen—yea, men of honour!—Lottery offices—another set of Capital Shavers! licensed gam-

bling houses good things enough though, as they enable a
few *honest industrious gentlemen* to humbug the people—
according to law—besides, if the people will be such fools,
whose fault is it but their own if they get *bit*?—Messrs. Paff
. . . beg pardon for putting them in such bad company, because they are a couple of fine fellows—mem.—to recommend Michael's antique snuff box to all amateurs *in the art.*—
Eagle singing Yankey-doodle—N. B.—Buffon, Pennant, and
the rest of the naturalists all *naturals*, not to know the eagle
was a singing bird—Linkum Fidelius knew better, and gives
a long description of a bald eagle that serenaded him once in
Canada—digression—particular account of the canadian indians—story about Areskou learning to make fishing nets of
a spider—don't believe it though, because, according to
Linkum, and many other learned authorities, Areskou is the
same as *Mars*, being derived from his greek name of *Ares*, and
if so he knew well enough what *a net* was without consulting
a spider—story of Arachne being changed into a spider as a
reward for having hanged herself—derivation of the word
spinster from spider—Colophon, now Altobosco, the birth
place of Arachne, remarkable for a famous breed of spiders to
this day—mem.—nothing like a little scholarship—make the
ignoramus' viz. the majority of my readers, stare like wild pigeons—return to New-York by a short cut—meet a dashing
belle, in a thick white veil—tried to get a peep at her face
. . . saw she squinted a little . . . thought so at first . . .
never saw a face covered with a veil that was worth looking
at . . . saw some ladies holding a conversation across the
street about going to church next Sunday . . . talked so loud
they frightened a cartman's horse, who ran away, and overset
a basket of gingerbread with a little boy under it . . . mem.
I dont much see the use of speaking trumpets now-a-days.

CHAP. V.

Bought a pair of gloves—dry-good stores the genuine
schools of politeness—true parisian manners there—got a
pair of gloves and a pistareen's worth of bows for a dollar—
dog cheap!—Courtlandt-street corner—famous place to see
the belles go by—quere, ever been shopping with a lady?—

some account of it—ladies go into all the shops in the city to
buy a pair of gloves—good way of spending time, if they
have nothing else to do.—Oswego-Market—looks very
much like a triumphal arch—some account of the manner of
erecting them in ancient times—digression to the *arch*-duke
Charles, and some account of the ancient germans.—N. B.
quote Tacitus on this subject.—Particular description of mar-
ket-baskets, butchers' blocks and wheelbarrows—mem. queer
things run upon one wheel!—Saw a cartman driving full-tilt
through Broadway—run over a child—good enough for it—
what business had it to be in the way?—Hint concerning the
laws against pigs, goats, dogs and cartmen—grand apostrophe to the sublime science of jurisprudence—comparison
between legislators and tinkers—quere, whether it requires
greater ability to mend a law than to mend a kettle?—inquiry
into the utility of making laws that are broken a hundred
times in a day with impunity—my lord Coke's opinion on
the subject—my lord a very great man—so was lord Bacon—good story about a criminal named Hog claiming relationship with him.—Hogg's porter-house—great haunt of
Will Wizard—Will put down there one night by a sea captain, in an argument concerning the area of the Chinese empire, Whang-po;—Hogg's a capital place for hearing the
same stories, the same jokes and the same songs every night
in the year—mem. except Sunday nights—fine school for
young politicians too—some of the longest and thickest
heads in the city come there to settle the nation.—Scheme of
Ichabod Fungus to restore the balance of Europe—digression—some account of the balance of Europe—comparison
between it, and a pair of scales, with the emperor Alexander
in one and the emperor Napoleon in the other—fine fellows—both of a weight, can't tell which will kick the beam
. . . mem. dont care much either . . . nothing to me . . .
Ichabod very unhappy about it . . . thinks Napoleon has an
eye on this country . . . capital place to pasture his horses,
and provide for the rest of his family . . . . Dey-street . . .
ancient dutch name of it, signifying murders'-valley—formerly the site of a great peach orchard . . . my grandmother's history of the famous *Peach war* . . . arose from an
indian stealing peaches out of this orchard . . . good cause

as need be for a war . . . just as good as the balance of power
. . . Anecdote of a war between two italian states about a
bucket . . . introduce some capital new *truisms* about the
folly of mankind, the ambition of kings, potentates and
princes, particularly Alexander, Caesar, Charles the XIIth, Napoleon, little king Pepin and the great Charlemagne . . . .
Conclude with an exhortation to the present race of sovereigns to keep the king's peace, and abstain from all those
deadly quarrels which produce battle, murder and sudden
death . . . Mem. ran my nose against lamp-post . . . conclude in great dudgeon.

FROM MY ELBOW-CHAIR.

Our cousin Pindar after having been confined for some
time past with a fit of the gout, which is a kind of keep-sake
in our family, has again set his mill going, as my readers will
perceive. On reading his piece I could not help smiling at the
high compliments which, contrary to his usual style, he has
lavished on the dear sex. The old gentleman unfortunately
observing my merriment, stumped out of the room with great
vociferation of crutch, and has not exchanged three words
with me since. I expect every hour to hear that he has packed
up his moveables, and, as usual in all cases of disgust, retreated to his old country house.

Pindar, like most of the old Cockloft heroes, is wonderfully
susceptible to the genial influence of warm weather. In winter
he is one of the most crusty old bachelors under heaven, and
is *wickedly* addicted to sarcastic reflections of every kind, particularly on the little enchanting foibles, and whim-whams of
women. But when the spring comes on, and the mild influence of the sun releases nature from her icy fetters, the ice of
his bosom dissolves into a gentle current, which reflects the
bewitching qualities of the fair, as, in some mild clear evening
when nature reposes in silence, the stream bears in its pure
bosom, all the starry magnificence of heaven. It is under the
controul of this influence he has written his piece, and I beg
the ladies in the plentitude of their harmless conceit not to
flatter themselves, that because the good Pindar has suffered
them to escape his censures, he had nothing more to censure.

It is but sunshine and zephyrs, which have wrought this wonderful change, and I am much mistaken, if the first North-
easter don't convert all his good nature into most exquisite
spleen.

FROM THE MILL OF

PINDAR COCKLOFT, ESQ.

How often I cast my reflections behind,
And call up the days of past youth to my mind!
When folly assails in habiliaments new,
When fashion obtrudes some fresh whim-wham to view
When the foplings of fashion bedazzle my sight,
Bewilder my feelings—my senses benight;
I retreat in disgust from the world of the day,
To commune with the world that has mouldered away
To converse with the shades of those friends of my love
Long gathered in peace to the angels above.
  In my rambles thro' life should I meet with annoy
From the bold beardless stripling—the turbid pert boy
One reared in the mode lately reckoned *genteel*,
Which neglecting the head, aims to perfect the heel,
Which completes the sweet fopling while yet in his teens,
And fits him for fashion's light changeable scenes;
Proclaims him *a man* to the near and the far,
Can he dance a cotillion or smoke a cygarr.
And tho' brainless and vapid as vapid can be,
To routs and to parties pronounces him free;—
Oh, I think on the beaux that existed of yore,
On those rules of the ton that exist now no more!
  I recal with delight how each yonker at first
In the cradle of science and virtue was nursed;
—How the graces of person and graces of mind,
The polish of learning and fashion combined,
Till soft'ned in manners and strength'ned in head,
By the classical lore of the living and dead,
Matured in person till manly in size,
He then was presented a beau to our eyes!
  My nieces of late have made frequent complaint
That they suffer vexation and painful constraint,

By having their circles too often distrest
By some three or four goslings just fledg'd in the nest,
Who propp'd by the credit their fathers sustain,
Alike tender in years, and in person and brain,
But plenteously stock'd with that substitute *brass*,
For true wits and critics would anxiously pass.
They complain of that empty sarcastical slang,
So common to all the coxcombical gang,
Who the fair with their shallow experience vex,
By thrumming forever their *weakness of sex*;
And who boast to themselves when they talk with proud air
Of MAN's mental ascendancy over the fair.

　Twas thus the young owlet, produced in the nest,
Where the eagle of Jove her young eaglets had prest
Pretended to boast of his royal descent,
And vaunted that force which to eagles is lent;
Tho' fated to shun with his dim visual ray,
The cheering delights, and the brilliance of day;
To forsake the fair regions of aether and light,
For dull moping caverns of darkness and night:
Still talked of that eagle like strength of the eye,
Which approaches unwinking the pride of the sky;
Of that wing which unwearied can hover and play
In the noon-tide effulgence and torrent of day.

　Dear girls, the sad evils of which ye complain,
Your sex *must* endure from the feeble and vain.
Tis the common place jest of the nursery scape-goat,
Tis the common place ballad that croaks from his throat.
He knows not that nature—that polish decrees,
That women should always endeavour to please:
That the law of their system has early imprest
The importance of fitting themselves to each guest;
And, of course, that full oft, when ye trifle and play,
Tis to gratify triflers who strut in your way.
The child might as well of its mother complain,
As wanting true wisdom and soundness of brain.
Because that, at times, while it hangs on her breast,
She with "lulla-by-baby" beguiles it to rest.
Tis its weakness of mind that induces the strain,
For wisdom to *infants* is prattled in vain.

Tis true at odd times, when in frolicksome fit,
In the midst of his gambols, the mischievous wit
May start some light foible that clings to the fair,
Like cobwebs that fasten to objects most rare—
In the play of his fancy will sportively say
Some delicate censure that pops in his way.
He may smile at your fashions, and frankly express
His dislike of a dance, or a flaming red dress;
Yet he blames not your want of man's physical force,
Nor complains though ye cannot in latin discourse.
He delights in the language of nature ye speak
Tho' not so refined as true classical greek.
He remembers that providence never designed
Our females like suns to bewilder and blind;
But like the mild star of pale evening serene,
Whose radiance illumines, yet softens the scene,
To light us with cheering and welcoming ray,
Along the rude path when the sun is away.
Nor e'er would he wish those fair beings to find
In places for *Di majorum gentium* designed;
But as *Dii penates* performing their part—
Receiving and claiming the vows of the heart—
Recalling affections long given to roam,
To centre at last in the bosom of HOME.
    I own in my scribblings I lately have named
Some faults of our fair which I gently have blamed
But be it forever by all understood
My censures were only pronounced for their good.
I delight in the sex, tis the pride of my mind
To consider them gentle, endearing, refin'd,
As our solace below in the journey of life
To smooth its rough passes—to soften its strife:
As objects intended our joys to supply
And to lead us in love to the temples on high.
How oft have I felt when two lucid blue eyes
As calm and as bright as the gems of the skies,
Have beam'd their soft radiance into my soul,
Impress'd with an awe like an angel's controul!
    Yes, fair ones, by this is forever defin'd,
The fop from the man of refinement and mind;

The latter believes ye in bounty were given
As a bond upon earth of our union with heaven:
And, if ye are weak and are frail in his view,
Tis to call forth fresh warmth, and his fondness renew.
Tis his joy to support these defects of your frame,
And his love at your weakness redoubles its flame,
He rejoices the gem is so rich and so fair,
And is proud that it claims his protection and care.

SALMAGUNDI NO. XIII

Friday, August 14, 1807.

FROM MY ELBOW-CHAIR.

I WAS NOT a little perplexed, a short time since, by the eccentric conduct of my knowing coadjutor, Will Wizard. For two or three days, he was completely in a quandary. He would come into old Cockloft's parlour ten times a day, swinging his ponderous legs along with his usual vast strides, clap his hands into his sides, contemplate the little shepherdesses on the mantle-piece for a few minutes, whistling all the while, and then sally out full sweep, without uttering a word. To be sure a *pish*, or a *pshaw* occasionally escaped him; and he was observed once to pull out his enormous tobacco box, drum for a moment upon its lid with his knuckles, and then return it into his pocket without taking a quid—'twas evident Will was full of some mighty idea—not that his restlessness was any way uncommon; for I have often seen Will throw himself almost into a fever of heat and fatigue—doing nothing. But his inflexible taciturnity set the whole family, as usual, a wondering, as Will seldom enters the house without giving one of his "one thousand and one" stories. For my part, I began to think that the late *fracas* at Canton had alarmed Will for the safety of his friends Kinglun, Chinqua and Consequa; or, that something had gone wrong in the alterations of the theatre—or that some new outrage at Norfolk had put him in a worry—in short, I did not know what to think; for Will is such an universal busybody, and meddles so much in every thing going forward, that you might as well attempt to conjecture what is going on in the north star, as in his precious pericranium. Even mrs. Cockloft who (like a worthy woman as she is) seldom troubles herself about any thing in this world—saving the affairs of her household, and the correct deportment of her female friends—was struck with the mystery of Will's behaviour. She happened, when he came in and went out the tenth time, to be busy darning the bottom of one of the old red damask chairs, and notwithstanding this is to her an affair of vast importance, yet, she could not help turning round and exclaiming "I *wonder* what can be the matter with mr. Wizard?"—"Nothing" replied old Christopher, "only we shall have an eruption soon." The old lady did not understand a word of this—neither did she care—she had expressed her wonder; and that, with her, is always sufficient.

I am so well acquainted with Will's peculiarities, that I can tell, even by his whistle, when he is about an essay for our paper, as certainly as a weather wiseacre knows that it is going to rain, when he sees a pig run squeaking about with his nose in the wind. I therefore, laid my account with receiving a communication from him before long, and sure enough, the evening before last I distinguished his free-mason knock at my door. I have seen many wise men in my time, philosophers, mathematicians, astronomers, politicians, editors, and almanack makers, but never did I see a man look half as wise as did my friend Wizard on entering the room. Had Lavater beheld him at that moment, he would have set him down to a certainty, as a fellow who had just discovered the longitude, or the philosopher's stone.

Without saying a word, he handed me a roll of paper, after which he lighted his cygarr, sat down, crossed his legs, folded his arms, and elevating his nose to an angle of about forty-five degrees, began to smoke like a steam-engine—Will delights in the picturesque. On opening his budget, and perceiving the motto, it struck me that Will had brought me one of his confounded chinese manuscripts, and I was forthwith going to dismiss it with indignation, but accidentally seeing the name of our oracle, the sage Linkum, (of whose inestimable folioes we pride ourselves upon being the sole possessors,) I began to think the better of it and looked round at Will to express my approbation. I shall never forget the figure he cut at that moment! He had watched my countenance, on opening his manuscript, with the argus eyes of an author, and perceiving some tokens of disapprobation, began, according to custom, to puff away at his cygarr with such vigour, that in a few minutes he had entirely involved himself in smoke, except his nose and one foot which were just visible, the latter wagging with great velocity. I believe I have hinted before—at least I ought to have done so—that Will's nose is a very goodly nose; to which it may be as well to add, that in his voyages under the tropics, it has acquired a copper complexion, which renders it very brilliant and luminous. You may imagine what a sumptuous appearance it made, projecting boldly, like the celebrated *promontorium nasidium* at Samos, with a light-house upon it, and surrounded on all sides with smoke and vapour. Had my gravity been like the chinese philosopher's "within one degree of absolute frigidity," here would have been a trial for it.—I could not stand it, but burst into such a laugh, as I do not indulge in above once in a hundred years—this was too much for Will—he emerged from his cloud, threw his cygarr into the fire-place, and strode out of the room pulling up his breeches, muttering something which, I verily believe, was nothing more or less than a horrible long chinese malediction.

He however left his manuscript behind him, which I now give to the world. Whether he is serious on the occasion, or only bantering, no one I believe can tell; for whether in speaking or writing, there is such an invincible gravity in his demeanour and style that even I, who have studied him as closely as an antiquarian studies an old manuscript or inscription, am frequently at a loss to know what the rogue would be at. I have seen him indulge in his favourite amusement of *quizzing* for hours together, without any one having the least suspicion of the matter, until he would suddenly twist his phiz into an expression that baffles all description, thrust his tongue in his cheek and *blow up* in a laugh almost as loud as a shout of the romans on a certain occasion, which honest Plutarch avers frightened several crows to such a degree that they fell down stone dead into the Campus Martius. Jeremy Cockloft the younger, who, like a true modern philosopher, delights in experiments that are of no kind of use, took the trouble to measure one of Will's risible explosions, and declared to me that, according to accurate measurement, it contained thirty feet square of solid laughter—what will the professors say to this?

PLANS FOR DEFENDING OUR HARBOUR.
BY WILLIAM WIZARD, ESQ.

> *Long-fong te-ko buzz tor-pe-do,*
> *Fudge* ——————   CONFUCIUS.
> *We'll blow the villains all sky high;*
> *But do it with econo*———— *my.*   LINK. FID.

Surely never was a town more subject to mid-summer fancies and dog-day whim-whams, than this most excellent of
cities:—Our notions, like our diseases, seem all epidemick;
and no sooner does a new disorder or a new freak seize one
individual but it is sure to run through all the community.
This is particularly the case when the summer is at the hottest,
and every body's head is in a vertigo, and his brain in a ferment—'tis absolutely necessary then the poor souls should
have some bubble to amuse themselves with, or they would
certainly run mad. Last year the *poplar worm* made its appearance most fortunately for our citizens, and every body was so
much in horror of being poisoned and devoured, and so busied in making humane experiments on cats and dogs, that we
got through the summer quite comfortably—the cats had the
worst of it—every mouser of them was shaved, and there was
not a whisker to be seen in the whole sisterhood. This summer every body has had full employment in planning fortifications for our harbour. Not a cobler or tailor in the city but
has left his awl and his thimble, become an engineer outright,
and aspired so magnanimously to the building of forts and
destruction of navies! Heavens! as my friend Mustapha would
say, on what great scale is every thing in this country!

Among the various plans that have been offered, the most
conspicuous is one devised and exhibited, as I am informed,
by that notable confederacy, THE NORTH RIVER SOCIETY.

Anxious to redeem their reputation from the foul suspicions that have for a long time overclouded it, these aquatic
incendiaries have come forward at the present alarming juncture, and announced a most potent discovery, which is to
guarantee our port from the visits of any foreign marauders.
The society have, it seems, invented a cunning machine,
shrewdly y'clep'd a *Torpedo*, by which the stoutest line of bat-

tle ship, even a *santissima trinidada* may be caught napping, and *decomposed* in a twinkling—a kind of sub-marine powder magazine to *swim* under water, like an aquatic mole, or water rat, and destroy the enemy in the moments of unsuspicious security.

This straw tickled the noses of all our dignitaries wonderfully—for, to do our government justice, it has no objection to injuring and exterminating its enemies in any manner—provided the thing can be done *economically*.

It was determined the experiment should be tried, and an old brig was purchased (for not more than twice its value,) and delivered over into the hands of its tormenters, the North River Society, to be tortured, and battered, and annihilated, *secundum artem*. A day was appointed for the occasion, when all the good citizens of the wonder loving city of Gotham were invited to the blowing up; like the fat inn-keeper in Rabelais, who requested all his customers to come on a certain day and see him burst.

As I have almost as great a veneration as the good mr. Walter Shandy, for all kinds of experiments that are ingeniously ridiculous, I made very particular mention of the one in question at the table of my friend Christopher Cockloft, but it put the honest old gentleman in a violent passion. He condemned it in toto, as an attempt to introduce a dastardly, and exterminating mode of warfare. "Already have we proceeded far enough" said he, "in the science of destruction; war is already invested with sufficient horrors and calamities—let us not increase the catalogue—let us not by these deadly artifices provoke a system of insidious and indiscriminate hostility, that shall terminate in laying our cities desolate, and exposing our women, our children, and our infirm, to the sword of pitiless recrimination." Honest old cavalier!—it was evident he did not reason as a true politician—but he felt as a christian and philanthropist, and that was, perhaps, just as well.

It may be readily supposed, that our citizens did not refuse the invitation of the society to the *blow up*—it was the first *naval* action ever exhibited in our port; and the good people all crowded to see the british navy blown up in effigy. The young ladies were delighted with the novelty of the show, and declared that if war could be conducted in this manner, it would become a fashionable amusement, and the destruction of a fleet be as pleasant as a ball or a tea party. The old folk were equally pleased with the spectacle—because it cost them nothing. Dear souls, how hard was it they should be disappointed! the brig most obstinately refused to be *decomposed*—the dinners grew cold, and the puddings were overboiled, throughout the renowned city of Gotham, and its sapient inhabitants, like the honest strasburghers, (from whom most of them are doubtless descended) who went out to see the courteous stranger and his nose, all returned home, after having threatened to pull down the flag-staff, by way of taking satisfaction for their disappointment.—By the way, there is not an animal in the world more discriminating in its vengeance than a free born *mob*.

In the evening I repaired to friend Hogg's, to smoke a sociable cygarr, but had scarcely entered the room when I was taken prisoner by my friend, mr. Ichabod Fungus, who I soon saw was at his usual trade of prying into mill-stones. The old gentleman informed me that the brig had actually blown up, after a world of manoeuvreing, and had nearly blown up the society with it—he seemed to entertain strong doubts as to the objects of the society in the invention of these infernal machines—hinted a suspicion of their wishing to set the river on fire, and that he should not be surprized on waking one of these mornings, to find the Hudson in a blaze. "Not that I disapprove of the plan," said he, "provided it has the end in view which they profess—no, no, an excellent plan of defence—no need of batteries, forts, frigates, and gun-boats:—observe, sir, all that's necessary is that the ships must come to anchor in a convenient place—watch must be asleep, or so complacent as not to disturb any boats paddling about them—fair wind and tide—no moonlight—machines well-directed—mustn't *flash in the pan*—bang's the word, and the vessel's blown up in a moment!" "Good," said I, "you remind me of a lubberly chinese who was flogged by an honest captain of my acquaintance, and who on being advised to retaliate, exclaimed—"Hi yah! spose two men hold fast him captain, den very mush me bamboo he!"

The old gentleman grew a little crusty, and insisted that I did not understand him—all that was requisite to render the effect certain, was that the enemy should enter into the project, or in other words, be *agreeable to the measure*, so that if the machine did not come to the ship, the ship should go to the machine, by which means he thought the success of the machine would be inevitable—provided it struck fire. "But do not you think," said I, doubtingly, "that it would be rather difficult to persuade the enemy into such an agreement? some people have an invincible antipathy to being blown up"— "not at all, not at all," replied he, triumphantly—"got an excellent notion for that—do with them as we have done with the brig; *buy* all the vessels we mean to destroy, and blow 'em up as best suits our convenience. I have thought deeply on that subject and have calculated to a certainty, that if our funds hold out, we may in this way distroy the whole british navy—by contract."

By this time all the quidnuncs of the room had gathered around us, each pregnant with some mighty scheme for the salvation of his country. One pathetically lamented that we had no such men among us as the famous Toujoursdort and Grossitout, who, when the celebrated captain Tranchemont, made war against the city of Kalacahabalaba, utterly discomfited the great king Big-staff, and blew up his whole army by sneezing. Another imparted a sage idea which seems to have occupied more heads than one—that is, that the best way of fortifying the harbour was to ruin it at once; choak the channel with rocks and blocks; strew it with *chevaux-de-frises* and torpedoes; and make it like a nursery-garden, full of mentraps and spring-guns. No vessel would then have the temerity to enter our harbour—we should not even dare to navigate it ourselves. Or if no cheaper way could be devised, let Governor's-Island be raised by levers and pulleys—floated with empty casks, &c. towed down to the Narrows, and dropped plump in the very mouth of the harbour!—"But," said I, " would not the prosecution of these whim-whams be rather expensive and dilatory?"—"Pshaw!" cried the other— " what's a million of money to an experiment—the true spirit of our economy requires that we should *spare no expense* in discovering the *cheapest* mode of defending ourselves; and then if all these modes should fail, why you know the worst we have to do is to return to the old-fashioned hum-drum mode of forts and batteries." "By which time," cried I, "the arrival of the enemy may have rendered their erection super-fluous."

A shrewd old gentleman, who stood listening by with a mischievously equivocal look, observed that the most effec-tual mode of repulsing a fleet from our ports would be to administer them a proclamation from time to time, *till it operated.*

Unwilling to leave the company without demonstrating my patriotism and ingenuity, I communicated a plan of defence, which in truth was suggested long since by that infallible or-acle MUSTAPHA, who had as clear a head for cobweb weav-ing, as ever dignified the shoulders of a projector. He thought the most effectual mode would be to assemble all the slang-whangers, great and small, from all parts of the state, and marshall them at the battery, where they should be exposed, point blank, to the enemy, and form a tremendous body of scolding infantry, similar to the *poissards* or doughty champi-ons of Billingsgate. They should be exhorted to fire away without pity or remorse, in sheets, half-sheets, columns, hand-bills or squibs—great canon, little canon, pica, german-text, stereotype—and to run their enemies through and through with sharp pointed italics. They should have orders to show no quarter—to blaze away in their loudest epithets —*"miscreants!" "murderers!" "barbarians!" "pirates!" "robbers!"* "BLACKGUARDS!" and to do away all fear of consequences they should be guaranteed from all dangers of pillory, kick-ing, cuffing, nose-pulling, whipping-post, or prosecution for libels. If, continued Mustapha, you wish men to fight well and valiantly, they must be allowed those weapons they have been used to handle. Your countrymen are notoriously adroit in the management of the tongue and the pen, and conduct all their battles by speeches or newspapers. Adopt, therefore, the plan I have pointed out, and rely upon it, that let any fleet, however large, be but once assailed by this battery of slang-whangers, and if they have not entirely lost the sense of hearing, or a regard for their own characters and feelings, they will, at the very first fire, slip their cables and retreat with as much precipitation as if they had unwarily entered into the atmosphere of the *Bohan upas.* In this manner may your wars be conducted with proper economy; and it will cost no more to drive off a fleet than to write *up* a party or write down a bashaw of three tails.

The sly old gentleman, I have before mentioned, was highly delighted with this plan, and proposed, as an improvement, that mortars should be placed on the battery, which, instead of throwing shells and such trifles, might be charged with newspapers, Tammany addresses, &c. by way of red-hot shot, which would undoubtedly be very potent in blowing up any powder magazine they might chance to come in contact with. He concluded by informing the company, that in the course of a few evenings he would have the honour to present them with a scheme for loading certain vessels with newspapers, resolutions of numerous and respectable meetings, and other combustibles, which vessels were to be blown directly in the midst of the enemy by the bellows of the slangwhangers, and he was much mistaken if they would not be more fatal than fire-ships, bomb-ketches, gun-boats, or even torpedoes.

These are but two or three specimens of the nature and efficacy of the innumerable plans with which this city abounds. Every body seems charged to the muzzle with gunpowder—every eye flashes fire-works and torpedoes, and every corner is occupied by knots of inflammatory projectors, not one of whom but has some preposterous mode of destruction which he has proved to be infallible by a previous experiment in a *tub of water!*

Even Jeremy Cockloft has caught the infection, to the great annoyance of the inhabitants of Cockloft-hall, whither he retired to make his experiments undisturbed. At one time all the mirrors in the house were unhung—their collected rays thrown into the hot-house, to try Archimedes' plan of burning-glasses; and the honest old gardener was almost knocked down by what he mistook for a stroke of the sun, but which turned out to be nothing more than a sudden attack of one of these tremendous *jack-o' lanterns*. It became dangerous to walk through the court-yard for fear of an explosion: and the whole family was thrown into absolute distress and consternation, by a letter from the old house-keeper to mrs. Cockloft, informing her of his having blown up a favorite chinese

gander, which I had brought from Canton, as he was majestically sailing in the duck-pond.

"In the multitude of counsellors there is safety"—if so, the
defenceless city of Gotham has nothing to apprehend;—but
much do I fear that so many excellent and infallible projects
will be presented, that we shall be at a loss which to adopt,
and the peaceable inhabitants fare like a famous projector of
my acquaintance, whose house was unfortunately plundered
while he was contriving a patent lock to secure the door.

FROM MY ELBOW-CHAIR.
A RETROSPECT,
OR, "WHAT YOU WILL."

Lolling in my Elbow-Chair this fine summer noon, I feel
myself insensibly yielding to that genial feeling of indolence
the season is so well fitted to inspire. Every one, who is
blessed with a little of the delicious languor of disposition
that delights in repose, must often have sported among the
faëry scenes, the golden visions, the voluptuous reveries, that
swim before the imagination at such moments—and which
so much resemble those blissful sensations a mussulman enjoys after his favourite indulgence of opium, which Will Wizard declares can be compared to nothing but "swimming in
an ocean of peacocks' feathers." In such a mood, every body
must be sensible it would be idle and unprofitable for a man
to send his wits a gadding on a voyage of discovery into futurity; or even to trouble himself with a laborious investigation of what is actually passing under his eye. We are, at such
times, more disposed to resort to the pleasures of memory,
than to those of the imagination; and like the way-faring traveller, reclining for a moment on his staff, had rather contemplate the ground we have travelled, than the region which is
yet before us.

I could here amuse myself and stultify my readers with a
most elaborate and ingenious parallel between authors and
travellers; but in this balmy season which makes men stupid
and dogs mad, and when doubtless many of our most strenuous admirers have great difficulty in keeping awake through
the day, it would be cruel to saddle them with the formidable

difficulty of putting two ideas together and drawing a conclusion, or in the learned phrase, forging *syllogisms in Baroco*—a
terrible undertaking for the Dog Days! To say the truth, my
observations were only intended to prove that this, of all others, is the most auspicious moment, and my present, the most
favourable mood for indulging in a retrospect. Whether, like
certain great personages of the day, in attempting to prove
one thing, I have exposed another; or whether like certain
other great personages, in attempting to prove a great deal, I
have proved nothing at all, I leave to my readers to decide,
provided they have the power and inclination so to do; but a
RETROSPECT will I take notwithstanding.

I am perfectly aware that in doing this I shall lay myself
open to the charge of imitation, than which a man might
better be accused of downright house-breaking, for it has
been a standing rule with many of my illustrious predecessors,
occasionally, and particularly at the conclusion of a volume,
to look over their shoulder and chuckle at the miracles they
had atchieved. But as I before professed, I am determined to
hold myself intirely independent of all manner of opinions
and criticisms, as the only method of getting on in this world
in any thing like a straight line. True it is, I may sometimes
seem to angle a little for the good opinion of mankind, by
giving them excellent reasons for doing unreasonable things;
but this is merely to show them, that although I may occasionally go wrong, it is not for want of knowing how to go
right: and here I will lay down a maxim, which will for ever
intitle me to the gratitude of my inexperienced readers—
namely, that a man always gets more credit in the eyes of this
naughty world for sinning wilfully, than for sinning through
sheer ignorance.

It will doubtless be insisted by many ingenious cavillers,
who will be meddling with what does not at all concern
them, that this retrospect should have been taken at the commencement of our second volume—it is usual, I know—
moreover it is natural. So soon as a writer has once accomplished a volume, he forthwith becomes wonderfully increased in altitude—he steps upon his book as upon a
pedestal, and is elevated in proportion to its magnitude. A
duodecimo makes him one inch taller; an octavo, three

inches; a quarto, six;—but he who, like mynheer, has written a book "as tick as a cheese" looks down upon his fellow creatures from such a fearful height, that, ten to one, the poor man's head is turned for ever afterwards. From such a lofty situation, therefore, it is natural an author should cast his eyes behind, and having reached the first landing place on the stairs of immortality, may reasonably be allowed to plead his privilege to look back over the height he has ascended. I have deviated a little from this venerable custom, merely that our retrospect might fall in the Dog Days—of all days in the year most congenial to the indulgence of a little self-sufficiency, inasmuch as people have then little to do but to retire within the sphere of self, and make the most of what they find there.

Let it not be supposed, however, that we think ourselves a whit the wiser or better since we have finished our volume than we were before; on the contrary, we seriously assure our readers that we were fully possessed of all the wisdom and morality it contains at the moment we commenced writing. It is the world which has grown wiser—not us; we have thrown our mite into the common stock of knowledge—we have shared our morsel with the ignorant multitude; and so far from elevating ourselves above the world, our sole endeavour has been to raise the world to our own level—and make it as wise as we, its disinterested benefactors.

To a moral writer like myself, who, next to his own comfort and entertainment, has the good of his fellow-citizens at heart, a retrospect is but a sorry amusement. Like the industrious husbandman, he often contemplates in silent disappointment his labours wasted on a barren soil, or the seed he has carefully sown, choaked by a redundancy of worthless weeds. I expected long ere this to have seen a complete reformation in manners and morals, atchieved by our united efforts. My fancy echoed to the applauding voices of a retrieved generation; I anticipated, with proud satisfaction, the period, not far distant, when our work would be introduced into the *Academies* with which every lane and alley of our cities abounds; when our precepts would be gently inducted into every unlucky urchin by force of birch, and my iron-bound physiognomy, as taken by Will Wizard, be as notorious as that of Noah Webster, junr. esq. or his no less renowned predecessor the illustrious Dilworth of spelling-book immortality. But, well-a-day! to let my readers into a profound secret—the expectations of man are like the varied hues that tinge the distant prospect—never to be realised, never to be enjoyed but in perspective. Luckless Launcelot! that the humblest of the many air castles thou hast erected should prove a "baseless fabrick!" Much does it grieve me to confess, that after all our lectures, precepts, and excellent admonitions, the people of New-York are nearly as much given to backsliding and ill-nature as ever; they are just as much abandoned to dancing and tea-drinking: and as to scandal, Will Wizard informs me that by a rough computation, since the last cargo of gunpowder-tea from Canton, no less than eighteen characters have been blown up, besides a number of others that have been woefully shattered.

The ladies still labour under the same scarcity of muslins, and delight in flesh-coloured silk stockings; it is evident, however, that our advice has had very considerable effect on them, as they endeavour to act as opposite to it as possible—this being what Evergreen calls *female independence*. As to Straddles, they abound as much as ever in Broadway, particularly on Sundays; and Wizard roundly asserts that he supped in company with a knot of them a few evenings since, when they *liquidated* a whole Birmingham consignment, in a batch of imperial champaign. I have furthermore, in the course of a month past, detected no less than three Giblet families making their first onset towards style and gentility, in the very manner we have heretofore reprobated. Nor have our utmost efforts been able to check the progress of that alarming epidemic, the rage for punning, which, though doubtless originally intended merely to ornament and enliven conversation by little sports of fancy, threatens to overrun and poison the whole, like the baneful ivy which destroys the useful plant it first embellished. Now I look upon an habitual punster as a depredator upon conversation; and I have remarked sometimes one of these offenders, sitting silent on the watch for an hour together, until some luckless wight, unfortunately for the ease and quiet of the company, dropped a phrase susceptible of a double meaning,—when—pop,—our punster would dart out like a veteran mouser from her covert, seize the unlucky word, and after worrying and mumbling at it until it was capable of no further marring, relapse again into silent watchfulness, and lie in wait for another opportunity. Even this might be borne with, by the aid of a little philosophy: but, the worst of it is, they are not content to manufacture puns and laugh heartily at them themselves; but they expect we should laugh with them—which I consider as an intolerable hardship, and a flagrant imposition on good nature. Let these gentlemen fritter away conversation with impunity, and deal out their wits in sixpenny bits if they please, but I beg I may have the choice of refusing currency to their small change. I am seriously afraid, however, that our junto is not quite free from the infection, nay, that it has even approached so near as to menace the tranquility of my elbow-chair: for, Will Wizard, as we were in caucus the other night, absolutely electrified Pindar and myself with a most palpable and perplexing pun—had it been a torpedo, it could not have more discomposed the fraternity. Sentence of banishment was unanimously decreed, but on his confessing that like many celebrated wits, he was merely retailing other men's wares on commission, he was for that once forgiven, on condition of refraining from such diabolical practices in future. Pindar is particularly outrageous against punsters; and quite astonished and put me to a nonplus a day or two since, by asking abruptly " whether I thought a punster could be a good christian?" He followed up his question triumphantly by offering to prove, by sound logic and historical fact, that the roman empire owed its decline and fall to a pun; and that nothing tended so much to demoralize the french nation, as their abominable rage for *jeux de mots*.

But what, above every thing else, has caused me much vexation of spirit, and displeased me most with this stiff-necked nation, is that in spite of all the serious and profound censures of the sage Mustapha, in his various letters—they *will talk!*—they will still wag their tongues, and chatter like very slang-whangers! This is a degree of obstinacy incomprehensible in the extreme; and is another proof, how alarming is the force of habit, and how difficult it is to reduce beings, accustomed to talk, to that state of silence which is the very acme of human wisdom.

We can only account for these disappointments in our moderate and reasonable expectations, by supposing the world so deeply sunk in the mire of delinquency, that not even Hercules, were he to put his shoulder to the axletree, would be able to extricate it. We comfort ourselves, however, by the reflection, that there are, at least, three good men left in this degenerate age, to benefit the world by example, should precept ultimately fail. And borrowing, for once, an example from certain sleepy writers, who, after the first emotions of surprise at finding their invaluable effusions neglected or despised, console themselves with the idea that 'tis a stupid age, and look forward to posterity for redress—we bequeath our first volume to future generations—and much good may it do them. Heaven grant they may be able to read it! for, if our fashionable mode of education continues to improve, as of late, I am under serious apprehensions that the period is not far distant, when the discipline of the dancing master will supersede that of the grammarian; crochets and quavers supplant the alphabet, and the heels, by an antipodean manoeuvre, obtain entire pre-eminence over the head. How does my heart yearn for poor dear posterity, when this work shall become as unintelligible to our grandchildren, as it seems to be to their grandfathers and grandmothers.

In fact (for I love to be candid) we begin to suspect that many people read our numbers, merely for their amusement, without paying any attention to the serious truths conveyed in every page. Unpardonable want of penetration! not that we wish to restrict our readers in the article of laughing, which we consider as one of the dearest prerogatives of man, and the distinguishing characteristic which raises him above all other animals: let them laugh therefore if they will, provided they profit at the same time, and do not mistake our object. It is one of our indisputable facts, that it is easier to laugh ten follies out of countenance than to coax, reason, or flog a man out of one. In this odd singular and indescribable age, which is neither the age of gold, silver, iron, brass, chivalry, or *pills* (as sir John Carr asserts) a grave writer who attempts to attack folly with the heavy artillery of moral reasoning, will fare like Smollet's honest pedant, who clearly demonstrated by angles &c., after the manner of Euclid, that it was wrong to do evil—and was laughed at for his pains. Take my word for it, a little well applied ridicule, like Hannibal's application of vinegar to rocks, will do more with certain hard heads and obdurate hearts, than all the logic or demonstrations in Longinus or Euclid. But the people of Gotham, wise souls! are so much accustomed to see morality approach them clothed in formidable wigs and sable garbs, "with leaden eye that loves the ground," that they can never recognize her when, drest in gay attire, she comes tripping towards them with smiles and sunshine in her countenance.— Well, let the rogues remain in happy ignorance, for "ignorance is bliss," as the poet says;—and I put as implicit faith in poetry as I do in the almanack or the newspaper—we *will* improve them, without their being the wiser for it, and they shall become better in spite of their teeth, and without their having the least suspicion of the reformation working within them.

Among all our manifold grievances, however, still some small, but vivid rays of sunshine occasionally brighten along our path, cheering our steps, and inviting us to persevere.

The publick have paid some little regard to a few articles of our advice—they have purchased our numbers freely—so much the better for our publisher—they have read them attentively—so much the better for themselves. The melancholy fate of my dear aunt Charity has had a wonderful effect, and I have now before me a letter from a gentleman who lives opposite to a couple of old ladies, remarkable for the interest they took in his affairs—his apartments were absolutely in a state of blockade, and he was on the point of changing his lodgings or capitulating, until the appearance of our ninth number, which he immediately sent over with his compliments—the good old ladies took the hint, and have scarcely appeared at their window since. As to the *wooden gentlemen*, our friend miss Sparkle assures me, they are wonderfully improved by our criticisms, and sometimes venture to make a remark or attempt a pun in company, to the great edification of all who happen to understand them. As to red shawls, they are intirely discarded from the fair shoulders of our ladies— ever since the last importation of finery—nor has any lady, since the cold weather, ventured to expose her elbows to the

admiring gaze of scrutinizing passengers. But there is one victory we have atchieved which has given us more pleasure than
to have written down the whole administration. I am assured
from unquestionable authority, that our young ladies, doubtless in consequence of our weighty admonitions, have not
once indulged in that intoxicating, inflammatory, and whirligig dance, the *waltz*—ever since hot weather commenced.
True it is, I understand an attempt was made to exhibit it by
some of the sable fair ones at the last *african ball*, but it was
highly disapproved of by all the respectable elderly ladies
present.

These are sweet sources of comfort to atone for the many
wrongs and misrepresentations heaped upon us by the
world—for even *we* have experienced its ill nature. How often have we heard ourselves reproached for the insidious applications of the uncharitable!—how often have we been
accused of emotions which never found an entrance into our
bosoms!—how often have our sportive effusions been
wrested to serve the purposes of particular enmity and bitterness!—Meddlesome spirits! little do they know our dispositions; we "lack gall" to wound the feelings of a single
innocent individual; we can even forgive *them* from the very
bottom of our souls—may they meet as ready a forgiveness
from their own consciences! Like true and independent bachelors, having no domestic cares to interfere with our general
benevolence, we consider it incumbent upon us to watch over
the welfare of society; and although we are indebted to the
world for little else than left-handed favours, yet we feel a
proud satisfaction in requiting evil with good, and the sneer
of illiberality with the unfeigned smile of good-humour. With
these mingled motives of selfishness and philanthropy we
commenced our work, and if we cannot solace ourselves with
the consciousness of having done much good, yet there is still
one pleasing consolation left, which the world can neither
give nor take away. There are moments—lingering moments
of listless indifference and heavy-hearted despondency—
when our best hopes and affections slipping, as they sometimes will, from their hold on those objects to which they
usually cling for support, seem abandoned on the wide waste
of cheerless existence, without a place to cast anchor—with-

out a shore in view to excite a single wish, or to give a momentary interest to contemplation. We look back with delight upon many of these moments of mental gloom, whiled away by the cheerful exercise of our pen, and consider every such triumph over the spleen, as retarding the furrowing hand of time, in its insidious encroachments on our brows. If, in addition to our own amusements, we have, as we jogged carelessly laughing along, brushed away one tear of dejection, and called forth a smile in its place; if we have brightened the pale countenance of a single child of sorrow; we shall feel almost as much joy and rejoicing as a slang-whanger does when he bathes his pen in the heart's-blood of a patron and factor; or sacrifices one more illustrious victim on the altar of *party animosity*.

TO READERS AND CORRESPONDENTS.

It is our misfortune to be frequently pestered, in our peregrinations about this learned city, by certain critical gad-flies, who buzz around and merely attack the skin, without ever being able to penetrate the body. The reputation of our promising *protégé*, Jeremy Cockloft the younger, has been assailed by these skin-deep critics; they have questioned his claims to originality, and even hinted that the ideas for his New-Jersey Tour were borrowed from a late work entitled "MY POCKETBOOK." As there is no literary offence more despicable in the eyes of the trio than *borrowing*, we immediately called Jeremy to an account; when he proved, by the dedication of the work in question, that it was first published in *London* in March 1807—and that his "Stranger in New-Jersey" had made its appearance on the 24th of the preceding February.

We were on the point of acquitting Jeremy with honour, on the ground that it was impossible, *knowing* as he is, to borrow from a foreign work *one month before* it was in existence, when Will Wizard suddenly took up the cudgels for the critics, and insisted that nothing was more probable, for he recollected reading of an ingenious dutch author, who plainly convicted the *antients* of stealing from his labours!— So much for *criticism*.

We have received a host of friendly and admonitory letters from different quarters, and among the rest a very loving epistle from George-town, Columbia, signed *Teddy M'Gundy*, who addresses us by the name of Saul M'Gundy, and insists that we are descended from the same irish progenitors, and nearly related. As friend Teddy seems to be an honest merry rogue, we are sorry that we cannot admit his claims to kindred; we thank him, however, for his good will, and should he ever be inclined to *favour* us with another epistle, we will hint to him, and at the same time to our other numerous correspondents, that their communications will be infinitely more acceptable if they will just recollect Tom Shuffleton's advice, "pay the post-boy, Muggins."

SALMAGUNDI NO. XIV

Saturday, September 19, 1807.

FROM MUSTAPHA RUB-A-DUB KELI KHAN,
To ASEM HACCHEM, *principal slave-driver to
his highness the Bashaw of Tripoli.*

HEALTH AND JOY to the friend of my heart!—May the
angel of peace ever watch over thy dwelling, and the
star of prosperity shed its benignant lustre on all thy under-
takings. Far other is the lot of thy captive friend—his brightest hopes extend but to a lengthened period of weary
captivity, and memory only adds to the measure of his griefs,
by holding up a mirror which reflects with redoubled charms
the hours of past felicity. In midnight slumbers my soul holds
sweet converse with the tender objects of its affections—it is
then the exile is restored to his country—it is then the wide
waste of waters that rolls between us disappears, and I clasp
to my bosom the companion of my youth. I awake, and find
it is but a vision of the night—the sigh will rise—the tear of
dejection will steal adown my cheek—I fly to my pen, and
strive to forget myself and my sorrows in conversing with my
friend.

In such a situation, my good Asem, it cannot be expected
that I should be able so wholly to abstract myself from my
own feelings, as to give thee a full and systematick account of
the singular people among whom my disastrous lot has been
cast. I can only find leisure from my own individual sorrows,
to entertain thee occasionally with some of the most prominent features of their character, and now and then a solitary
picture of their most preposterous eccentricities.

I have before observed that among the distinguishing char-
acteristicks of the people of this logocracy, is their invincible
love of talking; and that I could compare the nation to nothing but a mighty wind-mill. Thou art doubtless at a loss to
conceive how this mill is supplied with *grist*; or, in other
words, how it is possible to furnish subjects to supply the
perpetual motion of so many tongues.

The genius of the nation appears in its highest lustre in this particular, in the discovery, or rather the application, of a subject which seems to supply an inexhaustible mine of words. It is nothing more, my friend, than POLITICKS, a word, which I declare to thee, has perplexed me almost as much as the redoubtable one of *economy*. On consulting a dictionary of this language, I found it denoted the science of government, and the relations, situations and dispositions of states and empires.—Good, thought I, for a people who boast of governing themselves, there could not be a more important subject of investigation. I therefore listened attentively, expecting to hear from "the most enlightened people under the sun," (for so they modestly term themselves) sublime disputations on the science of legislation, and precepts of political wisdom, that would not have disgraced our great prophet and legislator himself—but alas, Asem! how continually are my expectations disappointed! how dignified a meaning does this word bear in the dictionary—how despicable its common application! I find it extending to every contemptible discussion of local animosity, and every petty altercation of insignificant individuals. It embraces alike all manner of concerns, from the organization of a divan, the election of a bashaw, or the levying of an army, to the appointment of a constable, the personal disputes of two miserable slang-whangers, the cleaning of the streets, or the economy of a dirt cart. A couple of politicians will quarrel with the most vociferous pertinacity, about the character of a bum-bailiff, whom nobody cares for, or the deportment of a little great man, whom nobody knows—and this is called talking *politicks*;—nay, it is but a few days since, that I was annoyed by a debate between two of my fellow lodgers, who were magnanimously employed in condemning a luckless wight to infamy, because he chose to wear a *red coat*, and to entertain certain erroneous opinions some thirty years ago. Shocked at their illiberal and vindictive spirit, I rebuked them for thus indulging in slander and uncharitablenesses, about the colour of a coat, which had doubtless for many years been worn out, or the belief in errors, which in all probability had been long since atoned for and abandoned; but they justified themselves by alledging that they were only engaged in *politicks*, and exerting that liberty of speech, and freedom of discussion, which was the glory and safeguard of their national independence. "Oh Mahomet!" thought I, "what a country must that be, which builds its political safety on ruined characters and the persecution of individuals!"

Into what transports of surprize and incredulity am I continually betrayed, as the character of this eccentrick people gradually developes itself to my observations. Every new research encreases the perplexities in which I am involved, and I am more than ever at a loss where to place them in the scale of my estimation. It is thus the philosopher, in pursuing truth through the labyrinth of doubt, error and misrepresentation, frequently finds himself bewildered in the maze of contradictory experience, and almost wishes he could quietly retrace his wandering steps, steal back into the path of honest ignorance, and jog on once more in contented indifference.

How fertile in these contradictions is this extensive logocracy! Men of different nations, manners and languages, live in this country in the most perfect harmony, and nothing is more common than to see individuals, whose respective governments are at variance, taking each other by the hand and exchanging the offices of friendship. Nay, even on the subject of religion, which, as it affects our dearest interests, our earliest opinions and prejudices, some warmth and heart-burnings might be excused, which even in *our* enlightened country is so fruitful in difference between man and man—even religion occasions no dissension among these people, and it has even been discovered by one of their *sages*, that believing in one God or twenty Gods, "neither breaks a man's leg, nor picks his pocket." The idolatrous persian may here bow down before his everlasting fire, and prostrate himself towards the glowing east. The chinese may adore his *Fo'* or his *Josh*—the egyptian his stork,—and the mussulman practise unmolested the divine precepts of our immortal prophet. Nay, even the forlorn, abandoned atheist, who lays down at night without committing himself to the protection of heaven, and rises in the morning without returning thanks for his safety—who hath no deity but his own will—whose soul, like the sandy desart, is barren of every flower of hope, to throw a solitary bloom over the dead level of sterility, and soften the wide extent of desolation—whose darkened views extend not beyond the horizon that bounds his cheerless existence—to whom no blissful perspective opens beyond the grave;—even he is suffered to indulge in his desperate opinions, without exciting one other emotion than pity or contempt. But this mild and tolerating spirit reaches not beyond the pale of religion:—once differ in *politicks*, in mere theories, visions and chimeras, the growth of interest, of folly, or madness, and deadly warfare ensues; every eye flashes fire, every tongue is loaded with reproach, and every heart is filled with gall and bitterness.

At this period several unjustifiable and serious injuries on the part of the barbarians of the british island, have given new impulse to the tongue and the pen, and occasioned a terrible wordy fever. Do not suppose, my friend, that I mean to condemn any proper and dignified expression of resentment for injuries. On the contrary, I love to see a word before a blow: for "in the fulness of the heart the tongue moveth." But my long experience has convinced me, that people who talk the most about taking satisfaction for affronts, generally content themselves with talking, instead of revenging the insult: like the street women of this country, who, after a prodigious scolding, quietly sit down and fan themselves cool as fast as possible. But to return—the rage for talking has now, in consequence of the aggressions I alluded to, increased to a degree far beyond what I have observed heretofore. In the gardens of his highness of Tripoli, are fifteen thousand bee-hives, three hundred peacocks, and a prodigious number of parrots and baboons—and yet I declare to thee, Asem, that their buzzing and squalling and chattering is nothing, compared to the wild uproar and war of words now raging within the bosom of this mighty and distracted *logocracy. Politicks* pervade every city, every village, every temple, every porter house— the universal question is, "what is the news?"—This is a kind of challenge to political debate, and as no two men think exactly alike, tis ten to one but before they finish, all the *polite* phrases in the language are exhausted, by way of giving fire and energy to argument. What renders this talking fever more alarming is, that the people appear to be in the unhappy state of a patient whose palate nauseates the medicine best calculated for the cure of his disease, and seem anxious to continue

in the full enjoyment of their chattering epidemick. They
alarm each other by direful reports and fearful apprehensions,
like I have seen a knot of old wives in this country, entertain
themselves with stories of ghosts and goblins, until their
imaginations were in a most agonizing panick. Every day begets some new tale big with agitation, and the busy *goddess*
rumour (to speak in the poetick language of the *christians*) is
constantly in motion. She mounts her rattling stage-waggon,
and gallops about the country, freighted with a load of
"hints" "informations" "extracts of letters from respectable
gentlemen" "observations of respectable correspondents," and
"unquestionable authorities," which her high priests, the
slang-whangers, retail to their sapient followers, with all the
solemnity and all the authenticity of oracles. True it is, the
unfortunate slang-whangers are sometimes at a loss for food
to supply this insatiable appetite for intelligence, and are not
unfrequently reduced to the necessity of manufacturing dishes
suited to the taste of the times, to be served up as morning
and evening repasts to their disciples.

When the hungry politician is thus full charged with important information, he sallies forth to give due exercise to
his tongue, and tell all he knows to every body he meets.
Now it is a thousand to one, that every person he meets is
just as wise as himself, charged with the same articles of information, and possessed of the same violent inclination to
give it vent, for in this country every man adopts some particular slang-whanger as the standard of his judgment, and reads
every thing he writes, if he reads nothing else—which is
doubtless the reason why the people of this logocracy are so
marvelously *enlightened*. So away they tilt at each other with
their borrowed lances, advancing to the combat with the
opinions and speculations of their respective slang-whangers
which in all probability, are diametrically opposite—here
then arises as fair an opportunity for a battle of words as heart
could wish; and thou mayest rely upon it, Asem, they do not
let it pass unimproved. They *sometimes* begin with argument,
but in process of time, as the tongue begins to wax wanton,
other auxiliaries become necessary—recrimination commences, reproach follows close at its heels—from political
abuse they proceed to personal, and thus often is a friendship

of years trampled down by this contemptible enemy; this gigantic dwarf of POLITICKS, the mongrel issue of grovelling ambition and aspiring ignorance!

There would be but little harm indeed in all this, if it ended merely in a broken head; for this might soon be healed, and the scar, if any remained, might serve as a warning ever after against the indulgence of political intemperance—at the worst, the loss of such heads as these would be a gain to the nation.—But the evil extends far deeper; it threatens to impair all social intercourse, and even to sever the sacred union of family and kindred. The convivial table is disturbed, the cheerful fire-side is invaded, the smile of social hilarity is chased away—the bond of social love is broken by the everlasting intrusion of this fiend of contention, who lurks in the sparkling bowl, crouches by the fire-side, growls in the friendly circle, infests every avenue to pleasure; and like the scowling Incubus, sits on the bosom of society, pressing down and smothering every throe and pulsation of liberal philanthropy.

But thou wilt perhaps ask, "What can these people dispute about? one would suppose that being all *free* and *equal*, they would harmonize as brothers; children of the same parent, and equal heirs of the same inheritance." This theory is most exquisite, my good friend, but in practice it turns out the very dream of a madman. Equality, Asem, is one of the most consummate scoundrels that ever crept from the brain of a political juggler. A fellow who thrusts his hand into the pocket of honest industry, or enterprising talent, and squanders their hard earned profit on profligate idleness or indolent stupidity. There will always be an inequality among mankind, so long as a portion of it is enlightened and industrious, and the rest idle and ignorant. The one will acquire a larger share of wealth, and its attendant comforts, refinements, and luxuries of life, and the influence and power which those will always possess who have the greatest ability of administering to the necessities of their fellow creatures. These advantages will inevitably excite envy, and envy as inevitably begets ill-will—hence arises that eternal warfare which the lower orders of society are waging against those who have raised themselves by their own merits, or have been raised by the merits of their

ancestors, above the common level. In a nation possessed of
quick feelings and impetuous passions, this hostility might
engender deadly broils, and bloody commotions; but here it
merely vents itself in high sounding words, which lead to
continual breaches of decorum; or in the insidious assassina-
tion of character, and a restless propensity among the base to
blacken every reputation which is fairer than their own.

I cannot help smiling sometimes to see the solicitude with
which the people of *America* (so called from the country having been first discovered by *Christopher Columbus*) battle
about them when any election takes place; as if *they* had the
least concern in the matter, or were to be benefitted by an
exchange of bashaws—they really seem ignorant, that none
but the *bashaws and their dependants* are at all interested in the
event, and that the people at large will not find their situation
altered in the least. I formerly gave thee an account of an
election, which took place under my eye. The result has been,
that the *people*, as some of the slang-whangers say, have obtained a glorious triumph, which however, is flatly denied by
the opposite slang-whangers, who insist that *their* party is
composed of the true sovereign people, and that the others
are all jacobins, frenchmen, and *irish rebels*. I ought to apprize
thee, that the last is a term of great reproach here, which
perhaps thou wouldst not otherwise imagine, considering
that it is not many years since this very people were engaged
in a revolution; the failure of which would have subjected
them to the same ignominious epithet, and a participation in
which, is now the highest recommendation to publick confidence. By Mahomet, but it cannot be denied that the *consistency* of this people, like every thing else appertaining to them
is on a prodigious *great scale*! To return, however, to the
event of the election.—The people triumphed—and much
good has it done them. I, for my part, expected to see wonderful changes, and most magical metamorphoses. I expected
to see the people all rich, that they would be all gentlemen
bashaws, riding in their coaches, and faring sumptuously
every day; emancipated from toil, and revelling in luxurious
ease. Wilt thou credit me, Asem, when I declare to thee, that
every thing remains exactly in the same state as it was before
the last wordy campaign? except a few noisy retainers who

have crept into office, and a few noisy patriots on the other side, who have been kicked out, there is not the least difference. The labourer still toils for his daily support; the beggar still lives on the charity of those who have any charity to bestow, and the only *solid* satisfaction the multitude have reaped, is that they have got a *new governor* (or bashaw) whom they will praise, idolize, and exalt for a while, and afterwards, notwithstanding the sterling merits he really possesses, in compliance with immemorial custom, they will abuse, calumniate, and trample under foot.

Such, my dear Asem, is the way in which the wise people, of "the most enlightened country under the sun," are amused with straws, and puffed up with mighty conceits: like a certain fish I have seen here, which having his belly tickled for a short time, will swell and puff himself up to twice his usual size, and become a mere bladder of wind and vanity.

The blessing of a true mussulman light on thee, good Asem,—ever while thou livest, be true to thy prophet, and rejoice, that though the boasting *political chatterers* of this logocracy cast upon thy countrymen the ignominious epithet of slaves; yet, thou livest in a country where the people, instead of being at the mercy of a tyrant with a *million of heads*, have nothing to do but submit to the will of a bashaw of *only three tails*.

ever thine,
MUSTAPHA.

COCKLOFT HALL.
BY LAUNCELOT LANGSTAFF, ESQ.

Those who pass their time immured in the smoky circumference of the city, amid the rattling of carts, the brawling of the multitude, and the variety of unmeaning and discordant sounds that prey insensibly upon the nerves, and beget a weariness of the spirits, can alone understand and feel that expansion of the heart, that physical renovation which a citizen experiences when he steals forth from his dusty prison, to breathe the free air of heaven, and enjoy the unsophisticated face of nature. Who that has rambled by the side of one of our majestic rivers, at the hour of sun-set, when the wildly

romantick scenery around is softened and tinted by the voluptuous mist of evening; when the bold and swelling outlines
of the distant mountain seem melting into the glowing horizon, and a rich mantle of refulgence is thrown over the whole
expanse of the heavens, but must have felt how abundant is
nature in sources of pure enjoyment; how luxuriant in all that
can enliven the senses or delight the imagination. The jocund
zephyr full freighted with native fragrance, sues sweetly to the
senses; the chirping of the thousand varieties of insects with
which our woodlands abound, forms a concert of simple melody; even the barking of the farm dog, the lowing of the
cattle, the tinkling of their bells, and the strokes of the wood-
man's axe from the opposite shore, seem to partake of the
softness of the scene and fall tunefully upon the ear; while the
voice of the villager, chaunting some rustick ballad, swells
from a distance, in the semblance of the very musick of harmonious love.

At such times I feel a sensation of a sweet tranquility—a
hallowed calm is diffused over my senses; I cast my eyes
around and every object is serene, simple, and beautiful; no
warring passion, no discordant string there vibrates to the
touch of ambition, self-interest, hatred or revenge—I am at
peace with the whole world, and hail all mankind as friends
and brothers.—Blissful moments! ye recal the careless days of
my boyhood, when mere existence was happiness, when hope
was certainty, this world a paradise, and every woman a ministering angel!—Surely man was designed for a tenant of the
universe, instead of being pent up in these dismal cages, these
dens of strife, disease and discord. We were created to range
the fields, to sport among the groves, to build castles in the
air, and have every one of them realized!

A whole legion of reflections like these, insinuated themselves into my mind, and stole me from the influence of the
cold realities before me, as I took my accustomed walk, a few
weeks since, on the Battery. Here watching the splendid mutations of one of our summer skies, which emulated the
boasted glories of an italian sun-set, I all at once discovered
that it was but to pack up my portmanteau; bid adieu for a
while to my elbow-chair, and in a little time I should be transported from the region of smoke and noise and dust, to the

enjoyment of a far sweeter prospect and a brighter sky. The next morning I was off full tilt to Cockloft-Hall, leaving my man Pompey to follow at his leisure with my baggage. I love to indulge in rapid transitions, which are prompted by the quick impulse of the moment—tis the only mode of guarding against that intruding and deadly foe to all parties of pleasure—anticipation.

Having now made good my retreat, until the black frosts commence, it is but a piece of civility due to my readers, who I trust are, ere this, my friends, to give them a proper introduction to my present residence. I do this as much to gratify them as myself, well knowing a reader is always anxious to learn how his author is lodged, whether in a garret or a cellar, a hovel or a palace—at least an author is generally vain enough to think so; and an author's vanity ought sometimes to be gratified—poor vagabond! it is often the only gratification he ever tastes in this world!

COCKLOFT-HALL is the country residence of the family, or rather the paternal mansion, which, like the mother country, sends forth whole colonies to populate the face of the earth. Pindar whimsically denominates it the *family hive*, and there is at least as much truth as humour in my cousin's epithet— for many a redundant swarm has it produced. I dont recollect whether I have at any time mentioned to my readers (for I seldom look back on what I have written) that the fertility of the Cocklofts is proverbial. The female members of the family are most incredibly fruitful; and to use a favourite phrase of old Cockloft, who is excessively addicted to backgammon, they seldom fail "to throw doublets every time." I myself have known three or four very industrious young men reduced to great extremities, with some of these capital breeders— heaven smiled upon their union, and enriched them with a numerous and hopeful offspring—who eat them out of doors.

But to return to the hall.—It is pleasantly situated on the bank of a sweet pastoral stream, not so near town as to invite an inundation of unmeaning, idle acquaintance, who come to lounge away an afternoon, nor so distant as to render it an absolute deed of charity or friendship to perform the journey. It is one of the oldest habitations in the country, and was built by my cousin Christopher's grandfather, who was also mine by the mother's side, in his latter days, to form, as the old gentleman expressed himself, "a snug retreat, where he meant to sit himself down *in his old days* and be comfortable *for the rest of his life*." He was at this time a few years over fourscore; but this was a common saying of his, with which he usually closed his airy speculations. One would have thought from the long vista of years through which he contemplated many of his projects, that the good man had forgot the age of the patriarchs had long since gone by, and calculated upon living a century longer at least. He was for a considerable time in doubt, on the question of roofing his house with shingles or slate—shingles would not last *above thirty* years; but then they were much cheaper than slates. He settled the matter by a kind of compromise, and determined to build with shingles first; "and when they are worn out," said the old gentleman, triumphantly, "twill be time enough for us to replace them with more durable materials:" But his contemplated improvements surpassed every thing; and scarcely had he a roof over his head, when he discovered a thousand things to be arranged before he could "sit down comfortably." In the first place every tree and bush on the place, was cut down or grubbed up by the roots because they were not placed to his mind; and a vast quantity of oaks, chesnuts and elms, set out in clumps and rows, and labyrinths, which he observed in about *five-and-twenty or thirty years* at most, would yield a very tolerable shade, and moreover, shut out all the surrounding country; for he was determined he said, to have all his views on his own land, and be beholden to no man for a prospect. This, my learned readers will perceive, was something very like the idea of Lorenzo de Medici, who gave as a reason for preferring one of his seats above all the others, "that all the ground within view of it, was his own:" now, whether my grandfather ever heard of the Medici, is more than I can say; I rather think however from the characteristic originality of the Cocklofts that it was a whim-wham of his own begetting. Another odd notion of the old gentleman, was to blow up a large bed of rocks for the purpose of having a fish-pond, although the river ran at about one hundred yards distance from the house, and was well stored with fish—but there was nothing he said like having things to oneself. So at it he went with all the ardour of a projector, who has just hit upon some splendid and useless whim-wham. As he proceeded, his views enlarged; he would have a summer-house built on the margin of the fish-pond; he would have it surrounded with elms and willows; and he would have a cellar dug under it, for some incomprehensible purpose, which remains a secret to this day. "In a few years," he observed, "it would be a delightful piece of wood and wa-ter, where he might ramble on a summer's noon, smoke his pipe and enjoy himself in his old days"—thrice honest old soul!—he died of an apoplexy in his ninetieth year, just as he had begun to blow up the fish-pond.

Let no one ridicule the whim-whams of my grandfather:— If—and of this there is no doubt, for wise men have said it —if life is but a dream, happy is he who can make the most of the illusion.

Since my grandfather's death, the hall has passed through the hands of a succession of true old cavaliers, like himself, who gloried in observing the golden rules of hospitality, which, according to the Cockloft principle, consist in giving a guest the freedom of the house, cramming him with beef and pudding, and if possible, laying him under the table with prime port, claret or London particular. The mansion appears to have been consecrated to the jolly god, and teems with monuments sacred to conviviality. Every chest of drawers, clothes-press and cabinet is decorated with enormous china punch-bowls, which mrs. Cockloft has paraded with much os-tentation, particularly in her favourite red damask bed-cham-ber, and in which a projector might with great satisfaction practise his experiments on fleets, diving-bells, and sub-marine boats.

I have before mentioned cousin Christopher's profound veneration for antique furniture; in consequence of which the old hall is furnished in much the same style with the house in town. Old fashioned bed-steads, with high testers, massy clothes-presses, standing most majestically on eagles' claws, and ornamented with a profusion of shining brass handles, clasps and hinges, and around the grand parlour are solemnly arranged a sett of high-backed leather-bottomed, massy mahogany chairs, that always remind me of the formal long-waisted belles who flourished in stays and buckram, about the time they were in fashion.

If I may judge from their height it was not the fashion for gentlemen in those days to loll over the back of a lady's chair, and whisper in her ear what—might be as well spoken aloud—at least they must have been patagonians to have effected it. Will Wizard declares that he saw a little fat german gallant attempt once to whisper miss Barbara Cockloft in this manner, but being unluckily caught by the chin, he dangled and kicked about for half a minute, before he could find terra firma—but Will is much addicted to hyperbole, by reason of his having been a great traveller.

But what the Cocklofts most especially pride themselves upon, is the possession of several family portraits, which exhibit as honest a square set of portly well fed looking gentlemen, and gentlewomen as ever grew and flourished under the pencil of a dutch painter. Old Christopher, who is a complete genealogist, has a story to tell of each, and dilates with copious eloquence on the great services of the general in large sleeves, during the old french war, and on the piety of the lady in blue velvet, who so attentively peruses her book, and was once so celebrated for a beautiful arm: But much as I reverence my illustrious ancestors, I find little to admire in their biography, except my cousin's excellent memory, which is most provokingly retentive of every uninteresting particular.

My allotted chamber in the hall is the same that was occupied in days of yore by my honoured uncle John. The room exhibits many memorials which recal to my remembrance the solid excellence and amiable eccentricities of that gallant old lad. Over the mantlepiece hangs the portrait of a young lady, dressed in a flaring long-waisted blue silk gown, be-flowered, and be-furbelowed, and be-cuffed in a most abundant manner—she holds in one hand a book, which she very complaisantly neglects, to turn and smile on the spectator; in the other, a flower, which I hope, for the honor of dame nature, was the sole production of the painter's imagination; and a little behind her is something tied to a blue ribbon, but whether a little dog, a monkey, or a pigeon, must be left to

the judgment of future commentators. This little damsel, tradition says, was my uncle John's third flame, and he would
infallibly have run away with her, could he have persuaded
her into the measure; but at that time, ladies were not quite
so easily run away with as Columbine; and my uncle failing
in the point, took a lucky thought, and with great gallantry
run off with her picture, which he conveyed in triumph to
Cockloft-hall, and hung up in his bed-chamber as a monument of his enterprising spirit. The old gentleman prided
himself mightily on this chivalrick manoeuvre; always chuckled, and pulled up his stock when he contemplated the picture, and never related the exploit without winding up
with—"I might, indeed, have carried off the original, had I
chose to dangle a little longer after her chariot-wheels—for,
to do the girl justice, I believe she had a liking for me, but I
always scorned to coax, my boy—always—'twas my way."
My uncle John was of a happy temperament—I would give
half I am worth for his talent at self-consolation.

The miss Cocklofts have made several spirited attempts to
introduce modern furniture into the hall, but with very indifferent success. Modern *style* has always been an object of great
annoyance to honest Christopher, and is ever treated by him
with sovereign contempt, as an upstart intruder. It is a common observation of his, that your old-fashioned substantial
furniture bespeaks the respectability of one's ancestors, and
indicates that the family has been used to hold up its head for
more than the present generation; whereas the fragile appen-
dages of modern style seemed to be emblems of mushroom
gentility, and to his mind predicted that the family dignity
would moulder away and vanish with the finery thus put on
of a sudden. The same whim-wham makes him averse to having his house surrounded with poplars, which he stigmatizes
as mere upstarts, just fit to ornament the shingle palaces of
modern gentry, and characteristick of the establishments they
decorate. Indeed, so far does he carry his veneration for all
the antique trumpery, that he can scarcely see the venerable
dust brushed from its resting place on the old-fashioned testers, or a grey-bearded spider dislodged from his antient inheritance, without groaning; and I once saw him in a
transport of passion, on Jeremy's knocking down a moulder-

ing martin-coop with his tennis-ball, which had been set up in the latter days of my grandfather. Another object of his peculiar affection is an old english cherry-tree, which leans against a corner of the hall, and whether the house supports it, or it supports the house, would be, I believe, a question of some difficulty to decide.

It is held sacred by friend Christopher, because he planted and reared it himself, and had once well nigh broke his neck, by a fall from one of its branches. This is one of his favourite stories; and there is reason to believe, that if the tree was out of the way, the old gentleman would forget the whole affair—which would be a great pity. The old tree has long since ceased bearing, and is exceedingly infirm—every tempest robs it of a limb, and one would suppose, from the lamentations of my old friend, on such occasions, that he had lost one of his own. He often contemplates it in a half-melancholy, half-moralizing humour—"together" he says "have we flourished, and together shall we wither away—a few years, and both our heads will be laid low; and, perhaps my mouldering bones, may one day or other, mingle with the dust of the tree I have planted." He often fancies, he says, that it rejoices to see him when he revisits the hall, and that its leaves assume a brighter verdure, as if to welcome his arrival. How whimsically are our tenderest feelings assailed! At one time the old tree had obtruded a withered branch before miss Barbara's window, and she desired her father to order the gardener to saw it off. I shall never forget the old man's answer, and the look that accompanied it. "What" cried he, "lop off the limbs of my cherry tree in its old age?—why do you not cut off the grey locks of your poor old father?"

Do my readers yawn at this long family detail?—they are welcome to throw down our work, and never resume it again. I have no care for such ungratified spirits, and will not throw away a thought on one of them—full often have I contributed to their amusement, and have I not a right for once to consult my own? Who is there that does not fondly turn at times, to linger round those scenes which were once the haunt of his boyhood ere his heart grew heavy, and his head waxed grey—and to dwell with fond affection on the friends who have twined themselves round his heart—mingled in all his enjoyments—contributed to all his felicities? If there be any, who cannot relish these enjoyments, let them despair—for they have been so soiled in their intercourse with the world, as to be incapable of tasting some of the purest pleasures, that survive the happy period of youth.

To such as have not yet lost the rural feeling, I address this simple family picture—and in the honest sincerity of a warm heart, I invite them to turn aside from bustle, care and toil, to tarry with me for a season in the hospitable mansion of the Cocklofts.

I was really apprehensive, on reading the following effusion of Will Wizard, that he still retained that pestilent hankering after *puns* of which we lately convicted him. He however declares, that he is fully authorized by the example of the most popular cricks and wits of the present age, whose manner and matter he has closely, and he flatters himself, successfully, copied in the subsequent essay.

THEATRICAL INTELLIGENCE.
BY WILLIAM WIZARD, ESQ.

The uncommon healthiness of the season (occasioned, as several learned physicians assure me, by the universal prevalence of the influenza) has encouraged the chieftain of our dramatick corps to marshal his forces, and commence the campaign at a much earlier day than usual. He has been induced to take the field thus suddenly, I am told, by the invasion of certain foreign marauders, who pitched their tents at Vauxhall-Garden during the warm months, and taking advantage of his army being disbanded and dispersed in *summer quarters*, committed sad depredations upon the borders of his territories—carrying off a considerable portion of his winter harvest, and *murdering* some of his most distinguished characters.

It is true, these hardy invaders have been reduced to great extremity by the late heavy rains, which injured and destroyed much of their camp equipage, besides spoiling the best part of their wardrobe. Two cities, a triumphal car, and a new moon for Cinderella, together with the barber's boy, who was employed every night to powder and make it shine white, have been entirely washed away, and the sea has become very wet and mouldy, insomuch that great apprehensions are entertained that it will never be dry enough for use. Add to this, the noble county Paris had the misfortune to tear his corduroy breeches in the scuffle with Romeo (by reason of the tomb being very wet, which occasioned him to slip) and he, and his noble rival, possessing but one poor pair of sattin ones between them, were reduced to considerable shifts to keep up the dignity of their respective houses. In spite of these disadvantages, and untoward circumstances, they continued to enact most intrepidly, performing with much ease and confidence, inasmuch as they were seldom pestered with an audience to criticise and put them out of countenance. It is rumored that the last heavy shower has absolutely *dissolved* the company, and that our manager has nothing further to apprehend from that quarter.

The theatre opened on Wednesday last with great *eclat*, (as we criticks say) and almost vied in brilliancy with that of my superb friend Consequa in Canton, where the castles were all ivory, the sea mother of pearl, the skies gold and silver leaf, and the outside of the boxes *inlaid* with scallop shell-work. Those who want a better description of the theatre, may as well go and see it, and then they can judge for themselves. For the gratification of a highly respectable class of readers, who love to see every thing on paper, I had indeed prepared a circumstantial and truly incomprehensible account of it, such as your traveller always fills his book with, and which I defy the most intelligent architect, even the great sir Christopher Wren, to understand. I had jumbled cornices, and pilasters, and pillars, and capitals, and trigliphs, and modules, and plinths, and volutes, and perspectives, and fore-shortenings, helter-skelter, and had set all the orders of architecture, doric, ionic, corinthian, &c. together by the ears, in order to work out a satisfactory description; but the manager, having sent me a polite note, requesting that I would not take off the sharp edge (as he whimsically expresses it) of publick curiosity, thereby diminishing the receipts of his house, I have willingly consented to oblige him, and have left my description at the store of our publisher, where any person may see it—provided he applies at a proper hour.

I cannot refrain here from giving vent to the satisfaction I received from the excellent performances of the different actors, one and all, and particularly the gentlemen who shifted the scenes, who acquitted themselves throughout with great celerity, dignity, pathos, and effect. Nor must I pass over the peculiar merits of my friend JOHN, who gallanted off the chairs and tables in the most dignified and circumspect manner. Indeed I have had frequent occasion to applaud the correctness with which this gentleman fulfills the parts allotted him, and consider him as one of the best general performers in the company. My friend the cockney, who Evergreen whimsically dubs my *Tender,* found considerable fault with the manner in which *John* shoved a huge rock from behind the scenes, maintaining that he should have put his left foot forward, and pushed it with his right hand, that being the method practised by his contemporaries of the royal theatres, and universally approved by their best criticks. He also took exception to *John's* coat, which he pronounced too short by a foot at least—particularly when he turned his back to the company. But I look upon these objections in the same light as new readings, and insist that *John* shall be allowed to manoeuvre his chairs and tables, shove his rocks, and wear his skirts in that style which his genius best effects. My hopes in the rising merit of this *favourite actor* daily increase; and I would hint to the manager the propriety of giving him a benefit, advertising in the usual style of play-bills, as a "springe to catch woodcocks," that between the play and farce *John* will MAKE A BOW—for that night only!

I am told that no pains have been spared to make the exhibitions of this season as splendid as possible. Several expert rat-catchers have been sent into different parts of the country to catch white mice for the grand pantomime of CINDER-ELLA. A nest full of little squab Cupids have been taken in the neighbourhood of Communipaw; they are as yet but half fledged, of the true *Holland* breed, and it is hoped will be able to fly about by the middle of October; otherwise they will be suspended about the stage by the waistband, like little alligators in an apothecaries shop, as the pantomime must positively be performed by that time. Great pains and expense have been incurred in the importation of one of the most portly pumpkins in New-England; and the publick may be assured there is now one on board a vessel from New-Haven, which will contain Cinderella's coach and six with perfect ease, were the white mice even ten times as large.

Also several barrels of hail, rain, brimstone, and gunpowder are in store for *melo-drames*, of which a number are to be played off this winter. It is furthermore whispered me that the great *thunder drum* has been new braced, and an expert performer on that instrument engaged, who will thunder in plain english, so as to be understood by the most illiterate hearer. This will be infinitely preferable to the miserable italian thunderer employed last winter by mr. Ciceri, who performed in such an unnatural and outlandish tongue, that none but the scholars of Signior Da Ponte could understand him. It will be a further gratification to the patriotic audience to know that the present thunderer is a fellow countryman, born at Dunderbarrack, among the echoes of the highlands—and that he thunders with peculiar emphasis and pompous enunciation, in the true style of a fourth of July orator.

In addition to all these additions, the manager has provided an entire new snow-storm the very sight of which will be quite sufficient to draw a shawl over every naked bosom in the theatre—the snow is perfectly fresh having been manufactured last August.

N. B. The outside of the theatre has been ornamented with a new chimney!!

SALMAGUNDI NO. XV

Thursday, October 1, 1807.

SKETCHES FROM NATURE.
BY ANTHONY EVERGREEN, GENT.

THE BRISK NORTH-WESTERS which prevailed not long since, had a powerful effect in arresting the progress of belles, beaux and wild-pigeons, in their fashionable northern tour, and turning them back to the more balmy region of the south. Among the rest I was encountered, full butt, by a blast, which set my teeth chattering, just as I doubled one of the frowning bluffs of the Mohawk mountains, in my route to Niagara, and facing about incontinently, I forthwith scud before the wind, and a few days since arrived at my old quarters in New-York. My first care on returning from so long an absence, was to visit the worthy family of the Cocklofts, whom I found safe burrowed in their country mansion. On inquiring for my highly respected coadjutor, Langstaff, I learned with great concern that he had relapsed into one of his eccentrick fits of the spleen, ever since the era of a turtle dinner, given by old Cockloft to some of the neighbouring squires, wherein the old gentleman had achieved a glorious victory in laying honest Launcelot fairly under the table. Langstaff, although fond of the social board and cheerful glass, yet abominates any excess, and has an invincible aversion to *getting mellow*, considering it a wilful outrage on the sanctity of imperial *mind*, a senseless abuse of the body, and an unpardonable, because a voluntary, prostration of both mental and personal dignity. I have heard him moralize on the subject, in a style that would have done honour to Michael Cassio himself; but I believe, if the truth were known, this antipathy rather arises from his having, as the phrase is, but a weak head, and nerves so extremely sensitive, that he is sure to suffer severely from a frolick, and will groan and make resolutions against it for a week afterwards. He therefore took this waggish exploit of old Christopher's, and the consequent quizzing which he underwent, in high dudgeon, had kept aloof from company for a fortnight, and appeared to be meditating some deep plan of retaliation upon his mischievous old crony. He had, however, for the last day or two, shown some symptoms of convalescence; had listened, without more than half a dozen twitches of impatience, to one of Christopher's unconscionable long stories, and even was seen to smile, for the one hundred and thirtieth time, at a venerable joke, originally borrowed from Joe Miller; but which by dint of long occupancy, and frequent repetition, the old gentleman now firmly believes happened to himself somewhere in New-England.

As I am well acquainted with Launcelot's haunts, I soon found him out. He was lolling on his favourite bench rudely constructed at the foot of an old tree, which is full of fantastical twists, and with its spreading branches forms a canopy of luxuriant foliage. This tree is a kind of chronicle of the short reigns of his uncle John's mistresses, and its trunk is sorely wounded with carvings of true lovers knots, hearts, darts, names, and inscriptions—frail memorials of the variety of fair dames who captivated the wandering fancy of that old cavalier in the days of his youthful romance. Launcelot holds this tree in particular regard, as he does every thing else connected with the memory of his good uncle John. He was reclining, in one of his usual brown studies, against its trunk, and gazing pensively upon the river that glided just by, washing the drooping branches of the dwarf willows that fringed its bank. My appearance roused him—he grasped my hand with his usual warmth, and with a tremulous but close pressure, which spoke that his heart entered into the salutation. After a number of affectionate inquiries and felicitations, such as friendship, not form, dictated, he seemed to relapse into his former flow of thought, and to resume the chain of ideas my appearance had broken for a moment.

"I was reflecting," said he, "my dear Anthony, upon some observations I made in our last number, and considering whether the sight of objects once dear to the affections, or of scenes where we have passed different happy periods of early life, really occasions most enjoyment or most regret. Renewing our acquaintance with well-known but long separated objects, revives, it is true, the recollection of former pleasures and touches the tenderest feelings of the heart, like the flavour of a delicious beverage will remain upon the palate long after the cup has parted from the lips. But on the other hand, my friend, these same objects are too apt to awaken us to a keener recollection of what *we were*, when they erst delighted us, and to provoke a mortifying and melancholy contrast with what we are at present. They act in a manner as milestones of existence, showing us how far we have travelled in the journey of life—how much of our weary but fascinating pilgrimage is accomplished. I look round me, and my eye fondly recognizes the fields I once sported over, the river in which I once swam, and the orchard I intrepidly robbed in the halcyon days of boyhood. The fields are still green, the river still rolls unaltered and undiminished, and the orchard is still flourishing and fruitful—it is I only am changed. The thoughtless flow of mad-cap spirits that nothing could depress—the elasticity of nerve that enabled me to bound over the field, to stem the stream, and climb the tree—the "sunshine of the breast" that beamed an illusive charm over every object, and created a paradise around me—where are they?—The thievish lapse of years has stolen them away, and left in return nothing but grey hairs, and a repining spirit." My friend Launcelot concluded his harangue with a sigh, and as I saw he was still under the influence of a whole legion of the *blues,* and just on the point of sinking into one of his whimsical, and unreasonable fits of melancholy abstraction, I proposed a walk—he consented, and slipping his left arm in mine, and waving in the other a gold-headed thorn cane, bequeathed him by his uncle John, we slowly rambled along the margin of the river.

Langstaff, though possessing great vivacity of temper, is most woefully subject to these "thick coming fancies;" and I do not know a man whose animal spirits do insult him with more jiltings, and coquetries, and slippery tricks. In these moods he is often visited by a whim-wham which he indulges in common with the Cocklofts. It is that of looking back with regret, conjuring up the phantoms of good old times, and decking them out in imaginary finery, with the spoils of his fancy, like a good lady widow, regretting the loss of the "poor dear man," for whom, while living, she cared not a rush. I have seen him and Pindar, and old Cockloft, amuse them-

selves over a bottle with their youthful days, until by the time
they had become what is termed *merry*, they were the most
miserable beings in existence. In a similar humour was Launcelot at present, and I knew the only way was to let him moralize himself out of it.

Our ramble was soon interrupted by the appearance of a
personage of no little importance at Cockloft-hall—for, to let
my readers into a family secret, friend Christopher is notoriously hen-pecked by an old negro, who has *whitened* on the
place, and is his master's almanack and counsellor. My readers, if haply they have sojourned in the country and become
conversant in rural manners, must have observed, that there
is scarce a little hamlet but has one of these old weatherbeaten wiseacres of negroes, who ranks among the great characters of the place. He is always resorted to as an oracle to
resolve any question about the weather, fishing, shooting,
farming and horse-doctoring; and on such occasions will
slouch his remnant of a hat on one side, fold his arms, roll
his white eyes and examine the sky, with a look as knowing
as Peter Pindar's magpie, when peeping into a marrow-bone.
Such a sage curmudgeon is *Old Caesar*, who acts as friend
Cockloft's prime minister, or grand vizier, assumes, when
abroad, his master's style and title, to wit, *Squire Cockloft*, and
is, in effect, absolute lord and ruler of the soil.

As he passed us, he pulled off his hat, with an air of something more than respect,—it partook, I thought, of affection.
"There, now, is another memento of the kind I have been
noticing," said Launcelot; "Caesar was a bosom friend and
chosen playmate of cousin Pindar and myself, when we were
boys. Never were we so happy as when stealing away on a
holiday to the hall, we ranged about the fields with honest
Caesar. He was particularly adroit in making our quail-traps
and fishing rods, was always the ring-leader in all the schemes
of frolicksome mischief perpetrated by the urchins of the
neighbourhood, considered himself on an equality with the
best of us, and many a hard battle have I had with him, about
a division of the spoils of an orchard, or the title to a bird's
nest. Many a summer evening do I remember when, huddled
together on the steps of the hall door, Caesar, with his stories
of ghosts, goblins, and witches, would put us all in a panick,

and people every lane, and church-yard, and solitary wood, with imaginary beings. In process of time, he became the constant attendant and *Man Friday* of cousin Pindar, whenever he went a *sparking* among the rosy country girls of the neighbouring farms; and brought up his rear at every rustick dance, when he would mingle in the sable group that always thronged the door of merriment, and it was enough to put to the rout a host of splenetick imps, to see his mouth gradually dilate from ear to ear, with pride and exultation, at seeing how neatly master Pindar footed it over the floor. Caesar was likewise the chosen confidant and special agent of Pindar in all his love affairs, until, as his evil stars would have it, on being entrusted with the delivery of a poetick billetdoux, to one of his patron's sweethearts, he took an unlucky notion to send it to his own sable dulcinea, who, not being able to read it, took it to her mistress—and so the whole affair was blown; Pindar was universally roasted, and Caesar discharged forever from his confidence.

"Poor Caesar!—he has now grown old like his young masters; but he still remembers old times, and will, now and then, remind me of them as he lights me to my room, and lingers a little while to bid me a good night—believe me, my dear Evergreen, the honest simple old creature has a warm corner in my heart—I dont see, for my part, why a body may not like a negro, as well as a white man!"

By the time these biographical anecdotes were ended, we had reached the stable, into which we involuntarily strolled, and found Caesar busily employed in rubbing down the horses, an office he would not entrust to any body else; having contracted an affection for every beast in the stable, from their being descendants of the old race of animals, his youthful contemporaries. Caesar was very particular in giving us their pedigrees, together with a panegyrick on the swiftness, bottom, blood, and spirit of their sires. From these he digressed into a variety of anecdotes in which Launcelot bore a conspicuous part, and on which the old negro dwelt with all the garrulity of age. Honest Langstaff stood leaning with his arm over the back of his favorite steed, old *Killdeer*, and I could perceive he listened to Caesar's simple details with that fond attention with which a feeling mind will hang over the narratives of boyish days. His eye sparkled with animation, a glow of youthful fire stole across his pale visage—he nodded with smiling approbation at every sentence—chuckled at every exploit—laughed heartily at the story of his once having smoked out a country singing-school with brimstone and assafoetida—and slipping a piece of money into old Caesar's hand to buy himself a new tobacco-box, he seized me by the arm and hurried out of the stable brimfull of good nature. "Tis a pestilent old rogue for talking, my dear fellow," cried he, "but you must not find fault with him—the creature means well." I knew at the very moment that he made this apology, honest Caesar could not have given him half the satisfaction, had he talked like a Cicero or a Solomon.

Launcelot returned to the house with me in the best possible humour:—the whole family, who in truth love and honour him from their very souls, were delighted to see the sunbeams once more play in his countenance. Every one seemed to vie who should talk the most, tell the longest stories and be most agreeable; and Will Wizard, who had accompanied me in my visit, declared, as he lighted his cygarr, which had gone out forty times in the course of one of his oriental tales—that he had not passed so pleasant an evening since the birth-night ball of the beauteous empress of Hayti.

[The following essay was written by my friend Langstaff, in one of the paroxysms of his splenetick complaint; and, for aught I know, may have been effectual in restoring him to good humour—A mental discharge of the kind has a remarkable tendency toward sweetening the temper—and Launcelot is at this moment one of the best natured men in existence.

                                        A. EVERGREEN.]

ON GREATNESS.
BY LAUNCELOT LANGSTAFF, ESQ.
————'Αχιλλεδς ωρτο.
THE HERO ROSE.   *Pope*.

We have, more than once in the course of our work, been most jocosely familiar with great personages; and, in truth, treated them with as little ceremony, respect, and consideration, as if they had been our most particular friends. Now, we would not suffer the mortification of having our readers even suspect us of an intimacy of the kind; assuring them we are extremely choice in our intimates, and uncommonly circumspect in avoiding connexion with all doubtful characters, particularly pimps, bailiffs, lottery-brokers, chevaliers of industry, and *great men*. The world in general is pretty well aware of what is to be understood by the former classes of delinquents; but as the latter has never, I believe, been specifically defined, and as we are determined to instruct our readers to the extent of our abilities, and their limited comprehension, it may not be amiss here, to let them know what we understand by a *great man*.

First, therefore, let us (editors and kings are always plural) premise, that there are two kinds of greatness—one conferred by *heaven*—the exalted nobility of the soul—the other, a spurious distinction engendered by the mob, and lavished upon its favourites. The former of these distinctions we have always contemplated with reverence; the latter, we will take this opportunity to strip naked before our unenlightened readers: so that if by chance any of them are held in ignominious thraldom by this base circulation of false coin, they may forthwith emancipate themselves from such inglorious delusion.

It is a fictitious value given to individuals by publick caprice, as bankers give an impression to a worthless slip of paper, thereby gaining it a currency for infinitely more than its intrinsick value. Every nation has its peculiar coin, and peculiar great men; neither of which will, for the most part, pass current out of the country where they are stamped. Your true mob-created great man, is like a note of one of the little New-England banks, and his value depreciates in proportion to the distance from home. In England, a great man is he who has most ribbonds and gew-gaws on his coat, most horses to his carriage, most slaves in his retinue, or most toad-eaters at his table; in France, he who can most dexterously flourish his heels above his head—*Duport* is most incontestably the greatest man in France, when the emperor is absent. The greatest man in China, is he who can trace his ancestry up to the moon; and in this country our great men may generally *hunt down* their pedigree until it burrows into the dirt like a rabbit. To be concise, our great men are those who are most expert at crawling on all-fours, and have the happiest facility in dragging and winding themselves along in the dirt like very reptiles. This may seem a paradox to many of my readers, who, with great good nature be it hinted, are too stupid to look beyond the mere surface of our invaluable writings, and often pass over the knowing allusion, and poignant meaning, that is slily couching beneath. It is for the benefit of such helpless ignorants, who have no other creed but the opinion of the mob, that I shall trace, as far as it is possible to follow him in his progress from insignificance—the rise, progress, and completion of a LITTLE GREAT MAN.

In a *logocracy* (to use the sage Mustapha's phrase) it is not absolutely necessary to the formation of a great man, that he should be either wise or valiant, upright, or honourable. On the contrary, daily experience shows, that these qualities rather impede his preferment; inasmuch as they are prone to render him too inflexibly erect, and are directly at variance with that willowy *suppleness*, which enables a man to wind and twist through all the nooks and turns, and dark winding passages that lead to greatness. The grand requisite for climbing the rugged hill of popularity—the summit of which is the seat of power—is to be useful. And here once more, for the sake of our readers, who are of course not so wise as ourselves, I must explain what we understand by *usefulness*. The horse, in his native state, is wild, swift, impetuous, full of majesty, and of a most generous spirit. It is then the animal is noble, exalted, and *useless*. But entrap him, manacle him, cudgel him, break down his lofty spirit, put the curb into his mouth, the load upon his back, and reduce him into servile obedience to the bridle and the lash, and it is then he becomes *useful*. Your jackass is one of the most *useful* animals in existence. If my readers do not now understand what I mean by usefulness, I give them all up for most absolute *nincoms*.

To rise in this country a man must first *descend*. The aspiring politician, may be compared to that indefatigable insect, called the *Tumbler*; (pronounced by a distinguished personage to be the only industrious animal in Virginia,) which buries itself in filth, and works ignobly in the dirt until it forms a little ball, which it rolls laboriously along, (like Diogenes his tub) sometimes head, sometimes tail foremost, pilfering from every rut and mud hole, and increasing its ball of greatness by the contributions of the kennel. Just so the candidate for greatness—he plunges into that mass of obscenity the *mob*, labours in dirt and oblivion, and makes unto himself the rudiments of a popular name from the admiration and praises of rogues, ignoramuses and blackguards. His name once started, onward he goes, struggling, and puffing, and pushing it before him, collecting new tributes from the dregs and offals of the land, as he proceeds, until having gathered together a mighty mass of popularity, he mounts it in triumph, is hoisted into office, and becomes a *great man*, and a ruler in the land—all this will be clearly illustrated by a sketch of a worthy of the kind, who sprung up under my eye, and was hatched from pollution by the broad rays of popularity, which, like the sun, can "breed maggots in a dead dog."

TIMOTHY DABBLE was a young man of very promising talents—for he wrote a fair hand, and had thrice won the silver medal at a country academy—he was also an orator, for he talked with emphatick volubility, and could argue a full hour, without taking either side, or advancing a single opinion—he had still farther requisites for eloquence—for he made very handsome gestures, had dimples in his cheeks when he smiled, and enunciated most harmoniously through his nose. In short, nature had certainly marked him out for a great man; for though he was not tall, yet he added at least half an inch to his stature by elevating his head, and assumed an amazing expression of dignity by turning up his nose and curling his nostrils, in a style of conscious superiority. Convinced by these unequivocal appearances, Dabble's friends in full caucus, one and all, declared that he was undoubtedly born to be a great man, and it would be his own fault if he were not one. Dabble was tickled with an opinion which coincided so happily with his own—for vanity, in a confidential whisper, had given him the like intimation—and he reverenced the judgment of his friends, because they thought so highly of himself—accordingly he sat out with a determination to become a great man, and to start in the scrub-race for

honour and renown. How to attain the desired prizes was
however the question. He knew by a kind of instinctive feeling, which seems peculiar to grovelling minds, that honour,
and its better part—profit, would never seek *him* out; that
they would never knock at his door and crave admittance, but
must be courted, and toiled after, and *earned*. He therefore
strutted forth into the highways, the market-places, and the
assemblies of the people—ranted like a true cockerel orator
about virtue, and patriotism, and liberty, and equality, and
himself. Full many a political wind-mill did he battle with;
and full many a time did he talk himself out of breath and his
hearers out of their patience. But Dabble found to his vast
astonishment, that there was not a notorious political pimp at
a ward meeting but could out-talk him; and what was still
more mortifying, there was not a notorious political pimp,
but was more noticed and caressed than himself. The reason
was simple enough, while he harangued about *principles*, the
others ranted about *men*; where he reprobated a political error, they blasted a political character—they were, consequently, the most *useful*: for the great object of our political
disputes is, not who shall have the *honour* of emancipating
the community from the leading-strings of delusion, but who
shall have the *profit* of holding the strings, and leading the
community by the nose.

Dabble was likewise very loud in his professions of integrity, incorruptibility, and disinterestedness, words which,
from being filtered and refined through newspapers and election handbills, have lost their original signification, and in the
political dictionary, are synonymous with empty pockets,
itching palms, and interested ambition. He, in addition to all
this, declared that he would support none but honest men—
but unluckily as but few of these offered themselves to be
supported, Dabble's services were seldom required. He
pledged himself never to engage in party schemes or party
politicks, but to stand up solely for the broad interests of his
country—so he stood alone, and what is the same thing, he
stood still; for, in this country, he who does not side with
either party, is like a body in a *vacuum* between two planets,
and must for ever remain motionless.

Dabble was immeasurably surprised that a man so honest,

so disinterested, and so sagacious withal—and one too, who had the good of his country so much at heart, should thus remain unnoticed and unapplauded. A little worldly advice whispered in his ear by a shrewd old politician, at once explained the whole mystery. "He who would become great," said he, "must serve an apprenticeship to greatness, and rise by regular gradation, like the master of a vessel, who commences by being scrub and cabin-boy. He must fag in the train of great men, echo all their sentiments, become their toad-eater and parasite—laugh at all their jokes, and above all, endeavour to make *them* laugh; if you only now and then make a great man laugh your fortune is made. Look but about you, youngster, and you will not see a single little great man of the day, but has his miserable herd of retainers, who yelp at his heels, come at his whistle, worry whoever he points his finger at, and think themselves fully rewarded by sometimes snapping up a crumb that falls from the great man's table. Talk of patriotism and virtue, and incorruptibility!—tut, man!—they are the very qualities that scare munificence, and keep patronage at a distance. You might as well attempt to entice crows with red rags and gunpowder. Lay all these scarecrow virtues aside, and let this be your maxim, that a candidate for political eminence is like a dried herring—he never becomes *luminous* until he is *corrupt*."

Dabble caught with hungry avidity these congenial doctrines, and turned into his pre-destined channel of action with the force and rapidity of a stream which has for awhile been restrained from its natural course. He became what nature had fitted him to be—his tone softened down from arrogant self-sufficiency, to the whine of fawning solicitation. He mingled in the *caucuses* of the sovereign people, adapted his dress to a similitude of dirty raggedness, argued most logically with those who were of his own opinion, and slandered with all the malice of impotence, exalted characters whose orbit he despaired ever to approach—just as that scoundred midnight thief, the owl, hoots at the blessed light of the sun, whose glorious lustre he dares never contemplate. He likewise applied himself to discharging faithfully the honourable duties of a partizan—he poached about for private slanders, and ribald anecdotes—he folded handbills—he even wrote one or two himself, which he carried about in his pocket and read to every body—he became a secretary at ward-meetings, set his hand to divers resolutions of patriotick import, and even once went so far as to make a speech, in which he proved that patriotism was a virtue—the *reigning bashaw* a great man—that this was a free country, and he himself an arrant and incontestible buzzard!

Dabble was now very frequent and devout in his visits to those temple of politicks, popularity and smoke, the ward porter-houses; those true dens of equality, where all ranks, ages, and talents, are brought down to the dead level of rude familiarity. 'Twas here his talents expanded, and his genius swelled up into its proper size, like the loathsome toad, which shrinking from balmy airs, and jocund sunshine, finds his congenial home in caves and dungeons, and there nourishes his venom, and bloats his deformity. 'Twas here he revelled with the swinish multitude in their debauches on patriotism and porter; and it became an even chance whether Dabble would turn out a great man, or a great drunkard. But Dabble in all this kept steadily in his eye the only deity he ever worshipped—his interest. Having by this familiarity ingratiated himself with the mob, he became wonderfully potent and industrious at elections, knew all the dens and cellars of profligacy and intemperance, brought more negroes to the polls, and knew to a greater certainty where votes could be bought for beer, than any of his contemporaries. His exertions in the cause, his persevering industry, his degrading compliance, his unresisting humility, his steadfast dependence, at length caught the attention of one of the leaders of the party, who was pleased to observe that Dabble was a very *useful* fellow, who would *go all lengths*. From that moment his fortune was made—he was hand and glove with orators and slang-whangers, basked in the sunshine of great mens' smiles, and had the honour, sundry times, of shaking hands with dignitaries, and drinking out of the same pot with them at a porterhouse!!

I will not fatigue myself with tracing this catterpillar in his slimy progress from worm to butterfly: suffice it to say that Dabble bowed and bowed, and fawned, and sneaked, and smirked, and libelled, until one would have thought perseverence itself would have settled down into despair. There was no knowing how long he might have lingered at a distance from his hopes, had he not luckily got *tarred and feathered* for some of his electioneering manoeuvres—this was the making of him!—Let not my readers stare—tarring and feathering here is equal to pillory and cropped ears in England, and either of these kinds of martyrdom will ensure a *patriot* the sympathy and support of his faction. His partizans (for even he had his partizans) took his case into consideration—he had been kicked and cuffed, and disgraced, and dishonoured in the cause—he had licked the dust at the feet of the mob—he was a faithful drudge, slow to anger, of invincible patience, of incessant assiduity—a thorough going tool, who could be curbed, and spurred, and directed at pleasure;—in short he had all the important qualifications for *a little great man*, and he was accordingly ushered into office amid the acclamations of the party. The leading men complimented his usefulness, the multitude his republican simplicity, and the slang-whangers vouched for his patriotism. Since his elevation he has discovered indubitable signs of having been destined for a great man. His nose has acquired an additional elevation of several degrees, so that now he appears to have bidden adieu to this world, and to have set his thoughts altogether *on things above*; and he has swelled and inflated himself to such a degree that his friends are under apprehensions that he will one day or other explode and blow up like a *torpedo*.

SALMAGUNDI NO. XVI

Thursday, October 15, 1807.

STYLE AT BALLSTON.
BY WILLIAM WIZARD, ESQ.

NOTWITHSTANDING Evergreen has never been abroad, nor had his understanding enlightened, or his views enlarged by that marvellous sharpener of the wits, a salt-water voyage; yet he is tolerably shrewd, and correct, in the limited sphere of his observations; and now and then astounds me with a right pithy remark, which would do no discredit even to a man who had made the grand tour.

In several late conversations at Cockloft-Hall, he has amused us exceedingly by detailing sundry particulars concerning that notorious slaughter-house of time, Ballston Springs, where he spent a considerable part of the last summer. The following is a summary of his observations.

Pleasure has passed through a variety of significations at Ballston. It originally meant nothing more than a relief from pain and sickness; and the patient who had journeyed many a weary mile to the Springs, with a heavy heart, and emaciated form, called it pleasure when he threw by his crutches, and danced away from them with renovated spirits and limbs jocund with vigour. In process of time pleasure underwent a refinement and appeared in the likeness of a sober unceremonious country-dance, to the flute of an amateur, or the three-stringed fiddle of an itinerant country musician. Still every thing bespoke that happy holiday which the spirits ever enjoy, when emancipated from the shackles of formality, ceremony and modern politeness: things went on cheerily, and Ballston was pronounced a charming hum-drum careless place of resort, where every one was at his ease, and might follow unmolested the bent of his humour—provided his wife was not there—when, lo! all of a sudden *Style* made its baneful appearance in the semblance of a gig and tandem, a pair of leather breeches, a liveried footman and a cockney!—since that fatal era pleasure has taken an entire new signification, and at present means nothing but STYLE.

286

The worthy, fashionable, dashing, good-for-nothing people of every state, who had rather suffer the martyrdom of a crowd, than endure the monotony of their own homes, and the stupid company of their own thoughts, flock to the Springs—not to enjoy the pleasures of society, or benefit by the qualities of the waters, but to exhibit their equipages and wardrobes, and to excite the admiration, or what is much more satisfactory, the *envy* of their fashionable competitors. This of course awakens a spirit of noble emulation between the eastern, middle and southern states, and every lady hereupon finding herself charged in a manner with the whole weight of her country's dignity and *style*, dresses, and dashes, and sparkles without mercy, at her competitors from other parts of the union. This kind of rivalship naturally requires a vast deal of preparation and prodigious quantities of supplies. A sober citizen's wife will break half a dozen milliners' shops, and sometimes starve her family a whole season, to enable herself to make the Springs campaign in *style*—she repairs to the seat of war with a mighty force of trunks and bandboxes, like so many ammunition chests, filled with caps, hats, gowns, ribbons, shawls, and all the various artillery of fashionable warfare. The lady of a southern planter will lay out the whole annual produce of a rice plantation in silver and gold muslins, lace veils, and new liveries, carry a hogshead of tobacco on her head, and trail a bale of sea-island cotton at her heels— while a lady of Boston or Salem will wrap herself up in the nett proceeds of a cargo of whale oil, and tie on her hat with a quintal of codfish.

The planters' ladies, however, have generally the advantage in this contest; for, as it is an incontestable fact, that whoever comes from the West or East Indies, or Georgia, or the Carolinas, or in fact any warm climate, is immensely rich, it cannot be expected that a simple cit of the north can cope with them in *style*. The planter, therefore, who drives four horses abroad, and a thousand negroes at home, and who flourishes up to the Springs followed by half a score of black-a-moors in gorgeous liveries, is unquestionably superiour to the northern merchant, who plods on in a carriage and pair; which being nothing more than is quite *necessary*, has no claim whatever to *style*. He, however, has his consolation in feeling superiour to the honest cit, who dashes about in a simple gig—he in return sneers at the country squire, who jogs along with his scrubby long-eared poney and saddle bags; and the squire, by way of taking satisfaction, would make no scruple to run over the unobtrusive pedestrian, were it not that the last, being the most independent of the whole, might chance to break his head by way of retort.

The great misfortune is, that this *style* is supported at such an expense as sometimes to encroach on the rights and privileges of the pocket, and occasion very awkward embarrassments to the tyro of fashion. Among a number of instances, Evergreen mentions the fate of a dashing blade from the south, who made his *entré* with a tandem and two outriders, by the aid of which he attracted the attention of all the ladies, and caused a coolness between several young couples, who, it was thought before his arrival, had a considerable kindness for each other. In the course of a fortnight his tandem disappeared!—the class of good folk who seem to have nothing to do in this world but pry into other people's affairs—began to stare!—in a little time longer an outrider was missing—this increased the alarm, and it was consequently whispered that he had eaten the horses, and drank the negro—(N. B. Southern gentlemen are very apt to do this on an emergency.)— Serious apprehensions were entertained about the fate of the remaining servant, which were soon verified, by his actually vanishing—and in "one little month" the dashing carolinian modestly took his departure in the *Stage-Coach!*—universally regretted by the friends who had generously released him from his cumbrous load of *style*.

Evergreen, in the course of his detail, gave very melancholy accounts of an alarming famine which raged with great violence at the Springs. Whether this was owing to the incredible appetites of the company, or the scarcity which prevailed at the inns, he did not seem inclined to say, but he declares, that he was for several days in imminent danger of starvation, owing to his being a little too dilatory in his attendance at the dinner-table. He relates a number of "moving accidents," which befel many of the polite company in their zeal to get a good seat at dinner, on which occasion a kind of scrub-race always took place, wherein a vast deal of jockeying and unfair

play was shown, and a variety of squabbles and unseemly altercations occurred. But when arrived at the scene of action,
it was truly an awful sight to behold the confusion, and to
hear the tumultuous uproar of voices crying out, some for
one thing, and some for another, to the tuneful accompany-
ment of knives and forks, rattling with all the energy of hungry impatience.—The feast of the Centaurs and the Lapithae
was nothing when compared with a dinner at the *Great
House*. At one time, an old gentleman, whose natural irasci-
bility was a little sharpened by the gout, had scalded his
throat, by gobbling down a bowl of hot soup in a vast hurry,
in order to secure the first fruits of a roasted partridge, before
it was snapped up by some hungry rival; when, just as he was
whetting his knife and fork preparatory for a descent on the
promised land, he had the mortification to see it transferred,
bodily, to the plate of a squeamish little damsel, who was
taking the waters for debility and loss of appetite. This was
too much for the patience of old Crusty; he longed his fork
into the partridge, whipt it into his dish, and cutting off a
wing of it,—"There, miss, there's more than you can eat—
Oons! what should such a little chalky-faced puppet as you
do with a whole partridge!"—At another time a mighty
sweet disposed old dowager, who loomed most magnificently
at the table, had a sauce-boat launched upon the capacious
lap of a silver-sprigged muslin gown, by the manoeuvring of
a little politick frenchman, who was dexterously attempting
to make a lodgement under the covered way of a chicken-
pie—Human nature could not bear it!—the lady bounced
round, and, with one box on the ear, drove the luckless wight
to utter annihilation.

But these little cross accidents are amply compensated by
the great variety of amusements which abounds at this charming resort of beauty and fashion. In the morning the company, each like a jolly bacchanalian, with glass in hand, sally
forth to the Spring; where the gentlemen, who wish to make
themselves agreeable, have an opportunity of *dipping* themselves into the good opinion of the ladies: and it is truly delectable to see with what grace and adroitness they perform
this ingratiating feat. Anthony says that it is peculiarly amazing to behold the quantity of water the ladies drink on this

occasion, for the purpose of getting an appetite for breakfast. He assures me he has been present when a young lady of unparalleled delicacy, tossed off in the space of a minute or two, one and twenty tumblers and a wine-glass full. On my asking Anthony whether the solicitude of the bye-standers was not greatly awakened as to what might be the *effects* of this *debauch*; he replied, that the ladies at Ballston had become such great sticklers for the doctrine of *evaporation*, that no gentleman ever ventured to remonstrate against this excessive drinking, for fear of bringing his philosophy into contempt. The most notorious water-drinkers in particular, were continually holding forth on the surprising aptitude with which the Ballston waters *evaporated*; and several gentlemen, who had the hardihood to question this female philosophy, were held in high displeasure.

After breakfast, every one chooses his amusement—some take a ride into the pine woods, and enjoy the varied and romantick scenery of burnt trees, post and rail fences, pine flats, potatoe patches, and log huts—others scramble up the surrounding sand hills, that look like the abodes of a gigantick race of ants—take a peep at other sand hills beyond them—and then—come down again; others who are romantick (and sundry young ladies insist upon being so whenever they visit the Springs, or go any where into the country) stroll along the borders of a little swampy brook that drags itself along like an alexandrine, and that, so lazily, as not to make a single murmur—watching the little tadpoles, as they frolick right flippantly in the muddy stream, and listening to the inspiring melody of the harmonious frogs that croak upon its borders. Some play at billiards, some play the fiddle, and some—play the fool—the latter being the most prevalent amusement at Ballston.

These, together with abundance of dancing, and a prodigious deal of sleeping of afternoons, make up the variety of pleasures at the Springs—a delicious life of alternate lassitude and fatigue, of laborious dissipation, and listless idleness, of sleepless nights, and days spent in that dozing insensibility which ever succeeds them. Now and then, indeed, the influenza, the fever-and-ague, or some such pale-faced intruder may happen to throw a momentary damp on the general felicity; but on the whole, Evergreen declares that Ballston wants only six things; to wit, good air, good wine, good living, good beds, good company, and good humour, to be the most enchanting place in the world—excepting Botany-bay, Musquito Cove, Dismal Swamp, and the Black-hole at Calcutta.

The following letter from the sage Mustapha, has cost us more trouble to decypher and render into tolerable english, than any hitherto published. It was full of blots and erasures, particularly the latter part, which we have no doubt was penned in a moment of great wrath and indignation. Mustapha has often a rambling mode of writing, and his thoughts take such unaccountable turns that it is difficult to tell one moment where he will lead you the next. This is particularly obvious in the commencement of his letters, which seldom bear much analogy to the subsequent parts—he sets off with a flourish, like a dramatick hero—assumes an air of great pomposity, and struts up to his subject, mounted most loftily *on stilts*.

L. LANGSTAFF.

FROM MUSTAPHA RUB-A-DUB KELI KHAN,
*To Asem Hacchem, principal slave-driver to
his highness the Bashaw of Tripoli.*

Among the variety of principles by which mankind are actuated, there is one, my dear Asem, which I scarcely know whether to consider as springing from grandeur and nobility of mind, or from a refined species of vanity and egotism. It is that singular, although almost universal, desire of living in the memory of posterity; of occupying a share of the world's attention, when we shall long since have ceased to be susceptible either of its praise or censure. Most of the passions of the mind are bounded by the grave—sometimes, indeed, an anxious hope or trembling fear, will venture beyond the clouds and darkness that rest upon our mortal horizon, and expatiate in boundless futurity: but it is only this active love of fame which steadily contemplates its fruition, in the applause or gratitude of future ages. Indignant at the narrow limits which

circumscribe existence, ambition is forever struggling to soar
beyond them—to triumph over space and time, and to bear
a name, at least, above the inevitable oblivion in which every
thing else that concerns us must be involved. It is this, my
friend, which prompts the patriot to his most heroick achievements; which inspires the sublimest strains of the poet, and
breathes ethereal fire into the productions of the painter and
the statuary.

For this the monarch rears the lofty column; the laurelled
conqueror claims the triumphal arch, while the obscure individual, who moved in an humbler sphere, asks but a plain and
simple stone to mark his grave, and bear to the next generation this important truth, that he was born, died—and was
buried. It was this passion which once erected the vast nu-
midian piles, whose ruins we have so often regarded with
wonder, as the shades of evening—fit emblems of oblivion!—
gradually stole over and enveloped them in darkness—It was
this which gave being to those sublime monuments of saracen
magnificence, which nod in mouldering desolation as the
blast sweeps over our deserted plains.—How futile are all our
efforts to evade the obliterating hand of time! As I traversed
the dreary wastes of Egypt, on my journey to Grand Cairo, I
stopped my camel for a while, and contemplated, in awful
admiration the stupendous pyramids—An appalling silence
prevailed around; such as reigns in the wilderness when the
tempest is hushed, and the beasts of prey have retired to their
dens. The myriads that had once been employed in rearing
these lofty mementoes of human vanity, whose busy hum
once enlivened the solitude of the desart—had all been swept
from the earth by the irresistible arm of death—all were mingled with their native dust—all were forgotten! Even the
mighty names which these sepulchres were designed to perpetuate, had long since faded from remembrance; history and
tradition afforded but vague conjectures, and the pyramids
imparted a humiliating lesson to the candidate for immortality.—Alas! alas! said I to myself, how mutable are the foundations on which our proudest hopes of future fame are
reposed. He who imagines he has secured to himself the meed
of deathless renown, indulges in deluding visions, which only
bespeak the vanity of the dreamer. The storied obelisk—the

triumphal arch—the swelling dome shall crumble into dust, and the names they would preserve from oblivion shall often pass away, before their own duration is accomplished.

Yet this passion for fame, however ridiculous in the eye of the philosopher, deserves respect and consideration from having been the source of so many illustrious actions; and, hence, it has been the practice in all enlightened governments to perpetuate by monuments, the memory of great men, as a testimony of respect for the illustrious dead, and to awaken in the bosoms of posterity an emulation to merit the same honourable distinction. The people of the american logocracy, who pride themselves upon improving on every precept or example of antient or modern governments, have discovered a new mode of exciting this love of glory—a mode by which they do honour to their great men, even in their life time!

Thou must have observed by this time, that they manage every thing in a manner peculiar to themselves; and doubtless in the best possible manner, seeing they have denominated themselves "the most enlightened people under the sun." Thou wilt therefore, perhaps, be curious to know how they contrive to honour the name of a living patriot, and what unheard of monument they erect, in memory of his achievements—By the fiery beard of the mighty Barbarossa, but I can scarcely preserve the sobriety of a true disciple of Mahomet while I tell thee!—Wilt thou not smile, oh, mussulman of invincible gravity, to learn that they honour their great men by *eating*, and that the only trophy erected to their exploits, is a *publick dinner!* But trust me, Asem, even in this measure whimsical as it may seem, the philosophick and considerate spirit of this people is admirably displayed. Wisely concluding that when the hero is dead, he becomes insensible to the voice of fame, the song of adulation, or the splendid trophy, they have determined that he shall enjoy his quantum of celebrity while living, and revel in the full enjoyment of a nine days immortality. The barbarous nations of antiquity immolated human victims to the memory of their lamented dead, but the enlightened americans offer up whole hecatombs of geese and calves, and oceans of wine in honour of the illustrious living; and the patriot has the felicity of hearing from every quarter the vast exploits in gluttony and revelling that have been celebrated to the glory of his name.

No sooner does a citizen signalize himself in a conspicuous manner in the service of his country, than all the gormandizers assemble and discharge the national debt of gratitude— by giving him a dinner—not that he really receives all the luxuries provided on this occasion—no my friend, it is ten chances to one that the great man does not taste a morsel from the table, and is, perhaps, five hundred miles distant; and, to let thee into a melancholy fact, a patriot, under this *economick* government, may be often in want of a dinner, while dozens are devoured in his praise. Neither are these repasts spread out for the hungry and necessitous, who might otherwise be filled with food and gladness, and inspired to shout forth the illustrious name, which had been the means of their enjoyment—far from this, Asem—it is the rich only who indulge in the banquet—those who pay for the dainties are alone privileged to enjoy them; so that, while opening their purses in honour of the patriot, they, at the same time, fulfill a great maxim, which in this country comprehends all the rules of prudence, and all the duties a man owes to *himself*—namely, *getting the worth of their money.*

In process of time this mode of testifying publick applause, has been found so marvellously agreeable, that they extend it to events as well as characters, and eat in triumph at the news of a treaty—at the anniversary of any grand national era, or at the gaining that splendid victory of the tongue—an *election.*—Nay, so far do they carry it, that certain days are set apart when the guzzlers, the gormandizers, and the wine bibbers meet together to celebrate a *grand indigestion*, in memory of some great event; and every man in the zeal of patriotism gets devoutly drunk—"as the act directs." Then, my friend, mayest thou behold the sublime spectacle of love of country, elevating itself from a sentiment into an *appetite*, whetted to the quick with the cheering prospect of tables loaded with the fat things of the land. On this occasion every man is anxious to fall to work, cram himself in honour of *the day*, and risk a surfeit in the glorious cause. Some, I have been told, actually fast for four and twenty hours preceding, that they may be enabled to do greater honour to the feast; and certainly, if eating and drinking are patriotick rites, he who eats and drinks most and proves himself the greatest glutton, is, undoubtedly, the most distinguished patriot. Such, at any rate, seems to be the opinion here; and they act up to it so rigidly, that by the time it is dark, every kennel in the neighbourhood teems with illustrious members of the sovereign people, wallowing in their congenial element of mud and mire.

These patriotick feasts, or rather national monuments, are patronized and promoted by certain inferior *Cadis*, called ALDERMEN, who are commonly complimented with their direction. These dignitaries, as far as I can learn, are generally appointed on account of their great talents for eating, a qualification peculiarly necessary in the discharge of their official duties. They hold frequent meetings at taverns and hotels, where they enter into solemn consultation for the benefit of lobsters and turtles—establish wholesome regulations for the safety and preservation of fish and wild-fowl—appoint the seasons most proper for eating oysters—inquire into the economy of taverns, the characters of publicans, and the abilities of their cooks, and discuss, most learnedly, the merits of a bowl of soup, a chicken-pie, or a haunch of venison: in a word, the alderman has absolute control in all matters of eating, and superintends the whole police—of the belly. Having in the prosecution of their important office, signalized themselves at so many public festivals; having gorged so often on patriotism and pudding, and entombed so many great names in their extensive maws, thou wilt easily conceive that they wax portly apace, that they fatten on the fame of mighty men, and that their rotundity, like the rivers, the lakes and the mountains of their country, must be *on a great scale!* Even so, my friend; and when I sometimes see a portly alderman, puffing along, and swelling as if he had the world under his waistcoat, I can not help looking upon him as a walking monument, and am often ready to exclaim—"Tell me, thou majestick mortal, thou breathing catacomb!—to what illustrious character, what mighty event, does that capacious carcass of thine bear testimony?"

But though the enlightened citizens of this logocracy *eat* in honour of their friends, yet they *drink* destruction to their enemies.—Yea, Asem, woe unto those who are doomed to undergo the publick vengeance, at a publick dinner. No sooner are the viands removed, than they prepare for merciless and exterminating hostilities. They drink the intoxicating juice of the grape, out of little glass cups, and over each draught pronounce a short sentence or prayer—not such a prayer as thy virtuous heart would dictate, thy pious lips give utterance to, my good Asem—not a tribute of thanks to all bountiful Allah, nor a humble supplication for his blessing on the draught—no, my friend, it is merely a *toast*, that is to say, a fulsome tribute of flattery to their demagogues—a laboured sally of affected sentiment or national egotism; or, what is more despicable, a malediction on their enemies, an empty threat of vengeance, or a petition for their destruction; for toasts thou must know are another kind of missive weapon in a logocracy, and are levelled from afar, like the annoying arrows of the tartars.

Oh Asem! couldst thou but witness one of these patriotick, these monumental dinners—how furiously the flame of patriotism blazes forth—how suddenly they vanquish armies, subjugate whole countries, and exterminate nations in a bumper, thou wouldst more than ever admire the force of that omnipotent weapon the tongue. At these moments every coward becomes a hero, every raggamuffin an invincible warrior; and the most zealous votaries of peace and quiet, forget for a while their cherished maxims and join in the furious attack. Toast succeeds toast—kings, emperors, bashaws, are like chaff before the tempest; the inspired patriot vanquishes fleets with a single gun-boat, and swallows down navies at a draught, until overpowered with victory and wine, he sinks upon the field of battle—dead drunk in his country's cause—Sword of the puissant Khalid! what a display of valour is here!—the sons of Africk are hardy, brave and enterprising; but they can achieve nothing like this.

Happy would it be if this mania for *toasting*, extended no farther than to the expression of national resentment. Though we might smile at the impotent vapouring and windy hyperbole, by which it is distinguished, yet we would excuse it as the unguarded overflowings of a heart, glowing with national injuries, and indignant at the insults offered to its country. But alas, my friend, private resentment, individual hatred, and

the illiberal *spirit of party*, are let loose on these festive occasions. Even *the names of individuals*, of unoffending fellow-
citizens, are sometimes dragged forth, to undergo the slanders
and execrations of a distempered herd of revellers.*—Head
of Mahomet!—how vindictive, how insatiably vindictive
must be that spirit, which can drug the mantling bowl with
gall and bitterness, and indulge an angry passion in the moment of rejoicing!—"Wine," say their poets, "is like sunshine
to the heart, which under its generous influence expands with
good will, and becomes the very temple of philanthropy."—
Strange, that in a temple consecrated to such a divinity, there
should remain a secret corner, polluted by the lurkings of
malice and revenge—strange, that in the full flow of social
enjoyment, these votaries of pleasure can turn aside to call
down curses on the head of a fellow-creature. Despicable
souls! ye are unworthy of being citizens of this "most enlightened country under the sun"—rather herd with the murderous savages who prowl the mountains of Tibesti; who stain
their midnight orgies with the blood of the innocent wanderer, and drink their infernal potations from the sculls of the
victims they have massacred.

And yet trust me, Asem, this spirit of vindictive cowardice
is not owing to any inherent depravity of soul, for, on other
occasions, I have had ample proof that this nation is mild and
merciful, brave and magnanimous—neither is it owing to any
defect in their political or religious precepts. The principles
inculcated by their rulers, on all occasions, breathe a spirit of
universal philanthropy; and as to their religion, much as I am
devoted to the Koran of our divine prophet, still I cannot but
acknowledge with admiration the mild forbearance, the ami-

*NOTE, BY WILLIAM WIZARD, ESQ.

It would seem that in this sentence, the sage Mustapha had reference to a
patriotick dinner, celebrated last fourth of July, by some *gentlemen* of Baltimore, when they righteously drank perdition to an unoffending individual,
and really thought "they had done the state some service." This amiable custom of "eating and drinking damnation" *to others*, is not confined to any
party:—for a month or two after the fourth of July, the different newspapers
file off their columns of *patriotick* toasts against each other, and take a pride
in showing how brilliantly their partizans can blackguard publick characters
in their cups—"they do but jest—poison in jest," as Hamlet says.

able benevolence, the sublime morality bequeathed them by the founder of their faith. Thou rememberest the doctrines of the mild Nazarine, who preached peace and good will to all mankind; who, when he was reviled, reviled not again; who blessed those who cursed him, and prayed for those who despightfully used and persecuted him! what then can give rise to this uncharitable, this inhuman custom among the disciples of a master, so gentle and forgiving?—It is that fiend POLITICKS, Asem—that baneful fiend, which bewildereth every brain, and poisons every social feeling; which intrudes itself at the festive banquet, and like the detestable harpy, pollutes the very viands of the table; which contaminates the refreshing draught while it is inhaled; which prompts the cowardly assassin to launch his poisoned arrows from behind the social board; and which renders the bottle, that boasted promoter of good fellowship and hilarity, an infernal engine, charged with direful combustion!

Oh Asem! Asem! how does my heart sicken when I contemplate these cowardly barbarities—let me, therefore, if possible, withdraw my attention from them forever. My feelings have borne me from my subject; and from the monuments of antient greatness, I have wandered to those of modern degradation. My warmest wishes remain with thee, thou most illustrious of slave-drivers; mayest thou ever be sensible of the mercies of our great prophet, who, in compassion to human imbecility, has prohibited his disciples from the use of the deluding beverage of the grape—that enemy to reason—that promoter of defamation—that auxilliary of POLITICKS.

ever thine,
MUSTAPHA.

SALMAGUNDI NO. XVII

Wednesday, November 11, 1807.

AUTUMNAL REFLECTIONS.
BY LAUNCELOT LANGSTAFF, ESQ.

WHEN A MAN is quietly journeying downwards into the valley of the shadow of departed youth, and begins to contemplate in a shortened perspective the end of his pilgrimage, he becomes more solicitous than ever that the remainder of his wayfaring should be smooth and pleasant, and the evening of his life, like the evening of a summer's day, fade away in mild uninterrupted serenity. If haply his heart has escaped uninjured through the dangers of a seductive world, it may then administer to the purest of his felicities, and its chords vibrate more musically for the trials they have sustained—like the viol, which yields a melody sweet in proportion to its age.

To a mind thus temperately harmonized, thus matured and mellowed by a long lapse of years, there is something truly congenial in the quiet enjoyment of our early autumn, amid the tranquillities of the country. There is a sober and chastened air of gaiety diffused over the face of nature, peculiarly interesting to an old man; and when he views the surrounding landscape withering under his eye, it seems as if he and nature were taking a last farewel of each other, and parting with a melancholy smile; like a couple of old friends, who having sported away the spring and summer of life together, part at the approach of winter, with a kind of prophetick fear that they are never to meet again.

It is either my good fortune or mishap, to be keenly susceptible to the influence of the atmosphere, and I can feel in the morning, before I open my window, whether the wind is easterly. It will not, therefore, I presume, be considered an extravagant instance of vain-glory when I assert, that there are few men who can discriminate more accurately in the different varieties of damps, fogs, scotch-mists, and north-east storms, than myself. To the great discredit of my philosophy I confess, I seldom fail to anathematize and excommunicate the weather, when it sports too rudely with my sensitive sys-

tem; but then I always endeavour to atone therefor, by eulo-
gizing it when deserving of approbation. And as most of my
readers—simple folk!—make but one distinction, to wit, rain
and sunshine—living in most honest ignorance of the various
nice shades which distinguish one fine day from another, I
take the trouble, from time to time, of letting them into some
of the secrets of nature—so will they be the better enabled to
enjoy her beauties, with the zest of connoisseurs, and derive
at least as much information from my pages, as from the
weather-wise lore of the almanack.

Much of my recreation, since I retreated to the Hall, has
consisted in making little excursions through the neighbourhood which abounds in the variety of wild, romantick, and
luxuriant landscape, that generally characterizes the scenery in
the vicinity of our rivers. There is not an eminence within a
circuit of many miles but commands an extensive range of
diversified and enchanting prospect.

Often have I rambled to the summit of some favourite hill,
and thence, with feelings sweetly tranquil as the lucid expanse
of the heavens that canopied me, have noted the slow and
almost imperceptible changes that mark the waning year.
There are many features peculiar to our autumn, and which
give it an individual character. The "green and yellow melancholy" that first steals over the landscape—the mild and
steady serenity of the weather, and the transparent purity of
the atmosphere speak not merely to the senses, but the
heart—it is the season of liberal emotions. To this succeeds a
fantastick gaiety, a motley dress which the woods assume,
where green and yellow, orange, purple, crimson and scarlet,
are whimsically blended together, like the hues in Joseph's
coat of many colours.—A sickly splendour this!—like the
wild and broken-hearted gaiety that sometimes precedes dissolution—or that childish sportiveness of superannuated age,
proceeding, not from a vigorous flow of animal spirits, but
from the decay and imbecility of the mind. We might, perhaps, be deceived by this gaudy garb of nature, were it not
for the rustling of the falling leaf, which, breaking on the
stillness of the scene, seems to announce in prophetick whispers the dreary winter that is approaching. When I have
sometimes seen a thrifty young oak, changing its hue of

sturdy vigour for a bright, but transient, glow of red it has recalled to my mind the treacherous bloom that once mantled the cheek of a friend who is now no more; and which, while it seemed to promise a long life of jocund spirits, was the sure precursor of premature decay. In a little while, and this ostentatious foliage disappears; the close of autumn leaves but one wide expanse of dusky brown, save where some rivulet steals along, bordered with little strips of green grass—the woodland echoes no more to the carols of the feathered tribes that sported in the leafy covert, and its solitude and silence is uninterrupted, except by the plaintive whistle of the quail, the barking of the squirrel, or the still more melancholy wintry wind, which rushing and swelling through the hollows of the mountains, sighs through the leafless branches of the grove, and seems to mourn the desolation of the year.

To one who, like myself, is fond of drawing comparisons between the different divisions of life, and those of the seasons, there will appear a striking analogy which connects the feelings of the aged with the decline of the year. Often as I contemplate the mild, uniform, and genial lustre with which the sun cheers and invigorates us in the month of October, and the almost imperceptible haze which, without obscuring, tempers all the asperities of the landscape, and gives to every object a character of stillness and repose, I cannot help comparing it with that portion of existence, when the spring of youthful hope, and the summer of the passions having gone by, reason assumes an undisputed sway, and lights us on with bright, but undazzling lustre adown the hill of life. There is a full and mature luxuriance in the fields that fills the bosom with generous and disinterested content. It is not the thoughtless extravagance of spring, prodigal only in blossoms, nor the languid voluptuousness of summer, feverish in its enjoyments, and teeming only with immature abundance—it is that certain fruition of the labours of the past— that prospect of comfortable realities, which those will be sure to enjoy who have improved the bounteous smiles of heaven, nor wasted away their spring and summer in empty trifling or criminal indulgence.

Cousin Pindar, who is my constant companion in these expeditions, and who still possesses much of the fire and energy of youthful sentiment, and a buxom hilarity of the spirits, often, indeed, draws me from these half-melancholy reveries, and makes me feel young again by the enthusiasm with which he contemplates, and the animation with which he eulogizes the beauties of nature displayed before him. His enthusiastick disposition never allows him to enjoy things by halves, and his feelings are continually breaking out in notes of admiration and ejaculations that sober reason might perhaps deem extravagant:—But for my part, when I see a hale, hearty old man, who has jostled through the rough path of the world, without having worn away the fine edge of his feelings, or blunted his sensibility to natural and moral beauty, I compare him to the evergreen of the forest, whose colours, instead of fading at the approach of winter, seem to assume additional lustre, when contrasted with the surrounding desolation— such a man is my friend Pindar—yet sometimes, and particularly at the approach of evening, even he will fall in with my humour; but he soon recovers his natural tone of spirits, and, mounting on the elasticity of his mind, like Ganymede on the eagle's wing, he soars to the ethereal regions of sunshine and fancy.

One afternoon we had strolled to the top of a high hill in the neighbourhood of the Hall, which commands an almost boundless prospect; and as the shadows began to lengthen around us, and the distant mountains to fade into mist, my cousin was seized with a moralizing fit. "It seems to me," said he, laying his hand lightly on my shoulder, "that there is just at this season, and this hour, a sympathy between us and the world we are now contemplating. The evening is stealing upon nature as well as upon us—the shadows of the opening day have given place to those of its close, and the only difference is, that in the morning they were before us, now they are behind, and that the first vanished in the splendours of noonday, the latter will be lost in the oblivion of night—our 'May of life' my dear Launce, has forever fled, our summer is over and gone—But," continued he, suddenly recovering himself and slapping me gaily on the shoulder,—"but why should we repine?—what though the capricious zephyrs of spring, the heats and hurricanes of summer, have given place to the sober sunshine of autumn—and though the woods begin to assume the dappled livery of decay—yet the prevailing colour is still green—gay, sprightly green.

"Let us then comfort ourselves with this reflection, that though the shades of the morning have given place to those of the evening—though the spring is past, the summer over, and the autumn come—still you and I go on our way rejoicing—and while, like the lofty mountains of our Southern America, our heads are covered with snow, still, like them, we feel the genial warmth of spring and summer playing upon our bosoms."

BY LAUNCELOT LANGSTAFF, ESQ.

In the description which I gave sometime since, of Cock-loft-hall, I totally forgot to make honourable mention of the library; which I confess was a most inexcusable oversight, for in truth it would bear a comparison, in point of usefulness and eccentricity, with the motley collection of the renowned hero of La Mancha.

It was chiefly gathered together by my grandfather, who spared neither pains nor expense to procure specimens of the oldest, most quaint, and insufferable books in the whole compass of english, scotch, and irish literature. There is a tradition in the family that the old gentleman once gave a grand entertainment in consequence of having got possession of a copy of a phillipick by archbishop Anselm, against the unseemly luxury of long toed shoes, as worn by the courtiers in the time of William Rufus, which he purchased of an honest brick-maker in the neighbourhood, for a little less than forty times its value. He had, undoubtedly, a singular reverence for old authors, and his highest eulogium on his library was, that it consisted of books not to be met with in any other collection, and as the phrase is, entirely out of print. The reason of which was, I suppose, that they were not worthy of being reprinted.

Cousin Christopher preserves these relicks with great care, and has added considerably to the collection; for with the hall he has inherited almost all the whim-whams of its former possessor. He cherishes a reverential regard for ponderous tomes in greek and latin, though he knows about as much of these

languages, as a young bachelor of arts does, a year or two
after leaving college. A worm-eaten work in eight or ten volumes he compares to an old family, more respectable for its
antiquity than its splendour—a lumbering folio he considers
as a duke—a sturdy quarto, as an earl, and a row of gilded
duodecimoes, as so many gallant knights of the garter. But as
to modern works of literature, they are thrust into trunks, and
drawers, as intruding upstarts, and regarded with as much
contempt, as mushroom nobility in England; who, having
risen to grandeur, merely by their talents and services, are regarded as utterly unworthy to mingle their blood with those
noble currents that can be traced without a single contami-
nation through a long line of, perhaps, useless and profligate
ancestors, up to William the bastard's cook, or butler, or
groom, or some one of Rollo's freebooters.

WILL WIZARD, whose studies are of a most uncommon
complexion, takes great delight in ransacking the library, and
has been, during his late sojournings at the hall, very constant
and devout in his visits to this receptacle of obsolete learning.
He seemed particularly tickled with the contents of the great
mahogany chest of drawers mentioned in the beginning of
this work. This venerable piece of architecture has frowned in
sullen majesty from a corner of the library, time out of mind,
and is filled with musty manuscripts, some in my grandfather's hand-writing, and others evidently written long before
his day.

It was a sight, worthy of a man's seeing, to behold Will,
with his outlandish phiz, poring over old scrawls that would
puzzle a whole society of antiquarians to expound, and diving
into receptacles of trumpery, which, for a century past, had
been undisturbed by mortal hand. He would sit for whole
hours, with a phlegmatick patience unknown in these degenerate days (except, peradventure, among the high dutch commentators) prying into the quaint obscurity of musty
parchments, until his whole face seemed to be converted into
a folio leaf of black-letter; and occasionally, when the whimsical meaning of an obscure passage flashed on his mind, his
countenance would curl up into an expression of gothick ris-
ibility, not unlike the physiognomy of a cabbage leaf wilting
before a hot fire.

At such times there was no getting Will to join in our walks, or take any part in our usual recreations—he hardly gave us an oriental tale in a week, and would smoke so inveterately that no one else dared enter the library under pain of suffocation. This was more especially the case when he encountered any knotty piece of writing; and he honestly confessed to me that one worm-eaten manuscript, written in a pestilent crabbed hand, had cost him a box of the best spanish cygarrs, before he could make it out, and after all, it was not worth a tobacco-stalk. Such is the turn of my knowing associate—only let him get fairly in the track of any odd, out of the way whim-wham, and away he goes, whip and cut, until he either runs down his game, or runs himself out of breath—I never in my life met with a man, who rode his hobby-horse more intolerably hard than Wizard.

One of his favourite occupations for some time past, has been the hunting of black-letter, which he holds in high regard, and he often hints that learning has been on the decline ever since the introduction of the roman alphabet. An old book printed three hundred years ago, is a treasure; and a ragged scroll, about one half unintelligible, fills him with rapture. Oh! with what enthusiasm will he dwell on the discovery of the Pandects of Justinian and Livy's history; and when he relates the pious exertions of the Medici in recovering the lost treasures of greek and roman literature, his eye brightens, and his face assumes all the splendour of an illuminated manuscript.

Will had vegitated for a considerable time in perfect tranquillity among dust and cobwebs, when one morning as we were gathered on the piazza, listening with exemplary patience to one of cousin Christopher's long stories about the revolutionary war, we were suddenly electrified by an explosion of laughter from the library.—My readers, unless, peradventure they have heard honest Will laugh, can form no idea of the prodigious uproar he makes. To hear him in a forest, you would imagine (that is to say if you were classical enough) that the satyrs and the dryads had just discovered a pair of rural lovers in the shade, and were deriding, with bursts of obstreperous laughter, the blushes of the nymph and

the indignation of the swain:—or if it were suddenly, as in
the present instance, to break upon the serene and pensive
silence of an autumnal morning, it would cause a sensation
something like that which arises from hearing a sudden clap
of thunder in a summer's day, when not a cloud is to be seen
above the horizon. In short, I recommend Will's laugh as a
sovereign remedy for the spleen; and if any of our readers are
troubled with that villanous complaint—which can hardly be,
if they make good use of our works—I advise them earnestly
to get introduced to him forthwith.

This outrageous merriment of Will's, as may be easily supposed, threw the whole family into a violent fit of *wondering*;
we all, with the exception of Christopher, who took this interruption in high dudgeon, silently stole up to the library,
and bolting in upon him, were fain at the first glance to join
in his inspiring roar. His face—but I despair to give an idea
of his appearance—and until his portrait, which is now in the
hands of an eminent artist, is engraved, my readers must be
content—I promise them they shall one day or other, have a
striking likeness of Will's indescribable phiz, in all its native
comeliness.

Upon my inquiring the occasion of his mirth, he thrust an
old, rusty, musty, and dusty manuscript into my hand, of
which I could not decypher one word out of ten, without
more trouble than it was worth. This task, however, he kindly
took off my hands, and in little more than eight and forty
hours, produced a translation into fair roman letters; though
he assured me it had lost a vast deal of its humour by being
modernized and degraded into plain english. In return for the
great pains he had taken, I could not do less than insert it in
our work. Will informs me that it is but one sheet of a stupendous bundle which still remains uninvestigated—who was
the author we have not yet discovered; but a note on the
back, in my grandfather's handwriting, informs us that it was
presented to him as a literary curiosity, by his particular
friend, the illustrious RYP VAN DAM, formerly lieutenant-gov-
ernor of the colony of NEW AMSTERDAM, and whose fame if
it has never reached these latter days, it is only because he was
too modest a man ever to do any thing worthy of being particularly recorded.

CHAP. CIX.
OF THE CHRONICLES OF THE RENOWNED
AND ANTIENT CITY OF GOTHAM.

How Gotham city conquered was,
And how the folk turned apes—because.   LINK. FID.

Albeit, much about this time it did fall out, that the thrice
renowned and delectable city of GOTHAM did suffer great discomfiture, and was reduced to perilous extremity, by the invasion and assaults of the HOPPINGTOTS. These are a people
inhabiting a far distant country, exceeding pleasaunte and fertile—but they being withal egregiously addicted to migration, do thence issue forth in mighty swarms, like the
Scythians of old, overrunning divers countries, and common-
wealths, and committing great devastations wheresoever they
do go, by their horrible and dreadful feats and prowesses.
They are specially noted for being right valorous in all exercises of the leg; and of them it hath been rightly affirmed that
no nation in all Christendom, or elsewhere, can cope with
them in the adroit, dexterous, and jocund shaking of the heel.
This engaging excellence doth stand unto them a sovereign
recommendation, by which they do insinuate themselves into
universal favour and good countenance; and it is a notable
fact that, let a Hoppingtot but once introduce a *foot* into
company, and it goeth hardly if he doth not contrive to flourish his whole body in thereafter. The learned Linkum Fidelius
in his famous and unheard-of treatise on man, whom he de-
fineth, with exceeding sagacity, to be a corn-cutting, tooth-
drawing animal, is particularly minute and elaborate in treating of the nation of the Hoppingtots, and betrays a little of
the pythagorean in his theory, inasmuch as he accounteth for
their being so wonderously adroit in pedestrian exercises, by
supposing that they did originally acquire this unaccountable
and unparalleled aptitude for huge and unmatchable feats of
the leg, by having heretofore been condemned for their numerous offences against that harmless race of bipeds—or
quadrupeds—(for herein the sage Linkum Fidelius appeareth
to doubt and waiver exceedingly) the frogs, to animate their
bodies for the space of one or two generations. He also giveth

it as his opinion, that the name of Hoppingtots is manifestly derivative from this transmigration. Be this, however, as it may, the matter (albeit it hath been the subject of controversie among the learned) is but little pertinent to the subject of this history, wherefore shall we treat and consider it as naughte.

Now these people being thereto impelled by a superfluity of appetite, and a plentiful deficiency of the wherewithal to satisfy the same, did take thought that the antient and venerable city of *Gotham*, was, peradventure, possessed of mighty treasures, and did, moreover, abound with all manner of fish and flesh, and eatables and drinkables, and such like delightsome and wholesome excellencies withal. Whereupon calling a council of the most active heeled warriors, they did resolve forthwith to put forth a mighty array, make themselves masters of the same, and revel in the good things of the land. To this were they hotly stirred up, and wickedly incited by two redoubtable and renowned warriors, hight PIROUET and RIGADOON, ycleped in such sort, by reason that they were two mighty, valiant, and invincible little men, utterly famous for the victories of the leg which they had, on divers illustrious occasions, right gallantly achieved.

These doughty champions did ambitiously and wickedly inflame the minds of their countrymen, with gorgeous descriptions, in the which they did cunninglie set forth the marvellous riches and luxuries of Gotham—where Hoppingtots might have garments for their bodies, shirts to their ruffles, and might riot most merrily every day in the week on beef, pudding, and such like lusty dainties. They (Pirouet and Rigadoon) did likewise hold out hopes of an easy conquest; forasmuch as the Gothamites were as yet but little versed in the mystery and science of handling the legs, and being, moreover, like unto that notable bully of antiquity, Achilles, most vulnerable to all attacks on the heel, would doubtless surrender at the very first assault.—Whereupon, on the hearing of this inspiriting council, the Hoppingtots did set up a prodigious great cry of joy, shook their heels in triumph, and were all impatience to dance on to Gotham and take it by storm.

The cunning Pirouet and the arch caitiff Rigadoon, knew

full well how to profit of this enthusiasm. They forthwith did order every man to arm himself with a certain pestilent little weapon, called a fiddle—to pack up in his knapsack a pair of silk breeches, the like of ruffles, a cocked hat of the form of a half moon, a bundle of cat-gut—and inasmuch as in marching to Gotham, the army might, peradventure, be smitten with scarcity of provision, they did account it proper that each man should take especial care to carry with him a bunch of right merchantable onions. Having proclaimed these orders by sound of fiddle, they (Pirouet and Rigadoon) did accordingly put their army behind them, and striking up the right jolly and sprightfull tune of *Ca Ira*, away they all capered towards the devoted city of Gotham, with a most horrible and appalling chattering of voices.

Of their first appearance before the beleaguered town, and of the various difficulties which did encounter them in their march, this history saith not, being that other matters of more weighty import require to be written. When that the army of the Hoppingtots did peregrinate within sight of Gotham, and the people of the city did behold the villanous and hitherto unseen capers, and grimaces, which they did make, a most horrifick panick was stirred up among the citizens; and the sages of the town fell into great despondency and tribulation, as supposing that these invaders were of the race of the Jig-hees, who did make men into baboons, when they achieved a conquest over them. The sages, therefore, called upon all the dancing men, and dancing women, and exhorted them with great vehemency of speech, to make *heel* against the invaders, and to put themselves upon such gallant defence, such glorious array, and such sturdy evolution, elevation, and transposition of the foot as might incontinently impester the legs of the Hoppingtots, and produce their complete discomfiture. But so it did happen by great mischance, that divers light-heeled youth of Gotham (more especially those who are descended from three wise men so renowned of yore, for having most venturesomely voyaged over sea in a bowl) were from time to time captured and inveigled into the camp of the enemy; where being foolishly cajoled and treated for a season with outlandish disports and pleasauntries, they were sent back to their friends, entirely changed, degenerated,

and turned topsy-turvy; insomuch that they thought thenceforth of nothing but their heels, always assaying to thrust
them into the most manifest point of view—and, in a word,
as might truly be affirmed, did forever after walk upon their
heads, outright.

And the Hoppingtots did day by day, and at late hours of
the night, wax more and more urgent in this their investment
of the city. At one time they would, in goodly procession,
make an open assault by sound of fiddle, in a tremendous
contra-dance—and anon they would advance by little detachments and manoeuvre to take the town by figuring in cotil-
lons. But truly their most cunning and devilish craft, and
subtilty, was made manifest in their strenuous endeavours to
corrupt the garrison, by a most insidious and pestilent dance
called the *Waltz*. This, in good truth, was a potent auxilliary,
for by it were the heads of the simple Gothamites most villan-
ously turned, their wits sent a wool-gathering, and themselves
on the point of surrendering at discretion, even unto the *very
arms* of their invading foemen.

At length the fortifications of the town began to give manifest symptoms of decay, inasmuch as the breastwork of decency was considerably broken down, and the curtain works
of propriety blown up. When that the cunning caitiff, Pirouet
beheld the ticklish and jeopardized state of the city—"Now
by my leg," quoth he—(he always swore by his leg, being
that it was an exceeding goodlie leg) "Now by my leg, quoth
he, but this is no great matter of recreation—I will show
these people a pretty, strange and new way forsooth, present-
lie, and will shake the dust off my pumps upon this most
obstinate and uncivilized town." Whereupon he ordered, and
did command his warriors, one and all, that they should put
themselves in readiness, and prepare to carry the town by a
GRAND BALL. They, in no wise to be daunted, do forthwith,
at the word, equip themselves for the assault, and in good
faith, truly, it was a gracious and glorious sight, a most triumphant and incomparable spectacle to behold them gallantly
arrayed in glossy and shining silk breeches, tied with abundance of ribbon; with silken hose of the gorgeous colour of
the salmon—right goodlie morocco pumps, decorated with
clasps or buckles of a most cunninge and secret contrivance,

inasmuch as they did of themselves grapple to the shoe without any aid of fluke or tongue, marvellously ensembling
witchcraft and necromancy. They had withal, exuberant chitterlings which puffed out at the neck and bosom, after a most
jolly fashion, like unto the beard of an antient he-turkey—
and cocked hats, the which they did carry not on their heads,
after the fashion of the Gothamites, but under their arms, as
a roasted fowl his gizzard.

Thus being equipped, and marshalled, they do attack, assault, batter and belabour the town with might and main—
most gallantly displaying the vigour of their legs, and shaking
their heels at it most emphatically. And the manner of their
attack was in this sort—first, they did thunder and gallop
forward in a *contre temps*—and anon, displayed column in a
cossack dance, a fandango, or a gavot. Whereat the Gothamites, in no wise understanding this unknown system of warfare, marvelled exceedinglie, and did open their mouths,
incontinently, the full distance of a bow shot (meaning a
cross-bow) in sore dismay and apprehension. Whereupon,
saith Rigadoon, flourishing his left leg with great expression
of valour, and most magnifick carriage—"my copesmates, for
what wait we here—are not the townsmen already won to
our favour—do not their women and young damsels wave to
us from the walls in such sort that, albeit there is some show
of defence, yet is it manifestly converted into our interests?"
so saying, he made no more ado, but leaping into the air
about a flight-shot, and crossing his feet six times after the
manner of the Hoppingtots, he gave a short *partridge run*,
and with mighty vigour and swiftness did bolt outright over
the walls with a *somerset*. The whole army of Hoppingtots
danced in after their valiant chieftain, with an enormous
squeaking of fiddles, and a horrifick blasting, and brattling of
horns, insomuch that the dogs did howl in the streets; so
hideously were their ears assailed. The Gothamites made
some semblance of defence, but their women having been all
won over into the interest of the enemy, they were shortly
reduced to make most abject submission, and delivered over
to the coercion of certain professors of the Hoppingtots, who
did put them under most ignominious durance, for the space
of a long time, until they had learned to turn out their toes,

and flourish their legs after the true manner of their conquerors. And thus, after the manner I have related, was the mighty and puissant city of Gotham circumvented, and taken by a *coup de pied*, or as it might be rendered, by *force of legs*.

The conquerors showed no mercy, but did put all ages, sexes, and conditions, to the fiddle and the dance, and, in a word, compelled and enforced them to become absolute Hoppingtots. "Habit," as the ingenious Linkum Fidelius, profoundly affirmeth, "is second nature." And this original and invaluable observation, hath been most aptly proved and illustrated, by the example of the Gothamites, ever since this disastrous and unlucky mischaunce. In process of time, they have waxed to be most flagrant, outrageous, and abandoned dancers; they do ponder on naughte but how to gallantize it at balls, routs, and fandangoes, insomuch that the like was and in no time or place ever observed before. They do, moreover, pitifully devote their nights to the jollification of the legs, and their days forsooth to the instruction and edification of the heel. And to conclude their young folk, who whilome did bestow a modicum of leisure upon the improvement of the head, have of late utterly abandoned this hopeless task, and have quietly, as it were, settled themselves down into mere machines, wound up by a tune, and set in motion by a *fiddle-stick*!

SALMAGUNDI NO. XVIII

Tuesday, November 24, 1807.

THE LITTLE MAN IN BLACK.
BY LAUNCELOT LANGSTAFF, ESQ.

THE FOLLOWING STORY has been handed down by family tradition for more than a century. It is one on which my cousin Christopher dwells with more than usual prolixity; and, being in some measure connected with a personage often quoted in our work, I have thought it worthy of being laid before my readers.

Soon after my grandfather, mr. Lemuel Cockloft, had quietly settled himself at the hall, and just about the time that the gossips of the neighbourhood, tired of prying into his affairs, were anxious for some new tea-table topick, the busy community of our little village was thrown into a grand turmoil of curiosity and conjecture; (a situation very common to little gossiping villages) by the sudden and unaccountable appearance of a mysterious individual.

The object of this solicitude was a little black looking man of a foreign aspect, who took possession of an old building, which having long had the reputation of being haunted, was in a state of ruinous desolation, and an object of fear to all true believers in ghosts. He usually wore a high sugar-loaf hat, with a narrow brim, and a little black cloak, which, short as he was, scarcely reached below his knees. He sought no intimacy or acquaintance with any one; appeared to take no interest in the pleasures or the little broils of the village, nor ever talked; except sometimes to himself in an outlandish tongue. He commonly carried a large book, covered with sheepskin, under his arm; appeared always to be lost in meditation, and was often met by the peasantry, sometimes watching the dawning of day, sometimes at noon seated under a tree poring over his volume, and sometimes at evening, gazing with a look of sober tranquility at the sun as it gradually sunk below the horizon.

The good people of the vicinity beheld something prodigiously singular in all this—a profound mystery seemed to hang about the stranger, which, with all their sagacity they could not penetrate, and in the excess of worldly charity they pronounced it a sure sign "that he was no better than he should be"—a phrase innocent enough in itself, but which, as applied in common, signifies nearly every thing that is bad. The young people thought him a gloomy misanthrope, because he never joined in their sports—the old men thought still more hardly of him, because he followed no trade, nor even seemed ambitious of earning a farthing—and as to the old gossips, baffled by the inflexible taciturnity of the stranger, they unanimously decreed that a man who could not or would not talk, was no better than a dumb beast. The little man in black, careless of their opinions, seemed resolved to maintain the liberty of keeping his own secret; and the consequence was that, in a little while, the whole village was in an uproar—for in little communities of this description, the members have always the privilege of being thoroughly versed, and even of meddling in all the affairs of each other.

A confidential conference was held one Sunday morning after sermon, at the door of the village church, and the character of the unknown fully investigated. The schoolmaster gave as his opinion that he was the wandering Jew—the sexton was certain that he must be a free-mason from his silence—a third maintained, with great obstinacy, that he was a high german doctor, and that the book which he carried about with him, contained the secrets of the black art; but the most prevailing opinion seemed to be that he was a *witch*—a race of beings at that time abounding in those parts; and a sagacious old matron from Connecticut proposed to ascertain the fact by sousing him into a kettle of hot water.

Suspicion, when once afloat, goes with wind and tide, and soon becomes certainty. Many a stormy night was the little man in black seen by the flashes of lightning, frisking and curveting in the air upon a broomstick; and it was always observed that at those times the storm did more mischief than at any other. The old lady in particular, who suggested the humane ordeal of the boiling kettle, lost on one of these occasions a fine brindled cow; which accident was entirely ascribed to the vengeance of the little man in black. If ever a mischievous hireling rode his master's favourite horse to a distant frolick, and the animal was observed to be lame and jaded in the morning—the little man in black was sure to be at the bottom of the affair, nor could a high wind howl through the village at night, but the old women shrugged up their shoulders and observed "the little man in black was in his *tantrums*." In short he became the bugbear of every house, and was as effectual in frightening little children into obedience and hystericks, as the redoubtable Raw-head-and-bloody-bones himself; nor could a house-wife of the village sleep in peace, except under the guardianship of a horse-shoe nailed to the door.

The object of these direful suspicions remained for some time totally ignorant of the wonderful quandary he had occasioned, but he was soon doomed to feel its effects. An individual who is once so unfortunate as to incur the odium of a village, is in a great measure outlawed and proscribed; and becomes a mark for injury and insult—particularly if he has not the power or the disposition to recriminate. The little venomous passions, which in the great world are dissipated and weakened by being widely diffused, act in the narrow limits of a country town with collected vigour, and become rancorous in proportion as they are confined in their sphere of action. The little man in black experienced the truth of this—every mischievous urchin returning from school, had full liberty to break his windows; and this was considered as a most daring exploit, for, in such awe did they stand of him, that the most adventurous schoolboy was never seen to approach his threshold, and at night would prefer going round by the cross-roads, where a traveller had been murdered by the indians, rather than pass by the door of his forlorn habitation.

The only living creature that seemed to have any care or affection for this deserted being, was an old turnspit—the companion of his lonely mansion and his solitary wanderings—the sharer of his scanty meals, and, sorry am I to say it—the sharer of his persecutions. The turnspit, like his master, was peaceable and inoffensive; never known to bark at a horse, to growl at a traveller, or to quarrel with the dogs of the neighbourhood. He followed close at his master's heels when he went out, and when he returned stretched himself in the sunbeams at the door, demeaning himself in all things like a civil and well disposed turnspit. But notwithstanding his exemplary deportment he fell likewise under the ill report of the village, as being the familiar of the little man in black, and the evil spirit that presided at his incantations. The old hovel was considered as the scene of their unhallowed rites, and its harmless tenants regarded with a detestation, which their inoffensive conduct never merited. Though pelted and jeered at by the brats of the village, and frequently abused by their parents, the little man in black never turned to rebuke them, and his faithful dog, when wantonly assaulted, looked up wistfully in his master's face, and there learned a lesson of patience and forbearance.

The movements of this inscrutable being had long been the subject of speculation at Cockloft-hall, for its inmates were full as much given to *wondering* as their descendants. The patience with which he bore his persecutions, particularly surprised them—for patience is a virtue but little known in the Cockloft family. My grandmother, who it appears was rather superstitious, saw in this humility nothing but the gloomy sullenness of a wizard, who restrained himself for the present, in hopes of midnight vengeance—the parson of the village, who was a man of some reading, pronounced it the stubborn insensibility of a stoick philosopher:—my grandfather, who, worthy soul, seldom wandered abroad in search of conclusions, took a data from his own excellent heart, and regarded it as the humble forgiveness of a christian. But however different were their opinions as to the character of the stranger, they agreed in one particular, namely, in never intruding upon his solitude; and my grandmother, who was at that time nursing my mother, never left the room, without wisely putting the large family bible in the cradle—a sure talisman, in her opinion, against witchcraft and necromancy.

One stormy winter night, when a bleak north-east wind moaned about the cottages, and howled around the village steeple, my grandfather was returning from club, preceded by a servant with a lantern. Just as he arrived opposite the desolate abode of the little man in black, he was arrested by the piteous howling of a dog which, heard in the pauses of the storm, was exquisitely mournful; and he fancied now and then, that he caught the low and broken groans of some one in distress. He stopped for some minutes, hesitating between the benevolence of his heart and a sensation of genuine delicacy, which in spite of his eccentricity he fully possessed— and which forbade him to pry into the concerns of his neighbours. Perhaps too, this hesitation might have been strengthened by a little taint of superstition; for surely, if the unknown had been addicted to witchcraft, this was a most propitious night for his vagaries. At length the old gentleman's philanthropy predominated; he approached the hovel and pushing open the door—for poverty has no occasion for locks and keys—beheld, by the light of the lantern, a scene that smote his generous heart to the core.

On a miserable bed, with pallid and emaciated visage and hollow eyes—in a room destitute of every convenience— without fire to warm, or friend to console him, lay this helpless mortal who had been so long the terror and wonder of the village. His dog was crouching on the scanty coverlet, and shivering with cold. My grandfather stepped softly and hesitatingly to the bed side, and accosted the forlorn sufferer in his usual accents of kindness. The little man in black seemed recalled by the tones of compassion from the lethargy into which he had fallen; for, though his heart was almost frozen, there was yet one chord that answered to the call of the good old man who bent over him—the tones of sympathy, so novel to his ear, called back his wandering senses and acted like a restorative to his solitary feelings.

He raised his eyes, but they were vacant and haggard—he put forth his hand, but it was cold—he essayed to speak, but the sound died away in his throat—he pointed to his mouth with an expression of dreadful meaning, and, sad to relate! my grandfather understood that the harmless stranger, deserted by society, was perishing with hunger!—With the quick impulse of humanity he dispatched the servant to the hall for refreshment. A little warm nourishment renovated him for a short time—but not long; it was evident his pilgrimage was drawing to a close, and he was about entering that peaceful asylum, where "the wicked cease from troubling."

His tale of misery was short and quickly told; infirmities

had stolen upon him, heightened by the rigours of the season: he had taken to his bed without strength to rise and ask for assistance—"and if I had," said he, in a tone of bitter despondency, "to whom should I have applied? I have no friend that I know of in the world!—the villagers avoid me as something loathsome and dangerous; and here, in the midst of christians, should I have perished without a fellow-being to soothe the last moments of existence, and close my dying eyes, had not the howlings of my faithful dog excited your attention."

He seemed deeply sensible of the kindness of my grand-father, and at one time as he looked up into his old benefactor's face, a solitary tear was observed to steal adown the parched furrows of his cheek—poor outcast!—it was the last tear he shed—but I warrant it was not the first by millions! My grandfather watched by him all night. Towards morning he gradually declined, and as the rising sun gleamed through the window, he begged to be raised in his bed that he might look at it for the last time. He contemplated it for a moment with a kind of religious enthusiasm, and his lips moved as if engaged in prayer. The strange conjectures concerning him rushed on my grandfather's mind: "he is an idolator!" thought he, "and is worshipping the sun!"—He listened a moment and blushed at his own uncharitable suspicion—he was only engaged in the pious devotions of a christian. His simple orison being finished, the little man in black withdrew his eyes from the east, and taking my grandfather's hand in one of his, and making a motion with the other, towards the sun—"I love to contemplate it," said he, "tis an emblem of the universal benevolence of a true christian—and it is the most glorious work of him, who is philanthropy itself!" My grandfather blushed still deeper at his ungenerous surmises; he had pitied the stranger at first, but now he revered him—he turned once more to regard him, but his countenance had undergone a change—the holy enthusiasm that had lighted up each feature had given place to an expression of mysterious import—a gleam of grandeur seemed to steal across his gothick visage, and he appeared full of some mighty secret which he hesitated to impart. He raised the tattered nightcap that had sunk almost over his eyes, and waving his withered hand with a slow and feeble expression of dignity,—"In me," said he, with laconick solemnity—"In me you behold the last descendant of the renowned Linkum Fidelius!" My grandfather gazed at him with reverence, for though he had never heard of the illustrious personage thus pompously announced, yet there was a certain black-letter dignity in the name, that peculiarly struck his fancy and commanded his respect.

"You have been kind to me," continued the little man in black, after a momentary pause, "and richly will I requite your kindness, by making you heir to my treasures! In yonder large deal box are the volumes of my illustrious ancestor, of which I alone am the fortunate possessor. Inherit them—ponder over them—and be wise!" He grew faint with the exertion he had made, and sunk back almost breathless on his pillow. His hand, which, inspired with the importance of his subject, he had raised to my grandfather's arm, slipped from its hold and fell over the side of the bed, and his faithful dog licked it, as if anxious to soothe the last moments of his master, and testify his gratitude to the hand that had so often cherished him. The untaught caresses of the faithful animal were not lost upon his dying master—he raised his languid eyes— turned them on the dog, then on my grandfather, and having given this silent recommendation—closed them forever.

The remains of the little man in black, notwithstanding the objections of many pious people, were decently interred in the church-yard of the village, and his spirit, harmless as the body it once animated, has never been known to molest a living being. My grandfather complied as far as possible with his last request—he conveyed the volumes of Linkum Fidelius to his library—he pondered over them frequently—but whether he grew wiser the tradition does not mention. This much is certain, that his kindness to the poor descendant of Fidelius, was amply rewarded by the approbation of his own heart, and the devoted attachment of the old turnspit, who transferring his affection from his deceased master to his benefactor, became his constant attendant, and was father to a long line of runty curs that still flourish in the family. And thus was the Cockloft library first enriched by the invaluable folioes of the sage LINKUM FIDELIUS.

LETTER
FROM MUSTAPHA RUB-A-DUB KELI KHAN,
To Asem Hacchem, principal slave-driver to
his highness the bashaw of Tripoli.

Though I am often disgusted, my good Asem, with the
vices and absurdities of the men of this country, yet the
women afford me a world of amusement. Their lovely prattle
is as diverting as the chattering of the red-tailed parrot; nor
can the green-headed monkey of Timandi equal them in
whim and playfulness. But, notwithstanding these valuable
qualifications, I am sorry to observe they are not treated with
half the attention bestowed on the before mentioned animals.
These infidels put their parrots in cages and chain their monkeys; but their women, instead of being carefully shut up in
harams and seraglioes, are abandoned to the direction of their
own reason, and suffered to run about in perfect freedom,
like other domestick animals:—this comes, Asem, of treating
their women as rational beings and allowing them souls. The
consequence of this piteous neglect may easily be imagined—
they have degenerated into all their native wildness, are seldom to be caught at home, and at an early age take to the
streets and highways, where they rove about in droves, giving
almost as much annoyance to the peaceable people, as the
troops of wild dogs that infest our great cities, or the flights
of locusts, that sometimes spread famine and desolation over
whole regions of fertility.

This propensity to relapse into pristine wildness, convinces
me of the untameable disposition of the sex, who may indeed
be partially domesticated by a long course of confinement and
restraint, but the moment they are restored to personal freedom, become wild as the young partridge of this country,
which, though scarcely half hatched, will take to the fields and
run about with the shell upon its back.

Notwithstanding their wildness, however, they are remarkably easy of access, and suffer themselves to be approached,
at certain hours of the day, without any symptoms of apprehension; and I have even happily succeeded in detecting them
at their domestick occupations. One of the most important of
these consists in thumping vehemently on a kind of musical

instrument, and producing a confused, hideous, and indefinable uproar, which they call the description of a battle—a jest, no doubt, for they are wonderfully facetious at times, and make great practise of passing jokes upon strangers. Sometimes they employ themselves in painting little caricatures of landscapes, wherein they will display their singular drollery in bantering nature fairly out of countenance—representing her tricked out in all the tawdry finery of copper skies, purple rivers, calico rocks, red grass, clouds that look like old clothes set adrift by the tempest, and foxy trees, whose melancholy foliage, drooping and curling most fantastically, reminds me of an undressed periwig that I have now and then seen hung on a stick in a barber's window. At other times they employ themselves in acquiring a smattering of languages spoken by nations on the other side of the globe, as they find their own language not sufficiently copious to supply their constant demands, and express their multifarious ideas. But their most important domestick avocation is to embroider on satin or muslin, flowers of a non-descript kind, in which the great art is to make them as unlike nature as possible—or to fasten little bits of silver, gold, tinsel and glass, on long strips of muslin, which they drag after them with much dignity whenever they go abroad—a fine lady, like a bird of paradise, being estimated by the length of her tail.

But do not, my friend, fall into the enormous error of supposing, that the exercise of these arts is attended with any useful or profitable result—believe me, thou couldst not indulge an idea more unjust and injurious; for it appears to be an established maxim among the women of this country that a lady loses her dignity when she condescends to be useful; and forfeits all rank in society the moment she can be convicted of earning a farthing. Their labours therefore, are directed not towards supplying their household but in decking their persons, and—generous souls!—they deck their persons, not so much to please themselves, as to gratify others, particularly strangers. I am confident thou wilt stare at this, my good Asem, accustomed as thou art to our eastern females, who shrink in blushing timidity even from the glances of a lover, and are so chary of their favours that they even seem fearful of lavishing their smiles too profusely on their husbands. Here, on the contrary, the stranger has the first place in female regard, and so far do they carry their hospitality, that I have seen a fine lady slight a dozen tried friends and real admirers, who lived in her smiles and made her happiness their study, merely to allure the vague and wandering glances of a stranger, who viewed her person with indifference and treated her advances with contempt—By the whiskers of our sublime bashaw, but this is highly flattering to a foreigner! and thou mayest judge how particularly pleasing to one who is, like myself, so ardent an admirer of the sex. Far be it from me to condemn this extraordinary manifestation of good will—let their own countrymen look to that.

Be not alarmed, I conjure thee, my dear Asem, lest I should be tempted by these beautiful barbarians to break the faith I owe to the three-and-twenty wives from whom my unhappy destiny has perhaps severed me for ever—no, Asem; neither time nor the bitter succession of misfortunes that pursues me, can shake from my heart the memory of former attachments. I listen with tranquil heart to the strumming and prattling of these fair syrens—their whimsical paintings touch not the tender chord of my affections; and I would still defy their fascinations, though they trailed after them trains as long as the gorgeous trappings which are dragged at the heels of the holy camel of Mecca: or as the tail of the great beast in our prophet's vision, which measured three hundred and forty-nine leagues, two miles, three furlongs, and a hand's breadth in longitude.

The dress of these women is, if possible, more eccentrick and whimsical than their deportment, and they take an inordinate pride in certain ornaments which are probably derived from their savage progenitors.—A woman of this country, dressed out for an exhibition, is loaded with as many ornaments as a circassian slave when brought out for sale. Their heads are tricked out with little bits of horn or shell, cut into fantastick shapes, and they seem to emulate each other in the number of these singular baubles—like the women we have seen in our journeys to Aleppo, who cover their heads with the entire shell of a tortoise, and thus equipped are the envy of all their less fortunate acquaintance. They also decorate their necks and ears with coral, gold chains, and glass beads, and load their fingers with a variety of rings; though, I must confess, I have never perceived that they wear any in their noses—as has been affirmed by many travellers. We have heard much of their painting themselves most hideously, and making use of bear's-grease in great profusion; but this, I solemnly assure thee, is a misrepresentation, civilization, no doubt, having gradually extirpated these nauseous practises. It is true, I have seen two or three of these females, who had disguised their features with paint; but then it was merely to give a tinge of red to their cheeks, and did not look very frightful—and as to ointment, they rarely use any now, except occasionally a little grecian oil for their hair, which gives it a glossy, greasy, and (as they think) very comely appearance. The last mentioned class of females, I take it for granted, have been but lately caught and still retain strong traits of their original savage propensities.

The most flagrant and inexcusable fault however, which I find in these lovely savages, is the shameless and abandoned exposure of their persons. Wilt thou not suspect me of exaggeration when I affirm—wilt thou not blush for them most discreet mussulman, when I declare to thee, that they are so lost to all sense of modesty as to expose the whole of their faces from the forehead to the chin, and that they even go abroad with their hands uncovered!—Monstrous indelicacy!—

But what I am going to disclose, will doubtless appear to thee still more incredible. Though I cannot forbear paying a tribute of admiration to the beautiful faces of these fair infidels, yet I must give it as my firm opinion that their persons are preposterously unseemly. In vain did I look around me on my first landing, for those divine forms of redundant proportions which answer to the true standard of eastern beauty—not a single fat fair one could I behold among the multitudes that thronged the streets; the females that passed in review before me, tripping sportively along, resembled a procession of shadows, returning to their graves at the crowing of the cock.

This meagreness I at first ascribed to their excessive volubility; for I have somewhere seen it advanced by a learned doctor, that the sex were endowed with a peculiar activity of tongue, in order that they might practise talking as a healthful exercise, necessary to their confined and sedentary mode of life. This exercise, it was natural to suppose, would be carried to great excess in a logocracy—"Too true" thought I "they have converted, what was undoubtedly meant as a beneficent gift, into a noxious habit that steals the flesh from their bones and the roses from their cheeks—they absolutely talk themselves thin!"—judge then of my surprise when I was assured not long since, that this meagreness was considered the perfection of personal beauty, and that many a lady starved herself, with all the obstinate perseverance of a pious dervise—into a fine figure!—"Nay more," said my informer, "they will often sacrifice their healths in this eager pursuit of skeleton beauty, and drink vinegar, eat pickles and smoke tobacco to keep themselves within the scanty outlines of the fashion."—Faugh! Allah preserve me from such beauties, who contaminate their pure blood with noxious recipes; who impiously sacrifice the best gift of heaven, to a preposterous and mistaken vanity.—Ere long I shall not be surprised to see them scarring their faces like the negroes of Congo, flattening their noses in imitation of the Hottentots, or like the barbarians of Ab-al Timar, distorting their lips and ears out of all natural dimensions. Since I received this information I cannot contemplate a fine figure, without thinking of a vinegar cruet; nor look at a dashing belle, without fancying her a pot of pickled cucumbers! What a difference, my friend, between these shades, and the plump beauties of Tripoli—what a contrast between an infidel fair one and my favourite wife, Fatima, whom I bought by the hundred weight, and had trundled home in a wheel-barrow!

But enough for the present; I am promised a faithful account of the arcana of a lady's toilette—a complete initiation into the arts, mysteries, spells and potions, in short the whole chemical process by which she reduces herself down to the most fashionable standard of insignificance; together with specimens of the strait waistcoats, the lacing, the bandages and the various ingenious instruments with which she puts nature to the rack, and tortures herself into a proper figure to be admired.

Farewel, thou sweetest of slave drivers! the echoes that repeat to a lover's ear the song of his mistress, are not more soothing than tidings from those we love. Let thy answers to my letters be speedy; and never, I pray thee, for a moment cease to watch over the prosperity of my house, and the welfare of my beloved wives. Let them want for nothing, my friend; but feed them plentifully on honey, boiled rice and water gruel, so that when I return to the blessed land of my fathers (if that can ever be!) I may find them improved in size and loveliness, and sleek as the graceful elephants that range the green valley of Abimar.

Ever thine.

MUSTAPHA.

SALMAGUNDI NO. XIX

FROM MY ELBOW CHAIR.

HAVING RETURNED to town, and once more formally taken possession of my elbow chair, it behoves me to discard the rural feelings, and the rural sentiments, in which I have for some time past indulged, and devote myself more exclusively to the edification of the town. As I feel at this moment a chivalrick spark of gallantry playing around my heart, and one of those dulcet emotions of cordiality, which an old bachelor will sometimes entertain toward the divine sex, I am determined to gratify the sentiment for once, and devote this number exclusively to the ladies. I would not, however, have our fair readers imagine that we wish to flatter ourselves into their good graces; devoutly as we adore them, (and what true cavalier does not) and heartily as we desire to flourish in the mild sunshine of their smiles, yet we scorn to insinuate ourselves into their favour; unless it be as honest friends, sincere well wishers, and disinterested advisers. If in the course of this number they find us rather prodigal of our encomiums, they will have the modesty to ascribe it to the excess of their own merits—if they find us extremely indulgent to their faults, they will impute it rather to the superabundance of our good nature, than to any servile and illiberal fear of giving offence.

The following letter of Mustapha falls in exactly with the current of my purpose. As I have before mentioned, that his letters are without dates, we are obliged to give them irregularly, without any regard to chronological order.

The present one, appears to have been written not long after his arrival, and antecedent to several already published. It is more in the familiar and colloquial style than the others. Will Wizard declares he has translated it with fidelity, excepting that he has omitted several remarks on the *waltz*, which the honest Mussulman eulogizes with great enthusiasm; comparing it to certain voluptuous dances of the seraglio. Will regretted exceedingly that the indelicacy of several of these observations compelled their total exclusion, as he wishes to give all possible encouragement to this popular and amiable exhibition.

LETTER
FROM MUSTAPHA RUB-A-DUB KELI KHAN,
to MULEY HELIM AL RAGGI, (*surnamed the agreeable Ragamuffin*) *chief mountebank and buffa-dancer to his highness.*

The numerous letters which I have written to our friend the *slave driver*, as well as those to thy kinsman THE SNORER, and which doubtless were read to thee, honest Muley, have in all probability awakened thy curiosity to know further particulars concerning the manners of the barbarians, who hold me in such ignominious captivity. I was lately at one of their publick ceremonies, which at first perplexed me exceedingly as to its object; but as the explanations of a friend have let me somewhat into the secret, and as it seems to bear no small analogy to thy profession, a description of it may contribute to thy amusement, if not to thy instruction.

A few days since, just as I had finished my coffee, and was perfuming my whiskers preparatory to a morning walk I was waited upon by an inhabitant of this place, a gay young infidel, who has of late cultivated my acquaintance. He presented me with a square bit of painted pasteboard, which he informed me would entitle me to admittance to the CITY ASSEMBLY. Curious to know the meaning of a phrase, which was entirely new to me, I requested an explanation; when my friend informed me that the assembly was a numerous concourse of young people of both sexes, who, on certain occasions, gathered together to dance about a large room with violent gesticulation, and try to out-dress each other.—"In short," said he, "if you wish to see *the natives* in all their glory, there's no place like the *City Assembly*; so you must go there, and sport your whiskers."—Though the matter of *sporting my whiskers*, was considerably above my apprehension, yet I now began, as I thought, to understand him. I had heard of the war dances of the natives, which are a kind of religious institution, and had little doubt but that this must be a solemnity of the kind—upon a prodigious great scale. Anxious as I am to contemplate these strange people in every situation, I willingly acceded to his proposal, and to be the more at ease, I determined to lay aside my turkish dress, and appear in plain garments of the fashion of this country—as is my custom whenever I wish to mingle in a crowd, without exciting the attention of the gaping multitude.

It was long after the shades of night had fallen, before my friend appeared to conduct me to the assembly. "These infidels," thought I, "shroud themselves in mystery, and seek the aid of gloom and darkness to heighten the solemnity of their pious orgies." Resolving to conduct myself with that decent respect, which every stranger owes to the customs of the land in which he sojourns, I chastised my features into an expression of sober reverence, and stretched my face into a degree of longitude suitable to the ceremony I was about to witness. Spite of myself, I felt an emotion of awe stealing over my senses as I approached the majestick pile. My imagination pictured something similar to a descent into the cave of Dom-Daniel, where the necromancers of the east are taught their infernal arts. I entered with the same gravity of demeanour that I would have approached the holy Temple at Mecca, and bowed my head three times, as I passed the threshold. "Head of the mighty Amrou!" thought I, on being ushered into a splendid saloon, " what a display is here! surely I am transported to the mansions of the Houris, the elysium of the faithful!"—How tame appeared all the descriptions of enchanted palaces in our arabian poetry!—wherever I turned my eyes, the quick glances of beauty dazzled my vision and ravished my heart—lovely virgins fluttered by me, darting imperial looks of conquest, or beaming such smiles of invitation, as did Gabriel when he beckoned our holy prophet to heaven. Shall I own the weakness of thy friend, good Muley?—while thus gazing on the enchanted scene before me, I for a moment forgot my country; and even the memory of my three-and-twenty wives faded from my heart—my thoughts were bewildered and led

astray by the charms of these bewitching savages, and I sunk
for awhile into that delicious state of mind where the senses,
all enchanted, and, all striving for mastery, produce an endless
variety of tumultuous, yet pleasing emotions. Oh, Muley,
never shall I again wonder that an infidel should prove a recreant to the single solitary wife allotted him, when even thy
friend, armed with all the precepts of Mahomet, can so easily
prove faithless to three-and-twenty!

"Whither have you led me?" said I at length to my companion, "and to whom do these beautiful creatures belong?
certainly this must be the seraglio of the grand bashaw of the
city, and a most happy bashaw must he be to possess treasures
which even his highness of Tripoli cannot parallel." "Have a
care," cried my companion, "how you talk about seraglioes,
or you'll have all these gentle nymphs about your ears; for
seraglio is a word which, beyond all others, they abhor;—
most of them," continued he, "have no lord and master, but
come here to catch one—they're *in the market*, as we term
it."—"Ah, hah!" said I, exultingly, "then you really have a
fair, or slave-market, such as we have in the east, where the
faithful are provided with the choicest virgins of Georgia and
Circassia?—by our glorious sun of Africk, but I should like
to select some ten or a dozen wives from so lovely an assemblage! pray, what would you suppose they might be bought
for?"—

Before I could receive an answer, my attention was attracted by two or three good looking middle sized men, who
being dressed in black, a colour universally worn in this country by the muftis and dervises, I immediately concluded to be
high priests, and was confirmed in my original opinion that
this was a religious ceremony. These reverend personages are
entitled *managers*, and enjoy unlimited authority in the assemblies, being armed with swords, with which I am told
they would infallibly put any lady to death, who infringed the
laws of the temple. They walked round the room with great
solemnity, and with an air of profound importance and mystery put a little piece of folded paper in each fair hand, which
I concluded were religious talismans. One of them dropped
on the floor, whereupon I slily put my foot on it, and watch-

ing an opportunity, picked it up unobserved and found it to contain some unintelligible words and the mystic number 9. What were its virtues I know not, except that I put it in my pocket, and have hitherto been preserved from my fit of the lumbago, which I generally have about this season of the year, ever since I tumbled into the well of Zim-zim on my pilgrimage to Mecca. I enclose it to thee in this letter, presuming it to be particularly serviceable against the dangers of thy profession.

Shortly after the distribution of these talismans, one of the high priests stalked into the middle of the room with great majesty, and clapped his hands three times; a loud explosion of musick succeeded from a number of black, yellow and white musicians perched in a kind of cage over the grand entrance. The company were thereupon thrown into great confusion and apparent consternation. They hurried to and fro about the room, and at length formed themselves into little groupes of eight persons, half male and half female—the musick struck into something like harmony, and in a moment to my utter astonishment and dismay, they were all seized with what I concluded to be a paroxysm of religious phrenzy, tossing about their heads in a ludicrous style from side to side and indulging in extravagant contortions of figure—now throwing their heels into the air, and anon whirling round with the velocity of the eastern idolators, who think they pay a grateful homage to the sun by imitating his motions. I expected every moment to see them fall down in convulsions, foam at the mouth, and shriek with fancied inspiration. As usual the females seemed most fervent in their religious exercises, and performed them with a melancholy expression of feature that was peculiarly touching; but I was highly gratified by the exemplary conduct of several male devotees, who, though their gesticulations would intimate a wild merriment of the feelings, maintained throughout as inflexible a gravity of countenance as so many monkeys of the island of Borneo at their anticks.

"And pray", said I, "who is the divinity that presides in this splendid mosque?"—"The divinity!—oh, I understand—you mean the *belle* of the evening; we have a new one every season; the one at present in fashion is that lady you see yonder, dressed in white, with pink ribbons, and a crowd of adorers around her." "Truly," cried I, "this is the pleasantest deity I have encountered in the whole course of my travels—so familiar, so condescending, and so merry withal—why, her very worshippers take her by the hand, and whisper in her ear."—"My good mussulman," replied my friend with great gravity, "I perceive you are completely in an error concerning the intent of this ceremony. You are now in a place of publick amusement, not of publick worship—and the pretty looking young men you see making such violent and grotesque distortions, are merely indulging in our favourite amusement of dancing." "I cry you mercy," exclaimed I, "these then are the dancing men and women of the town, such as we have in our principal cities, who hire themselves out for the entertainment of the wealthy—but, pray who pays them for this fatiguing exhibition?"—My friend regarded me for a moment with an air of whimsical perplexity, as if doubtful whether I was in jest or earnest.— " 'Sblood, man," cried he, "these are some of our greatest people, our fashionables, who are merely dancing here for amusement."—*Dancing for amusement!*—think of that, Muley—thou, whose greatest pleasure is to chew opium, smoke tobacco, loll on a couch, and doze thyself into the region of the Houris!—*Dancing for amusement!*—shall I never cease having occasion to laugh at the absurdities of these barbarians, who are laborious in their recreations, and indolent only in their hours of business?—*Dancing for amusement!*—the very idea makes my bones ache, and I never think of it without being obliged to apply my handkerchief to my forehead, and fan myself into some degree of coolness.

"And pray," said I, when my astonishment had a little subsided, "do these musicians also toil for amusement, or are they confined to their cage, like birds, to sing for the gratification of others?—I should think the former was the case, from the animation with which they flourish their elbows." "Not so," replied my friend, "they are well paid, which is no more than just, for I assure you they are the most important personages in the room. The fiddler puts the whole assembly in motion, and directs their movements, like the master of a puppet-show, who sets all his pasteboard gentry kicking by a jerk of his fingers:—there now—look at that dapper little gentleman yonder, who appears to be suffering the pangs of dislocation in every limb—he is the most expert puppet in the room, and performs, not so much for his own amusement, as for that of the bye-standers."—Just then, the little gentleman, having finished one of his paroxysms of activity, seemed to be looking round for applause from the spectators. Feeling myself really much obliged to him for his exertions, I made him a low bow of thanks, but nobody followed my example, which I thought a singular instance of ingratitude.

Thou wilt perceive, friend Muley, that the dancing of these barbarians is totally different from the *science* professed by thee in Tripoli;—the country, in fact, is afflicted by numerous epidemical diseases, which travel from house to house, from city to city, with the regularity of a caravan. Among these, the most formidable is this dancing mania, which prevails chiefly throughout the winter. It at first seized on a few people of fashion, and being indulged in moderation, was a cheerful exercise; but in a little time, by quick advances, it infected all classes of the community, and became a raging epidemick. The doctors immediately, as is their usual way, instead of devising a remedy, fell together by the ears, to decide whether it was native or imported, and the sticklers for the latter opinion traced it to a cargo of trumpery from France, as they had before hunted down the yellow-fever to a bag of coffee from the West-Indies. What makes this disease the more formidable, is that the patients seem infatuated with their malady, abandon themselves to its unbounded ravages, and expose their persons to wintry storms and midnight airs, more fatal in this capricious climate than the withering Simoom blast of the desert.

I know not whether it is a sight most whimsical or melancholy to witness a fit of this dancing malady. The lady hops up to the gentleman, who stands at the distance of about three paces, and then capers back again to her place—the gentleman of course does the same—then they skip one way, then they jump another—then they turn their backs to each other—then they seize each other and shake hands—then

they whirl round, and throw themselves into a thousand grotesque and ridiculous attitudes—sometimes on one leg,
sometimes on the other, and sometimes on no leg at all—and
this they call *exhibiting the graces!*—By the nineteen thousand
capers of the great mountebank of Damascus, but these *graces*
must be something like the crooked backed dwarf Shabrac,
who is sometimes permitted to amuse his highness by imitating the tricks of a monkey. These fits continue at short intervals from four to five hours, till at last the lady is led off,
faint, languid, exhausted, and panting, to her carriage—rattles home—passes a night of feverish restlessness, cold per-
spirations and troubled sleep—rises late next morning (if
she rises at all) is nervous, petulant, or a prey to languid indifference all day—a mere household spectre, neither giving
nor receiving enjoyment—in the evening hurries to another
dance—receives an unnatural exhilaration from the lights, the
musick, the crowd, and the unmeaning bustle—flutters, sparkles, and blooms for awhile, until, the transient delirium
being past, the infatuated maid droops and languishes into
apathy again—is again led off to her carriage, and the next
morning rises to go through exactly the same joyless routine.

And yet, wilt thou believe it, my dear Raggi, these are rational beings; nay, more, their countrymen would fain persuade me they have souls!—Is it not a thousand times to be
lamented that beings, endowed with charms that might warm
even the frigid heart of a dervise—with social and endearing
powers, that would render them the joy and pride of the
haram—should surrender themselves to a habit of heartless
dissipation, which preys imperceptibly on the roses of the
cheek—which robs the eye of its lustre, the mouth of its dimpled smile, the spirits of their cheerful hilarity, and the limbs
of their elastick vigour—which hurries them off in the
spring-time of existence; or, if they survive, yields to the arms
of a youthful bridegroom a frame wrecked in the storms of
dissipation, and struggling with premature infirmity. Alas,
Muley! may I not ascribe to this cause the number of little
old women I meet with in this country, from the age of eighteen to eight-and-twenty?

In sauntering down the room, my attention was attracted
by a smoky painting, which on nearer examination I found

consisted of two female figures crowning a bust with a wreath of laurel. "This, I suppose," cried I, "was some famous dancer in his time?"—"Oh, no," replied my friend, "he was *only* a general."—"Good; but then he must have been great at a cotillion, or expert at a fiddle-stick—or why is his memorial here?"—"Quite the contrary," answered my companion, "history makes no mention of his ever having flourished a fiddle-stick, or figured in a single dance. You have, no doubt, heard of him—he was the illustrious WASHINGTON, the father and deliverer of his country; and as our nation is remarkable for gratitude to great men, it always does honour to their memory, by placing their monuments over the doors of taverns or in the corners of dancing-rooms."

From thence my friend and I strolled into a small apartment adjoining the grand saloon, where I beheld a number of grave looking persons with venerable grey heads, (but without beards, which I thought very unbecoming) seated around a table, studying hieroglyphicks;—I approached them with reverence, as so many *magi*, or learned men, endeavouring to expound the mysteries of egyptian science: several of them threw down money, which I supposed was a reward proposed for some great discovery, when presently one of them spread his hieroglyphics on the table, exclaimed triumphantly "two bullets and a bragger!" and swept all the money into his pocket. He has discovered a key to the hieroglyphicks, thought I—happy mortal! no doubt his name will be immortalized. Willing, however, to be satisfied, I looked round on my companion with an inquiring eye—he understood me, and informed me that these were a company of *friends*, who had met together to win each other's money, and be agreeable. "Is that all?" exclaimed I, "why then, I pray you, make way, and let me escape from this temple of abominations, or who knows but these people, who meet together to toil, worry and fatigue themselves to death, and give it the name of pleasure—and who win each others money by way of being agreeable—may some one of them take a liking to me, and pick my pocket, or break my head in a paroxysm of hearty good-will!"

thy friend.
MUSTAPHA.

BY ANTHONY EVERGREEN, GENT

Nunc est bibendum, nunc pede libero
Pulsanda tellus. HOR.
Now is the tyme for wine and myrtheful sportes,
For daunce, and song, and disportes of syche sortes.

LINK FID.

The winter campaign has opened. Fashion has summoned her numerous legions at the sound of trumpet, tamborine and drum, and all the harmonious minstrelsy of the orchestra, to hasten from the dull, silent, and insipid glades and groves, where they have vegetated during the summer, recovering from the ravages of the last winter's campaign. Our fair ones have hurried to town eager to pay their devotions to this tutelary deity, and to make an offering at her shrine of the few pale and transient roses they gathered in their healthful retreat. The fiddler rosins his bow, the card-table devotee is shuffling her pack, the young ladies are industriously spangling muslins, and the tea-party heroes are airing their *chapeaux bras* and pease-blossom breeches, to prepare for figuring in the gay circle of smiles, and graces, and beauty. Now the fine lady forgets her country friends in the hurry of fashionable engagements, or receives the simple intruder who has foolishly accepted her thousand pressing invitations, with such *politeness* that the poor soul determines never to come again—now the gay buck who erst figured at Ballston and quaffed the pure spring, exchanges the sparkling water for still more sparkling champaign, and deserts the *nymph* of the fountain, to enlist under the standard of jolly Bacchus. In short, now is the important time of the year in which to harangue the bon-ton reader, and like some ancient hero in front of the battle, to spirit him up to deeds of noble daring, or still more noble suffering, in the ranks of fashionable warfare.

Such, indeed, has been my intention; but the number of cases which have lately come before me, and the variety of complaints I have received from a crowd of honest and well-meaning correspondents, call for more immediate attention. A host of appeals, petitions, and letters of advice are now before me; and I believe the shortest way to satisfy my petitioners, memorialists, and advisers will be to publish their letters, as I suspect the object of most of them is merely to get into print.

TO ANTHONY EVERGREEN, GENT.

Sir,

As you appear to have taken to yourself the trouble of meddling in the concerns of the beau monde, I take the liberty of appealing to you on a subject, which though considered merely as a very good joke, has occasioned me great vexation and expense. You must know I pride myself on being very *useful* to the ladies; that is, I take boxes for them at the theatre, go shopping with them, supply them with boquets, and furnish them with novels from the circulating library. In consequence of these attentions I am become a great favourite, and there is seldom a party going on in the city without my having an invitation. The grievance I have to mention, is the exchange of hats which takes place on these occasions; for, to speak my mind freely, there are certain young gentlemen who seem to consider fashionable parties as mere places to barter old clothes, and I am informed that a number of them manage by this great system of exchange to keep their crowns decently covered without their hatter *suffering* in the least by it.

It was but lately that I went to a private ball with a new hat, and on returning in the latter part of the evening, and asking for it, the scoundrel of a servant, with a broad grin informed me, that the new hats had been dealt out half an hour since, and they were then on the third quality; and I was in the end obliged to borrow a young lady's beaver rather than go home with any of the ragged remnants that were left.

Now I would wish to know, if there is no possibility of having these offenders punished by law—and whether it would not be advisable for ladies to mention in their cards of invitation, as a postscript, "stealing hats and shawls positively prohibited." At any rate, I would thank you mr. Evergreen, to discountenance the thing totally by publishing in your paper, that *stealing a hat is no joke*.

Your humble servant,
WALTER WITHERS.

My correspondent is informed that the police have determined to take this matter into consideration, and have set apart Saturday mornings for the cognizance of *fashionable larcenies*.

MR. EVERGREEN,
SIR,

Do you think a married woman may lawfully put her husband right in a story, before strangers, when she knows him to be in the wrong, and can any thing authorize a wife in the exclamation of—"lord, my dear, how can you say so!"

MARGARET TIMSON.

DEAR ANTHONY,

Going down Broadway this morning in a great hurry I ran full against an object which at first put me to a prodigious non plus. Observing it to be dressed in a man's hat, a cloth overcoat, and spatterdashes, I framed my apology accordingly, exclaiming "my dear *sir*, I ask ten thousand pardons—I assure you, *sir*, it was entirely accidental—pray excuse me *sir*, &c." At every one of these excuses, the thing answered me with a downright laugh; at which, I was not a little surprised until, on resorting to my pocket glass I discovered that it was no other than my old acquaintance Clarinda Trollop—I never was more chagrined in my life, for being an old bachelor I like to appear as young as possible, and am always boasting of the goodness of my eyes. I beg of you, mr. Evergreen, if you have any feeling for your cotemporaries, to discourage this hermaphrodite mode of dress; for really, if the fashion take, we poor bachelors will be utterly at a loss to distinguish a woman from a man. Pray let me know your opinion, sir, whether a lady who wears a man's hat and spatterdashes before marriage, may not be apt to usurp some other article of his dress afterwards.

Your humble servant,
RODERICK WORRY.

DEAR MR. EVERGREEN,

The other night, at Richard the Third, I sat behind three gentlemen, who talked very loud on the subject of Richard's wooing Lady Ann directly in the face of his crimes against

that lady. One of them declared such an unnatural scene
would be hooted at in China. Pray, sir, was that mr. Wizard?

SELINA BADGER.

P. S. The gentleman I allude to, had a pocket glass, and
wore his hair fastened behind by a tortoise shell comb, with
two teeth wanting.

MR. EVERGRIN,
SIR,

Being a little curious in the affairs of the toilette, I was
much interested by the sage Mustapha's remarks in your last
number, concerning the art of manufacturing a modern fine
lady. I would have you caution your fair readers, however, to
be very careful in the management of their machinery, as a
deplorable accident happened last assembly, in consequence
of the architecture of a lady's figure not being sufficiently
strong. In the middle of one of the cotillions the company
was suddenly alarmed by a tremendous crash at the lower end
of the room, and on crouding to the place, discovered that it
was a fine figure which had unfortunately broken down, from
too great exertion in a pigeon-wing. By great good luck I
secured the *corset*, which I carried home in triumph, and the
next morning had it publickly dissected and a lecture read on
it at Surgeon's Hall. I have since commenced a dissertation
on the subject, in which I shall treat of the superiority of
those figures manufactured by steel, stay-tape and whalebone, to those formed by dame nature. I shall show clearly
that the Venus de Medicis has no pretension to beauty of
form, as she never wore stays, and her waist is in exact proportion to the rest of her body. I shall inquire into the mysteries of compression, and how tight a *figure* can be laced
without danger of fainting; and whether it would not be adviseable for a lady when dressing for a ball, to be attended by
the family physician, as culprits are when tortured on the
rack—to know how much more nature will endure. I shall
prove that ladies have discovered the secret of that notorious
juggler who offered to squeeze himself into a quart bottle,
and I shall demonstrate to the satisfaction of every fashionable
reader, that there is a degree of heroism in purchasing a pre-

posterously slender waist at the expense of an old age of decrepitude and rheumaticks. This dissertation shall be published as soon as finished, and distributed gratis among boarding-school madams, and all worthy matrons who are ambitious that their daughters should sit straight, move like clockwork, and "do credit to their bringing up." In the mean time, I have hung up the skeleton of the corset in the Museum, beside a dissected weazel and a stuffed alligator, where it may be inspected by all those naturalists who are fond of studying the "human form divine."

Yours, &c.

JULIAN COGNOUS.

P. S. By accurate calculation I find it is dangerous for a fine figure, when full dressed, to pronounce a word of more than three syllables. Fine figure, if in love, may indulge in a gentle sigh, but a sob is hazardous. Fine figure may smile with safety, may even venture as far as a giggle, but must never risk a loud laugh. Figure must never play the part of a *confidante*; as at a tea-party some five evenings since, a young lady whose unparallelled impalpability of waist was the envy of the drawing-room, burst with an important secret, and had three ribs [of her corset] fractured on the spot.

MR. EVERGREEN,

SIR,

I am one of those industrious gemmen who labour hard to obtain currency in the fashionable world. I have went to great expense in little boots, short vests, and long breeches—my coat is regularly imported per stage from Philadelphia, duly insured against all risks, and my boots are smuggled from Bond-street. I have lounged in Broadway with one of the most crooked walking-sticks I could procure, and have sported a pair of salmon coloured small-clothes and flame coloured stockings, at every concert and ball to which I could purchase admission. Being affeared that I might possibly appear to less advantage as a pedestrian, in consequence of my being rather short and a little bandy, I have lately hired a tall horse with cropped ears and a cocked tail, on which I have joined the cavalcade of pretty gemmen, who exhibit bright

stirrups every fine morning in Broadway, and take a canter of
two miles per day, at the rate of 300 dollars per annum. But,
sir, all this expense has been laid out in vain, for I can scarcely
get a partner at an assembly, or an invitation to a tea-party.
Pray sir inform me what more I can do to acquire admission
into the true stylish circles, and whether it would not be
advisable to charter a curricle for a month and have my cy-
pher put on it, as is done by certain dashers of my acquaintance.

Yours to serve,
MALVOLIO DUBSTER.

TEA,
A POEM.
FROM THE MILL OF PINDAR COCKLOFT ESQ.
*and earnestly recommended to the attention of all
maidens of a certain age.*

Old time, my dear girls, is a knave who in truth
From the fairest of beauties will pilfer their youth;
Who by constant attention and wiley deceit
For ever is coaxing some grace to retreat;
And, like crafty seducer, with subtle approach,
The further indulged, will still further encroach.
Since this "thief of the world" has made off with your
    bloom,
And left you some score of stale years in its room—
Has deprived you of all those gay dreams that would dance,
In your brains at fifteen, and your bosoms entrance,
And has forced you almost to renounce in despair
The hope of a husband's affection and care—
Since such is the case, (and a case rather hard!)
Permit one who holds you in special regard,
To furnish such hints in your loveless estate
As may shelter your names from detraction and hate.
Too often our maidens grown aged, I ween,
Indulge to excess in the workings of spleen;
And at times, when annoyed by the slights of *man*-kind,
Work off their resentment by *speaking their mind*;
Assemble together in snuff taking clan,

And hold round the tea-urn a solemn divan,
A convention of tattling—a *tea party* hight,
   Which, like meeting of witches, is brewed up at night:
Where each matron arrives, fraught with tales of surprize,
With knowing suspicion and doubtful surmize,
Like the broomstick whirl'd hags that appear in Macbeth,
Each bearing some relick of venom or death,
"To stir up the toil and to double the trouble,
That fire may burn, and that cauldron may bubble."
   When the party commences, all starched and all glum,
They talk of the weather, their corns, or sit mum:
They will tell you of cambrick, of ribbons, of lace,
How cheap they were sold—and will name you the place.
They discourse of their colds, and they hem and they cough,
And complain of their servants to pass the time off;
Or list to the tale of some doating mamma
How her ten weeks old baby will laugh and say *taa*!
   But *tea*, that enlivener of wit and of soul
More loquacious by far than the draughts of the bowl,
Soon unloosens the tongue and enlivens the mind,
And enlightens their eyes to the faults of mankind.
It brings on the tapis their neighbours defects,
The faults of their friends or their wilful neglects;
Reminds them of many a good natured tale,
About those who are stylish or those who are frail,
Till the sweet tempered dames are converted by tea,
Into character manglers—Gunaikophagi.*

'Twas thus with the Pythia who served at the fount,
That flowed near the far famed parnassian mount:
While the steam she inhaled of the sulphuric spring,
Her vision expanded, her fancy took wing,
By its aid she pronounced the oracular will,
That Apollo commanded his sons to fulfill.
But alas! the sad vestal performing the rite

---

*I was very anxious that our friend Pindar, should give up this learned word, as being rather above the comprehension of his fair readers; but the old gentleman, according to custom, swore it was the finest point in his whole poem—so I knew it was in vain to say any more about it.

                               W. WIZARD.

Appeared like a demon—terrifick to sight,
E'en the priests of Apollo averted their eyes,
And the temple of Delphi resounded her cries.
But quitting the nymph of the tripod of yore,
We return to the dames of the tea-pot once more.

In harmless chit-chat an acquaintance they roast,
And serve up a friend, as they serve up a toast,
Some gentle *faux pas*, or some female *mistake*,
Is like sweetmeats delicious, or relished as cake;
A bit of broad scandal is like a dry crust,
It would stick in the throat, so they butter it first
With a little affected good-nature, and cry
"No body regrets the thing deeper than I."
Our young ladies nibble a good name in play
As for pastime they nibble a biscuit away:
While with shrugs and surmises, the toothless old dame,
As she mumbles a crust she will mumble a name.
And as the fell sisters astonished the scot,
In predicting of Banquo's descendants the lot,
Making shadows of kings, amid flashes of light,
To appear in array and to frown in his sight.
So they conjure up spectres all hideous in hue,
Which, as shades of their neighbours, are passed in review.

The wives of our cits of inferior degree,
Will soak up repute in a little *bohea*;
The potion is vulgar, and vulgar the slang
With which on their neighbours' defects they harangue.
But the scandal improves, (a refinement in wrong)
As our matrons are richer and rise to *souchong*.
With *hyson*—a beverage that's still more refined,
Our ladies of fashion enliven their mind,
And by nods, inuendos, and hints, and what not,
Reputations and tea send together to pot.
While madam in cambricks and laces arrayed;
With her plate and her liveries in splendid parade,
Will drink in *imperial* a friend at a sup,
Or in *gunpowder* blow them by dozens all up.
Ah me! how I groan when with full swelling sail,
Wafted stately along by the favouring gale,
A China ship proudly arrives in our bay,

Displaying her streamers and blazing away.
Oh! more fell to our port, is the cargo she bears,
Than granadoes, torpedoes, or warlike affairs:
Each chest is a bombshell thrown into our town
To shatter repute and bring characters down.
   Ye Samquas, ye Chinquas, ye Chouquas, so free,
Who discharge on our coast your cursed quantums of tea,
Oh think as ye waft the sad weed from your strand,
Of the plagues and vexations ye deal to our land.
As the Upas' dread breath o'er the plain where it flies,
Empoisons and blasts each green blade that may rise,
So wherever the leaves of your shrub find their way,
The social affections soon suffer decay:
Like to Java's drear waste they embarren the heart,
Till the blossoms of love and of friendship depart.
   Ah ladies, and was it by heaven designed,
That ye should be merciful, loving and kind!
Did it form you like angels, and send you below
To prophesy peace—to bid charity flow!
And have ye thus left your primeval estate,
And wandered so widely—so strangely of late?
Alas! the sad cause I too plainly can see—
These evils have all come upon you through *tea*:
Cursed weed that can make our fair spirits resign
The character mild of their mission divine,
That can blot from their bosoms that tenderness true,
Which from female to female forever is due!
Oh how nice is the texture—how fragile the frame
Of that delicate blossom, a female's fair fame!
Tis the sensitive plant, it recoils from the breath
And shrinks from the touch as if pregnant with death.
How often, how often, has innocence sigh'd;
Has beauty been reft of its honour—its pride;
Has virtue, though pure as an angel of light,
Been painted as dark as a demon of night:
All offer'd up victims, an *auto de fe*,
At the gloomy cabals—the dark orgies of tea.
   If I, in the remnant that's left me of life,
Am to suffer the torments of slanderous strife,
Let me fall I implore in the slang-whangers claw,

ere the evil is open, and subject to law.
nibbled and mumbled and put to the rack
ce sly underminings of tea party clack:
Condemn me, ye gods, to a newspaper roasting,
But spare me! oh spare me a tea table toasting!

SALMAGUNDI NO. XX

Monday, January 25, 1808.

FROM MY ELBOW-CHAIR.
Extremum hunc nihi concede laborem.   VIRG.
"Soft you, a word or two before we part."

IN THIS SEASON of festivity when the gate of time swings open on its hinges, and an honest rosy-faced New-Year comes waddling in, like a jolly fat-sided alderman, loaded with good wishes, good humour and minced pies—at this joyous era it has been the custom, from time immemorial, in this antient and respectable city, for periodical writers, from reverend, grave, and potent essayists like ourselves, down to the humble but industrious editors of magazines, reviews, and newspapers, to tender their subscribers the compliments of the season, and when they have slily thawed their hearts with a little of the sunshine of flattery, to conclude by delicately dunning them for their arrears of subscription money. In like manner the carriers of newspapers, who undoubtedly belong to the antient and honourable order of literati, do regularly at the commencement of the year, salute their patrons with abundance of excellent advice, conveyed in exceeding good poetry, for which the aforesaid good-natured patrons are well pleased to pay them exactly twenty-five cents. In walking the streets, I am every day saluted with good wishes from old grey-headed negroes, whom I never recollect to have seen before; and it was but a few days ago, that I was called out to receive the compliments of an ugly old woman, who last spring was employed by mrs. Cockloft to white-wash my room and put things in order: a phrase which, if rightly understood, means little else than huddling every thing into holes and corners, so that if I want to find any particular article, it is, in the language of an humble but expressive saying—"looking for a needle in a haystack." Not recognizing my visitor, I demanded by what authority she wished me a "Happy New-Year?" Her claim was one of the weakest she could have urged, for I have an innate and mortal antipathy to this custom of *putting things to rights*—so giving the old witch a pistareen, I desired her forthwith to mount her broomstick, and ride off as fast as possible.

Of all the various ranks of society, the bakers alone, to their immortal honour be it recorded, depart from this practice of making a market of congratulations; and, in addition to always allowing thirteen to the dozen, do, with great liberality, instead of drawing on the purses of their customers at the New-Year, present them with divers large, fair spiced cakes, which, like the shield of Achilles, or an egyptian obelisk, are adorned with figures of a variety of strange animals, that in their conformation, out-marvel all the wild wonders of nature.

This honest grey-beard custom of setting apart a certain portion of this good-for-nothing existence, for purposes of cordiality, social merriment, and good cheer, is one of the inestimable relicks handed down to us from our worthy dutch ancestors. In perusing one of the manuscripts from my worthy grandfather's mahogany chest of drawers, I find the new year was celebrated with great festivity during that golden age of our city, when the reins of government were held by the renowned Rip Van Dam, who always did honour to the season, by *seeing out the old year*, a ceremony which consisted of plying his guests with bumpers, until not one of them was capable of seeing. "Truely," observes my grandfather, who was generally of these parties—"Truely, he was a most stately and magnificent burgomaster, inasmuch, as he did right lustily carouse it with his friends, about new-year; roasting huge quantities of turkies; baking innumerable minced pies, and smacking the lips of all fair ladies the which he did meet, with such sturdy emphasis that the same might have been heard the distance of a stone's throw." In his days, according to my grandfather, were first invented those notable cakes, hight *new-year cookies*, which originally were impressed on one side with the honest burley countenance of the illustrious Rip, and on the other with that of the noted St. Nicholas, vulgarly called Santaclaus—of all the saints in the kalendar the most venerated by true hollanders, and their unsophisticated descendants. These cakes are to this time given on the first of January, to all visitors, together with a glass of cherry-bounce, or raspberry-brandy. It is with great regret, however, I observe that the simplicity of this venerable usage has been much violated by modern pretenders to style, and our respectable new-year cookies, and cherry-bounce, elbowed aside by plumb-cake and outlandish liqueurs, in the same way that our worthy old dutch families are out-dazzled by modern upstarts, and mushroom cockneys.

In addition to this divine origin of new-year festivity, there is something exquisitely grateful to a good-natured mind, in seeing every face dressed in smiles—in hearing the oft repeated salutations that flow spontaneously from the heart to the lips—in beholding the poor for once, enjoying the smiles of plenty, and forgetting the cares which press hard upon them, in the jovial revelry of the feelings—the young children decked out in their sunday clothes, and freed from their only cares, the cares of the school, tripping through the streets on errands of pleasure—and even the very negroes, those holiday-loving rogues, gorgeously arrayed in cast-off finery, collected in juntoes at corners, displaying their white teeth, and making the welkin ring with bursts of laughter, loud enough to crack even the icy cheek of old winter. There is something so pleasant in all this, that I confess it would give me a real pain, to behold the frigid influence of modern style, cheating us of this jubilee of the heart, and converting it, as it does every other article of social intercourse, into an idle, and unmeaning ceremony. 'Tis the annual festival of good-humour—it comes in the dead of winter, when nature is without a charm, when our pleasures are contracted to the fire-side, and where every thing that unlocks the icy fetters of the heart, and sets the genial current flowing, should be cherished, as a stray lamb found in the wilderness, or a flower blooming among thorns and briers.

Animated by these sentiments, it is with peculiar satisfaction I perceived that the last new-year was kept with more than ordinary enthusiasm. It seemed as if the good old times had rolled back again, and brought with them all the honest, unceremonious intercourse of those golden days, when people were more open and sincere, more moral, and more hospitable than now—when every object carried about it a charm which the hand of time has stolen away, or turned to a deformity—when the women were more simple, more domestick, more lovely, and more true; and when even the sun, like a hearty old blade, as he is, shone with a genial lustre, unknown in these degenerate days:—in short, those fairy times when I was a mad-cap boy, crowding every enjoyment into the present moment—making of the past an oblivion—of the future a heaven; and careless of all that was "over the hills and far away." Only one thing was wanting to make every part of the celebration accord with its antient simplicity.—The ladies, who (I write it with the most piercing regret) are generally at the head of all domestick innovations, most fastidiously refused that mark of good will, that chaste and holy salute which was so fashionable in the happy days of governor Rip and the patriarchs.—Even the miss Cocklofts, who belong to a family that is the last entrenchment behind which the manners of the good old school have retired, made violent opposition; and whenever a gentleman entered the room, immediately put themselves in a posture of defence;—this Will Wizard, with his usual shrewdness, insists was only to give the visitor a hint that they expected an attack, and declares he has uniformly observed, that the resistance of those ladies, who make the greatest noise and bustle, is most easily overcome. This sad innovation originated with my good aunt Charity, who was as arrant a tabby as ever wore whiskers; and I am not a little afflicted to find that she has found so many followers, even among the young and beautiful.

In compliance with an antient and venerable custom, sanctioned by time and our ancestors, and more especially by my own inclinations, I will take this opportunity to salute my readers with as many good wishes, as I can possibly spare; for in truth, I have been so prodigal of late, that I have but few remaining. I should have offered my congratulations sooner, but to be candid, having made the last new-year's campaign, according to custom under cousin Christopher, in which I have seen some pretty hard service, my head has been somewhat out of order of late, and my intellects rather cloudy for clear writing. Beside, I may allege as another reason, that I have deferred my greetings until this day, which is exactly one year since we introduced ourselves to the publick; and surely periodical writers have the same right of dating from the commencement of their works, that monarchs have from the time of their coronation, or our most puissant republick, from the declaration of its independence.

These good wishes are warmed into more than usual benevolence, by the thought that I am now perhaps addressing my old friends for the last time. That we should thus cut off our work in the very vigour of its existence, may excite some little matter of wonder in this enlightened community. Now though we could give a variety of good reasons, for so doing, yet it would be an ill-natured act to deprive the publick of such an admirable opportunity to indulge in their favourite amusement of conjecture—so we generously leave them to flounder in the smooth ocean of glorious uncertainty. Beside, we have ever considered it as beneath persons of our dignity, to account for our movements or caprices—thank heaven we are not like the unhappy rulers of this enlightened land, accountable to the mob for our actions, or dependant on their smiles for support:—this much, however, we will say, it is not for want of subjects that we stop our career. We are not in the situation of poor Alexander the Great, who wept, as well indeed he might, because there were no more worlds to conquer; for, to do justice to this queer, odd, rantipole city, and this whimsical country, there is matter enough in them, to keep our risible muscles, and our pens going until doomsday.

Most people, in taking a farewel which may perhaps be forever, are anxious to part on good terms, and it is usual in such melancholy occasions, for even enemies to shake hands, forget their previous quarrels, and bury all former animosities in parting regrets. Now because most people do this, I am determined to act in quite a different way; for as I have lived, so should I wish to die in my own way, without imitating any person, whatever may be his rank, talents, or reputation. Besides, if I know our trio, we have no enmities to obliterate, no hatchet to bury, and as to all injuries—those we have long since forgiven. At this moment, there is not an individual in the world, not even the Pope himself, to whom we have any personal hostility. But if, shutting their eyes to the many striking proofs of good-nature displayed through the whole course of this work, there should be any persons so singularly ridiculous as to take offence at our strictures, we heartily forgive their stupidity, earnestly intreating them to desist from

all manifestations of ill-humour, lest they should, peradventure, be classed under some one of the denominations of recreants, we have felt it our duty to hold up to public ridicule.
Even at this moment, we feel a glow of parting philanthropy
stealing upon us—a sentiment of cordial good will towards
the numerous host of readers that have jogged on at our heels
during the last year; and in justice to ourselves, must seriously
protest, that if at any time we have treated them a little un-
gently, it was purely in that spirit of hearty affection, with
which a schoolmaster drubs an unlucky urchin, or a humane
muleteer his recreant animal, at the very moment when his
heart is brim-full of loving kindness. If this is not considered
an ample justification, so much the worse; for in that case I
fear we shall remain forever unjustified—a most desperate extremity, and worthy of every man's commisseration!

One circumstance in particular, has tickled us mightily, as
we jogged along; and that is, the astonishing secrecy with
which we have been able to carry on our lucubrations! Fully
aware of the profound sagacity of the publick of Gotham, and
their wonderful faculty of distinguishing a writer by his style,
it is with great self-congratulation we find that suspicion has
never pointed to us as the authors of Salmagundi. Our grey-
beard speculations have been most bountifully attributed to
sundry smart young gentlemen, who, for aught we know,
have no beards at all; and we have often been highly amused,
when they were charged with the sin of writing what their
harmless minds never conceived, to see them affect all the
blushing modesty and beautiful embarrassment of detected
virgin authors. The profound and penetrating publick, having
so long been led away from truth and nature by a constant
perusal of those delectable histories, and romances, from beyond seas, in which human nature is for the most part
wickedly mangled and debauched, have never once imagined
this work was a genuine and most authentick history—that
the Cocklofts were a real family dwelling in the city—paying
scot and lot, entitled to the right of suffrage, and holding
several respectable offices in the corporation.—As little do
they suspect that there is a knot of merry old bachelors seated
snugly in the old-fashioned parlour of an old-fashioned dutch
house, with a weathercock on the top, that came from Hol-

land; who amuse themselves of an evening by laughing at their neighbours, in an honest way, and who manage to jog on through the streets of our antient and venerable city, without elbowing or being elbowed by a living soul.

When we first adopted the idea of discontinuing this work, we determined, in order to give the criticks a fair opportunity for dissection, to declare ourselves, one and all, absolutely defunct; for it is one of the rare and invaluable privileges of a periodical writer, that by an act of innocent suicide he may lawfully consign himself to the grave, and cheat the world of posthumous renown. But we abandoned this scheme for many substantial reasons. In the first place, we care but little for the opinion of criticks, who we consider a kind of freebooters in the republick of letters; who, like deer, goats, and divers other graminivorous animals, gain subsistence by gorging upon the buds and leaves of the young shrubs of the forest, thereby robbing them of their verdure, and retarding their progress to maturity. It also occurred to us that though an author might lawfully, in all countries, kill himself outright, yet this privilege did not extend to the raising himself from the dead, if he was ever so anxious; and all that is left him in such a case, is to take the benefit of the metempsychosis act, and revive under a new name and form.

Far be it, therefore, from us, to condemn ourselves to useless embarrassments, should we ever be disposed to resume the guardianship of this learned city of Gotham, and finish this invaluable work, which is yet but half completed. We hereby openly and seriously declare that we are not dead, but intend, if it pleases providence, to live for many years to come—to enjoy life with the genuine relish of honest souls, careless of riches, honours, and every thing but a good name, among good fellows; and with the full expectation of shuffling off the remnant of existence, after the excellent fashion of that merry grecian, who died laughing.

TO THE LADIES.
BY ANTHONY EVERGREEN, GENT.

Next to our being a knot of independent old bachelors, there is nothing on which we pride ourselves more highly, than upon possessing that true chivalrick spirit of gallantry, which distinguished the days of king Arthur, and his valiant peers of the Round-table. We cannot, therefore, leave the lists where we have so long been tilting at folly, without giving a farewel salutation to those noble dames and beauteous damsels who have honoured us with their presence at the tourney. Like true knights, the only recompense we crave is the smile of beauty, and the approbation of those gentle fair ones, whose smile and whose approbation far excels all the trophies of honour, and all the rewards of successful ambition. True it is that we have suffered infinite perils, in standing forth as their champions, from the sly attacks of sundry arch caitiffs, who in the overflowings of their malignity have even accused us of entering the lists as defenders of the very foibles and faults of the sex.—Would that we could meet with these recreants hand to hand—they should receive no more quarter than giants and enchanters in romance.

Had we a spark of vanity in our natures, here is a glorious occasion to show our skill in refuting these illiberal insinuations—but there is something manly, and ingenuous, in making an honest confession of ones offences when about retiring from the world—and so, without any more ado, we doff our helmets and thus publickly plead guilty to the deadly sin of GOOD NATURE; hoping and expecting forgiveness from our good natured readers—yet careless whether they bestow it or not. And in this we do but imitate sundry condemned criminals; who, finding themselves convicted of a capital crime, with great openness and candour, do generally in their last dying speech make a confession of all their previous offences, which confession is always read with great delight by all true lovers of biography.

Still, however, notwithstanding our notorious devotion to the gentle sex, and our indulgent partiality, we have endeavoured, on divers occasions, with all the polite and becoming delicacy of true respect, to reclaim them from many of those delusive follies and unseemly peccadilloes in which they are unhappily too prone to indulge. We have warned them against the sad consequences of encountering our midnight damps and withering wintry blasts—we have endeavoured, with pious hand, to snatch them from the wildering mazes of the waltz, and thus rescuing them from the arms of strangers, to restore them to the bosoms of their friends—to preserve them from the nakedness, the famine, the cobweb muslins, the vinegar cruet, the corset, the stay tape, the buckram, and all the other miseries and racks of a *fine figure*. But above all we have endeavoured to lure them from the mazes of a dissipated world, where they wander about careless of their value, until they lose their original worth—and to restore them before it is too late, to the sacred asylum of home, the soil most congenial to the opening blossom of female loveliness, where it blooms and expands in safety in the fostering sunshine of maternal affection, and where its heavenly sweets are best known and appreciated.

Modern philosophers may determine the proper destination of the sex—they may assign to them an extensive and brilliant orbit in which to revolve, to the delight of the million and the confusion of man's superior intellect; but when on this subject we disclaim philosophy, and appeal to the higher tribunal of the heart—and what heart that had not lost its better feelings, would ever seek to repose its happiness on the bosom of one, whose pleasures all lay without the threshold of home—who snatched enjoyment only in the whirlpool of dissipation, and amid the thoughtless and evanescent gaiety of a ball room. The fair one who is forever in the career of amusement, may for a while dazzle, astonish and entertain; but we are content with coldly admiring and fondly turn from glitter and noise, to seek the happy fire side of social life there to confide our dearest and best affections.

Yet some there are, and we delight to mention them, who mingle freely with the world, unsullied by its contaminations; whose brilliant minds, like the stars of the firmament, are destined to shed their light abroad, and gladden every beholder with their radiance—to withhold them from the world, would be doing it injustice—they are inestimable gems, which were never formed to be shut up in caskets; but to be the pride and ornament of elegant society.

We have endeavoured always to discriminate between a female of this superior order, and the thoughtless votary of pleasure; who, destitute of intellectual resources, is servilely dependant on others for every little pittance of enjoyment; who exhibits herself incessantly amid the noise, the giddy frolick and capricious variety of fashionable assemblages; dissipating her languid affections on a crowd—lavishing her ready smiles with indiscriminate prodigality on the worthy, or the undeserving; and listening, with equal vacancy of mind, to the conversation of the enlightened, the frivolity of the coxcomb, and the flourish of the fiddlestick.

There is a certain artificial polish—a common place vivacity acquired by perpetually mingling in the *beau-monde*; which, in the commerce of the world, supplies the place of natural suavity and good humour, but is purchased at the expense of all original and sterling traits of character. By a kind of fashionable discipline, the eye is taught to brighten, the lip to smile, and the whole countenance to emanate with the semblance of friendly welcome—while the bosom is unwarmed by a single spark of genuine kindness, or good will. This elegant simulation may be admired by the connoisseur of human character, as a perfection of art; but the heart is not to be deceived by the superficial illusion: it turns with delight to the timid retiring fair one, whose smile is the smile of nature; whose blush is the soft suffusion of delicate sensibility; and whose affections, unblighted by the chilling effects of dissipation, glow with all the tenderness and purity of artless youth. Her's is a singleness of mind, a native innocence of manners, and a sweet timidity, that steal insensibly upon the heart and lead it a willing captive—though venturing occasionally among the fairy haunts of pleasure, she shrinks from the broad glare of notoriety, and seems to seek refuge among her friends, even from the admiration of the world.

These observations bring to mind a little allegory in one of the manuscripts of the sage Mustapha, which being in some measure applicable to the subject of this essay, we transcribe for the benefit of our fair readers.

Among the numerous race of the Bedouins, who people the vast tracts of Arabia Deserta, is a small tribe, remarkable for their habits of solitude and love of independence. They are of a rambling disposition, roving from waste to waste, slaking their thirst at such scanty pools as are found in those cheerless plains, and glory in the unenvied liberty they enjoy.

A youthful arab of this tribe, a simple son of nature, at length growing weary of his precarious and unsettled mode of life, determined to set out in search of some permanent abode. "I will seek" said he "some happy region, some generous clime, where the dews of heaven diffuse fertility—I will find out some unfailing stream, and forsaking the joyless life of my forefathers, settle on its borders, dispose my mind to gentle pleasures and tranquil enjoyments, and never wander more."

Enchanted with this picture of pastoral felicity, he departed from the tents of his companions, and having journeyed during five days, on the sixth, as the sun was just rising in all the splendours of the east, he lifted up his eyes and beheld extended before him, in smiling luxuriance, the fertile regions of Arabia the Happy. Gently swelling hills, tufted with blooming groves, swept down into luxuriant vales, enamelled with flowers of never withering beauty. The sun, no longer darting his rays with torrid fervour, beamed with a genial warmth that gladdened and enriched the landscape. A pure and temperate serenity, an air of voluptuous repose, a smile of contented abundance pervaded the face of nature, and every zephyr breathed a thousand delicious odours. The soul of the youthful wanderer expanded with delight—he raised his eyes to heaven, and almost mingled with his tribute of gratitude a sigh of regret, that he had lingered so long amid the sterile solitudes of the desart.

With fond impatience he hastened to make choice of a stream where he might fix his habitation, and taste the promised sweets of this land of delight. But here commenced an unforseen perplexity; for, though he beheld innumerable streams on every side, yet not one could he find which completely answered his high raised expectations. One abounded with wild and picturesque beauty, but it was capricious and unsteady in its course; sometimes dashing its angry billows against the rocks, and often raging and overflowing its banks. Another flowed smoothly along, with out even a ripple or a murmur; but its bottom was soft and muddy, and its current dull and sluggish. A third was pure and transparent, but its waters were of a chilling coldness, and it had rocks and flints in its bosom. A fourth was dulcet in its tinklings, and graceful in its meanderings; but it had a cloying sweetness that palled upon the taste; while a fifth possessed a sparkling vivacity, and a pungency of flavour, that deterred the wanderer from repeating his draught.

The youthful Bedouin, began to weary with fruitless trials and repeated disappointments, when his attention was suddenly attracted by a lively brook, whose dancing waves glittered in the sunbeams, and whose prattling current communicated an air of bewitching gaiety to the surrounding landscape. The heart of the wayworn traveller beat with expectation; but on regarding it attentively in its course, he found that it constantly avoided the embowering shade, loitering with equal fondness, whether gliding through the rich valley, or over the barren sand—that the fragrant flower, the fruitful shrub, and worthless bramble were alike fostered by its waves, and that its current was often interrupted by unprofitable weeds. With idle ambition it expanded itself beyond its proper bounds, and spread into a shallow waste of water, destitute of beauty or utility, and babbling along with uninteresting vivacity and vapid turbulence.

The wandering son of the desert turned away with a sigh of regret, and pitied a stream which, if content within its natural limits, might have been the pride of the valley, and the object of all his wishes. Pensive, musing and disappointed, he slowly pursued his now almost hopeless pilgrimage, and had rambled for some time along the margin of a gentle rivulet, before he became sensible of its beauties. It was a simple pastoral stream, which, shunning the noonday glare, pursued its unobtrusive course through retired and tranquil vales—now dimpling among flowery banks and tufted shrubbery; now winding among spicy groves, whose aromatick foliage fondly bent down to meet the limpid wave. Sometimes, but not often, it would venture from its covert to stray through a flowery meadow, but quickly, as if fearful of being seen, stole back again into its more congenial shade, and there lingered with sweet delay. Wherever it bent its course, the face of nature brightened into smiles, and a perennial spring reigned upon its borders. The warblers of the woodland delighted to quit their recesses and carol among its bowers; while the turtle-dove, the timid fawn, the soft-eyed gazel, and all the rural populace who joy in the sequestered haunts of nature, resorted to its vicinity.—Its pure transparent waters rolled over snow-white sands, and heaven itself was reflected in its tranquil bosom.

The simple arab threw himself upon its verdant margin—he tasted the silver tide, and it was like nectar to his lips—he bounded with transport, for he had found the object of his wayfaring. "Here," cried he, " will I pitch my tent—here will I pass my days; for pure, oh fair stream, is thy gentle current; beauteous are the borders; and the grove must be a paradise that is refreshed by thy meanderings!"

> *Pendent opera interrupta.*   VIRG.
> *The work's all aback.*   LINK FID.

"How hard it is" exclaims the divine Con-fut-sé (better known among the illiterate by the name of Confucius) for a man to bite off his own nose! At this moment I, William Wizard, esq. feel the full force of this remark, and cannot but give vent to my tribulation at being obliged through the whim of friend Langstaff, to stop short in my literary career when at the very point of astonishing my country, and reaping the brightest laurels of literature. We daily hear of shipwrecks, of failures and bankruptcies, they are trifling mishaps which from their frequency excite but little astonishment or sympathy; but it is not often that we hear of a man's letting immortality slip through his fingers, and when he does meet with such a misfortune, who would deny him the comfort of bewailing his calamity?

Next to the embargo laid upon our commerce, the greatest publick annoyance is the embargo laid upon our work: in consequence of which the produce of my wits like that of my country must remain at home, and my ideas, like so many merchantmen in port or redoubtable frigates in the Potomac, moulder away in the mud of my own brain. I know of few things in this world more annoying than to be interrupted in the middle of a favourite story, at the most interesting part, where one expects to shine; or to have a conversation broken off just when you are about coming out with a score of excellent jokes, not one of which but was good enough to make every fine figure in corsets literally split her sides with laughter.—In some such predicament am I placed at present; and I do protest to you, my good-looking and well-beloved readers, by the chop-sticks of the immortal Josh, I was on the very brink of treating you with a full broadside of the most ingenious and instructive essays, that your precious noddles were ever bothered with.

In the first place, I had with infinite labour and pains, and by consulting the divine Plato, Sanconiathon, Appollonius Rhodius, sir John Harrington, Noah Webster, Linkum Fidelius and others, fully refuted all those wild theories respecting the first settlement of our venerable country; and proved, beyond contradiction, that America, so far from being, as the writers of upstart Europe denominate it, *the new world*, is at least as old as any country in existence, not excepting Egypt, China, or even the land of the Assiniboils, which, according to the traditions of that antient people, has already assisted at the funerals of thirteen suns, and four hundred and seventy thousand moons!

I had likewise written a long dissertation on certain hieroglyphicks discovered on those fragments of the moon which have lately fallen, with singular propriety, in a neighbouring state—and have thrown considerable light on the state of literature and the arts in that planet—showing that the universal language which prevails there is high dutch—thereby proving it to be the most antient and original tongue, and corroborating the opinion of a celebrated poet, that it is the language in which the serpent tempted our grandmother Eve.

To support the theatrick department, I had several very judicious critiques, ready written wherein no quarter was shown either to authors or actors; and I was only waiting to determine at what plays or performances they should be levelled. As to the grand spectacle of Cinderella, which is to be represented this season, I had given it a most unmerciful handling: showing that it was neither tragedy, comedy, nor farce; that the incidents were highly improbable, that the prince played like a perfect harlequin, that the white mice were merely powdered for the occasion, and that the new moon had a most outrageous copper nose.

But my most profound and erudite essay in embryo, is an

analytical, hypercritical, review of these Salmagundi lucubrations; which I had written partly in revenge for the many
waggish jokes played off against me by my confederates, and
partly for the purpose of saving much invaluable labour to
the Zoiluses and Dennises of the age, by detecting and exposing all the similarities, resemblances, synonimies, analogies,
coincidences, &c. which occur in this work.

I hold it downright plagiarism for any author to write or
even to think in the same manner with any other writer that
either did, doth, or may exist. It is a sage maxim of law—
"*Ignorantia neminem excusat*"—and the same has been extended to literature: so that if an author shall publish an idea
that has been ever hinted by another, it shall be no exculpa-
tion for him to plead ignorance of the fact. All, therefore, that
I had to do was to take a good pair of spectacles, or a mag-
nifying-glass, and with Salmagundi in hand and a table full of
books before me, to mouse over them alternately, in a corner
of Cockloft library: carefully comparing and contrasting all
odd ends and fragments of sentences. Little did honest
Launce suspect, when he sat lounging and scribbling in his
elbow-chair, with no other stock to draw upon than his own
brain, and no other authority to consult than the sage
Linkum Fidelius—little did he think that his careless, un-
studied effusions, would receive such scrupulous investigation.

By laborious researches, and patiently collating words,
where sentences and ideas did not correspond, I have detected
sundry sly disguises and metamorphoses of which, I'll be
bound, Langstaff himself is ignorant. Thus, for instance—
The Little Man in Black, is evidently no less a personage than
old Goody Blake, or goody something, filched from the Spectator, who confessedly filched her from Otway's " wrinkled
hag with age grown double." My friend Launce has taken the
honest old woman, dressed her up in the cast-off suit worn
by Twaits in Lampedo, and endeavoured to palm the impos-
ture upon the enlightened inhabitants of Gotham. No further
proof of the fact need be given, than that Goody Blake was
taken for a witch, and the little man in black for a conjuror,
and that they both lived in villages, the inhabitants of which
were distinguished by a most respectful abhorrence of hob-

goblins and broomsticks—to be sure the astonishing similarity ends here, but surely that is enough to prove that the little
man in black is no other than Goody Blake in the disguise of
a white witch.

Thus, also, the sage Mustapha, in mistaking a brag-party
for a convention of Magi studying hieroglyphicks, may pretend to originality of idea and to a familiar acquaintance with
the black-letter literati of the east—but this tripolitan trick
will not pass here—I refer those who wish to detect his lar-
ceny to one of those wholesale jumbles, or hodge-podge collections of science, which, like a tailor's pandemonium, or a
giblet-pie, are receptacles for scientifick fragments of all sorts
and sizes. The reader, learned in dictionary studies, will at
once perceive I mean an encyclopoedia. There, under the title
of magi, Egypt, cards, or hieroglyphicks, I forget which, will
be discovered an idea similar to that of Mustapha, as snugly
concealed as truth at the bottom of a well, or the misletoe
amid the shady branches of an oak:—and it may at any time
be drawn from its lurking-place, by those hewers of wood
and drawers of water, who labour in the humbler walks of
criticism. This is assuredly a most unpardonable error of the
sage Mustapha, who had been the captain of a ketch, and of
course, as your nautical men are for the most part very
learned, ought to have known better. But this is not the only
blunder of the grave mussulman who swears by the head of
Amrou, the beard of Barbarossa, and the sword of Khalid, as
glibly as our good christian soldiers anathematize body and
soul, or a sailor his eyes and odd limbs. Now, I solemnly
pledge myself to the world, that in all my travels through the
east, in Persia, Arabia, China and Egypt, I never heard man,
woman, or child, utter any of these preposterous and new
fangled asseverations; and that, so far from swearing by any
man's head, it is considered throughout the east, the greatest
insult that can be offered to either the living or dead, to meddle in any shape even with his beard. These are but two or
three specimens of the exposures I would have made—but I
should have descended still lower, nor would have spared the
most insignificant *and*, or *but*, or *nevertheless*, provided I
could have found a ditto in the Spectator or the dictionary—
but all these minutiae I bequeath to the lilliputian literati of

this sagacious community, who are fond of hunting "such small deer," and I earnestly pray they may find full employment for a twelvemonth to come.

But the most outrageous plagiarisms of friend Launcelot, are those made on sundry living personages. Thus; Tom Straddle has been evidently stolen from a distinguished *Brumagem* emigrant, since they both ride on horseback—Dabble, the great little man, has his origin in a certain aspiring counsellor, who is rising in the world as rapidly as the heaviness of his head will permit—Mine Uncle John will bear a tolerable comparison, particularly as it respects the sterling qualities of his heart, with a worthy yeoman of Westchester-county;—and to deck out Aunt Charity and the amiable Miss Cocklofts, he has rifled the charms of half the antient vestals in the city. Nay, he has taken unpardonable liberties with my own person—elevating me on the substantial pedestals of a worthy gentleman from China, and tricking me out with claret coats, tight breeches, and silver-sprigged dickeys, in such sort that I can scarcely recognize my own resemblance—whereas I absolutely declare that I am an exceeding good-looking man, neither too tall nor too short, too old nor too young, with a person indifferently robust, a head rather inclining to be large, an easy swing in my walk; and that I wear my own hair, neither queued, nor cropped, nor turned up, but in a fair, pendulous, oscillating club, tied with a yard of ninepenny black ribband.

And now having said all that occurs to me on the present pathetick occasion—having made my speech, wrote my eulogy, and drawn my portrait, I bid my readers an affectionate farewel; exhorting them to live honestly and soberly—paying their taxes and reverencing the state, the church and the corporation—reading diligently the bible, the almanack, the newspaper and Salmagundi—which is all the reading an honest citizen has occasion for—and eschewing all spirit of faction, discontent, irreligion and criticism.

which is all at present,
from their departed friend,
WILLIAM WIZARD.

A HISTORY
O F
NEW YORK,

From the Beginning of the World to the
End of the Dutch Dynasty.

CONTAINING

Among many Surprising and Curious Matters, the Unutterable Ponderings of WALTER THE DOUBTER, the Disastrous Projects of WILLIAM THE TESTY, and the
Chivalric Achievements of PETER THE HEADSTRONG, the
three Dutch Governors of NEW AMSTERDAM; being
the only Authentic History of the Times that ever
hath been, or ever will be Published.

BY DIEDRICH KNICKERBOCKER.

De waarheid die in duister lag,
Die komt met klaarheid aan den dag.

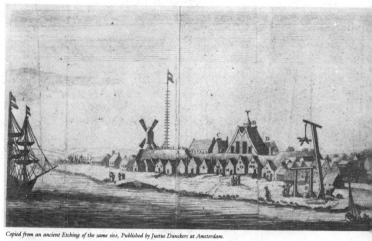

Copied from an ancient Etching of the same size, Published by Justus Danckers at Amsterdam.

A. The Fort.
B. Church of St. Nicholas.
C. The Jail
D. Governor's House

NEW AMSTERDAM
As it appeared about the year 1640

ₙow NEW-YORK).

ₑile under the Dutch Government.

E. *The Gallows.*
F. *The Pillory.*
G. *West India Companie's Stores.*
H. *City Tavern.*

Contents

BOOK VII.

Account of the Author

IT WAS SOMETIME, if I recollect right, in the early part of the Fall of 1808, that a stranger applied for lodgings at the Independent Columbian Hotel in Mulberry Street, of which I am landlord. He was a small brisk looking old gentleman, dressed in a rusty black coat, a pair of olive velvet breeches, and a small cocked hat. He had a few grey hairs plaited and clubbed behind, and his beard seemed to be of some four and twenty hours growth. The only piece of finery which he bore about him, was a bright pair of square silver shoe buckles, and all his baggage was contained in a pair of saddle bags which he carried under his arm. His whole appearance was something out of the common run, and my wife, who is a very shrewd body, at once set him down for some eminent country school-master.

As the Independent Columbian Hotel is a very small house, I was a little puzzled at first where to put him; but my wife, who seemed taken with his looks, would needs put him in her best chamber, which is genteely set off with the profiles of the whole family, done in black, by those two great painters Jarvis and Wood; and commands a very pleasant view of the new grounds on the Collect, together with the rear of the Poor house and Bridewell and the full front of the Hospital, so that it is the cheerfullest room in the whole house.

During the whole time that he stayed with us, we found him a very worthy good sort of an old gentleman, though a little queer in his ways. He would keep in his room for days together, and if any of the children cried or made a noise about his door, he would bounce out in a great passion, with his hands full of papers, and say something about "deranging his ideas," which made my wife believe sometimes that he was not altogether *compos*. Indeed there was more than one reason to make her think so, for his room was always covered with scraps of paper and old mouldy books, laying about at sixes and sevens, which he would never let any body touch; for he said he had laid them all away in their proper places, so that he might know where to find them; though for that matter, he was half his time worrying about the house in search of some book or writing which he had carefully put out of the way. I shall never forget what a pother he once made, because my wife cleaned out his room when his back was turned, and put every thing to rights; for he swore he should never be able to get his papers in order again in a twelvemonth— Upon this my wife ventured to ask him what he did with so many books and papers, and he told her that he was "seeking for immortality," which made her think more than ever, that the poor old gentleman's head was a little cracked.

He was a very inquisitive body, and when not in his room was continually poking about town, hearing all the news and prying into every thing that was going on; this was particularly the case about election time, when he did nothing but bustle about from poll to poll, attending all ward meetings and committee rooms; though I could never find that he took part with either side of the question. On the contrary he would come home and rail at both parties with great wrath— and plainly proved one day, to the satisfaction of my wife and three old ladies who were drinking tea with her, one of whom was as deaf as a post, that the two parties were like two rogues, each tugging at a skirt of the nation, and that in the end they would tear the very coat off of its back and expose its nakedness. Indeed he was an oracle among the neighbours, who would collect around him to hear him talk of an afternoon, as he smoaked his pipe on the bench before the door; and I really believe he would have brought over the whole neighbourhood to his own side of the question, if they could ever have found out what it was.

He was very much given to argue, or as he called it *philosophize*, about the most trifling matter, and to do him justice, I never knew any body that was a match for him, except it was a grave looking gentleman who called now and then to see him, and often posed him in an argument. But this is nothing surprising, as I have since found out this stranger is the city librarian, and of course must be a man of great learning; and I have my doubts, if he had not some hand in the following history.

As our lodger had been a long time with us, and we had never received any pay, my wife began to be somewhat uneasy, and curious to find out who, and what he was. She accordingly made bold to put the question to his friend, the librarian, who replied in his dry way, that he was one of the *Literati*; which she supposed to mean some new party in politics. I scorn to push a lodger for his pay, so I let day after day pass on without dunning the old gentleman for a farthing; but my wife, who always takes these matters on herself, and is as I said a shrewd kind of a woman, at last got out of patience, and hinted, that she thought it high time "some people should have a sight of some people's money." To which the old gentleman replied, in a mighty touchy manner, that she need not make herself uneasy, for that he had a treasure there (pointing to his saddle-bags) worth her whole house put together. This was the only answer we could ever get from him; and as my wife, by some of those odd ways in which women find out every thing, learnt that he was of very great connexions, being related to the Knickerbockers of Scaghtikoke, and cousin-german to the Congress-man of that name, she did not like to treat him uncivilly. What is more, she even offered, merely by way of making things easy, to let him live scot-free, if he would teach the children their letters; and to try her best and get the neighbours to send their children also; but the old gentleman took it in such dudgeon, and seemed so affronted at being taken for a school-master, that she never dared speak on the subject again.

About two month's ago, he went out of a morning, with a bundle in his hand—and has never been heard of since. All kinds of inquiries were made after him, but in vain. I wrote to his relations at Scaghtikoke, but they sent for answer, that he had not been there since the year before last, when he had a great dispute with the Congress-man about politics, and left the place in a huff, and they had neither heard nor seen any thing of him from that time to this. I must own I felt very much worried about the poor old gentleman, for I thought something bad must have happened to him, that he should be missing so long, and never return to pay his bill. I therefore advertised him in the news-papers, and though my melancholy advertisement was published by several humane printers, yet I have never been able to learn any thing satisfactory about him.

My wife now said it was high time to take care of ourselves, and see if he had left any thing behind in his room, that would pay us for his board and lodging. We found nothing however, but some old books and musty writings, and his pair of saddle bags, which being opened in presence of the librarian, contained only a few articles of worn out clothes, and a large bundle of blotted paper. On looking over this, the librarian told us, he had no doubt it was the treasure which the old gentleman had spoken about; as it proved to be a most excellent and faithful HISTORY OF NEW YORK, which he advised us by all means to publish: assuring us that it would be so eagerly bought up by a discerning public, that he had no doubt it would be enough to pay our arrears ten times over. Upon this we got a very learned school-master, who teaches our children, to prepare it for the press, which he accordingly has done, and has moreover, added to it a number of notes of his own; and an engraving of the city, as it was, at the time Mr. Knickerbocker writes about.

This, therefore, is a true statement of my reasons for having this work printed, without waiting for the consent of the author: and I here declare, that if he ever returns (though I much fear some unhappy accident has befallen him) I stand ready to account with him, like a true and honest man. Which is all at present—

From the public's humble servant,

SETH HANDASIDE.

Independent Columbian Hotel,
  New York.

To the Public

TO RESCUE from oblivion the memory of former incidents, and to render a just tribute of renown to the many great and wonderful transactions of our Dutch progenitors, Diedrich Knickerbocker, native of the city of New York, produces this historical essay."* Like the great Father of History whose words I have just quoted, I treat of times long past, over which the twilight of uncertainty had already thrown its shadows, and the night of forgetfulness was about to descend forever. With great solicitude had I long beheld the early history of this venerable and ancient city, gradually slipping from our grasp, trembling on the lips of narrative old age, and day by day dropping piece meal into the tomb. In a little while, thought I, and those venerable dutch burghers, who serve as the tottering monuments of good old times, will be gathered to their fathers; their children engrossed by the empty pleasures or insignificant transactions of the present age, will neglect to treasure up the recollections of the past, and posterity shall search in vain, for memorials of the days of the Patriarchs. The origin of our city will be buried in eternal oblivion, and even the names and atchievements of Wouter Van Twiller, William Kieft, and Peter Stuyvesant, be enveloped in doubt and fiction, like those of Romulus and Rhemus, of Charlemagne, King Arthur, Rinaldo, and Godfrey of Bologne.

Determined therefore, to avert if possible this threatening misfortune, I industriously sat myself to work, to gather together all the fragments of our infant history which still existed, and like my revered prototype Herodotus, where no written records could be found, I have endeavoured to continue the chain of history by well authenticated traditions.

In this arduous undertaking, which has been the whole business of a long and solitary life, it is incredible the number of learned authors I have consulted; and all to but little purpose. Strange as it may seem, though such multitudes of excellent works have been written about this country, there are

*Beloe's Herodotus.

none extant which give any full and satisfactory account of the early history of New York, or of its three first Dutch governors. I have, however, gained much valuable and curious matter from an elaborate manuscript written in exceeding pure and classic low dutch, excepting a few errors in orthography, which was found in the archives of the Stuyvesant family. Many legends, letters and other documents have I likewise gleaned, in my researches among the family chests and lumber garrets of our respectable dutch citizens, and I have gathered a host of well authenticated traditions from divers excellent old ladies of my acquaintance, who requested that their names might not be mentioned. Nor must I neglect to acknowledge, how greatly I have been assisted by that admirable and praiseworthy institution, the NEW YORK HISTORICAL SOCIETY, to which I here publicly return my sincere acknowledgements.

In the conduct of this inestimable work I have adopted no individual model, but on the contrary have simply contented myself with combining and concentrating the excellencies of the most approved ancient historians. Like Xenophon I have maintained the utmost impartiality, and the strictest adherence to truth throughout my history. I have enriched it after the manner of Sallust, with various characters of ancient worthies, drawn at full length, and faithfully coloured. I have seasoned it with profound political speculations like Thucydides, sweetened it with the graces of sentiment like Tacitus, and infused into the whole the dignity, the grandeur and magnificence of Livy.

I am aware that I shall incur the censure of numerous very learned and judicious critics, for indulging too frequently in the bold excursive manner of my favourite Herodotus. And to be candid, I have found it impossible always to resist the allurements of those pleasing episodes, which like flowery banks and fragrant bowers, beset the dusty road of the historian, and entice him to turn aside, and refresh himself from his wayfaring. But I trust it will be found, that I have always resumed my staff, and addressed myself to my weary journey with renovated spirits, so that both my readers and myself, have been benefited by the relaxation.

Indeed, though it has been my constant wish and uniform

endeavour, to rival Polybius himself, in observing the requisite unity of History, yet the loose and unconnected manner in which many of the facts herein recorded have come to hand, rendered such an attempt extremely difficult. This difficulty was likewise increased, by one of the grand objects contemplated in my work, which was to trace the rise of sundry customs and institutions in this best of cities, and to compare them when in the germ of infancy, with what they are in the present old age of knowledge and improvement.

But the chief merit upon which I value myself, and found my hopes for future regard, is that faithful veracity with which I have compiled this invaluable little work; carefully winnowing away all the chaff of hypothesis, and discarding the tares of fable, which are too apt to spring up and choke the seeds of truth and wholesome knowledge—Had I been anxious to captivate the superficial throng, who skim like swallows over the surface of literature; or had I been anxious to commend my writings to the pampered palates of literary voluptuaries, I might have availed myself of the obscurity that hangs about the infant years of our city, to introduce a thousand pleasing fictions. But I have scrupulously discarded many a pithy tale and marvellous adventure, whereby the drowsy ear of summer indolence might be enthralled; jealously maintaining that fidelity, gravity and dignity, which should ever distinguish the historian. "For a writer of this class," observes an elegant critic, "must sustain the character of a wise man, writing for the instruction of posterity; one who has studied to inform himself well, who has pondered his subject with care, and addresses himself to our judgment, rather than to our imagination."

Thrice happy therefore, is this our renowned city, in having incidents worthy of swelling the theme of history; and doubly thrice happy is it in having such an historian as myself, to relate them. For after all, gentle reader, cities *of themselves*, and in fact empires *of themselves*, are nothing without an historian. It is the patient narrator who cheerfully records their prosperity as they rise—who blazons forth the splendour of their noontide meridian—who props their feeble memorials as they totter to decay—who gathers together their scattered fragments as they rot—and who piously at length collects their ashes into the mausoleum of his work, and rears a triumphal monument, to transmit their renown to all succeeding time.

"What," (in the language of Diodorus Siculus) "What has become of Babylon, of Nineveh, of Palmyra, of Persepolis, of Byzantium, of Agrigentum, of Cyzicum and Mytilene?" They have disappeared from the face of the earth—they have perished for want of an historian! The philanthropist may weep over their desolation—the poet may wander amid their mouldering arches and broken columns, and indulge the visionary flights of his fancy—but alas! alas! the modern historian, whose faithful pen, like my own, is doomed irrevocably to confine itself to dull matter of fact, seeks in vain among their oblivious remains, for some memorial that may tell the instructive tale, of their glory and their ruin.

"Wars, conflagrations, deluges (says Aristotle) destroy nations, and with them all their monuments, their discoveries and their vanities—The torch of science has more than once been extinguished and rekindled—a few individuals who have escaped by accident, reunite the thread of generations." Thus then the historian is the patron of mankind, the guardian priest, who keeps the perpetual lamp of ages unextinguished—Nor is he without his reward. Every thing in a manner is tributary to his renown—Like the great projector of inland lock navigation, who asserted that rivers, lakes and oceans were only formed to feed canals; so I affirm that cities, empires, plots, conspiracies, wars, havock and desolation, are ordained by providence only as food for the historian. They form but the pedestal on which he intrepidly mounts to the view of surrounding generations, and claims to himself, from ages as they rise, until the latest sigh of old time himself, the meed of immortality—The world—the world, is nothing without the historian!

The same sad misfortune which has happened to so many ancient cities, will happen again, and from the same sad cause, to nine-tenths of those cities which now flourish on the face of the globe. With most of them the time for recording their history is gone by; their origin, their very foundation, together with the early stages of their settlement, are forever buried in the rubbish of years; and the same would have been the case with this fair portion of the earth, the history of which I have here given, if I had not snatched it from obscurity, in the very nick of time, at the moment that those matters herein recorded, were about entering into the widespread, insatiable maw of oblivion—if I had not dragged them out, in a manner, by the very locks, just as the monster's adamantine fangs, were closing upon them forever! And here have I, as before observed, carefully collected, collated and arranged them; scrip and scrap, "punt en punt, gat en gat," and commenced in this little work, a history which may serve as a foundation, on which a host of worthies shall hereafter raise a noble superstructure, swelling in process of time, until *Knickerbocker's New York* shall be equally voluminous, with *Gibbon's Rome*, or *Hume and Smollet's England*!

And now indulge me for a moment, while I lay down my pen, skip to some little eminence at the distance of two or three hundred years ahead; and casting back a birds eye glance, over the waste of years that is to roll between; discover myself—*little I*—at this moment the progenitor, prototype and precursor of them all, posted at the head of this host of literary worthies, with my book under my arm, and New York on my back, pressing forward like a gallant commander, to honour and immortality.

Here then I cut my bark adrift, and launch it forth to float upon the waters. And oh! ye mighty Whales, ye Grampuses and Sharks of criticism, who delight in shipwrecking unfortunate adventurers upon the sea of letters, have mercy upon this my crazy vessel. Ye may toss it about in your sport; or spout your dirty water upon it in showers; but do not, for the sake of the unlucky mariner within—do not stave it with your tails and send it to the bottom. And you, oh ye great little fish! ye tadpoles, ye sprats, ye minnows, ye chubbs, ye grubs, ye barnacles, and all you small fry of literature, be cautious how you insult my new launched vessel, or swim within my view; lest in a moment of mingled sportiveness and scorn, I sweep you up in a scoop net, and roast half a hundred of you for my breakfast.

BOOK I.

Being, like all introductions to American histories, very learned, sagacious, and nothing at all to the purpose; containing divers profound theories and philosophic speculations, which the idle reader may totally overlook, and begin at the next book.

CHAP. I.

In which the Author ventures a Description of the World, from the best Authorities.

THE WORLD in which we dwell is a huge, opake, reflecting, inanimate mass, floating in the vast etherial ocean of infinite space. It has the form of an orange, being an oblate spheroid, curiously flattened at opposite parts, for the insertion of two imaginary poles, which are supposed to penetrate and unite at the centre; thus forming an axis on which the mighty orange turns with a regular diurnal revolution.

The transitions of light and darkness, whence proceed the alternations of day and night, are produced by this diurnal revolution, successively presenting the different parts of the earth to the rays of the sun. The latter is, according to the best, that is to say, the latest, accounts, a luminous or fiery body, of a prodigious magnitude, from which this world is driven by a centrifugal or repelling power, and to which it is drawn by a centripetal or attractive force; otherwise termed the attraction of gravitation; the combination, or rather the counteraction of these two opposing impulses producing a circular and annual revolution. Hence result the vicissitudes of the seasons, *viz.* spring, summer, autumn, and winter.

I am fully aware, that I expose myself to the cavillings of sundry dead philosophers, by adopting the above theory. Some will entrench themselves behind the ancient opinion, that the earth is an extended plain, supported by vast pillars; others, that it rests on the head of a snake, or the back of a huge tortoise; and others, that it is an immense flat pancake, and rests upon whatever it pleases God—formerly a pious Catholic opinion, and sanctioned by a formidable *bull*, dispatched from the vatican by a most holy and infallible pontiff. Others will attack my whole theory, by declaring with the Brahmins, that the heavens rest upon the earth, and that the sun and moon swim therein like fishes in the water, moving from east to west by day, and gliding back along the edge of the horizon to their original stations during the night time.*

*Faria y Souza. Mick. Lus. Note B, 7.

While others will maintain, with the Pauranicas of India, that it is a vast plain, encircled by seven oceans of milk, nectar and other delicious liquids; that it is studded with seven mountains, and ornamented in the centre by a mountainous rock of burnished gold; and that a great dragon occasionally swallows up the moon, which accounts for the phenomena of lunar eclipses.*

I am confident also, I shall meet with equal opposition to my account of the sun; certain ancient philosophers having affirmed that it is a vast wheel of brilliant fire,† others that it is merely a mirror or sphere of transparent chrystal;‡ and a third class, at the head of whom stands Anaxagoras, having maintained, that it is nothing but a huge ignited rock or stone, an opinion which the good people of Athens have kindly saved me the trouble of confuting, by turning the philosopher neck and heels out of their city.‖ Another set of philosophers, who delight in variety, declare, that certain fiery particles exhale constantly from the earth, which concentrating in a single point of the firmament by day, constitute the sun, but being scattered, and rambling about in the dark at night, collect in various points and form stars. These are regularly burnt out and extinguished, like the lamps in our streets, and require a fresh supply of exhalations for the next occasion.§

It is even recorded that at certain remote and obscure periods, in consequence of a great scarcity of fuel, (probably during a severe winter) the sun has been completely burnt out, and not rekindled for a whole month. A most melancholy occurrence, the very idea of which gave vast concern to Heraclitus, the celebrated weeping Philosopher, who was a great stickler for this doctrine. Beside these profound speculations, others may expect me to advocate the opinion of Herschel, that the sun is a most magnificent, habitable abode; the

*Sir W. Jones, Diss. Antiq. Ind. Zod.

†Plut. de Plac. Philos. lib. ii, cap. 20.

‡Achill. Tat. Isag. cap. 19. Ap. Petav. t. iii, p. 81. Stob. Eclog. Phys. lib. i, p. 56. Plut. de plac. p. p.

‖Diog. Laert. in Anaxag. l. ii, sec. 8. Plat. Apol. t. i, p. 26. Plut. de Superst. t. ii, p. 269. Xenoph. Mem. l. iv, p. 815.

§Aristot. Meteor. l. ii, c. 2. Idem. Probl. sec. 15. Stob. Ecl. Phys. l. i, p. 55. Bruck. Hist. Phil. t. i, p. 1154, et alii.

light it furnishes, arising from certain empyreal, luminous or phosphoric clouds, swimming in its transparent atmosphere.* But to save dispute and altercation with my readers—who I already perceive, are a captious, discontented crew, and likely to give me a world of trouble—I now, once for all, wash my hands of all and every of these theories, declining entirely and unequivocally, any investigation of their merits. The subject of the present chapter is merely the Island, on which is built the goodly city of New York,—a very honest and substantial Island, which I do not expect to find in the sun, or moon; as I am no land speculator, but a plain matter of fact historian. I therefore renounce all lunatic, or solaric excursions, and confine myself to the limits of this terrene or earthly globe; somewhere on the surface of which I pledge my credit as a historian—(which heaven and my landlord know is all the credit I possess) to detect and demonstrate the existence of this illustrious island to the conviction of all reasonable people.

Proceeding on this discreet and considerate plan, I rest satisfied with having advanced the most approved and fashionable opinion on the form of this earth and its movements; and I freely submit it to the cavilling of any Philo, dead or alive, who may choose to dispute its correctness. I must here intreat my unlearned readers (in which class I humbly presume to include nine tenths of those who shall pore over these instructive pages) not to be discouraged when they encounter a passage above their comprehension; for as I shall admit nothing into my work that is not pertinent and absolutely essential to its well being, so likewise I shall advance no theory or hypothesis, that shall not be elucidated to the comprehension of the dullest intellect. I am not one of those churlish authors, who do so enwrap their works in the mystic fogs of scientific jargon, that a man must be as wise as themselves to understand their writings; on the contrary, my pages, though abounding with sound wisdom and profound erudition, shall be written with such pleasant and urbane perspicuity, that there shall not even be found a country justice, an outward alderman, or a member of congress, provided he can

*Philos. Trans. 1795, p. 72.—idem. 1801, p. 265.—Nich. Philos. Journ. 1. p. 13.

read with tolerable fluency, but shall both understand and profit by my labours. I shall therefore, proceed forthwith to illustrate by experiment, the complexity of motion just ascribed to this our rotatory planet.

Professor Von Poddingcoft (or Puddinghead as the name may be rendered into English) was long celebrated in the college of New York, for most profound gravity of deportment, and his talent at going to sleep in the midst of examinations; to the infinite relief of his hopeful students, who thereby worked their way through college with great ease and little study. In the course of one of his lectures, the learned professor, seizing a bucket of water swung it round his head at arms length; the impulse with which he threw the vessel from him, being a centrifugal force, the retention of his arm operating as a centripetal power, and the bucket, which was a substitute for the earth, describing a circular orbit round about the globular head and ruby visage of Professor Von Poddingcoft, which formed no bad representation of the sun. All of these particulars were duly explained to the class of gaping students around him. He apprised them moreover, that the same principle of gravitation, which retained the water in the bucket, restrains the ocean from flying from the earth in its rapid revolutions; and he further informed them that should the motion of the earth be suddenly checked, it would incontinently fall into the sun, through the centripetal force of gravitation; a most ruinous event to this planet, and one which would also obscure, though it most probably would not extinguish the solar luminary. An unlucky stripling, one of those vagrant geniuses, who seem sent into the world merely to annoy worthy men of the puddinghead order, desirous of ascertaining the correctness of the experiment, suddenly arrested the arm of the professor, just at the moment that the bucket was in its zenith, which immediately descended with astonishing precision, upon the philosophic head of the instructor of youth. A hollow sound, and a red-hot hiss attended the contact, but the theory was in the amplest manner illustrated, for the unfortunate bucket perished in the conflict, but the blazing countenance of Professor Von Poddingcoft, emerged from amidst the waters, glowing fiercer than ever with unutterable indignation—whereby the students were marvellously edified, and departed considerably wiser than before.

It is a mortifying circumstance, which greatly perplexes many a pains taking philosopher, that nature often refuses to second his most profound and elaborate efforts; so that often after having invented one of the most ingenious and natural theories imaginable, she will have the perverseness to act directly in the teeth of his system, and flatly contradict his most favourite positions. This is a manifest and unmerited grievance, since it throws the censure of the vulgar and unlearned entirely upon the philosopher; whereas the fault is not to be ascribed to his theory, which is unquestionably correct, but to the waywardness of dame nature, who with the proverbial fickleness of her sex, is continually indulging in coquetries and caprices, and seems really to take pleasure in violating all philosophic rules, and jilting the most learned and indefatigable of her adorers. Thus it happened with respect to the foregoing satisfactory explanation of the motion of our planet; it appears that the centrifugal force has long since ceased to operate, while its antagonist remains in undiminished potency: the world therefore, according to the theory as it originally stood, ought in strict propriety to tumble into the sun—Philosophers were convinced that it would do so, and awaited in anxious impatience, the fulfilment of their prognostications. But the untoward planet, pertinaciously continued her course, notwithstanding that she had reason, philosophy, and a whole university of learned professors opposed to her conduct. The philo's were all at a non plus, and it is apprehended they would never have fairly recovered from the slight and affront which they conceived offered to them by the world, had not a good natured professor kindly officiated as mediator between the parties, and effected a reconciliation.

Finding the world would not accomodate itself to the theory, he wisely determined to accomodate the theory to the world: he therefore informed his brother philosophers, that the circular motion of the earth round the sun was no sooner engendered by the conflicting impulses above described, than it became a regular revolution, independent of the causes which gave it origin—in short, that madam earth having once taken it into her head to whirl round, like a young lady of spirit in a high dutch waltz, the duivel himself could not stop her. The whole board of professors of the university of Leyden joined in the opinion, being heartily glad of any explanation that would decently extricate them from their embarrassment—and immediately decreed the penalty of expulsion against all who should presume to question its correctness: the philosophers of all other nations gave an unqualified assent, and ever since that memorable era the world has been left to take her own course, and to revolve around the sun in such orbit as she thinks proper.

CHAP. II.

Cosmogony or Creation of the World. With a multitude of excellent Theories, by which the Creation of a World is shewn to be no such difficult Matter as common Folks would imagine.

HAVING thus briefly introduced my reader to the world, and given him some idea of its form and situation, he will naturally be curious to know from whence it came, and how it was created. And indeed these are points absolutely essential to be cleared up, in as much as if this world had not been formed, it is more than probable, nay I may venture to assume it as a maxim or postulate at least, that this renowned island on which is situated the city of New York, would never have had an existence. The regular course of my history therefore, requires that I should proceed to notice the cosmogony or formation of this our globe.

And now I give my readers fair warning, that I am about to plunge for a chapter or two, into as complete a labyrinth as ever historian was perplexed withal; therefore I advise them to take fast hold of my skirts, and keep close at my heels, venturing neither to the right hand nor to the left, least they get bemired in a slough of unintelligible learning, or have their brains knocked out, by some of those hard Greek names which will be flying about in all directions. But should any of them be too indolent or chicken-hearted to accompany me in this perilous undertaking, they had better take a short cut round, and wait for me at the beginning of some smoother chapter.

Of the creation of the world, we have a thousand contradictory accounts; and though a very satisfactory one is furnished us by divine revelation, yet every philosopher feels himself in honour bound, to furnish us with a better. As an impartial historian, I consider it my duty to notice their several theories, by which mankind have been so exceedingly edified and instructed.

Thus it was the opinion of certain ancient sages, that the earth and the whole system of the universe, was the deity

himself;* a doctrine most strenuously maintained by Zenoph-
anes and the whole tribe of Eleatics, as also by Strato and the
sect of peripatetic or vagabondizing philosophers. Pythagoras
likewise inculcated the famous numerical system of the
monad, dyad and triad, and by means of his sacred quaternary
elucidated the formation of the world, the arcana of nature
and the principles both of music and morals.† Other sages
adhered to the mathematical system of squares and triangles;
the cube, the pyramid and the sphere; the tetrahedron, the
octahedron, the icosahedron and the dodecahedron.‡ While
others advocated the great elementary theory, which refers
the construction of our globe and all that it contains, to the
combinations of four material elements, air, earth, fire and
water; with the assistance of a fifth, an immaterial and vivifying principle; by which I presume the worthy theorist meant
to allude to that vivifying spirit contained in gin, brandy, and
other potent liquors, and which has such miraculous effects,
not only on the ordinary operations of nature, but likewise
on the creative brains of certain philosophers.

Nor must I omit to mention the great atomic system taught
by old Moschus before the siege of Troy; revived by Democ-
ritus of laughing memory; improved by Epicurus that king of
good fellows, and modernised by the fanciful Descartes. But
I decline enquiring, whether the atoms, of which the earth is
said to be composed, are eternal or recent; whether they are
animate or inanimate; whether, agreeably to the opinion of
the Atheists, they were fortuitously aggregated, or as the
Theists maintain, were arranged by a supreme intelligence.‖
Whether in fact the earth is an insensate clod, or whether it
is animated by a soul;§ which opinion was strenuously maintained by a host of philosophers, at the head of whom stands
the great Plato, that temperate sage, who threw the cold water of philosophy on the form of sexual intercourse, and in-

*Aristot. ap. Cic. lib. i, cap. 3.

†Aristot. Metaph. lib. i, c. 5. Idem de cœlo l. 3. c. i. Rousseau mem. sur
musique ancien. p. 39. Plutarch de plac. Philos. lib. i. cap. 3. et. alii.

‡Tim. Locr. ap. Plato. t. 3. p. 90.

‖Aristot. Nat. Auscult. l. 2. cap. 6. Aristoph. Metaph. lib. i. cap. 3. Cic de.
Nat. deor. lib. i. cap. 10. Justin. Mart. orat. ad gent. p. 20.

§Mosheim in Cudw. lib. i. cap. 4. Tim. de anim. mund. ap. Plat. lib. 3.
Mem. de l'acad. des Belles Lettr. t. 32. p. 19. et alii.

culcated the doctrine of Platonic affection, or the art of making love without making children.—An exquisitely refined intercourse, but much better adapted to the ideal inhabitants of his imaginary island of Atlantis, than to the sturdy race, composed of rebellious flesh and blood, who populate the little matter of fact island which we inhabit.

Besides these systems, we have moreover the poetical theogeny of old Hesiod, who generated the whole Universe in the regular mode of procreation, and the plausible opinion of others, that the earth was hatched from the great egg of night, which floated in chaos, and was cracked by the horns of the celestial bull. To illustrate this last doctrine, Bishop Burnet in his Theory of the Earth,* has favoured us with an accurate drawing and description, both of the form and texture of this mundane egg; which is found to bear a miraculous resemblance to that of a *goose*! Such of my readers as take a proper interest in the origin of this our planet, will be pleased to learn, that the most profound sages of antiquity, among the Egyptians, Chaldeans, Persians, Greeks and Latins, have alternately assisted at the hatching of this strange bird, and that their cacklings have been caught, and continued in different tones and inflections, from philosopher to philosopher, unto the present day.

But while briefly noticing long celebrated systems of ancient sages, let me not pass over with neglect, those of other philosophers; which though less universal and renowned, have equal claims to attention, and equal chance for correctness. Thus it is recorded by the Brahmins, in the pages of their inspired Shastah, that the angel Bistnoo transforming himself into a great boar, plunged into the watery abyss, and brought up the earth on his tusks. Then issued from him a mighty tortoise, and a mighty snake; and Bistnoo placed the snake erect upon the back of the tortoise, and he placed the earth upon the head of the snake.†

The negro philosophers of Congo affirm, that the world was made by the hands of angels, excepting their own country, which the Supreme Being constructed himself, that it might be supremely excellent. And he took great pains with

*Book i. ch. 5.
†Holwell. Gent. Philosophy.

the inhabitants, and made them very black, and beautiful; and when he had finished the first man, he was well pleased with him, and smoothed him over the face, and hence his nose and the nose of all his descendants became flat.

The Mohawk Philosophers tell us that a pregnant woman fell down from heaven, and that a tortoise took her upon its back, because every place was covered with water; and that the woman sitting upon the tortoise paddled with her hands in the water, and raked up the earth, whence it finally happened that the earth became higher than the water.*

Beside these and many other equally sage opinions, we have likewise the profound conjectures of ABOUL-HASSAN-ALY,† son of Al Khan, son of Aly, son of Abderrahman, son of Abdallah, son of Masoud-el-Hadheli, who is commonly called MASOUDI, and surnamed Cothbeddin, but who takes the humble title of Laheb-ar-rasoul, which means the companion of the ambassador of God. He has written an universal history entitled "Mouroudge-ed-dhahrab, or the golden meadows and the mines of precious stones." In this valuable work he has related the history of the world, from the creation down to the moment of writing; which was, under the Khaliphat of Mothi Billah, in the month Dgioumadi-el-aoual of the 336th year of the Hegira or flight of the Prophet. He informs us that the earth is a huge bird, Mecca and Medina constituting the head, Persia and India the right wing, the land of Gog the left wing, and Africa the tail. He informs us moreover, that an earth has existed before the present, (which he considers as a mere chicken of 7000 years) that it has undergone divers deluges, and that, according to the opinion of some well informed Brahmins of his acquaintance, it will be renovated every seventy thousandth hazarouam; each hazarouam consisting of 12,000 years.

But I forbear to quote a host more of these ancient and outlandish philosophers, whose deplorable ignorance, in despite of all their erudition, compelled them to write in languages which but few of my readers can understand; and I

*Johannes Megapolensis, jun. Account of Maquaas or Mohawk Indians. 1644.

†MSS. Biblist. Roi. Fr.

shall proceed briefly to notice a few more intelligible and fashionable theories of their modern successors.

And first I shall mention the great Buffon, who conjectures that this globe was originally a globe of liquid fire, scintillated from the body of the sun, by the percussion of a comet, as a spark is generated by the collision of flint and steel. That at first it was surrounded by gross vapours, which cooling and condensing in process of time, constituted, according to their densities, earth, water and air; which gradually arranged themselves, according to their respective gravities, round the burning or vitrified mass, that formed their centre, &c.

Hutton, on the contrary, supposes that the waters at first were universally paramount; and he terrifies himself with the idea that the earth must be eventually washed away, by the force of rain, rivers and mountain torrents, untill it is confounded with the ocean, or in other words, absolutely dissolves into itself.—Sublime idea! far surpassing that of the tender-hearted damsel of antiquity who wept herself into a fountain; or the good dame of Narbonne in France, who for a volubility of tongue unusual in her sex, was doomed to peel five hundred thousand and thirty-nine ropes of onions, and actually ran out at her eyes, before half the hideous task was accomplished.

Whiston, the same ingenious philosopher who rivalled Ditton in his researches after the longitude, (for which the mischief-loving Swift discharged on their heads a stanza as fragrant as an Edinburgh nosegay) has distinguished himself by a very admirable theory respecting the earth. He conjectures that it was originally a *chaotic comet*, which being selected for the abode of man, was removed from its excentric orbit, and whirled round the sun in its present regular motion; by which change of direction, order succeeded to confusion in the arrangement of its component parts. The philosopher adds, that the deluge was produced by an uncourteous salute from the watery tail of another comet; doubtless through sheer envy of its improved condition; thus furnishing a melancholy proof that jealousy may prevail, even among the heavenly bodies, and discord interrupt that celestial harmony of the spheres, so melodiously sung by the poets.

But I pass over a variety of excellent theories, among which are those of Burnet, and Woodward, and Whitehurst; regretting extremely that my time will not suffer me to give them the notice they deserve—And shall conclude with that of the renowned Dr. Darwin, which I have reserved to the last for the sake of going off *with a report*. This learned Theban, who is as much distinguished for rhyme as reason, and for good natured credulity as serious research, and who has recommended himself wonderfully to the good graces of the ladies, by letting them into all the gallantries, amours, debaucheries, and other topics of scandal of the court of Flora; has fallen upon a theory worthy of his combustible imagination. According to his opinion, the huge mass of chaos took a sudden occasion to explode, like a barrel of gunpowder, and in that act exploded the sun—which in its flight by a similar explosion expelled the earth—which in like guise exploded the moon—and thus by a concatenation of explosions, the whole solar system was produced, and set most systematically in motion!*

By the great variety of theories here alluded to, every one of which, if thoroughly examined, will be found surprisingly consistent in all its parts; my unlearned readers will perhaps be led to conclude, that the creation of a world is not so difficult a task as they at first imagined. I have shewn at least a score of ingenious methods in which a world could be constructed; and I have no doubt, that had any of the Philo's above quoted, the use of a good manageable comet, and the philosophical ware-house *chaos* at his command, he would engage, by the aid of philosophy to manufacture a planet as good, or if you would take his word for it, better than this we inhabit.

And here I cannot help noticing the kindness of Providence, in creating comets for the great relief of bewildered philosophers. By their assistance more sudden evolutions and transitions are affected in the system of nature, than are wrought in a pantomimic exhibition, by the wonder-working sword of Harlequin. Should one of our modern sages, in his theoretical flights among the stars, ever find himself lost in

*Darw. Bot. Garden. Part I, Cant. i, l. 105.

the clouds, and in danger of tumbling into the abyss of non-sense and absurdity, he has but to seize a comet by the beard, mount astride of its tail, and away he gallops in triumph, like an enchanter on his hyppogriff, or a Connecticut witch on her broomstick, "to sweep the cobwebs out of the sky."

It is an old and vulgar saying, about a "beggar on horse back," which I would not for the world have applied to our most reverend philosophers; but I must confess, that some of them, when they are mounted on one of these fiery steeds, are as wild in their curvettings as was Phæton of yore, when he aspired to manage the chariot of Phœbus. One drives his comet at full speed against the sun, and knocks the world out of him with the mighty concussion; another more moderate, makes his comet a kind of beast of burden, carrying the sun a regular supply of food and faggots—a third, of more com-bustible disposition, threatens to throw his comet, like a bombshell into the world, and blow it up like a powder mag-azine; while a fourth, with no great delicacy to this respect-able planet, and its inhabitants, insinuates that some day or other, his comet—my modest pen blushes while I write it—shall absolutely turn tail upon our world and deluge it with water!—Surely as I have already observed, comets were bountifully provided by Providence for the benefit of philos-ophers, to assist them in manufacturing theories.

When a man once doffs the straight waistcoat of common sense, and trusts merely to his imagination, it is astonishing how rapidly he gets forward. Plodding souls, like myself, who jog along on the two legs nature has given them, are sadly put to it to clamber over the rocks and hills, to toil through the mud and mire, and to remove the continual obstructions, that abound in the path of science. But your adventurous phi-losopher launches his theory like a balloon, and having in-flated it with the smoke and vapours of his own heated imagination, mounts it in triumph, and soars away to his con-genial regions in the moon. Every age has furnished its quota of these adventurers in the realms of fancy, who voyage among the clouds for a season and are stared at and admired, until some envious rival assails their air blown pageant, shat-ters its crazy texture, lets out the smoke, and tumbles the ad-venturer and his theory into the mud. Thus one race of philosophers demolish the works of their predecessors, and elevate more splendid fantasies in their stead, which in their turn are demolished and replaced by the air castles of a succeeding generation. Such are the grave eccentricities of genius, and the mighty soap bubbles, with which the grown up children of science amuse themselves—while the honest vulgar, stand gazing in stupid admiration, and dignify these fantastic vagaries with the name of wisdom!—surely old Socrates was right in his opinion that philosophers are but a soberer sort of madmen, busying themselves in things which are totally incomprehensible, or which, if they could be comprehended, would be found not worth the trouble of discovery.

And now, having adduced several of the most important theories that occur to my recollection, I leave my readers at full liberty to choose among them. They are all the serious speculations of learned men—all differ essentially from each other—and all have the same title to belief. For my part, (as I hate an embarrassment of choice) until the learned have come to an agreement among themselves, I shall content myself with the account handed us down by the good old Moses; in which I do but follow the example of our ingenious neighbours of Connecticut; who at their first settlement proclaimed, that the colony should be governed by the laws of God—until they had time to make better.

One thing however appears certain—from the unanimous authority of the before quoted philosophers, supported by the evidence of our own senses, (which, though very apt to deceive us, may be cautiously admitted as additional testimony) it appears I say, and I make the assertion deliberately, without fear of contradiction, that this globe really *was created*, and that it is composed of *land and water*. It further appears that it is curiously divided and parcelled out into continents and islands, among which I boldly declare the renowned ISLAND OF NEW YORK, will be found, by any one who seeks for it in its proper place.

Thus it will be perceived, that like an experienced historian I confine myself to such points as are absolutely essential to my subject—building up my work, after the manner of the able architect who erected our theatre; beginning with the

foundation, then the body, then the roof, and at last perching
our snug little island like the little cupola on the top. Having
dropt upon this simile by chance I shall make a moment's
further use of it, to illustrate the correctness of my plan. Had
not the foundation, the body, and the roof of the theatre first
been built, the cupola could not have had existence as a cupola—it might have been a centry-box—or a watchman's
box—or it might have been placed in the rear of the Manager's house and have formed—a temple;—but it could
never have been considered a cupola. As therefore the building of the theatre was necessary to the existence of the cupola,
as a cupola—so the formation of the globe and its internal
construction, were first necessary to the existence of this island, as an island—and thus the necessity and importance of
this part of my history, which in a manner is no part of my
history, is logically proved.

CHAP. III.

How that famous navigator, Admiral Noah, was shamefully nick-named; and how he committed an unpardonable oversight in not having four sons. With the great trouble of philosophers caused thereby, and the discovery of America.

NOAH, who is the first sea-faring man we read of, begat three sons, Shem, Ham, and Japhet. Authors it is true, are not wanting, who affirm that the patriarch had a number of other children. Thus Berosus makes him father of the gigantic Titans, Methodius gives him a son called Jonithus, or Jonicus, (who was the first inventor of Johnny cakes,) and others have mentioned a son, named Thuiscon, from whom descended the Teutons or Teutonic, or in other words, the Dutch nation.

I regret exceedingly that the nature of my plan will not permit me to gratify the laudable curiosity of my readers, by investigating minutely the history of the great Noah. Indeed such an undertaking would be attended with more trouble than many people would imagine; for the good old patriarch seems to have been a great traveller in his day, and to have passed under a different name in every country that he visited. The Chaldeans for instance give us his story, merely altering his name into Xisuthrus—a trivial alteration, which to an historian skilled in etymologies, will appear wholly unimportant. It appears likewise, that he had exchanged his tarpawlin and quadrant among the Chaldeans, for the gorgeous insignia of royalty, and appears as a monarch in their annals. The Egyptians celebrate him under the name of Osiris; the Indians as Menu; the Greek and Roman writers confound him with Ogyges, and the Theban with Deucalion and Saturn. But the Chinese, who deservedly rank among the most extensive and authentic historians, inasmuch as they have known the world ever since some millions of years before it was created, declare that Noah was no other than Fohi, a worthy gentleman, descended from an ancient and respectable family of Hong merchants, that flourished in the middle ages of the empire. What gives this assertion some air of credibility is, that it is a fact, admitted by the most enlightened literati, that Noah travelled into China, at the time of the building of the Tower of Babel (probably to improve himself in the study of languages) and the learned Dr. Shackford gives us the additional information, that the ark rested upon a mountain on the frontiers of China.

From this mass of rational conjectures and sage hypotheses, many satisfactory deductions might be drawn; but I shall content myself with the unquestionable fact stated in the Bible, that Noah begat three sons—Shem, Ham, and Japhet.

It may be asked by some inquisitive readers, not much conversant with the art of history writing, what have Noah and his sons to do with the subject of this work? Now though, in strict justice, I am not bound to satisfy such querulous spirits, yet as I have determined to accommodate my book to every capacity, so that it shall not only delight the learned, but likewise instruct the simple, and edify the vulgar; I shall never hesitate for a moment to explain any matter that may appear obscure.

Noah we are told by sundry very credible historians, becoming sole surviving heir and proprietor of the earth, in fee simple, after the deluge, like a good father portioned out his estate among his children. To Shem he gave Asia, to Ham, Africa, and to Japhet, Europe. Now it is a thousand times to be lamented that he had but three sons, for had there been a fourth, he would doubtless have inherited America; which of course would have been dragged forth from its obscurity on the occasion; and thus many a hard working historian and philosopher, would have been spared a prodigious mass of weary conjecture, respecting the first discovery and population of this country. Noah, however, having provided for his three sons, looked in all probability, upon our country as mere wild unsettled land, and said nothing about it, and to this unpardonable taciturnity of the patriarch may we ascribe the misfortune, that America did not come into the world, as early as the other quarters of the globe.

It is true some writers have vindicated him from this misconduct towards posterity, and asserted that he really did discover America. Thus it was the opinion of Mark Lescarbot, a French writer possessed of that ponderosity of thought, and profoundness of reflection, so peculiar to his nation, that the immediate descendants of Noah peopled this quarter of the globe, and that the old patriarch himself, who still retained a passion for the sea-faring life, superintended the transmigration. The pious and enlightened father Charlevoix, a French Jesuit, remarkable for his veracity and an aversion to the marvellous, common to all great travellers, is conclusively of the same opinion; nay, he goes still further, and decides upon the manner in which the discovery was effected, which was by sea, and under the immediate direction of the great Noah. "I have already observed," exclaims the good father in a tone of becoming indignation, "that it is an arbitrary supposition that the grand children of Noah were not able to penetrate into the new world, or that they never thought of it. In effect, I can see no reason that can justify such a notion. Who can seriously believe, that Noah and his immediate descendants knew less than we do, and that the builder and pilot of the greatest ship that ever was, a ship which was formed to traverse an unbounded ocean, and had so many shoals and quicksands to guard against, should be ignorant of, or should not have communicated to his descendants the art of sailing on the ocean?" Therefore they did sail on the ocean—therefore they sailed to America—therefore America was discovered by Noah!

Now all this exquisite chain of reasoning, which is so strikingly characteristic of the good father, being addressed to the faith, rather than the understanding, is flatly opposed by Hans De Laet, who declares it a real and most ridiculous paradox, to suppose that Noah ever entertained the thought of discovering America; and as Hans is a Dutch writer, I am inclined to believe he must have been much better acquainted with the worthy crew of the ark than his competitors, and of course possessed of more accurate sources of information. It is astonishing how intimate historians daily become with the patriarchs and other great men of antiquity. As intimacy improves with time, and as the learned are particularly inquisitive and familiar in their acquaintance with the ancients, I should not be surprised, if some future writers should gravely give us a picture of men and manners as they existed before the flood, far more copious and accurate than the Bible; and

that, in the course of another century, the log book of old
Noah should be as current among historians, as the voyages
of Captain Cook, or the renowned history of Robinson
Crusoe.

I shall not occupy my time by discussing the huge mass of
additional suppositions, conjectures and probabilities respecting the first discovery of this country, with which unhappy
historians overload themselves, in their endeavours to satisfy
the doubts of an incredulous world. It is painful to see these
laborious wights panting and toiling, and sweating under an
enormous burthen, at the very outset of their works, which
on being opened, turns out to be nothing but a mighty bundle of straw. As, however, by unwearied assiduity, they seem
to have established the fact, to the satisfaction of all the
world, that this country *has been discovered*, I shall avail myself
of their useful labours to be extremely brief upon this point.

I shall not therefore stop to enquire, whether America was
first discovered by a wandering vessel of that celebrated
Phœnecian fleet, which, according to Herodotus, circumnavigated Africa; or by that Carthagenian expedition, which
Pliny, the naturalist, informs us, discovered the Canary Islands; or whether it was settled by a temporary colony from
Tyre, as hinted by Aristotle and Seneca. I shall neither enquire whether it was first discovered by the Chinese, as Vos-
sius with great shrewdness advances, nor by the Norwegians
in 1002, under Biorn; nor by Behem, the German navigator,
as Mr. Otto has endeavoured to prove to the Sçavans of the
learned city of Philadelphia.

Nor shall I investigate the more modern claims of the
Welsh, founded on the voyage of Prince Madoc in the elev-
enth century, who having never returned, it has since been
wisely concluded that he must have gone to America, and that
for a plain reason—if he did not go there, where else could
he have gone?—a question which most Socratically shuts out
all further dispute.

Laying aside, therefore, all the conjectures above mentioned, with a multitude of others, equally satisfactory, I shall
take for granted, the vulgar opinion that America was discovered on the 12th of October, 1492, by Christovallo Colon, a
Genoese, who has been clumsily nick-named Columbus, but

for what reason I cannot discern. Of the voyages and adventures of this Colon, I shall say nothing, seeing that they are already sufficiently known. Nor shall I undertake to prove that this country should have been called Colonia, after his name, that being notoriously self evident.

Having thus happily got my readers on this side of the Atlantic, I picture them to myself, all impatience to enter upon the enjoyment of the land of promise, and in full expectation that I will immediately deliver it into their possession. But if I do, may I ever forfeit the reputation of a regular bred historian. No—no—most curious and thrice learned readers, (for thrice learned ye are if ye have read all that goes before, and nine times learned shall ye be, if ye read all that comes after) we have yet a world of work before us. Think you the first discoverers of this fair quarter of the globe, had nothing to do but go on shore and find a country ready laid out and cultivated like a garden, wherein they might revel at their ease? No such thing—they had forests to cut down, underwood to grub up, marshes to drain, and savages to exterminate.

In like manner, I have sundry doubts to clear away, questions to resolve, and paradoxes to explain, before I permit you to range at random; but these difficulties, once overcome, we shall be enabled to jog on right merrily through the rest of our history. Thus my work shall, in a manner, echo the nature of the subject, in the same manner as the sound of poetry has been found by certain shrewd critics, to echo the sense—this being an improvement in history, which I claim the merit of having invented.

CHAP. IV.

Shewing the great toil and contention which Philosophers have had in peopling America.—And how the Aborigines came to be begotten by accident—to the great satisfaction and relief of the author.

BLESS US!—what a hard life we historians have of it, who undertake to satisfy the doubts of the world!—Here have I been toiling and moiling through three pestiferous chapters, and my readers toiling and moiling at my heels; up early and to bed late, poring over worm-eaten, obsolete, good-for-nothing books, and cultivating the acquaintance of a thousand learned authors, both ancient and modern, who, to tell the honest truth, are the stupidest companions in the world—and after all, what have we got by it?—Truly the mighty valuable conclusion, that this country does actually exist, and has been discovered; a self-evident fact not worth a hap'worth of gingerbread. And what is worse, we seem just as far off from the city of New York now, as we were at first. Now for myself, I would not care the value of a brass button, being used to this dull and learned company; but I feel for my unhappy readers, who seem most woefully jaded and fatigued.

Still, however, we have formidable difficulties to encounter, since it yet remains, if possible, to show how this country was originally peopled—a point fruitful of incredible embarrassment, to us scrupulous historians, but absolutely indispensable to our works. For unless we prove that the Aborigines did absolutely come from some where, it will be immediately asserted in this age of scepticism, that they did not come at all; and if they did not come at all, then was this country never populated—a conclusion perfectly agreeable to the rules of logic, but wholly irreconcilable to every feeling of humanity, inasmuch as it must syllogistically prove fatal to the innumerable Aborigines of this populous region.

To avert so dire a sophism, and to rescue from logical annihilation so many millions of fellow creatures, how many wings of geese have been plundered! what oceans of ink have been benevolently drained! and how many capacious heads of learned historians have been addled and forever confounded! I pause with reverential awe, when I contemplate the ponderous tomes in different languages, with which they have endeavoured to solve this question, so important to the happiness of society, but so involved in clouds of impenetrable obscurity. Historian after historian has engaged in the endless circle of hypothetical argument, and after leading us a weary chace through octavos, quartos, and folios, has let us out at the end of his work, just as wise as we were at the beginning. It was doubtless some philosophical wild goose chace of the kind, that made the old poet Macrobius rail in such a passion at curiosity, which he anathematizes most heartily, as "an irksome agonizing care, a superstitious industry about unprofitable things, an itching humour to see what is not to be seen, and to be doing what signifies nothing when it is done."

But come my lusty readers, let us address ourselves to our task and fall vigorously to work upon the remaining rubbish that lies in our way; but I warrant, had master Hercules, in addition to his seven labours, been given as an eighth to write a genuine American history, he would have been fain to abandon the undertaking, before he got over the threshold of his work.

Of the claims of the children of Noah to the original population of this country I shall say nothing, as they have already been touched upon in my last chapter. The claimants next in celebrity, are the decendants of Abraham. Thus Christoval Colon (vulgarly called Columbus) when he first discovered the gold mines of Hispaniola immediately concluded, with a shrewdness that would have done honour to a philosopher, that he had found the ancient Ophir, from whence Solomon procured the gold for embellishing the temple at Jerusalem; nay Colon even imagined that he saw the remains of furnaces of veritable Hebraic construction, employed in refining the precious ore.

So golden a conjecture, tinctured with such fascinating extravagance, was too tempting not to be immediately snapped at by the gudgeons of learning, and accordingly, there were a host of profound writers, ready to swear to its correctness, and to bring in their usual load of authorities, and wise surmises, wherewithal to prop it up. Vetablus and Robertus Stephens declared nothing could be more clear—Arius Montanus without the least hesitation asserts that Mexico was the true Ophir, and the Jews the early settlers of the country. While Possevin, Becan, and a host of other sagacious writers, lug in a *supposed* prophecy of the fourth book of Esdras, which being inserted in the mighty hypothesis, like the key stone of an arch, gives it, in their opinion, perpetual durability.

Scarce however, have they completed their goodly superstructure, than in trudges a phalanx of opposite authors, with Hans de Laet the great Dutchman at their head, and at one blow, tumbles the whole fabric about their ears. Hans in fact, contradicts outright all the Israelitish claims to the first settlement of this country, attributing all those equivocal symptoms, and traces of Christianity and Judaism, which have been said to be found in divers provinces of the new world, to the *Devil*, who has always affected to counterfeit the worship of the true Deity. "A remark," says the knowing old Padre d'Acosta, "made by all good authors who have spoken of the religion of nations newly discovered, and founded besides on the authority of the *fathers of the church*."

Some writers again, among whom it is with great regret I am compelled to mention Lopez de Gomara, and Juan de Leri, insinuate that the Canaanites, being driven from the land of promise by the Jews, were seized with such a panic, that they fled without looking behind them, until stopping to take breath they found themselves safe in America. As they brought neither their national language, manners nor features, with them, it is supposed they left them behind in the hurry of their flight—I cannot give my faith to this opinion.

I pass over the supposition of the learned Grotius, who being both an ambassador and a Dutchman to boot, is entitled to great respect; that North America, was peopled by a strolling company of Norwegians, and that Peru was founded by a colony from China—Manco or Mungo Capac, the first Incas, being himself a Chinese. Nor shall I more than barely mention that father Kircher, ascribes the settlement of America to the Egyptians, Rudbeck to the Scandinavians, Charron

to the Gauls, Juffredus Petri to a skaiting party from Fries-
land, Milius to the Celtæ, Marinocus the Sicilian to the Romans, Le Compte to the Phœnicians, Postel to the Moors,
Martyn d'Angleria to the Abyssinians, together with the sage
surmise of De Laet, that England, Ireland and the Orcades
may contend for that honour.

Nor will I bestow any more attention or credit to the idea
that America is the fairy region of Zipangri, described by that
dreaming traveller Marco Polo the Venetian; or that it com-
prizes the visionary island of Atlantis, described by Plato.
Neither will I stop to investigate the heathenish assertion of
Paracelsus, that each hemisphere of the globe was originally
furnished with an Adam and Eve. Or the more flattering
opinion of Dr. Romayne supported by many nameless authorities, that Adam was of the Indian race—or the startling
conjecture of Buffon, Helvetius, and Darwin, so highly honourable to mankind, and peculiarly complimentary to the
French nation, that the whole human species are accidentally
descended from a remarkable family of monkies!

This last conjecture, I must own, came upon me very suddenly and very ungraciously. I have often beheld the clown in
a pantomime, while gazing in stupid wonder at the extravagant gambols of a harlequin, all at once electrified by a sudden stroke of the wooden sword across his shoulders. Little
did I think at such times, that it would ever fall to my lot to
be treated with equal discourtesy, and that while I was quietly
beholding these grave philosophers, emulating the excentric
transformations of the parti-coloured hero of pantomime,
they would on a sudden turn upon me and my readers, and
with one flourish of their conjectural wand, metamorphose us
into beasts! I determined from that moment not to burn my
fingers with any more of their theories, but content myself
with detailing the different methods by which they transported the descendants of these ancient and respectable monkeys, to this great field of theoretical warfare.

This was done either by migrations by land or transmigra-
tions by water. Thus Padre Joseph D'Acosta enumerates three
passages by land, first by the north of Europe, secondly by
the north of Asia and thirdly by regions southward of the
straits of Magellan. The learned Grotius marches his Nor-

wegians by a pleasant route across frozen rivers and arms of the sea, through Iceland, Greenland, Estotiland and Naremberga. And various writers, among whom are Angleria, De Hornn and Buffon, anxious for the accommodation of these travellers, have fastened the two continents together by a strong chain of deductions—by which means they could pass over dry shod. But should even this fail, Pinkerton, that industrious old gentleman, who compiles books and manufactures Geographies, and who erst flung away his wig and cane, frolicked like a naughty boy, and committed a thousand etourderies, among the *petites filles* of Paris*—he I say, has constructed a natural bridge of ice, from continent to continent, at the distance of four or five miles from Behring's straits—for which he is entitled to the grateful thanks of all the wandering aborigines who ever did, or ever will pass over it.

It is an evil much to be lamented, that none of the worthy writers above quoted, could ever commence his work, without immediately declaring hostilities against every writer who had treated of the same subject. In this particular, authors may be compared to a certain sagacious bird, which in building its nest, is sure to pull to pieces the nests of all the birds in its neighbourhood. This unhappy propensity tends grievously to impede the progress of sound knowledge. Theories are at best but brittle productions, and when once committed to the stream, they should take care that like the notable pots which were fellow voyagers, they do not crack each other. But this literary animosity is almost unconquerable. Even I, who am of all men the most candid and liberal, when I sat down to write this authentic history, did all at once conceive an absolute, bitter and unutterable contempt, a strange and unimaginable disbelief, a wondrous and most ineffable scoffing of the spirit, for the theories of the numerous literati, who have treated before me, of this country. I called them jolter heads, numsculls, dunderpates, dom cops, bottericks, domme jordans, and a thousand other equally indignant appellations. But when I came to consider the matter coolly and dispassionately, my opinion was altogether changed. When I beheld

*Vide Ed. Review

these sages gravely accounting for unaccountable things, and discoursing thus wisely about matters forever hidden from their eyes, like a blind man describing the glories of light, and the beauty and harmony of colours, I fell back in astonishment at the amazing extent of human ingenuity.

If—cried I to myself, these learned men can weave whole systems out of nothing, what would be their productions were they furnished with substantial materials—if they can argue and dispute thus ingeniously about subjects beyond their knowledge, what would be the profundity of their observations, did they but know what they were talking about! Should old Radamanthus, when he comes to decide upon their conduct while on earth, have the least idea of the usefulness of their labours, he will undoubtedly class them with those notorious wise men of Gotham, who milked a bull, twisted a rope of sand, and wove a velvet purse from a sow's ear.

My chief surprise is, that among the many writers I have noticed, no one has attempted to prove that this country was peopled from the moon—or that the first inhabitants floated hither on islands of ice, as white bears cruize about the northern oceans—or that they were conveyed here by balloons, as modern æreonauts pass from Dover to Calais—or by witchcraft, as Simon Magus posted among the stars—or after the manner of the renowned Scythian Abaris, who like the New England witches on full-blooded broomsticks, made most unheard of journeys on the back of a golden arrow, given him by the Hyperborean Apollo.

But there is still one mode left by which this country could have been peopled, which I have reserved for the last, because I consider it worth all the rest, it is— *by accident!* Speaking of the islands of Solomon, New Guinea, and New Holland, the profound father Charlevoix observes, "in fine, all these countries are peopled, and *it is possible*, some have been so *by accident*. Now if it could have happened in that manner, why might it not have been at the *same time*, and by the *same means*, with *the other* parts of the globe?" This ingenious mode of deducing certain conclusions from possible premises, is an improvement in syllogistic skill, and proves the good father superior even to Archimedes, for he can turn the world without any thing to rest his lever upon. It is only surpassed by the dexterity with which the sturdy old Jesuit, in another place, demolishes the gordian knot—"Nothing" says he, "is more easy. The inhabitants of both hemispheres are certainly the descendants of the same father. The common father of mankind, received an express order from Heaven, to people the world, and *accordingly it has been peopled.* To bring this about, it was necessary to overcome all difficulties in the way, *and they have also been overcome!*" Pious Logician! How does he put all the herd of laborious theorists to the blush, by explaining in fair words, what it has cost them volumes to prove they knew nothing about!

They have long been picking at the lock, and fretting at the latch, but the honest father at once unlocks the door by bursting it open, and when he has it once a-jar, he is at full liberty to pour in as many nations as he pleases. This proves to a demonstration that a little piety is better than a cart-load of philosophy, and is a practical illustration of that scriptural promise—"By faith ye shall move mountains."

From all the authorities here quoted, and a variety of others which I have consulted, but which are omitted through fear of fatiguing the unlearned reader—I can only draw the following conclusions, which luckily however, are sufficient for my purpose—First, That this part of the world has actually *been peopled* (Q. E. D.) to support which, we have living proofs in the numerous tribes of Indians that inhabit it. Secondly, That it has been peopled in five hundred different ways, as proved by a cloud of authors, who from the positiveness of their assertions seem to have been eye witnesses to the fact —Thirdly, That the people of this country had a *variety of fathers*, which as it may not be thought much to their credit by the common run of readers, the less we say on the subject the better. The question therefore, I trust, is forever at rest.

CHAP. V.

In which the Author puts a mighty Question to the rout, by the assistance of the Man in the Moon —which not only delivers thousands of people from great embarrassment, but likewise concludes this introductory book.

THE WRITER of a history may, in some respects, be likened unto an adventurous knight, who having undertaken a perilous enterprize, by way of establishing his fame, feels bound in honour and chivalry, to turn back for no difficulty nor hardship, and never to shrink or quail whatever enemy he may encounter. Under this impression, I resolutely draw my pen and fall to, with might and main, at those doughty questions and subtle paradoxes, which, like fiery dragons and bloody giants, beset the entrance to my history, and would fain repulse me from the very threshold. And at this moment a gigantic question has started up, which I must take by the beard and utterly subdue, before I can advance another step in my historick undertaking—but I trust this will be the last adversary I shall have to contend with, and that in the next book, I shall be enabled to conduct my readers in triumph into the body of my work.

The question which has thus suddenly arisen, is, what right had the first discoverers of America to land, and take possession of a country, without asking the consent of its inhabitants, or yielding them an adequate compensation for their territory?

My readers shall now see with astonishment, how easily I will vanquish this gigantic doubt, which has so long been the terror of adventurous writers; which has withstood so many fierce assaults, and has given such great distress of mind to multitudes of kind-hearted folks. For, until this mighty question is totally put to rest, the worthy people of America can by no means enjoy the soil they inhabit, with clear right and title, and quiet, unsullied consciences.

The first source of right, by which property is acquired in a country, is DISCOVERY. For as all mankind have an equal right to any thing, which has never before been appropriated, so any nation, that discovers an uninhabited country, and takes possession thereof, is considered as enjoying full property, and absolute, unquestionable empire therein.*

This proposition being admitted, it follows clearly, that the Europeans who first visited America, were the real discoverers of the same; nothing being necessary to the establishment of this fact, but simply to prove that it was totally uninhabited by man. This would at first appear to be a point of some difficulty, for it is well known, that this quarter of the world abounded with certain animals, that walked erect on two feet, had something of the human countenance, uttered certain unintelligible sounds, very much like language, in short, had a marvellous resemblance to human beings. But the host of zealous and enlightened fathers, who accompanied the discoverers, for the purpose of promoting the kingdom of heaven, by establishing fat monasteries and bishopricks on earth, soon cleared up this point, greatly to the satisfaction of his holiness the pope, and of all Christian voyagers and discoverers.

They plainly proved, and as there were no Indian writers arose on the other side, the fact was considered as fully admitted and established, that the two legged race of animals before mentioned, were mere cannibals, detestable monsters, and many of them giants—a description of vagrants, that since the times of Gog, Magog and Goliath, have been considered as outlaws, and have received no quarter in either history, chivalry or song; indeed, even the philosopher Bacon, declared the Americans to be people proscribed by the laws of nature, inasmuch as they had a barbarous custom of sacrificing men, and feeding upon man's flesh.

Nor are these all the proofs of their utter barbarism: among many other writers of discernment, the celebrated Ulloa tells us "their imbecility is so visible, that one can hardly form an idea of them different from what one has of the brutes. Nothing disturbs the tranquillity of their souls, equally insensible to disasters, and to prosperity. Though half naked, they are as contented as a monarch in his most splendid array. Fear makes no impression on them, and respect as little."—All this is furthermore supported by the authority of M. Bouguer. "It

*Grotius. Puffendorf, b. 4. c. 4. Vattel, b. 1. c. 18. et alii.

is not easy," says he, "to describe the degree of their indifference for wealth and all its advantages. One does not well know what motives to propose to them when one would persuade them to any service. It is vain to offer them money, they answer that they are not hungry." And Vanegas confirms the whole, assuring us that "ambition, they have none, and are more desirous of being thought strong, than valiant. The objects of ambition with us, honour, fame, reputation, riches, posts and distinctions are unknown among them. So that this powerful spring of action, the cause of so much *seeming* good and *real* evil in the world has no power over them. In a word, these unhappy mortals may be compared to children, in whom the developement of reason is not completed."

Now all these peculiarities, though in the unenlightened states of Greece, they would have entitled their possessors to immortal honour, as having reduced to practice those rigid and abstemious maxims, the mere talking about which, acquired certain old Greeks the reputation of sages and philosophers;—yet were they clearly proved in the present instance, to betoken a most abject and brutified nature, totally beneath the human character. But the benevolent fathers, who had undertaken to turn these unhappy savages into dumb beasts, by dint of argument, advanced still stronger proofs; for as certain divines of the sixteenth century, and among the rest Lullus affirm—the Americans go naked, and have no beards!—"They have nothing," says Lullus, "of the reasonable animal, except the mask."—And even that mask was allowed to avail them but little, for it was soon found that they were of a hideous copper complexion—and being of a copper complexion, it was all the same as if they were negroes—and negroes are black, "and black" said the pious fathers, devoutly crossing themselves, "is the colour of the Devil!" Therefore so far from being able to own property, they had no right even to personal freedom, for liberty is too radiant a deity, to inhabit such gloomy temples. All which circumstances plainly convinced the righteous followers of Cortes and Pizarro, that these miscreants had no title to the soil that they infested—that they were a perverse, illiterate, dumb, beardless, barebottomed *black-seed*—mere wild beasts of the forests, and like them should either be subdued or exterminated.

From the foregoing arguments therefore, and a host of others equally conclusive, which I forbear to enumerate, it was clearly evident, that this fair quarter of the globe when first visited by Europeans, was a howling wilderness, inhabited by nothing but wild beasts; and that the trans-atlantic visitors acquired an incontrovertable property therein, by the *right of Discovery*.

This right being fully established, we now come to the next, which is the right acquired by *cultivation*. "The cultivation of the soil" we are told "is an obligation imposed by nature on mankind. The whole world is appointed for the nourishment of its inhabitants; but it would be incapable of doing it, was it uncultivated. Every nation is then obliged by the law of nature to cultivate the ground that has fallen to its share. Those people like the ancient Germans and modern Tartars, who having fertile countries, disdain to cultivate the earth, and choose to live by rapine, are wanting to themselves, and *deserve to be exterminated as savage and pernicious beasts*."*

Now it is notorious, that the savages knew nothing of agriculture, when first discovered by the Europeans, but lived a most vagabond, disorderly, unrighteous life,—rambling from place to place, and prodigally rioting upon the spontaneous luxuries of nature, without tasking her generosity to yield them any thing more; whereas it has been most unquestionably shewn, that heaven intended the earth should be ploughed and sown, and manured, and laid out into cities and towns and farms, and country seats, and pleasure grounds, and public gardens, all which the Indians knew nothing about—therefore they did not improve the talents providence had bestowed on them—therefore they were careless stewards—therefore they had no right to the soil—therefore they deserved to be exterminated.

It is true the savages might plead that they drew all the benefits from the land which their simple wants required— they found plenty of game to hunt, which together with the roots and uncultivated fruits of the earth, furnished a sufficient variety for their frugal table;—and that as heaven

*Vattel—B.i, ch. 17. See likewise Grotius, Puffendorf, et alii.

merely designed the earth to form the abode, and satisfy the wants of man; so long as those purposes were answered, the will of heaven was accomplished.—But this only proves how undeserving they were of the blessings around them—they were so much the more savages, for not having more wants; for knowledge is in some degree an increase of desires, and it is this superiority both in the number and magnitude of his desires, that distinguishes the man from the beast. Therefore the Indians, in not having more wants, were very unreasonable animals; and it was but just that they should make way for the Europeans, who had a thousand wants to their one, and therefore would turn the earth to more account, and by cultivating it, more truly fulfil the will of heaven. Besides— Grotius and Lauterbach, and Puffendorff and Titius and a host of wise men besides, who have considered the matter properly, have determined, that the property of a country cannot be acquired by hunting, cutting wood, or drawing water in it—nothing but precise demarcation of limits, and the intention of cultivation, can establish the possession. Now as the savages (probably from never having read the authors above quoted) had never complied with any of these necessary forms, it plainly follows that they had no right to the soil, but that it was completely at the disposal of the first comers, who had more knowledge and more wants than themselves—who would portion out the soil, with churlish boundaries; who would torture nature to pamper a thousand fantastic humours and capricious appetites; and who of course were far more rational animals than themselves. In entering upon a newly discovered, uncultivated country therefore, the new comers were but taking possession of what, according to the aforesaid doctrine, was their own property— therefore in opposing them, the savages were invading their just rights, infringing the immutable laws of nature and counteracting the will of heaven—therefore they were guilty of impiety, burglary and trespass on the case,—therefore they were hardened offenders against God and man—therefore they ought to be exterminated.

But a more irresistible right then either that I have mentioned, and one which will be the most readily admitted by my reader, provided he is blessed with bowels of charity and philanthropy, is the right acquired by civilization. All the world knows the lamentable state in which these poor savages were found. Not only deficient in the comforts of life, but what is still worse, most piteously and unfortunately blind to the miseries of their situation. But no sooner did the benevolent inhabitants of Europe behold their sad condition than they immediately went to work to ameliorate and improve it. They introduced among them the comforts of life, consisting of rum, gin and brandy—and it is astonishing to read how soon the poor savages learnt to estimate these blessings—they likewise made known to them a thousand remedies, by which the most inveterate diseases are alleviated and healed, and that they might comprehend the benefits and enjoy the comforts of these medicines, they previously introduced among them the diseases, which they were calculated to cure. By these and a variety of other methods was the condition of these poor savages, wonderfully improved; they acquired a thousand wants, of which they had before been ignorant, and as he has most sources of happiness, who has most wants to be gratified, they were doubtlessly rendered a much happier race of beings.

But the most important branch of civilization, and which has most strenuously been extolled, by the zealous and pious fathers of the Roman Church, is the introduction of the Christian faith. It was truly a sight that might well inspire horror, to behold these savages, stumbling among the dark mountains of paganism, and guilty of the most horrible ignorance of religion. It is true, they neither stole nor defrauded, they were sober, frugal, continent, and faithful to their word; but though they acted right habitually, it was all in vain, unless they acted so from precept. The new comers therefore used every method, to induce them to embrace and practice the true religion—except that of setting them the example.

But notwithstanding all these complicated labours for their good, such was the unparalleled obstinacy of these stubborn wretches, that they ungratefully refused, to acknowledge the strangers as their benefactors, and persisted in disbelieving the doctrines they endeavoured to inculcate; most insolently alledging, that from their conduct, the advocates of Christianity did not seem to believe in it themselves. Was not this too much for human patience?—would not one suppose, that the foreign emigrants from Europe, provoked at their incredulity and discouraged by their stiff-necked obstinacy, would forever have abandoned their shores, and consigned them to their original ignorance and misery?—But no—so zealous were they to effect the temporal comfort and eternal salvation of these pagan infidels, that they even proceeded from the milder means of persuasion, to the more painful and troublesome one of persecution—Let loose among them, whole troops of fiery monks and furious blood-hounds—purified them by fire and sword, by stake and faggot; in consequence of which indefatigable measures, the cause of Christian love and charity were so rapidly advanced, that in a very few years, not one fifth of the number of unbelievers existed in South America, that were found there at the time of its discovery.

Nor did the other methods of civilization remain uninforced. The Indians improved daily and wonderfully by their intercourse with the whites. They took to drinking rum, and making bargains. They learned to cheat, to lie, to swear, to gamble, to quarrel, to cut each others throats, in short, to excel in all the accomplishments that had originally marked the superiority of their Christian visitors. And such a surprising aptitude have they shewn for these acquirements, that there is very little doubt that in a century more, provided they survive so long, the irresistible effects of civilization; they will equal in knowledge, refinement, knavery, and debauchery, the most enlightened, civilized and orthodox nations of Europe.

What stronger right need the European settlers advance to the country than this. Have not whole nations of uninformed savages been made acquainted with a thousand imperious wants and indispensible comforts of which they were before wholly ignorant—Have they not been literally hunted and smoked out of the dens and lurking places of ignorance and infidelity, and absolutely scourged into the right path. Have not the temporal things, the vain baubles and filthy lucre of this world, which were too apt to engage their worldly and selfish thoughts, been benevolently taken from them; and have they not in lieu thereof, been taught to set their affections on things above—And finally, to use the words of a reverend Spanish father, in a letter to his superior in Spain— "Can any one have the presumption to say, that these savage Pagans, have yielded any thing more than an inconsiderable recompense to their benefactors; in surrendering to them a little pitiful tract of this dirty sublunary planet, in exchange for a glorious inheritance in the kingdom of Heaven!"

Here then are three complete and undeniable sources of right established, any one of which was more than ample to establish a property in the newly discovered regions of America. Now, so it has happened in certain parts of this delightful quarter of the globe, that the right of discovery has been so strenuously asserted—the influence of cultivation so industriously extended, and the progress of salvation and civilization so zealously prosecuted, that, what with their attendant wars, persecutions, oppressions, diseases, and other partial evils that often hang on the skirts of great benefits—the savage aborigines have, some how or another, been utterly annihilated—and this all at once brings me to a fourth right, which is worth all the others put together—For the original claimants to the soil being all dead and buried, and no one remaining to inherit or dispute the soil, the Spaniards as the next immediate occupants entered upon the possession, as clearly as the hang-man succeeds to the clothes of the malefactor—and as they have Blackstone,* and all the learned expounders of the law on their side, they may set all actions of ejectment at defiance—and this last right may be entitled, the RIGHT BY EXTERMINATION, or in other words, the RIGHT BY GUNPOWDER.

But lest any scruples of conscience should remain on this head, and to settle the question of right forever, his holiness Pope Alexander VI, issued one of those mighty bulls, which bear down reason, argument and every thing before them; by which he generously granted the newly discovered quarter of the globe, to the Spaniards and Portuguese; who, thus having law and gospel on their side, and being inflamed with great spiritual zeal, shewed the Pagan savages neither favour nor affection, but prosecuted the work of discovery, colonization,

*Black. Com. B. II, c. i.

civilization, and extermination, with ten times more fury than ever.

Thus were the European worthies who first discovered America, clearly entitled to the soil; and not only entitled to the soil, but likewise to the eternal thanks of these infidel savages, for having come so far, endured so many perils by sea and land, and taken such unwearied pains, for no other purpose under heaven but to improve their forlorn, uncivilized and heathenish condition—for having made them acquainted with the comforts of life, such as gin, rum, brandy, and the small-pox; for having introduced among them the light of religion, and finally—for having hurried them out of the world, to enjoy its reward!

But as argument is never so well understood by us selfish mortals, as when it comes home to ourselves, and as I am particularly anxious that this question should be put to rest forever, I will suppose a parallel case, by way of arousing the candid attention of my readers.

Let us suppose then, that the inhabitants of the moon, by astonishing advancement in science, and by a profound insight into that ineffable lunar philosophy, the mere flickerings of which, have of late years, dazzled the feeble optics, and addled the shallow brains of the good people of our globe— let us suppose, I say, that the inhabitants of the moon, by these means, had arrived at such a command of their *energies*, such an enviable state of *perfectability*, as to controul the elements, and navigate the boundless regions of space. Let us suppose a roving crew of these soaring philosophers, in the course of an ærial voyage of discovery among the stars, should chance to alight upon this outlandish planet.

And here I beg my readers will not have the impertinence to smile, as is too frequently the fault of volatile readers, when perusing the grave speculations of philosophers. I am far from indulging in any sportive vein at present, nor is the supposition I have been making so wild as many may deem it. It has long been a very serious and anxious question with me, and many a time, and oft, in the course of my overwhelming cares and contrivances for the welfare and protection of this my native planet, have I lain awake whole nights, debating in my mind whether it was most probable we should first discover and civilize the moon, or the moon discover and civilize our globe. Neither would the prodigy of sailing in the air and cruising among the stars be a whit more astonishing and incomprehensible to us, than was the European mystery of navigating floating castles, through the world of waters, to the simple savages. We have already discovered the art of coasting along the ærial shores of our planet, by means of balloons, as the savages had, of venturing along their sea coasts in canoes; and the disparity between the former, and the ærial vehicles of the philosophers from the moon, might not be greater, than that, between the bark canoes of the savages, and the mighty ships of their discoverers. I might here pursue an endless chain of very curious, profound and unprofitable speculations; but as they would be unimportant to my subject, I abandon them to my reader, particularly if he is a philosopher, as matters well worthy his attentive consideration.

To return then to my supposition—let us suppose that the aerial visitants I have mentioned, possessed of vastly superior knowledge to ourselves; that is to say, possessed of superior knowledge in the art of extermination—riding on Hypogriffs, defended with impenetrable armour—armed with concentrated sun beams, and provided with vast engines, to hurl enormous moon stones: in short, let us suppose them, if our vanity will permit the supposition, as superior to us in knowledge, and consequently in power, as the Europeans were to the Indians, when they first discovered them. All this is very possible, it is only our self-sufficiency, that makes us think otherwise; and I warrant the poor savages, before they had any knowledge of the white men, armed in all the terrors of glittering steel and tremendous gun-powder, were as perfectly convinced that they themselves, were the wisest, the most virtuous, powerful and perfect of created beings, as are, at this present moment, the lordly inhabitants of old England, the volatile populace of France, or even the self-satisfied citizens of this most enlightened republick.

Let us suppose, moreover, that the aerial voyagers, finding this planet to be nothing but a howling wilderness, inhabited by us, poor savages and wild beasts, shall take formal possession of it, in the name of his most gracious and philosophic excellency, the man in the moon. Finding however, that their numbers are incompetent to hold it in complete subjection, on account of the ferocious barbarity of its inhabitants, they shall take our worthy President, the King of England, the Emperor of Hayti, the mighty little Bonaparte, and the great King of Bantam, and returning to their native planet, shall carry them to court, as were the Indian chiefs led about as spectacles in the courts of Europe.

Then making such obeisance as the etiquette of the court requires, they shall address the puissant man in the moon, in, as near as I can conjecture, the following terms:

"Most serene and mighty Potentate, whose dominions extend as far as eye can reach, who rideth on the Great Bear, useth the sun as a looking glass and maintaineth unrivalled controul over tides, madmen and sea-crabs. We thy liege subjects have just returned from a voyage of discovery, in the course of which we have landed and taken possession of that obscure little scurvy planet, which thou beholdest rolling at a distance. The five uncouth monsters, which we have brought into this august presence, were once very important chiefs among their fellow savages; for the inhabitants of the newly discovered globe are totally destitute of the common attributes of humanity, inasmuch as they carry their heads upon their shoulders, instead of under their arms—have two eyes instead of one—are utterly destitute of tails, and of a variety of unseemly complexions, particularly of a horrible whiteness—whereas all the inhabitants of the moon are pea green!

We have moreover found these miserable savages sunk into a state of the utmost ignorance and depravity, every man shamelessly living with his own wife, and rearing his own children, instead of indulging in that community of wives, enjoined by the law of nature, as expounded by the philosophers of the moon. In a word they have scarcely a gleam of true philosophy among them, but are in fact, utter heretics, ignoramuses and barbarians. Taking compassion therefore on the sad condition of these sublunary wretches, we have endeavoured, while we remained on their planet, to introduce among them the light of reason—and the comforts of the moon.—We have treated them to mouthfuls of moonshine and draughts of nitrous oxyde, which they swallowed with incredible voracity, particularly the females; and we have likewise endeavoured to instil into them the precepts of lunar Philosophy. We have insisted upon their renouncing the contemptible shackles of religion and common sense, and adoring the profound, omnipotent, and all perfect energy, and the extatic, immutable, immoveable perfection. But such was the unparalleled obstinacy of these wretched savages, that they persisted in cleaving to their wives and adhering to their religion, and absolutely set at naught the sublime doctrines of the moon—nay, among other abominable heresies they even went so far as blasphemously to declare, that this ineffable planet was made of nothing more nor less than green cheese!"

At these words, the great man in the moon (being a very profound philosopher) shall fall into a terrible passion, and possessing equal authority over things that do not belong to him, as did whilome his holiness the Pope, shall forthwith issue a formidable bull,—specifying, "That—whereas a certain crew of Lunatics have lately discovered and taken possession of that little dirty planet, called *the earth*—and that whereas it is inhabited by none but a race of two legged animals, that carry their heads on their shoulders instead of under their arms; cannot talk the lunatic language; have two eyes instead of one; are destitute of tails, and of a horrible whiteness, instead of pea green—therefore and for a variety of other excellent reasons—they are considered incapable of possessing any property in the planet they infest, and the right and title to it are confirmed to its original discoverers.— And furthermore, the colonists who are now about to depart to the aforesaid planet, are authorized and commanded to use every means to convert these infidel savages from the darkness of Christianity, and make them thorough and absolute lunatics."

In consequence of this benevolent bull, our philosophic benefactors go to work with hearty zeal. They seize upon our fertile territories, scourge us from our rightful possessions, relieve us from our wives, and when we are unreasonable enough to complain, they will turn upon us and say—miserable barbarians! ungrateful wretches!—have we not come thousands of miles to improve your worthless planet—have we not fed you with moon shine—have we not intoxicated you with nitrous oxyde—does not our moon give you light every night and have you the baseness to murmur, when we claim a pitiful return for all these benefits? But finding that we not only persist in absolute contempt to their reasoning and disbelief in their philosophy, but even go so far as daringly to defend our property, their patience shall be exhausted, and they shall resort to their superior powers of argument—hunt us with hypogriffs, transfix us with concentrated sun-beams, demolish our cities with moonstones; until having by main force, converted us to the true faith, they shall graciously permit us to exist in the torrid deserts of Arabia, or the frozen regions of Lapland, there to enjoy the blessings of civilization and the charms of lunar philosophy—in much the same manner as the reformed and enlightened savages of this country, are kindly suffered to inhabit the inhospitable forests of the north, or the impenetrable wildernesses of South America.

Thus have I clearly proved, and I hope strikingly illustrated, the right of the early colonists to the possession of this country—and thus is this gigantic question, completely knocked in the head—so having manfully surmounted all obstacles, and subdued all opposition, what remains but that I should forthwith conduct my impatient and way-worn readers, into the renowned city, which we have so long been in a manner besieging.—But hold, before I proceed another step, I must pause to take breath and recover from the excessive fatigue I have undergone, in preparing to begin this most accurate of histories. And in this I do but imitate the example of the celebrated Hans Von Dunderbottom, who took a start of three miles for the purpose of jumping over a hill, but having been himself out of breath by the time he reached the foot, sat himself quietly down for a few moments to blow, and then walked over it at his leisure.

END OF BOOK I.

BOOK II.

Treating of the first settlement of the province
of Nieuw Nederlandts.

CHAP. I.

*How Master Hendrick Hudson, voyaging in search of a
north-west passage discovered the famous bay of New York,
and likewise the great river Mohegan—and how he was
magnificently rewarded by the munificence of their High
Mightinesses.*

IN the ever memorable year of our Lord 1609, on the five
and twentieth day of March (O. S.)—a fine Saturday
morning, when jocund Phœbus, having his face newly
washed, by gentle dews and spring time showers, looked
from the glorious windows of the east, with a more than usually shining countenance—"that worthy and irrecoverable
discoverer, Master Henry Hudson" set sail from Holland in a
stout vessel,* called the Half Moon, being employed by the
Dutch East India Company, to seek a north-west passage to
China.

Of this celebrated voyage we have a narration still extant,
written with true log-book brevity, by master Robert Juet of
Lime house, mate of the vessel; who was appointed historian
of the voyage, partly on account of his uncommon literary
talents, but chiefly, as I am credibly informed, because he was
a countryman and schoolfellow of the great Hudson, with
whom he had often played truant and sailed chip boats, when
he was a little boy. I am enabled however to supply the deficiencies of master Juet's journal, by certain documents furnished me by very respectable Dutch families, as likewise by
sundry family traditions, handed down from my great great
Grandfather, who accompanied the expedition in the capacity
of cabin boy.

From all that I can learn, few incidents worthy of remark
happened in the voyage; and it mortifies me exceedingly that
I have to admit so noted an expedition into my work, without making any more of it.—Oh! that I had the advantages
of that most authentic writer of yore, Apollonius Rhodius,
who in his account of the famous Argonautic expedition, has

*Ogilvie calls it a frigate.

the whole mythology at his disposal, and elevates Jason and his compeers into heroes and demigods; though all the world knows them to have been a meer gang of sheep stealers, on a marauding expedition—or that I had the privileges of Dan Homer and Dan Virgil to enliven my narration, with giants and Lystrigonians; to entertain our honest mariners with an occasional concert of syrens and mermaids, and now and then with the rare shew of honest old Neptune and his fleet of frolicksome cruisers. But alas! the good old times have long gone by, when your waggish deities would descend upon the terraqueous globe, in their own proper persons, and play their pranks, upon its wondering inhabitants. Neptune has proclaimed an embargo in his dominions, and the sturdy tritons, like disbanded sailors, are out of employ, unless old Charon has charitably taken them into his service, to sound their conchs, and ply as his ferry-men. Certain it is, no mention has been made of them by any of our modern navigators, who are not behind their ancient predecessors in tampering with the marvellous—nor has any notice been taken of them, in that most minute and authentic chronicle of the seas, the New York Gazette edited by Solomon Lang. Even Castor and Pollux, those flaming meteors that blaze at the masthead of tempest tost vessels, are rarely beheld in these degenerate days—and it is but now and then, that our worthy sea captains fall in with that portentous phantom of the seas, that terror to all experienced mariners, that shadowy spectrum of the night—the flying Dutchman!

Suffice it then to say, the voyage was prosperous and tranquil—the crew being a patient people, much given to slumber and vacuity, and but little troubled with the disease of thinking—a malady of the mind, which is the sure breeder of discontent. Hudson had laid in abundance of gin and sour crout, and every man was allowed to sleep quietly at his post, unless the wind blew. True it is, some slight dissatisfaction was shewn on two or three occasions, at certain unreasonable conduct of Commodore Hudson. Thus for instance, he forbore to shorten sail when the wind was light, and the weather serene, which was considered among the most experienced dutch seamen, as certain *weather breeders*, or prognostics, that the weather would change for the worse. He acted, moreover, in direct contradiction to that ancient and sage rule of the dutch navigators, who always took in sail at night—put the helm a-port, and turned in—by which precaution they had a good night's rest—were sure of knowing where they were the next morning, and stood but little chance of running down a continent in the dark. He likewise prohibited the seamen from wearing more than five jackets, and six pair of breeches, under pretence of rendering them more alert; and no man was permitted to go aloft, and hand in sails, with a pipe in his mouth, as is the invariable Dutch custom, at the present day—All these grievances, though they might ruffle for a moment, the constitutional tranquillity of the honest Dutch tars, made but transient impression; they eat hugely, drank profusely, and slept immeasurably, and being under the especial guidance of providence, the ship was safely conducted to the coast of America; where, after sundry unimportant touchings and standings off and on, she at length, on the fourth day of September entered that majestic bay, which at this day expands its ample bosom, before the city of New York, and which had never before been visited by any European.

True it is—and I am not ignorant of the fact, that in a certain apocryphal book of voyages, compiled by one Hacluyt, is to be found a letter written to Francis the First, by one Giovanne, or John Verazzani, on which some writers are inclined to found a belief that this delightful bay had been visited nearly a century previous to the voyage of the enterprizing Hudson. Now this (albeit it has met with the countenance of certain very judicious and learned men) I hold in utter disbelief, and that for various good and substantial reasons—*First*, Because on strict examination it will be found, that the description given by this Verazzani, applies about as well to the bay of New York, as it does to my night cap—*Secondly*, Because that this John Verazzani, for whom I already begin to feel a most bitter enmity, is a native of Florence; and every body knows the crafty wiles of these losel Florentines, by which they filched away the laurels, from the arms of the immortal Colon, (vulgarly called Columbus) and bestowed them on their officious townsman, Amerigo Vespucci—and I make no doubt they are equally ready to rob

the illustrious Hudson, of the credit of discovering this beauteous island, adorned by the city of New York, and placing it
beside their usurped discovery of South America. And *thirdly*,
I award my decision in favour of the pretensions of Hendrick
Hudson, inasmuch as his expedition sailed from Holland,
being truly and absolutely a Dutch enterprize—and though
all the proofs in the world were introduced on the other side,
I would set them at naught as undeserving my attention. If
these three reasons are not sufficient to satisfy every burgher
of this ancient city—all I can say is, they are degenerate descendants from their venerable Dutch ancestors, and totally
unworthy the trouble of convincing. Thus, therefore, the title
of Hendrick Hudson, to his renowned discovery is fully vindicated.

It has been traditionary in our family, that when the great
navigator was first blessed with a view of this enchanting island, he was observed, for the first and only time in his life,
to exhibit strong symptoms of astonishment and admiration.
He is said to have turned to master Juet, and uttered these
remarkable words, while he pointed towards this paradise of
the new world—"see! there!"—and thereupon, as was always
his way when he was uncommonly pleased, he did puff out
such clouds of dense tobacco smoke, that in one minute the
vessel was out of sight of land, and master Juet was fain to
wait, until the winds dispersed this impenetrable fog.

It was indeed—as my great great grandfather used to say—
though in truth I never heard him, for he died, as might be
expected, before I was born.—"It was indeed a spot, on
which the eye might have revelled forever, in ever new and
never ending beauties." The island of Manna-hata, spread
wide before them, like some sweet vision of fancy, or some
fair creation of industrious magic. Its hills of smiling green
swelled gently one above another, crowned with lofty trees of
luxuriant growth; some pointing their tapering foliage towards the clouds, which were gloriously transparent; and
others, loaded with a verdant burthen of clambering vines,
bowing their branches to the earth, that was covered with
flowers. On the gentle declivities of the hills were scattered in
gay profusion, the dog wood, the sumach, and the wild briar,
whose scarlet berries and white blossoms glowed brightly

among the deep green of the surrounding foliage; and here and there, a curling column of smoke rising from the little glens that opened along the shore, seemed to promise the weary voyagers, a welcome at the hands of their fellow creatures. As they stood gazing with entranced attention on the scene before them, a red man crowned with feathers, issued from one of these glens, and after contemplating in silent wonder, the gallant ship, as she sat like a stately swan swimming on a silver lake, sounded the war-whoop, and bounded into the woods, like a wild deer, to the utter astonishment of the phlegmatic Dutchmen, who had never heard such a noise, or witnessed such a caper in their whole lives.

Of the transactions of our adventurers with the savages, and how the latter smoked copper pipes, and eat dried currants; how they brought great store of tobacco and oysters; how they shot one of the ship's crew, and how he was buried, I shall say nothing, being that I consider them unimportant to my history. After tarrying a few days in the bay, in order to smoke their pipes and refresh themselves after their seafaring, our voyagers weighed anchor, and adventurously ascended a mighty river which emptied into the bay. This river it is said was known among the savages by the name of the *Shatemuck*; though we are assured in an excellent little history published in 1674, by John Josselyn, Gent. that it was called the *Mohegan*,* and master Richard Blome, who wrote some time afterwards, asserts the same—so that I very much incline in favour of the opinion of these two honest gentlemen. Be this as it may, the river is at present denominated the Hudson; and up this stream the shrewd Hendrick had very little doubt he should discover the much looked for passage to China!

The journal goes on to make mention of divers interviews between the crew and the natives, in the voyage up the river, but as they would be impertinent to my history, I shall pass them over in silence, except the following dry joke, played off by the old commodore and his school-fellow Robert Juet; which does such vast credit to their experimental philosophy, that I cannot refrain from inserting it. "Our master and his

*This river is likewise laid down in Ogilvy's map as Manhattan—Noordt—Montaigne and Mauritius river.

mate determined to try some of the chiefe men of the countrey, whether they had any treacherie in them. So they tooke
them downe into the cabin and gave them so much wine and
aqua vitæ that they were all merrie; and one of them had his
wife with him, which sate so modestly, as any of our countrey
women would do in a strange place. In the end, one of them
was drunke, which had been aboarde of our ship all the time
that we had beene there, and that was strange to them, for
they could not tell how to take it."*

Having satisfied himself by this profound experiment, that
the natives were an honest, social race of jolly roysters, who
had no objection to a drinking bout, and were very merry in
their cups, the old commodore chuckled hugely to himself,
and thrusting a double quid of tobacco in his cheek, directed
master Juet to have it carefully recorded, for the satisfaction
of all the natural philosophers of the university of Leyden—
which done, he proceeded on his voyage, with great self-complacency. After sailing, however, above an hundred miles up
the river, he found the watery world around him, began to
grow more shallow and confined, the current more rapid and
perfectly fresh—phenomena not uncommon in the ascent of
rivers, but which puzzled the honest dutchmen prodigiously.
A consultation of our modern Argonauts was therefore called,
and having deliberated full six hours, they were brought to a
determination, by the ship's running aground—whereupon
they unanimously concluded, that there was but little chance
of getting to China in this direction. A boat, however, was
dispatched to explore higher up the river, which on its return,
confirmed the opinion—upon this the ship was warped off
and put about, with great difficulty, being like most of her
sex, exceedingly hard to govern; and the adventurous Hudson, according to the account of my great great grandfather,
returned down the river—with a prodigious flea in his ear!

Being satisfied that there was little likelihood of getting to
China, unless like the blind man, he returned from whence he
sat out and took a fresh start; he forthwith re-crossed the sea
to Holland, where he was received with great welcome by the
honourable East-India company, who were very much re-

*Juet's Journ. Purch. Pil.

joiced to see him come back safe—with their ship; and at a large and respectable meeting of the first merchants and burgomasters of Amsterdam, it was unanimously determined, that as a munificent reward for the eminent services he had performed, and the important discovery he had made, the great river Mohegan should be called after his name!—and it continues to be called Hudson river unto this very day.

CHAP. II.

Containing an account of a mighty Ark which floated, under the protection of St. Nicholas, from Holland to Gibbet Island—the descent of the strange Animals therefrom—a great victory, and a description of the ancient village of Communipaw.

THE DELECTABLE ACCOUNTS given by the great Hudson, and Master Juet, of the country they had discovered, excited not a little talk and speculation among the good people of Holland.—Letters patent were granted by government to an association of merchants, called the West-India company, for the exclusive trade on Hudson river, on which they erected a trading house called Fort Aurania, or Orange, at present the superb and hospitable city of Albany. But I forbear to dwell on the various commercial and colonizing enterprizes which took place; among which was that of Mynheer Adrian Block, who discovered and gave a name to Block Island, since famous for its cheese—and shall barely confine myself to that, which gave birth to this renowned city.

It was some three or four years after the return of the immortal Hendrick, that a crew of honest, well meaning, copper headed, low dutch colonists set sail from the city of Amsterdam, for the shores of America. It is an irreparable loss to history, and a great proof of the darkness of the age, and the lamentable neglect of the noble art of bookmaking, since so industriously cultivated by knowing sea-captains, and spruce super-cargoes, that an expedition so interesting and important in its results, should have been passed over in utter silence. To my great great grandfather am I again indebted, for the few facts, I am enabled to give concerning it—he having once more embarked for this country, with a full determination, as he said, of ending his days here—and of begetting a race of Knickerbockers, that should rise to be great men in the land.

The ship in which these illustrious adventurers set sail was called the *Goede Vrouw*, or Good Woman, in compliment to the wife of the President of the West India Company, who was allowed by every body (except her husband) to be a singularly sweet tempered lady, when not in liquor. It was in truth a gallant vessel, of the most approved dutch construction, and made by the ablest ship carpenters of Amsterdam, who it is well known, always model their ships after the fair forms of their country women. Accordingly it had one hundred feet in the keel, one hundred feet in the beam, and one hundred feet from the bottom of the stern post, to the tafferel. Like the beauteous model, who was declared the greatest belle in Amsterdam, it was full in the bows, with a pair of enormous cat-heads, a copper bottom, and withal, a most prodigious poop!

The architect, who was somewhat of a religious man, far from decorating the ship with pagan idols, such as Jupiter, Neptune, or Hercules (which heathenish abominations, I have no doubt, occasion the misfortunes and shipwrack of many a noble vessel) he I say, on the contrary, did laudably erect for a head, a goodly image of St. Nicholas, equipped with a low, broad brimmed hat, a huge pair of Flemish trunk hose, and a pipe that reached to the end of the bow-sprit. Thus gallantly furnished, the staunch ship floated sideways, like a majestic goose, out of the harbour of the great city of Amsterdam, and all the bells, that were not otherwise engaged, rung a triple bob-major on the joyful occasion.

My great great grandfather remarks, that the voyage was uncommonly prosperous, for being under the especial care of the ever-revered St. Nicholas, the Goede Vrouw seemed to be endowed with qualities, unknown to common vessels. Thus she made as much lee-way as head-way, could get along very nearly as fast with the wind a-head, as when it was a-poop— and was particularly great in a calm; in consequence of which singular advantages, she made out to accomplish her voyage in a very few months, and came to anchor at the mouth of the Hudson, a little to the east of Gibbet Island.*

Here lifting up their eyes, they beheld, on what is at present called the Jersey shore, a small Indian village, pleasantly embowered in a grove of spreading elms, and the natives all collected on the beach, gazing in stupid admiration at the Goede Vrouw. A boat was immediately dispatched to enter

*So called, because one Joseph Andrews, a pirate and murderer, was hanged in chains on that Island, the 23d May, 1769. EDITOR.

into a treaty with them, and approaching the shore, hailed them through a trumpet, in the most friendly terms; but so horribly confounded were these poor savages at the tremendous and uncouth sound of the low dutch language, that they one and all took to their heels, scampered over the Bergen hills, nor did they stop until they had buried themselves, head and ears, in the marshes, on the other side, where they all miserably perished to a man—and their bones being collected, and decently covered by the Tammany Society of that day, formed that singular mound, called *Rattle-snake-hill*, which rises out of the centre of the salt marshes, a little to the east of the Newark Causeway.

Animated by this unlooked-for victory our valiant heroes sprang ashore in triumph, took possession of the soil as conquerors in the name of their High Mightinesses the lords states general, and marching fearlessly forward, carried the village of *Communipaw* by storm—having nobody to withstand them, but some half a score of old squaws, and poppooses, whom they tortured to death with low dutch. On looking about them they were so transported with the excellencies of the place, that they had very little doubt, the blessed St. Nicholas, had guided them thither, as the very spot whereon to settle their colony. The softness of the soil was wonderfully adapted to the driving of piles; the swamps and marshes around them afforded ample opportunities for the constructing of dykes and dams; the shallowness of the shore was peculiarly favourable to the building of docks—in a word, this spot abounded with all the singular inconveniences, and aquatic obstacles, necessary for the foundation of a great dutch city. On making a faithful report therefore, to the crew of the Goede Vrouw, they one and all determined that this was the destined end of their voyage. Accordingly they descended from the Goede Vrouw, men women and children, in goodly groups, as did the animals of yore from the ark, and formed themselves into a thriving settlement, which they called by the Indian name *Communipaw*.

As all the world is perfectly acquainted with Communipaw, it may seem somewhat superfluous to treat of it in the present work; but my readers will please to recollect, that notwithstanding it is my chief desire to improve the present age, yet

I write likewise for posterity, and have to consult the understanding and curiosity of some half a score of centuries yet to come; by which time perhaps, were it not for this invaluable history, the great Communipaw, like Babylon, Carthage, Nineveh and other great cities, might be perfectly extinct—sunk and forgotten in its own mud—its inhabitants turned into oysters,* and even its situation a fertile subject of learned controversy and hardheaded investigation among indefatigable historians. Let me then piously rescue from oblivion, the humble reliques of a place, which was the egg from whence was hatched the mighty city of New York!

Communipaw is at present but a small village, pleasantly situated among rural scenery, on that beauteous part of the Jersey shore which was known in ancient legends by the name of Pavonia, and commands a grand prospect of the superb bay of New York. It is within but half an hour's sail of the latter place, provided you have a fair wind, and may be distinctly seen from the city. Nay, it is a well known fact, which I can testify from my own experience, that on a clear still summer evening, you may hear, from the battery of New York, the obstreperous peals of broad-mouthed laughter of the dutch negroes at Communipaw, who, like most other negroes, are famous for their risible powers. This is peculiarly the case on Sunday evenings; when, it is remarked by an ingenious and observant philosopher, who has made great discoveries in the neighbourhood of this city, that they always laugh loudest—which he attributes to the circumstance of their having their holliday clothes on.

These negroes, in fact, like the monks in the dark ages, engross all the knowledge of the place, and being infinitely more adventurous and more knowing than their masters, carry on all the foreign trade; making frequent voyages to town in canoes loaded with oysters, buttermilk and cabbages. They are great astrologers, predicting the different changes of weather almost as accurately as an almanack—they are moreover exquisite performers on three stringed fiddles: in whistling they almost boast the farfamed powers of Orpheus his lyre, for not a horse or an ox in the place, when at the plow

*"Men by inaction degenerate into Oysters." Kaimes.

or in the waggon, will budge a foot until he hears the well known whistle of his black driver and companion.—And from their amazing skill at casting up accounts upon their fingers, they are regarded with as much veneration as were the disciples of Pythagoras of yore, when initiated into the sacred quaternary of numbers.

As to the honest dutch burghers of Communipaw, like wise men, and sound philosophers, they never look beyond their pipes, nor trouble their heads about any affairs out of their immediate neighbourhood; so that they live in profound and enviable ignorance of all the troubles, anxieties and revolutions, of this distracted planet. I am even told that many among them do verily believe that Holland, of which they have heard so much from tradition, is situated somewhere on Long-Island—that *Spiking-devil* and *the Narrows* are the two ends of the world—that the country is still under the dominion of their high mightinesses, and that the city of New York still goes by the name of Nieuw Amsterdam. They meet every saturday afternoon, at the only tavern in the place, which bears as a sign, a square headed likeness of the prince of Orange; where they smoke a silent pipe, by way of promoting social conviviality, and invariably drink a mug of cider to the success of admiral Von Tromp, who they imagine is still sweeping the British channel, with a broom at his mast head.

Communipaw, in short, is one of the numerous little villages in the vicinity of this most beautiful of cities, which are so many strong holds and fastnesses, whither the primitive manners of our dutch forefathers have retreated, and where they are cherished with devout and scrupulous strictness. The dress of the original settlers is handed down inviolate, from father to son—the identical broad brimmed hat, broad skirted coat and broad bottomed breeches, continue from generation to generation, and several gigantic knee buckles of massy silver, are still in wear, that made such gallant display in the days of the patriarchs of Communipaw. The language likewise, continues unadulterated by barbarous innovations; and so critically correct is the village school-master in his dialect, that his reading of a low dutch psalm, has much the same effect on the nerves, as the filing of a hand saw.

CHAP. III.

*In which is set forth the true art of making a bargain, to-
gether with a miraculous escape of a great Metropolis in a
fog—and how certain adventurers departed from Communipaw on a perilous colonizing expedition.*

HAVING, in the trifling digression with which I concluded
my last chapter, discharged the filial duty, which the
city of New York owes to Communipaw, as being the mother
settlement; and having given a faithful picture of it as it
stands at present, I return, with a soothing sentiment of self-
approbation, to dwell upon its early history. The crew of the
Goede Vrouw being soon reinforced by fresh importations
from Holland, the settlement went jollily on, encreasing in
magnitude and prosperity. The neighbouring Indians in a
short time became accustomed to the uncouth sound of the
dutch language, and an intercourse gradually took place between them and the new comers. The Indians were much
given to long talks, and the Dutch to long silence—in this
particular therefore, they accommodated each other completely. The chiefs would make long speeches about the big
bull, the wabash and the great spirit, to which the others
would listen very attentively, smoke their pipes and grunt *yah
myn-her*—whereat the poor savages were wonderously delighted. They instructed the new settlers in the best art of
curing and smoking tobacco, while the latter in return, made
them drunk with true Hollands—and then learned them the
art of making bargains.

A brisk trade for furs was soon opened: the dutch traders
were scrupulously honest in their dealings, and purchased by
weight, establishing it as an invariable table of avoirdupoise,
that the hand of a dutchman weighed one pound, and his
foot two pounds. It is true, the simple Indians were often
puzzled at the great disproportion between bulk and weight,
for let them place a bundle of furs, never so large, in one
scale, and a dutchman put his hand or foot in the other, the
bundle was sure to kick the beam—never was a package of

furs known to weigh more than two pounds, in the market of Communipaw!

This is a singular fact—but I have it direct from my great great grandfather, who had risen to considerable importance in the colony, being promoted to the office of weigh master, on account of the uncommon heaviness of his foot.

The Dutch possessions in this part of the globe began now to assume a very thriving appearance, and were comprehended under the general title of Nieuw Nederlandts, on account, no doubt, of their great resemblance to the Dutch Netherlands—excepting that the former were rugged and mountainous, and the latter level and marshy. About this time the tranquility of the dutch colonists was doomed to suffer a temporary interruption. In 1614, captain Sir Samuel Argal, sailing under a commission from Dale, governor of Virginia, visited the dutch settlements on Hudson river, and demanded their submission to the English crown and Virginian dominion.—To this arrogant demand, as they were in no condition to resist it, they submitted for the time, like discreet and reasonable men.

It does not appear that the valiant Argal molested the settlement of Communipaw; on the contrary, I am told that when his vessel first hove in sight the worthy burghers were seized with such a panic, that they fell to smoking their pipes with astonishing vehemence; insomuch that they quickly raised a cloud, which combining with the surrounding woods and marshes, completely enveloped and concealed their beloved village; and overhung the fair regions of Pavonia—So that the terrible captain Argal passed on, totally unsuspicious that a sturdy little Dutch settlement lay snugly couched in the mud, under cover of all this pestilent vapour. In commemoration of this fortunate escape, the worthy inhabitants have continued to smoke, almost without intermission, unto this very day; which is said to be the cause of the remarkable fog that often hangs over Communipaw of a clear afternoon.

Upon the departure of the enemy, our magnanimous ancestors took full six months to recover their wind, having been exceedingly discomposed by the consternation and hurry of affairs. They then called a council of safety to smoke over the state of the province. After six months more of mature deliberation, during which nearly five hundred words were spoken, and almost as much tobacco was smoked, as would have served a certain modern general through a whole winter's campaign of hard drinking, it was determined, to fit out an armament of canoes, and dispatch them on a voyage of discovery; to search if peradventure some more sure and formidable position might not be found, where the colony would be less subject to vexatious visitations.

This perilous enterprize was entrusted to the superintendance of Mynheers Oloffe Van Kortlandt, Abraham Hardenbroek, Jacobus Van Zandt and Winant Ten Broek—four indubitably great men, but of whose history, though I have made diligent enquiry, I can learn but little, previous to their leaving Holland. Nor need this occasion much surprize; for adventurers, like prophets, though they make great noise abroad, have seldom much celebrity in their own countries; but this much is certain, that the overflowings and off scourings of a country, are invariably composed of the richest parts of the soil. And here I cannot help remarking how convenient it would be to many of our great men and great families of doubtful origin, could they have the privilege of the heroes of yore, who, whenever their origin was involved in obscurity, modestly announced themselves descended from a god— and who never visited a foreign country, but what they told some cock and bull stories, about their being kings and princes at home. This venial trespass on the truth, though it has occasionally been played off by some pseudo marquis, baronet, and other illustrious foreigner, in our land of good natured credulity, has been completely discountenanced in this sceptical, matter of fact age—And I even question whether any tender virgin, who was accidentally and unaccountably enriched with a bantling, would save her character at parlour fire-sides and evening tea-parties, by ascribing the phenomenon to a swan, a shower of gold or a river god.

Thus being totally denied the benefit of mythology and classic fable, I should have been completely at a loss as to the early biography of my heroes, had not a gleam of light been thrown upon their origin from their names.

By this simple means have I been enabled to gather some particulars, concerning the adventurers in question. Van Kortlandt for instance, was one of those peripatetic philosophers, who tax providence for a livelihood, and like Diogenes, enjoy a free and unincumbered estate in sunshine. He was usually arrayed in garments suitable to his fortune, being curiously fringed and fangled by the hand of time; and was helmeted with an old fragment of a hat which had acquired the shape of a sugar-loaf; and so far did he carry his contempt for the adventitious distinction of dress, that it is said, the remnant of a shirt, which covered his back, and dangled like a pocket handkerchief out of a hole in his breeches, was never washed, except by the bountiful showers of heaven. In this garb was he usually to be seen, sunning himself at noon day, with a herd of philosophers of the same sect, on the side of the great canal of Amsterdam. Like your nobility of Europe, he took his name of *Kortlandt* (or *lack land*) from his landed estate, which lay some where in Terra incognita.

Of the next of our worthies, might I have had the benefit of mythological assistance, the want of which I have just lamented—I should have made honourable mention, as boasting equally illustrious pedigree, with the proudest hero of antiquity. His name was *Van Zandt*, which freely translated, signifies *from the dirt*, meaning, beyond a doubt, that like Triptolemus, Themis—the Cyclops and the Titans, he sprung from dame Terra or the earth! This supposition is strongly corroborated by his size, for it is well known that all the progeny of mother earth were of a gigantic stature; and Van Zandt, we are told, was a tall raw-boned man, above six feet high—with an astonishingly hard head. Nor is this origin of the illustrious Van Zandt a whit more improbable or repugnant to belief, than what is related and universally admitted of certain of our greatest, or rather richest men; who we are told, with the utmost gravity, did originally spring from a dung-hill!

Of the third hero, but a faint description has reached to this time, which mentions, that he was a sturdy, obstinate, burley, bustling little man; and from being usually equipped with an old pair of buck-skins, was familiarly dubbed Harden broek, or *Tough Breeches*.

Ten Broek completed this junto of adventurers. It is a singular but ludicrous fact, which, were I not scrupulous in recording the whole truth, I should almost be tempted to pass over in silence, as incompatible with the gravity and dignity of my history, that this worthy gentleman should likewise have been nicknamed from the most whimsical part of his dress. In fact, the small clothes seems to have been a very important garment in the eyes of our venerated ancestors, owing in all probability to its really being the largest article of raiment among them. The name of Ten Broek, or Tin Broek is indifferently translated into Ten Breeches and Tin Breeches—the high dutch commentators incline to the former opinion; and ascribe it to his being the first who introduced into the settlement the ancient dutch fashion of wearing ten pair of breeches. But the most elegant and ingenious writers on the subject, declare in favour of Tin, or rather *Thin* Breeches; from whence they infer, that he was a poor, but merry rogue, whose galligaskins were none of the soundest, and who was the identical author of that truly philosophical stanza:

> "Then why should we quarrel for riches,
>   Or any such glittering toys;
> A light heart and *thin pair of breeches*,
>   Will go thorough the world my brave boys!"

Such was the gallant junto that fearlessly set sail at the head of a mighty armament of canoes, to explore the yet unknown country about the mouth of the Hudson—and heaven seemed to shine propitious on their undertaking.

It was that delicious season of the year, when nature, breaking from the chilling thraldom of old winter, like a blooming damsel, from the tyranny of a sordid old hunks of a father, threw herself blushing with ten thousand charms, into the arms, of youthful spring. Every tufted copse and blooming grove resounded with the notes of hymeneal love; the very insects as they sipped the morning dew, that gemmed the tender grass of the meadows, lifted up their little voices to join the joyous epithalamium—the virgin bud timidly put forth its blushes, and the heart of man dissolved away in tenderness. Oh sweet Theocritus! had I thy oaten reed, wherewith thou erst didst charm the gay Sicilian plains; or oh gentle

Bion! thy pastoral pipe, in which the happy swains of the Lesbian isle so much delighted; then would I attempt to sing, in soft Bucolic or negligent Idyllium, the rural beauties of the scene—But having nothing but this jaded goose quill, wherewith to wing my flight, I must fain content myself to lay aside these poetic disportings of the fancy and pursue my faithful narrative in humble prose—comforting myself with the reflection, that though it may not commend itself so sweetly to the imagination of my reader, yet will it insinuate itself with virgin modesty, to his better judgment, clothed as it is in the chaste and simple garb of truth.

In the joyous season of spring then, did these hardy adventurers depart on this eventful expedition, which only wanted another Virgil to rehearse it, to equal the oft sung story of the Eneid—Many adventures did they meet with and divers bitter mishaps did they sustain, in their wanderings from Communipaw to oyster Island—from oyster Island to gibbet island, from gibbet island to governors island, and from governors island through buttermilk channel, (a second streights of Pylorus) to the Lord knows where; until they came very nigh being ship wrecked and lost forever, in the tremendous vortexes of *Hell gate*,* which for terrors, and frightful perils, might laugh old Scylla and Charybdis to utter scorn—In all which cruize they encountered as many Lystrigonians and Cyclops and Syrens and unhappy Didos, as did ever the pious Eneas, in his colonizing voyage.

At length, after wandering to and fro, they were attracted by the transcendant charms of a vast island, which lay like a gorgeous stomacher, dividing the beauteous bosom of the bay, and to which the numerous mighty islands among which they had been wandering, seemed as so many foils and append-

---

*This is a fearful combination of rocks and whirlpools, in the sound above New York, dangerous to ships unless under the care of a skillful pilot. Certain wise men who instruct these modern days have softened this characteristic name into *Hurl gate*, on what authority, I leave them to explain. The name as given by our author is supported by Ogilvie's History of America published 1671, as also by a journal still extant, written in the 16th century, and to be found in Hazard's state papers. The original name, as laid down in all the Dutch manuscripts and maps, was *Helle gat*, and an old MS. written in French, speaking of various alterations in names about this city observes "De *Helle gat* trou d'Enfer, ils ont fait *Hell gate*, Porte d'Enfer."—Printer's Devil.

ages. Hither they bent their course, and old Neptune, as if anxious to assist in the choice of a spot, whereon was to be founded a city that should serve as his strong hold in this western world, sent half a dozen potent billows, that rolled the canoes of our voyagers, high and dry on the very point of the island, where at present stands the delectable city of New York.

The original name of this beautiful island is in some dispute, and has already undergone a vitiation, which is a proof of the melancholy instability of sublunary things, and of the industrious perversions of modern orthographers. The name which is most current among the vulgar (such as members of assembly and bank directors) is *Manhattan*—which is said to have originated from a custom among the squaws, in the early settlement, of wearing men's wool hats, as is still done among many tribes. "Hence," we are told by an old governor, somewhat of a wag, who flourished almost a century since, and had paid a visit to the wits of Philadelphia—"Hence arose the appellation of Man-hat-on, first given to the Indians, and afterwards to the island"—a stupid joke!—but well enough for a governor.

Among the more ancient authorities which deserve very serious consideration, is that contained in the valuable history of the American possessions, written by master Richard Blome in 1687, wherein it is called *Manhadaes*, or *Manahanent*; nor must I forget the excellent little book of that authentic historian, John Josselyn, Gent. who explicitly calls it *Manadaes*.

But an authority still more ancient, and still more deserving of credit, because it is sanctioned by the countenance of our venerated dutch ancestors, is that founded on certain letters still extant, which passed between the early governors, and their neighbour powers; wherein it is variously called the Monhattoes, Munhatos and Manhattoes—an unimportant variation, occasioned by the literati of those days having a great contempt for those spelling book and dictionary researches, which form the sole study and ambition of so many learned men and women of the present times. This name is said to be derived from the great Indian spirit Manetho, who was supposed to have made this island his favourite residence, on account of its uncommon delights. But the most venerable and indisputable authority extant, and one on which I place implicit confidence, because it confers a name at once melodious, poetical and significant, is that furnished by the before quoted journal of the voyage of the great Hudson, by Master Juet; who clearly and correctly calls it MANNA-HATA—that is to say, the island of Manna; or in other words—"a land flowing with milk and honey!"

CHAP. IV.

In which are contained divers very sound reasons why a man should not write in a hurry: together with the building of New Amsterdam, and the memorable dispute of Mynheers Ten Breeches and Tough Breeches thereupon.

M Y GREAT GRANDFATHER, by the mother's side, Hermanus Van Clattercop, when employed to build the large stone church at Rotterdam, which stands about three hundred yards to your left, after you turn off from the Boomkeys, and which is so conveniently constructed, that all the zealous Christians of Rotterdam prefer sleeping through a sermon there, to any other church in the city—My great grandfather, I say, when employed to build that famous church, did in the first place send to Delft for a box of long pipes; then having purchased a new spitting box and a hundred weight of the best Virginia, he sat himself down, and did nothing for the space of three months, but smoke most laboriously. Then did he spend full three months more in trudging on foot, and voyaging in Trekschuit, from Rotterdam to Amsterdam—to Delft—to Haerlem—to Leyden—to the Hague, knocking his head and breaking his pipe, against every church in his road. Then did he advance gradually, nearer and nearer to Rotterdam, until he came in full sight of the identical spot, whereon the church was to be built. Then did he spend three months longer in walking round it and round it; contemplating it, first from one point of view, and then from another—now would he be paddled by it on the canal—now would he peep at it through a telescope, from the other side of the Meuse, and now would he take a bird's eye glance at it, from the top of one of those gigantic wind mills, which protect the gates of the city. The good folks of the place were on the tiptoe of expectation and impatience—notwithstanding all the turmoil of my great grandfather, not a symptom of the church was yet to be seen; they even began to fear it would never be brought into the world, but that its great projector would lie down, and die in labour, of the mighty plan he had conceived. At length,

having occupied twelve good months in puffing and paddling, and talking and walking—having travelled over all
Holland, and even taken a peep into France and Germany—
having smoked five hundred and ninety-nine pipes, and three
hundred weight of the best Virginia tobacco; my great grandfather gathered together all that knowing and industrious
class of citizens, who prefer attending to any body's business
sooner than their own, and having pulled off his coat and five
pair of breeches, he advanced sturdily up, and laid the corner
stone of the church, in the presence of the whole multitude—
just at the commencement of the thirteenth month.

In a similar manner and with the example of my worthy
ancestor full before my eyes, have I proceeded in writing this
most authentic history. The honest Rotterdammers no doubt
thought my great grandfather was doing nothing at all to the
purpose, while he was making such a world of prefatory bustle, about the building of his church—and many of the ingenious inhabitants of this fair city, (whose intellects have
been thrice stimulated and quickened, by transcendant nitrous
oxyde, as were those of Chrysippus, with hellebore,) will unquestionably suppose that all the preliminary chapters, with
the discovery, population and final settlement of America,
were totally irrelevant and superfluous—and that the main
business, the history of New York, is not a jot more advanced,
than if I had never taken up my pen. Never were wise people
more mistaken in their conjectures; in consequence of going
to work slowly and deliberately, the church came out of my
grandfather's hands, one of the most sumptuous, goodly and
glorious edifices in the known world—excepting, that, like
our transcendant capital at Washington, it was begun on such
a grand scale, the good folks could not afford to finish more
than the wing of it.

In the same manner do I prognosticate, if ever I am enabled to finish this history, (of which in simple truth, I often
have my doubts,) that it will be handed down to posterity,
the most complete, faithful, and critically constructed work
that ever was read—the delight of the learned, the ornament
of libraries, and a model for all future historians. There is
nothing that gives such an expansion of mind, as the idea of
writing for posterity—And had Ovid, Herodotus, Polybius

or Tacitus, like Moses from the top of Mount Pisgah, taken a view of the boundless region over which their offspring were destined to wander—like the good old Israelite, they would have lain down and died contented.

I hear some of my captious readers questioning the correctness of my arrangement—but I have no patience with these continual interruptions—never was historian so pestered with doubts and queries, and such a herd of discontented quidnuncs! if they continue to worry me in this manner, I shall never get to the end of my work. I call Apollo and his whole seraglio of muses to witness, that I pursue the most approved and fashionable plan of modern historians; and if my readers are not pleased with my matter, and my manner, for God's sake let them throw down my work, take up a pen and write a history to suit themselves—for my part I am weary of their incessant interruptions, and beg once for all, that I may have no more of them.

The island of Manna-hata, Manhattoes, or as it is vulgarly called Manhattan, having been discovered, as was related in the last chapter; and being unanimously pronounced by the discoverers, the fairest spot in the known world, whereon to build a city, that should surpass all the emporiums of Europe, they immediately returned to Communipaw with the pleasing intelligence. Upon this a considerable colony was forthwith fitted out, who after a prosperous voyage of half an hour, arrived at Manna hata, and having previously purchased the land of the Indians, (a measure almost unparalleled in the annals of discovery and colonization) they settled upon the south-west point of the island, and fortified themselves strongly, by throwing up a mud battery, which they named FORT AMSTERDAM. A number of huts soon sprung up in the neighbourhood, to protect which, they made an enclosure of strong pallisadoes. A creek running from the East river, through what at present is called Whitehall street, and a little inlet from Hudson river to the bowling green formed the original boundaries; as though nature had kindly designated the cradle, in which the embryo of this renowned city was to be nestled. The woods on both sides of the creek were carefully cleared away, as well as from the space of ground now occupied by the bowling green.—These precautions were taken to protect the fort from either the open attacks or insidious advances of its savage neighbours, who wandered in hordes about the forests and swamps that extended over those tracts of country, at present called broad way, Wall street, William street and Pearl street.

No sooner was the colony once planted, than like a luxuriant vine, it took root and throve amazingly; for it would seem, that this thrice favoured island is like a munificent dung hill, where every thing finds kindly nourishment, and soon shoots up and expands to greatness. The thriving state of the settlement, and the astonishing encrease of houses, gradually awakened the leaders from a profound lethargy, into which they had fallen, after having built their mud fort. They began to think it was high time some plan should be devised, on which the encreasing town should be built; so taking pipe in mouth, and meeting in close divan, they forthwith fell into a profound deliberation on the subject.

At the very outset of the business, an unexpected difference of opinion arose, and I mention it with regret, as being the first internal altercation on record among the new settlers. An ingenious plan was proposed by Mynheer Ten Broek to cut up and intersect the ground by means of canals; after the manner of the most admired cities in Holland; but to this Mynheer Hardenbroek was diametrically opposed; suggesting in place thereof, that they should run out docks and wharves, by means of piles driven into the bottom of the river, on which the town should be built—By this means said he triumphantly, shall we rescue a considerable space of territory from these immense rivers, and build a city that shall rival Amsterdam, Venice, or any amphibious city in Europe. To this proposition, Ten Broek (or Ten breeches) replied, with a look of as much scorn as he could possibly assume. He cast the utmost censure upon the plan of his antagonist, as being preposterous, and against the very order of things, as he would leave to every true hollander. "For what," said he, "is a town without canals?—it is like a body without veins and arteries, and must perish for want of a free circulation of the vital fluid"—Tough breeches, on the contrary, retorted with a sarcasm upon his antagonist, who was somewhat of an arid, dry boned habit of body; he remarked that as to the circulation of the blood being necessary to existence, Mynheer Ten breeches was a living contradiction to his own assertion; for every body knew there had not a drop of blood circulated through his wind dried carcass for good ten years, and yet there was not a greater busy body in the whole colony. Personalities have seldom much effect in making converts in argument—nor have I ever seen a man convinced of error, by being convicted of deformity. At least such was not the case at present. Ten Breeches was very acrimonious in reply, and Tough Breeches, who was a sturdy little man, and never gave up the last word, rejoined with encreasing spirit—Ten Breeches had the advantage of the greatest volubility, but Tough Breeches had that invaluable coat of mail in argument called obstinacy—Ten Breeches had, therefore, the most mettle, but Tough Breeches the best bottom—so that though Ten Breeches made a dreadful clattering about his ears, and battered and belaboured him with hard words and sound arguments, yet Tough Breeches hung on most resolutely to the last. They parted therefore, as is usual in all arguments where both parties are in the right, without coming to any conclusion—but they hated each other most heartily forever after, and a similar breach with that between the houses of Capulet and Montague, had well nigh ensued between the families of Ten Breeches and Tough Breeches.

I would not fatigue my reader with these dull matters of fact, but that my duty as a faithful historian, requires that I should be particular—and in truth, as I am now treating of the critical period, when our city, like a young twig, first received the twists and turns, that have since contributed to give it the present picturesque irregularity for which it is celebrated, I cannot be too minute in detailing their first causes.

After the unhappy altercation I have just mentioned, I do not find that any thing further was said on the subject, worthy of being recorded. The council, consisting of the largest and oldest heads in the community, met regularly once a week, to ponder on this momentous subject.—But either they were deterred by the war of words they had witnessed, or they were naturally averse to the exercise of the tongue, and the consequent exercise of the brains—certain it is, the most profound silence was maintained—the question as usual lay on the table—the members quietly smoked their pipes, making but few laws, without ever enforcing any, and in the mean time the affairs of the settlement went on—as it pleased God.

As most of the council were but little skilled in the mystery of combining pot hooks and hangers, they determined most judiciously not to puzzle either themselves or posterity, with voluminous records. The secretary however, kept the minutes of each meeting with tolerable precision, in a large vellum folio, fastened with massy brass clasps, with a sight of which I have been politely favoured by my highly respected friends, the Goelets, who have this invaluable relique, at present in their possession. On perusal, however, I do not find much information—The journal of each meeting consists but of two lines, stating in dutch, that, "the council sat this day, and smoked twelve pipes, on the affairs of the colony."—By which it appears that the first settlers did not regulate their time by hours, but pipes, in the same manner as they measure distances in Holland at this very time; an admirably exact measurement, as a pipe in the mouth of a genuine dutchman is never liable to those accidents and irregularities, that are continually putting our clocks out of order.

In this manner did the profound council of NEW AMSTER-DAM smoke, and doze, and ponder, from week to week, month to month, and year to year, in what manner they should construct their infant settlement—mean while, the town took care of itself, and like a sturdy brat which is suf-fered to run about wild, unshackled by clouts and bandages, and other abominations by which your notable nurses and sage old women cripple and disfigure the children of men, encreased so rapidly in strength and magnitude, that before the honest burgomasters had determined upon a plan, it was too late to put it in execution—whereupon they wisely aban-doned the subject altogether.

CHAP. V.

In which the Author is very unreasonably afflicted about nothing.—Together with divers Anecdotes of the prosperity of New Amsterdam, and the wisdom of its Inhabitants.—And the sudden introduction of a Great Man.

G RIEVOUS, and very much to be commiserated, is the task of the feeling historian, who writes the history of his native land. If it falls to his lot to be the sad recorder of calamity or crime, the mournful page is watered with his tears—nor can he recal the most prosperous and blissful eras, without a melancholy sigh at the reflection, that they have passed away forever! I know not whether it be owing to an immoderate love for the simplicity of former times, or to a certain tenderness of heart, natural to a sentimental historian; but I candidly confess, I cannot look back on the halcyon days of the city, which I now describe, without a deep dejection of the spirits. With faultering hand I withdraw the curtain of oblivion, which veils the modest merits of our venerable dutch ancestors, and as their revered figures rise to my mental vision, humble myself before the mighty shades.

Such too are my feelings when I revisit the family mansion of the Knickerbockers and spend a lonely hour in the attic chamber, where hang the portraits of my forefathers, shrouded in dust like the forms they represent. With pious reverence do I gaze on the countenances of those renowned burghers, who have preceded me in the steady march of existence—whose sober and temperate blood now meanders through my veins, flowing slower and slower in its feeble conduits, until its lingering current shall soon be stopped forever!

These, say I to myself, are but frail memorials of the mighty men, who flourished in the days of the patriarchs; but who, alas, have long since mouldered in that tomb, towards which my steps are insensibly and irresistibly hastening! As I pace the darkened chamber and lose myself in melancholy musings, the shadowy images around me, almost seem to steal once more into existence—their countenances appear for an in-

stant to assume the animation of life—their eyes to pursue
me in every movement! carried away by the delusion of fancy,
I almost imagine myself surrounded by the shades of the
departed, and holding sweet converse with the worthies of
antiquity!—Luckless Diedrich! born in a degenerate age—
abandoned to the buffettings of fortune—a stranger and a
weary pilgrim in thy native land; blest with no weeping wife,
nor family of helpless children—but doomed to wander neglected through those crowded streets, and elbowed by foreign upstarts from those fair abodes, where once thine
ancestors held sovereign empire. Alas! alas! is then the dutch
spirit forever extinct? The days of the patriarchs, have they
fled forever? Return—return sweet days of simplicity and
ease—dawn once more on the lovely island of Manna hata!—
Bear with me my worthy readers, bear with the weakness of
my nature—or rather let us sit down together, indulge the
full flow of filial piety, and weep over the memories of our
great great grand-fathers.

Having thus gratified those feelings irresistibly awakened
by the happy scenes I am describing, I return with more composure to my history.

The town of New Amsterdam, being, as I before mentioned, left to its own course and the fostering care of providence, increased as rapidly in importance, as though it had
been burthened with a dozen panniers full of those sage laws,
which are usually heaped upon the backs of young cities—in
order to make them grow. The only measure that remains on
record of the worthy council, was to build a chapel within the
fort, which they dedicated to the great and good St. Nicholas, who immediately took the infant town of New Amsterdam under his peculiar patronage, and has ever since been,
and I devoutly hope will ever be, the tutelar saint of this excellent city. I am moreover told, that there is a little legendary
book somewhere extant, written in low dutch, which says that
the image of this renowned saint, which whilome graced the
bowsprit of the Goede Vrouw, was placed in front of this
chapel; and the legend further treats of divers miracles
wrought by the mighty pipe which the saint held in his
mouth; a whiff of which was a sovereign cure for an indigestion, and consequently of great importance in this colony of

huge feeders. But as, notwithstanding the most diligent search, I cannot lay my hands upon this little book, I entertain considerable doubt on the subject.

This much is certain, that from the time of the building of this chapel, the town throve with tenfold prosperity, and soon became the metropolis of numerous settlements, and an extensive territory. The province extended on the north, to Fort Aurania or Orange, now known by the name of Albany, situated about 160 miles up the Mohegan or Hudson River. Indeed the province claimed quite to the river St. Lawrence; but this claim was not much insisted on at the time, as the country beyond Fort Aurania was a perfect wilderness, reported to be inhabited by cannibals, and termed Terra Incognita. Various accounts were given of the people of these unknown parts; by some they are described as being of the race of the *Acephali*, such as Herodotus describes, who have no heads, and carry their eyes in their bellies. Others affirm they were of that race whom father Charlevoix mentions, as having but one leg; adding gravely, that they were exceedingly alert in running. But the most satisfactory account is that given by the reverend Hans Megapolensis, a missionary in these parts, who, in a letter still extant, declares them to be the Mohagues or Mohawks; a nation, according to his description, very loose in their morals, but withal most rare wags. "For," says he, "if theye can get to bedd with another mans wife, theye thinke it a piece of wit."* This excellent old gentleman gives moreover very important additional information, about this country of monsters; for he observes, "theye have plenty of tortoises here, and within land, from two and three to four feet long; some with two heads, very mischievous and addicted to biting."†

*Let. of I. Megapol. Hag. S. P.

†Ogilvie, in his excellent account of America, speaking of these parts, makes mention of Lions, which abounded on a high mountain, and likewise observes, "On the borders of Canada there is seen sometimes a kind of beast which hath some resemblance with a horse, having cloven feet, shaggy mayn, one horn just on the forehead, a tail like that of a wild hog, and a deer's neck." He furthermore gives a picture of this strange beast, which resembles exceedingly an unicorn.—It is much to be lamented by philosophers, that this miraculous breed of animals, like that of the horned frog, is totally extinct.

On the south the province reached to Fort Nassau, on the South River, since called the Delaware—and on the east it extended to Varshe (or Fresh) River, since called Connecticut River. On this frontier was likewise erected a mighty fort and trading house, much about the spot where at present is situated the pleasant town of Hartford; this port was called FORT GOED HOOP, or Good Hope, and was intended as well for the purpose of trade as defence; but of this fort, its valiant garrison, and staunch commander, I shall treat more anon, as they are destined to make some noise in this eventful and authentic history.

Thus prosperously did the province of New Nederlandts encrease in magnitude; and the early history of its metropolis, presents a fair page, unsullied by crime or calamity. Herds of painted savages still lurked about the tangled woods and the rich bottoms of the fair island of Manna-hata—the hunter still pitched his rude bower of skins and branches, beside the wild brooks, that stole through the cool and shady valleys; while here and there were seen on some sunny knoll, a group of indian wigwams, whose smoke rose above the neighbour-ing trees and floated in the clear expanse of heaven. The un-civilized tenants of the forest remained peaceable neighbours of the town of New Amsterdam; and our worthy ancestors endeavoured to ameliorate their situation as much as possible, by benevolently giving them gin, rum and glass beads, in ex-change for all the furs they brought; for it seems the kind hearted dutchmen had conceived a great friendship for their savage neighbours—on account of the facility with which they suffered themselves to be taken in. Not that they were deficient in understanding, for certain of their customs give tokens of great shrewdness, especially that mentioned by Ogilvie, who says, "for the least offence the bridegroom soundly beats the wife, and turns her out of doors and mar-ries another, insomuch that some of them have every year a new wife."

True it is, that good understanding between our worthy ancestors and their savage neighbours, was liable to occa-sional interruptions—and I recollect hearing my grand-mother, who was a very wise old woman, well versed in the history of these parts, tell a long story of a winter evening, about a battle between the New Amsterdammers and the Indians, which was known, but why, I do not recollect, by the name of the *Peach War*, and which took place near a peach orchard, in a dark and gloomy glen, overshadowed by cedars, oaks and dreary hemlocks. The legend of this bloody encounter, was for a long time current among the nurses, old women, and other ancient chroniclers of the place; and the dismal seat of war, went, for some generations, by the name of *Murderers' Valley*; but time and improvement have equally obliterated the tradition and the place of this battle, for what was once the blood-stained valley, is now in the centre of this populous city, and known by the name of *Dey-street*.*

For a long time the new settlement depended upon the mother country for most of its supplies. The vessels which sailed in search of a north west passage, always touched at New Amsterdam, where they unloaded fresh cargoes of adventurers, and unheard of quantities of gin, bricks, tiles, glass beads, gingerbread and other necessaries; in exchange for which they received supplies of pork and vegetables, and made very profitable bargains for furs and bear skins. Never did the simple islanders of the south seas, look with more impatience for the adventurous vessels, that brought them rich ladings of old hoops, spike nails and looking glasses, than did our honest colonists, for the vessels that brought them the comforts of the mother country. In this particular they resembled their worthy but simple descendants, who prefer depending upon Europe for necessaries, which they might produce or manufacture at less cost and trouble in their own country. Thus have I known a very shrewd family, who being removed to some distance from an inconvenient draw well, beside which they had long sojourned, always preferred to send to it for water, though a plentiful brook ran by the very door of their new habitation.

How long the growing colony might have looked to its parent Holland for supplies, like a chubby overgrown urchin,

*This battle is said by some to have happened much later than the date assigned by our historian. Some of the ancient inhabitants of our city, place it in the beginning of the last century. It is more than probable, however, that Mr. Knickerbocker is correct, as he has doubtless investigated the matter. — *Print. Dev.*

clinging to its mother's breast, even after it is breeched, I will not pretend to say, for it does not become an historian to indulge in conjectures—I can only assert the fact, that the inhabitants, being obliged by repeated emergencies, and frequent disappointments of foreign supplies, to look about them and resort to contrivances, became nearly as wise as people generally are, who are taught wisdom by painful experience. They therefore learned to avail themselves of such expedients as presented—to make use of the bounties of nature, where they could get nothing better—and thus became prodigiously enlightened, under the scourge of inexorable necessity; gradually opening one eye at a time, like the Arabian impostor receiving the bastinado.

Still however they advanced from one point of knowledge to another with characteristic slowness and circumspection, admitting but few improvements and inventions, and those too, with a jealous reluctance that has ever distinguished our respectable dutch yeomanry; who adhere, with pious and praiseworthy obstinacy, to the customs, the fashions, the manufactures and even the very utensils, however inconvenient, of their revered forefathers. It was long after the period of which I am writing, before they discovered the surprising secret, that it was more economic and commodious, to roof their houses with shingles procured from the adjacent forests, than to import tiles for the purpose from Holland; and so slow were they in believing that the soil of a young country, could possibly make creditable bricks; that even at a late period of the last century, ship loads have been imported from Holland, by certain of its most orthodox descendants.

The accumulating wealth and consequence of New Amsterdam and its dependencies, at length awakened the serious solicitude of the mother country; who finding it a thriving and opulent colony, and that it promised to yield great profit and no trouble; all at once became wonderfully anxious about its safety, and began to load it with tokens of regard; in the same manner that people are sure to oppress rich relations with their affection and loving kindness, who could do much better without their assistance.

The usual marks of protection shewn by mother countries to wealthy colonies, were forthwith evinced—the first care always being to send rulers to the new settlement, with orders to squeeze as much revenue from it as it will yield. Accordingly in the year of our Lord 1629 mynheer WOUTER VAN TWILLER was appointed governor of the province of Nieuw Nederlandts, under the controul of their High Mightinesses the lords states general of the United Netherlands, and the privileged West India company.

This renowned old gentleman arrived at New Amsterdam in the merry month of June, the sweetest month in all the year; when Dan Apollo seems to dance up the transparent firmament—when the robin, the black-bird, the thrush and a thousand other wanton songsters make the woods to resound with amorous ditties, and the luxurious little Boblincon revels among the clover blossoms of the meadows.—All which happy coincidence, persuaded the old ladies of New Amsterdam, who were skilled in the art of foretelling events, that this was to be a happy and prosperous administration.

But as it would be derogatory to the consequence of the first dutch governor of the great province of Nieuw Nederlandts, to be thus scurvily introduced at the end of a chapter, I will put an end to this second book of my history, that I may usher him in, with the more dignity in the beginning of my next.

END OF BOOK II.

BOOK III.

In which is recorded the golden reign of
Wouter Van Twiller.

CHAP. I.

Setting forth the unparalleled virtues of the renowned Wou-
ter Van Twiller, as likewise his unutterable wisdom in the
law case of Wandle Schoonhoven and Barent Bleecker—and
the great admiration of the public thereat.

THE RENOWNED Wouter (or Walter) Van Twiller, was descended from a long line of dutch burgomasters, who
had successively dozed away their lives and grown fat upon
the bench of magistracy in Rotterdam; and who had comported themselves with such singular wisdom and propriety,
that they were never either heard or talked of—which, next
to being universally applauded, should be the object of ambition of all sage magistrates and rulers.

His surname of Twiller, is said to be a corruption of the
original *Twijfler*, which in English means *doubter*; a name admirably descriptive of his deliberative habits. For though he
was a man, shut up within himself like an oyster, and of such
a profoundly reflective turn, that he scarcely ever spoke except
in monosyllables, yet did he never make up his mind, on any
doubtful point. This was clearly accounted for by his adherents, who affirmed that he always conceived every subject on
so comprehensive a scale, that he had not room in his head,
to turn it over and examine both sides of it, so that he always
remained in doubt, merely in consequence of the astonishing
magnitude of his ideas!

There are two opposite ways by which some men get into
notice—one by talking a vast deal and thinking a little, and
the other by holding their tongues and not thinking at all. By
the first many a vapouring, superficial pretender acquires the
reputation of a man of quick parts—by the other many a
vacant dunderpate, like the owl, the stupidest of birds, comes
to be complimented, by a discerning world, with all the attributes of wisdom. This, by the way, is a mere casual remark,
which I would not for the universe have it thought, I apply
to Governor Van Twiller. On the contrary he was a very wise
dutchman, for he never said a foolish thing—and of such invincible gravity, that he was never known to laugh, or even

to smile, through the course of a long and prosperous life. Certain however it is, there never was a matter proposed, however simple, and on which your common narrow minded mortals, would rashly determine at the first glance, but what the renowned Wouter, put on a mighty mysterious, vacant kind of look, shook his capacious head, and having smoked for five minutes with redoubled earnestness, sagely observed, that "he had his doubts about the matter"—which in process of time gained him the character of a man slow of belief, and not easily imposed on.

The person of this illustrious old gentleman was as regularly formed and nobly proportioned, as though it had been moulded by the hands of some cunning dutch statuary, as a model of majesty and lordly grandeur. He was exactly five feet six inches in height, and six feet five inches in circumference. His head was a perfect sphere, far excelling in magnitude that of the great Pericles (who was thence waggishly called *Schenocephalus*, or onion head)—indeed, of such stupendous dimensions was it, that dame nature herself, with all her sex's ingenuity, would have been puzzled to construct a neck, capable of supporting it; wherefore she wisely declined the attempt, and settled it firmly on the top of his back bone, just between the shoulders; where it remained, as snugly bedded, as a ship of war in the mud of the Potowmac. His body was of an oblong form, particularly capacious at bottom; which was wisely ordered by providence, seeing that he was a man of sedentary habits, and very averse to the idle labour of walking. His legs, though exceeding short, were sturdy in proportion to the weight they had to sustain; so that when erect, he had not a little the appearance of a robustious beer barrel, standing on skids. His face, that infallible index of the mind, presented a vast expanse perfectly unfurrowed or deformed by any of those lines and angles, which disfigure the human countenance with what is termed expression. Two small grey eyes twinkled feebly in the midst, like two stars of lesser magnitude, in a hazy firmament; and his full fed cheeks, which seemed to have taken toll of every thing that went into his mouth, were curiously mottled and streaked with dusky red, like a spitzenberg apple.

His habits were as regular as his person. He daily took his four stated meals, appropriating exactly an hour to each; he smoked and doubted eight hours, and he slept the remaining twelve of the four and twenty. Such was the renowned Wouter Van Twiller—a true philosopher, for his mind was either elevated above, or tranquilly settled below, the cares and perplexities of this world. He had lived in it for years, without feeling the least curiosity to know whether the sun revolved round it, or it round the sun; and he had even watched for at least half a century, the smoke curling from his pipe to the ceiling, without once troubling his head with any of those numerous theories, by which a philosopher would have perplexed his brain, in accounting for its rising above the surrounding atmosphere.

In his council he presided with great state and solemnity. He sat in a huge chair of solid oak hewn in the celebrated forest of the Hague, fabricated by an experienced Timmerman of Amsterdam, and curiously carved about the arms and feet, into exact imitations of gigantic eagle's claws. Instead of a sceptre he swayed a long turkish pipe, wrought with jasmin and amber, which had been presented to a stadtholder of Holland, at the conclusion of a treaty with one of the petty Barbary powers.—In this stately chair would he sit, and this magnificent pipe would he smoke, shaking his right knee with a constant motion, and fixing his eye for hours together upon a little print of Amsterdam, which hung in a black frame, against the opposite wall of the council chamber. Nay, it has ever been said, that when any deliberation of extraordinary length and intricacy was on the carpet, the renowned Wouter would absolutely shut his eyes for full two hours at a time, that he might not be disturbed by external objects—and at such times the internal commotion of his mind, was evinced by certain regular guttural sounds, which his admirers declared were merely the noise of conflict, made by his contending doubts and opinions.

It is with infinite difficulty I have been enabled to collect these biographical anecdotes of the great man under consideration. The facts respecting him were so scattered and vague, and divers of them so questionable in point of authenticity, that I have had to give up the search after many, and decline the admission of still more, which would have tended to heighten the colouring of his portrait.

I have been the more anxious to delineate fully, the person and habits of the renowned Van Twiller, from the consideration that he was not only the first, but also the best governor that ever presided over this ancient and respectable province; and so tranquil and benevolent was his reign, that I do not find throughout the whole of it, a single instance of any offender being brought to punishment:—a most indubitable sign of a merciful governor, and a case unparalleled, excepting in the reign of the illustrious King Log, from whom, it is hinted, the renowned Van Twiller was a lineal descendant.

The very outset of the career of this excellent magistrate, like that of Solomon, or to speak more appropriately, like that of the illustrious governor of Barataria, was distinguished by an example of legal acumen, that gave flattering presage of a wise and equitable administration. The very morning after he had been solemnly installed in office, and at the moment that he was making his breakfast from a prodigious earthen dish, filled with milk and Indian pudding, he was suddenly interrupted by the appearance of one Wandle Schoonhoven, a very important old burgher of New Amsterdam, who complained bitterly of one Barent Bleecker, inasmuch as he fraudulently refused to come to a settlement of accounts, seeing that there was a heavy balance in favour of the said Wandle. Governor Van Twiller, as I have already observed, was a man of few words, he was likewise a mortal enemy to multiplying writings—or being disturbed at his breakfast. Having therefore listened attentively to the statement of Wandle Schoonhoven, giving an occasional grunt, as he shovelled a mighty spoonful of Indian pudding into his mouth—either as a sign that he relished the dish, or comprehended the story—he called unto him his constable, and pulling out of his breeches pocket a huge jack-knife, dispatched it after the defendant as a summons, accompanied by his tobacco box as a warrant.

This summary process was as effectual in those simple days, as was the seal ring of the great Haroun Alraschid, among the true believers—the two parties, being confronted before him, each produced a book of accounts, written in a language and character that would have puzzled any but a High Dutch commentator, or a learned decypherer of Egyptian obelisks, to understand. The sage Wouter took them one after the other, and having poised them in his hands, and attentively counted over the number of leaves, fell straightway into a very great doubt, and smoked for half an hour without saying a word; at length, laying his finger beside his nose, and shutting his eyes for a moment, with the air of a man who has just caught a subtle idea by the tail, he slowly took his pipe from his mouth, puffed forth a column of tobacco smoke, and with marvellous gravity and solemnity pronounced—that having carefully counted over the leaves and weighed the books, it was found, that one was just as thick and as heavy as the other—therefore it was the final opinion of the court that the accounts were equally balanced—therefore Wandle should give Barent a receipt, and Barent should give Wandle a receipt—and the constable should pay the costs.

This decision being straightway made known, diffused general joy throughout New Amsterdam, for the people immediately perceived, that they had a very wise and equitable magistrate to rule over them. But its happiest effect was, that not another law suit took place throughout the whole of his administration—and the office of constable fell into such decay, that there was not one of those lossel scouts known in the province for many years. I am the more particular in dwelling on this transaction, not only because I deem it one of the most sage and righteous judgments on record, and well worthy the attention of modern magistrates, but because it was a miraculous event in the history of the renowned Wouter—being the only time he was ever known to come to a decision, in the whole course of his life.

CHAP. II.

Containing some account of the grand Council of New Am-
sterdam, as also divers especial good philosophical reasons why
an Alderman should be fat—with other particulars touching
the state of the Province.

IN TREATING of the early governors of the province, I must
caution my readers against confounding them, in point of
dignity and power, with those worthy gentlemen, who are
whimsically denominated governors, in this enlightened republic—a set of unhappy victims of popularity, who are in
fact the most dependant, hen-pecked beings in community:
doomed to bear the secret goadings and corrections of their
own party, and the sneers and revilings of the whole world
beside.—Set up, like geese, at christmas hollidays, to be
pelted and shot at by every whipster and vagabond in the
land. On the contrary, the dutch governors enjoyed that un-
controlled authority vested in all commanders of distant colonies or territories. They were in a manner, absolute despots
in their little domains, lording it, if so disposed, over both
law and gospel, and accountable to none but the mother
country; which it is well known is astonishingly deaf to all
complaints against its governors, provided they discharge the
main duty of their station—squeezing out a good revenue.
This hint will be of importance, to prevent my readers from
being seized with doubt and incredulity, whenever, in the
course of this authentic history, they encounter the uncommon circumstance, of a governor, acting with independence,
and in opposition to the opinions of the multitude.

To assist the doubtful Wouter, in the arduous business of
legislation, a board of magistrates was appointed, which presided immediately over the police. This potent body consisted
of a schout or bailiff, with powers between those of the present mayor and sheriff—five burgermeesters, who were equivalent to aldermen, and five schepens, who officiated as scrubs,
sub-devils, or bottle-holders to the burgermeesters, in the
same manner as do assistant aldermen to their principals at
the present day; it being their duty to fill the pipes of the

lordly burgermeesters—see that they were accommodated
with spitting boxes—hunt the markets for delicacies for corporation dinners, and to discharge such other little offices of
kindness, as were occasionally required. It was moreover, tacitly understood, though not specifically enjoined, that they
should consider themselves as butts for the blunt wits of the
burgermeesters, and should laugh most heartily at all their
jokes; but this last was a duty as rarely called in action in
those days, as it is at present, and was shortly remitted, in
consequence of the tragical death of a fat little Schepen—
who actually died of suffocation in an unsuccessful effort to
force a laugh, at one of Burgermeester Van Zandt's best
jokes.

In return for these humble services, they were permitted to
say *yes* and *no* at the council board, and to have that enviable
privilege, the run of the public kitchen—being graciously
permitted to eat, and drink, and smoke, at all those snug junkettings and public gormandizings, for which the ancient
magistrates were equally famous with their more modern successors. The post of Schepen therefore, like that of assistant
alderman, was eagerly coveted by all your burghers of a certain description, who have a huge relish for good feeding,
and a humble ambition to be great men, in a small way—
who thirst after a little brief authority, that shall render them
the terror of the alms house, and the bridewell—that shall
enable them to lord it over obsequious poverty, vagrant vice,
outcast prostitution, and hunger driven dishonesty—that
shall place in their hands the lesser, but galling scourge of the
law, and give to their beck a hound like pack of catchpoles
and bum bailiffs—tenfold greater rogues than the culprits
they hunt down!—My readers will excuse this sudden
warmth, which I confess is unbecoming of a grave historian—but I have a mortal antipathy to catchpoles, bum bailiffs, and little great men.

The ancient magistrates of this city, corresponded with
those of the present time, no less in form, magnitude and
intellect, than in prerogative and privilege. The burgomasters,
like our aldermen, were generally chosen by weight—and not
only the weight of the body, but likewise the weight of the
head. It is a maxim practically observed in all honest, plain

thinking, regular cities, that an alderman should be fat—and the wisdom of this can be proved to a certainty. That the body is in some measure an image of the mind, or rather that the mind is moulded to the body, like melted lead to the clay in which it is cast, has been insisted on by many men of science, who have made human nature their peculiar study— For as a learned gentleman of our city observes "there is a constant relation between the moral character of all intelligent creatures, and their physical constitution—between their habits and the structure of their bodies." Thus we see, that a lean, spare, diminutive body, is generally accompanied by a petulant, restless, meddling mind—either the mind wears down the body, by its continual motion; or else the body, not affording the mind sufficient house room, keeps it continually in a state of fretfulness, tossing and worrying about from the uneasiness of its situation. Whereas your round, sleek, fat, unwieldly periphery is ever attended by a mind, like itself, tranquil, torpid and at ease; and we may always observe, that your well fed, robustious burghers are in general very tenacious of their ease and comfort; being great enemies to noise, discord and disturbance—and surely none are more likely to study the public tranquillity than those who are so careful of their own—Who ever hears of fat men heading a riot, or herding together in turbulent mobs?—no—no—it is your lean, hungry men, who are continually worrying society, and setting the whole community by the ears.

The divine Plato, whose doctrines are not sufficiently attended to by philosophers of the present age, allows to every man three souls—one, immortal and rational, seated in the brain, that it may overlook and regulate the body—a second consisting of the surly and irascible passions, which like belligerent powers lie encamped around the heart—a third mortal and sensual, destitute of reason, gross and brutal in its propensities, and enchained in the belly, that it may not disturb the divine soul, by its ravenous howlings. Now, according to this excellent theory what can be more clear, than that your fat alderman, is most likely to have the most regular and well conditioned mind. His head is like a huge, spherical chamber, containing a prodigious mass of soft brains, whereon the rational soul lies softly and snugly couched, as on a feather bed; and the eyes, which are the windows of the bed chamber, are usually half closed that its slumberings may not be disturbed by external objects. A mind thus comfortably lodged, and protected from disturbance, is manifestly most likely to perform its functions with regularity and ease. By dint of good feeding, moreover, the mortal and malignant soul, which is confined in the belly, and which by its raging and roaring, puts the irritable soul in the neighbourhood of the heart in an intolerable passion, and thus renders men crusty and quarrelsome when hungry, is completely pacified, silenced and put to rest—whereupon a host of honest good fellow qualities and kind hearted affections, which had lain perdue, slily peeping out of the loop holes of the heart, finding this cerberus asleep, do pluck up their spirits, turn out one and all in their holliday suits, and gambol up and down the diaphragm—disposing their possessor to laughter, good humour and a thousand friendly offices towards his fellow mortals.

As a board of magistrates, formed on this model, think but very little, they are the less likely to differ and wrangle about favourite opinions—and as they generally transact business upon a hearty dinner, they are naturally disposed to be lenient and indulgent in the administration of their duties. Charlemagne was conscious of this, and therefore (a pitiful measure, for which I can never forgive him), ordered in his cartularies, that no judge should hold a court of justice, except in the morning, on an empty stomach.—A rule which, I warrant, bore hard upon all the poor culprits in his kingdom. The more enlightened and humane generation of the present day, have taken an opposite course, and have so managed that the aldermen are the best fed men in the community; feasting lustily on the fat things of the land, and gorging so heartily on oysters and turtles, that in process of time they acquire the activity of the one, and the form, the waddle, and the green fat of the other. The consequence is, as I have just said; these luxurious feastings do produce such a dulcet equanimity and repose of the soul, rational and irrational, that their transactions are proverbial for unvarying monotony—and the profound laws, which they enact in their dozing moments, amid the labours of digestion, are quietly suffered to remain as dead letters, and never enforced, when awake. In a word your fair round-bellied burgomaster, like a full fed mastiff, dozes quietly at the house-door, always at home, and always at hand to watch over its safety—but as to electing a lean, meddling candidate to the office, as has now and then been done, I would as leave put a grey-hound, to watch the house, or a race horse to drag an ox waggon.

The Burgo-masters then, as I have already mentioned, were wisely chosen by weight, and the Schepens, or assistant aldermen, were appointed to attend upon them, and *help them eat*; but the latter, in the course of time, when they had been fed and fattened into sufficient bulk of body and drowsiness of brain, became very eligible candidates for the Burgomasters' chairs, having fairly eaten themselves into office, as a mouse eats his way into a comfortable lodgement in a goodly, blue-nosed, skim'd milk, New England cheese.

Nothing could equal the profound deliberations that took place between the renowned Wouter, and these his worthy compeers, unless it be the sage divans of some of our modern corporations. They would sit for hours smoking and dozing over public affairs, without speaking a word to interrupt that perfect stillness, so necessary to deep reflection—faithfully observing an excellent maxim, which the good old governor had caused to be written in letters of gold, on the walls of the council chamber

Stille Seugen eten al den draf op.

which, being rendered into English for the benefit of modern legislatures, means—

> "The sow that's still
> Sucks all the swill."

Under the sober way, therefore, of the renowned Van Twiller, and the sage superintendance of his burgomasters, the infant settlement waxed vigorous apace, gradually emerging from the swamps and forests, and exhibiting that mingled appearance of town and country, customary in new cities, and which at this day may be witnessed in the great city of Washington; that immense metropolis, which makes such a glorious appearance—upon paper.

Ranges of houses began to give the idea of streets and lanes, and wherever an interval occurred, it was over-run by a wilderness of sweet smelling thorn apple, vulgarly called stinkweed. Amid these fragrant bowers, the honest burghers, like so many patriarchs of yore, sat smoking their pipes of a sultry afternoon, inhaling the balmy odours wafted on every gale, and listening with silent gratulation to the clucking of their hens, the cackling of their geese, or the sonorous gruntings of their swine; that combination of farm-yard melody, which may truly be said to have a silver sound, inasmuch as it conveys a certain assurance of profitable marketing.

The modern spectator, who wanders through the crowded streets of this populous city, can scarce form an idea, of the different appearance which every object presented, in those primitive times. The busy hum of commerce, the noise of revelry, the rattling equipages of splendid luxury, were unknown in the peaceful settlement of New Amsterdam. The bleating sheep and frolicksome calves sported about the verdant ridge, where now their legitimate successors, the Broadway loungers, take their morning's stroll; the cunning fox or ravenous wolf, skulked in the woods, where now are to be seen the dens of Gomez and his righteous fraternity of money brokers, and flocks of vociferous geese cackled about the field, where now the patriotic tavern of Martling echoes with the wranglings of the mob.* The whole island, at least such parts of it as were inhabited, bloomed like a second Eden; every dwelling had its own cabbage garden, and that esculent vegetable, while it gave promise of bounteous loads of sour crout, was also emblematic of the rapid growth and regular habits of the youthful colony.

Such are the soothing scenes presented by a fat government. The province of the New Netherlands, destitute of

*"De Vries mentions a place where they over-haul their ships, which he calls *Smits Vleye*, there is still to this day a place in New York called by that name, where a market is built called the Fly market."—Old MS.

There are few native inhabitants, I trow, of this great city, who when boys were not engaged in the renowned feuds of Broadway and Smith fly—the subject of so many fly market romances and schoolboy rhymes. EDITOR.

wealth, possessed a sweet tranquillity that wealth could never purchase. It seemed indeed as if old Saturn had again commenced his reign, and renewed the golden days of primeval simplicity. For the golden age, says Ovid, was totally destitute of gold, and for that very reason was called the golden age, that is, the happy and fortunate age—because the evils produced by the precious metals, such as avarice, covetuousness, theft, rapine, usury, banking, note-shaving, lottery-insuring, and the whole catalogue of crimes and grievances were then unknown. In the iron age there was abundance of gold, and on that very account it was called the iron age, because of the hardships, the labours, the dissentions, and the wars, occasioned by the thirst of gold.

The genial days of Wouter Van Twiller therefore, may truly be termed the golden age of our city. There were neither public commotions, nor private quarrels; neither parties, nor sects, nor schisms; neither prosecutions, nor trials, nor punishments; nor were there counsellors, attorneys, catch-poles or hangmen. Every man attended to what little business he was lucky enough to have, or neglect it if he pleased, without asking the opinion of his neighbour.—In those days nobody meddled with concerns above his comprehension, nor thrust his nose into other people's affairs; nor neglected to correct his own conduct, and reform his own character, in his zeal to pull to pieces the characters of others—but in a word, every respectable citizen eat when he was not hungry, drank when he was not thirsty, and went regularly to bed, when the sun set, and the fowls went to roost, whether he was sleepy or not; all which, being agreeable to the doctrines of Malthus, tended so remarkably to the population of the settlement, that I am told every dutiful wife throughout New Amsterdam, made a point of always enriching her husband with at least one child a year, and very often a brace—this superabundance of good things clearly constituting the true luxury of life, according to the favourite dutch maxim that "more than enough constitutes a feast." Every thing therefore went on exactly as it should do, and in the usual words employed by historians to express the welfare of a country, "the profoundest *tranquillity* and *repose* reigned throughout the province."

CHAP. III.

*How the town of New Amsterdam arose out of the mud, and
came to be marvellously polished and polite—together with a
picture of the manners of our great great Grandfathers.*

MANIFOLD are the tastes and dispositions of the enlightened literati, who turn over the pages of history.
Some there be whose hearts are brim full of the yeast of courage, and whose bosoms do work, and swell, and foam with
untried valour, like a barrel of new cider, or a train-band captain, fresh from under the hands of his taylor. This doughty
class of readers can be satisfied with nothing but bloody battles, and horrible encounters; they must be continually storming forts, sacking cities, springing mines, marching up to the
muzzles of cannons, charging bayonet through every page,
and revelling in gun-powder and carnage. Others, who are of
a less martial, but equally ardent imagination, and who,
withal, are a little given to the marvellous, will dwell with
wonderous satisfaction on descriptions of prodigies, unheard
of events, hair-breadth escapes, hardy adventures, and all
those astonishing narrations, that just amble along the boundary line of possibility.—A third class, who, not to speak
slightingly of them, are of a lighter turn, and skim over the
records of past times, as they do over the edifying pages of a
novel, merely for relaxation and innocent amusement; do singularly delight in treasons, executions, sabine rapes, tarquin
outrages, conflagrations, murders, and all the other catalogue
of hideous crimes, that like Cayenne in cookery, do give a
pungency and flavour, to the dull detail of history—while a
fourth class, of more philosophic habits, do diligently pore
over the musty chronicles of time, to investigate the operations of the human mind, and watch the gradual changes in
men and manners, effected by the progress of knowledge, the
vicissitudes of events, or the influence of situation.

If the three first classes find but little wherewithal to solace
themselves, in the tranquil reign of Wouter Van Twiller, I entreat them to exert their patience for a while, and bear with
the tedious picture of happiness, prosperity and peace, which

my duty as a faithful historian obliges me to draw; and I promise them, that as soon as I can possibly light upon any thing horrible, uncommon or impossible, it shall go hard, but I will make it afford them entertainment. This being premised, I turn with great complacency to the fourth class of my readers, who are men, or, if possible, women, after my own heart; grave, philosophical and investigating; fond of analyzing characters, of taking a start from first causes, and so hunting a nation down, through all the mazes of innovation and improvement. Such will naturally be anxious to witness the first developement of the newly hatched colony, and the primitive manners and customs, prevalent among its inhabitants, during the halcyon reign of Van Twiller or the doubter.

To describe minutely the gradual advances, from the rude log hut, to the stately dutch mansion, with a brick front, glass windows, and shingle roof—from the tangled thicket, to the luxuriant cabbage garden, and from the skulking Indian to the ponderous burgomaster, would probably be fatiguing to my reader, and certainly very inconvenient to myself; suffice it to say, trees were cut down, stumps grubbed up, bushes cleared away, until the new city rose gradually from amid swamps and stinkweeds, like a mighty fungus, springing from a mass of rotten wood.

The sage council, as has been mentioned in a preceding chapter, not being able to determine upon any plan for the building of their city—the cows, in a laudable fit of patriotism, took it under their particular charge, and as they went to and from pasture, established paths through the bushes, on each side of which the good folks built their houses; which is one cause of the rambling and picturesque turns and labyrinths, which distinguish certain streets of New York, at this very day.

Some, it must be noted, who were strenuous partizans of Mynheer Ten Breeches, (or Ten Broek) vexed that his plan of digging canals was not adopted, made a compromise with their inclinations, by establishing themselves on the margins of those creeks and inlets, which meandered through various parts of the ground laid out for improvement. To these may be particularly ascribed the first settlement of Broad street; which originally was built along a creek, that ran up, to what at present is called Wall street. The lower part soon became very busy and populous; and a ferry house* was in process of time established at the head of it; being at that day called "the head of inland navigation."

The disciples of Mynheer Toughbreeches, on the other hand, no less enterprising, and more industrious than their rivals, stationed themselves along the shore of the river, and laboured with unexampled perseverance, in making little docks and dykes, from which originated that multitude of mud traps with which this city is fringed. To these docks would the old Burghers repair, just at those hours when the falling tide had left the beach uncovered, that they might snuff up the fragrant effluvia of mud and mire; which they observed had a true wholesome smell, and reminded them of the canals of Holland. To the indefatigable labours, and praiseworthy example of this latter class of projectors, are we indebted for the acres of artificial ground, on which several of our streets, in the vicinity of the rivers are built; and which, if we may credit the assertions of several learned physicians of this city, have been very efficacious in producing the yellow fever.

The houses of the higher class, were generally constructed of wood, excepting the gable end, which was of small black and yellow dutch bricks, and always faced on the street, as our ancestors, like their descendants, were very much given to outward shew, and were noted for putting the best leg foremost. The house was always furnished with abundance of large doors and small windows on every floor, the date of its erection was curiously designated by iron figures on the front, and on the top of the roof was perched a fierce little weather cock, to let the family into the important secret, which way the wind blew. These, like the weather cocks on the tops of our steeples, pointed so many different ways, that every man could have a wind to his mind; and you would have thought old Eolus had set all his bags of wind adrift, pell mell, to gambol about this windy metropolis—the most staunch and

---

*This house has been several times repaired, and at present is a small yellow brick house, No. 23, Broad Street, with the gable end to the street, surmounted with an iron rod, on which, until within three or four years, a little iron ferry boat officiated as weather cock.

loyal citizens, however, always went according to the weather
cock on top of the governor's house, which was certainly the
most correct, as he had a trusty servant employed every morning to climb up and point it whichever way the wind blew.

In those good days of simplicity and sunshine, a passion
for cleanliness, was the grand desideratum in domestic economy and the universal test of an able housewife—a character
which formed the utmost ambition of our unenlightened
grandmothers. The front door, was never opened except on
marriages, funerals, new year's days, the festival of St. Nicholas, or some such great occasion.—It was ornamented with a
gorgeous brass knocker, curiously wrought, sometimes into
the device of a dog, and sometimes of a lion's head, and was
daily burnished with such religious zeal, that it was oft times
worn out, by the very precautions taken for its preservation.
The whole house was constantly in a state of inundation,
under the discipline of mops and brooms and scrubbing
brushes; and the good housewives of those days were a kind
of amphibious animal, delighting exceedingly to be dabbling
in water—insomuch that an historian of the day gravely tells
us, that many of his townswomen grew to have webbed fingers like unto a duck; and some of them, he had little doubt,
could the matter be examined into, would be found to have
the tails of mermaids—but this I look upon to be a mere
sport of fancy, or what is worse, a wilful misrepresentation.

The grand parlour was the sanctum sanctorum, where the
passion for cleaning was indulged without controul. In this
sacred apartment no one was permitted to enter, excepting
the mistress and her confidential maid, who visited it once a
week, for the purpose of giving it a thorough cleaning, and
putting things to rights—always taking the precaution of
leaving their shoes at the door, and entering devoutly, on
their stocking feet. After scrubbing the floor, sprinkling it
with fine white sand, which was curiously stroked into angles,
and curves, and rhomboids, with a broom—after washing the
windows, rubbing and polishing the furniture, and putting a
new bunch of evergreens in the fire-place—the window shutters were again closed to keep out the flies, and the room
carefully locked up until the revolution of time, brought
round the weekly cleaning day.

As to the family, they always entered in at the gate, and most generally lived in the kitchen. To have seen a numerous household assembled around the fire, one would have imagined that he was transported back to those happy days of primeval simplicity, which float before our imaginations like golden visions. The fire-places were of a truly patriarchal magnitude, where the whole family, old and young, master and servant, black and white, nay even the very cat and dog, enjoyed a community of privilege, and had each a prescriptive right to a corner. Here the old burgher would set in perfect silence, puffing his pipe, looking in the fire with half shut eyes, and thinking of nothing for hours together; the goede vrouw on the opposite side would employ herself diligently in spinning her yarn, or knitting stockings. The young folks would crowd around the hearth, listening with breathless attention to some old crone of a negro, who was the oracle of the family,—and who, perched like a raven in a corner of the chimney, would croak forth for a long winter afternoon, a string of incredible stories about New England witches— grisly ghosts—horses without heads—and hairbreadth scapes and bloody encounters among the Indians.

In those happy days a well regulated family always rose with the dawn, dined at eleven, and went to bed at sun down. Dinner was invariably a private meal, and the fat old burghers shewed incontestible symptoms of disapprobation and uneasiness, at being surprised by a visit from a neighbour on such occasions. But though our worthy ancestors were thus singularly averse to giving dinners, yet they kept up the social bands of intimacy by occasional banquettings, called tea parties.

As this is the first introduction of those delectable orgies which have since become so fashionable in this city, I am conscious my fair readers will be very curious to receive information on the subject. Sorry am I, that there will be but little in my description calculated to excite their admiration. I can neither delight them with accounts of suffocating crowds, nor brilliant drawing rooms, nor towering feathers, nor sparkling diamonds, nor immeasurable trains. I can detail no choice anecdotes of scandal, for in those primitive times the simple folk were either too stupid, or too good natured to pull each other's characters to pieces—nor can I furnish any whimsical anecdotes of brag—how one lady cheated, or another bounced into a passion; for as yet there was no junto of dulcet old dowagers, who met to win each other's money, and lose their own tempers at a card table.

These fashionable parties were generally confined to the higher classes, or noblesse, that is to say, such as kept their own cows, and drove their own waggons. The company commonly assembled at three o'clock, and went away about six, unless it was in winter time, when the fashionable hours were a little earlier, that the ladies might get home before dark. I do not find that they ever treated their company to iced creams, jellies or syllabubs; or regaled them with musty almonds, mouldy raisins, or sour oranges, as is often done in the present age of refinement.—Our ancestors were fond of more sturdy, substantial fare. The tea table was crowned with a huge earthen dish, well stored with slices of fat pork, fried brown, cut up into mouthfuls, and swimming in doup or gravy. The company being seated around the genial board, and each furnished with a fork, evinced their dexterity in launching at the fattest pieces in this mighty dish—in much the same manner as sailors harpoon porpoises at sea, or our Indians spear salmon in the lakes. Sometimes the table was graced with immense apple pies, or saucers full of preserved peaches and pears; but it was always sure to boast an enormous dish of balls of sweetened dough, fried in hog's fat, and called dough nuts, or oly koeks—a delicious kind of cake, at present, scarce known in this city, excepting in genuine dutch families; but which retains its pre-eminent station at the tea tables in Albany.

The tea was served out of a majestic delft tea-pot, ornamented with paintings of fat little dutch shepherds and shepherdesses, tending pigs—with boats sailing in the air, and houses built in the clouds, and sundry other ingenious dutch fantasies. The beaux distinguished themselves by their adroitness in replenishing this pot, from a huge copper tea kettle, which would have made the pigmy macaronies of these degenerate days, sweat, merely to look at it. To sweeten the beverage, a lump of sugar was laid beside each cup—and the company alternately nibbled and sipped with great decorum, until an improvement was introduced by a shrewd and economic old lady, which was to suspend a large lump directly over the tea table, by a string from the ceiling, so that it could be swung from mouth to mouth—an ingenious expedient, which is still kept up by some families in Albany; but which prevails without exception, in Communipaw, Bergen, Flat-Bush, and all our uncontaminated dutch villages.

At these primitive tea-parties the utmost propriety and dignity of deportment prevailed. No flirting nor coquetting—no gambling of old ladies nor hoyden chattering and romping of young ones—No self satisfied struttings of wealthy gentlemen with their brains in their pockets—nor amusing conceits, and monkey divertisements of smart young gentlemen, with no brains at all. On the contrary, the young ladies seated themselves demurely in their rush-bottomed chairs, and knit their own woollen stockings; nor ever opened their lips, excepting to say *yah Mynher*, or *yah, ya Vrouw*, to any question that was asked them; behaving in all things, like decent, well educated damsels. As to the gentlemen, each of them tranquilly smoked his pipe, and seemed lost in contemplation of the blue and white tiles, with which the fire-places were decorated; wherein sundry passages of scripture, were piously pourtrayed—Tobit and his dog figured to great advantage; Haman swung conspicuously on his gibbet, and Jonah appeared most manfully bouncing out of the whale, like Harlequin through a barrel of fire.

The parties broke up without noise and without confusion—for, strange as it may seem, the ladies and gentlemen were content to take their own cloaks and shawls and hats; not dreaming, simple souls! of the ingenious system of exchange established in modern days; by which those who first leave a party are authorized to choose the best shawl or hat they can find—a custom which has doubtless arisen in consequence of our commercial habits. They were carried home by their own carriages, that is to say, by the vehicles nature had provided them, excepting such of the wealthy, as could afford to keep a waggon. The gentlemen gallantly attended their fair ones to their respective abodes, and took leave of them with a hearty smack at the door: which as it was an established piece of etiquette, done in perfect simplicity and honesty of heart, occasioned no scandal at that time, nor should it at the present—if our great grandfathers approved of the custom, it would argue a great want of reverence in their descendants to say a word against it.

CHAP. IV.

Containing further particulars of the Golden Age, and what constituted a fine Lady and Gentleman in the days of Walter the Doubter.

I N THIS DULCET PERIOD of my history, when the beauteous island of Mannahata presented a scene, the very counterpart of those glowing pictures drawn by old Hesiod of the golden reign of Saturn, there was a happy ignorance, an honest simplicity prevalent among its inhabitants, which were I even able to depict, would be but little understood by the degenerate age for which I am doomed to write. Even the female sex, those arch innovaters upon the tranquillity, the honesty, and grey-beard customs of society, seemed for a while to conduct themselves with incredible sobriety and comeliness, and indeed behaved almost as if they had not been sent into the world, to bother mankind, baffle philosophy, and confound the universe.

Their hair untortured by the abominations of art, was scrupulously pomatomed back from their foreheads with a candle, and covered with a little cap of quilted calico, which fitted exactly to their heads. Their petticoats of linsey woolsey, were striped with a variety of gorgeous dyes, rivalling the many coloured robes of Iris—though I must confess these gallant garments were rather short, scarce reaching below the knee; but then they made up in the number, which generally equalled that of the gentlemen's small clothes; and what is still more praiseworthy, they were all of their own manufacture—of which circumstance, as may well be supposed, they were not a little vain.

These were the honest days, in which every woman staid at home, read the bible and wore pockets—aye, and that too of a goodly size, fashioned with patch-work into many curious devices, and ostentatiously worn on the outside. These in fact, were convenient receptacles, where all good housewives carefully stored away such things as they wished to have at hand; by which means they often came to be incredibly crammed— and I remember there was a story current when I was a boy, that the lady of Wouter Van Twiller, having occasion to empty her right pocket in search of a wooden ladle, the contents filled three corn baskets, and the utensil was at length discovered lying among some rubbish in one corner—but we must not give too much faith to all these stories; the anecdotes of these remote periods being very subject to exaggeration.

Beside these notable pockets, they likewise wore scissars and pincushions suspended from their girdles by red ribbands, or among the more opulent and shewy classes, by brass and even silver chains—indubitable tokens of thrifty housewives and industrious spinsters. I cannot say much in vindication of the shortness of the petticoats; it doubtless was introduced for the purpose of giving the stockings a chance to be seen, which were generally of blue worsted with magnificent red clocks—or perhaps to display a well turned ankle, and a neat, though serviceable foot; set off by a high-heel'd leathern shoe, with a large and splendid silver buckle. Thus we find, that the gentle sex in all ages, have shewn the same disposition to infringe a little upon the laws of decorum, in order to betray a lurking beauty, or gratify an innocent love of finery.

From the sketch here given it will be seen, that our good grandmothers differed considerably in their ideas of a fine figure, from their scantily dressed descendants of the present day. A fine lady, in those times, waddled under more clothes even on a fair summer's day, than would have clad the whole bevy of a modern ball room. Nor were they the less admired by the gentlemen in consequence thereof. On the contrary, the greatness of a lover's passion seemed to encrease in proportion to the magnitude of its object—and a voluminous damsel, arrayed in a dozen of petticoats, was declared by a low-dutch sonnetteer of the province, to be radiant as a sunflower, and luxuriant as a full blown cabbage. Certain it is, that in those days, the heart of a lover could not contain more than one lady at a time; whereas the heart of a modern gallant has often room enough to accommodate half a dozen—The reason of which I conclude to be, either that the hearts of the gentlemen have grown larger, or the persons of the ladies smaller—this however is a question for physiologists to determine.

But there was a secret charm in these petticoats, which no doubt entered into the consideration of the prudent gallant. The wardrobe of a lady was in those days her only fortune; and she who had a good stock of petticoats and stockings, was as absolutely an heiress, as is a Kamschatka damsel with a store of bear skins, or a Lapland belle with a plenty of rein deer. The ladies therefore, were very anxious to display these powerful attractions to the greatest advantage; and the best rooms in the house instead of being adorned with caricatures of dame nature, in water colours and needle work, were always hung round with abundance of homespun garments; the manufacture and property of the females—a piece of laudable ostentation that still prevails among the heiresses of our dutch villages. Such were the beauteous belles of the ancient city of New Amsterdam, rivalling in primæval simplicity of manners, the renowned and courtly dames, so loftily sung by Dan Homer—who tells us that the princess Nausicaa, washed the family linen, and the fair Penelope wove her own petticoats.

The gentlemen in fact, who figured in the circles of the gay world in these ancient times, corresponded in most particulars, with the beauteous damsels whose smiles they were ambitious to deserve. True it is, their merits would make but a very inconsiderable impression, upon the heart of a modern fair; they neither drove in their curricles nor sported their tandems, for as yet those gaudy vehicles were not even dreamt of—neither did they distinguish themselves by their brilliance at the table, and their consequent rencontres with watchmen, for our forefathers were of too pacific a disposition to need those guardians of the night, every soul throughout the town being in full snore before nine o'clock. Neither did they establish their claims by gentility at the expense of their taylors— for as yet those offenders against the pockets of society, and the tranquillity of all aspiring young gentlemen, were unknown in New Amsterdam; every good housewife made the clothes of her husband and family, and even the goede vrouw of Van Twiller himself, thought it no disparagement to cut out her husband's linsey woolsey galligaskins.

Not but what there were some two or three youngsters who manifested the first dawnings of what is called fire and spirit. Who held all labour in contempt; skulked about docks and market places; loitered in the sun shine; squandered what little money they could procure at hustle cap and chuck farthing, swore, boxed, fought cocks, and raced their neighbours' horses—in short who promised to be the wonder, the talk and abomination of the town, had not their stylish career been unfortunately cut short, by an affair of honour with a whipping post.

Far other, however, was the truly fashionable gentleman of those days—his dress, which served for both morning and evening, street and drawing room, was a linsey woolsey coat, made perhaps by the fair hands of the mistress of his affections, and gallantly bedecked with abundance of large brass buttons.—Half a score of breeches heightened the proportions of his figure—his shoes were decorated by enormous copper buckles—a low crowned broad brimmed hat overshadowed his burley visage, and his hair dangled down his back, in a prodigious queue of eel skin.

Thus equipped, he would manfully sally forth with pipe in mouth to besiege some fair damsel's obdurate heart—not such a pipe, good reader, as that which Acis did sweetly tune in praise of his Galatea, but one of true delft manufacture and furnished with a charge of fragrant Cow-pen tobacco. With this would he resolutely set himself down before the fortress, and rarely failed in the process of time to smoke the fair enemy into a surrender, upon honourable terms.

Such was the happy reign of Wouter Van Twiller, celebrated in many a long forgotten song as the real golden age, the rest being nothing but counterfeit copper-washed coin. In that delightful period, a sweet and holy calm reigned over the whole province. The Burgomaster smoked his pipe in peace—the substantial solace of his domestic house, his well petticoated *yffrouw*, after her daily cares were done, sat soberly at her door, with arms crossed over her apron of snowy white, without being insulted by ribald street walkers or vagabond boys—those unlucky urchins, who do so infest our streets, displaying under the roses of youth, the thorns and briars of iniquity. Then it was that the lover with ten breeches and the damsel with petticoats of half a score indulged in all the innocent endearments of virtuous love, without fear and without reproach—for what had that virtue to fear, which was defended by a shield of good linsey woolseys, equal at least to the seven bull hides of the invincible Ajax.

Thrice happy, and never to be forgotten age! when every thing was better than it has ever been since, or ever will be again—when Buttermilk channel was quite dry at low water—when the shad in the Hudson were all salmon, and when the moon shone with a pure and resplendent whiteness, instead of that melancholy yellow light, which is the consequence of her sickening at the abominations she every night witnesses in this degenerate city!

CHAP. V.

*In which the reader is beguiled into a delectable walk, which
ends very differently from what it commenced.*

IN THE YEAR of our Lord, one thousand eight hundred and
four, on a fine afternoon, in the mellow month of October, I took my customary walk upon the battery, which is at
once the pride and bulwark of this ancient and impregnable
city of New York. I remember well the season, for it immediately preceded that remarkably cold winter, in which our
sagacious corporation, in a spasm of economical philanthropy, pulled to pieces, at an expense of several hundred dollars, the wooden ramparts, which had cost them several
thousand; and distributed the rotten fragments, which were
worth considerably less than nothing, among the shivering
poor of the city—never, since the fall of the walls of Jericho,
or the heaven built battlements of Troy, had there been
known such a demolition—nor did it go unpunished; five
men, eleven old women and nineteen children, besides cats,
dogs and negroes, were blinded, in vain attempts to smoke
themselves warm, with this charitable substitute for firewood,
and an epidemic complaint of sore eyes was moreover produced, which has since recurred every winter; particularly
among those who undertake to burn rotten logs—who warm
themselves with the charity of others—or who use patent
chimnies.

On the year and month just designated, did I take my accustomed walk of meditation, on that same battery, which,
though at present, no battery, furnishes the most delightful
walk, and commands the noblest prospect, in the whole
known world. The ground on which I trod was hallowed by
recollections of the past, and as I slowly wandered through
the long alleys of poplars, which, like so many birch brooms
standing on end, diffused a melancholy and lugubrious shade,
my imagination drew a contrast between the surrounding scenery, and what it was in the classic days of our forefathers.
Where the government house by name, but the custom house
by occupation, proudly reared its brick walls and wooden

pillars; there whilome stood the low but substantial, red tiled mansion of the renowned Wouter Van Twiller. Around it the mighty bulwarks of fort Amsterdam frowned defiance to every absent foe; but, like many a whiskered warrior and gallant militia captain, confined their martial deeds to frowns alone—alas! those threatening bulwarks had long since been sapped by time, and like the walls of Carthage, presented no traces to the enquiring eye of the antiquarian. The mud breast works had long been levelled with the earth, and their scite converted into the green lawns and leafy alleys of the battery; where the gay apprentice sported his sunday coat, and the laborious mechanic, relieved from the dirt and drudgery of the week, poured his septennial tale of love into the half averted ear of the sentimental chambermaid. The capacious bay still presented the same expansive sheet of water, studded with islands, sprinkled with fishing boats, and bounded by shores of picturesque beauty. But the dark forests which once clothed these shores had been violated by the savage hand of cultivation, and their tangled mazes, and impracticable thickets, had degenerated into teeming orchards and waving fields of grain. Even Governors Island, once a smiling garden, appertaining to the sovereigns of the province, was now covered with fortifications, inclosing a tremendous block house—so that this once peaceful island resembled a fierce little warrior in a big cocked hat, breathing gunpowder and defiance to the world!

For some time did I indulge in this pensive train of thought; contrasting in sober sadness, the present day, with the hallowed years behind the mountains; lamenting the melancholy progress of improvement, and praising the zeal, with which our worthy burghers endeavour to preserve the wrecks of venerable customs, prejudices and errors, from the overwhelming tide of modern innovation—when by degrees my ideas took a different turn, and I insensibly awakened to an enjoyment of the beauties around me.

It was one of those rich autumnal days which heaven particularly bestows upon the beauteous island of Mannahata and its vicinity—not a floating cloud obscured the azure firmament—the sun, rolling in glorious splendour through his etherial course, seemed to expand his honest dutch countenance into an unusual expression of benevolence, as he smiled his evening salutation upon a city, which he delights to visit with his most bounteous beams—the very winds seemed to hold in their breaths in mute attention, lest they should ruffle the tranquillity of the hour—and the waveless bosom of the bay presented a polished mirror, in which nature beheld herself and smiled!—The standard of our city, which, like a choice handkerchief, is reserved for days of gala, hung motionless on the flag staff, which forms the handle to a gigantic churn; and even the tremulous leaves of the poplar and the aspen, which, like the tongues of the immortal sex, are seldom still, now ceased to vibrate to the breath of heaven. Every thing seemed to acquiesce in the profound repose of nature.—The formidable eighteen pounders slept in the embrazures of the wooden batteries, seemingly gathering fresh strength, to fight the battles of their country on the next fourth of July—the solitary drum on Governor's island forgot to call the garrison to their *shovels*—the evening gun had not yet sounded its signal, for all the regular, well meaning poultry throughout the country, to go to roost; and the fleet of canoes, at anchor between Gibbet Island and Communipaw, slumbered on their rakes, and suffered the innocent oysters to lie for a while unmolested, in the soft mud of their native banks!—My own feelings sympathized in the contagious tranquillity, and I should infallibly have dozed upon one of those fragments of benches, which our benevolent magistrates have provided for the benefit of convalescent loungers, had not the extraordinary inconvenience of the couch set all repose at defiance.

In the midst of this soothing slumber of the soul, my attention was attracted to a black speck, peering above the western horizon, just in the rear of Bergen steeple—gradually it augments and overhangs the would-be cities of Jersey, Harsimus and Hoboken, which, like three jockies, are starting cheek by jowl on the career of existence, and jostling each other at the commencement of the race. Now it skirts the long shore of ancient Pavonia, spreading its wide shadows from the high settlements at Weehawk quite to the lazaretto and quarantine, erected by the sagacity of our police, for the embarrassment of commerce—now it climbs the serene vault of heaven, cloud rolling over cloud, like successive billows, shrouding the orb of day, darkening the vast expanse, and bearing thunder and hail, and tempest in its bosom. The earth seems agitated at the confusion of the heavens—the late waveless mirror is lashed into furious waves, that roll their broken surges in hollow murmurs to the shore—the oyster boats that erst sported in the placid vicinity of Gibbet Island, now hurry affrighted to the shore—the late dignified, unbending poplar, writhes and twists, before the merciless blast—descending torrents of drenching rain and sounding hail deluge the battery walks, the gates are thronged by 'prentices, servant maids and little Frenchmen, with their pocket handkerchiefs over their hats, scampering from the storm—the late beauteous prospect presents one scene of anarchy and wild uproar, as though old chaos had resumed his reign, and was hurling back into one vast turmoil, the conflicting elements of nature. Fancy to yourself, oh reader! the awful combat sung by old Hesiod, of Jupiter, and the Titans—fancy to yourself the long rebellowing artillery of heaven, streaming at the heads of the gigantic sons of earth.—In short, fancy to yourself all that has ever been said or sung, of tempest, storm and hurricane—and you will save me the trouble of describing it.

Whether I fled from the fury of the storm, or remained boldly at my post, as our gallant train band captains, who march their soldiers through the rain without flinching, are points which I leave to the conjecture of the reader. It is possible he may be a little perplexed also, to know the reason why I introduced this most tremendous and unheard of tempest, to disturb the serenity of my work. On this latter point I will gratuitously instruct his ignorance. The panorama view of the battery was given, merely to gratify the reader with a correct description of that celebrated place, and the parts adjacent—secondly, the storm was played off, partly to give a little bustle and life to this tranquil part of my work, and to keep my drowsy readers from falling asleep—and partly to serve as a preparation, or rather an overture, to the tempestuous times, that are about to assail the pacific province of Nieuw Nederlandt—and that over-hang the slumbrous administration of the renowned Wouter Van Twiller. It is thus the experienced play-wright puts all the fiddles, the french horns, the kettle drums and trumpets of his orchestra in requisition, to usher in one of those horrible and brimstone uproars, called Melodrames—and it is thus he discharges his thunder, his lightening, his rosin and saltpetre, preparatory to the raising of a ghost, or the murdering of a hero—We will now proceed with our history.

Whatever Plato, Aristotle, Grotius, Puffendorf, Sydney, Thomas Jefferson or Tom Paine may say to the contrary, I insist that, as to nations, the old maxim that "honesty is the best policy," is a sheer and ruinous mistake. It might have answered well enough in the honest times when it was made; but in these degenerate days, if a nation pretends to rely merely upon the justice of its dealings, it will fare something like an honest man among thieves, who unless he has something more than his honesty to depend upon, stands but a poor chance of profiting by his company. Such at least was the case with the guileless government of the New Netherlands; which, like a worthy unsuspicious old burgher, quietly settled itself down into the city of New Amsterdam, as into a snug elbow chair—and fell into a comfortable nap—while in the mean time its cunning neighbours stepp'd in and picked its pockets. Thus may we ascribe the commencement of all the woes of this great province, and its magnificent metropolis, to the tranquil security, or to speak more accurately, to the unfortunate honesty of its government. But as I dislike to begin an important part of my history, towards the end of a chapter; and as my readers like myself must doubtless be exceedingly fatigued with the long walk we have taken, and the tempest we have sustained—I hold it meet we shut up the book, smoke a pipe and having thus refreshed our spirits; take a fair start in the next chapter.

CHAP. VI.

Faithfully describing the ingenious people of Connecticut and thereabouts —Shewing moreover the true meaning of liberty of conscience, and a curious device among these sturdy barbarians, to keep up a harmony of intercourse and promote population.

THAT MY READERS may the more fully comprehend the extent of the calamity, at this very moment impending over the honest, unsuspecting province of Nieuw Nederlandts, and its dubious Governor, it is necessary that I should give some account of a horde of strange barbarians, bordering upon the eastern frontier.

Now so it came to pass, that many years previous to the time of which we are treating, the sage cabinet of England had adopted a certain national creed, a kind of public walk of faith, or rather a religious turnpike in which every loyal subject was directed to travel to Zion—taking care to pay the *toll gatherers* by the way.

Albeit a certain shrewd race of men, being very much given to indulge their own opinions, on all manner of subjects (a propensity, exceedingly obnoxious to your free governments of Europe) did most presumptuously dare to think for themselves in matters of religion, exercising what they considered a natural and unextinguishable right—the liberty of conscience.

As however they possessed that ingenious habit of mind which always thinks aloud; which in a manner rides cock-a-hoop on the tongue, and is forever galloping into other people's ears, it naturally followed that their liberty of conscience likewise implied *liberty of speech*, which being freely indulged, soon put the country in a hubbub, and aroused the pious indignation of the vigilant fathers of the church.

The usual methods were adopted to reclaim them, that in those days were considered so efficacious in bringing back stray sheep to the fold; that is to say, they were coaxed, they were admonished, they were menaced, they were buffeted— line upon line, precept upon precept, lash upon lash, here a

493

little and there a great deal, were exhausted without mercy, but without success; until at length the worthy pastors of the church wearied out by their unparalleled stubbornness, were driven in the excess of their tender mercy, to adopt the scripture text, and literally "heaped live embers on their heads."

Nothing however could subdue that invincible spirit of independence which has ever distinguished this singular race of people, so that rather than submit to such horrible tyranny, they one and all embarked for the wilderness of America, where they might enjoy unmolested, the inestimable luxury of talking. No sooner did they land on this loquacious soil, than as if they had caught the disease from the climate, they all lifted up their voices at once, and for the space of one whole year, did keep up such a joyful clamour, that we are told they frightened every bird and beast out of the neighbourhood, and so completely dumb-founded certain fish, which abound on their coast, that they have been called *dumb-fish* ever since.

From this simple circumstance, unimportant as it may seem, did first originate that renowned privilege so loudly boasted of throughout this country—which is so eloquently exercised in news-papers, pamphlets, ward meetings, pot-house committees and congressional deliberations—which establishes the right of talking without ideas and without information—of misrepresenting public affairs; of decrying public measures—of aspersing great characters, and destroying little ones; in short, that grand palladium of our country, the *liberty of speech*; or as it has been more vulgarly denominated—the *gift of the gab*.

The simple aborigines of the land for a while contemplated these strange folk in utter astonishment, but discovering that they wielded harmless though noisy weapons, and were a lively, ingenious, good-humoured race of men, they became very friendly and sociable, and gave them the name of *Yanokies*, which in the Mais-Tchusaeg (or Massachusett) language signifies *silent men*—a waggish appellation, since shortened into the familiar epithet of YANKEES, which they retain unto the present day.

True it is, and my fidelity as an historian will not allow me to pass it over in silence, that the zeal of these good people, to maintain their rights and privileges unimpaired, did for a while betray them into errors, which it is easier to pardon than defend. Having served a regular apprenticeship in the school of persecution, it behoved them to shew that they had become proficients in the art. They accordingly employed their leisure hours in banishing, scourging or hanging, divers heretical papists, quakers and anabaptists, for daring to abuse the *liberty of conscience*; which they now clearly proved to imply nothing more, than that every man should think as he pleased in matters of religion—*provided* he thought *right*; for otherwise it would be giving a latitude to damnable heresies. Now as they (the majority) were perfectly convinced that *they alone* thought right, it consequently followed, that whoever thought different from them thought wrong—and whoever thought wrong and obstinately persisted in not being convinced and converted, was a flagrant violater of the inestimable liberty of conscience, and a corrupt and infectious member of the body politic, and deserved to be lopped off and cast into the fire.

Now I'll warrant, there are hosts of my readers, ready at once to lift up their hands and eyes, with that virtuous indignation with which we always contemplate the faults and errors of our neighbours, and to exclaim at these well meaning but mistaken people, for inflicting on others the injuries they had suffered themselves—for indulging the preposterous idea of convincing the mind by toasting the carcass, and establishing the doctrine of charity and forbearance, by intolerant persecution.—But soft you, my very captious sirs! what are we doing at this very day, and in this very enlightened nation, but acting upon the very same principle, in our political controversies. Have we not within but a few years released ourselves from the shackles of a government, which cruelly denied us the privilege of governing ourselves, and using in full latitude that invaluable member, the tongue? and are we not at this very moment striving our best to tyrannise over the opinions, tie up the tongues, or ruin the fortunes of one another? What are our great political societies, but mere political inquisitions—our pot-house committees, but little tribunals of denunciation—our news-papers but mere whipping posts and pillories, where unfortunate individuals are pelted with rotten eggs—and our council of appointment—but a grand *auto de fé*, where culprits are annually sacrificed for their political heresies?

Where then is the difference in principle between our measures and those you are so ready to condemn among the people I am treating of? There is none; the difference is merely circumstantial.—Thus we *denounce*, instead of banishing—We *libel* instead of scourging—we *turn out of office* instead of hanging—and where they burnt an offender in propria personæ—we either tar and feather or *burn him in effigy*—this political persecution being, some how or other, the grand palladium of our liberties, and an incontrovertible proof that this is *a free country!*

But notwithstanding the fervent zeal with which this holy war was prosecuted against the whole race of unbelievers, we do not find that the population of this new colony was in any wise hindered thereby; on the contrary they multiplied to a degree, which would be incredible to any man unacquainted with the marvellous fecundity of this growing country.

This amazing increase, may indeed be partly ascribed to a singular custom prevalent among them, and which was probably borrowed from the ancient republic of Sparta; where we are told the young ladies, either from being great romps and hoydens, or else like many modern heroines, very fond of meddling with matters that did not appertain to their sex, used frequently to engage with the men, in wrestling, and other athletic exercises of the gymnasium. The custom to which I allude was vulgarly known by the name of *bundling*—a superstitious rite observed by the young people of both sexes, with which they usually terminated their festivities; and which was kept up with religious strictness, by the more bigoted and vulgar part of the community. This ceremony was likewise, in those primitive times considered as an indispensible preliminary to matrimony; their courtships commencing, where ours usually finish—by which means they acquired that intimate acquaintance with each others good qualities before marriage, that has been pronounced by philosophers the sure basis of a happy union. Thus early did this cunning and ingenious people, display a shrewdness at making a bargain which has ever since distinguished them—

and a strict adherence to the good old vulgar maxim about "buying a pig in a poke."

To this sagacious custom, therefore, do I chiefly attribute the unparalleled increase of the yanokie or yankee tribe; for it is a certain fact, well authenticated by court records and parish registers, that wherever the practice of bundling prevailed, there was an amazing number of sturdy brats annually born unto the state, without the license of the law, or the benefit of clergy; and it is truly astonishing that the learned Malthus, in his treatise on population, has entirely overlooked this singular fact. Neither did the irregularity of their birth operate in the least to their disparagement. On the contrary they grew up a long sided, raw boned, hardy race of whoreson whalers, wood cutters, fishermen and pedlars, and strapping corn-fed wenches; who by their united efforts tended marvellously towards populating those notable tracts of country, called Nantucket, Piscataway and Cape Cod.

CHAP. VII.

How these singular barbarians turned out to be notorious squatters. How they built air castles, and attempted to initiate the Nederlanders in the mystery of bundling.

IN THE LAST CHAPTER, my honest little reader, I have given thee a faithful and unprejudiced account, of the origin of that singular race of people, inhabiting the country eastward of the Nieuw Nederlandts; but I have yet to mention certain peculiar habits which rendered them exceedingly obnoxious to our ever honoured dutch ancestors.

The most prominent of these was a certain rambling propensity, with which, like the sons of Ishmael, they seem to have been gifted by heaven, and which continually goads them on, to shift their residence from place to place, so that a Yankey farmer is in a constant state of migration; *tarrying* occasionally here and there; clearing lands for other people to enjoy, building houses for others to inhabit, and in a manner may be considered the wandering Arab of America.

His first thought, on coming to the years of manhood, is to *settle* himself in the world—which means nothing more nor less than to begin his rambles. To this end he takes unto himself for a wife, some dashing country heiress; that is to say, a buxom rosy cheeked wench, passing rich in red ribbands, glass beads and mock tortoise-shell combs, with a white gown and morocco shoes for Sunday, and deeply skilled in the mystery of making apple sweetmeats, long sauce and pumpkin pie.

Having thus provided himself, like a true pedlar with a heavy knapsack, wherewith to regale his shoulders through the journey of life, he literally sets out on the peregrination. His whole family, household furniture and farming utensils are hoisted into a covered cart; his own and his wife's wardrobe packed up in a firkin—which done, he shoulders his axe, takes staff in hand, whistles "yankee doodle" and trudges off to the woods, as confident of the protection of providence, and relying as cheerfully upon his own resources, as did ever a patriarch of yore, when he journeyed into a strange country of the Gentiles. Having buried himself in the wilderness, he builds himself a log hut, clears away a cornfield and potatoe patch, and, providence smiling upon his labours, is soon surrounded by a snug farm and some half a score of flaxen headed urchins, who by their size, seem to have sprung all at once out of the earth, like a crop of toad-stools.

But it is not the nature of this most indefatigable of speculators, to rest contented with any state of sublunary enjoyment—*improvement* is his darling passion, and having thus improved his lands the next care is to provide a mansion worthy the residence of a land holder. A huge palace of pine boards immediately springs up in the midst of the wilderness, large enough for a parish church, and furnished with windows of all dimensions, but so rickety and flimsy withal, that every blast gives it a fit of the ague.

By the time the outside of this mighty air castle is completed, either the funds or the zeal of our adventurer are exhausted, so that he barely manages to half finish one room within, where the whole family burrow together—while the rest of the house is devoted to the curing of pumpkins, or storing of carrots and potatoes, and is decorated with fanciful festoons of wilted peaches and dried apples. The outside remaining unpainted, grows venerably black with time: the family wardrobe is laid under contribution for old hats, petticoats and breeches to stuff into the broken windows, while the four winds of heaven keep up a whistling and howling about this aerial palace, and play as many unruly gambols, as they did of yore, in the cave of old Eolus.

The humble log hut, which whilome nestled this *improving* family snugly within its narrow but comfortable walls, stands hard by in ignominious contrast, degraded into a cow house or pig stye; and the whole scene reminds one forcibly of a fable, which I am surprised has never been recorded, of an aspiring snail who quit his humble habitation which he filled with great respectability, to crawl into the empty shell of a lobster—where he would no doubt have resided with great style and splendour, the envy and hate of all the pains-taking snails of his neighbourhood, had he not accidentally perished with cold, in one corner of his stupendous mansion.

Being thus completely settled, and to use his own words,

"to rights," one would imagine that he would begin to enjoy the comforts of his situation, to read newspapers, talk politics, neglect his own business, and attend to the affairs of the nation, like a useful and patriotic citizen; but now it is that his wayward disposition begins again to operate. He soon grows tired of a spot, where there is no longer any room for improvement—sells his farm, air castle, petticoat windows and all, reloads his cart, shoulders his axe, puts himself at the head of his family, and wanders away in search of new lands—again to fell trees—again to clear cornfields—again to build a shingle palace, and again to sell off, and wander.

Such were the people of Connecticut, who bordered upon the eastern frontier of Nieuw Nederlandts, and my readers may easily imagine what obnoxious neighbors this light hearted but restless tribe must have been to our tranquil progenitors. If they cannot, I would ask them, if they have ever known one of our regular, well organized, antediluvian dutch families, whom it hath pleased heaven to afflict with the neighbourhood of a French boarding house. The honest old burgher cannot take his afternoon's pipe, on the bench before his door, but he is persecuted with the scraping of fiddles, the chattering of women, and the squalling of children—he cannot sleep at night for the horrible melodies of some amateur, who chooses to serenade the moon, and display his terrible proficiency in *execution*, by playing demisemiquavers in alt on the clarionet, the hautboy, or some other soft toned instrument—nor can he leave the street door open, but his house is defiled by the unsavoury visits of a troop of pug dogs, who even sometimes carry their loathsome ravages into the sanctum sanctorum, the parlour!

If my readers have ever witnessed the sufferings of such a family, so situated, they may form some idea, how our worthy ancestors were distressed by their mercurial neighbours of Connecticut.

Gangs of these marauders we are told, penetrated into the New Netherland settlements and threw whole villages into consternation by their unparalleled volubility and their intolerable inquisitiveness—two evil habits hitherto unknown in those parts, or only known to be abhorred; for our ancestors were noted, as being men of truly spartan taciturnity, and who neither knew nor cared aught about any body's concerns but their own. Many enormities were committed on the high ways, where several unoffending burghers were brought to a stand, and so tortured with questions and guesses, that it was a miracle they escaped with their five senses.

Great jealousy did they likewise stir up, by their intermeddling and successes among the divine sex; for being a race of brisk, likely, pleasant tongued varlets, they soon seduced the light affections of the simple damsels, from their honest but ponderous dutch gallants. Among other hideous customs they attempted to introduce among them that of *bundling*, which the dutch lasses of the Nederlandts, with that eager passion for novelty and foreign fashions, natural to their sex, seemed very well inclined to follow, but that their mothers, being more experienced in the world, and better acquainted with men and things strenuously discountenanced all such outlandish innovations.

But what chiefly operated to embroil our ancestors with these strange folk, was an unwarrantable liberty which they occasionally took, of entering in hordes into the territories of the New Netherlands, and settling themselves down, without leave or licence, to *improve* the land, in the manner I have before noticed. This unceremonious mode of taking possession of *new land* was technically termed *squatting*, and hence is derived the appellation of *squatters*; a name odious in the ears of all great landholders, and which is given to those enterprizing worthies, who seize upon land first, and take their chance to make good their title to it afterwards.

All these grievances, and many others which were constantly accumulating, tended to form that dark and portentous cloud, which as I observed in a former chapter, was slowly gathering over the tranquil province of New Netherlands. The pacific cabinet of Van Twiller, however, as will be perceived in the sequel, bore them all with a magnanimity that redounds to their immortal credit—becoming by passive endurance inured to this increasing mass of wrongs; like the sage old woman of Ephesus, who by dint of carrying about a calf, from the time it was born, continued to carry it without difficulty, when it had grown to be an ox.

CHAP. VIII.

How the Fort Goed Hoop was fearfully beleaguered—how the renowned Wouter fell into a profound doubt, and how he finally evaporated.

B Y THIS TIME my readers must fully perceive, what an arduous task I have undertaken—collecting and collating with painful minuteness, the chronicles of past times, whose events almost defy the powers of research—raking in a little kind of Herculaneum of history, which had lain nearly for ages, buried under the rubbish of years, and almost totally forgotten—raking up the limbs and fragments of disjointed facts, and endeavouring to put them scrupulously together, so as to restore them to their original form and connection—now lugging forth the character of an almost forgotten hero, like a mutilated statue—now decyphering a half defaced inscription, and now lighting upon a mouldering manuscript, which after painful study, scarce repays the trouble of perusal.

In such case how much has the reader to depend upon the honour and probity of his author, lest like a cunning antiquarian, he either impose upon him some spurious fabrication of his own, for a precious relique from antiquity—or else dress up the dismembered fragment, with such false trappings, that it is scarcely possible to distinguish the truth from the fiction with which it is enveloped. This is a grievance which I have more than once had to lament, in the course of my wearisome researches among the works of my fellow historians; who have strangely disguised and distorted the facts respecting this country; and particularly respecting the great province of New Netherlands; as will be perceived by any who will take the trouble to compare their romantic effusions, tricked out in the meretricious gauds of fable, with this excellent little history—universally to be renowned for its severe simplicity and unerring truth.

I have had more vexations of the kind to encounter, in those parts of my history which treat of the transactions on the eastern border, than in any other, in consequence of the troops of historians who have infested these quarters, and have shewn the honest people of New Nederlandt no mercy in their works. Among the rest, Mr. Benjamin Trumbull arrogantly declares that "the Dutch were always mere intruders."—Now to this I shall make no other reply, than to proceed in the steady narration of my history, which will contain not only proofs that the Dutch had clear title and possession in the fair valleys of the Connecticut, and that they were wrongfully dispossessed thereof—but likewise that they have been scandalously maltreated ever since, by the misrepresentations of the crafty historians of New England. And in this I shall be guided by a spirit of truth and impartiality, and a regard to my immortal fame—for I would not wittingly dishonour my work by a single falsehood, misrepresentation or prejudice, though it should gain our forefathers the whole country of New England.

It was at an early period of the province, and previous to the arrival of the renowned Wouter—that the cabinet of Nieuw Nederlandts purchased the lands about the Connecticut, and established, for their superintendance and protection, a fortified post on the banks of the river, which was called Fort Goed Hoop, and was situated hard by the present fair city of Hartford. The command of this important post, together with the rank, title, and appointments of commissary, were given in charge to the gallant Jacobus Van Curlet, or as some historians will have it Van Curlis—a most doughty soldier of that stomachful class of which we have such numbers on parade days—who are famous for eating all they kill. He was of a very soldierlike appearance, and would have been an exceeding tall man, had his legs been in proportion to his body; but the latter being long, and the former uncommonly short, it gave him the uncouth appearance of a tall man's body, mounted upon a little man's legs. He made up for this turn-spit construction of body by throwing his legs to such an extent when he marched, that you would have sworn he had on the identical seven league boots of the farfamed Jack the giant killer; and so astonishingly high did he tread on any great military occasion, that his soldiers were oft times alarmed, lest the little man should trample himself under foot.

But notwithstanding the erection of this fort, and the appointment of this ugly little man of war as a commander, the intrepid Yankees, continued those daring interlopings which I have hinted at in my last chapter; and taking advantage of the character which the cabinet of Wouter Van Twiller soon acquired, for profound and phlegmatic tranquillity—did audaciously invade the territories of the Nieuw Nederlandts, and *squat* themselves down within the very jurisdiction of fort Goed Hoop.

On beholding this outrage, the long bodied Van Curlet proceeded as became a prompt and valiant officer. He immediately protested against these unwarrantable encroachments, in low dutch, by way of inspiring more terror, and forthwith dispatched a copy of the protest to the governor at New Amsterdam, together with a long and bitter account of the aggressions of the enemy. This done, he ordered his men, one and all to be of good cheer—shut the gate of the fort, smoked three pipes, went to bed and awaited the result with a resolute and intrepid tranquillity, that greatly animated his adherents, and no doubt struck sore dismay and affright into the hearts of the enemy.

Now it came to pass, that about this time, the renowned Wouter Van Twiller, full of years and honours, and council dinners, had reached that period of life and faculty which, according to the great Gulliver, entitle a man to admission into the ancient order of Struldbruggs. He employed his time in smoking his turkish pipe, amid an assemblage of sages, equally enlightened, and nearly as venerable as himself, and who for their silence, their gravity, their wisdom, and their cautious averseness to coming to any conclusion in business, are only to be equalled by certain profound corporations which I have known in my time. Upon reading the protest of the gallant Jacobus Van Curlet therefore, his excellency fell straightway into one of the deepest doubts that ever he was known to encounter; his capacious head gradually drooped on his chest,* he closed his eyes and inclined his ear to one side, as if listening with great attention to the discussion that was going on in his belly; which all who knew him, declared to be the huge court-house, or council chamber of his

---

*"Perplexed with vast affairs of state and town,
   His great head being overset, hangs down."
                                      Telecides, on Pericles.

thoughts; forming to his head what the house of representatives does to the senate. An inarticulate sound, very much resembling a snore, occasionally escaped him—but the nature of this internal cogitation, was never known, as he never opened his lips on the subject to man, woman or child. In the mean time, the protest of Van Curlet laid quietly on the table, where it served to light the pipes of the venerable sages assembled in council; and in the great smoke which they raised, the gallant Jacobus, his protest, and his mighty Fort Goed Hoop, were soon as completely beclouded and forgotten, as is a question of emergency swallowed up in the speeches and resolutions of a modern session of congress.

There are certain emergencies when your profound legislators and sage deliberative councils, are mightily in the way of a nation; and when an ounce of hair-brained decision, is worth a pound of sage doubt, and cautious discussion. Such at least was the case at present; for while the renowned Wouter Van Twiller was daily battling with his doubts, and his resolution growing weaker and weaker in the contest, the enemy pushed further and further into his territories, and assumed a most formidable appearance in the neighbourhood of Fort Goed Hoop. Here they founded the mighty town of *Pyquag*, or as it has since been called *Weathersfield*, a place which, if we may credit the assertions of that worthy historian John Josselyn, Gent. "hath been infamous by reason of the witches therein."—And so daring did these men of Pyquag become, that they extended those plantations of onions, for which their town is illustrious, under the very noses of the garrison of Fort Goed Hoop—insomuch that the honest dutchmen could not look toward that quarter, without tears in their eyes.

This crying injustice was regarded with proper indignation by the gallant Jacobus Van Curlet. He absolutely trembled with the amazing violence of his choler and the exacerbations of his valour; which seemed to be the more turbulent in their workings, from the length of the body, in which they were agitated. He forthwith proceeded to strengthen his redoubts, heighten his breastworks, deepen his fosse, and fortify his position with a double row of abbatis; after which valiant precautions, he with unexampled intrepidity, dispatched a fresh courier with tremendous accounts of his perilous situation. Never did the modern hero, who immortalized himself at the second Sabine war, shew greater valour in the art of letter writing, or distinguish himself more gloriously upon paper, than the heroic Van Curlet.

The courier chosen to bear these alarming dispatches, was a fat, oily little man, as being least liable to be worn out, or to lose leather on the journey; and to insure his speed, he was mounted on the fleetest waggon horse in the garrison; remarkable for his length of limb, largeness of bone, and hardness of trot; and so tall, that the little messenger was obliged to climb on his back by means of his tail and crupper. Such extraordinary speed did he make, that he arrived at Fort Amsterdam in little less than a month, though the distance was full two hundred pipes, or about 120 miles.

The extraordinary appearance of this portentous stranger would have thrown the whole town of New Amsterdam into a quandary, had the good people troubled themselves about any thing more than their domestic affairs. With an appearance of great hurry and business, and smoking a short travelling pipe, he proceeded on a long swing trot through the muddy lanes of the metropolis, demolishing whole batches of dirt pies, which the little dutch children were making in the road; and for which kind of pastry the children of this city have ever been famous—On arriving at the governor's house he climbed down from his steed in great trepidation; roused the grey headed door keeper, old Skaats who like his lineal decendant, and faithful representative, the venerable crier of our court, was nodding at his post—rattled at the door of the council chamber, and startled the members as they were dozing over a plan for establishing a public market.

At that very moment a gentle grunt, or rather a deep drawn snore was heard from the chair of the governor; a whiff of smoke was at the same instant observed to escape from his lips, and a slight cloud to ascend from the bowl of his pipe. The council of course supposed him engaged in deep sleep for the good of the community, and according to custom in all such cases established, every man bawled out silence, in order to maintain tranquillity; when of a sudden, the door flew open and the little courier straddled into the apartment, cased to the middle in a pair of Hessian boots, which he had got into for the sake of expedition. In his right hand he held forth the ominous dispatches, and with his left he grasped firmly the waist-band of his galligaskins; which had unfortunately given way, in the exertion of descending from his horse. He stumped resolutely up to the governor, and with more hurry than perspicuity delivered his message. But fortunately his ill tidings came too late, to ruffle the tranquillity of this most tranquil of rulers. His venerable excellency had just breathed and smoked his last—his lungs and his pipe having been exhausted together, and his peaceful soul, as Dan Homer would have said, having escaped in the last whiff that curled from his tobacco pipe.—In a word the renowned Wouter Van Twiller, alias Walter the Doubter, who had so often slumbered with his cotemporaries, now slept with his fathers, and Wilhelmus Kieft governed in his stead.

END OF BOOK III.

BOOK IV.

Containing the Chronicles of the reign of
William the Testy.

CHAP. I.

Exposing the craftiness and artful devices of those arch Free Booters, the Book Makers, and their trusty Squires, the Book Sellers. Containing furthermore, the universal acquirements of William the Testy, and how a man may learn so much as to render himself good for nothing.

IF EVER I HAD my readers completely by the button, it is at this moment. Here is a redoubtable fortress reduced to the greatest extremity; a valiant commander in a state of the most imminent jeopardy—and a legion of implacable foes thronging upon every side. The sentimental reader is preparing to indulge his sympathies, and bewail the sufferings of the brave. The philosophic reader, to come with his first principles, and coolly take the dimensions and ascertain the proportions of great actions, like an antiquary, measuring a pyramid with a two-foot rule—while the mere reader, for amusement, promises to regale himself after the monotonous pages through which he has dozed, with murders, rapes, ravages, conflagrations, and all the other glorious incidents, that give eclat to victory, and grace the triumph of the conqueror.

Thus every reader must press forward—he cannot refrain, if he has the least spark of curiosity in his disposition, from turning over the ensuing page. Having therefore gotten him fairly in my clutches—what hinders me from indulging in a little recreation, and varying the dull task of narrative by stultifying my readers with a drove of sober reflections about this, that and the other thing—by pushing forward a few of my own darling opinions; or talking a little about myself— all which the reader will have to peruse, or else give up the book altogether, and remain in utter ignorance of the mighty deeds, and great events, that are contained in the sequel.

To let my readers into a great literary secret, your experienced writers, who wish to instil peculiar tenets, either in religion, politics or morals, do often resort to this expedient— illustrating their favourite doctrines by pleasing fictions on established facts—and so mingling historic truth, and subtle speculation together, that the unwary million never perceive

the medley; but, running with open mouth, after an interesting story, are often made to swallow the most heterodox
opinions, ridiculous theories, and abominable heresies. This is
particularly the case with the industrious advocates of the
modern philosophy, and many an honest unsuspicious reader,
who devours their works under an idea of acquiring solid
knowledge, must not be surprised if, to use a pious quotation, he finds "his belly filled with the east wind."

This same expedient is likewise a literary artifice, by which
one sober truth, like a patient and laborious pack horse, is
made to carry a couple of panniers of rascally little conjectures
on its back. In this manner books are encreased, the pen is
kept going and trade flourishes; for if every writer were
obliged to tell merely what he knew, there would soon be an
end of great books, and Tom Thumb's folio would be considered as a gigantic production—A man might then carry his
library in his pocket, and the whole race of book makers,
book printers, book binders and book sellers might starve together; but by being entitled to tell every thing he thinks, and
every thing he does not think—to talk about every thing he
knows, or does not know—to conjecture, to doubt, to argue
with himself, to laugh with and laugh at his reader, (the latter
of which we writers do nine times out of ten—in our sleeves)
to indulge in hypotheses, to deal in dashes——and stars ****
and a thousand other innocent indulgencies—all these I say,
do marvelously concur to fill the pages of books, the pockets
of booksellers, and the hungry stomachs of authors—do contribute to the amusement and edification of the reader, and
redound to the glory, the encrease and the profit of the craft!

Having thus, therefore, given my readers the whole art and
mystery of book making, they have nothing further to do,
than to take pen in hand, set down and write a book for
themselves—while in the mean time I will proceed with my
history, without claiming any of the privileges above recited.

WILHELMUS KIEFT who in 1634 ascended the *Gubernato-
rial* chair, (to borrow a favourite, though clumsy appellation
of modern phraseologists) was in form, feature and character,
the very reverse of Wouter Van Twiller, his renowned predecessor. He was of very respectable descent, his father being
Inspector of Windmills in the ancient town of Saardam; and

our hero we are told made very curious investigations into the nature and operations of these machines when a little boy, which is one reason why he afterwards came to be so ingenious a governor. His name according to the most ingenious etymologists was a corruption of *Kyver*, that is to say a *wrangler* or *scolder*, and expressed the hereditary disposition of his family; which for nearly two centuries, had kept the windy town of Saardam in hot water, and produced more tartars and brimstones than any ten families in the place—and so truly did Wilhelmus Kieft inherit this family endowment, that he had scarcely been a year in the discharge of his government, before he was universally known by the appellation of WILLIAM THE TESTY.

He was a brisk, waspish, little old gentleman, who had dried and wilted away, partly through the natural process of years, and partly from being parched and burnt up by his fiery soul; which blazed like a vehement rush light in his bosom, constantly inciting him to most valourous broils, altercations and misadventures. I have heard it observed by a profound and philosophical judge of human nature, that if a woman waxes fat as she grows old, the tenure of her life is very precarious, but if haply she wilts, she lives forever—such likewise was the case with William the Testy, who grew tougher in proportion as he dried. He was some such a little dutchman as we may now and then see, stumping briskly about the streets of our city, in a broad skirted coat, with buttons nearly as large as the shield of Ajax, which makes such a figure in Dan Homer, an old fashioned cocked hat stuck on the back of his head, and a cane as high as his chin. His visage was broad, but his features sharp, his nose turned up with a most petulant curl; his cheeks, like the region of Terra del Fuego, were scorched into a dusky red—doubtless in consequence of the neighbourhood of two fierce little grey eyes, through which his torrid soul beamed as fervently, as a tropical sun blazing through a pair of burning glasses. The corners of his mouth were curiously modeled into a kind of fret work, not a little resembling the wrinkled proboscis of an irritable pug dog—in a word he was one of the most positive, restless, ugly little men, that ever put himself in a passion about nothing.

Such were the personal endowments of William the Testy, but it was the sterling riches of his mind that raised him to dignity and power. In his youth he had passed with great credit through a celebrated academy at the Hague, noted for producing finished scholars, with a dispatch unequalled, except by certain of our American colleges, which seem to manufacture bachelors of arts, by some patent machine. Here he skirmished very smartly on the frontiers of several of the sciences, and made such a gallant inroad into the dead languages, as to bring off captive a host of Greek nouns and Latin verbs, together with divers pithy saws and apothegms, all which he constantly paraded in conversation and writing, with as much vain glory as would a triumphant general of yore display the spoils of the countries he had ravaged. He had moreover puzzled himself considerably with logic, in which he had advanced so far as to attain a very familiar acquaintance, by name at least, with the whole family of syllogisms and dilemmas; but what he chiefly valued himself on, was his knowledge of metaphysics, in which, having once upon a time ventured too deeply, he came well nigh being smothered in a slough of unintelligible learning—a fearful peril, from the effects of which he never perfectly recovered.—In plain words, like many other profound intermeddlers in this abstruse bewildering science, he so confused his brain, with abstract speculations which he could not comprehend, and artificial distinctions which he could not realize, that he could never think clearly on any subject however simple, through the whole course of his life afterwards. This I must confess was in some measure a misfortune, for he never engaged in argument, of which he was exceeding fond, but what between logical deductions and metaphysical jargon, he soon involved himself and his subject in a fog of contradictions and perplexities, and then would get into a mighty passion with his adversary, for not being convinced gratis.

It is in knowledge, as in swimming, he who ostentatiously sports and flounders on the surface, makes more noise and splashing, and attracts more attention, than the industrious pearl diver, who plunges in search of treasures to the bottom. The "universal acquirements" of William Kieft, were the subject of great marvel and admiration among his countrymen—

he figured about at the Hague with as much vain glory, as does a profound Bonze at Pekin, who has mastered half the letters of the Chinese alphabet; and in a word was unanimously pronounced an *universal genius!*—I have known many universal geniuses in my time, though to speak my mind freely I never knew one, who, for the ordinary purposes of life, was worth his weight in straw—but for the purposes of government, a little sound judgment and plain common sense, is worth all the sparkling genius that ever wrote poetry, or invented theories.

Strange as it may sound therefore, the *universal acquirements* of the illustrious Wilhelmus, were very much in his way, and had he been a less learned little man, it is possible he would have been a much greater governor. He was exceedingly fond of trying philosophical and political experiments; and having stuffed his head full of scraps and remnants of ancient republics, and oligarchies, and aristocracies, and monarchies, and the laws of Solon and Lycurgus and Charondas, and the imaginary commonwealth of Plato, and the Pandects of Justinian, and a thousand other fragments of venerable antiquity, he was forever bent upon introducing some one or other of them into use; so that between one contradictory measure and another, he entangled the government of the little province of Nieuw Nederlandts in more knots during his administration, than half a dozen successors could have untied.

No sooner had this bustling little man been blown by a whiff of fortune into the seat of government, than he called together his council and delivered a very animated speech on the affairs of the province. As every body knows what a glorious opportunity a governor, a president, or even an emperor has, of drubbing his enemies in his speeches, messages and bulletins, where he has the talk all on his own side, they may be sure the high mettled William Kieft did not suffer so favourable an occasion to escape him, of evincing that gallantry of tongue, common to all able legislators. Before he commenced, it is recorded that he took out of his pocket a red cotton handkerchief, and gave a very sonorous blast of the nose, according to the usual custom of great orators. This in general I believe is intended as a signal trumpet, to call the attention of the auditors, but with William the testy it boasted a more classic cause, for he had read of the singular expedient of that famous demagogue Caius Gracchus, who when he harangued the Roman populace, modulated his tones by an oratorical flute or pitch-pipe—" which", said the shrewd Wilhelmus, "I take to be nothing more nor less, than an elegant and figurative mode of saying—he previously blew his nose."

This preparatory symphony being performed, he commenced by expressing a humble sense of his own want of talents—his utter unworthiness of the honour conferred upon him, and his humiliating incapacity to discharge the important duties of his new station—in short, he expressed so contemptible an opinion of himself, that many simple country members present, ignorant that these were mere words of course, always used on such occasions, were very uneasy, and even felt wrath that he should accept an office, for which he was consciously so inadequate.

He then proceeded in a manner highly classic, profoundly erudite, and nothing at all to the purpose, being nothing more than a pompous account of all the governments of ancient Greece, and the wars of Rome and Carthage, together with the rise and fall of sundry outlandish empires, about which the assembly knew no more than their great grand children who were yet unborn. Thus having, after the manner of your learned orators, convinced the audience that he was a man of many words and great erudition, he at length came to the less important part of his speech, the situation of the province—and here he soon worked himself into a fearful rage against the Yankees, whom he compared to the Gauls who desolated Rome, and the Goths and Vandals who overran the fairest plains of Europe—nor did he forget to mention, in terms of adequate opprobrium, the insolence with which they had encroached upon the territories of New Netherlands, and the unparalleled audacity with which they had commenced the town of New Plymouth, and planted the onion patches of Weathersfield under the very walls, or rather mud batteries of Fort Goed Hoop.

Having thus artfully wrought up his tale of terror to a climax, he assumed a self satisfied look, and declared, with a nod of knowing import, that he had taken measures to put a final stop to these encroachments—that he had been obliged to have recourse to a dreadful engine of warfare, lately invented, awful in its effects, but authorized by direful necessity. In a word, he was resolved to conquer the Yankees—by proclamation!

For this purpose he had prepared a tremendous instrument of the kind ordering, commanding and enjoining the intruders aforesaid, forthwith to remove, depart and withdraw from the districts, regions and territories aforesaid, under pain of suffering all the penalties, forfeitures, and punishments in such case made and provided, &c. This proclamation he assured them, would at once exterminate the enemy from the face of the country, and he pledged his valour as a governor, that within two months after it was published, not one stone should remain on another, in any of the towns which they had built.

The council remained for some time silent, after he had finished; whether struck dumb with admiration at the brilliancy of his project, or put to sleep by the length of his harangue, the history of the times doth not mention. Suffice it to say, they at length gave a universal grunt of acquiescence—the proclamation was immediately dispatched with due ceremony, having the great seal of the province, which was about the size of a buckwheat pancake, attached to it by a broad red ribband. Governor Kieft having thus vented his indignation, felt greatly relieved—adjourned the council *sine die*—put on his cocked hat and corduroy small clothes, and mounting a tall raw boned charger, trotted out to his country seat, which was situated in a sweet, sequestered swamp, now called Dutch street, but more commonly known by the name of Dog's Misery.

Here, like the good Numa, he reposed from the toils of legislation, taking lessons in government, not from the Nymph Egeria, but from the honoured wife of his bosom; who was one of that peculiar kind of females, sent upon earth a little after the flood, as a punishment for the sins of mankind, and commonly known by the appellation of *knowing women*. In fact, my duty as an historian obliges me to make known a circumstance which was a great secret at the time,

and consequently was not a subject of scandal at more than
half the tea tables in New Amsterdam, but which like many
other great secrets, has leaked out in the lapse of years—and
this was, that the great Wilhelmus the Testy, though one of
the most potent little men that ever breathed, yet submitted
at home to a species of government, neither laid down in
Aristotle, nor Plato; in short, it partook of the nature of a
pure, unmixed tyranny, and is familarly denominated *petticoat
government.*—An absolute sway, which though exceedingly
common in these modern days, was very rare among the ancients, if we may judge from the rout made about the domestic economy of honest Socrates; which is the only ancient case
on record.

The great Kieft however, warded off all the sneers and sar-
casms of his particular friends, who are ever ready to joke
with a man on sore points of the kind, by alledging that it
was a government of his own election, which he submitted to
through choice; adding at the same time that it was a profound maxim which he had found in an ancient author—"he
who would aspire to *govern*, should first learn to *obey*."

CHAP. II.

In which are recorded the sage Projects of a Ruler of universal Genius. —The art of Fighting by Proclamation, —and how that the valiant Jacobus Van Curlet came to be foully dishonoured at Fort Goed Hoop.

NEVER was a more comprehensive, a more expeditious, or, what is still better, a more economical measure devised, than this of defeating the Yankees by proclamation—an expedient, likewise, so humane, so gentle and pacific; there were ten chances to one in favour of its succeeding,—but then there was one chance to ten that it would not succeed—as the ill-natured fates would have it, that single chance carried the day! The proclamation was perfect in all its parts, well constructed, well written, well sealed and well published—all that was wanting to insure its effect, was that the Yankees should stand in awe of it; but, provoking to relate, they treated it with the most absolute contempt, applied it to an unseemly purpose, which shall be nameless, and thus did the first warlike proclamation come to a shameful end—a fate which I am credibly informed, has befallen but too many of its successors.

It was a long time before Wilhelmus Kieft could be persuaded by the united efforts of all his counsellors, that his war measure had failed in producing any effect.—On the contrary, he flew in a passion whenever any one dared to question its efficacy; and swore, that though it was slow in operating, yet when once it began to work, it would soon purge the land from these rapacious intruders. Time however, that tester of all experiments both in philosophy and politics, at length convinced the great Kieft, that his proclamation was abortive; and that notwithstanding he had waited nearly four years, in a state of constant irritation, yet he was still further off than ever from the object of his wishes. His implacable adversaries in the east became more and more troublesome in their encroachments, and founded the thriving colony of Hartford close upon the skirts of Fort Goed Hoop. They moreover commenced the fair settlement of Newhaven (alias the Red Hills) within the domains of their high mightinesses—while the onion patches of Pyquag were a continual eye sore to the garrison of Van Curlet. Upon beholding therefore the inefficacy of his measure, the sage Kieft like many a worthy practitioner of physic, laid the blame, not to the medicine, but the quantity administered, and resolutely resolved to double the dose.

In the year 1638 therefore, that being the fourth year of his reign, he fulminated against them a second proclamation, of heavier metal than the former; written in thundering long sentences, not one word of which was under five syllables. This, in fact, was a kind of non-intercourse bill, forbidding and prohibiting all commerce and connexion, between any and every of the said Yankee intruders, and the said fortified post of Fort Goed Hoop, and ordering, commanding and advising, all his trusty, loyal and well-beloved subjects, to furnish them with no supplies of gin, gingerbread or sour crout; to buy none of their pacing horses, meazly pork, apple brandy, Yankee rum, cyder water, apple sweetmeats, Weathersfield onions or wooden bowls, but to starve and exterminate them from the face of the land.

Another pause of a twelve month ensued, during which the last proclamation received the same attention, and experienced the same fate as the first—at the end of which term, the gallant Jacobus Van Curlet dispatched his annual messenger, with his customary budget of complaints and entreaties. Whether the regular interval of a year, intervening between the arrival of Van Curlet's couriers, was occasioned by the systematic regularity of his movements, or by the immense distance at which he was stationed from the seat of government is a matter of uncertainty. Some have ascribed it to the slowness of his messengers, who, as I have before noticed, were chosen from the shortest and fattest of his garrison, as least likely to be worn out on the road; and who, being pursy, short winded little men, generally travelled fifteen miles a day, and then laid by a whole week, to rest. All these, however, are matters of conjecture; and I rather think it may be ascribed to the immemorial maxim of this worthy country— and which has ever influenced all its public transactions—not to do things in a hurry.

The gallant Jacobus Van Curlet in his dispatches respectfully represented, that several years had now elapsed, since his first application to his late excellency, the renowned Wouter Van Twiller: during which interval, his garrison had been reduced nearly one-eighth, by the death of two of his most valiant, and corpulent soldiers, who had accidentally over eaten themselves on some fat salmon, caught in the Varsche river. He further stated that the enemy persisted in their inroads, taking no notice of the fort or its inhabitants; but squatting themselves down, and forming settlements all around it; so that, in a little while, he should find himself enclosed and blockaded by the enemy, and totally at their mercy.

But among the most atrocious of his grievances, I find the following still on record, which may serve to shew the bloody minded outrages of these savage intruders. "In the meane time, they of Hartford have not onely usurped and taken in the lands of Connecticott, although unrighteously and against the lawes of nations, but have hindered our nation in sowing theire owne purchased broken up lands, but have also sowed them with corne in the night, which the Netherlanders had broken up and intended to sowe: and have beaten the servants of the high and mighty the honored companie, which were labouring upon theire master's lands, from theire lands, with sticks and plow staves in hostile manner laming, and amongst the rest, struck Ever Duckings* a hole in his head, with a stick, soe that the blood ran downe very strongly downe upon his body!"

But what is still more atrocious—

"Those of Hartford sold a hogg, that belonged to the honored companie, under pretence that it had eaten of theire grounde grass, when they had not any foot of inheritance. They proferred the hogg for 5*s.* if the commissioners would have given 5*s.* for damage; which the commissioners denied, because noe mans owne hogg (as men use to say) can trespasse upon his owne master's grounde."†

---

*This name is no doubt misspelt. In some old Dutch MSS. of the time, we find the name of Evert Duyckingh, who is unquestionably the unfortunate hero above alluded to.

†Haz. Col. Stat. Paps.

The receipt of this melancholy intelligence incensed the whole community—there was something in it that spoke to the dull comprehension, and touched the obtuse feelings even of the puissant vulgar, who generally require a kick in the rear, to awaken their slumbering dignity. I have known my profound fellow citizens bear without murmur, a thousand essential infringements of their rights, merely because they were not immediately obvious to their senses—but the moment the unlucky Pearce was shot upon our coasts, the whole body politic was in a ferment—so the enlighted Nederlanders, though they had treated the encroachments of their eastern neighbours with but little regard, and left their quill valiant governor, to bear the whole brunt of war, with his single pen—yet now every individual felt his head broken in the broken head of Duckings—and the unhappy fate of their fellow citizen the hog; being impressed, carried and sold into captivity, awakened a grunt of sympathy from every bosom.

The governor and council, goaded by the clamours of the multitude, now set themselves earnestly to deliberate upon what was to be done. Proclamations had at length fallen into temporary disrepute; some were for sending the Yankees a tribute, as we make peace offerings to the petty Barbary powers, or as the Indians sacrifice to the devil. Others were for buying them out, but this was opposed, as it would be acknowledging their title to the land they had seized. A variety of measures were, as usual in such cases, proposed, discussed and abandoned, and the council had at last, to adopt the means, which being the most common and obvious, had been knowingly overlooked—for your amazing acute politicians, are forever looking through telescopes, which only enable them to see such objects as are far off, and unattainable; but which incapacitates them to see such things as are in their reach, and obvious to all simple folk, who are content to look with the naked eyes, heaven has given them. The profound council, as I have said, in their pursuit after Jack-o'-lanterns, accidentally stumbled on the very measure they were in need of; which was to raise a body of troops, and dispatch them to the relief and reinforcement of the garrison. This measure was carried into such prompt operation, that in less than twelve months, the whole expedition, consisting of a serjeant and twelve men, was ready to march; and was reviewed for that purpose, in the public square, now known by the name of the Bowling Green. Just at this juncture the whole community was thrown into consternation, by the sudden arrival of the gallant Jacobus Van Curlet; who came straggling into town at the head of his crew of tatterdemalions, and bringing the melancholy tidings of his own defeat, and the capture of the redoubtable post of Fort Goed Hope by the ferocious Yankees.

The fate of this important fortress, is an impressive warning to all military commanders. It was neither carried by storm, nor famine; no practicable breach was effected by cannon or mines; no magazines were blown up by red hot shot, nor were the barracks demolished, or the garrison destroyed, by the bursting of bombshells. In fact, the place was taken by a stratagem no less singular than effectual; and one that can never fail of success, whenever an opportunity occurs of putting it in practice. Happy am I to add, for the credit of our illustrious ancestors, that it was a stratagem, which though it impeached the vigilance, yet left the bravery of the intrepid Van Curlet and his garrison, perfectly free from reproach.

It appears that the crafty Yankees, having learned the regular habits of the garrison, watched a favourable opportunity and silently introduced themselves into the fort, about the middle of a sultry day; when its vigilant defenders having gorged themselves with a hearty dinner and smoaked out their pipes, were one and all snoring most obstreperously at their posts; little dreaming of so disasterous an occurrence. The enemy most inhumanly seized Jacobus Van Curlet, and his sturdy myrmidons by the nape of the neck, gallanted them to the gate of the fort, and dismissed them severally, with a kick on the crupper, as Charles the twelfth dismissed the heavy bottomed Russians, after the battle of Narva—only taking care to give two kicks to Van Curlet, as a signal mark of distinction.

A strong garrison was immediately established in the fort; consisting of twenty long sided, hard fisted Yankees; with Weathersfield onions stuck in their hats, by way of cockades and feathers—long rusty fowling pieces for muskets—hasty pudding, dumb fish, pork and molasses for stores; and a huge pumpkin was hoisted on the end of a pole, as a standard—liberty caps not having as yet come into fashion.

CHAP. III.

Containing the fearful wrath of William the Testy, and the great dolour of the New Amsterdammers, because of the affair of Fort Goed Hoop. —And moreover how William the Testy fortified the city by a Trumpeter—a Flagstaff, and a Wind-mill. —Together with the exploits of Stoffel Brinkerhoff.

LANGUAGE cannot express the prodigious fury, into which the testy Wilhelmus Kieft was thrown by this provoking intelligence. For three good hours the rage of the little man was too great for words, or rather the words were too great for him; and he was nearly choaked by some dozen huge, mis-shapen, nine cornered dutch oaths, that crowded all at once into his gullet. A few hearty thumps on the back, fortunately rescued him from suffocation—and shook out of him a bushel or two of enormous execrations, not one of which was smaller than "dunder and blixum!"—It was a matter of astonishment to all the bye standers, how so small a body, could have contained such an immense mass of words without bursting. Having blazed off the first broadside, he kept up a constant firing for three whole days—anathematizing the Yankees, man, woman, and child, body and soul, for a set of dieven, schobbejaken, deugenieten, twist-zoekeren, loozen-schalken, blaes-kaeken, kakken-bedden, and a thousand other names of which, unfortunately for posterity, history does not make particular mention. Finally he swore that he would have nothing more to do with such a squatting, bundling, guessing, questioning, swapping, pumpkin-eating, molasses-daubing, shingle-splitting, cider-watering, horse-jockeying, notion-peddling crew—that they might stay at Fort Goed Hoop and rot, before he would dirty his hands by attempting to drive them away; in proof of which he ordered the new raised troops, to be marched forthwith into winter quarters, although it was not as yet quite mid summer. Governor Kieft faithfully kept his word, and his adversaries as faithfully kept their post; and thus the glorious river Connecticut, and all the gay vallies through which it rolls, together with the salmon, shad and other fish within its waters, fell into the hands of the victorious Yankees, by whom they are held at this very day—and much good may they do them.

Great despondency seized upon the city of New Amsterdam, in consequence of these melancholly events. The name of Yankee became as terrible among our good ancestors, as was that of Gaul among the ancient Romans; and all the sage old women of the province, who had not read Miss Hamilton on education, used it as a bug-bear, wherewith to frighten their unruly brats into obedience.

The eyes of all the province were now turned upon their governor, to know what he would do for the protection of the common weal in these days of darkness and peril. Great apprehensions prevailed among the reflecting part of the community, especially the old women, that these terrible fellows of Connecticut, not content with the conquest of Fort Goed Hoop would incontinently march on to New Amsterdam and take it by storm—and as these old ladies, through means of the governor's spouse, who as has been already hinted, was "the better horse," had obtained considerable influence in public affairs, keeping the province under a kind of petticoat government, it was determined that measures should be taken for the effective fortification of the city.

Now it happened that at this time there sojourned in New Amsterdam one Anthony Van Corlear* a jolly fat dutch trumpeter, of a pleasant burley visage—famous for his long wind and his huge whiskers, and who as the story goes, could twang so potently upon his instrument, as to produce an effect upon all within hearing, as though ten thousand bagpipes were singing most lustly i' the nose. Him did the illustrious Kieft pick out as the man of all the world, most fitted to be the champion of New Amsterdam, and to garrison its fort; making little doubt but that his instrument would be as effectual and offensive in war as was that of the Paladin Astolpho, or the more classic horn of Alecto. It would have done one's heart good to have seen the governor snapping his

*David Pietrez *De Vries* in his "Reyze naer Nieuw Nederlandt onder het yaer 1640," makes mention of one *Corlear* a trumpeter in fort Amsterdam, who gave name to Corlear's Hook and who was doubtless this same champion, described by Mr. Knickerbocker.

fingers and fidgetting with delight, while his sturdy trumpeter strutted up and down the ramparts, fearlessly twanging his trumpet in the face of the whole world, like a thrice valorous editor daringly insulting all the principalities and powers—on the other side of the Atlantic.

Nor was he content with thus strongly garrisoning the fort, but he likewise added exceedingly to its strength by furnishing it with a formidable battery of quaker guns—rearing a stupendous flag-staff in the centre which overtopped the whole city—and moreover by building a great windmill on one of the bastions.* This last to be sure, was somewhat of a novelty in the art of fortification, but as I have already observed William Kieft was notorious for innovations and experiments, and traditions do affirm that he was much given to mechanical inventions—constructing patent smoke-jacks—carts that went before the horses, and especially erecting windmills, for which machines he had acquired a singular predilection in his native town of Saardam.

All these scientific vagaries of the little governor were cried up with ecstasy by his adherents as proofs of his universal genius—but there were not wanting ill natured grumblers who railed at him as employing his mind in frivolous pursuits, and devoting that time to smoke-jacks and windmills, which should have been occupied in the more important concerns of the province. Nay they even went so far as to hint once or twice, that his head was turned by his experiments, and that he really thought to manage his government, as he did his mills—by mere wind!—such is the illiberality and slander to which your enlightened rulers are ever subject.

Notwithstanding all the measures therefore of William the Testy to place the city in a posture of defence, the inhabitants continued in great alarm and despondency. But fortune, who seems always careful, in the very nick of time, to throw a bone for hope to gnaw upon, that the starveling elf may be kept alive; did about this time crown the arms of the province with success in another quarter, and thus cheered the droop-

*De Vries mentions that this windmill stood on the south-east bastion, and it is likewise to be seen, together with the flag-staff, in Justus Danker's View of New Amsterdam, which I have taken the liberty of prefixing to Mr. Knickerbocker's history.—EDITOR.

ing hearts of the forlorn Nederlanders; otherwise there is no knowing to what lengths they might have gone in the excess of their sorrowing—"for grief," says the profound historian of the seven champions of Christendom, "is companion with despair, and despair a procurer of infamous death!"

Among the numerous inroads of the Moss-troopers of Connecticut, which for some time past had occasioned such great tribulation, I should particularly have mentioned a settlement made on the eastern part of Long Island, at a place which, from the peculiar excellence of its shell fish, was called Oyster Bay. This was attacking the province in a most sensible part, and occasioned a great agitation at New Amsterdam.

It is an incontrovertible fact, well known to your skilful physiologists, that the high road to the affections, is through the throat; and this may be accounted for on the same principles which I have already quoted, in my strictures on fat aldermen. Nor is this fact unknown to the world at large; and hence do we observe, that the surest way to gain the hearts of the million, is to feed them well—and that a man is never so disposed to flatter, to please and serve another, as when he is feeding at his expense; which is one reason why your rich men, who give frequent dinners, have such abundance of sincere and faithful friends. It is on this principle that our knowing leaders of parties secure the affections of their partizans, by rewarding them bountifully with loaves and fishes; and entrap the suffrages of the greasy mob, by treating them with bull feasts and roasted oxen. I have known many a man, in this same city, acquire considerable importance in society, and usurp a large share of the good will of his enlightened fellow citizens, when the only thing that could be said in his eulogium was, that "he gave a good dinner, and kept excellent wine."

Since then the heart and the stomach are so nearly allied, it follows conclusively that what affects the one, must sympathetically affect the other. Now it is an equally incontrovertible fact, that of all offerings to the stomach, there is none more grateful than the testaceous marine animal, called by naturalists the Ostea, but known commonly by the vulgar name of Oyster. And in such great reverence has it ever been held, by my gormandizing fellow citizens, that temples have been dedicated to it, time out of mind, in every street, lane and alley throughout this well fed city. It is not to be expected therefore, that the seizing of Oyster Bay, a place abounding with their favourite delicacy, would be tolerated by the inhabitants of New Amsterdam. An attack upon their honour they might have pardoned; even the massacre of a few citizens might have been passed over in silence; but an outrage that affected the larders of the great city of New Amsterdam, and threatened the stomachs of its corpulent Burgomasters, was too serious to pass unrevenged. The whole council were unanimous in opinion, that the intruders should be immediately driven by force of arms, from Oyster Bay, and its vicinity, and a detachment was accordingly dispatched for the purpose, under command of one Stoffel Brinkerhoff, or Brinkerhoofd (*i.e.* Stoffel, the head-breaker) so called because he was a man of mighty deeds, famous throughout the whole extent of Nieuw Nederlandts for his skill at quarterstaff, and for size would have been a match for Colbrand, that famous Danish champion, slain by little Guy of Warwick.

Stoffel Brinckerhoff was a man of few words, but prompt actions—one of your straight going officers, who march directly forward, and do their orders without making any parade about it. He used no extraordinary speed in his movements, but trudged steadily on, through Nineveh and Babylon, and Jericho and Patchog, and the mighty town of Quag, and various other renowned cities of yore, which have by some unaccountable witchcraft of the Yankees, been strangely transplanted to Long Island, until he arrived in the neighbourhood of Oyster Bay.

Here was he encountered by a tumultuous host of valiant warriors, headed by Preserved Fish, and Habbakuk Nutter, and Return Strong, and Zerubbabel Fisk, and Jonathan Doolittle and Determined Cock!—at the sound of whose names the courageous Stoffel verily believed that the whole parliament of Praise God Barebones had been let loose to discomfit him. Finding however that this formidable body was composed merely of the "select men" of the settlement, armed with no other weapons but their tongues, and that they had issued forth with no other intent, than to meet him on the field of argument—he succeeded in putting them to the rout with little difficulty, and completely broke up their settlement. Without waiting to write an account of his victory on the spot, and thus letting the enemy slip through his fingers while he was securing his own laurels, as a more experienced general would have done, the brave Stoffel thought of nothing but completing his enterprize, and utterly driving the Yankees from the island. This hardy enterprize he performed in much the same manner as he had been accustomed to drive his oxen; for as the Yankees fled before him, he pulled up his breeches and trudged steadily after them, and would infallibly have driven them into the sea, had they not begged for quarter, and agreed to pay tribute.

The news of this achievement was a seasonable restorative to the spirits of the citizens of New Amsterdam. To gratify them still more, the governor resolved to astonish them with one of those gorgeous spectacles, known in the days of classic antiquity, a full account of which had been flogged into his memory, when a school-boy at the Hague. A grand triumph therefore was decreed to Stoffel Brinckerhoff, who made his triumphant entrance into town riding on a Naraganset pacer; five pumpkins, which like Roman eagles had served the enemy for standards, were carried before him—ten cart loads of oysters, five hundred bushels of Weathersfield onions, a hundred quintals of codfish, two hogsheads of molasses and various other treasures, were exhibited as the spoils and tribute of the Yankees; while three notorious counterfeiters of Manhattan notes,* were led captive to grace the hero's triumph. The procession was enlivened by martial music, from the trumpet of Antony Van Corlear the champion, accompanied by a select band of boys and negroes, performing on the national instruments of rattle bones and clam shells. The citizens devoured the spoils in sheer gladness of heart—every man did honour to the conqueror, by getting devoutly drunk on New England rum—and learned Wilhelmus Kieft

---

*This is one of those trivial anachronisms, that now and then occur in the course of this otherwise authentic history. How could Manhattan notes be counterfeited, when as yet Banks were unknown in this country—and our simple progenitors had not even dreamt of those inexhaustible mines of *paper opulence. Print. Dev.*

calling to mind, in a momentary fit of enthusiasm and generosity, that it was customary among the ancients to honour
their victorious generals with public statues, passed a gracious
decree, by which every tavernkeeper was permitted to paint
the head of the intrepid Stoffel on his sign!

CHAP. IV.

Philosophical reflections on the folly of being happy in time of prosperity. —Sundry troubles on the southern Frontiers. — How William the Testy by his great learning had well nigh ruined the province through a Cabalistic word. —As also the secret expeditions of Jan Jansen Alpenden, and his astonishing reward.

IF WE COULD but get a peep at the tally of dame Fortune, where, like a notable landlady, she regularly chalks up the debtor and creditor accounts of mankind, we should find that, upon the whole, good and evil are pretty nearly balanced in this world; and that though we may for a long while revel in the very lap of prosperity, the time will at length come, when we must ruefully pay off the reckoning. Fortune, in fact, is a pestilent shrew, and withal a most inexorable creditor; for though she may indulge her favourites in long credits, and overwhelm them with her favours; yet sooner or later, she brings up her arrears, with the rigour of an experienced publican, and washes out her scores with their tears. "Since," says good old Bœtius in his consolations of philosophy, "since no man can retain her at his pleasure, and since her flight is so deeply lamented, what are her favours but sure prognostications of approaching trouble and calamity."

There is nothing that more moves my contempt at the stupidity and want of reflection in my fellow men, than to behold them rejoicing, and indulging in security and self confidence, in times of prosperity. To a wise man, who is blessed with the light of reason, those are the very moments of anxiety and apprehension; well knowing that according to the system of things, happiness is at best but transient—and that the higher a man is elevated by the capricious breath of fortune, the lower must be his proportionate depression. Whereas, he who is overwhelmed by calamity, has the less chance of encountering fresh disasters, as a man at the bottom of a hill, runs very little risk of breaking his neck by tumbling to the top.

This is the very essence of true wisdom, which consists in

knowing when we ought to be miserable; and was discovered much about the same time with that invaluable secret, that "every thing is vanity and vexation of spirit;" in consequence of which maxim your wise men have ever been the unhappiest of the human race; esteeming it as an infallible mark of genius to be distressed without reason—since any man may be miserable in time of misfortune, but it is the philosopher alone who can discover cause for grief in the very hour of prosperity.

According to the principle I have just advanced, we find that the colony of New Netherlands, which under the reign of the renowned Van Twiller, had flourished in such alarming and fatal serenity; is now paying for its former welfare, and discharging the enormous debt of comfort which it contracted. Foes harass it from different quarters; the city of New Amsterdam, while yet in its infancy is kept in constant alarm; and its valiant commander little William the Testy answers the vulgar, but expressive idea of "a man in a peck of troubles."

While busily engaged repelling his bitter enemies the Yankees, on one side, we find him suddenly molested in another quarter, and by other assailants. A vagrant colony of Swedes, under the conduct of Peter Minnewits, and professing allegience to that redoubtable virago, Christina queen of Sweden; had settled themselves and erected a fort on south (or Delaware) river—within the boundaries, claimed by the Government of the New Netherlands. History is mute as to the particulars of their first landing, and their real pretensions to the soil, and this is the more to be lamented; as this same colony of Swedes will hereafter be found most materially to affect, not only the interests of the Nederlanders, but of the world at large!

In whatever manner therefore, this vagabond colony of Swedes first took possession of the country, it is certain that in 1638, they established a fort, and Minnewits, according to the off hand usage of his contemporaries, declared himself governor of all the adjacent country, under the name of the province of NEW SWEDEN. No sooner did this reach the ears of the choleric Wilhelmus, than, like a true spirited chieftan, he immediately broke into a violent rage, and calling together his council, belaboured the Swedes most lustily in the longest

speech that had ever been heard in the colony, since the memorable dispute of Ten breeches and Tough breeches. Having
thus given vent to the first ebullitions of his indignation, he
had resort to his favourite measure of proclamation, and dispatched one, piping hot, in the first year of his reign, informing Peter Minnewits that the whole territory, bordering on
the south river, had, time out of mind, been in possession of
the Dutch colonists, having been "beset with forts, and sealed
with their blood."

The latter sanguinary sentence, would convey an idea of
direful war and bloodshed; were we not relieved by the information that it merely related to a fray, in which some half a
dozen Dutchmen had been killed by the Indians, in their benevolent attempts to establish a colony and promote civilization. By this it will be seen that William Kieft, though a very
small man, delighted in big expressions, and was much given
to a praise-worthy figure in rhetoric, generally cultivated by
your little great men, called hyperbole. A figure which has
been found of infinite service among many of his class, and
which has helped to swell the grandeur of many a mighty self-
important, but windy chief magistrate. Nor can I resist in this
place, from observing how much my beloved country is indebted to this same figure of hyperbole, for supporting certain of her greatest characters—statesmen, orators, civilians
and divines; who by dint of big words, inflated periods, and
windy doctrines, are kept afloat on the surface of society, as
ignorant swimmers are buoyed up by blown bladders.

The proclamation against Minnewits concluded by ordering the self-dubbed governor, and his gang of Swedish adventurers, immediately to leave the country under penalty of the
high displeasure, and inevitable vengeance of the puissant
government of the Nieuw Nederlandts. This "strong measure," however, does not seem to have had a whit more effect
than its predecessors, which had been thundered against the
Yankees—the Swedes resolutely held on to the territory they
had taken possession of—whereupon matters for the present
remained in statu quo.

That Wilhelmus Kieft should put up with this insolent obstinacy in the Swedes, would appear incompatible with his
valourous temperament; but we find that about this time the

little man had his hands full; and what with one annoyance and another, was kept continually on the bounce.

There is a certain description of active legislators, who by shrewd management, contrive always to have a hundred irons on the anvil, every one of which must be immediately attended to; who consequently are ever full of temporary shifts and expedients, patching up the public welfare and cobbling the national affairs, so as to make nine holes where they mend one—stopping chinks and flaws with whatever comes first to hand, like the Yankees I have mentioned stuffing old clothes in broken windows. Of this class of statesmen was William the Testy—and had he only been blessed with powers equal to his zeal, or his zeal been disciplined by a little discretion, there is very little doubt but he would have made the greatest governor of his size on record—the renowned governor of the island of Barataria alone excepted.

The great defect of Wilhelmus Kieft's policy was, that though no man could be more ready to stand forth in an hour of emergency, yet he was so intent upon guarding the national pocket, that he suffered the enemy to break its head—in other words, whatever precaution for public safety he adopted, he was so intent upon rendering it cheap, that he invariably rendered it ineffectual. All this was a remote consequence of his profound education at the Hague—where having acquired a smattering of knowledge, he was ever after a great conner of indexes, continually dipping into books, without ever studying to the bottom of any subject; so that he had the scum of all kinds of authors fermenting in his pericranium. In some of these title page researches he unluckily stumbled over a grand political *cabalistic word*, which, with his customary facility he immediately incorporated into his great scheme of government, to the irretrievable injury and delusion of the honest province of Nieuw Nederlandts, and the eternal misleading, of all experimental rulers.

In vain have I pored over the Theurgia of the Chaldeans, the Cabala of the Jews, the Necromancy of the Arabians— The Magic of the Persians—the Hocus Pocus of the English, the Witch-craft of the Yankees, or the Pow-wowing of the Indians to discover where the little man first laid eyes on this terrible word. Neither the Sephir Jetzirah, that famous cabalistic volume, ascribed to the Patriarch Abraham; nor the pages of the Zohar, containing the mysteries of the cabala, recorded by the learned rabbi Simeon Jochaides, yield any light to my enquiries—Nor am I in the least benefited by my painful researches in the Shem-hamphorah of Benjamin, the wandering Jew, though it enabled Davidus Elm to make a ten days' journey, in twenty four hours. Neither can I perceive the slightest affinity in the Tetragrammaton, or sacred name of four letters, the profoundest word of the Hebrew Cabala; a mystery, sublime, ineffable and incommunicable—and the letters of which Jod-He-Vau-He, having been stolen by the Pagans, constituted their great Name Jao, or Jove. In short, in all my cabalistic, theurgic, necromantic, magical and astrological researches, from the Tetractys of Pythagoras, to the recondite works of Breslaw and mother Bunch, I have not discovered the least vestige of an origin of this word, nor have I discovered any word of sufficient potency to counteract it.

Not to keep my reader in any suspence, the word which had so wonderfully arrested the attention of William the Testy and which in German characters, had a particularly black and ominous aspect, on being fairly translated into the English is no other than *economy*—a talismanic term, which by constant use and frequent mention, has ceased to be formidable in our eyes, but which has as terrible potency as any in the arcana of necromancy.

When pronounced in a national assembly it has an immediate effect in closing the hearts, beclouding the intellects, drawing the purse strings and buttoning the breeches pockets of all philosophic legislators. Nor are its effects on the eye less wonderful. It produces a contraction of the retina, an obscurity of the christaline lens, a viscidity of the vitreous and an inspiration of the aqueous humours, an induration of the tunica sclerotica and a convexity of the cornea; insomuch that the organ of vision loses its strength and perspicuity, and the unfortunate patient becomes *myopes* or in plain English, purblind; perceiving only the amount of immediate expense without being able to look further, and regard it in connexion with the ultimate object to be effected.—"So that," to quote the words of the eloquent Burke, "a briar at his nose is of greater magnitude than an oak at five hundred yards distance." Such are its instantaneous operations, and the results are still more astonishing. By its magic influence seventy-fours, shrink into frigates—frigates into sloops, and sloops into gun-boats. As the defenceless fleet of Eneas, at the command of the protecting Venus, changed into sea nymphs, and protected itself by diving; so the mighty navy of America, by the cabalistic word economy, dwindles into small craft, and shelters itself in a mill-pond!

This all potent word, which served as his touchstone in politics, at once explains the whole system of proclamations, protests, empty threats, windmills, trumpeters, and paper war, carried on by Wilhelmus the Testy—and we may trace its operations in an armament which he fitted out in 1642 in a moment of great wrath; consisting of two sloops and *thirty* men, under the command of Mynheer Jan Jansen Alpendam, as admiral of the fleet, and commander in chief of the forces. This formidable expedition, which can only be paralleled by some of the daring cruizes of our infant navy, about the bay and up the sound; was intended to drive the Marylanders from the Schuylkill, of which they had recently taken possession—and which was claimed as part of the province of New Nederlandts—for it appears that at this time our infant colony was in that enviable state, so much coveted by ambitious nations, that is to say, the government had a vast extent of territory; part of which it enjoyed, and the greater part of which it had continually to quarrel about.

Admiral Jan Jansen Alpendam was a man of great mettle and prowess; and no way dismayed at the character of the enemy; who were represented as a gigantic gunpowder race of men, who lived on hoe cakes and bacon, drank mint juleps and brandy toddy, and were exceedingly expert at boxing, biting, gouging, tar and feathering, and a variety of other athletic accomplishments, which they had borrowed from their cousins german and prototypes the Virginians, to whom they have ever borne considerable resemblance—notwithstanding all these alarming representations, the admiral entered the Schuylkill most undauntedly with his fleet, and arrived without disaster or opposition at the place of destination.

Here he attacked the enemy in a vigorous speech in low dutch, which the wary Kieft had previously put in his pocket;

wherein he courteously commenced by calling them a pack of lazy, louting, dram drinking, cock fighting, horse racing, slave driving, tavern haunting, sabbath breaking, mulatto breeding upstarts—and concluded by ordering them to evacuate the country immediately—to which they most laconically replied in plain English (as was very natural for Swedes) "they'd see him d——d first."

Now this was a reply for which neither Jan Jansen Alpendam, nor Wilhelmus Kieft had made any calculation—and finding himself totally unprepared to answer so terrible a rebuff with suitable hostility he concluded, like a most worthy admiral of a modern English expedition, that his wisest course was to return home and report progress. He accordingly sailed back to New Amsterdam, where he was received with great honours, and considered as a pattern for all commanders; having achieved a most hazardous enterprize, at a trifling expense of treasure, and without losing a single man to the state!—He was unanimously called the deliverer of his country; (an appellation liberally bestowed on all great men) his two sloops having done their duty, were laid up (or dry docked) in a cove now called the Albany Bason, where they quietly rotted in the mud; and to immortalize his name, they erected, by subscription, a magnificent shingle monument on the top of Flatten barrack* Hill, which lasted three whole years; when it fell to pieces, and was burnt for fire-wood.

*A corruption of Varleth's bergh—or Varleth's hill, so called from one Varleth, who lived upon that hill in the early days of the settlement. EDITOR.

CHAP. V.

How William the Testy enriched the Province by a multitude of good-for-nothing laws, and came to be the Patron of Lawyers and Bum-Bailiffs. How he undertook to rescue the public from a grievous evil, and had well nigh been smoked to death for his pains. How the people became exceedingly enlightened and unhappy, under his instructions—with divers other matters which will be found out upon perusal.

AMONG THE MANY wrecks and fragments of exalted wisdom, which have floated down the stream of time, from venerable antiquity, and have been carefully picked up by those humble, but industrious wights, who ply along the shores of literature, we find the following sage ordinance of Charondas, the locrian legislator—Anxious to preserve the ancient laws of the state from the additions and improvements of profound "country members," or officious candidates for popularity, he ordained, that whoever proposed a new law, should do it with a halter about his neck; so that in case his proposition was rejected, he was strung up—and there the matter ended.

This salutary institution had such an effect, that for more than two hundred years there was only one trifling alteration in the criminal code—and the whole race of lawyers starved to death for want of employment. The consequence of this was, that the Locrians being unprotected by an overwhelming load of excellent laws, and undefended by a standing army of pettifoggers and sheriff's officers, lived very lovingly together, and were such a happy people, that we scarce hear any thing of them throughout the whole Grecian history—for it is well known that none but your unlucky, quarrelsome, rantipole nations make any noise in the world.

Well would it have been for William the Testy, had he happily, in the course of his "universal acquirements," stumbled upon this precaution of the good Charondas. On the contrary, he conceived that the true policy of a legislator was to multiply laws, and thus secure the property, the persons and the morals of the people, by surrounding them in a manner with men traps and spring guns, and besetting even the sweet sequestered walks of private life, with quick-set hedges, so that a man could scarcely turn, without the risk of encountering some of these pestiferous protectors. Thus was he continually coining petty laws for every petty offence that occurred, until in time they became too numerous to be remembered, and remained like those of certain modern legislators, in a manner dead letters—revived occasionally for the purpose of individual oppression, or to entrap ignorant offenders.

Petty courts consequently began to appear, where the law was administered with nearly as much wisdom and impartiality as in those august tribunals the aldermen's and justice shops of the present day. The plaintiff was generally favoured, as being a customer and bringing business to the shop; the offences of the rich were discreetly winked at—for fear of hurting the feelings of their friends;—but it could never be laid to the charge of the vigilant burgomasters, that they suffered vice to skulk unpunished, under the disgraceful rags of poverty.

About this time may we date the first introduction of capital punishments—a goodly gallows being erected on the water-side, about where Whitehall stairs are at present, a little to the east of the battery. Hard by also was erected another gibbet of a very strange, uncouth and unmatchable description, but on which the ingenious William Kieft valued himself not a little, being a punishment entirely of his own invention.*

It was for loftiness of altitude not a whit inferior to that of Haman, so renowned in bible history; but the marvel of the contrivance was, that the culprit instead of being suspended by the neck, according to venerable custom, was hoisted by the waistband, and was kept for an hour together, dangling and sprawling between heaven and earth—to the infinite entertainment and doubtless great edification of the multitude of respectable citizens, who usually attend upon exhibitions of the kind.

It is incredible how the little governor chuckled at beholding caitiff vagrants and sturdy beggars thus swinging by the breech, and cutting antic gambols in the air. He had a thou-

*Both the gibbets as mentioned above by our author, may be seen in the sketch of Justus Danker, which we have prefixed to the work.—EDITOR.

sand pleasantries, and mirthful conceits to utter upon the occasions. He called them his dandle-lions—his wild fowl—his
high flyers—his spread eagles—his goshawks—his scare-
crows and finally his *gallows birds*, which ingenious appellation, though originally confined to worthies who had taken
the air in this strange manner, has since grown to be a cant
name given to all candidates for legal elevation. This punishment, moreover, if we may credit the assertions of certain
grave etymologists, gave the first hint for a kind of harness-
ing, or strapping, by which our forefathers braced up their
multifarious breeches, and which has of late years been revived and continues to be worn at the present day. It still
bears the name of the object to which it owes its origin; being
generally termed a pair of *gallows-es*—though I am informed
it is sometimes vulgarly denominated *suspenders*.

Such were the admirable improvements of William Kieft in
criminal law—nor was his civil code less a matter of wonderment, and much does it grieve me that the limits of my work
will not suffer me to expatiate on both, with the prolixity they
deserve. Let it suffice then to say; that in a little while the
blessings of innumerable laws became notoriously apparent.
It was soon found necessary to have a certain class of men to
expound and confound them—divers pettifoggers accordingly made their appearance, under whose protecting care the
community was soon set together by the ears.

I would not here, for the whole world, be thought to insinuate any thing derogatory to the profession of the law, or to
its dignified members. Well am I aware, that we have in this
ancient city an innumerable host of worthy gentlemen, who
have embraced that honourable order, not for the sordid love
of filthy lucre, or the selfish cravings of renown, but through
no other motives under heaven, but a fervent zeal for the correct administration of justice, and a generous and disinterested devotion to the interests of their fellow citizens!—
Sooner would I throw this trusty pen into the flames, and
cork up my ink bottle forever (which is the worst punishment
a maggot brained author can inflict upon himself) than infringe even for a nail's breadth upon the dignity of this truly
benevolent class of citizens—on the contrary I allude solely
to that crew of caitiff scouts who in these latter days of evil

have become so numerous—who infest the skirts of the profession, as did the recreant Cornish knights the honourable order of chivalry—who, under its auspices, commit their depredations on society—who thrive by quibbles, quirks and chicanery, and like vermin swarm most, where there is most corruption.

Nothing so soon awakens the malevolent passions as the facility of gratification. The courts of law would never be so constantly crowded with petty, vexatious and disgraceful suits, were it not for the herds of pettifogging lawyers that infest them. These tamper with the passions of the lower and more ignorant classes; who, as if poverty was not a sufficient misery in itself, are always ready to heighten it, by the bitterness of litigation. They are in law what quacks are in medicine—exciting the malady for the purpose of profiting by the cure, and retarding the cure, for the purpose of augmenting the fees. Where one destroys the constitution, the other impoverishes the purse; and it may likewise be observed, that a patient, who has once been under the hands of a quack, is ever after dabbling in drugs, and poisoning himself with infallible remedies; and an ignorant man who has once meddled with the law under the auspices of one of these empyrics, is forever after embroiling himself with his neighbours, and impoverishing himself with successful law suits.—My readers will excuse this digression into which I have been unwarily betrayed; but I could not avoid giving a cool, unprejudiced account of an abomination too prevalent in this excellent city, and with the effects of which I am unluckily acquainted to my cost; having been nearly ruined by a law suit, which was unjustly decided against me—and my ruin having been completed, by another which was decided in my favour.

It is an irreparable loss to posterity, that of the innumerable laws enacted by William the Testy, which doubtless formed a code that might have vied with those of Solon, Lycurgus or Sancho Panza, but few have been handed down to the present day, among which the most important is one framed in an unlucky moment, to prohibit the universal practice of smoking. This he proved by mathematical demonstration, to be not merely a heavy tax upon the public pocket, but an incredible consumer of time, a hideous encourager of idleness, and of course a deadly bane to the morals of the people. Ill fated Kieft!—had he lived in this most enlightened and libel loving age, and attempted to subvert the inestimable liberty of the press, he could not have struck more closely, upon the sensibilities of the million.

The populace were in as violent a turmoil as the constitutional gravity of their deportment would permit—a mob of factious citizens had even the hardihood to assemble around the little governor's house, where setting themselves resolutely down, like a besieging army before a fortress, they one and all fell to smoking with a determined perseverance, that plainly evinced it was their intention, to funk him into terms with villainous Cow-pen mundungus!—Already was the stately mansion of the governor enveloped in murky clouds, and the puissant little man, almost strangled in his hole, when bethinking himself, that there was no instance on record, of any great man of antiquity perishing in so ignoble a manner (the case of Pliny the elder being the only one that bore any resemblance)—he was fain to come to terms, and compromise with the mob, on condition that they should spare his life, by immediately extinguishing their tobacco pipes.

The result of the armistice was, that though he continued to permit the custom of smoking, yet did he abolish the fair long pipes which prevailed in the days of Wouter Van Twiller, denoting ease, tranquillity and sobriety of deportment, and in place thereof introduced little captious short pipes, two inches in length; which he observed could be stuck in one corner of the mouth, or twisted in the hatband, and would not be in the way of business. But mark, oh reader! the deplorable consequences. The smoke of these villainous little pipes—continually ascending in a cloud about the nose, penetrated into and befogged the cerebellum, dried up all the kindly moisture of the brain, and rendered the people as vapourish and testy as their renowned little governor—nay, what is more, from a goodly burley race of folk, they became, like our honest dutch farmers, who smoke short pipes, a lanthorn-jawed, smoak-dried, leathern-hided race of men.

Indeed it has been remarked by the observant writer of the Stuyvesant manuscript, that under the administration of Wilhelmus Kieft the disposition of the inhabitants of New

Amsterdam experienced an essential change, so that they became very meddlesome and factious. The constant exacerbations of temper into which the little governor was thrown, by
the maraudings on his frontiers, and his unfortunate propensity to experiment and innovation, occasioned him to keep his
council in a continual worry—and the council being to the
people at large, what yeast or leaven is to a batch, they threw
the whole community into a ferment—and the people at
large being to the city, what the mind is to the body, the
unhappy commotions they underwent operated most disas-
trously, upon New Amsterdam—insomuch, that in certain of
their paroxysms of consternation and perplexity, they begat
several of the most crooked, distorted and abominable streets,
lanes and alleys, with which this metropolis is disfigured.

But the worst of the matter was, that just about this time
the mob, since called the sovereign people, like Balaam's ass,
began to grow more enlightened than its rider, and exhibited
a strange desire of governing itself. This was another effect of
the "universal acquirements" of William the Testy. In some of
his pestilent researches among the rubbish of antiquity, he
was struck with admiration at the institution of public tables
among the Lacedemonians, where they discussed topics of a
general and interesting nature—at the schools of the philosophers, where they engaged in profound disputes upon
politics and morals—where grey beards were taught the rudiments of wisdom, and youths learned to become little men,
before they were boys. "There is nothing" said the ingenious
Kieft, shutting up the book, "there is nothing more essential
to the well management of a country, than education among
the people; the basis of a good government, should be laid in
the public mind."—Now this was true enough, but it was
ever the wayward fate of William the Testy, that when he
thought right, he was sure to go to work wrong. In the present instance he could scarcely eat or sleep, until he had set on
foot brawling debating societies, among the simple citizens of
New Amsterdam. This was the one thing wanting to complete his confusion. The honest Dutch burghers, though in
truth but little given to argument or wordy altercation, yet by
dint of meeting often together, fuddling themselves with
strong drink, beclouding their brains with tobacco smoke,

and listening to the harangues of some half a dozen oracles, soon became exceedingly wise, and—as is always the case where the mob is politically enlightened—exceedingly discontented. They found out, with wonderful quickness of discernment, the fearful error in which they had indulged, in fancying themselves the happiest people in creation—and were fortunately convinced, that, all circumstances to the contrary notwithstanding, they were a very unhappy, deluded, and consequently, ruined people!

In a short time the quidnuncs of New Amsterdam formed themselves into sage juntos of political croakers, who daily met together to groan over public affairs, and make themselves miserable; thronging to these unhappy assemblages with the same eagerness, that your zealots have in all ages abandoned the milder and more peaceful paths of religion to crowd to the howling convocations of fanaticism. We are naturally prone to discontent, and avaricious after imaginary causes of lamentation—like lubberly monks we belabour our own shoulders, and seem to take a vast satisfaction in the music of our own groans. Nor is this said for the sake of paradox; daily experience shews the truth of these sage observations. It is next to a farce to offer consolation, or to think of elevating the spirits of a man, groaning under ideal calamities; but nothing is more easy than to render him wretched, though on the pinnacle of felicity; as it is an Herculean task to hoist a man to the top of a steeple, though the merest child can topple him off thence.

In the sage assemblages I have noticed, the philosophic reader will at once perceive the faint germs of those sapient convocations called popular meetings, prevalent at our day—Hither resorted all those idlers and "squires of low degree," who like rags, hang loose upon the back of society, and are ready to be blown away by every wind of doctrine. Coblers abandoned their stalls and hastened hither to give lessons on political economy—blacksmiths left their handicraft and suffered their own fires to go out, while they blew the bellows and stirred up the fire of faction; and even taylors, though but the shreds and patches, the ninth parts of humanity, neglected their own measures, to attend to the measures of government—Nothing was wanting but half a dozen newspapers and patriotic editors, to have completed this public illumination and to have thrown the whole province in an uproar!

I should not forget to mention, that these popular meetings were always held at a noted tavern; for houses of that description, have always been found the most congenial nurseries of politicks; abounding with those genial streams which give strength and sustenance to faction—We are told that the ancient Germans, had an admirable mode of treating any question of importance; they first deliberated upon it when drunk, and afterwards reconsidered it, when sober. The shrewder mobs of America, who dislike having two minds upon a subject, both determine and act upon it drunk; by which means a world of cold and tedious speculation is dispensed with—and as it is universally allowed that when a man is drunk he sees *double*, it follows most conclusively that he sees twice as well as his sober neighbours.

CHAP. VI.

Shewing the great importance of party distinctions, and the dolourous perplexities into which William the Testy was thrown, by reason of his having enlightened the multitude.

FOR SOME TIME however, the worthy politicians of New Amsterdam, who had thus conceived the sublime project of saving the nation, were very much perplexed by dissentions, and strange contrariety of opinions among themselves, so that they were often thrown into the most chaotic uproar and confusion, and all for the simple want of party classification. Now it is a fact well known to your experienced politicians, that it is equally necessary to have a distinct classification and nomenclature in politics, as in the physical sciences. By this means the several orders of patriots, with their breedings and cross breedings, their affinities and varieties may be properly distinguished and known. Thus have arisen in different quarters of the world the generic titles of Guelfs and Ghibbelins—Round heads and Cavaliers—Big endians and Little endians—Whig and Tory—Aristocrat and Democrat—Republican and Jacobin—Federalist and Antifederalist, together with a certain mongrel party called *Quid*; which seems to have been engendered between the two last mentioned parties, as a mule is produced between an horse and an ass—and like a mule it seems incapable of procreation, fit only for humble drudgery, doomed to bear successively the burthen of father and mother, and to be cudgelled soundly for its pains.

The important benefit of these distinctions is obvious. How many very strenuous and hard working patriots are there, whose knowledge is bounded by the political vocabulary, and who, were they not thus arranged in parties would never know their own minds, or which way to think on a subject; so that by following their own common sense the community might often fall into that unanimity, which has been clearly proved, by many excellent writers, to be fatal to the welfare of a republick. Often have I seen a very well meaning hero of seventy six, most horribly puzzled to make up his opinion about certain men and measures, and running a great risk of thinking right; until all at once he resolved his doubts by resorting to the old touch stone of *Whig* and *Tory*; which titles, though they bear about as near an affinity to the present parties in being, as do the robustious statues of Gog and Magog, to the worthy London Aldermen, who devour turtle under their auspices at Guild-Hall; yet are they used on all occasions by the sovereign people, as a pair of spectacles, through which they are miraculously enabled to see beyond their own noses, and to distinguish a hawk from a hand saw, or an owl from a turkey buzzard!

Well was it recorded in holy writ, "the horse knoweth his rider, and the ass his master's crib," for when the sovereign people are thus harnessed out, and properly yoked together, it is delectable to behold with what system and harmony they jog onward, trudging through mud and mire, obeying the commands of their drivers, and dragging the scurvy dung carts of faction at their heels. How many a patriotic member of congress have I known, loyally disposed to adhere to his party through thick and thin, but who would often, from sheer ignorance, or the dictates of conscience and common sense, have stumbled into the ranks of his adversaries, and advocated the opposite side of the question, had not the parties been thus broadly designated by generic titles.

The wise people of New Amsterdam therefore, after for some time enduring the evils of confusion, at length, like honest dutchmen as they were, soberly settled down into two distinct parties, known by the name of *Square head* and *Platter breech*—the former implying that the bearer was deficient in that rotundity of pericranium, which was considered as a token of true genius—the latter, that he was destitute of genuine courage, or *good bottom*, as it has since been technically termed—and I defy all the politicians of this great city to shew me where any two parties of the present day, have split upon more important and fundamental points.

These names, to tell the honest truth—and I scorn to tell any thing else—were not the mere progeny of whim or accident, as were those of Ten Breeches and Tough Breeches, in the days of yore, but took their origin in recondite and scientific deductions of certain Dutch philosophers. In a word,

they were the dogmas or elementary principia of those ingenious systems since supported in the physiognomical tracts of
Lavater, who gravely measures intellect by the length of a
nose, or detects it lurking in the curve of a lip, or the arch of
an eye-brow—The craniology of Dr. Gall, who has found out
the encampments and strong holds of the virtues and vices,
passions and habits among the protuberances of the skull, and
proves that your whorson jobbernowl, is your true skull of
genius—The *Linea Fascialis* of Dr. Petrus Camper, anatomical professor in the college of Amsterdam, which regulates
every thing by the relative position of the upper and lower
jaw; shewing the ancient opinion to be correct that the owl
is the wisest of animals, and that a pancake face is an unfailing
index of talents, and a true model of beauty—and finally, the
breechology of professor Higgenbottom, which teaches the
surprizing and intimate connection between the seat of honour, and the seat of intellect—a doctrine supported by experiments of pedagogues in all ages, who have found that
applications *a parte poste*, are marvellously efficacious in
quickening the perceptions of their scholars, and that the
most expeditious mode of instilling knowledge into their
heads, is to hammer it into their bottoms!

Thus then, the enlightened part of the inhabitants of
Nieuw Nederlandts, being comfortably arranged into parties,
went to work with might and main to uphold the common
wealth—assembling together in separate beer-houses, and
smoking at each other with implacable animosity, to the great
support of the state, and emolument of the tavern-keepers.
Some indeed who were more zealous than the rest went further, and began to bespatter one another with numerous very
hard names and scandalous little words, to be found in the
dutch language; every partizan believing religiously that he
was serving his country, when he besmutted the character,
or damaged the pocket of a political adversary. But however
they might differ between themselves, both parties agreed on
one point, to cavil at and condemn every measure of government whether right or wrong; for as the governor was by
his station independent of their power, and was not elected
by their choice, and as he had not decided in favour of
either faction, neither of them were interested in his suc-

cess, or the prosperity of the country while under his administration.

"Unhappy William Kieft!" exclaims the sage writer of the
Stuyvesant manuscript,—doomed to contend with enemies
too knowing to be entrapped, and to reign over people, too
wise to be governed! All his expeditions against his enemies
were baffled and set at naught, and all his measures for the
public safety, were cavilled at by the people. Did he propose
levying an efficient body of troops for internal defence, the
mob, that is to say, those vagabond members of the community who have nothing to lose, immediately took the alarm,
vociferated that their interests were in danger—that a standing army was a legion of moths, preying on the pockets of
society; a rod of iron in the hands of government; and that a
government with a military force at its command, would inevitably swell into a despotism. Did he, as was but too commonly the case, defer preparation until the moment of
emergency, and then hastily collect a handful of undisciplined
vagrants, the measure was hooted at, as feeble and inadequate, as trifling with the public dignity and safety, and as
lavishing the public funds on impotent enterprizes.—Did he
resort to the economic measure of proclamation, he was
laughed at by the Yankees, did he back it by non-intercourse,
it was evaded and counteracted by his own subjects. Whichever way he turned himself he was beleaguered and distracted
by petitions of "numerous and respectable meetings," consisting of some half a dozen scurvy pot-house politicians—all of
which he read, and what is worse, all of which he attended
to. The consequence was, that by incessantly changing his
measures, he gave none of them a fair trial; and by listening
to the clamours of the mob and endeavouring to do every
thing, he in sober truth did nothing.

I would not have it supposed however, that he took all
these memorials and interferences good naturedly, for such an
idea would do injustice to his valiant spirit; on the contrary
he never received a piece of advice in the whole course of his
life, without first getting into a passion with the giver. But I
have ever observed that your passionate little men, like small
boats with large sails, are the easiest upset or blown out of
their course; and this is demonstrated by governor Kieft, who

though in temperament as hot as an old radish, and with a mind, the territory of which was subjected to perpetual whirlwinds and tornadoes, yet never failed to be carried away by the last piece of advice that was blown into his ear. Lucky was it for him that his power was not dependant upon the greasy multitude, and that as yet the populace did not possess the important privilege of nominating their chief magistrate. They, however, like a true mob, did their best to help along public affairs; pestering their governor incessantly, by goading him on with harangues and petitions, and then thwarting his fiery spirit with reproaches and memorials, like a knot of sunday jockies, managing an unlucky devil of a hack horse— so that Wilhelmus Kieft, may be said to have been kept either on a worry or a hand gallop, throughout the whole of his administration.

CHAP. VII.

Containing divers fearful accounts of Border wars, and the flagrant outrages of the Moss troopers of Connecticut—With the rise of the great Amphyctionic Council of the east, and the decline of William the Testy.

AMONG THE MANY perils and mishaps that surround your hardy historian, there is one that in spite of my unspeakable delicacy, and unbounded good will towards all my fellow creatures, I have no hopes of escaping. While raking with curious hand, but pious heart, among the rotten remains of former days, I may fare somewhat like that doughty fellow Sampson, who in meddling with the carcass of a dead Lion, drew a swarm of bees about his ears. Thus I am sensible that in detailing the many misdeeds of the Yanokie, or Yankee tribe, it is ten chances to one but I offend the morbid sensibilities of certain of their unreasonable descendants, who will doubtless fly out, and raise such a buzzing about this unlucky pate of mine, that I shall need the tough hide of an Achilles, or an Orlando Furioso, to protect me from their stings. Should such be the case I should deeply and sincerely lament—not my misfortune in giving offence—but the wrongheaded perverseness of this most ill natured and uncharitable age, in taking offence at any thing I say.—My good, honest, testy sirs, how in heaven's name, can I help it, if your great grandfathers behaved in a scurvy manner to my great grandfathers?—I'm very sorry for it, with all my heart, and wish a thousand times, that they had conducted themselves a thousand times better. But as I am recording the sacred events of history, I'd not bate one nail's breadth of the honest truth, though I were sure the whole edition of my work, should be bought up and burnt by the common hangman of Connecticut.—And let me tell you, masters of mine! this is one of the grand purposes for which we impartial historians were sent into the world—to redress wrongs and render justice on the heads of the guilty—So that though a nation may wrong their neighbours, with temporary impunity, yet some time or another an historian shall spring up, who shall give them a hearty rib-roasting in return. Thus your ancestors, I warrant them, little thought, when they were kicking and cuffing the worthy province of Nieuw Nederlandts, and setting its unlucky little governor at his wits ends, that such an historian as I should ever arise, and give them their own, with interest—Body-o'me! but the very talking about it makes my blood boil! and I have as great a mind as ever I had for my dinner, to cut a whole host of your ancestors to mince meat, in my very next page!—but out of the bountiful affection which I feel towards their descendants, I forbear—and I trust when you perceive how completely I have them all in my power, and how, with one flourish of my pen I could make every mother's son of ye grandfatherless, you will not be able enough to applaud my candour and magnanimity.—To resume then, with my accustomed calmness and impartiality, the course of my history.

It was asserted by the wise men of ancient times, intimately acquainted with these matters, that at the gate of Jupiter's palace lay two huge tuns, the one filled with blessings, the other with misfortunes—and it verily seems as if the latter had been set a tap, and left to deluge the unlucky province of Nieuw Nederlandts. Among other causes of irritation, the incessant irruptions and spoliations of his eastern neighbours upon his frontiers, were continually adding fuel to the naturally inflammable temperament of William the Testy. Numerous accounts of them may still be found among the records of former days; for the commanders on the frontiers were especially careful to evince their vigilance and soldierlike zeal, by striving who should send home the most frequent and voluminous budgets of complaints, as your faithful servant is continually running with complaints to the parlour, of all the petty squabbles and misdemeanours of the kitchen.

All these valiant tale-bearings were listened to with great wrath by the passionate little governor, and his subjects, who were to the full as eager to hear, and credulous to believe these frontier fables, as are my fellow citizens to swallow those amusing stories with which our papers are daily filled, about British aggressions at sea, French sequestrations on shore, and Spanish infringements in the *promised land* of

Louisiana—all which proves what I have before asserted, that your enlightened people love to be miserable.

Far be it from me to insinuate however, that our worthy ancestors indulged in groundless alarms; on the contrary they were daily suffering a repetition of cruel wrongs, not one of which, but was a sufficient reason, according to the maxims of national dignity and honour, for throwing the whole universe into hostility and confusion.

From among a host of these bitter grievances still on record, I select a few of the most atrocious, and leave my readers to judge, if our progenitors were not justifiable in getting into a very valiant passion on the occasion.

"24 June 1641. Some of Hartford haue taken a hogg out of the vlact or common and shut it vp out of meer hate or other prejudice, causing it to starve for hunger in the stye!

26 July. The foremencioned English did againe driue the companies hoggs out of the vlact of Sicojoke into Hartford; contending daily with reproaches, blows, beating the people with all disgrace that they could imagine.

May 20, 1642. The English of Hartford haue violently cut loose a horse of the honored companies, that stood bound vpon the common or vlact.

May 9, 1643. The companies horses pastured vpon the companies ground, were driven away by them of Connecticott or Hartford, and the heardsman was lustily beaten with hatchets and sticks.

16. Again they sold a young Hogg belonging to the Companie which piggs had pastured on the Companies land."*

Oh ye powers! into what indignation did every one of these outrages throw the philosophic Kieft! Letter after letter; protest after protest; proclamation after proclamation; bad Latin,† worse English, and hideous low dutch were exhausted in vain upon the inexorable Yankees; and the four-and-twenty letters of the alphabet, which except his champion, the sturdy trumpeter Van Corlear, composed the only standing army he had at his command, were never off duty, throughout the whole of his administration.—Nor did Antony the trum-

*Haz. Collect. S. Pap.

†Certain of Wilhelmus Kieft's Latin letters are still extant in divers collections of state papers.

peter, remain a whit behind his patron, the gallant William in his fiery zeal; but like a faithful champion and preserver of the public safety, on the arrival of every fresh article of news, he was sure to sound his trumpet from the ramparts with most disasterous notes, throwing the people into violent alarms and disturbing their rest at all times and seasons—which caused him to be held in very great regard, the public paying and pampering him, as we do brawling editors, for similar important services.

Appearances to the eastward began now to assume a more formidable aspect than ever—for I would have you note that hitherto the province had been chiefly molested by its immediate neighbours, the people of Connecticut, particularly of Hartford, which, if we may judge from ancient chronicles, was the strong hold of these sturdy moss troopers; from whence they sallied forth, on their daring incursions, carrying terror and devastation into the barns, the hen-roosts and pig-styes of our revered ancestors.

Albeit about the year 1643, the people of the east country, inhabiting the colonies of Massachusetts, Connecticut, New Plymouth and New Haven, gathered together into a mighty conclave, and after buzzing and turmoiling for many days, like a political hive of bees in swarming time, at length settled themselves into a formidable confederation, under the title of the United Colonies of New England. By this union they pledged themselves to stand by one another in all perils and assaults, and to co-operate in all measures offensive and defensive against the surrounding savages, among which were doubtlessly included our honoured ancestors of the Manhattoes; and to give more strength and system to this confederation, a general assembly or grand council was to be annually held, composed of representatives from each of the provinces.

On receiving accounts of this puissant combination, the fiery Wilhelmus was struck with vast consternation, and for the first time in his whole life, forgot to bounce, at hearing an unwelcome piece of intelligence—which a venerable historian of the times observes, was especially noticed among the sage politicians of New Amsterdam. The truth was, on turning over in his mind all that he had read at the Hague, about leagues and combinations, he found that this was an exact imitation of the famous Amphyctionic council, by which the states of Greece were enabled to attain to such power and supremacy, and the very idea made his heart to quake for the safety of his empire at the Manhattoes.

He strenuously insisted, that the whole object of this confederation, was to drive the Nederlanders out of their fair domains; and always flew into a great rage if any one presumed to doubt the probability of his conjecture. Nor, to speak my mind freely, do I think he was wholly unwarranted in such a suspicion; for at the very first annual meeting of the grand council, held at Boston (which governor Kieft denominated the Delphos of this truly classic league) strong representations were made against the Nederlanders, for as much as that in their dealings with the Indians they carried on a traffic in "guns, powther and shott—a trade damnable and injurious to the colonists." Not but what certain of the Connecticut traders did likewise dabble a little in this "damnable traffic"— but then they always sold the Indians such scurvy guns, that they burst at the first discharge—and consequently hurt no one but these pagan savages.

The rise of this potent confederacy was a death blow to the glory of William the Testy, for from that day forward, it was remarked by many, he never held up his head, but appeared quite crest fallen. His subsequent reign therefore, affords but scanty food for the historic pen—we find the grand council continually augmenting in power, and threatening to overwhelm the mighty but defenceless province of Nieuw Nederlandts; while Wilhelmus Kieft kept constantly firing off his proclamations and protests, like a sturdy little sea captain, firing off so many carronades and swivels, in order to break and disperse a water spout—but alas! they had no more effect than if they had been so many blank cartridges.

The last document on record of this learned, philosophic, but unfortunate little man is a long letter to the council of the Amphyctions, wherein in the bitterness of his heart he rails at the people of New Haven, or red hills, for their uncourteous contempt of his protest levelled at them for squatting within the province of their high mightinesses. From this letter, which is a model of epistolary writing, abounding with pithy apophthegms and classic figures, my limits will barely allow me to extract the following recondite passage: — "Certainly when we heare the Inhabitants of New Hartford complayninge of us, we seem to heare Esop's wolfe complayninge of the lamb, or the admonition of the younge man, who cryed out to his mother, chideing with her neighboures, 'Oh Mother revile her, lest she first take up that practice against you.' But being taught by precedent passages we received such an answer to our protest from the inhabitants of New Haven as we expected: *the Eagle always despiseth the Beetle fly*; yet notwithstanding we doe undauntedly continue on our purpose of pursuing our own right, by just arms and righteous means, and doe hope without scruple to execute the express commands of our superiours." To shew that this last sentence was not a mere empty menace he concluded his letter, by intrepidly protesting against the whole council, as a horde of *squatters* and interlopers, inasmuch as they held their meeting at New Haven, or the Red Hills, which he claimed as being within the province of the New Netherlands.

Thus end the authenticated chronicles of the reign of William the Testy—for henceforth, in the trouble, the perplexities and the confusion of the times he seems to have been totally overlooked, and to have slipped forever through the fingers of scrupulous history. Indeed from some cause or another, which I cannot divine, there appears to have been a combination among historians to sink his very name into oblivion, in consequence of which they have one and all forborne even to speak of his exploits; and though I have disappointed the caitiffs in this their nefarious conspiracy, yet I much question whether some one or other of their adherents may not even yet have the hardihood to rise up, and question the authenticity of certain of the well established and incontrovertible facts, I have herein recorded—but let them do it at their peril; for may I perish, if ever I catch any slanderous incendiaries contradicting a word of this immaculate history, or robbing my heroes of any particle of that renown they have gloriously acquired, if I do not empty my whole inkhorn upon them—even though it should equal in magnitude that of the sage Gargantua; which according to the faithful chronicle of his miraculous atchievements, weighed seven thousand quintals.

It has been a matter of deep concern to me, that such darkness and obscurity should hang over the latter days of the illustrious Kieft—for he was a mighty and great little man worthy of being utterly renowned, seeing that he was the first potentate that introduced into this land, the art of fighting by proclamation; and defending a country by trumpeters, and windmills—an economic and humane mode of warfare, since revived with great applause, and which promises, if it can ever be carried into full effect, to save great trouble and treasure, and spare infinitely more bloodshed than either the discovery of gunpowder, or the invention of torpedoes.

It is true that certain of the early provincial poets, of whom there were great numbers in the Nieuw Nederlandts, taking advantage of the mysterious exit of William the Testy, have fabled, that like Romulus he was translated to the skies, and forms a very fiery little star, some where on the left claw of the crab; while others equally fanciful, declare that he had experienced a fate similar to that of the good king Arthur; who, we are assured by ancient bards, was carried away to the delicious abodes of fairy land, where he still exists, in pristine worth and vigour, and will one day or another return to rescue poor old England from the hands of paltry, flippant, pettifogging cabinets, and restore the gallantry, the honour and the immaculate probity, which prevailed in the glorious days of the Round Table.*

All these however are but pleasing fantasies, the cobweb visions of those dreaming varlets the poets, to which I would not have my judicious reader attach any credibility. Neither am I disposed to yield any credit to the assertion of an ancient and rather apocryphal historian, who alledges that the ingenious Wilhelmus was annihilated by the blowing down of one

---

*The old welsh bards believed that king Arthur was not dead but carried awaie by the fairies into some pleasant place, where he shold remaine for a time, and then returne againe and reigne in as great authority as ever. —HOLLINGSHED.

The Britons suppose that he shall come yet and conquere all Britaigne, for certes this is the prophicye of Merlyn—He say'd that his deth shall be doubteous; and said soth, for men thereof yet have doubte and shullen for ever more—for men wyt not whether that he lyveth or is dede.—DE LEEW. CHRON.

of his windmills—nor to that of a writer of later times, who affirms that he fell a victim to a philosophical experiment, which he had for many years been vainly striving to accomplish; having the misfortune to break his neck from the garret window of the Stadt house, in an ineffectual attempt to catch swallows, by sprinkling fresh salt upon their tails.

The most probable account, and to which I am inclined to give my implicit faith, is contained in a very obscure tradition, which declares, that what with the constant troubles on his frontiers, the incessant schemings, and projects going on in his own pericranium—the memorials, petitions, remonstrances and sage pieces of advice from divers respectable meetings of the sovereign people, together with the refractory disposition of his council, who were sure to differ from him on every point and uniformly to be in the wrong—all these I say, did eternally operate to keep his mind in a kind of furnace heat, until he at length became as completly burnt out, as a dutch family pipe which has passed through three generations of hard smokers. In this manner did the choleric but magnanimous William the Testy undergo a kind of animal combustion, consuming away like a farthing rush light—so that when grim death finally snuffed him out, there was scarce left enough of him to bury!

END OF BOOK IV.

BOOK V.

Containing the first part of the reign of Peter Stuyvesant
and his troubles with the Amphyctionic Council.

CHAP. I.

In which the death of a great man is shewn to be no such
inconsolable matter of sorrow—and how Peter Stuyvesant ac-
quired a great name from the uncommon strength
of his head.

To a profound philosopher, like myself, who am apt to
see clear through a subject, where the penetration of ordinary people extends but half way, there is no fact more simple and manifest, than that the death of a great man, is a
matter of very little importance. Much as we think of ourselves, and much as we may excite the empty plaudits of the
million, it is certain that the greatest among us do actually fill
but an exceeding small space in the world; and it is equally
certain, that even that small space is quickly supplied, when
we leave it vacant. "Of what consequence is it," said the elegant Pliny, "that individuals appear, or make their exit? the
world is a theatre whose scenes and actors are continually
changing." Never did philosopher speak more correctly, and
I only wonder, that so wise a remark could have existed so
many ages, and mankind not have laid it more to heart. Sage
follows on in the footsteps of sage; one hero just steps out of
his triumphant car, to make way for the hero who comes after
him; and of the proudest monarch it is merely said, that—
"he slept with his fathers, and his successor reigned in his
stead."

The world, to tell the private truth, cares but little for their
loss, and if left to itself would soon forget to grieve; and
though a nation has often been figuratively drowned in tears
on the death of a great man, yet it is ten chances to one if an
individual tear has been shed on the melancholy occasion, excepting from the forlorn pen of some hungry author. It is the
historian, the biographer, and the poet, who have the whole
burden of grief to sustain; who—unhappy varlets!—like un-
dertakers in England, act the part of chief mourners—who
inflate a nation with sighs it never heaved, and deluge it with
tears, it never dreamed of shedding. Thus while the patriotic
author is weeping and howling, in prose, in blank verse, and

in rhyme, and collecting the drops of public sorrow into his volume, as into a lachrymal vase, it is more than probable his fellow citizens are eating and drinking, fiddling and dancing; as utterly ignorant of the bitter lamentations made in their name, as are those men of straw, John Doe, and Richard Roe, of the plaintiffs for whom they are generously pleased on divers occasions to become sureties.

The most glorious and praise-worthy hero that ever desolated nations, might have mouldered into oblivion among the rubbish of his own monument, did not some kind historian take him into favour, and benevolently transmit his name to posterity—and much as the valiant William Kieft worried, and bustled, and turmoiled, while he had the destinies of a whole colony in his hand, I question seriously, whether he will not be obliged to this authentic history, for all his future celebrity.

His exit occasioned no convulsion in the city of New Amsterdam, or its vicinity: the earth trembled not, neither did any stars shoot from their spheres—the heavens were not shrowded in black, as poets would fain persuade us they have been, on the unfortunate death of a hero—the rocks (hard hearted vagabonds) melted not into tears; nor did the trees hang their heads in silent sorrow; and as to the sun, he laid abed the next night, just as long, and shewed as jolly a face when he arose, as he ever did on the same day of the month in any year, either before or since. The good people of New Amsterdam, one and all, declared that he had been a very busy, active, bustling little governor; that he was "the father of his country"—that he was "the noblest work of God"—that "he was a man, take him for all in all, they never should look upon his like again"—together with sundry other civil and affectionate speeches that are regularly said on the death of all great men; after which they smoked their pipes, thought no more about him, and Peter Stuyvesant succeeded to his station.

Peter Stuyvesant was the last, and like the renowned Wouter Van Twiller, he was also the best, of our ancient dutch governors. Wouter having surpassed all who preceded him; and Pieter, or Piet, as he was sociably called by the old dutch burghers, who were ever prone to familiarize names, having never been equalled by any successor. He was in fact the very man fitted by nature to retrieve the desperate fortunes of her beloved province, had not the fates or parcæ, Clotho, Lachesis and Atropos, those most potent, immaculate and unrelenting of all ancient and immortal spinsters, destined them to inextricable confusion.

To say merely that he was a hero would be doing him unparalleled injustice—he was in truth a combination of heroes—for he was of a sturdy, raw boned make like Ajax Telamon, so famous for his prowess in belabouring the little Trojans—with a pair of round shoulders, that Hercules would have given his hide for, (meaning his lion's hide) when he undertook to ease old Atlas of his load. He was moreover as Plutarch describes Coriolanus, not only terrible for the force of his arm, but likewise of his voice, which sounded as though it came out of a barrel; and like the self same warrior, he possessed a sovereign contempt for the sovereign people, and an iron aspect, which was enough of itself to make the very bowels of his adversaries quake with terror and dismay. All this martial excellency of appearance was inexpressibly heightened by an accidental advantage, with which I am surprised that neither Homer nor Virgil have graced any of their heroes, for it is worth all the paltry scars and wounds in the Iliad and Eneid, or Lucan's Pharsalia into the bargain. This was nothing less than a redoubtable wooden leg, which was the only prize he had gained, in bravely fighting the battles of his country; but of which he was so proud, that he was often heard to declare he valued it more than all his other limbs put together; indeed so highly did he esteem it, that he caused it to be gallantly enchased and relieved with silver devices, which caused it to be related in divers histories and legends that he wore a silver leg.*

Like that choleric warrior Achilles, he was somewhat subject to extempore bursts of passion, which were oft-times rather unpleasant to his favourites and attendants, whose perceptions he was apt to quicken, after the manner of his illustrious imitator, Peter the Great, by anointing their shoulders with his walking staff.

*See the histories of Masters Josselyn and Blome.

But the resemblance for which I most value him was that which he bore in many particulars to the renowned Charlemagne. Though I cannot find that he had read Plato, or Aristotle, or Hobbes, or Bacon, or Algernon Sydney, or Tom Paine, yet did he sometimes manifest a shrewdness and sagacity in his measures, that one would hardly expect from a man, who did not know Greek, and had never studied the ancients. True it is, and I confess it with sorrow, that he had an unreasonable aversion to experiments, and was fond of governing his province after the simplest manner—but then he contrived to keep it in better order than did the erudite Kieft, though he had all the philosophers ancient and modern, to assist and perplex him. I must likewise own that he made but very few laws, but then again he took care that those few were rigidly and impartially enforced—and I do not know but justice on the whole, was as well administered, as if there had been volumes of sage acts and statutes yearly made, and daily neglected and forgotten.

He was in fact the very reverse of his predecessors, being neither tranquil and inert like Walter the Doubter, nor restless and fidgetting, like William the Testy, but a man, or rather a governor, of such uncommon activity and decision of mind that he never sought or accepted the advice of others; depending confidently upon his single head, as did the heroes of yore upon their single arms, to work his way through all difficulties and dangers. To tell the simple truth he wanted no other requisite for a perfect statesman, than to think always right, for no one can deny that he always acted as he thought, and if he wanted in correctness he made up for it in perseverance—An excellent quality! since it is surely more dignified for a ruler to be persevering and consistent in error, than wavering and contradictory, in endeavouring to do what is right; this much is certain, and I generously make the maxim public, for the benefit of all legislators, both great and small, who stand shaking in the wind, without knowing which way to steer—a ruler who acts according to his own will is sure of pleasing himself, while he who seeks to consult the wishes and whims of others, runs a great risk of pleasing nobody. The clock that stands still, and points resolutely in one direction, is certain of being right twice in the four and twenty hours—while others may keep going continually, and continually be going wrong.

Nor did this magnanimous virtue escape the discernment of the good people of Nieuw Nederlandts; on the contrary so high an opinion had they of the independent mind and vigorous intellects of their new governor, that they universally called him *Hard-koppig Piet*, or PETER THE HEADSTRONG— a great compliment to his understanding!

If from all that I have said thou dost not gather, worthy reader, that Peter Stuyvesant was a tough, sturdy, valiant, weatherbeaten, mettlesome, leathernsided, lion hearted, generous spirited, obstinate, old "seventy six" of a governor, thou art a very numscull at drawing conclusions.

This most excellent governor, whose character I have thus attempted feebly to delineate, commenced his administration on the 29th of May 1647: a remarkably stormy day, distinguished in all the almanacks of the time, which have come down to us, by the name of *Windy Friday*. As he was very jealous of his personal and official dignity, he was inaugurated into office with great ceremony; the goodly oaken chair of the renowned Wouter Van Twiller, being carefully preserved for such occasions; in like manner as the chair and stone were reverentially preserved at Schone in Scotland, for the coronation of the caledonian monarchs.

I must not omit to mention that the tempestuous state of the elements, together with its being that unlucky day of the week, termed "hanging day," did not fail to excite much grave speculation, and divers very reasonable apprehensions, among the more ancient and enlightened inhabitants; and several of the sager sex, who were reputed to be not a little skilled in the science and mystery of astrology and fortune telling, did declare outright, that they were fearful omens of a disastrous administration—an event that came to be lamentably verified, and which proves, beyond dispute, the wisdom of attending to those preternatural intimations, furnished by dreams and visions, the flying of birds, falling of stones and cackling of geese, on which the sages and rulers of ancient times placed such judicious reliance—or to those shootings of stars, eclipses of the moon, howlings of dogs and flarings of candles, carefully noted and interpreted by the oracular old sybils of our day; who, in my humble opinion, are the legitimate possessors and preservers of the ancient science of divination. This much is certain, that governor Stuyvesant succeeded to the chair of state, at a turbulent period; when foes thronged and threatened from without; when anarchy and stiff necked opposition reigned rampant within; and when the authority of their high mightinesses the lords states general, though founded on the broad dutch bottom of unoffending imbecility; though supported by economy, and defended by speeches, protests, proclamations, flagstaffs, trumpeters and windmills—vacillated, oscillated, tottered, tumbled and was finally prostrated in the dirt, by british invaders, in much the same manner that our majestic, stupendous, butricketty shingle steeples, will some day or other be toppled about our ears by a brisk north wester.

CHAP. II.

Shewing how Peter the Headstrong bestirred himself among the rats and cobwebs on entering into office—And the perilous mistake he was guilty of, in his dealings with the Amphyctions.

THE VERY FIRST movements of the great Peter, on taking the reins of government, displayed the magnanimity of his mind, though they occasioned not a little marvel and uneasiness among the people of the Manhattoes. Finding himself constantly interrupted by the opposition and annoyed by the sage advice of his privy council, the members of which had acquired the unreasonable habit of thinking and speaking for themselves during the preceding reign; he determined at once to put a stop to such a grievous abomination. Scarcely therefore had he entered upon his authority than he kicked out of office all those meddlesome spirits that composed the factious cabinet of William the Testy, in place of whom he chose unto himself councillors from those fat, somniferous, respectable families, that had flourished and slumbered under the easy reign of Walter the Doubter. All these he caused to be furnished with abundance of fair long pipes, and to be regaled with frequent corporation dinners, admonishing them to smoke and eat and sleep for the good of the nation, while he took all the burden of government upon his own shoulders—an arrangement to which they all gave a hearty grunt of acquiescence.

Nor did he stop here, but made a hideous rout among the ingenious inventions and expedients of his learned predecessor—demolishing his flag-staffs and wind-mills, which like mighty giants, guarded the ramparts of New Amsterdam—pitching to the duyvel whole batteries of quaker guns—rooting up his patent gallows, where caitiff vagabonds were suspended by the breech, and in a word, turning topsy-turvy the whole philosophic, economic and wind-mill system of the immortal sage of Saardam.

The honest folk of New Amsterdam, began to quake now for the fate of their matchless champion Antony the trumpeter, who had acquired prodigious favour in the eyes of the women by means of his whiskers and his trumpet. Him did Peter the Headstrong, cause to be brought into his presence, and eyeing him for a moment from head to foot, with a countenance that would have appalled any thing else than a sounder of brass—"Prythee who and what art thou?" said he.— "Sire," replied the other in no wise dismayed,—"for my name, it is Antony Van Corlear—for my parentage, I am the son of my mother—for my profession I am champion and garrison of this great city of New Amsterdam."—"I doubt me much," said Peter Stuyvesant, "that thou art some scurvy costard-monger knave—how didst thou acquire this paramount honour and dignity?"—"Marry sir," replied the other, "like many a great man before me, simply *by sounding my own trumpet*."—"Aye, is it so?" quoth the governor, "why then let us have a relish of thy art." Whereupon he put his instrument to his lips and sounded a charge, with such a tremendous outset, such a delectable quaver, and such a triumphant cadence that it was enough to make your heart leap out of your mouth only to be within a mile of it. Like as a war-worn charger, while sporting in peaceful plains, if by chance he hears the strains of martial music, pricks up his ears, and snorts and paws and kindles at the noise, so did the heroic soul of the mighty Peter joy to hear the clangour of the trumpet; for of him might truly be said what was recorded of the renowned St. George of England, "there was nothing in all the world that more rejoiced his heart, than to hear the pleasant sound of war, and see the soldiers brandish forth their steeled weapons." Casting his eyes more kindly therefore, upon the sturdy Van Corlear, and finding him to be a jolly, fat little man, shrewd in his discourse, yet of great discretion and immeasurable wind, he straightway conceived an astonishing kindness for him; and discharging him from the troublesome duty of garrisoning, defending and alarming the city, ever after retained him about his person, as his chief favourite, confidential envoy and trusty squire. Instead of disturbing the city with disastrous notes, he was instructed to play so as to delight the governor, while at his repasts, as did the minstrels of yore in the days of glorious chivalry— and on all public occasions, to rejoice the ears of the people with warlike melody—thereby keeping alive a noble and martial spirit.

Many other alterations and reformations, both for the better and for the worse, did the governor make, of which my time will not serve me to record the particulars, suffice it to say, he soon contrived to make the province feel that he was its master, and treated the sovereign people with such tyrannical rigour, that they were all fain to hold their tongues, stay at home and attend to their business; insomuch that party feuds and distinctions were almost forgotten, and many thriving keepers of taverns and dram-shops, were utterly ruined for want of business.

Indeed the critical state of public affairs at this time, demanded the utmost vigilance, and promptitude. The formidable council of the Amphyctions, which had caused so much tribulation to the unfortunate Kieft, still continued augmenting its forces, and threatened to link within its union, all the mighty principalities and powers of the east. In the very year following the inauguration of governor Stuyvesant a grand deputation departed from the city of Providence (famous for its dusty streets, and beauteous women,) in behalf of the puissant plantation of Rhode Island, praying to be admitted into the league.

The following mention is made of this application in the records still extant, of that assemblage of worthies.*

"Mr. Will Cottington and captain Partridg of Rhoode Iland presented this insewing request to the commissioners in wrighting——

"Our request and motion is in behalfe of Rhoode Iland, that wee the Ilanders of Rhoode Iland may be rescauied into combination with all the united colonyes of New England in a firme and perpetuall league of friendship and amity of ofence and defence, mutuall advice and succor upon all just occasions for our mutuall safety and wellfaire, &c.

Will Cottington,
Alicxsander Partridg."

I confess the very sight of this fearful document, made me to quake for the safety of my beloved province. The name of

*Haz. Col. Stat. pap.

Alexander, however misspelt, has been warlike in every age, and though its fierceness is in some measure softened by being coupled with the gentle cognomen of Partridge, still, like the colour of scarlet, it bears an exceeding great resemblance to the sound of a trumpet. From the style of the letter, moreover, and the soldierlike ignorance of orthography displayed by the noble captain Alicxsander Partridg in spelling his own name, we may picture to ourselves this mighty man of Rhodes like a second Ajax, strong in arms, great in the field, but in other respects, (meaning no disparagement) as great a dom cop, as if he had been educated among that learned people of Thrace, who Aristotle most slanderously assures us, could not count beyond the number four.

But whatever might be the threatening aspect of this famous confederation, Peter Stuyvesant was not a man to be kept in a state of incertitude and vague apprehension; he liked nothing so much as to meet danger face to face, and take it by the beard. Determined therefore to put an end to all these petty maraudings on the borders, he wrote two or three categorical letters to the grand council, which though neither couched in bad latin, nor yet graced by rhetorical tropes about wolfs and lambs, and beetle flies, yet had more effect than all the elaborate epistles, protests and proclamations of his learned predecessor, put together. In consequence of his urgent propositions, the sage council of the amphyctions agreed to enter into a final adjustment of grievances and settlement of boundaries, to the end that a perpetual and happy peace might take place between the two powers. For this purpose governor Stuyvesant deputed two ambassadors, to negotiate with commissioners from the grand council of the league, and a treaty was solemnly concluded at Hartford. On receiving intelligence of this event, the whole community was in an uproar of exultation. The trumpet of the sturdy Van Corlear, sounded all day with joyful clangour from the ramparts of Fort Amsterdam, and at night the city was magnificently illuminated with two hundred and fifty tallow candles; besides a barrel of tar, which was burnt before the governor's house, on the cheering aspect of public affairs.

And now my worthy, but simple reader, is doubtless, like the great and good Peter, congratulating himself with the idea, that his feelings will no longer be molested by afflicting details of stolen horses, broken heads, impounded hogs, and all the other catalogue of heart-rending cruelties, that disgraced these border wars. But if my reader should indulge in such expectations, it is only another proof, among the many he has already given in the course of this work, of his utter ignorance of state affairs—and this lamentable ignorance on his part, obliges me to enter into a very profound dissertation, to which I call his attention in the next chapter—wherein I will shew that Peter Stuyvesant has already committed a great error in politics; and by effecting a peace, has materially jeopardized the tranquility of the province.

CHAP. III.

Containing divers philosophical speculations on war and ne-
gociations—and shewing that a treaty of peace is a great
national evil.

IT WAS the opinion of that poetical philosopher Lucretius,
that war was the original state of man; whom he described
as being primitively a savage beast of prey, engaged in a constant state of hostility with his own species, and that this ferocious spirit was tamed and ameliorated by society. The
same opinion has been advocated by the learned Hobbes, nor
have there been wanting a host of sage philosophers to admit
and defend it.

For my part, I am prodigiously fond of these valuable speculations so complimentary to human nature, and which are
so ingeniously calculated to make beasts of both writer and
reader; but in this instance I am inclined to take the proposition by halves, believing with old Horace,* that though war
may have been originally the favourite amusement and industrious employment of our progenitors, yet like many other
excellent habits, so far from being ameliorated, it has been
cultivated and confirmed by refinement and civilization, and
encreases in exact proportion as we approach towards that
state of perfection, which is the *ne plus ultra* of modern philosophy.

The first conflict between man and man was the mere exertion of physical force, unaided by auxiliary weapons—his
arm was his buckler, his fist was his mace, and a broken head
the catastrophe of his encounters. The battle of unassisted
strength, was succeeded by the more rugged one of stones
and clubs, and war assumed a sanguinary aspect. As man
advanced in refinement, as his faculties expanded, and his
sensibilities became more exquisite, he grew rapidly more

---

*Quum prorepserunt primis animalia terris,
 Mutum ac turpe pecus, glandem atque cubilia propter,
 Unguibus et pugnis, dein fustibus, atque ita porro
 Pugnabant armis, quæ post fabricaverat usus.

                              Hor. Sat. L. i. S 3.

ingenious and experienced, in the art of murdering his fellow
beings. He invented a thousand devices to defend and to assault—the helmet, the cuirass and the buckler; the sword, the
dart and the javelin, prepared him to elude the wound, as well
as to launch the blow. Still urging on, in the brilliant and
philanthropic career of invention, he enlarges and heightens
his powers of defence and injury—The Aries, the Scorpio,
the Balista and the Catapulta, give a horror and sublimity to
war, and magnify its glory, by encreasing its desolation. Still
insatiable; though armed with machinery that seemed to
reach the limits of destructive invention, and to yield a power
of injury, commensurate, even to the desires of revenge—still
deeper researches must be made in the diabolical arcana. With
furious zeal he dives into the bowels of the earth; he toils
midst poisonous minerals and deadly salts—the sublime discovery of gunpowder, blazes upon the world—and finally the
dreadful art of fighting by proclamation, seems to endow the
demon of war, with ubiquity and omnipotence!

By the hand of my body but this is grand!—this indeed
marks the powers of mind, and bespeaks that divine endowment of reason, which distinguishes us from the animals, our
inferiors. The unenlightened brutes content themselves with
the native force which providence has assigned them. The angry bull butts with his horns, as did his progenitors before
him—the lion, the leopard, and the tyger, seek only with
their talons and their fangs, to gratify their sanguinary fury;
and even the subtle serpent darts the same venom, and uses
the same wiles, as did his sire before the flood. Man alone,
blessed with the inventive mind, goes on from discovery to
discovery—enlarges and multiplies his powers of destruction;
arrogates the tremendous weapons of deity itself, and tasks
creation to assist him, in murdering his brother worm!

In proportion as the art of war has increased in improvement, has the art of preserving peace advanced in equal ratio.
But as I have already been very prolix to but little purpose, in
the first part of this truly philosophic chapter, I shall not fatigue my patient, but unlearned reader, in tracing the history
of the art of making peace. Suffice it to say, as we have discovered in this age of wonders and inventions, that proclamation is the most formidable engine in war, so have we

discovered the no less ingenious mode of maintaining peace by perpetual negociations.

A treaty, or to speak more correctly a negociation, therefore, according to the acceptation of your experienced statesmen, learned in these matters, is no longer an attempt to accommodate differences, to ascertain rights, and to establish an equitable exchange of kind offices; but a contest of skill between two powers, which shall over-reach and take in the other. It is a cunning endeavour to obtain by peaceful manœuvre, and the chicanery of cabinets, those advantages, which a nation would otherwise have wrested by force of arms.—In the same manner that a conscientious highwayman reforms and becomes an excellent and praiseworthy citizen contenting himself with cheating his neighbour out of that property he would formerly have seized with open violence.

In fact the only time when two nations can be said to be in a state of perfect amity, is when a negociation is open, and a treaty pending. Then as there are no stipulations entered into, no bonds to restrain the will, no specific limits to awaken that captious jealousy of right implanted in our nature, as both parties have some advantage to hope and expect from the other, then it is that the two nations are as gracious and friendly to each other, as two rogues making a bargain. Their ministers professing the highest mutual regard, exchanging billets-doux, making fine speeches and indulging in all those little diplomatic flirtations, coquetries and fondlings, that do so marvelously tickle the good humour of the respective nations. Thus it may paradoxically be said, that there is never so good an understanding between two nations, as when there is a little misunderstanding—and that so long as they are on no terms, they are on the best terms in the world!

As I am of all men in the world, particularly historians, the most candid and unassuming, I would not for an instant claim the merit of having made the above political discovery. It has in fact long been secretly acted upon by certain enlightened cabinets, and is, together with divers other notable theories, privately copied out of the common place book of an illustrious gentleman, who has been member of congress, and enjoyed the unlimited confidence of heads of department. To this principle may be ascribed the wonderful ingenuity that has been shewn of late years in protracting and interrupting negociations.—Hence the cunning measure of appointing as ambassador, some political pettifogger skilled in delays, sophisms, and misconstructions, and dexterous in the art of baffling argument—or some blundering statesman, whose stupid errors and misconstructions may be a plea for refusing to ratify his engagements. And hence too that most notable expedient, so popular with our government, of sending out a brace of ambassadors; who having each an individual will to consult, character to establish, and interest to promote, you may as well look for unanimity and concord between them, as between two lovers with one mistress, two dogs with one bone, or two naked rogues and one pair of breeches. This disagreement therefore is continually breeding delays and impediments, in consequence of which the negociation goes on swimmingly—inasmuch as there is no prospect of its ever coming to a close. Nothing is lost by these delays and obstacles but *time*, and in a negociation, according to the theory I have exposed, all time lost is in reality so much time gained— with what delightful paradoxes, does the modern arcana of political economy abound!

Now all that I have here advanced is so notoriously true, that I almost blush to take up the time of my readers, with treating of matters which must many a time have stared them in the face. But the proposition to which I would most earnestly call their attention is this, that though a negociation is the most harmonizing of all national transactions, yet a treaty of peace is a great political evil and one of the most fruitful sources of war.

I have rarely seen an instance in my time, of any special contract between individuals, that did not produce jealousies, bickerings, and often downright ruptures between them; nor did I ever know of a treaty between two nations, that did not keep them continually in hot water. How many worthy country neighbours have I known, who after living in peace and good fellowship for years, have been thrown into a state of distrust, cavilling and animosity, by some ill starred agreement about fences, runs of water, and stray cattle. And how many well meaning nations, who would otherwise have remained in the most amiable disposition towards each other, have been brought to loggerheads about the infringement, or misconstruction of some treaty, which in an evil hour they had constructed by way of making their amity more sure.

Treaties at best are but complied with so long as interest requires their fulfillment; consequently they are virtually binding on the weaker party only, or in other words, they are not really binding at all. No nation will wantonly go to war with another if it has nothing to gain thereby, and therefore needs no treaty to restrain it from violence; and if it has any thing to gain, I much question, from what I have witnessed of the righteous conduct of nations, whether any treaty could be made so strong, that it could not thrust the sword through— nay I would hold ten to one, the treaty itself, would be the very source to which resort would be had, to find a pretext for hostilities.

Thus therefore I sagely conclude—that though it is the best of all policies for a nation to keep up a constant negociation with its neighbours, it is the utmost summit of folly, for it ever to be beguiled into a treaty; for then comes on the non-fulfilment and infraction, then remonstrance, then altercation, then retaliation, then recrimination and finally open war. In a word, negociation is like courtship, a time of sweet words, gallant speeches, soft looks and endearing caresses, but the marriage ceremony is the signal for hostilities—and thus ends this very abstruse though very instructive chapter.

CHAP. IV.

*How Peter Stuyvesant was horribly belied by his adversaries
the Moss Troopers—and his conduct thereupon.*

IF my pains-taking reader, whose perception, it is a hundred
to one, is as obtuse as a beetle's, is not somewhat perplexed, in the course of the ratiocination of my last chapter;
he will doubtless, at one glance perceive, that the great Peter,
in concluding a treaty with his eastern neighbours, was guilty
of a most notable error and heterodoxy in politics. To this
unlucky agreement may justly be ascribed a world of little
infringements, altercations, negociations and bickerings,
which afterwards took place between the irreproachable Stuyvesant, and the evil disposed council of amphyctions; in all
which, with the impartial justice of an historian, I pronounce
the latter to have been invariably in the wrong. All these did
not a little disturb the constitutional serenity of the good and
substantial burghers of Mannahata—otherwise called Manhattoes, but more vulgarly known by the name of Manhattan.
But in sooth they were so very scurvy and pitiful in their
nature and effects, that a grave historian like me, who grudges
the time spent in any thing less than recording the fall of
empires, and the revolution of worlds, would think them unworthy to be recorded in his sacred page.

The reader is therefore to take it for granted, though I
scorn to waste in the detail, that time, which my furrowed
brow and trembling hand, inform me is invaluable, that all
the while the great Peter was occupied in those tremendous
and bloody contests, that I shall shortly rehearse, there was a
continued series of little, dirty, snivelling, pettifogging skirmishes, scourings, broils and maraudings made on the eastern
frontiers, by the notorious moss troopers of Connecticut. But
like that mirror of chivalry, the sage and valourous Don Quixote, I leave these petty contests for some future Sancho
Panza of an historian, while I reserve my prowess and my pen
for achievements of higher dignity.

Now did the great Peter conclude, that his labours had
come to a close in the east, and that he had nothing to do

but apply himself to the internal prosperity of his beloved Manhattoes. Though a man of great modesty, he could not help boasting that he had at length shut the temple of Janus, and that, were all rulers like a certain person who should be nameless, it would never be opened again. But the exultation of the worthy governor was put to a speedy check, for scarce was the treaty concluded, and hardly was the ink dried on the paper, before the crafty and discourteous council of the league sought a new pretence for reilluming the flames of discord.

In the year 1651, with a flagitious hardihood that makes my gorge to rise while I write, they accused the immaculate Peter—the soul of honour and heart of steel—that by divers gifts and promises he had been secretly endeavouring to instigate the Narrohigansett (or Narraganset) Mohaque and Pequot Indians, to surprize and massacre the English settlements. For, as the council maliciously observed, "the Indians round about for divers hundred miles cercute, seeme to have drunke deep of an intoxicating cupp, att or from the Monhatoes against the English, whoe have sought there good, both in bodily and sperituall respects." To support their most unrighteous accusation, they examined divers Indians, who all swore to the fact as sturdily as if they had been so many christian troopers. And to be more sure of their veracity, the knowing council previously made every mother's son of them devoutly drunk, remembering the old proverb— *In vino veritas.*

Though descended from a family which suffered much injury from the losel Yankees of those times; my great grandfather having had a yoke of oxen and his best pacer stolen, and having received a pair of black eyes and a bloody nose, in one of these border wars; and my grandfather, when a very little boy tending the pigs, having been kidnapped and severely flogged by a long sided Connecticut schoolmaster— Yet I should have passed over all these wrongs with forgiveness and oblivion—I could even have suffered them to have broken Evert Ducking's head, to have kicked the doughty Jacobus Van Curlet and his ragged regiment out of doors, carried every hog into captivity, and depopulated every hen roost, on the face of the earth with perfect impunity—But this wanton, wicked and unparalleled attack, upon one of the most gallant and irreproachable heroes of modern times, is too much even for me to digest, and has overset, with a single puff, the patience of the historian and the forbearance of the Dutchman.

Oh reader it was false!—I swear to thee it was false!—if thou hast any respect for my word—if the undeviating and unimpeached character for veracity, which I have hitherto borne throughout this work, has its due weight with thee, thou wilt not give thy faith to this tale of slander; for I pledge my honour and my immortal fame to thee, that the gallant Peter Stuyvesant, was not only innocent of this foul conspiracy, but would have suffered his right arm, or even his wooden leg to consume with slow and everlasting flames, rather than attempt to destroy his enemies in any other way, than open generous warfare—Beshrew those caitiff scouts, that conspired to sully his honest name by such an imputation!

Peter Stuyvesant, though he perhaps had never heard of a Knight Errant; yet had he as true a heart of chivalry as ever beat at the round table of King Arthur. There was a spirit of native gallantry, a noble and generous hardihood diffused through his rugged manners, which altogether gave unquestionable tokens of an heroic mind. He was, in truth, a hero of chivalry struck off by the hand of nature at a single heat, and though she had taken no further care to polish and refine her workmanship, he stood forth a miracle of her skill.

But not to be figurative, (a fault in historic writing which I particularly eschew) the great Peter possessed in an eminent degree, the seven renowned and noble virtues of knighthood; which, as he had never consulted authors, in the disciplining and cultivating of his mind, I verily believe must have been stowed away in a corner of his heart by dame nature herself— where they flourished, among his hardy qualities, like so many sweet wild flowers, shooting forth and thriving with redundant luxuriance among stubborn rocks. Such was the mind of Peter the Headstrong, and if my admiration for it, has on this occasion, transported my style beyond the sober gravity which becomes the laborious scribe of historic events, I can plead as an apology, that though a little, grey headed

Dutchman, arrived almost at the bottom of the down-hill of life, I still retain some portion of that celestial fire, which sparkles in the eye of youth, when contemplating the virtues and atchievements of ancient worthies. Blessed, thrice and nine times blessed, be the good St. Nicholas—that I have escaped the influence of that chilling apathy, which too often freezes the sympathies of age; which like a churlish spirit, sits at the portals of the heart, repulsing every genial sentiment, and paralyzing every spontaneous glow of enthusiasm.

No sooner then, did this scoundrel imputation on his honour reach the ear of Peter Stuyvesant, than he proceeded in a manner which would have redounded to his credit, even if he had studied for years, in the library of Don Quixote himself. He immediately dispatched his valiant trumpeter and squire, Antony Van Corlear, with orders to ride night and day, as herald, to the Amphyctionic council, reproaching them in terms of noble indignation, for giving ear to the slanders of heathen infidels, against the character of a Christian, a gentleman and a soldier—and declaring, that as to the treacherous and bloody plot alledged against him, whoever affirmed it to be true, he lied in his teeth!—to prove which he defied the president of the council and all of his compeers, or if they pleased, their puissant champion, captain Alicxsander Partridg that mighty man of Rhodes, to meet him in single combat, where he would trust the vindication of his innocence to the prowess of his arm.

This challenge being delivered with due ceremony, Antony Van Corlear sounded a trumpet of defiance before the whole council, ending with a most horrific and nasal twang, full in the face of captain Partridg, who almost jumped out of his skin in an extacy of astonishment, at the noise. This done he mounted a tall Flanders mare, which he always rode, and trotted merrily towards the Manhattoes—passing through Hartford, and Pyquag and Middletown and all the other border towns—twanging his trumpet like a very devil, so that the sweet vallies and banks of the Connecticut resounded with the warlike melody—and stopping occasionally to eat pumpkin pies, dance at country frolicks, and bundle with the beauteous lasses of those parts—whom he rejoiced exceedingly with his soul stirring instrument.

But the grand council being composed of considerate men, had no idea of running a tilting with such a fiery hero as the hardy Peter—on the contrary they sent him an answer, couched in the meekest, the most mild and provoking terms, in which they assured him that his guilt was proved to their perfect satisfaction, by the testimony of divers sage and respectable Indians, and concluding with this truly amiable paragraph.—"For youer confidant denialls of the Barbarous plott charged, will waigh little in ballance against such evidence, soe that we must still require and seeke due satisfaction and cecuritie, soe we rest,

Sir,

Youres in wayes of Righteousness, &c."

I am conscious that the above transaction has been differently recorded by certain historians of the east, and elsewhere; who seem to have inherited the bitter enmity of their ancestors to the brave Peter—and much good may their inheritance do them. These moss troopers in literature, whom I regard with sovereign scorn, as mere vampers up of vulgar prejudices and fabulous legends, declare, that Peter Stuyvesant requested to have the charges against him, enquired into, by commissioners to be appointed for the purpose; and yet that when such commissioners were appointed, he refused to submit to their examination. Now this is partly true—he did indeed, most gallantly offer, when that he found a deaf ear was turned to his challenge, to submit his conduct to the rigorous inspection of a court of honour—but then he expected to find it an august tribunal, composed of courteous gentlemen, the governors and nobility, of the confederate plantations, and of the province of New Netherlands; where he might be tried by his peers, in a manner worthy of his rank and dignity—whereas, let me perish, if they did not send on to the Manhattoes two lean sided hungry pettifoggers, mounted on Narraganset pacers, with saddle bags under their bottoms, and green satchels under their arms, as if they were about to beat the hoof from one county court to another—in search of a law suit.

The chivalric Peter, as well he might, took no notice of these cunning varlets; who with professional industry fell to prying and sifting about, in quest of *ex parte* evidence; bothering and perplexing divers simple Indians and old women, with their cross questioning, until they contradicted and forswore themselves most horribly—as is every day done in our courts of justice. Thus having dispatched their errand to their full satisfaction, they returned to the grand council with their satchels and saddle-bags stuffed full of the most scurvy rumours, apocryphal stories and outrageous heresies, that ever were heard—for all which the great Peter did not care a tobacco stopper; but I warrant me had they attempted to play off the same trick upon William the Testy, he would have treated them both to an ærial gambol on his patent gallows.

The grand council of the east, held a very solemn meeting on the return of their envoys, and after they had pondered a long time on the situation of affairs, were upon the point of adjourning without being able to agree upon anything. At this critical moment one of those little, meddlesome, indefatigable spirits, who endeavour to establish a character for patriotism by blowing the bellows of party, until the whole furnace of politics is red-hot with sparks and cinders—and who have just cunning enough to know, that there is no time so favourable for getting on the people's backs, as when they are in a state of turmoil, and attending to every body's business but their own—This aspiring imp of faction, who was called a great politician, because he had secured a seat in council by calumniating all his opponents—He I say, conceived this a fit opportunity to strike a blow that should secure his popularity among his constituents, who lived on the borders of Nieuw Nederlandt, and were the greatest poachers in Christendom, excepting the Scotch border nobles. Like a second Peter the hermit, therefore, he stood forth and preached up a crusade against Peter Stuyvesant, and his devoted city.

He made a speech which lasted three days, according to the ancient custom in these parts, in which he represented the dutch as a race of impious heretics, who neither believed in witchcraft, nor the sovereign virtues of horse shoes—who, left their country for the lucre of gain, not like themselves for the enjoyment of *liberty of conscience*—who, in short, were a race of mere cannibals and anthropophagi, inasmuch as they never eat cod-fish on saturdays, devoured swine's flesh without molasses, and held pumpkins in utter contempt.

This speech had the desired effect, for the council, being awakened by their serjeant at arms, rubbed their eyes, and declared that it was just and politic to declare instant war against these unchristian anti-pumpkinites. But it was necessary that the people at large should first be prepared for this measure, and for this purpose the arguments of the little orator were earnestly preached from the pulpit for several sundays subsequent, and earnestly recommended to the consideration of every good Christian, who professed, as well as practised the doctrine of meekness, charity, and the forgiveness of injuries. This is the first time we hear of the "Drum Ecclesiastic" beating up for political recruits in our country; and it proved of such signal efficacy, that it has since been called into frequent service throughout our union. A cunning politician is often found skulking under the clerical robe, with an outside all religion, and an inside all political rancour. Things spiritual and things temporal are strangely jumbled together, like poisons and antidotes on an apothecary's shelf, and instead of a devout sermon, the simple church-going folk, have often a political pamphlet, thrust down their throats, labeled with a pious text from Scripture.

CHAP. V.

How the New Amsterdammers became great in arms, and of the direful catastrophe of a mighty army—together with Peter Stuyvesant's measures to fortify the City—and how he was the original founder of the Battery.

B UT NOTWITHSTANDING that the grand council, as I have already shewn, were amazingly discreet in their proceedings respecting the New Netherlands, and conducted the whole with almost as much silence and mystery, as does the sage British cabinet one of its ill star'd *secret expeditions*—yet did the ever watchful Peter receive as full and accurate information of every movement, as does the court of France of all the notable enterprises I have mentioned.—He accordingly set himself to work, to render the machinations of his bitter adversaries abortive.

I know that many will censure the precipitation of this stout hearted old governor, in that he hurried into the expenses of fortification, without ascertaining whether they were necessary, by prudently waiting until the enemy was at the door. But they should recollect Peter Stuyvesant had not the benefit of an insight into the modern arcana of politics, and was strangely bigotted to certain obsolete maxims of the old school; among which he firmly believed, that, to render a country respected abroad, it was necessary to make it formidable at home—and that a nation should place its reliance for peace and security, more upon its own strength, than on the justice or good will of its neighbours.—He proceeded therefore, with all diligence, to put the province and metropolis in a strong posture of defence.

Among the few remnants of ingenious inventions which remained from the days of William the Testy, were those impregnable bulwarks of public safety, militia laws; by which the inhabitants were obliged to turn out twice a year, with such military equipments—as it pleased God; and were put under the command of very valiant taylors, and man milliners, who though on ordinary occasions, the meekest, pippen-hearted little men in the world, were very devils at parades and court-martials, when they had cocked hats on their heads, and swords by their sides. Under the instructions of these periodical warriors, the gallant train bands made marvellous proficiency in the mystery of gun-powder. They were taught to face to the right, to wheel to the left, to snap off empty firelocks without winking, to turn a corner without any great uproar or irregularity, and to march through sun and rain from one end of the town to the other without flinching—until in the end they became so valourous that they fired off blank cartridges, without so much as turning away their heads—could hear the largest field piece discharged, without stopping their ears or falling into much confusion—and would even go through all the fatigues and perils of a summer day's parade, without having their ranks much thinned by desertion!

True it is, the genius of this truly pacific people was so little given to war, that during the intervals which occurred between field days, they generally contrived to forget all the military tuition they had received; so that when they re-appeared on parade, they scarcely knew the butt end of the musket from the muzzle, and invariably mistook the right shoulder for the left—a mistake which however was soon obviated by shrewdly chalking their left arms. But whatever might be their blunders and aukwardness, the sagacious Kieft, declared them to be of but little importance—since, as he judiciously observed, one campaign would be of more instruction to them than a hundred parades; for though two-thirds of them might be food for powder, yet such of the other third as did not run away, would become most experienced veterans.

The great Stuyvesant had no particular veneration for the ingenious experiments and institutions of his shrewd predecessor, and among other things, held the militia system in very considerable contempt, which he was often heard to call in joke—for he was sometimes fond of a joke—governor Kieft's broken reed. As, however, the present emergency was pressing, he was obliged to avail himself of such means of defence as were next at hand, and accordingly appointed a general inspection and parade of the train bands. But oh! Mars and Bellona, and all ye other powers of war, both great and small, what a turning out was here!—Here came men without officers, and officers without men—long fowling pieces, and short blunderbusses—muskets of all sorts and sizes, some without bayonets, others without locks, others without stocks, and many without lock, stock, or barrel.— Cartridge-boxes, shot belts, powder-horns, swords, hatchets, snicker-snees, crow-bars, and broomsticks, all mingled higgledy, piggledy—like one of our continental armies at the breaking out of the revolution.

The sturdy Peter eyed this ragged regiment with some such rueful aspect, as a man would eye the devil; but knowing, like a wise man, that all he had to do was to make the best out of a bad bargain, he determined to give his heroes a seasoning. Having therefore drilled them through the manual exercise over and over again, he ordered the fifes to strike up a quick march, and trudged his sturdy boots backwards and forwards, about the streets of New Amsterdam, and the fields adjacent, till I warrant me, their short legs ached, and their fat sides sweated again. But this was not all; the martial spirit of the old governor caught fire from the sprightly music of the fife, and he resolved to try the mettle of his troops, and give them a taste of the hardships of iron war. To this end he encamped them as the shades of evening fell, upon a hill formerly called Bunker's hill, at some distance from the town, with a full intention of initiating them into the discipline of camps, and of renewing the next day, the toils and perils of the field. But so it came to pass, that in the night there fell a great and heavy rain, which descended in torrents upon the camp, and the mighty army of swing tails strangely melted away before it; so that when Gaffer Phœbus came to shed his morning beams upon the place, saving Peter Stuyvesant and his trumpeter Van Corlear, scarce one was to be found of all the multitude, that had taken roost there the night before.

This awful dissolution of his army would have appalled a commander of less nerve than Peter Stuyvesant; but he considered it as a matter of but small importance, though he thenceforward regarded the militia system with ten times greater contempt than ever, and took care to provide himself with a good garrison of chosen men, whom he kept in pay, of whom he boasted that they at least possessed the quality, indispensible in soldiers, of being *water proof*.

The next care of the vigilant Stuyvesant, was to strengthen and fortify New Amsterdam. For this purpose he reared a substantial barrier that reached across the island from river to river, being the distance of a full half a mile!—a most stupendous work, and scarcely to be rivalled in the opinion of the old inhabitants, by the great wall of China, or the Roman wall erected in Great Britain against the incursions of the Scots, or the wall of brass that Dr. Faustus proposed to build round Germany, by the aid of the devil.

The materials of which this wall was constructed are differently described, but from a majority of opinions I am inclined to believe that it was a picket fence of especial good pine posts, intended to protect the city, not merely from the sudden invasions of foreign enemies, but likewise from the incursions of the neighbouring Indians.

Some traditions it is true, have ascribed the building of this wall to a later period, but they are wholly incorrect; for a memorandum in the Stuyvesant manuscript, dated towards the middle of the governor's reign, mentions this wall particularly, as a very strong and curious piece of workmanship, and the admiration of all the savages in the neighbourhood. And it mentions moreover the alarming circumstance of a drove of stray cows, breaking through the grand wall of a dark night; by which the whole community of New Amsterdam was thrown into as great panic, as were the people of Rome, by the sudden irruptions of the Gauls, or the valiant citizens of Philadelphia, during the time of our revolution, by a fleet of empty kegs floating down the Delaware.*

But the vigilance of the governor was more especially manifested by an additional fortification which he erected as an out work to fort Amsterdam, to protect the sea bord, or water edge. I have ascertained by the most painful and minute investigation, that it was neither fortified according to the

*In an antique view of Nieuw Amsterdam, taken some few years after the above period, is an accurate representation of this wall, which stretched along the course of *Wall-street*, so called in commemoration of this great bulwark. One gate, called the *Land-poort* opened upon Broadway, hard by where at present stands the Trinity Church; and another called the *Water-poort*, stood about where the Tontine coffee house is at present—opening upon *Smits Vleye*, or as it is commonly called Smith fly; then a marshy valley, with a creek or inlet, extending up what we call maiden lane.

method of Evrard de Bar-le-duc, that earliest inventor of complete system; the dutch plan of Marollois; the French method invented by Antoine de Ville; the Flemish of Stevin de Bruges; the Polish of Adam de Treitach, or the Italian of Sardi.

He did not pursue either of the three systems of Pagan; the three of Vauban; the three of Scheiter; the three of Coehorn, that illustrious dutchman, who adapted all his plans to the defence of low and marshy countries—or the hundred and sixty methods, laid down by Francisco Marchi of Bologna.

The fortification did not consist of a Polygon, inscribed in a circle, according to Alain Manesson Maillet; nor with four long batteries, agreeably to the expensive system of Blondel; nor with the *fortification a rebours* of Dona Rosetti, nor the *Caponiere Couverte*, of the ingenious St. Julien; nor with angular polygons and numerous casemates, as recommended by Antoine d'Herbert; who served under the duke of Wirtemberg, grandfather to the second wife, and first queen of Jerome Bonaparte—otherwise called Jerry Sneak.

It was neither furnished with bastions, fashioned after the original invention of Zisca, the Bohemian; nor those used by Achmet Bassa, at Otranto in 1480; nor those recommended by San Micheli of Verona; neither those of triangular form, treated of by Specle, the high dutch engineer of Strasbourg, or the famous wooden bastions, since erected in this renowned city, the destruction of which, is recorded in a former chapter. In fact governor Stuyvesant, like the celebrated Montalembert, held bastions in absolute contempt; yet did he not like him substitute a *tenaille angulaire des polygons à ailerons*.

He did not make use of Myrtella towers, as are now erecting at Quebec; neither did he erect flagstaffs and windmills as was done by his illustrious predecessor of Saardam; nor did he employ circular castellated towers, or batteries with two tier of heavy artillery, and a third of columbiads on the top; as are now erecting for the defence of this defenceless city.

My readers will perhaps be surprized, that out of so many systems, governor Stuyvesant should find none to suit him; this may be tolerably accounted for, by the simple fact, that many of them were unfortunately invented long since his time; and as to the rest, he was as ignorant of them, as the child that never was and never will be born. In truth, it is more than probable, that had they all been spread before him, with as many more into the bargain; that same peculiarity of mind, that acquired him the name of Hard-koppig Piet, would have induced him to follow his own plans, in preference to them all. In a word, he pursued no system either past, present or to come; he equally disdained to imitate his predecessors, of whom he had never heard—his contemporaries, whom he did not know; or his unborn successors, whom, to say the truth, he never once thought of in his whole life. His great and capacious mind was convinced, that the simplest method is often the most efficient and certainly the most expeditious, he therefore fortified the water edge with a formidable mud breast work, solidly faced, after the manner of the dutch ovens common in those days, with clam shells.

These frowning bulwarks in process of time, came to be pleasantly overrun by a verdant carpet of grass and clover, and their high embankments overshadowed by wide spreading sycamores, among whose foliage the little birds sported about, making the air to resound with their joyous notes. The old burghers would repair of an afternoon to smoke their pipes under the shade of their branches, contemplating the golden sun as he gradually sunk into the west an emblem of that tranquil end toward which themselves were hastening—while the young men and the damsels of the town would take many a moonlight stroll among these favourite haunts, watching the silver beams of chaste Cynthia, tremble along the calm bosom of the bay, or light up the white sail of some gliding bark, and interchanging the honest vows of constant affection. Such was the origin of that renowned walk, *the Battery*, which though ostensibly devoted to the purposes of war, has ever been consecrated to the sweet delights of peace. The favourite walk of declining age—the healthful resort of the feeble invalid—the sunday refreshment of the dusty tradesman—the scene of many a boyish gambol—the rendezvous of many a tender assignation—the comfort of the citizen—the ornament of New York, and the pride of the lovely island of Mannahata.

CHAP. VI.

How the people of the east country were suddenly afflicted with a diabolical evil—and their judicious measures for the extirpation thereof.

HAVING thus provided for the temporary security of New Amsterdam, and guarded it against any sudden surprise, the gallant Peter took a hearty pinch of snuff, and snapping his fingers, set the great council of Amphyctions, and their champion, the doughty Alicxsander Partridg at defiance. It is impossible to say, notwithstanding, what might have been the issue of this affair, had not the great council been all at once involved in huge perplexity, and as much horrible dissension sown among its members, as of yore was stirred up in the camp of the brawling warriors of Greece.

The all potent council of the league, as I have shewn in my last chapter, had already announced its hostile determinations, and already was the mighty colony of New Haven and the puissant town of Pyquag, otherwise called Wethersfield—famous for its onions and its witches—and the great trading house of Hartford, and all the other redoubtable little border towns, in a prodigious turmoil, furbishing up their rusty fowling pieces and shouting aloud for war; by which they anticipated easy conquests, and gorgeous spoils, from the little fat dutch villages. But this joyous brawling was soon silenced by the conduct of the colony of Massachusetts. Struck with the gallant spirit of the brave old Peter, and convinced by the chivalric frankness and heroic warmth of his vindication, they refused to believe him guilty of the infamous plot most wrongfully laid at his door. With a generosity for which I would yield them immortal honour, they declared, that no determination of the grand council of the league, should bind the general court of Massachusetts, to join in an offensive war, which should appear to such general court to be unjust.*

This refusal immediately involved the colony of Massachu-

*Haz. Col. S. Pap.

setts and the other combined colonies, in very serious difficulties and disputes, and would no doubt have produced a
dissolution of the confederacy, but that the great council of
Amphyctions, finding that they could not stand alone, if mutilated by the loss of so important a member as Massachusetts, were fain to abandon for the present their hostile
machinations against the Manhattoes. Such is the marvellous
energy and puissance of those notable confederacies, composed of a number of sturdy, self-will'd, discordant parts,
loosely banded together by a puny general government. As it
is however, the warlike towns of Connecticut, had no cause
to deplore this disappointment of their martial ardour; for
by my faith—though the combined powers of the league
might have been too potent in the end, for the robustious
warriors of the Manhattoes—yet in the interim would the
lion hearted Peter and his myrmidons, have choaked the
stomachful heroes of Pyquag with their own onions, and
have given the other little border towns such a scouring,
that I warrant they would have had no stomach to squat on
the land, or invade the hen-roost of a New Nederlander for
a century to come.

Indeed there was more than one cause to divert the attention of the good people of the east, from their hostile purposes; for just about this time were they horribly beleagured
and harassed by the inroads of the prince of darkness, divers
of whose liege subjects they detected, lurking within their
camp, all of whom they incontinently roasted as so many
spies, and dangerous enemies. Not to speak in parables, we
are informed, that at this juncture, the unfortunate "east
countrie" was exceedingly troubled and confounded by multitudes of losel witches, who wrought strange devices to
beguile and distress the multitude; and notwithstanding numerous judicious and bloody laws had been enacted, against
all "solem conversing or compacting with the divil, by way of
conjuracon or the like,"* yet did the dark crime of witchcraft
continue to encrease to an alarming degree, that would almost transcend belief, were not the fact too well authenticated to be even doubted for an instant.

*New Plymouth record.

What is particularly worthy of admiration is, that this terrible art, which so long has baffled the painful researches, and abstruse studies of philosophers, astrologers, alchymists, theurgists and other sages, was chiefly confined to the most ignorant, decrepid, ugly, abominable old women in the community, who had scarcely more brains than the broomsticks they rode upon. Where they first acquired their infernal education—whether from the works of the ancient Theurgists—the demonology of the Egyptians—the belomancy, or divination by arrows of the Scythians—the spectrology of the Germans—the magic of the Persians—the enchantment of the Laplanders, or from the archives of the dark and mysterious caverns of the Dom Daniel, is a question pregnant with a host of learned and ingenious doubts—particularly as most of them were totally unversed in the occult mysteries of the alphabet.

When once an alarm is sounded, the public, who love dearly to be in a panic, are not long in want of proofs to support it—raise but the cry of yellow fever, and immediately every head-ache, and indigestion, and overflowing of the bile is pronounced the terrible epidemic—In like manner in the present instance, whoever was troubled with a cholic or lumbago, was sure to be bewitched, and woe to any unlucky old woman that lived in his neighbourhood. Such a howling abomination could not be suffered to remain long unnoticed, and it accordingly soon attracted the fiery indignation of the sober and reflective part of the community—more especially of those, who, whilome, had evinced so much active benevolence in the conversion of quakers and anabaptists. The grand council of the amphyctions publicly set their faces against so deadly and dangerous a sin, and a severe scrutiny took place after those nefarious witches, who were easily detected by devil's pinches, black cats, broomsticks, and the circumstance of their only being able to weep three tears, and those out of the left eye.

It is incredible the number of offences that were detected, "for every one of which," says the profound and reverend Cotton Mather, in that excellent work, the history of New England—"we have such a sufficient evidence, that no reasonable man in this whole country ever did question them; *and it will be unreasonable to do it in any other.*"*

Indeed, that authentic and judicious historian John Josselyn, Gent. furnishes us with unquestionable facts on this subject. "There are none," observes he, "that beg in this country, but there be witches too many—bottle bellied witches and others, that produce many strange apparitions, if you will believe report of a shalop at sea manned with women—and of a ship and great red horse standing by the main mast; the ship being in a small cove to the eastward vanished of a sudden," &c.

The number of delinquents, however, and their magical devices, were not more remarkable than their diabolical obstinacy. Though exhorted in the most solemn, persuasive and affectionate manner, to confess themselves guilty, and be burnt for the good of religion, and the entertainment of the public; yet did they most pertinaciously persist in asserting their innocence. Such incredible obstinacy was in itself deserving of immediate punishment, and was sufficient proof, if proof were necessary, that they were in league with the devil, who is perverseness itself. But their judges were just and merciful, and were determined to punish none that were not convicted on the best of testimony; not that they needed any evidence to satisfy their own minds, for, like true and experienced judges their minds were perfectly made up, and they were thoroughly satisfied of the guilt of the prisoners before they proceeded to try them; but still something was necessary to convince the community at large—to quiet those prying quid nuncs who should come after them—in short, the world must be satisfied. Oh the world—the world!—all the world knows the world of trouble the world is eternally occasioning!—The worthy judges therefore, like myself in this most authentic, minute and satisfactory of all histories, were driven to the necessity of sifting, detecting and making evident as noon day, matters which were at the commencement all clearly understood and firmly decided upon in their own own pericraniums—so that it may truly be said, that the witches were burnt, to gratify the populace of the day—but were

*Mather's hist. N. Eng B. 6. ch. 7.

tried for the satisfaction of the whole world that should come after them!

Finding therefore that neither exhortation, sound reason, nor friendly entreaty had any avail on these hardened offenders, they resorted to the more urgent arguments of the torture, and having thus absolutely wrung the truth from their stubborn lips—they condemned them to undergo the roasting due unto the heinous crimes they had confessed. Some even carried their perverseness so far, as to expire under the torture, protesting their innocence to the last; but these were looked upon as thoroughly and absolutely possessed, and governed by the devil, and the pious bye-standers, only lamented that they had not lived a little longer, to have perished in the flames.

In the city of Ephesus, we are told, that the plague was expelled by stoning a ragged old beggar to death, whom Appolonius pointed out as being the evil spirit that caused it, and who actually shewed himself to be a demon, by changing into a shagged dog. In like manner, and by measures equally sagacious, a salutary check was given to this growing evil. The witches were all burnt, banished or panic struck, and in a little while there was not an ugly old woman to be found throughout New England—which is doubtless one reason why all their young women are so handsome. Those honest folk who had suffered from their incantations gradually recovered, excepting such as had been afflicted with twitches and aches, which, however assumed the less alarming aspects of rheumatisms, sciatics and lumbagos—and the good people of New England, abandoning the study of the occult sciences, turned their attention to the more profitable hocus pocus of trade, and soon became expert in the legerdemain art of turning a penny. Still however, a tinge of the old leaven is discernable, even unto this day, in their characters—witches occasionally start up among them in different disguises, as physicians, civilians, and divines. The people at large shew a 'cuteness, a cleverness, and a profundity of wisdom, that savours strongly of witchcraft—and it has been remarked, that whenever any stones fall from the moon, the greater part of them are sure to tumble into New England!

CHAP. VII.

*Which records the rise and renown of a valiant commander,
shewing that a man, like a bladder, may be puffed up to
greatness and importance, by mere wind.*

WHEN TREATING of these tempestuous times, the unknown writer of the Stuyvesant manuscript, breaks out
into a vehement apostrophe, in praise of the good St. Nicholas; to whose protecting care he entirely ascribes the strange
dissentions that broke out in the council of the amphyctions,
and the direful witchcraft that prevailed in the east country—
whereby the hostile machinations against the Nederlanders
were for a time frustrated, and his favourite city of New Amsterdam, preserved from imminent peril and deadly warfare.
Darkness and lowering superstition hung over the fair valleys
of the east; the pleasant banks of the Connecticut, no longer
echoed with the sounds of rustic gaiety; direful phantoms
and portentous apparitions were seen in the air—gliding
spectrums haunted every wild brook and dreary glen—
strange voices, made by viewless forms, were heard in desart solitudes—and the border towns were so occupied in
detecting and punishing the knowing old women, that had
produced these alarming appearances, that for a while the
province of New Nederlandt and its inhabitants were totally
forgotten.

The great Peter therefore, finding that nothing was to be
immediately apprehended from his eastern neighbours,
turned himself about with a praiseworthy vigilance that ever
distinguished him, to put a stop to the insults of the Swedes.
These lossel freebooters my attentive reader will recollect had
begun to be very troublesome towards the latter part of the
reign of William the Testy, having set the proclamations of
that doughty little governor at naught, and put the intrepid
Jan Jansen Alpendam to a perfect non plus!

Peter Stuyvesant, however, as has already been shewn, was
a governor of different habits and turn of mind—without
more ado he immediately issued orders for raising a corps of
troops to be stationed on the southern frontier, under the

command of brigadier general Jacobus Von Poffenburgh. This illustrious warrior had risen to great importance during the reign of Wilhelmus Kieft, and if histories speak true, was second in command to the gallant Van Curlet, when he and his ragged regiment were inhumanly kicked out of Fort Good Hope by the Yankees. In consequence of having been in such a "memorable affair," and of having received more wounds on a certain honourable part that shall be nameless, than any of his comrades, he was ever after considered as a hero, who had "seen some service." Certain it is, he enjoyed the unlimited confidence and friendship of William the Testy; who would sit for hours and listen with wonder to his gunpowder narratives of surprising victories—he had never gained: and dreadful battles—from which he had run away; and the governor was once heard to declare that had he lived in ancient times, he might unquestionably have claimed the armour of Achilles—being not merely like Ajax, a mighty blustering man of battle, but in the cabinet a second Ulysses, that is to say, very valiant of speech and long winded—all which, as nobody in New Amsterdam knew aught of the ancient heroes in question, passed totally uncontradicted.

It was tropically observed by honest old Socrates, of henpecked memory, that heaven had infused into some men at their birth a portion of intellectual gold; into others of intellectual silver; while others were bounteously furnished out with abundance of brass and iron—now of this last class was undoubtedly the great general Von Poffenburgh, and from the great display he continually made, I am inclined to think that dame nature, who will sometimes be partial, had blessed him with enough of those valuable materials to have fitted up a dozen ordinary braziers. But what is most to be admired is, that he contrived to pass off all his brass and copper upon Wilhelmus Kieft, who was no great judge of base coin, as pure and genuine gold. The consequence was, that upon the resignation of Jacobus Van Curlet, who after the loss of fort Goed Hoop retired like a veteran general, to live under the shade of his laurels, the mighty "copper captain" was promoted to his station. This he filled with great importance, always styling himself "commander in chief of the armies of the New Netherlands;" though to tell the truth the armies, or rather army, consisted of a handful of half uniformed, hen stealing, bottle bruizing raggamuffins.

Such was the character of the warrior appointed by Peter Stuyvesant to defend his southern frontier, nor may it be uninteresting to my reader to have a glimpse of his person. He was not very tall, but notwithstanding, a huge, full bodied man, whose size did not so much arise from his being fat, as windy; being so completely inflated with his own importance, that he resembled one of those puffed up bags of wind, which old Eolus, in an incredible fit of generosity, gave to that vagabond warrior Ulysses.

His dress comported with his character, for he had almost as much brass and copper without, as nature had stored away within—His coat was crossed and slashed, and carbonadoed, with stripes of copper lace, and swathed round the body with a crimson sash, of a size and texture of a fishing net, doubtless to keep his valiant heart from bursting through his ribs. His head and whiskers were profusely powdered, from the midst of which his full blooded face glowed like a fiery furnace; and his magnanimous soul seemed ready to bounce out at a pair of large glassy blinking eyes, which projected like those of a lobster.

I swear to thee, worthy reader, if report belie not this great general, I would give half my fortune (which at this moment is not enough to pay the bill of my landlord) to have seen him accoutered cap-a-pie, in martial array—booted to the middle—sashed to the chin—collared to the ears—whiskered to the muzzle—crowned with an overshadowing cocked-hat, and girded with a leathern belt ten inches broad, from which trailed a faulchion of a length that I dare not mention.

Thus equipped, he strutted about, as bitter looking a man of war as the far-famed More of More Hall, when he sallied forth, armed at all points, to slay the Dragon of Wantley—

> "Had you but seen him in this dress
>   How fierce he look'd and how big;
> You would have thought him for to be
>   Some Egyptian Porcupig.
>
> He frighted all, cats, dogs and all,
>   Each cow, each horse, and each hog;

> For fear they did flee, for they took him to be
> Some strange outlandish hedge hog."*

Notwithstanding all the great endowments and transcendent qualities of this renowned general, I must confess he was not exactly the kind of man that the gallant Peter the Headstrong would have chosen to command his troops—but the truth is, that in those days the province did not abound, as at present, in great military characters; who like so many Cincinnatuses people every little village—marshalling out cabbages, instead of soldiers, and signalizing themselves in the corn field, instead of the field of battle. Who have surrendered the toils of war, for the more useful but inglorious arts of peace, and so blended the laurel with the olive, that you may have a general for a landlord, a colonel for a stage driver, and your horse shod by a valiant "captain of volunteers"—Neither had the great Stuyvesant an opportunity of choosing, like modern rulers, from a loyal band of editors of newspapers—no mention being made in the histories of the times, of any such class of mercenaries, being retained in pay by government, either as trumpeters, champions, or body guards. The redoubtable general Von Poffenburgh, therefore, was appointed to the command of the new levied troops; chiefly because there were no competitors for the station, and partly because it would have been a breach of military etiquette, to have appointed a younger officer over his head—an injustice, which the great Peter would rather have died than have committed.

No sooner did this thrice valiant copper captain receive marching orders, than he conducted his army undauntedly to the southern frontier; through wild lands and savage deserts; over insurmountable mountains, across impassable floods and through impenetrable forests; subduing a vast tract of uninhabited country, and overturning, discomfiting and making incredible slaughter of certain hostile hosts of grass-hoppers, toads and pismires, which had gathered together to oppose his progress—an achievement unequalled in the pages of history, save by the farfamed retreat of old Xenophon and his ten thousand Grecians. All this accomplished, he established on the South (or Delaware) river, a redoubtable redoubt, named FORT CASIMER, in honour of a favourite pair of brim-

*Ballad of Drag. of Want.

stone coloured trunk breeches of the governor's. As this fort
will be found to give rise to very important and interesting
events, it may be worth while to notice that it was afterwards
called Nieuw Amstel, and was the original germ of the present flourishing town of NEW CASTLE, an appellation erroneously substituted for *No Castle*, there neither being, nor
ever having been a castle, or any thing of the kind upon the
premises.

The Swedes did not suffer tamely this menacing movement
of the Nederlanders; on the contrary Jan Printz, at that time
governor of New Sweden, issued a sturdy protest against
what he termed an encroachment upon his jurisdiction.—But
the valiant Von Poffenburgh had become too well versed in
the nature of proclamations and protests, while he served under William the Testy, to be in any wise daunted by such
paper warfare. His fortress being finished, it would have done
any man's heart good to behold into what a magnitude he
immediately swelled. He would stride in and out a dozen
times a day, surveying it in front and in rear; on this side and
on that.—Then would he dress himself in full regimentals,
and strut backwards and forwards, for hours together, on the
top of his little rampart—like a vain glorious cock pidgeon
vapouring on the top of his coop. In a word, unless my readers have noticed, with curious eye, the petty commander of a
little, snivelling, military post, swelling with all the vanity of
new regimentals, and the pomposity derived from commanding a handful of tatterdemalions, I despair of giving them
any adequate idea of the prodigious dignity of general Von
Poffenburgh.

It is recorded in the delectable romance of Pierce Forest,
that a young knight being dubbed by king Alexander, did
incontinently gallop into an adjoining forest, and belaboured
the trees with such might and main, that the whole court
were convinced that he was the most potent and courageous
gentleman on the face of the earth. In like manner the great
general Von Poffenburgh would ease off that valourous
spleen, which like wind is so apt to grow unruly in the stomachs of new made soldiers, impelling them to box-lobby
brawls, and broken headed quarrels.—For at such times,
when he found his martial spirit waxing hot within him, he

would prudently sally forth into the fields, and lugging out his trusty sabre, of full two flemish ells in length, would lay about him most lustily, decapitating cabbages by platoons—hewing down whole phalanxes of sunflowers, which he termed gigantic Swedes; and if peradventure, he espied a colony of honest big bellied pumpkins quietly basking themselves in the sun, "ah caitiff Yankees," would he roar, "have I caught ye at last!"—so saying, with one sweep of his sword, he would cleave the unhappy vegetables from their chins to their waistbands: by which warlike havoc, his choler being in some sort allayed, he would return to his garrison with a full conviction, that he was a very miracle of military prowess.

The next ambition of general Von Poffenburgh was to be thought a strict disciplinarian. Well knowing that discipline is the soul of all military enterprize, he enforced it with the most rigorous precision; obliging every man to turn out his toes, and hold up his head on parade, and prescribing the breadth of their ruffles to all such as had any shirts to their backs.

Having one day, in the course of his devout researches in the bible, (for the pious Eneas himself, could not exceed him in outward religion) encountered the history of Absalom and his melancholy end; the general in an evil hour, issued orders for cropping the hair of both officers and men throughout the garrison. Now it came to pass, that among his officers was one Kildermeester; a sturdy old veteran, who had cherished through the course of a long life, a rugged mop of hair, not a little resembling the shag of a Newfoundland dog; terminating with an immoderate queue, like the handle of a frying pan; and queued so tightly to his head, that his eyes and mouth generally stood ajar, and his eye-brows were drawn up to the top of his forehead. It may naturally be supposed that the possessor of so goodly an appendage would resist with abhorrence, an order condemning it to the shears. Sampson himself could not have held his wig more sacred, and on hearing the general orders, he discharged a tempest of veteran, soldier-like oaths, and dunder and blixums—swore he would break any man's head who attempted to meddle with his tail—queued it stiffer than ever, and whisked it about the garrison, as fiercely as the tail of a crocodile.

The eel-skin queue of old Kildermeester, became instantly an affair of the utmost importance. The commander in chief was too enlightened an officer not to perceive, that the discipline of the garrison, the subordination and good order of the *armies* of the Nieuw Nederlandts, the consequent safety of the whole province, and ultimately the dignity and prosperity of their high mightinesses, the lords states general, but above all, the dignity of the great general Von Poffenburgh, all imperiously demanded the docking of that stubborn queue. He therefore patriotically determined that old Kildermeester should be publicly shorn of his glories in presence of the whole garrison—the old man as resolutely stood on the defensive—whereupon the general, as became a great man, was highly exasperated, and the offender was arrested and tried by a court martial for mutiny, desertion and all the other rigmarole of offences noticed in the articles of war, ending with a "videlicit, in wearing an eel-skin queue, three feet long, contrary to orders"—Then came on arraignments, and trials, and pleadings, and convictings, and the whole country was in a ferment about this unfortunate queue. As it is well known that the commander of a distant frontier post has the power of acting pretty much after his own will, there is little doubt but that the old veteran would have been hanged or shot at least, had he not luckily fallen ill of a fever, through mere chagrin and mortification—and most flagitiously deserted from all earthly command, with his beloved locks unviolated. His obstinacy remained unshaken to the very last moment, when he directed that he should be carried to his grave with his eel-skin queue sticking out of a knot hole in his coffin.

This magnanimous affair obtained the general great credit as an excellent disciplinarian, but it is hinted that he was ever after subject to bad dreams, and fearful visitations in the night—when the grizly spectrum of old Kildermeester would stand centinel by his bed side, erect as a pump, his enormous queue strutting out like the handle.

END OF BOOK V.

BOOK VI.

Containing the second part of the reign of Peter the Headstrong—
and his gallant atchievements on the Delaware.

CHAP. I.

In which is presented a warlike portrait of the Great Peter. —
And how General Von Poffenburgh gave a stout carousal, for
which he got more kicks than coppers.

HITHERTO most venerable and courteous reader, have I
shewn thee the administration of the valourous Stuyvesant, under the mild moonshine of peace; or rather the
grim tranquillity of awful preparation; but now the war drum
rumbles, the brazen trumpet brays its thrilling note, and the
rude clash of hostile arms, speaks fearful prophecies of coming troubles. The gallant warrior starts from soft repose, from
golden visions and voluptuous ease; where in the dulcet,
"piping time of peace," he sought sweet solace after all his
toils. No more in beauty's syren lap reclined, he weaves fair
garlands for his lady's brows; no more entwines with flowers
his shining sword, nor through the live-long lazy summers
day, chaunts forth his lovesick soul in madrigals. To manhood
roused, he spurns the amorous flute; doffs from his brawny
back the robe of peace, and clothes his pampered limbs in
panoply of steel. O'er his dark brow, where late the myrtle
waved; where wanton roses breathed enervate love, he rears
the beaming casque and nodding plume; grasps the bright
shield and shakes the pondrous lance; or mounts with eager
pride his fiery steed; and burns for deeds of glorious chivalry!

But soft, worthy reader! I would not have you go about to
imagine, that any *preux chevalier* thus hideously begirt with
iron existed in the city of New Amsterdam. — This is but a
lofty and gigantic mode in which we heroic writers always
talk of war, thereby to give it a noble and imposing aspect;
equipping our warriors with bucklers, helms and lances, and
a host of other outlandish and obsolete weapons, the like of
which perchance they had never seen or heard of; in the same
manner that a cunning statuary arrays a modern general or an
admiral in the accoutrements of a Cæsar or an Alexander. The
simple truth then of all this oratorical flourish is this. — That
the valiant Peter Stuyvesant all of a sudden found it necessary
to scour his trusty blade, which too long had rusted in its

scabbard, and prepare himself to undergo those hardy toils of war, in which his mighty soul so much delighted.

Methinks I at this moment behold him in my imagination—or rather I behold his goodly portrait, which still hangs up in the family mansion of the Stuyvesants—arrayed in all the terrors of a true dutch general. His regimental coat of German blue, gorgeously decorated with a goodly shew of large brass buttons, reaching from his waistband to his chin. The voluminous skirts turned up at the corners and separating gallantly behind, so as to display the seat of a sumptuous pair of brimstone coloured trunk breeches—a graceful style still prevalent among the warriors of our day, and which is in conformity to the custom of ancient heroes, who scorned to defend themselves in rear.—His face rendered exceeding terrible and warlike by a pair of black mustachios; his hair strutting out on each side in stiffly pomatumed ear locks and descending in a rat tail queue below his waist; a shining stock of black leather supporting his chin, and a little, but fierce cocked hat stuck with a gallant and fiery air, over his left eye. Such was the chivalric port of Peter the Headstrong; and when he made a sudden halt, planted himself firmly on his solid supporter, with his wooden leg, inlaid with silver, a little in advance, in order to strengthen his position; his right hand stuck a-kimbo, his left resting upon the pummel of his brass hilted sword; his head dressing spiritedly to the right, with a most appalling and hard favoured frown upon his brow—he presented altogether one of the most commanding, bitter looking, and soldierlike figures, that ever strutted upon canvass.—Proceed we now to enquire the cause of this warlike preparation.

The encroaching disposition of the Swedes, on the south, or Delaware river, has been duly recorded in the Chronicles of the reign of William the Testy. These encroachments having been endured with that heroic magnanimity, which is the corner stone, or according to Aristotle, the left hand neighbour of true courage, had been repeated and wickedly aggravated.

The Swedes, who, were of that class of cunning pretenders to Christianity, that read the Bible upside down, whenever it interferes with their interests, inverted the golden maxim, and when their neighbour suffered them to smite him on the one cheek, they generally smote him on the other also, whether it was turned to them or not. Their repeated aggressions had been among the numerous sources of vexation, that conspired to keep the irritable sensibilities of Wilhelmus Kieft, in a constant fever, and it was only owing to the unfortunate circumstance, that he had always a hundred things to do at once, that he did not take such unrelenting vengeance as their offences merited. But they had now a chieftan of a different character to deal with; and they were soon guilty of a piece of treachery, that threw his honest blood in a ferment, and precluded all further sufferance.

Printz, the governor of the province of New Sweden, being either deceased or removed, for of this fact some uncertainty exists; he was succeeded by Jan Risingh, a gigantic Swede, and who, had he not been rather in-kneed and splay-footed, might have served for the model of a Sampson, or a Hercules. He was no less rapacious than mighty, and withal as crafty as he was rapacious; so that in fact there is very little doubt, had he lived some four or five centuries before, he would have made one of those wicked giants, who took such a cruel pleasure in pocketing distressed damsels, when gadding about the world, and locking them up in enchanted castles, without a toilet, a change of linen, or any other convenience.—In consequence of which enormities they fell under the high displeasure of chivalry, and all true, loyal and gallant knights, were instructed to attack and slay outright any miscreant they might happen to find above six feet high; which is doubtless one reason that the race of large men is nearly extinct, and the generations of latter ages so exceeding small.

No sooner did governor Risingh enter upon his office, than he immediately cast his eyes upon the important post of Fort Casimer, and formed the righteous resolution of taking it into his possession. The only thing that remained to consider, was the mode of carrying his resolution into effect; and here I must do him the justice to say, that he exhibited a humanity rarely to be met with among leaders; and which I have never seen equalled in modern times, excepting among the English, in their glorious affair at Copenhagen. Willing to spare the effusion of blood, and the miseries of open warfare, he benevolently shunned every thing like avowed hostility or regular siege, and resorted to the less glorious, but more merciful expedient of treachery.

Under pretence therefore, of paying a sociable, neighbourly visit to general Von Poffenburgh, at his new post of Fort Casimer, he made requisite preparation, sailed in great state up the Delaware, displayed his flag with the most ceremonious punctilio, and honoured the fortress with a royal salute, previous to dropping anchor. The unusual noise awakened a veteran dutch centinel, who was napping faithfully on his post, and who after hammering his flint for good ten minutes, and rubbing its edge with the corner of his ragged cocked hat, but all to no purpose, contrived to return the compliment, by discharging his rusty firelock with the spark of a pipe, which he borrowed from one of his comrades. The salute indeed would have been answered by the guns of the fort, had they not unfortunately been out of order, and the magazine deficient in ammunition—accidents to which forts have in all ages been liable, and which were the more excusable in the present instance, as Fort Casimer had only been erected about two years, and general Von Poffenburgh, its mighty commander, had been fully occupied with matters of much greater self importance.

Risingh, highly satisfied with this courteous reply to his salute, treated the fort to a second, for he well knew its puissant and pompous leader, was marvellously delighted with these little ceremonials, which he considered as so many acts of homage paid unto his greatness. He then landed in great state, attended by a suite of thirty men—a prodigious and vain-glorious retinue, for a petty governor of a petty settlement, in those days of primitive simplicity; and to the full as great an army as generally swells the pomp and marches in the rear of our frontier commanders at the present day.

The number in fact might have awakened suspicion, had not the mind of the great Von Poffenburgh been so completely engrossed with an all pervading idea of himself, that he had not room to admit a thought besides. In fact he considered the concourse of Risingh's followers as a compliment to himself—so apt are great men to stand between themselves and the sun, and completely eclipse the truth by their own shadow.

It may readily be imagined how much general Von Poffenburgh was flattered by a visit from so august a personage; his only embarrassment was, how he should receive him in such a manner as to appear to the greatest advantage, and make the most advantageous impression. The main guard was ordered immediately to turn out, and the arms and regimentals (of which the garrison possessed full half a dozen suits) were equally distributed among the soldiers. One tall lank fellow, appeared in a coat intended for a small man, the skirts of which reached a little below his waist, the buttons were between his shoulders and the sleeves half way to his wrists, so that his hands looked like a couple of huge spades—and the coat not being large enough to meet in front, was linked together by loops, made of a pair of red worsted garters. Another had an old cocked hat, stuck on the back of his head and decorated with a bunch of cocks tails—a third had a pair of rusty gaiters hanging about his heels—while a fourth, who was a short duck legged little trojan, was equipped in a huge pair of the general's cast off breeches, which he held up with one hand, while he grasped his firelock with the other. The rest were accoutred in similar style, excepting three graceless raggamuffins, who had no shirts and but a pair and half of breeches between them, wherefore they were sent to the black hole, to keep them out of view. There is nothing in which the talents of a prudent commander are more completely testified, than in thus setting matters off to the greatest advantage; and it is for this reason that our frontier posts at the present day (that of Niagara in particular) display their best suit of regimentals on the back of the centinel who stands in sight of travellers.

His men being thus gallantly arrayed—those who lacked muskets shouldering shovels and pick axes, and every man being ordered to tuck in his shirt tail and pull up his brogues, general Von Poffenburgh first took a sturdy draught of foaming ale, which like the magnanimous More of More-hall* was his invariable practice on all great occasions—which done he

*"——as soon as he rose,
　To make him strong and mighty,
He drank by the tale, six pots of ale,
　And a quart of Aqua Vitæ."

put himself at their head, ordered the pine planks, which served as a draw bridge, to be laid down, and issued forth from his castle, like a mighty giant, just refreshed with wine. But when the two heroes met, then began a scene of warlike parade and chivalric courtesy, that beggars all description. Risingh, who, as I before hinted, was a shrewd, cunning politician, and had grown grey much before his time, in consequence of his craftiness, saw at one glance the ruling passion of the great Von Poffenburgh, and humoured him in all his valorous fantasies.

Their detachments were accordingly drawn up in front of each other; they carried arms and they presented arms; they gave the standing salute and the passing salute—They rolled their drums, they flourished their fifes and they waved their colours—they faced to the left, and they faced to the right, and they faced to the right about—They wheeled forward, and they wheeled backward, and they wheeled into *echellon*— They marched and they countermarched, by grand divisions, by single divisions and by sub-divisions—by platoons, by sections and by files—In quick time, in slow time and in no time at all; for, having gone through all the evolutions of two great armies, including the eighteen manœuvres of Dundas (which, not being yet invented they must have anticipated by intuition or inspiration) having exhausted all that they could recollect or imagine of military tactics, including sundry strange and irregular evolutions, the like of which were never seen before or since, excepting among certain of our newly raised drafts, the two great commanders and their respective troops, came at length to a dead halt, completely exhausted by the toils of war—Never did two valiant train band captains, or two buskin'd theatric heroes, in the renowned tragedies of Pizarro, Tom Thumb, or any other heroical and fighting tragedy, marshal their gallows-looking, duck-legged, heavy-heeled, sheep-stealing myrmidons with more glory and self-admiration.

These military compliments being finished, general Von Poffenburgh escorted his illustrious visitor, with great ceremony into the fort; attended him throughout the fortifications; shewed him the horn works, crown works, half moons, and various other outworks; or rather the places where they ought to be erected, and where they might be erected if he pleased; plainly demonstrating that it was a place of "great capability," and though at present but a little redoubt, yet that it evidently was a formidable fortress, in embryo. This survey over, he next had the whole garrison put under arms, exercised and reviewed, and concluded by ordering the three bridewell birds to be hauled out of the black hole, brought up to the halberts and soundly flogged, for the amusement of his visitor, and to convince him, that he was a great disciplinarian.

There is no error more dangerous than for a commander to make known the strength, or, as in the present case, the weakness of his garrison; this will be exemplified before I have arrived to an end of my present story, which thus carries its moral like a roasted goose his pudding in its very middle. The cunning Risingh, while he pretended to be struck dumb outright, with the puissance of the great Von Poffenburgh, took silent note of the incompetency of his garrison, of which he gave a hint to his trusty followers; who tipped each other the wink, and laughed most obstreperously—in their sleeves.

The inspection, review, and flogging being concluded, the party adjourned to the table; for among his other great qualities, the general was remarkably addicted to huge entertainments, or rather carousals, and in one afternoon's campaign would leave more *dead men* on the field, than he ever did in the whole course of his military career. Many bulletins of these bloodless victories do still remain on record; and the whole province was once thrown in amaze, by the return of one of his campaigns; wherein it was stated, that though like captain Bobadel, he had only twenty men to back him, yet in the short space of six months he had conquered and utterly annihilated sixty oxen, ninety hogs, one hundred sheep, ten thousand cabbages, one thousand bushels of potatoes, one hundred and fifty kilderkins of small beer, two thousand seven hundred and thirty five pipes, seventy eight pounds of sugar-plumbs, and forty bars of iron, besides sundry small meats, game, poultry and garden stuff. An atchievement unparalleled since the days of Pantagruel and his all devouring army, and which shewed that it was only necessary to let the great general Von Poffenburgh, and his garrison, loose in an enemies country, and in a little while they would breed a famine, and starve all the inhabitants.

No sooner therefore had the general received the first intimation of the visit of governor Risingh, than he ordered a big dinner to be prepared; and privately sent out a detachment of his most experienced veterans, to rob all the henroosts in the neighbourhood, and lay the pig-styes under contribution; a service to which they had been long enured, and which they discharged with such incredible zeal and promptitude, that the garrison table groaned under the weight of their spoils.

I wish with all my heart, my readers could see the valiant Von Poffenburgh, as he presided at the head of the banquet: it was a sight worth beholding—there he sat, in his greatest glory, surrounded by his soldiers, like that famous wine bibber Alexander, whose thirsty virtues he did most ably imitate—telling astounding stories of his hair-breadth adventures and heroic exploits, at which, though all his auditors knew them to be most incontinent and outrageous gasconadoes, yet did they cast up their eyes in admiration and utter many interjections of astonishment. Nor could the general pronounce any thing that bore the remotest semblance to a joke, but the stout Risingh would strike his brawny fist upon the table till every glass rattled again, throwing himself back in his chair, and uttering gigantic peals of laughter, swearing most horribly, it was the best joke he ever heard in his life.— Thus all was rout and revelry and hideous carousal within Fort Casimer, and so lustily did the great Von Poffenburgh ply the bottle, that in less than four short hours he made himself, and his whole garrison, who all sedulously emulated the deeds of their chieftain, dead drunk, in singing songs, quaffing bumpers, and drinking fourth of July toasts, not one of which, but was as long as a Welsh pedigree or a plea in chancery.

No sooner did things come unto this pass, than the crafty Risingh and his Swedes, who had cunningly kept themselves sober, rose on their entertainers, tied them neck and heels, and took formal possession of the fort, and all its dependencies, in the name of queen Christina, of Sweden: administering, at the same time, an oath of allegiance to all the dutch soldiers, who could be made sober enough to swallow it.

Risingh then put the fortifications in order, appointed his discreet and vigilant friend Suen Scutz, a tall, wind-dried, water drinking Swede, to the command, and departed bearing with him this truly amiable garrison, and their puissant commander; who when brought to himself by a sound drubbing, bore no little resemblance to a "deboshed fish;" or bloated sea monster, caught upon dry land.

The transportation of the garrison was done to prevent the transmission of intelligence to New Amsterdam; for much as the cunning Risingh exulted in his stratagem, he dreaded the vengeance of the sturdy Peter Stuyvesant; whose name spread as much terror in the neighbourhood, as did whilome that of the unconquerable Scanderbeg among his scurvy enemies the Turks.

CHAP. II.

*Shewing how profound secrets are strangely brought to light;
with the proceedings of Peter the Headstrong when he heard
of the misfortune of General Von Poffenburgh.*

WHOEVER first described common fame, or rumour, as
belonging to the sager sex, was a very owl for shrewdness. She has in truth certain feminine qualities to an astonishing degree; particularly that benevolent anxiety to take care
of the affairs of others, which keeps her continually hunting
after secrets, and gadding about, proclaiming them. Whatever
is done openly and in the face of the world, she takes but
transient notice of, but whenever a transaction is done in a
corner, and attempted to be shrouded in mystery, then her
goddesship is at her wit's end to find it out, and takes a most
mischievous and lady-like pleasure in publishing it to the
world. It is this truly feminine propensity that induces her
continually to be prying into cabinets of princes; listening at
the key holes of senate chambers, and peering through chinks
and crannies, when our worthy Congress are sitting with
closed doors, deliberating between a dozen excellent modes
of ruining the nation. It is this which makes her so obnoxious
to all wary statesmen and intriguing commanders—such a
stumbling block to private negociations and secret expeditions;
which she often betrays, by means and instruments which never
would have been thought of by any but a female head.

Thus it was in the case of the affair of Fort Casimer. No
doubt the cunning Risingh imagined, that by securing the
garrison, he should for a long time prevent the history of its
fate from reaching the ears of the gallant Stuyvesant; but his
exploit was blown to the world when he least expected it, and
by one of the last beings he would ever have suspected of
enlisting as trumpeter to the wide mouthed deity.

This was one Dirk Schuiler (or Skulker); a kind of hanger
on to the garrison; who seemed to belong to no body, and in
a manner to be self outlawed. One of those vagabond Cos-
mopolites, who shirk about the world, as if they had no right
or business in it, and who infest the skirts of society, like

poachers and interlopers. Every garrison and country village
has one or more scape goats of this kind, whose life is a kind of
enigma, whose existence is without motive, who comes from
the Lord knows where, who lives the Lord knows how, and
seems to be made for no other earthly purpose but to keep up
the antient and honourable order of idleness—This vagrant
philosopher was supposed to have some Indian blood in his
veins, which was manifested by a certain Indian complexion
and cast of countenance; but more especially by his propensities and habits. He was a tall, lank fellow, swift of foot and
long-winded. He was generally equipped in a half Indian dress,
with belt, leggings, and moccasons. His hair hung in straight
gallows locks, about his ears, and added not a little to his shirk-
ing demeanour. It is an old remark, that persons of Indian mixture are half civilized, half savage, and half devil, a third half
being expressly provided for their particular convenience. It is
for similar reasons, and probably with equal truth, that the
back-wood-men of Kentucky are styled half man, half horse
and half alligator, by the settlers on the Mississippi, and held
accordingly in great respect and abhorrence.

The above character may have presented itself to the garrison as applicable to Dirk Schuiler, whom they familiarly
dubbed Galgenbrok, or Gallows Dirk. Certain it is, he appeared to acknowledge allegiance to no one—was an utter
enemy to work, holding it in no manner of estimation—but
lounged about the fort, depending upon chance for a subsistence; getting drunk whenever he could get liquor, and stealing whatever he could lay his hands on. Every day or two he
was sure to get a sound rib-roasting for some of his misdemeanours, which however, as it broke no bones, he made
very light of, and scrupled not to repeat the offence, whenever another opportunity presented. Sometimes in consequence of some flagrant villainy, he would abscond from the
garrison, and be absent for a month at a time; skulking about
the woods and swamps, with a long fowling piece on his
shoulder, laying in ambush for game—or squatting himself
down on the edge of a pond catching fish for hours together,
and bearing no little resemblance to that notable bird ycleped
the Mud-poke. When he thought his crimes had been forgotten or forgiven, he would sneak back to the fort with a bun-

dle of skins, or a bunch of poultry which perchance he had stolen, and exchange them for liquor, with which, having well soaked his carcass, he would lay in the sun and enjoy all the luxurious indolence of that swinish philosopher Diogenes. He was the terror of all the farm yards in the country; into which he made fearful inroads; and sometimes he would make his sudden appearance at the garrison at day break, with the whole neighbourhood at his heels; like a scoundrel thief of a fox, detected in his maraudings and hunted to his hole. Such was this Dirk Schuiler; and from the total indifference he shewed to the world or its concerns, and from his true Indian stoicism and taciturnity, no one would ever have dreamt, that he would have been the publisher of the treachery of Risingh.

When the carousal was going on, which proved so fatal to the brave Von Poffenburgh and his watchful garrison, Dirk skulked about from room to room, being a kind of privileged vagrant, or useless hound, whom nobody noticed. But though a fellow of few words, yet like your taciturn people, his eyes and ears were always open, and in the course of his prowlings he overheard the whole plot of the Swedes. Dirk immediately settled in his own mind, how he should turn the matter to his own advantage. He played the perfect jack-of-both-sides—that is to say, he made a prize of every thing that came in his reach, robbed both parties, stuck the copper bound cocked hat of the puissant Von Poffenburgh, on his head, whipped a huge pair of Risingh's jack boots under his arm, and took to his heels, just before the denouement and confusion at the garrison.

Finding himself completely dislodged from his haunt in this quarter, he directed his flight towards his native place, New Amsterdam, from whence he had formerly been obliged to abscond precipitately, in consequence of misfortune in business—in other words, having been detected in the act of sheep stealing. After wandering many days in the woods, toiling through swamps, fording brooks, swimming various rivers, and encountering a world of hardships that would have killed any other being, but an Indian, a back-wood-man, or the devil, he at length arrived, half famished, and lank as a starved weazle at Communipaw, where he stole a canoe and paddled over to New Amsterdam. Immediately on landing, he repaired to governor Stuyvesant, and in more words than he had ever spoken before, in the whole course of his life, gave an account of the disastrous affair.

On receiving these direful tidings the valiant Peter started from his seat, as did the stout king Arthur when at "merry Carleile," the news was brought him of the uncourteous misdeeds of the "grim barone"—without uttering a word, he dashed the pipe he was smoking against the back of the chimney—thrust a prodigious quid of negro head tobacco into his left cheek—pulled up his galligaskins, and strode up and down the room, humming, as was customary with him, when in a passion a most hideous north-west ditty. But, as I have before shewn, he was not a man to vent his spleen in idle vapouring. His first measure after the paroxysm of wrath had subsided, was to stump up stairs, to a huge wooden chest, which served as his armoury, from whence he drew forth that identical suit of regimentals described in the preceding chapter. In these portentous habiliments he arrayed himself, like Achilles in the armour of Vulcan, maintaining all the while a most appalling silence; knitting his brows and drawing his breath through his clinched teeth. Being hastily equipped, he thundered down into the parlour like a second Magog—jerked down his trusty sword, from over the fire place, where it was usually suspended; but before he girded it on his thigh he drew it from its scabbard, and as his eye coursed along the rusty blade, a grim smile stole over his iron visage—It was the first smile that had visited his countenace for five long weeks; but every one who beheld it, prophesied that there would soon be warm work in the province!

Thus armed at all points, with grizly war depicted in each feature; his very cocked hat assuming an air of uncommon defiance; he instantly put himself on the alert, and dispatched Antony Van Corlear hither and thither, this way and that way, through all the muddy streets and crooked lanes of the city: summoning by sound of trumpet his trusty peers to assemble in instant council.—This done, by way of expediting matters, according to the custom of people in a hurry, he kept in continual bustle, thrusting his bottom into every chair, popping his head out of every window, and stumping up and down stairs with his wooden leg in such brisk and incessant motion, that, as I am informed by an authentic historian of the times, the continual clatter bore no small resemblance to the music of a cooper, hooping a flour barrel.

A summons so peremptory, and from a man of the governor's mettle, was not to be trifled with: the sages forthwith repaired to the council chamber, where the gallant Stuyvesant entered in martial style, and took his chair, like another Charlemagne, among his Paladins. The councillors seated themselves with the utmost tranquillity, and lighting their long pipes, gazed with unruffled composure on his excellency and his regimentals; being, as all councillors should be, not easily flustered, or taken by surprise. The governor, not giving them time to recover from the astonishment they did not feel, addressed them in a short, but soul stirring harangue.

I am extremely sorry, that I have not the advantages of Livy, Thucydides, Plutarch and others of my predecessors, who were furnished as I am told, with the speeches of all their great emperors, generals, and orators, taken down in short hand, by the most accurate stenographers of the time; whereby they were enabled wonderfully to enrich their histories, and delight their readers with sublime strains of eloquence. Not having such important auxiliaries, I cannot possibly pronounce, what was the tenor of governor Stuyvesant's speech. Whether he with maiden coyness hinted to his hearers that "there was a speck of war in the horison;"—that it would be necessary to resort to the "unprofitable trial of which could do each other the most harm,"—or any other delicate construction of language, whereby the odious subject of war, is handled so fastidiously and modestly by modern statesmen; as a gentleman volunteer handles his filthy saltpetre weapons with gloves, lest he should soil his dainty fingers.

I am bold however to say, from the tenor of Peter Stuyvesant's character, that he did not wrap his rugged subject in silks and ermines, and other sickly trickeries of phrase; but spoke forth, like a man of nerve and vigour, who scorned to shrink in words, from those dangers which he stood ready to encounter in very deed. This much is certain, that he concluded by announcing his determination of leading on his troops in person, and routing these costard-monger Swedes, from their usurped quarters at Fort Casimer. To this hardy resolution, such of his council as were awake, gave their usual signal of concurrence, and as to the rest, who had fallen asleep about the middle of the harangue (their "usual custom in the afternoon")—they made not the least objection.

And now was seen in the fair city of New Amsterdam, a prodigious bustle and preparation for iron war. Recruiting parties marched hither and thither, trailing long standards in the mud, with which as at the present day the streets were benevolently covered, for the benefit of those unfortunate wights who are aggrieved with corns. Thus did they lustily call upon and invite all the scrubs, the runagates and the tatterdemalions of the Manhattoes and its vicinity, who had any ambition of six pence a day, and immortal fame into the bargain, to enlist in the cause of glory. For I would have you note that your warlike heroes who trudge in the rear of conquerors, are generally of that illustrious class of gentlemen, who are equal candidates for the army or the bridewell—the halberts or the whipping post—for whom dame fortune has cast an even die whether they shall make their exit by the sword or the halter—and whose deaths shall, at all events, be a lofty example to their countrymen.

But notwithstanding all this martial rout and invitation, the ranks of honour were but scantily supplied; so averse were the peaceful burghers of New Amsterdam to enlist in foreign broils, or stir beyond that home, which rounded all their earthly ideas. Upon beholding this, the great Peter whose noble heart was all on fire with war and sweet revenge, determined to wait no longer for the tardy assistance of these oily citizens, but to muster up his merry men of the Hudson; who, brought up among woods and wilds and savage beasts, like our yeomen of Kentucky, delighted in nothing so much as desperate adventures and perilous expeditions through the wilderness. Thus resolving, he ordered his trusty squire Antony Van Corlear to have his state galley prepared and duly victualled; which being faithfully performed he attended public service at the great church of St. Nicholas, like a true and pious governor, and then leaving peremptory orders with his council to have the chivalry of the Manhattoes marshalled out and appointed against his return, departed upon his recruiting voyage, up the waters of the Hudson.

CHAP. III.

Containing Peter Stuyvesant's voyage up the Hudson, and the wonders and delights of that renowned river.

Now did the soft breezes of the south, steal sweetly over the beauteous face of nature, tempering the panting heats of summer into genial and prolific warmth: when that miracle of hardihood and chivalric virtue, the dauntless Peter Stuyvesant, spread his canvass to the wind, and departed from the fair island of Manna-hata. The galley in which he embarked was sumptuously adorned with pendants and streamers of gorgeous dyes, which fluttered gaily in the wind, or drooped their ends into the bosom of the stream. The bow and poop of this majestic vessel were gallantly bedight, after the rarest dutch fashion, with naked figures of little pursy cupids with periwigs on their heads, and bearing in their hands garlands of flowers, the like of which are not to be found in any book of botany; being the matchless flowers which flourished in the golden age, and exist no longer, unless it be in the imaginations of ingenious carvers of wood and discolourers of canvass.

Thus rarely decorated, in style befitting the state of the puissant potentate of the Manhattoes, did the galley of Peter Stuyvesant launch forth upon the bosom of the lordly Hudson; which as it rolled its broad waves to the ocean, seemed to pause for a while, and swell with pride, as if conscious of the illustrious burthen it sustained.

But trust me gentlefolk, far other was the scene presented to the contemplation of the crew, from that which may be witnessed at this degenerate day. Wildness and savage majesty reigned on the borders of this mighty river—the hand of cultivation had not as yet laid low the dark forests, and tamed the features of the landscape—nor had the frequent sail of commerce yet broken in upon the profound and awful solitude of ages. Here and there might be seen a rude wigwam perched among the cliffs of the mountains, with its curling column of smoke mounting in the transparent atmosphere—but so loftily situated that the whoopings of the savage children, gambolling on the margin of the dizzy heights, fell almost as faintly on the ear, as do the notes of the lark, when lost in the azure vault of heaven. Now and then from the beetling brow of some rocky precipice, the wild deer would look timidly down upon the splendid pageant as it passed below; and then tossing his branching antlers in the air, would bound away into the thickets of the forest.

Through such scenes did the stately vessel of Peter Stuyvesant pass. Now did they skirt the bases of the rocky heights of Jersey, which spring up like everlasting walls, reaching from the waves unto the heavens; and were fashioned, if tradition may be believed, in times long past, by the mighty spirit Manetho, to protect his favourite abodes from the unhallowed eyes of mortals. Now did they career it gaily across the vast expanse of Tappan bay, whose wide extended shores present a vast variety of delectable scenery—here the bold promontory, crowned with embowering trees advancing into the bay—there the long woodland slope, sweeping up from the shore in rich luxuriance, and terminating in the rude upland precipice—while at a distance a long waving line of rocky heights, threw their gigantic shades across the water. Now would they pass where some modest little interval, opening among these stupendous scenes, yet retreating as it were for protection into the embraces of the neighbouring mountains, displayed a rural paradise, fraught with sweet and pastoral beauties; the velvet tufted lawn—the bushy copse—the tinkling rivulet, stealing through the fresh and vivid verdure—on whose banks was situated some little Indian village, or peradventure, the rude cabin of some solitary hunter.

The different periods of the revolving day seemed each with cunning magic, to diffuse a different charm over the scene. Now would the jovial sun break gloriously from the east, blazing from the summits of the eastern hills and sparkling the landscape with a thousand dewy gems; while along the borders of the river were seen heavy masses of mist, which like midnight caitiffs, disturbed at his approach, made a sluggish retreat, rolling in sullen reluctance up the mountains. At such times all was brightness and life and gaiety—the atmosphere seemed of an indescribable pureness and transparency—the birds broke forth in wanton madrigals, and the freshening breezes wafted the vessel merrily on her course. But when the sun sunk amid a flood of glory in the west, mantling the heavens and the earth with a thousand gorgeous dyes—then all was calm and silent and magnificent. The late swelling sail hung lifelessly against the mast—the simple seaman with folded arms leaned against the shrouds, lost in that involuntary musing which the sober grandeur of nature commands in the rudest of her children. The vast bosom of the Hudson was like an unruffled mirror, reflecting the golden splendour of the heavens, excepting that now and then a bark canoe would steal across its surface, filled with painted savages, whose gay feathers glared brightly, as perchance a lingering ray of the setting sun, gleamed upon them from the western mountains.

But when the fairy hour of twilight spread its magic mists around, then did the face of nature assume a thousand fugitive charms, which to the worthy heart that seeks enjoyment in the glorious works of its maker, are inexpressibly captivating. The mellow dubious light that prevailed, just served to tinge with illusive colours, the softened features of the scenery. The deceived but delighted eye sought vainly to discern in the broad masses of shade, the separating line between the land and water; or to distinguish the fading objects that seemed sinking into chaos. Now did the busy fancy supply the feebleness of vision, producing with industrious craft a fairy creation of her own. Under her plastic wand the barren rocks frowned upon the watery waste, in the semblance of lofty towers and high embattled castles—trees assumed the direful forms of mighty giants, and the inaccessible summits of the mountains seemed peopled with a thousand shadowy beings.

Now broke forth from the shores the notes of an innumerable variety of insects, who filled the air with a strange but not inharmonious concert—while ever and anon was heard the melancholy plaint of the Whip-poor-will, who, perched on some lone tree, wearied the ear of night with his incessant moanings. The mind, soothed into a hallowed melancholy by the solemn mystery of the scene, listened with pensive stillness to catch and distinguish each sound, that vaguely echoed from the shore—now and then startled perchance by the whoop of some straggling savage, or the dreary howl of some caitiff wolf, stealing forth upon his nightly prowlings.

Thus happily did they pursue their course, until they entered upon those awful defiles denominated THE HIGHLANDS, where it would seem that the gigantic Titans had erst waged their impious war with heaven, piling up cliffs on cliffs, and hurling vast masses of rock in wild confusion. But in sooth very different is the history of these cloud-capt mountains.— These in ancient days, before the Hudson poured his waters from the lakes, formed one vast prison, within whose rocky bosom the omnipotent Manetho confined the rebellious spirits who repined at his controul. Here, bound in adamantine chains, or jammed in rifted pines, or crushed by ponderous rocks, they groaned for many an age.—At length the lordly Hudson, in his irresistible career towards the ocean, burst open their prison house, rolling his tide triumphantly through its stupendous ruins.

Still however do many of them lurk about their old abodes; and these it is, according to venerable legends, that cause the echoes which resound throughout these awful solitudes; which are nothing but their angry clamours when any noise disturbs the profoundness of their repose.—But when the elements are agitated by tempest, when the winds are up and the thunder rolls, then horrible is the yelling and howling of these troubled spirits—making the mountains to rebellow with their hideous uproar; for at such times it is said, they think the great Manetho is returning once more to plunge them in gloomy caverns and renew their intolerable captivity.

But all these fair and glorious scenes were lost upon the gallant Stuyvesant; naught occupied his active mind but thoughts of iron war, and proud anticipations of hardy deeds of arms. Neither did his honest crew trouble their vacant minds with any romantic speculations of the kind. The pilot at the helm quietly smoked his pipe, thinking of nothing either past present or to come—those of his comrades who were not industriously snoring under the hatches, were listening with open mouths to Antony Van Corlear; who, seated on the windlass, was relating to them the marvellous history of those myriads of fire flies, that sparkled like gems and spangles upon the dusky robe of night. These, according to

tradition, were originally a race of pestilent sempiternous bel-
dames, who peopled these parts long before the memory of
man; being of that abominated race emphatically called *brimstones*; and who for their innumerable sins against the children
of men, and to furnish an awful warning to the beauteous
sex, were doomed to infest the earth in the shape of these
threatening and terrible little bugs; enduring the internal torments of that fire, which they formerly carried in their hearts
and breathed forth in their words; but now are sentenced to
bear about forever—in their tails!

And now am I going to tell a fact, which I doubt me much
my readers will hesitate to believe; but if they do, they are
welcome not to believe a word in this whole history, for
nothing which it contains is more true. It must be known
then that the nose of Antony the trumpeter was of a very
lusty size, strutting boldly from his countenance like a mountain of Golconda; being sumptuously bedecked with rubies
and other precious stones—the true regalia of a king of good
fellows, which jolly Bacchus grants to all who bouse it heartily at the flaggon. Now thus it happened, that bright and
early in the morning, the good Antony having washed his
burley visage, was leaning over the quarter railing of the galley, contemplating it in the glassy wave below—Just at this
moment the illustrious sun, breaking in all his splendour from
behind one of the high bluffs of the Highlands, did dart one
of his most potent beams full upon the refulgent nose of the
sounder of brass—the reflection of which shot straightway
down, hissing hot, into the water, and killed a mighty sturgeon that was sporting beside the vessel! This huge monster
being with infinite labour hoisted on board, furnished a luxurious repast to all the crew, being accounted of excellent flavour, excepting about the wound, where it smacked a little of
brimstone—and this, on my veracity, was the first time that
ever sturgeon was eaten in these parts, by christian people.*

When this astonishing miracle came to be made known to
Peter Stuyvesant, and that he tasted of the unknown fish, he,

*Domine Hans Megapolensis, treating of the country about Albany in a
letter which was written some time after the settlement thereof, says, "There
is in the river, great plenty of Sturgeon, which we christians do not make use
of; but the Indians eate them greedilie."

as may well be supposed, marvelled exceedingly; and as a monument thereof, he gave the name of *Anthony's Nose* to a stout promontory in the neighbourhood—and it has continued to be called Anthony's nose ever since that time.

But hold—Whether am I wandering?—By the mass, if I attempt to accompany the good Peter Stuyvesant on this voyage, I shall never make an end, for never was there a voyage so fraught with marvellous incidents, nor a river so abounding with transcendent beauties, worthy of being severally recorded. Even now I have it on the point of my pen to relate, how his crew were most horribly frightened, on going on shore above the highlands, by a gang of merry roystering devils, frisking and curvetting on a huge flat rock, which projected into the river—and which is called the *Duyvel's Dans-Kamer* to this very day—But no! Diedrich Knickerbocker—it becomes thee not to idle thus in thy historic wayfaring.

Recollect that while dwelling with the fond garrullity of age, over these fairy scenes, endeared to thee, by the recollections of thy youth, and the charms of a thousand legendary tales which beguiled the simple ear of thy childhood; recollect that thou art trifling with those fleeting moments which should be devoted to loftier themes.—Is not time—relentless time!—shaking with palsied hand, his almost exhausted hour glass before thee?—hasten then to pursue thy weary task, lest the last sands be run, ere thou hast finished thy renowned history of the Manhattoes.

Let us then commit the dauntless Peter, his brave galley and his loyal crew, to the protection of the blessed St. Nicholas; who I have no doubt will prosper him in his voyage, while we await his return at the great city of New Amsterdam.

CHAP. IV.

Describing the powerful army that assembled at the city of New Amsterdam — together with the interview between Peter the Headstrong, and general Von Poffenburgh, and Peter's sentiments touching unfortunate great men.

WHILE thus the enterprizing Peter was coasting, with flowing sail up the shores of the lordly Hudson, and arousing all the phlegmatic little dutch settlements upon its borders, a great and puissant concourse of warriors was assembling at the city of New Amsterdam. And here that most invaluable fragment of antiquity, the Stuyvesant manuscript, is more than commonly particular; by which means I am enabled to record the illustrious host that encamped themselves in the public square, in front of the fort, at present denominated the Bowling Green.

In the centre then, was pitched the tent of the men of battle of the Manhattoes, who being the inmates of the metropolis, composed the life guards of the governor. These were commanded by the valiant Stoffel Brinkerhoff, who whilome had acquired such immortal fame at Oyster Bay—they displayed as a standard, a mighty beaver *rampant* on a field of orange; being the arms of the province, and denoting the persevering industry, and the amphibious origin of the valiant Nederlanders.*

Then might be seen on their right hand, the vassals of that renowned Mynheer, Michael Paw,† who lorded it over the fair regions of ancient Pavonia, and the lands away south,

---

*This was likewise the great seal of the New Netherlands, as may still be seen in ancient records.

†Besides what is mentioned by the Stuyvesant MS. I have found mention made of this illustrious Patroon in another manuscript, which says: "De Heer (or the Squire) Michael Paw, a dutch subject, about 10th Aug. 1630, by deed purchased Staten Island. N. B. The same Michael Paw had what the dutch call a colonie at Pavonia, on the Jersey shore opposite New York, and his overseer in 1636, was named Corns. Van Vorst—a person of same name in 1769, owned Pawles Hook, and a large farm at Pavonia, and is a lineal descendant from Van Vorst."

even unto the Navesink mountains,* and was moreover patroon of Gibbet Island. His standard was borne by his trusty
squire, Cornelius Van Vorst; consisting of a huge oyster *re-
cumbent* upon a sea-green field; being the armorial bearings
of his favourite metropolis, Communipaw. He brought to the
camp a stout force of warriors, heavily armed, being each clad
in ten pair of linsey woolsey breeches, and overshadowed by
broad brimmed beavers, with short pipes twisted in their hat-
bands. These were the men who vegetated in the mud along
the shores of Pavonia; being of the race of genuine copper-
heads, and were fabled to have sprung from oysters.

At a little distance was encamped the tribe of warriors who
came from the neighbourhood of Hell-gate. These were commanded by the Suy Dams, and the Van Dams, most incontinent hard swearers, as their names betoken—they were
terrible looking fellows, clad in broad skirted gaberdines, of
that curious coloured cloth, called thunder and lightning—
and bore as a standard three Devil's-darning-needles, *volant*,
in a flame coloured field.

Hard by was the tent of the men of battle from the marshy
borders of the Wael-bogtig,† and the country thereabouts—
these were of a sour aspect, by reason that they lived on crabs
which abound in these parts. They were the first institutors
of that honourable order of knighthood, called *Fly market
shirks*, and if tradition speak true, did likewise introduce the
far-famed step in dancing, called "double trouble." They were
commanded by the fearless Jacobus Varra Vanger, and had
moreover a jolly band of Brooklyn ferry-men, who performed
a brave concerto on conch shells.

But I refrain from pursuing this minute description, which
goes on to describe the warriors of Bloemen dael, and Weehawk, and Hoboken, and sundry other places, well known in
history and song—for now does the sound of martial music
alarm the people of New Amsterdam, sounding afar from be-

*So called from the Navesink tribe of Indians that inhabited these parts—
at present they are erroneously denominated the Neversink, or Neversunk
mountains.

†I. E. The *Winding Bay*, named from the winding of its shores. This has
since been corrupted by the vulgar into the *Wallabout*, and is the basin which
shelters our infant navy.

yond the walls of the city. But this alarm was in a little while relieved, for lo, from the midst of a vast cloud of dust, they recognized the brimstone coloured breeches, and splendid silver leg of Peter Stuyvesant, glaring in the sun beams; and beheld him approaching at the head of a formidable army, which he had mustered along the banks of the Hudson. And here the excellent, but anonymous writer of the Stuyvesant manuscript breaks out into a brave and glorious description of the forces, as they defiled through the principal gate of the city, that stood by the head of wall street.

First of all came the Van Bummels who inhabit the pleasant borders of the Bronx—These were short fat men, wearing exceeding large trunk breeches, and are renowned for feats of the trencher—they were the first inventors of Suppawn or Mush and milk—Close in their rear marched the Van Vlotens of Kaats kill, most horrible quaffers of new cyder, and arrant braggarts in their liquor—After them came the famous Van Pelts of Esopus, dextrous horsemen, mounted upon goodly switch tailed steeds of the Esopus breed—these were mighty hunters of minks and musk rats, whence came the word *Peltry*—Then the Van Nests of Kinderhook, valiant robbers of birds nests, as their name denotes; to these if report may be believed, are we indebted for the invention of slap jacks, or buck-wheat cakes.—Then the Van Grolls of Anthony's Nose, who carried their liquor in fair round little pottles, by reason they could not bouse it out of their canteens, having such rare long noses.—Then the Gardeniers of Hudson and thereabouts, distinguished by many triumphant feats, such as robbing water melon patches, smoking rabbits out of their holes and the like; and by being great lovers of roasted pigs tails; these were the ancestors of the renowned congress man of that name.—Then the Van Hoesens of Sing-Sing, great choristers and players upon the jews harp; these marched two and two, singing the great song of St. Nicholas.—Then the Counhovens, of Sleepy Hollow, these gave birth to a jolly race of publicans, who first discovered the magic artifice of conjuring a quart of wine into a pint bottle.—Then the Van Courtlandts who lived on the wild banks of the Croton, and were great killers of wild ducks, being much spoken of for their skill in shooting with the long bow.—Then the Bunschotens of Nyack and Kakiat who were the first that did ever kick with the left foot; they were gallant bush-whackers and hunters of racoons by moon-light.—Then the Van Winkles of Haerlem, potent suckers of eggs, and noted for running of horses and running up of scores at taverns; they were the first that ever winked with both eyes at once.—Lastly came the KNICKERBOCKERS of the great town of Scaghtikoke, where the folk lay stones upon the houses in windy weather, lest they should be blown away. These derive their name, as some say, from *Knicker* to shake, and *Beker* a goblet, indicating thereby that they were sturdy toss pots of yore; but in truth it was derived from *Knicker* to nod, and *Boeken* books; plainly meaning that they were great nodders or dozers over books—from them did descend the writer of this History.

Such was the legion of sturdy bush beaters that poured into the grand gate of New Amsterdam; the Stuyvesant manuscript indeed speaks of many more, whose names I omit to mention, seeing that it behoves me to hasten to matters of greater moment. Nothing could surpass the joy and martial pride of the lion hearted Peter as he reviewed this mighty host of warriors, and he determined no longer to defer the gratification of his much wished for revenge, upon the scoundrel Swedes at Fort Casimer.

But before I hasten on to record those unmatchable events, which will be found in the sequel of this renowned history, let me pause to notice the fate of Jacobus Von Poffenburgh, the discomfited commander in chief of the armies of the New Netherlands. Such is the inherent uncharitableness of human nature, that scarcely did the news become public of his deplorable discomfiture at Fort Casimer; than a thousand scurvy rumours were set afloat in New Amsterdam, wherein it was insinuated, that he had in reality a treacherous understanding with the Swedish commander; that he had long been in the practice of privately communicating with the Swedes, together with divers hints about "secret service money"—To all which deadly charges I do not give a jot more credit—than I think they deserve.

Certain it is, that the general vindicated his character by the most vehement oaths and protestations, and put every man out of the ranks of honour who dared to doubt his integrity. Moreover on returning to New Amsterdam, he paraded up and down the streets with a crew of hard swearers at his heels—sturdy bottle companions, whom he gorged and fattened, and who were ready to bolster him through all the courts of justice—Heroes of his own kidney, fierce whiskered, broad shouldered, colbrand looking swaggerers—not one of whom but looked as if he could eat up an ox, and pick his teeth with the horns. These life guard men quarreled all his quarrels, were ready to fight all his battles, and scowled at every man that turned up his nose at the general, as though they would devour him alive. Their conversation was interspersed with oaths like minute guns, and every bombastic rodomontade was rounded off by a thundering execration, like a patriotic toast honoured with a discharge of artillery.

All these valorous vapourings had a considerable effect in convincing certain profound sages, many of whom began to think the general a hero of most unutterable loftiness and magnanimity of soul, particularly as he was continually protesting *on the honour of a soldier*—a marvelously high sounding asseveration. Nay one of the members of the council went so far as to propose they should immortalize him by an imperishable statue of plaster of Paris!

But the vigilant Peter the Headstrong was not thus to be deceived—Sending privately for the commander in chief of all the armies, and having heard all his story, garnished with the customary pious oaths, protestations and ejaculations— "Harkee, *Metgelsel*," cried he, "though by your own account you are the most brave, upright and honourable man in the whole province, yet do you lie under the misfortune of being most damnably traduced, and immeasureably despised. Now though it is certainly hard to punish a man for his misfortunes, and though it is very possible you are totally innocent of the crimes laid to your charge, yet as heaven, at present, doubtless for some wise purpose, sees fit to withhold all proofs of your innocence, far be it from me to counteract its sovereign will. Beside, I cannot consent to venture my armies with a commander whom they despise, or to trust the welfare of my people to a champion whom they distrust. Retire therefore, my friend, from the irksome toils and cares of public life, with this comforting reflection—that if you are guilty, you are but enjoying your just reward—and if you are innocent, that you are not the first great and good man, who has most wrongfully been slandered and maltreated in this wicked world—doubtless to be better treated in a better world, where there shall be neither error, calumny nor persecution.—In the mean time let me never see your face again, for I have a horrible antipathy to the countenances of unfortunate great men like yourself."

CHAP. V.

In which the Author discourses very ingenuously of himself. —
After which is to be found much interesting history about
Peter the Headstrong and his followers.

———————————————————————

AS MY READERS and myself, are about entering on as many
perils and difficulties, as ever a confederacy of meddlesome knights-errant wilfully ran their heads into; it is meet
that like those hardy adventurers, we should join hands, bury
all differences, and swear to stand by one another, in weal or
woe, to the end of the enterprize. My readers must doubtless
perceive, how completely I have altered my tone and deportment, since we first set out together. I warrant they then
thought me a crabbed, cynical, impertinent little son of a
Dutchman; for I never gave them a civil word, nor so much
as touched my beaver, when I had occasion to address them.
But as we jogged along together, in the high-road of my history, I gradually began to relax, to grow more courteous, and
occasionally to enter into familiar discourse, until at length I
came to conceive a most social, companionable kind of regard
for them. This is just my way—I am always a little cold and
reserved at first, particularly to people about whom I neither
know nor care the value of a brass farthing or a Vermont
bank note, and am only to be completely won by long
intimacy.

Besides, why should I have been sociable to the host of
how-d'ye-do acquaintances, who flocked around me at my
first appearance? They were merely attracted by a new face;
many of them only stared me full in the title page, and then
walked off without saying a word; while others lingered
yawningly through the preface, and having gratified their
short-lived curiosity, soon dropped off one by one.—But
more especially to try their mettle, I had recourse to an expedient, similar to one which we are told was used, by that
peerless flower of chivalry, king Arthur; who before he admitted any knight to his intimacy, first required that he
should shew himself superior to danger or hardships, by encountering unheard of mishaps, slaying some dozen giants,

vanquishing wicked enchanters, not to say a word of dwarfs, hyppogriffs and fiery dragons. On a similar principle I cunningly led my readers, at the first sally, into two or three knotty chapters, where they were most woefully belaboured and buffetted, by a host of pagan philosophers and infidel writers. It did my midriff good, by reason of the excessive laughter into which I was thrown, at seeing the utter confusion and dismay of my valiant cavaliers—some dropped down dead (*asleep*) on the field; others threw down my book in the middle of the first chapter, took to their heels, and never ceased scampering until they had fairly run it out of sight; when they stopped to take breath, to tell their friends what troubles they had undergone, and to warn all others from venturing on so thankless an expedition. Every page thinned my ranks more and more; and of the mighty host that first set out, but a comparatively few made shift to survive, in exceedingly battered condition, through the five introductory chapters.

What then! would you have had me take such sun shine, faint hearted recreants to my bosom, at our first acquaintance? No—no. I reserved my friendship for those who deserved it; for those who undauntedly bore me company, in despite of difficulties, dangers and fatigues. And now as to those who adhere to me at present, I take them affectionately by the hand.—Worthy and thrice beloved readers! brave and well tried comrades! who have faithfully followed my footsteps through all my wanderings—I salute you from my heart—I pledge myself to stand by you to the last; and to conduct you, (so heaven speed this trusty weapon which I now hold between my fingers,) triumphantly to the end of this our stupenduous undertaking.

But hark! while we are thus talking, the city of New Amsterdam is in a constant bustle. The gallant host of warriors encamped in the bowling green are striking their tents; the brazen trumpet of Antony Van Corlear makes the welkin to resound with portentous clangour—the drums beat—the standards of the Manhattoes, of Hell-gate and of Michael Paw wave proudly in the air. And now behold where the mariners are busily prepared, hoisting the sails of yon top sail schooner, and those two clump built Albany sloops, which are to waft the army of the Nederlanders to gather immortal laurels on the Delaware!

The entire population of the city, man woman and child, turned out to behold the chivalry of New Amsterdam, as it paraded the streets previous to embarkation. Many a dirty pocket handkerchief was waved out of the windows; many a fair nose was blown in melodious sorrow, on the mournful occasion. The grief of the fair dames and beauteous damsels of Grenada, could not have been more vociferous on the banishment of the gallant tribe of Abencerrages, than was that of the kind hearted *Yfrouws* of New Amsterdam, on the departure of their intrepid warriors. Every love sick maiden fondly crammed the pockets of her hero with gingerbread and dough-nuts—many a copper ring was exchanged and crooked sixpence broken, in pledge of eternal constancy—and there remain extant to this day, some love verses written on that occasion, sufficiently crabbed and incomprehensible to confound the whole universe.

But it was a moving sight to see the buxom lasses, how they hung about the doughty Antony Van Corlear—for he was a jolly, rosy faced, lusty bachelor, and withal a great royster, fond of his joke and a desperate rogue among the women. Fain would they have kept him to comfort them while the army was away; for besides what I have said of him, it is no more than justice to add, that he was a kind hearted soul, noted for his benevolent attentions in comforting disconsolate wives during the absence of their husbands—and this made him to be very much regarded by the honest burghers of the city. But nothing could keep the valiant Antony from following the heels of the old governor, whom he loved as he did his very soul—so embracing all the young vrouws and giving every one of them that had good teeth and a clean mouth, a dozen hearty smacks—he departed loaded with their kind wishes.

Nor was the departure of the gallant Peter among the least causes of public distress. Though the old governor was by no means indulgent to the follies and waywardness of his subjects; and had turned over a complete "new leaf," from that which was presented in the days of William the Testy, yet some how or another he had become strangely popular among the people. There is something so captivating in personal bravery, that, with the common mass of mankind, it takes the lead of most other merits. The simple folk of New Amsterdam looked upon Peter Stuyvesant, as a prodigy of valour. His wooden leg, that trophy of his martial encounters, was regarded with reverence and admiration. Every old burgher had a budget of miraculous stories to tell about the exploits of Hard-koppig Piet, wherewith he regaled his children, of a long winter night, and on which he dwelt with as much delight and exaggeration, as do our honest country yeomen on the hardy adventures of old general Putnam (or as he is familiarly termed *Old Put,*) during our glorious revolution—Not an individual but verily believed the old governor was a match for Belzebub himself; and there was even a story told with great mystery, and under the rose, of his having shot the devil with a silver bullet one dark stormy night, as he was sailing in a canoe through Hell-gate—But this I do not record as being an absolute fact—perish the man, who would let fall a drop that should discolour the pure stream of history!

Certain it is, not an old woman in New Amsterdam, but considered Peter Stuyvesant as a tower of strength, and rested satisfied, that the public welfare was secure as long as he was in the city. It is not surprising then that they looked upon his departure as a sore affliction. With heavy hearts they draggled at the heels of his troop, as they marched down to the river side to embark. The governor from the stern of his schooner, gave a short, but truly patriarchal address to his citizens; wherein he recommended them to comport like loyal and peaceful subjects—to go to church regularly on sundays, and to mind their business all the week besides—That the women should be dutiful and affectionate to their husbands—looking after no bodies concerns but their own: eschewing all gossippings, and morning gaddings—and carrying short tongues and long petticoats. That the men should abstain from ward meetings and porter houses, entrusting the cares of government to the officers appointed to support them—staying home, like good citizens, making money for themselves, and getting children for the benefit of their country. That the burgomasters should look well to the public interest—not oppressing the poor, nor indulging the rich—not tasking their sagacity to devise new laws, but faithfully enforcing those which were already made—rather bending their attention to prevent evil than to punish it; ever recollecting that civil magistrates should consider themselves more as guardians of public morals, than rat catchers employed to entrap public delinquents. Finally, he exhorted them, one and all, high and low, rich and poor, to conduct themselves *as well as they could*; assuring them that if they faithfully and conscientiously complied with this golden rule there was no danger but that they would all conduct themselves well enough.—This done he gave them a paternal benediction; the sturdy Antony sounded a most loving farewell with his trumpet, the jolly crews put up a lusty shout of triumph, and the invincible armada swept off proudly down the bay.

The good people of New Amsterdam crowded down to the Battery—that blest resort, from whence so many a tender prayer has been wafted, so many a fair hand waved, so many a tearful look been cast by lovesick damsel, after the lessening bark, which bore her adventurous swain to distant climes!—Here the populace watched with straining eyes the gallant squadron, as it slowly floated down the bay, and when the intervening land at the Narrows shut it from their sight, gradually dispersed with silent tongues and downcast countenances.

A heavy gloom hung over the late bustling city—The honest burghers smoked their pipes in profound thoughtfulness, casting many a wistful look to the weather cock, on the church of St. Nicholas, and all the old women, having no longer the presence of Hard-koppig Piet to hearten them, gathered their children home, and barricadoed the doors and windows every evening at sun down.

In the mean while the armada of the sturdy Peter proceeded prosperously on its voyage, and after encountering about as many storms and water spouts and whales and other horrors and phenomena, as generally befall adventurous landsmen, in perilous voyages of the kind; after undergoing a severe scouring from that deplorable and unpitied malady called sea sickness; and suffering from a little touch of constipation or dispepsy, which was cured by a box of

Anderson's pills, the whole squadron arrived safely in the Delaware.

Without so much as dropping anchor and giving his wearied ships time to breathe after labouring so long in the ocean, the intrepid Peter pursued his course up the Delaware, and made a sudden appearance before Fort Casimer. Having summoned the astonished garrison by a terrific blast from the trumpet of the long winded Van Corlear, he demanded, in a tone of thunder, an instant surrender of the fort. To this demand Suen Scutz, the wind dried commandant, replied in a shrill, whiffling voice, which by reason of his extreme spareness, sounded like the wind whistling through a broken bellows—"that he had no very strong reasons for refusing, except that the demand was particularly disagreeable, as he had been ordered to maintain his post to the last extremity." He requested time therefore, to consult with governor Rising, and proposed a truce for that purpose.

The choleric Peter, indignant at having his rightful fort so treacherously taken from him, and thus pertinaceously withheld; refused the proposed armistice, and swore by the pipe of St. Nicholas, which like the sacred fire was never extinguished, that unless the fort was surrendered in ten minutes, he would incontinently storm the works, make all the garrison run the gauntlet, and split their scoundrel of a commander, like a pickled shad. To give this menace the greater effect, he drew forth his trusty sword, and shook it at them with such a fierce and vigorous motion, that doubtless, if it had not been exceedingly rusty, it would have lightened terror into the eyes and hearts of the enemy. He then ordered his men to bring a broadside to bear upon the fort, consisting of two swivels, three muskets, a long duck fowling piece and two brace of horse pistols.

In the mean time the sturdy Van Corlear marshalled all his forces, and commenced his warlike operations.—Distending his cheeks like a very Boreas, he kept up a most horrific twanging of his trumpet—the lusty choristers of Sing-Sing broke forth into a hideous song of battle—the warriors of Brooklyn and the Wael bogtig blew a potent and astounding blast on their conch shells, all together forming as outrageous a concerto, as though five thousand French orchestras were displaying their skill in a modern overture—at the hearing of which I warrant me not a Swede in the fortress but felt himself literally distilling away, with pure affright and bad music.

Whether the formidable front of war thus suddenly presented, smote the garrison with sore dismay—or whether the concluding terms of the summons, which mentioned that he should surrender *at discretion*, were mistaken by Suen Scutz, who though a Swede, was a very considerate easy tempered man—as a compliment to his discretion, I will not take upon me to say; certain it is, he found it impossible to resist so courteous a demand. Accordingly, in the very nick of time, just as the cabin boy had gone after a coal of fire, to discharge the swivels, a chamade was beat on the rampart, by the only drum in the garrison, to the no small satisfaction of both parties; who, notwithstanding their great stomach for fighting, had full as good an inclination, to eat a quiet dinner, as to exchange black eyes and bloody noses.

Thus did this impregnable fortress, once more return to the domination of their high mightinesses; Scutz, and his garrison of twenty men, were allowed to march out with the honours of war, and the victorious Peter, who was as generous as brave, permitted them to keep possession of all their arms and ammunition—the same on inspection being found totally unfit for service, having long rusted in the magazine of the fortress, even before it was wrested by the Swedes from the magnanimous, but windy Von Poffenburgh. But I must not omit to mention, that the governor was so well pleased with the services of his faithful squire Van Corlear, in the reduction of this great fortress, that he made him on the spot, lord of a goodly domain in the vicinity of New Amsterdam—which goes by the name of Corlear's Hook, unto this very day.*

The unexampled liberality of the valiant Stuyvesant, towards the Swedes, who certainly had used his government very scurvily—occasioned great surprize in the city of New Amsterdam—nay, certain of those factious individuals, who

*De Vriez, makes mention in one of his voyages of *Corlears Hoek*, and *Corlears Plantagie*, or *Bouwery*; and that too, at an earlier date than the one given by Mr. Knickerbocker—De Vriez, is no doubt a little incorrect in this particular. EDITOR.

had been enlightened by the political meetings, that prevailed during the days of William the Testy—but who had not dared to indulge their meddlesome habits, under the eye of their present ruler; now emboldened by his absence, dared even to give vent to their censures in the streets—Murmurs, equally loud with those uttered by that nation of genuine grumblers, the British, in consequence of the convention of Portugal; were heard in the very council chamber of New Amsterdam; and there is no knowing whether they would not have broken out into downright speeches and invectives, had not the sturdy Peter, privately sent home his walking staff, to be laid as a mace, on the table of the council chamber, in the midst of his councillors; who, like wise men took the hint, and forever after held their peace.

CHAP. VI.

In which is shewn the great advantage the Author has over his reader in time of battle—together with divers portentous movements—which betoken that something terrible is about to happen.

"STRIKE while the Iron is hot," was a favourite saying of Peter the Great, while an apprentice in a blacksmith's shop, at Amsterdam. It is one of those proverbial sayings, which speak a word to the ear, but a volume to the understanding—and contain a world of wisdom, condensed within a narrow compass—Thus every art and profession has thrown a gem of the kind, into the public stock, enriching society by some sage maxim and pithy apothegm drawn from its own experience; in which is conveyed, not only the arcana of that individual art or profession, but also the important secret of a prosperous and happy life. "Cut your coat according to your cloth," says the taylor—"Stick to your last," cries the cobler—"Make hay while the sun shines," says the farmer—"Prevention is better than cure," hints the physician—Surely a man has but to travel through the world, with open ears, and by the time he is grey, he will have all the wisdom of Solomon—and then he has nothing to do but to grow young again, and turn it to the best advantage.

"Strike while the Iron is hot," was not more invariably the saying of Peter the great, than it was the practice of Peter the Headstrong. Like as a mighty alderman, when at a corporation feast the first spoonful of turtle soup salutes his palate, feels his impatient appetite but ten fold quickened, and redoubles his vigorous attacks upon the tureen, while his voracious eyes, projecting from his head, roll greedily round devouring every thing at table—so did the mettlesome Peter Stuyvesant, feel that intolerable hunger for martial glory, which raged within his very bowels, inflamed by the capture of Fort Casimer, and nothing could allay it, but the conquest of all New Sweden. No sooner therefore had he secured his conquest, than he stumped resolutely on, flushed with success, to gather fresh laurels at Fort Christina.*

This was the grand Swedish post, established on a small river (or as it is termed, creek,) of the same name, which empties into the Delaware: and here that crafty governor Jan Risingh, like another Charles the twelfth, commanded his subjects in person.

Thus have I fairly pitted two of the most potent chieftans that ever this country beheld, against each other, and what will be the result of their contest, I am equally anxious with my readers to ascertain. This will doubtless appear a paradox to such of them, as do not know the way in which I write. The fact is, that as I am not engaged in a work of imagination, but a faithful and veritable history, it is not necessary, that I should trouble my head, by anticipating its incidents and catastrophe. On the contrary, I generally make it a rule, not to examine the annals of the times whereof I treat, further than exactly a page in advance of my own work; hence I am equally interested in the progress of my history, with him who reads it, and equally unconscious, what occurrence is next to happen. Darkness and doubt hang over each coming chapter—with trembling pen and anxious mind I conduct my beloved native city through the dangers and difficulties, with which it is continually surrounded; and in treating of my favourite hero, the gallant Peter Stuyvesant, I often shrink back with dismay, as I turn another page, lest I should find his undaunted spirit hurrying him into some dolorous misadventure.

Thus am I situated at present. I have just conducted him into the very teeth of peril—nor can I tell, any more than my reader, what will be the issue of this horrid din of arms, with which our ears are mutually assailed. It is true, I possess one advantage over my reader, which tends marvelously to soothe my apprehensions—which is, that though I cannot save the life of my favourite hero, nor absolutely contradict the event of a battle, (both of which misrepresentations, though much

*The formidable fortress and metropolis to which Mr. Knickerbocker alludes, is at present a flourishing little town called Christiana, about thirty seven miles from Philadelphia, on your route to Baltimore.—EDITOR.

practised by the French writers, of the present reign, I hold to be utterly unworthy of a scrupulous historian) yet I can now and then make him bestow on his enemy a sturdy back stroke, sufficient to fell a giant; though in honest truth he may never have done any thing of the kind—or I can drive his antagonist clear round and round the field, as did Dan Homer most falsely make that fine fellow Hector scamper like a poltroon around the walls of Troy; for which in my humble opinion the prince of Poets, deserved to have his head broken—as no doubt he would, had those terrible fellows the Edinburgh reviewers, existed in those days—or if my hero should be pushed too hard by his opponent, I can just step in, and with one dash of my pen, give him a hearty thwack over the sconce, that would have cracked the scull of Hercules himself—like a faithful second in boxing, who when he sees his principal down, and likely to be worsted, puts in a sly blow, that knocks the wind out of his adversary, and changes the whole state of the contest.

I am aware that many conscientious readers will be ready to cry out "foul play!" whenever I render such assistance— but I insist that it is one of those little privileges, strenuously asserted and exercised by historiographers of all ages—and one which has never been disputed. An historian, in fact, is in some measure bound in honour to stand by his hero—the fame of the latter is entrusted to his hands, and it is his duty to do the best by it he can. Never was there a general, an admiral or any other commander, who in giving an account of any battle he had fought, did not sorely belabour the enemy; and I have no doubt that, had my heroes written the history of their own atchievements, they would have hit much harder blows, than any I shall recount. Standing forth therefore, as the guardian of their fame, it behoves me to do them the same justice, they would have done themselves; and if I happen to be a little hard upon the Swedes, I give free leave to any of their descendants, who may write a history of the state of Delaware, to take fair retaliation, and thump Peter Stuyvesant as hard as they please.

Therefore stand by for broken heads and bloody noses! my pen has long itched for a battle—siege after siege have I carried on, without blows or bloodshed; but now I have at length got a chance, and I vow to heaven and St. Nicholas, that, let the chronicles of the times say what they please, neither Sallust, Livy, Tacitus, Polybius, or any other battle monger of them all, did ever record a fiercer fight, than that in which my valiant chieftans are now about to engage.

And thou, most excellent reader, who, for thy faithful adherence to my heels, I could lodge in the best parlour of my heart—be not uneasy—trust the fate of our favourite Stuyvesant to me—for by the rood, come what will, I'll stick by Hard-koppig Piet to the last; I'll make him drive about these lossels vile as did the renowned Launcelot of the lake, a herd of recreant cornish Knights—and if he does fall, let me never draw my pen to fight another battle, in behalf of a brave man, if I don't make these lubberly Swedes pay for it!

No sooner had Peter Stuyvesant arrived before fort Christina than he proceeded without delay to entrench himself, and immediately on running his first parallel, dispatched Antony Van Corlear, that incomparable trumpeter, to summon the fortress to surrender. Van Corlear was received with all due formality, hoodwinked at the portal, and conducted through a pestiferous smell of salt fish and onions, to the citadel, a substantial hut built of pine logs. His eyes were here uncovered, and he found himself in the august presence of governor Risingh, who, having been accidentally likened to Charles XII, the intelligent reader will instantly perceive, must have been a tall, robustious, able bodied, mean looking man, clad in a coarse blue coat with brass buttons, a shirt which for a week, had longed in vain for the wash-tub, a pair of foxey coloured jack boots—and engaged in the act of shaving his grizly beard, at a bit of broken looking glass, with a villainous patent Brummagem razor. Antony Van Corlear delivered in a few words, being a kind of short hand speaker, a long message from his excellency, recounting the whole history of the province, with a recapitulation of grievances, enumeration of claims, &c.&c. and concluding with a peremptory demand of instant surrender: which done, he turned aside, took his nose between his thumb and finger, and blew a tremendous blast, not unlike the flourish of a trumpet of defiance—which it had doubtless learned from a long and intimate neighbourhood with that melodious instrument.

Governor Risingh heard him through, trumpet and all, but with infinite impatience; leaning at times, as was his usual custom, on the pommel of his sword, and at times twirling a huge steel watch chain or snapping his fingers. Van Corlear having finished he bluntly replied, that Peter Stuyvesant and his summons might go to the D——l, whither he hoped to send him and his crew of raggamuffins before supper time. Then unsheathing his brass hilted sword, and throwing away the scabbard—"Fore gad," quod he, "but I will not sheathe thee again, until I make a scabbard of the smoke dried leathern hide, of this runegate Dutchman." Then having flung a fierce defiance in the teeth of his adversary, by the lips of his messenger, the latter was reconducted to the portal, with all the ceremonious civility due to the trumpeter, squire and ambassador of so great a commander, and being again unblinded, was courteously dismissed with a tweak of the nose, to assist him in recollecting his message.

No sooner did the gallant Peter receive this insolent reply, than he let fly a tremendous volley of red hot, four and forty pounder execrations, that would infallibly have battered down the fortifications and blown up the powder magazines, about the ears of the fiery Swede, had not the ramparts been remarkably strong, and the magazine bomb proof. Perceiving that the works withstood this terrific blast, and that it was utterly impossible (as it really was in those unphilosophic days) to carry on a war with words, he ordered his merry men all, to prepare for immediate assault. But here a strange murmur broke out among his troops, beginning with the tribe of the Van Bummels, those valiant trencher men of the Bronx, and spreading from man to man, accompanied with certain mutinous looks and discontented murmurs. For once in his life, and only for once, did the great Peter turn pale, for he verily thought his warriors were going to faulter in this hour of perilous trial, and thus tarnish forever the fame of the province of New Nederlands.

But soon did he discover to his great joy, that in this suspicion he deeply wronged this most undaunted army; for the cause of this agitation and uneasiness simply was, that the hour of dinner was at hand, and it would have almost broken the hearts of these regular dutch warriors, to have broken in upon the invariable routine of their habits. Beside it was an established rule among our valiant ancestors, always to fight upon a full stomach, and to this may be doubtless attributed the circumstance that they came to be so renowned in arms.

And now are the hearty men of the Manhattoes, and their no less hearty comrades, all lustily engaged under the trees, buffeting stoutly with the contents of their wallets, and taking such affectionate embraces of their canteens and pottles, as though they verily believed they were to be the last. And as I foresee we shall have hot work in a page or two, I advise my readers to do the same, for which purpose I will bring this chapter to a close; giving them my word of honour that no advantage shall be taken of this armistice, to surprise, or in any wise molest, the honest Nederlanders, while at their vigorous repast.

Before we part however, I have one small favour to ask of them; which is, that when I have set both armies by the ears in the next chapter, and am hurrying about, like a very devil, in the midst—they will just stand a little on one side, out of harms way—and on no account attempt to interrupt me by a single question or remonstrance. As the whole spirit, hurry and sublimity of the battle will depend on my exertions, the moment I should stop to speak, the whole business would stand still—wherefore I shall not be able to say a word to my readers, throughout the whole of the next chapter, but I promise them in the one after, I'll listen to all they have to say, and answer any questions they may ask.

CHAP. VII.

Containing the most horrible battle ever recorded in poetry or prose; with the admirable exploits of Peter the Headstrong.

Now had the Dutchmen snatch'd a huge repast," and finding themselves wonderfully encouraged and animated thereby, prepared to take the field. Expectation, says a faithful matter of fact dutch poet, whose works were unfortunately destroyed in the conflagration of the Alexandrian library—Expectation now stood on stilts. The world forgot to turn round, or rather stood still, that it might witness the affray; like a fat round bellied alderman, watching the combat of two chivalric flies upon his jerkin. The eyes of all mankind, as usual in such cases, were turned upon Fort Christina. The sun, like a little man in a crowd, at a puppet shew, scampered about the heavens, popping his head here and there, and endeavouring to get a peep between the unmannerly clouds, that obtruded themselves in his way. The historians filled their ink-horns—the poets went without their dinners, either that they might buy paper and goose-quills, or because they could not get any thing to eat—antiquity scowled sulkily out of its grave, to see itself outdone—while even posterity stood mute, gazing in gaping extacy of retrospection, on the eventful field!

The immortal deities, who whilome had seen service at the "affair" of Troy—now mounted their feather-bed clouds, and sailed over the plain, or mingled among the combatants in different disguises, all itching to have a finger in the pie. Jupiter sent off his thunderbolt to a noted coppersmiths, to have it furbished up for the direful occasion. Venus, swore by her chastity she'd patronize the Swedes, and in semblance of a blear eyed trull, paraded the battlements of Fort Christina, accompanied by Diana, as a serjeant's widow, of cracked reputation—The noted bully Mars, stuck two horse pistols into his belt, shouldered a rusty firelock, and gallantly swaggered at their elbow, as a drunken corporal—while Apollo trudged in their rear, as a bandy-legged fifer, playing most villainously out of tune.

On the other side, the ox-eyed Juno, who had won a pair of black eyes over night, in one of her curtain lectures with old Jupiter, displayed her haughty beauties on a baggage waggon—Minerva, as a brawny gin suttler, tucked up her skirts, brandished her fists, and swore most heroically, in exceeding bad dutch, (having but lately studied the language) by way of keeping up the spirits of the soldiers; while Vulcan halted as a club-footed blacksmith, lately promoted to be a captain of militia. All was silent horror, or bustling preparation; war reared his horrid front, gnashed loud his iron fangs, and shook his direful crest of bristling bayonets.

And now the mighty chieftans marshalled out their hosts. Here stood stout Risingh, firm as a thousand rocks—encrusted with stockades, and entrenched to the chin in mud batteries—His artillery consisting of two swivels and a carronade, loaded to the muzzle, the touch holes primed, and a whiskered bombardier stationed at each, with lighted match in hand, waiting the word. His valiant infantry, that had never turned back upon an enemy (having never seen any before)—lined the breast work in grim array, each having his mustachios fiercely greased, and his hair pomatomed back, and queued so stiffly, that he grinned above the ramparts like a grizly death's head.

There came on the intrepid Hard-koppig Piet,—a second Bayard, without fear or reproach—his brows knit, his teeth clenched, his breath held hard, rushing on like ten thousand bellowing bulls of Bashan. His faithful squire Van Corlear, trudging valiantly at his heels, with his trumpet gorgeously bedecked with red and yellow ribbands, the remembrances of his fair mistresses at the Manhattoes. Then came waddling on his sturdy comrades, swarming like the myrmidons of Achilles. There were the Van Wycks and the Van Dycks and the Ten Eycks—the Van Nesses, the Van Tassels, the Van Grolls; the Van Hœsens, the Van Giesons, and the Van Blarcoms—The Van Warts, the Van Winkles, the Van Dams; the Van Pelts, the Van Rippers, and the Van Brunts.—There were the Van Horns, the Van Borsums, the Van Bunschotens; the Van Gelders, the Van Arsdales, and the Van Bummels—The Vander Belts, the Vander Hoofs, the Vander Voorts, the Vander Lyns, the Vander Pools and the Vander

Spiegels.—There came the Hoffmans, the Hooglands, the Hoppers, the Cloppers, the Oothouts, the Quackenbosses, the Roerbacks, the Garrebrantzs, the Onderdonks, the Varra Vangers, the Schermerhorns, the Brinkerhoffs, the Bontecous, the Knickerbockers, the Hockstrassers, the Ten Breecheses and the Tough Breecheses, with a host more of valiant worthies, whose names are too crabbed to be written, or if they could be written, it would be impossible for man to utter—all fortified with a mighty dinner, and to use the words of a great Dutch poet

—"Brimful of wrath and cabbage!"

For an instant the mighty Peter paused in the midst of his career, and mounting on a rotten stump addressed his troops in eloquent low dutch, exhorting them to fight like *duyvels*, and assuring them that if they conquered, they should get plenty of booty—if they fell they should be allowed the unparalleled satisfaction, while dying, of reflecting that it was in the service of their country—and after they were dead, of seeing their names inscribed in the temple of renown and handed down, in company with all the other great men of the year, for the admiration of posterity.—Finally he swore to them, on the word of a governor (and they knew him too well to doubt it for a moment) that if he caught any mother's son of them looking pale, or playing craven, he'd curry his hide till he made him run out of it like a snake in spring time.—Then lugging out his direful snickersnee, he brandished it three times over his head, ordered Van Corlear to sound a tremendous charge, and shouting the word "St. Nicholas and the Manhattoes!" courageously dashed forwards. His warlike followers, who had employed the interval in lighting their pipes, instantly stuck them in their mouths, gave a furious puff, and charged gallantly, under cover of the smoke.

The Swedish garrison, ordered by the cunning Risingh not to fire until they could distinguish the whites of their assailants' eyes, stood in horrid silence on the covert-way; until the eager dutchmen had half ascended the glacis. Then did they pour into them such a tremendous volley, that the very hills quaked around, and were terrified even unto an incontinence of water, insomuch that certain springs burst forth from their sides, which continue to run unto the present day. Not a dutchman but would have bit the dust, beneath that dreadful fire, had not the protecting Minerva kindly taken care, that the Swedes should one and all, observe their usual custom of shutting their eyes and turning away their heads, at the moment of discharge.

But were not the muskets levelled in vain, for the balls, winged with unerring fate, went point blank into a flock of wild geese, which, like geese as they were, happened at that moment to be flying past—and brought down seventy dozen of them—which furnished a luxurious supper to the conquerors, being well seasoned and stuffed with onions.

Neither was the volley useless to the musqueteers, for the hostile wind, commissioned by the implacable Juno, carried the smoke and dust full in the faces of the dutchmen, and would inevitably have blinded them, had their eyes been open. The Swedes followed up their fire, by leaping the counterscarp, and falling tooth and nail upon the foe, with furious outcries. And now might be seen prodigies of valour, of which neither history nor song have ever recorded a parallel. Here was beheld the sturdy Stoffel Brinkerhoff brandishing his lusty quarter staff, like the terrible giant Blanderon his oak tree (for he scorned to carry any other weapon,) and drumming a horrific tune upon the heads of whole squadrons of Swedes. There were the crafty Van Courtlandts, posted at a distance, like the little Locrian archers of yore, and plying it most potently with the long bow, for which they were so justly renowned. At another place were collected on a rising knoll the valiant men of Sing-Sing, who assisted marvellously in the fight, by chaunting forth the great song of St. Nicholas. In a different part of the field might be seen the Van Grolls of Anthony's nose; but they were horribly perplexed in a defile between two little hills, by reason of the length of their noses. There were the Van Bunschotens of Nyack and Kakiat, so renowned for kicking with the left foot, but their skill availed them little at present, being short of wind in consequence of the hearty dinner they had eaten—and they would irretrievably have been put to rout, had they not been reinforced by a gallant corps of *Voltigeurs* composed of the Hoppers, who advanced to their assistance nimbly on one foot. At another place might you see the Van Arsdales, and the Van Bummels, who ever went together, gallantly pressing forward to bombard the fortress—but as to the Gardeniers of Hudson, they were absent from the battle, having been sent on a marauding party, to lay waste the neighbouring water-melon patches. Nor must I omit to mention the incomparable atchievement of Antony Van Corlear, who, for a good quarter of an hour waged horrid fight with a little pursy Swedish drummer, whose hide he drummed most magnificently; and had he not come into the battle with no other weapon but his trumpet, would infallibly have put him to an untimely end.

But now the combat thickened—on came the mighty Jacobus Varra Vanger and the fighting men of the Wael Bogtig; after them thundered the Van Pelts of Esopus, together with the Van Rippers and the Van Brunts, bearing down all before them—then the Suy Dams and the Van Dams, pressing forward with many a blustering oath, at the head of the warriors of Hell-gate, clad in their thunder and lighting gaberdines; and lastly the standard bearers and body guards of Peter Stuyvesant, bearing the great beaver of the Manhattoes.

And now commenced the horrid din, the desperate struggle, the maddening ferocity, the frantic desperation, the confusion and self abandonment of war. Dutchman and Swede commingled, tugged, panted and blowed. The heavens were darkened with a tempest of missives. Carcasses, fire balls, smoke balls, stink balls and hand grenades, jostling each other, in the air. Bang! went the guns—whack! struck the broad swords—thump! went the cudgels—crash! went the musket stocks—blows—kicks—cuffs—scratches—black eyes and bloody noses swelling the horrors of the scene! Thick-thwack, cut and hack, helter-skelter, higgledy-piggledy, hurley-burley, head over heels, klip-klap, slag op slag, bob over bol, rough and tumble!——Dunder and blixum! swore the dutchmen, splitter and splutter! cried the Swedes—Storm the works! shouted Hard-koppig Piet—fire the mine! roared stout Risingh—Tantara-ra-ra! twang'd the trumpet of Antony Van Corlear—until all voice and sound became unintelligible—grunts of pain, yells of fury, and shouts of triumph commingling in one hideous clamour. The earth shook as if struck with a paralytic stroke—The trees shrunk aghast, and wilted at the sight—The rocks burrowed in the ground like rabbits, and even Christina creek turned from its course, and ran up a mountain in breathless terror!

Nothing, save the dullness of their weapons, the damaged condition of their powder, and the singular accident of one and all striking with the flat instead of the edge of their swords, could have prevented a most horrible carnage—As it was, the sweat prodigiously streaming, ran in rivers on the field, fortunately without drowning a soul, the combatants being to a man, expert swimmers, and furnished with cork jackets for the occasion—but many a valiant head was broken, many a stubborn rib belaboured, and many a broken winded hero drew short breath that day!

Long hung the contest doubtful, for though a heavy shower of rain, sent by the "cloud compelling Jove," in some measure cooled their ardour, as doth a bucket of water thrown on a group of fighting mastiffs, yet did they but pause for a moment, to return with tenfold fury to the charge, belabouring each other with black and bloody bruises. Just at this juncture was seen a vast and dense column of smoke, slowly rolling towards the scene of battle, which for a while made even the furious combatants to stay their arms in mute astonishment—but the wind for a moment dispersing the murky cloud, from the midst thereof emerged the flaunting banner of the immortal Michael Paw. This noble chieftain came fearlessly on, leading a solid phalanx of oyster-fed Pavonians, who had remained behind, partly as a *corps de reserve*, and partly to digest the enormous dinner they had eaten. These sturdy yeomen, nothing daunted, did trudge manfully forward, smoking their pipes with outrageous vigour, so as to raise the awful cloud that has been mentioned; but marching exceedingly slow, being short of leg and of great rotundity in the belt.

And now the protecting deities of the army of New Amsterdam, having unthinkingly left the field and stept into a neighbouring tavern to refresh themselves with a pot of beer, a direful catastrophe had well nigh chanced to befall the Nederlanders. Scarcely had the myrmidons of the puissant Paw attained the front of battle, before the Swedes, instructed by the cunning Risingh, levelled a shower of blows, full at their tobacco pipes. Astounded at this unexpected assault, and totally discomfited at seeing their pipes broken by this "d—d nonsense," the valiant dutchmen fall in vast confusion—already they begin to fly—like a frightened drove of unwieldy Elephants they throw their own army in an uproar—bearing down a whole legion of little Hoppers—the sacred banner on which is blazoned the gigantic oyster of Communipaw is trampled in the dirt—The Swedes pluck up new spirits and pressing on their rear, apply their feet *a parte poste* with a vigour that prodigiously accelerates their motions—nor doth the renowned Paw himself, fail to receive divers grievous and intolerable visitations of shoe leather!

But what, Oh muse! was the rage of the gallant Peter, when from afar he saw his army yield? With a voice of thunder did he roar after his recreant warriors, putting up such a war whoop, as did the stern Achilles, when the Trojan troops were on the point of burning all his gunboats. The dreadful shout rung in long echoes through the woods—trees toppled at the noise; bears, wolves and panthers jumped out of their skins, in pure affright; several wild looking hills bounced clear over the Delaware; and all the small beer in Fort Christina, turned sour at the sound!

The men of the Manhattoes plucked up new courage when they heard their leader—or rather they dreaded his fierce displeasure, of which they stood in more awe than of all the Swedes in Christendom—but the daring Peter, not waiting for their aid, plunged sword in hand, into the thickest of the foe. Then did he display some such incredible atchievements, as have never been known since the miraculous days of the giants. Wherever he went the enemy shrunk before him— with fierce impetuosity he pushed forward, driving the Swedes, like dogs, into their own ditch—but as he fearlessly advanced, the foe, like rushing waves which close upon the scudding bark, thronged in his rear, and hung upon his flank with fearful peril. One desperate Swede, who had a mighty heart, almost as large as a pepper corn, drove his dastard sword full at the hero's heart. But the protecting power that watches over the safety of all great and good men turned aside the hostile blade, and directed it to a large side pocket, where reposed an enormous Iron Tobacco Box, endowed like the shield of Achilles with supernatural powers—no doubt in consequence of its being piously decorated with a portrait of the blessed St. Nicholas. Thus was the dreadful blow repelled, but not without occasioning to the great Peter a fearful loss of wind.

Like as a furious bear, when gored by worrying curs, turns fiercely round, shews his dread teeth, and springs upon the foe, so did our hero turn upon the treacherous Swede. The miserable varlet sought in flight, for safety—but the active Peter, seizing him by an immeasurable queue, that dangled from his head—"Ah Whoreson Caterpillar!" roared he, "here is what shall make dog's meat of thee!" So saying he whirled his trusty sword, and made a blow, that would have decapitated him, had he, like Briarcus, half a hundred heads, but that the pitying steel struck short and shaved the queue forever from his crown. At this very moment a cunning arquebusier, perched on the summit of a neighbouring mound, levelled his deadly instrument, and would have sent the gallant Stuyvesant, a wailing ghost to haunt the Stygian shore— had not the watchful Minerva, who had just stopped to tie up her garter, saw the great peril of her favourite chief, and dispatched old Boreas with his bellows; who in the very nick of time, just as the direful match descended to the pan, gave such a lucky blast, as blew all the priming from the touch hole!

Thus waged the horrid fight—when the stout Risingh, surveying the battle from the top of a little ravelin, perceived his faithful troops, banged, beaten and kicked by the invincible Peter. Language cannot describe the choler with which he was seized at the sight—he only stopped for a moment to disburthen himself of five thousand anathemas; and then drawing his immeasurable cheese toaster, straddled down to the field of combat, with some such thundering strides, as Jupiter is said by old Hesiod to have taken, when he strode down the spheres, to play off his sky rockets at the Titans.

No sooner did these two rival heroes come face to face, than they each made a prodigious start of fifty feet, (flemish measure) such as is made by your most experienced stage champions. Then did they regard each other for a moment, with bitter aspect, like two furious ram cats, on the very point of a clapper clawing. Then did they throw themselves in one attitude, then in another, striking their swords on the ground, first on the right side, then on the left, at last at it they went, like five hundred houses on fire! Words cannot tell the prodigies of strength and valour, displayed in this direful encounter—an encounter, compared to which the far famed battles of Ajax with Hector, of Eneas with Turnus, Orlando with Rodomont, Guy of Warwick with Colbrand the Dane, or of that renowned Welsh Knight Sir Owen of the mountains with the giant Guylon, were all gentle sports and holliday recreations. At length the valiant Peter watching his opportunity, aimed a fearful blow with the full intention of cleaving his adversary to the very chine; but Risingh nimbly raising his sword, warded it off so narrowly, that glancing on one side, it shaved away a huge canteen full of fourth proof brandy, that he always carried swung on one side; thence pursuing its tranchant course, it severed off a deep coat pocket, stored with bread and cheese—all which dainties rolling among the armies, occasioned a fearful scrambling between the Swedes and Dutchmen, and made the general battle to wax ten times more furious than ever.

Enraged to see his military stores thus woefully laid waste, the stout Risingh collecting all his forces, aimed a mighty blow, full at the hero's crest. In vain did his fierce little cocked hat oppose its course; the biting steel clove through the stubborn ram beaver, and would infallibly have cracked his gallant crown, but that the scull was of such adamantine hardness that the brittle weapon shivered into five and twenty pieces, shedding a thousand sparks, like beams of glory, round his grizly visage.

Stunned with the blow the valiant Peter reeled, turned up his eyes and beheld fifty thousand suns, besides moons and stars, dancing Scotch reels about the firmament—at length, missing his footing, by reason of his wooden leg, down he came, on his seat of honour, with a crash that shook the surrounding hills, and would infallibly have wracked his anatomical system, had he not been received into a cushion softer than velvet, which providence, or Minerva, or St. Nicholas, or some kindly cow, had benevolently prepared for his reception.

The furious Risingh, in despight of that noble maxim, cherished by all true knights, that "fair play is a jewel," hastened to take advantage of the hero's fall; but just as he was stooping to give the fatal blow, the ever vigilant Peter bestowed him a sturdy thwack over the sconce, with his wooden leg, that set some dozen chimes of bells ringing triple bob-majors in his cerebellum. The bewildered Swede staggered with the blow, and in the mean time the wary Peter, espying a pocket pistol lying hard by (which had dropped from the wallet of his faithful squire and trumpeter Van Corlear during his furious encounter with the drummer) discharged it full at the head of the reeling Risingh— Let not my reader mistake—it was not a murderous weapon loaded with powder and ball, but a little sturdy stone pottle, charged to the muzzle with a double dram of true dutch courage, which the knowing Van Corlear always carried about him by way of replenishing his valour. The hideous missive sung through the air, and true to its course, as was the mighty fragment of a rock, discharged at Hector by bully Ajax, encountered the huge head of the gigantic Swede with matchless violence.

This heaven directed blow decided the eventful battle. The ponderous pericranium of general Jan Risingh sunk upon his breast; his knees tottered under him; a deathlike torpor seized upon his Titan frame, and he tumbled to the earth with such tremendous violence, that old Pluto started with affright, lest he should have broken through the roof of his infernal palace.

His fall, like that of Goliah, was the signal for defeat and victory—The Swedes gave way—the Dutch pressed forward; the former took to their heels, the latter hotly pursued— Some entered with them, pell mell, through the sally port— others stormed the bastion, and others scrambled over the curtain. Thus in a little while the impregnable fortress of Fort Christina, which like another Troy had stood a siege of full ten *hours*, was finally carried by assault, without the loss of a single man on either side. Victory in the likeness of a gigantic ox fly, sat perched upon the little cocked hat of the gallant

Stuyvesant, and it was universally declared, by all the writers, whom he hired to write the history of his expedition, that on this memorable day he gained a sufficient quantity of glory to immortalize a dozen of the greatest heroes in Christendom!

CHAP. VIII.

*In which the author and reader, while reposing after the bat-
tle, fall into a very grave and instructive discourse—after
which is recorded the conduct of Peter Stuyvesant in respect to
his victory.*

THANKS to St. Nicholas! I have fairly got through this
tremendous battle: let us sit down, my worthy reader,
and cool ourselves, for truly I am in a prodigious sweat and
agitation—Body o'me, but this fighting of battles is hot
work! And if your great commanders, did but know what
trouble they give their historians, they would not have the
conscience to atchieve so many horrible victories. I already
hear my reader complaining, that throughout all this boasted
battle, there is not the least slaughter, nor a single individual
maimed, if we except the unhappy Swede, who was shorn of
his queue by the tranchant blade of Peter Stuyvesant—all
which is a manifest outrage on probability, and highly injurious to the interest of the narrative.

For once I candidly confess my captious reader has some
grounds for his murmuring—But though I could give a variety of substantial reasons for not having deluged my whole
page with blood, and swelled the cadence of every sentence
with dying groans, yet I will content myself with barely mentioning one; which if it be not sufficient to satisfy every reasonable man on the face of the earth, I will consent that my
book shall be cast into the flames—The simple truth then is
this, that on consulting every history, manuscript and tradition, which relates to this memorable, though long forgotten
battle, I cannot find that a single man was killed, or even
wounded, throughout the whole affair!

My readers, if they have any bowels, must easily feel the
distressing situation in which I was placed. I had already
promised to furnish them with a hideous and unparalleled
battle—I had made incredible preparations for the same—
and had moreover worked myself up into a most warlike and
blood-thirsty state of mind—my honour, as a historian, and
my feelings, as a man of spirit, were both too deeply engaged

in the business, to back out. Beside, I had transported a great
and powerful force of warriors from the Nederlandts, at vast
trouble and expense, and I could not reconcile it to my own
conscience, or to that reverence which I entertain for them,
and their illustrious descendants, to have suffered them to return home, like a renowned British expedition—with a flea
in their ears.

How to extract myself from this dilemma was truly perplexing. Had the inexorable fates only allowed me half a
dozen dead men, I should have been contented, for I would
have made them such heroes as abounded in the olden time,
but whose race is now unfortunately extinct. Men, who, if we
may believe those authentic writers, the poets, could drive
great armies like sheep before them, and conquer and desolate
whole cities by their single arm. I'd have given every mother's
son of them as many lives as a cat, and made them die hard,
I warrant you.

But seeing that I had not a single carcass at my disposal, all
that was left for me, was to make the most I could of my
battle, by means of kicks and cuffs, and bruises—black eyes,
and bloody noses, and such like ignoble wounds. My greatest
difficulty however, was, when I had once put my warriors in
a passion, and let them loose into the midst of the enemy; to
keep them from doing mischief. Many a time had I to restrain
the sturdy Peter, from cleaving a gigantic Swede, to the very
waist-band, or spitting half a dozen little fellows on his
sword, like so many sparrows—And when I had set some
hundreds of missives flying in the air, I did not dare to suffer
one of them to reach the ground, lest it should have put an
end to some unlucky Dutchman.

The reader cannot conceive how much I suffered from thus
in a manner having my hands tied, and how many tempting
opportunities I had to wink at, where I might have made as
fine a death blow, as any recorded in history or song.

From my own experience, I begin to doubt most potently
of the authenticity of many of Dan Homer's stories. I verily
believe, that when he had once launched one of his hearty
blades among a crowd of the enemy, he cut down many an
honest fellow, without any authority for so doing, excepting
that he presented a fair mark—and that often a poor devil

was sent to grim Pluto's domains, merely because he had a name that would give a sounding turn to a period. But I disclaim all such unprincipled liberties—let me but have truth and the law on my side, and no man would fight harder than myself—but since the various records I consulted did not warrant it, I had too much conscience to kill a single soldier.—By St. Nicholas, but it would have been a pretty piece of business! My enemies the critics, who I foresee will be ready enough to lay any crime they can discover, at my door, might have charged me with murder outright—and I should have esteemed myself lucky to escape, with no harsher verdict than manslaughter!

And now gentle reader that we are tranquilly sitting down here, smoking our pipes, permit me to indulge in a melancholy reflection which at this moment passes across my mind.—How vain, how fleeting, how uncertain are all those gaudy bubbles after which we are panting and toiling in this world of fair delusions. The wealthy store which the hoary miser has painfully amassed with so many weary days, so many sleepless nights, a spendthrift heir shall squander away in joyless prodigality—The noblest monuments which pride has ever reared to perpetuate a name, the hand of time shall shortly tumble into promiscuous ruins—and even the brightest laurels, gained by hardiest feats of arms, may wither and be forever blighted by the chilling neglect of mankind.— "How many illustrious heroes," says the good Boëtius, " who were once the pride and glory of the age, hath the silence of historians buried in eternal oblivion!" And this it was, that made the Spartans when they went to battle, solemnly to sacrifice to the muses, supplicating that their atchievements should be worthily recorded. Had not Homer tuned his lofty lyre, observes the elegant Cicero, the valour of Achilles had remained unsung.—And such too, after all the toils and perils he had braved, after all the gallant actions he had atchieved, such too had nearly been the fate of the chivalric Peter Stuyvesant, but that I fortunately stepped in and engraved his name on the indelible tablet of history, just as the caitiff Time was silently brushing it away forever!

The more I reflect, the more am I astonished to think, what important beings are we historians! We are the sovereign censors who decide upon the renown or infamy of our fellow mortals—We are the public almoners of fame, dealing out her favours according to our judgment or caprice—we are the benefactors of kings—we are the guardians of truth—we are the scourgers of guilt—we are the instructors of the world— we are—in short, what are we not!—And yet how often does the lofty patrician or lordly Burgomaster stalk contemptuously by the little, plodding, dusty historian like myself, little thinking that this humble mortal is the arbiter of his fate, on whom it shall depend whether he shall live in future ages, or be forgotten in the dirt, as were his ancestors before him. "Insult not the dervise" said a wise caliph to his son, "lest thou offend thine historian;" and many a mighty man of the olden time, had he observed so obvious a maxim, would have escaped divers cruel wipes of the pen, which have been drawn across his character.

But let not my readers think I am indulging in vain glorious boasting, from the consciousness of my own power and importance. On the contrary I shudder to think what direful commotions, what heart rending calamities we historians occasion in the world—I swear to thee, honest reader, as I am a man, I weep at the very idea!—Why, let me ask, are so many illustrious men daily tearing themselves away from the embraces of their distracted families—slighting the smiles of beauty—despising the allurements of fortune, and exposing themselves to all the miseries of war?—Why are renowned generals cutting the throats of thousands who never injured them in their lives?—Why are kings desolating empires and depopulating whole countries? in short, what induces all great men, of all ages and countries to commit so many horrible victories and misdeeds, and inflict so many miseries upon mankind and on themselves; but the mere hope that we historians will kindly take them into notice, and admit them into a corner of our volumes. So that the mighty object of all their toils, their hardships and privations is nothing but *immortal fame*—and what is immortal fame?——why, half a page of dirty paper!——alas! alas! how humiliating the idea— that the renown of so great a man as Peter Stuyvesant, should depend upon the pen of so little a man, as Diedrich Knickerbocker!

And now, having refreshed ourselves after the fatigues and perils of the field, it behoves us to return once more to the scene of conflict, and inquire what were the results of this renowned conquest. The Fortress of Christina being the fair metropolis and in a manner the Key to New Sweden, its capture was speedily followed by the entire subjugation of the province. This was not a little promoted by the gallant and courteous deportment of the chivalric Peter. Though a man terrible in battle, yet in the hour of victory was he endued with a spirit generous, merciful and humane—He vaunted not over his enemies, nor did he make defeat more galling by unmanly insults; for like that mirror of Knightly virtue, the renowned Paladin Orlando, he was more anxious to do great actions, than to talk of them after they were done. He put no man to death; ordered no houses to be burnt down; permitted no ravages to be perpetrated on the property of the vanquished, and even gave one of his bravest staff officers a severe rib-roasting, who was detected in the act of sacking a hen roost.

He moreover issued a proclamation inviting the inhabitants to submit to the authority of their high mightinesses; but declaring, with unexampled clemency, that whoever refused, should be lodged at the public expense, in a goodly castle provided for the purpose, and have an armed retinue to wait on them in the bargain. In consequence of these beneficent terms, about thirty Swedes stepped manfully forward and took the oath of allegiance; in reward for which they were graciously permitted to remain on the banks of the Delaware, where their descendants reside at this very day. But I am told by sundry observant travellers, that they have never been able to get over the chap-fallen looks of their ancestors, and do still unaccountably transmit from father to son, manifest marks of the sound drubbing given them by the sturdy Amsterdammers.

The whole country of New Sweden, having thus yielded to the arms of the triumphant Peter, was reduced to a colony called South River, and placed under the superintendance of a lieutenant governor; subject to the controul of the supreme government at New Amsterdam. This great dignitary, was called Mynheer William Beekman, or rather *Beck*man, who derived his surname, as did Ovidius Naso of yore, from the lordly dimensions of his nose, which projected from the centre of his countenance, like the beak of a parrot. Indeed, it is furthermore insinuated by various ancient records, that this was not only the origin of his name, but likewise the foundation of his fortune, for, as the city was as yet unprovided with a clock, the public made use of Mynheer Beckman's face, as a sun dial. Thus did this romantic, and truly picturesque feature, first thrust itself into public notice, dragging its possessor along with it, who in his turn dragged after him the whole Beckman family—These, as the story further adds, were for a long time among the most ancient and honourable families of the province, and gratefully commemorated the origin of their dignity, not as your noble families in England would do, by having a glowing proboscis emblazoned in their escutcheon, but by one and all, wearing a right goodly nose, stuck in the very middle of their faces.

Thus was this perilous enterprize gloriously terminated, with the loss of only two men; Wolfert Van Horne, a tall spare man, who was knocked overboard by the boom of a sloop, in a flaw of wind: and fat Brom Van Bummel, who was suddenly carried off by a villainous indigestion; both, however, were immortalized, as having bravely fallen, in the service of their country. True it is, Peter Stuyvesant had one of his limbs terribly fractured, being shattered to pieces in the act of storming the fortress; but as it was fortunately his wooden leg, the wound was promptly and effectually healed.

And now nothing remains to this branch of my history, but to mention, that this immaculate hero, and his victorious army, returned joyously to the Manhattoes, marching under the shade of their laurels, as did the followers of young Malcolm, under the moving forest of Dunsinane. Thus did they make a solemn and triumphant entry into New Amsterdam, bearing with them the conquered Risingh, and the remnant of his battered crew, who had refused allegiance. For it appears that the gigantic Swede, had only fallen into a swound, at the end of the battle, from whence he was speedily restored by a wholesome tweak of the nose.

These captive heroes were lodged, according to the promise of the governor, at the public expense, in a fair and spacious castle; being the prison of state, of which Stoffel Brinkerhoff, the immortal conqueror of Oyster Bay, was appointed Lord Lieutenant; and which has ever since remained in the possession of his descendants.*

It was a pleasant and goodly sight to witness the joy of the people of New Amsterdam, at beholding their warriors once more returned, from this war in the wilderness. The old women thronged round Antony Van Corlear, who gave the whole history of the campaign with matchless accuracy; saving that he took the credit of fighting the whole battle himself, and especially of vanquishing the stout Risingh, which he considered himself as clearly entitled to, seeing that it was effected by his own stone pottle. The schoolmasters throughout the town gave holliday to their little urchins, who followed in droves after the drums, with paper caps on their heads and sticks in their breeches, thus taking the first lesson in vagabondizing. As to the sturdy rabble they thronged at the heels of Peter Stuyvesant wherever he went, waving their greasy hats in the air, and shouting "Hard-koppig Piet forever!"

It was indeed a day of roaring rout and jubilee. A huge dinner was prepared at the Stadt-house in honour of the conquerors, where were assembled in one glorious constellation, the great and the little luminaries of New Amsterdam. There were the lordly Schout and his obsequious deputy—the Burgomasters with their officious Schepens at their elbows—the subaltern officers at the elbows of the Schepens, and so on to the lowest grade of illustrious hangers-on of police; every Tag having his Rag at his side, to finish his pipe, drink off his heel-taps, and laugh at his flights of immortal dullness. In short—for a city feast is a city feast all the world over, and has been a city feast ever since the creation—the dinner went off much the same as do our great corporation junkettings and fourth of July banquets. Loads of fish, flesh and fowl were devoured, oceans of liquor drank, thousands of pipes smoked, and many a dull joke honoured with much obstreperous fat sided laughter.

I must not omit to mention that to this far-famed victory

---

*This castle though very much altered and modernized is still in being. And stands at the corner of Pearl Street, facing Coentie's slip.

Peter Stuyvesant was indebted for another of his many titles—for so hugely delighted were the honest burghers with
his atchievements, that they unanimously honoured him with
the name of *Pieter de Groodt*, that is to say Peter the Great, or
as it was translated by the people of New Amsterdam, *Piet de
Pig*—an appellation which he maintained even unto the day
of his death.

END OF BOOK VI.

BOOK VII.

Containing the third part of the reign of Peter the Headstrong—his troubles with the British nation, and the decline and fall of the Dutch dynasty.

CHAP. I.

How Peter Stuyvesant relieved the sovereign people from the burthen of taking care of the nation—with sundry particulars of his conduct in time of peace.

THE HISTORY of the reign of Peter Stuyvesant, furnishes a melancholy picture of the incessant cares and vexations inseparable from government; and may serve as a solemn warning, to all who are ambitious of attaining the seat of power. Though crowned with victory, enriched by conquest, and returning in triumph to his splendid metropolis, his exultation was checked by beholding the sad abuses that had taken place during the short interval of his absence.

The populace, unfortunately for their own comfort, had taken a deep draught of the intoxicating cup of power, during the reign of William the Testy; and though, upon the accession of Peter Stuyvesant they felt, with a certain instinctive perception, which mobs as well as cattle possess, that the reins of government had passed into stronger hands, yet could they not help fretting and chafing and champing upon the bit, in restive silence. No sooner, therefore, was the great Peter's back turned, than the quid nuncs and pot-house politicians of the city immediately broke loose, and indulged in the most ungovernable freaks and gambols.

It seems by some strange and inscrutable fatality, to be the destiny of most countries, and (more especially of your enlightened republics,) always to be governed by the most incompetent man in the nation, so that you will scarcely find an individual throughout the whole community, but who shall detect to you innumerable errors in administration, and shall convince you in the end, that had he been at the head of affairs, matters would have gone on a thousand times more prosperously. Strange! that government, which seems to be so generally understood should invariably be so erroneously administered—strange, that the talent of legislation so prodigally bestowed, should be denied to the only man in the nation, to whose station it is requisite!

Thus it was in the present instance, not a man of all the

herd of pseudo politicians in New Amsterdam, but was an oracle on topics of state, and could have directed public affairs incomparably better than Peter Stuyvesant. But so perverse was the old governor in his disposition, that he would never suffer one of the multitude of able counsellors by whom he was surrounded, to intrude his advice and save the country from destruction.

Scarcely therefore had he departed on his expedition against the Swedes, than the old factions of William Kieft's reign began to thrust their heads above water, and to gather together in political meetings, to discuss "the state of the nation." At these assemblages the busy burgomasters and their officious schepens made a very considerable figure. These worthy dignitaries were no longer the fat, well fed, tranquil magistrates that presided in the peaceful days of Wouter Van Twiller—On the contrary, being elected by the people, they formed in a manner, a sturdy bulwark, between the mob and the administration. They were great candidates for popularity, and strenuous advocates for the rights of the rabble; resembling in disinterested zeal the wide mouthed tribunes of ancient Rome, or those virtuous patriots of modern days, emphatically denominated "the friends of the people."

Under the tuition of these profound politicians, it is astonishing how suddenly enlightened the swinish multitude became, in matters above their comprehensions. Coblers, Tinkers and Taylors all at once felt themselves inspired, like those religious ideots, in the glorious times of monkish illumination; and without any previous study or experience, became instantly capable of directing all the movements of government. Nor must I neglect to mention a number of superannuated, wrong headed old burghers, who had come over when boys, in the crew of the *Goede Vrouw*, and were held up as infallible oracles by the enlightened mob. To suppose a man who had helped to discover a country, did not know how it ought to be governed was preposterous in the extreme. It would have been deemed as much a heresy, as at the present day to question the political talents, and universal infallibility of our old "heroes of '76"—and to doubt that he who had fought for a government, however stupid he might naturally be, was not competent to fill any station under it.

But as Peter Stuyvesant had a singular inclination to govern his province without the assistance of his subjects, he felt highly incensed on his return to find the factious appearance they had assumed during his absence. His first measure therefore was to restore perfect order, by prostrating the dignity of the sovereign people in the dirt.

He accordingly watched his opportunity, and one evening when the enlightened mob was gathered together in full caucus, listening to a patriotic speech from an inspired cobbler, the intrepid Peter, like his great namesake of all the Russias, all at once appeared among them with a countenance, sufficient to petrify a mill stone. The whole meeting was thrown in consternation—the orator seemed to have received a paralytic stroke in the very middle of a sublime sentence, he stood aghast with open mouth and trembling knees, while the words horror! tyranny! liberty! rights! taxes! death! destruction! and a deluge of other patriotic phrases, came roaring from his throat, before he had power to close his lips. The shrewd Peter took no notice of the skulking throng around him, but advancing to the brawling bully-ruffian, and drawing out a huge silver watch, which might have served in times of yore as a town clock, and which is still retained by his decendants as a family curiosity, requested the orator to mend it, and set it going. The orator humbly confessed it was utterly out of his power, as he was unacquainted with the nature of its construction. "Nay, but," said Peter "try your ingenuity man, you see all the springs and wheels, and how easily the clumsiest hand may stop it and pull it to pieces; and why should it not be equally easy to regulate as to stop it." The orator declared that his trade was wholly different, he was a poor cobbler, and had never meddled with a watch in his life. There were men skilled in the art, whose business it was to attend to those matters, but for his part, he should only mar the workmanship, and put the whole in confusion——"Why harkee master of mine," cried Peter, turning suddenly upon him, with a countenance that almost petrified the patcher of shoes into a perfect lapstone—"dost thou pretend to meddle with the movements of government—to regulate and correct and patch and cobble a complicated machine, the principles of which are above thy comprehension, and its simplest operations too subtle for thy understanding; when thou canst not correct a trifling error in a common piece of mechanism, the whole mystery of which is open to thy inspection?—Hence with thee to the leather and stone, which are emblems of thy head; cobble thy shoes and confine thyself to the vocation for which heaven has fitted thee—But," elevating his voice until it made the welkin ring, "if ever I catch thee, or any of thy tribe, whether square-head, or platter breech, meddling with affairs of government; by St. Nicholas but I'll have every mother's bastard of ye flea'd alive, and your hides stretched for drum heads, that ye may henceforth make a noise to some purpose!"

This threat and the tremendous voice in which it was uttered, caused the whole multitude to quake with fear. The hair of the orator rose on his head like his own swine's bristles, and not a knight of the thimble present, but his mighty heart died within him, and he felt as though he could have verily escaped through the eye of a needle.

But though this measure produced the desired effect, in reducing the community to order, yet it tended to injure the popularity of the great Peter, among the enlightened vulgar. Many accused him of entertaining highly aristocratic sentiments, and of leaning too much in favour of the patricians. Indeed there was some appearance of ground for such a suspicion, for in his time did first arise that pride of family and ostentation of wealth, that has since grown to such a height in this city.* Those who drove their own waggons, kept their own cows, and possessed the fee simple of a cabbage garden, looked down, with the most gracious, though mortifying condescension, on their less wealthy neighbours; while those whose parents had been cabin passengers in the Goede Vrouw, were continually railing out, about the dignity of ancestry—Luxury began to make its appearance under divers forms, and even Peter Stuyvesant himself (though in truth his station required a little state and dignity) appeared with great

---

*In a work published many years after the time of which Mr. Knickerbocker treats (in 1701. By C. W. A. M.) it is mentioned "Frederick Philips was counted the richest Mynheer in New York, and was said to have *whole hogsheads of Indian money or wampum*; and had a son and daughter, who according to the Dutch custom should divide it equally."   EDITOR.

pomp of equipage on public occasions, and always rode to church in a yellow waggon with flaming red wheels!

From this picture my readers will perceive, how very faithfully many of the peculiarities of our ancestors have been retained by their descendants. The pride of purse still prevails among our wealthy citizens. And many a laborious tradesman, after plodding in dust and obscurity in the morning of his life, sits down out of breath in his latter days to enact the gentleman, and enjoy the dignity honestly earned by the sweat of his brow. In this he resembles a notable, but ambitious housewife, who after drudging and stewing all day in the kitchen to prepare an entertainment; flounces into the parlour of an evening, and swelters in all the magnificence of a maudlin fine lady.

It is astonishing, moreover, to behold how many great families have sprung up of late years, who pride themselves excessively on the score of ancestry. Thus he who can look up to his father without humiliation assumes not a little importance—he who can safely talk of his grandfather, is still more vain-glorious, but he who can look back to his great grandfather, without stumbling over a cobler's stall, or running his head against a whipping post, is absolutely intolerable in his pretensions to family—bless us! what a piece of work is here, between these mushrooms of an hour, and these mushrooms of a day!

For my part I look upon our old dutch families as the only local nobility, and the real lords of the soil—nor can I ever see an honest old burgher quietly smoking his pipe, but I look upon him with reverence as a dignified descendant from the Van Rensellaers, the Van Zandts, the Knickerbockers, and the Van Tuyls.

But from what I have recounted in the former part of this chapter, I would not have my reader imagine, that the great Peter was a tyrannical governor, ruling his subjects with a rod of iron—on the contrary, where the dignity of authority was not implicated, he abounded with generosity and courteous condescension. In fact he really believed, though I fear my more enlightened republican readers will consider it a proof of his ignorance and illiberality, that in preventing the cup of social life from being dashed with the intoxicating ingredient of politics, he promoted the tranquility and happiness of the people—and by detaching their minds from subjects which they could not understand, and which only tended to inflame their passions, he enabled them to attend more faithfully and industriously to their proper callings; becoming more useful citizens and more attentive to their families and fortunes.

So far from having any unreasonable austerity, he delighted to see the poor and the labouring man rejoice, and for this purpose was a great promoter of holidays and public amusements. Under his reign was first introduced the custom of cracking eggs at Paas or Easter. New year's day was also observed with extravagant festivity—and ushered in by the ringing of bells and firing of guns. Every house was a temple to the jolly god—Oceans of cherry brandy, true Hollands and mulled cyder were set afloat on the occasion; and not a poor man in town, but made it a point to get drunk, out of a principle of pure economy—taking in liquor enough to serve him for half a year afterwards.

It would have done one's heart good also to have seen the valiant Peter, seated among the old burghers and their wives of a saturday afternoon, under the great trees that spread their shade over the Battery, watching the young men and women, as they danced on the green. Here he would smoke his pipe, crack his joke, and forget the rugged toils of war, in the sweet oblivious festivities of peace. He would occasionally give a nod of approbation to those of the young men who shuffled and kicked most vigorously, and now and then give a hearty smack, in all honesty of soul, to the buxom lass that held out longest, and tired down all her competitors—infallible proofs of her being the best dancer. Once it is true the harmony of the meeting was rather interrupted. A young vrouw, of great figure in the gay world, and who, having lately come from Holland, of course led the fashions in the city, made her appearance in not more than half a dozen petticoats, and these too of most alarming shortness.—An universal whisper ran through the assembly, the old ladies all felt shocked in the extreme, the young ladies blushed, and felt excessively for the "poor thing," and even the governor himself was observed to be a little troubled in mind. To complete the astonishment of the good folks, she undertook in the course of a jig, to describe some astonishing figures in algebra, which she had learned from a dancing master at Rotterdam.—Whether she was too animated in flourishing her feet, or whether some vagabond Zephyr took the liberty of obtruding his services, certain it is that in the course of a grand evolution, that would not have disgraced a modern ball room, she made a most unexpected display—Whereat the whole assembly were thrown into great admiration, several grave country members were not a little moved, and the good Peter himself, who was a man of unparalleled modesty, felt himself grievously scandalized.

The shortness of the female dresses, which had continued in fashion, ever since the days of William Kieft, had long offended his eye, and though extremely averse to meddling with the petticoats of the ladies, yet he immediately recommended, that every one should be furnished with a flounce to the bottom. He likewise ordered that the ladies, and indeed the gentlemen, should use no other step in dancing, than shuffle and turn, and double trouble; and forbade, under pain of his high displeasure, any young lady thenceforth to attempt what was termed "exhibiting the graces."

These were the only restrictions he ever imposed upon the sex, and these were considered by them, as tyrannical oppressions, and resisted with that becoming spirit, always manifested by the gentle sex, whenever their privileges are invaded—In fact, Peter Stuyvesant plainly perceived, that if he attempted to push the matter any further, there was danger of their leaving off petticoats altogether; so like a wise man, experienced in the ways of women, he held his peace, and suffered them ever after to wear their petticoats and cut their capers, as high as they pleased.

CHAP. II.

How Peter Stuyvesant was much molested by the moss troopers of the East, and the Giants of Merry-land—and how a dark and horrid conspiracy was carried on in the British Cabinet, against the prosperity of the Manhattoes.

WE are now approaching towards what may be termed the very pith and marrow of our work, and if I am not mistaken in my forebodings, we shall have a world of business to dispatch, in the ensuing chapters. Thus far have I come on prosperously, and even beyond my expectations; for to let the reader into a secret (and truly we have become so extremely intimate, that I believe I shall tell him all my secrets before we part) when I first set out upon this marvellous, but faithful little history, I felt horribly perplexed to think how I should ever get through with it—and though I put a bold face on the matter, and vapoured exceedingly, yet was it naught but the blustering of a braggadocio at the commencement of a quarrel, which he feels sure he shall have to sneak out of in the end.

When I reflected, that this illustrious province, though of prodigious importance in the eyes of its inhabitants and its historian, had in sober sadness, but little wealth or other spoils to reward the trouble of assailing it, and that it had little to expect from running wantonly into war, save a sound drubbing—When I pondered all these things in my mind, I began utterly to despair, that I should find either battles, or bloodshed, or any other of those calamities, which give importance to a nation, to enliven my history withal.—I regarded this most amiable of provinces, in the light of an unhappy maiden, to whom Heaven had not granted sufficient charms, to excite the diabolical attempts of wicked man; who had no cruel father to persecute and oppress her, no abominable ravisher to run away with her, and who had not strength nor courage enough, of her own accord, to act the heroine, and go in "quest of adventures"—in short, who was doomed to vegetate, in a tranquil, unmolested, hopeless, howling state of virginity, and finally to die in peace, without bequeathing a single misery, or outrage, to those warehouses of sentimental woe, the circulating libraries.

But thanks to my better stars, they have decreed otherwise. It is with some communities, as it is with certain meddlesome individuals, they have a wonderful facility at getting into scrapes, and I have always remarked, that those are most liable to get in, who have the least talent at getting out again. This is doubtless occasioned by the excessive *valour* of those little states; for I have likewise noticed, that this rampant and ungovernable virtue, is always most unruly where most confined; which accounts for its raging and vapouring so amazingly in little states, little men, and ugly little women more especially. Thus this little province of Nieuw Nederlandts has already drawn upon itself a host of enemies; has had as many hard knocks, as would gratify the ambition of the most warlike nation; and is in sober sadness, a very forlorn, distressed, and woe begone little province!—all which was no doubt kindly ordered by providence, to give interest and sublimity, to this most pathetic of histories.

But I forbear to enter into a detail of the pitiful maraudings and harrassments, that for a long while after the victory on the Delaware, continued to insult the dignity and disturb the repose of the Nederlanders. Never shall the pen which has been gloriously wielded in the tremendous battle of Fort Christina, be drawn in scurvy border broils and frontier skirmishings—nor the historian who put to flight stout Risingh and his host, and conquered all New Sweden, be doomed to battle it in defence of a pig stye or a hen roost, and wage ignoble strife with squatters and moss troopers! Forbid it all ye muses, that a Knickerbocker should ever so far forget what is due to his family and himself!

Suffice it then in brevity to say, that the implacable hostility of the people of the east, which had so miraculously been prevented from breaking out, as my readers must remember, by the sudden prevalence of witchcraft, and the dissensions in the council of Amphyctions, now again displayed itself in a thousand grievous and bitter scourings upon the borders.

Scarcely a month passed but what the little dutch settlements on the frontiers were alarmed by the sudden appearance of an invading army from Connecticut. This would advance resolutely through the country, like a puissant caravan of the deserts, the women and children mounted in carts loaded with pots and kettles, as though they meant to boil the honest dutchmen alive, and devour them like so many lobsters. At the tail of these carts would stalk a crew of long limbed, lank sided varlets, with axes on their shoulders and packs on their backs, resolutely bent upon *improving* the country in despite of its proprietors. These settling themselves down, would in a little while completely dislodge the unfortunate Nederlanders; elbowing them out of those rich little bottoms and fertile valleys, in which your dutch yeomanry are so famous for nestling themselves—For it is notorious that wherever these shrewd men of the east get a footing, the honest dutchmen do gradually disappear, retiring slowly like the Indians before the whites; being totally discomfited by the talking, chaffering, swapping, bargaining disposition of their new neighbours.

All these audacious infringements on the territories of their high mightinesses were accompanied, as has before been hinted, by a world of rascally brawls, ribroastings and bundlings, which would doubtlessly have incensed the valiant Peter to wreak immediate chastisement, had he not at the very same time been perplexed by distressing accounts, from Mynheer Beckman, who commanded the territories at South river.

The rebellious Swedes who had so graciously been suffered to remain about the Delaware, already began to shew signs of mutiny and disaffection. But what was worse, a peremptory claim was laid to the whole territory, as the rightful property of lord Baltimore, by Fendal, a chieftain who ruled over the colony of Maryland, or Merry-land as it was anciently called, because that the inhabitants not having the fear of the Lord before their eyes, were notoriously prone to get fuddled and make *merry* with mint julep and apple toddy. Nay, so hostile was this bully Fendal, that he threatened, unless his claim was instantly complied with, to march incontinently at the head of a potent force of the roaring boys of Merryland, together with a great and mighty train of giants who infested the banks of the Susquehanna*—and to lay waste and depopulate the whole country of South river.

By this it is manifest that this boasted colony, like all great acquisitions of territory, soon became a greater evil to the conqueror, than the loss of it was to the conquered; and caused greater uneasiness and trouble, than all the territory of the New Netherlands besides. Thus providence wisely orders, that one evil shall balance another. The conqueror who wrests the property of his neighbour, who wrongs a nation and desolates a country, though he may acquire increase of empire, and immortal fame, yet ensures his own inevitable punishment. He takes to himself a cause of endless anxiety—he incorporates with his late sound domain, a loose part—a rotten disaffected member; which is an exhaustless source of internal treason and disunion, and external altercation and hostility—Happy is that nation, which compact, united, loyal in all its parts, and concentrated in its strength, seeks no idle acquisition of unprofitable and ungovernable territory—which, content to be prosperous and happy, has no ambition to be great. It is like a man well organized in all his system, sound in health, and full of vigour; unincumbered by useless trappings, and fixed in an unshaken attitude. But the nation, insatiable of territory, whose domains are scattered, feebly united, and weakly organized, is like a senseless miser sprawling among golden stores, open to every attack, and unable to defend the riches he vainly endeavours to overshadow.

At the time of receiving the alarming dispatches from South river, the great Peter was busily employed in quelling certain Indian troubles that had broken out about Esopus,

---

*We find very curious and wonderful accounts of these strange people (who were doubtless the ancestors of the present Marylanders) made by master Hariot, in his interesting history. "The Susquesahanocks"—observes he, "are a giantly people, strange in proportion, behaviour and attire—their voice sounding from them as if out a cave. Their tobacco pipes were three quarters of a yard long, carved at the great end with a bird, beare, or other device, sufficient to beat out the braines of a horse, (and how many asses braines are beaten out, or rather men's braines smoked out and asses brains haled in, by our lesser pipes at home.) The calfe of one of their legges was measured three quarters of a yard about, the rest of his limbs proportionable.

Master Hariot's Journ . . Purch. Pil.

and was moreover meditating how to relieve his eastern borders, on the Connecticut. He however sent word to Mynheer
Beckman to be of good heart, to maintain incessant vigilance,
and to let him know if matters wore a more threatening appearance; in which case he would incontinently repair with
his warriors of the Hudson, to spoil the merriment of these
Merry landers; for he coveted exceedingly to have a bout,
hand to hand, with some half a score of these giants—
having never encountered a giant in his whole life, unless we
may so call the stout Risingh, and he was but a little
one.

Nothing however appeared further to molest the tranquillity of Mynheer Beckman and his colony. Fendal and his Myrmidons remained at home, carousing it soundly upon hoe
cakes, bacon, and mint julep, and running horses, and fighting cocks, for which they were greatly renowned. At hearing
of this Peter Stuyvesant was highly rejoiced, for notwithstanding his inclination to measure weapons with these monstrous
men of the Susquehanna, yet he had already as much employment nearer home, as he could turn his hands to. Little did
he think, worthy soul, that this southern calm, was but the
deceitful prelude to a most terrible and fatal storm, then
brewing, which was soon to burst forth and overwhelm the
unsuspecting city of New Amsterdam!

Now so it was, that while this excellent governor was, like
a second Cato, giving his little senate laws, and not only giving them, but enforcing them too—while he was incessantly
travelling the rounds of his beloved province—posting from
place to place to redress grievances, and while busy at one
corner of his dominions all the rest getting into an uproar—
At this very time, I say, a dark and direful plot was hatching
against him, in that nursery of monstrous projects, the British
Cabinet. The news of his atchievements on the Delaware, according to a sage old historian of New Amsterdam, had occasioned not a little talk and marvel in the courts of Europe.
And the same profound writer assures us that the cabinet of
England began to entertain great jealousy and uneasiness at
the encreasing power of the Manhattoes, and the valour of its
sturdy yeomanry.

Agents we are told, were at work from the Amphyctionic

council of the East, earnestly urging the cabinet to assist them in subjugating this fierce and terrible little province, and that sagacious cabinet, which ever likes to be dabbling in dirty water, had already began to lend an ear to their importunities. Just at this time Lord Baltimore, whose bullying agent, as has before been mentioned, had so alarmed Mynheer Beckman, laid his claim before the cabinet to the lands of South river, which he complained were unjustly and forcibly detained from him, by these daring usurpers of the New Nederlandts.

At this it is said his majesty Charles II, who though Defender of the Faith, was an arrant, lounging, rake-helly roystering wag of a Prince, settled the whole matter by a dash of the pen, by which he made a present of a large tract of North America, including the province of New Netherlands, to his brother the duke of York—a donation truly loyal, since none but great monarchs have a right to give away, what does not belong to them.

That this munificent gift might not be merely nominal, his majesty on the 12th of March 1664, ordered that a gallant armament should be forthwith prepared, to invade the city of New Amsterdam by land and water, and put his brother in complete possession of the premises.

Thus critically are situated the affairs of the New Netherlanders. The honest burghers, so far from thinking of the jeopardy in which their interests are placed, are soberly smoking their pipes and thinking of nothing at all—the privy councillors of the province, are at this moment snoring in full quorum, like the drones of five hundred bagpipes, while the active Peter, who takes all the labour of thinking and acting upon himself, is busily devising some method of bringing the grand council of Amphyctions to terms. In the mean while an angry cloud is darkly scowling on the horizon—soon shall it rattle about the ears of these dozing Nederlanders and put the mettle of their stout hearted governor completely to the trial.

But come what may, I here pledge my veracity, that in all warlike conflicts and subtle perplexities, he shall still acquit himself with the gallant bearing and spotless honour of a noble minded obstinate old cavalier—Forward then to the charge!—shine out propitious stars on the renowned city of the Manhattoes; and may the blessing of St. Nicholas go with thee—honest Peter Stuyvesant!

CHAP. III.

Of Peter Stuyvesant's expedition into the east Country, shew-
ing that though an old bird, he did not understand trap.

G REAT NATIONS resemble great men in this particular,
that their greatness is seldom known, until they get in
trouble; adversity has therefore, been wisely denominated the
ordeal of true greatness, which like gold, can never receive its
real estimation until it has passed through the furnace. In proportion therefore as a nation, a community or an individual
(possessing the inherent quality of greatness) is involved in
perils and misfortunes, in proportion does it rise in grandeur—and even when sinking under calamity, like a house on
fire, makes a more glorious display, than ever it did, in the
fairest period of its prosperity.

The vast empire of China, though teeming with population
and imbibing and concentrating the wealth of nations, has
vegetated through a succession of drowsy ages; and were it
not for its internal revolution, and the subversion of its
ancient government by the Tartars, might have presented
nothing but an uninteresting detail of dull, monotonous
prosperity. Pompeia and Herculaneum might have passed
into oblivion, with a herd of their contemporaries, had they
not been fortunately overwhelmed by a volcano. The renowned city of Troy has acquired celebrity only from its ten
years distress, and final conflagration—Paris rises in importance, by the plots and massacres, which have ended in the
exaltation of the illustrious Napoleon—and even the mighty
London itself, has skulked through the records of time, celebrated for nothing of moment, excepting the Plague, the
great fire and Guy Faux's gunpowder plot! Thus cities and
empires seem to creep along, enlarging in silent obscurity under the pen of the historian, until at length they burst forth
in some tremendous calamity—and snatch as it were, immortality from the explosion!

The above principle being plainly advanced, strikingly illustrated, and readily admitted, my reader will need but little
discernment to perceive, that the city of New Amsterdam and

its dependent province, are on the high road to greatness. Dangers and hostilities threaten them from every side, and it is really a matter of astonishment to me, how so small a state, has been able in so short a time, to entangle itself in so many difficulties. Ever since the province was first taken by the nose, at the fort of Good Hope, in the tranquil days of Wouter Van Twiller, has it been gradually encreasing in historic importance; and never could it have had a more appropriate chieftain to conduct it to the pinnacle of grandeur, than Peter Stuyvesant.

He was an iron headed old veteran, in whose fiery heart sat enthroned all those five kinds of courage described by Aristotle, and had the philosopher mentioned five hundred more to the back of them, I verily believe, he would have been found master of them all—The only misfortune was, that he was deficient in the better part of valour called discretion, a cold blooded virtue which could not exist in the tropical climate of his mighty soul. Hence it was he was continually hurrying into those unheard of enterprises that gave an air of chivalric romance to all his history, and hence it was that he now conceived a project, the very thought of which makes me to tremble while I write.

This was no other than to repair in person to the mighty council of the Amphyctions, bearing the sword in one hand and the olive branch in the other—to require immediate reparation for the innumerable violations of that treaty which in an evil hour he had formed—to put a stop to those repeated maraudings on the eastern borders—or else to throw his gauntlet and appeal to arms for satisfaction.

On declaring this resolution in his privy council, the venerable members were seized with vast astonishment, for once in their lives they ventured to remonstrate, setting forth the rashness of exposing his sacred person, in the midst of a strange and barbarous people, with sundry other weighty remonstrances—all which had about as much influence upon the determination of the headstrong Peter, as though you were to endeavour to turn a rusty weather cock, with a broken winded bellows.

Summoning therefore to his presence, his trusty follower Antony Van Corlear, he commanded him to hold himself in readiness to accompany him the following morning, on this his hazardous enterprise. Now Antony the trumpeter was a little stricken in years, yet by dint of keeping up a good heart, and having never known care or sorrow (having never been married) he was still a hearty, jocund rubicond, gamesome wag, and of great capacity in the doublet. This last was ascribed to his living a jolly life on those domains at the Hook, which Peter Stuyvesant had granted to him, for his gallantry at Fort Casimer.

Be this as it may, there was nothing that more delighted Antony, than this command of the great Peter, for he could have followed the stout hearted old governor to the world's end, with love and loyalty—and he moreover still remembered the frolicking and dancing and bundling, and other disports of the east country, and entertained dainty recollection of numerous kind and buxom lasses, whom he longed exceedingly again to encounter.

Thus then did this mirror of hardihood set forth, with no other attendant but his trumpeter, upon one of the most perilous enterprises ever recorded in the annals of Knight errantry.—For a single warrior to venture openly among a whole nation of foes; but above all, for a plain downright dutchman to think of negociating with the whole council of New England—never was there known a more desperate undertaking!—Ever since I have entered upon the chronicles of this peerless but hitherto uncelebrated chieftain, has he kept me in a state of incessant action and anxiety with the toils and dangers he is constantly encountering—Oh! for a chapter of the tranquil reign of Wouter Van Twiller, that I might repose on it as on a feather bed!

Is it not enough Peter Stuyvesant, that I have once already rescued thee from the machinations of these terrible Amphyctions, by bringing the whole powers of witchcraft to thine aid?—Is it not enough, that I have followed thee undaunted, like a guardian spirit, into the midst of the horrid battle of Fort Christina?—That I have been put incessantly to my trumps to keep thee safe and sound—now warding off with my single pen the shower of dastard blows that fell upon thy rear—now narrowly shielding thee from a deadly thrust, by a mere tobacco box—now casing thy dauntless scull with adamant, when even thy stubborn ram beaver failed to resist the sword of the stout Risingh—and now, not merely bringing thee off alive, but triumphant, from the clutches of the gigantic Swede, by the desperate means of a paltry stone pottle?—Is not all this enough, but must thou still be plunging into new difficulties and jeopardizing in headlong enterprises, thyself, thy trumpeter, and thy historian!

But all this is empty talk. What influence can I expect to have, when even his councillors, who never before attempted to advise him in their lives, have spoken to no effect. All that remains is quietly to take up my pen, as did Antony his trumpet, and faithfully follow at his heels—and I swear that, like the latter, so truly do I love the hairbrained valour of this fierce old Cavalier, that I feel as if I could follow him through the world, even though (which Heaven forefend) he should lead me through another volume of adventures.

And now the ruddy faced Aurora, like a buxom chambermaid, draws aside the sable curtains of the night, and out bounces from his bed the jolly red haired Phœbus, startled at being caught so late in the embraces of Dame Thetis. With many a stable oath, he harnesses his brazen footed steeds, and whips and lashes, and splashes up the firmament, like a loitering post boy, half an hour behind his time. And now behold that imp of fame and prowess the headstrong Peter, bestriding a raw boned, switch tailed charger, gallantly arrayed in full regimentals, and bracing on his thigh that trusty brass hilted sword, which had wrought such fearful deeds on the banks of the Delaware.

Behold hard after him his doughty trumpeter Van Corlear, mounted on a broken winded, wall eyed, calico mare; his sturdy stone pottle which had laid low the mighty Risingh, slung under his arm, and his trumpet displayed vauntingly in his right hand, decorated with a gorgeous banner, on which is emblazoned the great beaver of the Manhattoes. See them proudly issuing out of the city gate, like an iron clad hero of yore, with his faithful squire at his heels, the populace following them with their eyes, and shouting many a parting wish, and hearty cheering.—Farewel, Hardkoppig-Piet! Farewel honest Antony!—Pleasant be your wayfaring—prosperous your return! The stoutest hero that ever drew a sword, and the worthiest trumpeter that ever trod shoe leather!

Legends are lamentably silent about the events that befel our adventurers, in this their adventurous travel, excepting the Stuyvesant Manuscript, which gives the substance of a pleasant little heroic poem, written on the occasion by Domine Ægidius Luyck,* who appears to have been the poet-laureat of New Amsterdam. This inestimable manuscript assures us, that it was a rare spectacle to behold the great Peter and his loyal follower, hailing the morning sun, and rejoicing in the clear countenance of nature, as they pranced it through the pastoral scenes of Bloemen Dael;† which in those days was a sweet and rural valley, beautified with many a bright wild flower, refreshed by many a pure streamlet, and enlivened here and there by a delectable little dutch cottage, sheltered under some gently swelling hill, and almost buried in embowering trees.

Now did they enter upon the confines of Connecticut, where they encountered many grievous difficulties and perils. At one place they were assailed by some half a score of country squires and militia colonels, who, mounted on goodly steeds, hung upon their rear for several miles, harassing them exceedingly with guesses and questions, more especially the worthy Peter, whose silver chas'd leg excited not a little marvel. At another place hard by the renowned town of Stamford, they were set upon by a great and mighty legion of church deacons, who imperiously demanded of them five shillings, for travelling on Sunday, and threatened to carry them captive to a neighbouring church whose steeple peer'd above the trees; but these the valiant Peter put to rout with little difficulty, insomuch that they bestrode their canes and gallopped off in horrible confusion, leaving their cocked hats behind in the hurry of their flight. But not so easily did he escape from the hands of a crafty man of Pyquag; who with undaunted perseverance, and repeated onsets, fairly bargained him out of his goodly switch-tailed charger, leaving

*This Luyck, was moreover, rector of the Latin school in Nieuw Nederlandt, 1663. There are two pieces of verses to Ægidius Luyck in D. Selyn's MSS. of poesies, upon his marriage with Judith Van Isendoorn.   Old MS.

†Now called Blooming Dale, about four miles from New York.

in place thereof a villainous, spavined, foundered Narraganset pacer.

But maugre all these hardships, they pursued their journey
cheerily, along the course of the soft flowing Connecticut,
whose gentle waves, says the song, roll through many a fertile
vale, and sunny plain; now reflecting the lofty spires of the
bustling city, and now the rural beauties of the humble hamlet; now echoing with the busy hum of commerce, and now
with the cheerful song of the peasant.

At every town would Peter Stuyvesant, who was noted for
warlike punctilio, order the sturdy Antony to sound a courteous salutation; though the manuscript observes, that the inhabitants were thrown into great dismay, when they heard of
his approach. For the fame of his incomparable atchievements
on the Delaware, had spread throughout the East country,
and they dreaded lest he had come to take vengeance on their
manifold transgressions.

But the good Peter rode through these towns with a smiling aspect; waving his hand with inexpressible majesty and
condescension; for he verily believed that the old clothes
which these ingenious people had thrust into their broken
windows, and the festoons of dried apples and peaches which
ornamented the fronts of their houses, were so many decorations in honour of his approach; as it was the custom in days
of chivalry, to compliment renowned heroes, by sumptuous
displays of tapestry and gorgeous furniture. The women
crowded to the doors to gaze upon him as he passed, so
much does prowess in arms, delight the gentle sex. The little
children too ran after him in troops, staring with wonder at
his regimentals, his brimstone breeches, and the silver garni-
ture of his wooden leg. Nor must I omit to mention the joy
which many strapping wenches betrayed, at beholding the jovial Van Corlear, who had whilome delighted them so much
with his trumpet, when he bore the great Peter's challenge to
the Amphyctions. The kind-hearted Antony alighted from his
calico mare, and kissed them all with infinite loving kindness—and was right pleased to see a crew of little trumpeters
crowding around him for his blessing; each of whom he pat-
ted on the head, bade him be a good boy, and gave him a
penny to buy molasses candy.

The Stuyvesant manuscript makes but little further mention of the governor's adventures upon this expedition, excepting that he was received with extravagant courtesy and respect by the great council of the Amphyctions, who almost talked him to death with complimentary and congratulatory harangues. Of his negociations with the grand council I shall say nothing, as there are more important matters which call for the attention of myself, my readers, and Peter Stuyvesant. Suffice it to mention, it was like all other negociations—a great deal was said, and very little done: one conversation led to another—one conference begat misunderstandings which it took a dozen conferences to explain; at the end of which the parties found themselves just where they were at first; excepting that they had entangled themselves in a host of questions of etiquette, and conceived a cordial distrust of each other that rendered their future negociations ten times more difficult than ever.*

In the midst of all these perplexities, which bewildered the brain and incensed the ire of the sturdy Peter, who was of all men in the world, perhaps, the least fitted for diplomatic wiles, he privately received the first intimation of the dark conspiracy which had been matured in the Cabinet of England. To this was added the astounding intelligence that a hostile squadron had already sailed from England, destined to reduce the province of New Netherlands, and that the grand council of Amphyctions had engaged to co-operate, by sending a great army to invade New Amsterdam by land.

Unfortunate Peter! did I not enter with sad forebodings upon this ill starred expedition! did I not tremble when I saw thee, with no other councillor but thine own head, with no other armour but an honest tongue, a spotless conscience and a rusty sword! with no other protector but St. Nicholas—and no other attendant but a brokenwinded trumpeter—Did I not tremble when I beheld thee thus sally forth, to contend with all the knowing powers of New England.

Oh how did the sturdy old warrior rage and roar, when he

*For certain of the particulars of this ancient negociation see Haz. Col. State Pap. It is singular that Smith is entirely silent with respect to the memorable expedition of Peter Stuyvesant above treated of by Mr. Knickerbocker. EDITOR.

found himself thus entrapped, like a lion in the hunter's toil. Now did he determine to draw his trusty sword, and manfully to fight his way through all the countries of the east. Now did he resolve to break in upon the council of the Amphyctions and put every mother's son of them to death.—At length, as his direful wrath subsided, he resorted to safer though less glorious expedients.

Concealing from the council his knowledge of their machinations, he privately dispatched a trusty messenger, with missives to his councillors at New Amsterdam, apprizing them of the impending danger, commanding them immediately to put the city in a posture of defence, while in the mean time he endeavoured to elude his enemies and come to their assistance. This done he felt himself marvellously relieved, rose slowly, shook himself like a rhinoceros, and issued forth from his den, in much the same manner as giant Despair is described to have issued from Doubting castle, in the chivalric history of the Pilgrim's Progress.

And now much does it grieve me that I must leave the gallant Peter in this perilous jeopardy: but it behoves us to hurry back and see what is going on at New Amsterdam, for greatly do I fear that city is already in a turmoil. Such was ever the fate of Peter Stuyvesant, while doing one thing with heart and soul, he was too apt to leave every thing else at sixes and sevens. While, like a potentate of yore, he was absent attending to those things in person, which in modern days are trusted to generals and ambassadors, his little territory at home was sure to get in an uproar—All which was owing to that uncommon strength of intellect, which induced him to trust to nobody but himself, and which had acquired him the renowned appellation of Peter the Headstrong.

CHAP. IV.

How the people of New Amsterdam, were thrown into a great panic, by the news of a threatened invasion, and how they fortified themselves very strongly—with resolutions.

THERE is no sight more truly interesting to a philosopher, than to contemplate a community, where every individual has a voice in public affairs, where every individual thinks himself the atlas of the nation, and where every individual thinks it his duty to bestir himself for the good of his country—I say, there is nothing more interesting to a philosopher, than to see such a community in a sudden bustle of war. Such a clamour of tongues—such a bawling of patriotism—such running hither and thither—every body in a hurry—every body up to the ears in trouble—every body in the way, and every body interrupting his industrious neighbour—who is busily employed in doing nothing! It is like witnessing a great fire, where every man is at work like a hero—some dragging about empty engines—others scampering with full buckets, and spilling the contents into the boots of their neighbours—and others ringing the church bells all night, by way of putting out the fire. Little firemen—like sturdy little knights storming a breach, clambering up and down scaling ladders, and bawling through tin trumpets, by way of directing the attack.—Here one busy fellow, in his great zeal to save the property of the unfortunate, catches up an anonymous chamber utensil, and gallants it off with an air of as much self-importance, as if he had rescued a pot of money—another throws looking glasses and china, out of the window, by way of saving them from the flames, while those who can do nothing else, to assist in the great calamity run up and down the streets with open throats, keeping up an incessant cry of *Fire! Fire! Fire!*

"When the news arrived at Corinth," says the grave and profound Lucian—though I own the story is rather trite, "that Philip was about to attack them, the inhabitants were thrown into violent alarm. Some ran to furbish up their arms; others rolled stones to build up the walls—every body in short, was employed, and every body was in the way of his neighbour. Diogenes alone, was the only man who could find nothing to do—whereupon determining not to be idle when the welfare of his country was at stake, he tucked up his robe, and fell to rolling his tub with might and main, up and down the Gymnasium." In like manner did every mother's son, in the patriotic community of New Amsterdam, on receiving the missives of Peter Stuyvesant, busy himself most mightily in putting things in confusion, and assisting the general uproar. "Every man"—saith the Stuyvesant Manuscript—"flew to arms!"—by which is meant, that not one of our honest dutch citizens would venture to church or to market, without an old fashioned spit of a sword, dangling at his side, and a long dutch fowling piece on his shoulder—nor would he go out of a night without a lanthorn; nor turn a corner, without first peeping cautiously round, lest he should come unawares upon a British army—And we are informed, that Stoffel Brinkerhoff, who was considered by the old women, almost as brave a man as the governor himself—actually had two one pound swivels mounted in his entry, one pointing out at the front door, and the other at the back.

But the most strenuous measure resorted to on this aweful occasion, and one which has since been found of wonderful efficacy, was to assemble popular meetings. These brawling convocations, I have already shewn, were extremely obnoxious to Peter Stuyvesant, but as this was a moment of unusual agitation, and as the old governor was not present to repress them, they broke out with intolerable violence. Hither therefore, the orators and politicians repaired, and there seemed to be a competition among them, who should bawl the loudest, and exceed the other in hyperbolical bursts of patriotism, and in resolutions to uphold and defend the government. In these sage and all powerful meetings it was determined *nem. con.* that they were the most enlightened, the most dignified, the most formidable and the most ancient community upon the face of the earth—and finding that this resolution was so universally and readily carried, another was immediately proposed—whether it was not possible and politic to exterminate Great Britain? upon which sixty nine members spoke most eloquently in the affirmative, and only one arose to suggest some doubts—who as a punishment for his treasonable presumption, was immediately seized by the mob and tarred and feathered—which punishment being equivalent to the Tarpeian Rock, he was afterwards considered as an outcast from society and his opinion went for nothing—The question therefore, being unanimously carried in the affirmative, it was recommended to the grand council to pass it into a law; which was accordingly done—By this measure the hearts of the people at large were wonderfully encouraged, and they waxed exceeding choleric and valourous—Indeed the first paroxysm of alarm having in some measure subsided; the old women having buried all the money they could lay their hands on; and their husbands daily getting fuddled with what was left—the community began even to stand on the offensive. Songs were manufactured in low dutch and sung about the streets, wherein the English were most woefully beaten, and shewn no quarter, and popular addresses were made, wherein it was proved to a certainty, that the fate of old England depended upon the will of the New Amsterdammers.

Finally, to strike a violent blow at the very vitals of Great Britain, a grand caucus of the wiser inhabitants assembled; and having purchased all the British manufactures they could find, they made thereof a huge bonfire—and in the patriotic glow of the moment, every man present, who had a hat or breeches of English workmanship, pulled it off and threw it most undauntedly into the flames—to the irreparable detriment, loss and ruin of the English manufacturers. In commemoration of this great exploit, they erected a pole on the spot, with a device on the top intended to represent the province of Nieuw Nederlandts destroying Great Britain, under the similitude of an Eagle picking the little Island of Old England out of the globe; but either through the unskillfulness of the sculptor, or his ill timed waggery, it bore a striking resemblance to a goose, vainly striving to get hold of a dumpling.

CHAP. V.

Shewing how the grand Council of the New Netherlands came to be miraculously gifted with long tongues. — Together with a great triumph of Economy.

IT WILL NEED but very little witchcraft on the part of my enlightened reader—particularly if he is in any wise acquainted with the ways and habits of that most potent and blustering monarch, the sovereign people—to discover, that notwithstanding all the incredible bustle and talk of war that stunned him in the last chapter, the renowned city of New Amsterdam is in sad reality, not a whit better prepared for defence than before. Now, though the people, having got over the first alarm, and finding no enemy immediately at hand, had with that valour of tongue, for which your illustrious rabble is so famous, run into the opposite extreme, and by dint of gallant vapouring and rodomontado had actually talked themselves into the opinion that they were the bravest and most powerful people under the sun, yet were the privy councillors of Peter Stuyvesant somewhat dubious on that point. They dreaded moreover lest that stern hero should return and find, that instead of obeying his peremptory orders, they had wasted their time in listening to the valiant hectorings of the mob, than which they well knew there was nothing he held in more exalted contempt.

To make up therefore as speedily as possible for lost time, a grand divan of the councillors and robustious Burgomasters was convened, to talk over the critical state of the province and devise measures for its safety. Two things were unanimously agreed upon in this venerable assembly: first, that the city required to be put in a state of defence—and secondly, that as the danger was imminent, there should no time be lost—which points being settled, they immediately fell to making long speeches and belabouring one another in endless and intemperate disputes. For about this time was this unhappy city first visited by that talking endemic so universally prevalent in this country, and which so invariably evinces itself, wherever a number of wise men assemble together;

breaking out in long, windy speeches, caused, as physicians suppose, by the foul air which is ever generated in a crowd. Now it was, moreover, that they first introduced the ingenious method of measuring the merits of an harangue by the hour-glass; he being considered the ablest orator who spoke longest on a question—For which excellent invention it is recorded, we are indebted to the same profound dutch critic who judged of books by their bulk, and gave a prize medal to a stupendous volume of flummery—because it was "as tick as a cheese."

The reporters of the day, therefore, in publishing the debates of the grand council, seem merely to have noticed the length of time each member was on the floor—and the only record I can find of the proceedings in the important business of which we are treating, mentions, that "Mynheer —— made a very animated speech of six hours and a half, in favour of fortification—He was followed by Mynheer —— on the other side, who spoke with great clearness and precision for about eight hours—Mynheer —— suggested an amendment of the bill by substituting in the eighth line, the words '*four and twenty*,' instead of 'twenty four,' in support of which he offered a few remarks, which only took up three hours and a quarter—and was followed by Mynheer Windroer in a most pithy, nervous, concise, elegant, ironical, argumentative strain of eloquence, superior to any thing which ever issued from the lips of a Cicero, a Demosthenes, or any orator, either of antient or modern times—he occupied the floor the whole of yesterday; this morning he arose in continuation, and is in the middle of the second branch of his discourse, at this present writing; having already carried the council through their second nap—We regret," concludes this worthy reporter, "that the irresistable propensity of our Stenographer to nod, will prevent us from giving the substance of this truly luminous and *lengthy* speech."

This sudden passion for endless harangues, so little consonant with the customary gravity and taciturnity of our sage forefathers, is supposed by certain learned philosophers of the time, to have been imbibed, together with divers other barbarous propensities, from their savage neighbours; who were peculiarly noted for their *long talks* and *council fires*; and who would never undertake any affair of the least importance, without previous debates and harangues among their chiefs and *old men*. But let its origin be what it may, it is without doubt a cruel and distressing disease, which has never been eradicated from the body politic to this day; but is continually breaking out, on all occasions of great agitation, in alarming and obnoxious flatulencies, whereby the said body politic is grievously afflicted, as with a wind cholic.

Thus then did Madam Wisdom, (who for some unaccountable, but doubtlessly whimsical reason, the wits of antiquity have represented under the form of a woman) seem to take a mischievous pleasure in jilting the grave and venerable councillors of New Amsterdam. The old factions of Square heads and Platter Breeches, which had been almost strangled by the herculean grasp of Peter Stuyvesant, now sprung up with tenfold violence—To complete the public confusion and bewilderment, the fatal word *Economy*, which one would have thought was dead and buried with William the Testy, was once more set afloat, like the apple of discord, in the grand council of the New Nederlandts—according to which sound principle of policy, it was deemed more expedient to throw away twenty thousand guilders upon an inefficient plan of defence, than thirty thousand on a good and substantial one—the province thus making a clear saving of ten thousand guilders.

But when they came to discuss the mode of defence, then began a war of words that baffles all description. The members being, as I observed, drawn out into opposite parties, were enabled to proceed with amazing system and regularity in the discussion of the questions before them. Whatever was proposed by a Square head, was opposed by the whole tribe of Platter breeches, who like true politicians, considered it their first duty to effect the downfall of the Square heads—their second, to elevate themselves, and their third, to consult the welfare of the country. This at least was the creed of the most upright among the party, for as to the great mass, they left the third consideration out of the question altogether.

In this great collision of hard heads, it is astonishing the number of projects for defence, that were struck out, not one of which had ever been heard of before, nor has been heard of since, unless it be in very modern days—projects that threw the windmill system of the ingenious Kieft completely in the back ground—Still, however, nothing could be decided on, for as fast as a formidable host of air castles were reared by one party, they were demolished by the other—the simple populace stood gazing in anxious expectation of the mighty egg, that was to be hatched, with all this cackling, but they gazed in vain, for it appeared that the grand council was determined to protect the province as did the noble and gigantic Pantagruel his army—by covering it with his tongue.

Indeed there was a magnanimous portion of the members, fat, self important old burghers, who smoked their pipes and said nothing, excepting to negative every plan of defence that was offered. These were of that class of wealthy old citizens who having amassed a fortune, button up their pockets, shut their mouths, look rich and are good for nothing all the rest of their lives. Like some phlegmetic oyster, which having swallowed a pearl, closes its shell, settles down in the mud and parts with its life sooner than its treasure. Every plan of defence seemed to these worthy old gentlemen pregnant with ruin. An armed force was a legion of locusts, preying upon the public property—to fit out a naval armament was to throw their money into the sea—to build fortifications was to bury it in the dirt. In short they settled it as a sovereign maxim, so long as their pockets were full, no matter how much they were drubbed—A kick left no scar—a broken head cured itself—but an empty purse was of all maladies the slowest to heal, and one in which nature did nothing for the patient.

Thus did this venerable assembly of *sages*, lavish away that time which the urgency of affairs rendered invaluable, in empty brawls and long winded arguments, without even agreeing, except on the point with which they started, namely, that there was no time to be lost, and delay was ruinous. At length St. Nicholas, taking compassion on their distracted situation, and anxious to preserve them from total anarchy, so ordered, that in the midst of one of their most noisy and patriotic debates, when they had nearly fallen to loggerheads in consequence of not being able to convince each other, the question was happily settled by a messenger, who bounced into the chamber and informed them, that the hostile fleet had arrived, and was actually advancing up the bay!

Thus was all further necessity of either fortifying or disputing completely obviated, and thus was the grand council saved a world of words, and the province a world of expense—a most absolute and glorious triumph of economy!

CHAP. VI.

*In which the troubles of New Amsterdam appear to thicken —
Shewing the bravery in time of peril, of a people who defend
themselves by resolutions.*

LIKE a ward committee of politic cats, who, when engaged
in clamorous gibberings, and catterwaulings, eyeing one
another with hideous grimaces, spitting in each other's faces,
and on the point of breaking forth into a general clapper-
clawing, are suddenly put to scampering rout and confusion
by the startling appearance of a house-dog—So was the no
less vociferous council of New Amsterdam, amazed, astounded, and totally dispersed, by the sudden arrival of the
enemy. Every member made the best of his way home, waddling along as fast as his short legs could fag under their
heavy burthen, and wheezing as he went with corpulency and
terror. When he arrived at his castle, he barricadoed the street
door, and buried himself in the cider cellar, without daring to
peep out, lest he should have his head carried off by a cannon
ball.

The sovereign people all crowded into the market place,
herding together with the instinct of sheep who seek for
safety in each others company, when the shepherd and his
dog are absent and the wolf is prowling round the fold. Far
from finding relief however, they only encreased each others
terrors. Each man looked ruefully in his neighbour's face, in
search of encouragement, but only found in its woe begone
lineaments, a confirmation of his own dismay. Not a word
now was to be heard of conquering Great Britain, not a whisper about the sovereign virtues of economy—while the old
women heightened the general gloom by clamorously bewailing their fate, and incessantly calling for protection on St.
Nicholas and Peter Stuyvesant.

Oh how did they bewail the absence of the lion hearted
Peter!—and how did they long for the comforting presence
of Antony Van Corlear! Indeed a gloomy uncertainty hung
over the fate of these adventurous heroes. Day after day had
elapsed since the alarming message from the governor, with-

out bringing any further tidings of his safety. Many a fearful conjecture was hazarded as to what had befallen him and his loyal squire. Had they not been devoured alive by the Cannibals of Piscataway and Cape Cod?—were they not put to the question by the great council of Amphyctions?—were they not smothered in onions by the terrible men of Pyquag?—In the midst of this consternation and perplexity, when horror like a mighty night-mare sat brooding upon the little, fat, plethoric city of New Amsterdam, the ears of the multitude were suddenly startled by a strange and distant sound—it approached—it grew louder and louder—and now it resounded at the city gate. The public could not be mistaken in the well known sound—A shout of joy burst from their lips as the gallant Peter, covered with dust, and followed by his faithful trumpeter, came galloping into the market place.

The first transports of the populace having subsided, they gathered round the honest Antony, as he dismounted from his horse, overwhelming him with greetings and congratulations. In breathless accents he related to them the marvellous adventures through which the old governor and himself had gone, in making their escape from the clutches of the terrible Amphyctions. But though the Stuyvesant Manuscript, with its customary minuteness where any thing touching the great Peter is concerned, is very particular, as to the incidents of this masterly retreat, yet the critical state of the public affairs, will not allow me to indulge in a full recital thereof. Let it suffice to say, that while Peter Stuyvesant was anxiously revolving in his mind, how he could make good his escape with honour and dignity, certain of the ships sent out for the conquest of the Manhattoes touched at the Eastern ports, to obtain needful supplies, and to call on the grand council of the league, for its promised co-operation. Upon hearing of this, the vigilant Peter, perceiving that a moment's delay was fatal, made a secret and precipitate decampment, though much did it grieve his lofty soul, to be obliged to turn his back even upon a nation of foes. Many hair-breadth scapes and divers perilous mishaps, did they sustain, as they scoured, without sound of trumpet, through the fair regions of the east. Already was the country in an uproar with hostile preparation—and they were obligated to take a large circuit in their flight, lurking along, through the woody mountains of the Devil's back bone; from whence the valiant Peter sallied forth one day, like a lion, and put to route a whole legion of squatters, consisting of three generations of a prolific family, who were already on their way to take possession of some corner of the New Netherlands. Nay, the faithful Antony had great difficulty at sundry times, to prevent him in the excess of his wrath, from descending down from the mountains, and falling sword in hand, upon certain of the border towns, who were marshalling forth their draggle-tailed militia.

The first movements of the governor on reaching his dwelling, was to mount the roof, from whence he contemplated with rueful aspect the hostile squadron. This had already come to anchor in the bay, and consisted of two stout frigates, having on board, as John Josselyn, gent. informs us, three hundred valiant red coats. Having taken this survey, he sat himself down, and wrote an epistle to the commander, demanding the reason of his anchoring in the harbour without obtaining previous permission so to do. This letter was couched in the most dignified and courteous terms, though I have it from undoubted authority, that his teeth were clinched, and he had a bitter sardonic grin upon his visage, all the while he wrote. Having dispatched his letter, the grim Peter stumped to and fro about the town, with a most warbetokening countenance, his hands thrust into his breeches pockets, and whistling a low dutch psalm tune, which bore no small resemblance to the music of a north east wind, when a storm is brewing—the very dogs as they eyed him skulked away in dismay—while all the old and ugly women of New Amsterdam, ran howling at his heels, imploring him to save them from murder, robbery, and piteous ravishment!

The reply of Col. Nichols, who commanded the invaders, was couched in terms of equal courtesy with the letter of the governor—declaring the right and title of his British Majesty to the province; where he affirmed the dutch to be mere interlopers; and demanding that the town, forts, &c. should be forthwith rendered into his majesty's obedience and protection—promising at the same time, life, liberty, estate and free trade, to every dutch denizen, who should readily submit to his majesty's government.

Peter Stuyvesant read over this friendly epistle with some such harmony of aspect as we may suppose a crusty farmer, who has long been fattening upon his neighbour's soil, reads the loving letter of John Stiles, that warns him of an action of ejectment. The old governor however, was not to be taken by surprize, but thrusting, according to custom, a huge quid of tobacco into his cheek, and cramming the summons into his breeches pocket, promised to answer it the next morning. In the mean time he called a general council of war of his privy councillors and Burgomasters, not for the purpose of asking their advice, for that, as has been already shewn, he valued not a rush; but to make known unto them his sovereign determination, and require their prompt adherence.

Before, however, he convened his council he resolved upon three important points; *first*, never to give up the city without a little hard fighting, for he deemed it highly derogatory to the dignity of so renowned a city, to suffer itself to be captured and stripped, without receiving a few kicks into the bargain. *Secondly*, that the majority of his grand council were a crew of arrant platter breeches, utterly destitute of true bottom—and *thirdly*—that he would not therefore suffer them to see the summons of Col. Nichols, lest the easy terms it held out, might induce them to clamour for a surrender.

His orders being duly promulgated, it was a piteous sight to behold the late valiant Burgomasters, who had demolished the whole British empire in their harangues; peeping ruefully out of their nests, and then crawling cautiously forth, dodging through narrow lanes and alleys; starting at every little dog that barked, as if it had been a discharge of artillery— mistaking lamp posts for British grenadiers, and in the excess of their panic, metamorphosing pumps into formidable soldiers, levelling blunderbusses at their bosoms! Having however, in despite of numerous perils and difficulties of the kind, arrived safe, without the loss of a single man, at the hall of assembly, they took their seats and awaited in fearful silence the arrival of the governor. In a few moments the wooden leg of the intrepid Peter, was heard in regular and stout-hearted thumps upon the stair case—He entered the chamber, arrayed in full suit of regimentals, a more than ordinary quantity of flour shook into his ear locks, and carrying his trusty toledo, not girded on his thigh, but tucked under his arm. As the governor never equipped himself in this portentous manner, unless something of martial nature was working within his fearless pericranium, his council regarded him ruefully as a very Janus bearing fire and sword in his iron countenance— and forgot to light their pipes in breathless suspence.

The great Peter was as eloquent as he was valorous—indeed these two rare qualities seemed to go hand in hand in his composition; and, unlike most great statesmen, whose victories are only confined to the bloodless field of argument, he was always ready to enforce his hardy words, by no less hardy deeds. Like another Gustavus addressing his Dalecarlians, he touched upon the perils and hardships he had sustained in escaping from his inexorable foes—He next reproached the council for wasting in idle debate and impertinent personalities that time which should have been devoted to their country—he then recalled the golden days of former prosperity, which were only to be regained by manfully withstanding their enemies—endeavoured to rouse their martial fire, by reminding them of the time, when, before the frowning walls of fort Christina, he led them on to victory—when they had subdued a whole army of fifty Swedes—and subjugated an immense extent of uninhabited territory.—He strove likewise to awaken their confidence, by assuring them of the protection of St. Nicholas; who had hitherto maintained them in safety; amid all the savages of the wilderness, the witches and squatters of the east, and the giants of Merry land. Finally he informed them of the insolent summons he had received, to surrender, but concluded by swearing to defend the province as long as heaven was on his side, and he had a wooden leg to stand upon. Which noble sentence he emphasized by a tremendous thwack with the broad side of his sword upon the table, that totally electrified his auditors.

The privy councillors, who had long been accustomed to the governor's way, and in fact had been brought into as perfect discipline, as were ever the soldiers of the great Frederick; saw that there was no use in saying a word—so lighted their pipes and smoked away in silence, like fat and discreet councillors. But the Burgomasters being less under the governor's controul—considering themselves as representatives of the sovereign people, and being moreover inflated with considerable importance and self-sufficiency, which they had acquired at those notable schools of wisdom and morality, the popular meetings; (whereof in fact I am told certain of them had been chairmen) these I say, were not so easily satisfied. Mustering up fresh spirit, when they found there was some chance of escaping from their present perilous jeopardy, without the disagreeable alternative of fighting, they arrogantly requested a copy of the summons to surrender, that they might shew it to a general meeting of the people.

So insolent and mutinous a request would have been enough to have roused the gorge of the tranquil Van Twiller himself—what then must have been its effect upon the great Stuyvesant, who was not only a Dutchman, a Governor, and a valiant wooden legged soldier to boot, but withal a man of the most stomachful and gunpowder disposition. He burst forth into a blaze of heroical indignation, to which the famous rage of Achilles was a mere pouting fit—swore not a mother's son of them should see a syllable of it—that they deserved, every one of them, to be hung, drawn and quartered, for traitorously daring to question the infallibility of government—that as to their advice or concurrence, he did not care a whiff of tobacco for either—that he had long been harrassed and thwarted by their cowardly councils; but that they might henceforth go home, and go to bed like old women; for he was determined to defend the colony himself, without the assistance of them or their adherents! So saying he tucked his sword under his arm, cocked his hat upon his head, and girding up his loins, stumped indignantly out of the council chamber—every body making room for him as he passed.

No sooner had he gone than the sturdy Burgomasters called a public meeting in front of the Stadt-house, where they appointed as chairman one Dofue Roerback, a mighty gingerbread baker in the land, and formerly of the cabinet of William the Testy. He was looked up to, with great reverence by the populace, who considered him a man of dark knowledge, seeing he was the first that imprinted new year cakes with the mysterious hieroglyphics of the Cock and Breeches, and such like magical devices.

This great Burgomaster, who still chewed the cud of ill will against the valiant Stuyvesant, in consequence of having been ignominiously kicked out of his cabinet—addressed the greasy multitude in an exceeding long-winded speech, in which he informed them of the courteous summons to surrender—of the governor's refusal to comply therewith—of his denying the public a sight of the summons, which he had no doubt, from the well known liberality, humanity, and forbearance, of the British nation, contained conditions highly to the honour and advantage of the province.

He then proceeded to speak of his excellency in high sounding terms, suitable to the dignity and grandeur of his station, comparing him to Nero, Caligula, and other great men of yore, of whom he had often heard William the Testy discourse in his learned moods—Assuring the people, that the history of the world did not contain a despotic outrage to equal the present, for atrocity, cruelty, tyranny, blood-thirstiness, battle, murder, and sudden death—that it would be recorded in letters of fire, on the blood-stained tablet of history! that ages would roll back with sudden horror, when they came to view it! That the womb of time—(by the way your orators and writers take strange liberties with the womb of time, though some would fain have us believe that time is an old gentleman) that the womb of time, pregnant as it was with direful horrors, would never produce a parallel enormity!—that posterity would be struck dumb with petrifying astonishment, and howl in unavailing indignation, over the records of irremediable barbarity!—With a variety of other heart-rending, soul stirring tropes and figures, which I cannot enumerate—Neither indeed need I, for they were exactly the same that are used in all popular harangues and fourth of July orations at the present day, and may be classed in rhetoric under the general title of RIGMAROLE.

The patriotic address of Burgomaster Roerback had a wonderful effect upon the populace, who, though a race of sober phlegmatic Dutchmen, were amazing quick at discerning insults; for your ragged rabble, though it may bear injuries without a murmur, yet is always marvellously jealous of its

sovereign dignity. They immediately fell into the pangs of tumultuous labour, and brought forth, not only a string of right
wise and valiant resolutions, but likewise a most resolute memorial, addressed to the governor, remonstrating at his conduct—which he no sooner received than he handed it into
the fire; and thus deprived posterity of an invaluable document, that might have served as a precedent to the enlightened coblers and taylors, of the present day, in their sage
intermeddlings with politics.

CHAP. VII.

*Containing a doleful disaster of Antony the Trumpeter —
And how Peter Stuyvesant, like a second Cromwell suddenly
dissolved a rump Parliament.*

Now did the high minded Pieter *de Groodt*, shower down a pannier load of benedictions upon his Burgomasters, for a set of self-willed, obstinate, headstrong varlets, who would neither be convinced nor persuaded; and determined henceforth to have nothing more to do with them, but to consult merely the opinion of his privy councillors, which he knew from experience to be the best in the world — inasmuch as it never differed from his own. Nor did he omit, now that his hand was in, to bestow some thousand left-handed compliments upon the sovereign people; whom he railed at for a herd of arrant poltroons, who had no relish for the glorious hardships and illustrious misadventures of battle — but would rather stay at home, and eat and sleep in ignoble ease, than gain immortality and a broken head, by valiantly fighting in a ditch!

Resolutely bent however upon defending his beloved city, in despite even of itself, he called unto him his trusty Van Corlear, who was his right hand man in all times of emergency. Him did he adjure to take his war denouncing trumpet, and mounting his horse, to beat up the country, night and day — Sounding the alarm along the pastoral borders of the Bronx — startling the wild solitudes of Croton, arousing the rugged yeomanry of Weehawk and Hoboken — the mighty men of battle of Tappan Bay* — and the brave boys of Tarry town and Sleepy hollow — together with all the other warriors of the country round about; charging them one and all, to sling their powder horns, shoulder their fowling pieces, and march merrily down to the Manhattoes.

Now there was nothing in all the world, the divine sex excepted, that Antony Van Corlear loved better than errands of this kind. So just stopping to take a lusty dinner, and bracing

*A corruption of Top-paun; so called from a tribe of Indians which boasted 150 fighting men. See Ogilvie. EDITOR.

to his side his junk bottle, well charged with heart inspiring Hollands, he issued jollily from the city gate, that looked out upon what is at present called Broadway; sounding as usual a farewell strain, that rung in sprightly echoes through the winding streets of New Amsterdam—Alas! never more were they to be gladdened by the melody of their favourite trumpeter!

It was a dark and stormy night when the good Antony arrived at the famous creek (sagely denominated Hærlem *river*) which separates the island of Manna-hata from the main land. The wind was high, the elements were in an uproar, and no Charon could be found to ferry the adventurous sounder of brass across the water. For a short time he vapoured like an impatient ghost upon the brink, and then, bethinking himself of the urgency of his errand, took a hearty embrace of his stone bottle, swore most valourously that he would swim across, *en spijt den Duyvel* (in spite of the devil!) and daringly plunged into the stream.—Luckless Antony! scarce had he buffetted half way over, when he was observed to struggle most violently as if battling with the spirit of the waters—instinctively he put his trumpet to his mouth and giving a vehement blast—sunk forever to the bottom!

The potent clangour of his trumpet, like the ivory horn of the renowned Paladin Orlando, when expiring in the glorious field of Roncesvalles, rung far and wide through the country, alarming the neighbours round, who hurried in amazement to the spot—Here an old Dutch burgher, famed for his veracity, and who had been a witness of the fact, related to them the melancholy affair; with the fearful addition (to which I am slow of giving belief) that he saw the duyvel, in the shape of a huge Moss-bonker with an invisible fiery tail, and vomiting boiling water, seize the sturdy Antony by the leg, and drag him beneath the waves. Certain it is, the place, with the adjoining promontory, which projects into the Hudson, has been called *Spijt den duyvel*, or *Spiking devil*, ever since—the restless ghost of the unfortunate Antony still haunts the surrounding solitudes, and his trumpet has often been heard by the neighbours, of a stormy night, mingling with the howling of the blast. No body ever attempts to swim over the creek after dark; on the contrary, a bridge has been built to guard against such melancholy accidents in future—and as to Moss-bonkers, they are held in such abhorrence, that no true Dutchman will admit them to his table, who loves good fish, and hates the devil.

Such was the end of Antony Van Corlear—a man deserving of a better fate. He lived roundly and soundly, like a true and jolly batchelor, until the day of his death; but though he was never married, yet did he leave behind some two or three dozen children, in different parts of the country—fine, chubby, brawling, flatulent little urchins, from whom, if legends speak true, (and they are not apt to lie) did descend the innumerable race of editors, who people and defend this country, and who are bountifully paid by the people for keeping up a constant alarm—and making them miserable. Would that they inherited the worth, as they do the wind, of their renowned progenitor!

The tidings of this lamentable catastrophe imparted a severer pang to the bosom of Peter Stuyvesant, than did even the invasion of his beloved Amsterdam. It came ruthlessly home to those sweet affections that grow close around the heart, and are nourished by its warmest current. As some lorn pilgrim wandering in trackless wastes, while the rude tempest whistles through his hoary locks, and dreary night is gathering around, sees stretched cold and lifeless, his faithful dog—the sole companion of his lonely journeying, who had shared his solitary meal, who had so often licked his hand in humble gratitude, who had lain in his bosom, and been unto him as a child—So did the generous hearted hero of the Manhattoes contemplate the untimely end of his faithful Antony. He had been the humble attendant of his footsteps—he had cheered him in many a heavy hour, by his honest gaiety, and had followed him in loyalty and affection, through many a scene of direful peril and mishap—he was gone forever—and that too, at a moment when every mongrel cur seemed skulking from his side—This—Peter Stuyvesant—this was the moment to try thy magnanimity; and this was the moment, when thou didst indeed shine forth—Peter *the Headstrong!*

The glare of day had long dispelled the horrors of the last stormy night; still all was dull and gloomy. The late jovial Apollo hid his face behind lugubrious clouds, peeping out now and then, for an instant, as if anxious, yet fearful, to see what was going on, in his favourite city. This was the eventful morning, when the great Peter was to give his reply, to the audacious summons of the invaders. Already was he closetted with his privy council, sitting in grim state, brooding over the fate of his favourite trumpeter, and anon boiling with indignation as the insolence of his recreant Burgomasters flashed upon his mind. While in this state of irritation, a courier arrived in all haste from Winthrop, the subtle governor of Connecticut, councilling him in the most affectionate and disinterested manner to surrender the province, and magnifying the dangers and calamities to which a refusal would subject him.—What a moment was this to intrude officious advice upon a man, who never took advice in his whole life!—The fiery old governor strode up and down the chamber, with a vehemence, that made the bosoms of his councillors to quake with awe—railing at his unlucky fate, that thus made him the constant butt of factious subjects, and jesuitical advisers.

Just at this ill chosen juncture, the officious Burgomasters, who were now completely on the watch, and had got wind of the arrival of mysterious dispatches, came marching in a resolute body, into the room, with a legion of Schepens and toad-eaters at their heels, and abruptly demanded a perusal of the letter. Thus to be broken in upon by what he esteemed a "rascal rabble," and that too at the very moment he was grinding under an irritation from abroad, was too much for the spleen of the choleric Peter. He tore the letter in a thousand pieces*—threw it in the face of the nearest Burgomaster—broke his pipe over the head of the next—hurled his spitting box at an unlucky Schepen, who was just making a masterly retreat out at the door, and finally dissolved the whole meeting *sine die*, by kicking them down stairs with his wooden leg!

As soon as the Burgomasters could recover from the confusion into which their sudden exit had thrown them, and had taken a little time to breathe, they protested against the conduct of the governor, which they did not hesitate to pro-

*Smith's History of N. Y.

nounce tyrannical, unconstitutional, highly indecent, and somewhat disrespectful. They then called a public meeting, where they read the protest, and addressing the assembly in a set speech related at full length, and with appropriate colouring and exaggeration, the despotic and vindictive deportment of the governor; declaring that, for their own parts, they did not value a straw the being kicked, cuffed, and mauled by the timber toe of his excellency, but they felt for the dignity of the sovereign people, thus rudely insulted by the outrage committed on the seats of honour of their representatives. The latter part of the harangue had a violent effect upon the sensibility of the people, as it came home at once, to that delicacy of feeling and jealous pride of character, vested in all true mobs: and there is no knowing to what act of resentment they might have been provoked, against the redoubtable Hard-koppig Piet—had not the greasy rogues been somewhat more afraid of their sturdy old governor, than they were of St. Nicholas, the English—or the D——l himself.

CHAP. VIII.

Shewing how Peter Stuyvesant defended the city of New Amsterdam for several days, by dint of the strength of his head.

PAUSE, oh most considerate reader! and contemplate for a moment the sublime and melancholy scene, which the present crisis of our history presents! An illustrious and venerable little town—the metropolis of an immense extent of flourishing but unenlightened, because uninhabited country—Garrisoned by a doughty host of orators, chairmen, committee-men, Burgomasters, Schepens and old women—governed by a determined and strong headed warrior, and fortified by mud batteries, pallisadoes and resolutions.—blockaded by sea, beleaguered by land, and threatened with direful desolation from without; while its very vitals are torn, and griped, and becholiced with internal faction and commotion! Never did the historic pen record a page of more complicated distress, unless it be the strife that distracted the Israelites during the siege of Jerusalem—where discordant parties were cutting each others throats, at the moment when the victorious legions of Titus had toppled down their bulwarks, and were carrying fire and sword, into the very sanctum sanctorum of the temple.

Governor Stuyvesant having triumphantly, as has been recorded, put his grand council to the rout, and thus delivered himself from a multitude of impertinent advisers, dispatched a categorical reply to the commanders of the invading squadron; wherein he asserted the right and title of their High Mightinesses the lords States general to the province of New Netherlands, and trusting in the righteousness of his cause, set the whole British nation at defiance! My anxiety to extricate my readers, and myself, from these disastrous scenes, prevents me from giving the whole of this most courteous and gallant letter, which concluded in these manly and affectionate terms.

"As touching the threats in your conclusion, we have nothing to answer, only that we fear nothing but what God, (who is as just as merciful) shall lay upon us; all things being in his

712

gracious disposal, and we may as well be preserved by him with small forces, as by a great army; which makes us to wish you all happiness and prosperity, and recommend you to his protection—My lords your thrice humble and affectionate servant and friend

P. Stuyvesant."

Thus having resolutely thrown his gauntlet, the brave Hard-koppig Piet stuck a huge pair of horse pistols in his belt, girded an immense powder horn on his side—thrust his sound leg into a Hessian boot, and clapping his fierce little war hat on top of his head—paraded up and down in front of his house, determined to defend his beloved city to the last.

While all these woeful struggles and dissensions were prevailing in the unhappy little city of New Amsterdam, and while its worthy but ill starred governor was framing the above quoted letter, the English commanders did not remain idle. They had agents secretly employed to foment the fears and clamours of the populace, and moreover circulated far and wide through the adjacent country a proclamation, repeating the terms they had already held out in their summons to surrender, and beguiling the simple Nederlanders with the most crafty and conciliating professions. They promised every man who voluntarily submitted to the authority of his British majesty, that he should retain peaceable possession of his house, his vrouw and his cabbage garden. That he should be suffered to smoke his pipe, speak dutch, wear as many breeches as he pleased, and import bricks, tiles and stone jugs from Holland, instead of manufacturing them on the spot— That he should on no account be compelled to learn the English language, or keep accounts in any other way than by casting them up upon his fingers, and chalking them down upon the crown of his hat; as is still observed among the dutch yeomanry at the present day. That every man should be allowed quietly to inherit his father's hat, coat, shoe-buckles, pipe, and every other personal appendage, and that no man should be obliged to conform to any improvements, inventions, or any other modern innovations, but on the contrary should be permitted to build his house, follow his trade, manage his farm, rear his hogs, and educate his children, pre-

cisely as his ancestors did before him since time immemorial—Finally, that he should have all the benefits of free trade,
and should not be required to acknowledge any other saint in
the calendar than saint Nicholas, who should thenceforward,
as before, be considered the tutelar saint of the city.

These terms, as may be supposed, appeared very satisfactory to the people; who had a great disposition to enjoy their
property unmolested, and a most singular aversion to engage
in a contest, where they could gain little more than honour
and broken heads—the first of which they held in philosophic indifference, the latter in utter detestation. By these
insidious means, therefore, did the English succeed in alien-
ating the confidence and affections of the populace from their
gallant old governor, whom they considered as obstinately
bent upon running them into hideous misadventures, and did
not hesitate to speak their minds freely, and abuse him most
heartily—behind his back.

Like as a mighty grampus, who though assailed and buffeted by roaring waves and brawling surges, still keeps on an
undeviating course; and though overwhelmed by boisterous
billows, still emerges from the troubled deep, spouting and
blowing with tenfold violence—so did the inflexible Peter
pursue, unwavering, his determined career, and rise contemptuous, above the clamours of the rabble.

But when the British warriors found by the tenor of his
reply that he set their power at defiance, they forthwith dispatched recruiting officers to Jamaica, and Jericho, and
Nineveh, and Quag, and Patchog, and all those redoubtable
towns which had been subdued of yore by the immortal Stoffel Brinkerhoff, stirring up the valiant progeny of Preserved
Fish, and Determined Cock, and those other illustrious squatters, to assail the city of New Amsterdam by land. In the
mean while the hostile ships made awful preparation to commence a vehement assault by water.

The streets of New Amsterdam now presented a scene of
wild dismay and consternation. In vain did the gallant Stuyvesant order the citizens to arm and assemble in the public
square or market place. The whole party of Platter breeches
in the course of a single night had changed into arrant old
women—a metamorphosis only to be paralleled by the prod-

igies recorded by Livy as having happened at Rome at the approach of Hannibal, when statues sweated in pure affright, goats were converted into sheep, and cocks turning into hens ran cackling about the streets.

The harrassed Peter, thus menaced from without and tormented from within—baited by the burgomasters and hooted at by the rabble, chafed and growled and raged like a furious bear tied to a stake and worried by a legion of scoundrel curs. Finding however that all further attempt to defend the city was in vain, and hearing that an irruption of borderers and moss troopers was ready to deluge him from the east, he was at length compelled, in spite of his mighty heart, which swelled in his throat until it had nearly choked him, to consent to a treaty of surrender.

Words cannot express the transports of the people, on receiving this agreeable intelligence; had they obtained a conquest over their enemies, they could not have indulged greater delight—The streets resounded with their congratulations—they extolled their governor as the father and deliverer of his country—they crowded to his house to testify their gratitude, and were ten times more noisy in their plaudits, than when he returned, with victory perched upon his beaver, from the glorious capture of Fort Christina—But the indignant Peter shut up his doors and windows and took refuge in the innermost recesses of his mansion, that he might not hear the ignoble rejoicings of the rabble.

In consequence of this consent of the governor, a parley was demanded of the besieging forces to treat of the terms of surrender. Accordingly a deputation of six commissioners was appointed on both sides, and on the 27th August, 1664, a capitulation highly favourable to the province, and honourable to Peter Stuyvesant, was agreed to by the enemy, who had conceived a high opinion of the valour of the men of the Manhattoes, and the magnanimity and unbounded discretion of their governor.

One thing alone remained, which was, that the articles of surrender should be ratified, and signed by the chivalric Peter—When the commissioners respectfully waited upon him for this purpose, they were received by the hardy old warrior, with the most grim and bitter courtesy. His warlike accoutrements were laid aside—an old India night gown was wrapped around his rugged limbs, a red woollen night cap overshadowed his frowning brow, and an iron grey beard, of three days growth, heightened the grizly terrors of his visage. Thrice did he seize a little worn out stump of a pen, and essay to sign the loathesome paper—thrice did he clinch his teeth, and make a most horrible countenance, as though a pestiferous dose of rhubarb, senna, and ipecacuanha, had been offered to his lips, at length dashing it from him, he seized his brass hilted sword, and jerking it from the scabbard, swore by St. Nicholas, he'd sooner die than yield to any power under heaven.

In vain was every attempt to shake this sturdy resolution—menaces, remonstrances, revilings were exhausted to no purpose—for two whole days was the house of the valiant Peter besieged by the clamourous rabble, and for two whole days did he betake himself to his arms, and persist in a magnanimous refusal to ratify the capitulation—thus, like a second Horatius Cocles, bearing the whole brunt of war, and defending this modern Rome, with the prowess of his single arm!

At length the populace finding that boisterous measures, did but incense more determined opposition, bethought themselves of a humble expedient, by which haply, the governor's lofty ire might be soothed, and his resolution undermined. And now a solemn and mournful procession, headed by the Burgomasters, and Schepens, and followed by the enlightened vulgar, moves slowly to the governor's dwelling—bearing the unfortunate capitulation. Here they found the stout old hero, drawn up like a giant into his castle—the doors strongly barricadoed, and himself in full regimentals, with his cocked hat on his head, firmly posted with a blunderbuss at the garret window.

There was something in this formidable position that struck even the ignoble vulgar, with awe and admiration. The brawling multitude could not but reflect with self abasement, upon their own degenerate conduct, when they beheld their hardy but deserted old governor, thus faithful to his post, like a forlorn hope, and fully prepared to defend his ungrateful city to the last. These compunctions however, were soon overwhelmed, by the recurring tide of public apprehension.

The populace arranged themselves before the house, taking off their hats, with most respectful humility—One of the Burgomasters, of that popular class of orators, who, as old Sallust observes, are "talkative rather than eloquent" stepped forth and addressed the governor in a speech of three hours length; detailing in the most pathetic terms the calamitous situation of the province, and urging him in a constant repetition of the same arguments and words, to sign the capitulation.

The mighty Peter eyed him from his little garret window in grim silence—now and then his eye would glance over the surrounding rabble, and an indignant grin, like that of an angry mastiff, would mark his iron visage—But though he was a man of most undaunted mettle—though he had a heart as big as an ox, and a head that would have set adamant to scorn—yet after all he was a mere mortal:—wearied out by these repeated oppositions and this eternal haranguing, and perceiving that unless he complied, the inhabitants would follow their inclinations, or rather their fears, without waiting for his consent, he testily ordered them to hand him up the paper. It was accordingly hoisted to him on the end of a pole, and having scrawled his name at the bottom of it, he excommunicated them all for a set of cowardly, mutinous, degenerate platter-breeches—threw the capitulation at their heads, slammed down the window, and was heard stumping down the stairs with the most vehement indignation. The rabble incontinently took to their heels; even the Burgomasters were not slow in evacuating the premises, fearing lest the sturdy Peter might issue from his den, and greet them with some unwelcome testimonial of his displeasure.

CHAP. IX.

Containing reflections on the decline and fall of empires, with the final extinction of the Dutch Dynasty.

AMONG the numerous events, which are each in their turn the most direful and melancholy of all possible occurrences, in your interesting and authentic history; there is none that occasions such heart rending grief to your historian of sensibility, as the decline and fall of your renowned and mighty empires! Like your well disciplined funeral orator, whose feelings are properly tutored to ebb and flow, to blaze in enthusiastic eulogy, or gush in overwhelming sorrow—who has reduced his impetuous grief to a kind of manual—has prepared to slap his breast at a comma, strike his forehead at a semicolon; start with horror at a dash—and burst into an ungovernable paroxysm of despair at a note of admiration! Like unto him your woe begone historian ascends the rostrum; bends in dumb pathos over the ruins of departed greatness; casts an upbraiding eye to heaven, a glance of indignant misery on the surrounding world; settles his features into an expression of unutterable agony, and having by this eloquent preparation, invoked the whole animate and inanimate creation to unite with him in sorrow, draws slowly his white handkerchief from his pocket, and as he applies it to his face, seems to sob to his readers, in the words of a most tear shedding dutch author, "You who have noses, prepare to blow them now!"—or rather, to quote more literally "let every man blow his own nose!"

Where is the reader who can contemplate without emotion, the disastrous events by which the great dynasties of the world have been extinguished? When wandering, with mental eye amid the awful and gigantic ruins of kingdoms, states and empires—marking the tremendous convulsions that shook their foundations and wrought their lamentable downfall—the bosom of the melancholy enquirer swells with sympathy, commensurate to the sublimity of the surrounding horrors—each petty feeling—each private misery, is overpowered and forgotten; like a helpless mortal struggling under the night mare; so the unhappy reader pants and groans, and labours, under one stupendous grief—one vast immoveable idea—one immense, one mountainous—one overwhelming mass of woe!

Behold the great Assyrian Empire, founded by Nimrod, that mighty hunter, extending its domains over the fairest portion of the globe—encreasing in splendour through a long lapse of fifteen centuries, and terminating ingloriously in the reign of the effeminate Sardinapalus, consumed in the conflagration of his capital by the Median Arbaces.

Behold its successor, the Median Empire, augmented by the warlike power of Persia, under the sceptre of the immortal Cyrus, and the Egyptian conquests of the desert-braving Cambyses—accumulating strength and glory during seven centuries—but shook to its centre, and finally overthrown, in the memorable battles of the Granicus, the Issus, and the plains of Arbela, by the all conquering arm of Alexander.

Behold next the Grecian Empire; brilliant, but brief, as the warlike meteor with which it rose and descended—existing but seven years, in a blaze of glory—and perishing, with its hero, in a scene of ignominious debauchery.

Behold next the Roman Eagle, fledged in her Ausonean aerie, but wheeling her victorious flight over the fertile plains of Asia—the burning desarts of Africa, and at length spreading wide her triumphant wings, the mistress of the world! But mark her fate—view the imperial Rome, the emporium of taste and science—the paragon of cities—the metropolis of the universe—ravaged, sacked and overturned by successive hordes of fierce barbarians—and the unwieldly empire, like a huge but over ripe pumpkin, splitting into the western empire of the renowned Charlemagne, and the eastern or Greek Empire of Leo the Great—which latter, after enduring through six long centuries, is dismembered by the unhallowed hands of the Saracens.

Behold the Saracenic empire, swayed by the puissant Gengis Khan, lording it over these conquered domains, and, under the reign of Tamerlane subduing the whole Eastern region. Then cast an eye towards the Persian mountains. Mark how the fiery shepherd Othman, with his fierce compeers, descend like a whirlwind on the Nicomedian plains.

Lo! the late fearless Saracen succumbs—he flies! he falls! His dynasty is destroyed, and the Ottoman crescent is reared triumphant on its ruins!

Behold——but why should we behold any more? Why should we rake among the ashes of extinguished greatness?—Kingdoms, Principalities, and Powers, have each had their rise, their progress, and their fall—each in its turn has swayed a mighty sceptre—each has returned to its primeval nothingness. And thus did it fare with the empire of their High Mightinesses, at the illustrious metropolis of the Manhattoes, under the peaceful reign of Walter the Doubter—the fractious reign of William the Testy, and the chivalric reign of Peter Stuyvesant—alias, Pieter de Groodt—alias, Hardkoppig-Piet—which meaneth Peter the Headstrong!

The patron of refinement, hospitality, and the elegant arts, it shone resplendent, like a jewel in a dunghill, deriving additional lustre from the barbarism of the savage tribes, and European hordes, by which it was surrounded. But alas! neither virtue, nor talents, eloquence, nor economy, can avert the inavertable stroke of fate. The Dutch Dynasty, pressed, and assailed on every side, approached to its destined end. It had been puffed, and blown up from small beginnings, to a most corpulent rotundity—it had resisted the constant incroachments of its neighbouring foes, with phlegmatic magnanimity—but the sudden shock of invasion was too much for its strength.

Thus have I seen a crew of truant urchins, beating and belabouring a distended bladder, which maintained its size, uninjured by their assaults—At length an unlucky brat, more knowing than the rest, collecting all his might, bounces down with his bottom upon the inflated globe—The contact of contending spheres is aweful and destructive—the bloated membrane yields—it bursts, it explodes with a noise strange and equivocal, wonderfully resembling thunder—and is no more.

And now nought remains but sadly and reluctantly to deliver up this excellent little city into the hands of its invaders. Willingly would I, like the impetuous Peter, draw my trusty weapon and defend it through another volume; but truth, unalterable truth forbids the rash attempt, and what is more imperious still, a phantom, hideous, huge and black, forever haunts my mind, the direful spectrum of my landlord's bill—which like a carrion crow hovers around my slow expiring history, impatient of its death, to gorge upon its carcass.

Suffice it then in brevity to say, that within three hours after the surrender, a legion of British beef fed warriors poured into New Amsterdam, taking possession of the fort and batteries. And now might be heard the busy sound of hammers made by the old Dutch burghers, who industriously nailed up their doors and windows to protect their vrouws from these fierce barbarians; whom they contemplated in silent sullenness from the attic story, as they paraded through the streets.

Thus did Col. Richard Nichols, the commander of the British force enter into quiet possession of the conquered realm as *locum tenant* for the duke of York. The victory was attended with no other outrage than that of changing the name of the province and its metropolis, which thenceforth were denominated NEW YORK, and so have continued to be called unto the present day. The inhabitants according to treaty were allowed to maintain quiet possession of their property, but so inveterately did they retain their abhorrence to the British nation, that in a private meeting of the leading citizens, it was unanimously determined never to ask any of their conquerors to dinner.

Such was the fate of the renowned province of New Netherlands, and it formed but one link in a subtle chain of events, originating at the capture of Fort Casimer, which has produced the present convulsions of the globe!—Let not this assertion excite a smile of incredulity, for extravagant as it may seem, there is nothing admits of more conclusive proof—Attend then gentle reader to this plain deduction, which if thou are a king, an emperor, or other powerful potentate, I advise thee to treasure up in thy heart—though little expectation have I that my work will fall into such hands, for well I know the care of crafty ministers, to keep all grave and edifying books of the kind out of the way of unhappy monarchs—lest peradventure they should read them and learn wisdom.

By the treacherous surprisal of Fort Casimer, then, did the

crafty Swedes enjoy a transient triumph; but drew upon their heads the vengeance of Peter Stuyvesant, who wrested all New Sweden from their hands—By the conquest of New Sweden Peter Stuyvesant aroused the claims of Lord Baltimore, who appealed to the cabinet of Great Britain, who subdued the whole province of New Netherlands—By this great atchievement the whole extent of North America from Nova Scotia to the Floridas, was rendered one entire dependency upon the British crown—but mark the consequence—The hitherto scattered colonies being thus consolidated, and having no rival colonies to check or keep them in awe, waxed great and powerful, and finally becoming too strong for the mother country, were enabled to shake off its bonds, and by a glorious revolution became an independent empire——But the chain of effects stopped not here; the successful revolution in America produced the sanguinary revolution in France, which produced the puissant Buonaparte who produced the French Despotism, which has thrown the whole world in confusion!—Thus have these great powers been successively punished for their ill-starred conquests—and thus, as I asserted, have all the present convulsions, revolutions and disasters that overwhelm mankind, originated in the capture of little Fort Casimer, as recorded in this eventful history.

Let then the potentates of Europe, beware how they meddle with our beloved country. If the surprisal of a comparatively insignificant fort has overturned the economy of empires, what (reasoning from analogy) would be the effect of conquering a vast republic?—It would set all the stars and planets by the ears—the moon would go to loggerheads with the sun—the whole system of nature would be hurled into chaos—unless it was providentially rescued by the Millenium!

CHAP. X.

Containing the dignified retirement, and mortal surrender
of Peter the Headstrong.

THUS THEN have I concluded this renowned historical enterprize; but before I lay aside my weary pen, there yet remains to be performed one pious duty. If among the incredible host of readers that shall peruse this book, there should haply be found any of those souls of true nobility, which glow with celestial fire, at the history of the generous and the brave, they will doubtless be anxious to know the fate of the gallant Peter Stuyvesant. To gratify one such sterling heart of gold I would go more lengths, than to instruct the cold blooded curiosity of a whole fraternity of philosophers.

No sooner had that high mettled cavalier signed the articles of capitulation than, determined not to witness the humiliation of his favourite city, he turned his back upon its walls and made a growling retreat to his *Bouwery*, or country seat, which was situated about two miles off, where he passed the remainder of his days in patriarchal retirement. There he enjoyed that tranquillity of mind, which he had never known amid the distracting cares of government, and tasted the sweets of absolute and uncontrouled authority, which his factious subjects had so often dashed with the bitterness of opposition.

No persuasions could ever induce him to revisit the city—on the contrary he would always have his great arm chair placed with its back to the windows, which looked in that direction; until a thick grove of trees planted by his own hand grew up and formed a screen, that effectually excluded it from the prospect. He railed continually at the degenerate innovations and improvements introduced by the conquerors—forbade a word of their detested language to be spoken in his family, a prohibition readily obeyed, since none of the household could speak any thing but dutch—and even ordered a fine avenue to be cut down in front of his house, because it consisted of English cherry trees.

The same incessant vigilance, that blazed forth when he had

a vast province under his care, now shewed itself with equal vigour, though in narrower limits. He patrolled with unceasing watchfulness around the boundaries of his little territory; repelled every encroachment with intrepid promptness; punished every vagrant depredation upon his orchard or his farm yard with inflexible severity—and conducted every stray hog or cow in triumph to the pound. But to the indigent neighbour, the friendless stranger, or the weary wanderer, his spacious door was ever open, and his capacious fire place, that emblem of his own warm and generous heart, had always a corner to receive and cherish them. There was an exception to this, I must confess, in case the ill starred applicant was an Englishman or a Yankee, to whom, though he might extend the hand of assistance, he could never be brought to yield the rites of hospitality. Nay, if peradventure some straggling merchant of the east, should stop at his door with his cart load of tin ware or wooden bowls, the fiery Peter would issue forth like a giant from his castle, and make such a furious clattering among his pots and kettles, that the vender of *"notions"* was fain to betake himself to instant flight.

His ancient suit of regimentals, worn threadbare by the brush, were carefully hung up in the state bed chamber, and regularly aired the first fair day of every month—and his cocked hat and trusty sword, were suspended in grim repose, over the parlour mantle-piece, forming supporters to a full length portrait of the renowned admiral Von Tromp. In his domestic empire he maintained strict discipline, and a well organized, despotic government; but though his own will was the supreme law, yet the good of his subjects was his constant object. He watched over, not merely, their immediate comforts, but their morals, and their ultimate welfare; for he gave them abundance of excellent admonition, nor could any of them complain, that when occasion required, he was by any means niggardly in bestowing wholesome correction.

The good old Dutch festivals, those periodical demonstrations of an overflowing heart and a thankful spirit, which are falling into sad disuse among my fellow citizens, were faithfully observed in the mansion of governor Stuyvesant. New year was truly a day of open handed liberality, of jocund revelry, and warm hearted congratulation—when the bosom

seemed to swell with genial good-fellowship—and the plenteous table, was attended with an unceremonious freedom,
and honest broad mouthed merriment, unknown in these
days of degeneracy and refinement. Paas and Pinxter were
scrupulously observed throughout his dominions; nor was
the day of St. Nicholas suffered to pass by, without making
presents, hanging the stocking in the chimney, and complying
with all its other ceremonies.

Once a year, on the first day of April, he used to array
himself in full regimentals, being the anniversary of his triumphal entry into New Amsterdam, after the conquest of New
Sweden. This was always a kind of saturnalia among the domestics, when they considered themselves at liberty in some
measure, to say and do what they pleased; for on this day
their master was always observed to unbend, and become exceeding pleasant and jocose, sending the old greyheaded negroes on April fools errands for pigeons milk; not one of
whom but allowed himself to be taken in, and humoured his
old master's jokes; as became a faithful and well disciplined
dependant. Thus did he reign, happily and peacefully on his
own land—injuring no man—envying no man—molested
by no outward strifes; perplexed by no internal commotions—and the mighty monarchs of the earth, who were
vainly seeking to maintain peace, and promote the welfare of
mankind, by war and desolation, would have done well to
have made a voyage to the little island of Manna-hata, and
learned a lesson in government, from the domestic economy
of Peter Stuyvesant.

In process of time, however, the old governor, like all other
children of mortality, began to exhibit evident tokens of decay. Like an aged oak, which though it long has braved the
fury of the elements, and still retains its gigantic proportions,
yet begins to shake and groan with every blast—so the gallant Peter, though he still bore the port and semblance of
what he was, in the days of his hardihood and chivalry, yet
did age and infirmity begin to sap the vigour of his frame—
but his heart, that most unconquerable citadel, still triumphed
unsubdued. With matchless avidity, would he listen to every
article of intelligence, concerning the battles between the English and Dutch—Still would his pulse beat high, whenever

he heard of the victories of De Ruyter—and his countenance lower, and his eye brows knit, when fortune turned in favour of the English. At length, as on a certain day, he had just smoked his fifth pipe, and was napping after dinner, in his arm chair, conquering the whole British nation in his dreams, he was suddenly aroused by a most fearful ringing of bells, rattling of drums, and roaring of cannon, that put all his blood in a ferment. But when he learnt, that these rejoicings were in honour of a great victory obtained by the combined English and French fleets, over the brave De Ruyter, and the younger Von Tromp, it went so much to his heart, that he took to his bed, and in less than three days, was brought to death's door, by a violent cholera morbus! But even in this extremity, he still displayed the unconquerable spirit of Peter *the Headstrong*; holding out, to the last gasp, with most inflexible obstinacy, against a whole army of old women, who were bent upon driving the enemy out of his bowels, after a true Dutch mode of defence, by inundating the seat of war, with catnip and penny royal.

While he thus lay, lingering on the verge of dissolution; news was brought him, that the brave De Ruyter, had suffered but little loss—had made good his retreat—and meant once more to meet the enemy in battle. The closing eye of the old warrior kindled at the words—he partly raised himself in bed—a flash of martial fire beamed across his visage— he clinched his withered hand, as if he felt within his gripe that sword which waved in triumph before the walls of Fort Christina, and giving a grim smile of exultation, sunk back upon his pillow, and expired.

Thus died Peter Stuyvesant, a valiant soldier—a loyal subject—an upright governor, and an honest Dutchman—who wanted only a few empires to desolate, to have been immortalized as a hero!

His funeral obsequies were celebrated with the utmost grandeur and solemnity. The town was perfectly emptied of its inhabitants, who crowded in throngs to pay the last sad honours to their good old governor. All his sterling qualities rushed in full tide upon their recollections, while the memory of his foibles, and his faults, had expired with him. The ancient burghers contended who should have the privilege of bearing the pall; the populace strove who should walk nearest to the bier—and the melancholy procession was closed by a number of grey headed negroes, who had wintered and summered in the household of their departed master, for the greater part of a century.

With sad and gloomy countenances the multitude gathered round the grave. They dwelt with mournful hearts, on the sturdy virtues, the signal services and the gallant exploits of the brave old veteran. They recalled with secret upbraidings, their own factious oppositions to his government—and many an ancient burgher, whose phlegmatic features had never been known to relax, nor his eyes to moisten—was now observed to puff a pensive pipe, and the big drop to steal down his cheek—while he muttered with affectionate accent and melancholy shake of the head—"Well den—Hard-koppig Piet ben gone at last!"

His remains were deposited in the family vault, under a chapel, which he had piously erected on his estate and dedicated to St. Nicholas—and which stood on the identical spot at present occupied by St. Mark's church, where his tomb stone is still to be seen. His estate, or *Bouwery*, as it was called, has ever continued in the possession of his descendants, who by the uniform integrity of their conduct, and their strict adherence to the customs and manners that prevailed in the *good old times*, have proved themselves worthy of their illustrious ancestor. Many a time and oft, has the farm been haunted at night by enterprizing money-diggers, in quest of pots of gold, said to have been buried by the old governor—though I cannot learn that any of them have ever been enriched by their researches—and who is there, among my native born fellow citizens, that does not remember, when in the mischievous days of his boyhood, he conceived it a great exploit, to rob "Stuyvesant's orchard" on a holliday afternoon.

At this strong hold of the family may still be seen certain memorials of the immortal Peter. His full length portrait frowns in martial terrors from the parlour wall—his cocked hat and sword still hang up in the best bed room—His brimstone coloured breeches were for a long while suspended in the hall, until some years since they occasioned a dispute between a new married couple—and his silver mounted wooden leg is still treasured up in the store room as an invaluable relique.

———————

And now worthy reader, ere I take a sad farewell—which alas! must be forever—willingly would I part in cordial fellowship, and bespeak thy kind hearted remembrance. That I have not written a better history of the days of the patriarchs is not my fault—had any other person written one, as good I should not have attempted it at all.—That many will hereafter spring up and surpass me in excellence, I have very little doubt, and still less care; well knowing, that when the great Christovallo Colon (who is vulgarly called Columbus) had once stood his egg upon its end, every one at table could stand his up a thousand times more dexterously.—Should any reader find matter of offence in this history, I should heartily grieve, though I would on no account question his penetration by telling him he is mistaken—his good nature by telling him he is captious—or his pure conscience by telling him he is startled at a shadow.—Surely if he is so ingenious in finding offence where none is intended, it were a thousand pities he should not be suffered to enjoy the benefit of his discovery.

I have too high an opinion of the understanding of my fellow citizens, to think of yielding them any instruction, and I covet too much their good will, to forfeit it by giving them good advice. I am none of those cynics who despise the world, because it despises them—on the contrary, though but low in its regard I look up to it with the most perfect good nature, and my only sorrow is, that it does not prove itself worthy of the unbounded love I bear it.

If however in this my historic production—the scanty fruit of a long and laborious life—I have failed to gratify the dainty palate of the age, I can only lament my misfortune—for it is too late in the season for me even to hope to repair it. Already has withering age showered his sterile snows upon my brow; in a little while, and this genial warmth which still lingers around my heart, and throbs—worthy reader— throbs kindly towards thyself, shall be chilled forever. Haply this frail compound of dust, which while alive may have given birth to naught but unprofitable weeds, may form a humble sod of the valley, from whence shall spring many a sweet wild flower, to adorn my beloved island of Manna-hata!

FINIS.

THE SKETCH BOOK
OF
GEOFFREY CRAYON, GENT.

Contents

THE SKETCH BOOK
OF
GEOFFREY CRAYON, GENT.

"I have no wife nor children, good or bad, to provide for. A
mere spectator of other men's fortunes and adventures, and how
they play their parts; which methinks are diversely presented
unto me, as from a common theatre or scene."

BURTON

Preface to the Revised Edition

THE FOLLOWING PAPERS, with two exceptions, were written in England, and formed but part of an intended series for which I had made notes and memorandums. Before I could mature a plan, however, circumstances compelled me to send them piecemeal to the United States, where they were published from time to time in portions or numbers. It was not my intention to publish them in England, being conscious that much of their contents could be interesting only to American readers, and in truth, being deterred by the severity with which American productions had been treated by the British press.

By the time the contents of the first volume had appeared in this occasional manner, they began to find their way across the Atlantic, and to be inserted, with many kind encomiums, in the London Literary Gazette. It was said, also, that a London bookseller intended to publish them in a collective form. I determined, therefore, to bring them forward myself, that they might at least have the benefit of my superintendence and revision. I accordingly took the printed numbers which I had received from the United States, to Mr. John Murray, the eminent publisher, from whom I had already received friendly attentions, and left them with him for examination, informing him that should he be inclined to bring them before the public, I had materials enough on hand for a second volume. Several days having elapsed without any communication from Mr. Murray, I addressed a note to him, in which I construed his silence into a tacit rejection of my work, and begged that the numbers I had left with him might be returned to me. The following was his reply.

MY DEAR SIR,

I entreat you to believe that I feel truly obliged by your kind intentions towards me, and that I entertain the most unfeigned respect for your most tasteful talents. My house is completely filled with workpeople at this time, and I have only an office to transact business in; and yesterday I was wholly occupied, or I should have done myself the pleasure of seeing you.

If it would not suit me to engage in the publication of your present work, it is only because I do not see that scope in the nature of it which would enable me to make those satisfactory accounts between us, without which I really feel no satisfaction in engaging—but I will do all I can to promote their circulation, and shall be most ready to attend to any future plan of yours.

With much regard, I remain, dear sir,
Your faithful servant,
John Murray.

This was disheartening, and might have deterred me from any further prosecution of the matter, had the question of republication in Great Britain rested entirely with me; but I apprehended the appearance of a spurious edition. I now thought of Mr. Archibald Constable as publisher, having been treated by him with much hospitality during a visit to Edinburgh; but first I determined to submit my work to Sir Walter (then Mr.) Scott, being encouraged to do so by the cordial reception I had experienced from him at Abbotsford a few years previously, and by the favourable opinion he had expressed to others of my earlier writings. I accordingly sent him the printed numbers of the Sketch Book in a parcel by coach, and at the same time wrote to him, hinting that since I had had the pleasure of partaking of his hospitality, a reverse had taken place in my affairs which made the successful exercise of my pen all important to me; I begged him, therefore, to look over the literary articles I had forwarded to him, and, if he thought they would bear European republication, to ascertain whether Mr. Constable would be inclined to be the publisher.

The parcel containing my work went by coach to Scott's address in Edinburgh; the letter went by mail to his residence in the country. By the very first post I received a reply, before he had seen my work.

"I was down at Kelso," said he, "when your letter reached Abbotsford. I am now on my way to town, and will

converse with Constable, and do all in my power to forward your views—I assure you nothing will give me more
pleasure."

The hint, however, about a reverse of fortune had struck
the quick apprehension of Scott, and, with that practical and
efficient good will which belonged to his nature, he had already devised a way of aiding me. A weekly periodical, he
went on to inform me, was about to be set up in Edinburgh,
supported by the most respectable talents, and amply furnished with all the necessary information. The appointment
of the editor, for which ample funds were provided, would
be five hundred pounds sterling a year, with the reasonable
prospect of further advantages. This situation, being apparently at his disposal, he frankly offered to me. The work,
however, he intimated, was to have somewhat of a political
bearing, and he expressed an apprehension that the tone it
was desired to adopt might not suit me. "Yet I risk the question," added he, "because I know no man so well qualified for
this important task, and perhaps because it will necessarily
bring you to Edinburgh. If my proposal does not suit, you
need only keep the matter secret and there is no harm done.
'And for my love I pray you wrong me not.' If on the
contrary you think it could be made to suit you, let me know
as soon as possible, addressing Castle street, Edinburgh."

In a postscript, written from Edinburgh, he adds, "I am
just come here, and have glanced over the Sketch Book. It is
positively beautiful, and increases my desire to *crimp* you, if
it be possible. Some difficulties there always are in managing
such a matter, especially at the outset; but we will obviate
them as much as we possibly can."

The following is from an imperfect draught of my reply,
which underwent some modifications in the copy sent.

"I cannot express how much I am gratified by your letter.
I had begun to feel as if I had taken an unwarrantable liberty;
but, somehow or other, there is a genial sunshine about you
that warms every creeping thing into heart and confidence.
Your literary proposal both surprises and flatters me, as it
evinces a much higher opinion of my talents than I have myself."

I then went on to explain that I found myself peculiarly unfitted for the situation offered to me, not merely by my political opinions, but by the very constitution and habits of my mind. "My whole course of life," I observed, "has been desultory, and I am unfitted for any periodically recurring task, or any stipulated labor of body or mind. I have no command of my talents, such as they are, and have to watch the varyings of my mind as I would those of a weather cock. Practice and training may bring me more into rule; but at present I am as useless for regular service as one of my own country Indians, or a Don Cossack.

"I must, therefore, keep on pretty much as I have begun; writing when I can, not when I would. I shall occasionally shift my residence and write whatever is suggested by objects before me, or whatever rises in my imagination; and hope to write better and more copiously by and by.

"I am playing the egotist, but I know no better way of answering your proposal than by showing what a very good for nothing kind of being I am. Should Mr. Constable feel inclined to make a bargain for the wares I have on hand, he will encourage me to further enterprise; and it will be something like trading with a gipsy for the fruits of his prowlings, who may at one time have nothing but a wooden bowl to offer, and at another time a silver tankard."

In reply, Scott expressed regret, but not surprise, at my declining what might have proved a troublesome duty. He then recurred to the original subject of our correspondence; entered into a detail of the various terms upon which arrangements were made between authors and booksellers, that I might take my choice; expressing the most encouraging confidence of the success of my work, and of previous works which I had produced in America. "I did no more," added he, "than open the trenches with Constable; but I am sure if you will take the trouble to write to him, you will find him disposed to treat your overtures with every degree of attention. Or, if you think it of consequence in the first place to see me, I shall be in London in the course of a month, and whatever my experience can command is most heartily at your command. But I can add little to what I have said above, except my earnest recommendation to Constable to enter into the negotiation."*

Before the receipt of this most obliging letter, however, I had determined to look to no leading bookseller for a launch, but to throw my work before the public at my own risk, and let it sink or swim according to its merits. I wrote to that effect to Scott, and soon received a reply:

"I observe with pleasure that you are going to come forth in Britain. It is certainly not the very best way to publish on one's own accompt; for the booksellers set their face against the circulation of such works as do not pay an amazing toll to themselves. But they have lost the art of altogether damming up the road in such cases between the author and the public, which they were once able to do as effectually as Diabolus in John Bunyan's Holy War closed up the windows of my Lord Understanding's mansion. I am sure of one thing, that you have only to be known to the British public to be admired by them, and I would not say so unless I really was of that opinion.

"If you ever see a witty but rather local publication called Blackwood's Edinburgh Magazine, you will find some notice of your works in the last number: the author is a friend of mine, to whom I have introduced you in your literary capacity. His name is Lockhart, a young man of very considerable talent, and who will soon be intimately connected with my family. My faithful friend Knickerbocker is to be next exam-

---

*I cannot avoid subjoining in a note a succeeding paragraph of Scott's letter, which, though it does not relate to the main subject of our correspondence, was too characteristic to be omitted. Some time previously I had sent Miss Sophia Scott small duodecimo American editions of her father's poems published in Edinburgh in quarto volumes; showing the "nigromancy" of the American press, by which a quart of wine is conjured into a pint bottle. Scott observes: "In my hurry, I have not thanked you in Sophia's name for the kind attention which furnished her with the American volumes. I am not quite sure I can add my own, since you have made her acquainted with much more of papa's folly than she would ever otherwise have learned; for I had taken special care they should never see any of those things during their earlier years. I think I told you that Walter is sweeping the firmament with a feather like a maypole and indenting the pavement with a sword like a scythe—in other words, he has become a whiskered hussar in the 18th dragoons."

ined and illustrated. Constable was extremely willing to enter into consideration of a treaty for your works, but I foresee will be still more so when

> Your name is up, and may go
> From Toledo to Madrid.

——And that will soon be the case. I trust to be in London about the middle of the month, and promise myself great pleasure in once again shaking you by the hand."

The first volume of the Sketch Book was put to press in London as I had resolved, at my own risk, by a bookseller unknown to fame, and without any of the usual arts by which a work is trumpeted into notice. Still some attention had been called to it by the extracts which had previously appeared in the Literary Gazette, and by the kind word spoken by the editor of that periodical, and it was getting into fair circulation, when my worthy bookseller failed before the first month was over, and the sale was interrupted.

At this juncture Scott arrived in London. I called to him for help, as I was sticking in the mire, and, more propitious than Hercules, he put his own shoulder to the wheel. Through his favourable representations, Murray was quickly induced to undertake the future publication of the work which he had previously declined. A further edition of the first volume was struck off and the second volume was put to press, and from that time Murray became my publisher, conducting himself in all his dealings with that fair, open, and liberal spirit which had obtained for him the well merited appellation of the Prince of Booksellers.

Thus, under the kind and cordial auspices of Sir Walter Scott, I began my literary career in Europe; and I feel that I am but discharging, in a trifling degree, my debt of gratitude to the memory of that golden hearted man in acknowledging my obligations to him.—But who of his literary contemporaries ever applied to him for aid or counsel that did not experience the most prompt, generous, and effectual assistance!

W.I.

Sunnyside, 1848.

The Author's Account of Himself

I am of this mind with Homer, that as the snaile that crept out of her shel was turned eftsoones into a Toad, and thereby was forced to make a stoole to sit on; so the traveller that stragleth from his owne country is in a short time transformed into so monstrous a shape that he is faine to alter his mansion with his manners and to live where he can, not where he would.

Lyly's Euphues

I WAS ALWAYS fond of visiting new scenes and observing strange characters and manners. Even when a mere child I began my travels and made many tours of discovery into foreign parts and unknown regions of my native city; to the frequent alarm of my parents and the emolument of the town cryer. As I grew into boyhood I extended the range of my observations. My holyday afternoons were spent in rambles about the surrounding country. I made myself familiar with all its places famous in history or fable. I knew every spot where a murder or robbery had been committed or a ghost seen. I visited the neighbouring villages and added greatly to my stock of knowledge, by noting their habits and customs, and conversing with their sages and great men. I even journeyed one long summer's day to the summit of the most distant hill, from whence I stretched my eye over many a mile of terra incognita, and was astonished to find how vast a globe I inhabited.

This rambling propensity strengthened with my years. Books of voyages and travels became my passion, and in devouring their contents I neglected the regular exercises of the school. How wistfully would I wander about the pier heads in fine weather, and watch the parting ships, bound to distant climes. With what longing eyes would I gaze after their lessening sails, and waft myself in imagination to the ends of the earth.

Further reading and thinking, though they brought this vague inclination into more reasonable bounds, only served to make it more decided. I visited various parts of my own country, and had I been merely a lover of fine scenery, I should have felt little desire to seek elsewhere its gratification, for on no country have the charms of nature been more prodigally lavished. Her mighty lakes, like oceans of liquid silver; her mountains with their bright aerial tints; her valleys teeming with wild fertility; her tremendous cataracts thundering in their solitudes; her boundless plains waving with spontaneous verdure; her broad deep rivers, rolling in solemn silence to the ocean; her trackless forests, where vegetation puts forth all its magnificence; her skies kindling with the magic of summer clouds and glorious sunshine—no, never need an American look beyond his own country for the sublime and beautiful of natural scenery.

But Europe held forth the charms of storied and poetical association. There were to be seen the masterpieces of art, the refinements of highly cultivated society, the quaint peculiarities of ancient and local custom. My native country was full of youthful promise; Europe was rich in the accumulated treasures of age. Her very ruins told the history of times gone by, and every mouldering stone was a chronicle. I longed to wander over the scenes of renowned achievement—to tread as it were in the footsteps of antiquity—to loiter about the ruined castle—to meditate on the falling tower—to escape in short, from the commonplace realities of the present, and lose myself among the shadowy grandeurs of the past.

I had, beside all this, an earnest desire to see the great men of the earth. We have, it is true, our great men in America— not a city but has an ample share of them. I have mingled among them in my time, and been almost withered by the shade into which they cast me; for there is nothing so baleful to a small man as the shade of a great one, particularly the great man of a city. But I was anxious to see the great men of Europe; for I had read in the works of various philosophers, that all animals degenerated in America, and man among the number. A great man of Europe, thought I, must therefore be as superior to a great man of America, as a peak of the Alps to a highland of the Hudson; and in this idea I was confirmed by observing the comparative importance and swelling magnitude of many English travellers among us; who, I was assured, were very little people in their own country.—I will visit this land of wonders, thought I, and see the gigantic race from which I am degenerated.

It has been either my good or evil lot to have my roving passion gratified. I have wandered through different countries and witnessed many of the shifting scenes of life. I cannot say that I have studied them with the eye of a philosopher, but rather with the sauntering gaze with which humble lovers of the picturesque stroll from the window of one print shop to another; caught sometimes by the delineations of beauty, sometimes by the distortions of caricature and sometimes by the loveliness of landscape. As it is the fashion for modern tourists to travel pencil in hand, and bring home their portfolios filled with sketches, I am disposed to get up a few for the entertainment of my friends. When I look over, however, the hints and memorandums I have taken down for the purpose, my heart almost fails me at finding how my idle humour has led me aside from the great objects studied by every regular traveller who would make a book. I fear I shall give equal disappointment with an unlucky landscape painter, who had travelled on the continent, but following the bent of his vagrant inclination, had sketched in nooks and corners and bye places. His sketch book was accordingly crowded with cottages, and landscapes, and obscure ruins; but he had neglected to paint St. Peter's or the Coliseum; the cascade of Terni or the Bay of Naples; and had not a single Glacier or Volcano in his whole collection.

The Voyage

Ships, ships, I will descrie you
    Amidst the main,
I will come and try you
What you are protecting
And projecting,
    What's your end and aim.
One goes abroad for merchandize and trading,
Another stays to keep his country from invading,
A third is coming home with rich and wealthy lading.
    Hallo my fancie, whither wilt thou go?

Old Poem

To an American visiting Europe the long voyage he has to make is an excellent preparative. The temporary absence of worldly scenes and employments produces a state of mind peculiarly fitted to receive new and vivid impressions. The vast space of waters, that separates the hemispheres is like a blank page in existence. There is no gradual transition by which as in Europe the features and population of one country blend almost imperceptibly with those of another. From the moment you lose sight of the land you have left, all is vacancy until you step on the opposite shore, and are launched at once into the bustle and novelties of another world.

In travelling by land there is a continuity of scene and a connected succession of persons and incidents, that carry on the story of life, and lessen the effect of absence and separation. We drag, it is true, "a lengthening chain" at each remove of our pilgrimage; but the chain is unbroken—we can trace it back link by link; and we feel that the last still grapples us to home. But a wide sea voyage severs us at once.—It makes us conscious of being cast loose from the secure anchorage of settled life and sent adrift upon a doubtful world. It interposes a gulph, not merely imaginary, but real, between us and our homes—a gulph subject to tempest and fear and uncertainty, rendering distance palpable and return precarious.

Such at least was the case with myself. As I saw the last

blue line of my native land fade away like a cloud in the horizon, it seemed as if I had closed one volume of the world and its concerns, and had time for meditation before I opened another. That land too, now vanishing from my view; which contained all that was most dear to me in life; what vicissitudes might occur in it—what changes might take place in me, before I should visit it again.—Who can tell when he sets forth to wander, whither he may be driven by the uncertain currents of existence; or when he may return; or whether it may ever be his lot to revisit the scenes of his childhood?

I said that at sea all is vacancy—I should correct the expression. To one given to day dreaming and fond of losing himself in reveries, a sea voyage is full of subjects for meditation: but then they are the wonders of the deep and of the air, and rather tend to abstract the mind from worldly themes. I delighted to loll over the quarter railing or climb to the main top of a calm day, and muse for hours together, on the tranquil bosom of a summer's sea. To gaze upon the piles of golden clouds just peering above the horizon; fancy them some fairy realms and people them with a creation of my own. To watch the gently undulating billows, rolling their silver volumes as if to die away on those happy shores.

There was a delicious sensation of mingled security and awe with which I looked down from my giddy height on the monsters of the deep at their uncouth gambols. Shoals of porpoises tumbling about the bow of the ship; the grampus slowly heaving his huge form above the surface, or the ravenous shark darting like a spectre through the blue waters. My imagination would conjure up all that I had heard or read of the watery world beneath me. Of the finny herds that roam its fathomless valleys; of the shapeless monsters that lurk among the very foundations of the earth and of those wild phantasms that swell the tales of fishermen and sailors.

Sometimes a distant sail, gliding along the edge of the ocean would be another theme of idle speculation. How interesting this fragment of a world, hastening to rejoin the great mass of existence. What a glorious monument of human invention; which has in a manner triumphed over wind and wave; has brought the ends of the earth into communion; has established an interchange of blessings,—pouring into the sterile regions of the north all the luxuries of the south; has diffused the light of knowledge and the charities of cultivated life, and has thus bound together those scattered portions of the human race, between which nature seemed to have thrown an insurmountable barrier.

We one day described some shapeless object drifting at a distance. At sea every thing that breaks the monotony of the surrounding expanse attracts attention. It proved to be the mast of a ship that must have been completely wrecked; for there were the remains of handkerchiefs, by which some of the crew had fastened themselves to this spar to prevent their being washed off by the waves. There was no trace by which the name of the ship could be ascertained. The wreck had evidently drifted about for many months: clusters of shell fish had fastened about it; and long sea weeds flaunted at its sides.

But where, thought I, is the crew!—Their struggle has long been over—they have gone down amidst the roar of the tempest—their bones lie whitening among the caverns of the deep. Silence—oblivion, like the waves, have closed over them, and no one can tell the story of their end. What sighs have been wafted after that ship; what prayers offered up at the deserted fireside of home. How often has the mistress, the wife, the mother pored over the daily news to catch some casual intelligence of this rover of the deep. How has expectation darkened into anxiety—anxiety into dread and dread into despair. Alas! not one memento may ever return for love to cherish. All that may ever be known is, that she sailed from her port, "and was never heard of more!"

The sight of this wreck, as usual, gave rise to many dismal anecdotes. This was particularly the case in the evening when the weather, which had hitherto been fair began to look wild and threatening, and gave indications of one of those sudden storms which will sometimes break in upon the serenity of a summer voyage. As we sat round the dull light of a lamp in the cabin, that made the gloom more ghastly, every one had his tale of shipwreck and disaster. I was peculiarly struck with a short one related by the captain.

"As I was once sailing," said he, "in a fine stout ship across the banks of Newfoundland, one of those heavy fogs which prevail in those parts rendered it impossible for us to see far ahead even in the day time; but at night the weather was so thick that we could not distinguish any object at twice the length of the ship. I kept lights at the mast head and a constant watch forward to look out for fishing smacks, which are accustomed to lie at anchor on the banks. The wind was blowing a smacking breeze and we were going at a great rate through the water. Suddenly the watch gave the alarm of 'a sail ahead!'—it was scarcely uttered before we were upon her. She was a small schooner at anchor, with the broad side toward us. The crew were all asleep and had neglected to hoist a light. We struck her just a mid-ships. The force, the size and weight of our vessel bore her down below the waves—we passed over her and were hurried on our course. As the crashing wreck was sinking beneath us I had a glimpse of two or three halfnaked wretches, rushing from her cabin—they just started from their beds to be swallowed shrieking by the waves. I heard their drowning cry mingling with the wind. The blast that bore it to our ears swept us out of all further hearing—I shall never forget that cry!—It was some time before we could put the ship about; she was under such headway. We returned as nearly as we could guess to the place where the smack had anchored. We cruised about for several hours in the dense fog. We fired signal guns and listened if we might hear the halloo of any survivors; but all was silent—we never saw or heard any thing of them more!—"

I confess these stories for a time put an end to all my fine fancies. The storm encreased with the night. The sea was lashed up into tremendous confusion. There was a fearful sullen sound of rushing waves and broken surges. Deep called unto deep. At times the black volume of clouds over head seemed rent asunder by flashes of lightning which quivered along the foaming billows, and made the succeeding darkness doubly terrible. The thunders bellowed over the wild waste of waters and were echoed and prolonged by the mountain waves. As I saw the ship staggering and plunging among these roaring caverns, it seemed miraculous that she regained her balance or preserved her buoyancy. Her yards would dip into the water; her bow was almost buried beneath the waves. Sometimes an impending surge appeared ready to overwhelm

her, and nothing but a dextrous movement of the helm preserved her from the shock.

When I retired to my cabin the awful scene still followed
me. The whistling of the wind through the rigging sounded
like funereal wailings. The creaking of the masts; the straining
and groaning of bulk heads as the ship laboured in the wel-
tering sea were frightful. As I heard the waves rushing along
the side of the ship and roaring in my very ear, it seemed as
if death were raging round this floating prison, seeking for
his prey—the mere starting of a nail—the yawning of a seam
might give him entrance.

A fine day, however, with a tranquil sea and favouring
breeze soon put all these dismal reflections to flight. It is impossible to resist the gladdening influence of fine weather and
fair wind at sea. When the ship is decked out in all her canvass, every sail swelled, and careering gaily over the curling
waves, how lofty, how gallant she appears—how she seems
to lord it over the deep!

I might fill a volume with the reveries of a sea voyage, for
with me it is almost a continual reverie—but it is time to get
to shore.

It was a fine sunny morning when the thrilling cry of Land!
was given from the mast head. None but those who have
experienced it can form an idea of the delicious throng of
sensations which rush into an American's bosom, when he
first comes in sight of Europe. There is a volume of associations with the very name. It is the land of promise, teeming
with every thing of which his childhood has heard, or on
which his studious years have pondered.

From that time until the moment of arrival it was all feverish excitement. The ships of war that prowled like guardian
giants along the coast—the headlands of Ireland stretching
out into the channel—the Welsh mountains towering into
the clouds, all were objects of intense interest. As we sailed
up the Mersey I reconnoitered the shores with a telescope.
My eye dwelt with delight on neat cottages with their trim
shrubberies and green grass plots. I saw the mouldering ruin
of an abbey over run with ivy, and the taper spire of a village
church rising from the brow of a neighbouring hill—all were
characteristic of England.

The tide and wind were so favourable that the ship was enabled to come at once to the pier. It was thronged with people; some idle lookers-on, others eager expectants of friends or relatives. I could distinguish the merchant to whom the ship was consigned. I knew him by his calculating brow and restless air. His hands were thrust into his pockets; he was whistling thoughtfully and walking to and fro, a small space having been accorded him by the crowd in deference to his temporary importance. There were repeated cheerings and salutations interchanged between the shore and the ship, as friends happened to recognize each other. I particularly noticed one young woman of humble dress, but interesting demeanour. She was leaning forward from among the crowd; her eye hurried over the ship as it neared the shore, to catch some wished for countenance. She seemed disappointed and agitated; when I heard a faint voice call her name. It was from a poor sailor who had been ill all the voyage and had excited the sympathy of every one on board. When the weather was fine his messmates had spread a mattress for him on deck in the shade, but of late his illness had so encreased, that he had taken to his hammock, and only breathed a wish that he might see his wife before he died. He had been helped on deck as we came up the river, and was now leaning against the shrouds, with a countenance so wasted, so pale, so ghastly that it was no wonder even the eye of affection did not recognize him. But at the sound of his voice her eye darted on his features—it read at once a whole volume of sorrow—she clasped her hands; uttered a faint shriek and stood wringing them in silent agony.

All now was hurry and bustle. The meetings of acquaintances—the greetings of friends—the consultations of men of business. I alone was solitary and idle. I had no friend to meet, no cheering to receive. I stepped upon the land of my forefathers—but felt that I was a stranger in the land.

Roscoe

—In the service of mankind to be
A guardian god below; still to employ
The mind's brave ardour in heroic aims,
Such as may raise us o'er the groveling herd,
And make us shine forever—that is life.

Thomson

ONE OF THE FIRST places to which a stranger is taken in Liverpool is the Athenæum. It is established on a liberal and judicious plan; contains a good library and spacious reading room and is the great literary resort of the place. Go there at what hour you may, you are sure to find it filled with grave looking personages, deeply absorbed in the study of newspapers.

As I was once visiting this haunt of the learned my attention was attracted to a person just entering the room. He was advanced in life, tall, and of a form that might once have been commanding, but it was a little bowed by time—perhaps by care. He had a noble Roman style of countenance; a head that would have pleased a painter; and though some slight furrows on his brow shewed that wasting thought had been busy there, yet his eye still beamed with the fire of a poetic soul. There was something in his whole appearance that indicated a being of a different order from the bustling race around him.

I inquired his name and was informed that it was Roscoe. I drew back with an involuntary feeling of veneration. This then was an Author of celebrity; this was one of those men, whose voices have gone forth to the ends of the earth; with whose minds I have communed even in the solitudes of America. Accustomed as we are in our country to know European writers only by their works, we cannot conceive of them, as of other men, engrossed by trivial or sordid pursuits, and jostling with the crowd of common minds in the dusty paths of life. They pass before our imaginations like superior beings, radiant with the emanations of their genius, and surrounded by a halo of literary glory.

To find, therefore, the elegant historian of the Medici, mingling among the busy sons of traffic at first shocked my poetical ideas; but it is from the very circumstances and situation in which he has been placed, that Mr. Roscoe derives his highest claims to admiration. It is interesting to notice how some minds seem almost to create themselves; springing up under every disadvantage, and working their solitary but irresistible way through a thousand obstacles. Nature seems to delight in disappointing the assiduities of art, with which it would rear legitimate dullness to maturity, and to glory in the vigour and luxuriance of her chance productions. She scatters the seeds of genius to the winds, and though some may perish among the stony places of the world, and some be choked by the thorns and brambles of early adversity, yet others will now and then strike root even in the clefts of the rock, struggle bravely up into sunshine, and spread over their sterile birth place all the beauties of vegetation.

Such has been the case with Mr. Roscoe. Born in a place apparently ungenial to the growth of literary talent; in the very market place of trade; without fortune, family connexions or patronage; self prompted, self sustained and almost self taught, he has conquered every obstacle, achieved his way to eminence, and having become one of the ornaments of the nation, has turned the whole force of his talents and influence to advance and embellish his native town.

Indeed it is this last trait in his character which has given him the greatest interest in my eyes, and induced me particularly to point him out to my countrymen. Eminent as are his literary merits, he is but one among the many distinguished authors of this intellectual nation. They, however, in general live but for their own fame, or their own pleasures. Their private history presents no lesson to the world, or perhaps a humiliating one of human frailty and inconsistency. At best, they are prone to steal away from the bustle and commonplace of busy existence; to indulge in the selfishness of lettered ease, and to revel in scenes of mental but exclusive enjoyment.

Mr. Roscoe on the contrary has claimed none of the accorded privileges of talent. He has shut himself up in no garden of thought nor elysium of fancy; but has gone forth into

the highways and thoroughfares of life; he has planted bowers by the wayside for the refreshment of the pilgrim and the
sojourner, and has opened pure fountains where the labouring man may turn aside from the dust and heat of the day,
and drink of the living streams of knowledge. There is a
"daily beauty in his life," on which mankind may meditate
and grow better. It exhibits no lofty and almost useless, because inimitable example of excellence; but presents a picture
of active yet simple and imitable virtues, which are within
every man's reach, but which, unfortunately, are not exercised
by many, or this world would be a paradise.

But his private life is peculiarly worthy the attention of the
citizens of our young and busy country, where literature and
the elegant arts must grow up side by side with the coarser
plants of daily necessity; and must depend for their culture,
not on the exclusive devotion of time and wealth, nor the
quickening rays of titled patronage, but on hours and seasons
snatched from the pursuit of worldly interests, by intelligent
and public spirited individuals.

He has shown how much may be done for a place in hours
of leisure, by one master spirit, and how completely it can
give its own impress to surrounding objects. Like his own
Lorenzo De Medici, on whom he seems to have fixed his eye
as on a pure model of antiquity, he has interwoven the history
of his life with the history of his native town, and has made
the foundations of its fame the monuments of his virtues.
Wherever you go in Liverpool you perceive traces of his footsteps in all that is elegant and liberal. He found the tide of
wealth flowing merely in the channels of traffic, he has diverted from it invigorating rills to refresh the gardens of literature. By his own example and constant exertions he has
effected that union of commerce and the intellectual pursuits
so eloquently recommended in one of his latest writings;*
and has practically proved how beautifully they may be
brought to harmonize and to benefit each other. The noble
institutions for literary and scientific purposes, which reflect
such credit on Liverpool, and are giving such an impulse to
the public mind, have mostly been originated, and have all

*Address on the opening of the Liverpool Institution.

been effectively promoted by Mr. Roscoe; and when we consider the rapidly encreasing opulence and magnitude of that town, which promises to vie in commercial importance with the metropolis; it will be perceived that in awakening an ambition of mental improvement among its inhabitants, he has effected a great benefit to the cause of British literature.

In America we know Mr. Roscoe only as the Author—in Liverpool he is spoken of as the Banker, and I was told of his having been unfortunate in business. I could not pity him as I heard some rich men do. I considered him far above the reach of my pity. Those who live only for the world and in the world, may be cast down by the frowns of adversity; but a man like Roscoe is not to be overcome by the reverses of fortune. They do but drive him in upon the resources of his own mind, to the superior society of his own thoughts, which the best of men are apt sometimes to neglect, and to roam abroad in search of less worthy associates. He is independent of the world around him. He lives with antiquity and with posterity. With antiquity, in the sweet communions of studious retirement, and with posterity in the generous aspirings after future renown. The solitude of such a mind is its state of highest enjoyment. It is then visited by those elevated meditations which are the proper aliment of noble souls, and are like manna, sent from heaven in the wilderness of this world.

While my feelings were yet alive on the subject it was my fortune to light on further traces of Mr. Roscoe. I was riding out with a gentleman to view the environs of Liverpool when he turned off through a gate into some ornamented grounds. After riding a short distance we came to a spacious mansion of freestone, built in the Grecian style. It was not in the purest taste, yet it had an air of elegance and the situation was delightful. A fine lawn sloped away from it, studded with clumps of trees, so disposed as to break a soft fertile country into a variety of Landscapes. The Mersey was seen winding a broad quiet sheet of water through an expanse of green meadow land, while the Welsh mountains, blending with clouds and melting into distance, bordered the horizon.

This was Roscoe's favourite residence during the days of his prosperity. It had been the seat of elegant hospitality and literary retirement—The house was now silent and deserted.

I saw the windows of the study, which looked out upon the soft scenery I have mentioned. The windows were closed—the library was gone. Two or three ill favoured beings were loitering about the place, whom my fancy pictured into retainers of the law. It was like visiting some classic fountain that had once welled its pure waters in a sacred shade, but finding it dry and dusty, with the lizard and the toad brooding over the shattered marbles.

I enquired after the fate of Mr. Roscoe's library which had consisted of scarce and foreign books, from many of which he had drawn the materials for his Italian histories. It had passed under the hammer of the auctioneer and was dispersed about the country. The good people of the vicinity thronged like wreckers to get some part of the noble vessel that had been driven on shore. Did such a scene admit of ludicrous associations, we might imagine something whimsical in this strange irruption into the regions of learning. Pigmies rummaging the armoury of a giant, and contending for the possession of weapons which they could not wield. We might picture to ourselves some knot of speculators debating with calculating brow over the quaint binding and illuminated margin of an obsolete author; or the air of intense but baffled sagacity with which some successful purchaser attempted to dive into the black letter bargain he had secured.

It is a beautiful incident in the story of Mr. Roscoe's misfortunes, and one which cannot fail to interest the studious mind, that the parting with his books seems to have touched upon his tenderest feelings; and to have been the only circumstance that could provoke the notice of his muse. The scholar only knows how dear these silent, yet eloquent companions of pure thoughts and innocent hours become in the season of adversity. When all that is worldly turns to dross around us, these only retain their steady value. When friends grow cold and the converse of intimates languishes into vapid civility and commonplace, these only continue the unaltered countenance of happier days, and cheer us with that true friendship which never deceived hope nor deserted sorrow.

I do not wish to censure, but surely if the people of Liverpool had been properly sensible of what was due to Mr. Roscoe and themselves, his library would never have been sold.

Good worldly reasons may doubtless be given for the circumstance, which it would be difficult to combat with others that might seem merely fanciful; but it certainly appears to me such an opportunity as seldom occurs, of cheering a noble mind, struggling under misfortunes, by one of the most delicate but most expressive tokens of public sympathy. It is difficult, however, to estimate a man of genius properly, who is daily before our eyes. He becomes mingled up and confounded with other men. His great qualities lose their novelty and we become too familiar with the common materials which form the basis even of the loftiest character. Some of Mr. Roscoe's townsmen may regard him merely as a man of business; others as a politician; all find him engaged like themselves in ordinary occupations and surpassed, perhaps, by themselves on some points of worldly wisdom. Even that amiable and unostentatious simplicity of character, which gives the nameless grace to real excellence, may cause him to be undervalued by some coarse minds, who do not know that true worth is always void of glare and pretension. But the man of letters who speaks of Liverpool, speaks of it as the residence of Roscoe. The intelligent traveller who visits it, enquires where Roscoe is to be seen. He is the literary land mark of the place, indicating its existence to the distant Scholar. He is like Pompey's column at Alexandria, towering alone in classic dignity.

The following sonnet, addressed by Mr. Roscoe to his books on parting with them, is alluded to in the preceding article. If any thing can add effect to the pure feeling and elevated thought here displayed, it is the conviction, that the whole is no effusion of fancy, but a faithful transcript from the writer's heart.

To My Books

As one, who, destined from his friends to part,
Regrets his loss, but hopes again erewhile
To share their converse and enjoy their smile,
And tempers as he may, affliction's dart;

Thus, loved associates, chiefs of elder art,
Teachers of wisdom, who could once beguile
My tedious hours and lighten every toil—
I now resign you; nor with fainting heart;

For pass a few short years, or days, or hours,
And happier seasons may their dawn unfold,
And all your sacred fellowship restore;
When, freed from earth, unlimited its powers,
Mind shall with mind direct communion hold,
And kindred spirits meet to part no more.

The Wife

The treasures of the deep are not so precious
As are the conceal'd comforts of a man
Lock'd up in woman's love. I scent the air
Of blessings, when I come but near the house.
What a delicious breath marriage sends forth,
The violet bed's not sweeter!

Middleton

I HAVE OFTEN had occasion to remark the fortitude with which women sustain the most overwhelming reverses of fortune. Those disasters which break down the spirits of a man, and prostrate him in the dust, seem to call forth all the energies of the softer sex, and give such intrepidity and elevation to their character, that at times it approaches to sublimity. Nothing can be more touching than to behold a soft and tender female, who had been all weakness and dependence, and alive to every trivial roughness while treading the prosperous paths of life, suddenly rising in mental force, to be the comforter and supporter of her husband under misfortune, and abiding, with unshrinking firmness, the bitterest blasts of adversity.

As the vine which has long twined its graceful foliage about the oak, and been lifted by it into sunshine, will, when the hardy plant is rifted by the thunderbolt, cling round it with its carressing tendrils and bind up its shattered boughs; so is it beautifully ordered by providence, that woman, who is the mere dependent and ornament of man in his happier hours, should be his stay and solace when smitten with sudden calamity, winding herself into the rugged recesses of his nature; tenderly supporting the drooping head, and binding up the broken heart.

I was once congratulating a friend, who had around him a blooming family knit together in the strongest affection. "I can wish you no better lot," said he, with enthusiasm, "than to have a wife and children. If you are prosperous, there they are to share your prosperity; and if otherwise, there they are to comfort you.—" And indeed I have observed that a married man falling into misfortune, is more apt to retrieve his situation in the world than a single one; partly because he is more stimulated to exertion by the necessities of the helpless and beloved beings who depend upon him for subsistence; but chiefly because his spirits are soothed and relieved by domestic endearments, and his self respect kept alive by finding, that though all abroad is darkness and humiliation, yet there is still a little world of love at home, of which he is the monarch. Whereas a single man is apt to run to waste and self neglect; to fancy himself lonely and abandoned, and his heart to fall to ruin like some deserted mansion for want of an inhabitant.

These observations call to mind a little domestic story, of which I was once a witness. My intimate friend Leslie had married a beautiful and accomplished girl, who had been brought up in the midst of fashionable life. She had, it is true, no fortune, but that of my friend was ample and he delighted in the anticipation of indulging her in every elegant pursuit; and administering to those delicate tastes and fancies, that spread a kind of witchery about the sex—"her life," said he, "shall be like a fairy tale."

The very difference in their characters produced an harmonious combination. He was of a romantic and somewhat serious cast; she was all life and gladness. I have often noticed the mute rapture with which he would gaze upon her in company, of which her sprightly powers made her the delight; and how in the midst of applause, her eye would still turn to him, as if there alone she sought favour and acceptance. When leaning on his arm her slender form contrasted finely with his tall, manly person. The fond confiding air with which she looked up to him, seemed to call forth a flush of triumphant pride and cherishing tenderness; as if he doted on his lovely burthen, for its very helplessness.—Never did a couple set forward on the flowery path of early and well suited marriage, with a fairer prospect of felicity.

It was the misfortune of my friend, however, to have embarked his property in large speculations, and he had not been married many months, when, by a succession of sudden disasters, it was swept from him, and he found himself reduced almost to penury. For a time he kept his situation to himself and went about with a haggard countenance and a breaking heart. His life was but a protracted agony, and what rendered it more insupportable was the necessity of keeping up a smile in the presence of his wife; for he could not bring himself to overwhelm her with the news. She saw, however, with the quick eyes of affection, that all was not well with him. She marked his altered looks and stifled sighs, and was not to be deceived by his sickly and vapid attempts at cheerfulness. She tasked all her sprightly powers and tender blandishments to win him back to happiness; but she only drove the arrow deeper into his soul—the more he saw cause to love her the more torturing was the thought that he was soon to make her wretched. A little while, thought he, and the smile will vanish from that cheek—the song will die away from those lips— the lustre of those eyes will be quenched with sorrow; and the happy heart which now beats lightly in that bosom, will be weighed down like mine by the cares and miseries of the world.

At length he came to me, one day, and related his whole situation in a tone of the deepest despair. When I had heard him through I enquired, "Does your wife know all this?"— at the question he burst into an agony of tears—"For God's sake!" cried he, "if you have any pity on me don't mention my wife—it is the thought of her that drives me almost to madness!"

"And why not?" said I, "she must know it sooner or later: you cannot keep it long from her, and the intelligence may break upon her in a more startling manner than if imparted by yourself; for the accents of those we love soften the harshest tidings. Besides you are depriving yourself of the comforts of her sympathy and not merely that, but also endangering the only bond that can keep hearts together, an unreserved community of thought and feeling. She will soon perceive that something is secretly preying upon your mind, and true love will not brook reserve: it feels undervalued and outraged when even the sorrows of those it loves are concealed from it."

"Oh but my friend! to think what a blow I am to give to all her future prospects—how I am to strike her very soul to the earth, by telling her that her husband is a beggar!—That she is to forego all the elegancies of life—all the pleasures of society—to shrink with me into indigence and obscurity!—To tell her that I have dragged her down from the sphere in which she might have continued to move in constant brightness—the light of every eye—the admiration of every heart!——How can she bear poverty!—she has been brought up in all the refinements of opulence.—How can she bear neglect!—she has been the idol of society—oh, it will break her heart!—it will break her heart!—"

I saw his grief was eloquent and I let it have its flow, for sorrow relieves itself by words. When his paroxysm had subsided and he had relapsed into moody silence, I resumed the subject gently, and urged him to break his situation at once to his wife. He shook his head mournfully, but positively.

"But how are you to keep it from her? It is necessary she should know it, that you may take the steps proper to the alteration of your circumstances. You must change your style of living——nay," observing a pang to pass across his countenance—"don't let that afflict you. I am sure you have never placed your happiness in outward shew—you have yet friends, warm friends, who will not think the worse of you for being less splendidly lodged;—and surely it does not require a palace to be happy with Mary—"

"I could be happy with her," cried he convulsively, "in a hovel!—I could go down with her into poverty and the dust!—I could—I could——God bless her!—God bless her!—" cried he, bursting into a transport of grief and tenderness.

"And believe me my friend," said I stepping up and grasping him warmly by the hand—"believe me, she can be the same with you. Aye, more—it will be a source of pride and triumph to her—it will call forth all the latent energies and fervent sympathies of her nature; for she will rejoice to prove that she loves you for yourself. There is in every true woman's heart a spark of heavenly fire which lies dormant in the broad daylight of prosperity; but which kindles up, and beams and blazes in the dark hour of adversity. No man knows what the wife of his bosom is—no man knows what a ministering angel she is—until he has gone with her through the fiery trials of this world."

There was something in the earnestness of my manner, and the figurative style of my language that caught the excited imagination of Leslie. I knew the auditor I had to deal with; and following up the impression I had made, I finished by persuading him to go home and unburthen his sad heart to his wife.

I must confess, notwithstanding all I had said, I felt some little solicitude for the result. Who can calculate on the fortitude of one whose whole life has been a round of pleasures?—Her gay spirits might revolt at the dark downward path of low humility suddenly pointed out before her, and might cling to the sunny regions in which they had hitherto revelled. Besides, ruin in fashionable life is accompanied by so many galling mortifications to which in other ranks it is a stranger—in short, I could not meet Leslie the next morning without trepidation. He had made the disclosure.

—"And how did she bear it?"

"Like an angel! It seemed rather to be a relief to her mind, for she threw her arms round my neck, and asked if this was all that had lately made me unhappy—but, poor girl,"—added he, "she cannot realize the change we must undergo. She has no idea of poverty but in the abstract—she has only read of it in poetry, where it is allied to love. She feels as yet no privation—she suffers no loss of accustomed conveniences nor elegancies. When we come practically to experience its sordid cares, its paltry wants, its petty humiliations—then will be the real trial."

"But," said I, "now that you have got over the severest task, that of breaking it to her, the sooner you let the world into the secret the better. The disclosure may be mortifying, but then it is a single misery and soon over, whereas you otherwise suffer it in anticipation, every hour in the day. It is not poverty so much as pretence, that harrasses a ruined man. The struggle between a proud mind and an empty purse—the keeping up a hollow shew that must soon come to an end. Have the courage to appear poor and you disarm poverty of its sharpest sting."—On this point I found Leslie perfectly prepared. He had no false pride himself, and as to his wife she was only anxious to conform to their altered fortunes.

Some days afterwards he called upon me in the evening.

He had disposed of his dwelling house and taken a small cottage in the country, a few miles from town. He had been busied all day in sending out furniture. The new establishment required few articles, and those of the simplest kind. All the splendid furniture of his late residence had been sold excepting his wife's Harp. That, he said, was too closely associated with the idea of herself—it belonged to the little story of their loves—for some of the sweetest moments of their courtship were those when he had leant over that instrument and listened to the melting tones of her voice.—I could not but smile at this instance of romantic gallantry in a doting husband.

He was now going out to the cottage, where his wife had been all day, superintending its arrangement. My feelings had become strongly interested in the progress of this family story and as it was a fine evening I offered to accompany him.

He was wearied with the fatigues of the day, and as we walked out, fell into a fit of gloomy musing.

"Poor Mary!" at length broke with a heavy sigh from his lips.

"And what of her," asked I, "has any thing happened to her?"

"What," said he, darting an impatient glance, "is it nothing to be reduced to this paltry situation—to be caged in a miserable cottage—to be obliged to toil almost in the menial concerns of her wretched habitation?"

"Has she then repined at the change?"

"Repined!—she has been nothing but sweetness and good humour. Indeed she seems in better spirits than I have ever known her—she has been to me all love and tenderness and comfort!"

"Admirable girl!" exclaimed I. "You call yourself poor my friend; you never were so rich—you never knew the boundless treasures of excellence you possessed in that woman."

"Oh, but my friend—if this first meeting at the cottage were over—I think I could then be comfortable. But this is her first day of real experience. She has been introduced into our humble dwelling. She has been employed all day in arranging its miserable equipments. She has for the first time known the fatigues of domestic employment—She has for the first time looked around her on a home destitute of every thing elegant,—almost of every thing convenient, and may now be sitting down exhausted and spiritless, brooding over a prospect of future poverty."

There was a degree of probability in this picture that I could not gainsay—so we walked on in silence.

After turning from the main road up a narrow lane so thickly shaded by forest trees as to give it a complete air of seclusion, we came in sight of the cottage. It was humble enough in its appearance for the most pastoral poet; and yet it had a pleasing rural look. A wild vine had over run one end with a profusion of foliage—a few trees threw their branches gracefully over it, and I observed several pots of flowers taste-fully disposed about the door and on the grass plot in front. A small wicket gate opened upon a foot path that wound through some shrubbery to the door. Just as we approached we heard the sound of music.—Leslie grasped my arm—we paused and listened. It was Mary's voice singing, in a style of the most touching simplicity, a little air of which her husband was peculiarly fond.

I felt Leslie's hand tremble on my arm. He stepped forward to hear more distinctly—His step made a noise on the gravel walk—a bright beautiful face glanced out at the window and vanished—a light footstep was heard, and Mary came trip-ping forth to meet us. She was in a pretty, rural dress of white; a few wild flowers were twisted in her fine hair; a fresh bloom was on her cheek; her whole countenance beamed with smiles—I had never seen her look so lovely.

"My dear George," cried she, "I am so glad you are come— I've been watching and watching for you; and running down the lane, and looking out for you. I've set out a table under a beautiful tree behind the cottage—and I've been gathering some of the most delicious strawberries, for I know you are fond of them—and we have such excellent cream—and every thing is so sweet and still here—Oh!" said she, putting her arm within his, and looking up brightly in his face—"oh, we shall be so happy!"

Poor Leslie was overcome—He caught her to his bosom— he folded his arms round her—he kissed her again and again—he could not speak, but the tears gushed into his eyes—And he has often assured me that though the world has since gone prosperously with him, and his life has, indeed, been a happy one; yet never has he experienced a moment of more exquisite felicity.

Rip Van Winkle

The following Tale was found among the papers of the late Diedrich Knickerbocker, an old gentleman of New York, who was very curious in the Dutch history of the province, and the manners of the descendants from its primitive settlers. His historical researches, however, did not lie so much among books, as among men; for the former are lamentably scanty on his favourite topics; whereas he found the old burghers, and still more, their wives, rich in that legendary lore so invaluable to true history. Whenever, therefore, he happened upon a genuine Dutch family, snugly shut up in its low roofed farm house, under a spreading sycamore, he looked upon it as a little clasped volume of black letter, and studied it with the zeal of a bookworm.

The result of all these researches was a history of the province, during the reign of the Dutch governors, which he published some years since. There have been various opinions as to the literary character of his work and, to tell the truth, it is not a whit better than it should be. Its chief merit is its scrupulous accuracy, which indeed was a little questioned on its first appearance, but has since been completely established; and it is now admitted into all historical collections as a book of unquestionable authority.

The old gentleman died shortly after the publication of his work, and now that he is dead and gone, it cannot do much harm to his memory to say that his time might have been much better employed in weightier labours. He, however, was apt to ride his hobby his own way; and though it did now and then kick up the dust a little in the eyes of his neighbours, and grieve the spirit of some friends for whom he felt the truest deference and affection; yet his errors and follies are remembered "more in sorrow than in anger," and it begins to be suspected that he never intended to injure or offend. But however his memory may be appreciated by criticks, it is still held dear by many folk whose good opinion is well worth having; particularly by certain biscuit bakers, who have gone so far as to imprint his likeness on their new year cakes, and have thus given him a chance for immortality, almost equal to being stamped on a Waterloo medal, or a Queen Anne's farthing.

Rip Van Winkle

A Posthumous Writing of Diedrich Knickerbocker

By Woden, God of Saxons,
From whence comes Wensday, that is Wodensday,
Truth is a thing that ever I will keep
Unto thylke day in which I creep into
My sepulchre—

Cartwright

WHOEVER has made a voyage up the Hudson must remember the Kaatskill mountains. They are a dismembered branch of the great Appalachian family, and are seen away to the west of the river swelling up to noble height and lording it over the surrounding country. Every change of season, every change of weather, indeed every hour of the day, produces some change in the magical hues and shapes of these mountains, and they are regarded by all the good wives far and near as perfect barometers. When the weather is fair and settled they are clothed in blue and purple, and print their bold outlines on the clear evening sky; but sometimes, when the rest of the landscape is cloudless, they will gather a hood of grey vapours about their summits, which, in the last rays of the setting sun, will glow and light up like a crown of glory.

At the foot of these fairy mountains the voyager may have descried the light smoke curling up from a village, whose shingle roofs gleam among the trees, just where the blue tints of the upland melt away into the fresh green of the nearer landscape. It is a little village of great antiquity, having been founded by some of the Dutch colonists in the early times of the province, just about the beginning of the government of the good Peter Stuyvesant, (may he rest in peace!) and there were some of the houses of the original settlers standing within a few years; built of small yellow bricks brought from Holland, having latticed windows and gable fronts, surmounted with weathercocks.

In that same village, and in one of these very houses (which to tell the precise truth was sadly time worn and weather beaten) there lived many years since, while the country was yet a province of Great Britain, a simple good natured fellow of the name of Rip Van Winkle. He was a descendant of the Van Winkles who figured so gallantly in the chivalrous days of Peter Stuyvesant, and accompanied him to the siege of Fort Christina. He inherited, however, but little of the martial character of his ancestors. I have observed that he was a simple good natured man; he was moreover a kind neighbour, and an obedient, henpecked husband. Indeed to the latter circumstance might be owing that meekness of spirit which gained him such universal popularity; for those men are most apt to be obsequious and conciliating abroad, who are under the discipline of shrews at home. Their tempers doubtless are rendered pliant and malleable in the fiery furnace of domestic tribulation, and a curtain lecture is worth all the sermons in the world for teaching the virtues of patience and long suffering. A termagant wife may therefore in some respects be considered a tolerable blessing—and if so, Rip Van Winkle was thrice blessed.

Certain it is that he was a great favourite among all the good wives of the village, who as usual with the amiable sex, took his part in all family squabbles, and never failed, whenever they talked those matters over in their evening gossippings, to lay all the blame on Dame Van Winkle. The children of the village too would shout with joy whenever he approached. He assisted at their sports, made their play things, taught them to fly kites and shoot marbles, and told them long stories of ghosts, witches and Indians. Whenever he went dodging about the village he was surrounded by a troop of them hanging on his skirts, clambering on his back and playing a thousand tricks on him with impunity; and not a dog would bark at him throughout the neighbourhood.

The great error in Rip's composition was an insuperable aversion to all kinds of profitable labour. It could not be from the want of assiduity or perseverance; for he would sit on a wet rock, with a rod as long and heavy as a Tartar's lance, and fish all day without a murmur, even though he should not be encouraged by a single nibble. He would carry a fowling piece on his shoulder for hours together, trudging through woods, and swamps and up hill and down dale, to shoot a few squirrels or wild pigeons; he would never refuse to assist a neighbour even in the roughest toil, and was a foremost man at all country frolicks for husking Indian corn, or building stone fences; the women of the village too used to employ him to run their errands and to do such little odd jobs as their less obliging husbands would not do for them— in a word Rip was ready to attend to any body's business but his own; but as to doing family duty, and keeping his farm in order, he found it impossible.

In fact he declared it was of no use to work on his farm; it was the most pestilent little piece of ground in the whole country; every thing about it went wrong and would go wrong in spite of him. His fences were continually falling to pieces; his cow would either go astray or get among the cabbages, weeds were sure to grow quicker in his fields than any where else; the rain always made a point of setting in just as he had some outdoor work to do. So that though his patrimonial estate had dwindled away under his management, acre by acre until there was little more left than a mere patch of Indian corn and potatoes, yet it was the worst conditioned farm in the neighbourhood.

His children too were as ragged and wild as if they belonged to nobody. His son Rip, an urchin begotten in his own likeness, promised to inherit the habits with the old clothes of his father. He was generally seen trooping like a colt at his mother's heels, equipped in a pair of his father's cast off galligaskins, which he had much ado to hold up with one hand, as a fine lady does her train in bad weather.

Rip Van Winkle, however, was one of those happy mortals of foolish, well oiled dispositions, who take the world easy, eat white bread or brown, whichever can be got with least thought or trouble, and would rather starve on a penny than work for a pound. If left to himself, he would have whistled life away in perfect contentment, but his wife kept continually dinning in his ears about his idleness, his carelessness and the ruin he was bringing on his family. Morning noon and night her tongue was incessantly going, and every thing he said or did was sure to produce a torrent of household eloquence. Rip had but one way of replying to all lectures of the kind, and that by frequent use had grown into a habit. He shrugged his shoulders, shook his head, cast up his eyes, but said nothing. This, however, always provoked a fresh volley from his wife, so that he was fain to draw off his forces and take to the outside of the house—the only side which in truth belongs to a henpecked husband.

Rip's sole domestic adherent was his dog Wolf who was as much henpecked as his master, for Dame Van Winkle regarded them as companions in idleness, and even looked upon Wolf with an evil eye as the cause of his master's going so often astray. True it is, in all points of spirit befitting an honourable dog, he was as courageous an animal as ever scoured the woods—but what courage can withstand the ever during and all besetting terrors of a woman's tongue? The moment Wolf entered the house his crest fell, his tail drooped to the ground or curled between his legs, he sneaked about with a gallows air, casting many a sidelong glance at Dame Van Winkle, and at the least flourish of a broomstick or ladle he would fly to the door with yelping precipitation.

Times grew worse and worse with Rip Van Winkle as years of matrimony rolled on; a tart temper never mellows with age, and a sharp tongue is the only edged tool that grows keener with constant use. For a long while he used to console himself when driven from home, by frequenting a kind of perpetual club of the sages, philosophers and other idle personages of the village which held its sessions on a bench before a small inn, designated by a rubicund portrait of his majesty George the Third. Here they used to sit in the shade, through a long lazy summer's day, talking listlessly over village gossip, or telling endless sleepy stories about nothing. But it would have been worth any statesman's money to have heard the profound discussions that sometimes took place, when by chance an old newspaper fell into their hands from some passing traveller. How solemnly they would listen to the contents as drawled out by Derrick Van Bummel the schoolmaster, a dapper, learned little man, who was not to be daunted by the most gigantic word in the dictionary; and how sagely they would deliberate upon public events some months after they had taken place.

The opinions of this junto were completely controlled by

Nicholaus Vedder, a patriarch of the village, and landlord of the inn, at the door of which he took his seat from morning till night, just moving sufficiently to avoid the sun and keep in the shade of a large tree; so that the neighbours could tell the hour by his movements as accurately as by a sun dial. It is true he was rarely heard to speak, but smoked his pipe incessantly. His adherents, however (for every great man has his adherents), perfectly understood him and knew how to gather his opinions. When any thing that was read or related displeased him, he was observed to smoke his pipe vehemently and to send forth short, frequent and angry puffs; but when pleased he would inhale the smoke slowly and tranquilly and emit it in light and placid clouds, and sometimes taking the pipe from his mouth and letting the fragrant vapour curl about his nose, would gravely nod his head in token of perfect approbation.

From even this strong hold the unlucky Rip was at length routed by his termagant wife who would suddenly break in upon the tranquility of the assemblage and call the members all to naught; nor was that august personage Nicholaus Vedder himself sacred from the daring tongue of this terrible virago, who charged him outright with encouraging her husband in habits of idleness.

Poor Rip was at last reduced almost to despair; and his only alternative to escape from the labour of the farm and the clamour of his wife, was to take gun in hand and stroll away into the woods. Here he would sometimes seat himself at the foot of a tree and share the contents of his wallet with Wolf, with whom he sympathised as a fellow sufferer in persecution. "Poor Wolf," he would say, "thy mistress leads thee a dog's life of it, but never mind my lad, whilst I live thou shalt never want a friend to stand by thee!" Wolf would wag his tail, look wistfully in his master's face, and if dogs can feel pity I verily believe he reciprocated the sentiment with all his heart.

In a long ramble of the kind on a fine autumnal day, Rip had unconsciously scrambled to one of the highest parts of the Kaatskill mountains. He was after his favourite sport of squirrel shooting and the still solitudes had echoed and re-echoed with the reports of his gun. Panting and fatigued he threw himself, late in the afternoon, on a green knoll, covered with mountain herbage, that crowned the brow of a precipice. From an opening between the trees he could overlook all the lower country for many a mile of rich woodland. He saw at a distance the lordly Hudson, far, far below him, moving on its silent but majestic course, with the reflection of a purple cloud, or the sail of a lagging bark here and there sleeping on its glassy bosom, and at last losing itself in the blue highlands.

On the other side he looked down into a deep mountain glen, wild, lonely and shagged, the bottom filled with fragments from the impending cliffs and scarcely lighted by the reflected rays of the setting sun. For some time Rip lay musing on this scene, evening was gradually advancing, the mountains began to throw their long blue shadows over the valleys, he saw that it would be dark, long before he could reach the village, and he heaved a heavy sigh when he thought of encountering the terrors of Dame Van Winkle.

As he was about to descend he heard a voice from a distance hallooing "Rip Van Winkle! Rip Van Winkle!" He looked around, but could see nothing but a crow winging its solitary flight across the mountain. He thought his fancy must have deceived him and turned again to descend, when he heard the same cry ring through the still evening air: "Rip Van Winkle! Rip Van Winkle!"—at the same time Wolf bristled up his back and giving a low growl, skulked to his master's side, looking fearfully down into the glen. Rip now felt a vague apprehension stealing over him; he looked anxiously in the same direction and perceived a strange figure slowly toiling up the rocks and bending under the weight of something he carried on his back. He was surprised to see any human being in this lonely and unfrequented place, but supposing it to be some one of the neighbourhood in need of his assistance he hastened down to yield it.

On nearer approach he was still more surprised at the singularity of the stranger's appearance. He was a short, square built old fellow, with thick bushy hair and a grizzled beard. His dress was of the antique Dutch fashion, a cloth jerkin strapped round the waist, several pair of breeches, the outer one of ample volume decorated with rows of buttons down the sides and bunches at the knees. He bore on his shoulder

a stout keg that seemed full of liquor, and made signs for Rip
to approach and assist him with the load. Though rather shy
and distrustful of this new acquaintance Rip complied with
his usual alacrity, and mutually relieving each other they clam-
bered up a narrow gully apparently the dry bed of a mountain
torrent. As they ascended Rip every now and then heard long
rolling peals like distant thunder, that seemed to issue out of
a deep ravine or rather cleft between lofty rocks, toward
which their rugged path conducted. He paused for an instant,
but supposing it to be the muttering of one of those transient
thunder showers which often take place in mountain heights,
he proceeded. Passing through the ravine they came to a hollow like a small amphitheatre, surrounded by perpendicular
precipices, over the brinks of which impending trees shot
their branches, so that you only caught glimpses of the azure
sky and the bright evening cloud. During the whole time Rip
and his companion had laboured on in silence, for though the
former marvelled greatly what could be the object of carrying
a keg of liquor up this wild mountain, yet there was something strange and incomprehensible about the unknown, that
inspired awe and checked familiarity.

On entering the amphitheatre new objects of wonder presented themselves. On a level spot in the centre was a company of odd looking personages playing at ninepins. They
were dressed in a quaint outlandish fashion—some wore
short doublets, others jerkins with long knives in their belts
and most of them had enormous breeches of similar style with
that of the guide's. Their visages too were peculiar. One had
a large head, broad face and small piggish eyes. The face of
another seemed to consist entirely of nose, and was surmounted by a white sugarloaf hat, set off with a little red
cock's tail. They all had beards of various shapes and colours.
There was one who seemed to be the Commander. He was a
stout old gentleman, with a weatherbeaten countenance. He
wore a laced doublet, broad belt and hanger, high crowned
hat and feather, red stockings and high heel'd shoes with
roses in them. The whole group reminded Rip of the figures
in an old Flemish painting, in the parlour of Dominie Van
Schaick the village parson, and which had been brought over
from Holland at the time of the settlement.

What seemed particularly odd to Rip was, that though these folks were evidently amusing themselves, yet they maintained the gravest faces, the most mysterious silence, and were, withal, the most melancholy party of pleasure he had ever witnessed. Nothing interrupted the stillness of the scene, but the noise of the balls, which, whenever they were rolled, echoed along the mountains like rumbling peals of thunder.

As Rip and his companion approached them they suddenly desisted from their play and stared at him with such fixed statue like gaze, and such strange uncouth, lack lustre countenances, that his heart turned within him, and his knees smote together. His companion now emptied the contents of the keg into large flagons and made signs to him to wait upon the company. He obeyed with fear and trembling; they quaffed the liquor in profound silence and then returned to their game.

By degrees Rip's awe and apprehension subsided. He even ventured, when no eye was fixed upon him, to taste the beverage, which he found had much of the flavour of excellent hollands. He was naturally a thirsty soul and was soon tempted to repeat the draught. One taste provoked another, and he reiterated his visits to the flagon so often that at length his senses were overpowered, his eyes swam in his head—his head gradually declined and he fell into a deep sleep.

On awaking he found himself on the green knoll from whence he had first seen the old man of the glen. He rubbed his eyes—it was a bright, sunny morning. The birds were hopping and twittering among the bushes, and the eagle was wheeling aloft and breasting the pure mountain breeze. "Surely," thought Rip, "I have not slept here all night." He recalled the occurrences before he fell asleep. The strange man with a keg of liquor—the mountain ravine—the wild retreat among the rocks—the woe begone party at ninepins—the flagon—"ah! that flagon! that wicked flagon!" thought Rip—"what excuse shall I make to Dame Van Winkle?"

He looked round for his gun, but in place of the clean well oiled fowling piece he found an old firelock lying by him, the barrel encrusted with rust; the lock falling off and the stock worm eaten. He now suspected that the grave roysters of the mountain had put a trick upon him, and having dosed him with liquor, had robbed him of his gun. Wolf too had disappeared, but he might have strayed away after a squirrel or partridge. He whistled after him and shouted his name—but all in vain; the echoes repeated his whistle and shout, but no dog was to be seen.

He determined to revisit the scene of the last evening's gambol, and if he met with any of the party, to demand his dog and gun. As he arose to walk he found himself stiff in the joints and wanting in his usual activity. "These mountain beds do not agree with me," thought Rip, "and if this frolick should lay me up with a fit of the rheumatism, I shall have a blessed time with Dame Van Winkle." With some difficulty he got down into the glen; he found the gully up which he and his companion had ascended the preceding evening, but to his astonishment a mountain stream was now foaming down it; leaping from rock to rock, and filling the glen with babbling murmurs. He, however, made shift to scramble up its sides working his toilsome way through thickets of birch, sassafras and witch hazel, and sometimes tripped up or entangled by the wild grape vines that twisted their coils and tendrils from tree to tree, and spread a kind of net work in his path.

At length he reached to where the ravine had opened through the cliffs, to the amphitheatre—but no traces of such opening remained. The rocks presented a high impenetrable wall over which the torrent came tumbling in a sheet of feathery foam, and fell into a broad deep basin black from the shadows of the surrounding forest. Here then poor Rip was brought to a stand. He again called and whistled after his dog—he was only answered by the cawing of a flock of idle crows, sporting high in air about a dry tree that overhung a sunny precipice; and who, secure in their elevation seemed to look down and scoff at the poor man's perplexities.

What was to be done? The morning was passing away and Rip felt famished for want of his breakfast. He grieved to give up his dog and gun; he dreaded to meet his wife; but it would not do to starve among the mountains. He shook his head, shouldered the rusty fire lock and with a heart full of trouble and anxiety, turned his steps homeward.

As he approached the village he met a number of people,

but none whom he knew, which somewhat surprised him, for he had thought himself acquainted with every one in the country round. Their dress too was of a different fashion from that to which he was accustomed. They all stared at him with equal marks of surprise, and whenever they cast their eyes upon him, invariably stroked their chins. The constant recurrence of this gesture induced Rip involuntarily to do the same, when to his astonishment he found his beard had grown a foot long!

He had now entered the skirts of the village. A troop of strange children ran at his heels, hooting after him and pointing at his grey beard. The dogs too, not one of which he recognized for an old acquaintance, barked at him as he passed. The very village was altered—it was larger and more populous. There were rows of houses which he had never seen before, and those which had been his familiar haunts had disappeared. Strange names were over the doors—strange faces at the windows—every thing was strange. His mind now misgave him; he began to doubt whether both he and the world around him were not bewitched. Surely this was his native village which he had left but the day before. There stood the Kaatskill mountains—there ran the silver Hudson at a distance—there was every hill and dale precisely as it had always been—Rip was sorely perplexed—"That flagon last night," thought he, "has addled my poor head sadly!"

It was with some difficulty that he found the way to his own house, which he approached with silent awe, expecting every moment to hear the shrill voice of Dame Van Winkle. He found the house gone to decay—the roof fallen in, the windows shattered and the doors off the hinges. A half starved dog that looked like Wolf was skulking about it. Rip called him by name but the cur snarled, shewed his teeth and passed on. This was an unkind cut indeed—"My very dog," sighed poor Rip, "has forgotten me!"

He entered the house, which, to tell the truth, Dame Van Winkle had always kept in neat order. It was empty, forlorn and apparently abandoned. This desolateness overcame all his connubial fears—he called loudly for his wife and children—the lonely chambers rung for a moment with his voice, and then all again was silence.

He now hurried forth and hastened to his old resort, the village inn—but it too was gone. A large, ricketty wooden building stood in its place, with great gaping windows, some of them broken, and mended with old hats and petticoats, and over the door was printed "The Union Hotel, by Jonathan Doolittle." Instead of the great tree, that used to shelter the quiet little Dutch inn of yore, there now was reared a tall naked pole with something on top that looked like a red night cap, and from it was fluttering a flag on which was a singular assemblage of stars and stripes—all this was strange and incomprehensible. He recognized on the sign, however, the ruby face of King George under which he had smoked so many a peaceful pipe, but even this was singularly metamorphosed. The red coat was changed for one of blue and buff; a sword was held in the hand instead of a sceptre; the head was decorated with a cocked hat, and underneath was printed in large characters GENERAL WASHINGTON.

There was as usual a crowd of folk about the door; but none that Rip recollected. The very character of the people seemed changed. There was a busy, bustling disputatious tone about it, instead of the accustomed phlegm and drowsy tranquility. He looked in vain for the sage Nicholaus Vedder with his broad face, double chin and fair long pipe, uttering clouds of tobacco smoke instead of idle speeches. Or Van Bummel the schoolmaster doling forth the contents of an ancient newspaper. In place of these a lean bilious looking fellow with his pockets full of hand bills, was haranguing vehemently about rights of citizens—elections—members of Congress—liberty—Bunker's hill—heroes of seventy six—and other words which were a perfect babylonish jargon to the bewildered Van Winkle.

The appearance of Rip with his long grizzled beard, his rusty fowling piece his uncouth dress and an army of women and children at his heels soon attracted the attention of the tavern politicians. They crowded around him eying him from head to foot, with great curiosity. The orator bustled up to him, and drawing him partly aside, enquired "on which side he voted?"—Rip stared in vacant stupidity. Another short but busy little fellow, pulled him by the arm and rising on tiptoe, enquired in his ear " whether he was Federal or Democrat?"—

Rip was equally at a loss to comprehend the question—when a knowing, self important old gentleman, in a sharp cocked hat, made his way through the crowd, putting them to the right and left with his elbows as he passed, and planting himself before Van Winkle, with one arm akimbo, the other resting on his cane, his keen eyes and sharp hat penetrating as it were into his very soul, demanded in an austere tone—" what brought him to the election with a gun on his shoulder and a mob at his heels, and whether he meant to breed a riot in the village?"—"Alas gentlemen," cried Rip, somewhat dismayed, "I am a poor quiet man, a native of the place, and a loyal subject of the King—God bless him!"

Here a general shout burst from the byestanders—"A tory! a tory! a spy! a Refugee! hustle him! away with him!"—It was with great difficulty that the self important man in the cocked hat restored order; and having assumed a ten fold austerity of brow demanded again of the unknown culprit, what he came there for and whom he was seeking. The poor man humbly assured him that he meant no harm; but merely came there in search of some of his neighbours, who used to keep about the tavern.

"—Well—who are they?—name them."

Rip bethought himself a moment and enquired, "Where's Nicholaus Vedder?"

There was a silence for a little while, when an old man replied, in a thin, piping voice, "Nicholaus Vedder? why he is dead and gone these eighteen years! There was a wooden tombstone in the church yard that used to tell all about him, but that's rotted and gone too."

"Where's Brom Dutcher?"

"Oh he went off to the army in the beginning of the war; some say he was killed at the storming of Stoney Point—others say he was drowned in a squall at the foot of Antony's Nose—I don't know—he never came back again."

"Where's Van Bummel the schoolmaster?"

"He went off to the wars too—was a great militia general, and is now in Congress."

Rip's heart died away at hearing of these sad changes in his home and friends, and finding himself thus alone in the world—every answer puzzled him too by treating of such enormous lapses of time and of matters which he could not understand—war—Congress, Stoney Point—he had no courage to ask after any more friends, but cried out in despair, "Does nobody here know Rip Van Winkle?"

"Oh. Rip Van Winkle?" exclaimed two or three—"oh to be sure!—that's Rip Van Winkle—yonder—leaning against the tree."

Rip looked and beheld a precise counterpart of himself, as he went up the mountain: apparently as lazy and certainly as ragged! The poor fellow was now completely confounded. He doubted his own identity, and whether he was himself or another man. In the midst of his bewilderment the man in the cocked hat demanded who he was,—what was his name?

"God knows," exclaimed he, at his wit's end, "I'm not myself.—I'm somebody else—that's me yonder—no—that's somebody else got into my shoes—I was myself last night; but I fell asleep on the mountain—and they've changed my gun—and every thing's changed—and I'm changed—and I can't tell what's my name, or who I am!"

The byestanders began now to look at each other, nod, wink significantly and tap their fingers against their foreheads. There was a whisper also about securing the gun, and keeping the old fellow from doing mischief—at the very suggestion of which, the self important man in the cocked hat retired with some precipitation. At this critical moment a fresh likely looking woman pressed through the throng to get a peep at the greybearded man. She had a chubby child in her arms, which frightened at his looks began to cry. "Hush Rip," cried she, "hush you little fool, the old man won't hurt you." The name of the child, the air of the mother, the tone of her voice all awakened a train of recollections in his mind. "What is your name my good woman?" asked he.

"Judith Gardenier."

"And your father's name?"

"Ah, poor man, Rip Van Winkle was his name, but it's twenty years since he went away from home with his gun and never has been heard of since—his dog came home without him—but whether he shot himself, or was carried away by the Indians no body can tell. I was then but a little girl."

Rip had but one question more to ask, but he put it with a faltering voice—

"Where's your mother?"—

Oh she too had died but a short time since—she broke a blood vessel in a fit of passion at a New England pedlar.—

There was a drop of comfort at least in this intelligence. The honest man could contain himself no longer—he caught his daughter and her child in his arms.—"I am your father!" cried he—"Young Rip Van Winkle once—old Rip Van Winkle now!—does nobody know poor Rip Van Winkle!"

All stood amazed, until an old woman tottering out from among the crowd put her hand to her brow and peering under it in his face for a moment exclaimed—"Sure enough!—it is Rip Van Winkle—it is himself—welcome home again old neighbour—why, where have you been these twenty long years?"

Rip's story was soon told, for the whole twenty years had been to him but as one night. The neighbours stared when they heard it; some were seen to wink at each other and put their tongues in their cheeks, and the self important man in the cocked hat, who when the alarm was over had returned to the field, screwed down the corners of his mouth and shook his head—upon which there was a general shaking of the head throughout the assemblage.

It was determined, however, to take the opinion of old Peter Vanderdonk, who was seen slowly advancing up the road. He was a descendant of the historian of that name, who wrote one of the earliest accounts of the province. Peter was the most ancient inhabitant of the village and well versed in all the wonderful events and traditions of the neighbourhood. He recollected Rip at once, and corroborated his story in the most satisfactory manner. He assured the company that it was a fact handed down from his ancestor the historian, that the Kaatskill mountains had always been haunted by strange beings. That it was affirmed that the great Hendrick Hudson, the first discoverer of the river and country, kept a kind of vigil there every twenty years, with his crew of the Half Moon— being permitted in this way to revisit the scenes of his enterprize and keep a guardian eye upon the river and the great city called by his name. That his father had once seen them in their old Dutch dresses playing at nine pins in a hollow of the mountain; and that he himself had heard one summer afternoon the sound of their balls, like distant peals of thunder.

To make a long story short—the company broke up, and returned to the more important concerns of the election. Rip's daughter took him home to live with her; she had a snug well furnished house, and a stout cheery farmer for a husband whom Rip recollected for one of the urchins that used to climb upon his back. As to Rip's son and heir, who was the ditto of himself seen leaning against the tree; he was employed to work on the farm; but evinced an hereditary disposition to attend to any thing else but his business.

Rip now resumed his old walks and habits; he soon found many of his former cronies, though all rather the worse for the wear and tear of time; and preferred making friends among the rising generation, with whom he soon grew into great favour. Having nothing to do at home, and being arrived at that happy age when a man can be idle, with impunity, he took his place once more on the bench at the inn door and was reverenced as one of the patriarchs of the village and a chronicle of the old times "before the war." It was some time before he could get into the regular track of gossip, or could be made to comprehend the strange events that had taken place during his torpor. How that there had been a revolutionary war—that the country had thrown off the yoke of Old England and that instead of being a subject of his majesty George the Third, he was now a free citizen of the United States. Rip in fact was no politician; the changes of states and empires made but little impression on him; but there was one species of despotism under which he had long groaned and that was petticoat government. Happily that was at an end—he had got his neck out of the yoke of matrimony, and could go in and out whenever he pleased without dreading the tyranny of Dame Van Winkle. Whenever her name was mentioned, however, he shook his head, shrugged his shoulders and cast up his eyes; which might pass either for an expression of resignation to his fate or joy at his deliverance.

He used to tell his story to every stranger that arrived at Mr. Doolittle's Hotel. He was observed at first to vary on some points, every time he told it, which was doubtless owing to his having so recently awaked. It at last settled down precisely to the tale I have related and not a man woman or child in the neighbourhood but knew it by heart. Some always pretended to doubt the reality of it, and insisted that Rip had been out of his head, and that this was one point on which he always remained flighty. The old Dutch inhabitants, however, almost universally gave it full credit— Even to this day they never hear a thunder storm of a summer afternoon about the Kaatskill, but they say Hendrick Hudson and his crew are at their game of nine pins; and it is a common wish of all henpecked husbands in the neighbourhood, when life hangs heavy on their hands, that they might have a quieting draught out of Rip Van Winkle's flagon.

NOTE

The foregoing tale one would suspect had been suggested to Mr. Knickerbocker by a little German superstition about the emperor Frederick *der Rothbart* and the Kypphauser Mountain; the subjoined note, however, which he had appended to the tale, shews that it is an absolute fact, narrated with his usual fidelity.—

"The story of Rip Van Winkle may seem incredible to many, but nevertheless I give it my full belief, for I know the vicinity of our old Dutch settlements to have been very subject to marvellous events and appearances. Indeed I have heard many stranger stories than this, in the villages along the Hudson; all of which were too well authenticated to admit of a doubt. I have even talked with Rip Van Winkle myself, who when last I saw him was a very venerable old man and so perfectly rational and consistent on every other point, that I think no conscientious person could refuse to take this into the bargain—nay I have seen a certificate on the subject taken before a country justice and signed with a cross in the justice's own hand writing. The story therefore is beyond the possibility of doubt.

D.K."

POSTSCRIPT

The following are travelling notes from a memorandum book of Mr. Knickerbocker.

The Kaatsberg or Catskill mountains have always been a region full of fable. The Indians considered them the abode of spirits who influenced the weather, spreading sunshine or clouds over the landscape and sending good or bad hunting seasons. They were ruled by an old squaw spirit, said to be their mother. She dwelt on the highest peak of the Catskills and had charge of the doors of day and night to open and shut them at the proper hour. She hung up the new moons in the skies and cut up the old ones into stars. In times of drought, if properly propitiated, she would spin light summer clouds out of cobwebs and morning dew, and send them off, from the crest of the mountain, flake after flake, like flakes of carded cotton to float in the air: until, dissolved by the heat of the sun, they would fall in gentle showers, causing the grass to spring, the fruits to ripen and the corn to grow an inch an hour. If displeased, however, she would brew up clouds black as ink, sitting in the midst of them like a bottle bellied spider in the midst of its web; and when these clouds broke—woe betide the valleys!

In old times say the Indian traditions, there was a kind of Manitou or Spirit, who kept about the wildest recesses of the Catskill mountains, and took a mischievous pleasure in wreaking all kinds of evils and vexations upon the red men. Sometimes he would assume the form of a bear a panther or a deer, lead the bewildered hunter a weary chace through tangled forests and among rugged rocks; and then spring off with a loud ho! ho! leaving him aghast on the brink of a beetling precipice or raging torrent.

The favorite abode of this Manitou is still shewn. It is a great rock or cliff in the loneliest part of the mountains, and, from the flowering vines which clamber about it, and the wild flowers which abound in its neighborhood, is known by the name of the Garden Rock. Near the foot of it is a small lake the haunt of the solitary bittern, with water snakes basking in the sun on the leaves of the pond lillies which lie on the surface. This place was held in great awe by the Indians, insomuch that the boldest hunter would not pursue his game within its precincts. Once upon a time, however, a hunter who had lost his way, penetrated to the garden rock where he beheld a number of gourds placed in the crotches of trees. One of these he seized and made off with it, but in the hurry of his retreat he let it fall among the rocks, when a great stream gushed forth which washed him away and swept him down precipices where he was dashed to pieces, and the stream made its way to the Hudson and continues to flow to the present day; being the identical stream known by the name of the Kaaters-kill.

English Writers on America

Methinks I see in my mind a noble and puissant nation rousing herself, like a strong man after sleep, and shaking her invincible locks: methinks I see her as an eagle mewing her mighty youth, and kindling her endazzled eyes at the full midday beam.

Milton, on the Liberty of the Press

I T IS WITH FEELINGS of deep regret that I observe the literary animosity daily growing up between England and America. Great curiosity has been awakened of late with respect to the United States, and the London press has teemed with volumes of travels through the republic; but they seem intended to diffuse error rather than knowledge; and so successful have they been, that, notwithstanding the constant intercourse between the nations, there is no people concerning whom the great mass of the British public have less pure information, or entertain more numerous prejudices.

English travellers are the best, and the worst in the world. Where no motives of pride or interest intervene, none can equal them for profound and philosophical views of society, or faithful, and graphical descriptions of external objects; but when either the interest or reputation of their own country comes in collision with that of another, they go to the opposite extreme, and forget their usual probity and candour in the indulgence of splenetic remark and an illiberal spirit of ridicule.

Hence their travels are more honest and accurate the more remote the country described. I would place implicit confidence in an Englishman's description of the regions beyond the cataracts of the Nile; of unknown islands in the Yellow Sea; of the interior of India, or of any other tract which other travellers might be apt to picture out with the illusions of their fancies; but I would cautiously receive his account of his immediate neighbours, and of those nations with which he is in habits of most frequent intercourse. However I might be disposed to trust his probity I dare not trust his prejudices.

It has also been the peculiar lot of our country to be visited by the worst kind of English travellers. While men of philosophical spirit and cultivated minds have been sent from England to ransack the poles, to penetrate the deserts, and to study the manners and customs of barbarous nations, with which she can have no permanent intercourse of profit or pleasure; it has been left to the broken down tradesman, the scheming adventurer, the wandering mechanic, the Manchester and Birmingham agent, to be her oracles respecting America. From such sources she is content to receive her information respecting a country in a singular state of moral and physical development; a country in which one of the greatest political experiments in the history of the world is now performing, and which presents the most profound and momentous studies to the statesman and the philosopher.

That such men should give prejudiced accounts of America is not a matter of surprize. The themes it offers for contemplation are too vast and elevated for their capacities. The national character is yet in a state of fermentation: it may have its frothings and sediment, but its ingredients are sound and wholesome; it has already given proofs of powerful and generous qualities, and the whole promises to settle down into something substantially excellent. But the causes which are operating to strengthen and ennoble it, and its daily indications of admirable properties, are all lost upon these pur-blind observers; who are only affected by the little asperities incident to its present situation. They are capable of judging only of the surface of things; of those matters which come in contact with their private interests and personal gratifications. They miss some of the snug conveniences and petty comforts which belong to an old, highly finished, and overpopulous state of society, where the ranks of useful labour are crowded, and many earn a painful and servile subsistence, by studying the very caprices of appetite and self indulgence. These minor comforts, however, are all important in the estimation of narrow minds, which either do not perceive, or will not acknowledge, that they are more than counterbalanced among us, by great and generally diffused blessings.

They may, perhaps, have been disappointed in some unreasonable expectation of sudden gain. They may have pictured America to themselves, an El Dorado, where gold and silver abounded, and the natives were lacking in sagacity; and where they were to become strangely and suddenly rich, in some unforeseen, but easy manner. The same weakness of mind that indulges absurd expectations, produces petulance in disappointment. Such persons become embittered against the country on finding that there, as every where else, a man must sow before he can reap; must win wealth by industry and talent; and must contend with the common difficulties of nature, and the shrewdness of an intelligent and enterprizing people.

Perhaps, through mistaken, or ill directed hospitality, or from the prompt disposition to cheer and countenance the stranger, prevalent among my countrymen, they may have been treated with unwonted respect in America; and having been accustomed all their lives to consider themselves below the surface of good society; and brought up in a servile feeling of inferiority; they become arrogant on the common boon of civility; they attribute to the lowliness of others, their own elevation; and under rate a society, where there are no artificial distinctions, and where, by any chance, such individuals as themselves can rise to consequence.

One would suppose, however, that information coming from such sources, on a subject where the truth is so desirable, would be received with caution by the censors of the press. That the motives of these men, their veracity, their opportunities of enquiry and observation and their capacities for judging correctly would be rigorously scrutinized, before their evidence was admitted in such sweeping extent, against a kindred nation. The very reverse, however, is the case, and it furnishes a striking instance of human inconsistency. Nothing can surpass the vigilance with which English critics will examine the credibility of the traveller, who publishes an account of some distant, and comparatively unimportant, country. How warily will they compare the measurements of a pyramid, or the descriptions of a ruin, and how sternly will they censure any inaccuracy in these contributions of merely curious knowledge; while they will receive, with eagerness and unhesitating faith, the gross misrepresentations of coarse and obscure writers, concerning a country with which their own is placed in the most important and delicate relations. Nay, they will even make these apocryphal volumes text books, on which to enlarge, with a zeal and an ability worthy of a more generous cause.

I shall not, however, dwell on this irksome and hackney'd topic; nor should I have adverted to it but for the undue interest apparently taken in it by my countrymen, and certain injurious effects, which I apprehended it might produce upon the national feeling. We attach too much consequence to these attacks. They cannot do us any essential injury. The tissue of misrepresentations attempted to be woven round us are like cobwebs, woven round the limbs of an infant giant. Our country continually outgrows them. One falsehood after another falls off of itself. We have but to live on, and every day we live a whole volume of refutation. All the writers of England united, if we could for a moment suppose their great minds stooping to so unworthy a combination, could not conceal our rapidly growing importance and matchless prosperity. They could not conceal that these are owing, not merely to physical and local, but also to moral causes. To the political liberty, the general diffusion of knowledge, the prevalence of sound moral and religious principles, which give force and sustained energy to the character of a people; and which, in fact have been the acknowledged and wonderful supporters of their own national power and glory.

But why are we so exquisitely alive to the aspersions of England? Why do we suffer ourselves to be so affected by the contumely she has endeavoured to cast upon us? It is not in the opinion of England alone that honor lives and reputation has its being. The world at large is the arbiter of a nation's fame; with its thousand eyes it witnesses a nation's deeds, and from their collective testimony is national glory or national disgrace established.

For ourselves, therefore, it is comparatively of but little importance whether England does us justice or not—it is perhaps of far more importance to herself. She is instilling anger and resentment into the bosom of a youthful nation, to grow with its growth and strengthen with its strength. If in America, as some of her writers are labouring to convince her, she is hereafter to find an invidious rival and a gigantic foe, she may thank those very writers, for having provoked rivalship, and irritated hostility. Every one knows the all pervading influence of literature at the present day, and how much the opinions and passions of mankind are under its control. The mere contests of the sword are temporary; their wounds are but in the flesh, and it is the pride of the generous to forgive and forget them: but the slanders of the pen pierce to the heart; they rankle longest in the noblest spirits; they dwell ever present in the mind; and render it morbidly sensitive to the most trifling collision. It is but seldom that any one overt act produces hostilities between two nations; there exists, most commonly, a previous jealousy and ill will; a predisposition to take offence. Trace these to their cause, and how often will they be found to originate in the mischievous effusions of mercenary writers, who, secure in their closets, and for ignominious bread, concoct and circulate the venom, that is to inflame the generous and the brave.

I am not laying too much stress upon this point; for it applies most emphatically to our particular case. Over no nation does the press hold a more absolute control than over the people of America; for the universal education of the poorest classes, makes every individual a reader. There is nothing published in England on the subject of our country that does not circulate through every part of it. There is not a calumny dropt from an English pen, nor an unworthy sarcasm uttered by an English statesman, that does not go to blight good will and add to the mass of latent resentment. Possessing then as England does, the fountain head from whence the literature of the language flows, how completely is it in her power, and how truly is it her duty, to make it the medium of amiable and magnanimous feeling—a stream where the two nations might meet together and drink in peace and kindness. Should she, however, persist in turning it to waters of bitterness, the time may come when she may repent her folly. The present friendship of America may be of but little moment to her; but the future destinies of that country do not admit of a doubt; over those of England there lower some shadows of uncertainty. Should then a day of gloom arrive; should those reverses overtake her, from which the proudest empires have not been exempt, she may look back with regret at her infatuation, in repulsing from her side a nation she might have grappled to her bosom, and thus destroying her only chance for real friendship beyond the boundaries of her own dominions.

There is a general impression in England that the people of the United States are inimical to the parent country. It is one of the errors which has been diligently propagated by designing writers. There is doubtless considerable political hostility, and a general soreness at the illiberality of the English press, but, generally speaking, the prepossessions of the people are strongly in favour of England. Indeed at one time they amounted, in many parts of the union, to an absurd degree of bigotry. The bare name of Englishman was a passport to the confidence and hospitality of every family, and too often gave a transient currency to the worthless and the ungrateful. Throughout the country there was something of enthusiasm connected with the idea of England. We looked to it with a hallowed feeling of tenderness and veneration as the land of our forefathers—the august repository of the monuments and antiquities of our race—the birth place and mausoleum of the sages and heroes of our paternal history. After our own country there was none in whose glory we more delighted—none whose good opinion we were more anxious to possess—none towards which our hearts yearned with such throbbings of warm consanguinity. Even during the late war, whenever there was the least opportunity for kind feelings to spring forth it was the delight of the generous spirits of our country to shew that in the midst of hostilities they still kept alive the sparks of future friendship.

Is all this to be at an end? Is this golden band of kindred sympathies, so rare between nations, to be broken forever?—Perhaps it is for the best—It may dispel an illusion which might have kept us in mental vassallage; which might have interfered occasionally with our true interests, and prevented the growth of proper national pride. But it is hard to give up the kindred tie!—and there are feelings dearer than interest—closer to the heart than pride—that will still make us cast back a look of regret, as we wander farther and farther from the paternal roof, and lament the waywardness of the parent, that would repel the affections of the child.

Short sighted and injudicious, however, as the conduct of England may be in this system of aspersion, recrimination on our part would be equally ill judged. I speak not of prompt and spirited vindication of our country, nor the keenest castigation of her slanderers—but I allude to a disposition to retaliate in kind; to retort sarcasm and inspire prejudice, which seems to be spreading widely among our writers. Let us guard particularly against such a temper, for it would double the evil instead of redressing the wrong. Nothing is so easy and inviting as the retort of abuse and sarcasm; but it is a paltry and an unprofitable contest. It is the alternative of a morbid mind fretted into petulance rather than warmed into indignation. If England is willing to permit the mean jealousies of trade or the rancorous animosities of politics to deprave the integrity of her press, and poison the fountain of public opinion, let us beware of her example. She may deem it her interest to diffuse error and engender antipathy, for the purpose of checking emigration; we have no purpose of the kind to serve. Neither have we any spirit of national jealousy to gratify, for as yet, in all our rivalships with England we are the rising and the gaining party. There can be no end to answer, therefore, but the gratification of resentment; a mere spirit of retaliation, and even that is impotent. Our retorts are never republished in England; they fall short, therefore, of their aim—but they foster a querulous and peevish temper among our writers—they sour the sweet flow of our early literature, and sow thorns and brambles among its blossoms. What is still worse they circulate through our own country, and, as far as they have effect, excite virulent national prejudices. This last is the evil most especially to be deprecated. Governed as we are entirely by public opinion, the utmost care should be taken to preserve the purity of the public mind. Knowledge is power, and truth is knowledge; whoever therefore knowingly propagates a prejudice, wilfully saps the foundation of his country's strength.

The members of a republic, above all other men, should be candid and dispassionate. They are individually portions of the sovereign mind and sovereign will, and should be enabled to come to all questions of national concern with calm and unbiassed judgements. From the peculiar nature of our relations with England, we must have more frequent questions of a difficult and delicate character with her, than with any other nation; questions that affect the most acute and excitable feelings; and as in the adjusting of these, our national measures must ultimately be determined by popular sentiment, we cannot be too anxiously attentive to purify it from all latent passion or prepossession.

Opening too, as we do, an asylum for strangers from every portion of the earth, we should receive all with impartiality. It should be our pride to exhibit an example of one nation at least, destitute of national antipathies, and exercising, not merely the overt acts of hospitality but those more rare and noble courtesies which spring from liberality of opinion.

What have we to do with national prejudices? They are the inveterate diseases of old countries, contracted in rude and ignorant ages, when nations knew but little of each other, and looked beyond their own boundaries with distrust and hostility. We, on the contrary, have sprung into national existence in an enlightened and philosophic age; when the different parts of the habitable world, and the various branches of the human family, have been indefatigably studied and made known to each other; and we forego the advantages of our birth, if we do not shake off the national prejudices, as we would the local superstitions, of the old world.

But above all, let us not be influenced by any angry feelings so far as to shut our eyes to the perception of what is really excellent and amiable in the English character. We are a young people, necessarily an imitative one, and must take our examples and models, in a great degree, from the existing nations of Europe. There is no country more worthy of our study than England. The spirit of her constitution is most analogous to ours. The manners of her people,—their intellectual activity—their freedom of opinion—their habits of thinking on those subjects which concern the dearest interests and most sacred charities of private life, are all congenial to the American character; and in fact are all intrinsically excellent: for it is in the moral feeling of the people that the deep foundations of British prosperity are laid; and however the superstructure may be time worn, or over run by abuses, there must be something solid in the basis, admirable in the materials, and stable in the structure of an edifice that so long has towered unshaken amidst the tempests of the world.

Let it be the pride of our writers, therefore, discarding all feelings of irritation and disdaining to retaliate the illiberality of British authors, to speak of the English nation without prejudice, and with determined candour. While they rebuke the undiscriminating bigotry with which some of our countrymen admire and imitate every thing english, merely because it is english, let them frankly point out what is really worthy of approbation. We may thus place England before us as a perpetual volume of reference, wherein are recorded sound deductions from ages of experience; and while we avoid the errors and absurdities which may have crept into the page, we may draw from thence golden maxims of practical wisdom, wherewith to strengthen and to embellish our national character.

Rural Life in England

Oh! friendly to the best pursuits of man,
Friendly to thought, to virtue and to peace,
Domestic life in rural pleasure pass'd!

Cowper

THE STRANGER who would form a correct opinion of the English character must not confine his observations to the metropolis. He must go forth into the country; he must sojourn in villages and hamlets; he must visit castles, villas, farm houses, cottages; he must wander through parks and gardens; along hedges and green lanes; he must loiter about country churches, attend wakes and fairs and other rural festivals, and cope with the people in all their conditions, and all their habits and humours.

In some countries the large cities absorb the wealth and fashion of the nation; they are the only fixed abodes of elegant and intelligent society and the country is inhabited almost entirely by boorish peasantry. In England, on the contrary, the metropolis is a mere gathering place, or general rendezvous of the polite circles, where they devote a small portion of the year to a hurry of gaiety and dissipation, and having indulged this kind of carnival, return again to the apparently more congenial habits of rural life. The various orders of society are therefore diffused over the whole surface of the kingdom, and the most retired neighbourhoods afford specimens of the different ranks.

The English, in fact, are strongly gifted with the rural feeling. They possess a quick sensibility to the beauties of nature, and a keen relish for the pleasures and employments of the country. This passion seems inherent in them. Even the inhabitants of cities born and brought up among brick walls and bustling streets, enter with facility into rural habits and evince a tact for rural occupation. The merchant has his snug retreat in the vicinity of the metropolis, where he often displays as much pride and zeal in the cultivation of his flower garden and the maturing of his fruits as he does in the conduct of his business and the success of a commercial enterprise. Even those less fortunate individuals, who are doomed to pass their lives in the midst of din and traffic, contrive to have something that shall remind them of the green aspect of nature. In the most dark and dingy quarters of the city, the drawing room window resembles frequently a bank of flowers; every spot capable of vegetation, has its grass plot and flower bed; and every square its mimic park, laid out with picturesque taste, and gleaming with refreshing verdure.

Those who see the Englishman only in town are apt to form an unfavourable opinion of his social character. He is either absorbed in business, or distracted by the thousand engagements that dissipate time, thought and feeling, in this huge metropolis. He has therefore too commonly a look of hurry and abstraction. Wherever he happens to be, he is on the point of going somewhere else; at the moment he is talking on one subject his mind is wandering to another; and while paying a friendly visit, he is calculating how he shall economize time so as to pay the other visits allotted in the morning. An immense metropolis like London is calculated to make men selfish and uninteresting. In their casual and transient meetings they can but deal briefly in commonplaces. They present but the cold superficies of character—its rich and genial qualities have no time to be warmed into a flow.

It is in the country that the Englishman gives scope to his natural feelings. He breaks loose gladly from the cold formalities and negative civilities of town; throws off his habits of shy reserve, and becomes joyous and freehearted. He manages to collect around him all the conveniencies and elegancies of polite life, and to banish its restraints. His country seat abounds with every requisite either for studious retirement, tasteful gratification or rural exercise. Books, paintings, music, horses, dogs, and sporting implements of all kinds are at hand. He puts no constraint either upon his guests or himself, but in the true spirit of hospitality, provides the means of enjoyment, and leaves every one to partake according to his inclination.

The taste of the English in the cultivation of land and in what is called landscape gardening is unrivalled. They have studied nature intently and discover an exquisite sense of her beautiful forms and harmonious combinations. Those charms which in other countries she lavishes in wild solitudes are here assembled round the haunts of domestic life. They seem to have caught her coy and furtive graces, and spread them, like witchery, about their rural abodes.

Nothing can be more imposing than the magnificence of English park scenery. Vast lawns that extend like sheets of vivid green, with here and there clumps of gigantic trees heaping up rich piles of foliage. The solemn pomp of groves and woodland glades, with the deer trooping in silent herds across them, the hare bounding away to the covert or the pheasant suddenly bursting upon the wing. The brook, taught to wind in natural meanderings or expand into a glassy lake—The sequestered pool reflecting the quivering trees, with the yellow leaf sleeping on its bosom, and the trout roaming fearlessly about its limpid waters, while some rustic temple, or sylvan statue grown green and dank with age, gives an air of classic sanctity to the seclusion.

These are but a few of the features of park scenery; but what most delights me is the creative talent with which the English decorate the unostentatious abodes of middle life. The rudest habitation; the most unpromising and scanty portion of land, in the hands of an Englishman of taste, becomes a little paradise. With a nicely discriminating eye he seizes at once upon its capabilities, and pictures in his mind the future landscape. The sterile spot grows into loveliness under his hand; and yet the operations of art which produce the effect are scarcely to be perceived. The cherishing and training of some trees; the cautious pruning of others; the nice distribution of flowers and plants of tender and graceful foliage; the introduction of a green slope of velvet turf; the partial opening to a peep of blue distance or silver gleam of water—all these are managed with a delicate tact, a pervading yet quiet assiduity, like the magic touchings with which a painter finishes up a favourite picture.

The residence of people of fortune and refinement in the country has diffused a degree of taste and elegance in rural economy, that descends to the lowest class. The very labourer, with his thatched cottage and narrow slip of ground, attends to their embellishment. The trim hedge, the grass plot before the door, the little flower bed bordered with snug box; the

woodbine trained up against the wall and hanging its blossoms about the lattice; the pot of flowers in the window; the
holly providently planted about the house to cheat winter of
its dreariness, and to throw in a semblance of green summer
to cheer the fire side—all these bespeak the influence of taste,
flowing down from high sources, and pervading the lowest
levels of the public mind. If ever love, as poets sing, delights
to visit a cottage, it must be the cottage of an English peasant.

The fondness for rural life among the higher classes of the
English has had a great and salutary effect upon the national
character. I do not know a finer race of men than the English
gentlemen. Instead of the softness and effeminacy which char-
acterize the men of rank in most countries, they exhibit a
union of elegance and strength, a robustness of frame and
freshness of complexion, which I am inclined to attribute to
their living so much in the open air, and pursuing so eagerly
the invigorating recreations of the country. These hardy exercises produce also a healthful tone of mind and spirits, a
manliness and simplicity of manners, which even the follies
and dissipations of the town cannot easily pervert, and can
never entirely destroy. In the country too, the different orders
of society seem to approach more freely, to be more disposed
to blend and operate favourably upon each other. The distinctions between them do not appear to be so marked and
impassable as in the cities. The manner in which property has
been distributed into small estates and farms has established a
regular gradation from the nobleman, through the classes of
gentry, small landed proprietors, and substantial farmers,
down to the labouring peasantry; and while it has thus
banded the extremes of society together, has infused in each
intermediate rank a spirit of independence. This, it must be
confessed, is not so universally the case at present as it was
formerly; the larger estates having in late years of distress,
absorbed the smaller, and in some parts of the country almost
annihilated the sturdy race of small farmers. These, however,
I believe, are but casual breaks in the general system I have
mentioned.

In rural occupation there is nothing mean and debasing. It
leads a man forth among scenes of natural grandeur and
beauty; it leaves him to the workings of his own mind oper-

ated upon by the purest and most elevating of external influences. Such a man may be simple and rough, but he cannot be vulgar. The man of refinement, therefore, finds nothing revolting in an intercourse with the lower orders in rural life, as he does when he casually mingles with the lower orders of cities. He lays aside his distance and reserve, and is glad to wave the distinctions of rank, and to enter into the honest heartfelt enjoyments of common life. Indeed the very amusements of the country bring men more and more together; and the sound of hound and horn blend all feelings into harmony. I believe this is one great reason why the nobility and gentry are more popular among the inferior orders in England than they are in any other country; and why the latter have endured so many excessive pressures and extremities, without repining more generally at the unequal distribution of fortune and privilege.

To this mingling of cultivated and rustic society may also be attributed the rural feeling that runs through British literature: the frequent use of illustrations from rural life: those incomparable descriptions of nature that abound in the British poets; that have continued down from "The Flower and the Leaf" of Chaucer, and have brought into our closets all the freshness and fragrance of the dewy landscape. The pastoral writers of other countries appear as if they had paid nature an occasional visit, and become acquainted with her general charms; but the British poets have lived and revelled with her—they have wooed her in her most secret haunts, they have watched her minutest caprices. A spray could not tremble in the breeze; a leaf could not rustle to the ground; a diamond drop could not patter in the stream; a fragrance could not exhale from the humble violet, nor a daisy unfold its crimson tints to the morning, but it has been noticed by these impassioned and delicate observers, and wrought up into some beautiful morality.

The effect of this devotion of elegant minds to rural occupations has been wonderful on the face of the country. A great part of the island is rather level, and would be monotonous were it not for the charms of culture, but it is studded and gemmed, as it were, with castles and palaces, and embroidered with parks and gardens. It does not abound in grand and sublime prospects, but rather in little, home scenes of rural repose and sheltered quiet. Every antique farm house and moss grown cottage is a picture, and as the roads are continually winding, and the view shut in by groves and hedges, the eye is delighted by a continual succession of small landscapes of captivating loveliness.

The great charm, however, of English scenery is the moral feeling that seems to pervade it. It is associated in the mind with ideas of order, of quiet, of sober well established principles, of hoary usage and reverend custom. Every thing seems to be the growth of ages of regular, and peaceful existence. The old church of remote architecture, with its low massive portal; its gothic tower; its windows rich with tracery and painted glass in scrupulous preservation; its stately monuments of warriors and worthies of the olden time, ancestors of the present lords of the soil; its tombstones recording successive generations of sturdy yeomanry, whose progeny still plow the same fields and kneel at the same altar. The parsonage, a quaint irregular pile, partly antiquated, but repaired and altered in the tastes of various ages and occupants. The style and footpath leading from the church yard, across pleasant fields and along shady hedge rows, according to an immemorial right of way. The neighbouring village, with its venerable cottages, its public green sheltered by trees under which the forefathers of the present race have sported. The antique family mansion, standing apart in some little rural domain, but looking down with a protecting air on the surrounding scene.—All these common features of English landscape evince a calm and settled security, and hereditary transmission of home bred virtues and local attachments, that speak deeply and touchingly for the moral character of the nation.

It is a pleasing sight of a Sunday morning, when the bell is sending its sober melody across the quiet fields, to behold the peasantry in their best finery, with ruddy faces and modest cheerfulness, thronging tranquilly along the green lanes to church: but it is still more pleasing to see them in the evenings, gathering about their cottage doors, and appearing to exult in the humble comforts and embellishments, which their own hands have spread around them.

It is this sweet home feeling; this settled repose of affection in the domestic scene, that is, after all, the parent of the steadiest virtues and purest enjoyments, and I cannot close these desultory remarks better, than by quoting the words of a modern English poet, who has depicted it with remarkable felicity.

> Through each gradation, from the castled hall,
> The city dome, the villa crown'd with shade,
> But chief from modest mansions numberless,
> In town or hamlet shelt'ring middle life,
> Down to the cottag'd vale and straw-roof'd shed,
> This western isle hath long been fam'd for scenes
> Where bliss domestic finds a dwelling place:
> Domestic bliss, that, like a harmless dove,
> (Honour and sweet endearment keeping guard)
> Can centre in a little quiet nest
> All that desire would fly for through the earth;
> That can, the world eluding, be itself
> A world enjoy'd; that wants no witnesses
> But its own sharers, and approving heaven.
> That, like a flower deep hid in rocky cleft,
> Smiles, though 'tis looking only at the sky.*

*From a poem on the death of the Princess Charlotte, by the Reverend Rann Kennedy, A. M.

The Broken Heart

I never heard
Of any true affection but 'twas nipt
With care, that, like the caterpillar, eats
The leaves of the spring's sweetest book, the rose.

Middleton

IT IS A COMMON practice with those who have outlived the susceptibility of early feeling, or have been brought up in the gay heartlessness of dissipated life, to laugh at all love stories, and to treat the tales of romantic passion as mere fictions of novelists and poets. My observations on human nature have induced me to think otherwise. They have convinced me, that however the surface of the character may be chilled and frozen by the cares of the world, or cultivated into mere smiles by the arts of society, still there are dormant fires lurking in the depths of the coldest bosom, which, when once enkindled, become impetuous and are sometimes desolating in their effects. Indeed, I am a true believer in the blind deity, and go to the full extent of his doctrines—Shall I confess it?—I believe in broken hearts and the possibility of dying of disappointed love!—I do not, however, consider it a malady often fatal to my own sex; but I firmly believe that it withers down many a lovely woman into an early grave.

Man is the creature of interest and ambition. His nature leads him forth into the struggle and bustle of the world. Love is but the embellishment of his early life, or a song piped in the intervals of the acts. He seeks for fame, for fortune, for space in the world's thought, and dominion over his fellow men. But a woman's whole life is a history of the affections. The heart is her world: it is there her ambition strives for empire: it is there her avarice seeks for hidden treasures. She sends forth her sympathies on adventure; she embarks her whole soul in the traffic of affection, and if shipwrecked her case is hopeless, for it is a bankruptcy of the heart.

To a man the disappointment of love may occasion some bitter pangs—it wounds some feelings of tenderness—it blasts some prospects of felicity; but he is an active being—he may dissipate his thoughts in the whirl of varied occupation; or may plunge into the tide of pleasure. Or if the scene of disappointment be too full of painful associations, he can shift his abode at will, and, taking as it were the wings of the morning, can "fly to the uttermost parts of the earth and be at rest."

But woman's is comparatively a fixed, a secluded, and a meditative life. She is more the companion of her own thoughts and feelings; and if they are turned to ministers of sorrow, where shall she look for consolation! Her lot is to be wooed and won; and if unhappy in her love, her heart is like some fortress that has been captured, and sacked, and abandoned and left desolate.

How many bright eyes grow dim—how many soft cheeks grow pale—how many lovely forms fade away into the tomb, and none can tell the cause that blighted their loveliness. As the dove will clasp its wings to its side, and cover and conceal the arrow that is preying on its vitals; so is it the nature of woman to hide from the world the pangs of wounded affection. The love of a delicate female is always shy and silent. Even when fortunate, she scarcely breathes it to herself; but when otherwise, she buries it in the recesses of her bosom, and there lets it cower and brood among the ruins of her peace. With her the desire of the heart has failed. The great charm of existence is at an end. She neglects all the cheerful exercises which gladden the spirits, quicken the pulses and send the tide of life in healthful currents through the veins. Her rest is broken—the sweet refreshment of sleep is poisoned by melancholy dreams—"dry sorrow drinks her blood," until her enfeebled frame sinks under the slightest external injury. Look for her, after a little while, and you find friendship weeping over her untimely grave, and wondering that one, who but lately glowed with all the radiance of health and beauty, should so speedily be brought down to "darkness and the worm." You will be told of some wintry chill, some casual indisposition that laid her low—but no one knows of the mental malady which previously sapped her strength and made her so easy a prey to the spoiler.

She is like some tender tree, the pride and beauty of the

grove; graceful in its form; bright in its foliage, but with the worm preying at its heart. We find it suddenly withering when it should be most fresh and luxuriant. We see it drooping its branches to the earth and shedding leaf by leaf; until wasted and perished away, it falls even in the stillness of the forest; and as we muse over the beautiful ruin, we strive in vain to recollect the blast or thunderbolt that could have smitten it with decay.

I have seen many instances of women running to waste and self neglect, and disappearing gradually from the earth, almost as if they had been exhaled to heaven; and have repeatedly fancied that I could trace their deaths through the various declensions of consumption, cold, debility, languor, melancholy, until I reached the first symptom of disappointed love. But an instance of the kind was lately told to me; the circumstances are well known in the country where they happened, and I shall but give them in the manner in which they were related.

Every one must recollect the tragical story of young E—— the Irish patriot; it was too touching to be soon forgotten. During the troubles in Ireland he was tried, condemned and executed on a charge of treason. His fate made a deep impression on public sympathy. He was so young— so intelligent—so generous—so brave—so every thing that we are apt to like in a young man. His conduct under trial too was so lofty and intrepid. The noble indignation with which he repelled the charge of treason against his country— the eloquent vindication of his name, his pathetic appeal to posterity in the hopeless hour of condemnation—all these entered deeply into every generous bosom, and even his enemies lamented the stern policy that dictated his execution.

But there was one heart, whose anguish it would be impossible to describe. In happier days and fairer fortunes he had won the affections of a beautiful and interesting girl, the daughter of a late celebrated Irish Barrister. She loved him with the disinterested fervour of a woman's first and early love. When every worldly maxim arrayed itself against him; when blasted in fortune, and disgrace and danger darkened around his name, she loved him the more ardently for his very sufferings. If then his fate could awaken the sympathy even of his foes, what must have been the agony of her whose whole soul was occupied by his image! Let those tell who have had the portals of the tomb suddenly closed between them, and the being they most loved on earth—who have sat at its threshold, as one shut out in a cold and lonely world, from whence all that was most lovely and loving had departed.

But then the horrors of such a grave! so frightful—so dishonoured!—There was nothing for memory to dwell on that could soothe the pang of separation—none of those tender though melancholy circumstances which endear the parting scene—nothing to melt sorrow into those blessed tears, sent like the dews of heaven, to revive the heart in the parching hour of anguish.

To render her widowed situation more desolate, she had incurred her father's displeasure by her unfortunate attachment, and was an exile from the paternal roof. But could the sympathy and kind offices of friends have reached a spirit so shocked and driven in by horror, she would have experienced no want of consolation, for the Irish are a people of quick and generous sensibilities. The most delicate and cherishing attentions were paid her by families of wealth and distinction. She was led into society; and they tried by all kinds of occupations and amusements to dissipate her grief and wean her from the tragical story of her loves. But it was all in vain. There are some strokes of calamity which scathe and scorch the soul; which penetrate to the vital seat of happiness, and blast it, never again to put forth bud or blossom. She never objected to frequent the haunts of pleasure, but was as much alone there, as in the depths of solitude; walking about in a sad reverie, apparently unconscious of the world around her. She carried with her an inward woe that mocked at all the blandishments of friendship, and "heeded not the song of the charmer, charm he never so wisely."

The person who told me her story had seen her at a masquerade. There can be no exhibition of far gone wretchedness more striking and painful than to meet it in such a scene. To find it wandering like a spectre, lonely and joyless, where all around is gay—To see it dressed out in the trappings of mirth, and looking so wan and woe begone, as if it had tried in vain to cheat the poor heart into a momentary forgetfulness of sorrow. After strolling through the splendid rooms and giddy crowd with an air of utter abstraction, she sat herself down on the steps of an orchestra, and looking about for some time with a vacant air that shewed her insensibility to the garish scene, she began, with the capriciousness of a sickly heart, to warble a little plaintive air. She had an exquisite voice; but on this occasion it was so simple, so touching, it breathed forth such a soul of wretchedness, that she drew a crowd mute and silent around her, and melted every one into tears.

The story of one so true and tender could not but excite great interest in a country remarkable for enthusiasm. It completely won the heart of a brave officer, who paid his addresses to her, and thought that one so true to the dead, could not but prove affectionate to the living. She declined his attentions, for her thoughts were irrevocably engrossed by the memory of her former lover. He, however, persisted in his suit. He solicited not her tenderness, but her esteem. He was assisted by her conviction of his worth, and her sense of her own destitute and dependent situation, for she was existing on the kindness of friends—In a word he at length succeeded in gaining her hand, though with the solemn assurance that her heart was unalterably another's.

He took her with him to Sicily, hoping that a change of scene might wear out the remembrance of early woes. She was an amiable and exemplary wife, and made an effort to be a happy one; but nothing could cure the silent and devouring melancholy that had entered into her very soul. She wasted away in a slow but hopeless decline, and at length sunk into the grave, the victim of a broken heart.

It was on her that Moore the distinguished Irish poet composed the following lines.

> She is far from the land where her young hero sleeps,
>   And lovers around her are sighing;
> But coldly she turns from their gaze and weeps,
>   For her heart in his grave is lying.
>
> She sings the wild song of her dear native plains,
>   Every note which he lov'd awaking—
> Ah! little they think, who delight in her strains,
>   How the heart of the minstrel is breaking!

He had liv'd for his love, for his country he died;
　　They were all that to life had entwin'd him—
Nor soon shall the tears of his country be dried,
　　Nor long will his love stay behind him!

Oh! make her a grave where the sunbeams rest,
　　When they promise a glorious morrow;
They'll shine o'er her sleep, like a smile from the west,
　　From her own lov'd island of sorrow!

The Art of Book Making

If that severe doom of Synesius be true, "it is a greater offence to steal dead men's labors, than their clothes," what shall become of most writers?

Burton's Anatomy of Melancholy

I HAVE often wondered at the extreme fecundity of the press, and how it comes to pass that so many heads, on which nature seemed to have inflicted the curse of barrenness, should teem with voluminous productions. As a man travels on, however, in the journey of life his objects of wonder daily diminish, and he is continually finding out some very simple cause, for some great matter of marvel. Thus have I chanced, in my peregrinations about this great metropolis, to blunder upon a scene which unfolded to me some of the mysteries of the bookmaking craft, and at once put an end to my astonishment.

I was one summer's day loitering through the great saloons of the British Museum, with that listlessness with which one is apt to saunter about a museum in warm weather; sometimes lolling over the glass cases of minerals, sometimes studying the hieroglyphics on an Egyptian Mummy, and sometimes trying, with nearly equal success, to comprehend the allegorical paintings on the lofty ceilings. Whilst I was gazing about in this idle way my attention was attracted to a distant door, at the end of a suite of apartments. It was closed, but every now and then it would open and some strange favoured being, generally clothed in black, would steal forth and glide through the rooms without noticing any of the surrounding objects. There was an air of mystery about this that piqued my languid curiosity, and I determined to attempt the passage of that strait and to explore the unknown regions beyond. The door yielded to my hand, with that facility with which the portals of enchanted castles yield to the adventurous Knight errant. I found myself in a spacious chamber, surrounded with great cases of venerable books. Above the cases, and just under the cornice, were arranged a great number of black looking portraits of ancient authors.

About the room were placed long tables, with stands for read-ing and writing, at which sat many pale, studious personages, poring intently over dusty volumes, rummaging among mouldy manuscripts, and taking copious notes of their con-tents. A hushed stillness reigned through this mysterious apartment, excepting that you might hear the racing of pens over sheets of paper; or occasionally the deep sigh of one of these sages as he shifted his position to turn over the page of an old folio; doubtless arising from that hollowness and flat-ulency incident to learned research.

Now and then one of these personages would write some-thing on a small slip of paper and ring a bell, whereupon a familiar would appear, take the paper in profound silence, glide out of the room and return shortly loaded with ponder-ous tomes, upon which the other would fall, tooth and nail, with famished voracity. I had no longer a doubt that I had happened upon a body of Magi, deeply engaged in the study of occult sciences. The scene reminded me of an old Arabian tale, of a philosopher shut up in an enchanted library, in the bosom of a mountain, which opened only once a year; where he made the spirits of the place bring him books of all kinds of dark knowledge, so that at the end of the year, when the magic portal once more swung open on its hinges, he issued forth so versed in forbidden lore, as to be able to soar above the heads of the multitude, and to control the powers of nature.

My curiosity being now fully aroused I whispered to one of the familiars, as he was about to leave the room, and begged an interpretation of the strange scene before me. A few words were sufficient for the purpose. I found that these mysterious personages whom I had mistaken for Magi, were principally authors and in the very act of manufacturing books. I was, in fact, in the reading room of the great British library, an immense collection of volumes of all ages and lan-guages, many of which are now forgotten, and most of which are seldom read: one of these sequestered pools of obsolete literature, to which modern authors repair, and draw buckets full of classic lore, or "pure English undefiled" wherewith to swell their own scanty rills of thought.

Being now in possession of the secret, I sat down in a

corner and watched the process of this book manufactory. I noticed one lean, bilious looking wight, who sought none but the most worm eaten volumes, printed in black letter. He was evidently constructing some work of profound erudition, that would be purchased by every man who wished to be thought learned, placed upon a conspicuous shelf of his library, or laid open upon his table—but never read. I observed him now and then draw a large fragment of biscuit out of his pocket, and gnaw; whether it was his dinner, or whether he was endeavouring to keep off that exhaustion of the stomach, produced by much pondering over dry works, I leave to harder students than myself to determine.

There was one dapper little gentleman in bright coloured clothes, with a chirping, gossipping expression of countenance, who had all the appearance of an author on good terms with his bookseller. After considering him attentively, I recognized in him a diligent getter up of miscellaneous works, which bustled off well with the trade. I was curious to see how he manufactured his wares. He made more stir and shew of business than any of the others; dipping into various books, fluttering over the leaves of manuscripts, taking a morsel out of one, a morsel out of another, line upon line, precept upon precept, here a little and there a little. The contents of his book seemed to be as heterogeneous as those of the witches' cauldron in Macbeth. It was, here a finger and there a thumb; toe of frog and blind worm's sting, with his own gossip poured in like "baboon's blood," to make the medley "slab and good."

After all, thought I, may not this pilfering disposition be implanted in authors for wise purposes; may it not be the way in which providence has taken care that the seeds of knowledge and wisdom shall be preserved from age to age, in spite of the inevitable decay of the works in which they were first produced. We see that nature has wisely, though whimsically, provided for the conveyance of seeds from clime to clime in the maws of certain birds; so that animals which in themselves are little better than carrion, and apparently the lawless plunderers of the orchard and the corn field, are in fact nature's carriers to disperse and perpetuate her blessings. In like manner the beauties and fine thoughts of ancient and obsolete writers, are caught up by these flights of predatory authors, and cast forth again to flourish and bear fruit in a remote and distant tract of time. Many of their works, also, undergo a kind of metempsychosis and spring up under new forms. What was formerly a ponderous history, revives in the shape of a romance—an old legend changes into a modern play, and a sober philosophical treatise, furnishes the body for a whole series of bouncing and sparkling essays. Thus it is in the clearing of our American woodlands; where we burn down a forest of stately pines, a progeny of dwarf oaks start up in their place; and we never see the prostrate trunk of a tree, mouldering into soil, but it gives birth to a whole tribe of fungi.

Let us not then lament over the decay and oblivion into which ancient writers descend; they do but submit to the great law of nature, which declares that all sublunary shapes of matter shall be limited in their duration, but which decrees also that their elements shall never perish. Generation after generation, both in animal and vegetable life, passes away, but the vital principle is transmitted to posterity, and the species continues to flourish. Thus also do authors beget authors, and having produced a numerous progeny, in a good old age they sleep with their fathers; that is to say, with the authors who preceded them—and from whom they had stolen.

Whilst I was indulging in these rambling fancies I had leaned my head against a pile of reverend folios. Whether it was owing to the soporific emanations from these works, or to the profound quiet of the room; or to the lassitude arising from much wandering, or to an unlucky habit of napping at improper times and places, with which I am grievously afflicted, so it was that I fell into a doze. Still however my imagination continued busy, and indeed the same scene remained before my mind's eye, only a little changed in some of the details. I dreamt that the chamber was still decorated with the portraits of ancient authors, but that the number was encreased. The long tables had disappeared and in place of the sage Magi I beheld a ragged, thread bare throng, such as may be seen plying about the great repository of cast off clothes Monmouth Street. Whenever they seized upon a book, by one of those incongruities common to dreams, methought it turned into a garment of foreign or antique fashion, with which they proceeded to equip themselves. I noticed, however, that no one pretended to clothe himself from any particular suit, but took a sleeve from one, a cape from another, a skirt from a third, thus decking himself out piece meal, while some of his original rags would peep out from among his borrowed finery.

There was a portly, rosy, well fed parson whom I observed ogling several mouldy polemical writers through an eye glass. He soon contrived to slip on the voluminous mantle of one of the old fathers, and having purloined the grey beard of another, endeavoured to look exceeding wise, but the smirking commonplace of his countenance set at naught all the trappings of wisdom. One sickly looking gentleman was busied embroidering a very flimsy garment with gold thread drawn out of several old court dresses of the reign of Queen Elizabeth. Another had trimmed himself magnificently from an illuminated manuscript, had stuck a nosegay in his bosom, culled from "The Paradise of dainty Devices," and having put Sir Philip Sidney's hat on one side of his head, strutted off with an exquisite air of vulgar elegance. A third, who was but of puny dimensions, had bolstered himself out bravely with the spoils from several obscure tracts of philosophy, so that he had a very imposing front, but he was lamentably tattered in rear, and I perceived that he had patched his small clothes with scraps of parchment from a Latin author.

There were some well dressed gentlemen, it is true, who only helped themselves to a gem or so, which sparkled among their own ornaments, without eclipsing them. Some too, seemed to contemplate the costumes of the old writers merely to imbibe their principles of taste, and catch their air and spirit; but I grieve to say that too many were apt to array themselves from top to toe, in the patch work manner I have mentioned. I should not omit to speak of one genius in drab breeches and gaiters, and an arcadian hat, who had a violent propensity to the pastoral, but whose rural wanderings had been confined to the classic haunts of Primrose hill and the solitudes of the Regent's Park. He had decked himself in wreaths and ribbands from all the old pastoral poets, and hanging his head on one side, went about with a fantastical, lack-a-daisical air, "babbling about green fields." But the personage that most struck my attention was a pragmatical old gentleman in clerical robes, with a remarkably large and square, but bald head. He entered the room wheezing and puffing, elbowed his way through the throng with a look of sturdy self confidence, and having laid hands upon a thick Greek quarto, clapped it upon his head, and swept majestically away in a formidable frizzled wig.

In the height of this literary masquerade a cry suddenly resounded from every side of "Thieves! Thieves!" I looked, and lo the portraits about the walls became animated! The old authors thrust out first a head, then a shoulder from the canvass, looked down curiously for an instant upon the motley throng, and then descended, with fury in their eyes, to claim their rifled property. The scene of scampering and hubbub that ensued baffles all description. The unhappy culprits endeavoured in vain to escape with their plunder. On one side might be seen half a dozen old monks stripping a modern professor—on another there was sad devastation carried into the ranks of modern dramatic writers. Beaumont and Fletcher side by side, raged round the field like Castor and Pollux, and sturdy Ben Jonson enacted more wonders than when a volunteer with the army in Flanders. As to the dapper little compiler of farragoes mentioned sometime since, he had arrayed himself in as many patches and colours as harlequin, and there was as fierce a contention of claimants about him, as about the dead body of Patroclus. I was grieved to see many men, to whom I had been accustomed to look up with awe and reverence, fain to steal off with scarce a rag to cover their nakedness. Just then my eye was caught by the pragmatical old gentleman in the Greek grizzled wig, who was scrambling away in sore affright with half a score of authors in full cry after him. They were close upon his haunches; in a twinkling off went his wig; at every turn some strip of raiment was peeled away, until in a few moments, from his domineering pomp, he shrunk into a little, pursy "chopped bald shot," and made his exit with only a few tags and rags fluttering at his back.

There was something so ludicrous in the catastrophe of this learned Theban that I burst into an immoderate fit of laughter, which broke the whole illusion. The tumult and the scuffle were at an end. The chamber resumed its usual appearance. The old authors shrunk back into their picture frames and hung in shadowy solemnity along the walls. In short, I found myself wide awake in my corner, with the whole assemblage of Bookworms gazing at me with astonishment. Nothing of the dream had been real but my burst of laughter, a sound never before heard in that grave sanctuary, and so abhorrent to the ears of wisdom as to electrify the fraternity.

The librarian now stepped up to me and demanded whether I had a card of admission. At first I did not comprehend him, but I soon found that the library was a kind of literary "preserve," subject to game laws, and that no one must presume to hunt there without special licence and permission. In a word, I stood convicted of being an arrant poacher, and was glad to make a precipitate retreat, lest I should have a whole pack of authors let loose upon me.

A Royal Poet

Though your body be confin'd,
  And soft love a prisoner bound,
Yet the beauty of your mind,
  Neither check nor chain hath found.
    Look out nobly, then, and dare
    Even the fetters that you wear.

Fletcher

O N A SOFT sunny morning in the genial month of May, I
made an excursion to Windsor castle. It is a place full of
storied and poetical associations. The very external aspect of
the proud old pile is enough to inspire high thought. It rears
its irregular walls and massive towers, like a mural crown,
round the brow of a lofty ridge, waves its royal banner in the
clouds, and looks down, with a lordly air, upon the surrounding world.

On this morning the weather was of that voluptuous vernal
kind, which calls forth all the latent romance of a man's temperament, filling his mind with musick, and disposing him to
quote poetry and dream of beauty. In wandering through the
magnificent saloons, and long echoing galleries of the castle,
I passed with indifference by whole rows of portraits of warriors and statesmen, but lingered in the chamber, where hang
the likenesses of the beauties that graced the gay court of
Charles the Second; and as I gazed upon them, depicted with
amorous, half dishevelled tresses, and the sleepy eye of love, I
blessed the pencil of Sir Peter Lely which had thus enabled
me to bask in the reflected rays of beauty. In traversing also
the "large green courts," with sunshine beaming on the gray
walls, and glancing along the velvet turf, my mind was engrossed with the image of the tender, the gallant, but hapless
Surrey, and his account of his loiterings about them in his
stripling days when enamoured of the Lady Geraldine—

"With eyes cast up unto the maiden's tower,
  With easie sighs, such as men draw in love."

In this mood of mere poetical susceptibility, I visited the ancient Keep of the Castle, where James the First of Scotland, the pride and theme of Scottish poets and historians, was for many years of his youth detained a prisoner of state. It is a large gray tower, that has stood the brunt of ages, and is still in good preservation. It stands on a mound, which elevates it above the other parts of the castle, and a great flight of steps leads to the interior. In the armoury, which is a gothic hall furnished with weapons of various kinds and ages, I was shewn a coat of armour hanging against the wall, which had once belonged to James. From hence I was conducted up a staircase to a suite of apartments of faded magnificence, hung with storied tapestry, which formed his prison, and the scene of that passionate and fanciful amour, which has woven into the web of his story the magical hues of poetry and fiction.

The whole history of this amiable but unfortunate prince is highly romantic. At the tender age of eleven he was sent from home by his father, Robert III. and destined for the French court, to be reared under the eye of the French monarch, secure from the treachery and danger that surrounded the royal house of Scotland. It was his mishap in the course of his voyage to fall into the hands of the English, and he was detained prisoner by Henry IV., notwithstanding that a truce existed between the two countries.

The intelligence of his capture, coming in the train of many sorrows and disasters, proved fatal to his unhappy father. "The news," we are told, " was brought to him while at supper, and did so overwhelm him with grief, that he was almost ready to give up the ghost into the hands of the servants that attended him. But being carried to his bed chamber, he abstained from all food, and in three days died of hunger and grief, at Rothesay."*

James was detained in captivity above eighteen years; but, though deprived of personal liberty, he was treated with the respect due to his rank. Care was taken to instruct him in all the branches of useful knowledge cultivated at that period, and to give him those mental and personal accomplishments

*Buchanan.

deemed proper for a prince. Perhaps, in this respect, his imprisonment was an advantage, as it enabled him to apply himself the more exclusively to his improvement, and quietly to imbibe that rich fund of knowledge, and to cherish those elegant tastes, which have given such a lustre to his memory. The picture drawn of him in early life, by the Scottish historians, is highly captivating, and seems rather the description of a hero of romance, than of a character in real history. He was well learnt, we are told, "to fight with the sword, to joust, to tournay, to wrestle, to sing and dance; he was an expert mediciner, right crafty in playing both of lute and harp and sundry other instruments of musick, and was expert in grammar, oratory, and poetry."*

With this combination of manly and delicate accomplishments, fitting him to shine both in active and elegant life, and calculated to give him an intense relish for joyous existence, it must have been a severe trial, in an age of bustle and chivalry, to pass the spring time of his years in monotonous captivity. It was the good fortune of James, however, to be gifted with a powerfully poetic fancy, and to be visited in his prison by the choicest inspirations of the muse. Some minds corrode and grow inactive, under the loss of personal liberty; others grow morbid and irritable; but it is the nature of the poet to become tender and imaginative in the loneliness of confinement. He banquets upon the honey of his own thoughts, and, like the captive bird, pours forth his soul in melody.

> Have you not seen the nightingale
>   A pilgrim coop'd into a cage,
> How doth she chant her wonted tale,
>   In that her lonely hermitage!
> Even there her charming melody doth prove
> That all her boughs are trees, her cage a grove.†

Indeed, it is the divine attribute of the imagination, that it is irrepressible, unconfinable. That when the real world is shut out, it can create a world for itself, and with a necromantic power, can conjure up glorious shapes and forms, and bril-

*Ballenden's Translation of Hector Boyce.
†Roger l'Estrange.

liant visions, to make solitude populous, and irradiate the
gloom of the dungeon. Such was the world of pomp and
pageant that lived round Tasso in his dismal cell at Ferrara,
when he conceived the splendid scenes of his Jerusalem; and
we may consider the "King's Quair," composed by James
during his captivity at Windsor, as another of those beautiful
breakings forth of the soul from the restraint and gloom of
the prison house.

The subject of the poem is his love for the Lady Jane Beau-
fort, daughter of the Earl of Somerset, and a princess of the
blood royal of England, of whom he became enamoured in
the course of his captivity. What gives it peculiar value is, that
it may be considered a transcript of the royal bard's true feelings, and the story of his real loves and fortunes. It is not
often that sovereigns write poetry, or that poets deal in fact.
It is gratifying to the pride of a common man, to find a monarch thus suing, as it were, for admission into his closet, and
seeking to win his favour by administering to his pleasures. It
is a proof of the honest equality of intellectual competition,
which strips off all the trappings of factitious dignity, brings
the candidate down to a level with his fellow men, and
obliges him to depend on his own native powers for distinction. It is curious, too, to get at the history of a monarch's
heart, and to find the simple affections of human nature
throbbing under the ermine. But James had learnt to be a
poet before he was a king: he was schooled in adversity, and
reared in the company of his own thoughts. Monarchs have
seldom time to parley with their hearts, or meditate their
minds into poetry; and had James been brought up amidst
the adulation and gaiety of a court, we should never, in all
probability, have had such a poem as the Quair.

I have been particularly interested by those parts of the
poem which breathe his immediate thoughts concerning his
situation, or which are connected with the apartment in the
tower. They have thus a personal and local charm, and are
given with such circumstantial truth, as to make the reader
present with the captive in his prison, and the companion of
his meditations.

Such is the account which he gives of his weariness of
spirit, and of the incident which first suggested the idea of

writing the poem. It was the still mid-watch of a clear moon-light night; the stars, he says, were twinkling as fire in the high vault of heaven; and "Cynthia rinsing her golden locks in Aquarius." He lay in bed, wakeful and restless, and took a book to beguile the tedious hours. The book he chose was Boetius' Consolations of Philosophy, a work popular among the writers of that day, and which had been translated by his great prototype Chaucer. From the high eulogium in which he indulges, it is evident this was one of his favourite volumes while in prison; and indeed it is an admirable text book for meditation under adversity. It is the legacy of a noble and enduring spirit, purified by sorrow and suffering, bequeathing to its successors in calamity, the maxims of sweet morality, and the trains of eloquent but simple reasoning, by which it was enabled to bear up against the various ills of life. It is a talisman, which the unfortunate may treasure up in his bosom, or like the good King James, lay upon his nightly pillow.

After closing the volume, he turns its contents over in his mind, and gradually falls into a fit of musing on the fickleness of fortune, the vicissitudes of his own life, and the evils that had overtaken him even in his tender youth. Suddenly he hears the bell ringing to matins; but its sound chiming in with his melancholy fancies, seems to him like a voice exhorting him to write his story. In the spirit of poetic errantry he determines to comply with this intimation; he therefore takes pen in hand, makes with it a sign of the cross to implore a benediction, and sallies forth into the fairy land of poetry. There is something extremely fanciful in all this, and it is interesting as furnishing a striking and beautiful instance of the simple manner in which whole trains of poetical thought are sometimes awakened, and literary enterprises suggested to the mind.

In the course of his poem he more than once bewails the peculiar hardness of his fate; thus doomed to lonely and inactive life, and shut up from the freedom and pleasure of the world, in which the meanest animal indulges unrestrained. There is a sweetness however in his very complaints; they are the lamentations of an amiable and social spirit at being denied the indulgence of its kind and generous propensities;

there is nothing in them harsh nor exaggerated; they flow with a natural and touching pathos, and are perhaps rendered more touching by their simple brevity. They contrast finely with those elaborate and iterated repinings, which we sometimes meet with, in poetry;—the effusions of morbid minds, sickening under miseries of their own creating, and venting their bitterness upon an unoffending world. James speaks of his privations with acute sensibility, but having mentioned them passes on, as if his manly mind disdained to brood over unavoidable calamities. When such a spirit breaks forth into complaint, however brief, we are aware how great must be the suffering that extorts the murmur. We sympathize with James, a romantic, active, and accomplished prince, cut off in the lustihood of youth from all the enterprise, the noble uses, and vigorous delights of life; as we do with Milton, alive to all the beauties of nature and glories of art, when he breathes forth brief, but deep toned lamentations, over his perpetual blindness.

Had not James evinced a deficiency of poetic artifice, we might almost have suspected that these lourings of gloomy reflection were meant as preparative to the brightest scene of his story; and to contrast with that refulgence of light and loveliness, that exhilarating accompaniment of bird and song, and foliage and flower, and all the revel of the year, with which he ushers in the lady of his heart. It is this scene in particular, which throws all the magic of romance about the old castle keep. He had risen, he says, at day break, according to custom, to escape from the dreary meditations of a sleepless pillow. "Bewailing in his chamber thus alone," despairing of all joy and remedy, "fortired of thought and wo begone," he had wandered to the window, to indulge the captive's miserable solace of gazing wistfully upon the world from which he is excluded. The window looked forth upon a small garden which lay at the foot of the tower. It was a quiet, sheltered spot, adorned with arbours and green alleys, and protected from the passing gaze by trees and hawthorn hedges.

> Now was there made fast by the tower's wall,
>   A garden faire, and in the corners set,
> An arbour green with wandis long and small

Railed about, and so with leaves beset
Was all the place and hawthorn hedges knet,
　That lyf* was none, walkyng there forbye,
　That might within scarce any wight espye.

So thick the branches and the leves grene,
　Beshaded all the alleys that there were,
And midst of every arbour might be seen
　The sharpe, grene, sweet juniper,
Growing so fair, with branches here and there,
　That as it seemed to a lyf without,
　The boughs did spread the arbour all about.

And on the small grene twistis† set
　The lytel swete nightingales and sung
So loud and clere, the hymnis consecrate
　Of lovis use, now soft, now loud among,
That all the garden and the wallis rung
Right of their song——

It was the month of May, when every thing was in bloom;
and he interprets the song of the nightingale into the language of his enamoured feeling:

Worship all ye that lovers be this May,
　For of your bliss the kalends are begun,
And sing with us, away, winter away,
　Come, summer come, the sweet season and sun.

As he gazes on the scene, and listens to the notes of the
birds, he gradually lapses into one of those tender and undefinable reveries, which fill the youthful bosom in this delicious
season. He wonders what this love may be, of which he has
so often read, and which thus seems breathed forth in the
quickening breath of May, and melting all nature into ecstacy
and song. If it really be so great a felicity, and if it be a boon

*_Lyf,_ person.
†_Twistis,_ small boughs or twigs.
Note.—The language of the quotations is generally modernized.

thus generally dispensed to the most insignificant beings, why is he alone cut off from its enjoyments?

> Oft would I think, O Lord, what, may this be
>   That love is of such noble myght and kynde?
> Loving his folk, and such prosperitee
> Is it of him, as we in books do find:
>   May he oure hertes setten* and unbynd:
> Hath he upon our hertes such maistrye?
> Or is all this but feynit fantasye?
>
> For giff he be of so grete excellence,
>   That he of every wight hath care and charge,
> What have I gilt† to him, or done offense?
>   That I am thral'd, and birdis go at large.

In the midst of his musing, as he casts his eye downward, he beholds "the fairest and the freshest young floure," that ever he had seen. It is the lovely lady Jane walking in the garden to enjoy the beauty of that "fresh May morrowe." Breaking thus suddenly upon his sight in the moment of loneliness and excited susceptibility, she at once captivates the fancy of the romantic prince, and becomes the object of his wandering wishes, the sovereign of his ideal world.

There is, in this charming scene, an evident resemblance to the early part of Chaucer's Knight's Tale; where Palamon and Arcite fall in love with Emilia, whom they see walking in the garden of their prison. Perhaps the similarity of the actual fact to the incident which he had read in Chaucer, may have induced James to dwell on it in his poem. His description of the Lady Jane is given in the picturesque and minute manner of his master; and being doubtless taken from the life, is a perfect portrait of a beauty of that day. He dwells, with the fondness of a lover, on every article of her apparel, from the net of pearl, splendent with emeralds and sapphires, that confined her golden hair, even to the "goodly chaine of small orfeverye‡" about her neck, whereby there hung a ruby in

---

* *Setten,* incline.
† *Gilt,* what injury have I done, &c.
‡Wrought gold.

shape of a heart, that seemed, he says, like a spark of fire burning upon her white bosom. Her dress of white tissue was looped up to enable her to walk with more freedom. She was accompanied by two female attendants, and about her sported a little hound decorated with bells; probably the small Italian hound of exquisite symmetry, which was a parlour favourite and pet among the fashionable dames of ancient times. James closes his description by a burst of general eulogium.

> In her was youth, beauty, with humble port,
>   Bountee, richesse, and womanly feature;
> God better knows than my pen can report,
>   Wisdom, largesse,* estate,† and cunning‡ sure,
> In every point so guided her mesure,
>   In word, in deed, in shape, in countenance,
>   That nature might no more her child advance.

The departure of the lady Jane from the garden, puts an end to this transient riot of the heart. With her departs the amorous illusion that had shed a temporary charm over the scene of his captivity, and he relapses into loneliness, now rendered tenfold more intolerable by this passing beam of unattainable beauty. Through the long and weary day he repines at his unhappy lot, and when evening approaches, and Phœbus, as he beautifully expresses it, had "bad farewell to every leaf and flower," he still lingers at the window, and laying his head upon the cold stone, gives vent to a mingled flow of love and sorrow, until gradually lulled by the mute melancholy of the twilight hour, he lapses "half sleeping, half swoon," into a vision which occupies the remainder of the poem, and in which is allegorically shadowed out the history of his passion.

When he wakes from his trance, he rises from his stony pillow, and, pacing his apartment, full of dreary reflections, questions his spirit whither it has been wandering; whether, indeed, all that has passed before his dreaming fancy, has been conjured up by preceding circumstances; or whether it

* *Largesse,* bounty.
† *Estate,* dignity.
‡ *Cunning,* discretion.

is a vision, intended to comfort and assure him in his despondency. If the latter, he prays that some token may be sent to confirm the promise of happier days, given him in his slumbers. Suddenly a turtle dove, of the purest whiteness, comes flying in at the window and alights upon his hand, bearing in her bill a branch of red gilliflower, on the leaves of which is written, in letters of gold, the following sentence:

> Awake! awake! I bring, lover, I bring
> The newis glad that blissful is, and sure
> Of thy comfort; now laugh, and play, and sing,
> For in the heaven decretit is thy cure.

He receives the branch with mingled hope and dread; reads it with rapture: and this, he says, was the first token of his succeeding happiness. Whether this is a mere poetic fiction, or whether the Lady Jane did actually send him a token of her favour in this romantic way, remains to be determined according to the faith or fancy of the reader. He concludes his poem, by intimating that the promise conveyed in the vision and by the flower, is fulfilled, by his being restored to liberty, and made happy in the possession of the sovereign of his heart.

Such is the poetical account given by James of his love adventures in Windsor Castle. How much of it is absolute fact, and how much the embellishment of fancy, it is fruitless to conjecture: let us not, however, reject every romantic incident as incompatible with real life; but let us sometimes take a poet at his word. I have noticed merely those parts of the poem immediately connected with the Tower, and have passed over a large part, written in the allegorical vein, so much cultivated at that day. The language, of course, is quaint and antiquated, so that the beauty of many of its golden phrases will scarcely be perceived at the present day; but it is impossible not to be charmed with the genuine sentiment, the delightful artlessness and urbanity, which prevail throughout it. The descriptions of nature, too, with which it is embellished, are given with a truth, a discrimination, and a freshness, worthy of the most cultivated periods of the art.

As an amatory poem it is edifying, in these days of coarser

thinking, to notice the nature, refinement, and exquisite delicacy which pervade it; banishing every gross thought or immodest expression, and presenting female loveliness, clothed in all its chivalrous attributes of almost supernatural purity and grace.

James flourished nearly about the time of Chaucer and Gower, and was evidently an admirer and studier of their writings. Indeed in one of his stanzas he acknowledges them as his masters; and in some parts of his poem we find traces of similarity to their productions, more especially to those of Chaucer. There are always, however, general features of resemblance in the works of contemporary authors, which are not so much borrowed from each other as from the times. Writers, like bees, toll their sweets in the wide world; they incorporate with their own conceptions the anecdotes and thoughts current in society; and thus each generation has some features in common, characteristic of the age in which it lives.

James belongs to one of the most brilliant eras of our literary history, and establishes the claims of his country to a participation in its primitive honours. Whilst a small cluster of English writers are constantly cited as the fathers of our verse, the name of their great Scottish compeer is apt to be passed over in silence; but he is evidently worthy of being enrolled in that little constellation of remote but never failing luminaries, who shine in the highest firmament of literature, and who, like morning stars, sang together at the bright dawning of British poesy.

Such of my readers as may not be familiar with Scottish history (though the manner in which it has of late been woven with captivating fiction, has made it a universal study), may be curious to learn something of the subsequent history of James, and the fortunes of his love. His passion for the Lady Jane, as it was the solace of his captivity, so it facilitated his release, it being imagined by the court that a connection with the blood royal of England would attach him to its interests. He was ultimately restored to his liberty and crown, having previously espoused the Lady Jane, who accompanied him to Scotland, and made him a most tender and devoted wife.

He found his kingdom in great confusion, the feudal chieftains having taken advantage of the troubles and irregularities
of a long interregnum to strengthen themselves in their possessions, and place themselves above the power of the laws.
James sought to found the basis of his power in the affections
of his people. He attached the lower orders to him by the
reformation of abuses, the temperate and equable administration of justice, the encouragement of the arts of peace, and
the promotion of every thing that could diffuse comfort,
competency, and innocent enjoyment through the humblest
ranks of society. He mingled occasionally among the common
people in disguise; visited their fire sides; entered into their
cares, their pursuits, and their amusements; informed himself
of the mechanical arts, and how they could best be patronized
and improved; and was thus an all pervading spirit, watching
with a benevolent eye over the meanest of his subjects. Having in this generous manner, made himself strong in the
hearts of the common people, he turned himself to curb the
power of the factious nobility; to strip them of those dangerous immunities which they had usurped; to punish such as
had been guilty of flagrant offences; and to bring the whole
into proper obedience to the crown. For some time they bore
this with outward submission, but secret impatience and
brooding resentment. A conspiracy was at length formed
against his life, at the head of which was his own uncle, Robert Stewart Earl of Athol, who, being too old himself for the
perpetration of the deed of blood, instigated his grandson Sir
Robert Stewart, together with Sir Robert Graham, and others of less note, to commit the deed. They broke into his bed
chamber at the Dominican Convent near Perth, where he was
residing, and barbarously murdered him by oft repeated
wounds. His faithful queen rushing to throw her tender body
between him and the sword, was twice wounded in the ineffectual attempt to shield him from the assassin, and it was not
until she had been forcibly torn from his person, that the
murder was accomplished.

It was the recollection of this romantic tale of former times,
and of the golden little poem which had its birth place in this
tower, that made me visit the old pile with more than common interest. The suit of armour hanging up in the hall,

richly gilt and embellished as if to figure in the tournay, brought the image of the gallant and romantic prince vividly before my imagination. I paced the deserted chambers where he had composed his poem; I leaned upon the window and endeavoured to persuade myself it was the very one where he had been visited by his vision; I looked out upon the spot where he had first seen the Lady Jane. It was the same genial and joyous month; the birds were again vying with each other in strains of liquid melody; every thing was bursting into vegetation, and budding forth the tender promise of the year. Time, which delights to obliterate the sterner memorials of human pride, seems to have passed lightly over this little scene of poetry and love, and to have withheld his desolating hand. Several centuries have gone by, yet the garden still flourishes at the foot of the tower. It occupies what was once the moat of the keep; and though some parts have been separated by dividing walls, yet others have still their arbours and shaded walks, as in the days of James, and the whole is sheltered, blooming, and retired. There is a charm about a spot that has been printed by the footsteps of departed beauty, and consecrated by the inspirations of the poet, which is heightened, rather than impaired, by the lapse of ages. It is, indeed, the gift of poetry to hallow every place in which it moves; to breathe round nature an odour more exquisite than the perfume of the rose, and to shed over it a tint more magical than the blush of morning.

Others may dwell on the illustrious deeds of James as a warrior and a legislator; but I have delighted to view him merely as the companion of his fellow man, the benefactor of the human heart, stooping from his high estate to sow the sweet flowers of poetry and song in the paths of common life. He was the first to cultivate the vigorous and hardy plant of Scottish genius, which has since become so prolific of the most wholesome and highly flavoured fruit. He carried with him into the sterner regions of the north, all the fertilizing arts of southern refinement. He did every thing in his power to win his countrymen to the gay, the elegant, and gentle arts, which soften and refine the character of a people, and wreathe a grace round the loftiness of a proud and warlike spirit. He wrote many poems, which, unfortunately for the fullness of

his fame, are now lost to the world; one which is still preserved, called "Christ's Kirk of the Green," shews how diligently he had made himself acquainted with the rustic sports
and pastimes, which constitute such a source of kind and social feeling among the Scottish peasantry; and with what simple and happy humour he could enter into their enjoyments.
He contributed greatly to improve the national music; and
traces of his tender sentiment, and elegant taste, are said to
exist in those witching airs, still piped among the wild mountains and lonely glens of Scotland. He has thus connected his
image with whatever is most gracious and endearing in the
national character; he has embalmed his memory in song, and
floated his name to after ages in the rich stream of Scottish
melody. The recollection of these things was kindling at my
heart, as I paced the silent scene of his imprisonment. I have
visited Vaucluse with as much enthusiasm as a pilgrim would
visit the shrine at Loretto; but I have never felt more poetical
devotion than when contemplating the old tower and the little garden at Windsor, and musing over the romantic loves of
the Lady Jane and the Royal Poet of Scotland.

The Country Church

A gentleman?
What, o'the woolpack? or the sugar chest?
Or lists of velvet? which is't pound, or yard,
You vend your gentry by?

Beggar's Bush

THERE ARE FEW places more favourable to the study of character than an English country church. I was once passing a few weeks at the seat of a friend who resided in the vicinity of one the appearance of which particularly struck my fancy. It was one of those rich morsels of quaint antiquity which give such a peculiar charm to English landscape. It stood in the midst of a county filled with ancient families, and contained within its cold and silent aisles, the congregated dust of many noble generations. The interior walls were encrusted with monuments of every age and style. The light streamed through windows dimmed with armorial bearings, richly emblazoned in stained glass. In various parts of the church were tombs of knights and high born dames of gorgeous workmanship, with their effigies in coloured marble. On every side the eye was struck with some instance of aspiring mortality; some haughty memorial which human pride had erected over its kindred dust, in this temple of the most humble of all religions.

The congregation was composed of the neighbouring people of rank, who sat in pews sumptuously lined and cushioned, furnished with richly gilded prayer books, and decorated with their arms upon the pew doors;—the villagers and peasantry, who filled the back seats, and a small gallery beside the organ, and the poor of the parish, who were ranged on benches in the aisles.

The service was performed by a snuffling well fed vicar, who had a snug dwelling near the church. He was a privileged guest at all the tables of the neighbourhood and had been the keenest foxhunter in the county, until age and good living had disabled him from doing any thing more than ride to see the hounds throw off, and make one at the hunting dinner.

Under the ministry of such a pastor I found it impossible to get into the train of thought suitable to the time and place, so having, like many other feeble christians, compromised with my conscience by laying the sin of my own delinquency at another person's threshold, I occupied myself by making observations of my neighbours.

I was as yet a stranger in England, and curious to notice the manners of its fashionable classes. I found, as usual, that there was the least pretension where there was the most acknowledged title to respect. I was particularly struck for instance, with the family of a nobleman of high rank, consisting of several sons and daughters. Nothing could be more simple and unassuming than their appearance. They generally came to church in the plainest equipage, and often on foot. The young ladies would stop and converse in the kindest manner with the peasantry, caress the children, and listen to the stories of the humble cottagers. Their countenances were open, beautifully fair, with an expression of high refinement, but at the same time a frank cheerfulness and an engaging affability. Their brothers were tall and elegantly formed. They were dressed fashionably but simply; with strict neatness and propriety, but without any mannerism or foppishness. Their whole demeanour was easy and natural, with that lofty grace and noble frankness, which bespeak free born souls that have never been checked in their growth by feelings of inferiority. There is a healthful hardiness about real dignity, that never dreads contact and communion with others, however humble. It is only spurious pride that is morbid and sensitive and shrinks from every touch. I was pleased to see the manner in which they would converse with the peasantry about those rural concerns and field sports, in which the gentlemen of this country so much delight. In these conversations there was neither haughtiness on the one part, nor servility on the other; and you were only reminded of the difference of rank by the habitual respect of the peasant.

In contrast to these was the family of a wealthy citizen, who had amassed a vast fortune, and having purchased the estate and mansion of a ruined nobleman in the neighbourhood, was endeavouring to assume all the style and dignity of an hereditary lord of the soil. The family always came to church *en prince*. They were rolled majestically along in a carriage emblazoned with arms. The crest glittered in silver radiance from every part of the harness where a crest could possibly be placed. A fat coachman in a three cornered hat, richly laced, and a flaxen wig, curling close around his rosy face, was seated on the box, with a sleek Danish dog beside him. Two footmen in gorgeous liveries, with huge boquets and gold headed canes lolled behind. The carriage rose and sunk on its long springs with peculiar stateliness of motion. The very horses champed their bits, arched their necks and glanced their eyes more proudly than common horses, either because they had caught a little of the family feeling, or were reined up more tightly than ordinary.

I could not but admire the style with which this splendid pageant was brought up to the gate of the church yard. There was a vast effect produced at the turning of an angle of the wall. A great cracking of the whip—straining and scrambling of the horses—glistering of harness and flashing of wheels through gravel. This was the moment of triumph and vain glory to the Coachman. The horses were urged and checked until they were fretted into a foam. They threw out their feet in a prancing trot, dashing about pebbles at every step. The crowd of villagers sauntering quietly to church opened precipitately to the right and left, gaping in vacant admiration—On reaching the gate the horses were pulled up with a suddenness that produced an immediate stop and almost threw them on their haunches.

There was an extraordinary hurry of the footmen to alight, open the door, pull down the steps and prepare every thing for the descent on earth of this august family. The old citizen first emerged his round red face from out the door, looking about him with the pompous air of a man accustomed to rule on change and shake the stock market with a nod. His consort, a fine, fleshy, comfortable dame followed him. There seemed, I must confess, but little pride in her composition. She was the picture of broad, honest, vulgar enjoyment. The world went well with her—and she liked the world. She had fine clothes, a fine house, a fine carriage, fine children, every thing was fine about her: it was nothing but driving about, and visiting, and feasting. Life was to her a perpetual revel; it was one long, lord mayor's day.

Two daughters succeeded to this goodly couple. They certainly were handsome but had a supercilious air, that chilled admiration and disposed the spectator to be critical. They were ultra-fashionables in dress, and though no one could deny the richness of their decorations, yet their appropriateness might be questioned amidst the simplicity of a country church. They descended loftily from the carriage and moved up the line of peasantry, with a step that seemed dainty of the soil it trod on. They cast an excursive glance around that passed coldly over the burly faces of the peasantry, until they met the eyes of the nobleman's family, when their countenances immediately brightened into smiles and they made the most profound and elegant courtsies; which were returned in a manner that shewed they were but slight acquaintances.

I must not forget the two sons of this aspiring citizen, who came to church in a dashing curricle with outriders. They were arrayed in the extremity of the mode, with all that pedantry of dress, which marks the man of questionable pretensions to style. They kept entirely by themselves, eying every one askance that came near them; as if measuring his claims to respectability; yet they were without conversation, except the exchange of an occasional cant phrase. They even moved artificially, for their bodies, in compliance with the caprice of the day, had been disciplined into the absence of all ease and freedom. Art had done every thing to accomplish them as men of fashion, but nature had denied the nameless grace. They were vulgarly shaped, like men formed for the common purposes of life and had that air of supercilious assumption which is never seen in the true gentleman.

I have been rather minute in drawing the pictures of these two families, because I considered them specimens of what is often to be met with in this country—the unpretending great and the arrogant little. I have no respect for titled rank, unless it be accompanied by true nobility of soul; but I have remarked, in all countries where artificial distinctions exist, the very highest classes are always the most courteous and unassuming—Those who are well assured of their own standing are least apt to trespass on that of others; whereas nothing is so offensive as the aspirings of vulgarity, which thinks to elevate itself by humiliating its neighbour.

As I have brought these families into contrast I must notice their behaviour in church. That of the nobleman's family was quiet, serious and attentive. Not that they appeared to have any fervour of devotion but rather a respect for sacred things and sacred places, inseparable from good breeding. The others on the contrary were in a perpetual flutter and whisper; they betrayed a continual consciousness of finery, and a sorry ambition of being the wonders of a rural congregation.

The old gentleman was the only one really attentive to the service. He took the whole burthen of family devotion upon himself; standing bolt upright and uttering the responses with a loud voice that might be heard all over the church. It was evident that he was one of those thorough Church and King men who connect the idea of devotion and loyalty; who consider the deity somehow or other, of the government party, and religion "a very excellent sort of thing that ought to be countenanced and kept up."

When he joined so loudly in the service it seemed more by way of example to the lower orders, to shew them, that though so great and wealthy, he was not above being religious, as I have seen a turtle fed alderman swallow publicly a basin of charity soup, smacking his lips at every mouthful and pronouncing it "excellent food for the poor."

When the service was at an end I was curious to witness the several exits of my groups. The young noblemen and their sisters as the day was fine preferred strolling home across the fields, chatting with the country people as they went. The others departed as they came, in grand parade. Again were the equipages wheeled up to the gate. There was again the smacking of whips, the clattering of hoofs and the glittering of harness. The horses started off almost at a bound; the villagers again hurried to right and left; the wheels threw up a cloud of dust, and the aspiring family was rapt out of sight in a whirlwind.

The Widow and Her Son

Pittie olde age, within whose silver haires
Honour and reverence ever more have raign'd.
Marlowe's Tamburlaine

THOSE WHO ARE in the habit of remarking such matters
must have noticed the pensive quiet of an English landscape on Sunday. The clacking of the mill, the regularly recurring stroke of the flail; the din of the blacksmith's
hammer; the whistling of the plowman; the rattling of the
cart, and all other sounds of rural labor are suspended. The
very farm dogs bark less frequently, being less disturbed by
passing travellers. At such times I have almost fancied the
winds sunk into quiet and that the sunny landscape, with its
fresh green tints melting into blue haze, enjoyed the hallowed
calm.

> Sweet day, so pure, so calm, so bright,
> The bridal of the earth and sky.

Well was it ordained that the day of devotion should be a day
of rest. The holy repose which reigns over the face of nature,
has its moral influence; every restless passion is charmed
down, and we feel the natural religion of the soul gently
springing up within us. For my part there are feelings that
visit me, in a country church, amid the beautiful serenity of
nature, which I experience no where else; and if not a more
religious, I think I am a better man on Sunday than on any
other day of the seven.

During my recent residence in the country I used frequently to attend at the old village church. Its shadowy aisles;
its mouldering monuments; its dark oaken panelling, all reverend with the gloom of departed years, seemed to fit it for
the haunt of solemn meditation; but being in a wealthy aristocratic neighborhood, the glitter of fashion penetrated even
into the sanctuary; and I felt myself continually thrown back
upon the world by the frigidity and pomp of the poor worms
around me. The only being in the whole congregation who

834

appeared thoroughly to feel the humble and prostrate piety of a true christian, was a poor, decrepid old woman, bending under the weight of years and infirmities. She bore the traces of something better than abject poverty. The lingerings of decent pride were visible in her appearance. Her dress, though humble in the extreme, was scrupulously clean. Some trivial respect too had been awarded her, for she did not take her seat among the village poor, but sat alone on the steps of the altar. She seemed to have survived all love, all friendship, all society, and to have nothing left her but the hopes of heaven. When I saw her feebly rising and bending her aged form in prayer; habitually conning her prayer book, which her palsied hand and failing eyes would not permit her to read, but which she evidently knew by heart—I felt persuaded that the faltering voice of that poor woman arose to heaven far before the responses of the clerk, the swell of the organ or the chaunting of the choir.

I am fond of loitering about country churches, and this was so delightfully situated that it frequently attracted me. It stood on a knoll, round which a small stream made a beautiful bend and then wound its way through a long reach of soft meadow scenery. The church was surrounded by yew trees, which seemed almost coeval with itself. Its tall gothic spire shot up lightly from among them, with rooks and crows generally wheeling about it. I was seated there one still sunny morning watching two labourers who were digging a grave. They had chosen one of the most remote and neglected corners of the church yard, where, from the number of nameless graves around, it would appear that the indigent and friendless were huddled into the earth. I was told that the new made grave was for the only son of a poor widow. While I was meditating on the distinctions of worldly rank, which extend thus down into the very dust, the toll of the bell announced the approach of the funeral. They were the obsequies of poverty, with which pride had nothing to do. A coffin of the plainest materials, without pall or other covering, was borne by some of the villagers. The sexton walked before with an air of cold indifference. There were no mock mourners in the trappings of affected woe, but there was one real mourner who feebly tottered after the corpse. It was the aged mother of the deceased—the poor old woman whom I had seen seated on the steps of the altar. She was supported by a humble friend, who was endeavouring to comfort her. A few of the neighbouring poor had joined the train, and some children of the village were running, hand in hand, now shouting with unthinking mirth, and now pausing to gaze with childish curiosity on the grief of the mourner.

As the funeral train approached the grave the parson issued from the church porch arrayed in the surplice, with prayer book in hand and attended by the clerk. The service, however, was a mere act of charity. The deceased had been destitute and the survivor was penniless. It was shuffled through, therefore, in form, but coldly and unfeelingly. The well fed priest moved but a few steps from the church door—his voice could scarcely be heard at the grave, and never did I hear the funeral service, that sublime and touching ceremony, turned into such a frigid mummery of words.

I approached the grave. The coffin was placed on the ground. On it were inscribed the name and age of the deceased. "George Somers, aged 26 Years." The poor mother had been assisted to kneel down at the head of it. Her withered hands were clasped as if in prayer, but I could perceive by a feeble rocking of the body, and a convulsive motion of the lips, that she was gazing on the last reliques of her son with the yearnings of a mother's heart.

Preparations were made to deposit the coffin in the earth. There was that bustling stir, which breaks so harshly on the feelings of grief and affection—directions given in the cold tones of business—the striking of spades into sand and gravel, which, at the grave of those we love, is of all sounds the most withering. The bustle around seemed to awaken the mother from a wretched reverie. She raised her glazed eyes, and looked about, with a faint wildness. As the men approached with cords to lower the coffin into the grave she wrung her hands and broke into an agony of grief. The poor woman who attended her took her by the arm, endeavouring to raise her from the earth and to whisper something like consolation—"Nay now—nay now—don't take it so sorely to heart—" She could only shake her head and wring her hands, as one not to be comforted.

As they lowered the body into the earth the creaking of the cords seemed to agonize her; but when, on some accidental obstruction there was a justling of the coffin, all the tenderness of the mother burst forth; as if any harm could come to him, who was far beyond the reach of worldly suffering.

I could see no more—my heart swelled into my throat—my eyes filled with tears—I felt as if I were acting a barbarous part in standing by and gazing idly on this scene of maternal anguish. I wandered to another part of the church yard where I remained until the funeral train had dispersed.

When I saw the mother slowly and painfully quitting the grave, leaving behind her the remains of all that was dear to her on earth, and returning to silence and destitution, my heart ached for her—What, thought I, are the distresses of the rich!—they have friends to soothe; pleasures to beguile; a world to divert and dissipate their griefs—What are the sorrows of the young! Their growing minds soon close above the wound—their elastic spirits soon rise beneath the pressure—their green and ductile affections soon twine around new objects—But the sorrows of the poor, who have no outward appliances to soothe—the sorrows of the aged with whom life at best is but a wintry day, and who can look for no aftergrowth of joy—the sorrows of a widow, aged, solitary, destitute, mourning over an only son the last solace of her years—these are indeed sorrows which make us feel the impotency of consolation.

It was some time before I left the church yard—on my way homeward I met with the woman who had acted as comforter: she was just returning from accompanying the mother to her lonely habitation, and I drew from her some particulars connected with the affecting scene I had witnessed.

The parents of the deceased had resided in the village from childhood. They had inhabited one of the neatest cottages, and by various rural occupations and the assistance of a small garden, had supported themselves creditably and comfortably, and led a happy and a blameless life. They had one son who had grown up to be the staff and pride of their age—"Oh sir!" said the good woman, "he was such a likely lad; so sweet tempered; so kind to every one round him; so dutiful to his parents! It did one's heart good to see him of a Sunday, drest out in his best, so tall, so straight, so cheery—supporting his old mother to church—for she was always fonder of leaning on George's arm than on her good man's—and, poor soul, she might well be proud of him, for a finer lad, there was not in the country round."

Unfortunately the son was tempted during a year of scarcity and agricultural hardship, to enter into the service of one of the small craft that plied on a neighbouring river. He had not been long in this employ when he was entrapped by a press gang and carried off to sea. His parents received tidings of his seizure, but beyond that they could learn nothing. It was the loss of their main prop. The father who was already infirm, grew heartless and melancholy and sunk into his grave. The widow left lonely in her age and feebleness could no longer support herself, and came upon the parish. Still there was a kind feeling towards her throughout the village and a certain respect as being one of the oldest inhabitants. As no one applied for the cottage in which she had passed so many happy days, she was permitted to remain in it, where she lived solitary and almost helpless—The few wants of nature were chiefly supplied from the scanty productions of her little garden, which the neighbours would now and then cultivate for her. It was but a few days before the time at which these circumstances were told me, that she was gathering some vegetables for her repast, when she heard the cottage door which faced the garden suddenly opened. A stranger came out and seemed to be looking eagerly and wildly around. He was dressed in seaman's clothes, was emaciated and ghastly pale, and bore the air of one broken by sickness and hardships. He saw her and hastened towards her, but his steps were faint and faltering—he sank on his knees before her and sobbed like a child. The poor woman gazed upon him with a vacant and wondering eye—"Oh my dear-dear mother! don't you know your son!—your poor boy George!" It was indeed the wreck of her once noble lad; who, shattered by wounds, by sickness and foreign imprisonment, had at length dragged his wasted limbs homeward to repose among the scenes of his childhood.

I will not attempt to detail the particulars of such a meeting, where joy and sorrow were so completely blended—Still he was alive!—he was come home!—he might yet live to comfort and cherish her old age!—Nature, however, was exhausted in him, and if any thing had been wanting to finish the work of fate, the desolation of his native cottage would have been sufficient. He stretched himself on the pallet on which his widowed mother had passed many a sleepless night, and he never rose from it again.

The villagers, when they heard that George Somers had returned, crowded to see him, offering every comfort and assistance that their humble means afforded. He was too weak, however, to talk—he could only look his thanks. His mother was his constant attendant; and he seemed unwilling to be helped by any other hand.

There is something in sickness that breaks down the pride of manhood; that softens the heart and brings it back to the feelings of infancy. Who that has languished, even in advanced life, in sickness and despondency—who that has pined on a weary bed in the neglect and loneliness of a foreign land—but has thought on the mother "that looked on his childhood," that smoothed his pillow and administered to his helplessness.—Oh! there is an enduring tenderness in the love of a mother to her son that transcends all other affections of the heart. It is neither to be chilled by selfishness—nor daunted by danger—nor weakened by worthlessness—nor stifled by ingratitude. She will sacrifice every comfort to his convenience—she will surrender every pleasure to his enjoyment—she will glory in his fame and exult in his prosperity. And if misfortune overtake him he will be the dearer to her from misfortune—and if disgrace settle upon his name, she will still love and cherish him in spite of his disgrace—and if all the world beside cast him off, she will be all the world to him—

Poor George Somers had known what it was to be in sickness and none to soothe, lonely and in prison and none to visit him. He could not endure his mother from his sight—if she moved away, his eye would follow her. She would sit for hours by his bed watching him as he slept. Sometimes he would start from a feverish dream, and look anxiously up until he saw her bending over him, when he would take her hand, lay it on his bosom and fall asleep with the tranquility of a child—In this way he died.

My first impulse on hearing this humble tale of affliction, was to visit the cottage of the mourner and administer pecuniary assistance, and, if possible comfort. I found, however, on enquiry, that the good feelings of the villagers had prompted them to do every thing that the case admitted: and as the poor know best how to console each other's sorrows, I did not venture to intrude.

The next Sunday I was at the village church; when to my surprize, I saw the poor old woman tottering down the aisle to her accustomed seat on the steps of the altar.

She had made an effort to put on something like mourning for her son; and nothing could be more touching than this struggle between pious affection and utter poverty—A black ribband, or so—a faded black handkerchief—and one or two more such humble attempts to express by outward signs that grief which passes shew—When I looked round upon the storied monuments—the stately hatchments—the cold marble pomp, with which grandeur mourned magnificently over departed pride; and turned to this poor widow bowed down by age and sorrow at the altar of her god, and offering up the prayers and praises of a pious, though a broken heart, I felt that this living monument of real grief was worth them all.

I related her story to some of the wealthy members of the congregation and they were moved by it. They exerted themselves to render her situation more comfortable, and to lighten her afflictions. It was, however, but smoothing a few steps to the grave. In the course of a Sunday or two after she was missed from her usual seat at church, and before I left the neighbourhood I heard with a feeling of satisfaction that she had quietly breathed her last, and had gone to rejoin those she loved, in that world where sorrow is never known, and friends are never parted.

A Sunday in London[*]

I N A PRECEDING paper I have spoken of an English Sunday in the country and its tranquilizing effect upon the landscape; but where is its sacred influence more strikingly apparent than in the very heart of that great Babel, London? On this sacred day the gigantic monster is charmed into repose. The intolerable din and struggle of the week are at an end. The shops are shut. The fires of forges and manufactories are extinguished; and the sun, no longer obscured by murky clouds of smoke, pours down a sober yellow radiance into the quiet streets. The few pedestrians we meet, instead of hurrying forward with anxious countenances, move leisurely along; their brows are smoothed from the wrinkles of business and care; they have put on their Sunday looks, and Sunday manners, with their Sunday clothes, and are cleansed in mind as well as in person.

And now the melodious clangor of bells from church towers summons their several flocks to the fold. Forth issues from his mansion the family of the decent tradesman; the small children in the advance; then the citizen and his comely spouse, followed by the grown up daughters, with small morocco bound prayerbooks laid in the folds of their pocket-handkerchiefs. The housemaid looks after them from the window, admiring the finery of the family, and receiving, perhaps, a nod and smile from her young mistresses, at whose toilette she has assisted.

Now rumbles along the carriage of some magnate of the city; peradventure an Alderman or a Sheriff; and now the patter of many feet announces a procession of charity scholars in uniforms of antique cut, and each with a prayerbook under his arm.

The ringing of bells is at an end; the rumbling of the carriage has ceased; the pattering of feet is heard no more: the flocks are folded in ancient churches cramped up in bye lanes and corners of the crowded city; where the vigilant beadle keeps watch, like the shepherd's dog, round the threshhold of the sanctuary. For a time every thing is hushed; but soon is

[*]Part of a sketch omitted in the preceding editions.

heard the deep pervading sound of the organ, rolling and vi-
brating through the empty lanes and courts; and the sweet
chaunting of the choir making them resound with melody
and praise. Never have I been more sensible of the sanctifying
effect of church music than when I have heard it thus poured
forth, like a river of joy through the inmost recesses of this
great metropolis, cleansing it, as it were, from all the sordid
pollutions of the week; and bearing the poor world worn soul
on a tide of triumphant harmony to heaven.

The morning service is at an end. The streets are again alive
with the congregations returning to their homes, but soon
again relapse into silence. Now comes on the Sunday dinner,
which to the city tradesman, is a meal of some importance.
There is more leisure for social enjoyment at the board. Members of the family can now gather together, who are separated
by the laborious occupations of the week. A school boy may
be permitted on that day to come to the paternal home; an
old friend of the family takes his accustomed Sunday seat at
the board, tells over his well known stories and rejoices young
and old with his well known jokes.

On Sunday afternoon the city pours forth its legions to
breathe the fresh air and enjoy the sunshine of the parks and
rural environs. Satyrists may say what they please about the
rural enjoyments of a London citizen on Sunday, but to me
there is something delightful in beholding the poor prisoner
of the crowded and dusty city enabled thus to come forth
once a week and throw himself upon the green bosom of
nature. He is like a child restored to the mother's breast; and
they who first spread out these noble parks and magnificent
pleasure grounds which surround this huge metropolis, have
done at least as much for its health and morality as if they
had expended the amount of cost in hospitals, prisons and
penitentiaries.

The Boar's Head Tavern, East Cheap

A Shakespearian Research

A tavern is the rendezvous, the Exchange, the staple of good fellows. I have heard my great grandfather tell, how his great, great grandfather should say, that it was an old proverb when his great grandfather was a child, that "it was a good wind that blew a man to the wine."

Mother Bombie

IT IS A PIOUS custom in some Catholic countries to honour the memory of saints, by votive lights burnt before their pictures. The popularity of a saint, therefore, may be known by the number of these offerings. One perhaps is left to moulder in the darkness of his little chapel; another may have a solitary lamp to throw its blinking rays athwart his effigy; while the whole blaze of adoration is lavished at the shrine of some beatified father of renown. The wealthy devotee brings his huge luminary of wax, the eager zealot his seven branched candlestick, and even the mendicant pilgrim is by no means satisfied that sufficient light is thrown upon the deceased, unless he hang up his little lamp of smoking oil. The consequence is, that in the eagerness to enlighten they are often apt to obscure; and I have occasionally seen an unlucky saint, almost smoked out of countenance by the officiousness of his followers.

In like manner has it fared with the immortal Shakespeare. Every writer considers it his bounden duty to light up some portion of his character or works, and to rescue some merit from oblivion. The commentator, opulent in words, produces vast tomes of dissertations; the common herd of editors send up mists of obscurity from their notes at the bottom of each page, and every casual scribbler brings his farthing rush light of eulogy or research, to swell the cloud of incense and of smoke.

As I honour all established usages of my brethren of the quill, I thought it but proper to contribute my mite of homage to the memory of the illustrious bard. I was for some time, however, sorely puzzled in what way I should discharge this duty. I found myself anticipated in every attempt at a new reading; every doubtful line had been explained a dozen different ways and perplexed beyond the reach of elucidation; and as to fine passages, they had all been amply praised by previous admirers; nay, so completely had the bard of late been overlarded with panegyrick by a great German critick, that it was difficult now to find even a fault that had not been argued into a beauty.

In this perplexity I was one morning turning over his pages, when I casually opened upon the comic scenes of Henry the Fourth, and was in a moment completely lost in the mad cap revelry of the Boar's head Tavern. So vividly and naturally are these scenes of humour depicted, and with such force and consistency are the characters sustained, that they become mingled up in the mind with the facts and personages of real life. To few readers does it occur that these are all ideal creations of a poet's brain, and that, in sober truth, no such knot of merry roysters ever enlivened the dull neighbourhood of East cheap.

For my part I love to give myself up to the illusions of poetry. A Hero of fiction who never existed, is just as valuable to me as a hero of history who existed a thousand years since; and, if I may be excused such an insensibility to the common ties of human nature, I would not give up fat Jack, for half the great men of ancient chronicle. What have the heroes of yore done for me, or men like me?—They have conquered countries of which I do not enjoy an acre—or they have gained laurels of which I do not inherit a leaf—or they have furnished examples of hairbrained prowess, which I have neither the opportunity nor the inclination to follow. But old Jack Falstaff!—kind Jack Falstaff!—sweet Jack Falstaff!—has enlarged the boundaries of human enjoyment; he has added vast regions of wit and good humour, in which the poorest man may revel; and has bequeathed a never failing inheritance of jolly laughter to make mankind merrier and better to the latest posterity.

A thought suddenly struck me—"I will make a pilgrimage to East cheap," said I, closing the book, "and see if the old Boar's head Tavern still exists. Who knows but I may light upon some legendary traces of Dame Quickly and her guests;

at any rate, there will be a kindred pleasure in treading the halls once vocal with their mirth, to that the toper enjoys, in smelling to the empty cask, once filled with generous wine."

The resolution was no sooner formed than put in execution. I forbear to treat of the various adventures and wonders I encountered in my travels—of the haunted regions of Cock-lane—of the faded glories of Little Britain and the parts adjacent; what perils I ran in Cateaton Street and Old Jewry; of the renowned Guildhall and its two stunted Giants, the pride and wonder of the city and the terror of all unlucky urchins—and how I visited London Stone and struck my staff upon it in imitation of that arch rebel Jack Cade.

Let it suffice to say, that I at length arrived in merry East cheap, that ancient region of wit and wassail, where the very names of the streets relished of good cheer, as Pudding Lane bears testimony even at the present day. For East cheap says old Stow, "was always famous for its convivial doings. The cookes cried hot ribbes of beef rosted, pies well baked and other victuals: there was clattering of pewter pots, harpe, pipe and sawtrie." Alas! how sadly is the scene changed since the roaring days of Falstaff and old Stow. The mad cap royster has given place to the plodding tradesman—the clattering of pots and the sound of "harp and sawtry" to the din of carts and the accursed dinging of the dustman's bell; and no song is heard save haply the strain of some syren from Billingsgate chaunting the eulogy of deceased mackrel.

I sought in vain for the ancient abode of Dame Quickly. The only relique of it is a boar's head carved in relief in stone, which formerly served as the sign, but at present is built into the parting line of two houses which stand on the scite of the renowned old Tavern.

For the history of this little empire of good fellowship I was referred to a Tallow chandler's widow opposite, who had been born and brought up on the spot, and was looked up to as the indisputable chronicler of the neighbourhood. I found her seated in a little back parlour, the window of which looked out upon a yard about eight feet square, laid out as a flower garden; while a glass door opposite afforded a distant peep of the street through a vista of soap and tallow candles: the two views which comprised in all probability her prospects of life, and the little world in which she had lived, and moved, and had her being, for the better part of a century.

To be versed in the history of East cheap, great and little, from London Stone even unto the Monument, was doubtless in her opinion to be acquainted with the history of the universe. Yet with all this she possessed the simplicity of true wisdom, and that liberal, communicative disposition, which I have generally remarked in intelligent old ladies, knowing in the concerns of their neighbourhood.

Her information, however, did not extend far back into antiquity. She could throw no light upon the history of the Boar's head from the time that Dame Quickly espoused the valiant Pistol, until the great fire of London, when it was unfortunately burnt down. It was soon rebuilt, and continued to flourish under the old name and sign, until a dying Landlord, struck with remorse for double scores, bad measures, and other iniquities which are incident to the sinful race of Publicans, endeavoured to make his peace with heaven by bequeathing the tavern to St. Michael's church, Crooked Lane, towards the supporting of a chaplain. For some time the vestry meetings were regularly held there, but it was observed that the old Boar never held up his head under church government. He gradually declined, and finally gave his last gasp about thirty years since. The tavern was then turned into shops, but she informed me that a picture of it was still preserved in St. Michael's church, which stood just in the rear. To get a sight of this picture was now my determination, so having informed myself of the abode of the sexton I took my leave of the venerable chronicler of East cheap, my visit having doubtless raised greatly her opinion of her legendary lore, and furnished an important incident in the history of her life.

It cost me some difficulty and much curious enquiry to ferret out the humble hanger on to the church. I had to explore Crooked Lane and divers little alleys and elbows and dark passages, with which this old city is perforated, like an ancient cheese, or a worm eaten chest of drawers. At length I traced him to a corner of a small court, surrounded by lofty houses, where the inhabitants enjoy about as much of the face of heaven, as a community of frogs at the bottom of a well. The sexton was a meek acquiescing little man, of a bowing lowly habit; yet he had a pleasant twinkle in his eye, and if encouraged would now and then hazard a small pleasantry, such as a man of his low estate might venture to make in the company of high church wardens, and other mighty men of the earth. I found him in company with the deputy organist, seated apart, like Milton's angels discoursing no doubt on high doctrinal points, and settling the affairs of the church over a friendly pot of ale—for the lower classes of English seldom deliberate on any weighty matter without the assistance of a cool tankard to clear their understandings. I arrived at the moment when they had finished their ale and their argument, and were about to repair to the church to put it in order, so having made known my wishes I received their gracious permission to accompany them.

The church of St. Michael, Crooked Lane, standing a short distance from Billingsgate, is enriched with the tombs of many Fishmongers of renown, and as every profession has its galaxy of glory and its constellation of great men, I presume the monument of a mighty Fishmonger of the olden time, is regarded with as much reverence by succeeding generations of the craft as poets feel on contemplating the tomb of Virgil, or soldiers the monument of a Marlborough or a Turenne.

I cannot but turn aside, while thus speaking of illustrious men, to observe that St. Michael's Crooked Lane contains also the ashes of that doughty champion William Walworth, knight, who so manfully clove down the sturdy wight Wat Tyler in Smithfield, a hero worthy of honorable blazon as almost the only Lord Mayor on record, famous for deeds of arms:—the Sovereigns of Cockney being generally renowned, as the most pacific of all potentates.*

*NOTE

The following was the ancient inscription on the monument of this worthy—which unhappily was destroyed in the great conflagration—

> Hereunder lyth a man of Fame
> William Walworth callyd by name:
> Fishmonger he was in Lyfftime here
> And twise Lord Maior, as in Books appere;
> Who with courage stout and manly myght
> Slew Jackstraw in King Richards syght.
> For which act done and trew Entent
> The Kyng made him Knyght incontinent;

Adjoining the church, in a small cemetery, immediately under the back windows of what was once the Boar's head stands the tomb stone of Robert Preston, whilom drawer at the Tavern. It is now nearly a century since this trusty drawer of good liquor closed his bustling career, and was thus quietly deposited within call of his customers. As I was clearing away the weeds from his epitaph the little sexton drew me on one side with a mysterious air, and informed me in a low voice, that once upon a time on a dark wintry night, when the wind was unruly, howling and whistling, banging about doors and windows and twirling weather cocks so that the living were frightened out of their beds and even the dead could not sleep quietly in their graves, the ghost of honest Preston, which happened to be airing itself in the church yard, was attracted by the well known call of "waiter" from the Boar's head, and made its sudden appearance in the midst of a roaring club, just as the parish clerk was singing a stave from the "mirrie garland of captain Death"—to the discomfiture of sundry train-band captains and the conversion of an infidel attorney, who became a zealous christian on the spot and was never known to twist the truth afterwards except in the way of business.

I beg it may be remembered that I do not pledge myself for the authenticity of this anecdote, though it is well known that the church yards and bye corners of this old metropolis are very much infested with perturbed spirits and every one must have heard of the Cock Lane Ghost, and the apparition that guards the regalia in the Tower, which has frightened so many bold sentinels almost out of their wits.

> And gave him armes, as here you see,
> To declare his Fact and chivaldrie.
> He left this Lyff the yere of our God
> Thirteen hondred fourscore and three odd.

An error in the foregoing inscription has been corrected by the venerable Stow—"Whereas," saith he, "it hath been far spread abroad by vulgar opinion, that the rebel smitten down so manfully by Sir William Walworth, the then worthy Lord Maior was named Jack Straw and not Wat Tyler, I thought good to reconcile this rash conceived doubt by such testimony as I find in ancient and good records. The principal Leaders or captains of the commons were Wat Tyler as the first man; the second was John or Jack Straw &c &c." Stow's London.

Be all this as it may, this Robert Preston seems to have been a worthy successor to the nimble tongued Francis who attended upon the revels of Prince Hal, to have been equally prompt with his "anon, anon, sir" and to have transcended his predecessor in honesty, for Falstaff, the veracity of whose taste no man will venture to impeach, flatly accuses Francis of putting lime in his sack: whereas honest Preston's epitaph lauds him for the sobriety of his conduct, the soundness of his wine and the fairness of his measure.* The worthy dignitaries of the church, however, did not appear much captivated by the sober virtues of the Tapster; the deputy organist, who had a moist look out of the eye, made some shrewd remark on the abstemiousness of a man brought up among full hogsheads, and the little sexton corroborated his opinion by a significant wink and a dubious shake of the head.

Thus far my researches, though they threw much light on the history of Tapsters, Fishmongers and Lord Mayors, yet disappointed me in the great object of my quest, the picture of the Boar's head Tavern. No such painting was to be found in the church of St. Michael. "Marry and amen!" said I, "here endeth my research!" So I was giving the matter up with the air of a baffled antiquary, when my friend the sexton, perceiving me to be curious in every thing relative to the old Tavern, offered to shew me the choice vessels of the vestry, which had been handed down from remote times, when the parish meetings were held at the Boar's head. These were deposited in the Parish club room, which had been transferred, on the de-

*Note.

As this inscription is rife with excellent morality, I transcribe it for the admonition of delinquent Tapsters. It is no doubt the production of some choice spirit who once frequented the Boar's head.

> "Bacchus to give the toping world surprize
> Produced one sober son, and here he lies.
> Though rear'd among full hogsheads he defy'd
> The charms of wine, and every one beside.
> O reader if to justice thou'rt inclin'd
> Keep honest Preston daily in thy mind.
> He drew good wine, took care to fill his pots
> Had sundry virtues that excus'd his faults.
> You that on Bacchus have the like dependance,
> Pray copy Bob, in measure and attendance."

cline of the ancient establishment, to a tavern in the neighbourhood.

A few steps brought us to the house which stands No. 12.
Miles Lane, bearing the title of The Mason's arms, and is kept
by Master Edward Honeyball, the "bully Rock" of the establishment. It is one of those little taverns which abound in the
heart of the city and form the centre of gossip and intelligence
of the neighbourhood.

We entered the bar room, which was narrow and darkling;
for in these close lanes but few rays of reflected light are enabled to struggle down to the inhabitants, whose broad day
is at best but a tolerable twilight. The room was partitioned
into boxes, each containing a table spread with a clean white
cloth ready for dinner. This shewed that the guests were of
the good old stamp, and divided their day equally; for it was
but just one O'clock. At the lower end of the room was a
clear coal fire, before which a breast of lamb was roasting. A
row of bright brass candlesticks and pewter mugs glistened
along the mantle piece, and an old fashioned clock ticked in
one corner. There was something primitive in this medley of
Kitchen, Parlour and Hall, that carried me back to earlier
times and pleased me. The place indeed was humble, but
every thing had that look of order and neatness which bespeaks the superintendance of a notable English housewife. A
group of amphibious looking beings, who might be either
fishermen or sailors were regaling themselves in one of the
boxes. As I was a visitor of rather higher pretensions I was
ushered into a little misshapen back room having at least nine
corners. It was lighted by a sky light, furnished with antiquated leathern chairs and ornamented with the portrait of a
fat pig. It was evidently appropriated to particular customers,
and I found a shabby gentleman, in a red nose and oil cloth
hat, seated in one corner, meditating on a half empty pot of
porter.

The old sexton had taken the landlady aside and with an
air of profound importance imparted to her my errand.
Dame Honeyball was a likely, plump, bustling little woman,
and no bad substitute for that paragon of hostesses Dame
Quickly. She seemed delighted with an opportunity to
oblige, and hurrying up stairs to the archives of her house,

where the precious vessels of the parish club were deposited, she returned smiling and curtseying with them in her hands.

The first she presented me was a japanned iron Tobacco box of gigantic size, out of which I was told the vestry had smoked at their stated meetings since time immemorial; and which was never suffered to be profaned by vulgar hands or used on common occasions. I received it with becoming reverence, but what was my delight on beholding on its cover the identical painting of which I was in quest. There was displayed the outside of the Boar's head Tavern, and before the door was to be seen the whole convivial group at table in full revel; pictured with that wonderful fidelity and force, with which the portraits of renowned generals and commodores are illustrated on Tobacco boxes, for the benefit of posterity. Lest, however, there should be any mistake, the cunning limner had warily inscribed the names of Prince Hal and Falstaff on the bottoms of their chairs.

On the inside of the cover was an inscription, nearly obliterated, recording that this box was the gift of Sir Richard Gore, for the use of the vestry meetings at the Boar's head Tavern, and that it was "repaired and beautified by his successor Mr. John Packard 1767." Such is a faithful description of this august and venerable relique, and I question whether the learned Scriblerius contemplated his Roman shield, or the Knights of the Round Table the long sought san-greal with more exultation.

While I was meditating on it with enraptured gaze, Dame Honeyball, who was highly gratified by the interest it excited, put in my hands a drinking cup or goblet, which also belonged to the vestry, and was descended from the old Boar's head. It bore the inscription of having been the gift of Francis Wythers, Knight, and was held, she told me, in exceeding great value, being considered very "antyke." This last opinion was strengthened by the shabby gentleman in the red nose and oil cloth hat, and whom I strongly suspected of being a lineal descendant from the valiant Bardolph. He suddenly aroused from his meditation on the pot of porter, and casting a knowing look at the goblet exclaimed—"Aye-aye, the head don't ache now, that made that there article."—

The great importance attached to this memento of ancient revelry by modern church wardens, at first puzzled me; but there is nothing sharpens the apprehension so much as antiquarian research; for I immediately perceived that this could be no other than the identical "parcel-gilt goblet" on which Falstaff made his loving but faithless vow to Dame Quickly; and which would of course be treasured up with care among the regalia of her domains, as a testimony of that solemn contract.*

Mine hostess indeed gave me a long history how the goblet had been handed down from generation to generation. She also entertained me with many particulars concerning the worthy vestrymen who have seated themselves thus quietly on the stools of the ancient roysters of East cheap, and, like so many commentators, utter clouds of smoke in honour of Shakespeare. These I forbear to relate, lest my readers should not be as curious in these matters as myself. Suffice it to say, the neighbours one and all about East cheap, believe that Falstaff and his merry crew actually lived and revelled there. Nay there are several legendary anecdotes concerning him still extant among the oldest frequenters of the Mason's arms; which they give, as transmitted down from their forefathers; and Mr. McKash, an Irish hair dresser, whose shop stands on the scite of the old Boar's head, has several dry jokes of Fat Jack's, not laid down in the books, with which he makes his customers ready to die of laughter.

I now turned to my friend the sexton to make some further enquiries, but I found him sunk in pensive meditation. His head had declined a little on one side—a deep sigh heaved from the very bottom of his stomach, and though I could not see a tear trembling in his eye, yet a moisture was evidently stealing from a corner of his mouth. I followed the direction of his eye through the door which stood open and found it

---

*NOTE.

Thou didst swear to me, upon a *parcel-gilt goblet*, sitting in my Dolphin chamber, at the round table, by a sea coal fire, on Wednesday in Whitsun-week, when the prince broke thy head for likening his father to a singing man of Windsor; thou didst swear to me then, as I was washing thy wound, to marry me, and make me my lady thy wife. Canst thou deny it? II.ᵈ Part. Henry IV.

fixed wistfully on the savoury breast of lamb, roasting in dripping richness before the fire.

I now called to mind, that in the eagerness of my recondite investigation I was keeping the poor man from his dinner. My bowels yearned with sympathy, and, putting in his hand a small token of my gratitude and good will, I departed with a hearty benediction on him, Dame Honeyball and the parish club of Crooked Lane—not forgetting my shabby, but sententious friend, in the oil cloth hat and copper nose.

Thus have I given a "tedious brief" account of this interesting research, for which, if it prove too short and unsatisfactory, I can only plead my inexperience in this branch of literature so deservedly popular at the present day. I am aware that a more skillful illustrator of the immortal bard would have swelled the materials I have but touched upon, to a good merchantable bulk—comprizing the biographies of William Walworth, Jack Straw and Robert Preston—some notice of the Eminent Fishmongers of St. Michael's—the history of East cheap, great and little—private anecdotes of Dame Honeyball and her pretty daughter, whom I have not even mentioned, to say nothing of a damsel tending the breast of lamb (and whom, by the way, I remarked to be a comely lass, with a neat foot and ancle)—the whole enlivened by the riots of Wat Tyler, and illuminated by the great fire of London.

All this I leave as a rich mine to be worked by future commentators; nor do I despair of seeing the Tobacco box and the "parcel-gilt goblet" which I have thus brought to light, the subjects of future engravings and almost as fruitful of voluminous dissertations and disputes as the shield of Achilles, or the far famed Portland vase.

The
Mutability of Literature

A Colloquy in Westminster Abbey

> I know that all beneath the moon decays,
> And what by mortals in this world is brought,
> In time's great period shall return to nought.
> I know that all the muses' heavenly layes,
> With toil of sprite which are so dearly bought,
> As idle sounds of few or none are sought,
> That there is nothing lighter than mere praise.
>
> *Drummond of Hawthornden*

THERE ARE CERTAIN half dreaming moods of mind, in which we naturally steal away from noise and glare, and seek some quiet haunt, where we may indulge our reveries and build our air castles undisturbed. In such a mood I was loitering about the old gray cloisters of Westminster Abbey, enjoying that luxury of wandering thought which one is apt to dignify with the name of reflection, when suddenly an irruption of madcap boys from Westminster school playing at football broke in upon the monastic stillness of the place, making the vaulted passages and mouldering tombs echo with their merriment. I sought to take refuge from their noise by penetrating still deeper into the solitudes of the pile, and applied to one of the vergers for admission to the library. He conducted me through a portal rich with the crumbling sculpture of former ages, which opened upon a gloomy passage leading to the chapter house and the chamber in which doomsday book is deposited. Just within the passage is a small door on the left. To this the verger applied a key; it was double locked, and opened with some difficulty, as if seldom used. We now ascended a dark narrow staircase, and passing through a second door, entered the library.

I found myself in a lofty antique hall, the roof supported by massive joists of old English oak. It was soberly lighted by a row of Gothic windows at a considerable height from the floor, and which apparently opened upon the roofs of the cloisters. An ancient picture of some reverend dignitary of the church in his robes hung over the fire place. Around the hall and in a small gallery were the books, arranged in carved oaken cases. They consisted principally of old polemical writers, and were much more worn by time than use. In the centre of the library was a solitary table with two or three books on it; an inkstand without ink, and a few pens parched by long disuse. The place seemed fitted for quiet study and profound meditation. It was buried deep among the massive walls of the abbey, and shut up from the tumult of the world. I could only hear now and then the shouts of the schoolboys faintly swelling from the cloister, and the sound of a bell tolling for prayers, echoing soberly along the roofs of the abbey. By degrees the shouts of merriment grew fainter and fainter, and at length died away. The bell ceased to toll, and a profound silence reigned through the dusky hall.

I had taken down a little thick quarto, curiously bound in parchment, with brass clasps, and seated myself at the table in a venerable elbow chair. Instead of reading, however, I was beguiled by the solemn monastic air, and lifeless quiet of the place, into a train of musing. As I looked around upon the old volumes in their mouldering covers, thus ranged on the shelves, and apparently never disturbed in their repose, I could not but consider the library a kind of literary catacomb, where authors, like mummies, are piously entombed, and left to blacken and moulder in dusty oblivion.

How much, thought I, has each of these volumes, now thrust aside with such indifference, cost some aching head; how many weary days—how many sleepless nights. How have their authors buried themselves in the solitude of cells and cloisters; shut themselves up from the face of man, and the still more blessed face of nature, and devoted themselves to painful research and intense reflection. And all for what! to occupy an inch of dusty shelf—to have the title of their works read now and then in a future age, by some drowsy churchman, or casual straggler like myself; and in another age to be lost, even to remembrance. Such is the amount of this boasted immortality.—A mere temporary rumour, a local sound, like the tone of that bell which has just tolled among these towers, filling the ear for a moment—lingering transiently in echo—and then passing away, like a thing that was not!

While I sat half murmuring, half meditating these unprofitable speculations, with my head resting on my hand, I was thrumming with the other hand upon the quarto, until I accidentally loosened the clasps, when, to my utter astonishment, the little book gave two or three yawns, like one awakening from a deep sleep; then a husky hem, and at length began to talk. At first its voice was very hoarse and broken, being much troubled by a cobweb which some studious spider had woven across it; and having probably contracted a cold from long exposure to the chills and damps of the abbey. In a short time, however, it became more distinct, and I soon found it an exceedingly fluent conversable little tome. Its language, to be sure, was rather quaint and obsolete, and its pronunciation, what, in the present day, would be deemed barbarous; but I shall endeavour, as far as I am able, to render it in modern parlance.

It began with railings about the neglect of the world—about merit being suffered to languish in obscurity, and other such common place topics of literary repining, and complained bitterly that it had not been opened for more than two centuries. That the Dean only looked now and then into the library, sometimes took down a volume or two, trifled with them for a few moments, and then returned them to their shelves. "What a plague do they mean," said the little quarto, which I began to perceive was somewhat choleric, "what a plague do they mean by keeping several thousand volumes of us shut up here, and watched by a set of old vergers like so many beauties in a harem, merely to be looked at now and then by the Dean? Books were written to give pleasure and to be enjoyed; and I would have a rule passed that the Dean should pay each of us a visit at least once a year; or if he is not equal to the task, let them once in a while turn loose the whole school of Westminster among us, that at any rate we may now and then have an airing."

"Softly, my worthy friend," replied I, "you are not aware how much better you are off than most books of your generation. By being stored away in this ancient library, you are like the treasured remains of those saints and monarchs which lie enshrined in the adjoining chapels, while the remains of your contemporary mortals, left to the ordinary course of nature, have long since returned to dust."

"Sir," said the little tome, ruffling his leaves and looking big, "I was written for all the world, not for the bookworms of an abbey. I was intended to circulate from hand to hand, like other great contemporary works; but here have I been clasped up for more than two centuries, and might have silently fallen a prey to these worms that are playing the very vengeance with my intestines, if you had not by chance given me an opportunity of uttering a few last words before I go to pieces."

"My good friend," rejoined I, "had you been left to the circulation of which you speak, you would long ere this have been no more. To judge from your physiognomy, you are now well stricken in years: very few of your contemporaries can be at present in existence; and those few owe their longevity to being immured like yourself in old libraries; which, suffer me to add, instead of likening to harems, you might more properly and gratefully have compared to those infirmaries attached to religious establishments, for the benefit of the old and decrepid, and where, by quiet fostering and no employment, they often endure to an amazingly good for nothing old age. You talk of your contemporaries as if in circulation—where do we meet with their works? what do we hear of Robert Grosteste of Lincoln? No one could have toiled harder than he for immortality. He is said to have written nearly two hundred volumes. He built, as it were, a pyramid of books to perpetuate his name: but, alas! the pyramid has long since fallen, and only a few fragments are scattered in various libraries, where they are scarcely disturbed even by the antiquarian. What do we hear of Gyraldus Cambrensis, the historian, antiquary, philosopher, theologian, and poet? He declined two bishoprics that he might shut himself up and write for posterity; but posterity never inquires after his labours. What of Henry of Huntingdon, who, beside a learned history of England, wrote a treatise on the contempt of the world, which the world has revenged by forgetting him. What is quoted of Joseph of Exeter, styled the miracle of his age in classical composition? Of his three great heroic poems one is lost forever, excepting a mere fragment; the others are

known only to a few of the curious in literature, and as to his
love verses and epigrams, they have entirely disappeared.
What is in current use of John Wallis, the Franciscan, who
acquired the name of the tree of life? Of William of Malms-
bury;—of Simeon of Durham; of Benedict of Peterborough;
of John Hanvill of St. Albans; of ——"

"Prithee, friend," cried the quarto in a testy tone, "how old
do you think me? You are talking of authors that lived long
before my time, and wrote either in Latin or French, so that they
in a manner expatriated themselves, and deserved to be forgotten;* but I, sir, was ushered into the world from the press of
the renowned Wynkyn de Worde. I was written in my own native tongue at a time when the language had become fixed, and
indeed I was considered a model of pure and elegant English."

(I should observe that these remarks were couched in such
intolerably antiquated terms, that I have had infinite difficulty
in rendering them into modern phraseology.)

"I cry you mercy," said I, "for mistaking your age; but it
matters little; almost all the writers of your time have likewise
passed into forgetfulness; and De Worde's publications are
mere literary rarities among book collectors. The purity and
stability of language, too, on which you found your claims to
perpetuity, have been the fallacious dependence of authors of
every age, even back to the times of the worthy Robert of
Gloucester, who wrote his history in rhymes of mongrel
Saxon.† Even now, many talk of Spenser's ' well of pure English undefiled,' as if the language ever sprang from a well or
fountain head, and was not rather a mere confluence of var-

---

*In Latin and French hath many soueraine wittes had great delyte to en-
dite, and have many noble thinges fulfilde, but certes there ben some that
speaken their poisye in French, of which speche the French men have as good
a fantasye as we have in heryng of Frenchemen's Englishe. *Chaucer's Testament of Love.*

†Holinshed, in his Chronicle, observes, "afterward, also, by diligent travell
of Geffray Chaucer and John Gowre, in the time of Richard the second, and
after them of John Scogan and John Lydgate, monke of Berrie, our said
toong was brought to an excellent passe, notwithstanding that it never came
unto the type of perfection until the time of Queen Elizabeth, wherein John
Jewell, Bishop of Sarum, John Fox, and sundrie learned and excellent writers,
have fully accomplished the ornature of the same, to their great praise and
immortal commendation."

ious tongues, perpetually subject to changes and intermixtures. It is this which has made English literature so extremely mutable, and the reputation built upon it so fleeting. Unless thought can be committed to something more permanent and unchangeable than such a medium, even thought must share the fate of every thing else, and fall into decay. This should serve as a check upon the vanity and exultation of the most popular writer. He finds the language in which he has embarked his fame gradually altering, and subject to the dilapidations of time and the caprice of fashion. He looks back and beholds the early authors of his country, once the favourites of their day, supplanted by modern writers. A few short ages have covered them with obscurity, and their merits can only be relished by the quaint taste of the bookworm. And such, he anticipates, will be the fate of his own work, which, however it may be admired in its day, and held up as a model of purity, will in the course of years grow antiquated and obsolete, until it shall become almost as unintelligible in its native land as an Egyptian obelisk, or one of those Runic inscriptions said to exist in the deserts of Tartary. I declare," added I with some emotion, " when I contemplate a modern library, filled with new works in all the bravery of rich gilding and binding, I feel disposed to sit down and weep, like the good Xerxes when he surveyed his army, pranked out in all the splendour of military array, and reflected that in one hundred years not one of them would be in existence!"

"Ah," said the little quarto, with a heavy sigh, "I see how it is; these modern scribblers have superseded all the good old authors. I suppose nothing is read now-a-days but Sir Philip Sidney's Arcadia, Sackville's stately plays, and Mirror for Magistrates, or the fine spun euphuisms of the "unparalelled John Lyly."

"There you are again mistaken," said I, "the writers whom you suppose in vogue, because they happened to be so when you were last in circulation, have long since had their day. Sir Philip Sydney's Arcadia, the immortality of which was so fondly predicted by his admirers,* and which, in truth, is full

*Live ever sweete booke; the silver image of his gentle witt, and the golden pillar of his noble courage; and ever notify unto the world that thy writer was the secretary of eloquence, the breath of the muses, the honey bee

of noble thoughts, delicate images, and graceful turns of language, is now scarcely ever mentioned. Sackville has strutted into obscurity; and even Lyly, though his writings were once the delight of a court, and apparently perpetuated by a proverb, is now scarcely known even by name. A whole crowd of authors who wrote and wrangled at the time, have likewise gone down with all their writings and their controversies. Wave after wave of succeeding literature has rolled over them, until they are buried so deep, that it is only now and then that some industrious diver after the fragments of antiquity brings up a specimen for the gratification of the curious.

"For my part," I continued, "I consider this mutability of language a wise precaution of Providence for the benefit of the world at large, and of authors in particular. To reason from analogy, we daily behold the varied and beautiful tribes of vegetables springing up, flourishing, adorning the fields for a short time, and then fading into dust, to make way for their successors. Were not this the case, the fecundity of nature would be a grievance instead of a blessing. The earth would groan with rank and excessive vegetation, and its surface become a tangled wilderness. In like manner, the works of genius and learning decline and make way for subsequent productions. Language gradually varies, and with it fade away the writings of authors who have flourished their allotted time; otherwise the creative powers of genius would overstock the world, and the mind would be completely bewildered in the endless mazes of literature. Formerly there were some restraints on this excessive multiplication. Works had to be transcribed by hand, which was a slow and laborious operation; they were written either on parchment, which was expensive, so that one work was often erased to make way for another; or on papyrus, which was fragile and extremely perishable. Authorship was a limited and unprofitable craft, and pursued chiefly by monks in the leisure and solitude of their

---

of the dayntiest flowers of witt and arte, the pith of morale and intellectual virtues, the arme of Bellona in the field, the tongue of Suada in the chamber, the spirite of Practise in esse, and the paragon of excellency in print. *Harvey's Pierce's Supererogation.*

cloisters. The accumulation of manuscripts was slow and costly, and confined almost entirely to monasteries. To these circumstances it may in some measure be owing that we have not been inundated by the intellect of antiquity; that the fountains of thought have not been broken up, and modern genius drowned in the deluge. But the inventions of paper and the press have put an end to all these restraints. They have made every one a writer, and enabled every mind to pour itself into print, and diffuse itself over the whole intellectual world. The consequences are alarming. The stream of literature has swoln into a torrent—augmented into a river—expanded into a sea. A few centuries since, five or six hundred manuscripts constituted a great library; but what would you say to libraries, such as actually exist, containing three and four hundred thousand volumes; legions of authors at the same time busy, and the press going on with fearfully increasing activity, to double and quadruple the number? Unless some unforeseen mortality should break out among the progeny of the muse, now that she has become so prolific, I tremble for posterity. I fear the mere fluctuation of language will not be sufficient. Criticism may do much; it increases with the increase of literature, and resembles one of those salutary checks on population spoken of by economists. All possible encouragement, therefore, should be given to the growth of critics, good or bad. But I fear all will be in vain; let criticism do what it may, writers will write, printers will print, and the world will inevitably be overstocked with good books. It will soon be the employment of a life time merely to learn their names. Many a man of passable information at the present day reads scarce any thing but reviews, and before long a man of erudition will be little better than a mere walking catalogue."

"My very good sir," said the little quarto, yawning most drearily in my face, "excuse my interrupting you, but I perceive you are rather given to prose. I would ask the fate of an author who was making some noise just as I left the world. His reputation, however, was considered quite temporary. The learned shook their heads at him, for he was a poor half educated varlet, that knew little of Latin, and nothing of Greek, and had been obliged to run the country for deer stealing. I think his name was Shakspeare. I presume he soon sunk into oblivion."

"On the contrary," said I, "it is owing to that very man that the literature of his period has experienced a duration beyond the ordinary term of English literature. There arise authors now and then, who seem proof against the mutability of language, because they have rooted themselves in the unchanging principles of human nature. They are like gigantic trees that we sometimes see on the banks of a stream; which, by their vast and deep roots, penetrating through the mere surface, and laying hold on the very foundations of the earth, preserve the soil around them from being swept away by the everflowing current, and hold up many a neighbouring plant, and, perhaps, worthless weed, to perpetuity. Such is the case with Shakspeare, whom we behold, defying the encroachments of time, retaining in modern use the language and literature of his day, and giving duration to many an indifferent author, merely from having flourished in his vicinity. But even he, I grieve to say, is gradually assuming the tint of age, and his whole form is overrun by a profusion of commentators, who, like clambering vines and creepers, almost bury the noble plant that upholds them."

Here the little quarto began to heave his sides and chuckle, until at length he broke out into a short plethoric fit of laughter that had well nigh choked him, by reason of his excessive corpulency. "Mighty well!" cried he, as soon as he could recover breath, "mighty well! and so you would persuade me that the literature of an age is to be perpetuated by a vagabond deer stealer! by a man without learning! by a poet, forsooth—a poet!" And here he wheezed forth another fit of laughter.

I confess I felt somewhat nettled at this rudeness, which, however, I pardoned on account of his having flourished in a less polished age. I determined, nevertheless, not to give up my point.

"Yes," resumed I positively, "a poet; for of all writers he has the best chance for immortality. Others may write from the head, but he writes from the heart, and the heart will always understand him. He is the faithful portrayer of nature, whose features are always the same, and always interesting.

Prose writers are voluminous and unwieldy; their pages are crowded with common places, and their thoughts expanded into tediousness. But with the true poet every thing is terse, touching, or brilliant. He gives the choicest thoughts in the choicest language. He illustrates them by every thing that he sees most striking in nature and art. He enriches them by pictures of human life, such as it is passing before him. His writings, therefore, contain the spirit, the aroma, if I may use the phrase, of the age in which he lives. They are caskets which inclose within a small compass the wealth of the language—its family jewels, which are thus transmitted in a portable form to posterity. The setting may occasionally be antiquated, and require now and then to be renewed, as in the case of Chaucer; but the brilliancy and intrinsic value of the gems continue unaltered. Cast a look back over the long reach of literary history. What vast valleys of dulness, filled with monkish legends and academical controversies. What bogs of theological speculations; what dreary wastes of metaphysics. Here and there only do we behold the heaven illumined bards, elevated like beacons on their widely separated heights, to transmit the pure light of poetical intelligence from age to age."*

I was just about to launch forth into eulogiums upon the poets of the day, when the sudden opening of the door caused me to turn my head. It was the verger, who came to inform me that it was time to close the library. I sought to have a parting word with the quarto, but the worthy little tome was silent; the clasps were closed, and it looked per-

*Thorow earth, and waters deepe,
 The pen by skill doth passe:
And featly nyps the worldes abuse,
 And shoes us in a glasse,
The vertu and the vice
 Of every wight alyve;
The honey combe that bee doth make,
 Is not so sweete in hyve,
As are the golden leves
 That drop from poets head:
Which doth surmount our common talke
 As farre as dros doth lead.
      CHURCHYARD.

fectly unconscious of all that had passed. I have been to the library two or three times since, and have endeavoured to draw it into farther conversation, but in vain. And whether all this rambling colloquy actually took place, or whether it was another of those odd day dreams to which I am subject, I have never, to this moment, been able to discover.

Rural Funerals

Here's a few flowers; but about midnight more:
The herbs that have on them cold dew o' the night
Are strewings fitt'st for graves.——
You were as flowers now wither'd: even so
These herb'lets shall, which we upon you strow.

Cymbeline

AMONG THE BEAUTIFUL and simple hearted customs of rural life which still linger in some parts of England, are those of strewing flowers before the funerals, and planting them at the graves, of departed friends. These, it is said, are the remains of some of the rites of the primitive church; but they are of still higher antiquity, having been observed among the Greeks and Romans, and frequently mentioned by their writers, and were no doubt the spontaneous tributes of unlettered affection, originating long before art had tasked itself to modulate sorrow into song, or story it on the monument. They are now only to be met with in the most distant and retired places of the kingdom, where fashion and innovation have not been able to throng in, and trample out all the curious and interesting traces of the olden time.

In Glamorganshire, we are told, the bed whereon the corpse lies, is covered with flowers, a custom alluded to in one of the wild and plaintive ditties of Ophelia:

> White his shroud as the mountain snow
> Larded all with sweet flowers;
> Which be-wept to the grave did go,
> With true-love showers.

There is also a most delicate and beautiful rite observed in some of the remote villages of the south, at the funeral of a female who has died young and unmarried. A chaplet of white flowers is borne before the corpse by a young girl nearest in age, size, and resemblance, and is afterwards hung up in the church over the accustomed seat of the deceased. These chaplets are sometimes made of white paper, in imitation of flowers, and inside of them is generally a pair of white gloves. They are intended as emblems of the purity of the deceased, and the crown of glory which she has received in heaven.

In some parts of the country, also, the dead are carried to the grave with the singing of psalms and hymns: a kind of triumph, "to show," says Bourne, "that they have finished their course with joy, and are become conquerors." This, I am informed, is observed in some of the northern counties, particularly in Northumberland, and it has a pleasing, though melancholy effect, to hear, of a still evening, in some lonely country scene, the mournful melody of a funeral dirge swelling from a distance, and to see the train slowly moving along the landscape.

> Thus, thus, and thus, we compass round
> Thy harmlesse and unhaunted ground,
> And as we sing thy dirge, we will
> > The Daffodill,
> And other flowers lay upon
> The altar of our love, thy stone.*

There is also a solemn respect paid by the traveller to the passing funeral in these sequestered places, for such spectacles, occurring among the quiet abodes of nature, sink deep into the soul. As the mourning train approaches, he pauses, uncovered, to let it go by; he then follows silently in the rear; sometimes quite to the grave, at other times for a few hundred yards, and having paid this tribute of respect to the deceased, turns and resumes his journey.

The rich vein of melancholy which runs through the English character, and gives it some of its most touching and ennobling graces, is finely evidenced in these pathetic customs, and in the solicitude shown by the common people for an honoured and a peaceful grave. The humblest peasant, whatever may be his lowly lot while living, is anxious that some little respect may be paid to his remains. Sir Thomas Overbury, describing the "faire and happy milkmaid," ob-

*Herrick

serves, "thus lives she, and all her care is, that she may die in
the spring time, to have store of flowers stucke upon her
winding sheet." The poets, too, who always breathe the feeling of a nation, continually advert to this fond solicitude
about the grave. In "The Maid's Tragedy," by Beaumont and
Fletcher, there is a beautiful instance of the kind, describing
the capricious melancholy of a broken hearted girl:

> When she sees a bank
> Stuck full of flowers, she, with a sigh, will tell
> Her servants, what a pretty place it were
> To bury lovers in; and make her maids
> Pluck 'em, and strew her over like a corse.

The custom of decorating graves was once universally prevalent: osiers were carefully bent over them to keep the turf
uninjured, and about them were planted evergreens and flowers. "We adorn their graves," says Evelyn, in his Sylva, " with
flowers and redolent plants, just emblems of the life of man,
which has been compared in holy scriptures to those fading
beauties, whose roots being buried in dishonour, rise again in
glory." This usage has now become extremely rare in England; but it may still be met with in the church yards of
retired villages, among the Welsh mountains; and I recollect
an instance of it at the small town of Ruthen, which lies at
the head of the beautiful vale of Clewyd. I have been told also
by a friend, who was present at the funeral of a young girl in
Glamorganshire, that the female attendants had their aprons
full of flowers, which, as soon as the body was interred, they
stuck about the grave. He noticed several graves which had
been decorated in the same manner. As the flowers had been
merely stuck in the ground, and not planted, they had soon
withered, and might be seen in various states of decay; some
drooping others quite perished. They were afterwards to be
supplanted by holly, rosemary, and other evergreens; which
on some graves had grown to great luxuriance, and overshadowed the tomb stones.

There was formerly a melancholy fancifulness in the arrangement of these rustic offerings that had something in it
truly poetical. The rose was sometimes blended with the lily,

to form a general emblem of frail mortality. "This sweet flower," says Evelyn, "borne on a branch set with thorns, and accompanied with the lily, are natural hieroglyphics of our fugitive, umbratile, anxious, and transitory life, which, making so fair a shew for a time, is not yet without its thorns and crosses." The nature and colour of the flowers, and of the ribbands with which they were tied, had often a particular reference to the qualities or story of the deceased, or were expressive of the feelings of the mourner. In an old poem, entitled "Corydon's Doleful Knell," a lover specifies the decorations he intends to use:

> A garland shall be framed
>   By art and nature's skill,
> Of sundry-coloured flowers,
>   In token of good will.
>
> And sundry-coloured ribbands
>   On it I will bestow;
> But chiefly blacke and yellowe
>   With her to grave shall go.
>
> I'll deck her tomb with flowers
>   The rarest ever seen;
> And with my tears as showers
>   I'll keepe them fresh and green.

The white rose, we are told, was planted at the grave of a virgin; her chaplet was tied with white ribbands, in token of her spotless innocence, though sometimes black ribbands were intermingled, to bespeak the grief of the survivors. The red rose was occasionally used in remembrance of such as had been remarkable for benevolence; but roses in general were appropriated to the graves of lovers. Evelyn tells us that the custom was not altogether extinct in his time, near his dwelling in the county of Surrey, "where the maidens yearly planted and decked the graves of their defunct sweethearts with rose-bushes." And Camden, likewise, remarks in his Britannia: "Here is also a certain custom, observed time out of mind, of planting rose trees upon the graves, especially by the young men and maids who have lost their loves; so that this church yard is now full of them."

When the deceased had been unhappy in their loves, emblems of a more gloomy character were used, such as the yew and cypress; and if flowers were strewn they were of the most melancholy colours. Thus, in poems by Thomas Stanley, Esq. (published in 1651) is the following stanza:

> Yet strew
> Upon my dismall grave
> Such offerings as you have,
> Forsaken cypresse and sad yewe;
> For kinder flowers can take no birth
> Or growth from such unhappy earth.

In "The Maid's Tragedy," a pathetic little air is introduced, illustrative of this mode of decorating the funerals of females who had been disappointed in love:

> Lay a garland on my hearse
> Of the dismall yew,
> Maidens willow branches wear,
> Say I died true.
>
> My love was false, but I was firm
> From my hour of birth,
> Upon my buried body lie
> Lightly, gentle earth.

The natural effect of sorrow over the dead is to refine and elevate the mind, and we have a proof of it in the purity of sentiment and the unaffected elegance of thought which pervaded the whole of these funereal observances. Thus, it was an especial precaution, that none but sweet scented evergreens and flowers should be employed. The intention seems to have been to soften the horrors of the tomb, to beguile the mind from brooding over the disgraces of perishing mortality, and to associate the memory of the deceased with the most delicate and beautiful objects in nature. There is a dismal process going on in the grave, ere dust can return to its kindred dust, which the imagination shrinks from contemplating; and we seek still to think of the form we have loved, with those refined associations which it awakened when blooming before us in youth and beauty. "Lay her i' the earth," says Laertes of his virgin sister,

> And from her fair and unpolluted flesh
> May violets spring!

Herrick, also, in his "Dirge of Jeptha," pours forth a fragrant flow of poetical thought and image, which in a manner embalms the dead in the recollections of the living.

> Sleep in thy peace, thy bed of spice,
> And make this place all Paradise:
> May sweets grow here! and smoke from hence,
>   Fat frankinscence.
> Let balme and cassia send their scent
> From out thy maiden monument.
>
>   *   *   *   *   *
>
> May all shie maids at wonted hours
> Come forth to strew thy tombe with flowers;
> May virgins when they come to mourn,
>   Male incense burn
> Upon thine altar! then return
> And leave thee sleeping in thine urn.

I might crowd my pages with extracts from the older British poets, who wrote when these rites were more prevalent, and delighted frequently to allude to them; but I have already quoted more than is necessary. I cannot however refrain from giving a passage from Shakspeare, even though it should appear trite, which illustrates the emblematical meaning often conveyed in these floral tributes, and at the same time possesses that magic of language and appositeness of imagery for which he stands pre-eminent:

> With fairest flowers,
> Whilst summer lasts, and I live here, Fidele,
> I'll sweeten thy sad grave; thou shalt not lack
> The flower that's like thy face, pale primrose; nor

The azur'd harebell like thy veins; no, nor
The leaf of eglantine; whom not to slander,
Outsweetened not thy breath.

There is certainly something more affecting in these prompt and spontaneous offerings of nature, than in the most costly monuments of art; the hand strews the flower while the heart is warm, and the tear falls on the grave as affection is binding the osier around the sod; but pathos expires under the slow labour of the chisel, and is chilled among the cold conceits of sculptured marble.

It is greatly to be regretted, that a custom so truly elegant and touching has disappeared from general use, and exists only in the most remote and insignificant villages. But it seems as if poetical custom always shuns the walks of cultivated society. In proportion as people grow polite they cease to be poetical. They talk of poetry, but they have learnt to check its free impulses, to distrust its sallying emotions, and to supply its most affecting and picturesque usages, by studied form and pompous ceremonial. Few pageants can be more stately and frigid than an English funeral in town. It is made up of show and gloomy parade: mourning carriages, mourning horses, mourning plumes, and hireling mourners, who make a mockery of grief. "There is a grave digged," says Jeremy Taylor, "and a solemn mourning, and a great talk in the neighbourhood, and when the daies are finished, they shall be, and they shall be remembered no more." The associate in the gay and crowded city is soon forgotten; the hurrying succession of new intimates and new pleasures effaces him from our minds, and the very scenes and circles in which he moved are incessantly fluctuating. But funerals in the country are solemnly impressive. The stroke of death makes a wider space in the village circle, and is an awful event in the tranquil uniformity of rural life. The passing bell tolls its knell in every ear; it steals with its pervading melancholy over hill and vale, and saddens all the landscape.

The fixed and unchanging features of the country also, perpetuate the memory of the friend with whom we once enjoyed them, who was the companion of our most retired walks, and gave animation to every lonely scene. His idea is associated with every charm of nature; we hear his voice in the echo which he once delighted to awaken; his spirit haunts the grove which he once frequented; we think of him in the wild upland solitude, or amidst the pensive beauty of the valley. In the freshness of joyous morning, we remember his beaming smiles and bounding gayety; and when sober evening returns with its gathering shadows and subduing quiet, we call to mind many a twilight hour of gentle talk and sweet souled melancholy.

> Each lonely place shall him restore,
>   For him the tear be duly shed,
> Belov'd till life can charm no more,
>   And mourn'd, till pity's self be dead.

Another cause that perpetuates the memory of the deceased in the country, is, that the grave is more immediately in sight of the survivors. They pass it on their way to prayer; it meets their eyes when their hearts are softened by the exercises of devotion; they linger about it on the sabbath, when the mind is disengaged from worldly cares, and most disposed to turn aside from present pleasures and present loves, and to sit down among the solemn mementos of the past. In North Wales the peasantry kneel and pray over the graves of their deceased friends for several Sundays after the interment; and where the tender rite of strewing and planting flowers is still practised, it is always renewed on Easter, Whitsuntide, and other festivals, when the season brings the companion of former festivity more vividly to mind. It is also invariably performed by the nearest relatives and friends; no menials nor hirelings are employed, and if a neighbour yields assistance, it would be deemed an insult to offer compensation.

I have dwelt upon this beautiful rural custom, because, as it is one of the last, so is it one of the holiest offices of love. The grave is the ordeal of true affection. It is there that the divine passion of the soul manifests its superiority to the instinctive impulse of mere animal attachment. The latter must be continually refreshed and kept alive by the presence of its object, but the love that is seated in the soul can live on long remembrance. The mere inclinations of sense languish and decline with the charms which excited them, and turn with shuddering disgust from the dismal precincts of the tomb; but it is thence that truly spiritual affection rises purified from every sensual desire, and returns, like a holy flame, to illumine and sanctify the heart of the survivor.

The sorrow for the dead is the only sorrow from which we refuse to be divorced. Every other wound we seek to heal—every other affliction to forget; but this wound we consider it a duty to keep open—this affliction we cherish and brood over in solitude. Where is the mother who would willingly forget the infant that perished like a blossom from her arms, though every recollection is a pang? Where is the child that would willingly forget the most tender of parents, though to remember be but to lament? Who, even in the hour of agony, would forget the friend over whom he mourns? Who, even when the tomb is closing upon the remains of her he most loved, when he feels his heart, as it were, crushed in the closing of its portal, would accept of consolation that must be bought by forgetfulness?—No, the love which survives the tomb is one of the noblest attributes of the soul. If it has its woes, it has likewise its delights; and when the overwhelming burst of grief is calmed into the gentle tear of recollection; when the sudden anguish and the convulsive agony over the present ruins of all that we most loved, is softened away into pensive meditation on all that it was in the days of its loveliness—who would root out such a sorrow from the heart? Though it may sometimes throw a passing cloud over the bright hour of gayety; or spread a deeper sadness over the hour of gloom; yet who would exchange it even for the song of pleasure, or the burst of revelry? No, there is a voice from the tomb sweeter than song. There is a remembrance of the dead to which we turn even from the charms of the living. Oh the grave!—the grave!—It buries every error—covers every defect—extinguishes every resentment. From its peaceful bosom spring none but fond regrets and tender recollections. Who can look down upon the grave even of an enemy, and not feel a compunctious throb, that he should ever have warred with the poor handful of earth that lies mouldering before him!

But the grave of those we loved—what a place for meditation! There it is that we call up in long review the whole

history of virtue and gentleness, and the thousand endearments lavished upon us almost unheeded in the daily intercourse of intimacy;—there it is that we dwell upon the
tenderness, the solemn, awful tenderness of the parting
scene—the bed of death, with all its stifled griefs, its noiseless
attendance, its mute, watchful assiduities—the last testimo-
nies of expiring love—the feeble, fluttering, thrilling, oh!
how thrilling! pressure of the hand—the faint, faltering
accents struggling in death to give one more assurance of
affection—the last fond look of the glazing eye, turning upon
us even from the threshold of existence!

Aye, go to the grave of buried love, and meditate! There
settle the account with thy conscience for every past benefit
unrequited—every past endearment unregarded, of that departed being, who can never—never—never return to be
soothed by thy contrition!

If thou art a child, and hast ever added a sorrow to the
soul, or a furrow to the silvered brow of an affectionate parent—if thou art a husband, and hast ever caused the fond
bosom that ventured its whole happiness in thy arms, to
doubt one moment of thy kindness or thy truth—if thou art
a friend, and hast ever wronged, in thought, or word, or
deed, the spirit that generously confided in thee—if thou art
a lover, and hast ever given one unmerited pang to that true
heart which now lies cold and still beneath thy feet;—then
be sure that every unkind look, every ungracious word, every
ungentle action, will come thronging back upon thy memory,
and knocking dolefully at thy soul—then be sure that thou
wilt lie down sorrowing and repentant on the grave, and utter
the unheard groan, and pour the unavailing tear, more deep,
more bitter, because unheard and unavailing.

Then weave thy chaplet of flowers, and strew the beauties
of nature about the grave; console thy broken spirit, if thou
canst, with these tender, yet futile tributes of regret;—but
take warning by the bitterness of this thy contrite affliction
over the dead, and henceforth be more faithful and affectionate in the discharge of thy duties to the living.

———————

In writing the preceding article, it was not intended to give a
full detail of the funeral customs of the English peasantry, but

merely to furnish a few hints and quotations illustrative of
particular rites; to be appended, by way of note, to another
paper, which has been withheld. The article swelled insensibly
into its present form, and this is mentioned as an apology for
so brief and casual a notice of these usages, after they have
been amply and learnedly investigated in other works.

I must observe, also, that I am well aware that this custom
of adorning graves with flowers prevails in other countries
besides England. Indeed, in some it is much more general,
and is observed even by the rich and fashionable, but it is
then apt to lose its simplicity, and to degenerate into affectation. Bright, in his travels in Lower Hungary, tells of monuments of marble, with recesses formed for retirement, with
seats placed among bowers of green house plants; and that
the graves generally are covered with the gayest flowers of the
season. He gives a casual picture of filial piety, which I cannot
but transcribe; for I trust it is as useful as it is delightful to
illustrate the amiable virtues of the sex. "When I was at Ber-
lin," says he, "I followed the celebrated Iffland to the grave.
Mingled with some pomp, you might trace much real feeling.
In the midst of the ceremony, my attention was attracted by
a young woman who stood on a mound of earth, newly covered with turf, which she anxiously protected from the feet of
the passing crowd. It was the tomb of her parent; and the
figure of this affectionate daughter presented a monument
more striking than the most costly work of art."

I will barely add an instance of sepulchral decoration that I
once met with among the mountains of Switzerland. It was
at the village of Gersau, which stands on the borders of the
lake of Lucerne, at the foot of Mount Rigi. It was once the
capital of a miniature republic, shut up between the Alps and
the lake, and accessible on the land side only by foot paths.
The whole force of the republic did not exceed six hundred
fighting men; and a few miles of circumference, scooped out
as it were from the bosom of the mountains, comprised its
territory. The village of Gersau seemed separated from the
rest of the world, and retained the golden simplicity of a
purer age. It had a small church, with a burying ground adjoining. At the heads of the graves were placed crosses of
wood or iron. On some were affixed miniatures, rudely exe-

cuted, but evidently attempts at likenesses of the deceased. On the crosses were hung chaplets of flowers, some withering, others fresh, as if occasionally renewed. I paused with interest at this scene; I felt that I was at the source of poetical description, for these were the beautiful but unaffected offerings of the heart which poets are fain to record. In a gayer and more populous place, I should have suspected them to have been suggested by factitious sentiment, derived from books; but the good people of Gersau knew little of books; there was not a novel nor a love poem in the village; and I question whether any peasant of the place dreamt, while he was twining a fresh chaplet for the grave of his mistress, that he was fulfilling one of the most fanciful rites of poetical devotion, and that he was practically a poet.

The Inn Kitchen

Shall I not take mine ease in mine inn?
Falstaff

DURING A JOURNEY that I once made through the Netherlands, I had arrived one evening at the *Pomme d'Or*, the principal inn of a small Flemish village. It was after the hour of the *table d'hote*, so that I was obliged to make a solitary supper from the reliques of its ampler board. The weather was chilly; I was seated alone in one end of a great gloomy dining room, and my repast being over, I had the prospect before me of a long dull evening, without any visible means of enlivening it. I summoned mine host, and requested something to read; he brought me the whole literary stock of his household, a Dutch family bible, an almanack in the same language, and a number of old Paris newspapers. As I sat dozing over one of the latter, reading old news and stale criticisms, my ear was now and then struck with bursts of laughter which seemed to proceed from the kitchen. Every one that has travelled on the continent, must know how favourite a resort the kitchen of a country inn is to the middle and inferior order of travellers, particularly in that equivocal kind of weather, when a fire becomes agreeable toward evening. I threw aside the newspaper, and explored my way to the kitchen, to take a peep at the group that appeared to be so merry. It was composed partly of travellers who had arrived some hours before in a diligence, and partly of the usual attendants and hangers on of inns. They were seated around a great burnished stove, that might have been mistaken for an altar, at which they were worshipping. It was covered with various kitchen vessels of resplendent brightness; among which steamed and hissed a huge copper tea kettle. A large lamp threw a strong mass of light upon the group, bringing out many odd features in strong relief. Its yellow rays partially illumined the spacious kitchen, dying duskily away into remote corners, except where they settled in mellow radiance on the broad side of a flitch of bacon, or were reflected back from well scoured utensils, that gleamed from the midst of obscurity. A strapping Flemish lass, with long golden pendants in her ears, and a necklace with a golden heart suspended to it, was the presiding priestess of the temple.

Many of the company were furnished with pipes, and most of them with some kind of evening potation. I found their mirth was occasioned by anecdotes which a little swarthy Frenchman, with a dry weazen face and large whiskers, was giving of his love adventures; at the end of each of which there was one of those bursts of honest unceremonious laughter, in which a man indulges in that temple of true liberty, an Inn.

As I had no better mode of getting through a tedious blustering evening, I took my seat near the stove, and listened to a variety of travellers' tales, some very extravagant, and most very dull. All of them, however, have faded from my treacherous memory except one, which I will endeavour to relate. I fear, however, it derived its chief zest from the manner in which it was told, and the peculiar air and appearance of the narrator. He was a corpulent old Swiss, who had the look of a veteran traveller. He was dressed in a tarnished green travelling jacket, with a broad belt round his waist, and a pair of overalls, with buttons from the hips to the ankles. He was of a full, rubicund countenance, with a double chin, aquiline nose, and a pleasant twinkling eye. His hair was light, and curled from under an old green velvet travelling cap stuck on one side of his head. He was interrupted more than once by the arrival of guests, or the remarks of his auditors; and paused now and then to replenish his pipe; at which times he had generally a roguish leer, and a sly joke for the buxom kitchen maid.

I wish my readers could imagine the old fellow lolling in a huge arm chair, one arm akimbo, the other holding a curiously twisted tobacco pipe, formed of genuine *écume de mer*, decorated with silver chain and silken tassel—his head cocked on one side, and a whimsical cut of the eye occasionally, as he related the following story.

The Spectre Bridegroom

A Traveller's Tale*

> He that supper for is dight,
> He lyes full cold, I trow, this night!
> Yestreen to chamber I him led,
> This night Gray-steel has made his bed!
> *Sir Eger, Sir Grahame, and Sir Gray-steel*

O N THE SUMMIT of one of the heights of the Odenwald, a wild and romantic tract of upper Germany, that lies not far from the confluence of the Main and the Rhine, there stood, many, many years since, the Castle of the Baron Von Landshort. It is now quite fallen to decay, and almost buried among beech trees and dark firs, above which, however, its old watch tower may still be seen struggling, like the former possessor I have mentioned, to carry a high head, and look down upon the neighbouring country.

The Baron was a dry branch of the great family of Katzen-ellenbogen,† and inherited the reliques of the property, and all the pride of his ancestors. Though the warlike disposition of his predecessors had much impaired the family possessions, yet the Baron still endeavoured to keep up some show of former state. The times were peaceable, and the German nobles, in general, had abandoned their inconvenient old castles, perched like eagles' nests among the mountains, and had built more convenient residences in the valleys: still the Baron remained proudly drawn up in his little fortress, cherishing with hereditary inveteracy, all the old family feuds; so that he was on ill terms with some of his nearest neighbours, on account of disputes that had happened between their great great grandfathers.

The Baron had but one child, a daughter; but nature, when

---

*The erudite reader, well versed in good for nothing lore, will perceive that the above tale must have been suggested to the old Swiss by a little French anecdote, of a circumstance said to have taken place at Paris.

† *i.e.* CATSELBOW. The name of a family of those parts very powerful in former times. The appellation, we are told, was given in compliment to a peerless dame of the family, celebrated for a fine arm.

she grants but one child, always compensates by making it a prodigy; and so it was with the daughter of the Baron. All the nurses, gossips, and country cousins, assured her father that she had not her equal for beauty in all Germany; and who should know better than they. She had, moreover, been brought up with great care under the superintendance of two maiden aunts, who had spent some years of their early life at one of the little German courts, and were skilled in all the branches of knowledge necessary to the education of a fine lady. Under their instructions, she became a miracle of accomplishments. By the time she was eighteen she could embroider to admiration, and had worked whole histories of the saints in tapestry, with such strength of expression in their countenances, that they looked like so many souls in purgatory. She could read without great difficulty, and had spelled her way through several church legends, and almost all the chivalric wonders of the Heldenbuch. She had even made considerable proficiency in writing, could sign her own name without missing a letter, and so legibly, that her aunts could read it without spectacles. She excelled in making little elegant good for nothing lady like nick-nacks of all kinds; was versed in the most abstruse dancing of the day; played a number of airs on the harp and guitar; and knew all the tender ballads of the Minne-lieders by heart.

Her aunts, too, having been great flirts and coquettes in their younger days, were admirably calculated to be vigilant guardians and strict censors of the conduct of their niece; for there is no duenna so rigidly prudent, and inexorably decorous, as a superannuated coquette. She was rarely suffered out of their sight; never went beyond the domains of the castle, unless well attended, or rather, well watched; had continual lectures read to her about strict decorum and implicit obedience; and, as to the men—pah!—she was taught to hold them at such distance and in such absolute distrust, that, unless properly authorized, she would not have cast a glance upon the handsomest cavalier in the world—no, not if he were even dying at her feet!

The good effects of this system were wonderfully apparent. The young lady was a pattern of docility and correctness. While others were wasting their sweetness in the glare of the world, and liable to be plucked and thrown aside by every hand, she was coyly blooming into fresh and lovely womanhood under the protection of those immaculate spinsters, like a rose bud blushing forth among guardian thorns. Her aunts looked upon her with pride and exultation, and vaunted that though all the other young ladies in the world might go astray, yet thank heaven, nothing of the kind could happen to the heiress of Katzenellenbogen.

But, however scantily the Baron Von Landshort might be provided with children, his household was by no means a small one, for providence had enriched him with abundance of poor relations. They, one and all, possessed the affectionate disposition common to humble relatives: were wonderfully attached to the Baron, and took every possible occasion to come in swarms and enliven the castle. All family festivals were commemorated by these good people at the Baron's expense; and when they were filled with good cheer, they would declare that there was nothing on earth so delightful as these family meetings, these jubilees of the heart.

The Baron, though a small man, had a large soul, and it swelled with satisfaction at the consciousness of being the greatest man in the little world about him. He loved to tell long stories about the stark old warriors whose portraits looked grimly down from the walls around, and he found no listeners equal to those who fed at his expense. He was much given to the marvellous, and a firm believer in all those supernatural tales with which every mountain and valley in Germany abounds. The faith of his guests exceeded even his own: they listened to every tale of wonder with open eyes and mouth, and never failed to be astonished, even though repeated for the hundredth time. Thus lived the Baron Von Landshort, the oracle of his table, the absolute monarch of his little territory, and happy above all things, in the persuasion that he was the wisest man of the age.

At the time of which my story treats, there was a great family gathering at the Castle, on an affair of the utmost importance. It was to receive the destined bridegroom of the Baron's daughter. A negotiation had been carried on between the father, and an old nobleman of Bavaria, to unite the dignity of their houses by the marriage of their children. The preliminaries had been conducted with proper punctilio. The young people were betrothed without seeing each other, and the time was appointed for the marriage ceremony. The young Count Von Altenburg had been recalled from the army for the purpose, and was actually on his way to the Baron's to receive his bride. Missives had even been received from him, from Wurtzburg, where he was accidentally detained, mentioning the day and hour when he might be expected to arrive.

The castle was in a tumult of preparation to give him a suitable welcome. The fair bride had been decked out with uncommon care. The two aunts had superintended her toilet, and quarrelled the whole morning about every article of her dress. The young lady had taken advantage of their contest to follow the bent of her own taste; and fortunately it was a good one. She looked as lovely as youthful bridegroom could desire; and the flutter of expectation heightened the lustre of her charms.

The suffusions that mantled her face and neck, the gentle heaving of the bosom, the eye now and then lost in reverie, all betrayed the soft tumult that was going on in her little heart. The aunts were continually hovering around her; for maiden aunts are apt to take great interest in affairs of this nature. They were giving her a world of staid counsel how to deport herself, what to say, and in what manner to receive the expected lover.

The Baron was no less busied in preparations. He had, in truth, nothing exactly to do; but he was naturally a fuming, bustling little man, and could not remain passive when all the world was in a hurry. He worried from top to bottom of the castle, with an air of infinite anxiety; he continually called the servants from their work to exhort them to be diligent, and buzzed about every hall and chamber, as idly restless and importunate as a blue bottle fly of a warm summer's day.

In the mean time, the fatted calf had been killed; the forests had rung with the clamour of the huntsmen; the kitchen was crowded with good cheer; the cellars had yielded up whole oceans of *Rhein-wein* and *Ferne-wein*, and even the great Heidelberg tun had been laid under contribution. Every thing was ready to receive the distinguished guest with *Saus und*

Braus in the true spirit of German hospitality—but the guest delayed to make his appearance. Hour rolled after hour. The sun that had poured his downward rays upon the rich forests of the Odenwald, now just gleamed along the summits of the mountains. The Baron mounted the highest tower, and strained his eyes in hopes of catching a distant sight of the Count and his attendants. Once he thought he beheld them; the sound of horns came floating from the valley, prolonged by the mountain echoes. A number of horsemen were seen far below, slowly advancing along the road; but when they had nearly reached the foot of the mountain, they suddenly struck off in a different direction. The last ray of sunshine departed—the bats began to flit by in the twilight—the road grew dimmer and dimmer to the view; and nothing appeared stirring in it, but now and then a peasant lagging homeward from his labour.

While the old castle of Landshort was in this state of perplexity, a very interesting scene was transacting in a different part of the Odenwald.

The young Count Von Altenburg was tranquilly pursuing his route in that sober jog trot way in which a man travels towards matrimony, when his friends have taken all the trouble and uncertainty of courtship off his hands, and a bride is waiting for him, as—certainly as a dinner, at the end of his journey. He had encountered, at Wurtzburg, a youthful companion in arms, with whom he had seen some service on the frontiers; Herman Von Starkenfaust, one of the stoutest hands, and worthiest hearts, of German chivalry, who was now returning from the army. His father's castle was not far distant from the old fortress of Landshort, although an hereditary feud rendered the families hostile, and strangers to each other.

In the warm hearted moment of recognition, the young friends related all their past adventures and fortunes, and the count gave the whole history of his intended nuptials with a young lady whom he had never seen, but of whose charms he had received the most enrapturing descriptions.

As the route of the friends lay in the same direction, they agreed to perform the rest of their journey together; and that they might do it the more leisurely, set off from Wurtzburg at an early hour, the count having given directions for his retinue to follow and overtake him.

They beguiled their wayfaring with recollections of their military scenes and adventures; but the count was apt to be a little tedious, now and then, about the reputed charms of his bride, and the felicity that awaited him.

In this way they had entered among the mountains of the Odenwald, and were traversing one of its most lonely and thickly wooded passes. It is well known that the forests of Germany have always been as much infested by robbers as its castles by spectres; and, at this time, the former were particularly numerous from the hordes of disbanded soldiers wandering about the country. It will not appear extraordinary, therefore, that the cavaliers were attacked by a gang of these stragglers, in the midst of the forest. They defended themselves with bravery, but were nearly overpowered, when the count's retinue arrived to their assistance. At sight of them the robbers fled, but not until the count had received a mortal wound. He was slowly and carefully conveyed back to the city of Wurtzburg, and a friar summoned from a neighbouring convent, who was famous for his skill in administering to both soul and body. But half of his skill was superfluous; the moments of the unfortunate count were numbered.

With his dying breath he entreated his friend to repair instantly to the castle of Landshort, and explain the fatal cause of his not keeping his appointment with his bride. Though not the most ardent of lovers, he was one of the most punctilious of men; and appeared earnestly solicitous that this mission should be speedily and courteously executed. "Unless this is done," said he, "I shall not sleep quietly in my grave!" He repeated these last words with peculiar solemnity. A request, at a moment so impressive, admitted no hesitation. Starkenfaust endeavoured to soothe him to calmness, promised faithfully to execute his wish, and gave him his hand in solemn pledge. The dying man pressed it in acknowledgment, but soon lapsed into delirium—raved about his bride—his engagement—his plighted word; ordered his horse, that he might ride to the castle of Landshort, and expired in the fancied act of vaulting into the saddle.

Starkenfaust bestowed a sigh, and a soldier's tear, on the

untimely fate of his comrade; and then pondered on the awkward mission he had undertaken. His heart was heavy, and his head perplexed; for he was to present himself an unbidden guest among hostile people, and to damp their festivity with tidings fatal to their hopes. Still there were certain whisperings of curiosity in his bosom to see this far famed beauty of Katzenellenbogen, so cautiously shut up from the world; for he was a passionate admirer of the sex, and there was a dash of eccentricity and enterprize in his character that made him fond of all singular adventure.

Previous to his departure, he made all due arrangements with the holy fraternity of the convent for the funeral solemnities of his friend, who was to be buried in the cathedral of Wurtzburg, near some of his illustrious relatives; and the mourning retinue of the count took charge of his remains.

It is now high time that we should return to the ancient family of Katzenellenbogen, who were impatient for their guest, and still more for their dinner; and to the worthy little Baron, whom we left airing himself on the watch tower.

Night closed in, but still no guest arrived. The Baron descended from the tower in despair. The banquet, which had been delayed from hour to hour could no longer be postponed. The meats were already overdone; the cook in an agony; and the whole household had the look of a garrison that had been reduced by famine. The Baron was obliged reluctantly to give orders for the feast without the presence of the guest. All were seated at table, and just on the point of commencing, when the sound of a horn from without the gate gave notice of the approach of a stranger. Another long blast filled the old courts of the castle with its echoes, and was answered by the warder from the walls. The Baron hastened to receive his future son in law.

The drawbridge had been let down, and the stranger was before the gate. He was a tall gallant cavalier, mounted on a black steed. His countenance was pale, but he had a beaming, romantic eye, and an air of stately melancholy. The Baron was a little mortified that he should have come in this simple, solitary style. His dignity for a moment was ruffled, and he felt disposed to consider it a want of proper respect for the important occasion, and the important family with which he was

to be connected. He, however, pacified himself with the conclusion that it must have been youthful impatience which had
induced him thus to spur on sooner than his attendants.

"I am sorry," said the stranger, "to break in upon you thus
unseasonably—"

Here the Baron interrupted him with a world of compliments and greetings; for, to tell the truth, he prided himself
upon his courtesy and his eloquence. The stranger attempted,
once or twice, to stem the torrent of words, but in vain, so
he bowed his head and suffered it to flow on. By the time the
Baron had come to a pause, they had reached the inner court
of the castle; and the stranger was again about to speak, when
he was once more interrupted by the appearance of the female
part of the family, leading forth the shrinking and blushing
bride. He gazed on her for a moment as one entranced; it
seemed as if his whole soul beamed forth in the gaze, and
rested upon that lovely form. One of the maiden aunts whispered something in her ear; she made an effort to speak; her
moist blue eye was timidly raised, gave a shy glance of inquiry
on the stranger, and was cast again to the ground. The words
died away; but there was a sweet smile playing about her lips,
and a soft dimpling of the cheek, that showed her glance had
not been unsatisfactory. It was impossible for a girl of the
fond age of eighteen, highly predisposed for love and matrimony, not to be pleased with so gallant a cavalier.

The late hour at which the guest had arrived, left no time
for parley. The Baron was peremptory, and deferred all particular conversation until the morning, and led the way to the
untasted banquet.

It was served up in the great hall of the castle. Around the
walls hung the hard favoured portraits of the heroes of the
house of Katzenellenbogen, and the trophies which they had
gained in the field and in the chase. Hacked corslets; splin-
tered jousting spears, and tattered banners, were mingled
with the spoils of sylvan warfare: the jaws of the wolf, and
the tusks of the boar, grinned horribly among cross bows and
battle axes, and a huge pair of antlers branched immediately
over the head of the youthful bridegroom.

The cavalier took but little notice of the company, or the
entertainment. He scarce tasted the banquet, but seemed ab-

sorbed in admiration of his bride. He conversed in a low tone that could not be overheard—for the language of love is never loud; but where is the female ear so dull that it cannot catch the softest whisper of the lover? There was a mingled tenderness and gravity in his manner, that appeared to have a powerful effect upon the young lady. Her colour came and went as she listened with deep attention. Now and then she made some blushing reply, and when his eye was turned away, she would steal a side long glance at his romantic countenance, and heave a gentle sigh of tender happiness. It was evident that the young couple were completely enamoured. The aunts, who were deeply versed in the mysteries of the heart, declared that they had fallen in love with each other at first sight.

The feast went on merrily, or at least noisily, for the guests were all blessed with those keen appetites that attend upon light purses and mountain air. The Baron told his best and longest stories, and never had he told them so well, or with such great effect. If there was any thing marvellous, his auditors were lost in astonishment; and if any thing facetious, they were sure to laugh exactly in the right place. The Baron, it is true, like most great men, was too dignified to utter any joke but a dull one; it was always enforced, however, by a bumper of excellent Hoch-heimer; and even a dull joke at one's own table, served up with jolly old wine, is irresistible. Many good things were said by poorer and keener wits, that would not bear repeating, except on similar occasions; many sly speeches whispered in ladies' ears, that almost convulsed them with suppressed laughter; and a song or two roared out by a poor, but merry and broad faced cousin of the Baron, that absolutely made the maiden aunts hold up their fans.

Amidst all this revelry, the stranger guest maintained a most singular and unseasonable gravity. His countenance assumed a deeper cast of dejection as the evening advanced, and, strange as it may appear, even the Baron's jokes seemed only to render him the more melancholy. At times he was lost in thought, and at times there was a perturbed and restless wandering of the eye that bespoke a mind but ill at ease. His conversations with the bride became more and more earnest and mysterious. Lowering clouds began to steal over the fair serenity of her brow, and tremors to run through her tender frame.

All this could not escape the notice of the company. Their gayety was chilled by the unaccountable gloom of the bridegroom; their spirits were infected; whispers and glances were interchanged, accompanied by shrugs and dubious shakes of the head. The song and the laugh grew less and less frequent; there were dreary pauses in the conversation, which were at length succeeded by wild tales, and supernatural legends. One dismal story produced another still more dismal, and the Baron nearly frightened some of the ladies into hysterics with the history of the goblin horseman that carried away the fair Leonora; a dreadful, but true story, which has since been put into excellent verse, and is read and believed by all the world.

The bridegroom listened to this tale with profound attention. He kept his eyes steadily fixed on the Baron, and as the story drew to a close, began gradually to rise from his seat, growing taller and taller, until, in the Baron's entranced eye, he seemed almost to tower into a giant. The moment the tale was finished, he heaved a deep sigh, and took a solemn farewell of the company. They were all amazement. The Baron was perfectly thunderstruck.

"What! going to leave the castle at midnight? why, every thing was prepared for his reception: a chamber was ready for him if he wished to retire."

The stranger shook his head mournfully, and mysteriously; "I must lay my head in a different chamber tonight!"

There was something in this reply, and the tone in which it was uttered, that made the Baron's heart misgive him; but he rallied his forces and repeated his hospitable entreaties.

The stranger shook his head silently, but positively, at every offer, and waving his farewell to the company, stalked slowly out of the hall. The maiden aunts were absolutely petrified— the bride hung her head, and a tear stole to her eye.

The Baron followed the stranger to the great court of the castle, where the black charger stood pawing the earth, and snorting with impatience. When they had reached the portal, whose deep archway was dimly lighted by a cresset, the stranger paused, and addressed the Baron in a hollow tone of voice, which the vaulted roof rendered still more sepulchral.

"Now that we are alone," said he, "I will impart to you the reason of my going. I have a solemn, an indispensable engagement—"

"Why," said the Baron, "cannot you send some one in your place?"

"It admits of no substitute—I must attend it in person—I must away to Wurtzburg cathedral—"

"Aye," said the Baron, plucking up spirit, "but not until tomorrow—tomorrow you shall take your bride there."

"No! no!" replied the stranger, with tenfold solemnity, "my engagement is with no bride—the worms! the worms expect me! I am a dead man—I have been slain by robbers—my body lies at Wurtzburg—at midnight I am to be buried—the grave is waiting for me—I must keep my appointment!"

He sprang on his black charger, dashed over the drawbridge, and the clattering of his horse's hoofs was lost in the whistling of the night blast.

The Baron returned to the hall in the utmost consternation, and related what had passed. Two ladies fainted outright, others sickened at the idea of having banquetted with a spectre. It was the opinion of some, that this might be the wild huntsman famous in German legend. Some talked of mountain sprites, of wood demons, and of other supernatural beings, with which the good people of Germany have been so grievously harassed since time immemorial. One of the poor relations ventured to suggest that it might be some sportive evasion of the young cavalier, and that the very gloominess of the caprice seemed to accord with so melancholy a personage. This, however, drew on him the indignation of the whole company, and especially of the Baron, who looked upon him as little better than an infidel; so that he was fain to abjure his heresy as speedily as possible, and come into the faith of the true believers.

But, whatever may have been the doubts entertained, they were completely put to an end by the arrival, next day, of regular missives, confirming the intelligence of the young Count's murder, and his interment in Wurtzburg cathedral.

The dismay at the castle may well be imagined. The Baron shut himself up in his chamber. The guests who had come to rejoice with him, could not think of abandoning him in his distress. They wandered about the courts, or collected in groups in the hall, shaking their heads and shrugging their shoulders, at the troubles of so good a man; and sat longer than ever at table, and ate and drank more stoutly than ever, by way of keeping up their spirits. But the situation of the widowed bride was the most pitiable. To have lost a husband before she had even embraced him—and such a husband! if the very spectre could be so gracious and noble, what must have been the living man! She filled the house with lamentations.

On the night of the second day of her widowhood she had retired to her chamber, accompanied by one of her aunts, who insisted on sleeping with her. The aunt, who was one of the best tellers of ghost stories in all Germany, had just been recounting one of her longest, and had fallen asleep in the very midst of it. The chamber was remote, and overlooked a small garden. The niece lay pensively gazing at the beams of the rising moon, as they trembled on the leaves of an aspen tree before the lattice. The castle clock had just tolled midnight, when a soft strain of music stole up from the garden. She rose hastily from her bed, and stepped lightly to the window. A tall figure stood among the shadows of the trees. As it raised its head, a beam of moonlight fell upon the countenance. Heaven and earth! she beheld the Spectre Bridegroom! A loud shriek at that moment burst upon her ear, and her aunt, who had been awakened by the music, and had followed her silently to the window, fell into her arms. When she looked again, the spectre had disappeared.

Of the two females, the aunt now required the most soothing, for she was perfectly beside herself with terror. As to the young lady, there was something, even in the spectre of her lover, that seemed endearing. There was still the semblance of manly beauty; and though the shadow of a man is but little calculated to satisfy the affections of a love sick girl, yet, where the substance is not to be had, even that is consoling. The aunt declared she would never sleep in that chamber again; the niece, for once, was refractory, and declared as strongly that she would sleep in no other in the castle: the consequence was, that she had to sleep in it alone; but she drew a promise from her aunt not to relate the story of the

spectre, lest she should be denied the only melancholy pleasure left her on earth—that of inhabiting the chamber over
which the guardian shade of her lover kept its nightly vigils.

How long the good old lady would have observed this
promise is uncertain, for she dearly loved to talk of the marvellous, and there is a triumph in being the first to tell a
frightful story; it is, however, still quoted in the neighbourhood, as a memorable instance of female secrecy, that she
kept it to herself for a whole week, when she was suddenly
absolved from all further restraint, by intelligence brought to
the breakfast table one morning, that the young lady was not
to be found. Her room was empty—the bed had not been
slept in—the window was open, and the bird had flown!

The astonishment and concern with which the intelligence
was received, can only be imagined by those who have witnessed the agitation which the mishaps of a great man cause
among his friends. Even the poor relations paused for a moment from the indefatigable labours of the trencher; when the
aunt, who had at first been struck speechless, wrung her
hands, and shrieked out, "the goblin! the goblin! she's carried
away by the goblin!"

In a few words, she related the fearful scene of the garden,
and concluded that the spectre must have carried off his bride.
Two of the domestics corroborated the opinion, for they had
heard the clattering of a horse's hoofs down the mountain
about midnight, and had no doubt that it was the spectre on
his black charger, bearing her away to the tomb. All present
were struck with the direful probability; for events of the kind
are extremely common in Germany, as many well authenticated histories bear witness.

What a lamentable situation was that of the poor Baron!
What a heartrending dilemma for a fond father, and a member of the great family of Katzenellenbogen! His only daughter had either been rapt away to the grave, or he was to have
some wood demon for a son in law, and, perchance, a troop
of goblin grand children. As usual, he was completely bewildered, and all the castle in an uproar. The men were ordered
to take horse, and to scour every road, and path, and glen of
the Odenwald. The Baron himself had just drawn on his jack
boots, girded on his sword, and was about to mount his

steed to sally forth on the doubtful quest, when he was brought to a pause by a new apparition. A lady was seen approaching the castle, mounted on a palfrey, attended by a cavalier on horseback. She galloped up to the gate, sprang from her horse, and falling at the Baron's feet, embraced his knees. It was his lost daughter, and her companion—the Spectre Bridegroom! The Baron was astounded. He looked at his daughter, then at the Spectre, and almost doubted the evidence of his senses. The latter, too, was wonderfully improved in his appearance, since his visit to the world of spirits. His dress was splendid, and set off a noble figure of manly symmetry. He was no longer pale and melancholy. His fine countenance was flushed with the glow of youth, and joy rioted in his large dark eye.

The mystery was soon cleared up. The cavalier (for in truth, as you must have known all the while, he was no goblin) announced himself as Sir Herman Von Starkenfaust. He related his adventure with the young Count. He told how he had hastened to the castle to deliver the unwelcome tidings, but that the eloquence of the Baron had interrupted him in every attempt to tell his tale. How the sight of the bride had completely captivated him, and that to pass a few hours near her, he had tacitly suffered the mistake to continue. How he had been sorely perplexed in what way to make a decent retreat, until the Baron's goblin stories had suggested his eccentric exit. How, fearing the feudal hostility of the family, he had repeated his visits by stealth—had haunted the garden beneath the young lady's window—had wooed—had won— had borne away in triumph—and, in a word, had wedded the fair.

Under any other circumstances, the Baron would have been inflexible, for he was tenacious of paternal authority, and devoutly obstinate in all family feuds; but he loved his daughter; he had lamented her as lost; he rejoiced to find her still alive; and, though her husband was of a hostile house, yet, thank heaven, he was not a goblin. There was something, it must be acknowledged, that did not exactly accord with his notions of strict veracity, in the joke the knight had passed upon him of his being a dead man; but several old friends present, who had served in the wars, assured him that every stratagem was excusable in love, and that the cavalier was entitled to especial privilege, having lately served as a trooper.

Matters, therefore, were happily arranged. The Baron pardoned the young couple on the spot. The revels at the castle were resumed. The poor relations overwhelmed this new member of the family with loving kindness; he was so gallant, so generous, and so rich. The aunts, it is true, were somewhat scandalized that their system of strict seclusion, and passive obedience, should be so badly exemplified, but attributed it all to their negligence in not having the windows grated. One of them was particularly mortified at having her marvellous story marred, and that the only spectre she had ever seen should turn out a counterfeit; but the niece seemed perfectly happy at having found him substantial flesh and blood—and so the story ends.

Westminster Abbey

When I behold, with deepe astonishment,
To famous Westminster how there resorte,
Living in brasse or stoney monyment,
The princes and the worthies of all sorte:
Doe not I see reformde nobilitie,
Without contempt, or pride, or ostentation,
And looke upon offenselesse majesty,
Naked of pompe or earthly domination?
And how a play-game of a painted stone,
Contents the quiet now and silent sprites,
Whome all the world which late they stood upon,
Could not content nor quench their appetites.
 Life is a froste of cold felicitie
 And death the thaw of all our vanitie.
Christolero's Epigrams, by T. B. 1598

ON ONE OF THOSE sober and rather melancholy days, in the latter part of Autumn, when the shadows of morning and evening almost mingle together, and throw a gloom over the decline of the year, I passed several hours in rambling about Westminster Abbey. There was something congenial to the season in the mournful magnificence of the old pile; and as I passed its threshold, it seemed like stepping back into the regions of antiquity, and losing myself among the shades of former ages.

I entered from the inner court of Westminster School, through a long, low, vaulted passage, that had an almost subterranean look, being dimly lighted in one part by circular perforations in the massy walls. Through this dark avenue I had a distant view of the cloisters, with the figure of an old verger, in his black gown, moving along their shadowy vaults, and seeming like a spectre from one of the neighbouring tombs. The approach to the abbey through these gloomy monastic remains prepares the mind for its solemn contemplation. The cloisters still retain something of the quiet and seclusion of former days. The grey walls are discoloured by damps, and crumbling with age; a coat of hoary moss has gathered over the inscriptions of the mural monuments, and obscured the death's heads, and other funereal emblems. The sharp touches of the chisel are gone from the rich tracery of the arches; the roses which adorned the key stones have lost their leafy beauty; every thing bears marks of the gradual dilapidations of time, which yet has something touching and pleasing in its very decay.

The sun was pouring down a yellow autumnal ray into the square of the cloisters; beaming upon a scanty plot of grass in the centre, and lighting up an angle of the vaulted passage with a kind of dusty splendour. From between the arcades the eye glanced up to a bit of blue sky or a passing cloud; and beheld the sun gilt pinnacles of the abbey towering into the azure heaven.

As I paced the cloisters, sometimes contemplating this mingled picture of glory and decay, and sometimes endeavouring to decipher the inscriptions on the tombstones, which formed the pavement beneath my feet, my eye was attracted to three figures, rudely carved in relief, but nearly worn away by the footsteps of many generations. They were the effigies of three of the early abbots; the epitaphs were entirely effaced; the names alone remained, having no doubt been renewed in later times; (Vitalis. Abbas. 1082, and Gislebertus Crispinus. Abbas. 1114, and Laurentius. Abbas. 1176). I remained some little while, musing over these casual reliques of antiquity, thus left like wrecks upon this distant shore of time, telling no tale but that such beings had been, and had perished; teaching no moral but the futility of that pride which hopes still to exact homage in its ashes, and to live in an inscription. A little longer and even these faint records will be obliterated, and the monument will cease to be a memorial. Whilst I was yet looking down upon these gravestones, I was roused by the sound of the abbey clock, reverberating from buttress to buttress, and echoing among the cloisters. It is almost startling to hear this warning of departed time sounding among the tombs, and telling the lapse of the hour, which like a billow has rolled us onward towards the grave.

I pursued my walk to an arched door opening to the interior of the abbey. On entering here, the magnitude of the building breaks fully upon the mind, contrasted with the vaults of the cloisters. The eye gazes with wonder at clustered columns of gigantic dimensions, with arches springing from them to such an amazing height; and man wandering about their bases, shrunk into insignificance in comparison with his own handywork. The spaciousness and gloom of this vast edifice produce a profound and mysterious awe. We step cautiously and softly about, as if fearful of disturbing the hallowed silence of the tomb; while every footfall whispers along the walls, and chatters among the sepulchres, making us more sensible of the quiet we have interrupted.

It seems as if the awful nature of the place presses down upon the soul, and hushes the beholder into noiseless reverence. We feel that we are surrounded by the congregated bones of the great men of past times; who have filled history with their deeds, and the earth with their renown. And yet it almost provokes a smile at the vanity of human ambition, to see how they are crowded together and justled in the dust: what parsimony is observed in doling out a scanty nook; a gloomy corner; a little portion of earth, to those, whom, when alive, kingdoms could not satisfy: and how many shapes, and forms and artifices, are devised to catch the casual notice of the passenger, and save from forgetfulness, for a few short years, a name which once aspired to occupy ages of the world's thought and admiration.

I passed some time in Poets' Corner, which occupies an end of one of the transepts or cross aisles of the Abbey. The monuments are generally simple; for the lives of literary men afford no striking themes for the sculptor. Shakespeare and Addison have statues erected to their memories; but the greater part have busts, medallions, and sometimes mere inscriptions. Notwithstanding the simplicity of these memorials, I have always observed that the visitors to the abbey remain longest about them. A kinder and fonder feeling takes place of that cold curiosity or vague admiration with which they gaze on the splendid monuments of the great and the heroic. They linger about these as about the tombs of friends and companions; for indeed there is something of companionship between the author and the reader. Other men are known to posterity only through the medium of history, which is continually growing faint and obscure; but the intercourse between the author and his fellow men is ever new, active and immediate. He has lived for them more than for himself; he has sacrificed surrounding enjoyments, and shut himself up from the delights of social life, that he might the more intimately commune with distant minds and distant ages. Well may the world cherish his renown; for it has been purchased, not by deeds of violence and blood, but by the diligent dispensation of pleasure. Well may posterity be grateful to his memory; for he has left it an inheritance, not of empty names and sounding actions, but whole treasures of wisdom, bright gems of thought, and golden veins of language.

From Poets' Corner I continued my stroll towards that part of the abbey which contains the sepulchres of the kings. I wandered among what once were chapels, but which are now occupied by the tombs and monuments of the great. At every turn I met with some illustrious name; or the cognizance of some powerful house renowned in history. As the eye darts into these dusky chambers of death, it catches glimpses of quaint effigies; some kneeling in niches, as if in devotion; others stretched upon the tombs, with hands piously pressed together; warriors in armour, as if reposing after battle; prelates with croziers and mitres; and nobles in robes and coronets, lying as it were in state. In glancing over this scene, so strangely populous, yet where every form is so still and silent, it seems almost as if we were treading a mansion of that fabled city, where every being had been suddenly transmuted into stone.

I paused to contemplate a tomb on which lay the effigy of a knight in complete armour. A large buckler was on one arm; the hands were pressed together in supplication upon the breast; the face was almost covered by the morion; the legs were crossed in token of the warrior's having been engaged in the holy war. It was the tomb of a crusader; of one of those military enthusiasts, who so strangely mingled religion and romance, and whose exploits form the connecting link between fact and fiction; between the history and the fairy tale. There is something extremely picturesque in the tombs of these adventurers, decorated as they are with rude armorial bearings and gothic sculpture. They comport with the antiquated chapels in which they are generally found; and in considering them, the imagination is apt to kindle with the legendary associations, the romantic fictions, the chivalrous pomp and pageantry which poetry has spread over the wars for the Sepulchre of Christ. They are the reliques of times utterly gone by; of beings passed from recollection; of customs and manners with which ours have no affinity. They are like objects from some strange and distant land, of which we have no certain knowledge, and about which all our conceptions are vague and visionary. There is something extremely solemn and awful in those effigies on gothic tombs, extended as if in the sleep of death, or in the supplication of the dying hour. They have an effect infinitely more impressive on my feelings than the fanciful attitudes, the overwrought conceits, and allegorical groups, which abound on modern monuments. I have been struck, also, with the superiority of many of the old sepulchral inscriptions. There was a noble way, in former times, of saying things simply, and yet saying them proudly; and I do not know an epitaph that breathes a loftier consciousness of family worth and honourable lineage, than one which affirms, of a noble house, that "all the brothers were brave, and all the sisters virtuous."

In the opposite transept to Poets' Corner stands a monument which is among the most renowned achievements of modern art; but which, to me, appears horrible rather than sublime. It is the tomb of Mrs. Nightingale, by Roubillac. The bottom of the monument is represented as throwing open its marble doors, and a sheeted skeleton is starting forth. The shroud is falling from his fleshless frame as he launches his dart at his victim. She is sinking into her affrighted husband's arms, who strives, with vain and frantic effort, to avert the blow. The whole is executed with terrible truth and spirit; we almost fancy we hear the gibbering yell of triumph, bursting from the distended jaws of the spectre.—But why should we thus seek to clothe death with unnecessary terrors, and to spread horrors round the tomb of those we love? The grave should be surrounded by every thing that might inspire tenderness and veneration for the dead; or that might win the living to virtue. It is the place, not of disgust and dismay, but of sorrow and meditation.

While wandering about these gloomy vaults and silent

aisles, studying the records of the dead, the sound of busy existence from without occasionally reaches the ear;—the rumbling of the passing equipage; the murmur of the multitude; or perhaps the light laugh of pleasure. The contrast is striking with the deathlike repose around: and it has a strange effect upon the feelings, thus to hear the surges of active life hurrying along and beating against the very walls of the sepulchre.

I continued in this way to move from tomb to tomb, and from chapel to chapel. The day was gradually wearing away; the distant tread of loiterers about the abbey grew less and less frequent; the sweet tongued bell was summoning to evening prayers; and I saw at a distance the choristers, in their white surplices, crossing the aisle and entering the choir. I stood before the entrance to Henry the Seventh's chapel. A flight of steps leads up to it, through a deep and gloomy, but magnificent arch. Great gates of brass, richly and delicately wrought, turn heavily upon their hinges, as if proudly reluctant to admit the feet of common mortals into this most gorgeous of sepulchres.

On entering, the eye is astonished by the pomp of architecture, and the elaborate beauty of sculptured detail. The very walls are wrought into universal ornament, encrusted with tracery, and scooped into niches, crowded with the statues of saints and martyrs. Stone seems, by the cunning labour of the chisel, to have been robbed of its weight and density, suspended aloft, as if by magic, and the fretted roof achieved with the wonderful minuteness and airy security of a cobweb.

Along the sides of the chapel are the lofty stalls of the Knights of the Bath, richly carved of oak, though with the grotesque decorations of gothic architecture. On the pinnacles of the stalls are affixed the helmets and crests of the knights, with their scarfs and swords; and above them are suspended their banners, emblazoned with armorial bearings, and contrasting the splendour of gold and purple and crimson, with the cold grey fretwork of the roof. In the midst of this grand mausoleum stands the sepulchre of its founder,—his effigy, with that of his queen, extended on a sumptuous tomb, and the whole surrounded by a superbly wrought brazen railing.

There is a sad dreariness in this magnificence; this strange mixture of tombs and trophies; these emblems of living and aspiring ambition, close beside mementos which show the dust and oblivion in which all must sooner or later terminate. Nothing impresses the mind with a deeper feeling of loneliness, than to tread the silent and deserted scene of former throng and pageant. On looking round on the vacant stalls of the knights and their esquires; and on the rows of dusty but gorgeous banners that were once borne before them, my imagination conjured up the scene when this hall was bright with the valour and beauty of the land; glittering with the splendour of jewelled rank and military array; alive with the tread of many feet and the hum of an admiring multitude. All had passed away: the silence of death had settled again upon the place; interrupted only by the casual chirping of birds, which had found their way into the chapel, and built their nests among its friezes and pendants—sure signs of solitariness and desertion.

When I read the names inscribed on the banners, they were those of men scattered far and wide about the world; some tossing upon distant seas; some under arms in distant lands; some mingling in the busy intrigues of courts and cabinets: all seeking to deserve one more distinction in this mansion of shadowy honours; the melancholy reward of a monument.

Two small aisles on each side of this chapel present a touching instance of the equality of the grave; which brings down the oppressor to a level with the oppressed, and mingles the dust of the bitterest enemies together. In one is the sepulchre of the haughty Elizabeth, in the other is that of her victim, the lovely and unfortunate Mary. Not an hour in the day but some ejaculation of pity is uttered over the fate of the latter, mingled with indignation at her oppressor. The walls of Elizabeth's sepulchre continually echo with the sighs of sympathy heaved at the grave of her rival.

A peculiar melancholy reigns over the aisle where Mary lies buried. The light struggles dimly through windows darkened by dust. The greater part of the place is in deep shadow, and the walls are stained and tinted by time and weather. A marble figure of Mary is stretched upon the tomb, round which is an iron railing, much corroded, bearing her national emblem the thistle. I was weary with wandering, and sat down to rest myself by the monument, revolving in my mind the chequered and disastrous story of poor Mary.

The sound of casual footsteps had ceased from the abbey. I could only hear, now and then, the distant voice of the priest repeating the evening service, and the faint responses of the choir; these paused for a time, and all was hushed. The stillness, the desertion and obscurity that were gradually prevailing around, gave a deeper and more solemn interest to the place:

> For in the silent grave no conversation,
> No joyful tread of friends, no voice of lovers,
> No careful father's counsel—nothing's heard,
> For nothing is, but all oblivion,
> Dust and an endless darkness.

Suddenly the notes of the deep labouring organ burst upon the ear, falling with doubled and redoubled intensity, and rolling, as it were, huge billows of sound. How well do their volume and grandeur accord with this mighty building! With what pomp do they swell through its vast vaults, and breathe their awful harmony through these caves of death, and make the silent sepulchre vocal!—And now they rise in triumphant acclamation, heaving higher and higher their accordant notes, and piling sound on sound.—And now they pause, and the soft voices of the choir break out into sweet gushes of melody; they soar aloft, and warble along the roof, and seem to play about these lofty vaults like the pure airs of heaven. Again the pealing organ heaves its thrilling thunders, compressing air into music, and rolling it forth upon the soul. What long drawn cadences! What solemn sweeping concords! It grows more and more dense and powerful—it fills the vast pile, and seems to jar the very walls—the ear is stunned—the senses are overwhelmed. And now it is winding up in full jubilee—it is rising from the earth to heaven—the very soul seems rapt away and floated upwards on this swelling tide of harmony!

I sat for some time lost in that kind of reverie which a strain of music is apt sometimes to inspire: the shadows of evening were gradually thickening around me; the monuments began to cast deeper and deeper gloom; and the distant clock again gave token of the slowly waning day.

I rose and prepared to leave the abbey. As I descended the flight of steps which lead into the body of the building, my eye was caught by the shrine of Edward the Confessor, and I ascended the small staircase that conducts to it, to take from thence a general survey of this wilderness of tombs. The shrine is elevated upon a kind of platform, and close around it are the sepulchres of various kings and queens. From this eminence the eye looks down between pillars and funeral trophies to the chapels and chambers below, crowded with tombs; where warriors, prelates, courtiers and statesmen lie mouldering in their "beds of darkness." Close by me stood the great chair of coronation, rudely carved of oak, in the barbarous taste of a remote and gothic age. The scene seemed almost as if contrived, with theatrical artifice, to produce an effect upon the beholder. Here was a type of the beginning and the end of human pomp and power; here it was literally but a step from the throne to the sepulchre. Would not one think that these incongruous mementos had been gathered together as a lesson to living greatness?—to show it, even in the moment of its proudest exaltation, the neglect and dishonour to which it must soon arrive; how soon that crown which encircles its brow must pass away; and it must lie down in the dust and disgraces of the tomb, and be trampled upon by the feet of the meanest of the multitude. For, strange to tell, even the grave is here no longer a sanctuary. There is a shocking levity in some natures, which leads them to sport with awful and hallowed things; and there are base minds, which delight to revenge on the illustrious dead the abject homage and grovelling servility which they pay to the living. The coffin of Edward the Confessor has been broken open, and his remains despoiled of their funeral ornaments; the sceptre has been stolen from the hand of the imperious Elizabeth, and the effigy of Henry the Fifth lies headless. Not a royal monument but bears some proof how false and fugitive is the homage of mankind. Some are plundered; some mutilated; some covered with ribaldry and insult—all more or less outraged and dishonoured!

The last beams of day were now faintly streaming through the painted windows in the high vaults above me: the lower parts of the abbey were already wrapped in the obscurity of twilight. The chapels and aisles grew darker and darker. The effigies of the kings faded into shadows; the marble figures of the monuments assumed strange shapes in the uncertain light; the evening breeze crept through the aisles like the cold breath of the grave; and even the distant footfall of a verger, traversing the Poets' Corner, had something strange and dreary in its sound. I slowly retraced my morning's walk, and as I passed out at the portal of the cloisters, the door, closing with a jarring noise behind me, filled the whole building with echoes.

I endeavoured to form some arrangement in my mind of the objects I had been contemplating, but found they were already falling into indistinctness and confusion. Names, inscriptions, trophies, had all become confounded in my recollection, though I had scarcely taken my foot from off the threshold. What, thought I, is this vast assemblage of sepulchres but a treasury of humiliation; a huge pile of reiterated homilies on the emptiness of renown, and the certainty of oblivion! It is, indeed, the empire of death; his great shadowy palace; where he sits in state, mocking at the reliques of human glory, and spreading dust and forgetfulness on the monuments of princes. How idle a boast, after all, is the immortality of a name! Time is ever silently turning over his pages; we are too much engrossed by the story of the present, to think of the characters and anecdotes that gave interest to the past; and each age is a volume thrown aside to be speedily forgotten. The idol of today pushes the hero of yesterday out of our recollection; and will, in turn, be supplanted by his successor of tomorrow. "Our fathers," says Sir Thomas Brown, "find their graves in our short memories, and sadly tell us how we may be buried in our survivors." History fades into fable; fact becomes clouded with doubt and controversy; the inscription moulders from the tablet; the statue falls from the pedestal. Columns, arches, pyramids, what are they but heaps of sand; and their epitaphs, but characters written in the dust? What is the security of a tomb, or the perpetuity of an embalmment? The remains of Alexander the Great have been scattered to the wind, and his empty sarcophagus is now the mere curiosity of a museum. "The Egyptian mummies, which Cambyses or time hath spared, avarice now consumeth; Mizraim cures wounds, and Pharaoh is sold for balsams."*

*Sir T. Brown.

What then is to insure this pile which now towers above me from sharing the fate of mightier mausoleums? The time must come when its gilded vaults, which now spring so loftily, shall lie in rubbish beneath the feet; when, instead of the sound of melody and praise, the wind shall whistle through the broken arches, and the owl hoot from the shattered tower—when the garish sun beam shall break into those gloomy mansions of death; and the ivy twine round the fallen column; and the fox glove hang its blossoms about the nameless urn, as if in mockery of the dead. Thus man passes away; his name perishes from record and recollection; his history is as a tale that is told, and his very monument becomes a ruin.

NOTES CONCERNING WESTMINSTER ABBEY

Toward the end of the sixth century when Britain, under the dominion of the Saxons, was in a state of barbarism and idolatry Pope Gregory the Great, struck with the beauty of some Anglo Saxon youths, exposed for sale in the Market place at Rome, conceived a fancy for the race and determined to send missionaries to preach the Gospel among these comely but benighted islanders. He was encouraged to this by learning that Ethelbert King of Kent and the most potent of the Anglo Saxon princes, had married Bertha a christian princess, only daughter of the King of Paris, and that she was allowed by stipulation, the full exercise of her religion.

The shrewd Pontiff knew the influence of the sex in matters of religious faith. He forthwith dispatched Augustine a Roman Monk with forty associates to the Court of Ethelbert at Canterbury, to effect the conversion of the King and to obtain through him a foothold in the island.

Ethelbert received them warily and held a conference in the open air; being distrustful of foreign priest craft, and fearful of spells and magic. They ultimately succeeded in making him as good a christian as his wife; the conversion of the King of course produced the conversion of his loyal subjects. The zeal and success of Augustine were rewarded by his being made archbishop of Canterbury and being endowed with authority over all the British churches.

One of the most prominent converts was Segebert or Sebert, King of the East Saxons a nephew of Ethelbert. He reigned at London, of which Mellitus, one of the Roman Monks who had come over with Augustine was made bishop.

Sebert, in 605, in his religious zeal founded a monastery by the river side to the west of the city on the ruins of a temple of Apollo, being in fact the origin of the present pile of Westminster Abbey. Great preparations were made for the consecration of the church which was to be dedicated to St. Peter. On the morning of the appointed day Mellitus the bishop proceeded with great pomp and solemnity to perform the ceremony. On approaching the edifice he was met by a fisherman who informed him that it was needless to proceed as the ceremony was over. The bishop stared with surprise when the fisherman went on to relate that the night before, as he was in his boat on the Thames St. Peter appeared to him and told him that he intended to consecrate the church himself that very night. The Apostle accordingly went into the church which suddenly became illuminated. The ceremony was performed in sumptuous style accompanied by strains of heavenly music and clouds of fragrant incense. After this the Apostle came onto the boat and ordered the fisherman to cast his net. He did so and had a miraculous draft of fishes; one of which he was commanded to present to the Bishop, and to signify to him that the Apostle had relieved him from the necessity of consecrating the church.

Mellitus was a wary man, slow of belief, and required confirmation of the fisherman's tale. He opened the church doors and beheld wax candles, crosses, holy water; oil sprinkled in various places and various other traces of a grand ceremonial. If he had still any lingering doubts they were completely removed on the fisherman's producing the identical fish which he had been ordered by the Apostle to present to him. To resist this would have been to resist ocular demonstration. The good bishop accordingly was convinced that the church had actually been consecrated by St. Peter in person; so he reverently abstained from proceeding further in the business.

The foregoing tradition is said to be the reason why King Edward the Confessor chose this place as the scite of a religious house which he meant to endow. He pulled down the old church and built another in its place in 1045. In this his remains were deposited in a magnificent shrine.

The sacred edifice again underwent modifications if not a reconstruction by Henry III in 1220 and began to assume its present appearance.

Under Henry VIII it lost its conventual character, that monarch turning the monks away and seizing upon the revenues.

RELIQUES OF EDWARD THE CONFESSOR

A curious narrative was printed in 1688 by one of the choiristers of the Cathedral, who appears to have been the Paul Pry of the sacred edifice, giving an account of his rummaging among the bones of Edward the Confessor, after they had quietly reposed in their sepulchre upwards of six hundred years, and of his drawing forth the crucifix and golden chain of the deceased monarch. During eighteen years that he had officiated in the choir it had been a common tradition, he says, among his brother choiristers and the grey headed servants of the abbey that the body of King Edward was deposited in a kind of chest or coffin which was indistinctly seen in the upper part of the shrine erected to his memory. None of the abbey gossips, however, had ventured upon a nearer inspection, until the worthy narrator to gratify his curiosity mounted to the coffin by the aid of a ladder and found it to be made of wood, apparently very strong and firm, being secured by bands of iron.

Subsequently, in 1685, on taking down the scaffolding used in the coronation of James II, the coffin was found to be broken, a hole appearing in the lid, probably made through accident, by the workmen. No one ventured, however, to meddle with the sacred depository of royal rest, until, several weeks afterwards, the circumstance came to the knowledge of the aforesaid choirister. He forthwith repaired to the abbey in company with two friends of congenial tastes who were desirous of inspecting the tombs. Procuring a ladder he again mounted to the coffin and found, as had been represented, a hole in the lid about six inches long and four inches broad, just in front of the left breast. Thrusting in his hand and groping among the bones he drew from underneath the shoulder a crucifix, richly adorned and enamelled affixed to a gold chain twenty four inches long. These he shewed to his inquisitive friends, who were equally surprized with himself.

"At the time," says he, "when I took the cross and chain out of the coffin, *I drew the head to the hole and viewed it,* being very sound and firm with the upper and nether jaws whole and full of teeth, and a list of gold above an inch broad, in the nature of a coronet, surrounding the temples. There was also in the coffin, white linen and gold coloured flowered silk, that looked indifferent fresh but the least stress put thereto shewed it was well nigh perished. There were all his bones and much dust likewise which I left as I found." It is difficult to conceive a more grotesque lesson to human pride than the scull of Edward the Confessor thus irreverently pulled about in its coffin by a prying choirister, and brought to grin face to face with him through a hole in the lid!

Having satisfied his curiosity the choirister put the crucifix and chain back again into the coffin and sought the Dean, to apprize him of his discovery. The Dean not being accessible at the time; and fearing that the "holy treasure" might be taken away by other hands, he got a brother choirister to accompany him to the shrine about two or three hours afterwards and in his presence again drew forth the reliques. These he afterwards delivered on his knees to King James. The King subsequently had the old coffin enclosed in a new one of great strength: "each plank being two inches thick and cramped together with large iron wedges, where it now remains (1688) as a testimony of his pious care that no abuse might be offered to the sacred ashes therein reposited."

As the history of this shrine is full of moral I subjoin a description of it in modern times. "The solitary and forlorn shrine," says a British writer, "now stands a mere skeleton of what it was. A few faint traces of its sparkling decorations inlaid on solid mortar catch the rays of the sun, forever set on its splendor * * * * Only two of the spiral pillars remain. The wooden Ionic top is much broken and covered with dust. The mosaic is picked away in every part within reach, only the lozenges of about a foot square and five circular pieces of the rich marble remain."

Malcolm. Lond. Rediv.

Inscription on a monument alluded to in the Sketch.

Here lyes the Loyal Duke of Newcastle, and his Dutchess his second wife, by whom he had no issue. Her name was Margaret Lucas, youngest sister to the Lord Lucas of Colchester, a noble Family; for all the brothers were valiant and all the sisters virtuous. This Dutchess was a wise, witty, and learned Lady, which her many Bookes do well testify: she was a most virtuous, and loving and careful wife, and was with her lord all the time of his banishment and miseries, and when he came home, never parted from him in his solitary retirements.

In the winter time, when the days are short, the service in the afternoon is performed by the light of tapers. The effect is fine of the choir partially lighted up; while the main body of the cathedral and the transepts are in profound and cavernous darkness. The white dresses of the choiristers gleam amidst the deep brown of the oaken slatts and canopies; the partial illumination makes enormous shadows from columns and screens, and darting into the surrounding gloom catches here and there upon a sepulchral decoration, or monumental effigy. The swelling notes of the organ accord well with the scene.

When the service is over the Dean is lighted to his dwelling, in the old conventual part of the pile, by the boys of the choir in their white dresses, bearing tapers, and the procession passes through the abbey and along the shadowy cloisters, lighting up angles and arches and grim sepulchral monuments and leaving all behind in darkness.

On entering the cloisters at night from what is called the Dean's Yard the eye ranging through a dark vaulted passage catches a distant view of a white marble figure reclining on a tomb, on which a strong glare thrown by a gas light, has quite a spectral effect. It is a mural monument of one of the Pultneys.

The cloisters are well worth visiting by moonlight, when the moon is in the full.

Christmas

But is old, old, good old Christmas gone? Nothing but the hair of his good, gray old head and beard left? Well, I will have that, seeing I cannot have more of him.

Hue and Cry after Christmas

Christmas

A man might then behold
  At Christmas, in each hall,
Good fires to curb the cold,
  And meat for great and small:
The neighbours were friendly bidden,
  And all had welcome true,
The poor from the gates were not chidden,
  When this old cap was new.

Old Song

NOTHING in England exercises a more delightful spell over my imagination, than the lingerings of the holyday customs and rural games of former times. They recall the pictures my fancy used to draw in the May morning of life, when as yet I only knew the world through books, and believed it to be all that poets had painted it; and they bring with them the flavour of those honest days of yore, in which, perhaps with equal fallacy, I am apt to think the world was more homebred, social, and joyous, than at present. I regret to say that they are daily growing more and more faint, being gradually worn away by time, but still more obliterated by modern fashion. They resemble those picturesque morsels of Gothic architecture, which we see crumbling in various parts of the country, partly dilapidated by the waste of ages, and partly lost in the additions and alterations of latter days. Poetry, however, clings with cherishing fondness about the rural game and holyday revel, from which it has derived so many of its themes—as the ivy winds its rich foliage about the gothic arch and mouldering tower, gratefully repaying their support, by clasping together their tottering remains, and, as it were, embalming them in verdure.

Of all the old festivals, however, that of Christmas awakens the strongest and most heartfelt associations. There is a tone of solemn and sacred feeling that blends with our conviviality, and lifts the spirit to a state of hallowed and elevated enjoyment. The services of the church about this season are extremely tender and inspiring. They dwell on the beautiful story of the origin of our faith, and the pastoral scenes that accompanied its announcement. They gradually increase in fervour and pathos during the season of Advent, until they break forth in full jubilee on the morning that brought peace and good will to men. I do not know a grander effect of music on the moral feelings, than to hear the full choir and the pealing organ performing a Christmas anthem in a cathedral, and filling every part of the vast pile with triumphant harmony.

It is a beautiful arrangement, also, derived from days of yore, that this festival, which commemorates the announcement of the religion of peace and love, has been made the season for gathering together of family connexions, and drawing closer again those bands of kindred hearts, which the cares and pleasures and sorrows of the world are continually operating to cast loose; of calling back the children of a family, who have launched forth in life, and wandered widely asunder, once more to assemble about the paternal hearth, that rallying place of the affections, there to grow young and loving again among the endearing mementos of childhood.

There is something in the very season of the year that gives a charm to the festivity of Christmas. At other times we derive a great portion of our pleasures from the mere beauties of nature. Our feelings sally forth and dissipate themselves over the sunny landscape, and we "live abroad and every where." The song of the bird, the murmur of the stream, the breathing fragrance of spring, the soft voluptuousness of summer, the golden pomp of autumn, earth with its mantle of refreshing green, and heaven with its deep delicious blue and its cloudy magnificence, all fill us with mute but exquisite delight, and we revel in the luxury of mere sensation. But in the depth of winter, when nature lies despoiled of every charm, and wrapped in her shroud of sheeted snow, we turn for our gratifications to moral sources. The dreariness and desolation of the landscape, the short gloomy days and darksome nights, while they circumscribe our wanderings, shut in our feelings also from rambling abroad, and make us more keenly disposed for the pleasures of the social circle. Our thoughts are more concentrated, our friendly sympathies more aroused. We feel more sensibly the charm of each other's society, and are brought more closely together by dependence on each other for enjoyment. Heart calleth unto heart, and we draw our pleasures from the deep wells of living kindness which lie in the quiet recesses of our bosoms, and which, when resorted to, furnish forth the pure element of domestic felicity.

The pitchy gloom without, makes the heart dilate on entering the room filled with the glow and warmth of the evening fire. The ruddy blaze diffuses an artificial summer and sunshine through the room, and lights up each countenance into a kindlier welcome. Where does the honest face of hospitality expand into a broader and more cordial smile—where is the shy glance of love more sweetly eloquent—than by the winter fireside;—and as the hollow blast of wintry wind rushes through the hall, claps the distant door, whistles about the casement, and rumbles down the chimney—what can be more grateful than that feeling of sober and sheltered security, with which we look round upon the comfortable chamber, and the scene of domestic hilarity?

The English, from the great prevalence of rural habits throughout every class of society, have always been fond of those festivals and holydays which agreeably interrupt the stillness of country life; and they were, in former days, particularly observant of the religious and social rites of Christmas. It is inspiring to read even the dry details which some antiquaries have given of the quaint humours, the burlesque pageants, the complete abandonment to mirth and good fellowship, with which this festival was celebrated. It seemed to throw open every door, and unlock every heart. It brought the peasant and the peer together, and blended all ranks in one warm generous flow of joy and kindness. The old halls of castles and manor houses resounded with the harp and the Christmas carol, and their ample boards groaned under the weight of hospitality. Even the poorest cottage welcomed the festive season with green decorations of bay and holly— the cheerful fire glanced its rays through the lattice, inviting the passenger to raise the latch, and join the gossip knot huddled round the hearth, beguiling the long evening with legendary jokes, and oft told Christmas tales.

One of the least pleasing effects of modern refinement is

the havoc it has made among the hearty old holyday customs. It has completely taken off the sharp touchings and spirited reliefs of these embellishments of life, and has worn down society into a more smooth and polished, but certainly a less characteristic surface. Many of the games and ceremonials of Christmas have entirely disappeared, and, like the sherris sack of old Falstaff, are become matters of speculation and dispute among commentators. They flourished in times full of spirit and lustihood, when men enjoyed life roughly, but heartily and vigorously: times wild and picturesque, which have furnished poetry with its richest materials, and the drama with its most attractive variety of characters and manners. The world has become more worldly. There is more of dissipation, and less of enjoyment. Pleasure has expanded into a broader, but a shallower stream, and has forsaken many of those deep and quiet channels where it flowed sweetly through the calm bosom of domestic life. Society has acquired a more enlightened and elegant tone; but it has lost many of its strong local peculiarities, its homebred feelings, its honest fireside delights. The traditionary customs of golden hearted antiquity, its feudal hospitalities, and lordly wassailings, have passed away with the baronial castles and stately manor houses in which they were celebrated. They comported with the shadowy hall, the great oaken gallery, and the tapestried parlour, but were unfitted to the light showy saloons and gay drawing rooms of the modern villa.

Shorn, however, as it is, of its ancient and festive honours, Christmas is still a period of delightful excitement in England. It is gratifying to see that home feeling completely aroused which holds so powerful a place in every English bosom. The preparations making on every side for the social board that is again to unite friends and kindred—the presents of good cheer passing and repassing, those tokens of regard and quickeners of kind feelings—the evergreens distributed about houses and churches, emblems of peace and gladness—all these have the most pleasing effect in producing fond associations, and kindling benevolent sympathies. Even the sound of the Waits, rude as may be their minstrelsy, breaks upon the midwatches of a winter night with the effect of perfect harmony. As I have been awakened by them in that still and solemn hour " when deep sleep falleth upon man," I have listened with a hushed delight, and connecting them with the sacred and joyous occasion, have almost fancied them into another celestial choir, announcing peace and good will to mankind.

How delightfully the imagination, when wrought upon by these moral influences, turns every thing to melody and beauty. The very crowing of the cock, heard sometimes in the profound repose of the country, "telling the night watches to his feathery dames," was thought by the common people to announce the approach of this sacred festival:

> Some say that ever 'gainst that season comes
> Wherein our Saviour's birth is celebrated,
> This bird of dawning singeth all night long:
> And then, they say, no spirit dares stir abroad;
> The nights are wholesome—then no planets strike,
> No fairy takes, no witch hath power to charm,
> So hallowed and so gracious is the time.

Amidst the general call to happiness, the bustle of the spirits, and stir of the affections, which prevail at this period, what bosom can remain insensible? It is, indeed, the season of regenerated feeling—the season for kindling not merely the fire of hospitality in the hall, but the genial flame of charity in the heart.

The scene of early love again rises green to memory beyond the sterile waste of years, and the idea of home, fraught with the fragrance of home dwelling joys, reanimates the drooping spirit—as the Arabian breeze will sometimes waft the freshness of the distant fields to the weary pilgrim of the desert.

Stranger and sojourner as I am in the land—though for me no social hearth may blaze, no hospitable roof throw open its doors, nor the warm grasp of friendship welcome me at the threshold—yet I feel the influence of the season beaming into my soul from the happy looks of those around me. Surely happiness is reflective, like the light of heaven; and every countenance bright with smiles, and glowing with innocent enjoyment, is a mirror transmitting to others the rays of a supreme and ever shining benevolence. He who can turn churlishly away from contemplating the felicity of his fellow beings, and can sit down darkling and repining in his loneliness when all around is joyful, may have his moments of strong excitement and selfish gratification, but he wants the genial and social sympathies which constitute the charm of a merry Christmas.

The Stage Coach

Omne benè
Sine poenâ
Tempus est ludendi.
Venit hora
Absque morâ
Libros deponendi.
Old Holyday School Song

IN THE PRECEDING paper I have made some general observations on the Christmas festivities of England, and am
tempted to illustrate them by some anecdotes of a Christmas
passed in the country: in perusing which, I would most courteously invite my reader to lay aside the austerity of wisdom,
and to put on that genuine holyday spirit, which is tolerant
of folly, and anxious only for amusement.

In the course of a December tour in Yorkshire, I rode
for a long distance in one of the public coaches, on the day preceding Christmas. The coach was crowded, both inside
and out, with passengers, who, by their talk, seemed principally
bound to the mansions of relations or friends, to eat the
Christmas dinner. It was loaded also with hampers of game,
and baskets and boxes of delicacies; and hares hung dangling
their long ears about the coachman's box, presents from distant friends for the impending feast. I had three fine rosy
cheeked school boys for my fellow passengers inside, full of
the buxom health and manly spirit which I have observed in
the children in this country. They were returning home for
the holydays, in high glee, and promising themselves a world
of enjoyment. It was delightful to hear the gigantic plans of
pleasure of the little rogues, and the impracticable feats they
were to perform during their six weeks' emancipation from
the abhorred thraldom of book, birch, and pedagogue. They
were full of anticipations of the meeting with the family and
household, down to the very cat and dog, and of the joy they
were to give their little sisters by the presents with which
their pockets were crammed; but the meeting to which they
seemed to look forward with the greatest impatience was with

Bantam, which I found to be a pony, and, according to their talk, possessed of more virtues than any steed since the days of Bucephalus. How he could trot! how he could run! and then such leaps as he would take—there was not a hedge in the whole country that he could not clear.

They were under the particular guardianship of the coachman, to whom, whenever an opportunity presented, they addressed a host of questions, and pronounced him one of the best fellows in the whole world. Indeed, I could not but notice the more than ordinary air of bustle and importance of the coachman, who wore his hat a little on one side, and had a large bunch of Christmas greens stuck in the button hole of his coat. He is always a personage full of mighty care and business, but he is particularly so during this season, having so many commissions to execute in consequence of the great interchange of presents. And here, perhaps, it may not be unacceptable to my untravelled readers, to have a sketch that may serve as a general representation of this very numerous and important class of functionaries, who have a dress, a manner, a language, an air, peculiar to themselves, and prevalent throughout the fraternity, so that, wherever an English stage coachman may be seen, he cannot be mistaken for one of any other craft or mystery.

He has commonly a broad full face, curiously mottled with red, as if the blood had been forced by hard feeding into every vessel of the skin; he is swelled into jolly dimensions by frequent potations of malt liquors, and his bulk is still further increased by a multiplicity of coats, in which he is buried like a cauliflower, the upper one reaching to his heels. He wears a broad brimmed low crowned hat, a huge roll of coloured handkerchief about his neck, knowingly knotted and tucked in at the bosom, and has in summer time a large boquet of flowers in his buttonhole, the present, most probably of some enamoured country lass. His waistcoat is commonly of some bright colour, striped, and his small clothes extend far below the knees, to meet a pair of jockey boots which reach about half way up his legs.

All this costume is maintained with much precision; he has a pride in having his clothes of excellent materials, and notwithstanding the seeming grossness of his appearance, there is still discernible that neatness and propriety of person, which is almost inherent in an Englishman. He enjoys great consequence and consideration along the road; has frequent conferences with the village housewives, who look upon him as a man of great trust and dependence; and he seems to have a good understanding with every bright eyed country lass. The moment he arrives where the horses are to be changed, he throws down the reins with something of an air, and abandons the cattle to the care of the hostler: his duty being merely to drive them from one stage to another. When off the box, his hands are thrust in the pockets of his great coat, and he rolls about the inn yard with an air of the most absolute lordliness. Here he is generally surrounded by an admiring throng of hostlers, stable boys, shoeblacks, and those nameless hangers on, that infest inns and taverns, and run errands, and do all kind of odd jobs, for the privilege of battening on the drippings of the kitchen and the leakage of the tap room. These all look up to him as to an oracle; treasure up his cant phrases; echo his opinions about horses and other topics of jockey lore; and above all, endeavour to imitate his air and carriage. Every ragamuffin that has a coat to his back, thrusts his hands in the pockets, rolls in his gait, talks slang, and is an embryo Coachey.

Perhaps it might be owing to the pleasing serenity that reigned in my own mind, that I fancied I saw cheerfulness in every countenance throughout the journey. A Stage Coach, however, carries animation always with it, and puts the world in motion as it whirls along. The horn, sounded at the entrance of a village, produces a general bustle. Some hasten forth to meet friends; some with bundles and bandboxes to secure places, and in the hurry of the moment can hardly take leave of the group that accompanies them. In the mean time, the coachman has a world of small commissions to execute; sometimes he delivers a hare or pheasant; sometimes jerks a small parcel or newspaper to the door of a public house, and sometimes, with knowing leer, and words of sly import, hands to some half blushing, half laughing housemaid, an odd shaped billet-doux from some rustic admirer. As the Coach rattles through the village, every one runs to the window, and you have glances on every side of fresh country faces, and blooming, giggling girls. At the corners are assembled juntos of village idlers and wise men, who take their stations there for the important purpose of seeing company pass: but the sagest knot is generally at the blacksmith's, to whom the passing of the coach is an event fruitful of much speculation. The smith, with the horse's heel in his lap, pauses as the vehicle whirls by; the cyclops round the anvil suspend their ringing hammers, and suffer the iron to grow cool; and the sooty spectre in brown paper cap, labouring at the bellows, leans on the handle for a moment, and permits the asthmatic engine to heave a long drawn sigh, while he glares through the murky smoke and sulphureous gleams of the smithy.

Perhaps the impending holyday might have given a more than usual animation to the country, for it seemed to me as if every body was in good looks and good spirits; game, poultry, and other luxuries of the table, were in brisk circulation in the villages; the grocer's, butcher's, and fruiterer's shops were thronged with customers. The housewives were stirring briskly about, putting their dwellings in order, and the glossy branches of holly, with their bright red berries, began to appear at the windows. The scene brought to mind an old writer's account of Christmas preparations. "Now capons and hens, besides turkeys, geese, and ducks, with beef and mutton—must all die—for in twelve days a multitude of people will not be fed with a little. Now plums and spice, sugar and honey, square it among pies and broath. Now or never must music be in tune, for the youth must dance and sing to get them a heat, while the aged sit by the fire. The country maid leaves half her market, and must be sent againe, if she forgets a pack of cards on Christmas even. Great is the contention of Holly and Ivy, whether master or dame wears the breeches. Dice and cards benefit the butler; and if the cook do not lack wit, he will sweetly lick his fingers."

I was roused from this fit of luxurious meditation, by a shout from my little travelling companions. They had been looking out of the coach windows for the last few miles, recognising every tree and cottage as they approached home, and now there was a general burst of joy. "There's John! and there's old Carlo! and there's Bantam!" cried the happy little rogues, clapping their hands.

At the head of a lane there was an old sober looking servant in livery, waiting for them; he was accompanied by a super-annuated pointer, and by the redoubtable Bantam, a little old rat of a pony, with a shagged mane and long rusty tail, who stood dozing quietly by the road side, little dreaming of the bustling times that awaited him.

I was pleased to see the fondness with which the little fellows leaped about the steady old footman, and hugged the pointer, who wriggled his whole body for joy. But Bantam was the great object of interest; all wanted to mount at once, and it was with some difficulty that John arranged that they should ride by turns, and the eldest should ride first.

Off they set at last, one on the pony with the dog bounding and barking before him, and the others holding John's hands, both talking at once, and overpowering him with questions about home, and with school anecdotes. I looked after them with a feeling in which I do not know whether pleasure or melancholy predominated; for I was reminded of those days when, like them, I had neither known care nor sorrow, and a holyday was the summit of earthly felicity. We stopped a few moments afterwards to water the horses; and on resuming our route, a turn of the road brought us in sight of a neat country seat. I could just distinguish the forms of a lady and two young girls in the portico, and I saw my little comrades, with Bantam, Carlo, and old John, trooping along the carriage road. I leaned out of the coach window, in hopes of witnessing the happy meeting, but a grove of trees shut it from my sight.

In the evening we reached a village where I had determined to pass the night. As we drove into the great gateway of the inn, I saw on one side, the light of a rousing kitchen fire beaming through a window. I entered and admired, for the hundredth time, that picture of convenience, neatness, and broad honest enjoyment, the kitchen of an English inn. It was of spacious dimensions, hung round with copper and tin vessels highly polished, and decorated here and there with a Christmas green. Hams, tongues, and flitches of bacon, were suspended from the ceiling; a smoke jack made its ceaseless clanking beside the fire place, and a clock ticked in one corner. A well scoured deal table extended along one side of the kitchen, with a cold round of beef, and other hearty viands, upon it, over which two foaming tankards of ale seemed mounting guard. Travellers of inferior order were preparing to attack this stout repast, whilst others sat smoking and gossipping over their ale on two high backed oaken seats beside the fire. Trim housemaids were hurrying backwards and forwards under the directions of a fresh bustling landlady; but still seizing an occasional moment to exchange a flippant word, and have a rallying laugh, with the group around the fire. The scene completely realized Poor Robin's humble idea of the comforts of mid-winter:

> Now trees their leafy hats do bare
> To reverence Winter's silver hair;
> A handsome hostess, merry host,
> A pot of ale now and a toast,
> Tobacco and a good coal fire,
> Are things this season doth require.*

I had not been long at the inn when a post chaise drove up to the door. A young gentleman stepped out, and by the light of the lamps I caught a glimpse of a countenance which I thought I knew. I moved forward to get a nearer view, when his eye caught mine. I was not mistaken; it was Frank Bracebridge, a sprightly good humoured young fellow, with whom I had once travelled on the continent. Our meeting was extremely cordial, for the countenance of an old fellow traveller always brings up the recollection of a thousand pleasant scenes, odd adventures, and excellent jokes. To discuss all these in a transient interview at an inn was impossible, and finding that I was not pressed for time, and was merely making a tour of observation, he insisted that I should give him a day or two at his father's country seat, to which he was going to pass the Holydays, and which lay at a few miles distance. "It is better than eating a solitary Christmas dinner at an inn," said he, "and I can assure you of a hearty welcome in something of the old fashioned style." His reasoning was cogent, and I must confess the preparation I had seen for

*Poor Robin's Almanack, 1684.

universal festivity and social enjoyment, had made me feel a little impatient of my loneliness. I closed, therefore, at once with his invitation; the chaise drove up to the door, and in a few moments I was on my way to the family mansion of the Bracebridges.

Christmas Eve

Saint Francis and Saint Benedight
Blesse this house from wicked wight;
From the night-mare and the goblin,
That is hight good fellow Robin;
Keep it from all evil spirits,
Fairies, weezels, rats, and ferrets:
>From curfew-time
>To the next prime.

Cartwright

IT WAS a brilliant moonlight night, but extremely cold: our chaise whirled rapidly over the frozen ground; the post boy cracked his whip incessantly, and a part of the time his horses were upon a gallop. "He knows where he is going," said my companion, laughing, "and is eager to arrive in time for some of the merriment and good cheer of the servants' hall. My father, you must know, is a bigoted devotee of the old school, and prides himself upon keeping up something of old English hospitality. He is a tolerable specimen of what you will rarely meet with now-a-days in its purity, the old English country gentleman; for our men of fortune spend so much of their time in town, and fashion is carried so much into the country, that the strong rich peculiarities of ancient rural life are almost polished away. My father, however, from early years, took honest Peacham* for his text book, instead of Chesterfield; he determined in his own mind, that there was no condition more truly honourable and enviable than that of a country gentleman on his paternal lands, and, therefore, passes the whole of his time on his estate. He is a strenuous advocate for the revival of the old rural games and holyday observances, and is deeply read in the writers, ancient and modern, who have treated of the subject. Indeed, his favourite range of reading is among the authors who flourished at least two centuries since, who, he insists, wrote and thought more like true Englishmen than any of their successors. He even regrets sometimes that he had not been born a few centuries

---

*Peacham's Compleat Gentleman, 1622.

earlier, when England was itself, and had its peculiar manners and customs. As he lives at some distance from the main road, in rather a lonely part of the country, without any rival gentry near him, he has that most enviable of all blessings to an Englishman, an opportunity of indulging the bent of his own humour, without molestation. Being representative of the oldest family in the neighbourhood, and a great part of the peasantry being his tenants, he is much looked up to, and, in general, is known simply by the appellation of 'The Squire;' a title which has been accorded to the head of the family since time immemorial. I think it best to give you these hints about my worthy old father, to prepare you for any little eccentricities that might otherwise appear absurd."

We had passed for some time along the wall of a park, and at length the chaise stopped at the gate. It was in a heavy magnificent old stile; of iron bars, fancifully wrought at top into flourishes and flowers. The huge square columns that supported the gate were surmounted by the family crest. Close adjoining was the porter's lodge, sheltered under dark fir trees, and almost buried in shrubbery.

The post boy rung a large porter's bell, which resounded through the still frosty air, and was answered by the distant barking of dogs, with which the mansion house seemed garrisoned. An old woman immediately appeared at the gate. As the moonlight fell strongly upon her, I had a full view of a little primitive dame, dressed very much in the antique taste, with a neat kerchief and stomacher, and her silver hair peeping from under a cap of snowy whiteness. She came curtseying forth, with many expressions of simple joy at seeing her young master. Her husband, it seemed, was up at the house keeping Christmas eve, in the servants' hall; they could not do without him, as he was the best hand at a song and story in the household.

My friend proposed that we should alight and walk through the park to the hall, which was at no great distance, while the chaise should follow on. Our road wound through a noble avenue of trees, among the naked branches of which the moon glittered as she rolled through the deep vault of a cloudless sky: the lawn beyond was sheeted with a slight covering of snow, which here and there sparkled as the moon beams caught a frosty chrystal; and at a distance might be seen a thin transparent vapour, stealing up from the low grounds, and threatening gradually to shroud the landscape.

My companion looked round him with transport:—"How often," said he, "have I scampered up this avenue, on returning home on school vacations. How often have I played under these trees when a boy. I feel a degree of filial reverence for them as we look up to those who have cherished us in childhood. My father was always scrupulous in exacting our holydays, and having us around him on family festivals. He used to direct and superintend our games with the strictness that some parents do the studies of their children. He was very particular that we should play the old English games according to their original form, and consulted old books for precedent and authority for every 'merrie disport.' Yet I assure you there never was pedantry so delightful. It was the policy of the good old gentleman to make his children feel that home was the happiest place in the world, and I value this delicious home feeling as one of the choicest gifts a parent could bestow."

We were interrupted by the clamour of a troop of dogs of all sorts and sizes, "mongrel, puppy, whelp and hound, and curs of low degree," that, disturbed by the ringing of the porter's bell, and the rattling of the chaise, came bounding open mouthed across the lawn.

> ——The little dogs and all,
> Tray, Blanch and Sweetheart, see, they bark at me!

cried Bracebridge, laughing. At the sound of his voice, the bark was changed into a yelp of delight, and in a moment he was surrounded and almost overpowered by the caresses of the faithful animals.

We had now come in full view of the old family mansion, partly thrown in deep shadow, and partly lit up by the cold moonshine. It was an irregular building of some magnitude, and seemed to be of the architecture of different periods. One wing was evidently very ancient, with heavy stone shafted bow windows jutting out and over run with ivy, from among the foliage of which the small diamond shaped panes of glass glittered with the moonbeams. The rest of the house was in the

French taste of Charles the Second's time, having been repaired and altered, as my friend told me, by one of his ancestors, who returned with that monarch at the restoration. The grounds about the house were laid out in the old formal manner of artificial flower beds, clipped shrubberies, raised terraces, with heavy stone ballustrades, ornamented with urns, a leaden statue or two, and a jet of water. The old gentleman, I was told, was extremely careful to preserve this obsolete finery in all its original state. He admired this fashion in gardening; it had an air of magnificence, was courtly and noble, and befitting good old family style. The boasted imitation of nature in modern gardening had sprung up with modern republican notions, but did not suit a monarchical government; it smacked of the levelling system. I could not help smiling at this introduction of politics into gardening, though I expressed some apprehension that I should find the old gentleman rather intolerant in his creed. Frank assured me, however, that it was almost the only instance in which he had ever heard his father meddle with politics, and he believed that he had got this notion from a member of parliament who once passed a few weeks with him. The Squire was glad of any argument to defend his clipped yew trees and formal terraces, which had been occasionally attacked by modern landscape gardeners.

As we approached the house, we heard the sound of music, and now and then a burst of laughter, from one end of the building. This, Bracebridge said, must proceed from the servants' hall, where a great deal of revelry was permitted, and even encouraged, by the Squire, throughout the twelve days of Christmas, provided every thing was done conformably to ancient usage. Here were kept up the old games of hoodman blind, shoe the wild mare, hot cockles, steal the white loaf, Bob apple, and snap dragon: the Yule clog, and Christmas candle, were regularly burnt, and the misletoe, with its white berries, hung up, to the imminent peril of all the pretty housemaids.*

So intent were the servants upon their sports, that we had

*The misletoe is still hung up in farm houses and kitchens at Christmas; and the young men have the privilege of kissing the girls under it, plucking each time a berry from the bush. When the berries are all plucked, the privilege ceases.

to ring repeatedly before we could make ourselves heard. On our arrival being announced, the Squire came out to receive us, accompanied by his two other sons; one a young officer of the army, home on leave of absence, the other an Oxonian, just from the university. The Squire was a fine healthy looking old gentleman, with silver hair curling lightly round an open florid countenance, in which a physiognomist, with the advantage, like myself, of a previous hint or two, might discover a singular mixture of whim and benevolence.

The family meeting was warm and affectionate; as the evening was far advanced, the Squire would not permit us to change our travelling dresses, but ushered us at once to the company, which was assembled in a large old fashioned hall. It was composed of different branches of a numerous family connexion, where there were the usual proportions of old uncles and aunts, comfortable married dames, superannuated spinsters, blooming country cousins, half fledged striplings, and bright eyed boarding school hoydens. They were variously occupied: some at a round game of cards; others conversing around the fire place; at one end of the hall was a group of the young folks, some nearly grown up, others of a more tender and budding age, fully engrossed by a merry game; and a profusion of wooden horses, penny trumpets, and tattered dolls, about the floor, showed traces of a troop of little fairy beings, who, having frolicked through a happy day, had been carried off to slumber through a peaceful night.

While the mutual greetings were going on between young Bracebridge and his relatives, I had time to scan the apartment. I have called it a hall, for so it had certainly been in old times, and the Squire had evidently endeavoured to restore it to something of its primitive state. Over the heavy projecting fire place was suspended a picture of a warrior in armour, standing by a white horse, and on the opposite wall hung a helmet, buckler and lance. At one end an enormous pair of antlers were inserted in the wall, the branches serving as hooks on which to suspend hats, whips and spurs; and in the corners of the apartment were fowling pieces, fishing rods, and other sporting implements. The furniture was of the cumbrous workmanship of former days, though some articles of modern convenience had been added, and the oaken floor had been carpeted, so that the whole presented an odd mixture of parlour and hall.

The grate had been removed from the wide overwhelming fire place, to make way for a fire of wood, in the midst of which was an enormous log glowing and blazing, and sending forth a vast volume of light and heat: this I understood was the Yule clog, which the Squire was particular in having brought in and illumined on a Christmas eve, according to ancient custom.*

It was really delightful to see the old Squire, seated in his hereditary elbow chair, by the hospitable fireside of his ancestors, and looking around him like the sun of a system, beaming warmth and gladness to every heart. Even the very dog that lay stretched at his feet, as he lazily shifted his position and yawned, would look fondly up in his master's face, wag his tail against the floor, and stretch himself again to sleep, confident of kindness and protection. There is an emanation from the heart in genuine hospitality, which cannot be described, but is immediately felt, and puts the stranger at once at his ease. I had not been seated many minutes by the comfortable hearth of the worthy old cavalier, before I

---

*The *Yule clog* is a great log of wood, sometimes the root of a tree, brought into the house with great ceremony, on Christmas eve, laid in the fire place, and lighted with the brand of the last year's clog. While it lasted, there was great drinking, singing, and telling of tales. Sometimes it was accompanied by Christmas candles; but in the cottages the only light was from the ruddy blaze of the great wood fire. The Yule clog was to burn all night; if it went out it was considered a sign of ill luck.

Herrick mentions it in one of his songs:

> Come bring with a noise,
> My merrie, merrie boyes,
> The Christmas Log to the firing;
> While my good dame, she
> Bids ye all be free,
> And drink to your hearts desiring.

The Yule clog is still burnt in many farm houses and kitchens in England, particularly in the north, and there are several superstitions connected with it among the peasantry. If a squinting person come to the house while it is burning, or a person bare footed, it is considered an ill omen. The brand remaining from the Yule clog is carefully put away to light the next year's Christmas fire.

found myself as much at home as if I had been one of the family.

Supper was announced shortly after our arrival. It was served up in a spacious oaken chamber, the pannels of which shone with wax, and around which were several family portraits decorated with holly and ivy. Besides the accustomed lights, two great wax tapers, called Christmas candles, wreathed with greens, were placed on a highly polished beaufet among the family plate. The table was abundantly spread with substantial fare; but the Squire made his supper of frumenty, a dish made of wheat cakes, boiled in milk with rich spices; being a standing dish in old times, for Christmas eve. I was happy to find my old friend, minced pie, in the retinue of the feast, and finding him to be perfectly orthodox, and that I need not be ashamed of my predilection, I greeted him with all the warmth wherewith we usually greet an old and very genteel acquaintance.

The mirth of the company was greatly promoted by the humours of an eccentric personage whom Mr. Bracebridge always addressed with the quaint appellation of Master Simon. He was a tight brisk little man, with the air of an arrant old Bachelor. His nose was shaped like the bill of a parrot; his face slightly pitted with the small pox, with a dry perpetual bloom on it, like a frost bitten leaf in autumn. He had an eye of great quickness and vivacity, with a drollery and lurking waggery of expression that was irresistible. He was evidently the wit of the family, dealing very much in sly jokes and innuendoes with the ladies, and making infinite merriment by harpings upon old themes, which, unfortunately, my ignorance of the family chronicles did not permit me to enjoy. It seemed to be his great delight during supper, to keep a young girl next him in a continual agony of stifled laughter, in spite of her awe of the reproving looks of her mother, who sat opposite. Indeed, he was the idol of the younger part of the company, who laughed at every thing he said or did, and at every turn of his countenance. I could not wonder at it; for he must have been a miracle of accomplishments in their eyes. He could imitate Punch and Judy; make an old woman of his hand, with the assistance of a burnt cork and pocket handkerchief; and cut an orange into such a ludicrous caricature, that the young folks were ready to die with laughing.

I was let briefly into his history by Frank Bracebridge. He was an old bachelor, of a small independent income, which, by careful management, was sufficient for all his wants. He revolved through the family system like a vagrant comet in its orbit, sometimes visiting one branch, and sometimes another quite remote, as is often the case with gentlemen of extensive connexions and small fortunes, in England. He had a chirping, buoyant disposition, always enjoying the present moment; and his frequent change of scene and company prevented his acquiring those rusty, unaccommodating habits, with which old bachelors are so uncharitably charged. He was a complete family chronicle, being versed in the genealogy, history, and intermarriages of the whole house of Bracebridge, which made him a great favourite with the old folks; he was a beau of all the elder ladies and superannuated spinsters, among whom he was habitually considered rather a young fellow, and he was master of the revels among the children; so that there was not a more popular being in the sphere in which he moved, than Mr. Simon Bracebridge. Of late years, he had resided almost entirely with the Squire, to whom he had become a factotum, and whom he particularly delighted by jumping with his humour in respect to old times, and by having a scrap of an old song to suit every occasion. We had presently a specimen of his last mentioned talent; for no sooner was supper removed, and spiced wines and other beverages peculiar to the season introduced, than Master Simon was called on for a good old Christmas song. He bethought himself for a moment, and then, with a sparkle of the eye, and a voice that was by no means bad, excepting that it ran occasionally into a falsetto, like the notes of a split reed, he quavered forth a quaint old ditty.

> Now Christmas is come,
> Let us beat up the drum,
> And call all our neighbours together;
> And when they appear,
> Let us make them such cheer,
> As will keep out the wind and the weather. &c.

The supper had disposed every one to gayety, and an old harper was summoned from the servants' hall, where he had been strumming all the evening, and to all appearance comforting himself with some of the Squire's home brewed. He was a kind of hanger on, I was told, of the establishment, and though ostensibly a resident of the village, was oftener to be found in the Squire's kitchen than his own home; the old gentleman being fond of the sound of "Harp in hall."

The dance, like most dances after supper, was a merry one: some of the older folks joined in it, and the Squire himself figured down several couple with a partner with whom he affirmed he had danced at every Christmas for nearly half a century. Master Simon, who seemed to be a kind of connecting link between the old times and the new, and to be withal a little antiquated in the taste of his accomplishments, evidently piqued himself on his dancing, and was endeavouring to gain credit by the heel and toe, rigadoon, and other graces of the ancient school; but he had unluckily assorted himself with a little romping girl from boarding school, who, by her wild vivacity, kept him continually on the stretch, and defeated all his sober attempts at elegance:—such are the ill sorted matches to which antique gentlemen are unfortunately prone!

The young Oxonian, on the contrary, had led out one of his maiden aunts, on whom the rogue played a thousand little knaveries with impunity; he was full of practical jokes, and his delight was to tease his aunts and cousins; yet, like all mad cap youngsters, he was a universal favourite among the women. The most interesting couple in the dance was the young officer, and a ward of the Squire's, a beautiful blushing girl of seventeen. From several shy glances which I had noticed in the course of the evening, I suspected there was a little kindness growing up between them; and, indeed, the young soldier was just the hero to captivate a romantic girl. He was tall, slender, and handsome; and, like most young British officers of late years, had picked up various small accomplishments on the continent—he could talk French and Italian—draw landscapes—sing very tolerably—dance divinely; but, above all, he had been wounded at Waterloo:— what girl of seventeen, well read in poetry and romance, could resist such a mirror of chivalry and perfection!

The moment the dance was over, he caught up a guitar, and lolling against the old marble fire place, in an attitude which I am half inclined to suspect was studied, began the little French air of the Troubadour. The Squire, however, exclaimed against having any thing on Christmas eve but good old English; upon which the young minstrel, casting up his eye for a moment, as if in an effort of memory, struck into another strain, and with a charming air of gallantry, gave Herrick's "night piece to Julia."

> Her eyes the glow-worm lend thee,
> The shooting stars attend thee,
>   And the elves also,
>   Whose little eyes glow
> Like the sparks of fire, befriend thee.
>
> No Will o' th' Wisp mislight thee;
> Nor snake or slow worm bite thee;
>   But on, on thy way,
>   Not making a stay,
> Since ghost there is none to affright thee.
>
> Then let not the dark thee cumber;
> What though the moon does slumber?
>   The stars of the night
>   Will lend thee their light,
> Like tapers clear without number.
>
> Then Julia, let me woo thee,
> Thus, thus, to come unto me;
>   And when I shall meet
>   Thy silvery feet,
> My soul I'll pour into thee.

The song might or might not have been intended in compliment to the fair Julia, for so I found his partner was called: she, however, was certainly unconscious of any such application; for she never looked at the singer, but kept her eyes cast upon the floor; her face was suffused, it is true, with a beautiful blush, and there was a gentle heaving of the bosom, but all that was doubtless caused by the exercise of the dance: indeed, so great was her indifference, that she was amusing herself with plucking to pieces a choice boquet of hot house flowers, and by the time the song was concluded, the nosegay lay in ruins on the floor.

The party now broke up for the night with the kind hearted old custom of shaking hands. As I passed through the hall, on my way to my chamber, the dying embers of the yule clog still sent forth a dusky glow, and had it not been the season when "no spirit dares stir abroad," I should have been half tempted to steal from my room at midnight, and peep, whether the fairies might not be at their revels about the hearth.

My chamber was in the old part of the mansion, the ponderous furniture of which might have been fabricated in the days of the giants. The room was pannelled, with cornices of heavy carved work, in which flowers and grotesque faces were strangely intermingled, and a row of black looking portraits stared mournfully at me from the walls. The bed was of rich, though faded damask, with a lofty tester, and stood in a niche opposite a bow window. I had scarcely got into bed when a strain of music seemed to break forth in the air just below the window. I listened, and found it proceeded from a band, which I concluded to be the waits from some neighbouring village. They went round the house, playing under the windows. I drew aside the curtains to hear them more distinctly. The moon beams fell through the upper part of the casement, partially lighting up the antiquated apartment. The sounds as they receded, became more soft and aerial, and seemed to accord with the quiet and moon light. I listened and listened—they became more and more tender and remote, and as they gradually died away, my head sunk upon the pillow, and I fell asleep.

Christmas Day

Dark and dull night flie hence away,
And give the honour to this day
That sees December turn'd to May.

*   *   *   *

Why does the chilling winter's morne
Smile like a field beset with corne?
Or smell like to a meade new-shorne,
Thus on the sudden?—Come and see
The cause why things thus fragrant be.

Herrick

WHEN I AWOKE the next morning, it seemed as if all the events of the preceding evening had been a dream, and nothing but the identity of the ancient chamber convinced me of their reality. While I lay musing on my pillow, I heard the sound of little feet pattering outside of the door, and a whispering consultation. Presently a choir of small voices chaunted forth an old Christmas carol, the burden of which was

Rejoice, our Saviour he was born
On Christmas day in the morning.

I rose softly, slipt on my clothes, opened the door suddenly, and beheld one of the most beautiful little fairy groups that a painter could imagine. It consisted of a boy and two girls, the eldest not more than six, and lovely as seraphs. They were going the rounds of the house and singing at every chamber door, but my sudden appearance frightened them into mute bashfulness. They remained for a moment playing on their lips with their fingers, and now and then stealing a shy glance from under their eyebrows, until as if by one impulse, they scampered away, and as they turned an angle of the gallery, I heard them laughing in triumph at their escape.

Every thing conspired to produce kind and happy feelings in this strong hold of old fashioned hospitality. The window of my chamber looked out upon what in summer would have been a beautiful landscape. There was a sloping lawn, a fine stream winding at the foot of it, and a tract of park beyond, with noble clumps of trees, and herds of deer. At a distance was a neat hamlet, with the smoke from the cottage chimneys hanging over it; and a church with its dark spire in strong relief against the clear cold sky. The house was surrounded with evergreens, according to the English custom, which would have given almost an appearance of summer; but the morning was extremely frosty; the light vapour of the preceding evening had been precipitated by the cold, and covered all the trees and every blade of grass with its fine chrystalizations. The rays of a bright morning sun had a dazzling effect among the glittering foliage. A robin perched upon the top of a mountain ash that hung its clusters of red berries just before my window, was basking himself in the sunshine, and piping a few querulous notes, and a peacock was displaying all the glories of his train, and strutting with the pride and gravity of a Spanish grandee on the terrace walk below.

I had scarce dressed myself, when a servant appeared to invite me to family prayers. He showed me the way to a small chapel in the old wing of the house, where I found the principal part of the family already assembled in a kind of gallery, furnished with cushions, hassocks, and large prayer books; the servants were seated on benches below. The old gentleman read prayers from a desk in front of the gallery, and Master Simon acted as clerk and made the responses, and I must do him the justice to say that he acquitted himself with great gravity and decorum.

The service was followed by a Christmas carol, which Mr. Bracebridge himself had constructed from a poem of his favourite author, Herrick; and it had been adapted to an old church melody by Master Simon. As there were several good voices among the household, the effect was extremely pleasing; but I was particularly gratified by the exaltation of heart, and sudden sally of grateful feeling, with which the worthy Squire delivered one stanza, his eye glistening, and his voice rambling out of all the bounds of time and tune.

'Tis thou that crown'st my glittering hearth
    With guiltlesse mirth,
And giv'st me Wassaile Bowles to drink
    Spic'd to the brink.
Lord, 'tis thy plenty-dropping hand
    That soiles my land;
And giv'st me, for my bushell sowne,
    Twice ten for one.

I afterwards understood that early morning service was read on every Sunday and saint's day throughout the year, either by Mr. Bracebridge or by some member of the family. It was once almost universally the case at the seats of the nobility and gentry of England, and it is much to be regretted that the custom is falling into neglect; for the dullest observer must be sensible of the order and serenity prevalent in those households, where the occasional exercise of a beautiful form of worship in the morning gives, as it were, the key note to every temper for the day, and attunes every spirit to harmony.

Our breakfast consisted of what the Squire denominated true old English fare. He indulged in some bitter lamentations over modern breakfasts of tea and toast, which he censured as among the causes of modern effeminacy and weak nerves, and the decline of old English heartiness: and though he admitted them to his table to suit the palates of his guests, yet there was a brave display of cold meats, wine, and ale, on the sideboard.

After breakfast, I walked about the grounds with Frank Bracebridge and Master Simon, or Mr. Simon, as he was called by every body but the Squire. We were escorted by a number of gentleman like dogs, that seemed loungers about the establishment, from the frisking spaniel to the steady old stag hound, the last of which was of a race that had been in the family time out of mind: they were all obedient to a dog whistle which hung at Master Simon's button hole, and in the midst of their gambols would glance an eye occasionally upon a small switch he carried in his hand.

The old mansion had a still more venerable look in the yellow sunshine than by pale moonlight; and I could not but feel the force of the Squire's idea, that the formal terraces, heavily moulded ballustrades, and clipped yew trees, carried with them an air of proud aristocracy. There appeared to be an unusual number of peacocks about the place, and I was making some remarks upon what I termed a flock of them that were basking under a sunny wall, when I was gently corrected in my phraseology by Master Simon, who told me that, according to the most ancient and approved treatise on hunting, I must say a *muster* of peacocks. "In the same way," added he, with a slight air of pedantry, " we say a flight of doves or swallows, a bevy of quails, a herd of deer, of wrens or cranes, a skulk of foxes, or a building of rooks." He went on to inform me that, according to Sir Anthony Fitzherbert, we ought to ascribe to this bird "both understanding and glory; for, being praised, he will presently set up his tail, chiefly against the sun, to the intent you may the better behold the beauty thereof. But at the fall of the leaf, when his tail falleth, he will mourn and hide himself in corners, till his tail come again as it was."

I could not help smiling at this display of small erudition on so whimsical a subject; but I found that the peacocks were birds of some consequence at the hall; for Frank Bracebridge informed me that they were great favourites with his father, who was extremely careful to keep up the breed, partly because they belonged to chivalry, and were in great request at the stately banquets of the olden time; and partly because they had a pomp and magnificence about them, highly becoming an old family mansion. Nothing, he was accustomed to say, had an air of greater state and dignity than a peacock perched upon an antique stone ballustrade.

Master Simon had now to hurry off, having an appointment at the parish church with the village choristers, who were to perform some music of his selection. There was something extremely agreeable in the cheerful flow of animal spirits of the little man; and I confess I had been somewhat surprised at his apt quotations from authors, who certainly were not in the range of every day reading. I mentioned this last circumstance to Frank Bracebridge, who told me with a smile that Master Simon's whole stock of erudition was confined to some half a dozen old authors, which the Squire had put into his hands, and which he read over and over, whenever he had a studious fit, as he sometimes had of a rainy day, or a long winter evening. Sir Anthony Fitzherbert's book of Husbandry; Markham's Country Contentments; the Tretyse of Hunting, by Sir Thomas Cockayne, Knight; Isaac Walton's Angler, and two or three more such ancient worthies of the pen, were his standard authorities; and, like all men who know but a few books, he looked up to them with a kind of idolatry, and quoted them on all occasions. As to his songs, they were chiefly picked out of old books in the Squire's library, and adapted to tunes that were popular among the choice spirits of the last century. His practical application of scraps of literature, however, had caused him to be looked upon as a prodigy of book knowledge by all the grooms, huntsmen, and small sportsmen of the neighbourhood.

While we were talking, we heard the distant toll of the village bell, and I was told that the Squire was a little particular in having his household at church on Christmas morning; considering it a day of pouring out of thanks and rejoicing, for, as old Tusser observed,

At Christmas be merry, *and thankful withal*,
And feast thy poor neighbours, the great with the small.

"If you are disposed to go to church," said Frank Bracebridge, "I can promise you a specimen of my cousin Simon's musical achievements. As the church is destitute of an organ, he has formed a band from the village amateurs, and established a musical club for their improvement; he has also sorted a choir, as he sorted my father's pack of hounds, according to the directions of Jervaise Markham, in his Country Contentments; for the bass he has sought out all the 'deep, solemn mouths,' and for the tenor the 'loud ringing mouths' among the country bumpkins; and for 'sweete mouths,' he has culled with curious taste among the prettiest lasses in the neighbourhood, though these last, he affirms, are the most difficult to keep in tune, your pretty female singer being exceedingly wayward and capricious, and very liable to accident."

As the morning, though frosty, was remarkably fine and

clear, the most of the family walked to the church, which was a very old building of grey stone, and stood near a village, about half a mile from the park gate. Adjoining it was a low snug parsonage, which seemed coeval with the church. The front of it was perfectly matted with a yew tree, that had been trained against its walls; through the dense foliage of which, apertures had been formed to admit light into the small antique lattices. As we passed this sheltered nest, the parson issued forth, and preceded us.

I had expected to see a sleek well conditioned pastor, such as is often found in a snug living in the vicinity of a rich patron's table, but I was disappointed. The parson was a little, meagre, black looking man, with a grizzled wig that was too wide, and stood off from each ear, so that his head seemed to have shrunk away within it, like a dried filbert in its shell. He wore a rusty coat with great skirts and pockets that would have held the church bible and prayer book; and his small legs seemed still smaller, from being planted in large shoes, decorated with enormous buckles.

I was informed by Frank Bracebridge, that the parson had been a chum of his father's at Oxford, and had received this living shortly after the latter had come to his estate. He was a complete black letter hunter, and would scarcely read a work printed in the Roman character. The editions of Caxton and Wynkin de Worde were his delight, and he was indefatigable in his researches after such old English writers as have fallen into oblivion from their worthlessness. In deference, perhaps, to the notions of Mr. Bracebridge, he had made diligent investigations into the festive rites and holyday customs of former times, and had been as zealous in the inquiry, as if he had been a boon companion; but it was merely with that plodding spirit, with which men of adust temperament follow up any track of study, merely because it is denominated learning, indifferent to its intrinsic nature, whether it be the illustration of the wisdom or of the ribaldry and obscenity of antiquity. He had pored over these old volumes so intensely, that they seemed to have been reflected into his countenance, which, if the face be, indeed, an index of the mind, might be compared to a title page of black letter.

On reaching the church porch, we found the parson rebuking the gray headed sexton for having used misletoe among the greens with which the church was decorated. It was, he observed, an unholy plant; profaned by having been used by the Druids in their mystic ceremonies, and though it might be innocently employed in the festive ornamenting of halls and kitchens, yet it had been deemed by the fathers of the church as unhallowed, and totally unfit for sacred purposes. So tenacious was he on this point, that the poor sexton was obliged to strip down a great part of the humble trophies of his taste, before the parson would consent to enter upon the service of the day.

The interior of the church was venerable, but simple: on the walls were several mural monuments of the Bracebridges; and just beside the altar was a tomb of ancient workmanship, on which lay the effigy of a warrior in armour, with his legs crossed, a sign of his having been a crusader. I was told it was one of the family who had signalized himself in the holy land, and the same whose picture hung over the fire place in the hall.

During service, Master Simon stood up in the pew, and repeated the responses very audibly; evincing that kind of ceremonious devotion punctually observed by a gentleman of the old school, and a man of old family connexions. I observed, too, that he turned over the leaves of a folio prayer book with something of a flourish, possibly to show off an enormous seal ring which enriched one of his fingers, and which had the look of a family relique. But he was evidently most solicitous about the musical part of the service, keeping his eye fixed intently on the choir, and beating time with much gesticulation and emphasis.

The orchestra was in a small gallery, and presented a most whimsical grouping of heads, piled one above the other, among which I particularly noticed that of the village taylor, a pale fellow with a retreating forehead and chin, who played on the clarionet, and seemed to have blown his face to a point; and there was another, a short pursy man, stooping and labouring at a bass viol, so as to show nothing but the top of a round bald head, like the egg of an ostrich. There were two or three pretty faces among the female singers, to which the keen air of a frosty morning had given a bright rosy tint; but the gentlemen choristers had evidently been chosen, like old Cremona fiddles, more for tone than looks; and as several had to sing from the same book, there were clusterings of odd physiognomies, not unlike those groups of cherubs we sometimes see on country tombstones.

The usual services of the choir were managed tolerably well, the vocal parts generally lagging a little behind the instrumental, and some loitering fiddler now and then making up for lost time by travelling over a passage with prodigious celerity, and clearing more bars than the keenest fox hunter, to be in at the death. But the great trial was an anthem that had been prepared and arranged by Master Simon, and on which he had founded great expectations. Unluckily, there was a blunder at the very outset; the musicians became flurried; Master Simon was in a fever; every thing went on lamely and irregularly until they came to a chorus beginning "Now let us sing with one accord," which seemed to be a signal for parting company: all became discord and confusion, each shifted for himself, and got to the end as well, or, rather, as soon as he could, excepting one old chorister in a pair of horn spectacles, bestriding and pinching a long sonorous nose, who, happening to stand a little apart, and being wrapped up in his own melody, kept on a quavering course, wriggling his head, ogling his book, and winding all up by a nasal solo of at least three bars duration.

The parson gave us a most erudite sermon on the rites and ceremonies of Christmas, and the propriety of observing it, not merely as a day of thanksgiving, but of rejoicing; supporting the correctness of his opinions by the earliest usages of the church, and enforcing them by the authorities of Theophilus of Cesarea, St. Cyprian, St. Chrysostom, St. Augustine, and a cloud more of saints and fathers, from whom he made copious quotations. I was a little at a loss to perceive the necessity of such a mighty array of forces to maintain a point which no one present seemed inclined to dispute; but I soon found that the good man had a legion of ideal adversaries to contend with, having, in the course of his researches on the subject of Christmas, got completely embroiled in the sectarian controversies of the revolution, when the Puritans made such a fierce assault upon the ceremonies of the church,

and poor old Christmas was driven out of the land by proclamation of Parliament.* The worthy parson lived but with
times past, and knew but little of the present.

Shut up among worm eaten tomes in the retirement of his
antiquated little study, the pages of old times were to him as
the gazettes of the day; while the era of the Revolution was
mere modern history. He forgot that nearly two centuries had
elapsed since the fiery persecution of poor Mince pie throughout the land; when plum porridge was denounced as "mere
popery," and roast beef as antichristian; and that Christmas
had been brought in again triumphantly with the merry court
of King Charles at the restoration. He kindled into warmth
with the ardour of his contest, and the host of imaginary foes
with whom he had to combat; had a stubborn conflict with
old Prynne and two or three other forgotten champions of
the round heads, on the subject of Christmas festivity; and
concluded by urging his hearers, in the most solemn and affecting manner, to stand to the traditionary customs of their
fathers, and feast and make merry on this joyful anniversary
of the church.

I have seldom known a sermon attended apparently with
more immediate effects; for on leaving the church the congregation seemed one and all possessed with the gayety of spirit
so earnestly enjoined by their pastor. The elder folks gathered
in knots in the church yard, greeting and shaking hands, and
the children ran about crying Ule! Ule! and repeating some
uncouth rhymes,† which the parson, who had joined us, informed me had been handed down from days of yore. The

*From "The Flying Eagle," a small Gazette published December 24th,
1652.—"The House spent much time this day about the businesse of the
Navy for settling the affairs at sea, and before they rose were presented with
a terrible remonstrance against Christmas day, grounded upon divine Scriptures, 2 Cor. v. 16. 1 Cor. xv. 14.17; and in honour of the Lord's day,
grounded upon these Scriptures, John, xx. 1. Rev. i. 10. Psalms, cxviii. 24.
Lev. xxiii. 7.11. Mark. xvi. 8. Psalms, lxxxiv. 10. In which Christmas is called
Antichrist's masse, and those Masse-mongers and Papists who observe it, &c.
In consequence of which Parliament spent some time in consultation about
the abolition of Christmas day, passed orders to that effect, and resolved to
sit on the following day, which was commonly called Christmas day."

†"Ule! Ule!
   Three puddings in a pule;
   Crack nuts and cry ule!"

villagers doffed their hats to the Squire as he passed, giving him the good wishes of the season with every appearance of heartfelt sincerity, and were invited by him to the hall, to take something to keep out the cold of the weather; and I heard blessings uttered by several of the poor, which convinced me that, in the midst of his enjoyments, the worthy old cavalier had not forgotten the true Christmas virtue of charity.

On our way homeward, his heart seemed overflowing with generous and happy feelings. As we passed over a rising ground which commanded something of a prospect, the sounds of rustic merriment now and then reached our ears; the Squire paused for a few moments, and looked around with an air of inexpressible benignity. The beauty of the day was, of itself, sufficient to inspire philanthropy. Notwithstanding the frostiness of the morning, the sun in his cloudless journey had acquired sufficient power to melt away the thin covering of snow from every southern declivity, and to bring out the living green which adorns an English landscape even in mid winter. Large tracts of smiling verdure, contrasted with the dazzling whiteness of the shaded slopes and hollows. Every sheltered bank, on which the broad rays rested, yielded its silver rill of cold and limpid water, glittering through the dripping grass; and sent up slight exhalations to contribute to the thin haze that hung just above the surface of the earth. There was something truly cheering in this triumph of warmth and verdure over the frosty thraldom of winter: it was, as the Squire observed, an emblem of Christmas hospitality breaking through the chills of ceremony and selfishness, and thawing every heart into a flow. He pointed with pleasure to the indications of good cheer reeking from the chimneys of the comfortable farm houses, and low thatched cottages. "I love," said he, "to see this day well kept by rich and poor; it is a great thing to have one day in the year at least, when you are sure of being welcome wherever you go, and of having, as it were, the world all thrown open to you; and I am almost disposed to join with poor Robin, in his malediction on every churlish enemy to this honest festival."

Those who at Christmas do repine
And would fain hence despatch him,
May they with old duke Humphry dine,
Or else may Squire Ketch catch 'em.

The Squire went on to lament the deplorable decay of the games and amusements which were once prevalent at this season among the lower orders, and countenanced by the higher. When the old halls of castles and manor houses were thrown open at daylight; when the tables were covered with brawn, and beef, and humming ale; when the harp and the carol resounded all day long, and when rich and poor were alike welcome to enter and make merry.* "Our old games and local customs," said he, "had a great effect in making the peasant fond of his home, and the promotion of them by the gentry made him fond of his lord. They made the times merrier, and kinder, and better, and I can truly say with one of our old poets,

I like them well—the curious preciseness
And all pretended gravity of those
That seek to banish hence these harmless sports,
Have thrust away much ancient honesty.

"The nation," continued he, "is altered; we have almost lost our simple, true hearted peasantry. They have broken asunder from the higher classes, and seem to think their interests are separate. They have become too knowing, and begin to read newspapers, listen to ale house politicians, and talk of reform. I think one mode to keep them in good humour in these hard times, would be for the nobility and gentry to pass more time on their estates, mingle more among the country people, and set the merry old English games going again."

*"An English gentleman at the opening of the great day, i.e. on Christmas day in the morning, had all his tenants and neighbours enter his hall by day break. The strong beer was broached, and the black jacks went plentifully about with toast, sugar, nutmeg, and good Cheshire cheese. The Hackin (the great sausage) must be boiled by daybreak, or else two young men must take the maiden (i.e. the cook,) by the arms and run her round the market place till she is ashamed of her laziness."—*Round about our Sea-coal Fire*.

Such was the good Squire's project for mitigating public discontent: and, indeed, he had once attempted to put his doctrine in practice, and a few years before had kept open house during the holydays in the old style. The country people, however, did not understand how to play their parts in the scene of hospitality: many uncouth circumstances occurred; the manor was overrun by all the vagrants of the country, and more beggars drawn into the neighbourhood in one week than the parish officers could get rid of in a year. Since then, he had contented himself with inviting the decent part of the neighbouring peasantry to call at the hall on Christmas day, and with distributing beef, and bread, and ale, among the poor, that they might make merry in their own dwellings.

We had not been long home when the sound of music was heard from a distance. A band of country lads without coats, their shirt sleeves fancifully tied with ribands, their hats decorated with greens, and clubs in their hands, were seen advancing up the avenue, followed by a large number of villagers and peasantry. They stopped before the hall door, where the music struck up a peculiar air, and the lads performed a curious and intricate dance, advancing, retreating, and striking their clubs together, keeping exact time to the music; while one, whimsically crowned with a fox's skin, the tail of which flaunted down his back, kept capering round the skirts of the dance, and rattling a Christmas box with many antic gesticulations.

The Squire eyed this fanciful exhibition with great interest and delight, and gave me a full account of its origin, which he traced to the times when the Romans held possession of the island, plainly proving that this was a lineal descendant of the sword dance of the ancients. "It was now," he said, "nearly extinct, but he had accidentally met with traces of it in the neighbourhood, and had encouraged its revival, though, to tell the truth, it was too apt to be followed up by rough cudgel play, and broken heads, in the evening."

After the dance was concluded, the whole party was entertained with brawn and beef, and stout home brewed. The Squire himself mingled among the rustics, and was received with awkward demonstrations of deference and regard. It is true, I perceived two or three of the younger peasants, as they were raising their tankards to their mouths, when the Squire's back was turned, making something of a grimace, and giving each other the wink, but the moment they caught my eye they pulled grave faces, and were exceedingly demure. With Master Simon, however, they all seemed more at their ease. His varied occupations and amusements had made him well known throughout the neighbourhood. He was a visiter at every farm house and cottage, gossipped with the farmers and their wives, romped with their daughters, and like that type of a vagrant bachelor, the humble bee, tolled the sweets from all the rosy lips of the country round.

The bashfulness of the guests soon gave way before good cheer and affability. There is something genuine and affectionate in the gayety of the lower orders, when it is excited by the bounty and familiarity of those above them; the warm glow of gratitude enters into their mirth, and a kind word, and a small pleasantry frankly uttered by a patron, gladdens the heart of the dependant more than oil and wine. When the Squire had retired, the merriment increased, and there was much joking and laughter; particularly between Master Simon and a hale ruddy faced white headed farmer, who appeared to be the wit of the village, for I observed all his companions to wait with open mouths for his retorts, and burst into a gratuitous laugh before they could well understand them.

The whole house indeed seemed abandoned to merriment: as I passed to my room to dress for dinner, I heard the sound of music in a small court, and looking through a window that commanded it, I perceived a band of wandering musicians with pandean pipes and tambourine: a pretty coquettish housemaid was dancing a jig with a smart country lad, while several of the other servants were looking on. In the midst of her sport the girl caught a glimpse of my face at the window, and colouring up, ran off with an air of roguish affected confusion.

The Christmas Dinner

Lo, now is come our joyful'st feast!
  Let every man be jolly,
Eache roome with yvie leaves is drest,
  And every post with holly.
Now all our neighbours' chimneys smoke
  And Christmas blocks are burning;
Their ovens they with bak't meats choke,
  And all their spits are turning.
    Without the door let sorrow lie,
      And if, for cold, it hap to die,
    Wee'le bury 't in a Christmas pye,
    And ever more be merry.
            Withers' Juvenilia

I HAD FINISHED my toilet, and was loitering with Frank Bracebridge in the library, when we heard a distant thwacking sound, which he informed me was a signal for the serving up of the dinner. The Squire kept up old customs in kitchen as well as hall, and the rolling pin struck upon the dresser by the cook, summoned the servants to carry in the meats.

    Just in this nick the cook knock'd thrice,
    And all the waiters in a trice
      His summons did obey;
    Each serving man, with dish in hand,
    March'd boldly up, like our train band,
      Presented, and away.*

The dinner was served up in the great hall, where the Squire always held his Christmas banquet. A blazing, crackling fire of logs had been heaped on to warm the spacious apartment, and the flame went sparkling and wreathing up the wide mouthed chimney. The great picture of the crusader and his white horse had been profusely decorated with greens for the occasion, and holly and ivy had likewise been

*Sir John Suckling.

wreathed round the helmet and weapons on the opposite wall, which I understood were the arms of the same warrior. I must own, by the by, I had strong doubts about the authenticity of the painting and armour as having belonged to the crusader, they certainly having the stamp of more recent days; but I was told that the painting had been so considered time out of mind; and that, as to the armour, it had been found in a lumber room, and elevated to its present situation by the Squire, who at once determined it to be the armour of the family hero; and as he was absolute authority on all such subjects in his own household, the matter had passed into current acceptation. A sideboard was set out just under this chivalric trophy, on which was a display of plate that might have vied (at least in variety) with Belshazzar's parade of the vessels of the temple: "flagons, cans, cups, beakers, goblets, basins, and ewers;" the gorgeous utensils of good companionship, that had gradually accumulated through many generations of jovial housekeepers; before these stood the two yule candles beaming like two stars of the first magnitude; other lights were distributed in branches, and the whole array glittered like a firmament of silver.

We were ushered into this banqueting scene with the sound of minstrelsy; the old harper being seated on a stool beside the fireplace, and twanging his instrument, with a vast deal more power than melody. Never did Christmas board display a more goodly and gracious assemblage of countenances; those who were not handsome, were, at least, happy; and happiness is a rare improver of your hard favoured visage. I always consider an old English family as well worth studying as a collection of Holbein's portraits or Albert Durer's prints. There is much antiquarian lore to be acquired; much knowledge of the physiognomies of former times. Perhaps it may be from having continually before their eyes those rows of old family portraits, with which the mansions of this country are stocked; certain it is, that the quaint features of antiquity are often most faithfully perpetuated in these ancient lines; and I have traced an old family nose through a whole picture gallery, legitimately handed down from generation to generation, almost from the time of the conquest. Some-

thing of the kind was to be observed in the worthy company around me. Many of their faces had evidently originated in a gothic age, and been merely copied by succeeding
generations; and there was one little girl in particular, of
staid demeanour, with a high Roman nose, and an antique
vinegar aspect, who was a great favourite of the Squire's,
being, as he said, a Bracebridge all over, and the very counterpart of one of his ancestors who figured in the court of
Henry VIII.

The parson said grace, which was not a short familiar one,
such as is commonly addressed to the deity, in these unceremonious days; but a long, courtly, well worded one, of the
ancient school. There was now a pause, as if something was
expected, when suddenly the Butler entered the hall, with
some degree of bustle: he was attended by a servant on each
side with a large wax light, and bore a silver dish, on which
was an enormous pig's head, decorated with rosemary, with
a lemon in its mouth, which was placed with great formality
at the head of the table. The moment this pageant made its
appearance, the harper struck up a flourish; at the conclusion
of which the young Oxonian, on receiving a hint from the
Squire, gave, with an air of the most comic gravity, an old
carol, the first verse of which was as follows:

> Caput apri defero
> Reddens laudes Domino.
> The boar's head in hand bring I,
> With garlands gay and rosemary.
> I pray you all synge merily
> Qui estis in convivio.

Though prepared to witness many of these little eccentricities,
from being apprized of the peculiar hobby of mine host; yet,
I confess, the parade with which so odd a dish was introduced, somewhat perplexed me, until I gathered from the
conversation of the Squire and the parson, that it was meant
to represent the bringing in of the boar's head, a dish formerly served up with much ceremony, and the sound of minstrelsy and song, at great tables on Christmas day. "I like the
old custom," said the Squire, "not merely because it is stately

and pleasing in itself, but because it was observed at the college at Oxford, at which I was educated. When I hear the old
song chanted, it brings to mind the time when I was young
and gamesome—and the noble old college hall—and my fellow students loitering about it in their black gowns, many of
whom, poor lads, are now in their graves!"

The parson, however, whose mind was not haunted by
such associations, and who was always more taken up with
the text than the sentiment, objected to the Oxonian's version
of the carol, which he affirmed was different from that sung at
college. He went on with the dry perseverance of a commentator, to give the college reading, accompanied by sundry anno-
tations, addressing himself at first to the company at large;
but finding their attention gradually diverted to other talk and
other objects, he lowered his tone as his number of auditors
diminished, until he concluded his remarks in an under voice,
to a fat headed old gentleman next him, who was silently
engaged in the discussion of a huge plate full of turkey.*

The table was literally loaded with good cheer, and presented an epitome of country abundance, in this season of

*The old ceremony of serving up the boar's head on Christmas day is still
observed in the hall of Queen's College Oxford. I was favoured by the parson
with a copy of the carol as now sung, and as it may be acceptable to such of
my readers as are curious in these grave and learned matters, I give it entire.

> The boar's head in hand bear I,
> Bedeck'd with bays and rosemary;
> And I pray you, my masters, be merry
>   Quot estis in convivio.
>   Caput apri defero
>   Reddens laudes Domino.
>
> The boar's head, as I understand,
> Is the rarest dish in all this land,
> Which thus bedeck'd with a gay garland
>   Let us servire cantico.
>   Caput apri defero, &c.
>
> Our steward hath provided this
> In honour of the King of bliss,
> Which on this day to be served is
>   In Reginensi Atrio.
>   Caput apri defero,
>   &c. &c. &c.

overflowing larders. A distinguished post was allotted to "ancient sirloin," as mine host termed it, being, as he added, "the standard of old English hospitality, and a joint of goodly presence, and full of expectation." There were several dishes quaintly decorated, and which had evidently something traditionary in their embellishments, but about which, as I did not like to appear over curious, I asked no questions.

I could not, however, but notice a pie, magnificently decorated with peacock's feathers, in imitation of the tail of that bird, which overshadowed a considerable tract of the table. This the Squire confessed, with some little hesitation, was a pheasant pie, though a peacock pie was certainly the most authentical; but there had been such a mortality among the peacocks this season, that he could not prevail upon himself to have one killed.*

It would be tedious, perhaps, to my wiser readers, who may not have that foolish fondness for odd and obsolete things to which I am a little given, were I to mention the other make shifts of this worthy old humourist, by which he was endeavouring to follow up, though at humble distance, the quaint customs of antiquity. I was pleased, however, to see the respect shown to his whims by his children and relatives, who, indeed, entered readily into the full spirit of them, and seemed all well versed in their parts, having doubtless been present at many a rehearsal. I was amused, too, at the air of profound gravity with which the

*The peacock was anciently in great demand for stately entertainments. Sometimes it was made into a pie, at one end of which the head appeared above the crust in all its plumage, with the beak richly gilt; at the other end the tail was displayed. Such pies were served up at the solemn banquets of chivalry, when Knights errant pledged themselves to undertake any perilous enterprize, whence came the ancient oath, used by Justice Shallow, "by cock and pye."

The peacock was also an important dish for the Christmas feast, and Massinger in his City Madam gives some idea of the extravagance with which this, as well as other dishes, was prepared for the gorgeous revels of the olden times:—

Men may talk of Country-Christmasses,
Their thirty pound butter'd eggs, their pies of carps' tongues;
Their pheasants drench'd with ambergris; *the carcasses of three fat wethers bruised for gravy to make sauce for a single peacock!*

butler and other servants executed the duties assigned them, however eccentric. They had an old fashioned look, having, for the most part, been brought up in the household, and grown into keeping with the antiquated mansion, and the humours of its lord, and most probably looked upon all his whimsical regulations, as the established laws of honourable housekeeping.

When the cloth was removed, the butler brought in a huge silver vessel of rare and curious workmanship, which he placed before the Squire. Its appearance was hailed with acclamation; being the Wassail Bowl, so renowned in Christmas festivity. The contents had been prepared by the Squire himself; for it was a beverage in the skilful mixture of which he particularly prided himself; alleging that it was too abstruse and complex for the comprehension of an ordinary servant. It was a potation, indeed, that might well make the heart of a toper leap within him; being composed of the richest and raciest wines, highly spiced and sweetened, with roasted apples bobbing about the surface.*

The old gentleman's whole countenance beamed with a serene look of indwelling delight, as he stirred this mighty bowl. Having raised it to his lips, with a hearty wish of a merry Christmas to all present, he sent it brimming round the board, for every one to follow his example, according to the primitive style; pronouncing it, "the ancient fountain of good feeling, where all hearts met together."†

*The Wassail Bowl was sometimes composed of ale instead of wine; with nutmeg, sugar, toast, ginger, and roasted crabs: in this way the nut brown beverage is still prepared in some old families, and round the hearths of substantial farmers at Christmas. It is also called Lamb's wool, and is celebrated by Herrick in his Twelfth Night:

> Next crowne the bowle full
> With gentle Lamb's wooll,
> Add sugar, nutmeg, and ginger,
> With store of ale too;
> And thus ye must doe
> To make the Wassaile a swinger.

†"The custom of drinking out of the same cup gave place to each having his cup. When the steward came to the doore with the Wassel, he was to cry three times *Wassel, Wassel, Wassel*, and then the chappel (chaplain) was to answer with a song." ARCHÆOLOGIA.

There was much laughing and rallying as the honest emblem of Christmas joviality circulated, and was kissed rather coyly by the ladies. When it reached Master Simon he raised it in both hands, and with the air of a boon companion struck up an old Wassail chanson:

>The brown bowle,
>The merry brown bowle,
>As it goes round about-a,
>>Fill
>>Still
>Let the world say what it will
>And drink your fill all out-a.
>
>The deep canne,
>The merry deep canne,
>As thou dost freely quaff-a,
>>Sing
>>Fling
>Be as merry as a king,
>And sound a lusty laugh-a.*

Much of the conversation during dinner turned upon family topics, to which I was a stranger. There was, however, a great deal of rallying of Master Simon about some gay widow, with whom he was accused of having a flirtation. This attack was commenced by the ladies; but it was continued throughout the dinner by the fat headed old gentleman next the parson, with the persevering assiduity of a slow hound; being one of those long winded jokers, who, though rather dull at starting game, are unrivalled for their talents in hunting it down. At every pause in the general conversation, he renewed his bantering in pretty much the same terms; winking hard at me with both eyes, whenever he gave Master Simon what he considered a home thrust. The latter, indeed, seemed fond of being teased on the subject, as old bachelors are apt to be, and he took occasion to inform me, in an under

*From Poor Robin's Almanack.

tone, that the lady in question was a prodigiously fine woman, and drove her own curricle.

The dinner time passed away in this flow of innocent hilarity, and though the old hall may have resounded in its time with many a scene of broader rout and revel, yet I doubt whether it ever witnessed more honest and genuine enjoyment. How easy it is for one benevolent being to diffuse pleasure around him; and how truly is a kind heart a fountain of gladness, making every thing in its vicinity to freshen into smiles. The joyous disposition of the worthy Squire was perfectly contagious; he was happy himself, and disposed to make all the world happy; and the little eccentricities of his humour did but season, in a manner, the sweetness of his philanthropy.

When the ladies had retired, the conversation, as usual, became still more animated: many good things were broached which had been thought of during dinner, but which would not exactly do for a lady's ear; and though I cannot positively affirm that there was much wit uttered, yet I have certainly heard many contests of rare wit produce much less laughter. Wit, after all, is a mighty tart, pungent ingredient, and much too acid for some stomachs; but honest good humour is the oil and wine of a merry meeting, and there is no jovial companionship equal to that, where the jokes are rather small, and the laughter abundant.

The Squire told several long stories of early college pranks and adventures, in some of which the parson had been a sharer; though in looking at the latter, it required some effort of imagination to figure such a little dark anatomy of a man, into the perpetrator of a mad cap gambol. Indeed, the two college chums presented pictures of what men may be made by their different lots in life: the Squire had left the university to live lustily on his paternal domains, in the vigorous enjoyment of prosperity and sunshine, and had flourished on to a hearty and florid old age, whilst the poor parson, on the contrary, had dried and withered away, among dusty tomes, in the silence and shadows of his study. Still there seemed to be a spark of almost extinguished fire, feebly glimmering in the bottom of his soul; and as the Squire hinted at a sly story of the parson and a pretty milkmaid whom they once met on the banks of the Isis, the old gentleman made an "alphabet of faces," which, as far as I could decypher his physiognomy, I verily believe was indicative of laughter;—indeed, I have rarely met with an old gentleman that took absolute offence at the imputed gallantries of his youth.

I found the tide of wine and wassail fast gaining on the dry land of sober judgment. The company grew merrier and louder as their jokes grew duller. Master Simon was in as chirping a humour as a grasshopper filled with dew; his old songs grew of a warmer complexion, and he began to talk maudlin about the widow. He even gave a long song about the wooing of a widow, which he informed me he had gathered from an excellent black letter work entitled "Cupid's Solicitor for Love;" containing store of good advice for Bachelors, and which he promised to lend me; the first verse was to this effect:

> He that will woo a widow must not dally,
>   He must make hay while the sun doth shine;
> He must not stand with her, shall I, shall I,
>   But boldly say, Widow thou must be mine.

This song inspired the fat headed old gentleman, who made several attempts to tell a rather broad story out of Joe Miller, that was pat to the purpose; but he always stuck in the middle, every body recollecting the latter part except himself. The parson, too, began to show the effects of good cheer, having gradually settled down into a doze, and his wig setting most suspiciously on one side. Just at this juncture we were summoned to the drawing room, and I suspect, at the private instigation of mine host, whose joviality seemed always tempered with a proper love of decorum.

After the dinner table was removed, the hall was given up to the younger members of the family, who, prompted to all kind of noisy mirth, by the Oxonian and Master Simon, made its old walls ring with their merriment, as they played at romping games. I delight in witnessing the gambols of children, and particularly at this happy holiday season, and could not help stealing out of the drawing room on hearing one of their peals of laughter. I found them at the game of blind-man's-buff. Master Simon, who was the leader of their revels, and seemed on all occasions to fulfil the office of that ancient potentate, the Lord of Misrule,* was blinded in the midst of the hall. The little beings were as busy about him as the mock fairies about Falstaff, pinching him, plucking at the skirts of his coat, and tickling him with straws. One fine blue eyed girl of about thirteen, with her flaxen hair all in beautiful confusion, her frolick face in a glow, her frock half torn off her shoulders, a complete picture of a romp, was the chief tormentor; and from the slyness with which Master Simon avoided the smaller game, and hemmed this wild little nymph in corners, and obliged her to jump shrieking over chairs, I suspected the rogue of being not a whit more blinded than was convenient.

When I returned to the drawing room, I found the company seated round the fire, listening to the parson, who was deeply ensconced in a high backed oaken chair, the work of some cunning artificer of yore, which had been brought from the library for his particular accommodation. From this venerable piece of furniture, with which his shadowy figure and dark weazen face so admirably accorded, he was dealing forth strange accounts of the popular superstitions, and legends of the surrounding country, with which he had become acquainted in the course of his antiquarian researches. I am half inclined to think that the old gentleman was himself somewhat tinctured with superstition, as men are very apt to be, who live a recluse and studious life in a sequestered part of the country, and pore over black letter tracts, so often filled with the marvellous and supernatural. He gave us several anecdotes of the fancies of the neighbouring peasantry, concerning the effigy of the crusader, which lay on the tomb by the church altar. As it was the only monument of the kind in that part of the country, it had always been regarded with feelings of superstition by the good wives of the village. It was said to get up from the tomb and walk the rounds of the church yard of stormy nights, particularly when it

---

*At christmasse there was in the Kinges house, wheresoever hee was lodged, a lorde of misrule, or mayster of merie disportes, and the like had ye in the house of every nobleman of honor, or good worshippe, were he spirituall or temporall. STOW.

thundered; and one old woman whose cottage bordered on the church yard had seen it, through the windows of the church, when the moon shone, slowly pacing up and down the aisles. It was the belief that some wrong had been left unredressed by the deceased, or some treasure hidden, which kept the spirit in a state of trouble and restlessness. Some talked of gold and jewels buried in the tomb, over which the spectre kept watch; and there was a story current of a sexton in old times who endeavoured to break his way to the coffin at night; but just as he reached it, received a violent blow from the marble hand of the effigy, which stretched him senseless on the pavement. These tales were often laughed at by some of the sturdier among the rustics, yet when night came on, there were many of the stoutest unbelievers that were shy of venturing alone in the footpath that led across the church yard.

From these and other anecdotes that followed, the crusader appeared to be the favourite hero of ghost stories throughout the vicinity. His picture, which hung up in the hall, was thought by the servants to have something supernatural about it; for they remarked that, in whatever part of the hall you went, the eyes of the warrior were still fixed on you. The old porter's wife too, at the lodge, who had been born and brought up in the family, and was a great gossip among the maid servants, affirmed, that in her young days she had often heard say, that on midsummer eve, when it is well known all kinds of ghosts, goblins, and fairies, become visible and walk abroad, the crusader used to mount his horse, come down from his picture, ride about the house, down the avenue, and so to the church to visit the tomb; on which occasion the church door most civilly swung open of itself: not that he needed it; for he rode through closed gates and even stone walls, and had been seen by one of the dairy maids to pass between two bars of the great park gate, making himself as thin as a sheet of paper.

All these superstitions I found had been very much countenanced by the Squire, who, though not superstitious himself, was very fond of seeing others so. He listened to every goblin tale of the neighbouring gossips with infinite gravity, and held the porter's wife in high favour on account of her talent for the marvellous. He was himself a great reader of old legends and romances, and often lamented that he could not believe in them, for a superstitious person, he thought, must live in a kind of fairy land.

Whilst we were all attention to the parson's stories, our ears were suddenly assailed by a burst of heterogeneous sounds from the hall, in which were mingled something like the clang of rude minstrelsy, with the uproar of many small voices and girlish laughter. The door suddenly flew open, and a train came trooping into the room, that might almost have been mistaken for the breaking up of the court of Fairy. That indefatigable spirit, Master Simon, in the faithful discharge of his duties, as lord of misrule, had conceived the idea of a Christmas mummery, or masqueing; and having called in to his assistance the Oxonian and the young officer, who were equally ripe for any thing that should occasion romping and merriment, they had carried it into instant effect. The old housekeeper had been consulted; the antique clothes presses and wardrobes rummaged, and made to yield up the reliques of finery that had not seen the light for several generations; the younger part of the company had been privately convened from parlour and hall, and the whole had been bedizened out, into a burlesque imitation of an antique masque.*

Master Simon led the van, as "Ancient Christmas," quaintly apparelled in a ruff, a short cloak, which had very much the aspect of one of the old housekeeper's petticoats, and a hat that might have served for a village steeple, and must indubitably have figured in the days of the Covenanters. From under this his nose curved boldly forth, flushed with a frost bitten bloom, that seemed the very trophy of a December blast. He was accompanied by the blue eyed romp, dished up as "Dame Mince Pie," in the venerable magnificence of faded brocade, long stomacher, peaked hat, and high heeled shoes. The young officer appeared as Robin Hood, in a sporting

*Masquings or mummeries were favourite sports at Christmas in old times; and the wardrobes at halls and manor houses were often laid under contribution to furnish dresses and fantastic disguisings. I strongly suspect Master Simon to have taken the idea of his from Ben Jonson's Masque of Christmas.

dress of Kendal green, and a foraging cap with a gold tassel. The costume, to be sure, did not bear testimony to deep research, and there was an evident eye to the picturesque, natural to a young gallant in the presence of his mistress. The fair Julia hung on his arm in a pretty rustic dress, as "Maid Marian." The rest of the train had been metamorphosed in various ways; the girls trussed up in the finery of the ancient belles of the Bracebridge line, and the striplings bewhiskered with burnt cork, and gravely clad in broad skirts, hanging sleeves, and full bottomed wigs, to represent the characters of Roast Beef, Plum Pudding, and other worthies celebrated in ancient masquings. The whole was under the control of the Oxonian, in the appropriate character of Misrule; and I observed that he exercised rather a mischievous sway with his wand over the smaller personages of the pageant.

The irruption of this motley crew, with beat of drum, according to ancient custom, was the consummation of uproar and merriment. Master Simon covered himself with glory by the stateliness with which, as Ancient Christmas, he walked a minuet with the peerless, though giggling, Dame Mince Pie. It was followed by a dance of all the characters, which, from its medley of costumes, seemed as though the old family portraits had skipped down from their frames to join in the sport. Different centuries were figuring at cross hands and right and left; the dark ages were cutting pirouettes and rigadoons; and the days of Queen Bess jigging merrily down the middle, through a line of succeeding generations.

The worthy Squire contemplated these fantastic sports, and this resurrection of his old wardrobe, with the simple relish of childish delight. He stood chuckling and rubbing his hands, and scarcely hearing a word the parson said, notwithstanding that the latter was discoursing most authentically on the ancient and stately dance of the Paon, or peacock, from which he conceived the minuet to be derived.* For my part, I was in a continual excitement from the varied scenes of whim and innocent gayety passing before me.

*Sir John Hawkins, speaking of the dance called the Pavon, from pavo, a peacock, says, "It is a grave and majestic dance; the method of dancing it anciently was by gentlemen, dressed with caps and swords, by those of the

It was inspiring to see wild eyed frolick and warm hearted hospitality breaking out from among the chills and glooms of winter, and old age throwing off its apathy, and catching once more the freshness of youthful enjoyment. I felt also an interest in the scene, from the consideration that these fleeting customs were posting fast into oblivion, and that this was, perhaps, the only family in England in which the whole of them was still punctiliously observed. There was a quaintness too, mingled with all this revelry that gave it a peculiar zest: it was suited to the time and place; and as the old manor house almost reeled with mirth and wassail, it seemed echoing back the joviality of long departed years.*

But enough of Christmas and its gambols: it is time for me to pause in this garrulity. Methinks I hear the question asked by my graver readers, "To what purpose is all this—how is the world to be made wiser by this talk?" Alas! is there not wisdom enough extant for the instruction of the world? And if not, are there not thousands of abler pens labouring for its improvement?—It is so much pleasanter to please than to instruct—to play the companion rather than the preceptor. What, after all, is the mite of wisdom that I could throw into the mass of knowledge; or how am I sure that my sagest deductions may be safe guides for the opinions of others? But in writing to amuse, if I fail, the only evil is my own disappointment. If, however, I can by any lucky chance, in these days of evil, rub out one wrinkle from the brow of care, or beguile the heavy heart of one moment of sorrow; if I can now and then penetrate through the gathering film of misanthropy, prompt a benevolent view of human nature, and

---

long robe in their gowns, by the peers in their mantles, and by the ladies in gowns with long trains, the motion whereof, in dancing, resembled that of a peacock." HISTORY OF MUSIC.

*At the time of the first publication of this paper, the picture of an old fashioned Christmas in the country was pronounced by some as out of date. The author had afterwards an opportunity of witnessing almost all the customs above described, existing in unexpected vigor on the skirts of Derbyshire and Yorkshire, where he passed the Christmas Holydays. The reader will find some notice of them in the author's account of his sojourn at Newstead Abbey.

make my reader more in good humour with his fellow beings and himself, surely, surely, I shall not then have written entirely in vain.

London Antiques

———I do walk
Methinks like Guido Vaux, with my dark lanthorn,
Stealing to set the town o' fire; i' th' country
I should be taken for William o' the Wisp,
Or Robin Goodfellow.

Fletcher

I AM SOMEWHAT of an antiquity hunter and am fond of exploring London in quest of the reliques of old times. These are principally to be found in the depths of the city, swallowed up and almost lost in a wilderness of brick and mortar; but deriving poetical and romantic interest from the commonplace prosaic world around them. I was struck with an instance of the kind in the course of a recent summer ramble into the city; for the city is only to be explored to advantage in summer time; when free from the smoke and fog, and rain and mud of winter. I had been buffeting for some time against the current of population setting through Fleet Street. The warm weather had unstrung my nerves and made me sensitive to every jar and jostle and discordant sound. The flesh was weary, the spirit faint and I was getting out of humor with the bustling busy throng through which I had to struggle, when in a fit of desperation I tore my way through the crowd, plunged into a bye lane, and after passing through several obscure nooks and angles emerged into a quaint and quiet court with a grass plot in the centre overhung by elms, and kept perpetually fresh and green by a fountain with its sparkling jet of water. A student with book in hand was seated on a stone bench, partly reading, partly meditating on the movements of two or three trim nursery maids with their infant charges.

I was like an Arab who had suddenly come upon an oasis amid the panting sterility of the desert. By degrees the quiet and coolness of the place soothed my nerves and refreshed my spirit. I pursued my walk and came, hard by, to a very ancient chapel with a low browed saxon portal of massive and rich architecture. The interior was circular and lofty, and lighted from above. Around were monumental tombs of ancient date, on which were extended the marble effigies of warriors in armour. Some had the hands devoutly crossed upon the breast; others grasped the pummel of the sword—menacing hostility even in the tomb!—while the crossed legs of several indicated soldiers of the Faith who had been on crusades to the Holy Land.

I was in fact, in the chapel of the Knights Templars, strangely situated in the very centre of sordid traffic; and I do not know a more impressive lesson for the man of the world than thus suddenly to turn aside from the high way of busy money seeking life, and sit down among these shadowy sepulchres, where all is twilight, dust and forgetfulness.

In a subsequent tour of observation I encountered another of these reliques of a "foregone world" locked up in the heart of the city. I had been wandering for some time through dull monotonous streets, destitute of any thing to strike the eye or excite the imagination, when I beheld before me a gothic gate way of mouldering antiquity. It opened into a spacious quadrangle forming the court yard of a stately gothic pile the portal of which stood "invitingly open."

It was apparently a public edifice, and as I was antiquity hunting I ventured in, though with dubious steps. Meeting no one either to oppose or rebuke my intrusion I continued on until I found myself in a great hall with a lofty arched roof and oaken gallery, all of gothic architecture. At one end of the hall was an enormous fireplace with wooden settles on each side; at the other end was a raised platform or dais, the seat of state, above which was the portrait of a man in antique garb, with a long robe, a ruff and a venerable grey beard.

The whole establishment had an air of monastic quiet and seclusion, and what gave it a mysterious charm was, that I had not met with a human being since I had passed the threshold.

Encouraged by this loneliness I seated myself in a recess of a large bow window which admitted a broad flood of yellow sunshine, checquered here and there by tints from panes of colored glass; while an open casement let in the soft summer air. Here leaning my head on my hand and my arm on an old oaken table I indulged in a sort of reverie about what might

have been the ancient uses of this edifice. It had evidently
been of monastic origin; perhaps one of those collegiate establishments built of yore for the promotion of learning,
where the patient monk, in the ample solitude of the cloister,
added page to page and volume to volume, emulating in
the productions of his brain the magnitude of the pile he inhabited.

As I was seated in this musing mood a small panneled door
in an arch at the upper end of the hall was opened and a
number of grey headed old men, clad in long black cloaks,
came forth one by one; proceeding in that manner through
the hall, without uttering a word, each turning a pale face on
me as he passed, and disappearing through a door at the
lower end.

I was singularly struck with their appearance; their black
cloaks and antiquated air comported with the style of this
most venerable and mysterious pile. It was as if the ghosts of
the departed years about which I had been musing were passing in review before me. Pleasing myself with such fancies, I
set out, in the spirit of Romance, to explore what I pictured
to myself a realm of shadows, existing in the very centre of
substantial realities.

My ramble led me through a labyrinth of interior courts
and corridors and delapidated cloisters, for the main edifice
had many additions and dependencies, built at various times
and in various styles; in one open space a number of boys
who evidently belonged to the establishment, were at their
sports; but every where I observed those mysterious old grey
men in black mantles, sometimes sauntering alone; sometimes
conversing in groups: they appeared to be the pervading genii
of the place. I now called to mind what I had read of certain
colleges in old times where judicial astrology, geomancy, necromancy and other forbidden and magical sciences were
taught. Was this an establishment of the kind—and were
these black cloaked old men really professors of the black art?

These surmises were passing through my mind as my eye
glanced into a chamber, hung round with all kinds of strange
and uncouth objects: implements of savage warfare; strange
idols and stuffed alligators; bottled serpents and monsters
decorated the mantelpiece; while on the high tester of an old

fashioned bed stead grinned a human scull, flanked on each side by a dried cat.

I approached to regard more narrowly this mystic chamber, which seemed a fitting laboratory for a necromancer, when I was startled at beholding a human countenance staring at me from a dusky corner. It was that of a small, shrivelled old man, with thin cheeks, bright eyes, and grey wiry projecting eyebrows. I at first doubted whether it were not a mummy curiously preserved, but it moved and I saw that it was alive. It was another of these black cloaked old men, and, as I regarded his quaint physiognomy, his obsolete garb, and the hideous and sinister objects by which he was surrounded, I began to persuade myself that I had come upon the Arch Mago, who ruled over this magical fraternity.

Seeing me pausing before the door he rose and invited me to enter. I obeyed, with singular hardihood, for how did I know whether a wave of his wand might not metamorphose me into some strange monster, or conjure me into one of the bottles on his mantel piece. He proved, however, to be any thing but a conjuror, and his simple garrulity soon dispelled all the magic and mystery with which I had enveloped this antiquated pile and its no less antiquated inhabitants.

It appeared that I had made my way into the centre of an ancient asylum for superannuated tradesmen and decayed householders, with which was connected a school for a limited number of boys. It was founded upwards of two centuries since on an old monastic establishment, and retained somewhat of the conventual air and character. The shadowy line of old men in black mantles who had passed before me in the hall, and whom I had elevated into magi, turned out to be the pensioners returning from morning service in the chapel.

John Hallum the little collector of curiosities whom I had made the arch magician, had been for six years a resident of the place, and had decorated this final nestling place of his old age with reliques and rarities picked up in the course of his life. According to his own account he had been somewhat of a traveller; having been once in France and very near making a visit to Holland. He regretted not having visited the latter country, "as then he might have said he had been there."— He was evidently a traveller of the simple kind.

He was aristocratical too in his notions; keeping aloof, as I found, from the ordinary run of pensioners. His chief associates were a blind man who spoke Latin and Greek, of both which languages Hallum was profoundly ignorant; and a broken down gentleman who had run through a fortune of forty thousand pounds left him by his father, and ten thousand pounds, the marriage portion of his wife. Little Hallum seemed to consider it an indubitable sign of gentle blood as well as of lofty spirit to be able to squander such enormous sums.

P.S. The picturesque remnant of old times into which I have thus beguiled the reader is what is called the Charter House, originally the Chartreuse. It was founded in 1611 on the remains of an ancient convent by Sir Thomas Sutton, being one of those noble charities set on foot by individual munificence, and kept up with the quaintness and sanctity of ancient times amidst the modern changes and innovations of London. Here eighty broken down men, who have seen better days, are provided, in their old age, with food, clothing, fuel and a yearly allowance for private expenses. They dine together as did the monks of old, in the hall which had been the refectory of the original convent. Attached to the establishment is a school for forty four boys.

Stow, whose work I have consulted on the subject; speaking of the obligations of the grey headed pensioners, says, "They are not to intermeddle with any business touching the affairs of the hospital; but to attend only to the service of God, and take thankfully what is provided for them, without muttering, murmuring or grudging. None to wear weapon, long hair, colored boots, spurs or colored shoes; feathers in their hats, or any ruffian like or unseemly apparel, but such as becomes hospital men to wear." "And in truth," adds Stow, "happy are they that are so taken from the cares and sorrows of the world, and fixed in so good a place as these old men are; having nothing to care for, but the good of their souls, to serve God and to live in brotherly love."

For the amusement of such as have been interested by the preceding sketch, taken down from my own observation, and who may wish to know a little more about the mysteries of London, I subjoin a modicum of local history, put into my hands by an odd looking old gentleman in a small brown wig and a snuff colored coat, with whom I became acquainted shortly after my visit to the Charter House. I confess I was a little dubious at first, whether it was not one of those apocryphal tales often passed off upon inquiring travellers like myself; and which have brought our general character for veracity into such unmerited reproach. On making proper inquiries, however, I have received the most satisfactory assurances of the author's probity; and, indeed, have been told that he is actually engaged in a full and particular account of the very interesting region in which he resides; of which the following may be considered merely as a foretaste.

Little Britain

What I write is most true. * * * * I have a whole booke of cases lying by me, which if I should sette foorth, some grave auntients (within the hearing of Bow bell) would bee out of charity with me.

Nashe

IN THE CENTRE of the great City of London lies a small neighbourhood, consisting of a cluster of narrow streets and courts, of very venerable and debilitated houses, which goes by the name of LITTLE BRITAIN. Christ Church School and St. Bartholomew's Hospital bound it on the west; Smith Field and Long Lane on the north; Aldersgate Street, like an arm of the sea, divides it from the eastern part of the city; whilst the yawning gulph of Bull and Mouth Street separates it from Butcher Lane, and the regions of New Gate. Over this little territory, thus bounded and designated, the great dome of St. Paul's, swelling above the intervening houses of Paternoster Row, Amen Corner, and Ave-Maria Lane, looks down with an air of motherly protection.

This quarter derives its appellation from having been, in ancient times, the residence of the Dukes of Britany. As London increased, however, rank and fashion rolled off to the west, and trade creeping on at their heels, took possession of their deserted abodes. For some time Little Britain became the great mart of learning, and was peopled by the busy and prolific race of booksellers: these also gradually deserted it, and emigrating beyond the great strait of New Gate Street, settled down in Paternoster Row and St. Paul's Church Yard; where they continue to increase and multiply even at the present day.

But though thus fallen into decline, Little Britain still bears traces of its former splendour. There are several houses, ready to tumble down, the fronts of which are magnificently enriched with old oaken carvings of hideous faces, unknown birds, beasts, and fishes; and fruits and flowers which it would perplex a naturalist to classify. There are also, in Aldersgate Street, certain remains of what were once spacious and lordly family mansions, but which have in latter days been subdivided into several tenements. Here may often be found the family of a petty tradesman, with its trumpery furniture, burrowing among the relics of antiquated finery, in great rambling time stained apartments, with fretted ceilings, gilded cornices, and enormous marble fireplaces. The lanes and courts also contain many smaller houses, not on so grand a scale, but, like your small ancient gentry, sturdily maintaining their claims to equal antiquity. These have their gable ends to the street; great bow windows, with diamond panes set in lead; grotesque carvings; and low arched door ways.*

In this most venerable and sheltered little nest have I passed several quiet years of existence; comfortably lodged in the second floor of one of the smallest, but oldest edifices. My sitting room is an old wainscotted chamber, with small pannels, and set off with a miscellaneous array of furniture. I have a particular respect for three or four high backed claw footed chairs, covered with tarnished brocade; which bear the marks of having seen better days; and have doubtless figured in some of the old palaces of Little Britain. They seem to me to keep together, and to look down with sovereign contempt upon their leathern bottomed neighbours; as I have seen decayed gentry carry a high head among the plebeian society with which they were reduced to associate. The whole front of my sitting room is taken up with a bow window; on the panes of which are recorded the names of previous occupants for many generations; mingled with scraps of very indifferent, gentleman like poetry, written in characters which I can scarcely decipher; and which extol the charms of many a beauty of Little Britain, who has long, long since, bloomed, faded, and passed away. As I am an idle personage, with no apparent occupation, and pay my bill regularly every week, I am looked upon as the only independent gentleman of the neighbourhood; and being curious to learn the internal state of a community so apparently shut up within itself, I have managed to work my way into all the concerns and secrets of the place.

Little Britain may truly be called the heart's core of the

*It is evident that the author of this interesting communication has included in his general title of Little Britain, many of those little lanes and courts that belong immediately to Cloth Fair.

city; the strong hold of true John Bullism. It is a fragment of London as it was in its better days, with its antiquated folks and fashions. Here flourish in great preservation many of the holyday games and customs of yore. The inhabitants most religiously eat pan cakes on Shrove Tuesday; hot cross buns on Good Friday, and roast goose at Michaelmas: they send love letters on Valentine's Day; burn the Pope on the Fifth of November, and kiss all the girls under the misletoe at Christmas. Roast beef and plum pudding are also held in superstitious veneration, and port and sherry maintain their grounds as the only true English wines; all others being considered vile outlandish beverages.

Little Britain has its long catalogue of city wonders, which its inhabitants consider the wonders of the world; such as the great bell of St. Paul's, which sours all the beer when it tolls; the figures that strike the hours at St. Dunstan's clock; the Monument; the lions in the Tower; and the wooden giants in Guildhall. They still believe in dreams and fortune telling, and an old woman that lives in Bull and Mouth Street makes a tolerable subsistence by detecting stolen goods, and promising the girls good husbands. They are apt to be rendered uncomfortable by comets and eclipses; and if a dog howls dolefully at night, it is looked upon as a sure sign of a death in the place. There are even many ghost stories current, particularly concerning the old mansion houses; in several of which it is said strange sights are sometimes seen. Lords and ladies, the former in full bottomed wigs, hanging sleeves and swords, the latter in lappets, stays, hoops, and brocade, have been seen walking up and down the great waste chambers, on moonlight nights; and are supposed to be the shades of the ancient proprietors in their court dresses.

Little Britain has likewise its sages and great men. One of the most important of the former is a tall dry old gentleman, of the name of Skryme, who keeps a small apothecary's shop. He has a cadaverous countenance, full of cavities and projections; with a brown circle round each eye, like a pair of horn spectacles. He is much thought of by the old women, who consider him as a kind of conjuror, because he has two or three stuffed alligators hanging up in his shop, and several snakes in bottles. He is a great reader of almanacks and news-

papers, and is much given to pore over alarming accounts of
plots, conspiracies, fires, earthquakes, and volcanic eruptions;
which last phenomena he considers as signs of the times. He
has always some dismal tale of the kind to deal out to his
customers, with their doses; and thus at the same time puts
both soul and body into an uproar. He is a great believer in
omens and predictions; and has the prophecies of Robert
Nixon and Mother Shipton by heart. No man can make so
much out of an eclipse, or even an unusually dark day; and
he shook the tail of the last comet over the heads of his customers and disciples until they were nearly frightened out of
their wits. He has lately got hold of a popular legend or
prophecy, on which he has been unusually eloquent. There
has been a saying current among the ancient Sybils, who treasure up these things, that when the grasshopper on the top
of the Exchange shook hands with the dragon on the top of
Bow Church steeple, fearful events would take place. This
strange conjunction, it seems, has as strangely come to pass.
The same architect has been engaged lately on the repairs of
the cupola of the Exchange, and the steeple of Bow Church;
and, fearful to relate, the dragon and the grasshopper actually
lie, cheek by jole, in the yard of his workshop!

"Others," as Mr. Skryme is accustomed to say, "may go star
gazing, and look for conjunctions in the heavens, but here is
a conjunction on the earth, near at home, and under our own
eyes, which surpasses all the signs and calculations of astrologers." Since these portentous weathercocks have thus laid
their heads together, wonderful events had already occurred.
The good old king, notwithstanding that he had lived eighty
two years, had all at once given up the ghost; another king
had mounted the throne; a royal duke had died suddenly—
another, in France, had been murdered; there had been radi-
cal meetings in all parts of the kingdom; the bloody scenes at
Manchester; the great plot in Cato Street;—and, above all,
the Queen had returned to England! All these sinister events
are recounted by Mr. Skryme with a mysterious look, and a
dismal shake of the head; and, being taken with his drugs,
and associated in the minds of his auditors with stuffed sea
monsters, bottled serpents, and his own visage, which is a
title page of tribulation, they have spread great gloom

through the minds of the people in Little Britain. They shake their heads whenever they go by Bow Church, and observe, that they never expected any good to come of taking down that steeple, which in old times told nothing but glad tidings, as the history of Wittington and his Cat bears witness.

The rival oracle of Little Britain is a substantial cheesemonger, who lives in a fragment of one of the old family mansions, and is as magnificently lodged as a round bellied mite in the midst of one of his own Cheshires. Indeed he is a man of no little standing and importance; and his renown extends through Huggin Lane, and Lad Lane, and even unto Aldermanbury. His opinion is very much taken in affairs of state, having read the Sunday papers for the last half century, together with the Gentleman's Magazine, Rapin's History of England, and the Naval Chronicle. His head is stored with invaluable maxims which have borne the test of time and use for centuries. It is his firm opinion that "it is a moral impossible," so long as England is true to herself, that any thing can shake her: and he has much to say on the subject of the national debt; which, some how or other, he proves to be a great national bulwark and blessing. He passed the greater part of his life in the purlieus of Little Britain, until of late years, when, having become rich, and grown into the dignity of a Sunday cane, he begins to take his pleasure and see the world. He has therefore made several excursions to Hampstead, Highgate, and other neighbouring towns, where he has passed whole afternoons in looking back upon the metropolis through a telescope and endeavouring to descry the steeple of St. Bartholomew's. Not a stage coachman of Bull and Mouth Street, but touches his hat as he passes; and he is considered quite a patron at the coach office of the Goose and Gridiron, St. Paul's Church yard. His family have been very urgent for him to make an expedition to Margate, but he has great doubts of those new gim-cracks the steam boats, and indeed thinks himself too advanced in life to undertake sea voyages.

Little Britain has occasionally its factions and divisions, and party spirit ran very high at one time in consequence of two rival "Burial Societies" being set up in the place. One held its meeting at the Swan and Horse Shoe, and was patronized by the cheesemonger; the other at the Cock and Crown, under the auspices of the apothecary: it is needless to say that the latter was the most flourishing. I have passed an evening or two at each, and have acquired much valuable information as to the best mode of being buried; the comparative merits of church yards; together with diverse hints on the subject of patent iron coffins. I have heard the question discussed in all its bearings as to the legality of prohibiting the latter on account of their durability. The feuds occasioned by these societies have happily died of late; but they were for a long time prevailing themes of controversy, the people of Little Britain being extremely solicitous of funeral honours and of lying comfortably in their graves.

Besides these two funeral societies there is a third of quite a different cast, which tends to throw the sunshine of good humour over the whole neighbourhood. It meets once a week at a little old fashioned house, kept by a jolly publican of the name of Wagstaff, and bearing for insignia a resplendent half moon, with a most seductive bunch of grapes. The whole edifice is covered with inscriptions to catch the eye of the thirsty wayfarer; such as "Truman, Hanbury, and Co's. Entire," "Wine, Rum, and Brandy Vaults," "Old Tom, Rum and Compounds, &c." This indeed has been a temple of Bacchus and Momus from time immemorial. It has always been in the family of the Wagstaffs, so that its history is tolerably preserved by the present landlord. It was much frequented by the gallants and cavalieros of the reign of Elizabeth, and was looked into now and then by the wits of Charles the Second's day. But what Wagstaff principally prides himself upon, is, that Henry the Eighth, in one of his nocturnal rambles, broke the head of one of his ancestors with his famous walking staff. This however is considered as rather a dubious and vain glorious boast of the landlord.

The club which now holds its weekly sessions here, goes by the name of "the Roaring Lads of Little Britain." They abound in old catches, glees and choice stories, that are traditional in the place, and not to be met with in any other part of the metropolis. There is a mad cap undertaker who is inimitable at a merry song; but the life of the club, and indeed the prime wit of Little Britain, is bully Wagstaff himself. His ancestors were all wags before him, and he has inherited with the inn a large stock of songs and jokes, which go with it from generation to generation as heir looms. He is a dapper little fellow, with bandy legs and pot belly, a red face with a moist merry eye, and a little shock of grey hair behind. At the opening of every club night he is called in to sing his "Confession of Faith," which is the famous old drinking trowl from Gammer Gurton's Needle. He sings it, to be sure with many variations, as he received it from his father's lips; for it has been a standing favourite at the Half Moon and Bunch of Grapes ever since it was written; nay, he affirms that his pre-decessors have often had the honour of singing it before the nobility and gentry at Christmas mummeries, when Little Britain was in all its glory.*

It would do one's heart good to hear on a club night the

---

*As mine host of the Half moon's Confession of Faith may not be familiar to the majority of readers, and as it is a specimen of the current songs of Little Britain, I subjoin it in its original orthography. I would observe that the whole club always join in the chorus with a fearful thumping on the table and clattering of pewter pots.

> I cannot eate but lytle meate,
>   My stomacke is not good,
> But sure I thinke that I can drinke
>   With him that weares a hood.
> Though I go bare take ye no care,
>   I nothing am a colde,
> I stuff my skyn so full within,
>   Of joly good ale and olde.

> *Chorus.* Backe and syde go bare, go bare,
>   Booth foote and hand go colde,
> But belly, God send thee good ale ynoughe,
>   Whether it be new or olde.

> I love no rost, but a nut browne toste,
>   And a crab laid in the fyre;
> A little breade shall do me steade,
>   Much breade I not desyre.
> No frost nor snow, nor winde, I trowe,
>   Can hurte mee if I wolde,
> I am so wrapt and throwly lapt
>   Of joly good ale and olde.

> *Chorus.* Back and syde go bare, go bare, &c.

shouts of merriment, the snatches of song, and now and then the choral bursts of half a dozen discordant voices, which issue from this jovial mansion. At such times the street is lined with listeners, who enjoy a delight equal to that of gazing into a confectioner's window, or snuffing up the steams of a cook shop.

There are two annual events which produce great stir and sensation in Little Britain; these are St. Bartholomew's Fair, and the Lord Mayor's day. During the time of the Fair, which is held in the adjoining regions of Smithfield, there is nothing going on but gossiping and gadding about. The late quiet streets of Little Britain are overrun with an irruption of strange figures and faces, every tavern is a scene of rout and revel. The fiddle and the song are heard from the tap room, morning, noon, and night; and at each window may be seen some group of boon companions, with half shut eyes, hats on one side, pipe in mouth and tankard in hand, fondling, and prozing, and singing maudlin songs over their liquor. Even the sober decorum of private families, which I must say is rigidly kept up at other times among my neighbours, is no proof against this saturnalia. There is no such thing as keeping maid servants within doors. Their brains are absolutely

---

And Tyb my wife, that, as her lyfe,
  Loveth well good ale to seeke,
Full oft drynkes shee, tyll ye may see,
  The teares run downe her cheeke.
Then doth shee trowle to me the bowle,
  Even as a mault-worme sholde,
And sayth, sweete harte, I tooke my parte
  Of this joly good ale and olde.

Chorus. Back and syde go bare, go bare, &c.

Now let them drynke, tyll they nod and winke,
  Even as goode fellowes should doe,
They shall not mysse to have the blisse,
  Good ale doth bring men to.
And all poore soules that have scowred bowles,
  Or have them lustily trolde,
God save the lyves of them and their wives,
  Whether they be yonge or olde.

Chorus. Back and syde go bare, go bare, &c.

set madding with Punch and the Puppet Show; the Flying Horses; Signior Polito; the Fire Eater; the celebrated Mr. Paap; and the Irish Giant. The children too lavish all their holyday money in toys and gilt ginger bread, and fill the house with the Lilliputian din of drums, trumpets and penny whistles.

But the Lord Mayor's day is the great anniversary. The Lord Mayor is looked up to by the inhabitants of Little Britain as the greatest potentate upon earth; his gilt coach with six horses as the summit of human splendour; and his procession, with all the Sheriffs and Aldermen in his train, as the grandest of earthly pageants. How they exult in the idea, that the King himself dare not enter the city, without first knocking at the gate of Temple Bar, and asking permission of the Lord Mayor: for if he did, heaven and earth! there is no knowing what might be the consequence. The man in armour who rides before the Lord Mayor, and is the city champion, has orders to cut down every body that offends against the dignity of the city; and then there is the little man with a velvet porringer on his head, who sits at the window of the state coach and holds the city sword, as long as a pike staff—Od's blood! If he once draws that sword, Majesty itself is not safe!

Under the protection of this mighty potentate, therefore, the good people of Little Britain sleep in peace. Temple Bar is an effectual barrier against all interior foes; and as to foreign invasion, the Lord Mayor has but to throw himself into the tower, call in the train bands, and put the standing army of Beef eaters under arms, and he may bid defiance to the world!

Thus wrapped up in its own concerns, its own habits, and its own opinions, Little Britain has long flourished as a sound heart to this great fungous metropolis. I have pleased myself with considering it as a chosen spot, where the principles of sturdy John Bullism were garnered up, like seed corn, to renew the national character, when it had run to waste and degeneracy. I have rejoiced also in the general spirit of harmony that prevailed throughout it; for though there might now and then be a few clashes of opinion between the adherents of the cheesemonger and the apothecary, and an occasional feud between the burial societies, yet these were but transient clouds, and soon passed away. The neighbours met with good will, parted with a shake of the hand, and never abused each other except behind their backs.

I could give rare descriptions of snug junketting parties at which I have been present; where we played at All-Fours, Pope-Joan, Tom-come-tickle-me, and other choice old games; and where we sometimes had a good old English country dance to the tune of Sir Roger de Coverly. Once a year also the neighbours would gather together and go on a gypsey party to Epping Forest. It would have done any man's heart good to see the merriment that took place here as we banqueted on the grass under the trees. How we made the woods ring with bursts of laughter at the songs of little Wagstaff and the merry undertaker! After dinner too, the young folks would play at blind-man's-buff and hide and seek; and it was amusing to see them tangled among the briars, and to hear a fine romping girl now and then squeak from among the bushes. The elder folks would gather round the cheesemonger and the apothecary, to hear them talk politics; for they generally brought out a newspaper in their pockets, to pass away time in the country. They would now and then, to be sure, get a little warm in argument; but their disputes were always adjusted by reference to a worthy old umbrella maker in a double chin, who, never exactly comprehending the subject, managed, some how or other, to decide in favour of both parties.

All empires, however, says some philosopher or historian, are doomed to changes and revolutions. Luxury and innovation creep in; factions arise; and families now and then spring up, whose ambition and intrigues throw the whole system into confusion. Thus in latter days has the tranquillity of Little Britain been grievously disturbed, and its golden simplicity of manners threatened with total subversion by the aspiring family of a retired butcher.

The family of the Lambs had long been among the most thriving and popular in the neighbourhood: the Miss Lambs were the belles of Little Britain, and every body was pleased when Old Lamb had made money enough to shut up shop, and put his name on a brass plate on his door. In an evil hour, however, one of the Miss Lambs had the honour of being a lady in attendance on the Lady Mayoress, at her grand annual ball, on which occasion she wore three towering ostrich feathers on her head. The family never got over it; they were immediately smitten with a passion for high life; set up a one horse carriage, put a bit of gold lace round the errand boy's hat, and have been the talk and detestation of the whole neighbourhood ever since. They could no longer be induced to play at Pope-Joan or blind-man's-buff; they could endure no dances but quadrilles, which no body had ever heard of in Little Britain; and they took to reading novels, talking bad French, and playing upon the piano. Their brother too, who had been articled to an attorney, set up for a dandy and a critic, characters hitherto unknown in these parts; and he confounded the worthy folks exceedingly by talking about Kean, the Opera and the Edinbro' Review.

What was still worse, the Lambs gave a grand ball, to which they neglected to invite any of their old neighbours; but they had a great deal of genteel company from Theobald's Road, Red lion Square, and other parts towards the west. There were several beaux of their brother's acquaintance from Grays inn Lane and Hatton Garden; and not less than three Aldermen's ladies with their daughters. This was not to be forgotten or forgiven. All Little Britain was in an uproar with the smacking of whips, the lashing of miserable horses, and the rattling and jingling of hackney coaches. The gossips of the neighbourhood might be seen popping their night caps out at every window, watching the crazy vehicles rumble by; and there was a knot of virulent old crones, that kept a look out from a house just opposite the retired butcher's, and scanned and criticized every one that knocked at the door.

This dance was a cause of almost open war, and the whole neighbourhood declared they would have nothing more to say to the Lambs. It is true that Mrs. Lamb, when she had no engagements with her quality acquaintance, would give little hum drum tea junkettings to some of her old cronies, "quite," as she would say, "in a friendly way;" and it is equally true that her invitations were always accepted, in spite of all previous vows to the contrary. Nay the good ladies would sit and be delighted with the music of the Miss Lambs, who would condescend to strum an Irish melody for them on the piano; and they would listen with wonderful interest to Mrs.

Lamb's anecdotes of Alderman Plunket's family of Portsoken ward, and the Miss Timberlakes, the rich heiresses of Crutched Friars; but then they relieved their consciences, and averted the reproaches of their confederates, by canvassing at the next gossiping convocation every thing that had passed, and pulling the Lambs and their rout all to pieces.

The only one of the family that could not be made fashionable was the retired butcher himself. Honest Lamb, in spite of the meekness of his name, was a rough hearty old fellow, with the voice of a lion, a head of black hair like a shoe brush, and a broad face mottled like his own beef. It was in vain that the daughters always spoke of him as "the old gentleman," addressed him as "papa," in tones of infinite softness, and endeavoured to coax him into a dressing gown and slippers, and other gentlemanly habits. Do what they might, there was no keeping down the butcher. His sturdy nature would break through all their glozings. He had a hearty vulgar good humour that was irrepressible. His very jokes made his sensitive daughters shudder; and he persisted in wearing his blue cotton coat of a morning, dining at two o'clock, and having a "bit of sausage with his tea."

He was doomed, however, to share the unpopularity of his family. He found his old comrades gradually growing cold and civil to him; no longer laughing at his jokes; and now and then throwing out a fling at "some people," and a hint about "quality binding." This both nettled and perplexed the honest butcher; and his wife and daughters, with the consummate policy of the shrewder sex, taking advantage of the circumstance, at length prevailed upon him to give up his afternoon's pipe and tankard at Wagstaff's; to sit after dinner by himself and take his pint of port—a liquor he detested—and to nod in his chair in solitary and dismal gentility.

The Miss Lambs might now be seen flaunting along the streets in French bonnets, with unknown beaux; and talking and laughing so loud that it distressed the nerves of every good lady within hearing. They even went so far as to attempt patronage, and actually induced a French dancing master to set up in the neighbourhood; but the worthy folks of Little Britain took fire at it, and did so persecute the poor Gaul, that he was fain to pack up fiddle and dancing pumps, and decamp with such precipitation, that he absolutely forgot to pay for his lodgings.

I had flattered myself, at first, with the idea that all this fiery indignation on the part of the community, was merely the overflowing of their zeal for good old English manners, and their horror of innovation; and I applauded the silent contempt they were so vociferous in expressing, for upstart pride, French fashions, and the Miss Lambs. But I grieve to say that I soon perceived the infection had taken hold; and that my neighbours, after condemning, were beginning to follow their example. I overheard my landlady importuning her husband to let their daughters have one quarter at French and music, and that they might take a few lessons in the quadrille. I even saw, in the course of a few Sundays, no less than five French bonnets, precisely like those of the Miss Lambs, parading about Little Britain.

I still had my hopes that all this folly would gradually die away; that the Lambs might move out of the neighbourhood; might die, or might run away with attornies' apprentices; and that quiet and simplicity might be again restored to the community. But unluckily a rival power arose. An opulent oil man died and left a widow with a large jointure and a family of buxom daughters. The young ladies had long been repining in secret at the parsimony of a prudent father which kept down all their elegant aspirings. Their ambition being now no longer restrained broke out into a blaze, and they openly took the field against the family of the butcher. It is true that the Lambs, having had the first start, had naturally an advantage of them in the fashionable career. They could speak a little bad French, play the piano, dance quadrilles, and had formed high acquaintances; but the Trotters were not to be distanced. When the Lambs appeared with two feathers in their hats, the Miss Trotters mounted four, and of twice as fine colours. If the Lambs gave a dance, the Trotters were sure not to be behind hand; and though they might not boast of as good company, yet they had double the number and were twice as merry.

The whole community has at length divided itself into fashionable factions, under the banners of these two families. The old games of Pope-Joan and Tom-come-tickle-me are entirely discarded; there is no such thing as getting up an honest country dance; and, on my attempting to kiss a young lady under the misletoe last Christmas, I was indignantly repulsed; the Miss Lambs having pronounced it "shocking vulgar." Bitter rivalry has also broken out as to the most fashionable part of Little Britain; the Lambs standing up for the dignity of Cross Keys Square, and the Trotters for the vicinity of St. Bartholomew's.

Thus is this little territory torn by factions and internal dissensions, like the great empire whose name it bears; and what will be the result would puzzle the apothecary himself, with all his talent at prognostics, to determine; though I apprehend that it will terminate in the total downfall of genuine John Bullism.

The immediate effects are extremely unpleasant to me. Being a single man, and, as I observed before, rather an idle good for nothing personage, I have been considered the only gentleman by profession in the place. I stand therefore in high favour with both parties, and have to hear all their cabinet counsels and mutual backbitings. As I am too civil not to agree with the ladies on all occasions, I have committed myself most horribly with both parties, by abusing their opponents. I might manage to reconcile this to my conscience, which is a truly accommodating one, but I cannot to my apprehension—if the Lambs and Trotters ever come to a reconciliation and compare notes, I am ruined!

I have determined, therefore, to beat a retreat in time, and am actually looking out for some other nest in this great city, where old English manners are still kept up; where French is neither eaten, drunk, danced nor spoken; and where there are no fashionable families of retired tradesmen. This found, I will, like a veteran rat, hasten away before I have an old house about my ears; bid a long, though a sorrowful adieu to my present abode, and leave the rival factions of the Lambs and the Trotters, to divide the distracted empire of LITTLE BRITAIN.

Stratford-on-Avon

Thou soft flowing Avon, by the silver stream,
Of things more than mortal sweet Shakespeare would dream;
The fairies by moonlight dance round his green bed,
For hallowed the turf is which pillowed his head.

Garrick

To a homeless man, who has no spot on this wide world which he can truly call his own, there is a momentary feeling of something like independence and territorial consequence, when, after a weary day's travel, he kicks off his boots, thrusts his feet into slippers, and stretches himself before an inn fire. Let the world without go as it may; let kingdoms rise or fall, so long as he has the wherewithal to pay his bill, he is, for the time being, the very monarch of all he surveys. The arm chair is his throne; the poker his sceptre, and the little parlour of some twelve feet square, his undisputed empire. It is a morsel of certainty, snatched from the midst of the uncertainties of life; it is a sunny moment gleaming out kindly on a cloudy day; and he who has advanced some way on the pilgrimage of existence, knows the importance of husbanding even morsels and moments of enjoyment. "Shall I not take mine ease in mine inn?" thought I, as I gave the fire a stir, lolled back in my elbow chair, and cast a complacent look about the little parlour of the Red Horse, at Stratford-on-Avon.

The words of sweet Shakespeare were just passing through my mind as the clock struck midnight from the tower of the church in which he lies buried. There was a gentle tap at the door, and a pretty chamber maid, putting in her smiling face, inquired, with a hesitating air, whether I had rung. I understood it as a modest hint that it was time to retire. My dream of absolute dominion was at an end; so abdicating my throne, like a prudent potentate, to avoid being deposed, and putting the Stratford Guide Book under my arm, as a pillow companion, I went to bed, and dreamt all night of Shakespeare, the Jubilee, and David Garrick.

The next morning was one of those quickening mornings which we sometimes have in early spring; for it was about the middle of March. The chills of a long winter had suddenly given way; the north wind had spent its last gasp; and a mild air came stealing from the west, breathing the breath of life into nature, and wooing every bud and flower to burst forth into fragrance and beauty.

I had come to Stratford on a poetical pilgrimage. My first visit was to the house where Shakespeare was born, and where, according to tradition, he was brought up to his father's craft of wool combing. It is a small mean looking edifice of wood and plaster, a true nestling place of genius, which seems to delight in hatching its offspring in bye corners. The walls of its squalid chambers are covered with names and inscriptions, in every language, by pilgrims of all nations, ranks, and conditions, from the prince to the peasant; and present a simple, but striking instance of the spontaneous and universal homage of mankind to the great poet of nature.

The house is shown by a garrulous old lady in a frosty red face, lighted up by a cold blue anxious eye, and garnished with artificial locks of flaxen hair, curling from under an exceedingly dirty cap. She was peculiarly assiduous in exhibiting the relics with which this, like all other celebrated shrines, abounds. There was the shattered stock of the very matchlock with which Shakespeare shot the deer, on his poaching exploit. There, too, was his tobacco box; which proves that he was a rival smoker of Sir Walter Raleigh; the sword also with which he played Hamlet; and the identical lanthorn with which Friar Laurence discovered Romeo and Juliet at the tomb! There was an ample supply also of Shakespeare's mulberry tree, which seems to have as extraordinary powers of self multiplication as the wood of the true cross; of which there is enough extant to build a ship of the line.

The most favourite object of curiosity, however, is Shakespeare's chair. It stands in the chimney nook of a small gloomy chamber, just behind what was his father's shop. Here he may many a time have sat when a boy, watching the slowly revolving spit with all the longing of an urchin; or of an evening, listening to the crones and gossips of Stratford, dealing forth church yard tales and legendary anecdotes of the troublesome times of England. In this chair it is the custom of every one that visits the house to sit: whether this be done with the hope of imbibing any of the inspiration of the bard I am at a loss to say, I merely mention the fact; and mine hostess privately assured me, that though built of solid oak, such was the fervent zeal of devotees, that the chair had to be new bottomed at least once in three years. It is worthy of notice also, in the history of this extraordinary chair, that it partakes something of the volatile nature of the Santa Casa of Loretto, or the flying chair of the Arabian enchanter, for though sold some few years since to a northern princess, yet, strange to tell, it has found its way back again to the old chimney corner.

I am always of easy faith in such matters, and am ever willing to be deceived, where the deceit is pleasant, and costs nothing. I am therefore a ready believer in relics, legends, and local anecdotes of goblins and great men; and would advise all travellers who travel for their gratification to be the same. What is it to us whether these stories be true or false, so long as we can persuade ourselves into the belief of them, and enjoy all the charm of the reality? There is nothing like resolute good humoured credulity in these matters; and on this occasion I went even so far as willingly to believe the claims of mine hostess to a lineal descent from the poet, when, unluckily for my faith, she put into my hands a play of her own composition, which set all belief in her consanguinity at defiance.

From the birth place of Shakespeare a few paces brought me to his grave. He lies buried in the chancel of the parish church, a large and venerable pile, mouldering with age, but richly ornamented. It stands on the banks of the Avon, on an embowered point, and separated by adjoining gardens from the suburbs of the town. Its situation is quiet and retired: the river runs murmuring at the foot of the church yard, and the elms which grow upon its banks droop their branches into its clear bosom. An avenue of limes, the boughs of which are curiously interlaced, so as to form in summer an arched way of foliage, leads up from the gate of the yard to the church porch. The graves are overgrown with grass; the grey tombstones, some of them nearly sunk into the earth, are half covered with moss, which has likewise tinted the reverend old building. Small birds have built their nests among the cor-

nices and fissures of the walls, and keep up a continual flutter
and chirping; and rooks are sailing and cawing about its lofty
grey spire.

In the course of my rambles I met with the grey headed
sexton, Edmonds, and accompanied him home to get the key
of the church. He had lived in Stratford, man and boy, for
eighty years, and seemed still to consider himself a vigorous
man, with the trivial exception that he had nearly lost the use
of his legs for a few years past. His dwelling was a cottage,
looking out upon the Avon and its bordering meadows; and
was a picture of that neatness, order, and comfort, which pervade the humblest dwellings in this country. A low white
washed room, with a stone floor carefully scrubbed, served
for parlour, kitchen, and hall. Rows of pewter and earthen
dishes glittered along the dresser. On an old oaken table, well
rubbed and polished, lay the family Bible and Prayer book,
and the drawer contained the family library, composed of
about half a score of well thumbed volumes. An ancient clock,
that important article of cottage furniture, ticked on the opposite side of the room; with a bright warming pan hanging
on one side of it, and the old man's horn handled Sunday
cane on the other. The fireplace, as usual, was wide and deep
enough to admit a gossip knot within its jambs. In one corner
sat the old man's grand daughter sewing, a pretty blue eyed
girl,—and in the opposite corner was a superannuated crony,
whom he addressed by the name of John Ange, and who, I
found, had been his companion from childhood. They had
played together in infancy; they had worked together in manhood; they were now tottering about and gossiping away the
evening of life; and in a short time they will probably be buried together in the neighbouring church yard. It is not often
that we see two streams of existence running thus evenly and
tranquilly side by side; it is only in such quiet "bosom scenes"
of life that they are to be met with.

I had hoped to gather some traditionary anecdotes of the
bard from these ancient chroniclers; but they had nothing new
to impart. The long interval during which Shakespeare's writings lay in comparative neglect has spread its shadow over his
history; and it is his good or evil lot that scarcely any thing remains to his biographers but a scanty handful of conjectures.

The sexton and his companion had been employed as carpenters on the preparations for the celebrated Stratford jubilee, and they remembered Garrick, the prime mover of the fête, who superintended the arrangements, and who, according to the sexton, was "a short punch man very lively and bustling." John Ange had assisted also in cutting down Shakespeare's mulberry tree, of which he had a morsel in his pocket for sale; no doubt a sovereign quickener of literary conception.

I was grieved to hear these two worthy wights speak very dubiously of the eloquent dame who shows the Shakespeare house. John Ange shook his head when I mentioned her valuable and inexhaustible collection of relics, particularly her remains of the mulberry tree; and the old sexton even expressed a doubt as to Shakespeare having been born in her house. I soon discovered that he looked upon her mansion with an evil eye, as a rival to the poet's tomb; the latter having comparatively but few visitors. Thus it is that historians differ at the very outset, and mere pebbles make the stream of truth diverge into different channels even at the fountain head.

We approached the church through the avenue of limes, and entered by a gothic porch, highly ornamented, with carved doors of massive oak. The interior is spacious, and the architecture and embellishments superior to those of most country churches. There are several ancient monuments of nobility and gentry, over some of which hang funeral escutcheons, and banners dropping piecemeal from the walls. The tomb of Shakespeare is in the chancel. The place is solemn and sepulchral. Tall elms wave before the pointed windows, and the Avon, which runs at a short distance from the walls, keeps up a low perpetual murmur. A flat stone marks the spot where the bard is buried. There are four lines inscribed on it, said to have been written by himself, and which have in them something extremely awful. If they are indeed his own, they show that solicitude about the quiet of the grave, which seems natural to fine sensibilities and thoughtful minds:

> Good friend, for Jesus' sake, forbeare
> To dig the dust encloased here.

> Blessed be the man that spares these stones,
> And curst be he that moves my bones.

Just over the grave, in a niche of the wall, is a bust of Shakespeare, put up shortly after his death, and considered as a resemblance. The aspect is pleasant and serene, with a finely arched forehead; and I thought I could read in it clear indications of that cheerful, social disposition, by which he was as much characterized among his cotemporaries as by the vastness of his genius. The inscription mentions his age at the time of his decease—fifty three years; an untimely death for the world: for what fruit might not have been expected from the golden autumn of such a mind, sheltered as it was from the stormy vicissitudes of life, and flourishing in the sunshine of popular and royal favour.

The inscription on the tombstone has not been without its effect. It has prevented the removal of his remains from the bosom of his native place to Westminster Abbey, which was at one time contemplated. A few years since also, as some labourers were digging to make an adjoining vault, the earth caved in, so as to leave a vacant space almost like an arch, through which one might have reached into his grave. No one, however, presumed to meddle with his remains, so awfully guarded by a malediction; and lest any of the idle or the curious, or any collector of relics, should be tempted to commit depredations, the old sexton kept watch over the place for two days, until the vault was finished and the aperture closed again. He told me that he had made bold to look in at the hole, but could see neither coffin nor bones; nothing but dust. It was something, I thought, to have seen the dust of Shakespeare.

Next to this grave are those of his wife, his favourite daughter Mrs. Hall, and others of his family. On a tomb close by, also, is a full length effigy of his old friend John Combe, of usurious memory; on whom he is said to have written a ludicrous epitaph. There are other monuments around, but the mind refuses to dwell on any thing that is not connected with Shakespeare. His idea pervades the place: the whole pile seems but as his mausoleum. The feelings, no longer checked and thwarted by doubt, here indulge in perfect confidence:

other traces of him may be false or dubious, but here is palpable evidence and absolute certainty. As I trod the sounding pavement, there was something intense and thrilling in the idea, that, in very truth, the remains of Shakespeare were mouldering beneath my feet. It was a long time before I could prevail upon myself to leave the place; and as I passed through the church yard I plucked a branch from one of the yew trees, the only relic that I have brought from Stratford.

I had now visited the usual objects of a pilgrim's devotion, but I had a desire to see the old family seat of the Lucys at Charlecot, and to ramble through the park where Shakespeare, in company with some of the roysters of Stratford, committed his youthful offence of deer stealing. In this harebrained exploit we are told that he was taken prisoner, and carried to the keeper's lodge, where he remained all night in doleful captivity. When brought into the presence of Sir Thomas Lucy, his treatment must have been galling and humiliating, for it so wrought upon his spirit as to produce a rough pasquinade, which was affixed to the park gate at Charlecot.*

This flagitious attack upon the dignity of the Knight so incensed him, that he applied to a lawyer at Warwick to put the severity of the laws in force against the rhyming deer stalker. Shakespeare did not wait to brave the united puissance of a Knight of the Shire and a country attorney. He forthwith abandoned the pleasant banks of the Avon and his paternal trade; wandered away to London; became a hanger on to the theatres; then an actor; and, finally, wrote for the stage; and thus, through the persecution of Sir Thomas Lucy,

*The following is the only stanza extant of this lampoon: —

> A parliament member, a justice of peace,
> At home a poor scarecrow, at London an asse,
> If lowsie is Lucy, as some volke miscalle it,
> Then Lucy is lowsie, whatever befall it.
> > He thinks himself great;
> > Yet an asse in his state,
> We allow, by his ears, but with asses to mate.
> If Lucy is lowsie, as some volke miscall it,
> Then sing lowsie Lucy whatever befall it.

Stratford lost an indifferent wool comber and the world gained an immortal poet. He retained, however, for a long time, a sense of the harsh treatment of the Lord of Charlecot, and revenged himself in his writings; but in the sportive way of a good natured mind. Sir Thomas is said to be the original of Justice Shallow, and the satire is slyly fixed upon him by the Justice's armorial bearings, which, like those of the Knight, had white luces* in the quarterings.

Various attempts have been made by his biographers to soften and explain away this early transgression of the poet; but I look upon it as one of those thoughtless exploits natural to his situation and turn of mind. Shakespeare, when young, had doubtless all the wildness and irregularity of an ardent, undisciplined, and undirected genius. The poetic temperament has naturally something in it of the vagabond. When left to itself it runs loosely and wildly, and delights in every thing eccentric and licentious. It is often a turn up of a die, in the gambling freaks of fate, whether a natural genius shall turn out a great rogue or a great poet; and had not Shakespeare's mind fortunately taken a literary bias, he might have as daringly transcended all civil, as he has all dramatic laws.

I have little doubt that, in early life, when running, like an unbroken colt, about the neighbourhood of Stratford, he was to be found in the company of all kinds of odd anomalous characters; that he associated with all the mad caps of the place, and was one of those unlucky urchins, at mention of whom old men shake their heads, and predict that they will one day come to the gallows. To him the poaching in Sir Thomas Lucy's park was doubtless like a foray to a Scottish Knight, and struck his eager, and as yet untamed, imagination, as something delightfully adventurous.†

The old mansion of Charlecot and its surrounding park still remain in the possession of the Lucy family, and are pecu-

*The luce is a pike, or jack, and abounds in the Avon about Charlecot.

†A proof of Shakespeare's random habits and associates in his youthful days, may be found in a traditionary anecdote, picked up at Stratford by the elder Ireland, and mentioned in his "Picturesque Views on the Avon."

About seven miles from Stratford lies the thirsty little market town of Bedford, famous for its ale. Two societies of the village yeomanry used to meet, under the appellation of the Bedford topers, and to challenge the lovers of good ale of the neighbouring villages, to a contest of drinking. Among others,

liarly interesting from being connected with this whimsical but eventful circumstance in the scanty history of the bard. As the house stood at little more than three miles distance from Stratford, I resolved to pay it a pedestrian visit, that I might stroll leisurely through some of those scenes from which Shakespeare must have derived his earliest ideas of rural imagery.

The country was yet naked and leafless; but English scenery is always verdant, and the sudden change in the temperature of the weather was surprising in its quickening effects upon the landscape. It was inspiring and animating to witness this first awakening of spring. To feel its warm breath stealing over the senses; to see the moist mellow earth beginning to put forth the green sprout and the tender blade; and the trees and shrubs, in their reviving tints and bursting buds, giving the promise of returning foliage and flower. The cold snow drop, that little borderer on the skirts of winter, was to be seen with its chaste white blossoms in the small gardens before the cottages. The bleating of the new dropt lambs was faintly heard from the fields. The sparrow twittered about the thatched eaves and budding hedges; the robin threw a livelier note into his late querulous wintry strain; and the lark,

---

the people of Stratford were called out to prove the strength of their heads; and in the number of the champions was Shakespeare, who, in spite of the proverb, that "they who drink beer will think beer," was as true to his ale as Falstaff to his sack. The chivalry of Stratford was staggered at the first onset, and sounded a retreat while they had yet legs to carry them off the field. They had scarcely marched a mile, when, their legs failing them, they were forced to lie down under a crab tree, where they passed the night. It is still standing, and goes by the name of Shakespeare's tree.

In the morning his companions awakened the bard, and proposed returning to Bedford, but he declined, saying he had had enough, having drank with

> Piping Pebworth, Dancing Marston,
> Haunted Hillbro', Hungry Grafton,
> Dudging Exhall, Papist Wicksford,
> Beggarly Broom, and Drunken Bedford.

"The villages here alluded to," says Ireland, "still bear the epithets thus given them; the people of Pebworth are still famed for their skill on the pipe and tabor: Hillborough is now called Haunted Hillborough: and Grafton is famous for the poverty of its soil."

springing up from the reeking bosom of the meadow, towered away into the bright fleecy cloud, pouring forth torrents
of melody. As I watched the little songster, mounting up
higher and higher, until his body was a mere speck on the
white bosom of the cloud, while the ear was still filled with
his music, it called to mind Shakespeare's exquisite little song
in Cymbeline:

> Hark! hark! the lark at heav'n's gate sings,
>   And Phœbus 'gins arise,
> His steeds to water at those springs,
>   On chaliced flowers that lies.
>
> And winking mary-buds begin,
>   To ope their golden eyes;
> With every thing that pretty bin,
>   My lady sweet arise!

Indeed the whole country about here is poetic ground:
every thing is associated with the idea of Shakespeare. Every
old cottage that I saw, I fancied into some resort of his boyhood, where he had acquired his intimate knowledge of rustic
life and manners, and heard those legendary tales and wild
superstitions which he has woven like witchcraft into his dra-
mas. For in his time, we are told, it was a popular amusement
in winter evenings "to sit round the fire, and tell merry tales
of errant knights, queens, lovers, lords, ladies, giants, dwarfs,
thieves, cheaters, witches, fairies, goblins, and friars."*
My route for a part of the way lay in sight of the Avon,
which made a variety of the most fanciful doublings and
windings through a wide and fertile valley; sometimes glittering from among willows, which fringed its borders; sometimes disappearing among groves, or beneath green banks;

---

*Scot, in his "Discoverie of Witchcraft," enumerates a host of these fireside
fancies. "And they have so fraid us with bull-beggars, spirits, witches, urchins, elves, hags, fairies, satyrs, pans, faunes, syrens, kit with the can'sticke,
tritons, centaurs, dwarfes, giantes, imps, calcars, conjurors, nymphes, change-
lings, incubus, Robin-good-fellow, the spoorne, the mare, the man in the
oke, the hell-waine, the fier drake, the puckle, Tom Thombe, hobgoblins,
Tom Tumbler, boneless, and such other bugs, that we were afraid of our own
shadowes."

and sometimes rambling out into full view, and making an azure sweep round a slope of meadow land. This beautiful bosom of country is called the vale of the Red Horse. A distant line of undulating blue hills seems to be its boundary, whilst all the soft intervening landscape lies in a manner enchained in the silver links of the Avon.

After pursuing the road for about three miles, I turned off into a footpath, which led along the borders of fields and under hedge rows to a private gate of the park; there was a style, however, for the benefit of the pedestrian; there being a public right of way through the grounds. I delight in these hospitable estates, in which every one has a kind of property—at least as far as the footpath is concerned. It in some measure reconciles a poor man to his lot, and what is more, to the better lot of his neighbour, thus to have parks and pleasure grounds thrown open for his recreation. He breathes the pure air as freely, and lolls as luxuriously under the shade, as the lord of the soil; and if he has not the privilege of calling all that he sees his own, he has not, at the same time, the trouble of paying for it, and keeping it in order.

I now found myself among noble avenues of oaks and elms, whose vast size bespoke the growth of centuries. The wind sounded solemnly among their branches, and the rooks cawed from their hereditary nests in the tree tops. The eye ranged through a long lessening vista, with nothing to interrupt the view but a distant statue; and a vagrant deer stalking like a shadow across the opening.

There is something about these stately old avenues that has the effect of gothic architecture, not merely from the pretended similarity of form, but from their bearing the evidence of long duration, and of having had their origin in a period of time with which we associate ideas of romantic grandeur. They betoken also the long settled dignity, and proudly concentrated independence of an ancient family; and I have heard a worthy but aristocratic old friend observe, when speaking of the sumptuous palaces of modern gentry, that "money could do much with stone and mortar, but thank heaven there was no such thing as suddenly building up an avenue of oaks."

It was from wandering in early life among this rich scenery, and about the romantic solitudes of the adjoining park of Ful-broke, which then formed a part of the Lucy estate, that some of Shakespeare's commentators have supposed he derived his noble forest meditations of Jaques, and the enchanting wood-land pictures in "As you like it." It is in lonely wanderings through such scenes, that the mind drinks deep but quiet draughts of inspiration, and becomes intensely sensible of the beauty and majesty of nature. The imagination kindles into reverie and rapture; vague but exquisite images and ideas keep breaking upon it; and we revel in a mute and almost incommunicable luxury of thought. It was in some such mood, and perhaps under one of those very trees before me, which threw their broad shades over the grassy banks and quivering waters of the Avon, that the poet's fancy may have sallied forth into that little song which breathes the very soul of a rural voluptuary:

> Under the green wood tree,
> Who loves to lie with me,
> And tune his merry throat
> Unto the sweet bird's note,
> Come hither, come hither, come hither,
>> Here shall he see
>> No enemy,
> But winter and rough weather.

I had now come in sight of the house. It is a large building of brick, with stone quoins, and is in the gothic style of Queen Elizabeth's day, having been built in the first year of her reign. The exterior remains very nearly in its original state, and may be considered a fair specimen of the residence of a wealthy country gentleman of those days. A great gate-way opens from the park into a kind of court yard in front of the house, ornamented with a grass plot, shrubs, and flower beds. The gateway is in imitation of the ancient barbican; being a kind of outpost, and flanked by towers; though evi-dently for mere ornament, instead of defence. The front of the house is completely in the old style; with stone shafted casements, a great bow window of heavy stone work, and a portal with armorial bearings over it, carved in stone. At each corner of the building is an octagon tower, surmounted by a gilt ball and weathercock.

The Avon, which winds through the park, makes a bend just at the foot of a gently sloping bank, which sweeps down from the rear of the house. Large herds of deer were feeding or reposing upon its borders; and swans were sailing majestically upon its bosom. As I contemplated the venerable old mansion, I called to mind Falstaff's encomium on Justice Shallow's abode, and the affected indifference and real vanity of the latter:

> "*Falstaff.*   You have here a goodly dwelling and a rich.
>   *Shallow.*   Barren, barren, barren; beggars all, beggars all, Sir John:—marry, good air."

Whatever may have been the joviality of the old mansion in the days of Shakespeare, it had now an air of stillness and solitude. The great iron gateway that opened into the court yard was locked; there was no show of servants bustling about the place; the deer gazed quietly at me as I passed, being no longer harried by the moss troopers of Stratford. The only sign of domestic life that I met with, was a white cat stealing with wary look and stealthy pace towards the stables, as if on some nefarious expedition. I must not omit to mention the carcass of a scoundrel crow which I saw suspended against the barn wall, as it shows that the Lucys still inherit that lordly abhorrence of poachers, and maintain that rigorous exercise of territorial power which was so strenuously manifested in the case of the bard.

After prowling about for some time, I at length found my way to a lateral portal which was the every day entrance to the mansion. I was courteously received by a worthy old housekeeper, who, with the civility and communicativeness of her order, showed me the interior of the house. The greater part has undergone alterations, and been adapted to modern tastes and modes of living: there is a fine old oaken staircase; and the great hall, that noble feature in an ancient manor house, still retains much of the appearance it must have had in the days of Shakespeare. The ceiling is arched and lofty; and at one end is a gallery, in which stands an organ. The weapons and trophies of the chace, which formerly adorned the hall of a country gentleman, have made way for family portraits. There is a wide hospitable fireplace, calculated for an ample old fashioned wood fire, formerly the rallying place of winter festivity. On the opposite side of the hall is the huge gothic bow window, with stone shafts, which looks out upon the court yard. Here are emblazoned in stained glass the armorial bearings of the Lucy family for many generations, some being dated in 1558. I was delighted to observe in the quarterings the three *white luces* by which the character of Sir Thomas was first identified with that of Justice Shallow. They are mentioned in the first scene of the Merry Wives of Windsor, where the Justice is in a rage with Falstaff for having "beaten his men, killed his deer, and broken into his lodge." The poet had no doubt the offences of himself and his comrades in mind at the time, and we may suppose the family pride and vindictive threats of the puissant Shallow to be a caricature of the pompous indignation of Sir Thomas.

"Shallow.   Sir Hugh, persuade me not: I will make a Star-Chamber matter of it; if he were twenty Sir John Falstaffs, he shall not abuse Robert Shallow, Esq.

Slender.   In the county of Gloster, justice of peace, and *coram.*

Shallow.   Ay, cousin Slender, and *custalorum.*

Slender.   Ay, and *ratalorum* too; and a gentleman born, master parson; who writes himself *Armigero* in any bill, warrant, quittance, or obligation, *Armigero.*

Shallow.   Ay, that I do; and have done any time these three hundred years.

Slender.   All his successors gone before him have done't, and all his ancestors that come after him may: they may give the dozen *white luces* in their coat. * * * * *

Shallow.   The council shall hear it; it is a riot.

Evans.   It is not meet the council hear of a riot; there is no fear of Got in a riot; the council, hear you, shall desire to hear the fear of Got, and not to hear a riot; take your vizaments in that.

Shallow. Ha! o' my life, if I were young again, the sword
should end it!"

Near the window thus emblazoned, hung a portrait by Sir
Peter Lely of one of the Lucy family, a great beauty of the
time of Charles the Second; the old housekeeper shook her
head as she pointed to the picture, and informed me that this
lady had been sadly addicted to cards, and had gambled away
a great portion of the family estate, among which was that
part of the park where Shakespeare and his comrades had
killed the deer. The lands thus lost had not been entirely regained by the family even at the present day. It is but justice
to this recreant dame to confess that she had a surpassingly
fine hand and arm.

The picture which most attracted my attention was a great
painting over the fire place, containing likenesses of a Sir
Thomas Lucy and his family who inhabited the hall in the
latter part of Shakespeare's life time. I at first thought that it
was the vindictive knight himself, but the housekeeper assured me that it was his son; the only likeness extant of the
former being an effigy upon his tomb in the church of the
neighbouring hamlet of Charlecot.* The picture gives a lively
idea of the costume and manners of the time. Sir Thomas is
dressed in ruff and doublet; white shoes with roses in them;

---

*This effigy is in white marble, and represents the Knight in complete
armor. Near him lies the effigy of his wife, and on her tomb is the following
inscription; which, if really composed by her husband, places him quite
above the intellectual level of Master Shallow:

Here lyeth the Lady Joyce Lucy wife of Sr Thomas Lucy of Charlecot in
ye county of Warwick, Knight, Daughter and heir of Thomas Acton of Sutton in ye county of Worcester Esquire who departed out of this wretched
world to her heavenly kingdom ye 10 day of February in ye yeare of our
Lord God 1595 and of her age 60 and three. All the time of her lyfe a true
and faythful servant of her good God, never detected of any cryme or vice.
In religion most sounde, in love to her husband most faythful and true. In
friendship most constant; to what in trust was committed unto her most
secret. In wisdom excelling. In governing of her house, bringing up of youth
in ye fear of God that did converse with her moste rare and singular. A great
maintayner of hospitality. Greatly esteemed of her betters; misliked of none
unless of the envyous. When all is spoken that can be saide a woman so
garnished with virtue as not to be bettered and hardly to be equalled by any.
As shee lived most virtuously so shee died most Godly. Set downe by him yt
best did knowe what hath byn written to be true. Thomas Lucye.

and has a peaked yellow, or, as Master Slender would say, "a cane coloured beard." His lady is seated on the opposite side of the picture in wide ruff and long stomacher, and the children have a most venerable stiffness and formality of dress. Hounds and spaniels are mingled in the family group; a hawk is seated on his perch in the foreground, and one of the children holds a bow;—all intimating the knight's skill in hunting, hawking, and archery—so indispensable to an accomplished gentleman in those days.*

I regretted to find that the ancient furniture of the hall had disappeared; for I had hoped to meet with the stately elbow chair of carved oak, in which the country Squire of former days was wont to sway the sceptre of empire over his rural domains; and in which it might be presumed the redoubted Sir Thomas sat enthroned in awful state when the recreant Shakespeare was brought before him. As I like to deck out pictures for my entertainment, I pleased myself with the idea that this very hall had been the scene of the unlucky bard's examination on the morning after his captivity in the lodge. I fancied to myself the rural potentate, surrounded by his body guard of butler, pages, and blue coated serving men with their badges; while the luckless culprit was brought in, bedrooped and chapfallen; in the custody of game keepers, huntsmen and whippers in, and followed by a rabble rout of country clowns. I fancied bright faces of curious housemaids peeping from the half open doors, while from the gallery the fair daughters of the Knight leaned gracefully forward, eyeing the youthful prisoner with that pity "that dwells in womanhood."—Who would have thought that this poor varlet, thus trembling before the brief authority of a country Squire, and

---

*Bishop Earle, speaking of the country gentleman of his time, observes, "his housekeeping is seen much in the different families of dogs, and serving men attendant on their kennels; and the deepness of their throats is the depth of his discourse. A hawk he esteems the true burden of nobility, and is exceedingly ambitious to seem delighted with the sport, and have his fist gloved with his jesses." And Gilpin, in his description of a Mr. Hastings remarks, "he kept all sorts of hounds that run buck, fox, hare, otter and badger; and had hawks of all kinds both long and short winged. His great hall was commonly strewed with marrow-bones, and full of hawk perches, hounds, spaniels and terriers. On a broad hearth paved with brick, lay some of the choicest terriers, hounds and spaniels."

the sport of rustic boors, was soon to become the delight of princes; the theme of all tongues and ages; the dictator to the human mind; and was to confer immortality on his oppressor by a caricature and a lampoon!

I was now invited by the butler to walk into the garden, and I felt inclined to visit the orchard and arbour where the Justice treated Sir John Falstaff and Cousin Silence, "to a last year's pippen of his own graffing, with a dish of carraways;" but I had already spent so much of the day in my ramblings that I was obliged to give up any further investigations. When about to take my leave I was gratified by the civil entreaties of the housekeeper and butler, that I would take some refreshment: an instance of good old hospitality, which I grieve to say we castle hunters seldom meet with in modern days. I make no doubt it is a virtue which the present representative of the Lucys inherits from his ancestor; for Shakespeare, even in his caricature, makes Justice Shallow importunate in this respect, as witness his pressing instances to Falstaff:

> "By cock and pye, Sir, you shall not away to night
> * * * *. I will not excuse you; you shall not be excused;
> excuses shall not be admitted; there is no excuse shall serve;
> you shall not be excused * * * * * *. Some pigeons, Davy;
> a couple of shortlegged hens; a joint of mutton; and any
> pretty little tiny kickshaws, tell William Cook."

I now bade a reluctant farewell to the old hall. My mind had become so completely possessed by the imaginary scenes and characters connected with it, that I seemed to be actually living among them. Every thing brought them, as it were, before my eyes; and as the door of the dining room opened, I almost expected to hear the feeble voice of Master Silence quavering forth his favourite ditty:

> " 'Tis merry in hall, when beards wag all,
> And welcome merry Shrove-tide!"

On returning to my inn, I could not but reflect on the singular gift of the poet; to be able thus to spread the magic of his mind over the very face of nature; to give to things and places a charm and character not their own, and to turn this

" working day world" into a perfect fairy land. He is indeed the true enchanter, whose spell operates not upon the senses, but upon the imagination and the heart. Under the wizard influence of Shakespeare I had been walking all day in a complete delusion. I had surveyed the landscape through the prism of poetry, which tinged every object with the hues of the rainbow. I had been surrounded with fancied beings; with mere airy nothings, conjured up by poetic power; yet which, to me, had all the charm of reality. I had heard Jaques soliloquize beneath his oak; had beheld the fair Rosalind and her companion adventuring through the woodlands; and, above all, had been once more present in spirit with fat Jack Falstaff, and his contemporaries, from the august Justice Shallow, down to the gentle Master Slender, and the sweet Anne Page. Ten thousand honours and blessings on the bard who has thus gilded the dull realities of life with innocent illusions; who has spread exquisite and unbought pleasures in my chequered path; and beguiled my spirit, in many a lonely hour, with all the cordial and cheerful sympathies of social life!

As I crossed the bridge over the Avon on my return, I paused to contemplate the distant church in which the poet lies buried, and could not but exult in the malediction, which has kept his ashes undisturbed in its quiet and hallowed vaults. What honour could his name have derived from being mingled in dusty companionship with the epitaphs and escutcheons and venal eulogiums of a titled multitude. What would a crowded corner in Westminster Abbey have been, compared with this reverend pile, which seems to stand in beautiful loneliness as his sole mausoleum! The solicitude about the grave may be but the offspring of an overwrought sensibility; but human nature is made up of foibles and prejudices; and its best and tenderest affections are mingled with these factitious feelings. He who has sought renown about the world, and has reaped a full harvest of worldly favour, will find, after all, that there is no love, no admiration, no applause, so sweet to the soul as that which springs up in his native place. It is there that he seeks to be gathered in peace and honour among his kindred and his early friends. And when the weary heart and failing head begin to warn him that the evening of life is drawing on, he turns as fondly as does the infant to the mother's arms, to sink to sleep in the bosom of the scene of his childhood.

How would it have cheered the spirit of the youthful bard, when, wandering forth in disgrace upon a doubtful world, he cast back a heavy look upon his paternal home; could he have foreseen that, before many years, he should return to it covered with renown; that his name should become the boast and glory of his native place; that his ashes should be religiously guarded as its most precious treasure; and that its lessening spire, on which his eyes were fixed in tearful contemplation, should one day become the beacon, towering amidst the gentle landscape, to guide the literary pilgrim of every nation to his tomb.

Traits of Indian Character

"I appeal to any white man if ever he entered Logan's cabin hungry, and he gave him not to eat; if ever he came cold and naked, and he clothed him not."

Speech of an Indian Chief

T HERE IS SOMETHING in the character and habits of the North American savage, taken in connexion with the scenery over which he is accustomed to range, its vast lakes, boundless forests, majestic rivers and trackless plains, that is, to my mind, wonderfully striking and sublime. He is formed for the wilderness, as the Arab is for the desert. His nature is stern, simple and enduring; fitted to grapple with difficulties, and to support privations. There seems but little soil in his heart for the growth of the kindly virtues; and yet, if we would but take the trouble to penetrate through that proud stoicism and habitual taciturnity, which lock up his character from casual observation, we should find him linked to his fellow man of civilized life by more of those sympathies and affections than are usually ascribed to him.

It has been the lot of the unfortunate aborigines of America, in the early periods of colonization, to be doubly wronged by the white men. They have been dispossessed of their hereditary possessions by mercenary and frequently wanton warfare; and their characters have been traduced by bigoted and interested writers. The colonist has often treated them like beasts of the forest; and the author has endeavoured to justify him in his outrages. The former found it easier to exterminate than to civilize; the latter to vilify than to discriminate. The appellations of savage and pagan were deemed sufficient to sanction the hostilities of both; and thus the poor wanderers of the forest were persecuted and defamed, not because they were guilty, but because they were ignorant.

The rights of the savage have seldom been properly appreciated or respected by the white man. In peace he has too often been the dupe of artful traffic; in war he has been regarded as a ferocious animal, whose life or death was a question of mere precaution and convenience. Man is cruelly wasteful of life when his own safety is endangered, and he is sheltered by impunity; and little mercy is to be expected from him when he feels the sting of the reptile and is conscious of the power to destroy.

The same prejudices which were indulged thus early, exist in common circulation at the present day. Certain learned societies have, it is true, with laudable diligence, endeavoured to investigate and record the real characters and manners of the Indian tribes; the American government too, has wisely and humanely exerted itself to inculcate a friendly and forbearing spirit towards them, and to protect them from fraud and injustice.* The current opinion of the Indian character, however, is too apt to be formed from the miserable hordes which infest the frontiers, and hang on the skirts of the settlements. These are too commonly composed of degenerate beings, corrupted and enfeebled by the vices of society, without being benefited by its civilization. That proud independence, which formed the main pillar of savage virtue, has been shaken down, and the whole moral fabric lies in ruins. Their spirits are humiliated and debased by a sense of inferiority, and their native courage cowed and daunted by the superior knowledge and power of their enlightened neighbours. Society has advanced upon them like one of those withering airs that will sometimes breathe desolation over a whole region of fertility. It has enervated their strength, multiplied their diseases, and superinduced upon their original barbarity the low vices of artificial life. It has given them a thousand superfluous wants, whilst it has diminished their means of mere existence. It has driven before it the animals of the chase, who fly from the sound of the axe and the smoke of the settlement, and seek refuge in the depths of remoter forests and yet untrodden wilds. Thus do we too often find the Indians on our frontiers to be mere wrecks and remnants of

*The American government has been indefatigable in its exertions to ameliorate the situation of the Indians, and to introduce among them the arts of civilization, and civil and religious knowledge. To protect them from the frauds of the white traders, no purchase of land from them by individuals is permitted; nor is any person allowed to receive lands from them as a present, without the express sanction of government. These precautions are strictly enforced.

once powerful tribes, who have lingered in the vicinity of the settlements, and sunk into precarious and vagabond existence. Poverty, repining and hopeless poverty, a canker of the mind unknown in savage life, corrodes their spirits and blights every free and noble quality of their natures. They become drunken, indolent, feeble, thievish and pusillanimous. They loiter like vagrants about the settlements, among spacious dwellings, replete with elaborate comforts, which only render them sensible of the comparative wretchedness of their own condition. Luxury spreads its ample board before their eyes, but they are excluded from the banquet. Plenty revels over the fields, but they are starving in the midst of its abundance; the whole wilderness has blossomed into a garden; but they feel as reptiles that infest it.

How different was their state while yet the undisputed lords of the soil. Their wants were few, and the means of gratification within their reach. They saw every one round them sharing the same lot, enduring the same hardships, feeding on the same aliments, arrayed in the same rude garments. No roof then rose, but was open to the homeless stranger; no smoke curled among the trees, but he was welcome to sit down by its fire and join the hunter in his repast. "For," says an old historian of New England, "their life is so void of care, and they are so loving also, that they make use of those things they enjoy as common goods, and are therein so compassionate, that rather than one should starve through want, they would starve all; thus do they pass their time merrily, not regarding our pomp, but are better content with their own, which some men esteem so meanly of." Such were the Indians whilst in the pride and energy of their primitive natures; they resemble those wild plants which thrive best in the shades of the forest, but shrink from the hand of cultivation, and perish beneath the influence of the sun.

In discussing the savage character, writers have been too prone to indulge in vulgar prejudice and passionate exaggeration, instead of the candid temper of true philosophy. They have not sufficiently considered the peculiar circumstances in which the Indians have been placed, and the peculiar principles under which they have been educated. No being acts more rigidly from rule than the Indian. His whole conduct is regulated according to some general maxims early implanted in his mind. The moral laws that govern him are, to be sure, but few; but then he conforms to them all;—the white man abounds in laws of religion, morals and manners, but how many does he violate!

A frequent ground of accusation against the Indians is their disregard of treaties, and the treachery and wantonness with which, in time of apparent peace, they will suddenly fly to hostilities. The intercourse of the white men with the Indians, however, is too apt to be cold, distrustful, oppressive, and insulting. They seldom treat them with that confidence and frankness which are indispensable to real friendship; nor is sufficient caution observed not to offend against those feelings of pride or superstition, which often prompt the Indian to hostility quicker than mere considerations of interest. The solitary savage feels silently, but acutely. His sensibilities are not diffused over so wide a surface as those of the white man; but they run in steadier and deeper channels. His pride, his affections, his superstitions, are all directed towards fewer objects; but the wounds inflicted on them are proportionably severe, and furnish motives of hostility which we cannot sufficiently appreciate. Where a community is also limited in number, and forms one great patriarchal family, as in an Indian tribe, the injury of an individual is the injury of the whole; and the sentiment of vengeance is almost instantaneously diffused. One council fire is sufficient for the discussion and arrangement of a plan of hostilities. Here all the fighting men and sages assemble. Eloquence and superstition combine to inflame the minds of the warriors. The orator awakens their martial ardour, and they are wrought up to a kind of religious desperation, by the visions of the prophet and the dreamer.

An instance of one of those sudden exasperations, arising from a motive peculiar to the Indian character, is extant in an old record of the early settlement of Massachusetts. The planters of Plymouth had defaced the monuments of the dead at Passonagessit, and had plundered the grave of the Sachem's mother of some skins with which it had been decorated. The Indians are remarkable for the reverence which they entertain for the sepulchres of their kindred. Tribes, that

have passed generations exiled from the abodes of their ancestors, when by chance they have been travelling in the vicinity,
have been known to turn aside from the high way, and,
guided by wonderfully accurate tradition, have crossed the
country for miles to some tumulus, buried perhaps in woods,
where the bones of their tribe were anciently deposited; and
there have passed hours in silent meditation. Influenced by
this sublime and holy feeling, the Sachem, whose mother's
tomb had been violated, gathered his men together, and addressed them in the following beautifully simple and pathetic
harangue; a curious specimen of Indian eloquence, and an
affecting instance of filial piety in a savage.

"When last the glorious light of all the sky was underneath
this globe, and birds grew silent, I began to settle, as my custom is, to take repose. Before mine eyes were fast closed,
methought I saw a vision, at which my spirit was much troubled; and, trembling at that doleful sight, a spirit cried aloud,
'Behold, my son, whom I have cherished, see the breasts that
gave thee suck, the hands that lapped thee warm, and fed thee
oft! Canst thou forget to take revenge of those wild people,
who have defaced my monument in a despiteful manner, disdaining our antiquities and honourable customs. See now, the
Sachem's grave lies like the common people, defaced by an
ignoble race. Thy mother doth complain, and implores thy
aid against this thievish people, who have newly intruded on
our land. If this be suffered, I shall not rest quiet in my everlasting habitation.' This said, the spirit vanished, and I, all in
a sweat, not able scarce to speak, began to get some strength,
and recollect my spirits that were fled, and determined to demand your counsel and assistance."

I have adduced this anecdote at some length, as it tends to
show, how these sudden acts of hostility, which have been
attributed to caprice and perfidy, may often arise from deep
and generous motives, which our inattention to Indian character and customs prevents our properly appreciating.

Another ground of violent outcry against the Indians is
their barbarity to the vanquished. This had its origin partly in
policy and partly in superstition. The tribes, though sometimes called nations, were never so formidable in their numbers, but that the loss of several warriors was sensibly felt;

this was particularly the case when they had been frequently engaged in warfare; and many an instance occurs in Indian history, where a tribe that had long been formidable to its neighbours, has been broken up and driven away, by the capture and massacre of its principal fighting men. There was a strong temptation, therefore, to the victor to be merciless; not so much to gratify any cruel revenge, as to provide for future security. The Indians had also the superstitious belief, frequent among barbarous nations, and prevalent also among the ancients, that the manes of their friends who had fallen in battle, were soothed by the blood of the captives. The prisoners, however, who are not thus sacrificed, are adopted into their families in place of the slain, and are treated with the confidence and affection of relatives and friends; nay, so hospitable and tender is their entertainment, that when the alternative is offered them they will often prefer to remain with their adopted brethren, rather than return to the home and the friends of their youth.

The cruelty of the Indians towards their prisoners has been heightened since the colonization of the whites. What was formerly a compliance with policy and superstition, has been exasperated into a gratification of vengeance. They cannot but be sensible that the white men are the usurpers of their ancient dominion, the cause of their degradation, and the gradual destroyers of their race. They go forth to battle, smarting with injuries and indignities which they have individually suffered, and they are driven to madness and despair by the wide spreading desolation, and the overwhelming ruin of European warfare. The whites have too frequently set them an example of violence, by burning their villages and laying waste their slender means of subsistence; and yet they wonder that savages do not show moderation and magnanimity towards those, who have left them nothing but mere existence and wretchedness.

We stigmatize the Indians, also, as cowardly and treacherous, because they use stratagem in warfare, in preference to open force; but in this they are fully justified by their rude code of honour. They are early taught that stratagem is praiseworthy: the bravest warrior thinks it no disgrace to lurk in silence, and take every advantage of his foe: he triumphs in the superior craft and sagacity by which he has been enabled to surprize and destroy an enemy. Indeed man is naturally more prone to subtilty than open valour, owing to his physical weakness in comparison with other animals. They are endowed with natural weapons of defence; with horns, with tusks, with hoofs and talons; but man has to depend on his superior sagacity. In all his encounters with these, his proper enemies, he resorts to stratagem; and when he perversely turns his hostility against his fellow man, he at first continues the same subtle mode of warfare.

The natural principle of war is to do the most harm to our enemy with the least harm to ourselves; and this of course is to be effected by stratagem. That chivalrous courage which induces us to despise the suggestions of prudence, and to rush in the face of certain danger, is the offspring of society, and produced by education. It is honourable, because it is in fact the triumph of lofty sentiment over an instinctive repugnance to pain, and over those yearnings after personal ease and security, which society has condemned as ignoble. It is kept alive by pride and the fear of shame; and thus the dread of real evil is overcome by the superior dread of an evil which exists but in the imagination. It has been cherished and stimulated also by various means. It has been the theme of spirit stirring song and chivalrous story. The poet and minstrel have delighted to shed round it the splendours of fiction; and even the historian has forgotten the sober gravity of narration, and broken forth into enthusiasm and rhapsody in its praise. Triumphs and gorgeous pageants have been its reward: monuments, on which art has exhausted its skill, and opulence its treasures, have been erected to perpetuate a nation's gratitude and admiration. Thus artificially excited, courage has arisen to an extraordinary and factitious degree of heroism; and, arrayed in all the glorious "pomp and circumstance of war," this turbulent quality has even been able to eclipse many of those quiet, but invaluable virtues, which silently ennoble the human character, and swell the tide of human happiness.

But if courage intrinsically consists in the defiance of danger and pain, the life of the Indian is a continual exhibition of it. He lives in a state of perpetual hostility and risk. Peril and adventure are congenial to his nature; or rather seem necessary to arouse his faculties and to give an interest to his existence. Surrounded by hostile tribes, whose mode of warfare is by ambush and surprisal, he is always prepared for fight, and lives with his weapons in his hands. As the ship careers in fearful singleness through the solitudes of ocean;—as the bird mingles among clouds, and storms, and wings its way, a mere speck, across the pathless fields of air;—so the Indian holds his course, silent, solitary, but undaunted, through the boundless bosom of the wilderness. His expeditions may vie in distance and danger with the pilgrimage of the devotee, or the crusade of the knight errant. He traverses vast forests, exposed to the hazards of lonely sickness, of lurking enemies and pining famine. Stormy lakes, those great inland seas, are no obstacles to his wanderings: in his light canoe of bark he sports, like a feather, on their waves, and darts, with the swiftness of an arrow, down the roaring rapids of the rivers. His very subsistence is snatched from the midst of toil and peril. He gains his food by the hardships and dangers of the chase; he wraps himself in the spoils of the bear, the panther, and the buffalo, and sleeps among the thunders of the cataract.

No hero of ancient or modern days can surpass the Indian in his lofty contempt of death, and the fortitude with which he sustains its cruelest infliction. Indeed we here behold him rising superior to the white man, in consequence of his peculiar education. The latter rushes to glorious death at the cannon's mouth; the former calmly contemplates its approach, and triumphantly endures it, amidst the varied torments of surrounding foes and the protracted agonies of fire. He even takes a pride in taunting his persecutors, and provoking their ingenuity of torture; and as the devouring flames prey on his very vitals, and the flesh shrinks from the sinews, he raises his last song of triumph, breathing the defiance of an unconquered heart, and invoking the spirits of his fathers to witness that he dies without a groan.

Notwithstanding the obloquy with which the early historians have overshadowed the characters of the unfortunate natives, some bright gleams occasionally break through, which throw a degree of melancholy lustre on their memories. Facts are occasionally to be met with in the rude annals of the eastern provinces, which, though recorded with the colouring of prejudice and bigotry, yet speak for themselves; and will be dwelt on with applause and sympathy, when prejudice shall have passed away.

In one of the homely narratives of the Indian wars in New England, there is a touching account of the desolation carried into the tribe of the Pequod Indians. Humanity shrinks from the cold blooded detail of indiscriminate butchery. In one place we read of the surprisal of an Indian fort in the night, when the wigwams were wrapped in flames, and the miserable inhabitants shot down and slain in attempting to escape, "all being dispatched and ended in the course of an hour." After a series of similar transactions, "our soldiers," as the historian piously observes, "being resolved by God's assistance to make a final destruction of them," the unhappy savages being hunted from their homes and fortresses, and pursued with fire and sword, a scanty but gallant band, the sad remnant of the Pequod warriors, with their wives and children, took refuge in a swamp.

Burning with indignation, and rendered sullen by despair; with hearts bursting with grief at the destruction of their tribe, and spirits galled and sore at the fancied ignominy of their defeat, they refused to ask their lives at the hands of an insulting foe, and preferred death to submission.

As the night drew on they were surrounded in their dismal retreat, so as to render escape impracticable. Thus situated, their enemy "plied them with shot all the time, by which means many were killed and buried in the mire." In the darkness and fog that preceded the dawn of day some few broke through the besiegers and escaped into the woods: "the rest were left to the conquerors, of which many were killed in the swamp, like sullen dogs who would rather, in their self willedness and madness, sit still and be shot through, or cut to pieces," than implore for mercy. When the day broke upon this handful of forlorn but dauntless spirits, the soldiers, we are told, entering the swamp, "saw several heaps of them sitting close together, upon whom they discharged their pieces, laden with ten or twelve pistol bullets at a time; putting the muzzles of their pieces under the boughs, within a few yards of them; so as, besides those that were found dead, many more were killed and sunk into the mire, and never were minded more by friend or foe."

Can any one read this plain unvarnished tale, without admiring the stern resolution, the unbending pride, the loftiness of spirit, that seemed to nerve the hearts of these self taught heroes, and to raise them above the instinctive feelings of human nature? When the Gauls laid waste the city of Rome, they found the senators clothed in their robes and seated with stern tranquillity in their curule chairs; in this manner they suffered death without resistance or even supplication. Such conduct was, in them, applauded as noble and magnanimous; in the hapless Indians it was reviled as obstinate and sullen. How truly are we the dupes of show and circumstance! How different is virtue, clothed in purple and enthroned in state, from virtue naked and destitute, and perishing obscurely in a wilderness.

But I forbear to dwell upon these gloomy pictures. The eastern tribes have long since disappeared; the forests that sheltered them have been laid low, and scarce any traces remain of them in the thickly settled states of New England, excepting here and there the Indian name of a village or a stream. And such must sooner or later be the fate of those other tribes which skirt the frontiers, and have occasionally been inveigled from their forests to mingle in the wars of white men. In a little while, and they will go the way that their brethren have gone before. The few hordes which still linger about the shores of Huron and Superior, and the tributary streams of the Mississippi, will share the fate of those tribes that once spread over Massachusetts and Connecticut, and lorded it along the proud banks of the Hudson; of that gigantic race said to have existed on the borders of the Susquehanna; and of those various nations that flourished about the Patowmac and the Rappahanoc, and that peopled the forests of the vast valley of Shenandoah. They will vanish like a vapour from the face of the earth; their very history will be lost in forgetfulness; and "the places that now know them will know them no more for ever." Or if, perchance, some dubious memorial of them should survive, it may be in the romantic dreams of the poet, to people in imagination his glades and groves, like the fauns and satyrs and sylvan deities of antiquity. But should he venture upon the dark story of their wrongs and wretchedness; should he tell how they were invaded, corrupted, despoiled; driven from their native abodes and the sepulchres of their fathers; hunted like wild beasts about the earth; and sent down with violence and butchery to the grave; posterity will either turn with horror and incredulity from the tale, or blush with indignation at the inhumanity of their forefathers.—"We are driven back," said an old warrior, "until we can retreat no further—our hatchets are broken, our bows are snapped, our fires are nearly extinguished—a little longer and the white man will cease to persecute us—for we shall cease to exist!"

Philip of Pokanoket

An Indian Memoir

> As monumental bronze unchanged his look:
> A soul that pity touch'd, but never shook:
> Train'd, from his tree-rock'd cradle to his bier,
> The fierce extremes of good and ill to brook
> Impassive—fearing but the shame of fear—
> A stoic of the woods—a man without a tear.
> *Campbell*

IT IS TO BE regretted that those early writers who treated of the discovery and settlement of America, have not given us more particular and candid accounts of the remarkable characters that flourished in savage life. The scanty anecdotes which have reached us are full of peculiarity and interest; they furnish us with nearer glimpses of human nature, and show what man is in a comparatively primitive state, and what he owes to civilization. There is something of the charm of discovery in lighting upon these wild and unexplored tracts of human nature; in witnessing, as it were, the native growth of moral sentiment; and perceiving those generous and romantic qualities which have been artificially cultivated by society, vegetating in spontaneous hardihood and rude magnificence.

In civilized life, where the happiness, and indeed almost the existence, of man depends so much upon the opinion of his fellow men, he is constantly acting a studied part. The bold and peculiar traits of native character are refined away, or softened down by the levelling influence of what is termed good breeding; and he practises so many petty deceptions, and affects so many generous sentiments, for the purposes of popularity, that it is difficult to distinguish his real, from his artificial character. The Indian, on the contrary, free from the restraints and refinements of polished life, and, in a great degree, a solitary and independent being, obeys the impulses of his inclination or the dictates of his judgment; and thus the attributes of his nature, being freely indulged, grow singly great and striking. Society is like a lawn, where every roughness is smoothed, every bramble eradicated, and where the eye is delighted by the smiling verdure of a velvet surface; he, however, who would study nature in its wildness and variety, must plunge into the forest, must explore the glen, must stem the torrent, and dare the precipice.

These reflections arose on casually looking through a volume of early colonial history, wherein are recorded, with great bitterness, the outrages of the Indians, and their wars with the settlers of New England. It is painful to perceive, even from these partial narratives, how the footsteps of civilization may be traced in the blood of the aborigines; how easily the colonists were moved to hostility by the lust of conquest; how merciless and exterminating was their warfare. The imagination shrinks at the idea, how many intellectual beings were hunted from the earth; how many brave and noble hearts, of nature's sterling coinage, were broken down and trampled in the duts.

Such as the fate of PHILIP OF POKANOKET, an Indian warrior, whose name was once a terror throughout Massachusetts and Connecticut. He was the most distinguished of a number of cotemporary Sachems who reigned over the Pequods, the Narrhagansets, the Wampanoags, and the other Eastern tribes, at the time of the first settlement of New England: a band of native untaught heroes; who made the most generous struggle of which human nature is capable; fighting to the last gasp in the cause of their country, without a hope of victory or a thought of renown. Worthy of an age of poetry, and fit subjects for local story and romantic fiction, they have left scarcely any authentic traces on the page of history, but stalk, like gigantic shadows in the dim twilight of tradition.*

When the pilgrims, as the Plymouth settlers are called by their descendants, first took refuge on the shores of the New World, from the religious persecutions of the Old, their situation was to the last degree gloomy and disheartening. Few in number, and that number rapidly perishing away through sickness and hardships; surrounded by a howling wilderness

*While correcting the proof sheets of this article, the author is informed, that a celebrated English poet has nearly finished an heroic poem on the story of Philip of Pokanoket.

and savage tribes; exposed to the rigours of an almost arctic winter, and the vicissitudes of an every shifting climate; their minds were filled with doleful forebodings, and nothing preserved them from sinking into despondency but the strong excitement of religious enthusiasm. In this forlorn situation they were visited by Massasoit, chief Sagamore of the Wampanoags, a powerful chief, who reigned over a great extent of country. Instead of taking advantage of the scanty number of the strangers, and expelling them from his territories into which they had intruded, he seemed at once to conceive for them a generous friendship, and extended towards them the rites of primitive hospitality. He came early in the spring to their settlement of New Plymouth, attended by a mere handful of followers; entered into a solemn league of peace and amity; sold them a portion of the soil, and promised to secure for them the good will of his savage allies. Whatever may be said of Indian of perfidy, it is certain that the integrity and good faith of Massasoit, have never been impeached. He continued a firm and magnanimous friend of the white men; suffering them to extend their possessions and to strengthen themselves in the land; and betraying no jealousy of their increasing power and prosperity. Shortly before his death he came once more to New Plymouth, with his son Alexander, for the purpose of renewing the covenant of peace, and of securing it to his posterity.

At this conference he endeavoured to protect the religion of his forefathers from the encroaching zeal of the missionaries; and stipulated that no further attempt should be made to draw off his people from their ancient faith; but, finding the English obstinately opposed to any such condition, he mildly relinquished the demand. Almost the last act of his life was to bring his two sons, Alexander and Philip (as they had been named by the English,) to the residence of a principal settler, recommending mutual kindness and confidence; and entreating that the same love and amity which had existed between the white men and himself, might be continued afterwards with his children. The good old Sachem died in peace, and was happily gathered to his fathers before sorrow came upon his tribe; his children remained behind to experience the ingratitude of white men.

His eldest son, Alexander, succeeded him. He was of a

quick and impetuous temper, and proudly tenacious of his hereditary rights and dignity. The intrusive policy and dictatorial conduct of the strangers excited his indignation; and he beheld with uneasiness their exterminating wars with the neighbouring tribes. He was doomed soon to incur their hostility, being accused of plotting with the Narrhagansets to rise against the English and drive them from the land. It is impossible to say whether this accusation was warranted by facts, or was grounded on mere suspicions. It is evident, however, by the violent and overbearing measures of the settlers, that they had by this time begun to feel conscious of the rapid increase of their power, and to grow harsh and inconsiderate in their treatment of the natives. They dispatched an armed force to seize at once upon Alexander, and to bring him before their court. He was traced to his woodland haunts, and surprised at a hunting house, where he was reposing with a band of his followers, unarmed, after the toils of the chase. The suddenness of his arrest, and the outrage offered to his sovereign dignity, so preyed upon the irascible feelings of this proud savage, as to throw him into a raging fever; he was permitted to return home on condition of sending his son as a pledge for his reappearance; but the blow he had received was fatal, and before he reached his home he fell a victim to the agonies of a wounded spirit.

The successor of Alexander was Metamocet, or King Philip, as he was called by the settlers, on account of his lofty spirit and ambitious temper. These, together with his well known energy and enterprise, had rendered him an object of great jealousy and apprehension, and he was accused of having always cherished a secret and implacable hostility towards the whites. Such may very probably, and very naturally, have been the case. He considered them as originally but mere intruders into the country, who had presumed upon indulgence, and were extending an influence baneful to savage life. He saw the whole race of his countrymen melting before them from the face of the earth; their territories slipping from their hands, and their tribes becoming feeble, scattered and dependent. It may be said that the soil was originally purchased by the settlers; but who does not know the nature of Indian purchases, in the early periods of colonization? The

Europeans always made thrifty bargains through their superior adroitness in traffic; and they gained vast accessions of territory, by easily provoked hostilities. An uncultivated savage is never a nice inquirer into the refinements of law, by which an injury may be gradually and legally inflicted. Leading facts are all by which he judges; and it was enough for Philip to know, that before the intrusion of the Europeans his countrymen were lords of the soil, and that now they were becoming vagabonds in the land of their fathers.

But whatever may have been his feelings of general hostility, and his particular indignation at the treatment of his brother, he suppressed them for the present; renewed the contract with the settlers; and resided peaceably for many years at Pokanoket, or, as it was called by the English, Mount Hope,* the ancient seat of dominion of his tribe. Suspicions, however, which were at first but vague and indefinite, began to acquire form and substance; and he was at length charged with attempting to instigate the various eastern tribes to rise at once, and by a simultaneous effort, to throw off the yoke of their oppressors. It is difficult at this distant period to assign the proper credit due to these early accusations against the Indians. There was a proneness to suspicion, and an aptness to acts of violence, on the part of the whites, that gave weight and importance to every idle tale. Informers abounded where tale bearing met with countenance and reward; and the sword was readily unsheathed when its success was certain and it carved out empire.

The only positive evidence on record against Philip is the accusation of one Sausaman, a renegado Indian, whose natural cunning had been quickened by a partial education which he had received among the settlers. He changed his faith and his allegiance two or three times, with a facility that evinced the looseness of his principles. He had acted for some time as Philip's confidential secretary and councillor, and had enjoyed his bounty and protection. Finding, however, that the clouds of adversity were gathering round his patron, he abandoned his service and went over to the whites; and in order to gain their favour, charged his former benefactor with plotting

*Now Bristol, Rhode Island.

against their safety. A rigorous investigation took place. Philip and several of his subjects submitted to be examined, but nothing was proved against them. The settlers, however, had now gone too far to retract; they had previously determined that Philip was a dangerous neighbour; they had publicly evinced their distrust; and had done enough to ensure his hostility; according, therefore, to the usual mode of reasoning in these cases, his destruction had become necessary to their security. Sausaman, the treacherous informer, was shortly after found dead in a pond, having fallen a victim to the vengeance of his tribe. Three Indians, one of whom was a friend and councillor of Philip, were apprehended and tried, and on the testimony of one very questionable witness, were condemned and executed as the murderers.

This treatment of his subjects, and ignominious punishment of his friend, outraged the pride and exasperated the passions of Philip. The bolt which had fallen thus at his very feet awakened him to the gathering storm, and he determined to trust himself no longer in the power of the white men. The fate of his insulted and broken hearted brother still rankled in his mind; and he had a further warning in the tragical story of Miantonimo, a great Sachem of the Narrhagansets, who, after manfully facing his accusers before a tribunal of the colonists, exculpating himself from a charge of conspiracy, and receiving assurances of amity, had been perfidiously dispatched at their instigation. Philip, therefore, gathered his fighting men about him; persuaded all strangers that he could, to join his cause; sent the women and children to the Narrhagansets for safety; and wherever he appeared, was continually surrounded by armed warriors.

When the two parties were thus in a state of distrust and irritation, the least spark was sufficient to set them in a flame. The Indians, having weapons in their hands, grew mischievous, and committed various petty depredations. In one of their maraudings a warrior was fired upon and killed by a settler. This was the signal for open hostilities; the Indians pressed to revenge the death of their comrade, and the alarm of war resounded through the Plymouth colony.

In the early chronicles of these dark and melancholy times we meet with many indications of the diseased state of the public mind. The gloom of religious abstraction, and the wildness of their situation, among trackless forests, and savage tribes, had disposed the colonists to superstitious fancies, and had filled their imaginations with the frightful chimeras of witchcraft and spectrology. They were much given also to a belief in omens. The troubles with Philip and his Indians were preceded, we are told, by a variety of those awful warnings which forerun great and public calamities. The perfect form of an Indian bow appeared in the air at New Plymouth, which was looked upon by the inhabitants as a "prodigious apparition." At Hadley, Northampton, and other towns in their neighbourhood, "was heard the report of a great piece of ordnance, with a shaking of the earth and a considerable echo."* Others were alarmed on a still sunshiny morning by the discharge of guns and muskets; bullets seemed to whistle past them, and the noise of drums resounded in the air, seeming to pass away to the westward: others fancied that they heard the galloping of horses over their heads; and certain monstrous births which took place about the time, filled the superstitious in some towns with doleful forebodings. Many of these portentous sights and sounds may be ascribed to natural phenomena. To the northern lights which occur vividly in those latitudes; the meteors which explode in the air; the casual rushing of a blast through the top branches of the forest; the crash of falling trees or disruptured rocks; and to those other uncouth sounds and echoes which will sometimes strike the ear so strangely amidst the profound stillness of woodland solitudes. These may have startled some melancholy imaginations, may have been exaggerated by the love for the marvellous, and listened to, with that avidity with which we devour whatever is fearful and mysterious. The universal currency of these superstitious fancies, and the grave record made of them by one of the learned men of the day, are strongly characteristic of the times.

The nature of the contest that ensued was such as too often distinguishes the warfare between civilized men and savages. On the part of the whites it was conducted with superior skill and success; but with a wastefulness of the blood, and a dis-

*The Rev. Increase Mather's History.

regard of the natural rights of their antagonists: on the part of the Indians it was waged with the desperation of men fearless of death, and who had nothing to expect from peace, but humiliation, dependence and decay.

The events of the war are transmitted to us by a worthy clergyman of the time; who dwells with horror and indignation on every hostile act of the Indians, however justifiable, whilst he mentions with applause the most sanguinary atrocities of the whites. Philip is reviled as a murderer and a traitor; without considering that he was a true born prince, gallantly fighting at the head of his subjects to avenge the wrongs of his family; to retrieve the tottering power of his line; and to deliver his native land from the oppression of usurping strangers.

The project of a wide and simultaneous revolt, if such had really been formed, was worthy of a capacious mind, and, had it not been prematurely discovered, might have been overwhelming in its consequences. The war that actually broke out was but a war of detail; a mere succession of casual exploits and unconnected enterprizes. Still it sets forth the military genius and daring prowess of Philip; and wherever, in the prejudiced and passionate narrations that have been given of it, we can arrive at simple facts, we find him displaying a vigorous mind; a fertility in expedients; a contempt of suffering and hardship; and an unconquerable resolution; that command our sympathy and applause.

Driven from his paternal domains at Mount Hope, he threw himself into the depths of those vast and trackless forests that skirted the settlements and were almost impervious to any thing but a wild beast, or an Indian. Here he gathered together his forces, like the storm accumulating its stores of mischief in the bosom of the thunder cloud, and would suddenly emerge at a time and place least expected, carrying havoc and dismay into the villages. There were now and then indications of these impending ravages, that filled the minds of the colonists with awe and apprehension. The report of a distant gun would perhaps be heard from the solitary woodland, where there was known to be no white man; the cattle which had been wandering in the woods, would sometimes return home wounded; or an Indian or two would be seen lurking about the skirts of the forests, and suddenly disappearing; as the lightning will sometimes be seen playing silently about the edge of the cloud that is brewing up the tempest.

Though sometimes pursued and even surrounded by the settlers, yet Philip as often escaped almost miraculously from their toils, and plunging into the wilderness would be lost to all search or inquiry, until he again emerged at some far distant quarter, laying the country desolate. Among his strong holds were the great swamps or morasses, which extend in some parts of New England; composed of loose bogs of deep black mud; perplexed with thickets, brambles, rank weeds, the shattered and mouldering trunks of fallen trees, and overshadowed by lugubrious hemlocks. The uncertain footing and the tangled mazes of these shagged wilds, render them almost impracticable to the white man, though the Indian could thrid their labyrinths with the agility of a deer. Into one of these, the great swamp of Pocasset Neck, was Philip once driven with a band of his followers. The English did not dare to pursue him, fearing to venture into these dark and frightful recesses, where they might perish in fens and miry pits, or be shot down by lurking foes. They therefore invested the entrance to the neck, and began to build a fort, with the thought of starving out the foe; but Philip and his warriors wafted themselves on a raft over an arm of the sea, in the dead of night, leaving the women and children behind; and escaped away to the westward, kindling the flames of war among the tribes of Massachusetts and the Nipmuck country, and threatening the colony of Connecticut.

In this way Philip became a theme of universal apprehension. The mystery in which he was enveloped exaggerated his real terrors. He was an evil that walked in darkness; whose coming none could foresee, and against which none knew when to be on the alert. The whole country abounded with rumours and alarms. Philip seemed almost possessed of ubiquity; for, in whatever part of the widely extended frontier an irruption from the forest took place, Philip was said to be its leader. Many superstitious notions also were circulated concerning him. He was said to deal in necromancy, and to be attended by an old Indian witch or prophetess, whom he consulted, and who assisted him by her charms and incantations. This indeed was frequently the case with Indian chiefs; either through their own credulity, or to act upon that of their followers: and the influence of the prophet and the dreamer over Indian superstition has been fully evidenced in recent instances of savage warfare.

At the time that Philip effected his escape from Pocasset, his fortunes were in a desperate condition. His forces had been thinned by repeated fights, and he had lost almost the whole of his resources. In this time of adversity he found a faithful friend in Canonchet, Chief Sachem of all the Narrhagansets. He was the son and heir of Miantonimo, the great Sachem, who, as already mentioned, after an honourable acquittal of the charge of conspiracy, had been privately put to death at the perfidious instigations of the settlers. "He was the heir," says the old chronicler, "of all his father's pride and insolence, as well as of his malice towards the English;"—he certainly was the heir of his insults and injuries, and the legitimate avenger of his murder. Though he had forborne to take an active part in this hopeless war, yet he received Philip and his broken forces with open arms; and gave them the most generous countenance and support. This at once drew upon him the hostility of the English; and it was determined to strike a signal blow that should involve both the sachems in one common ruin. A great force was, therefore, gathered together from Massachusetts, Plymouth, and Connecticut, and was sent into the Narrhaganset country in the depth of winter, when the swamps, being frozen and leafless, could be traversed with comparative facility, and would no longer afford dark and impenetrable fastnesses to the Indians.

Apprehensive of attack, Canonchet had conveyed the greater part of his stores, together with the old, the infirm, the women and children of his tribe, to a strong fortress; where he and Philip had likewise drawn up the flower of their forces. This fortress, deemed by the Indians impregnable, was situated upon a rising mound or kind of island, of five or six acres, in the midst of a swamp; it was constructed with a degree of judgment and skill vastly superior to what is usually displayed in Indian fortification, and indicative of the martial genius of these two chieftains.

Guided by a renegado Indian, the English penetrated, through December snows, to this strong hold, and came upon the garrison by surprize. The fight was fierce and tumultuous. The assailants were repulsed in their first attack, and several of their bravest officers were shot down in the act of storming the fortress, sword in hand. The assault was renewed with greater success. A lodgement was effected. The Indians were driven from one post to another. They disputed their ground inch by inch, fighting with the fury of despair. Most of their veterans were cut to pieces; and after a long and bloody battle, Philip and Canonchet, with a handful of surviving warriors, retreated from the fort, and took refuge in the thickets of the surrounding forest.

The victors set fire to the wigwams and the fort; the whole was soon in a blaze; many of the old men, the women and the children perished in the flames. This last outrage overcame even the stoicism of the savage. The neighbouring woods resounded with the yells of rage and despair, uttered by the fugitive warriors as they beheld the destruction of their dwellings, and heard the agonizing cries of their wives and offspring. "The burning of the wigwams," says a contemporary writer, "the shrieks and cries of the women and children, and the yelling of the warriors, exhibited a most horrible and affecting scene, so that it greatly moved some of the soldiers." The same writer cautiously adds, "they were in *much doubt* then, and afterwards seriously inquired, whether burning their enemies alive could be consistent with humanity, and the benevolent principles of the Gospel."*

The fate of the brave and generous Canonchet is worthy of particular mention: the last scene of his life is one of the noblest instances on record of Indian magnanimity.

Broken down in his power and resources by this signal defeat, yet faithful to his ally and to the hapless cause which he had espoused, he rejected all overtures of peace, offered on condition of betraying Philip and his followers, and declared that "he would fight it out to the last man, rather than become a servant to the English." His home being destroyed; his country harassed and laid waste by the incursions of the

---

*MS. of the Rev. W. Ruggles.

conquerors; he was obliged to wander away to the banks of the Connecticut; where he formed a rallying point to the whole body of western Indians, and laid waste several of the English settlements.

Early in the spring he departed on a hazardous expedition, with only thirty chosen men, to penetrate to Seaconk, in the vicinity of Mount Hope, and procure seed corn to plant for the sustenance of his troops. This little band of adventurers had passed safely through the Pequod country, and were in the centre of the Narrhaganset, resting at some wigwams near Pautucket river, when an alarm was given of an approaching enemy. Having but seven men by him at the time, Canonchet dispatched two of them to the top of a neighbouring hill, to bring intelligence of the foe.

Panic struck by the appearance of a troop of English and Indians rapidly advancing, they fled in breathless terror past their chieftain, without stopping to inform him of the danger. Canonchet sent another scout, who did the same. He then sent two more, one of whom, hurrying back in confusion and affright, told him that the whole British army was at hand. Canonchet saw there was no choice but immediate flight. He attempted to escape round the hill, but was perceived and hotly pursued by the hostile Indians and a few of the fleetest of the English. Finding the swiftest pursuer close upon his heels, he threw off, first his blanket, then his silver laced coat and belt of peag, by which his enemies knew him to be Canonchet, and redoubled the eagerness of pursuit. At length, in dashing through the river, his foot slipped upon a stone, and he fell so deep as to wet his gun. This accident so struck him with despair, that, as he afterwards confessed, "his heart and his bowels turned within him, and he became like a rotten stick, void of strength."

To such a degree was he unnerved, that, being seized by a Pequod Indian within a short distance of the river, he made no resistance, though a man of great vigour of body and boldness of heart. But on being made prisoner the whole pride of his spirit arose within him; and from that moment we find, in the anecdotes given by his enemies, nothing but repeated flashes of elevated and prince like heroism. Being questioned by one of the English who first came up with him, and who had not attained his twenty second year, the proud hearted warrior, looking with lofty contempt upon his youthful countenance, replied, "You are a child—you cannot understand matters of war—let your brother or your chief come—him will I answer."

Though repeated offers were made to him of his life, on condition of submitting, with his nation, to the English, yet he rejected them with disdain, and refused to send any proposals of the kind to the great body of his subjects; saying, that he knew none of them would comply. Being reproached with his breach of faith towards the whites; his boast that he would not deliver up a Wampanoag, nor the paring of a Wampanoag's nail; and his threat that he would burn the English alive in their houses; he disdained to justify himself, haughtily answering that others were as forward for the war as himself, "and he desired to hear no more thereof."

So noble and unshaken a spirit, so true a fidelity to his cause and his friend, might have touched the feelings of the generous and the brave: but Canonchet was an Indian; a being towards whom war had no courtesy, humanity no law, religion no compassion—he was condemned to die. The last words of his that are recorded, are worthy of the greatness of his soul. When sentence of death was passed upon him, he observed "that he liked it well, for he should die before his heart was soft, or he had spoken any thing unworthy of himself." His enemies gave him the death of a soldier, for he was shot at Stonington, by three young sachems of his own rank.

The defeat at the Narrhaganset fortress, and the death of Canonchet, were fatal blows to the fortunes of King Philip. He made an ineffectual attempt to raise a head of war, by stirring up the Mohawks to take arms; but though possessed of the native talents of a statesman, his arts were counteracted by the superior arts of his enlightened enemies, and the terror of their warlike skill began to subdue the resolution of the neighbouring tribes. The unfortunate chieftain saw himself daily stripped of power, and his ranks rapidly thinning around him. Some were suborned by the whites; others fell victims to hunger and fatigue, and to the frequent attacks by which they were harassed. His stores were all captured; his chosen friends were swept away from before his eyes; his uncle was shot down by his side; his sister was carried into captivity; and in one of his narrow escapes he was compelled to leave his beloved wife and only son to the mercy of the enemy. "His ruin," says the historian, "being thus gradually carried on, his misery was not prevented, but augmented thereby; being himself made acquainted with the sense and experimental feeling of the captivity of his children, loss of friends, slaughter of his subjects, bereavement of all family relations, and being stripped of all outward comforts, before his own life should be taken away."

To fill up the measure of his misfortunes, his own followers began to plot against his life, that by sacrificing him they might purchase dishonourable safety. Through treachery a number of his faithful adherents, the subjects of Wetamoe, an Indian princess of Pocasset, a near kinswoman and confederate of Philip, were betrayed into the hands of the enemy. Wetamoe was among them at the time, and attempted to make her escape by crossing a neighbouring river: either exhausted by swimming, or starved with cold and hunger, she was found dead and naked near the water side. But persecution ceased not at the grave. Even death, the refuge of the wretched, where the wicked commonly cease from troubling, was no protection to this outcast female, whose great crime was affectionate fidelity to her kinsman and her friend. Her corpse was the object of unmanly and dastardly vengeance; the head was severed from the body and set upon a pole, and was thus exposed at Taunton, to the view of her captive subjects. They immediately recognised the features of their unfortunate queen, and were so affected at this barbarous spectacle, that we are told they broke forth into the "most horrid and diabolical lamentations."

However Philip had borne up against the complicated miseries and misfortunes that surrounded him, the treachery of his followers seemed to wring his heart, and reduce him to despondency. It is said that "he never rejoiced afterwards, nor had success in any of his designs." The spring of hope was broken—the ardour of enterprise was extinguished—he looked around, and all was danger and darkness; "there was no eye to pity, nor any arm that could bring deliverance." With a scanty band of followers, who still remained true to his desperate fortunes, the unhappy Philip wandered back to the vicinity of Mount Hope, the ancient dwelling of his fathers. Here he lurked about, like a spectre, among the desolated scenes of former power and prosperity, now bereft of home, of family, and friend. There needs no better picture of his destitute and piteous situation than that furnished by the homely pen of the chronicler, who is unwarily enlisting the feelings of the reader in favour of the hapless warrior whom he reviles. "Philip," he says, "like a savage wild beast, having been hunted by the English forces through the woods above a hundred miles backward and forward, at last was driven to his own den upon Mount Hope, where he retired with a few of his best friends, into a swamp, which proved but a prison to keep him fast till the messengers of death came by divine permission to execute vengeance upon him."

Even in this last refuge of desperation and despair a sullen grandeur gathers round his memory. We picture him to ourselves seated among his care worn followers, brooding in silence over his blasted fortunes, and acquiring a savage sublimity from the wildness and dreariness of his lurking place. Defeated, but not dismayed—crushed to the earth, but not humiliated—he seemed to grow more haughty beneath disaster, and to experience a fierce satisfaction in draining the last dregs of bitterness. Little minds are tamed and subdued by misfortune; but great minds rise above it. The very idea of submission awakened the fury of Philip, and he smote to death one of his followers, who proposed an expedient of peace. The brother of the victim made his escape, and in revenge betrayed the retreat of his chieftain. A body of white men and Indians were immediately despatched to the swamp where Philip lay crouched, glaring with fury and despair. Before he was aware of their approach, they had begun to surround him. In a little while he saw five of his trustiest followers laid dead at his feet; all resistance was vain; he rushed forth from his covert, and made a headlong attempt at escape, but was shot through the heart by a renegado Indian of his own nation.

Such is the scanty story of the brave, but unfortunate King Philip; persecuted while living, slandered and dishonoured when dead. If, however, we consider even the prejudiced anecdotes furnished us by his enemies, we may perceive in them traces of amiable and lofty character, sufficient to awaken sympathy for his fate, and respect for his memory. We find, that amidst all the harassing cares and ferocious passions of constant warfare, he was alive to the softer feelings of connubial love and paternal tenderness, and to the generous sentiment of friendship. The captivity of his "beloved wife and only son" are mentioned with exultation, as causing him poignant misery: the death of any near friend is triumphantly recorded as a new blow on his sensibilities; but the treachery and desertion of many of his followers, in whose affections he had confided, is said to have desolated his heart, and to have bereaved him of all further comfort. He was a patriot attached to his native soil—a prince true to his subjects, and indignant of their wrongs—a soldier, daring in battle, firm in adversity, patient of fatigue, of hunger, of every variety of bodily suffering, and ready to perish in the cause he had espoused. Proud of heart, and with an untameable love of natural liberty, he preferred to enjoy it among the beasts of the forests, or in the dismal and famished recesses of swamps and morasses, rather than bow his haughty spirit to submission, and live dependent and despised in the ease and luxury of the settlements. With heroic qualities and bold achievements that would have graced a civilized warrior, and have rendered him the theme of the poet and the historian; he lived a wanderer and a fugitive in his native land, and went down, like a lonely bark foundering amid darkness and tempest—without a pitying eye to weep his fall, or a friendly hand to record his struggle.

John Bull

An old song, made by an aged old pate,
Of an old worshipful gentleman who had a great estate,
That kept a brave old house at a bountiful rate,
And an old porter to relieve the poor at his gate.

With an old study fill'd full of learned old books,
With an old reverend chaplain, you might know him by his looks,
With an old buttery-hatch worn quite off the hooks,
And an old kitchen that maintained half-a-dozen old cooks,
　　　　　　　　　　Like an old courtier, &c.

Old Song

THERE IS NO species of humour in which the English more excel, than that which consists in caricaturing and giving ludicrous appellations, or nick names. In this way they have whimsically designated, not merely individuals, but nations; and in their fondness for pushing a joke, they have not spared even themselves. One would think, that in personifying itself, a nation would be apt to picture something grand, heroic, and imposing; but it is characteristic of the peculiar humour of the English, and of their love for what is blunt, comic, and familiar, that they have embodied their national oddities in the figure of a sturdy, corpulent old fellow, with a three cornered hat, red waistcoat, leather breeches, and stout oaken cudgel. Thus they have taken a singular delight in exhibiting their most private foibles in a laughable point of view, and have been so successful in their delineations, that there is scarcely a being in actual existence more absolutely present to the public mind, than that eccentric personage, John Bull.

Perhaps the continual contemplation of the character thus drawn of them, has contributed to fix it upon the nation; and thus to give reality to what at first may have been painted in a great measure from the imagination. Men are apt to acquire peculiarities that are continually ascribed to them. The common orders of English seem wonderfully captivated with the *beau ideal* which they have formed of John Bull, and endeavour to act up to the broad caricature that is perpetually before their eyes. Unluckily, they sometimes make their boasted Bull-ism an apology for their prejudice or grossness; and this I have especially noticed among those truly home-bred and genuine sons of the soil, who have never migrated beyond the sound of Bow bells. If one of these should be a little uncouth in speech, and apt to utter impertinent truths, he confesses that he is a real John Bull, and always speaks his mind. If he now and then flies into an unreasonable burst of passion about trifles, he observes, that John Bull is a choleric old blade, but then his passion is over in a moment, and he bears no malice. If he betrays a coarseness of taste, and an insensibility to foreign refinements, he thanks heaven for his ignorance—he is a plain John Bull, and has no relish for frip-pery and nick-nacks. His very proneness to be gulled by strangers, and to pay extravagantly for absurdities, is excused under the plea of munificence—for John is always more gen-erous than wise.

Thus, under the name of John Bull, he will contrive to ar-gue every fault into a merit, and will frankly convict himself of being the honestest fellow in existence.

However little, therefore, the character may have suited in the first instance, it has gradually adapted itself to the nation, or rather, they have adapted themselves to each other; and a stranger who wishes to study English peculiarities, may gather much valuable information from the innumerable portraits of John Bull, as exhibited in the windows of the caricature shops. Still, however, he is one of those fertile humourists, that are continually throwing out new portraits, and presenting different aspects from different points of view; and often as he has been described, I cannot resist the temp-tation to give a slight sketch of him, such as he has met my eye.

John Bull, to all appearance, is a plain, downright, matter of fact fellow, with much less of poetry about him than rich prose. There is little of romance in his nature, but a vast deal of strong natural feeling. He excels in humour, more than in wit; is jolly, rather than gay; melancholy, rather than morose; can easily be moved to a sudden tear, or surprised into a broad laugh; but he loathes sentiment, and has no turn for light pleasantry. He is a boon companion, if you allow him to have his humour, and to talk about himself; and he will stand by a friend in a quarrel, with life and purse, however soundly he may be cudgelled.

In this last respect, to tell the truth, he has a propensity to be somewhat too ready. He is a busy minded personage, who thinks not merely for himself and family, but for all the country round, and is most generously disposed to be every body's champion. He is continually volunteering his services to settle his neighbours' affairs, and takes it in great dudgeon if they engage in any matter of consequence without asking his advice, though he seldom engages in any friendly office of the kind without finishing by getting into a squabble with all parties, and then railing bitterly at their ingratitude. He unluckily took lessons in his youth in the noble science of defence, and having accomplished himself in the use of his limbs and his weapons, and become a perfect master at boxing and cudgel play, he has had a troublesome life of it ever since. He cannot hear of a quarrel between the most distant of his neighbours, but he begins incontinently to fumble with the head of his cudgel, and consider whether his interest or honour does not require that he should meddle in the broil. Indeed, he has extended his relations of pride and policy so completely over the whole country, that no event can take place, without infringing some of his finely spun rights and dignities. Couched in his little domain, with these filaments stretching forth in every direction, he is like some choleric, bottle bellied old spider, who has woven his web over a whole chamber, so that a fly cannot buzz, nor a breeze blow, without startling his repose, and causing him to sally forth wrathfully from his den.

Though really a good hearted, good tempered old fellow at bottom, yet he is singularly fond of being in the midst of contention. It is one of his peculiarities, however, that he only relishes the beginning of an affray: he always goes into a fight with alacrity, but comes out of it grumbling even when victorious; and though no one fights with more obstinacy to carry a contested point, yet, when the battle is over, and he comes to the reconciliation, he is so much taken up with the mere shaking of hands, that he is apt to let his antagonist pocket all that they have been quarrelling about. It is not, therefore, fighting that he ought so much to be on his guard against, as making friends. It is difficult to cudgel him out of a farthing, but put him in a good humour, and you may bargain him out of all the money in his pocket. He is like a stout ship, which will weather the roughest storm uninjured, but roll its masts overboard in the succeeding calm.

He is a little fond of playing the magnifico abroad; of pulling out a long purse; flinging his money bravely about at boxing matches, horse races, and cock fights, and carrying a high head among "gentlemen of the fancy;" but immediately after one of these fits of extravagance, he will be taken with violent qualms of economy; stop short at the most trivial expenditure; talk desperately of being ruined, and brought upon the parish; and in such moods, will not pay the smallest tradesman's bill, without violent altercation. He is, in fact, the most punctual and discontented paymaster in the world; drawing his coin out of his breeches' pocket with infinite reluctance, paying to the uttermost farthing, but accompanying every guinea with a growl.

With all his talk of economy, however, he is a bountiful provider, and a hospitable housekeeper. His economy is of a whimsical kind, its chief object being to devise how he may afford to be extravagant, for he will begrudge himself a beef steak and pint of port one day, that he may roast an ox whole, broach a hogshead of ale, and treat all his neighbours, on the next.

His domestic establishment is enormously expensive, not so much from any great outward parade, as from the great consumption of solid beef and pudding, the vast number of followers he feeds and clothes, and his singular disposition to pay hugely for small services. He is a most kind and indulgent master, and, provided his servants humour his peculiarities, flatter his vanity a little now and then, and do not peculate grossly on him before his face, they may manage him to perfection. Every thing that lives on him seems to thrive and grow fat. His house servants are well paid, and pampered, and have little to do. His horses are sleek and lazy, and prance slowly before his state carriage, and his house dogs sleep quietly about the door, and will hardly bark at a house breaker.

His family mansion is an old castellated manor house, grey

with age, and of a most venerable though weather beaten appearance. It has been built upon no regular plan, but is a vast accumulation of parts, erected in various tastes and ages. The centre bears evident traces of Saxon architecture, and is as solid as ponderous stone and old English oak can make it. Like all the reliques of that style, it is full of obscure passages, intricate mazes, and dusky chambers; and though these have been partially lighted up in modern days, yet there are many places where you must still grope in the dark. Additions have been made to the original edifice from time to time, and great alterations have taken place; towers and battlements have been erected during wars and tumults; wings built in times of peace, and outhouses, lodges, and offices, run up according to the whim or convenience of different generations, until it has become one of the most spacious, rambling tenements imaginable. An entire wing is taken up with the family chapel, a reverend pile that must once have been exceedingly sumptuous, and, indeed, in spite of having been altered and simplified at various periods, has still a look of solemn religious pomp. Its walls within are storied with the monuments of John's ancestors, and it is snugly fitted up with soft cushions and well lined chairs, where such of his family as are inclined to church services, may doze comfortably in the discharge of their duties.

To keep up this chapel has cost John much money; but he is staunch in his religion, and piqued in his zeal, from the circumstance that many dissenting chapels have been erected in his vicinity, and several of his neighbours, with whom he has had quarrels, are strong papists.

To do the duties of the chapel, he maintains, at a large expense, a pious and portly family chaplain. He is a most learned and decorous personage, and a truly well bred christian, who always backs the old gentleman in his opinions, winks discreetly at his little peccadilloes, rebukes the children when refractory, and is of great use in exhorting the tenants to read their bibles, say their prayers, and above all, to pay their rents punctually, and without grumbling.

The family apartments are in a very antiquated taste, somewhat heavy, and often inconvenient, but full of the solemn magnificence of former times; fitted up with rich though faded tapestry, unwieldy furniture, and loads of massy gorgeous old plate. The vast fire places, ample kitchens, extensive cellars, and sumptuous banquetting halls, all speak of the roaring hospitality of days of yore, of which the modern festivity at the manor house is but a shadow. There are, however, complete suites of rooms apparently deserted and time worn; and towers and turrets that are tottering to decay, so that in high winds there is danger of their tumbling about the ears of the household.

John has frequently been advised to have the old edifice thoroughly overhauled, and to have some of the useless parts pulled down, and the others strengthened with their materials; but the old gentleman always grows testy on this subject. He swears the house is an excellent house—that it is tight and weather proof, and not to be shaken by tempests—that it has stood for several hundred years, and, therefore, is not likely to tumble down now—that as to its being inconvenient, his family is accustomed to the inconveniences, and would not be comfortable without them—that as to its unwieldy size and irregular construction, these result from its being the growth of centuries, and being improved by the wisdom of every generation—that an old family, like his, requires a large house to dwell in; new, upstart families may live in modern cottages and snug boxes, but an old English family should inhabit an old English manor house. If you point out any part of the building as superfluous, he insists that it is material to the strength or decoration of the rest, and the harmony of the whole, and swears, that the parts are so built into each other, that if you pull down one, you run the risk of having the whole about your ears.

The secret of the matter is, that John has a great disposition to protect and patronize. He thinks it indispensable to the dignity of an ancient and honourable family, to be bounteous in its appointments, and to be eaten up by dependants; and so, partly from pride, and partly from kind heartedness, he makes it a rule always to give shelter and maintenance to his superannuated servants.

The consequence is, that like many other venerable family establishments, his manor is incumbered by old retainers whom he cannot turn off, and an old style which he cannot lay down. His mansion is like a great hospital of invalids, and, with all its magnitude, is not a whit too large for its inhabitants. Not a nook or corner but is of use in housing some useless personage. Groups of veteran beef eaters, gouty pensioners, and retired heroes of the buttery and the larder, are seen lolling about its walls, crawling over its lawns, dozing under its trees, or sunning themselves upon the benches at its doors. Every office and out house is garrisoned by these supernumeraries and their families, for they are amazingly prolific; and when they die off, are sure to leave John a legacy of hungry mouths to be provided for. A mattock cannot be struck against the most mouldering, tumble down tower, but out pops, from some cranny or loop hole, the gray pate of some superannuated hanger on, who has lived at John's expense all his life, and makes the most grievous outcry, at their pulling down the roof from over the head of a worn out servant of the family. This is an appeal that John's honest heart never can withstand; so that a man, who has faithfully eaten his beef and pudding all his life, is sure to be rewarded with a pipe and tankard in his old days.

A great part of his park, also, is turned into paddocks, where his broken down chargers are turned loose, to graze undisturbed for the remainder of their existence—a worthy example of grateful recollection, which, if some of his neighbours were to imitate, would not be to their discredit. Indeed, it is one of his great pleasures to point out these old steeds to his visiters, to dwell on their good qualities, extol their past services, and boast, with some little vain glory, of the perilous adventures and hardy exploits, through which they have carried him.

He is given, however, to indulge his veneration for family usages, and family incumbrances, to a whimsical extent. His manor is infested by gangs of gipsies, yet he will not suffer them to be driven off, because they have infested the place time out of mind, and been regular poachers upon every generation of the family. He will scarcely permit a dry branch to be lopped from the great trees that surround the house, lest it should molest the rooks, that have bred there for centuries. Owls have taken possession of the dovecote; but they are hereditary owls, and must not be disturbed. Swallows have nearly choked up every chimney with their nests; martins build in every frieze and cornice; crows flutter about the towers, and perch on every weather cock; and old gray headed rats may be seen in every quarter of the house, running in and out of their holes undauntedly, in broad daylight. In short, John has such a reverence for every thing that has been long in the family, that he will not hear even of abuses being reformed, because they are good old family abuses.

All these whims and habits have concurred wofully to drain the old gentleman's purse; and as he prides himself on punctuality in money matters, and wishes to maintain his credit in the neighbourhood, they have caused him great perplexity in meeting his engagements. This too has been increased, by the altercations and heartburnings which are continually taking place in his family. His children have been brought up to different callings, and are of different ways of thinking; and as they have always been allowed to speak their minds freely, they do not fail to exercise the privilege most clamorously in the present posture of his affairs. Some stand up for the honour of the race, and are clear that the old establishment should be kept up in all its state, whatever may be the cost; others, who are more prudent and considerate, entreat the old gentleman to retrench his expenses, and to put his whole system of housekeeping on a more moderate footing. He has, indeed, at times seemed inclined to listen to their opinions, but their wholesome advice has been completely defeated by the obstreperous conduct of one of his sons. This is a noisy rattle pated fellow, of rather low habits, who neglects his business to frequent ale houses—is the orator of village clubs, and a complete oracle among the poorest of his father's tenants. No sooner does he hear any of his brothers mention reform or retrenchment, than up he jumps, takes the words out of their mouths, and roars out for an overturn. When his tongue is once going, nothing can stop it. He rants about the room, hectors the old man about his spendthrift practices, ridicules his tastes and pursuits, insists that he shall turn the old servants out of doors, give the broken down horses to the hounds, send the fat chaplain packing, and take a field preacher in his place—nay, that the whole family mansion shall be levelled with the ground, and a plain one of brick and mortar built in its place. He rails at every social entertainment and family festivity, and skulks away growling to the ale house whenever an equipage drives up to the door. Though constantly complaining of the emptiness of his purse, yet he scruples not to spend all his pocket money in these tavern convocations, and even runs up scores for the liquor over which he preaches about his father's extravagance.

It may readily be imagined, how little such thwarting agrees with the old cavalier's fiery temperament. He has become so irritable, from repeated crossings, that the mere mention of retrenchment or reform is a signal for a brawl between him and the tavern oracle. As the latter is too sturdy and refractory for paternal discipline, having grown out of all fear of the cudgel, they have frequent scenes of wordy warfare, which at times run so high, that John is fain to call in the aid of his son Tom, an officer who has served abroad, but is at present living at home, on half pay. This last is sure to stand by the old gentleman, right or wrong; likes nothing so much as a racketing, roystering life, and is ready, at a wink or nod, to out sabre, and flourish it over the orator's head, if he dares to array himself against paternal authority.

These family dissensions, as usual, have got abroad, and are rare food for scandal in John's neighbourhood. People begin to look wise, and shake their heads, whenever his affairs are mentioned. They all "hope that matters are not so bad with him as represented; but when a man's own children begin to rail at his extravagance, things must be badly managed. They understand he is mortgaged over head and ears, and is continually dabbling with money lenders. He is certainly an open handed old gentleman, but they fear he has lived too fast; indeed, they never knew any good come of this fondness for hunting, racing, revelling, and prize fighting. In short, Mr. Bull's estate is a very fine one, and has been in the family a long while; but for all that, they have known many finer estates come to the hammer."

What is worst of all, is the effect which these pecuniary embarrassments and domestic feuds have had on the poor man himself. Instead of that jolly round corporation, and smug rosy face, which he used to present, he has of late become as shrivelled and shrunk as a frost bitten apple. His scarlet gold laced waistcoat, which bellied out so bravely in those prosperous days when he sailed before the wind, now hangs loosely about him like a mainsail in a calm. His leather breeches are all in folds and wrinkles, and apparently have much ado to hold up the boots that yawn on both sides of his once sturdy legs.

Instead of strutting about, as formerly, with his three cornered hat on one side, flourishing his cudgel, and bringing it down every moment with a hearty thump upon the ground, looking every one sturdily in the face, and trolling out a stave of a catch or a drinking song, he now goes about, whistling thoughtfully to himself, with his head drooping down, his cudgel tucked under his arm, and his hands thrust to the bottom of his breeches' pockets, which are evidently empty.

Such is the plight of honest John Bull at present; yet for all this, the old fellow's spirit is as tall and as gallant as ever. If you drop the least expression of sympathy or concern, he takes fire in an instant; swears that he is the richest and stoutest fellow in the country; talks of laying out large sums to adorn his house, or to buy another estate; and, with a valiant swagger and grasping of his cudgel, longs exceedingly to have another bout at quarter staff.

Though there may be something rather whimsical in all this, yet I confess I cannot look upon John's situation, without strong feelings of interest. With all his odd humours, and obstinate prejudices, he is a sterling hearted old blade. He may not be so wonderfully fine a fellow as he thinks himself, but he is at least twice as good as his neighbours represent him. His virtues are all his own; all plain, homebred and unaffected. His very faults smack of the raciness of his good qualities. His extravagance savours of his generosity; his quarrelsomeness of his courage; his credulity of his open faith; his vanity of his pride; and his bluntness of his sincerity. They are all the redundancies of a rich and liberal character. He is like his own oak; rough without, but sound and solid within; whose bark abounds with excrescences in proportion to the growth and grandeur of the timber; and whose branches make a fearful groaning and murmuring in the least storm, from their very magnitude and luxuriance. There is something, too, in the appearance of his old family mansion, that is extremely poetical and picturesque; and as long as it can be rendered comfortably habitable, I should almost tremble to see it meddled with during the present conflict of tastes and opinions. Some of his advisors are no doubt good architects that might be of service; but many I fear are mere levellers, who when they had once got to work with their mattocks on the venerable edifice, would never stop until they had brought it to the ground, and perhaps buried themselves among the ruins. All that I wish is, that John's present troubles may teach him more prudence in future. That he may cease to distress his mind about other people's affairs; that he may give up the fruitless attempt to promote the good of his neighbours, and the peace and happiness of the world, by dint of the cudgel; that he may remain quietly at home; gradually get his house into repair; cultivate his rich estate according to his fancy; husband his income, if he thinks proper; bring his unruly children into order if he can; renew the jovial scenes of ancient prosperity, and long enjoy, on his paternal lands, a green, an honourable, and a merry old age.

The Pride of the Village

May no wolf howle; no screech owle stir
A wing about thy sepulchre!
No boysterous winds or stormes come hither,
To starve or wither
Thy soft sweet earth! but like a spring
Love keep it ever flourishing.

Herrick

IN THE COURSE of an excursion through one of the remote counties of England, I had struck into one of those cross roads that lead through the more secluded parts of the country, and stopped one afternoon at a village, the situation of which was beautifully rural and retired. There was an air of primitive simplicity about its inhabitants, not to be found in the villages which lie on the great coach roads. I determined to pass the night there, and having taken an early dinner, strolled out to enjoy the neighbouring scenery.

My ramble, as is usually the case with travellers, soon led me to the church, which stood at a little distance from the village. Indeed, it was an object of some curiosity, its old tower being completely overrun with ivy, so that only here and there a jutting buttress, an angle of grey wall, or a fantastically carved ornament, peered through the verdant covering. It was a lovely evening. The early part of the day had been dark and showery, but in the afternoon it had cleared up, and though sullen clouds still hung over head, yet there was a broad tract of golden sky in the west, from which the setting sun gleamed through the dripping leaves, and lit up all nature into a melancholy smile. It seemed like the parting hour of a good christian, smiling on the sins and sorrows of the world, and giving, in the serenity of his decline, an assurance that he will rise again in glory.

I had seated myself on a half sunken tombstone, and was musing, as one is apt to do at this sober thoughted hour, on past scenes, and early friends—on those who were distant, and those who were dead—and indulging in that kind of melancholy fancying, which has in it something sweeter even than pleasure. Every now and then, the stroke of a bell from the neighbouring tower fell on my ear; its tones were in unison with the scene, and instead of jarring, chimed in with my feelings, and it was some time before I recollected, that it must be tolling the knell of some new tenant of the tomb.

Presently I saw a funeral train moving across the village green; it wound slowly along a lane, was lost, and reappeared through the breaks of the hedges, until it passed the place where I was sitting. The pall was supported by young girls, dressed in white, and another, about the age of seventeen, walked before, bearing a chaplet of white flowers; a token that the deceased was a young and unmarried female. The corpse was followed by the parents. They were a venerable couple of the better order of peasantry. The father seemed to repress his feelings; but his fixed eye, contracted brow, and deeply furrowed face, showed the struggle that was passing within. His wife hung on his arm, and wept aloud with the convulsive bursts of a mother's sorrow.

I followed the funeral into the church. The bier was placed in the centre aisle, and the chaplet of white flowers, with a pair of white gloves, were hung over the seat which the deceased had occupied.

Every one knows the soul subduing pathos of the funeral service; for who is so fortunate as never to have followed some one he has loved to the tomb; but when performed over the remains of innocence and beauty, thus laid low in the bloom of existence—what can be more affecting? At that simple, but most solemn consignment of the body to the grave—"Earth to earth—ashes to ashes—dust to dust!" the tears of the youthful companions of the deceased flowed unrestrained. The father still seemed to struggle with his feelings, and to comfort himself with the assurance, that the dead are blessed which die in the Lord; but the mother only thought of her child as a flower of the field, cut down and withered in the midst of its sweetness; she was like Rachel, "mourning over her children, and would not be comforted."

On returning to the inn, I learnt the whole story of the deceased. It was a simple one, and such as has often been told. She had been the beauty and pride of the village. Her father had once been an opulent farmer, but was reduced in circumstances. This was an only child, and brought up entirely at home, in the simplicity of rural life. She had been the pupil of the village pastor, the favourite lamb of his little flock. The good man watched over her education with paternal care; it was limited, and suitable to the sphere in which she was to move, for he only sought to make her an ornament to her station in life, not to raise her above it. The tenderness and indulgence of her parents, and the exemption from all ordinary occupations, had fostered a natural grace and delicacy of character, that accorded with the fragile loveliness of her form. She appeared like some tender plant of the garden, blooming accidentally amid the hardier natives of the fields.

The superiority of her charms was felt and acknowledged by her companions, but without envy, for it was surpassed by the unassuming gentleness and winning kindness of her manners. It might be truly said of her,

> "This is the prettiest low-born lass, that ever
> Ran on the green-sward: nothing she does or seems,
> But smacks of something greater than herself;
> Too noble for this place."

The village was one of those sequestered spots, which still retain some vestiges of old English customs. It had its rural festivals and holyday pastimes, and still kept up some faint observance of the once popular rites of May. These, indeed, had been promoted by its present pastor; who was a lover of old customs, and one of those simple Christians that think their mission fulfilled by promoting joy on earth and good will among mankind. Under his auspices the May pole stood from year to year in the centre of the village green; on May day it was decorated with garlands and streamers; and a queen or lady of the May was appointed, as in former times, to preside at the sports, and distribute the prizes and rewards. The picturesque situation of the village, and the fancifulness of its rustic fetes would often attract the notice of casual visitors. Among these, on one May day, was a young officer, whose regiment had been recently quartered in the neighbourhood. He was charmed with the native taste that pervaded this village pageant; but, above all, with the dawning loveliness of the queen of May. It was the village favourite, who was crowned with flowers, and blushing and smiling in all the beautiful confusion of girlish diffidence and delight. The artlessness of rural habits enabled him readily to make her acquaintance; he gradually won his way into her intimacy; and paid his court to her in that unthinking way in which young officers are too apt to trifle with rustic simplicity.

There was nothing in his advances to startle or alarm. He never even talked of love; but there are modes of making it, more eloquent than language, and which convey it subtilely and irresistibly to the heart. The beam of the eye, the tone of voice, the thousand tendernesses which emanate from every word, and look, and action—these form the true eloquence of love, and can always be felt and understood, but never described. Can we wonder that they should readily win a heart, young, guileless, and susceptible? As to her, she loved almost unconsciously; she scarcely inquired what was the growing passion that was absorbing every thought and feeling, or what were to be its consequences. She, indeed, looked not to the future. When present, his looks and words occupied her whole attention; when absent, she thought but of what had passed at their recent interview. She would wander with him through the green lanes and rural scenes of the vicinity. He taught her to see new beauties in nature: he talked in the language of polite and cultivated life, and breathed into her ear the witcheries of romance and poetry.

Perhaps there could not have been a passion, between the sexes, more pure than this innocent girl's. The gallant figure of her youthful admirer, and the splendour of his military attire, might at first have charmed her eye; but it was not these that had captivated her heart. Her attachment had something in it of idolatry. She looked up to him as to a being of a superior order. She felt in his society the enthusiasm of a mind naturally delicate and poetical, and now first awakened to a keen perception of the beautiful and grand. Of the sordid distinctions of rank and fortune, she thought nothing; it was the difference of intellect, of demeanor, of manners, from those of the rustic society to which she had been accustomed, that elevated him in her opinion. She would listen to him with charmed ear and downcast look of mute delight, and her cheek would mantle with enthusiasm; or if ever she ventured a shy glance of timid admiration, it was as quickly withdrawn, and she would sigh and blush at the idea of her comparative unworthiness.

Her lover was equally impassioned; but his passion was mingled with feelings of a coarser nature. He had begun the connexion in levity; for he had often heard his brother officers boast of their village conquests, and thought some triumph of the kind necessary to his reputation as a man of spirit. But he was too full of youthful fervour. His heart had not yet been rendered sufficiently cold and selfish by a wandering and a dissipated life: it caught fire from the very flame it sought to kindle; and before he was aware of the nature of his situation, he became really in love.

What was he to do? There were the old obstacles which so incessantly occur in these heedless attachments. His rank in life—the prejudices of titled connexions—his dependance upon a proud and unyielding father—all forbad him to think of matrimony:—but when he looked down upon this innocent being, so tender and confiding, there was a purity in her manners, a blamelessness in her life, and a beseeching modesty in her looks, that awed down every licentious feeling. In vain did he try to fortify himself, by a thousand heartless examples of men of fashion, and to chill the glow of generous sentiment, with that cold derisive levity with which he had heard them talk of female virtue; whenever he came into her presence, she was still surrounded by that mysterious, but impassive charm of virgin purity, in whose hallowed sphere no guilty thought can live.

The sudden arrival of orders for the regiment to repair to the continent, completed the confusion of his mind. He remained for a short time in a state of the most painful irresolution; he hesitated to communicate the tidings, until the day for marching was at hand; when he gave her the intelligence in the course of an evening ramble.

The idea of parting had never before occurred to her. It broke in at once upon her dream of felicity; she looked upon it as a sudden and insurmountable evil, and wept with the guileless simplicity of a child. He drew her to his bosom, and kissed the tears from her soft cheek, nor did he meet with a repulse, for there are moments of mingled sorrow and tenderness, which hallow the caresses of affection. He was naturally impetuous, and the sight of beauty apparently yielding in his arms, the confidence of his power over her, and the dread of losing her forever, all conspired to overwhelm his better feelings—he ventured to propose that she should leave her home, and be the companion of his fortunes.

He was quite a novice in seduction, and blushed and faltered at his own baseness; but so innocent of mind was his intended victim, that she was at first at a loss to comprehend his meaning;—and why she should leave her native village, and the humble roof of her parents. When at last the nature of his proposals flashed upon her pure mind, the effect was withering. She did not weep—she did not break forth into reproach—she said not a word—but she shrunk back aghast as from a viper, gave him a look of anguish that pierced to his very soul, and clasping her hands in agony, fled, as if for refuge, to her father's cottage.

The officer retired, confounded, humiliated, and repentant. It is uncertain what might have been the result of the conflict of his feelings, had not his thoughts been diverted by the bustle of departure. New scenes, new pleasures, and new companions, soon dissipated his self reproach, and stifled his tenderness. Yet, amidst the stir of camps, the revelries of garrisons, the array of armies, and even the din of battles, his thoughts would sometimes steal back to the scene of rural quiet and village simplicity—the white cottage—the footpath along the silver brook and up the hawthorn hedge, and the little village maid loitering along it, leaning on his arm, and listening to him with eyes beaming with unconscious affection.

The shock which the poor girl had received, in the destruction of all her ideal world, had indeed been cruel. Faintings and hystericks had at first shaken her tender frame, and were succeeded by a settled and pining melancholy. She had beheld from her window the march of the departing troops. She had seen her faithless lover borne off, as if in triumph, amidst the sound of drum and trumpet, and the pomp of arms. She strained a last aching gaze after him, as the morning sun glittered about his figure, and his plume waved in the breeze: he passed away like a bright vision from her sight, and left her all in darkness.

It would be trite to dwell on the particulars of her after story. It was, like other tales of love, melancholy. She avoided society, and wandered out alone in the walks she had most frequented with her lover. She sought, like the stricken deer, to weep in silence and loneliness, and brood over the barbed sorrow that rankled in her soul. Sometimes she would be seen late of an evening sitting in the porch of the village church; and the milkmaids, returning from the fields, would now and then overhear her singing some plaintive ditty in the hawthorn walk. She became fervent in her devotions at church, and as the old people saw her approach, so wasted away, yet with a hectic bloom, and that hallowed air which melancholy diffuses round the form, they would make way for her, as for something spiritual, and, looking after her, would shake their heads in gloomy foreboding.

She felt a conviction that she was hastening to the tomb, but looked forward to it as a place of rest. The silver cord that had bound her to existence was loosed, and there seemed to be no more pleasure under the sun. If ever her gentle bosom had entertained resentment against her lover, it was extinguished. She was incapable of angry passions, and in a moment of saddened tenderness, she penned him a farewell letter. It was couched in the simplest language; but touching from its very simplicity. She told him that she was dying, and did not conceal from him that his conduct was the cause. She even depicted the sufferings which she had experienced; but concluded with saying, that she could not die in peace, until she had sent him her forgiveness and her blessing.

By degrees her strength declined, and she could no longer leave the cottage. She could only totter to the window, where, propped up in her chair, it was her enjoyment to sit all day and look out upon the landscape. Still she uttered no complaint, nor imparted to any one the malady that was preying on her heart. She never even mentioned her lover's name; but would lay her head on her mother's bosom and weep in silence. Her poor parents hung, in mute anxiety, over this fading blossom of their hopes, still flattering themselves that it might again revive to freshness, and that the bright unearthly bloom which sometimes flushed her cheek might be the promise of returning health.

In this way she was seated between them one Sunday afternoon; her hands were clasped in theirs, the lattice was thrown open, and the soft air that stole in, brought with it the fragrance of the clustering honeysuckle, which her own hands had trained round the window.

Her father had just been reading a chapter in the bible; it spoke of the vanity of worldly things, and of the joys of heaven; it seemed to have diffused comfort and serenity through her bosom. Her eye was fixed on the distant village church—the bell had tolled for the evening service—the last villager was lagging into the porch—and every thing had sunk into that hallowed stillness peculiar to the day of rest. Her parents were gazing on her with yearning hearts. Sickness and sorrow, which pass so roughly over some faces, had given to hers the expression of a seraph's. A tear trembled in her soft blue eye.—Was she thinking of her faithless lover?—or were her thoughts wandering to that distant church yard, into whose bosom she might soon be gathered?

Suddenly the clang of hoofs was heard—a horseman gallopped to the cottage—he dismounted before the window—the poor girl gave a faint exclamation, and sunk back in her chair:—it was her repentant lover! He rushed into the house, and flew to clasp her to his bosom; but her wasted form—her death like countenance—so wan, yet so lovely in its desolation, smote him to the soul, and he threw himself in an agony at her feet. She was too faint to rise—she attempted to extend her trembling hand—her lips moved as if she spoke, but no word was articulated—she looked down upon him with a smile of unutterable tenderness, and closed her eyes forever.

Such are the particulars which I gathered of this village story. They are but scanty, and I am conscious have little novelty to recommend them. In the present rage also for strange incident and high seasoned narrative, they may appear trite and insignificant, but they interested me strongly at the time; and, taken in connexion with the affecting ceremony which I had just witnessed, left a deeper impression on my mind than many circumstances of a more striking nature. I have passed through the place since, and visited the church again from a better motive than mere curiosity. It was a wintry evening; the trees were stripped of their foliage; the church yard looked naked and mournful, and the wind rustled coldly through the dry grass. Evergreens, however, had been planted about the grave of the village favourite, and osiers were bent over it to keep the turf uninjured.

The church door was open, and I stepped in. There hung the chaplet of flowers and the gloves, as on the day of the funeral: the flowers were withered, it is true, but care seemed to have been taken that no dust should soil their whiteness. I have seen many monuments, where art has exhausted its powers to awaken the sympathy of the spectator, but I have met with none that spoke more touchingly to my heart, than this simple, but delicate memento of departed innocence.

The Angler

This day dame Nature seemed in love,
The lusty sap began to move,
Fresh juice did stir th' embracing vines,
And birds had drawn their valentines.
The jealous trout that low did lie,
Rose at a well dissembled flie,
There stood my friend, with patient skill,
Attending of his trembling quill.
                                    Sir H. Wotton

IT IS SAID that many an unlucky urchin is induced to run away from his family, and betake himself to a seafaring life, from reading the history of Robinson Crusoe; and I suspect that, in like manner, many of those worthy gentlemen, who are given to haunt the sides of pastoral streams with angle rods in hand, may trace the origin of their passion to the seductive pages of honest Izaak Walton. I recollect studying his "Complete Angler" several years since, in company with a knot of friends in America, and moreover that we were all completely bitten with the angling mania. It was early in the year; but as soon as the weather was auspicious, and that the spring began to melt into the verge of summer, we took rod in hand and sallied into the country, as stark mad as was ever Don Quixote from reading books of chivalry.

One of our party had equalled the Don in the fullness of his equipments; being attired cap-a-pie for the enterprize. He wore a broad skirted fustian coat, perplexed with half a hundred pockets; a pair of stout shoes, and leathern gaiters; a basket slung on one side for fish; a patent rod; a landing net, and a score of other inconveniencies, only to be found in the true angler's armoury. Thus harnessed for the field, he was as great a matter of stare and wonderment among the country folk, who had never seen a regular angler, as was the steel clad hero of La Mancha among the goatherds of the Sierra Morena.

Our first essay was along a mountain brook, among the highlands of the Hudson; a most unfortunate place for the execution of those piscatory tactics which had been invented along the velvet margins of quiet English rivulets. It was one of those wild streams that lavish, among our romantic solitudes, unheeded beauties, enough to fill the sketch book of a hunter of the picturesque. Sometimes it would leap down rocky shelves, making small cascades, over which the trees threw their broad balancing sprays, and long nameless weeds hung in fringes from the impending banks, dripping with diamond drops. Sometimes it would brawl and fret along a ravine in the matted shade of a forest, filling it with murmurs; and after this termagant career, would steal forth into open day with the most placid demure face imaginable; as I have seen some pestilent shrew of a housewife, after filling her home with uproar and ill humour, come dimpling out of doors, swimming and curtseying, and smiling upon all the world.

How smoothly would this vagrant brook glide, at such times, through some bosom of green meadow land among the mountains; where the quiet was only interrupted by the occasional tinkling of a bell from the lazy cattle among the clover, or the sound of a woodcutter's axe from the neighbouring forest.

For my part, I was always a bungler at all kinds of sport that required either patience or adroitness, and had not angled above half an hour, before I had completely "satisfied the sentiment," and convinced myself of the truth of Izaak Walton's opinion, that angling is something like poetry—a man must be born to it. I hooked myself instead of the fish; tangled my line in every tree; lost my bait; broke my rod; until I gave up the attempt in despair, and passed the day under the trees, reading old Izaak; satisfied that it was his fascinating vein of honest simplicity and rural feeling that had bewitched me, and not the passion for angling. My companions, however, were more persevering in their delusion. I have them at this moment before my eyes, stealing along the border of the brook, where it lay open to the day, or was merely fringed by shrubs and bushes. I see the bittern rising with hollow scream as they break in upon his rarely invaded haunt; the kingfisher watching them suspiciously from his dry tree that overhangs the deep black mill pond, in the gorge of the hills; the tortoise letting himself slip sideways from off the stone or log on which he is sunning himself; and the panic struck frog plumping in headlong as they approach, and spreading an alarm throughout the watery world around.

I recollect also, that, after toiling and watching and creeping about for the greater part of a day, with scarcely any success, in spite of all our admirable apparatus, a lubberly country urchin came down from the hills with a rod made from a branch of a tree; a few yards of twine; and, as heaven shall help me! I believe a crooked pin for a hook, baited with a vile earth worm—and in half an hour caught more fish than we had nibbles throughout the day!

But above all, I recollect the "good, honest, wholesome, hungry" repast, which we made under a beech tree just by a spring of pure sweet water that stole out of the side of a hill; and how, when it was over, one of the party read old Izaak Walton's scene with the milkmaid, while I lay on the grass and built castles in a bright pile of clouds, until I fell asleep. All this may appear like mere egotism, yet I cannot refrain from uttering these recollections, which are passing like a strain of music over my mind and have been called up by an agreeable scene which I witnessed not long since.

In a morning's stroll along the banks of the Alun, a beautiful little stream which flows down from the Welsh hills and throws itself into the Dee, my attention was attracted to a group seated on the margin. On approaching, I found it to consist of a veteran angler and two rustic disciples. The former was an old fellow with a wooden leg, with clothes very much but very carefully patched, betokening poverty, honestly come by, and decently maintained. His face bore the marks of former storms, but present fair weather; its furrows had been worn into an habitual smile; his iron grey locks hung about his ears, and he had altogether the good humoured air of a constitutional philosopher, who was disposed to take the world as it went. One of his companions was a ragged wight, with the skulking look of an arrant poacher, and I'll warrant could find his way to any gentleman's fish pond in the neighbourhood in the darkest night. The other was a tall, awkward, country lad, with a lounging gait, and apparently somewhat of a rustic beau. The old man was busy in examining the maw of a trout which he had just killed, to discover by its contents what insects were seasonable for bait; and was lecturing on the subject to his companions, who appeared to listen with infinite deference. I have a kind feeling towards all "brothers of the angle," ever since I read Izaak Walton. They are men, he affirms, of a "mild, sweet and peaceable spirit"; and my esteem for them has been encreased since I met with an old "Tretyse of fishing with the Angle," in which are set forth many of the maxims of their inoffensive fraternity. "Take good hede," sayth this honest little tretyse, "that in going about your disportes ye open no man's gates but that ye shet them again. Also ye shall not use this forsayd crafti disport for no covetousness to the encreasing and sparing of your money only, but principally for your solace and to cause the helth of your body and specyally of your soule."*

I thought that I could perceive in the veteran angler before me an exemplification of what I had read; and there was a chearful contentedness in his looks that quite drew me towards him. I could not but remark the gallant manner in which he stumped from one part of the brook to another; waving his rod in the air, to keep the line from dragging on the ground, or catching among the bushes; and the adroitness with which he would throw his fly to any particular place; sometimes skimming it lightly along a little rapid; sometimes casting it into one of those dark holes made by a twisted root or overhanging bank, in which the large trout are apt to lurk. In the meanwhile he was giving instructions to his two disciples; showing them the manner in which they should handle their rods, fix their flies, and play them along the surface of the stream. The scene brought to my mind the instructions of the sage Piscator to his scholar. The country around was of that pastoral kind which Walton is fond of describing. It

---

*From this same treatise, it would appear that angling is a more industrious and devout employment than it is generally considered.—"For when ye purpose to go on your disportes in fishynge ye will not desyre greatlye many persons with you, which might let you of your game. And that ye may serve God devoutly in sayinge effectually your customable prayers. And thus doying, ye shall eschew and also avoyde many vices, as ydelnes, which is principall cause to induce man to many other vices, as it is right well known."

was a part of the great plain of Cheshire, close by the beautiful vale of Gessford, and just where the inferior Welsh hills begin to swell up from among fresh sweet smelling meadows. The day, too, like that recorded in his work, was mild and sunshiny; with now and then a soft dropping shower, that sowed the whole earth with diamonds.

I soon fell into conversation with the old angler, and was so much entertained, that, under pretext of receiving instructions in his art, I kept company with him almost the whole day; wandering along the banks of the stream, and listening to his talk. He was very communicative, having all the easy garrulity of cheerful old age; and I fancy was a little flattered by having an opportunity of displaying his piscatory lore; for who does not like now and then to play the sage?

He had been much of a rambler in his day; and had passed some years of his youth in America, particularly in Savannah, where he had entered into trade and had been ruined by the indiscretion of a partner. He had afterwards experienced many ups and downs in life, until he got into the navy, where his leg was carried away by a cannon ball, at the battle of Camperdown. This was the only stroke of real good fortune he had ever experienced, for it got him a pension, which, together with some small paternal property, brought him in a revenue of nearly forty pounds. On this he retired to his native village, where he lived quietly and independently, and devoted the remainder of his life to the "noble art of angling."

I found that he had read Izaak Walton attentively, and he seemed to have imbibed all his simple frankness and prevalent good humour. Though he had been sorely buffeted about the world, he was satisfied that the world, in itself, was good and beautiful. Though he had been as roughly used in different countries as a poor sheep, that is fleeced by every hedge and thicket, yet he spoke of every nation with candour and kindness, appearing to look only on the good side of things; and above all, he was almost the only man I had ever met with, who had been an unfortunate adventurer in America, and had honesty and magnanimity enough, to take the fault to his own door, and not to curse the country. The lad that was receiving his instructions I learnt was the son and heir apparent of a fat old widow who kept the village inn, and of course a youth of some expectation, and much courted by the idle, gentleman like personages of the place. In taking him under his care, therefore, the old man had probably an eye to a privileged corner in the tap room, and an occasional cup of cheerful ale free of expense.

There is certainly something in angling, if we could forget, which anglers are apt to do, the cruelties and tortures inflicted on worms and insects, that tends to produce a gentleness of spirit, and a pure serenity of mind. As the English are methodical even in their recreations, and are the most scientific of sportsmen, it has been reduced among them to perfect rule and system. Indeed it is an amusement peculiarly adapted to the mild and highly cultivated scenery of England, where every roughness has been softened away from the landscape. It is delightful to saunter along those limpid streams which wander, like veins of silver, through the bosom of this beautiful country; leading one through a diversity of small home scenery; sometimes winding through ornamented grounds; sometimes brimming along through rich pasturage, where the fresh green is mingled with sweet smelling flowers; sometimes venturing in sight of villages and hamlets; and then running capriciously away into shady retirements. The sweetness and serenity of nature, and the quiet watchfulness of the sport, gradually bring on pleasant fits of musing; which are now and then agreeably interrupted by the song of a bird; the distant whistle of the pheasant; or perhaps the vagary of some fish, leaping out of the still water, and skimming transiently about its glassy surface. "When I would beget content," says Izaak Walton, "and increase confidence in the power and wisdom and providence of Almighty God, I will walk the meadows by some gliding stream, and there contemplate the lilies that take no care, and those very many other little living creatures that are not only created, but fed (man knows not how) by the goodness of the God of nature, and therefore trust in him."

I cannot forbear to give another quotation from one of those ancient champions of angling which breathes the same innocent and happy spirit:

Let me live harmlessly, and near the brink
  Of Trent or Avon have a dwelling-place;
Where I may see my quill, or cork, down sink,
  With eager bite of pike, or bleak, or dace;
And on the world and my creator think:
  Whilst some men strive ill-gotten goods t' embrace;
And others spend their time in base excess
  Of wine, or worse, in war or wantonness.

Let them that will, these pastimes still pursue,
  And on such pleasing fancies feed their fill;
So I the fields and meadows green may view
  And daily by fresh rivers walk at will,
Among the daisies and the violets blue,
  Red hyacinth and yellow daffodil.*

On parting with the old angler I inquired after his place of
abode, and happening to be in the neighbourhood of the village a few evenings afterwards, I had the curiosity to seek him
out. I found him living in a small cottage, containing only
one room, but a perfect curiosity in its method and arrangement. It was on the skirts of the village, on a green bank, a
little back from the road, with a small garden in front, stocked
with kitchen herbs, and adorned with a few flowers. The
whole front of the cottage was overrun with a honeysuckle.
On the top was a ship for a weathercock. The interior was
fitted up in a truly nautical style, his ideas of comfort and
convenience having been acquired on the birth deck of a man
of war. A hammock was slung from the ceiling, which, in the
day time was lashed up so as to take but little room. From
the centre of the chamber hung a model of a ship of his own
workmanship. Two or three chairs, a table, and a large sea
chest, formed the principal moveables. About the walls were
stuck up naval ballads, such as Admiral Hosier's Ghost, All
in the Downs, and Tom Bowling, intermingled with pictures
of sea fights, among which the battle of Camperdown held a
distinguished place. The mantle piece was decorated with sea
shells; over which hung a quadrant, flanked by two woodcuts
of most bitter looking naval commanders. His implements for

*J. Davors.

angling were carefully disposed on nails and hooks about the room. On a shelf was arranged his library, containing a work on angling, much worn; a bible covered with canvass; an odd volume or two of voyages; a nautical almanack; and a book of songs.

His family consisted of a large black cat with one eye, and a parrot which he had caught and tamed, and educated himself, in the course of one of his voyages; and which uttered a variety of sea phrases with the hoarse brattling tone of a veteran boatswain. The establishment reminded me of that of the renowned Robinson Crusoe;—it was kept in neat order, every thing being "stowed away" with the regularity of a ship of war; and he informed me that he "scowred the deck every morning, and swept it between meals."

I found him seated on a bench before the door, smoking his pipe in the soft evening sunshine. His cat was purring soberly on the threshold, and his parrot describing some strange evolutions in an iron ring that swung in the centre of his cage. He had been angling all day, and gave me a history of his sport with as much minuteness as a general would talk over a campaign; being particularly animated in relating the manner in which he had taken a large trout, which had completely tasked all his skill and wariness, and which he had sent as a trophy to mine hostess of the Inn.

How comforting it is to see a cheerful and contented old age; and to behold a poor fellow, like this, after being tempest tost through life, safely moored in a snug and quiet harbour in the evening of his days. His happiness, however, sprung from within himself, and was independent of external circumstances; for he had that inexhaustible good nature, which is the most precious gift of heaven; spreading itself like oil over the troubled sea of thought, and keeping the mind smooth and equable in the roughest weather.

On inquiring further about him, I learnt that he was a universal favourite in the village, and the oracle of the tap room; where he delighted the rustics with his songs, and, like Sindbad, astonished them with his stories of strange lands, and shipwrecks, and sea fights. He was much noticed too by gentlemen sportsmen of the neighbourhood; had taught several of them the art of angling; and was a privileged visitor to their kitchens. The whole tenor of his life was quiet and in-offensive, being principally passed about the neighbouring streams when the weather and season were favourable; at other times he employed himself at home, preparing his fishing tackle for the next campaign, or manufacturing rods, nets, and flies for his patrons and pupils among the gentry.

He was a regular attendant at church on Sundays, though he generally fell asleep during the sermon. He had made it his particular request that when he died he should be buried in a green spot, which he could see from his seat in church, and which he had marked out ever since he was a boy, and had thought of when far from home on the raging sea, in danger of being food for the fishes—it was the spot where his father and mother had been buried.

I have done, for I fear that my reader is growing weary; but I could not refrain from drawing the picture of this worthy "brother of the angle;" who has made me more than ever in love with the theory, though I fear I shall never be adroit in the practice of his art: and I will conclude this rambling sketch, in the words of honest Izaak Walton, by craving the blessing of St. Peter's master upon my reader, "and upon all that are true lovers of virtue; and dare trust in his providence; and be quiet; and go a angling."

The Legend of Sleepy Hollow

(Found among the Papers
of the late Diedrich Knickerbocker)

A pleasing land of drowsy head it was,
Of dreams that wave before the half-shut eye;
And of gay castles in the clouds that pass,
Forever flushing round a summer sky.

Castle of Indolence

IN THE BOSOM of one of those spacious coves which indent the eastern shore of the Hudson, at that broad expansion of the river denominated by the ancient Dutch navigators the Tappaan Zee, and where they always prudently shortened sail, and implored the protection of St. Nicholas when they crossed, there lies a small market town or rural port, which by some is called Greensburgh, but which is more generally and properly known by the name of Tarry Town. This name was given, we are told, in former days, by the good housewives of the adjacent country, from the inveterate propensity of their husbands to linger about the village tavern on market days. Be that as it may, I do not vouch for the fact, but merely advert to it, for the sake of being precise and authentic. Not far from this village, perhaps about two miles, there is a little valley, or rather lap of land among high hills, which is one of the quietest places in the whole world. A small brook glides through it, with just murmur enough to lull one to repose, and the occasional whistle of a quail, or tapping of a woodpecker, is almost the only sound that ever breaks in upon the uniform tranquillity.

I recollect that when a stripling, my first exploit in squirrel shooting was in a grove of tall walnut trees that shades one side of the valley. I had wandered into it at noon time, when all nature is peculiarly quiet, and was startled by the roar of my own gun, as it broke the sabbath stillness around, and was prolonged and reverberated by the angry echoes. If ever I should wish for a retreat, whither I might steal from the world and its distractions, and dream quietly away the remnant of a troubled life, I know of none more promising than this little valley.

From the listless repose of the place, and the peculiar character of its inhabitants, who are descendants from the original Dutch settlers, this sequestered glen has long been known by the name of SLEEPY HOLLOW, and its rustic lads are called the Sleepy Hollow Boys throughout all the neighbouring country. A drowsy, dreamy influence seems to hang over the land, and to pervade the very atmosphere. Some say that the place was bewitched by a high German doctor during the early days of the settlement; others, that an old Indian chief, the prophet or wizard of his tribe, held his powwows there before the country was discovered by Master Hendrick Hudson. Certain it is, the place still continues under the sway of some witching power, that holds a spell over the minds of the good people, causing them to walk in a continual reverie. They are given to all kinds of marvellous beliefs; are subject to trances and visions, and frequently see strange sights, and hear music and voices in the air. The whole neighbourhood abounds with local tales, haunted spots, and twilight superstitions; stars shoot and meteors glare oftener across the valley than in any other part of the country, and the night mare, with her whole nine fold, seems to make it the favourite scene of her gambols.

The dominant spirit, however, that haunts this enchanted region, and seems to be commander in chief of all the powers of the air, is the apparition of a figure on horseback without a head. It is said by some to be the ghost of a Hessian trooper, whose head had been carried away by a cannon ball, in some nameless battle during the revolutionary war, and who is ever and anon seen by the country folk, hurrying along in the gloom of night, as if on the wings of the wind. His haunts are not confined to the valley, but extend at times to the adjacent roads, and especially to the vicinity of a church at no great distance. Indeed, certain of the most authentic historians of those parts, who have been careful in collecting and collating the floating facts concerning this spectre, allege, that the body of the trooper having been buried in the church yard, the ghost rides forth to the scene of battle in nightly quest of his head, and that the rushing speed with which he sometimes passes along the hollow, like a midnight blast, is owing to his being belated, and in a hurry to get back to the church yard before day break.

Such is the general purport of this legendary superstition, which has furnished materials for many a wild story in that region of shadows; and the spectre is known, at all the country firesides, by the name of The Headless Horseman of Sleepy Hollow.

It is remarkable, that the visionary propensity I have mentioned is not confined to the native inhabitants of the valley, but is unconsciously imbibed by every one who resides there for a time. However wide awake they may have been before they entered that sleepy region, they are sure, in a little time, to inhale the witching influence of the air, and begin to grow imaginative—to dream dreams, and see apparitions.

I mention this peaceful spot with all possible laud; for it is in such little retired Dutch valleys, found here and there embosomed in the great state of New York, that population, manners, and customs, remain fixed, while the great torrent of migration and improvement, which is making such incessant changes in other parts of this restless country, sweeps by them unobserved. They are like those little nooks of still water, which border a rapid stream, where we may see the straw and bubble riding quietly at anchor, or slowly revolving in their mimic harbour, undisturbed by the rush of the passing current. Though many years have elapsed since I trod the drowsy shades of Sleepy Hollow, yet I question whether I should not still find the same trees and the same families vegetating in its sheltered bosom.

In this by place of nature there abode, in a remote period of American history, that is to say, some thirty years since, a worthy wight of the name of Ichabod Crane, who sojourned, or, as he expressed it, "tarried," in Sleepy Hollow, for the purpose of instructing the children of the vicinity. He was a native of Connecticut, a state which supplies the Union with pioneers for the mind as well as for the forest, and sends forth yearly its legions of frontier woodmen and country schoolmasters. The cognomen of Crane was not inapplicable to his person. He was tall, but exceedingly lank, with narrow shoulders, long arms and legs, hands that dangled a mile out of his sleeves, feet that might have served for shovels, and his whole frame most loosely hung together. His head was small, and flat at top, with huge ears, large green glassy eyes, and a long snipe nose, so that it looked like a weathercock perched upon his spindle neck, to tell which way the wind blew. To see him striding along the profile of a hill on a windy day, with his clothes bagging and fluttering about him, one might have mistaken him for the genius of famine descending upon the earth, or some scarecrow eloped from a cornfield.

His school house was a low building of one large room, rudely constructed of logs; the windows partly glazed, and partly patched with leaves of old copy books. It was most ingeniously secured at vacant hours, by a withe twisted in the handle of the door, and stakes set against the window shutters; so that though a thief might get in with perfect ease, he would find some embarrassment in getting out; an idea most probably borrowed by the architect, Yost Van Houten, from the mystery of an eelpot. The school house stood in a rather lonely but pleasant situation, just at the foot of a woody hill, with a brook running close by, and a formidable birch tree growing at one end of it. From hence the low murmur of his pupils' voices conning over their lessons, might be heard of a drowsy summer's day, like the hum of a bee hive; interrupted now and then by the authoritative voice of the master, in the tone of menace or command, or peradventure, by the appalling sound of the birch, as he urged some tardy loiterer along the flowery path of knowledge. Truth to say, he was a conscientious man, and ever bore in mind the golden maxim, "spare the rod and spoil the child."—Ichabod Crane's scholars certainly were not spoiled.

I would not have it imagined, however, that he was one of those cruel potentates of the school, who joy in the smart of their subjects; on the contrary, he administered justice with discrimination rather than severity; taking the burthen off the backs of the weak, and laying it on those of the strong. Your mere puny stripling, that winced at the least flourish of the rod, was passed by with indulgence; but the claims of justice were satisfied, by inflicting a double portion on some little, tough, wrong headed, broad skirted Dutch urchin, who sulked and swelled and grew dogged and sullen beneath the birch. All this he called "doing his duty by their parents;" and he never inflicted a chastisement without following it by the assurance, so consolatory to the smarting urchin, that "he would remember it and thank him for it the longest day he had to live."

When school hours were over, he was even the companion and playmate of the larger boys; and on holyday afternoons would convoy some of the smaller ones home, who happened to have pretty sisters, or good housewives for mothers, noted for the comforts of the cupboard. Indeed, it behooved him to keep on good terms with his pupils. The revenue arising from his school was small, and would have been scarcely sufficient to furnish him with daily bread, for he was a huge feeder, and though lank, had the dilating powers of an Anaconda; but to help out his maintenance, he was, according to country custom in those parts, boarded and lodged at the houses of the farmers, whose children he instructed. With these he lived successively a week at a time, thus going the rounds of the neighbourhood, with all his worldly effects tied up in a cotton handkerchief.

That all this might not be too onerous on the purses of his rustic patrons, who are apt to consider the costs of schooling a grievous burthen, and schoolmasters as mere drones, he had various ways of rendering himself both useful and agreeable. He assisted the farmers occasionally in the lighter labours of their farms, helped to make hay, mended the fences, took the horses to water, drove the cows from pasture, and cut wood for the winter fire. He laid aside, too, all the dominant dignity and absolute sway, with which he lorded it in his little empire, the school, and became wonderfully gentle and ingratiating. He found favour in the eyes of the mothers, by petting the children, particularly the youngest, and like the lion bold, which whilome so magnanimously the lamb did hold, he would sit with a child on one knee, and rock a cradle with his foot, for whole hours together.

In addition to his other vocations, he was the singing master of the neighbourhood, and picked up many bright shillings by instructing the young folks in psalmody. It was a matter of no little vanity to him on Sundays, to take his station in front of the church gallery, with a band of chosen singers; where, in his own mind, he completely carried away the palm from the parson. Certain it is, his voice resounded far above all the rest of the congregation, and there are peculiar quavers still to be heard in that church, and which may even be heard half a mile off, quite to the opposite side of the mill pond, of a still Sunday morning, which are said to be legitimately descended from the nose of Ichabod Crane. Thus, by diverse little make shifts, in that ingenious way which is commonly denominated "by hook and by crook," the worthy pedagogue got on tolerably enough, and was thought, by all who understood nothing of the labour of headwork, to have a wonderfully easy life of it.

The schoolmaster is generally a man of some importance in the female circle of a rural neighbourhood, being considered a kind of idle gentleman like personage, of vastly superior taste and accomplishments to the rough country swains, and, indeed, inferior in learning only to the parson. His appearance, therefore, is apt to occasion some little stir at the tea table of a farm house, and the addition of a supernumerary dish of cakes or sweetmeats, or, peradventure, the parade of a silver tea pot. Our man of letters, therefore, was peculiarly happy in the smiles of all the country damsels. How he would figure among them in the church yard, between services on Sundays; gathering grapes for them from the wild vines that overrun the surrounding trees; reciting for their amusement all the epitaphs on the tombstones, or sauntering, with a whole bevy of them, along the banks of the adjacent mill pond; while the more bashful country bumpkins hung sheepishly back, envying his superior elegance and address.

From his half itinerant life, also, he was a kind of travelling gazette, carrying the whole budget of local gossip from house to house; so that his appearance was always greeted with satisfaction. He was, moreover, esteemed by the women as a man of great erudition, for he had read several books quite through, and was a perfect master of Cotton Mather's History of New England Witchcraft, in which, by the way, he most firmly and potently believed.

He was, in fact, an odd mixture of small shrewdness and simple credulity. His appetite for the marvellous, and his powers of digesting it, were equally extraordinary; and both had been increased by his residence in this spell bound region. No tale was too gross or monstrous for his capacious swallow. It was often his delight, after his school was dismissed of an afternoon, to stretch himself on the rich bed of clover, bordering the little brook that whimpered by his school house, and there con over old Mather's direful tales, until the gathering dusk of evening made the printed page a mere mist before his eyes. Then, as he wended his way, by swamp and stream and awful woodland, to the farm house where he happened to be quartered, every sound of nature, at that witching hour, fluttered his excited imagination: the moan of the whip-poor-will* from the hill side; the boding cry of the tree toad, that harbinger of storm; the dreary hooting of the screech owl; or the sudden rustling in the thicket, of birds frightened from their roost. The fire flies, too, which sparkled most vividly in the darkest places, now and then startled him, as one of uncommon brightness would stream across his path; and if, by chance, a huge blockhead of a beetle came winging his blundering flight against him, the poor varlet was ready to give up the ghost, with the idea that he was struck with a witch's token. His only resource on such occasions, either to drown thought, or drive away evil spirits, was to sing psalm tunes;—and the good people of Sleepy Hollow, as they sat by their doors of an evening, were often filled with awe, at hearing his nasal melody, "in linked sweetness long drawn out," floating from the distant hill, or along the dusky road.

Another of his sources of fearful pleasure was, to pass long winter evenings with the old Dutch wives, as they sat spinning by the fire, with a row of apples roasting and sputtering along the hearth, and listen to their marvellous tales of ghosts and goblins, and haunted fields and haunted brooks, and haunted bridges and haunted houses, and particularly of the headless horseman, or galloping Hessian of the Hollow, as they sometimes called him. He would delight them equally by his anecdotes of witchcraft, and of the direful omens and portentous sights and sounds in the air, which prevailed in the earlier times of Connecticut; and would frighten them wo-

*The whip-poor-will is a bird which is only heard at night. It receives its name from its note which is thought to resemble those words.

fully with speculations upon comets and shooting stars, and with the alarming fact that the world did absolutely turn round, and that they were half the time topsy-turvy!

But if there was a pleasure in all this, while snugly cuddling in the chimney corner of a chamber that was all of a ruddy glow from the crackling wood fire, and where, of course, no spectre dared to show its face, it was dearly purchased by the terrors of his subsequent walk homewards. What fearful shapes and shadows beset his path, amidst the dim and ghastly glare of a snowy night!—With what wistful look did he eye every trembling ray of light streaming across the waste fields from some distant window!—How often was he appalled by some shrub covered with snow, which like a sheeted spectre beset his very path!—How often did he shrink with curdling awe at the sound of his own steps on the frosty crust beneath his feet; and dread to look over his shoulder, lest he should behold some uncouth being tramping close behind him!—and how often was he thrown into complete dismay by some rushing blast, howling among the trees, in the idea that it was the gallopping Hessian on one of his nightly scourings.

All these, however, were mere terrors of the night, phantoms of the mind, that walk in darkness; and though he had seen many spectres in his time, and been more than once beset by Satan in diverse shapes, in his lonely perambulations, yet daylight put an end to all these evils; and he would have passed a pleasant life of it, in despite of the Devil and all his works, if his path had not been crossed by a being that causes more perplexity to mortal man, than ghosts, goblins, and the whole race of witches put together, and that was—a woman.

Among the musical disciples who assembled, one evening in each week, to receive his instructions in psalmody, was Katrina Van Tassel, the daughter and only child of a substantial Dutch farmer. She was a blooming lass of fresh eighteen; plump as a partridge; ripe and melting and rosy cheeked as one of her father's peaches, and universally famed, not merely for her beauty, but her vast expectations. She was withal a little of a coquette, as might be perceived even in her dress, which was a mixture of ancient and modern fashions, as most suited to set off her charms. She wore the ornaments of pure yellow gold, which her great great grandmother had brought over from Saardam; the tempting stomacher of the olden time, and withal a provokingly short petticoat, to display the prettiest foot and ankle in the country round.

Ichabod Crane had a soft and foolish heart toward the sex; and it is not to be wondered at, that so tempting a morsel soon found favour in his eyes, more especially after he had visited her in her paternal mansion. Old Baltus Van Tassel was a perfect picture of a thriving, contented, liberal hearted farmer. He seldom, it is true, sent either his eyes or his thoughts beyond the boundaries of his own farm; but within those every thing was snug, happy, and well conditioned. He was satisfied with his wealth, but not proud of it, and piqued himself upon the hearty abundance, rather than the style in which he lived. His strong hold was situated on the banks of the Hudson, in one of those green, sheltered, fertile nooks, in which the Dutch farmers are so fond of nestling. A great elm tree spread its broad branches over it, at the foot of which bubbled up a spring of the softest and sweetest water, in a little well, formed of a barrel, and then stole sparkling away through the grass, to a neighbouring brook, that babbled along among elders and dwarf willows. Hard by the farm house was a vast barn, that might have served for a church; every window and crevice of which seemed bursting forth with the treasures of the farm; the flail was busily resounding within it from morning to night; swallows and martins skimmed twittering about the eaves, and rows of pigeons, some with one eye turned up, as if watching the weather, some with their heads under their wings, or buried in their bosoms, and others, swelling, and cooing, and bowing about their dames, were enjoying the sunshine on the roof. Sleek unwieldy porkers were grunting in the repose and abundance of their pens, from whence sallied forth, now and then, troops of sucking pigs, as if to snuff the air. A stately squadron of snowy geese were riding in an adjoining pond, convoying whole fleets of ducks; regiments of turkeys were gobbling through the farm yard, and guinea fowls fretting about it like ill tempered housewives, with their peevish discontented cry. Before the barn door strutted the gallant cock, that pattern of a husband, a warrior, and a fine gentleman, clapping his burnished wings, and crowing in the pride and gladness of his heart—sometimes tearing up the earth with his feet, and then generously calling his ever hungry family of wives and children to enjoy the rich morsel which he had discovered.

The pedagogue's mouth watered, as he looked upon this sumptuous promise of luxurious winter fare. In his devouring mind's eye, he pictured to himself every roasting pig running about with a pudding in his belly, and an apple in his mouth; the pigeons were snugly put to bed in a comfortable pie, and tucked in with a coverlet of crust; the geese were swimming in their own gravy; and the ducks pairing cosily in dishes, like snug married couples, with a decent competency of onion sauce; in the porkers he saw carved out the future sleek side of bacon, and juicy relishing ham; not a turkey, but he beheld daintily trussed up, with its gizzard under its wing, and, per-adventure, a necklace of savoury sausages; and even bright chanticleer himself lay sprawling on his back, in a side dish, with uplifted claws, as if craving that quarter, which his chivalrous spirit disdained to ask while living.

As the enraptured Ichabod fancied all this, and as he rolled his great green eyes over the fat meadow lands, the rich fields of wheat, of rye, of buckwheat, and Indian corn, and the orchards burthened with ruddy fruit, which surrounded the warm tenement of Van Tassel, his heart yearned after the damsel who was to inherit these domains, and his imagination expanded with the idea, how they might be readily turned into cash, and the money invested in immense tracts of wild land, and shingle palaces in the wilderness. Nay, his busy fancy already realized his hopes, and presented to him the blooming Katrina, with a whole family of children, mounted on the top of a waggon loaded with household trumpery, with pots and kettles dangling beneath; and he beheld himself bestriding a pacing mare, with a colt at her heels, setting out for Kentucky, Tennessee, or the Lord knows where!

When he entered the house, the conquest of his heart was complete. It was one of those spacious farm houses, with high ridged, but lowly sloping roofs, built in the style handed down from the first Dutch settlers. The low, projecting eaves formed a piazza along the front, capable of being closed up in bad weather. Under this were hung flails, harness, various utensils of husbandry, and nets for fishing in the neighbouring river. Benches were built along the sides for summer use; and a great spinning wheel at one end, and a churn at the other, showed the various uses to which this important porch might be devoted. From this piazza the wondering Ichabod entered the hall, which formed the centre of the mansion, and the place of usual residence. Here, rows of resplendent pewter, ranged on a long dresser, dazzled his eyes. In one corner stood a huge bag of wool ready to be spun; in another a quantity of linsey-woolsey just from the loom; ears of Indian corn, and strings of dried apples and peaches, hung in gay festoons along the walls, mingled with the gaud of red peppers; and a door left ajar, gave him a peep into the best parlour, where the claw footed chairs, and dark mahogany tables, shone like mirrors; andirons, with their accompanying shovel and tongs, glistened from their covert of asparagus tops; mock oranges and conch shells decorated the mantlepiece; strings of various coloured birds' eggs were suspended above it; a great ostrich egg was hung from the centre of the room, and a corner cupboard, knowingly left open, displayed immense treasures of old silver and well mended china.

From the moment Ichabod laid his eyes upon these regions of delight, the peace of his mind was at an end, and his only study was how to gain the affections of the peerless daughter of Van Tassel. In this enterprize, however, he had more real difficulties than generally fell to the lot of a knight errant of yore, who seldom had any thing but giants, enchanters, fiery dragons, and such like easily conquered adversaries, to contend with; and had to make his way merely through gates of iron and brass, and walls of adamant, to the castle keep, where the lady of his heart was confined; all which he achieved as easily as a man would carve his way to the centre of a Christmas pie, and then the lady gave him her hand as a matter of course. Ichabod, on the contrary, had to win his way to the heart of a country coquette, beset with a labyrinth of whims and caprices, which were for ever presenting new difficulties and impediments, and he had to encounter a host of fearful adversaries of real flesh and blood, the numerous rustic admirers, who beset every portal to her heart, keeping a watchful and angry eye upon each other, but ready to fly out in the common cause against any new competitor.

Among these, the most formidable, was a burly, roaring, roystering blade, of the name of Abraham, or, according to the Dutch abbreviation, Brom Van Brunt, the hero of the country round, which rung with his feats of strength and hardihood. He was broad shouldered and double jointed, with short curly black hair, and a bluff, but not unpleasant countenance, having a mingled air of fun and arrogance. From his Herculean frame and great powers of limb, he had received the nick name of BROM BONES, by which he was universally known. He was famed for great knowledge and skill in horsemanship, being as dexterous on horseback as a Tartar. He was foremost at all races and cock fights, and with the ascendancy which bodily strength acquires in rustic life, was the umpire in all disputes, setting his hat on one side, and giving his decisions with an air and tone admitting of no gainsay or appeal. He was always ready for either a fight or a frolick; but had more mischief than ill will in his composition; and with all his overbearing roughness, there was a strong dash of waggish good humour at bottom. He had three or four boon companions, who regarded him as their model, and at the head of whom he scoured the country, attending every scene of feud or merriment for miles round. In cold weather he was distinguished by a fur cap, surmounted with a flaunting fox's tail, and when the folks at a country gathering descried this well known crest at a distance, whisking about among a squad of hard riders, they always stood by for a squall. Sometimes his crew would be heard dashing along past the farm houses at midnight, with whoop and halloo, like a troop of Don Cossacks, and the old dames, startled out of their sleep, would listen for a moment till the hurry scurry had clattered by, and then exclaim, "aye, there goes Brom Bones and his gang!" The neighbours looked upon him with a mixture of awe, admiration, and good will; and when any mad cap prank, or rustic brawl, occurred in the vicinity, always shook their heads, and warranted Brom Bones was at the bottom of it.

This rantipole hero had for some time singled out the blooming Katrina for the object of his uncouth gallantries, and though his amorous toyings were something like the gentle caresses and endearments of a bear, yet it was whispered that she did not altogether discourage his hopes. Certain it is, his advances were signals for rival candidates to retire, who felt no inclination to cross a lion in his amours; insomuch, that when his horse was seen tied to Van Tassel's paling, of a Sunday night, (a sure sign that his master was courting, or, as it is termed, "sparking," within,) all other suitors passed by in despair, and carried the war into other quarters.

Such was the formidable rival with whom Ichabod Crane had to contend, and, considering all things, a stouter man than he would have shrunk from the competition, and a wiser man would have despaired. He had, however, a happy mixture of pliability and perseverance in his nature; he was in form and spirit like a supple jack—yielding, but tough; though he bent, he never broke; and though he bowed beneath the slightest pressure, yet, the moment it was away— jerk!—he was as erect, and carried his head as high as ever.

To have taken the field openly against his rival, would have been madness; for he was not a man to be thwarted in his amours, any more than that stormy lover, Achilles. Ichabod, therefore, made his advances in a quiet and gently insinuating manner. Under cover of his character of singing master, he made frequent visits at the farm house; not that he had any thing to apprehend from the meddlesome interference of parents, which is so often a stumbling block in the path of lovers. Balt Van Tassel was an easy indulgent soul; he loved his daughter better even than his pipe, and like a reasonable man, and an excellent father, let her have her way in every thing. His notable little wife too, had enough to do to attend to her housekeeping and manage her poultry, for, as she sagely observed, ducks and geese are foolish things, and must be looked after, but girls can take care of themselves. Thus while the busy dame bustled about the house, or plied her spinning wheel at one end of the piazza, honest Balt would sit smoking his evening pipe at the other, watching the achievements of a little wooden warrior, who, armed with a sword in each hand, was most valiantly fighting the wind on the pinnacle of the barn. In the mean time, Ichabod would carry on his suit with the daughter by the side of the spring under the great elm, or sauntering along in the twilight, that hour so favourable to the lover's eloquence.

I profess not to know how women's hearts are wooed and won. To me they have always been matters of riddle and admiration. Some seem to have but one vulnerable point, or door of access; while others have a thousand avenues, and may be captured in a thousand different ways. It is a great triumph of skill to gain the former, but a still greater proof of generalship to maintain possession of the latter, for a man must battle for his fortress at every door and window. He who wins a thousand common hearts, is therefore entitled to some renown; but he who keeps undisputed sway over the heart of a coquette, is indeed a hero. Certain it is, this was not the case with the redoutable Brom Bones; and from the moment Ichabod Crane made his advances, the interests of the former evidently declined; his horse was no longer seen tied at the palings on Sunday nights, and a deadly feud gradually arose between him and the preceptor of Sleepy Hollow.

Brom, who had a degree of rough chivalry in his nature, would fain have carried matters to open warfare, and have settled their pretensions to the lady, according to the mode of those most concise and simple reasoners, the knights errant of yore—by single combat; but Ichabod was too conscious of the superior might of his adversary to enter the lists against him; he had overheard a boast of Bones, that he would "double the schoolmaster up, and lay him on a shelf of his own school house;" and he was too wary to give him an opportunity. There was something extremely provoking in this obstinately pacific system; it left Brom no alternative but to draw upon the funds of rustic waggery in his disposition, and to play off boorish practical jokes upon his rival. Ichabod became the object of whimsical persecution to Bones, and his gang of rough riders. They harried his hitherto peaceful domains; smoked out his singing school, by stopping up the chimney; broke into the school house at night, in spite of its formidable fastenings of withe and window stakes, and turned every thing topsy-turvy, so that the poor schoolmaster began to think all the witches in the country held their meetings there. But what was still more annoying, Brom took all opportunities of turning him into ridicule in presence of his mistress, and had a scoundrel dog, whom he taught to whine in the most ludicrous manner, and introduced as a rival of Ichabod's, to instruct her in psalmody.

In this way, matters went on for some time, without producing any material effect on the relative situations of the contending powers. On a fine autumnal afternoon, Ichabod, in pensive mood, sat enthroned on the lofty stool from whence he usually watched all the concerns of his little literary realm. In his hand he swayed a ferule, that sceptre of despotic power; the birch of justice reposed on three nails, behind the throne, a constant terror to evil doers; while on the desk before him might be seen sundry contraband articles and prohibited weapons, detected upon the persons of idle urchins, such as half munched apples, popguns, whirligigs, fly cages, and whole legions of rampant little paper game cocks. Apparently there had been some appalling act of justice recently inflicted, for his scholars were all busily intent upon their books, or slyly whispering behind them with one eye kept upon the master; and a kind of buzzing stillness reigned throughout the school room. It was suddenly interrupted by the appearance of a negro in tow cloth jacket and trowsers, a round crowned fragment of a hat, like the cap of Mercury, and mounted on the back of a ragged, wild, half broken colt, which he managed with a rope by way of halter. He came clattering up to the school door with an invitation to Ichabod to attend a merry making, or "quilting frolick," to be held that evening at Mynheer Van Tassel's, and having delivered his message with that air of importance, and effort at fine language, which a negro is apt to display on petty embassies of the kind, he dashed over the brook, and was seen scampering away up the hollow, full of the importance and hurry of his mission.

All was now bustle and hubbub in the late quiet school room. The scholars were hurried through their lessons, without stopping at trifles; those who were nimble, skipped over half with impunity, and those who were tardy, had a smart application now and then in the rear, to quicken their speed,

or help them over a tall word. Books were flung aside, without being put away on the shelves; inkstands were overturned, benches thrown down, and the whole school was turned loose an hour before the usual time; bursting forth like a legion of young imps, yelping and racketing about the green, in joy at their early emancipation.

The gallant Ichabod now spent at least an extra half hour at his toilet, brushing and furbishing up his best, and indeed only suit of rusty black, and arranging his looks by a bit of broken looking glass, that hung up in the school house. That he might make his appearance before his mistress in the true style of a cavalier, he borrowed a horse from the farmer with whom he was domiciliated, a choleric old Dutchman, of the name of Hans Van Ripper, and thus gallantly mounted, issued forth like a knight errant in quest of adventures. But it is meet I should, in the true spirit of romantic story, give some account of the looks and equipments of my hero and his steed. The animal he bestrode was a broken down plough horse, that had outlived almost every thing but his viciousness. He was gaunt and shagged, with a ewe neck and a head like a hammer; his rusty mane and tail were tangled and knotted with burrs; one eye had lost its pupil, and was glaring and spectral, but the other had the gleam of a genuine devil in it. Still he must have had fire and mettle in his day, if we may judge from the name he bore of Gunpowder. He had, in fact, been a favourite steed of his master's, the cholerick Van Ripper, who was a furious rider, and had infused, very probably, some of his own spirit into the animal, for, old and broken down as he looked, there was more of the lurking devil in him than in any young filly in the country.

Ichabod was a suitable figure for such a steed. He rode with short stirrups, which brought his knees nearly up to the pommel of the saddle; his sharp elbows stuck out like grasshoppers'; he carried his whip perpendicularly in his hand, like a sceptre, and as his horse jogged on, the motion of his arms was not unlike the flapping of a pair of wings. A small wool hat rested on the top of his nose, for so his scanty strip of forehead might be called, and the skirts of his black coat fluttered out almost to the horse's tail. Such was the appearance of Ichabod and his steed, as they shambled out of the gate of Hans Van Ripper, and it was altogether such an apparition as is seldom to be met with in broad day light.

It was, as I have said, a fine autumnal day, the sky was clear and serene, and nature wore that rich and golden livery which we always associate with the idea of abundance. The forests had put on their sober brown and yellow, while some trees of the tenderer kind had been nipped by the frosts into brilliant dyes of orange, purple, and scarlet. Streaming files of wild ducks began to make their appearance high in the air; the bark of the squirrel might be heard from the groves of beech and hickory nuts, and the pensive whistle of the quail at intervals from the neighbouring stubble field.

The small birds were taking their farewell banquets. In the fullness of their revelry, they fluttered, chirping and frolicking, from bush to bush, and tree to tree, capricious from the very profusion and variety around them. There was the honest cock robin, the favourite game of stripling sportsmen, with its loud querulous note; and the twittering blackbirds flying in sable clouds; and the golden winged woodpecker, with his crimson crest, his broad black gorget, and splendid plumage; and the cedar bird, with its red tipt wings and yellow tipt tail, and its little monteiro cap of feathers; and the blue jay, that noisy coxcomb, in his gay light blue coat and white under clothes, screaming and chattering, nodding, and bobbing, and bowing, and pretending to be on good terms with every songster of the grove.

As Ichabod jogged slowly on his way, his eye, ever open to every symptom of culinary abundance, ranged with delight over the treasures of jolly autumn. On all sides he beheld vast store of apples, some hanging in oppressive opulence on the trees, some gathered into baskets and barrels for the market, others heaped up in rich piles for the cider press. Further on he beheld great fields of Indian corn, with its golden ears peeping from their leafy coverts, and holding out the promise of cakes and hasty pudding; and the yellow pumpkins lying beneath them, turning up their fair round bellies to the sun, and giving ample prospects of the most luxurious of pies; and anon he passed the fragrant buckwheat fields, breathing the odour of the bee hive, and as he beheld them, soft anticipations stole over his mind of dainty slap jacks, well buttered, and garnished with honey or treacle, by the delicate little dimpled hand of Katrina Van Tassel.

Thus feeding his mind with many sweet thoughts and "sugared suppositions," he journeyed along the sides of a range of hills which look out upon some of the goodliest scenes of the mighty Hudson. The sun gradually wheeled his broad disk down into the west. The wide bosom of the Tappaan Zee lay motionless and glassy, excepting that here and there a gentle undulation waved and prolonged the blue shadow of the distant mountain: a few amber clouds floated in the sky, without a breath of air to move them. The horizon was of a fine golden tint, changing gradually into a pure apple green, and from that into the deep blue of the mid-heaven. A slanting ray lingered on the woody crests of the precipices that overhung some parts of the river, giving greater depth to the dark grey and purple of their rocky sides. A sloop was loitering in the distance, dropping slowly down with the tide, her sail hanging uselessly against the mast, and as the reflection of the sky gleamed along the still water, it seemed as if the vessel was suspended in the air.

It was toward evening that Ichabod arrived at the castle of the Heer Van Tassel, which he found thronged with the pride and flower of the adjacent country. Old farmers, a spare, leathern faced race, in homespun coats and breeches, blue stockings, huge shoes and magnificent pewter buckles. Their brisk withered little dames in close crimped caps, long waisted short gowns, homespun petticoats, with scissors and pincushions, and gay calico pockets, hanging on the outside. Buxom lasses, almost as antiquated as their mothers, excepting where a straw hat, a fine ribband, or perhaps a white frock, gave symptoms of city innovation. The sons, in short square skirted coats with rows of stupendous brass buttons, and their hair generally queued in the fashion of the times, especially if they could procure an eel skin for the purpose, it being esteemed throughout the country as a potent nourisher and strengthener of the hair.

Brom Bones, however, was the hero of the scene, having come to the gathering on his favourite steed Daredevil, a creature, like himself, full of mettle and mischief, and which no one but himself could manage. He was in fact noted for preferring vicious animals, given to all kinds of tricks, which kept the rider in constant risk of his neck, for he held a tractable well broken horse as unworthy of a lad of spirit.

Fain would I pause to dwell upon the world of charms that burst upon the enraptured gaze of my hero, as he entered the state parlour of Van Tassel's mansion. Not those of the bevy of buxom lasses, with their luxurious display of red and white: but the ample charms of a genuine Dutch country tea table, in the sumptuous time of autumn. Such heaped up platters of cakes of various and almost indescribable kinds, known only to experienced Dutch housewives. There was the doughty dough nut, the tenderer oly koek, and the crisp and crumbling cruller; sweet cakes and short cakes, ginger cakes and honey cakes, and the whole family of cakes. And then there were apple pies and peach pies and pumpkin pies; besides slices of ham and smoked beef; and moreover delectable dishes of preserved plums, and peaches, and pears, and quinces; not to mention broiled shad and roasted chickens; together with bowls of milk and cream, all mingled higgledy-piggledy, pretty much as I have enumerated them, with the motherly tea pot sending up its clouds of vapour from the midst—Heaven bless the mark! I want breath and time to discuss this banquet as it deserves, and am too eager to get on with my story. Happily, Ichabod Crane was not in so great a hurry as his historian, but did ample justice to every dainty.

He was a kind and thankful creature, whose heart dilated in proportion as his skin was filled with good cheer, and whose spirits rose with eating, as some men's do with drink. He could not help, too, rolling his large eyes round him as he ate, and chuckling with the possibility that he might one day be lord of all this scene of almost unimaginable luxury and splendour. Then, he thought, how soon he'd turn his back upon the old school house; snap his fingers in the face of Hans Van Ripper, and every other niggardly patron, and kick any itinerant pedagogue out of doors that should dare to call him comrade!

Old Baltus Van Tassel moved about among his guests with a face dilated with content and good humour, round and jolly as the harvest moon. His hospitable attentions were brief, but expressive, being confined to a shake of the hand, a slap on the shoulder, a loud laugh, and a pressing invitation to "fall to, and help themselves."

And now the sound of the music from the common room or hall, summoned to the dance. The musician was an old grey headed negro, who had been the itinerant orchestra of the neighbourhood for more than half a century. His instrument was as old and battered as himself. The greater part of the time he scraped away on two or three strings, accompanying every movement of the bow with a motion of the head; bowing almost to the ground, and stamping with his foot whenever a fresh couple were to start.

Ichabod prided himself upon his dancing as much as upon his vocal powers. Not a limb, not a fibre about him was idle, and to have seen his loosely hung frame in full motion, and clattering about the room, you would have thought Saint Vitus himself, that blessed patron of the dance, was figuring before you in person. He was the admiration of all the negroes, who, having gathered, of all ages and sizes, from the farm and the neighbourhood, stood forming a pyramid of shining black faces at every door and window, gazing with delight at the scene, rolling their white eye balls, and showing grinning rows of ivory from ear to ear. How could the flogger of urchins be otherwise than animated and joyous; the lady of his heart was his partner in the dance; and smiling graciously in reply to all his amorous oglings, while Brom Bones, sorely smitten with love and jealousy, sat brooding by himself in one corner.

When the dance was at an end, Ichabod was attracted to a knot of the sager folks, who, with old Van Tassel, sat smoking at one end of the piazza, gossipping over former times, and drawling out long stories about the war.

This neighbourhood, at the time of which I am speaking, was one of those highly favoured places which abound with chronicle and great men. The British and American line had run near it during the war; it had, therefore, been the scene of marauding, and been infested with refugees, cow boys, and all kinds of border chivalry. Just sufficient time had elapsed to enable each story teller to dress up his tale with a little becoming fiction, and in the indistinctness of his recollection, to make himself the hero of every exploit.

There was the story of Doffue Martling, a large, blue bearded Dutchman, who had nearly taken a British frigate with an old iron nine pounder from a mud breastwork, only that his gun burst at the sixth discharge. And there was an old gentleman who shall be nameless, being too rich a mynheer to be lightly mentioned, who in the battle of Whiteplains, being an excellent master of defence, parried a musket ball with a small sword, insomuch that he absolutely felt it whiz round the blade, and glance off at the hilt: in proof of which, he was ready at any time to show the sword, with the hilt a little bent. There were several more who had been equally great in the field, not one of whom but was persuaded that he had a considerable hand in bringing the war to a happy termination.

But all these were nothing to the tales of ghosts and apparitions that succeeded. The neighbourhood is rich in legendary treasures of the kind. Local tales and superstitions thrive best in these sheltered, long settled retreats; but are trampled under foot, by the shifting throng that forms the population of most of our country places. Besides, there is no encouragement for ghosts in most of our villages, for they have scarce had time to finish their first nap, and turn themselves in their graves, before their surviving friends have travelled away from the neighbourhood, so that when they turn out of a night to walk the rounds, they have no acquaintance left to call upon. This is perhaps the reason why we so seldom hear of ghosts except in our long established Dutch communities.

The immediate cause, however, of the prevalence of supernatural stories in these parts, was doubtless owing to the vicinity of Sleepy Hollow. There was a contagion in the very air that blew from that haunted region; it breathed forth an atmosphere of dreams and fancies infecting all the land. Several of the Sleepy Hollow people were present at Van Tassel's, and, as usual, were doling out their wild and wonderful legends. Many dismal tales were told about funeral trains, and mournful cries and wailings heard and seen about the great tree where the unfortunate Major André was taken, and which stood in the neighbourhood. Some mention was made also of the woman in white, that haunted the dark glen at Raven Rock, and was often heard to shriek on winter nights before a storm, having perished there in the snow. The chief part of the stories, however, turned upon the favourite spectre of Sleepy Hollow, the headless horseman, who had been heard several times of late, patroling the country; and it was said, tethered his horse nightly among the graves in the church yard.

The sequestered situation of this church seems always to have made it a favourite haunt of troubled spirits. It stands on a knoll, surrounded by locust trees and lofty elms, from among which its decent, whitewashed walls shine modestly forth, like Christian purity, beaming through the shades of retirement. A gentle slope descends from it to a silver sheet of water, bordered by high trees, between which, peeps may be caught at the blue hills of the Hudson. To look upon its grass grown yard, where the sunbeams seem to sleep so quietly, one would think that there at least the dead might rest in peace. On one side of the church extends a wide woody dell, along which raves a large brook among broken rocks and trunks of fallen trees. Over a deep black part of the stream, not far from the church, was formerly thrown a wooden bridge; the road that led to it, and the bridge itself, were thickly shaded by overhanging trees, which cast a gloom about it, even in the day time; but occasioned a fearful darkness at night. Such was one of the favourite haunts of the headless horseman, and the place where he was most frequently encountered. The tale was told of old Brouwer, a most heretical disbeliever in ghosts, how he met the horseman returning from his foray into Sleepy Hollow, and was obliged to get up behind him; how they gallopped over bush and brake, over hill and swamp, until they reached the bridge, when the horseman suddenly turned into a skeleton, threw old Brouwer into the brook, and sprang away over the tree tops with a clap of thunder.

This story was immediately matched by a thrice marvellous adventure of Brom Bones, who made light of the gallopping Hessian as an arrant jockey. He affirmed, that on returning one night from the neighbouring village of Sing-Sing, he had been overtaken by this midnight trooper; that he had offered to race with him for a bowl of punch, and should have won it too, for Daredevil beat the goblin horse all hollow, but just as they came to the church bridge, the Hessian bolted, and vanished in a flash of fire.

All these tales, told in that drowsy under tone with which men talk in the dark, the countenances of the listeners only now and then receiving a casual gleam from the glare of a pipe, sunk deep in the mind of Ichabod. He repaid them in kind with large extracts from his invaluable author, Cotton Mather, and added many very marvellous events that had taken place in his native state of Connecticut, and fearful sights which he had seen in his nightly walks about Sleepy Hollow.

The revel now gradually broke up. The old farmers gathered together their families in their wagons, and were heard for some time rattling along the hollow roads, and over the distant hills. Some of the damsels, mounted on pillions behind their favourite swains, and their light hearted laughter mingling with the clatter of hoofs, echoed along the silent woodlands, sounding fainter and fainter until they gradually died away—and the late scene of noise and frolick was all silent and deserted. Ichabod only lingered behind, according to the custom of country lovers, to have a tête-a-tête with the heiress; fully convinced that he was now on the high road to success. What passed at this interview I will not pretend to say, for in fact I do not know. Something, however, I fear me, must have gone wrong, for he certainly sallied forth, after no very great interval, with an air quite desolate and chopfallen—Oh these women! these women! Could that girl have been playing off any of her coquettish tricks?—Was her encouragement of the poor pedagogue all a mere sham to secure her conquest of his rival?—Heaven only knows, not I!—Let it suffice to say, Ichabod stole forth with the air of one who had been sacking a hen roost, rather than a fair lady's heart. Without looking to the right or left to notice the scene of rural wealth, on which he had so often gloated, he went straight to the stable, and with several hearty cuffs and kicks, roused his steed most uncourteously from the comfortable quarters in which he was soundly sleeping, dreaming of mountains of corn and oats, and whole valleys of timothy and clover.

It was the very witching time of night that Ichabod, heavy hearted and crest fallen, pursued his travel homewards, along the sides of the lofty hills which rise above Tarry Town, and which he had traversed so cheerily in the afternoon. The hour was as dismal as himself. Far below him the Tappaan Zee spread its dusky and indistinct waste of waters, with here and there the tall mast of a sloop, riding quietly at anchor under the land. In the dead hush of midnight, he could even hear the barking of the watch dog from the opposite shore of the Hudson; but it was so vague and faint as only to give an idea of his distance from this faithful companion of man. Now and then, too, the long drawn crowing of a cock, accidentally awakened, would sound far, far off, from some farm house away among the hills—but it was like a dreaming sound in his ear. No signs of life occurred near him, but occasionally the melancholy chirp of a cricket, or perhaps the guttural twang of a bull frog, from a neighbouring marsh, as if sleeping uncomfortably, and turning suddenly in his bed.

All the stories of ghosts and goblins that he had heard in the afternoon, now came crowding upon his recollection. The night grew darker and darker; the stars seemed to sink deeper in the sky, and driving clouds occasionally hid them from his sight. He had never felt so lonely and dismal. He was, moreover, approaching the very place where many of the scenes of the ghost stories had been laid. In the centre of the road stood an enormous tulip tree, which towered like a giant above all the other trees of the neighbourhood, and formed a kind of land mark. Its limbs were gnarled, and fantastic, large enough to form trunks for ordinary trees, twisting down almost to the earth, and rising again into the air. It was connected with the tragical story of the unfortunate André, who had been taken prisoner hard by; and was universally known by the name of Major André's tree. The common people regarded it with a mixture of respect and superstition, partly out of sympathy for the fate of its ill starred namesake, and partly from the tales of strange sights, and doleful lamentations, told concerning it.

As Ichabod approached this fearful tree, he began to whistle; he thought his whistle was answered: it was but a blast sweeping sharply through the dry branches. As he approached a little nearer, he thought he saw something white, hanging in the midst of the tree: he paused and ceased whistling; but on looking more narrowly, perceived that it was a place where the tree had been scathed by lightning, and the white wood laid bare. Suddenly he heard a groan—his teeth chattered, and his knees smote against the saddle: it was but the rubbing of one huge bough upon another, as they were swayed about by the breeze. He passed the tree in safety, but new perils lay before him.

About two hundred yards from the tree, a small brook crossed the road, and ran into a marshy and thickly wooded glen, known by the name of Wiley's Swamp. A few rough logs, laid side by side, served for a bridge over this stream. On that side of the road where the brook entered the wood, a group of oaks and chestnuts, matted thick with wild grape vines, threw a cavernous gloom over it. To pass this bridge, was the severest trial. It was at this identical spot that the unfortunate André was captured, and under the covert of those chestnuts and vines were the sturdy yeomen concealed who surprised him. This has ever since been considered a haunted stream, and fearful are the feelings of the schoolboy who has to pass it alone after dark.

As he approached the stream, his heart began to thump; he, however, summoned up all his resolution, gave his horse half a score of kicks in the ribs, and attempted to dash briskly across the bridge; but instead of starting forward, the perverse old animal made a lateral movement, and ran broadside against the fence. Ichabod, whose fears increased with the delay, jerked the reins on the other side, and kicked lustily with the contrary foot: it was all in vain; his steed started, it is true, but it was only to plunge to the opposite side of the road into a thicket of brambles and alder bushes. The schoolmaster now bestowed both whip and heel upon the starvelling ribs of old Gunpowder, who dashed forward, snuffling and snorting, but came to a stand just by the bridge with a suddenness that had nearly sent his rider sprawling over his head. Just at this moment a plashy tramp by the side of the bridge caught the sensitive ear of Ichabod. In the dark shadow of the grove, on the margin of the brook, he beheld something huge, misshapen, black and towering. It stirred not, but seemed gathered up in the gloom, like some gigantic monster ready to spring upon the traveller.

The hair of the affrighted pedagogue rose upon his head with terror. What was to be done? To turn and fly was now too late; and besides, what chance was there of escaping ghost or goblin, if such it was, which could ride upon the wings of the wind? Summoning up, therefore, a show of courage, he demanded in stammering accents—"who are you?" He received no reply. He repeated his demand in a still more agitated voice.—Still there was no answer. Once more he cudgelled the sides of the inflexible Gunpowder, and shutting his eyes, broke forth with involuntary fervour into a psalm tune. Just then the shadowy object of alarm put itself in motion, and with a scramble and a bound, stood at once in the middle of the road. Though the night was dark and dismal, yet the form of the unknown might now in some degree be ascertained. He appeared to be a horseman of large dimensions, and mounted on a black horse of powerful frame. He made no offer of molestation or sociability, but kept aloof on one side of the road, jogging along on the blind side of old Gunpowder, who had now got over his fright and waywardness.

Ichabod, who had no relish for this strange midnight companion, and bethought himself of the adventure of Brom Bones with the gallopping Hessian, now quickened his steed, in hopes of leaving him behind. The stranger, however, quickened his horse to an equal pace; Ichabod pulled up, and fell into a walk, thinking to lag behind—the other did the same. His heart began to sink within him; he endeavoured to resume his psalm tune, but his parched tongue clove to the roof of his mouth, and he could not utter a stave. There was something in the moody and dogged silence of this pertinacious companion, that was mysterious and appalling. It was soon fearfully accounted for. On mounting a rising ground, which brought the figure of his fellow traveller in relief against the sky, gigantic in height, and muffled in a cloak, Ichabod was horror struck, on perceiving that he was headless! but his horror was still more increased, on observing, that the head, which should have rested on his shoulders, was carried before him on the pommel of the saddle! His terror rose to desperation; he rained a shower of kicks and blows upon Gunpowder, hoping, by a sudden movement, to give his companion the slip—but the spectre started full jump with him. Away, then, they dashed, through thick and thin; stones flying, and sparks flashing, at every bound. Ichabod's flimsy garments fluttered in the air, as he stretched his long lank body away over his horse's head, in the eagerness of his flight.

They had now reached the road which turns off to Sleepy Hollow; but Gunpowder, who seemed possessed with a demon, instead of keeping up it, made an opposite turn, and plunged headlong down hill to the left. This road leads through a sandy hollow shaded by trees for about a quarter of a mile, where it crosses the bridge famous in goblin story, and just beyond swells the green knoll on which stands the whitewashed church.

As yet the panic of the steed had given his unskilful rider an apparent advantage in the chace, but just as he had got half way through the hollow, the girths of the saddle gave way, and he felt it slipping from under him; he seized it by the pommel, and endeavoured to hold it firm, but in vain; and had just time to save himself by clasping old Gunpowder round the neck, when the saddle fell to the earth, and he heard it trampled under foot by his pursuer. For a moment the terror of Hans Van Ripper's wrath passed across his mind—for it was his Sunday saddle; but this was no time for petty fears: the goblin was hard on his haunches; and (unskilful rider that he was!) he had much ado to maintain his seat; sometimes slipping on one side, sometimes on another, and sometimes jolted on the high ridge of his horse's back bone, with a violence that he verily feared would cleave him asunder.

An opening in the trees now cheered him with the hopes that the Church Bridge was at hand. The wavering reflection of a silver star in the bosom of the brook told him that he was not mistaken. He saw the walls of the church dimly glaring under the trees beyond. He recollected the place where Brom Bones' ghostly competitor had disappeared. "If I can but reach that bridge," thought Ichabod, "I am safe." Just then he heard the black steed panting and blowing close behind him; he even fancied that he felt his hot breath. Another convulsive kick in the ribs, and old Gunpowder sprung upon the bridge; he thundered over the resounding planks; he gained the opposite side, and now Ichabod cast a look behind to see if his pursuer should vanish, according to rule, in a flash of fire and brimstone. Just then he saw the goblin rising in his stirrups, and in the very act of hurling his head at him. Ichabod endeavoured to dodge the horrible missile, but too late. It encountered his cranium with a tremendous crash— he was tumbled headlong into the dust, and Gunpowder, the black steed, and the goblin rider, passed by like a whirl-wind.——

The next morning the old horse was found without his sad-dle, and with the bridle under his feet, soberly cropping the grass at his master's gate. Ichabod did not make his appear-ance at breakfast—dinner hour came, but no Ichabod. The boys assembled at the schoolhouse, and strolled idly about the banks of the brook; but no schoolmaster. Hans Van Ripper now began to feel some uneasiness about the fate of poor Ichabod, and his saddle. An inquiry was set on foot, and after diligent investigation they came upon his traces. In one part of the road leading to the church, was found the saddle tram-pled in the dirt; the tracks of horses' hoofs deeply dented in the road, and evidently at furious speed, were traced to the bridge, beyond which, on the bank of a broad part of the brook, where the water ran deep and black, was found the hat of the unfortunate Ichabod, and close beside it a shattered pumpkin.

The brook was searched, but the body of the schoolmaster was not to be discovered. Hans Van Ripper, as executor of his estate, examined the bundle which contained all his worldly effects. They consisted of two shirts and a half; two stocks for the neck; a pair or two of worsted stockings; an old pair of corduroy small clothes; a rusty razor; a book of psalm tunes, full of dog's ears; and a broken pitch pipe. As to the books and furniture of the schoolhouse, they belonged to the community, excepting Cotton Mather's History of Witchcraft, a New England Almanack, and a book of dreams and fortune telling, in which last was a sheet of foolscap much scribbled and blotted, in several fruitless attempts to make a copy of verses in honour of the heiress of Van Tassel. These magic books and the poetic scrawl were forthwith consigned to the flames by Hans Van Ripper, who from that time forward determined to send his children no more to school, observing, that he never knew any good come of this same reading and writing. Whatever money the schoolmaster possessed, and he had received his quarter's pay but a day or two before, he must have had about his person at the time of his disappearance.

The mysterious event caused much speculation at the Church on the following Sunday. Knots of gazers and gossips were collected in the church yard, at the bridge, and at the spot where the hat and pumpkin had been found. The stories of Brouwer, of Bones, and a whole budget of others, were called to mind; and when they had diligently considered them all, and compared them with the symptoms of the present case, they shook their heads, and came to the conclusion, that Ichabod had been carried off by the gallopping Hessian. As he was a bachelor, and in nobody's debt, nobody troubled his head any more about him, the school was removed to a different quarter of the hollow, and another pedagogue reigned in his stead.

It is true, an old farmer, who had been down to New York on a visit several years after, and from whom this account of the ghostly adventure was received, brought home the intelligence that Ichabod Crane was still alive; that he had left the neighbourhood partly through fear of the goblin and Hans Van Ripper, and partly in mortification at having been suddenly dismissed by the heiress; that he had changed his quarters to a distant part of the country; had kept school and studied law at the same time; had been admitted to the bar, turned politician, electioneered, written for the newspapers, and finally had been made a Justice of the Ten Pound Court. Brom Bones too, who, shortly after his rival's disappearance, conducted the blooming Katrina in triumph to the altar, was observed to look exceedingly knowing whenever the story of Ichabod was related, and always burst into a hearty laugh at the mention of the pumpkin; which led some to suspect that he knew more about the matter than he chose to tell.

The old country wives, however, who are the best judges

of these matters, maintain to this day, that Ichabod was spirited away by supernatural means; and it is a favourite story often told about the neighbourhood round the winter evening fire. The bridge became more than ever an object of superstitious awe, and that may be the reason why the road has been altered of late years, so as to approach the church by the border of the millpond. The schoolhouse being deserted, soon fell to decay, and was reported to be haunted by the ghost of the unfortunate pedagogue; and the plough boy, loitering homeward of a still summer evening, has often fancied his voice at a distance, chanting a melancholy psalm tune among the tranquil solitudes of Sleepy Hollow.

POSTSCRIPT

Found in the Handwriting of Mr. Knickerbocker

The preceding Tale is given, almost in the precise words in which I heard it related at a corporation meeting of the ancient city of Manhattoes, at which were present many of its sagest and most illustrious burghers. The narrator was a pleasant, shabby, gentlemanly old fellow, in pepper and salt clothes, with a sadly humourous face, and one whom I strongly suspected of being poor, he made such efforts to be entertaining. When his story was concluded, there was much laughter and approbation, particularly from two or three deputy aldermen, who had been asleep the greater part of the time. There was, however, one tall, dry looking old gentleman, with beetling eye brows, who maintained a grave and rather severe face throughout; now and then folding his arms, inclining his head, and looking down upon the floor, as if turning a doubt over in his mind. He was one of your wary men, who never laugh but upon good grounds—when they have reason and the law on their side. When the mirth of the rest of the company had subsided, and silence was restored, he leaned one arm on the elbow of his chair, and sticking the other akimbo, demanded, with a slight, but exceedingly sage motion of the head, and contraction of the brow, what was the moral of the story, and what it went to prove.

The story teller, who was just putting a glass of wine to his lips, as a refreshment after his toils, paused for a moment, looked at his inquirer with an air of infinite deference, and lowering the glass slowly to the table, observed, that the story was intended most logically to prove,

"That there is no situation in life but has its advantages and pleasures, provided we will but take a joke as we find it:

"That, therefore, he that runs races with goblin troopers, is likely to have rough riding of it:

"Ergo, for a country schoolmaster to be refused the hand of a Dutch heiress, is a certain step to high preferment in the state."

The cautious old gentleman knit his brows tenfold closer after this explanation, being sorely puzzled by the ratiocination of the syllogism; while methought the one in pepper and salt eyed him with something of a triumphant leer. At length he observed, that all this was very well, but still he thought the story a little on the extravagant—there were one or two points on which he had his doubts.

"Faith, sir," replied the story teller, "as to that matter, I don't believe one half of it myself."

D.K.

L'Envoy*

Go, little booke, God send thee good passage,
And specially let this be thy prayere,
Unto them all that thee will read or hear,
Where thou art wrong, after their help to call,
Thee to correct in any part or all.
                    Chaucer's Belle Dame sans Mercie

IN CONCLUDING a second volume of the Sketch Book, the
Author cannot but express his deep sense of the indulgence with which his first has been received, and of the
liberal disposition that has been evinced to treat him with
kindness as a stranger. Even the critics, whatever may be
said of them by others, he has found to be a singularly
gentle and good natured race: it is true that each has in
turn objected to some one or two articles,—and that these
individual exceptions, taken in the aggregate, would
amount almost to a total condemnation of his work; but
then he has been consoled by observing, that what one has
particularly censured, another has as particularly praised;
and thus, the encomiums being set off against the objections, he finds his work, upon the whole, commended far
beyond its deserts.

He is aware that he runs a risk of forfeiting much of this
kind favour by not following the counsel that has been liberally bestowed upon him; for where abundance of valuable advice is given gratis, it may seem a man's own fault if he should
go astray. He can only say, in his vindication, that he faithfully determined, for a time, to govern himself in his second
volume by the opinions passed upon his first; but he was
soon brought to a stand by the contrariety of excellent counsel. One kindly advised him to avoid the ludicrous; another
to shun the pathetic; a third assured him that he was tolerable
at description, but cautioned him to leave narrative alone;
while a fourth declared that he had a very pretty knack at
turning a story, and was really entertaining when in a pensive

*Closing the second volume of the London edition.

mood, but was grievously mistaken if he imagined himself to possess a spirit of humour.

Thus perplexed by the advice of his friends, who each in turn closed some particular path, but left him all the world beside to range in, he found that to follow all their counsels would, in fact, be to stand still. He remained for a time sadly embarrassed; when, all at once, the thought struck him to ramble on even as he had begun: that his work being miscellaneous, and written for different humours, it could not be expected that any one would be pleased with the whole; but that if it should contain something to suit each reader, his end would be completely answered. Few guests sit down to a varied table with an equal appetite for every dish. One has an elegant horror of a roasted pig; another holds a curry or a devil in utter abomination; a third cannot tolerate the ancient flavour of venison and wild fowl; and a fourth, of truly masculine stomach, looks with sovereign contempt on those knick-knacks, here and there dished up for the ladies. Thus each article is condemned in its turn; and yet, amidst this variety of appetites, seldom does a dish go away from the table without being tasted and relished by some one or other of the guests.

With these considerations he ventures to serve up this second volume in the same heterogeneous way with his first; simply requesting the reader, if he should find here and there something to please him, to rest assured that it was written expressly for intelligent readers like himself; but intreating him, should he find any thing to dislike, to tolerate it, as one of those articles which the author has been obliged to write for readers of a less refined taste.

To be serious.—The author is conscious of the numerous faults and imperfections of his work; and well aware how little he is disciplined and accomplished in the arts of authorship. His deficiencies are also increased by a diffidence arising from his peculiar situation. He finds himself writing in a strange land, and appearing before a public which he has been accustomed, from childhood, to regard with the highest feelings of awe and reverence. He is full of solicitude to deserve their approbation, yet finds that very solicitude continually embarrassing his powers, and depriving him of that ease and confidence which are necessary to successful exertion. Still the kindness with which he is treated encourages him to go on, hoping that in time he may acquire a steadier footing; and thus he proceeds, half venturing, half shrinking, surprized at his own good fortune, and wondering at his own temerity.

THE END.

Chronology

1783   Born April 3 at 131 William St., New York City, youngest of eleven children of Deacon William Irving, middle-class merchant of Scotch Presbyterian birth, and Sarah Sanders Irving, granddaughter of an English curate. Mother names him for George Washington. Soon after the Revolution ends, family moves across the street to what becomes their permanent home at 128 William St. Father is strictly religious, reads the Bible aloud to the family every evening, takes them to three sermons on Sundays, and makes the children study the catechism on Thursday afternoons. Irving feels closer to his mother and is the favorite of the four brothers (William, Peter, Ebenezer, John) and three sisters (Ann, Catharine, Sarah) who survive infancy.

1787   Attends Mrs. Ann Kilmaster's kindergarten.

1789   Takes a walk on Broadway one day in summer with Scottish nurse, Lizzie; she sees George Washington in a shop and asks him to bless his namesake.

1789–96   Attends school of Benjamin Romaine, old soldier and strict disciplinarian. Reads romances and travel books, *Robinson Crusoe*, and *Sinbad the Sailor*. Wanders among the wharves and watches the ships sail out to sea. Begins to attend theaters and pantomimes, sneaking out through the window and over the rooftop at night.

1797–98   After Romaine retires, studies at the seminary of Josiah Henderson, author of *The Well-Bred Scholar* and an authority on theater. Continues to read travel books such as *The World Displayed* and particularly enjoys the hyperbolic descriptions of New England in Jedidiah Morse's *Geography*. In December 1797, begins to study Latin at Jonathan Fiske's school. Attends dancing school, takes long exploratory walks in the open country above Broadway and Bridewell, goes hunting for squirrels along the Hudson River. Spends much time with his brothers and friends. Studies drawing with Archibald Robinson.

1799   Unlike his brothers, does not attend Columbia College. Enters law offices of Henry Masterton in preference to the family import business. Remains close friends with brother Peter, a doctor and literary man-about-town, and William, a businessman who writes verse.

1800   Takes first extended trip up the Hudson River to visit sisters Ann and Catharine near Albany.

1801   Transfers to office of well-known attorney Brockholst Livingston.

1802   Clerks for Judge Josiah Hoffman, former Attorney General of New York, and becomes an intimate of his family. Begins publishing letters under pseudonym "Jonathan Oldstyle, Gent." for the *Morning Chronicle*, edited by Peter. These attract generally favorable notice. Also writes for Peter's anonymous Burrite sheet, *The Corrector*.

1803   Accompanies Hoffman family on a trip through wilderness of upper New York State and Canada, traveling through forests and across rivers and streams. Hunts deer for the first time and encounters Indians.

1804–05 Embarks for Bordeaux May 19; brothers, concerned over his health and general well-being, finance his trip. Travels through France, Italy (where his ship, bound for Sicily, is captured by pirates), Switzerland, Belgium, Holland, and England. Participates in social life of Americans and English abroad. Studies history of Naples with Virginian Joseph Cabell; begins lifelong friendship with American artist Washington Allston and briefly considers becoming a painter; meets Mme. de Staël at a dinner given by Baron Humboldt. Attends theaters throughout Europe, especially in England, where he develops a passion for old English drama.

1806   Sails for New York January 17, arriving March 24. Returns to Hoffman law offices. Passes bar examination in November. Writes verse, essays, does translations, and begins to figure prominently in New York society and literary circles. Becomes a member of "lads of Kilkenny" or "nine worthies," a social and literary club. Develops friendship with young John Howard Payne, actor and author.

1807–08   Co-authors *Salmagundi*, which receives much praise, with William Irving and James Kirke Paulding. Is a sympathetic spectator at the trial of Aaron Burr in Richmond. Makes periodic visits to Philadelphia. Father dies October 1807; sister Ann Dodge dies May 1808. Continues to visit the Hoffman household and falls in love with Matilda Hoffman. With Peter Irving, conceives the idea of a burlesque historical guidebook to New York. Begins work on it June 1808.

1809   Seventeen-year-old Matilda Hoffman dies of consumption April 26, and Irving, who was present throughout her three-day agony, retires to the country in deep mourning. Works on *A History of New York*. Perpetrates newspaper hoax concerning disappearance of "Diedrich Knickerbocker" in October and November. Knickerbocker's *History of New York*, published December 6, becomes an instant success.

1810   Passes through a period of lethargy. Visits the Hoffmans, travels in Hudson Valley, keeps notebooks, and writes brief introduction to poems of Thomas Campbell. Brothers make him inactive partner in the family import business, P. & E. Irving, based in Liverpool and New York, giving him one-fifth interest. Enjoys being a literary celebrity in New York.

1811   Sent to Washington by family, lobbies for the interests of New York merchants in Congress. Appears uninvited at Dolly Madison's ball; participates in Washington social life; hears Clay, Cheves, and Calhoun speak. Returns to New York in May and shares living quarters with Henry Brevoort. *Salmagundi* published in book form in London, with introduction by John Lambert but otherwise unsigned.

1812   War against England is declared June 18. Firm of P. & E. Irving, believing 1807 embargo inactive, brings ship laden with English imports back to New York, where they are confiscated. Irving sent back to Washington as member of Committee of Merchants to petition for legislative relief, strengthens his friendship with Dolly Madison, meets the Albert Gallatins, attends patriotic dinners. Corrects and reprints *History*. Accepts editorship of *Select Reviews*.

1813–14	Writes a regular column, biographical sketches, and liter-
ary criticism, but dislikes editing and is relieved when firm
publishing *Select Reviews* (renamed *Analectic Magazine*)
fails. Swears never to edit again. Patriotism, aroused by
British burning of Washington in August 1814, leads him
to enlist as aide-de-camp with rank of colonel to Governor
Daniel Tompkins of New York. Serves on the Canadian
front but sees no actual combat.

1815–16	Feeling restless after peace treaty is ratified February 15,
resolves to travel abroad. Arrives in Liverpool late June on
the *Mexico* ("mewed up together for thirty days in dirty
cabins"). Sees brother Peter, now suffering from rheumatism, for the first time in seven years. Visits sister Sarah
Van Wart and her family in Birmingham, travels through
the English countryside, but further plans to travel to
France, Italy, and perhaps Greece, are changed when he
discovers that the firm of P. & E. Irving, troubled by lack
of American demand for English articles and by Peter's
overpurchasing, is failing. Peter's health worsens, and Irving begins long, unhappy effort ("anxious days and
sleepless nights") to redeem the firm's debts and the family name.

1817	Mother dies April 9. Stays in Liverpool until early sum-
mer when Peter's health improves. Takes lodgings in London near Trafalgar Square and begins to write ("to raise
myself from the degradation into which I considered myself fallen"). Late in August, interrupts his work to travel
for the first and last time in Scotland. Visits Sir Walter
Scott at Abbotsford in a memorable first meeting; is invited to stay for a few days. Irving is amazed at "being
under the roof of Scott; of being on the banks of the
Tweed, in the very centre of that region which had for
some time past been the favorite scene of romantic fiction." Scott reads aloud from *Le Morte d'Arthur* and intro-
duces him to German legend and literature. Returns to
Liverpool in September but takes occasional trips to London. Dines with publisher John Murray and various writers. Visits Coleridge. Renews friendship with Washington
Allston. Meets artists Charles Leslie and Gilbert Stuart
Newton, who become close friends. Chooses pen name
of "Geoffrey Crayon." Keeps notebooks assiduously.

1818   P. & E. Irving declares bankruptcy March 14. Immerses himself in notebooks, studies German, begins "Rip Van Winkle" in June. Leaves Liverpool and visits sister in Birmingham. Returns to London in mid-August. Declines position as clerk in Navy arranged by William, and editorship offered by Scott, to devote himself to writing.

1819–20   *The Sketch Book of Geoffrey Crayon, Gent.* is published serially in England and America and later in three volumes in London. Enthusiastic reviews on both sides of the Atlantic establish his reputation as American man of letters and give him financial independence. Attends afternoon gatherings at his publisher Murray's home where he meets many of the writers and reviewers of the day. Dines out frequently in the homes of fashionable London society.

1820–21   Visits France with Peter in late August. Invests money in steamboat venture on the Seine and South American mines (both are losses). Meets and becomes friends with Thomas Moore, John Jacob Astor, and the tragedian Talma in Paris. Visited by young George Bancroft. Agrees to act as theatrical agent for Payne, who is now living in Paris. Leslie illustrates a new edition of *A History of New York*. Begins writing *Bracebridge Hall* and returns to England to work. William Irving dies November 9, 1821, and Irving calls it "one of dismallest events" of his life. Suffers from severely inflamed ankles.

1822   *Bracebridge Hall* published. Worried by bad health, leaves English social life to travel in Germany, studying history and folklore. *Bracebridge Hall* is translated into German, and his presence hailed as an event in Dresden when he arrives for an eight-month stay in November.

1823   Becomes close friends with Mrs. John Foster of England and her family, with whom he acts in amateur theatricals. Grows deeply attached to eighteen-year-old Emily Foster. Travels with the family to Rotterdam on their way back to England, then returns to Paris to work on *Tales of a Traveller*. Begins collaboration on plays with Payne. Leads active social life.

1824   Returns to England. Mary Wollstonecraft Shelley accompanies him to see first performance of *Charles II*, a play written in collaboration with Payne. Lack of success causes him to stop writing plays in May. *Tales of a Traveller* published in August; reviewers call it imitative, indecent, and sycophantic.

1825   Depressed by reviews, visits friends in Paris. Studies Spanish for distraction. Reads Calderón, Lope de Vega, and Spanish history. With Peter, visits friends at the Chateau Margaux near Bordeaux. Pressured by creditors of Payne, with whom he has been sharing a flat in Paris, and financially hurt by earlier bad investments, realizes he must write to earn more money. Works on earlier unpublished essays about America.

1826   Alexander H. Everett secures him an appointment to the American Legation in Madrid as translator of Martín Fernández de Navarrete's monumental work on Columbus' voyages. Leaves Bordeaux with Peter in February. In Madrid, begins research at the extensive private library of Obadiah Rich. Decides that for artistic and financial reasons a direct translation of Navarrete's scholarly work would be a mistake, and undertakes to write instead a popular biography of Columbus. Begins planning another book, *Conquest of Granada*, in August. Presented to King Ferdinand VII of Spain by Everett.

1827   Leads quiet life, researching and writing *Columbus*, using Navarrete's books as source. Young Henry Wadsworth Longfellow visits him in Spain.

1828   *Life and Voyages of Columbus* published. Tours Spain with Prince Dimitri Dolgorouki, stays for a time in Seville and works on *Granada*. Meets German scholar Böhl von Faber and his daughter Cecilia Caballero Fernan, Spanish novelist and folklorist.

1829   *Conquest of Granada* published and quickly translated into French and German. Elected to Spanish Royal Academy of History. In April visits Granada with Prince Dolgorouki. Settles in the Alhambra from May to July ("It absolutely appears to me like a dream; or as if I am spell bound in some fairy palace"). Continues research in Spanish history and legend, takes notes and begins writing *The Alhambra*. Reluctantly leaves Spain in late July to accept secretaryship at the American Legation in London.

1830   Proves able diplomat (salary $2,000 a year), first under Louis McLane and then Martin Van Buren. His literary fame and gentle manners are helpful both in negotiations and social relations. Presented gold medal by the Royal Society of Literature. Sponsors William Cullen Bryant's poetry in England.

1831   *Voyages and Discoveries of the Companions of Columbus* published. Receives honorary Doctorate of Civil Law at Oxford. Dines with Walter Scott in London. Troubled by rumors of his permanent expatriation, decides to return to America. Resigns his position at end of year and refuses a diplomatic post in Naples.

1832   *The Alhambra* published. Takes a three-week excursion in the countryside with Van Buren; bids Peter farewell at Le Havre; arrives in New York May 21 to an enthusiastic reception and official dinner in his honor May 30. Soon after, takes trip to Washington where he dines with President Jackson and Vice President Van Buren. Visits Saratoga Springs and the White Mountains. In September, with Charles Joseph Latrobe, accompanies Commissioner Henry Ellsworth on trip west to superintend resettlement of Indians. Survives steamboat crash, sees defeated chief Black Hawk in St. Louis, lives and travels "almost Indian like," hunts buffalo, fords rivers, eats skunk, is exhilarated by frontier. Returns via New Orleans; reaches Washington early December.

1833   Becomes unofficial adviser to Vice President Van Buren on foreign and domestic affairs. Begins *A Tour on the Prairies*.

1834   John Jacob Astor suggests the idea of *Astoria*, to be written by Geoffrey Crayon. Begins collaborating with brother William's son, Pierre Irving.

1835 Lives with Pierre at Astor estate, writing and researching. *The Crayon Miscellany* published, consisting of *Abbotsford and Newstead Abbey*, *Legends of the Conquest of Spain*, and *A Tour on the Prairies*, the last an enormous success. Buys Sunnyside, a cottage on the Hudson near Tarrytown, and begins remodeling it.

1836 Publication of *Astoria* raises questions about Irving's association with Astor and with business interests, but work receives enthusiastic reviews in England. Occupies Sunnyside with Peter, Ebenezer, five nieces, and visiting relatives. Grows especially fond of Sarah, daughter of sister Catharine.

1837 *Adventures of Captain Bonneville, U.S.A.* published. Enjoys family life at Sunnyside. Visited by Louis Napoleon, later Napoleon III.

1838 Begins work on a history of Mexico. Declines Tammany Hall nomination as mayoral candidate and secretaryship of the Navy offered by President Van Buren. Deaths of brothers, Judge John Irving in March and Peter, his closest brother, in June. Worries about lack of money to support the family at Sunnyside. Brother Ebenezer's business failing.

1839 Unsuccessful in securing Ebenezer a government job. Gives up cherished history of Mexico when he learns W. H. Prescott is working on same project. Signs contract as permanent contributor to *Knickerbocker* in February. Averages an essay every three weeks for two years.

1840 Disagreements end friendship with Van Buren and Democratic affiliation; becomes Whig. Writes long, biographical introductory sketch for an edition of Oliver Goldsmith's works. Reprints biography of Campbell. Collected edition of his works issued with only respectable sales.

1841 *Biography and Poetical Remains of the Late Margaret Miller Davidson* published and goes into second printing; profits go to the mother of the young consumptive poet. Sarah, his favorite niece, marries and leaves for Paris in March.

1842   Appointed Minister to Spain by President Tyler. Meets an
               admiring Charles Dickens several times before sailing
               April 10 to London. Presented to Queen Victoria. Visits
               Sarah in Paris, and is presented to King Louis Philippe.
               Finds himself well-known and well-received in Madrid,
               although the country is in political turmoil, with many
               factions fighting for control of the twelve-year-old un-
               crowned Isabella II, daughter of exiled Queen Marie
               Christina. Irving maneuvers skillfully among all factions.
               His dispatches to Secretary of State Daniel Webster de-
               scribe the political drama in which ministers are "transient
               functionaries."

1843   Spain is in insurrection; Madrid besieged. Irving ill, but
               remains an avid observer. In September, sick and lonely,
               visits Sarah in Paris. Returns to Spain in November to
               find Isabella II crowned.

1844   Feels better and takes greater part in social life. Maria
               Christina, reunited with her daughter Isabella II, plans her
               marriage; Irving continues to follow fate of "the little
               queen" closely. Works on a life of George Washington.
               Visits Sarah in Paris, the Van Warts in Birmingham,
               England.

1845   Champions Spain's possession of Cuba against English
               and French threats. Endeavors to further American trade
               interests in Cuba. Rift between Maria Christina and cur-
               rent regent Narváez exacerbated over choice of Isabella
               II's husband; Irving maintains friendship with both sides
               but tires of intrigues. Continues work on life of Washing-
               ton and begins work on a life of Mahomet. In September
               visits Paris and sends his resignation to Washington in De-
               cember. Waits seven months for his replacement.

1846   Goes to London at the request of McLane to help nego-
               tiate the Oregon treaty. Hears Gansevoort Melville read
               Typee aloud and later recommends its publication. Returns
               to Madrid. In March sees Narváez ousted. To the great
               regret of Spanish court and government, leaves Spain per-
               manently in August, never having revisited the Alhambra.
               Arrives in New York in September; goes directly to
               Sunnyside.

1847   Lives with nieces, nephew Pierre, and brother Ebenezer. Adds tower to his "snuggery" to accommodate guests and family. Continues work on *Washington*. Develops close friendship with John Pendleton Kennedy, an early disciple.

1848   Acts as pallbearer for John Jacob Astor and is made an executor of his will. Signs with Putnam for complete edition of his works. Four revised volumes appear by December 1.

1849   New expanded version of *Oliver Goldsmith: A Biography* receives glowing reviews. Becomes honorary member of the Smithsonian, and president of Trustees of the Astor Library.

1850   *Mahomet and his Successors* published in two volumes.

1851–53 Works on the *Life of Washington*, using twenty-five years of notes and relying on historical data from Jared Sparks's 1834 biography. Travels in Washington's footsteps, researches public archives of the capital, tracks down anecdotes. Develops friendship with President and Mrs. Fillmore. Attends levees of President Pierce. Is guest of honor at dinner for Thackeray in 1853.

1855   Publication of *Wolfert's Roost*, a miscellany from the *Knickerbocker*, which Irving calls "garret trumpery," is loved by readers. First two volumes of *Life of Washington* published ("If I can only live to finish it, I would be willing to die the next moment").

1856–59 With Pierre's help, continues work on *Washington*. Often ill, he seldom leaves Sunnyside; receives stream of admiring visitors. Finishes fifth and final volume March 15, 1859, and collapses. Dies at Sunnyside November 28, surrounded by family.

Note on the Texts

This volume presents Washington Irving's first four works, three of them in versions established by modern textual scholarship, and one from the original edition.

Between November 15, 1802, and February 1, 1803, the New York *Morning Chronicle*, a Democratic newspaper edited by Peter Irving, published nine letters by the editor's nineteen-year-old brother Washington, each signed "Jonathan Old-style." All but the first of these were reprinted immediately in the *Chronicle Express*, the country edition of the paper, with minor corrections and revisions. Irving omitted the *Letters* from the Author's Revised Edition of his works, prepared for Putnam in 1848, and their only appearance in book form during his life was in two pirated editions in 1824, derived from the *Chronicle Express*, which first gave the series its present title, *Letters of Jonathan Oldstyle, Gent*. The modern scholarly edition prepared by Bruce I. Granger and Martha Hartzog for the edition of Irving's Complete Works (Boston: Twayne Publishers, 1977) follows the nine-part serial from the *Morning Chronicle*, emending obvious printer's errors and accepting a few minor variants from the text of the *Chronicle Express*. This Granger-Hartzog edition, which received the seal of the Center for Editions of American Authors, provides the text reproduced in this volume.

Salmagundi; or The Whim-Whams and Opinions of Launcelot Langstaff, Esq. & Others, a collaborative effort of Washington Irving, William Irving, and James Kirke Paulding, was first issued serially in twenty paperbound numbers between January 24, 1807, and January 25, 1808, by the American publisher David Longworth. Each of these installments subsequently appeared in various resettings or sub-editions, so that all of the numbers exist in several forms—the first number alone is known to exist in no fewer than nine different settings. In 1808 Longworth brought out a two-volume bound collection which incorporated different settings of the individual pieces. In 1811 J. M. Richardson of London published an English edition, prepared by John Lambert, and in 1814 David Longworth published a second American edition incorporating revisions by one of the authors, probably Washington Irving. In 1824, while Irving was in Paris, A. and W. Galignani of Paris brought out *Salmagundi* in an edition revised by Irving. This edition was reprinted in 1834 by Baudry in the French edition of Irving's complete works. Paulding added his own revisions to the French 1824 text and Harpers in New York published it as volumes I and II of the Works of James Kirke Paulding in 1835. Irving refused to include *Salmagundi* in his Author's Revised Edition of 1848, but in 1860 it was published by Putnam in an edition prepared by Evert Duyckinck that followed the original serial text and incorporated revisions from the 1834 Paris edition. In preparing their critical edition of *Salmagundi* for the modern Complete Works, editors Granger and Hartzog have followed the first setting of each of the twenty serial imprints and have incorporated Irving's revisions from subsequent settings of the serial and from the second American and first French editions. This modern scholarly edition provides the text used in this volume.

Although the authorship of the various parts of *Salmagundi* cannot be established absolutely, Hartzog and Granger attribute the following pieces to Washington Irving: "New-York Assembly" and probably "Theatrics" in No. I; the Elbow-Chair essay in No. II; "Fashions" in No. III; the Elbow-Chair essay in No. IV; "Will Wizard at a Ball" in No. V; the Elbow-Chair essay and "Theatrics" in No. VI; "Character of Launcelot Langstaff," "On Style," and "Answer to Certain Meddling Correspondents" in No. VIII; "My Aunt Charity" in No. IX; "The Stranger in Pennsylvania" in No. X; the Mustapha letter in No. XI; the Elbow-Chair essay and "Plans for Defending Our Harbor" in No. XIII; "Cockloft Hall" and "Theatrical Intelligence" in No. XIV; probably "On Greatness" in No. XV; the Mustapha letter in No. XVI; "Chronicles of the City of Gotham" in No. XVII; "The Little Man in Black" in No. XVIII; the Mustapha letter in No. XIX; and probably "To the Ladies" and the Will Wizard essay in No. XX.

A History of New York, by "Diedrich Knickerbocker," went through many editions, translations, revisions, and reprintings during Irving's lifetime. It was first published December 6, 1809, by Inskeep and Bradford of Philadelphia, and was an instant success. In 1812 Irving negotiated with Inskeep for the first of many revised editions, which corrected some misprints from the 1809 edition, altered spelling and punctuation throughout, eliminated various allusions to chivalry and the classics, condensed the comic preamble on world history, and deleted many references to Knickerbocker's problems as an historian. Irving dropped, in all, one-tenth of the narrative and added a like amount, keeping the book at about one hundred and thirty thousand words. Among the additions were a "Further Account of the Author," chapters iv and v of Book II (which narrate the exploration for the New Amsterdam settlement and Oloffe's dream), and the history of the Long Pipes and Short Pipes in chapter vi of Book IV (a satire of American political parties which replaced the quarrel of the Squareheads and Platterbreeches). In 1815 Irving apparently conceived the idea of a third edition of *A History of New York*, this time to be illustrated by the drawings of Washington Allston and C. R. Leslie. Irving continued to revise the *History* periodically over the next thirty years, until the Author's Revised Edition, G. P. Putnam's collected edition of his writings, in 1848. Although a subsequent edition in 1854 contained a number of minor corrections and revisions supplied by Irving, and a Grolier Club edition in 1886, after Irving's death, reprinted *A History of New York* with additional small changes based on Irving's 1848 manuscript, for all practical purposes the last major form of the text was the 1848 Author's Revised Edition. For it, Irving revised Books V, VI, and VII, reworked the Peter Stuyvesant section, added material on Van Rensselaer, deleted the allusions to Jefferson's policies, deleted passages regarded as "coarse," softened the satire of the Dutch, polished the style, and added "The Author's Apology," making this 1848 text some seven thousand words longer overall than previous editions. Much more important, however, were the further alterations of tone which these final revisions produced. The 1809 version was published when Irving was twenty-six and relatively unknown. In 1848 he was sixty-five, a revered American man of letters, a diplomat, and an international celebrity. *A History of New York* in 1848 is a vastly different book from the 1809 version he wrote as a young man. To retain the book's original flavor, the first edition of 1809 is the text chosen for reproduction here.

The Sketch Book of Geoffrey Crayon, Gent. was first published in seven paperbound numbers by C. S. Van Winkle in New York (and simultaneously in Boston, Philadelphia, and Baltimore) between June 23, 1819, and September 13, 1820. Irving was living in England at the time, and to insure his American copyright he sent parcels of manuscript to his friend Henry Brevoort in New York who oversaw their publication. As Irving received the printed numbers, he sent back corrections and alterations which were incorporated in the second editions of the individual issues. Meanwhile, he contracted with John Miller in London to publish an English edition in two volumes which would incorporate additional material, specifically the sketches "Philip of Pokanoket" and "Traits of Indian Character," which had originally appeared in the *Analectic Magazine* in 1814, and the new "Advertisement" and "L'Envoy." Miller published only the first volume before his business failed in 1820, but Irving, with help from Sir Walter Scott, persuaded John Murray to take over the publication. Murray bought Miller's stock of unbound sheets of Volume I, which he issued with a new title page, reading second edition, and bearing his own imprint. He also published the second volume, and then purchased the copyright from Irving and printed an entirely new edition (reprinted in 1821) incorporating numerous revisions by the author. Two years later, in 1822, Murray published another "New Edition" with further revisions by Irving, the text of which was published the following year in Paris by Baudry and Didot (some copies, dated 1824, also bear the imprint of A. and W. Galignani). Meanwhile the text of Murray's earlier edition (1821) was published (with additional changes) in Dresden, Germany, in 1823, by Montucci with Irving's permission. Finally, Irving made further additions and revisions in *The Sketch Book* for his Author's Revised Edition issued by Putnam in New York in 1848. Haskell Springer, who prepared the critical edition of *The Sketch Book* for the Complete Works (Boston: Twayne Publishers, 1978), has taken his text from the original manuscript where extant, from the first American edition, the first

English edition, the Author's Revised Edition, and from additional manuscript material from 1848. Springer has collated these texts against the many revised editions prepared by Irving and accepted emendations from those sources. This volume follows the text established by Springer, and for particular variants and discussions of emendations the reader is referred to his edition.

The standards for American English continue to fluctuate and in some ways were conspicuouly different in earlier periods from what they are now. In nineteenth-century writings, for example, a word might be spelled in more than one way, even in the same work, and such variations might be carried into print. Commas were sometimes used expressively to suggest the movements of voice, and capitals were sometimes meant to give significances to a word beyond those it might have in its uncapitalized form. Since modernization would remove such effects, this volume has preserved the spelling, punctuation, capitalization, and wording of the first edition of *A History of New York* and of the Twayne Publishers' editions of *Letters of Jonathan Oldstyle, Gent.*, *Salmagundi*, and *The Sketch Book*, which strive to be as faithful to Irving's usage as surviving evidence permits. Some changes, however, have been made: a table of contents has been added for *A History of New York* and typographical errors have been corrected throughout. The following is a list of those errors by page and line number: 53.35, use; 57.23, *flam* (english-town); 58.2, *occurences*; 98.20, mobility; 108.36, *Hellion*. "A; 110.19, men and; 141.29–30, "shook . . . Jove."; 173.12, at time; 176.2, inquirites; 193.13, doodle,; 212.21, Ae; 246.2, follew; 250.13, newapaper; 251.31, philanthrophy; 252.2, comtemplation; 272.24, August; 277.17, univerally; 278.9, pesilent; 289.2, occured; 300.30, blendid; 306.31–32, studendous; 311.6, thir; 333.16, exhiliration; 338.23, dessertation; 358.27, gandmother; 360.11, pandimonium; 360.29, myelf; 363.10, Achievments; 374.1, seach; 381.17, a head; 386.1–2, that is; 394.25, than; 396.5, renowed; 402.11, observed,; 402.12, that; 407.40, Budbeck; 409.4, acommodation; 423.2–3, contemptable; 423.33, sieze; 423.34, territories; 425.3, Nederlants; 429.23, aprocryphal; 431.25, Bloome; 432.4, acqua; 444.34, characterestic; 448.30, began; 453.3, *Ancedotes*; 458.22, discoverd; 476.34, Brock;

485.27, rencoutres; 492.22, acribe; 495.14, them though; 511.5, *aud*; 518.6, at at; 521.8, rivier; 525.24, loozen-schalken; 536.11, Van; 537.22, Nederlants; 541.12, continue; 544.31, now; 554.38, Hag.; 564.5, John,; 567.4, Nederlants; 569.22, then; 570.11, Stuyvesant," that; 570.15, why; 581.29, particularly) eschew; 588.24, dicipline; 589.27, revolution:; 591.20, foilage; 592.8, aud; 598.3, Wihelmus Keift; 600.36, Xenephon; 601.4, Neiuw; 603.36, END OF BOOK V. [added]; 610.2, seige; 610.20, Casimir; 610.22, wish; 614.33, pedigee; 617.32–33, consequenee; 640.5, whether tbe; 649.17, whiskerd; 649.33, Nesses; 650.3, Garrebrantzs; 650.3, Onderdonks; 659.21, deluded; 680.2, so; 694.31, That; 700.4, where; 700.5, where; 703.38, dicipline; 717.19, ther inclinations; 719.6, hunter,;; 865.31, did.

Notes

For more detailed notes, references to other studies, and further biographical background, see Volumes VI, VIII, and IX of The Complete Works of Washington Irving (Boston: Twayne Publishers, 1977 & 1978), from which many of the notes below have been derived; and for *A History of New York*, see the edition by Stanley Williams and Tremaine McDowell (New Haven, 1927), Edwin Greenlaw's 1909 edition, McDowell's "General James Wilkinson in the Knickerbocker *History of New York*" (*Modern Language Notes*, June 1926), and Clarence M. Webster, "Irving's Expurgation of the 1809 *History of New York*" (*American Literature*, November 1933). In the notes below, numbers refer to page and line of this volume (the line count includes chapter headings). No note is made for material included in a standard desk-reference book. Notes at the foot of the page in the text are Irving's own.

LETTERS OF JONATHAN OLDSTYLE, GENT.

6.15   copperplate speeches]   Engravings made on polished plates of copper were commonly used for eighteenth-century illustrations. Here the term implies elaborate, ornate, old-fashioned compliments.

6.34   OLDSTYLE]   Pseudonyms of this sort were often used by periodic contributors in Addisonian journals. "Oldstyle" here also suggests the Old Style or Julian calendar which was replaced by the New Style or Gregorian calendar in 1752.

10.10   THE BATTLE . . . *old.*]   By George Colman the Younger, written in 1798, this romantic comedy set during the War of the Roses was performed at the Park Theater in New York on November 24, 1802.

11.32   *The Tripolitan Prize*]   Comic opera based on Samuel James Arnold's *The Veteran Tar* (1801); the play was a patriotic piece concerning the war between the United States and Tripoli.

13.6   the gods]   The "gallery gods," playgoers seated in the upper gallery near the cloud-painted ceiling.

17.37   *harp . . . mirror*]   The curtain was of blue mohair, and in the center was a lyre with the motto: "To hold the Mirror up to Nature."

20.14   the *white lion*]   The Earl of Warwick in *The Battle of Hexham*.

20.33   *slab shabs*]   Possibly from the Dutch *slabbaerd*, a glutton or foulmouthed person, and the slang *shab*, a low fellow or mean trickster.

21.5   Suwarrow boots]   Cavalry boots named for the Russian field marshall A. V. Suvorov (1729–1800).

23.10   my wounded shin]   The *Morning Chronicle* of two days before had
carried the following item: "We have received a note from our correspondent
Jonathan Oldstyle. The old gentleman . . . states that he has been confined
to his house since the famous Battle of Hexham, in which engagement he
received a broken shin, in a skirmish with some impudent boys, who assailed
him for his check of admittance during the interval between the play and the
farce."

25.39   *club* it]   Make into a knot or tail, a hairstyle common for men in
the late eighteenth century.

27.12–13   the Shakspeare]   The Shakespeare box, located at the front of
the second tier in the Park Theater.

29.21   the play]   Sir John Vanbrugh's *The Provoked Husband* (1728), performed at the Park Theater on January 14, 1803.

SALMAGUNDI

49.4   *Psalmanazar*]   George Psalmanazar (1679?–1763), real name unknown, was a French emigrant in London who perpetrated numerous literary
hoaxes, including the presentation to Bishop Compton of a catechism in
"Formosan," a language he invented (cf. 79.1). His posthumous *Memoirs* were
published in 1764.

54.2–3   Bull's-head]   A tavern in Bowery Lane.

54.38   mr. COOPER]   Thomas Abthorpe Cooper (1776–1849), English
lead actor and manager of the Park Theater.

54.39   mrs. OLDMIXON]   English singer and actress who performed at the
Park Theater.

54.40   mrs. DARLEY]   Mrs. John Darley (1779–1848), nee Ellen Westray,
American actress.

57.24   MRS. VILLIERS]   Born Elizabeth Westray, sister of Mrs. John
Darley.

57.37   *Glumdalca*]   From Henry Fielding's play *Tom Thumb* (1730).

58.9   *sorry sight*]   On January 1, 1807, *The Town* had complained, "She
seems not to understand, that *sorry* here signifies *sad*. We presume that she
interprets it, *a sight to cause repentance*; but the meaning is, *a sight sad or
melancholy*. Lady Macbeth says that this is a foolish thought, because, in her
estimation, the sight is joyful."

59.24   mr. Jefferson's *****]   In his note to the 1811 English edition of

Salmagundi, John Lambert explains: "These Shandean stars mean neither more nor less than the late President's *breeches*, which are of *red* velvet; and, it is said, were always worn by him on levee-days, and other particular occasions."

59.26   smellfungi]   Smollett's complaints about travel accommodations in his *Travels through France and Italy* prompted Laurence Sterne to refer to him in *A Sentimental Journey* as "Smelfungus." By extension, "smellfungi" are stay-at-home bookworms who cannot tolerate public conditions.

59.39   cockney]   Irving here means any Englishman.

60.20–21   "North-river society."]   "An imaginary association, the object of which was to set the North-river (the Hudson) on fire. A number of young men of some fashion, little talent, and great pretension, were ridiculed as members." (Irving's note to the 1824 Paris edition.)

63.22   London particular]   A Madeira wine imported for the London market.

65.26   Dilworth]   Thomas Dilworth's *School-master's Assistant* (New York, 1793).

66.19   JOSSELIN]   John Josselyn (1638–75), English author of *New-England Rarities Discovered* (1672) and *An Account of Two Voyages to New England* (1674), both which related much historical and botanical misinformation.

67.18   lord Burleigh nod]   An unfathomable gesture which can be variously interpreted. The expression derives from Richard Sheridan's *The Critic*, III, i.

68.17   Paff's musical tree]   A poplar tree in front of the music shop of Michael and John Paff at the City Hotel, on which was hung the complete history of music.

69.14   M'Sychophant]   Sir Pertinax MacSycophant in Charles Macklin's comedy *The Man of the World*.

70.8   yellow cover]   "The numbers of Salmagundi were originally published in this form." (Irving's note to the 1824 Paris edition.)

73.4   bishop'd]   Wearing a bustle.

73.5   callash'd]   *Calash*: a woman's adjustable hood, supported by hoops of cane or whalebone, projecting beyond the face but capable of being folded far back on the head.

73.7   O'Brallagan's mistress]   Charlotte Goodchild, courted by the Irish soldier Sir Callaghan O'Brallaghan in Charles Macklin's *Love à-la-mode* (1759).

76.6   good-natured villainy]   "The manuscript had characterized [the *Salmagundi* authors'] satirical pleasantries as 'good-natured raillery,' which last word, by an expressive blunder, the printer converted into 'villainy.' Whether the blunder was felicitous or not, there was something waggishly descriptive in the epithet which hit the humor of Washington, and he resolved at once to retain it." Pierre M. Irving, *The Life and Letters of Washington Irving* (New York, 1862), I, 177.

78.28   tripolitan prisoners]   Seven Tripolitan prisoners of war were brought to New York aboard the U.S.S. *John Adams* in February 1805.

81.16   present bashaw]   Thomas Jefferson's aversion to ceremony and his interest in science were often ridiculed by the Federalists.

85.6   Dat . . . Columbas.]   "Our censor absolves the raven and passes judgment on the doves." Juvenal, *Satires,* II. 63.

87.31   Dr. Christopher Costive, L.L.D. &c.]   "Christopher Caustic" was the pen name of Thomas Green Fessenden (1771–1837), American satirist and inventor, author of two Hudibrastic poems, *Terrible Tractorian* (1803) and *Democracy Unveiled: or Tyranny Stripped of the Garb of Patriotism* (1805). Offended by verses alluding to his poetry in the February 4 issue of *Salmagundi*—"As to dull Hudibrastic, so boasted of late, / The doggrel discharge of some muddle brain'd pate," (74.8–9)—Fessenden, editor of the *Weekly Inspector*, printed a retort three days later: "Pray, Messrs. Caterers of Salmagundi, give us a little *bubble and squeak*, or *topsy-turvy*, by way of variety, or a little plain plum-pudding, if you have it at hand. But, in the name of all the gods of gormandizing, spare us your whipped syllabub, if you have nothing but *flummery* to substitute." The *Salmagundi* authors replied with a Hudibrastic poem, "Flummery," in their fourth issue on February 24 (pp. 101–02).

88.14   Dr. Lampedo]   A comic figure in John Tobin's *The Honey Moon* (1805).

94.36   Carr's Stranger in Ireland]   Sir John Carr, *The Stranger in Ireland* (Hartford, 1806). The reference to the man in the moon, as well as other allusions that follow, may be inventions.

95.37   Moore . . . Priest]   John Moore, *A View of Society and Manners in France, Switzerland and Germany* (London, 1781); Richard Parkinson, *A Tour of America in 1798, 1799, and 1800* (London, 1805); William Priest, *Travels in the United States of America* (London, 1802).

97.26   splac-nuncs]   *Splacknuck*: an imaginary animal of Brobdingnag in *Gulliver's Travels.*

98.30   Justice Bridlegoose]   In Rabelais' *Gargantua and Pantagruel,* III.

109.30   LLOYD]   Robert Lloyd (1733–64), "A Familiar Epistle. To a Friend Who Sent the Author a Hamper of Wine."

110.28   "THE ECHO"]   A collection of verse satires published in Hartford in 1807 by the Federalist authors Theodore Dwight, Richard Alsop, Lemuel

Hopkins, E. H. Smith, and Mason Cogswell, known as the "Connecticut Wits."

133.28   soup-maigre]   Watery soup, made from vegetables or fish.

138.4   Fennel]   James Fennell (1766–1816), English actor who emigrated to America in 1794, author of *The Wheel of Truth* (1803) described in *Jonathan Oldstyle*, letter VII.

138.14–15   Strasburgh . . . nose,]   In *Tristram Shandy*, Book IV, Slawkenbergius tells the story of a stranger whose appearance disrupted the town of Strasburgh, dividing the inhabitants into factions and causing scholarly controversy between the universities over whether his enormous nose was real or artificial.

138.28   WOOD and CAIN]   William B. Wood (1779–1861) and Alexander Cain (dates unknown) were both popular actors.

140.13   General Washington's life]   A reference to John Marshall's five-volume *Life of George Washington* (1804–07).

140.25–26   predilection . . . day.]   Thomas Jefferson was alleged to have a black mistress.

142.12   *secundum artem*]   Following the rules of art.

146.2   *anti-deluvian*]   Thomas Paine, who denied the historicity of the Flood and other scriptural miracles. In 1801 Jefferson offered him free passage from France to America aboard the government ship *Maryland*.

146.24   langrage]   Shot used in naval cannon which destroyed sails and rigging.

149.31–32   citizen . . . power,]   In 1806 the English frigate *Leander*, blockading New York harbor, accidentally killed an American merchant seaman, John Pierce, when it fired across the bow of his vessel.

149.33–150.2   insurrection . . . existence.]   In 1806 Jefferson, warned of Aaron Burr's plot to seize Spanish possessions on the lower Mississippi, issued a proclamation, never naming Burr, which enjoined all citizens to withdraw from the illegal enterprise.

152.36   MORSE]   A New England actor at the Park Theater.

155.7   *Fair Penitent*]   Nicholas Rowe's *The Fair Penitent* (1703) was performed at the Park Theater on February 18, 1807.

156.4–7   "In . . . thee."]   Translation of Martial's *Epigrams*, XII, 47, based on Ovid's *Amores*, III.

162.23   Blair's lectures]   Hugh Blair (1718–1800), *Lectures on Rhetoric and Belles-Lettres* (1783).

166.29   lodoiska]   John Philip Kemble's musical *Lodoiska* (1794) was first performed in New York on June 13, 1808. It became immensely popular in America.

170.20–21   the lady . . . lobster,]   The calcareous structure in the stomach of a lobster, serving for the trituration of its food; fancifully supposed to resemble the outline of a seated female figure.

172.18   latonian feat]   Latona, mother of Apollo, was prevented by Juno from throwing herself into a pool to refresh herself.

173.24   *Hutchin's improved*]   John Nathan Hutchins, teacher of mathematics in New York, wrote a series of almanacs with this title.

177.5   "Fire . . . hand."]   From Alexander Pope's "Epistle to Dr. Arbuthnot."

180.38–181.1   they . . . meetings!]   President Jefferson notified Congress on December 15, 1806, that the south wing of the Capitol needed repairs and would not be ready for congressional sessions. A three-month debate ensued over the $20,000 appropriations request.

182.4–6   warrior . . . Derne,]   William Eaton, United States Navy Agent for the Barbary Regencies in Egypt, directed the assault and capture of the city of Derne in 1805.

183.21   *in querpo*]   In undress; without clothing.

190.16–17   American . . . *dished.*]   The "American Ticket" was the derisive name given by Republicans to the losing Federalist slate in the New York election of 1807.

193.29   Communipaw]   Early name of Jersey City.

193.39   Solomon Lang]   John Lang, publisher of the *New-York Gazette*, was often outwitted by designing persons, and so earned the ironic nickname "Solomon."

196.11   play . . . Philadelphia]   Charles Breck's (1782–1822) sentimental comedy *The Fox Chase* (1808).

198.2   *doup*]   English *dope*: gravy or sauce.

199.40   Trim's argument]   Corporal Trim in *Tristram Shandy*.

202.28   horeback]   Here, and at 206.5, the editors of the Complete Works follow the first setting of the first American edition (1807). Later printings of that edition and all revised editions correct both readings to "horseback."

211.36   Eclipse colt]   The famous English racehorse Eclipse was foaled during the sun's eclipse of 1764. By implication, any fast horse.

217.34   bob-majors]   Changes rung on a set of eight bells.

217.38–39   Abel Drugger . . . Major Sturgeon]   Abel Drugger in Ben

Jonson's *The Alchemist* (1610) and Major Sturgeon in Samuel Foote's *The Mayor of Garratt* (1763) do not figure in each other's plays.

218.36   Guthrie's Geography]   *A New Geographical, Historical and Commercial Grammar, and Present State of the Several Kingdoms of the World* (London, 1770) by William Guthrie (1708–70).

220.26   Philip's ass]   "When [Philip of Macedon] was desirous of capturing a certain stronghold, his scouts reported that it was altogether difficult and quite impregnable, whereupon he asked if it were so difficult that not even an ass laden with money could approach it." (Plutarch, *Moralia*, III.)

223.16–17   "a Picture of New-York,"]   Dr. Samuel L. Mitchell's *Picture of New-York* (1807), later parodied in *A History of New York*.

227.15–16   *otium cum dignitate*]   Peace with honor.

228.36   pistareen's worth]   Pistareens were Spanish-American silver coins circulating at a debased rate.

229.20   Hogg's porter-house]   Tavern at 11 Nassau Street owned by John Hogg (1770–1813), a comic actor at the Park Theater.

235.22–26   *fracas* . . . Norfolk]   British warships repeatedly impressed seamen from American ships, alleging they were English deserters. The *fracas* at Canton in late 1806 involved the *Beaver*, an American vessel engaged in the China trade; the outrage at Norfolk involved the American navy frigate *Chesapeake*, which was fired upon and disabled by the British ship *Leopard* on June 22, 1807, for refusing to surrender four seamen.

238.1   PLANS . . . HARBOUR.]   Robert Fulton's submarine, one of many ingenious engines of war, was first demonstrated in New York harbor in July of 1807.

238.16   *poplar worm*]   "The foot-paths of Broadway, and some other streets, in New York, are planted with poplars, which afford an agreeable shade from the sun in summer. In 1806, the inhabitants were alarmed by a large species of caterpillar, or worm, which bred in great numbers on the poplars, and were supposed to be venomous. Various experiments were tried; and cats and dogs were made to swallow them. It was reported that many of the animals died in consequence; but the whole proved to be a false alarm. . . ." (Lambert's note to the 1811 English edition.)

245.2   *syllogisms in Baroco*]   "Baroco" is a mnemonic word in logic, representing by its vowels the fourth mood of the second figure of syllogisms, in which the premises are a universal affirmative and a particular negative, and the conclusion is a particular negative.

247.1   Dilworth]   Thomas Dilworth's spelling book, *New Guide to the English Tongue* (1740), was eventually replaced by Webster's *Grammatical Institute* (1783).

250.2–3   Hannibal's . . . rocks]   Livy relates *(Ab urbe condita)* that Hannibal's troops cut a road through the Alps by heating the rocks with fire and pouring vinegar over them to make them crumble.

256.28–29   "neither . . . pocket."]   The phrase is Jefferson's; cf. *Notes on the State of Virginia*, Query XVII.

269.26–27   Vauxhall-Garden]   Fashionable outdoor theater and gardens.

272.12   Ciceri]   Charles Ciceri, scene painter and machinist at the Park Theater.

272.17   Dunderbarrack]   Dunderberg, or "Thunder Mountain," in Rockland County, New York.

279.31–32   note . . . banks,]   "In the United States . . . bank-notes . . . are current for their full value only in the state where they are created; in all the rest they either will not pass at all or are current only at a very considerable discount." (Lambert's note to the 1811 English edition.)

289.7   feast . . . Lapithae]   The marriage feast of Peirithous, king of the Lapithae, to which he had invited the Centaurs, erupted in a bloody fight.

289.18   longed]   Obsolete form of "lunged."

334.23–24   "two . . . bragger!"]   In the card game "brag," two aces and a jack, the second highest possible hand.

345.4   *Extremum . . . laborem.*]   "My last task this—vouchsafe me it." From Virgil's *Eclogues*, X, 1; *nihi* is a misprint for *mihi*.

357.11   *Pendent opera interrupta.*]   "The works are broken off." Virgil, *Aeneid*, IV, 88.

357.27   the embargo]   The controversial Embargo Act of December 1807 forbade certain types of commerce with England.

359.35   Twaits in Lampedo]   The English actor William Twaits (1781–1814) played Lampedo in *The Honey Moon* at the Park Theater on November 5, 1806. See note at 88.14.

A HISTORY OF NEW YORK

373.1   Account of the Author]   On October 26, 1809, six weeks before the publication of *A History of New York* on December 6, this advertisement appeared in the New York *Evening Post*:

DISTRESSING

Left his lodgings some time since, and has not since been heard of, a small elderly gentleman, dressed in an old black coat and cocked hat, by the name of KNICKERBOCKER. As there are some reasons for believing he is not entirely in his right mind, and as great anxiety is entertained about him, any information concerning him left either at the Columbian Hotel, Mulberry-street, or at the Office of this paper will be thankfully received.

P.S. Printers of Newspapers would be aiding the cause of humanity, in giving an insertion to the above.

On November 6, a reply appeared:

To the Editor of the Evening Post.

SIR, Having read in your paper of the 26th Oct. last a paragraph respecting an old gentleman by the name of *Knickerbocker,* who was missing from his lodgings; if it would be any relief to his friends, or furnish them with any clue to discover where he is, you may inform them, that a person answering the description given was seen by the passengers of the Albany Stage early in the morning, about four or five weeks since, resting himself by the side of the road, a little above Kingsbridge—He had in his hand a small bundle tied in a red bandana handkerchief; he appeared to be travelling northward, and was very much fatigued and exhausted.

A TRAVELLER.

On November 16, "Seth Handaside, landlord of the Columbian Hotel," advertised the discovery of Knickerbocker's manuscript:

A very curious kind of a written book has been found in his room, in his own handwriting. Now I wish you to notice him, if he is still alive, that if he does not return and pay off his bill for boarding and lodging, I shall have to dispose of the book to satisfy me for the same.

373.21   Jarvis and Wood]   John Wesley Jarvis (1781–1839) and Joseph Wood (1778?–1832?) of Park Row in New York were famous for their silhouettes and miniatures. Jarvis painted a portrait of Irving in 1809.

378.4–7   manuscript . . . Stuyvesant family.]   While most of Irving's allusions and footnotes are genuine, many are his own inventions. There is no known Stuyvesant manuscript (also referred to on pages 550, 597, 628 and 628 *note,* 630, 687, and 689), nor any known French manuscript (444 *note*), nor a D. Selyn manuscript of poesies (687 *note*). The major sources of Irving's erudition in the first four chapters are: for classical lore, Diogenes Laertius, *De Clararum Philosophorum Vitis, Dogmatibus et Apophthegmatibus* (3rd century A.D.), available in a 1688 translation; Ralph Cudworth's *The True Intellectual System of the Universe* (London, 1678); and an English condensation (Dublin, 1792) of J. J. Brucker's *Historia Critica Philosophiae* (Leipzig, 1742–67). For historical background Irving used the only extant history of New York, William Smith's *History of the Province of New York* (London, 1757); Hazard's *Historical Collections* (New York, 1794); Samuel Purchas, *Purchas His Pilgrimes* (London, 1625); a translation of Pierre de Charlevoix entitled *Journal of a Voyage to North America* (London, 1761); a manuscript account of New Amsterdam by David De Vries in the Philadelphia Library; John Ogilby's *America* (London, 1671); Richard Blome's *Present State of His Majesty's Isles and*

Territories (London, 1687); and two works by John Josselyn, *An Account of Two Voyages to New England* and *Chronological Observations of America* (both London, 1674). Irving's contemporary sources included William Jones, *Dissertations and Miscellaneous Pieces* (London, 1792); the *Journal of Natural Philosophy* (London, 1797); Camoens' *Lusiad*, translated and annotated by Mickle (London, 1778); Erasmus Darwin's poem *Botanic Garden* (London, 1791); and Samuel Shuckford's *The Sacred and Profane History of the World Connected* (London, 1808).

393.12–13   Bishop Burnet] Thomas Burnet, not Bishop Gilbert Burnet, wrote *The Sacred Theory of the Earth* (London, 1726). Irving corrected this error for the 1812 edition.

401.4   Dr. Shackford] Actually Samuel Shuckford. See note 378.4–7.

427.36   *Ogilvie] Irving consistently misspells the name of John Ogilby. See note 378.4–7.

428.21   Solomon Lang] See note 193.39.

429.23–24   Hacluyt] Richard Hakluyt (1552?–1616), *The Principal Navigations, Voyages, Traffics, and Discoveries of the English Nation* (1598–1600).

431.25   Blome] Richard Blome. See note 378.4–7.

444.41   Printer's Devil] Here, and elsewhere in the footnotes, Irving invents a printer's devil, or apprentice typesetter, who adds to Knickerbocker's text on his own authority.

466.11   King Log] In Aesop's fable, when the frogs prayed to Jove to send them a king, he responded by throwing a log into their pool. Initially fearful of their new king because of the tremendous splash he made, the frogs grew derisive when they discovered they could jump on his back with impunity.

469.30   bum bailiffs] A bailiff close at a debtor's back, who catches him from behind.

473.24   Gomez] A rich banker in Dryden's *The Spanish Fryar* (1681).

486.17   eel skin] The queue or braid was wrapped in eelskin.

504.23–24   Gulliver . . . Struldbruggs] In Swift's *Gulliver's Travels* the Struldbruggs never die.

512.35   WILHELMUS KIEFT] Readers of 1809 noted many parallels between Wilhelmus Kieft and Thomas Jefferson.

520.12   non-intercourse bill] A reference to Jefferson's 1806 non-importation act.

521.38   Evert Duyckingh] After the appearance of *A History of New York*, "Diedrich Knickerbocker" complained in the *American Mercury* of January 23,

1810, of the premature publication of his manuscript by landlord Seth Handaside: "I regret exceedingly this last premature step, and particularly its having been published by Messrs. Inskeep and Bradford, instead of my much
esteemed friend Evert Duyckingh, who is a lineal descendant from one of the
ancient heroes of the Manhattoes, and whose grand father and my grand
father were just like brothers. As, however, I trust that Messrs. Inskeep and
Bradford, though not Dutchmen, are still very honest good sort of men, I
expect that they will account with me for my lawful share of the profits."

522.9   Pearce] See note 149.31–32.

524.3   liberty caps] Conical red caps worn by French and American rev-
olutionaries, said to be derived from the Phrygian bonnets worn by emancipated slaves among the Romans.

525.23–24   dieven . . . kakken-bedden] *Dieven*: thieves; *schobbejaken*:
scaly-coated; *deugenieten*: good-for-nothings; *twist-zoekeren*: quarrelers; *loozen-
schalken*: sly rascals; *blaes-kaeker*: wind-bags; *kakken-bedden*: bed-shitters.

526.34–35   Astolpho . . . Alecto.] Astolpho, in Ariosto's *Orlando Furioso*, possessed a magic horn whose sound inspired panic in all who heard it.
Alecto, one of the Furies, instigated strife between the Latins and the Trojans. See Virgil, *Aeneid*, VII, 286.

527.8   quaker guns] Logs painted black to resemble cannon.

529.32–36   Preserved . . . Barebones] Biblical and allegorical names were
commonly bestowed by Puritans on their children. Praise-God Barebones
(c.1596–1680), a London minister and leather merchant in Cromwell's Parliament of 1653, was the source of the derisive name "Barebones Parliament."

539.4   *Bum-Bailiffs*] See note 469.30

542.2   Cornish knights] Followers of the cowardly and treacherous King
Mark in the legends of King Arthur.

567.12   "seventy-six" of a governor] Resembling a veteran of the Revolutionary War.

574.33–36   Quum . . . usus.] "When living creatures crawled forth upon
primeval earth, dumb, shapeless beasts, they fought for their acorns and lairs
with nails and fists, then with clubs, and so on step by step with the weapons
which need later forged." Translated by H. Rushton Fairclough (New York,
1926).

580.3   shut . . . Janus] The doors of the Roman temple of Janus were
closed in time of peace and opened in time of war.

598.1   Jacobus Von Poffenburgh] A satiric portrait of General James Wilkinson, chief witness against Aaron Burr.

601.30   Pierce Forest] *Perceforest*, a romance published in French in the
sixteenth century.

602.24   cropping the hair]   In 1801 General Wilkinson ordered men in the United States Army to cut their hair, an innovation that was strongly resisted.

612.32   Pizarro]   By August von Kotzebue (1761–1819).

612.32   Tom Thumb]   See note 57.37.

629.22   crabs]   Crab-apples.

632.28   *Metgelsel*]   Comrades.

637.15   under the rose]   *Sub rosa*, or in confidence.

655.30   ravelin]   A fortified earthwork.

702.6   John Stiles]   A fictitious name, formerly used by lawyers, comparable to John Doe.

725.4   Paas and Pinxter]   Dutch names for Easter and Pentecost.

725.6   day of St. Nicholas]   December 6. The patron saint of children, Nicholas (d. 326) was bishop of Myra in Asia Minor. His name was later corrupted to Santa Claus.

THE SKETCH BOOK

735.4–8   "I have . . . BURTON]   Robert Burton, *The Anatomy of Melancholy* (1621).

737.1   Preface . . . Edition]   This preface was prepared for the Author's Revised Edition published by Putnam in 1848. The first three American editions began with the following "Prospectus":

PROSPECTUS

The following writings are published on experiment; should they please they may be followed by others. The writer will have to contend with some disadvantages. He is unsettled in his abode, subject to interruptions, and has his share of cares and vicissitudes. He cannot therefore promise a regular plan, nor regular periods of publication. Should he be encouraged to proceed, much time may elapse between the appearance of his numbers; and their size must depend on the materials he has on hand. His writings will partake of the fluctuations of his own thoughts and feelings; sometimes treating of scenes before him; sometimes of others purely imaginary, and sometimes wandering back with his recollections to his native country. He will not be able to give them that tranquil attention necessary to finished composition, and as they must be transmitted across the Atlantic for publication, he must trust to others to correct the frequent errors of the press. Should his writings, however, with all their imperfections, be well received, he cannot conceal that it would be a source of the purest gratification; for though he does not aspire to those high honours that are the rewards of loftier intellects; yet it is the dearest wish of his heart to have a secure, and cherished, though humble, corner in the good opinions and kind feelings of his countrymen.

London, 1819

The English and other American editions commenced with this "Advertisement":

ADVERTISEMENT

The following desultory papers are part of a series written in this country, but published in America. The author is aware of the austerity with which the writings of his countrymen have hitherto been treated by British critics: he is conscious, too, that much of the contents of his papers can be interesting only in the eyes of American readers. It was not his intention, therefore, to have them reprinted in this country. He has, however, observed several of them from time to time inserted in periodical works of merit, and has understood that it was probable they would be republished in a collective form. He has been induced, therefore, to revise and bring them forward himself, that they may at least come correctly before the public. Should they be deemed of sufficient importance to attract the attention of critics, he solicits for them that courtesy and candour which a stranger has some right to claim, who presents himself at the threshold of a hospitable nation.

February, 1820.

752.2–7   —In the . . . *Thomson*] James Thomson (1700–48), *Sophonisba*, II, i.

756.12–13   dispersed . . . country] Irving was unaware that friends of William Roscoe (1753–1831) had purchased a large portion of the auctioned books and had offered to restore them to him. Roscoe refused the gift, and the books were donated to the Liverpool Athenaeum.

759.2–8   The treasures . . . *Middleton*] Thomas Middleton (1570–1627), *Women Beware Women*, III, i.

767.36   Waterloo medal] Commemorative silver medal presented to all British soldiers who served against Napoleon at Waterloo, June 16–18, 1815.

767.36   Queen Anne's farthing] Pattern-farthings struck late in the reign of Queen Anne, not intended for circulation although they subsequently came into use as coinage. Once thought to be rare, they had become quite common by Irving's time.

779.8–9   red . . . cap] See note 524.3.

784.17   Frederick . . . Mountain] Frederick Barbarossa, Holy Roman Emperor (1152–90), sleeps, according to legend, in a cave in the Kyffhäuser mountains of Thuringia. When his beard has grown three times around the stone table at which he sits sleeping, he will awake and lead Germany to preeminence in the world.

795.2–5   Oh! . . . *Cowper*]   William Cowper (1731–96), *The Task*, Book III, 290–92.

799.21–22   "The Flower and the Leaf"]   Dryden attributed it to Chaucer, but its authorship is uncertain.

802.2–6   I never . . . *Middleton*]   *Blurt, Master Constable*, III, i. See note 759.2–8.

804.19–20   young E——]   Robert Emmet (1778–1803), who mounted an armed attack on the Dublin Castle.

804.35   daughter . . . Barrister]   Sarah Curran, daughter of John Philpot Curran (1750–1817).

806.32–807.8   She is . . . sorrow!]   Thomas Moore, *Irish Melodies*.

815.32–35   Surrey . . . love."]   Henry Howard, earl of Surrey (c. 1517–47), was beheaded for treason. The lines of verse are from his "Prisoned in Windsor."

816.39   *Buchanan]   George Buchanan (1506–82), *Rerum Scotticarum Historia*, Book X.

817.37   *Ballenden's . . . Boyce]   Translation by John Ballenden or Ballentyne (1533–87) of a Latin work by Hector Boece or Boethius (1465–1536), XVI, 16.

817.38   †Roger l'Estrange]   "Loyalty Confined," questionably attributed to Sir Roger l'Estrange (1616–1704).

828.16   Vaucluse]   The home of Petrarch, near Avignon.

828.17   shrine at Loretto]   Said to be the house in which the Virgin Mary lived at the time of the Annunciation, miraculously transported to Italy when the Turks threatened the Holy Land.

829.2–6   A gentleman? . . . *Bush*]   By John Fletcher (1579–1625) and Philip Massinger (1593–1640), II, iii.

843.3–8   A tavern . . . *Bombie*]   By John Lyly (1554–1606).

845.6–7   haunted . . . Cock-lane]   In 1762 the ghost of Cock Lane was shown by Dr. Johnson to be a hoax.

845.8   Cateaton . . . Jewry]   Now Gresham Street; site of the Jewish quarter before the expulsion of the Jews from England in 1290.

845.17   old Stow]   John Stowe's *Survey of London* (1598) was a principal source of Irving's knowledge of London history.

846.4   Monument]   Sir Christopher Wren's monument, a stone column

202 feet high, commemorating the fire of 1666, which virtually destroyed London.

851.25   Scriblerius] The Scriblerus Club, which included Pope, Swift, Gay, and Arbuthnot, produced the burlesque *Memoirs of the Extraordinary Life, Works, and Discoveries of Martinus Scriblerus* (1741).

854.4–11   I know . . . *Hawthornden*] From an untitled sonnet by William Drummond of Hawthornden (1585–1646) in *Poems* (1616).

858.32–33   *Chaucer's Testament of Love*] Actually by Chaucer's contemporary, Thomas Usk.

866.15–20   Thus, . . . stone.*] "The Dirge of Jephthah's Daughter," in *Noble Numbers*, by Robert Herrick (1591–1674).

870.32–871.3   With . . . breath.] *Cymbeline*, IV, ii.

875.12   Bright . . . Hungary] Richard Bright (1789–1858), *Travels from Vienna through Lower Hungary* (1818).

878.33   *écume de mer*] Meerschaum; literally, "sea foam."

880.17   the Heldenbuch] "The Book of Heroes," a collection of thirteenth-century German epic poetry.

880.24   Minne-lieders] The love songs sung by the *Minnesingers*, medieval German troubadors.

882.40–883.1   *Saus und Braus*] Revelry and riotous living.

894.2–16   When . . . *1598*] Thomas Bastard (1566–1618), *Chrestoleros: Seven Bookes of Epigrams*.

901.8–12   For . . . darkness.] Beaumont and Fletcher, *Thierry and Theodoret*, IV, i.

906.9   curious narrative] *A True and Perfect Narrative of the Strange and Unexpected Finding the Crucifix and Gold-Chain of that Pious Prince, St. Edward, The King and Confessor, which was found after 620 Years' Interment: and Presented to His Most Sacred Majesty, King James the Second*, by Charles Taylour, Gent. (London, 1688).

907.39   Malcolm. Lond. Rediv.] James Peller Malcolm, *Londinium Redivivum* (1802), I. 94.

909.5   *Hue . . . Christmas*] An anonymous pamphlet, "Arraignment, Conviction and Imprisoning of Christmas: . . . with An Hue and Cry after Christmas . . ." (London, 1645).

915.12–18   Some . . . time.] *Hamlet*, I, i.

917.2–7   Omne benè . . . deponendi.] "Every pleasure / No more pain /

Now it's time for play. / The hour has come / To set aside / Our book without delay."

920.22–33   "Now . . . fingers."] From the "December" section of Nicholas Breton's *The Fantasticks* (1626).

920.32   Dice . . . butler;] Players traditionally gave part of their winnings to the butler.

924.2–10   Saint . . . *Cartwright*] William Cartwright (1611–43), *The Ordinary*, II, i.

929.30–35   Come . . . desiring.] "Ceremonies for Christmasse," in Robert Herrick, *Hesperides*.

935.2–10   Dark . . . *Herrick*] "A Christmas *Carol* sung to the King in his Presence at *White-Hall*," in *Noble Numbers*.

937.1–8   'Tis . . . one.] "A Thanksgiving to God, for His House," in *Noble Numbers*.

945.3   duke Humphry] To "dine with Duke Humphry" is to fast.

945.4   Squire Ketch] The name of John ("Jack") Ketch, Esq., the common executioner in London 1663–86, was adopted for the hangman in the Punch puppet shows and soon became a common appellation for the hangman or executioner.

945.37   —*Round . . . Fire.*] An eighteenth-century pamphlet.

946.26   Christmas box] Earthenware box in which contributions were collected by apprentices and servants; it was broken and its contents shared on Boxing Day, the day after Christmas.

948.2–14   Lo, . . . *Juvenilia*] George Wither or Withers (1588–1667), "A Christmas Carol," *Juvenilia* (1622), III.

948.22–27   Just . . . away.*] "A Ballad upon a Wedding," *Fragmenta Aurea* (1646).

953.28   roasted crabs] Crab-apples.

956.17–20   He . . . mine.] Richard Crimsall (c.1640).

969.2–6   What . . . *Nashe*] Thomas Nashe (1567–1601), *Christ's Tears Over Jerusalem. Whereunto is annexed a comparative admonition to London* (1593).

971.7–8   Fifth of November] Guy Fawkes Day.

971.17   Monument] See note 846.4

972.15–16   grasshopper . . . Exchange] Erected in honor of Sir Thomas Gresham, founder of the Royal Exchange, whose coat of arms bore the figure of a grasshopper.

972.29–31   old king . . . throne;]   King George III died January 29, 1820, and was succeeded by his son, George IV.

972.31   a royal duke]   Edward, duke of Kent, son of George III and father of Queen Victoria, died January 23, 1820.

972.32   another . . . murdered;]   The Duc de Berri was murdered in Paris on February 14, 1820.

972.33–34   bloody . . . Manchester]   In the "Peterloo Massacre" of August 16, 1819, cavalry troops charged and dispersed a mass meeting of workers demanding Parliamentary reform, killing twelve and injuring hundreds.

972.34   plot . . . Street]   Arthur Thistlewood led an unsuccessful conspiracy to assassinate the members of the Cabinet on February 23, 1820.

972.35   Queen . . . England]   Caroline (1768–1821), wife of the Prince of Wales (later George IV), had been estranged from her profligate husband for many years, and lived abroad. On the death of George III in 1820, she returned to England to assume her place as queen, refused a settlement that would have relinquished her title, defeated her husband's attempt to secure a bill of divorce from the House of Lords, and aroused great popular support in sympathy for her wrongs.

975.33   crab]   See note 629.22.

976.28   mault-worme]   A lover of malt liquor.

983.2–6   Thou . . . *Garrick*]   David Garrick (1717–79), "Ode" (1769).

985.8–9   Casa of Loretto]   See note 828.17.

1002.2–5   "I . . . *Chief*.]   "Logan's Speech." Logan, or Tahgahjute (c.1725–80), a Cayuga chief whose family was murdered by a party of whites, led a series of attacks on Western settlements until his warriors were defeated by the Virginia militia in 1774. Logan refused to attend the council of peace and instead sent a message to be delivered to Lord Dunmore. Transcribed and translated by General John Gibson, the speech was widely circulated as an example of Indian eloquence. Cf. Thomas Jefferson, *Notes on the State of Virginia*, Query VI and Appendix 4.

1004.22–29   "For . . . meanly of."]   Thomas Morton, *New English Canaan* (1637), Book I, p. 178.

1005.35–1006.30   record . . . assistance."]   *Ibid.*, III, 169–71.

1010.6–8   narratives . . . Indians.]   William Hubbard (1621–1704), *A Narrative of the Troubles with the Indians in New-England* (Boston, 1677).

1013.3–9   As monumental . . . *Campbell*]   Thomas Campbell (1774–1844), "Gertrude of Wyoming" (1809).

1014.39   English poet]   Robert Southey (1774–1843).

1024.26   peag]   Beads made from shell, strung together, and used as money by the Indians; wampum.

1037.16   Tom, an officer]   "Thomas Atkins" or "Tommy" is the familiar name for the British soldier.

1040.2–8   May . . . *Herrick*]   "The Dirge of Jephthah's Daughter," stanza 12; see note 866.15–20.

1042.18–21   "This is . . . place."]   *The Winter's Tale*, IV, iv.

1049.2–10   This day . . . *Wotton*]   Sir Henry Wotton (1568–1639), *Reliquae Wottonianae*. Izaak Walton quotes these lines in *The Compleat Angler* (1653).

1052.8   "Tretyse . . . Angle,"]   *A Tretyse of Fysshynge wyth an Angle*, by Dame Juliana Berners, the first manual of fishing in England, printed in 1496.

1054.30–37   "When I . . . him."]   *The Compleat Angler*, Part I, Chapter 21.

1055.1–14   Let . . . daffodil.*]   Lines from John Dennys (d.1609)—not J. Davors—quoted in *The Compleat Angler*.

1058.4–8   A pleasing . . . *Indolence*]   By James Thomson; canto I.

1084.38–39   "If I . . . safe."]   Popular superstition held that supernatural beings could not cross running water.

1089.2–7   Go . . . Mercie]   A mid-fifteenth-century translation by Sir Richard Ros of a poem by Alain Chartier, formerly thought to have been written by Chaucer.

Library of Congress Cataloging in Publication Data

Irving, Washington, 1783–1859.
  History, tales and sketches.

  (The Library of America; 16)
  Edited by James W. Tuttleton.
  Contents: Letters of Jonathan Oldstyle, Gent.—Salmagundi—A
history of New York—The sketch book.
  I. Tuttleton, James W. II. Title. III. Series.
PS2052   1983   818'.209   83-5474
ISBN 0-940450-14-3

This book is set in 10 point Linotron Galliard, a face designed for photocomposition by Matthew Carter and based on the sixteenth-century face Granjon. The paper is Olin Nyalite and conforms to guidelines adopted by the Committee on Book Longevity of the Council on Library Resources. The binding material is Brillianta, a 100% rayon cloth made by Van Heek-Scholco Textielfabrieken, Holland. Composition by Haddon Craftsmen, Inc. and The Clarinda Company. Printing and binding by R. R. Donnelley & Sons Company. Designed by Bruce Campbell.